JOHN O'HARA
From The Terrace

Introduction by
Budd Schulberg

Carroll & Graf Publishers, Inc.
New York

To: Miss Katie Carpenter
God bless her.

Copyright © 1958 by John O'Hara
Introduction copyright © 1993 by Budd Schulberg

Reprinted by arrangement by Random House, Inc.

First Carroll & Graf edition 1984
Second and Fourth Carroll & Graf edition 1993

Carroll & Graf Publishers, Inc.
260 Fifth Avenue
New York, NY 10001

ISBN 0-88184-971-5

Manufactured in the United States of America

Introduction

This introduction, if my daughter's godfather John O'Hara were to see it, would infuriate him. It is also the last thing I would have expected myself to have to do—defend or even help to rebuild O'Hara's reputation. And yet would even the successful, gifted and embattled O'Hara deny that in 1993—just as in 1958 when this 900-page-turner was first published—it needed champions?

This was to be the biggest, grandest, greatest of all his novels, his calling card on immortality, his entrée to the special place on high allotted to America's twentieth-century literary hierarchy, from Wharton, Cather and Dreiser to Fitzgerald, Hemingway, Faulkner and Steinbeck.

Literary success in America, this introducer noted in assaying the careers of six famous authors he knew, is a wild roller coaster ride, and no one rode it with more zeal, dedication and desperation than John O'Hara. Like Scott Fitzgerald, whom he idolized and with whom he sometimes compared himself, O'Hara won instant fame with a dazzling first novel, *Appointment in Samarra*. But unlike Fitzgerald, in his early years there was to be no major triumph like *The Great Gatsby*. The books that followed were cruelly labeled "Disappointment in O'Hara." When Fitzgerald published *Tender is the Night* nine years after *Gatsby*, the social-minded critics of the thirties failed to appreciate Fitzgerald's gifts. When O'Hara returned from an eleven-year hiatus to publish *A Rage to Live*, most critics were equally disparaging. Fitzgerald endured his critics in personal anguish. Not so O'Hara, the most thin-skinned man I ever knew. One bad line in an otherwise favorable review would be enough for John to cross you off his list. So the barbs for his novels of the mid-fifties, when he himself was approaching the sensitive half-century mark, pierced the thin, raw skin of an author selling in the hundreds of thousands and growing quietly rich on his storytelling expertise, but inwardly hungry for the literary recognition he felt his work deserved.

O'Hara was comfortably ensconced in "Limebrook," his Princeton, New Jersey, home, with a fleet of expensive automobiles, including one Rolls that would be reserved for his riding off to the airport on his way to the Nobel Prize. Poor John and his Nobel. Writing best-sellers to respectful if nagging reviews wasn't nearly enough. The Nobel was his grail. Like being accepted in the Academy, the inner circle of the American Institute of Arts and Letters, another prize denied him. Slashing at his enemy, the literary elite, and almost pathetically embracing the faithful handful, like Charles Poore and John Hutchens of *The New York Times,* who held to their conviction that he was a Master, he braced himself for *the* novel of his life, a work he had been researching as only O'Hara could research, and digest, for years.

We all know the repartee of Scott Fitzgerald and Ernest Hemingway:

> SF: The rich are different from us.
> EH: Yes, they have more money.

"Papa" was quipping, and Scott was mythicizing the rich, but neither of them had an inkling of what the rich were really up to. O'Hara did. His friends could laugh at him about his obsession with Ivy League fraternities, subtle differences among expensive cars, and what seems a snob-obsession to be admitted to the best gentlemen's clubs. He judged his friends by the clubs they were permitted to join, those social shrines. One of his most bitter disappointments was that, try as he might, he would never make New York City's oh-so-exclusive Racquet Club. But O'Hara's gift was to transmute what may seem to us a silly social foible into a profound understanding of the rich that was beyond the pen of Fitzgerald or Hemingway.

O'Hara's "hero," or focus, in *From the Terrace,* is Alfred Eaton, born rich as the inheritor of a steel mill in "Port Jefferson," Pennsylvania. Young Eaton is the kind of small-town American who would seem to get what he wants in his life, the best schools, the prettiest girls to bed, the "perfect" beautiful, well-bred but sexy wife, the contacts to move East and go into banking—oh, the least of *his* troubles is making the Racquet Club—up and up he moves, in the world of finance, and though his marriage turns sour he puts up with it in what O'Hara implies is the American Way of Upper Class Wedlock. When it comes to the art of marriage and divorce, fidelity and adultery among the American rich, nobody has done this more accurately, more attentive to every last erotic detail, than John O'Hara. Critics of the body-of-work have complained that O'Hara writes excessively if not obsessively of bodily details. His work has been banned in such capitals of impeccable morality as Detroit and Albany. But, in the world of O'Hara sex, and occasionally romantic love, help to remind us that these millionaires, these Yalies, these upper-uppers who still call the turn for the rest of us, are horny and frigid, jealous and tolerant, armored and vulnerable.

In short, they are *people,* with all their warts, and O'Hara has never been accused of airbrushing out the flaws. Indeed, Alfred Eaton, chronicled from before World War I to post-World War II, is brought to life as much through his failures as his accomplishments. With an intimacy that makes us feel we are eavesdropping on his most secret affairs, we get to know Alfred Eaton, an Eastern tycoon, who acquires millions of dollars, finally divorces his flawed-beauty, socialite wife to marry the mistress he's truly loved, serves his country patriotically and yet is left with a terrible sense of emptiness and the probing question, What went wrong?

At the end of a "Who's Who" professional career and an intense personal life that brings him temptingly and frustratingly close to the very top rung of the American political and social ladder, he's left in an anticlimatic vacuum with nothing to do. Even his lifetime devoted "girl"/mistress/wife is beginning to hate him. This long and searching book ends not with the bang Eaton had worked for, but with a whimper. The background music could be ''What's It All About, Alfie?'' Or Peggy Lee's ''Is That All There Is?''

Alfred Eaton's declining years never add up to an American tragedy. Nor was that ever O'Hara's intention. His effects are more muted. If you feel a little sorry for Alfred Eaton, that's all this master of exactness asks. But critics can't help calling O'Hara a social historian. This fifty-year canvas of American experience from a Pennsylvania steel town to the Big Apple, the Hamptons, Washington, D.C., in the heady war years of '41–'45, and finally on to a far-West retreat (and that nagging sense of failure) in Beverly Hills—all that material in the hands of an uncanny observer like O'Hara can't help becoming social history.

But social history is only a by-product of O'Hara's laid-back and clinical approach. Alfred Eaton is not a prototype of American capitalism, he's an individual. ''Read the book, for its story, its people, its dialogue, its inevitable parade of events, and make of it what you will,'' O'Hara asks implicitly.

Reading it one way, Robert Kirsch, late editor of the *Los Angeles Times*, called the book ''a masterpiece that should have entitled O'Hara to the cherished Nobel.'' Filtered through another sensibility, *The New Yorker* reviewer, John Wain, considered it ''merely an attempt at a masterpiece.'' The critical jury was divided when O'Hara's most ambitious novel appeared, and thirty-five years later O'Hara's reputation still seems curiously suspended in controversy: in the golden circle with Hemingway, Fitzgerald and Faulkner to some, but to others, several notches lower with the talented popularizers. That special Rolls-Royce, speaking figuratively, is still in the garage, still awaiting the magical call from Stockholm.

But for the multitude of readers who were eagerly there for *From the Terrace* the first time around, and for a host of new readers born since its publication in 1958, Carroll & Graf provide both literary service and pleasure with this rich serving of O'Hara for the nineties. ''Nobel me no Nobel,'' the first Tom Wolfe might have said. ''Just O'Hara me O'Hara.''

—Budd Schulberg
1993

*T*HERE ARE ALIVE today hundreds of men who saw Samuel Eaton, who accepted wages from him, envied him, hated him, laughed at him behind his back, worked hard for him, cheated him, and never addressed him except as Mr. Eaton or Mr. Samuel. There are now fewer than a dozen men alive who ate with him, drank with him, played cards or went gunning with him, and who called him Samuel or Sam. At no single time in his life were there ever more than a dozen men on a first-name basis with him, and among them there were always more men who thus addressed him than were similarly addressed by him. If it had been easier to remember numbers than names he would have so called the men and women on his payrolls, and among his intimates it was not always a sign of affection or closeness when he used their Christian names. Even in social intercourse with his friends it was usually he who spoke first, and when another man spoke first Samuel Eaton often would not bother to reply, nor bother to pretend he had not heard.

He had a hard and heavy voice, resonant but not extremely deep. It was as though he had an instinct for pitching his voice at a different level from all other voices in his vicinity. In business and in society he made no effort to lower or soften his voice for the casual intimacies or confidences, and consequently he was reputed to be unusually outspoken. A small compliment to a woman, an unfavorable criticism of a workman, these could be overheard without strain by the listeners; but they were given disproportionate importance because of the quality of Samuel Eaton's voice, and no one profited by the overhearing. Samuel Eaton was more sure than anyone else that what he did not want heard was not heard. Inevitably a by-product of his manner of speaking was also a reputation for candor, and from that a reputation for sincerity, and from that a reputation for foolishness. But the noise that Samuel Eaton made when speaking was a true indication of nothing more than the character of his vocal cords and his chest tones and head tones. If men and women wanted to fool themselves, that was their hard luck.

Away from home, Samuel Eaton's Pennsylvania twang was an added factor in the self-deception of his listeners. An

1

illiterate New Englander speaks in the accents of a Dartmouth theologian, and the citizenry have learned not to underestimate the craftiness of an Alabaman; but the twang of Eastern Pennsylvania is a subtler thing with a subtler effect, vaguely strange and unidentifiable to most ears and giving to the words a sound that is not wholly unpleasant but not fully adult, as though no one who speaks that way can be altogether serious or quite grown up. It is a local sound, seldom comically imitated and therefore rarely recognized as an indigenous accent. At home, Samuel Eaton talked like everyone else, but louder; away, he talked louder than anyone else, and oddly.

Even after his death at an age that was considerably short of the century that he had planned to live, it was not often remarked that Samuel Eaton had been a man of many secrets and a secretive man. In the momentary mercifulness that people call upon at a man's death they repeated the old commonplace that had him an outspoken man, a man of candor. And again, after he was buried and a sensible attitude resumed, the people who had reason to know that he had not been merely a virile fellow with a large voice still failed to profit by what they might have learned from a more careful examination of one of his outstanding characteristics. They took the obvious, as they usually do, and some indeed went so far as to lament a future in which Sam's voice no longer would be heard. It was strange, too, that at his death, as during his life, no one thought to comment that Samuel Eaton's voice had never been associated with song.

As will soon become apparent, this is not the story of Samuel Eaton but of his second son, Raymond Alfred Eaton, who at this writing still lives. But a son's influence on the father is always less strong and less final than the father's influence on the son, and particularly in this case the son's story could not be told with any completeness without careful consideration of the father's influence. A father may love his son inordinately or hate him, but of the two lives, the father's life is already made and while the father lives (and sometimes after he dies), the son's life is still in the making. This, therefore, is Alfred Eaton's story, of which Samuel Eaton's story is a part. It is not a pretty story, but every life has some moments of beauty, and Alfred Eaton would be the first to point to such moments in his own life, even in his present anguish.

We have a long way to go before coming to the recognizable beginnings of the present anguish of Alfred Eaton, and if we had for our purpose nothing more than an adequate characterization of Alfred Eaton, that might be achieved deftly but without depth. And it could be an honest characterization and satisfactory, although hazardous, since Alfred Eaton was and is a simple man, and the hazardousness would lie in the in-

2

clination or temptation to make an attractive, handsome man more complicated than he is. And yet in spite of the known danger, we are reluctant to avoid the temptation to character-ize him briefly. It might be entertaining, for instance, to go over the life of Alfred Eaton for the purpose of selecting half a dozen items of information that would tell how he behaved in various circumstances, and to use other items by which he consciously or inadvertently revealed what he thought. As it happens, however, our purpose is not only to characterize Alfred Eaton; it is something more ambitious than that, and more ambitious than the characterization of the men and women and children whose lives he touched, whose lives touched his. But we cannot know until we have completed this chronicle how well we have succeeded or to what degree we have failed, and so we must refrain now from a statement of our purpose, until we come to the end of our work and can examine something that has been done. It is a scheme which is preferable to an early statement of our purpose, which might tend to make us too constantly aware of the purpose. It is more desirable for us to forget that we have a purpose, or to become less conscious of it, and to engage our attention with the lives and events that are to follow.

When the wind was right, that is to say when there was not much of it, and the day was clear and not too warm and not too cool, the whistle on the roof of the 18-inch mill at the Eaton Iron & Steel Company could easily be heard over a radius of two and a half miles. Under some conditions it could be heard as much as five miles away. Normally it was audible everywhere in the town of Port Johnson, a fact which was a cause of some annoyance to some of the citizens, but was no accident on the part of the owners of the Company or the borough council or the substantial men of the town. In installing their whistle the Company officials had had as their principal intent the summoning of the hands to work in the morning and their release at the end of the working day, but in 1890, when the whistle was first being seriously considered, Port Johnson was without adequate fire warning. The town had grown so that the bell in the borough hall belfry was not always heard, and since Port Johnson had a volunteer fire department of four companies, the idea of a general alarm met with enthusiastic approval. A few citizens, who lived near the E. I. & S., objected to the whistle, especially after the preliminary tests, which went on intermittently for half-hour periods, but their objections were answered with the comment that it was for the common good, that they would get used to it, and to those who more persistently objected went the suggestion that they move elsewhere.

3

It was agreed that the whistle would be blown to summon the men to work, which meant that it was sounded at five o'clock for the six o'clock starting time; at noon and at twelve-thirty for the beginning and end of the lunch hour; and at six o'clock for the closing of the regular working day. It was furthermore agreed that in the event of fire the whistle would be given one long blast of thirty seconds, followed by a shorter blast or blasts to indicate the number of the ward in which the fire was discovered. There were six wards in the borough. Four ten-second blasts in rapid succession meant that a fire had got out of control and that all able-bodied men in the town were expected to offer their help, regardless of their membership or non-membership in a hose company.

As the whistle became a part of the daily-except-Sunday life of the community it was, as predicted, something the citizens got used to and in many cases depended upon. It was not advisable to use the whistle as a standard time signal where railroad-watch accuracy was essential, since the whistle had been known to be a full minute ahead of time in the morning and as much as two minutes off at the end of the working day. But for most citizens and their children in the public and parochial schools it was a convenience. The whistle was not always blown synchronously with the tolling of the Angelus by Henry Heilbrunner, sexton of St. John's German Catholic Church, who rang his bell in conformity with the time shown on his own silver pocket watch. It became a common saying among the citizens that "The Pope says it's six o'clock but Eaton says it's only five fifty-eight."

For nearly four years the whistle at the E. I. & S., or "Eaton's," kept to its schedule; morning, noon, and evening except Sundays, Christmas, and the Fourth of July, and at odd times only when there was an alarm of fire. When, therefore, it was blown at nine o'clock on the night of August 21 in the year 1894 it was not a welcome sound. Most small boys, the only ones who took pleasure in an alarm of fire, had gone to bed; many of them were already asleep, and those who were awake took only a minimum of pleasure in the sound, since they would not be allowed to run to the fire at such a late hour. To others it meant interrupted rest, danger, loss of money, a friend in trouble—or, in the case of the volunteer firemen, a summons to extra effort after a muggy, sticky day during which the drawing of breath had been an effort.

Now a volunteer fireman's pride in his organization was often as fierce as his patriotism or his religious zeal. The horses and the rolling-stock were given the best of care constantly, the fire-fighting equipment was always at peak efficiency, and the buildings owned by the various companies

4

were as neat and clean as any housewife's kitchen, since the buildings not only housed the animals and equipment but also provided club facilities for the members. The second story of every hose-house contained a small bedroom for the single paid hand, and a larger room for the pool table and bar. The rivalry among the four companies was intense in such matters as neatness and comfort in the clubrooms as well as promptness in getting to the scene of fires. The house in which he dwelt, the place where he earned his living, and the hose company to which he belonged were in that order the most important structures in the lives of some three hundred Port Johnson men—and it was a common wifely plaint that "He spends more of his time at the hose company than he does in his own home." It was not, then, so remarkable that when Eaton's whistle blew at nine o'clock that night there were small gatherings of men at the hose companies, sitting on camp chairs on the brick ramps before the large double doors, fanning themselves with palm-frond fans while thirstier brothers were upstairs in the clubroom, enjoying the good clean beer.

The fire-alarm system in Port Johnson was fairly new and simple. Throughout the town boxes were mounted on light-company poles and when a lever in the box was pulled the location of the box was shown on an instrument in each of the hose companies and on similar instruments in Borough Hall and in the watchman's room in the 18-inch mill at Eaton's. As the location of the box was shown on the instruments a bell was sounded and continued to ring until it was turned off. Ideally the bell in the watchman's room at Eaton's would summon him so that he would blow the whistle to warn the town before a fire had gained headway.

On the night of August 21, 1894, the scene at the Phoenix Hook & Ladder Company Number 1 was duplicated in the three other hose-houses. The men with their fans, downstairs, and the men with their beer, upstairs, were startled to hear Eaton's whistle blow a long blast that was not the regulation thirty seconds' duration but only about ten seconds long, and followed by blasts of four seconds, three seconds, six seconds and short two-second toots. The men looked at each other in mystification. The Phoenix president, Walter B. Eck, looked at the instrument and said: "They aint nothing on here."

"Maybe old Charlie Nunemacher goes crazy with the heat yet," said a member, referring to the night watchman at Eaton's.

"Or dronk," said another member.

"No, Charlie is Temperance. He don't touch, taste nor hantle," said a comrade.

Lights began going on in the houses of the town, and firemen began to show up at their headquarters. Walter Eck was about to send a man to inquire at Borough Hall when Jim Muldoon, the patrolman on night duty, arrived at the Phoenix building, as mystified as Eck and his men. To the mounting confusion was added the behavior of Billy, Bobby and Benny, the beautifully matched Phoenix greys, whinnying and pawing in their box-stalls. "Will we leave them out?" said a member.

"What for? We don't know where we're going," said another member.

"Hitch them up and we'll go over to Eaton's," said Muldoon. "It's the quickest way we'll find out what the hell."

Someone opened the stall doors and the horses ran to their places in front of the hook-and-ladder, the hanging harness was lowered upon the horses and snapped into place, and with Eli Fenstermacher at the reins, Joe Kelly at the tiller and nine members hanging on at the sides, the apparatus was under way, headed for Eaton's.

The main gate at Eaton's was closed, barring entrance of the equipment, but Walter Eck and Jim Muldoon entered through the small door at the side of the gate and trotted to the watchman's shack near the 18-inch mill, while the big whistle continued to blow. "Here, you take my billy," said Muldoon. "I got my revolver. I think it's somebody went crazy."

Outside the watchman's shack they halted. Inside were two men, and one of them was tugging away at the whistle cord while the other was laughing.

When he saw the men Muldoon put away his revolver, and Eck handed back the club. "For Christ's sake," said Muldoon.

"I'm a son of a bitch," said Eck.

The man at the whistle cord turned and saw them and motioned to them to enter. He could not be heard above the whistle blasts. Eck and Muldoon went in.

"Mr. Eaton?" said Muldoon.

Samuel Eaton pointed to a whiskey bottle.

Muldoon shouted at him: "You got the whole town worried!"

"Take a drink, Muldoon. Eck, take a drink," Eaton shouted at them.

"You gotta cut that out, Mr. Eaton. It's against the law," said Muldoon.

"I don't hear you," said Eaton. He was laughing, and he took a gulp of whiskey and handed the bottle to Muldoon, while continuing to jerk the whistle cord. Muldoon hesitated once more, then grasped Eaton's wrists and pulled him away and out of reach of the cord.

6

"Get the hell off my property, you stupid Irish bastard," said Eaton.

"I can't help it, Mr. Eaton. You're violatin' the law. You got the whole town in an uproar."

"What the hell do you think I was trying to do?" said Eaton.

"I could arrest you," said Muldoon.

"You couldn't arrest a cold," said Eaton. "Go on, get out before I throw you out."

"You could have me fired, but you'll never see the day you could throw me out. Put up your mitts, you drunken bum."

"No rough-housing," said Eck. "No fist-fighting. Mr. Eaton, what's going on? The whole town . . ."

"I have a son, you stupid Dutch bastard. I have a son!"

"A baby boy at eight o'clock tonight," said Charlie Nunemacher.

"A son? Oh," said Eck. "Celebrating. Oh."

"The whole God damn town's gonna know it, the whole God damn county. Lemme have that whistle," said Eaton.

"You'll do no more blowing of that whistle, son or no son. I got my duty to perform, and I'll perform it. If you wanta celebrate, hire a brass band, but this whistle is intended for other purposes and I'll see to it."

"A brass band!" said Eaton, pointing his finger at Charlie Nunemacher. "I'm going to round up a brass band!" He ran out of the watchman's room, then turned and came back. "Where's my horse?" he said to Nunemacher.

"You sent the carriage home," said Nunemacher.

"The hell with it," said Eaton. He went out again, followed by Eck and Muldoon. When he saw the Phoenix apparatus he called to the mystified men: "Fire's out, boys, fire's out. We're all going to the Exchange Hotel. Drinks are on me. You, Fenstermacher? I'll drive. Let me have those reins."

"No sir. I got my orders."

"Well, the hell with that. I'll hang on here. Come on, Fenstermacher. Exchange Hotel. And ring that bell."

Fenstermacher looked at Eck, who nodded, and with the bell ringing the apparatus turned about and proceeded to the Exchange Hotel, which was soon filled with men and some women celebrating the quickly spreading news of the birth of William Eaton, the first child, the first son of Mr. and Mrs. Samuel Eaton.

The party lasted all night. After the first hour the owner and the bartender at the hotel made no attempt to serve drinks. Instead each man and each woman was given a bottle of whiskey for himself. When the beer ceased to flow from taps the bartender was already too drunk to go down-cellar and start another barrel, and it thus became entirely a whiskey

7

party in a beer-drinking town. Muldoon stayed away from the hotel and left the fighters to their fighting. The women raised their price to five dollars but were kept busy all night. The other women, the wives, stayed home with their disgust and their dread of the their men's return, and cursed the new baby for what he had started. In the morning at the main gate of Eaton's there was a sign that read: No Work Today Holiday With Full Pay By Order Samuel Eaton Pres. It had been the most spectacular birth in the sixty-year history of the town and the hundred-year history of the settlement.

It was a day that would have several causes to be remembered in years to come. All employes at Eaton's had reason to remember it for the same reason they had to remember the birthday of Christ: only on Christmas was an Eaton employe given the day off with full pay. Then there was the special reason that the comparatively few whiskey drinkers had: a whiskey drinker employed by Eaton's usually confined his pleasure to the Saturday nights. But the Eaton baby was born on a Tuesday, the second day of the work week, and the free bottles that were handed out at the Exchange Hotel made Tuesday seem like Saturday, and on the next day, when they realized that they had the day off and were being paid for it, many of the whiskey drinkers made straight for the saloons and drank up a day's pay before noon. On River Street, where most of the workmen's saloons were concentrated, there had never been so many drunken men in the middle of the day. They sat on beer kegs and on the curbstones. A few lay on the brick sidewalk and others leaned against the iron pipe that supported the roofing that covered the sidewalks of most of the business section of Port Johnson. The three men of the daytime police force abandoned River Street to the drunken men and did what they could to keep them from wandering up Montgomery Street, the principal business thoroughfare. Farmers, drummers and strangers who were unaware of the celebration were amused and shocked at what they saw and there were those few who had reasons other than fastidiousness to be shocked when one of the wandering drunks stumbled on the Reading Railway tracks and was cut in half by the switching engine.

The police of Port Johnson never arrested a man for drunkenness if they knew he had a steady job. On Saturday nights they would command his friends to get him home where the wife would punish him in her own way. Now, on this Wednesday, it would have taken a platoon of the militia to rid River Street of the drunken men, but so long as they remained in the saloon area no attempt was made to control them. A Protestant clergyman asked the chief of police, Louis Wehinger, to close the saloons and put an end to the Bacchanalian revel, as he called it.

"Reverend, I don't have the authority," said Wehinger.

"But it's a clear violation of the law, that's all the authority you need," said the clergyman.

"Reverend, do you know who started all this?"

"I'm afraid I do," said the clergyman.

"So do I. If you was to speak to him maybe he'd listen to you. Maybe he'd tell the Chief Burgess to order me to close the saloons. Then I would, but not so's it is."

"Unfortunately the gentleman isn't one of my parishioners."

"Yeah, and he wouldn't like it anyway, if he *was* one of your parishioners. He don't like to be told what to do."

The clergyman shook his head. "It's an unholy, disgraceful way to welcome a new-born babe."

"It's worse than that if you think about that poor—that poor fellow down in the freight yard. Did you see him, Reverend?"

"No, I—no, I didn't."

"Well, I did, Reverend, I seen him."

"Frightful. Frightful."

"Yes, I see near every frightful thing that happens in Port Johnson. I guess it's best if you go home and pray for them and I'll try to keep them outa the yards. Yes?"

"A dreadful welcome to a new-born babe," said the clergyman.

But in other parts of the town the occasion was being observed in a fashion that would not have given the clergyman so much pain. Six squares away, at the corner of Sixth and Montgomery Streets, the callers came and went all afternoon, considerately remaining only long enough to leave cards and flowers, but in every case departing with the pleased expression that meant that all was well, that mother and son were doing fine.

The house at Sixth and Montgomery was the Raymond Johnson residence, one of three houses in the block between Sixth and Seventh Streets, rather plain and old-fashioned when compared with its newer neighbors. It was, indeed, fifty years old and at one time had been alone on the crest of the hill, surrounded then by thirty acres of its own grounds, before the numbered streets had begun to cut across Montgomery Road. It was a large, square house, set well back from the streets, with driveway entrances on Montgomery and on Sixth, with a stable in the northeast corner of the plot, a building that had been erected after The Mansion had ceased to be the only residence in that section of the township, and consequently the stable not only looked new, but The Mansion looked old,

9

although the combined ages of the two buildings totaled less than seventy years. (The old stable remained as part of the Dockwiler establishment at Seventh and Montgomery, looking old and making the Dockwiler residence look new.) There was about The Mansion at first glance an elusive inappropriateness that was not satisfactorily explained by the obvious fact that it was a country house in a town district. The property still had more ground than any other residence in the town, and the walnuts, the elms and, at the rear, the apple and cherry trees relieved the eye from the startling view of the plain yellow box that would be one way to describe the house. A longer examination gave the clues to the eye's rejection of this house in this setting, and the clues were small. Where once had been a herd of iron deer there were now only a stag and hind; the summer house on the Miller property, which adjoined the Johnson property, clearly belonged as part of the Johnson property; the apple trees behind The Mansion had once been members of an orchard that was continued on the Miller and Dockwiler properties; the grape arbor at the rear of the Johnson property was so short that it only indicated that it had once been much longer, as indeed it had been until the Miller family tore down their section of it. The Mansion had been built as a home in the country, and some of the original intention persisted in asserting itself.

But the faults in The Mansion and its setting were not noticed or at least were of no consequence to the citizens of Port Johnson. Only a few, a very few citizens could remember when there had been no Mansion. Most of the citizens had grown up with an awareness of the house as a dwelling-place and as a symbol. As a dwelling-place it was the home of the Johnson family, for whom the town had been named, or re-named. Before the digging of the Canal the village had been called Johnson's Falls because an early Johnson farmed the bottom land at the point of the Falls. The village had consisted of a tavern, a blacksmith's shop, a flour mill, a Lutheran church, and the houses that were needed by the families of the men in charge of those enterprises. When the Canal was being built, but far from completion, a draughtsman, who knew that a series of locks was to be built near Johnson's Falls, gave that place the name of Port Johnson for his own convenience: Johnson's Falls was on the map, and by calling the new installation *Port* Johnson he made it easier to remember. By the time the locks were being installed, the civil engineers had long since accepted the name Port Johnson, and as the new community began to flourish as a result of the location of the locks and the Canal warehouse-station, Port Johnson became the name without further discussion. The anonymous

Vespucci was never called upon to explain why or how he had named the new town, and in any case the Johnsons had as much right to the distinction as any other family in the vicinity. And as the family prospered, through farming, banking, quarrying, and suitable intermarriages, no other family was in a good position to dispute the Johnsons' unuttered claim. Then, too, in time the old village of Johnson's Falls was assimilated by the more recent Port Johnson, a process which only strengthened the family's claim, and the subject of a different name for the town never came up.

The earlier Johnsons reversed the usual American trend in that they moved from west to east; from the farm on the west bank of the River to the top of the slope of the east bank, and there they built The Mansion, which was always known as The Mansion to the citizens of Port Johnson but was never so called by members of the Johnson family. Their frugality and business acumen enabled them to build The Mansion, and they saw no reason not to enjoy the best; but it was quite another matter—and a vulgar, ostentatious one—to speak of their house as *a*, or *the*, mansion. Indeed, they never named the house at all, not even while it was still eligible to the designation of gentleman's country estate. Their modesty, however, could not prevent their friends and the townsfolk from bestowing on the place the grand name. Every town of any size had at least one mansion, and in Port Johnson it was the Johnsons'.

As the proper people—those who were fully confident of the degree of intimacy they shared with the Johnson family— made their more or less formal calls on the second day of the new baby's life, Samuel Eaton had not made himself available to receive the visitors' good wishes. Besides suffering from the large quantity and low quality of the whiskey he had drunk the previous night, he was uncomfortable in the house of his parents-in-law, he was unwilling to submit himself to the mild or hearty joshings (or unspoken disapproval) that were bound to result from the blowing of the whistle, and he was impatient to take his wife and child out of this house and to his own. In the midst of his joy of anticipation and now of realization of his fatherhood he was plagued by the vital, statistical fact that his son had not been born in his own house. Samuel and Martha Eaton made their home on their small farm a few miles north of town. Samuel Eaton had inherited the house from his father and had been born there. It had never occurred to Samuel Eaton that his own son would be born anywhere else. But the doctor, Fred Chansellor, announced one day in Martha's seventh month that he "would feel better about it" if Martha had the baby in town.

"What for? She's all right, isn't she?"

11

"She's fine. But this is her first baby, Sam, and her pelvic structure, her bones—"

"What's the matter with her bones? There isn't a damn thing wrong with her bones."

"I didn't say there was anything the matter with her bones. Let me explain, and don't interrupt me, please. Suppose it's two o'clock in the morning and the baby wants to come. You'd have to get someone from the farm to hitch up or saddle a horse and come in and get me. I'd have to put on some clothes, hitch up, drive out to the farm. It's possible I might be out on a call, or I just might get there too late. And I want to *be* there."

"What the hell is the matter with you, Fred? Babies are born on farms every day of the week."

"Yes. To farmers' wives, and usually without a doctor."

"Yes, and they're damn healthy," said Samuel Eaton. "The whole idea is nonsense."

"They're damn healthy, as far as *you* know, but you're not a doctor. Martha's a friend of mine, and I don't want her to have her baby without a doctor. You can get another doctor if you like, but you make sure and get one that'll be there when the baby's being born. If you want to treat your wife the way some of those farmers treat theirs, you do it on your own responsibility. I'm not interested in your pig-headed insistence on having the baby born on your property."

"So does Martha."

"Martha will do anything you say, that's just the trouble. So it's up to you."

Samuel Eaton did not discuss the subject with Martha, but he had another discussion, and that one with Raymond Johnson.

He had never liked Raymond Johnson, and did not deceive himself that Raymond Johnson liked him. He considered Raymond Johnson a rather ugly, ignorant little man, who had some money and knew how to make it, but with nothing else to recommend him. He had been outside the Commonwealth of Pennsylvania only twice in his life, and what he had seen had not made him want to see more. He was a man who walked to and from his office twice a day except Saturday, and went to the Presbyterian Church every Sunday morning and read Scriptures every Sunday afternoon.

"Samuel, I've had a talk with Doctor Fred Chansellor."

"Fred Chansellor. Yes," said Samuel Eaton.

"Doctor Fred Chansellor. This was on a medical matter. Not a social matter. A medical matter. And it concerns you. At least it concerns you as the husband of my daughter Martha. I want the baby to be born here, and I don't want you standing in the way."

"Well, now wait a minute, Mr. Johnson."

"I'm not going to wait a minute. I'm not going to wait anything. That farm of yours, how long's it been in your family? One generation, that's all. Well, I want you to stop thinking it's some royal palace, because it isn't. I want you to stop thinking of yourself as some duke or lord that has to have their child born in the—the—the palace. I want my daughter to have her baby in advantageous circumstances, with a doctor and a nurse and every medical precaution. And *that's* all I'm going to say about it."

"Well, maybe I have something to say about it."

"Don't make any fuss, young fellow. Don't—you—make—any—fuss."

"Are you threatening me?"

"You bet your life I'm threatening you. And that's what you *would* be betting, too. That's *all* I have to say to *you*."

Samuel Eaton made no mention of the conversation with his father-in-law, nor could he bring himself to announce his change of mind to Martha directly. Instead he told Chanseilor he would agree to let Martha have the baby at The Mansion. He secretly admitted that he had taken an untenable position, but he secretly swore that the baby would grow up as a stranger to its Johnson grandparents. And now that the baby was a living being and its mother, in spite of the medical alarms, a well and happy person, Samuel Eaton wanted to get the two of them out of this house and begin his program of a life that would exclude the Raymond Johnsons.

He made his second visit of the day to his wife's old bedroom.

"How do you feel?" he said.

"Fine. A little tired, but I guess that's natural," she said.

"When do you think we can go home?"

"I don't know. I guess Fred will let me go home in a few days."

"Fred. If we ever have another baby we're going to have some other doctor."

"You mustn't be cross with Fred. I know why you're cross. Because he wanted me to stay here when the baby was born. But I have so much confidence in him."

"I've heard of women falling in love with their doctors. Is that happening to you?"

"Oh, Sam. I won't like it if you say things like that. If I weren't so tired I could get quite cross with you. Honestly I could. Please tell me you're sorry you said that."

"I'm sorry," said Samuel Eaton.

"And mean it. I want you to mean it."

"All right. I mean it."

"I wouldn't think of having another doctor—not that I'm

13

thinking of having another baby. You wouldn't either, not today, not if you were me. All I want to do is look at my baby and go to sleep and wake up and see my baby."

"Aren't we going to have any more children?"

"I suppose we are. But not for a long time."

"Oh, well. I was afraid you meant you didn't want any more."

"Is there no satisfying you, Sam? I've given you a son, I haven't recovered from that, and already you're making plans for more."

"No, I just misunderstood, that's all. For a minute I was afraid you were going to be one of those women that have one child and then don't want any more."

"I don't think any woman wants more the day after she's just given birth."

"Then how do you feel about me?"

"How do I feel about you? The same as I always do. I love you, you're my husband."

"Yes, but you don't seem very anxious to be husband and wife again."

"What *you* mean—the very thought of that is so far from my mind that I don't even want to talk about it. Not that I ever want to talk about it, but especially now."

"Don't you feel anything for me?"

"That way, I confess I don't. Let's not talk about it, any more. Really, there's something quite—common—talking about that now. Let's talk about something else, or if you can't, then I'd much rather you went downstairs . . . See, you make me say things I don't want to say."

"I'd better go, then."

"Give me a nice, gentle kiss, and then go have a cigar with Papa."

Samuel Eaton kissed his wife's forehead and left her. He went downstairs and in obedience to her suggestion, joined Raymond Johnson in the den.

"Care for a cigar?" said Johnson, pointing to the massive humidor.

"Yes, thanks, I will."

"The ones on the right, they're the ones from the Union League Club."

"I didn't know you belonged to the Union League. When did that happen?"

"It never did and it never will," said Raymond Johnson. "But I like a good cigar and I get those through a friend of mine. I have no use for clubs."

"You haven't? I have."

"Yes, I know you have, but you and I are different."

14

"In fact, I was thinking of putting my son up for a club that I just joined."

"Why don't you wait and see if he *wants* to join it?"

"He will," said Samuel Eaton.

The older man chuckled. "That, I must say . . . I heard of men entering their sons in a college . . . Have you done that yet?"

"No, but I will, right away. Do you mind if I use your writing paper?"

"Go right ahead, if it's for a college. Princeton, I daresay."

"Yes."

"But I just as soon you used your own stationery if it's to put him up for a club. A college is an altogether different matter. In fact I'd be willing to start a trust fund for his education, if that's all right with you."

"It isn't all right with me, thank you. And since the point's been raised, Mr. Johnson, let's have an understanding that everything my son gets, he gets from me."

"Well, I hope you have no objection if I leave him something in my will."

"Ah, but I do have an objection."

"You don't want me to leave him anything in my will?"

"Not a cent," said Samuel Eaton.

"Well, now there I don't think you're acting in the boy's best interests. You may not like me or my money, but the boy might. When he's ready to start out in the world, I'll bet he'll want all the money he can lay his hands on. Don't look down your nose at my money. It's clean. My money, that is, not your nose. I don't know anything about your nose, and care less. But I'm not going to let how you feel about me interfere with my grandson's finances. So in spite of your objections, I'm putting him in my will. If he doesn't want the money, he can give it to somebody else. But I know a lot more about this world than you do, and I'll bet he accepts my legacy. And he may even like me, you know. Young people like their grandparents, often as not."

"Sometimes they do, sometimes they don't."

"Correct. Sometimes they do, sometimes they don't. Sometimes they do in spite of what their own fathers or mothers may feel. Now for instance I don't expect you to encourage any affectionate feeling between the boy and me. That I don't expect at all. Quite the contrary. But don't be so all-fired sure that everything's going to turn out the way you want it to. A lot of sons don't like their father, and I notice when that happens, the young fellow often likes the grandfather, sometimes better than he likes the father."

"When that happens it's usually the father's fault, unless

15

the grandfather interferes and tries to spoil the boy. I've heard of that, too. Grandfathers trying to spoil their grandsons, turn them against their fathers."

"Maybe. I was thinking more of boys that just didn't like their fathers worth a hoot. Some boys are natured that way. No other explanation for it. I've seen fathers give the boy everything he could ask for, but the boy just can't get to like the father."

"Well, that wasn't the case with my father and I. He loved me and I loved him."

"Yes, if that hadn't been the case I never would of given my consent to Martha marrying you. Bill Eaton was a fine man. That's what you're calling the baby, isn't it? William Eaton?"

"We sure are."

"Well, if the boy lives up to his name he'll be a good man. Too bad Bill didn't live to see his grandson. He sees him, that I firmly believe, but it would have been a great joy to him on earth. Mm-hmm. Are you going to be here for supper?"

"If I'm expected."

"You're expected," said Raymond Johnson. "By the way, there's a lot of cards out in the hall, people stopped in. If you want to take a look at them you'll know who was here."

"Save them for Martha, if you don't mind."

"Well, I had an idea maybe you'd like to know too. Some of them asked to see you. By the way, did you know about the man killed in the freight yard?"

"What man?"

"One of those Rothermels on Maple Street. Four brothers of them."

"Yes, I know them. Why are you telling me? He didn't work for me. They all work for the packing-house."

"So they do. But the one that was killed, he was one of that crowd celebrating the birth of your son. I don't know if you realize it, but you started something scandalous last night. It's a wonder more weren't killed. They tell me that River Street was a positive disgrace today, men lying in the gutter."

"Rothermel wasn't one of my men. What happened to him?"

"He fell under the shifter in the Reading yards."

"What are you proposing I do? If he was one of my men— but do you expect me to go around and give his family some money?"

"No. I thought it would be better if you did it anonymously."

"Well I'll be damned if I see where I have any responsibility, if a man from the packing-house gets drunk."

"And killed. I'm going to give them something. I'm thinking of the baby upstairs. I don't like to think of him starting life

16

under any cloud. So I'm giving them something through their minister."

"That's your privilege."

"You're not going to help them at all?"

"No," said Samuel Eaton.

"Your father would have."

"You can't say what my father would have done. You didn't know him that well."

"Oh, yes I did. I knew the good things. Never mind."

"Never mind? I was never going to mind."

"I know. Do as you please," said Raymond Johnson.

"Mr. Johnson, all I want to do is take my wife and son and go to our own home and live our own life together."

"Young fellow, you can't do that any too soon for me."

The circumstances attending the birth of Samuel and Martha Eaton's second child were so different from the occurrences at the first that almost nothing was repeated. Raymond Alfred Eaton was born three years after his older brother. During those years Martha had overcome her own distaste for the act of love-making, or so she told her husband. In reality she never had been the cold, maidenly girl who suffered the attentions of her husband during the first year of their marriage. She was willing enough and curious, but throughout the first year, and until the first baby was born, she considered herself a bride, and the brides of her acquaintance were unwilling to trust each other with such confidences as a candid admission of enjoyment of any love-making that was advanced beyond the kiss on the lips, the close embrace in the moonlight. Martha Eaton was the mother of a son before she realized that she was not the only girl in Port Johnson who was living through the experience of passion with a man. Publicly, Martha and her friends maintained their virginity as long as they could, and when their size proclaimed their pregnancy they still had no language for the communication of details of their experience. When the baby was three months old (but not before) Martha permitted her husband to sleep with her again and they enjoyed each other. What had happened to her was that she unconsciously abandoned the public virginity and, again unconsciously, began to function as a woman. It was believed at that time that the act of giving birth made a physical difference in the young wife's capacity for enjoyment of love-making. Actually it was nothing more than the relaxation that came with the realization that no one else cared whether she slept with her husband or not: she was a married woman and it was taken for granted.

In those years between the birth of the first and the second babies Samuel and Martha Eaton were completely in love, and when she found herself pregnant for the second time it was she who announced that the new baby would be born on the farm. Her visits to The Mansion had been frequent, but timed so that they took place while Samuel Eaton was at the mill. Her father came home at noon every day, and he would see his daughter and his grandson. As for encounters with his son-in-law, there would often be stretches of two months during which Raymond Johnson did not lay eyes on Samuel Eaton. Samuel Eaton did not come home for lunch; he ate the noon meal at Schoffstal's Café, an oyster house and saloon that served the best restaurant food and catered to the richest men in town, and was the nearest thing to a gentlemen's club that Port Johnson had in the nineteenth century. Martha's arrangement was, of course, satisfactory all around: to the men, because it made it easy for them to avoid each other, and for Martha, because she was able to see her family without putting the peace in jeopardy.

Her announcement of the second pregnancy was not treated by her or her husband with the solemnity or drawn-out subtlety of the first. "I'm going to have another baby," she said.

He laughed. "Well, I guess we're not surprised at *that*," he said, and she laughed with him.

The baby was born without the blowing of whistles and ringing of bells and orgiastic celebration on River Street that had greeted the arrival of the first Eaton son. The father treated the next day's lunch crowd at Schoffstal's to champagne wine and good cigars, but the workmen at Eaton's were not given the day off, with or without pay. It was still an Eaton baby, and the occasion was potentially more important to the towns-folk than the dropping of a foal on one of the neighboring stock farms, but the celebration for the first baby remained unique in the town history, no less so than in the Eaton family.

Samuel Eaton now knew that when William was born he had secretly been at least as much concerned about the baby as he had been about its mother. This time his attitude was changed. He wanted nothing to happen to his wife, and if it had come to the point of making a decision he would un-hesitatingly have chosen Martha to be the survivor.

In the early days of the new baby's life Samuel Eaton spent far more time with Martha than with his second son, which had not been the case with William. Moreover, he also spent more time with the three-year-old William than with the new child. William was a husky blond child who was among other things a living refutation of Raymond Johnson's notions of the father-and-son relationship.

IN THE DAYS immediately preceding and following William's burial there was not much for Alfred to do. He had been out of school for nearly three weeks, but it was not like a real holiday. There was no other boy to play with, not even on Saturday and Sunday, since the parents of his friends at Professor Phillipson's were terrified by the danger of contagion, a fear which was not diminished by the attitude of the Port Johnson medical men. In later years as he looked back on those days, Alfred Eaton described himself as feeling suddenly naked, exposed: for eleven years as William's younger brother and for nine years as older brother to Sally and seven years as older brother to Constance he had lived in a kind of obscurity, which had not always been pleasant, but seemed pleasant in retrospect now that he was suddenly the oldest child, and conspicuous. He had never been close to William; the three-year difference in ages is likely to be enormous when both children are under ten. He had admired William and sometimes envied him, but William had only tolerated Alfred. To William, Alfred was a nuisance, someone he was ordered to be nice to, and belonging to a separate branch of the family that consisted of Alfred, Sally, and Constance. If William slapped Alfred or otherwise punished him, the difference in ages was always mentioned while William himself was being punished; and each time that that occurred the age separation contributed to a strengthening of the separation that was already there because of, among other considerations, the two distinct personalities. William had always spoken up with older people. There was no timidity about his questions or in the way he asked them, and when he was censured for being disobedient or disrespectful he defended himself as against equals. "A manly boy . . . he speaks right up to you . . . he looks you straight in the eye . . . he's not afraid of anyone . . ." Those were some of the comments inspired by William. In their attempts at a fair distribution of compliments the same people would say of Alfred: "Beautiful manners . . . the thoughtful type . . . quite aristocratic-looking, but none of the overbearing, if you know what I mean."

At the age of eleven Alfred was not able to describe his new position as only son. He would not have been able to say to anyone that he felt naked or exposed, any more than he would have been able to reveal that in the first eleven years of his life he had been content in his obscurity. It is barely possible that if the proper questions had been asked, he might have

19

been able at eleven to come forth with answers that would reveal his previous state of mind in regard to his brother: that since nothing was expected of him and everything was expected of William, he had accepted the situation. But no one was sufficiently interested in what Alfred Eaton felt to formulate the proper questions.

Nevertheless, the nakedness, the feeling of being exposed and, more serious, the abrupt removal of the protection that he had enjoyed in obscurity were real if undefined. For three weeks all thought and activity on the farm had been concentrated on William and his condition. Alfred was called in the morning, given his breakfast with the girls, and told to go out and play, but not to wander off the farm, and not to get dirty. He and his sisters were dressed as if for school; each morning Alfred put on his school suit and an Eton collar, on instructions from Nellie, the maid. So it had been for three weeks, and so it continued until the day immediately following William's burial.

On that morning Nellie came to the boys' room—now suddenly Alfred's room exclusively—and found him already dressed. "Oh, you're up. Well, if you're up why didn't you go down to breakfast and save me the trip?"

He made no answer; it would have been futile to try to explain to Nellie that he was waiting for some sign from his father or his mother; some sign, some word that would tell him what to expect in the future—or indeed, in the present. His brother was buried, buried deep in the ground, and would never be seen again, never again heard. Things were different now, with no William, and there *must* be *some* things his mother and father wanted to tell him. It was not clear in his mind what kind of things, but they *must* want to talk to him.

"Where is my mother?" he said.

"She's with your father," said Nellie.

"Where's my *father*?"

"They're in their room."

"Did *they* have *their* breakfast?"

"They had a cup of tea," said Nellie. "But don't you go bothering them, if that's what you were thinking of doing."

"Isn't my father going to the mill?"

"I don't know if he is or if he isn't."

"Aren't they going to have breakfast with us?"

"That's something I don't know either."

"Oh, Nellie, didn't they *tell* you?"

"They did not."

"Are their places set?"

"Yes, their places are set."

"Then they must be going to have breakfast with us."

20

"I wouldn't count on it if I was you. But that don't say they aint, either. I'm not privileged to know their intentions. But you scurry on down, Mister Questions. The sooner you're done the sooner I can clear the table. I have a lot of work to do."

He went down to the diningroom and ate his oatmeal and toast and strawberry jam and drank his milk. His sisters were already eating when he arrived. He ate rapidly and in silence.

"Are we going to school tomorrow?" said Sally.

"I don't know," said Alfred.

"What *do* you know?" said Sally.

"Oh, Smarty," said Alfred.

"That's rude," said Constance.

"Oh, rude, rude," said Alfred. "Eat your slop and shut up."

"If Mother heard you!" said Constance.

He got up. *"Dear* Miss Eaton, may I *please* be excused?"

"Not till you roll up your napkin and put it in the ring, dear Mr. Slop Eaton," said Sally.

"Where are you going?" said Constance.

"I'm going out to the pig-pen and get you some more slop," said Alfred.

"Rude, rude, rude, rude, rude, rude, rude, rude," said Constance.

"Listen to the little baby, she can only say one word," said Alfred.

"Rude, rude, rude, rude, rude, rude, rude," said Constance.

"She hasn't learned to talk yet," said Alfred.

"Rude, rude, rude, rude," said Constance.

"Oh, dear me, I thought it was a human being but I was wrong. It's a little pig with oatmeal all over her chin."

"Slop, slop, slop, slop, slop," said Constance.

"There, I made you say something else," said Alfred.

"You did not," said Constance.

"I did so," said Alfred, and left the room.

He left the house and walked to the stable, where there might be some things to do, where at least there was George Fry to listen to.

In the stable-yard the chestnut mare Missy was standing tied and harnessed up except for her bridle, while George Fry was carrying forkfuls of old bedding to the manure pit.

"Hello," said Alfred.

"Now keep out of my way or I'm liable to get you all over horse-shit and you wouldn't want that, all dressed up for fair. But don't stand too near that mare or you're liable to get a kick that'll send you into the middle of next week. Now mind, I warned you."

"She won't kick me," said Alfred. He patted the animal's neck. "Will you, Missy? No, you wouldn't kick me."

"Now don't go putting your hand in her mouth or you're liable to go home missing all your fingers."

"I wasn't putting my hand in her mouth."

"You don't think you were, but it's liable to be in there before you know it. She took a snap at your brother Wi—" He did not finish the name. "Sit over on the fence. No, don't. You're liable to get whitewash on your breeches and I'd be the one to blame."

"Is my father driving in to town?"

"Well, there's the mare, harnessed up, and there's the cut-under. That's the way it looks."

"When is he going?"

"When he's ready."

"But he always says what time he'll be ready," said Alfred.

"No, he don't. He didn't this morning. He said to have it ready about ha' past nine."

"Are you going with him?"

"Do I look as if I was going with him?"

An electric bell on the stable wall sounded three times.

"There he is," said George Fry. "Hold up the shafts." He put on the bridle and backed the mare into the cut-under, and Alfred automatically helped with the harness. "Two laps," said George Fry. "Do you want a ride to the house?"

"Yes," said Alfred. He got in and sat on the edge of the cushion. He saw his father at the front door, pulling on his yellow gloves. His father looked in their direction, then suddenly turned away and continued to look away until the carriage stopped.

"Good morning, sir," said Fry.

"Good morning, George. Good morning, son," said Samuel Eaton.

"Father?" said the boy.

"What?"

"Take me?" said the boy.

The father walked around the carriage to the right-hand side and picked up the reins, which Fry had wound around the whip.

"Father, will you?"

"Will I what?"

"Take me?" said the boy.

"I can't," said Samuel Eaton. He did not look at the boy, but turned his head in the boy's direction, telling him without words to get out of the carriage. The boy obeyed the unspoken order and went inside the house without looking back.

"All right, George, thanks," said Samuel Eaton.

Fry stood away from the mare and Samuel Eaton drove off. Fry watched the carriage turning the corner of the driveway.

"You son of a bitch, how could you do that to a little boy?"
he muttered.

He went to the front door and opened it and called out:
"Alfred? Come help me with the—with the things. D'ye hear
me, Alfred?"

When lunch-time came that day Martha Eaton was at her
place at table as the girls, then Alfred, went in.

"Hands clean?" said Martha.

"Mine are," said Constance.

"So're mine," said Sally.

"Alfred?"

The boy looked at his hands.

"I meant washed. The girls knew what I meant, *and so did
you,* Alfred." She spoke pleasantly and as though she and
Alfred were having a little joke.

"Do I have to go upstairs and wash them?" said Alfred.

"You may wash them in the kitchen, but if you *had* washed
in the trough you wouldn't have to wash them now, and then
you wouldn't be getting in Josephine's way and holding up
our lunch." The tone continued to be pleasant, but all the
words had been critical, and it was not a good beginning for
their first meal together in such a long, long while.

He went out to the kitchen and turned on the water. "A lick
and a promise," said Josephine. She never failed to say exactly that. "And don't rub all the dirt off on my towel." He
dried his hands on the roller towel and returned to the diningroom.

"Well, that was quick. May I see?" said Martha Eaton.

He showed her his hands.

"Those nails. After lunch you and I are going to have a
manicure," said Martha.

"Alfred's in mourning. He has black under his fingernails,"
said Sally, in sing-song.

"I don't think that's a very nice thing to say," said Martha,
and then as she studied the faces of the three children she
realized that Sally's remark had not had any double meaning
to them. She was quite prepared to be affected herself. "Constance, I'll let you ring."

"Oh, goody!" said Constance. She swung the bell, vigorously.

"They heard you," said Alfred. "They could hear you in
Reading."

"That will do, thank you, Constance," said Martha. "Can
anyone guess what we're having for lunch?"

"Brussels sprouts, I smelt them," said Sally.

"Blanc mange," said Constance.

"How do you know?" said Alfred.

"Nellie," said Constance.

Nellie appeared with the first tray.

"Nellie, are we having blanc mange?" said Alfred.

"I'm sure I don't know," said Nellie, winking at Martha.

"You told me we were," said Constance.

"Who knows, that may have been for dinner," said Martha Eaton.

"Or tomorrow breakfast," said Nellie.

"Oh, who ever heard of blanc mange at breakfast," said Constance.

"Some people eat pie for breakfast," said Alfred.

"They do not. Pie for breakfast. Who ever heard of pie for breakfast!" said Constance.

"Alfred's right. Grandfather Johnson used to eat pie for breakfast," said Martha.

"Did you ever eat pie for breakfast?" said Constance.

"Yes, often," said Martha.

"Well, I wish we could have it," said Constance.

"Oatmeal is much better for you," said Martha.

"Mother," said Alfred.

"Yes, dear?"

"Why can't we have pie for breakfast?"

"Oatmeal is healthier," said Martha.

"But we have apple dumplings sometimes on Sunday and that's the same as pie. It's just dough and apples."

"Where did you put Billy's napkin ring?" said Sally.

"Me?" said Nellie.

"Or Mother," said Sally.

"I have it upstairs, dear. It isn't lost," said Martha.

"Won't Billy *ever* come back? *Ever?*" said Constance.

"I told you he wouldn't," said Sally.

"No, he's in heaven with the little Lord Jesus," said Martha.

"He doesn't know the little Lord Jesus," said Constance.

"But the little Lord Jesus knows him," said Martha. "They're very happy together."

"How do you know?" said Constance.

"Because everybody is happy with the little Lord Jesus."

"I'm not. I don't know Him. I never saw Him," said Constance.

"Well, you know what He looks like," said Sally. "You've seen pictures of Him."

"They're all different," said Constance.

"It's religion," said Alfred. "Don't you go to Sunday School?"

"Yes, but . . ." Constance paused to think.

"But what?" said Alfred.

"I don't understand it," said Constance.

"What don't you understand, dear?" said Martha.

"The whole thing."

24

"Well, there's a lot to learn and you can't learn it all at once. The little Lord Jesus sent for Billy, and so Billy went to heaven."

"But I don't think that was nice of the little Lord Jesus to make him so sick. Billy had to throw up—"

"Not at the table," said Sally.

"And why did He send for Billy? Why didn't He send for Alfred?"

The boy looked at his mother.

"Because—" she began.

"He wanted Billy," said Alfred.

"No," said Martha. "Not because he *preferred* Billy, but perhaps because, you see we don't always understand what God does, and the little Lord Jesus—*I* know! At least I think He wanted Alfred to stay here and take care of all of us. And that's what Alfred will do, too, won't you, dear?"

"I guess so. I don't know," said the boy.

"Isn't Father going to take care of us any more?" said Constance.

"Oh, yes, of course. All of us. But Alfred is the older brother now, and he'll take care of his younger sisters, and me."

"What if I don't want him to?" said Constance.

"Then he will anyway," said Sally.

"No I won't," said Alfred. "If you don't want me to take care of you, I won't."

"When is he going to take care of us? What's he going to do?"

"Well, we can all begin by turning over a new leaf," said Martha. "All try to be nicer to each other and loving each other like real brothers and sisters should. And now I'd like to change the subject and tell you about a surprise I have for you."

"What?" said Constance.

"It depends on the weather, but—"

"A picnic!" said Constance.

"That's a very good guess," said Martha. "Yes, if it stays like this till supper-time I thought it would be nice if all four of us each took our own basket and had early supper in the grove."

"Isn't Father coming?" said Constance.

"No, he's not coming home till late. He has a lot of things to do."

"Can I have a banana?" said Constance.

"Not before you go to bed," said Sally.

"I didn't ask you, Sally," said Constance.

"A half," said Martha.

"I don't want a half, I want a whole one or I don't want any."

25

"Let her have a whole one and give her the gripes," said Alfred.

"Alfred!" said Martha. "I don't like that one bit, and besides, that isn't the way you're supposed to act now."

"All right, I don't care what she has," said Alfred.

"Well, I'm not sure we have any, so that'll take care of that," said Martha.

"We can get some," said Constance.

"Oh, Constance, this picnic isn't only for you," said Sally.

"I didn't say it was," said Constance.

"A person'd think it was," said Alfred. "Mother?"

"What, dear?"

"When are we going back to school?"

"Oh, are you anxious to get back to school? I'm glad to hear that. Next Monday."

"Not till then?" said Alfred.

"No, there's no use starting again in the middle of the week. Your father is speaking to Professor Phillipson today, if he remembers to with all those things on his mind. And children, when you go back?"

"What?" said Sally.

"Just be like everyone else, don't behave any differently than anyone else."

"Why should we behave any differently than anyone else, Mother?" said Constance.

"*Billy*, you ignoramus," said Alfred.

"Alfred, how many times must I remind you? Now let's see what else we'd like to have on our picnic. What kinds of sandwiches would we all like?"

A late afternoon shower made picnicking in the grove inadvisable. The festivities, such as they were, took place on the side porch and were scarcely different from having a meal in the diningroom, the only notable differences being the fare and the absence of the husband-and-father. A family meal without Samuel Eaton's attendance was conducted in a lighter atmosphere than otherwise, an atmosphere that was not made heavy by his voice. With Samuel Eaton at his rightful place at table the child or children to his right sat as though they had their heads ever so slightly turned leftward, ready to look at him if addressed; and similarly for the child or children to his left with their heads attentive rightward. He was apt to interrupt himself in a long story with a quick observation of what a child was doing with its food; not simply a comment on *what* the child was eating or not eating, but *how* the food was being eaten or spurned: "Alfred found a snake in his cauliflower . . . Sally's still digging for more potatoes. They're all gone, Sally. You can have some more if you ask . . ." He was blessed with exceptionally good teeth and

26

mastication was quick, so that his table talk was practically continual. Through the years it never occurred to him that one reason for the sparsity of communication between himself and his children was that he had not taken advantage and they had not been able to take advantage of meal-time as an occasion for two-way or three-way conversation. If he felt like talking, he dominated; if he was disturbed or distracted and uncommunicative, he made no effort at all, and discouraged the efforts of others. Forensically, the meal-times were wasted. The picnic on the porch was physically too close to the dining-room and in time too near the customary hour for Samuel Eaton's return home. It was not a success, and they all blamed the rain.

It was customary for Alfred to have the privilege of staying up a half hour longer than Sally and Constance, whose hours were alike. "Off to bed, young ladies, and I'll be up in a little while," said Martha.

The girls obeyed.

"I'm going, too," said Alfred.

Martha was suddenly alarmed. "Don't you feel well, dear?"

"I'm not sick, Mother. I'm all right, honestly I am."

"But you don't have to go up yet, you can wait till your father gets home."

"I don't want to," said the boy.

"Why? You haven't done something wrong, have you?"

"No."

"Just very, very tired?" said Martha.

"Uh-huh."

Martha readily accepted the explanation that she was more than willing to accept. "All right, dear. You get yourself ready for bed and I'll be up after I've tucked the girls in."

The three children mounted the stairs to the second story. The girls turned off to their own room and Alfred continued on his way to the third floor by way of the enclosed stairway with its doors at the bottom and at the top.

Billy's bed had not been taken out of the boys' room. It was covered over with a bedspread, under which there was a single pillow and no other bedclothes. Something had been said about burning the mattress, but nothing had been done. Alfred sat on the edge of Billy's bed while taking off his shoes. The room contained more of Billy's possessions than of Alfred's: an ash bow and a canvas quiver that George Fry had made; photographs of battleships; an unframed tacked-up certificate for school attendance; a small sword and scabbard that had been made by one of the blacksmiths at the mill (and which the boys had been forbidden to use as a plaything); a Civil War fieldpiece model from the same source; an Indian war canoe made of buckskin; a football nose guard that had once been worn by a member of the Princeton team; a fine scale model of a P. & R. camelback locomotive that had been a gift to Samuel Eaton. There were many more souvenirs and presents, which had preempted most of the available space. In all likelihood they would remain undisturbed until it was time for Alfred to go to boarding-school, but it was not a prospect that bothered Alfred. He liked most of the articles, and their removal would have left the room strangely bare, just as the removal of Billy's bed would have acted upon him more forcibly as a reminder of his brother's death than the real presence of the bed did now.

The room was lighted by a single weak incandescent bulb suspended from the center of the slanted ceiling, directly above the foot of the boys' beds. The bulb gave off only enough light to keep you from stumbling into the furniture, and not enough to read by, but Billy had never complained.

Alfred hung up his clothes in his closet, not so much from habit as from the knowledge that his mother would be visiting him shortly. For the same reason he brushed his teeth at the washstand, knowing that the toothbrush would be examined for moisture. Martha Eaton was a long time coming to his room, or so it seemed to Alfred, but then he heard the muffled beat of her feet on the steps and the click of the latch on the top door.

"Still awake?" she said.

"Uh-huh," he said.

"Brush your teeth and everything?"

"Uh-huh."

"Do you want anything before I say goodnight?"

"No thanks," said the boy.

"Very tired, aren't you? Well, it has been a long day, the first day . . ." She was forcing herself not to look at the other bed. "I hope we have better weather tomorrow, then we can have our picnic. I was thinking downstairs, I said to the girls we might have a picnic *lunch* tomorrow instead of supper. That way we won't wait all day and then be disappointed. Unless, of course, if it rains around noon."

"Mother?"

"Yes dear?"

"How old do I have to be before I go away to school?"

"How old? Do you mean how old or what grade?"

"Well, either one. When am I going?"

"Well, you're in fifth grade. Three more years at the earliest. That will make you fourteen. Do you want to go, or don't you? That is, are you looking forward to it, or not?"

"I guess I am."

"Oh," said Martha Eaton. "I was going to say, if you weren't

28

looking forward to it we might wait till tenth grade. But you *are* looking *forward* to it?"

"Yes, I guess so."

"Billy would have been going next fall," said Martha Eaton.

"Am I going to the same school?"

"I don't know. St. Paul's. Do you want to?"

"No," said the boy.

"Oh? Why not? Too far away?"

"I guess so."

She brightened a little. "Well, that's all right, because there's a new school down near Norristown. Knox School. It was started by a friend of your father's from Princeton, and we had a letter from him last year saying he'd like us to consider it. Billy was already entered in St. Paul's so we had to tell Mr.— I forget his name. But your father said he'd keep it in mind when it came time to send you. It might be a very good idea if we were to write to him. Then next year or the year after we could all go over and have a look at it. Wouldn't that be nice?"

"Uh-huh."

"I know the place they bought. It used to be owned by a friend of Grandfather Johnson's. It has a lot of ground around it and they grow their own vegetables, or they used to. I don't know how it is now."

"Do they have swimming?"

"Let me think. I went there once when I was about fifteen, just for the day. I remember crossing a bridge, a small bridge, so they must have had a brook."

"Is it very near Norristown?"

"Not within walking distance, at least I remember we took the train to Norristown and then had a quite a long drive from there. I don't like schools to be too near a town. Now I'm going to turn out the light and you can go right to sleep."

She had remained standing all during her visit, although in times past she had always sat on one of the boys' beds. She leaned down and kissed Alfred but did not touch him with her hands. "Snug as a bug?"

"Uh-huh."

"Goodnight, dear," she said.

"G'night," said the boy.

She reached up and turned the switch and left the darkened room. He heard her close the top stairway door, and her steps on the stairs and, faintly, the bottom stairway door being closed. Then he got out of bed and turned on the light. He lay there and listened to all the familiar sounds, so familiar that they had become unheard, but now he gave a bit of attention to each: the rustle of leaves in the trees, the signals of insects and birds in the early evening, hoofbeats in the distance, a

29

long train of coal cars and the locomotive whistle, shriller than the whistle of a passenger locomotive; and always somewhere a suspicious dog. It was so long since he had given individual attention to these sounds; it may have been a lifetime, his own, since he had consciously listened to them. But then there came one that he recognized and could even guess with accuracy how long it would last: the sound of his father with Missy and the cut-under, coming up the lane, going past the house and out to the stable-yard. Then there would be the hard beat of his father's heels on the flagstone walk through the garden.

Now he would be entering the house, now exchanging greetings with his wife, talking to her in the den.

Then, surprisingly, his mother on the enclosed stairs and entering his room.

"Alfred?" she said.

"What?"

"The light. Didn't I turn it out? I'm sure I did. Did you turn it on again?"

"Yes, Mother."

"But why? You know that's not allowed."

"I wasn't sleepy."

"You weren't sleepy? You could hardly hold your head up, you were so sleepy. Are you all right?"

"Yes."

"Then please go to sleep, and don't you turn it on again or I'll be very cross. Your father had no *idea* what was going on up here. Hadn't been for him *I* never would have known. Now off to sleep and no more funny business." She snapped out the light and went downstairs again.

Alfred Eaton was never able to remember truthfully whether he had turned on the light to dispel the darkness, or to have it burning in the hope that his father might come to his room. In any case he now went to sleep and when he awoke Nellie was standing over him, holding a glass kerosene lamp and wearing a bathrobe over her muslin nightgown.

"What is it, boy?" she said. "What's the matter?"

"I don't know," he said.

"Was it a nightmare you had?" She put down the lamp and sat on the edge of his bed. "I could hear you in my room."

"I don't know."

"It's twelve o'clock at night, boy. Do you want to go to the toilet?"

"No."

"I know, it was a nightmare. Them cheese sandwiches give it to you."

He put out his arms to her and with some hesitation she put her arms around him and held him to her. "Get rid of the

30

bad dreams, boy, get rid of the bad dreams." She made it into toneless song and continued to hold him, then she stopped and looked at him. "Do you know what you're doing, Alfred?"

"Hold on to me," he said.

"Is it the teat you want?"

He nodded, and she undid the string over her nightgown. "Don't ever let on," she said. "You must promise me that." He kissed her with tenderness and then with strength and then lay back.

"Did you?"

"Did I what?"

"Yes, you did," she said. "Now go to sleep and don't never breathe a word of this. This is a sin for me, a mortal sin. Will you sleep in peace now, child. But God forgive me for my own thoughts and desires. There, now. There, now." He was asleep, and she left him.

Nellie had been a widow for twelve of her thirty-one years; childless, thick-set, strong, humorless and manless. The death of her husband in a Lantenengo County mining accident had been the most dramatic moment of her life. Her marriage to him had removed her from the totally rejected; she was *Mrs.* But no other man had come along and there was no probability that one would, since Nellie offered neither comeliness nor money, and since her job offered little opportunity to make the acquaintance of a man who could discover her companionship, her warmth, and her willingness to work.

On the day and the days after she comforted Alfred Eaton she conscientiously gave him no look that could be interpreted as inviting. Indeed, she could hardly wait for Saturday afternoon when she and Josephine were taken to Port Johnson to make their confession. And while she was behaving so austerely toward Alfred, the boy was unconsciously cooperating by seeing nothing but her plainness and wondering—dishonestly—whether the experience had been something besides a dream. What he did not know was that she was as terrified as he that their secret might not be kept. She had no reason for fear on that score. It was a secret he wanted to keep, and it was his first and for a long while the only secret of that nature that he possessed. It was not unusual for boys of his acquaintance to have had experiences with servants as a result of their own curiosity or the near-celibate living conditions of the maids. But Alfred had always felt some disgust with the boys and their stories, and in any event his own story was not one that would make him seem manly in the telling: the experience had come about because he had been frightened in a dream, and there was no other way to tell the story than to reveal that he had been afraid like a baby.

He had another reason, or two other reasons, for wanting to

bury his secret. He was in love with a girl nearly his own age and he loved another girl who was considerably older. Victoria Dockwiler was the same age as Sally Eaton and in the same grade, and was one of Sally's close friends, but Sally's friendship did not make Victoria more accessible. Alfred saw her only at dancing school and at the infrequent children's parties. She was an extremely quiet girl with large brown eyes, unusually smooth and remarkably white skin and with delicate features already formed so that it was easy to imagine how she would look when she grew up. Her lips were thin but curving, and her mouth was usually closed. She often substituted a nod for a spoken word, and her eyes seemed to be taking in everything but withholding expression of anything, as though nothing surprised her and she possessed the wisdom of a grandmother. He was sure that some day he would marry her, to look at her face and to be with her for all time. He had nothing much to say to her, and she had nothing much to say to anyone. His conversations with her were skeletally factual: "Can I have the pleasure of this dance? . . . Merry Christmas if I don't see you . . . Don't bother about the door, I'll close it . . . Here's your ice cream . . ." He could not think of her as belonging to the same sexual organization as his sisters, who also wore skirts and curls, nor to the same race of animal as Nellie. There was a faded photograph of his mother in an oval walnut frame that showed points of resemblance between Victoria and his mother at the same age, but the resemblance was neither strong nor remarkable, since Martha Eaton and Victoria's mother were related within the third degree of kindred. And to a boy of eleven a girlhood photograph of his mother was a picture of someone he had never known, while Victoria was a living and beautiful creature, and really what had happened to him with Nellie had happened to someone else, because it was not the same person who loved Victoria Dockwiler.

His other love was Norma Budd, who was eighteen or nineteen and who could scarcely be called a Port Johnson girl, although she was born in the town. She would come home for Christmas and for a few days at the beginning of summer, but her family had a house in Locust Street in Philadelphia and her mother was the first woman whom Alfred ever heard described as a social climber, a term which meant nothing to him. Norma herself was said to be "just a wee bit too vivacious," but she had a quick and broad smile and large white teeth for it, and she always, without fail, shook his hand and said, "How is my friend Alfred Eaton?" in a way that he could not distrust. She had once sent him a postcard from London, England, and on her return she had brought him a leaden representation of a member of the Household Cavalry, one of the few possessions he was able to keep in his room. He never stopped to question what she saw in him; such friendliness was not to be questioned. And he loved her, and always would.

It was, therefore, many years, many years, before Alfred Eaton told anyone about his experience with Nellie, and he never told it to another man.

The Eaton children went back to school that Monday and the boys at Professor Phillipson's were unexpectedly considerate and kind, influenced perhaps by the professor himself. At morning assembly he concluded the announcements with the remark that "We are glad to have back with us Alfred Eaton, fifth grade, whose beloved brother as we all know passed away. The school has already expressed sympathy to the parents of our schoolmate—both schoolmates—and I'm sure we welcome Alfred back in the true spirit of fellowship that, uh, that prevails, or I like to think prevails in our school. Whilst he was kept out of school by doctor's orders Alfred was given home work to do, and, uh, I'm sure he will have no great difficulty, uh, catching up with his class. And, uh, that will be all for this morning. By twos, eighth grade first and so on down."

Seneca Phillipson had originally made a living by teaching music, principally piano and principally to the daughters of Montgomery Street. He added to his small income by taking on tutoring jobs for boys of preparatory-school age who were having difficulty with Latin, Greek, and French. One day he saw the opportunity to earn a more dependable income and to give up the onerous chores with the Port Johnson young ladies, and by the following September he had established a boys' private school and practically overnight he had become a respected as well as a respectable member of the community. He retained the title of professor, which was by common consent given to any man who taught music, and about which he felt some uneasiness because his own father was a bona fide professor at Amherst College. But he ran a good school, assisted in the lower grades by two young normal-school graduates, and was planning for the day when he would be headmaster of a full-scale preparatory institution with—who could tell?—boarders as well as day scholars. At the moment he was contended with the success of his school and with the knowledge that he could go home at night and play Franz Liszt only when it pleased him. He paid himself $1500 a year, and the trustees of the school, who were the richest and most worthwhile men in Port Johnson, administered the other financial affairs. He had a good thing, and it would be a good thing so long as his wife was able to recognize certain symptoms in time and hustle him to New York for his three-day bouts with the bottle. Ironically, in his present prosperous days it was easier to go to New York "to buy books" than it had been in the music-teaching period, when a canceled lesson meant no pay as well as the danger of discovery. Between book-buying sprees he was straight as a die, not even dependent on one of the 40 percent alcohol nostrums that were so popular among men and women who had their own good and sufficient reasons for shunning whiskey. Straight as a die, he was, and proud of his strength of character as demonstrated by the lengthening of the periods between New York trips. In that connection his wife felt it inadvisable to point out that when he did go, he stayed longer. She was playing a game with time, hoping that soon he would be able to have a few drinks, frequently, with men on his board of trustees, before any of them found out the real purpose of the trips to New York. It would be a nice life if Seneca could have a couple of drinks a day, openly, but in her heart she knew that with the coming of a certain wildly morose look in his eye, he would always have to drink himself unconscious, that the second day would demand another large amount of whiskey to get over the first day's effects, and the third or the fourth day's drinking was necessary to enable him to face reality again. In another day he had been able to blame the ungifted young ladies of Port Johnson, but with the school such a success and his plans for it so great he no longer had an excuse nor sought to invent one. She had a horrid suspicion, but she felt that the suspicion made her an evil person for entertaining it, and she had no real reason for entertaining it. And whatever he was, he worked hard, and he was good to her.

By the end of the school day the boys at Professor Phillipson's had become accustomed to Alfred Eaton again. For a while they would occasionally miss Billy, when there would be something to remind them of him, especially in the eighth and seventh grades. But there were fewer than eighty boys in the entire school and before three-thirty all of them had seen Alfred and all those whom he normally spoke to had spoken to him. There were no expressions of sympathy and no explicit words of welcome. A few boys had said, "Hello, Alfred," more softly than was their custom, and that was the extent of their ability to express themselves sentimentally. As to the teachers, one of them even forgot that Alfred was not expected to hand in any home work that day, and the entire class reminded him in chorus: "Alfred wasn't here Friday," and there was some laughter at the teacher's forgetfulness.

"Well, everybody forgets sometime," said the teacher.

A week since Billy died; two weeks since Billy died; one month ago today Billy died. Then that stretch of time until they would be able to say, "One year ago today Billy died."

The girls were the first to let their brother slip into the past. On a day in early summer Constance said to her sister: "Do you remember Billy?"

"Of course I remember him," said Sally. "He only died in —April. April the—whatever it was."

"I don't remember him," said Constance.

"You do so or you wouldn't be talking about him."

"Oh, I *remember* him, but I can't remember what his face looked like."

"Then go look at his pictures in Mother and Father's room."

"Later," said Constance.

The conversation remained with Sally and when she was able to be alone with her mother she said: "Alfred doesn't look like Billy, does he, Mother?"

"Not very much, at least not now. Why? Have you been thinking about Billy, dear? I don't want you to feel badly. After all, you have a life of—"

Sally interrupted her. "He didn't look much like that picture, either, did he?"

"No, I'm afraid not, it isn't a very good likeness, which reminds me we must all have our pictures taken. We must make a habit of it at least once a year," said Martha. Then: "But surely you remember what Billy looked like."

"I guess so."

But for Martha to have expected continuing grief was inconsistent with her own experience. With the death of the child there had come an enormous sorrow and a void and a practical sense of wasted pain and wasted effort and wasted love, but the enormous sorrow was becoming a sufficient and satisfactory thing, as large in her life as a living child and not nearly so much trouble. In fact, no trouble at all. Martha Eaton now had a sorrow instead of a living son called William. The politeness of the day practically forbade any but the most infrequent and most delicate reference to a recently deceased, and oddly enough the custom in many instances had the desired effect of sparing the bereaved any pain, but more than that, it had the unintended effect of making the bereaved forget the inspiration for the sorrow and retain only the sorrow itself. But none of this held true for Samuel Eaton.

It might be obvious to someone else but it was not obvious to Samuel Eaton that he was grieving for a part of himself, and since he knew only what he knew and was a man who had little truck with the souls of other men, the grief was, for him, an active, real, omnipresent emotion; a tremendous, loving pity for a boy whose life had been taken away. Yet, that was indeed it: he felt sorry for a bright and happy boy who was not allowed to go on living. And since that was what Samuel Eaton believed, for him it was the truth. Samuel Eaton now had a sorrow *and* a living son called William who was dead. What he believed was, for him, the truth and it was what he functioned on. He lived in and was a product of a time in which the palpable emotions and motives were not questioned. Some people grieved more than some other people, and the difference was taken to mean that the people who grieved the most, felt most deeply. A man could love one child more than he loved another child, as everyone has always known to be true, and if the better loved child died, the man suffered greater grief, and without examination by himself or by his contemporaries of the reasons for the greater love or the greater grief. Samuel Eaton lived in the iron age and in his time it was no more difficult to explain him than it was to explain iron. Not only was it not difficult; it was not a problem. It was the last time in the history of the world when hate, envy, greed, heroism, kindness and love were acceptable in themselves without further scrutiny.

He was now forty-six years old, Samuel Eaton. His time for raising children had passed—that is, for having new children. He wanted no infants about the house, even taking for granted that he and Martha could have another. They were in the habit of taking precautions against having any more, and they would continue the habit. Martha was yet to express any desire to have a new baby to keep the balance of children at two boys and two girls, but there was no need to discuss the matter since the precautions were taken by him. Even if he could be guaranteed a son, he wanted no more. He had a son, who would grow up and continue the family name (Samuel hated his own first name; the hayseed jokes in the periodicals and on the stage always had a Samuel). Children were for the young, for the early years of marriage. As a man approached fifty he wanted more quiet and an orderly household. Constance was too young, and though he loved her next after Billy, he often wished he could hasten her growth. She was getting heavy on his knee, and in their evening chats between his supper and his dinner she could not seem to realize that he had been up since six in the morning and been on the go all day. He had been able to discontinue the custom of carrying her upstairs. ("Just be firm with her two or three nights and she'll know you mean it," Martha had said.) He was thinking of installing a toilet and washstand on the main floor so that when he came home from work he could save himself the climb to his own bathroom. A man did a good day's work and he was entitled to come home and see his children, but then they ought to let him have his glass of whiskey and a look at the paper in peace. Martha was arranging things to just that end, and she was pretty good at it, but Martha could handle some things without a slip, even a complicated thing; then she had a way of following it up by making a botch of something simple that would just about take all the good out of the other thing.

Martha announced one day that she had made all the arrangements for the downstairs lavatory. She had spoken to Mr. Tillman, the carpenter, and they could use some of the space in the vestibule, which would make the vestibule that much smaller, but it was too large anyway. They could balance off the space on the other side by putting in a new coat closet while they were at it. She also had spoken to Mr. Jackson, the plumber, and he thought he could put in the necessary pipes without too much tearing out of walls and flooring. The whole thing would cost a little over a hundred dollars. Samuel gave his approval and the work was completed in such short order that he complimented her on her efficiency. "I guess I would have kept putting it off and putting it off," he said.

"It *is* a great convenience," she said. "It is for me, too, you know. I don't know how many times a day I climb those stairs just to go to the bathroom."

"Not *that* often, I hope. Don't tell me you're getting kidney trouble," said Samuel Eaton.

"Please," said Martha. "We don't discuss such subjects."

"Well, anyway, I'm glad it's in. Now the next thing is getting the children accustomed to me not going upstairs when I come home. You know, when I'm later than usual and I go up and say goodnight to them. Now that I don't have to go upstairs to wash."

"We can let them come down and kiss you goodnight."

"That's what I mean," he said. "No more dawdling and making excuses so I'm up there sometimes a half an hour."

"I'm in favor," said Martha. "Which brings up something else. Alfred."

"What about him?"

"Well, he's eleven, and you remember when Billy got to be ten you allowed him to have dinner with us. Alfred asked me last winter when he was going to be allowed to have dinner with us, remember, and you said put him off for a while. Well, I did, but now I think it's too noticeable that we haven't promoted him to dinner in the evening."

"No."

"But why not? He's eleven going on twelve now."

"What if he is? We probably started Billy too early."

"Oh, now, Sam, you don't believe that. You don't believe that at all."

"Are you inferring that I'm a liar?"

"I'm not inferring anything, but Alfred knows that when Billy was ten he was allowed to have dinner with us, and Alfred has just as much right."

"There's no such thing as right. Since when does an eleven-year-old boy have the right to dictate where he's going to have his meals? Not in my house, no boy of eleven or twelve or *twenty-one* can dictate to me where he has his supper, or his lunch or his breakfast or anything else. If that's the way he feels, he's going to be sadly disappointed, because now I've made up my mind that I won't even discuss the matter for at least another year."

She looked at him steadily. "You can be very cruel, Sam Eaton. You don't have to take it out on Alfred just because he isn't Billy."

"What do you mean by that statement? Exactly what do you mean?"

"I couldn't clarify it any more than what I said." She looked down into the palms of her hands, then quickly raised her head and turned her face toward the door. "If you're finished your appetizer, dinner's ready." She stood up and went out and waited for him in the hall, where she heard him utter a single word.

"I heard what you said," she said.

"You didn't hear anything. You're hearing things."

"Do you want me to repeat what you said?"

"No."

"Thank you, at least you don't want *me* to use language that *you* use. But kindly remember, I don't like to hear it from you any more than you like to hear it from me. Kindly remember that."

The well-to-do, the well-off people of Port Johnson shrank from the words *rich* and *wealth*, and the other word, *wealthy*, was not in common usage in the United States. It was used only to refer to the multimillionaires of New York and Philadelphia (hardly anyone in Port Johnson knew anything at all about Chicago), who existed only in print, saw only one another, and that lived only to try to outdo one another in extravagance that was made possible by inexhaustible resources that always seemed to have some connection with railroads. A few Port Johnson citizens had actually shaken hands with Mr. Stotesbury and he was therefore real, but no Port Johnson person had ever met a Vanderbilt or a Harriman and therefore anything any Vanderbilt or any Harriman did was possible and completely credible in much the same way that the lives of the Kaiser and the Czar were foreign but fact. The Philadelphia & Reading and the Pennsylvania both had right of way and stations in Port Johnson, and their schedules and performance had their effects on the daily lives of the citizens of the town; but Fritz Diefenderfer, the Morse operator at the P. & R. station, never for a moment thought that his living could depend on a decision made by J. Pierpont Morgan, elder or younger. For most people in Port Johnson the railroads were simply there, and they would go on being there. The even-numbered mixed freights arrived and left at their scheduled time; so did the odd-numbered, and the passenger trains. The loaded "westbound" coal trains passed through on their southward journey, the empty "eastbounds" went north. There would be excursions to Willow Grove and Cape May and New York and Washington, D. C. The pay car would stop on its way through and never was robbed in the history of either railroad. The crossing gate at the foot of Montgomery Street would hold up vehicular traffic for as much as half an hour without formal protest, although the pedestrians, male and female, would be inconvenienced only to the extent that they would have to climb and descend the steps of the platforms of passenger cars. The division superintendents and even higher officials would provide some other-world excitement when they arrived in their shiny, polished office cars and would lay over for a couple of hours on company business. The visit of a division superintendent was always recorded in the local press; his name, his title, the name and number of his car, the number and arrival time of the train that brought him in, the number and departure time of the train that took him away. The Port Johnson *Beacon* carried railroad news as it was handed out, and with no more deviation than was permitted in the publication of the Court Circular in the London *Times*. The Railroad, by which was meant both competing lines, was there forever, a part of the town that was a little more substantial than the banks and just a little less substantial than the churches, which after all operated by Divine franchise. The respective station agents might try to attract business away from the competing line, but it was a superior brand of competition, not to be compared with the small survival struggle between two clothing stores or two grocery stores. The Railroad would never go out of business, no matter what the wealthy did at Newport, a place in Rhode Island that no one from Port Johnson had ever been to.

The well-to-do, the well-off people of Port Johnson made their money in ways that could be seen, and in most cases made money that a Port Johnson citizen could touch. On payday at Eaton's a man lined up with other men in front of the paymaster's window, and each man, as his turn came, would put down a brass check with his number stamped on (the check shiny, the number easily legible because of the grime deposit). The assistant paymaster would call out the number, another assistant paymaster would repeat the call, consult the pay-sheet for the name, and call out the amount of money due the workman. The first assistant would then hand the workman a small envelope containing his pay in cash, and with it return the brass check. It was not customary for the workman to make any signature, although most of the men at Eaton's were able to do so. If a man had a complaint he was told that any error would show up in a day or so and be corrected. And it always was, although it was the man who suffered while a $5 mistake in distribution was correcting itself. For the average worker at Eaton's, $5 was two and a half days' pay. He was not considered one of the well-to-do, but if his job was steady he was considered well-off.

He had no bank account, but his credit was good, if limited. A man who was determined to save money could do so only with the day-to-day, meal-to-meal cooperation of his woman. She baked her own bread and tried to have some meat between the thick slices that she put in his lunch can. If he was young and had his teeth she would try to provide an apple for his noon meal. He had a ketchup bottle, with a patent porcelain stopper, that contained his coffee, in which there was enough sugar to taste, but no milk or cream. Some of the women breast-fed their children as long as anything would come out, and perhaps a little money was saved that way. The frugal workman did not smoke or drink beer, but he made dandelion wine for sicknesses and celebrations. The children were allowed to pick coal off the railroad tracks so long as they stayed off the cars. The railway police discouraged the theft of coal from the cars. The children likewise were sent on foraging expeditions to fruit orchards so that their mothers could cook apple sauce, which to some men was almost as satisfactory as meat in their sandwiches. Nothing was wasted, and nothing was store-bought that could be made at home: the women made soap, the men were cobblers, the women were tailors as well as dressmakers, the men were carpenters of a sort, the boys went fishing for catties and perch, the daughters learned to be handy with the needle and the dustpan and brush and broom, and the fathers and the daughters and the sons took on extra work when it was to be had. A boy would help to deliver groceries, a girl would do ironing after school, a father would repair a fence in the early evening. And clean and neat and full of self-respect they would attend church on Sunday, with a nickel from each of the parents for the plate offering, and a penny from each of the children at Sunday School.

The children who got through their first five years were likely to get through the second. The third five years were another test of their stamina, and during that period the boys would be ready to leave school and get some kind of work, preferably the learning of a trade. The girls would go into domestic service or take a job in the stocking factory. The money that the determined father had saved was not available for the education of the children beyond the eighth grade. High school was not for the children of an Eaton's workman. It was for the children of the Montgomery Street merchants, the sons and daughters of the clergy and the professional men, and the children of a few foremen and shop superintendents at Eaton's. The money that a workman had put by over a period of fifteen or twenty years was a disaster fund, and seldom amounted to more than a thousand dollars. An Eaton's workman, unlike a railroader, could not look forward to a pension. If he lived beyond his earning years his support was taken care of by his children. At his death his savings would pass on to his wife, and at her death the children inherited what was left. A workman at Eaton's had no "future" but only a continuing present. A serious injury, whether it occurred at the mill or away from it, meant no pay until he was able to return to work, and during that time the workman and his family subsisted on the disaster fund and on the kindness of their neighbors. A long illness, a crippling injury that used up the savings was also the end of that family as a unit. The young would be distributed among relatives or sent to the Children's Home; the mother would scrub floors in the stores and saloons, and the father would lie in their bed in the rented room until his woman's health gave out and he could be certified for the almshouse, she for the county hospital.

And yet a man with such a history seldom considered himself to be one of the poor. Until his accident or illness he had lived in a neighborhood of men in the same position: men who had steady jobs, wives and children. In a row of houses that were home to such families the yards were planted for vegetables, often with topsoil that had been brought by wheelbarrow from land a good distance away. The downstairs windows at the front of the house were treated with soap and water. The roofs did not leak. The kids had a wooden sled that hung on the back porch the year round, and there was an iron hoop hanging beside it that had been rolled by the older brothers and sisters. The woman spent scarce pennies for stove polish that the man also used on his shoes before going to church on Sunday. There was a clock in the kitchen and all the front-room furniture had fringes on it, and was sat in only at weddings and funerals and in the course of the annual visit by the clergyman. These were not the houses of the poor.

The poor were the people who had no steady jobs, who lived in shacks near the town dump. Some of the shacks were built entirely of discarded doors and covered with tarpaper. There were not many of the real poor in Port Johnson. The children of the Eaton's workmen were afraid of the children of the real poor, and not without reason; it was the children of the Eaton's workmen that the children of the poor stole

41

from, and not from the children of the well-to-do. The children of the poor rarely set foot on lower Montgomery Street, and when they did they were chased away by the police and the merchants. Likewise, the truant officer stayed away from the people of the shacks near the dump. He did not know their names. The women of the poor made most of the little cash their families ever saw. They would stand in front of a store on Montgomery Street until the store-owner would come out and attempt to shoo them away, but they would not budge until the merchant gave them a nickel or a dime. Their food was scraps from the packing house and the two Port Johnson meat markets, and stale bread from the bakeries, bruised fruit and vegetables from the produce house. A child of the poor had once stabbed a child of an Eaton's workman with a pen-knife, and thenceforth the poor and all their children were hated and feared by the families of the men with steady jobs.

Alfred Eaton at eleven had never been inside the house of an Eaton's workman. In some well-to-do families it was the custom for a servant to take her mistress's children home on her day off. It was a custom that was not uniformly successful, whatever its purpose. The chambermaid's family would behave toward the child with more obsequiousness than the child was accustomed to, or they would ply him with sweets and pastries, or they would make remarks that the child would know were naughty without clearly understanding the language. Martha Eaton's servants, Josephine and Nellie, had no relatives in Port Johnson and the Eaton children therefore were not called upon to conform to the custom. But it is also doubtful whether Samuel Eaton would have given his approval of a visit by his children to the home of one of his men, even in the extremely unlikely event that an invitation had been forthcoming. Samuel Eaton knew by name all the men at the mill, but only officials of the company above the rank of superintendent had ever been to his house or he to theirs. Samuel Eaton obeyed his father's rule: "Don't get too familiar with the men. You're not a friend of theirs, so don't pretend you are." The secretary-treasurer of the Company, Edmund Barlow, was unmarried and lived with his mother; the chief engineer, Walter Overton, had five children but his wife was a Catholic who was sending all the children to the parochial school, and the social relations between the Overtons and the Eatons were kept at an absolute minimum. Alfred Eaton did not even know the names of the younger members of the Overton brood, and since the parochial schoolchildren were dismissed half an hour earlier than the boys at Professor Phillipson's, Alfred Eaton seldom saw the Overton boys of his own age. His father, in truth, while having no use for Catholics, secretly acknowledged a small debt to Mary Overton, whose ideas on her children's education created a separation between the two families for which no one was responsible but the Pope of Rome. The Eatons had the Overton parents to dinner annually, prefatory to the Charity Ball, and Martha Eaton's attendance at Mary Overton's ladies' luncheon in the spring was considered to be the other half of the exchange of compliments. Michael and Desmond Overton came to the Eatons' picnics for children of Alfred's age, and he saw them and one younger Overton child at dancing school, but Samuel Eaton had no cause to be disturbed by the risk of mixing business and away-from-the-mill relations.

There were Johnsons white and black who were not related to Martha Eaton, but in Port Johnson there were no other Eatons, and consequently anyone who bore the name was known to be a member of the mill family, regardless of age. A boy less sensitive than Alfred Eaton would have noticed, as Alfred had noticed, that when his mother took him shopping and the proprietor of the store would greet her by name, other people in the store, customers and clerks, would turn their heads to inspect the bearers of the name. Martha as a Johnson was not stylish as the Budds and the Millers were stylish, but she was a Port Johnson Johnson and an Eaton, and she could easily have made a strong bid for the leadership of Port Johnson society. As it was, there were more citizens who knew exactly who she was than knew her when they saw her.

Eaton's was the largest single employer of manpower in the town without being the largest industry; the two breweries together employed more than the three hundred men who normally worked at the mill. Eaton, therefore, was the most prominent single man in Port Johnson industry, and in Port Johnson nothing else counted; there were no great land-owning family names, no famous politicians, no fifth-generation aristocracy, no local college or university. The main street of the town was named for a family that belonged in another county. And Eaton was now only a third-generation name, but its prominence was assured by the size of the mill payroll, and Alfred Eaton could not grow up without a rather early consciousness of that prominence.

He had eyes, and he could see what children begin to see very early: the differences between how his family lived and other families lived. As has been the case for centuries, the most easily read symbol for opulence was a family's means of transportation. In Port Johnson there were friends of Alfred Eaton's whose fathers had more horses and more carriages, larger stables and more men working in them. The human limit in Port Johnson was a coachman and a groom, and the Eatons' George Fry was both. The Eatons' stable had six box-stalls, now occupied by a matched pair; and Missy, for saddle and harness; and a Shetland. For them there were a landau, a Stanhope, a surrey, a cut-under, and a light wagon; and for the pony a governess cart and a dog-cart. Of these the landau and Stanhope had been passed down from Alfred's grandfather. Other families had more rolling stock, and while George Fry was given a livery, it was simple dark grey whipcord, with a square bowler, not an impressive turnout in the company of some coachmen who had boots and cockaded hats and starched white stocks. George was expert, quick with the wicker fender for the rear wheel when Martha Eaton alighted; but two Port Johnson families—the Budds and the Millers—had footmen for that attention. Alfred's Grandfather Johnson had even less in his stable, a pair and three carriages, but his grandfather was *old*.

"We're not the richest in town, are we, Mother?" Alfred had once said.

"Heavens, no! Far from it, and it isn't nice to talk about it."

"But who is?"

"Well, not us. The Millers are very well-to-do, and the Budds. I think the Millers *have* more, but the Budds *spend* more. But it's what people are, not how much money they have. That's what counts."

"No, money in the bank is what counts, that's what Grandfather Johnson says."

"Well—I think he must have been talking about business. He might have been talking about some business proposition that sounded shaky."

"*He's* rich."

"Grandfather Johnson? He wouldn't like to hear you say that."

"He is all the same."

"Well-off," said Martha. "You don't say rich or words like that. You don't discuss how much money you have. Ever. Not even in business."

"Then how are you going to find out how much money you have?"

"Oh, you don't have to talk about it. You know."

"Does Father know?"

"Of course."

"Why won't he tell you?"

"Why won't he tell me? I suppose he would if I asked him."

"But I'm going to be rich some day, am I not?"

"Who have you been talking to that fills you full of these nonsensical ideas?"

"You don't like us to tattle."

"That's true, but whoever it is—and I suspect George— you tell him it's none of his business and it's not good manners to talk about money."

"But we're not *poor*, are we, Mother?"

44

"Well hardly that. No, we have nothing to worry about in that line."

The conversation was one he could not have had with his father. Instinctively he knew that his father would have regarded any doubts of their financial position as a criticism of his ability to provide. Samuel Eaton was not a man to encourage any criticism of any kind; but in matters of business he did not even permit comment. If something went wrong at the mill he would tell about it at home, but Martha knew, and the children were learning, that at such times he wanted only silence. If something good happened, he permitted his wife to congratulate him, but not to go into detail. "I'm so glad . . . Isn't that fine?" were all right, but he did not want her to ask questions or to itemize his sagacity. It was a great convenience for him that the mill was of necessity dirty and smoky and dangerous. It kept her away, and made it easy for him to avoid the task of explaining the business to her. She consequently had as little knowledge of what went on at Eaton's as her children had—her living children. Billy had known, because Billy had been taught, taken to the mill, introduced to the key workmen, watched the pulling of a heat, given rides on the narrow-gauge railway and even sat in the cab of the overhead traveling cranes.

To Alfred the mill was like a third grandfather, who would have to be big, old, strong, rich, usually invisible but often heard. There was the land and there were the buildings, the high smokestacks and chimneys; and there were the crowds of men leaving at quitting-time. But there was something else that he was a long time in understanding and did not begin to understand until much later, when he had been away at school and college. As a boy of eleven he was not afraid of the mill and never had been, but he was continually aware of its existence while knowing so little about it.

What he did know was that because of the mill, because it was Eaton's mill, his father and mother were accorded respect that was not given to all the fathers and mothers of the boys he played with. He saw, too, that it was politeness and nothing more or worse that was behind his parents' show of respect for their contemporaries. As a boy of eleven he had already noticed that some of the fathers and mothers of his friends would contradict themselves if they expressed views that conflicted with those of his own parents. ("Such a lovely day!" "A little too warm for my taste." "Well, yes, it is rather close.") At eleven he felt embarrassment but no sympathy for men and women who could be bullied in small things. The sympathy did not come until he was able to see those people as so much like himself. But that was much later indeed. At eleven he only saw that his father and mother were rich and assured, and seeing that and seeing how it affected other people was as far as he could go.

It was far. It was also not good. The conversations with his mother removed all doubts and fears that had to do with money, and since he was not yet old enough to be conscious of social values, he had neither timidity nor arrogance on that score. But knowing that his last name carried weight with adults, whether they were friends of his mother's or the servants of his friends, he had begun to realize that the only condition where his name meant so little that he was on his own was in the time he spent at school and with his schoolmates. As a result he was compelled to take himself at their estimate. Adults treated him with almost precisely the same respect as they did his parents, but at school he earned what he got. It was an ideal system for the other boys, but not for a boy who was intelligent enough to notice how often and how much the adults became sycophants.

He had not earned much, and he had fallen heir to a tradition that was only three years older than he was. Billy had been one of the best fist-fighters in the school, and in another day he would have been called a natural athlete, well coordinated. Moreover, Billy had made good marks through regular study. One difference between the brothers was that Billy had an outspoken curiosity that, his teacher incorrectly surmised, emanated from a hunger for learning; while Alfred's curiosity was more easily satisfied, or could be temporarily satisfied, by a teacher's words and his own reflections on them. He had never been able to defend himself against his brother except by covering up with his hands and arms, and when he got into fights in school he reacted out of that experience. He would strike a blow in anger, but upon retaliation he would assume the old protective attitude while the other boy beat him. His father, then, was not compelled to accept him as a fighter or as a student, and it was as a student that Alfred had been expected to excel. Samuel Eaton was prepared to concede, however reluctantly, that his younger son was the better in studies, but when Alfred continued to remain in the middle or lower half of his class, Samuel Eaton could righteously complain that the boy wasn't much good at anything. And the boy was not helped out of his mediocrity by his schoolmasters' awareness of the father's feelings. It was not lost on them, from Seneca Phillipson down, that the father had a preference between his two sons.

As a boy Alfred Eaton was not one to keep on enemy terms for long. Boys who had licked him in fights were to be avoided for a while, a week, two weeks, and the relationship was, on Alfred's part, a nervous one while he was conscious of the aftereffects on his standing among his fellows. But there would be a new fight between other boys that would make his schoolmates forget his fight, and when his fight (and his licking) became ancient history, it would be only a question of time before he could again play with his conqueror. He would be careful not to repeat the offense that had caused the fight, and in his relief at the resumption of peaceful relations he was careful not to lose his temper and strike the first blow that would start another fight. He counted most of the world on his side rather than against him. Grownups could be strict, and other boys could be mean, and girls could be sneaky, but the strictness and the meanness and the sneakiness did not last; they seldom outlasted the next pleasure, favor, cheerful experience, pleasant surprise, triumph, occasion for laughter. He was living without a philosophy, but he had learned that his father did not love him and did love Billy, and his father's love was just something he could not have. It was only when his father deprived him of something real that he wanted to cry. If his father did not love him, that was not taking away something real. But when his father took away something real because he did not love him—*that* was real, *that* made him miserable. He could live without his father's love, because he had to. Alfred did not know at what time he first realized that his father did not love him, but at eleven he realized that he never had. But the knowledge did not keep him from wondering what you did to make your father love you.

The named places touching the borough boundaries of Port Johnson were Eatontown, Prosperity, Stone Fence, Farrier's Corners, Eckburg and Rothermel's Landing. Nearby were also Eck's Mills and the village of Rothermel, and elsewhere in the county there was a hamlet known as Rother Mill, which was thought to be a corruption of the name Rothermel. If Alfred Eaton at the age of eleven had had any curiosity about the name he would have found in Boyd's Directory eleven listings under Rothermel, representing, at that time, some sixty-five Rothermels ranging in age from a couple of months to ninety-four years. He would not have found the name on any of the bank directorates or in the membership of the Merchants Association. By far the greater number of Rothermels worked with their hands, a few in jobs that required training and skill, but most of them were engaged in occupations that involved manual labor performed under the direction of foremen. It was almost as though they were determined as a family to remain obscure, which, of course, was not the case; but in Port Johnson the name had come to mean a stodgy respectability, a dependable mediocrity. The Rothermel who was killed in the railroad yards during the celebration of William Eaton's birth was the only member of the family in two decades whose name appeared in the newspaper because of a matter with which the police might be concerned. And in that same period no Rothermel had been publicized for special accomplishment or distinction. They had, as many Pennsylvania families had, a Family Association, but the Port Johnson Rothermels were seldom represented at the Association picnics in the neighboring counties. There was no Rothermel in Port Johnson who assumed or was accorded leadership of the local contingent, with the result that they were not unified, for picnics or anything else. They walked around with a common name, and they had place names to remind them of some past distinction, but in 1908 they had nothing but their numerical presence to make them noteworthy in the life of the borough. Among them there was a young Rothermel who was on his way, but he was as yet only eleven years old, rather early for anyone to identify his struggles and restlessness as signs of hope.

Tom Rothermel and Alfred Eaton had a speaking acquaintance and nothing more. They had never been anywhere together, done anything together. They had in common only the number of years each had been on this earth, which was a mutuality just sufficient, in a town the size of Port Johnson, for two boys to become aware of each other. The circumstances of their daily lives, their personal conditions, never let the acquaintance go beyond the combination of curiosity, suspicion, semi-hostility, semi-friendliness that they felt. In Alfred's case, he knew that a certain boy was Tom Rothermel; in Tom's case, a certain boy was named Alfred Eaton, whose father was the boss of Eaton's.

Tom Rothermel's father owned the clothes he wore, the furniture in his house, the tools for his small garden, the plot in the cemetery, and little more. He had a gold watch and chain, and gold cuff buttons, and these treasures had been inherited. In the course of a year's time he had thousands of contacts with his fellow townsmen, and he handled many thousands of dollars, nearly all of it in cash, but he was not the richer for either experience. He was a quiet man, whose conversations at home were hardly more voluble than the necessary exchanges that took place in the office of the Port Johnson Gas Company. Throughout the years of his manhood he had worked for one employer; first as a meter reader, then as clerk and bookkeeper-cashier. Men did not often change their jobs in Port Johnson, and a man in a job like Jonas Rothermel's was not even considered settled in it if he had held it less than ten years. Whatever a man did became his life work, just as his wife became his life partner; the house he lived in, his permanent home; his habits fixed; his identity established by his name, his face, his job, his wife, his children, his house, and the manner in which he conducted himself within the permissible limits. Jonas Rothermel opened the Gas Company office in the morning at eleven or ten minutes before eight o'clock, and closed it in the evening at a few minutes past six. Every day he carried his lunch in one of the paper bags his wife saved from the groceries. She sliced her bread thinner than the hunks that the Eaton's workmen's wives gave their husbands, and the Eaton's workmen got more meat than Jonas Rothermel did. Jonas Rothermel ate his lunch in the rear of the Gas Company office; it did not do to have him seen from the street, and it also kept the nosy ones from finding out that between the slices of bread there was sometimes only ketchup and hardly ever more than cheese.

Jonas Rothermel was not a robust man, a fact, however, which did not prevent him from occasionally wishing that he could change places with some of the "workmen," who made more money and did not have to put on a clean collar every day. A workman's overalls would have saved wear on Jonas Rothermel's suit, but by remaining standing at his desk he avoided the wear on the seat of the pants that some office workers found costly. When the superintendent of the Gas Company asked him why he didn't avail himself of the high stool the company provided, Jonas Rothermel explained that he had to be up and down all day tending to customers, and didn't mind standing. The lives of the Jonas Rothermel family were full of economies that Elsie Rothermel considered worthwhile, since they made it possible for her husband to be something better than a common laborer. *Her* husband wore a necktie to work.

Elsie was a farm girl, and the memories of her first twenty-one years on earth made the next twenty seem like a life of ease. She had abandoned the farm forever, with its five-in-the-morning rising and the milking of the cows in whatever kind of weather the morning brought; the walk to and from school, three miles each way, during the months of November, December, January, February and March, and then the months of work that was hers to do because her mother had not borne any sons. Every year it would take months to get rid of the black stripe on the back of her neck, put there by the reins of the horse while she plowed the fields. She wore shoes like her father's and her hands and her arms developed like a man's. When she married Jonas Rothermel there was no kind of man's farm work that she had not done, and she was determined never to do any of it again. She became fat, cheerful, and lazy— lazy by her own standards; her house was scrubbed and dusted as no other house in The Row.

Jonas Rothermel never had seen her with the horse's reins hanging around her neck, or spreading manure on a winter

Saturday, or leading a cow to be serviced by the neighbor's bull. He had seen her only on Wednesdays, Farmer's Day, when the farmers brought their spring-wagons to town and sold vegetables door-to-door. He had proposed marriage to two other young women of the town and been turned down; and it was time for him to marry, a little past time since he was twenty-five years old and not getting any younger. His own mother was the matchmaker. "Elsie Angstadt would make a good wife, so strong and healthy-looking, and a hard worker," said his mother.

"Elsie Angstadt?"

"And Lutheran. The Angstadts are all Lutheran. You want I ask her momma?"

"No, Momma."

"I ask her momma. I find out is there any sickness inside. Then you go courtin'."

"I can't. I don't have a horse."

"The livery stable. Fifty cents for Sunday afternoon. Four Sundays this summer. I give you two dollars, you marry before next winter."

There was resistance by Father Angstadt, but the advantages of having Elsie supported by a man prevailed over the disadvantages of losing a farm hand, and so Elsie with her quilts and preserves and a good bed and a complete outfit of town clothes became a Rothermel. Jonas, who was a virgin, was at first overwhelmed by her willingness and superior knowledge of the consummating act, especially since she was likewise a virgin, but he soon learned to accept it for the pleasure it gave him at the time, and for the knowledge throughout the day that he could have that pleasure every night and it would cost him nothing.

They never spoke of love as an emotion they felt for each other. Away from the bedroom they never kissed. But Elsie knew that Jonas loved the children, and because they were half hers she accepted his love for them as evidence of his unspoken love for her.

They had two daughters who lived, followed by a son and a daughter born dead, and Thomas was born in 1897, given little hope to live because he was so small—barely five pounds.

The pennies that Jonas and Elsie Rothermel saved were put in the bank for one purpose and one purpose alone: the children's education. Elsie had stopped school at the sixth grade and she had not always been willing to make sacrifices for schooling that would not even begin for many years, but on that one point Jonas was not to be opposed. "If I would have had some education I'd be making more now. What can a man do if he isn't big and muscular? He can use what's in

50

here"—tapping his head—"but it don't get put in there without education."

"That's a man. The girls aint going to be a man."

"The girls are going to teach school, and make more than some men."

After Thomas was born, and lived, and was at first a frail child, Elsie allowed herself to be convinced of the need for an education for a son who was not going to be big and muscular. But even if she had not been convinced, she had already had to yield to Jonas in money matters. She had never owned a dollar bill until she married Jonas, and the whole subject of money was so unfamiliar to her that she was unable to discuss it with a husband who handled thousands of dollars every month, as against her having to be shown on paper how much change she was entitled to after making a cash purchase. Education therefore was a subject of conversation and an influence in the Rothermel household to a degree that money itself was talked about in the kitchens of their neighbors. It affected the very quality and amount of food they ate and clothes they wore, and Elsie Rothermel, in the process of completely changing her attitude toward schooling, learned to adopt the future education of her children as pridefully as she assumed the status of wife to a man who wore a necktie on the job. It was almost as though the future of her children were retroactively making her too an educated woman.

Now, in 1908, Jean Rothermel was already attending the normal school at West Chester, her sister Eudora was in high school, and Tom Rothermel, having skipped a grade, was in seventh grade at Third Street. The little man at the Gas Company would have been indignant at being called a gambler, but with a daughter at Normal and another in third year High he was already seeing some of his bets paying off: the years of ketchup sandwiches washed down by tap water were one bet; another bet was in his decision not to take out insurance. The money that would have paid for insurance went into the savings account, and he was gambling that he would educate his children before his life ran out. And never for a second did he doubt that education was all his children needed to have a better life than he had had. After all, he was convinced that only the lack of an education had kept him from acquiring a million of those dollars that he fingered so briefly.

Tom Rothermel was not allowed to take odd jobs that might interfere with his punctuality or attendance at Third Street School, but after school and on Saturdays and in the summer and Christmas vacations he was kept busy, always gainfully. The rich East Montgomery Street people had servants to perform such tasks as the shoveling of snow and the pulling of weeds and the running of errands that Tom did for the people who lived on the streets off Montgomery. In his own neighborhood the people shoveled their own snow, pulled their own weeds and ran their own errands, but for his neighbors Tom sharpened knives more cheaply and just about as well as the Italian who came around twice a year; and he salvaged nails after the carpenters were finished with a building job; he had a Sunday job the year round, watering and feeding the horse that Mr. Pickering, the grocer, fed and watered the rest of the week; he opened shipping cases of dry goods and notions for Miss McReynolds, who did not like to go down-cellar at her store because there were rats; he was sometimes summoned to push Mr. Tupper's wheelchair. His father did not permit him to take work in which he might rupture himself, but so long as a job or a chore did not interfere with his schooling, Tom was available wherever an honest penny could be turned. He seemed to have outgrown his early frailty and from the age of seven he brought some money into the home. The Rothermel children were so well disciplined in such matters that they never considered that money they earned belonged to them or was to be spent on them. They were not a family for games, but the acquiring of money was almost a game to them. The day on which Tom found a fifty-cent piece, wedged between the bricks of the River Street sidewalk, became a reference point in the family calendar. They expressed pity for the unknown person who had suffered the loss, but long after the pity had been forgotten they could stimulate their imagination by saying: "Remember the day Tom found the fifty cents?"

Tom's devotion to cash was regarded sympathetically by other merchants than Miss McReynolds and Mr. Pickering, and he was often offered jobs that he could not take. At eleven he was already in demand, not merely for his services but because of himself. In his own small world (but the only one he knew) he was considered honest, bright, quick, and thorough. Already they were saying of him, as they more usually said of boys much older, "He's going to amount to something." On Lower Montgomery Street, for a boy of eleven that was praise unprecedented and unique.

Money, as has already been shown, was not a lively topic of conversation in the Samuel Eaton family; as a topic it was considered to be in bad taste. At Jonas Rothermel's house it was unifying, like a common friend and a common enemy, an ambition and an elusive gain. Those conditions did not produce, among the Eaton children, the fascination of mystery that surrounds a forbidden topic. If it had been forbidden for some other reason than good taste versus bad taste, there might have been that fascination. Instead it became merely a rule created by taste, like the rule that a boy did not wear one brown shoe and one black shoe, that a young girl did not wear jewelry, that the things you ate with a fork you did not eat with a spoon. Then, too, there was still more to the difference between the two boys in the matter of money: Alfred Eaton, the child of abundance, was not allowed to work; Tom Rothermel was not encouraged to play. And the subtlest difference, which never was apparent to Samuel and Martha Eaton, was that their heir was growing up in ignorance of the values of money, while a Tom Rothermel, who handled some money or had a money transaction every day of his young life, was already an experienced merchant, who knew what to ask for his services, who knew how to make change, who in a few instances had learned about slow pay and bad debts, and, perhaps most important of all, was continually experiencing the satisfaction of tangible reward for his efforts. Comparatively, Tom Rothermel knew everything about money, and Alfred Eaton, nothing. A silver dollar was to Alfred Eaton a shiny, heavy coin that Grandfather Johnson gave you on your birthday and that you were allowed to spend as you liked. A silver dollar to Tom Rothermel—he had never owned one—would have represented fifty kitchen knives sharpened, or ten hours in Miss McReynolds's cellar, or pushing Mr. Tupper's wheelchair to and from the drug store twenty times.

In that year of 1908 and that age of eleven the two boys were growing out of their boyhood, and it is a good point in our chronicle from which to take note of another way in which their boyhood was equipping them for later life. If childhood is a time which children should spend with children, Tom Rothermel had been cheated. If, on the other hand, childhood is to be considered only as the earliest years of a continuing preparation for later life, Tom Rothermel had already gained a tremendous advantage over Alfred Eaton. Alfred Eaton's life was so regulated as to keep him in the company of other children: his brother and sisters, his schoolmates, his playmates; and to keep him away from and out of the way of grownups. He had his parents and his grandfather, the servants, and the intimate adult friends of those relatives, and scarcely any other contact or communication with older people. His teachers did not count; a boy's teachers belong to school life, and school life is children. The nearest thing he had to a relaxed and friendly companionship with an adult was his relationship with George Fry, which was conducted with gruffness by George and teasing by Alfred, but with a tacit understanding of a mutual liking that if tested could prove to be affection. If childhood is a time which children should spend with children, the advantage was Alfred Eaton's. Tom Rothermel usually had a paying chore to do before school and always chores after school and on Saturdays and Sundays, and he grew up with older people. Growing up with them, he lost his awe of them and a great deal of the respect for them that is expected of a boy of eleven for no better reason than that he is younger. After some indeterminate point when he was ten or eleven he was never again to be impressed by age *per se*, and when he began to question that superiority he was unconsciously getting himself ready to question other verities. If a man was not your superior although he happened to be older, then another man might not be holy although he was a preacher, another man might not know everything although he was a teacher, a woman need not be considered a fine lady although she wore satin and exuded cologne. And he had discovered the heresy that the possession of money did not make the possessors better people. When Mr. Tupper thought he was not being observed he spent much time in the examination of his private parts; Miss McReynolds had two brass tacks on her dry-goods counter that were supposed to be a yard apart but measured a fraction under thirty-six inches; Mr. Pickering took a scoopful of flour out of every twelve-pound sack until he had an extra sackful to sell; Mr. Habe at the bank regularly met a classmate of Tom's in the woods across the river and they would lie together with all their clothes off; the son of Mr. Budd had a sickness that he had caught from a girl on River Street and that he got medicine for for a whole year; Mr. Budd himself was often carried home from the Exchange Hotel after dark; Mrs. Streiber got fits on the sidewalk. But Tom had heard the same kinds of things about people who were not any better off than his own family, and he no more attributed the evils and misfortunes to the possession of money than he believed that the possession of money gave people immunity to the consequences of sin. Money was money, and people were people. Money was money, and people were *only* people. He was still years away from the development of his eventual philosophical attitude toward people and money, but he had made a start.

In the fall of 1911 Alfred Eaton was enrolled in the Knox School. It was not much more than thirty miles by train and carriage from Port Johnson to the school, but Samuel Eaton had not been able to find it convenient to make the inspection trip that Martha had mentioned to Alfred, so that when he arrived to begin his residence Alfred was seeing the place for the first time. The founder, headmaster and old Princeton friend of Samuel Eaton's was James Clement McCready, a tall, rather alarmingly thin man with a prominent and active Adam's apple. His study-office had once been the smoking-room of the converted manor house that was the school's main building. The room was paneled in mahogany and the

54

furniture was high-backed ecclesiastical oak chairs and a massive mahogany desk. There could be no doubt about the headmaster's university affiliation; the room contained a dozen group photographs of Princeton teams and a smaller number of larger pen-and-ink sketches of Princeton scenes, as well as a 10" x 12" Phi Beta Kappa key made of gilded tin, and a bronze Princeton coat of arms. A lawn-tennis racquet in a canvas cover stood in one corner of the room and there were two slightly tarnished silver cups on the mantelpiece which Alfred correctly assumed to be trophies of McCready's ability on the court. They were indeed just that: they had been won in 1900, McCready's best year competitively at the New Jersey seashore resort where McCready passed his summers.

"Welcome to Knox, Eaton," said McCready, and turning to Martha: "No doubt he's used to Alfred at home, but here the masters address all the boys by their last names. I'm sorry Samuel couldn't make the journey, Martha, but it's bully to see you again. Bully."

"Thank you, that's very nice of you."

"Eaton, I suppose I don't need to ask you whether you've paid careful attention to the R and R?"

"I don't know, sir."

"The R and R, the Rules and Regulations? Surely we sent you one last spring. What you may and may not do."

"That booklet," said Martha. "Oh, yes."

"Some of our boys I'm afraid irreverently refer to it as The Bible. Not in my presence, of course, but you see, Eaton, even the headmaster knows what's going on. Have you any questions, Martha?"

"No, I don't think so, thanks."

"He understands that he's to write home at least once a week, either parent, just so one gets a letter. The boys usually find time to do that in study period, but unfortunately that's against Regs and a boy found writing letters in study period most always has an additional piece of news to write home, namely, 'I was soaked ten lines—ten lines of Latin—for writing letters in study period.' Have you more than five dollars in your pocket, Eaton?"

"No sir."

"Well, that's good, because you'd have to turn it over to the bursar. Five dollars is expected to last you until Thanksgiving. If you visit the Jigger Shop too often—"

"What is that, the Jigger Shop?" said Martha.

"Well, they have one at Lawrenceville. Ours isn't as pretentious. Here a boy can buy Peter's milk chocolate, sourballs and licorice sticks, but no sodas or ice cream. It's open only twice a day, after dinner and after supper. You might call it a canteen. You can buy other things like shoelaces, tooth-brushes, although I'm afraid most boys who lose their tooth-brushes prefer to go without scrubbing their teeth until they can get the family to send one from home, that way saving ten cents of their own money."

"I see," said Martha.

"There again, a violation. A boy *must* brush his teeth twice a day. But all these things are in the R and R. Of course you may write as often as you like, Martha, and Samuel, and did I understand you to say there are three sisters?"

"Two," said Martha.

"Well, in that case this boy ought to get a full share of the mail. We don't open the mail, but we don't encourage the boys to correspond with other females, only the family. Mothers, sisters, grandmothers, aunts. And bona fide cousins. Preferably first cousins, not sixteenth cousins, if you get my meaning."

"Oh, yes."

"Can't I write to any other girl but my sisters?"

"Perhaps once or twice a term, but no mushy stuff, coming or going. We have nobody here that's old enough to be engaged, so we don't look with favor on *affaires de coeur*. I trust you're not engaged, Eaton?"

"No sir."

"But you asked. Why did you ask?" said McCready.

"Because a girl said she was going to write to me," said Alfred.

"And I think I know who that is," said Martha, and to Mc-Cready: "An awfully nice girl."

"But you *don't* know who it is, Mother."

"Not Victoria Dockwiler?"

"We had a Dockwiler here three years ago," said McCready. "I know the Dockwilers and they're a first-rate family, first-rate!"

"No. Somebody else," said Alfred.

"Someone I can vouch for, I hope," said Martha.

"If your mother can't vouch for her . . ."

"Oh, heck. It's Norma Budd."

"Norma *Budd?*" said Martha. "She's a young lady in her twenties."

"I know a lot of Budds," said McCready. "Fine people, those that I know, but I hope you're not planning to invite a lady in her twenties to Spring Day. Of course you couldn't have her anyway till you're in Four, and that's a long way to go, three years after this one, and this one is only beginning. Now then, Martha, to get back to letter-writing and Miss Budd. Do you approve?"

"Oh, I suppose so."

"Well, then that's settled. Jennie is expecting you for a cup of tea, and while you ladies are chatting I'll take this boy around and have him meet some of the masters."

The boy and the headmaster marched through the halls, passing other boys who would greet McCready with the word, "Sir," and were quickly sizing up the new arrival. McCready did not introduce any of the boys, but did introduce each master briefly until they encountered a short stout master in a Norfolk jacket and knickerbockers that made him seem like a man dressed for a fancy dress party. "Mr. Deland, this is Eaton, Alfred Eaton, one of the new boys."

"Well, Eaton," said Deland. 'Welcome to Knox. Home town?"

"Port Johnson, P A," said Alfred. "Thank you, sir."

"Oh, sure. Up the river. I believe your father went to Princeton with the Head, here. Well, we can't hold that against you."

"Mr. Deland attended a small educational institution in Philadelphia, the name of which escapes me."

"All you have to do is remember what state Philadelphia is in, but"—he pretended to whisper to Alfred—"headmasters aren't very good at geography. Well, shall I show Eaton to his room?"

"Would you please? Then have him come down to the parlor and say goodbye to his mother."

"This way, Eaton," said Deland. "Let me see now, you went to a day school in Port Johnson, Phillipson's?"

"Yes sir."

"Fair, pretty fair, in everything but math. Correct?"

"Yes sir."

"Father in the steel business. Town named after your mother's family. Had the usual contagious diseases, vaccinated for smallpox. Favorite exercise, swimming."

"Yes sir."

"Mine, too, now that I've got this corporation. Well, you see I know quite a lot about you already, but by the time June rolls around I expect to know a great deal more, and you'll know a great deal more about me. The Head didn't say so, but I'm the master for your hall. We're on the top floor, three flights up. You'll be rooming with a boy named Chauncey Moore. Philadelphia. He arrives tomorrow, a day late because he just had his tonsils out. I haven't seen him, but his brother graduated from here two years ago. His brother won the hundred-yard dash in his last year here, and of course was on the track team. Our track team and our baseball team are the only ones that compete against other schools, so we consider it a big honor to be on one of them. We play Germantown Academy, Chestnut Hill Academy, and the Hill School scrubs, and if you get in any two games you get your letter.

In any one year, that is. Next year we're going to start football. Now here's where I stop and get my breath. I have to go up and down these stairs ten times a day, if not more. Oh, dear. If I didn't try to talk and walk at one and the same time —I might not get so out of breath. Let's just sit a minute, shall we?"

"Yes sir."

" 'Gan losing my wind . . . got out of college . . . put on weight . . . eat too much . . . gave up smoking . . . big an appetite . . . my size . . . flight too many . . . two stories . . . not three . . . next year . . . damned stairs . . ." He got to his feet and they mounted the last flight step by step and without conversation, and Deland led the way to Alfred's room.

"Your home for the next ten months," said Deland. "Toilets are at the end of the hall, shower baths in the basement. I have to warn you, the one thing the boys steal around here is soap. Soap is everybody's property. If you haven't got a soap dish to keep your soap in, I advise you to buy one at the Jigger Shop. Did you read The Bible?"

"Yes sir."

"Good, then you know about the Jigger Shop. It doesn't do any good to steal each other's clothes or things like that, or things that are marked, but soap, and of course milk chocolate, they disappear the minute you turn your head. A few pictures and pennants will make this room a lot more habitable. Nice view, though, isn't it?"

"Yes sir. Very nice."

"Have you ever been away from home before?"

"No sir."

"Then you've never been homesick."

"But I'm not very far from home," said Alfred.

"It's not the distance, my boy. Have you got a jail in your town?"

"Yes sir."

"Those men get homesick, and they're not far from home. It isn't the distance, it isn't even home. It's being unable to get away. When that happens to you, come down and see me."

"Oh, I'll be all right."

"I hope so, but if it does happen, just come and tell me you're homesick. It's no disgrace. I get homesick, and I've been a teacher all my life. Isn't that astonishing? True, though. Anything else bothers you, tell me about it. Anything."

"I will, sir. Thank you."

"Ever had your appendix out?"

"No sir."

"Then if you ever get bad pains in your belly, don't be a brave soldier. Come and tell me."

Alfred could not tell whether Deland's cordiality was for him especially or routine for all new boys, but for the time being he was glad that he had come to Knox, a school which all new boys and no old boys called Hard Knox; just as they referred to Deland's floor as Deland ob de free and de home ob de brave. It took Alfred about a week to get accustomed to having his meals with a lot of other boys, and about that long to being awakened in the morning, going to the dining hall three times a day, to classes, study hall and to bed—all at the signal of an unnecessarily loud bell. But then he stopped thinking about the bell and eating in a group.

He had the advantage of a single day's residence over his roommate, which meant little enough to Alfred but a great deal to Chauncey Moore. They were introduced by Deland and left alone together immediately.

"Did you go here last year?" said Chauncey Moore.

"No, I'm new."

"Oh, are you? My brother went here. Did any of your brothers go here?"

"I only had one brother and he died. He was going to go to St. Paul's."

"Up in New Hampshire?"

"Yes."

"I have a cousin there. He lives in New York. Was your brother killed or anything?"

"No, but he had spinal meningitis."

"Oh, I knew somebody that had that."

"Did they die?"

"No."

"Then I guess it wasn't spinal meningitis. You always die of that."

"You do? Then I guess he had something that sounded like it. What was the name of it?"

"Spinal meningitis."

"Spinal?"

"Men-in-gitis."

"Spinal meningitis. I guess it was something else. What class are you in?"

"One."

"So am I. My brother said this is the hardest year. He said if you study like hell the first year you make a good impression and then they don't bother you any more. What does your father do?"

"He owns a steel mill."

"Owns it? The whole thing?"

"Yes. My grandfather started it."

"Have your family got an automobile?"

"No."

"No? Did you ever hear of a Packard?"

"Yes."

"That's what we have. I'm learning to drive."

"You are?"

"Not by myself, but I'm allowed to hold the steering-wheel. When I graduate my father's going to give me a car of my own."

"When you graduate from here?"

"No. College."

"Oh, I thought you meant when you graduated from here."

"Oh, that's nothing. A friend of my brother's has a car and he just graduated from prep school. Don't you have a car at all?"

"My grandfather has."

"What make?"

"Pierce-Arrow."

"If I owned a steel mill you can be sure I'd own a car."

"My father's getting one in the spring."

"What make?"

"I guess a Pierce-Arrow."

"My father had a demonstration in the Pierce-Arrow but he liked the Packard better. He said the Pierce-Arrow isn't very good on hills."

"My grandfather's is."

"Have you got any other brothers and sisters?"

"I have two sisters."

"What are their names?"

"Sally, and Constance."

"Have you got any pictures of them?"

"No."

"How old are they?"

"One is twelve and the other is ten or eleven."

"Did you ever kiss a girl? I don't mean your sisters."

"Maybe I did and maybe I didn't."

"I kissed at least six of them. I loved one up, too. Did you ever love one up?"

"Maybe I did, and maybe I didn't."

"That's more fun than kissing, *I'll tell you*. If you ever come to visit me I'll get one to love you up. Do you know what that is?"

"What?"

"It's when she lets you squeeze her tits and behind. She lets anybody do it. The trouble is she isn't very pretty, but she'll let you love her up. Oh, I could tell you a thing or two about her. One boy—no, I guess I can't tell you about that. I swore on my word of honor. What's that bell for?"

"Supper. We're supposed to wash and then the bell rings

60

again in five minutes and we're supposed to be in the dining hall."

"Wash? Where do we wash?"

"There, in your washbasin. You pour the water out of that pitcher."

"There's no water in my pitcher."

"I'll pour you some out of mine."

"No thanks, I'll go without it. They won't know the difference."

In a few weeks Alfred Eaton hated Chauncey Moore as he never had hated anyone, and the hatred was part of his education, the feeling itself and the things that caused it. Chauncey talked incessantly, regardless of Alfred's lack of interest and in spite of Alfred's frequent contradictions of Chauncey's facts, and after lights were out he still went on talking until Alfred feigned snoring. He borrowed freely—soap, clean towels, socks, handkerchiefs, tablets, pencils. Then Alfred discovered that if he told Moore to shut up, he would shut up; if he refused the loan of his soap, Moore would borrow from someone else, and in neither case was he offended. For Alfred the discovery was important because in a new environment, away from whatever influence his family might have, he became one boy's superior, and while the boy was an inferior boy, it was a new experience for Alfred, who had never given much thought to superiority and inferiority among his schoolmates. He had accepted the role of inferior to his brother, and now he was learning that as Eaton, on his own, he could command a boy to stop talking and be obeyed, to respect his property and be obeyed. In this new environment, among a group of boys who were all new to each other and to the environment, and starting on equal terms, and with no one there who had known his brother Billy, he was acquiring a new self-confidence that actually had its source in the total and mutual lack of self-confidence that afflicted all the members of his class in its early weeks. There were some members of the class who acquired self-confidence more quickly, and more of it, but Alfred Eaton, or Eaton of Class One, was measuring himself against his peers and finding he was as good as most and better than some.

He had never played football at Phillipson's, where the game was not on the sports program. Because he was one of the taller boys in his class he was made a tackle and played in the three games between Class One and Class Two. Class Two won the rubber game, but in the game that Class One won, Eaton, in spite of getting a bloody nose twice in the first half and once in the second, recovered a Two fumble during a guards-back play, and One made the winning touchdown two rushes later. He was spoken of as promising material for the next season, which was to be the school's first year in inter-scholastic competition.

Most of the students came from Philadelphia, with the others from Wilmington, Baltimore, Lancaster, Reading, Fort Penn and nearby smaller towns. The school closed over the Thanksgiving holiday and Alfred Eaton went home.

"I understand you went out for football," his father said at the Thanksgiving dinner.

"Yes."

"How did you like it?"

"Fine. I liked it."

"You did, or do you have to pretend you did?"

"I liked it. I don't have to pretend anything."

"Did you play in any games?"

"Yes, I played in all three."

"Did you win?"

"Alfred's team won one out of three. Very good, I think, considering that most of the boys had never played before."

"Who was it you played against?"

"Class Two."

"Oh, in the same school."

"Next year we're going to play other schools."

"What schools?"

"Chestnut Hill, Germantown, Haverford, maybe some more."

"Are you going out for the varsity?"

"Yes, they asked me to."

"Aren't you pretty light for teams like Haverford?"

"Maybe I am now, but they told me to put on weight."

"Well, here's some turkey, that'll put some on you."

"You didn't ask me if I played well."

"Well, did you?"

"In one game I recovered a fumble—"

"Whose fumble? Not your own, I trust."

"Theirs, the Class Two's."

"What is this, oysters in the stuffing?"

"Yes," said Martha. "We've always had bread or chestnut, and I thought oysters would be nice for a change."

"I'd rather have my oysters on the half shell."

"Go on, Alfred, you were telling us about a fumble."

"Oh, never mind."

"If we're going to have some boasting, I think we can do without that."

"Well, that's what I was going to do. Boast."

"Oh, you made a touchdown?" said Samuel Eaton.

"No, but I recovered the fumble."

"You recovered the fumble, somebody else made the touchdown. How many points did you get for recovering the fumble?"

"None, but the—"

"Well then I'd let the other boy do the boasting, the one that made the touchdown."

"All right, but he said I really won the game."

"That was very nice of him and I admire him for his sportsmanship—and modesty. Constance, I think you have a preference for the drumstick."

"A tackle doesn't get much chance to make touchdowns, and that's what I played. Right tackle."

"I'm afraid your mother and your sisters don't know that much about football, so let's talk about something we can all join in."

"I want to hear about Alfred's bloody nose," said Constance.

"Well, you go right ahead and ask him about it after we've left the table."

"But Father, maybe I'll forget."

"If you do, I'm sure Alfred will remind you."

Alfred was not disposed to remind his ten-year-old sister of her interest in his bloodied nose. Now she was less offensive to him and toward him, but also more remote. He had become the brother home from school, who had played football and made the acquaintance of city boys. The brother she had teased and snapped at as recently as the past summer was changed into a boy who had actually spoken up to his father, as in the exchange about boasting. She was full of respectful curiosity, but the new attitude did not make him forget all the years of picking on him. But he felt very friendly toward Sally.

He had arrived home the night before Thanksgiving. His mother and Sally were at the station with Grandfather Johnson's Pierce-Arrow and chauffeur. He sat between them on the way home, covered with a buffalo robe. It was a cold, damp evening without being cold enough or damp enough to put up the side curtains, and the air felt good after the stuffy train. His mother asked him questions that were easy to answer, and Sally sat silent until they were inside the house.

"I'm glad you're home," said Sally.

"Well, thanks. I'm glad to *be* home."

"Somebody else will be glad, too," said Sally.

"Oh, who?"

"V. D."

"V. D.?"

"You know."

"Victoria Dockwiler," said Alfred. "Did she say anything?"

"She asked me not to tell you."

"Oh, come on, Sally."

"If you promise not to tell her?"

"I won't say anything."

"She asked me to ask Mother if I could invite her to lunch on Friday. *You* know *why.*"

"Why?"

"So she can see *you.*"

"Is she coming Friday?"

"Yes," said Sally. "I know something else, too."

"What?"

"She has a real case on you. She really has, Alfred. She asked about you all the time you were away."

"Oh, that's only politeness."

"Not with V. D. Do you know what?"

"What?"

"She asked her mother to let her stay home from dancing school."

"Dancing school! Good old dancing school. Gone but not forgotten."

"But do you know why?"

"No."

"Because she didn't want to go any more because you weren't there. She told me that in those exact words, Alfred. I only hope one thing."

"What?"

"Well, you seem older."

"Do I? Well, I am. I'm September, October, November older. And I weigh more."

"I meant in other ways. You really seem at least a year older. You're more like fifteen or sixteen."

"Well, I guess I seem that way because I've been living with a lot of fellows, and most of them *are* fifteen or sixteen or seventeen or eighteen. One boy is nineteen. He was *expelled* from Lawrenceville."

"A *friend* of yours?"

"Oh, you couldn't call him a friend of mine, but you couldn't call him an enemy. Charlie Fentriss? No, he's not a friend of mine. One and Three are supposed to be friends, and he's in Four. But he's a Black and so am I. The whole school is one half Blacks and the other half Oranges. They're our rivals, the Oranges."

"Oh."

"What were you saying before that?"

"You do seem older."

"Well, I guess you do too."

"Do I? I don't to myself. In some ways, I guess, but not really till I put my hair up."

"Well, you're only twelve."

64

"So is V. D.," said Sally. "If you go out to lunch on Friday will you tell me? I wouldn't want V. D. to be disappointed."

Alfred made no plans that would cause his absence from home on the day after Thanksgiving. He accepted an invitation to attend the football game between Port Johnson High and Eckburg; three o'clock Thanksgiving afternoon, and to be followed by supper at the home of Joe Teasdale, a Phillipson classmate who was host at the football game. There would be a dance on Friday evening for present and former members of the dancing class, and on Saturday the boys and girls in Alfred's age group were going to a chicken-and-waffle supper at the Farmers Hotel in Prosperity. These engagements provided for entertainment while leaving time for the young people to make informal plans of their own.

The Teasdale party was the first get-together for the boys who were at boarding school. It was a success except for the slight envy Alfred felt at seeing three of his Phillipson classmates in the grey greatcoats and black tarbuckets of their military school and, all too visible at the supper when they took off the greatcoat, the military schoolboys' long pants that were part of the uniform but not yet a part of Alfred's wardrobe. He did not look forward to the dance wearing knickerbockers while three boys who were shorter than he wore dazzling uniforms that included long trousers.

He met the knickerbocker problem on Friday morning by putting on his old riding breeches and leather puttees and casually announcing that he was going for a ride after lunch. The breeches were tight at the waist and the knee and he left the top waist buttons and calf buttons undone; his jacket would cover the waist and the puttees would hide the legs. He was uncomfortable, but at least he was not dressed like a damn twelve-year-old kid.

He heard the high groan of the Dockwilers' car in the driveway. He stood at the hall window on the second story until Victoria got out of the car and he could hear her in the front hall. Sometimes when she visited Sally the two girls would go directly to Sally's room, but now they seemed to have gone into the sittingroom, which was a relief to him as he had not planned to greet her upstairs. He waited a few moments and then went downstairs and entered the sittingroom, making straight for a copy of *The Literary Digest* on the table.

"Alfred, here's Victoria," said Sally.

"Oh, hello, Victoria. I didn't see you there."

"Hello, Alfred. Did you go horseback riding?" said Victoria.

"Well at least aren't you going to shake hands?" said Sally.

65

"The gentleman is supposed to wait till the lady offers her hand," said Alfred.

"Hello, Alfred," said Victoria, offering her hand. "Or at least welcome home."

"Well, hello again, Victoria. Thank you. It's such a good day for a ride, I guess I'll take Missy for a few miles this afternoon."

"You can't. Missy's lame," said Sally.

"I didn't know that. Then I went to all this trouble of donning my equestrian garments for naught?"

"You should have asked George. Missy's going to be put out to pasture. Father went to see a new horse last week in Philadelphia."

"Oh, well, I guess I'd be stiff tomorrow. I use different muscles playing football."

Sally looked at her friend and at her brother. "Excuse me but I have to go upstairs and get a handkerchief."

"I'll go with you," said Victoria.

"No, you don't have to, Victoria. Alfred will talk to you while I'm just a minute." She left.

"You in seventh grade now?" said Alfred, when they were alone.

"Yes, seventh."

"That's right. You're in the same grade as Sally. Still go to dancing school?"

"Yes."

"Well, it helps to occupy the time."

"I don't like it any more."

"No? Why? You used to."

"I've changed."

"Oh, well, you have to expect that."

"I don't like to change."

"You don't like to change? Everybody changes sometime. Old people change, young people change, everybody changes. Would you want to stay in seventh grade the rest of your life?"

"Yes."

"It is to laugh," said Alfred. "I'll bet you don't mean that."

"I do, though. Excuse me." She got up and left him. He waited in the sittingroom but they did not come down again until lunch was announced. At the table his mother made an effort, but her only conversational support came from Constance. Sally and Victoria spoke only when asked direct questions, and Alfred, unable to understand why Victoria had left him so abruptly, eventually decided that she was young and not very interesting. He asked to be excused as soon as he ate his dessert, and went up to his room. He tried to do some home work, but gave up after finding it impossible to concentrate. He got out the clothes that would no longer fit him and put them in a pile as his mother had requested. He found other such things to do until he heard the car come to take Victoria away.

Not greatly to his surprise, Sally came to his room.

"Did you say anything to Victoria?" she asked.

"I conversed with her."

"But you must have said something."

"I said numerous things."

"I think you hurt her feelings."

"If anybody should have hurt feelings it's I. All of a sudden she just jumped up and ran upstairs. Don't ask me why, because I don't know. You females!"

"Victoria doesn't get hurt feelings over nothing. She has too much sense."

"Well, what did she say?"

"Not what she said, but she was almost crying."

"Lord deliver us. Crying."

"Not crying, but close to it. Victoria never cries. She didn't even cry when she had her broken arm."

"I didn't know she had a broken arm."

"Well, she did."

"When?"

"After you went away to school. She fainted during recess and fell off a swing. She had to have her arm in a plaster cast."

"Well, I'm sorry she broke her arm, but my goodness, I didn't say anything. Maybe her arm was hurting her today."

"No, it was something different."

"What did she *say?*"

"Nothing."

"She must have said *something.*"

"Not that had anything to do with you."

"Well, that had something to do with anything?"

"The only thing she said was—oh."

"She said oh?"

"I said oh. I just realized. Oh, now I know. Did you say anything about seventh grade?"

"Yes."

"Oh. She said she liked being in seventh grade, and never wanted to leave it. Did you tease her about that?"

"Not tease her, but I said something."

"She knew you've changed. It didn't take *her* long."

"Well, I'm not supposed to stay the same, am I? Everybody changes, older people change, young people change."

"Yes, but she didn't want you to change. She wanted you to be the same, and you're not. You're my brother, but you're not as nice as you used to be, Alfred. Not nearly as nice."

"A fat lot I care what a couple of seventh-graders think I am."

Sally turned and said no more.

He lay down on his bed and stared up at the ceiling. At first he was angry in his disappointment; all those nights and some days at Knox when he would have given anything to hear one word spoken from those thin, curving lips, and to stand as close to her and be looked at by those eyes, and to be able to tell her all the new things that were happening to him. And all of it, everything about her, kept to himself because he would not so much as mention her name to Chauncey Moore. It added to his anger to realize that he had been hoping she would not change—the same hope that she had entertained in her thoughts of him. And she had not changed, but he had, and now he knew that what his sister had told him was just as though she had been speaking for Victoria: he was not as nice as he used to be, not nearly as nice. Now all the fun of school had been spoiled: the games, the new friends. And exactly when he was going to enjoy it by reliving it in the telling of it to Victoria Dockwiler, a little girl who would not grow up and wanted no one else to.

She had taken all the pleasure out of vacation, and here it was only Friday afternoon and he wished it was Sunday and he could be back at school. He got up and gave the discarded clothes a kick and scattered them over the rug. He got out of his riding habit and put on the clothes he had worn home for the holiday, his new suit from Jacob Reed's, the new shoes from Geuting's. He remembered that there was a cake with chocolate icing on top of vanilla icing that should be in the cake-box and this was the time of day when both Josephine and Nellie were apt to be out of the kitchen.

He carefully opened and closed the top door of the stairway, carefully opened and closed the bottom door and was walking across the second-floor hall when he heard his mother's voice. What she said was indistinct, but he thought she was calling him. She had heard him in spite of his precautions.

He went to her door, which was not quite closed, and listened to make sure. "Oh, my darling," she said. "My darling." It was not in any voice she had ever used to him or to his father or to his sisters, and as he gently pushed the door open he suddenly knew that the words were not meant for him, for his father, for his sisters. They were meant for a man, and she was weeping for a man.

She was lying on the bed, dressed in the clothes she had worn at lunch. The bedspread was in place, but her face was deep in the covered pillow. There was no one else in the room, but Alfred had not expected there would be. The sounds she made were a call to someone who was nowhere near, and then maybe they were not a call to anyone, but to love that could not hear. And Alfred knew there was pity in it, too.

He retreated without a sound, and quietly went downstairs and through the house to the side door, turning the knob slowly, and opening and closing the door like a thief.

He walked around for a while, avoiding the stable and George Fry, but soon he began to feel the cold and he made his way to the tackroom, where there was a stove. He warmed his hands and turned his back to get the heat from the stove and was standing that way when George Fry came in.

"I didn't see you come in," said George Fry.

"Didn't you?"

"I just finished saying I didn't. What's the matter? You hear the bad news too?"

"What bad news?"

"Mr. Miller."

"What about Mr. Miller?" said Alfred.

"Well, I guess you're old anough to be told these things. Mr. Miller shot himself this morning. Shot himself in the head with a pistol. No earthly reason for it. A man that had everything to live for, everything you could name. It'll be a great shock to your father and mother, they were closer than if they were related. No earthly reason on God's earth. He left no note, he was in no trouble, didn't drink enough to give anybody any concern. No money troubles, not in that family. What would a man like that want to take his own life for?"

"He had some reason."

"Of course he had some reason. You don't do a thing like that if you don't have a reason. To put a gun to your head and pull the trigger, that calls for a desperate reason. Well, I guess we'll never know."

"I hope not," said Alfred.

"I hope not too if that's the way the poor man wanted it, but at the same time, the public are entitled to know, if it's humanly possible."

"They are not."

"I say they are. It isn't a good thing to have people talking and speculating. A man ought to leave a note, to forestall rumors and gossip and the like of that. And who are you to have all these large opinions on the subject? A minute ago I wasn't even sure I'd mention the matter to such a young whelp, and in no time you're stating your opinions as if you knew a single God damn thing about it. This school you're at's making you very cocky indeed. The next thing'll be long pants and then I guess not even your father will be able to hold you in. I can see you're not going to be much help to me today in them clothes, but here's a lump of sugar you can give to poor old Missy. You heard about her?"

"Yes."

He took the lump of sugar and fed it to the mare.

"So long," he called to George.

"So long," said George. "You're not going away mad?"

"No. I have to go back to the house."

His mother, with Constance, was in the sittingroom. She had on a different dress and her hair was brushed back in place and if he had not seen and heard what he had seen and heard he would not have been able to detect a faint redness in her eyes.

"Alfred, have you been out all this time without a coat and hat?"

"I was inside part of the time."

"With George, I should imagine. But even so, this is the kind of weather, and you don't want to go back to school with the sniffles. Wouldn't that be awful, Constance, if we sent our boy back from his first vacation with the sniffles?"

"Oh, yes."

"They'd say, 'We take better care of your boy than you do.' "

"One thing wrong with that argument is I don't *have* the sniffles," said Alfred.

"Not now, but I do hope you won't go around any more without your coat and hat, or you'll spend the next week in the infirmary. And then what will Mr. McCready think? He'll think I'm not a very good mother."

He had a flashing temptation to say, "Are you?" But he had never spoken rudely to her—angrily, but not with the kind of rudeness that some boys showed when they were exasperated by their mothers. And he had no reason, or no evidence, on which to base even a mildly sarcastic accusation. Accusation of what? He had found her crying and saying "Darling" in a tone that he had never heard her use before. Then he had gone out to the stable and heard that a friend of hers and his father's had committed suicide. And what if she *was* weeping for Mr. Miller and calling him "darling"? What if she was? Even though she had never called him "darling" while he was alive, his sudden, shocking death could be enough to make her say things she ordinarily did not say. Mr. and Mrs. Miller were his father-and-mother's closest friends. And yet he could not convincingly accuse himself of holding a nasty suspicion unjustly. For whatever instinct was worth, it was telling him that he was correctly relating his mother's tears to the bad news about Mr. Miller, and he knew that his mother had loved Mr. Miller in a way that she never would admit.

For the remainder of his vacation he studied her behavior, trying fairly to compare it with the way she normally behaved. He thought, but he could not be fairly sure, that she talked more, was more vivacious than usual; but that could be put down to the holiday spirit, having him home for his first vacation, party plans. He could not bring himself to ask her to sit down with him alone; he had no excuse to make what would have been such an unusual request. With his father she seemed to act no differently. And through the rest of Friday, Saturday and Sunday he never again detected any sign of the kind of unhappiness he had seen and heard in her bedroom.

It was not the sort of thing you talked about with a friend, but he kept wishing he had a friend whom he could talk to. In the surprising experience of discovering that his mother was in love with a man, he had been diverted from his disappointment with Victoria. She was more beautiful than ever, but now she had become—had *become*—a child. She had not been only a child while he was still a child, but she had become one when he became something else. He had never kissed her, but now he no longer hoped to, not for the present. She had become a child, and he was relegating her to the future, when she would be a young lady and he would be a man. And it was at that point in his thinking that he made a discovery that was valuable: in Port Johnson he had no real friend; he had always been the brother of Billy Eaton, in the family and out of it; while at Knox he was himself, in a place where Billy Eaton had never been heard of; and it explained why he was getting along so well at Knox. Knox was *his*, and not Billy's. He had been anxious to make good in order to elevate himself in the estimation of his father. But now he also wanted to make good because Knox was, secretly, his. It was not so much that Knox had provided a couple of friends who he was sure would remain his friends; it was the school life, what it took him away from, what it gave him. It was pleasant to be able to go to the pantry for a piece of cake whenever he felt like it, and not to be ordered about by the ringing of bells, but he would go back to school without regret.

His holiday was turning out to be something more, and not necessarily better, than the easy long weekend of good times that he had anticipated. There was the unexpected hero worship by his sisters; his impulsive sarcasm to his father; his disappointment in Victoria, and the unconfirmed but convincing suspicion of his mother. There remained one more surprise.

He had read in the *Beacon* that Norma Budd was attending the Penn-Cornell football game at Franklin Field, and he inferred that she would be gone from Port Johnson all during his holiday. But on Saturday morning, as he was going down Montgomery Street for a soda, Norma, in the yellow trap drawn by one of their sorrels, pulled up beside him. "Good morning, Mr. Alfred Eaton," said Norma. "Can I give you a lift?"

"Sure. Sure," he said, and climbed up on the seat beside her.

He took off his cap and shook hands with her, grinning and feeling that he was blushing.

"How are you? It's so nice to see you, Alfred. I was afraid I wouldn't."

"I know," he said.

"You know? What do you know? Do you know my innermost secret thoughts?"

"Oh, not that, but I saw in the paper you were going to the game."

"Yes, I saw that, too. Don't believe everything you see in print. My escort—I hate that word—had an attack of appendicitis and had to be operated on at the German Hospital. I had a special delivery from his sister and he's coming along nicely, but I missed the big game. I hear *you've* become a gridiron star."

"Oh, not a star. Only a tackle."

"But you were a *good* tackle. Now who told me that? It's always nice to know who—is your roommate a boy named Moore?"

"Chauncey Moore."

"Well, then that's how I heard it. His sister is a friend of mine, and she read me a letter from her brother. Chauncey. Are you wondering why she would read me a letter from her brother?"

"Yes."

"Do you like Chauncey?"

"Not very much, no."

"Then I'll tell you. She read the letter because it was so funny and full of mistakes, but he did say that Eaton, his roommate, won some game. That's how I knew."

"I don't think that's very nice of her, his sister."

"To read his letter? No, but it was a funny letter, and she wasn't mean about it. And that's one of the things I like about you. You're fair. Are you on your way to Sterling's? If you are, and you haven't got a heavy date, I'll have a phosphate with you. I noticed you were coming from the direction of your grandfather's, so I'll bet you're rich."

"I haven't spent a cent since I've been home."

"Will you spend five on me?"

"Sure. You've often spent more than that on me, and I've never spent anything on you."

"No, but last year you bought a tag from me on Tag Day and that was just about the same thing. Hospital Tag Day. Do you remember that?"

"Sure. I still have it," he said.

She suddenly looked at him and frowned. "Alfred!" she said, and he thought she was going to cry.

72

"I have everything you gave me. The British soldier, and the sailboat from Maine. And all your postcards."

"Do you know, Alfred, I'm not really surprised. If you gave me anything I'd keep it, too."

She tied the horse in front of Sterling's drug store and they went in and sat at one end of the soda fountain. "You order," she said.

"Lemon phosphate and chocolate soda, please," he said.

"Lemon phos, and one dark," said the man behind the counter, a stranger to Norma and Alfred. He went to prepare the order.

"Showing off for you," said Alfred.

Norma laughed. "I know." They smiled at each other in the back-bar mirror.

"Have you been having a good time on your first vacation?"

"Pretty good."

"Not altogether good. How is Victoria?"

"Oh—I don't know."

"But you've seen her?"

"Twice. But I don't know. She got her feelings hurt because she took the wrong meaning at something I said. I can't help it if I'm getting older. And I wouldn't want to stop it even if I could. I'm tired of being just a kid."

"Well, you won't be much longer, if that's any consolation. That's why I hope you have a good time now, because getting older doesn't mean everything gets better." She touched a gold badge on her shirtwaist, a device formed of two Greek letters.

"Is that a fraternity pin?"

"Yes," she said. "He's the one that was operated on. I ought not to be wearing it. We're not engaged. But he asked me to wear it, and I do. But it doesn't make me feel engaged. I really ought not to wear it, because I'm not *going* to be engaged, to him. You see, Alfred? Problems just the same, and I'm almost twenty-one. At least when I'm twenty-one I'll be able to do as I please, at least I'll have the money to. If you were twenty-five and I were twenty-one I'd ask you to marry me, and that would solve everything, wouldn't it, Alfred?"

"Pretty nearly."

"Not everything? Is there something else besides Victoria? There is, isn't there?"

"Yes."

"At school?"

"No."

"Oh, at home. But you don't want to talk about it?"

"I want to, but I wouldn't know how to start."

73

"You were going to write to me but you never did, except one postcard. Do you want to write it to me?"

"Write it? That would be worse," said the boy.

"If it'll make you feel better, write it and I'll promise to tear it up."

"Then I might . . . No, I guess not."

He finished the rest of his soda. On the way out a boy of Alfred's age held the door open for Norma Budd. "Hello, Alfred. Home for Thanksgiving?"

"Hello, Tom. Uh-huh. Home for Thanksgiving. Going to have a soda?"

"No, I work here," said Tom Rothermel. "So long."

"So long," said Alfred.

"If you wait a minute or two I'll drive you back to your grandfather's," said Norma Budd.

"Do you want me to carry any bundles?"

"I won't have any big enough to carry." She went to the jewelry store. Her purchase took five minutes, and she returned to the trap.

"Is that all the shopping you had?"

"That's all. Didn't even have that when I left home. I just wanted to get some fresh air—without walking," she said. "But I'm glad I saw you."

"I'm glad I saw you, too."

"I know," she said. "It's nice to be able to say things right out. Do you know what a coquette is?"

"A flirt, isn't it?"

"Yes. I guess I'm coquettish sometimes—I know I am. I flirt. But then I always wish I hadn't. When I get home I'm going to take this pin off and never wear it again."

"I don't think you like him anyway."

She nodded. "I wish I had you around to advise me. I *don't* like him, at least not enough to wear his fraternity pin. It should mean something, and it doesn't."

They were off the cobblestones of Lower Montgomery Street and on the safer dirt of East Montgomery. "Do you want to drive?" she said.

"Sure!" he said.

"We'll change places," she said. In so doing he moved too slowly or she moved too quickly, and as she sat down her whole upper leg gently crushed down on his. He could feel the softness of her under her skirt and petticoats, and the excitement sent his heart pumping. It was as if he had stolen a thrill from her, and from this moment on she would be the great repository of imagined touches.

"Let him trot, it'll do him good," she said.

The bob-tailed sorrel sensed the different hands on the russet reins and stepped out with a high, fast action as though he had been waiting all morning for the chance. The excitement of the nearness of the exciting girl and the gelding's response and the cold air made the boy into a different being from the one Norma Budd had always known, and without knowing all the reasons for his excitement, she felt some of it being communicated to her.

"Go all the way out, don't stop at your grandfather's," she said.

They drove out East Montgomery Street, past the built-up section and the borough limits and into the farming country until they came to a junction of three roads known locally as Five Points and used as a turnabout by people who wanted to breeze their horses.

"Shall we turn around at Five Points?" said Alfred.

"I don't want to, but it's getting close to lunch-time."

"Do you want to take the reins?"

"No, you keep them till we get to Mr. Johnson's. But I have something for you, and I want to give it to you now," said Norma. She handed him a small package. "It's something to take back to school."

"Shall I open it?"

"If you want to."

"Will you hold the reins, please?"

She took the reins while he undid the package and saw her present, a silver-mounted fountain pen, the first fountain pen he had owned.

"Oh! This is for me?"

"I expect at least one letter from you. Not the one we talked about. Just a letter. I hope you haven't got one."

"I've never had one. There's only one boy in my class has one. This is more like Christmas than Thanksgiving. *Thank* you, ever so much."

"Do you know how to fill it?"

"Sure. I'm going to fill it as soon as I get home."

"But don't show it to your family," said Norma Budd.

"Don't you want me to?"

"It'd be better if you didn't. I'm not old enough to give you presents, and I'm too old. When you were a little boy it was different, but you're not a little boy any more."

"No."

"Alfred?"

"What?"

"Is that why you don't like Victoria any more?"

"Yes."

"I thought so. Wait a few years, maybe only one year. You'll like her again, because she'll like you."

"I don't think I'll ever like her again, not as much."

"Why?"

"I like you better."

"Because you want to kiss me?"

"Yes."

"I'm sorry, Alfred, but you can't. It'd be all right for you, but not for me."

"If it's all right for me, why isn't it all right for you?"

"Because I'm too much older than you."

"Don't say that!"

"I have to say it because it's true."

He suddenly put his hand on her neck and roughly kissed her on the mouth, and in her surprise she raised her hands and the sorrel leapt forward. The boy and Norma were thrown against the back of the seat but she held on to the reins and was able to bring the horse down to a walk. They rode in silence for a while.

"I apologize," said the boy.

"I'm not cross," she said. She smiled. "Maybe I would have been if we'd been thrown out. But we weren't. But I think we'd better change places now."

The driver's cushion was slanted forward and higher than the other seat, and this time as Alfred slid over and down to his original seat their legs did not touch. She was a good and stylish driver, and she took the whip out of the socket and held it poised with the reins, and kept her eyes on the road, automatically checking the harness and the horse as they headed home.

"Don't feel badly, Alfred," she said.

"I don't know why I did that."

"But I do. You wanted to kiss me. A lady has no right to complain about that, if a gentleman wants to kiss her."

"Gentleman!"

"Yes, gentlemen kiss ladies, and not always when the ladies want them to. Something comes over them, I guess."

"You're just trying to make me feel better."

"Well, I don't want you to feel badly, but it's true, gentlemen don't always ask the lady for a kiss. And I'll tell you a secret, if you don't know it already. Ladies like to be kissed. Some day I'll let you kiss me, Alfred. Maybe when I'm twenty-eight and you're twenty-one. If you still want to."

"I'll always want to, but you won't, not after this."

"There you're wrong. And do you realize what I said? I practically said I wanted to kiss you now."

He was silent for a noticeable length of time.

"It's all right, Alfred. We're still friends."

"Norma?"

"Yes?"

"If you were twenty-eight, you'd be married, wouldn't you?"

"Well, I should hope so."

"But you'd kiss me, even if you were married?"

"Yes, I think I would."

"But without telling your husband."

"No, I don't think that would be a good idea. When I'm married, mind you, I don't expect to kiss other gentlemen, but I think I'd make an exception for you."

"Do you know any married people that do kiss other men and women?"

"I know some men who do."

"Any ladies?"

"I've heard of some."

"Do you know of any here in town?"

"Not ladies. Why?"

"I just wondered."

"Wondered what? Whether ladies do things behind their husband's back? If that's what you want to know, you're awfully young to be told so, but they do. In Philadelphia I've heard of some. Well—two."

"But you never heard of anybody in Port Johnson?"

"No."

"What happened to the ladies in Philadelphia?"

"One of them moved away. The other one's still there."

"Didn't her husband do anything to her?"

"You mean beat her, or something like that?"

"Anything."

"I don't think he'd dare, because everybody knows he's worse than she is."

"Why did the other one move away?"

"They say she was—I don't really know. It's just gossip."

"Because she didn't only kiss him? Is that why?"

"You know too much for your age."

"I know that people more than kiss."

"Do they?"

"You know it too—don't you?"

"Well, yes, I do."

"Is that what the lady did that moved away?"

"Alfred—yes, that's what they say."

"And the other one that stayed, you said her husband was worse than she was, but that means she was doing the same thing only not as much."

"I suppose that's what I meant."

"Would everybody know about it if it happened to a lady in Port Johnson?"

"It would be hard to keep it a secret in Port Johnson. They gossip here for less than that. You suspect somebody in Port Johnson, don't you?"

"I guess so."

"I don't want to know her name, but is it someone you like? And it isn't me?"

"No, it isn't you, but it's someone I like."

"In that case, the nicest thing you can do for her is never to say any more about it. Are other people suspicious of her?"

"I don't think so."

"Well, I can count on you to keep her secret. And if your suspicions are true, even if they're true, it may not be her fault."

"I'll keep her secret."

"When I'm twenty-eight and you're twenty-one and you want to kiss me, I'm going to ask you if you kept this secret."

"And if I don't keep it you won't let me kiss you."

"You hit the nail right on the head," she said.

"Goodbye, Alfred," she said. They were at The Mansion, and she put out her hand. "I won't be here for Christmas. We're going abroad to see some specialist about my brother's rheumatism. So I won't see you for a long, long time. But I'll let you know where I am so you can write to me."

"I'll write to you. How much does it cost to send a letter to Europe? What kind of a stamp do you put on?"

"Five cents, I think. Not any more than that."

"If I just put two twos and a one?"

"That's all you'll need." She looked down at him, standing with his cap off, and smiled. "You're going to be a handsome man."

"Me handsome? Huh."

"Oh, that's not all you'll be. You can be almost anything you decide, but you're going to be handsome, no mistake about that."

"You embarrass me," he said.

"I know, and we'll both be late for lunch, so goodbye, Alfred, and the very best of luck at school."

"Goodbye, and thank you for the fountain pen."

Parents had been instructed to return their sons to Knox on trains that would have them back in time for Sunday supper, and the train taken by Alfred also transported two school-mates from Reading, one from Fort Penn, and one from Gibbsville. The boys already on the train greeted Alfred with noisy friendliness and he was in effect back at school before the train had pulled out of the Port Johnson yards. None of the boys had been among his closest friends at Knox, but as the newest arrival on the train he was the object of the questions they had asked each other earlier (without waiting for answers). They had been away only since Wednesday evening, but for Alfred and two others it had been their first boarding-school vacation, and now to go back seemed to establish them more firmly as members of the school. They were glad to be going back, even those boys who had said, "If I ever get out of this place it's the last they'll ever see of me." And there would be only three more weeks before Christmas.

Mr. Deland did not enforce the no-visiting rule on the first night, but as an experienced schoolmaster he knew that the period between Thanksgiving and Christmas holidays was one in which it was difficult to get his charges to settle down. He was, therefore, stricter in the succeeding days and nights, and at the end of the first week he summoned Alfred to his room.

"Eaton, you've wasted a whole week since you came back from Thanksgiving. What's the trouble?"

"Sir?"

"Did the love-bug bite you instead of you biting the turkey? In my classes, and the same holds true of the other masters, you haven't been prepared. During free-time I've noticed you lying on your bed, with your shoes on, against R and R, gazing intently at the ceiling. Is it *l'amour?*"

"No sir."

"Then what is it? Any trouble at home?"

"No sir."

"Constipated?"

"No sir."

"Nothing wrong. Absolutely nothing wrong. And yet you have spring fever in December, or all the symptoms. Well, you're not going to confide in me, that's obvious, so you may go."

"Yes sir."

"But heed my warning. You're going to be back here next week if there isn't an improvement. Don't be one of those boys that believe they can make a good showing the first few months and never have to do any more. That is a great fallacy. I'm the kind of master that's more likely to forget the good past and pay more attention to the lazy present. You may go."

A week later Alfred was recalled by Deland. "Well, here we are again, Eaton."

"Yes sir."

"Latin down, English down, Civics down, French down, Algebra down, late for chapel twice, late for meals three times, hands not washed twice, and, unofficially, I suspect you of smoking cigarettes. If you were at school in England you'd be getting what they call ten of the very best, which would make your hands bleed. But here we don't administer corporal punishment. More's the pity, in some cases. Have you any excuses for all this?"

"No sir."

"Good, because there are no excuses. But I'm afraid there's an explanation. I'm not going to ask you, because you'd lie to me anyway, but I'm going to tell you what I think. I think you're committing a certain secret sin. You know what I'm talking about. Is there anyone else committing it with you?"

"No sir."

" 'No sir.' If there is, we'll find out about it, and when we find out, you and the other boy or boys will be sent home in disgrace. Are you fully aware of that?"

"Yes sir."

"You'll find it just about impossible to get into any other school, and it'll be on your record for the rest of your life. Do you understand that?"

"Yes sir."

"All right, then. Do you want to ruin your life? Do you want to lose your manhood? Do you want to become a nervous wreck? Do you want to become a slave to a habit that will make you unable to fall in love with some fine girl? Don't you look forward to the day when you'll marry the girl of your choice and have children? Then I tell you, Eaton, stop this habit now. Look me in the eye and tell me you're going to stop it."

Alfred met his gaze. "Yes sir."

"I suppose you came here expecting punishment, but I'm not going to punish you. When you go to bed tonight I want you to pray to the Lord for the courage and strength to resist temptation, to conquer this secret and sinful habit. It's His help you need, and not punishment from me. But if He doesn't hear your prayer, if He turns a deaf ear because He knows you are not beseeching Him for help and guidance, then that will be your worst punishment. That's all for the time being, but you know now that I've been watching you for the tell-tale signs. You may go."

Unfortunately for the force of Deland's argument he seemed not to have noticed tell-tale signs in two boys down the hall who committed the secret sin together whenever they were in the shower-room, and who made no effort to keep the sin a secret from the other boys. But Deland's lecture frightened Alfred out of the mood he had been in since Thanksgiving holiday. There had been too many things all at once. He had seen for the first time that his father was an ineffectual bully. He had discovered, in reverse order of their importance, that his mother was in love with another man and could *be* in love with another man. He had found that the girl he had loved had retrogressed to childhood. And he had had two experiences with Norma Budd that not even she knew all about, and which he tried to recapture and fulfill in the secret sin. Under her clothes she was surely like the pictures that

80

Chauncey Moore helped to circulate in the school, but Alfred had a demanding curiosity that could only be appeased in his own imagination. And in his thoughts of her he had reached the belief that she would be a willing partner to the excitement. The imagined moments with her became for a time the most precious interludes in his life, and for that reason, and not because of Deland's moral utterances, he exerted himself in his public conduct in the classroom and elsewhere.

He was so successful in his deception of Deland that on the day of departure for the Christmas holiday the master called him to his office and said: "Eaton, I hope I'm not speaking too soon, but I'd like you to know I've noticed a great improvement. Maybe our talk did some good, do you think?"

"Yes sir."

"And I only hope it'll be permanent. Merry Christmas, have a jolly good vacation and don't eat too much plum pudding."

"Thank you, sir, and the same to you."

Alfred remembered that Christmas as a continuation of the Thanksgiving holiday, rather than as a separate period of its own. In his four years at Knox he had the customary three interruptions of the school year: at Thanksgiving, at Christmas, and in the spring; and since he lived so near, he was always able to go home. In going back from maturity into the recollections of his Knox vacations he was quite likely to place an event of the 1912-1913 Christmas in the 1913-1914 school year. He was always able to recall in ample detail the small and greater triumphs and failures of prep school, and as a test of his memory he once wrote down the names of 100 boys he had known at the school; classmates and boys ahead of and behind him, then as a further test he tried to identify each boy as an Orange or a Black. In that part of the test he was more successful than in putting them in the proper class. It was easier to remember that a boy had been an Orange than that he had been two classes ahead of him or three classes behind him. He also had less trouble remembering articles that he had lost (or had been stolen) than presents without any more history than that they had been presents. His memory of Knox days contained such items as one happy dance with a girl he had known for a few days, and the time he was knocked unconscious by a pitched ball, and a runaway dray on Market Street, Philadelphia, but of a hundred or a thousand such memories there was none that came to mind without a topical reminder. In maturity he had no close friendship that had been created in prep school, although there were men, Knox schoolmates, whom he would have been glad to see again for the favorable impression they had made in his teens. As a man he always thought of Knox as the four-year period in which the outstanding and continuing concern was what had happened and was happening—and *if* it had happened and was happening—to his mother. It was in truth even more outstanding than the fact that in his fourth year at the school he once again fell in love with Victoria Dockwiler.

Spring Day in his last year at Knox was an occasion which had some aspects of the lawn fete, some of the sports carnival, and some of an inspection by a friendly Board of Visitors. It was all three. It was also the one day of the year on which Knox boys (of the upper two classes) were permitted to invite young ladies to be their chaperoned guests between the hours of ten A.M. and six P.M. All parents were invited to subscribe, and the subscription fee of ten dollars nicely covered the luncheon under a marquee, of which the young lady guests partook without financial demands on the boys. The fee also took care of the sprucing up of the grounds and the cost of the medals and cups for the sports events, and always left a small balance which McCready found some use for. Spring Day never *lost* money.

The sports program, entirely intra-mural, got under way at ten o'clock of a warm and sunny morning. In almost every case the chaperon for the young lady guest was a boy's mother, and the girl and the woman sat together under the mother's parasol, applauding, whenever possible at the right moment during the running and jumping and tossing down on the field. Boys who were not participating in the athletic contests were designated ushers and wore orange-and-black brassards to distinguish them from the members of Classes One and Two. Members of the teaching staff wore white flannel trousers and blue coats and it was correctly assumed that the marks of the years would distinguish them from the boys of One and Two.

Alfred took second place in the high jump, the only event he had entered, with a not particularly spectacular scissors with the bar at 4'11½". He waved to his mother and Victoria Dockwiler, trotted to the shower and dressed, and joined them within the hour.

"Think of being able to jump—what was it, dear?"

"Four-eleven and a half. Under five feet."

"But only half an inch under five feet. Why, that means he could jump over your head, Victoria."

"No I couldn't, Mother," said Alfred. "How tall are you, Victoria?"

"I'm five feet two inches."

"Then if I tried to jump over her head I'd kick the top of it."

"Well, I'm sure you wouldn't want to do that, and I don't think Victoria would care for it much either, but it was

82

almost five feet. I'm going to tell people it was five feet. And you get a medal, don't you?"

"Yes."

"Do you know what would be nice?"

"What?"

"If you gave Victoria the medal."

"Oh, Mother! I was going to, and now she'll think I did it because you suggested it."

"Oh, I think you ought to have it, Mrs. Eaton," said Victoria.

"I wish you'd let me have some say in the matter," said Alfred.

"I was only making a suggestion, dear. I'm sure Victoria and I agree that you may do exactly what you please with it, don't we, Victoria?"

"Yes, I do."

"When do you get the medal, dear?"

"At the presentation. Don't you remember last year?"

"I don't remember any presentation."

"That's because I didn't get a medal."

"Where do we go for that, and when is it?"

"At the end of this business. You don't have to wait if you don't want to. I'll get my medal."

"I wouldn't miss it for the world," said his mother.

They watched the few remaining events, then one of the masters announced through a megaphone that if everyone would remain seated, the presentation of trophies was about to commence. Mr. McCready went into his speech immediately, thereby trapping the parents of the not-to-be-decorated. He spoke, in highly complimentary terms, of Theodore Roosevelt and the strenuous life, with tactful emphasis on Teddy's youthful frailty as compared with his later vigor. The *Lusitania* was sailing that day on her final voyage, but while McCready was no more prescient than any other schoolmaster, he did not overlook the opportunity to remind the parents that we were living in dangerous times, when fitness in body and mind, such as was maintained at Knox, ought to be encouraged. Without committing us to the conflict in Europe he rather neatly suggested that there might be some connection between strong American youth, firm neutrality, and the new gymnasium for which estimates were being prepared. He closed with a pardonable reference to the playing fields of Eton and began the pleasant task of distributing the prizes.

"A lovely speech," said Martha Eaton. "Much better than last year."

"He didn't mean us, Mother."

"Now I don't know what *you* mean."

"The playing fields of Eton."

"Oh, ridiculous, Alfred. *I* knew that. I heard all those jokes about Eton School, and eat-ing, before you were born. Your father told me that every generation has to hear them all over again."

"Second prize, high jump. Eaton, Class Four," the headmaster called.

"There you are, dear," said Martha.

Alfred left them to accept his medal, and when he returned his mother asked him what McCready had said.

"He said, 'Good work, congratulations.' The same thing he said to all the others."

"I wish your father could—" Martha stopped herself.

"Well, he couldn't," said Alfred.

"But he'll be here for commencement."

"Do you want to bet? He's never been here, not once in four years."

Martha nudged him hard. "Well, Victoria, we have a few minutes to freshen up before luncheon. Would you like to come with me?"

"Oh, excuse me," said Alfred. "I almost forgot. Here, and I'm not giving it to you because Mother suggested it. Word of honor."

"Oh, thank you, Alfred." She looked at the bronze medal, with its stamped figure of a running athlete. "Is this the right one? This man isn't jumping, he's running."

"They're all the same, except some are silver and some are this. Bronze. We're supposed to have them engraved. I can get this engraved and send it to you."

"I'd rather keep it the way it is. Maybe engrave it later."

"Isn't she sweet?" said Martha. She patted Victoria on the shoulder. "Where shall we meet you, Alfred? We're off to freshen up."

"I'll wait for you at the canopy."

They left him and repaired to the first-floor toilet, temporarily restricted to ladies and so posted with a large sign. His mother's uncompleted *faux pas* about his father's absence had been forgotten in his presentation of the medal to Victoria, but now it came back to him. He wished his mother had not spoken to him of his father and his father's lame excuse about last-minute business. There would be something—last-minute business would do—to prevent his appearance at commencement, and now Alfred wanted it to be so. He wanted to be able some time to remind his father that in four years he had never appeared at Knox, and he did not want that record of indifference spoiled. All the living fathers of boys at Knox had visited them at school at least once a year. Two or three times in his school career he had been asked, "Is your father dead?" Especially during the football season, at the games with other schools, the fathers would appear, but Alfred Eaton, a letter man, had never embarrassed his father or made him proud, because his father never came for a game. It only made it worse when two of the men who had gone to Princeton with his father would ask Alfred to give their best regards to old Sam Eaton.

"Who are you hating?"

He turned and saw Victoria smiling. "Do I look as if I were hating somebody?"

"If it wasn't some *body* it was some *thing*, and I think it was some*body.*"

"No. Where's Mother?"

"Talking to a lady I think is the headmaster's wife."

"Or listening, most likely. Are we to wait for her?"

"No, she said to sit down and start our lunch and she'd be along. She wants us to have a chance to be together."

"Did she say that?"

"No, but I know."

He grinned. "You know everything."

"No, but she's glad you and I—we've taken up where we left off."

"No we didn't. We made a new start."

"Yes, I guess that's better."

"Are you glad we did?"

"Don't you know the answer to that, Alfred?"

"Yes. At least as far as I'm concerned."

"Don't be modest. You know it as far as I'm concerned too."

"Do you want to go inside?"

"No, then we'll be sitting next to people and have to make conversation. Unless you do."

"I don't want to," he said. "Victoria."

"What?"

"I wish I could kiss you."

"Here in front of everybody?"

"I wouldn't care."

"I would."

"I guess I would too, but I want to."

"I want to."

"Do you?"

"Yes. I'm sending you a kiss, now."

"Touch me. As if you were accidentally turning around or something."

Very elaborately she leaned forward as though looking for someone inside the marquee, and held her shoulder against his chest.

"I love you," he said.

"They're not here yet," she said. "I wonder if they're over that way?" She leaned against him again. "No, not there, either."

85

"I love you," he said.

"Don't look at me. People can tell."

"I wish you could be here for commencement."

"You'll be home the next day, won't you?"

"Maybe the same night."

"That's even better," she said.

"Will you miss me till then?"

"I miss you all the time."

"I can see you every day this summer."

"You're going away."

"I'll try to get out of it."

"I'm going away, too. All the entire month of August."

"To the shore?"

"No, not this summer. They're going to some new lake in New Hampshire."

"New *Hamp*shire? Why did they pick New Hampshire?"

"I don't know. They don't tell me why they do anything. They just do it."

"Yes."

"Do you know what your mother said on the train?"

"No."

"She said you're more entitled to happiness than most boys."

"Well, I guess that's natural."

"It is, but she meant something more than that. Why does she think you're more entitled to it?"

"I know what she meant. I'll tell you this summer."

"Oh."

"Why 'oh'?"

"I know what she meant, too."

"What?"

"I'll tell you this summer, too. Here she comes."

"You two shouldn't have waited for me. But Victoria has the best manners of any girl I've ever known."

"Thank you, Mrs. Eaton."

"You're very welcome," said Martha.

They queued up for their lunch of excellent potato salad, excellent baked ham, excellent summer sausage, excellent bologna, excellent cold chicken and choice of milk, tea, or coffee. Alfred, in the line, saw Mrs. McCready waving to him, signaling to him, and he smiled and pretended not to understand her signal, which he understood only too well. She wanted him to steer his mother and Victoria to the headmaster's table, but for four years at Knox he had been treated like everyone else, and he was damned if he was going to let his mother and himself in for the same kind of fawning-over that he had observed in bygone years in the shops of Lower Montgomery Street. The other boys at the headmaster's table were not outstanding athletes or scholars; they came from Main Line families, and their mothers had arrived in Pierce-Arrows. For four years, partly by his conscious efforts and partly through his father's neglect, he had been on his own. Nobody among the students had any positive information as to whether he came from a family that was rich, very rich, or moderately well-off (at Knox there were no boys below the moderately well-off grade), and as a matter of fact he was quite surprised to see one or two of his classmates at the headmaster's table, having had no previous knowledge of their families' financial standing. But it was a rather well-known thing among the boys that when Mrs. McCready put herself out for a boy's mother, the boy's father was presumed to have plenty of spondulix. Alfred had one month to go at Knox, and he was determined to keep Knox as something of *his*, irrespective of what his family were or possessed. *If* his father decided to appear at commencement, *if* he did, he could arrive in a foreign car painted gold, and hand out ten-dollar bills; but by that time Knox would be over and no damage could be done. Alfred was already well aware that Princeton was full of boys whose fathers had many times more money than Samuel Eaton had (an item of information he had been given by his father). At Princeton he would come prepared to be lost in the shuffle of millionaires' sons.

They seated themselves for luncheon in the three last camp chairs on their side of the table (planks on horses), and Martha adroitly maneuvered it so that Alfred was at the end and Victoria in the middle.

"I'm Mrs. Tinkham. I remember you from last year," said a bright little woman. "But I don't remember your name."

"I'm Mrs. Eaton, this is our friend Miss Victoria Dockwiler, and my son, Alfred," said Martha.

"And this is *my* son, Donald Tinkham."

"How do you do, Donald," said Martha.

"How do you do, Donald, I'm awfully pleased to meet you. I've heard so much about you," said Alfred.

"Oh, are you the famous Alfred Eaton?" said Donald Tinkham.

"Why, yes I am," said Alfred.

"Boys," said Martha.

"*The* famous Alfred Eaton?" said Donald.

"Donald," said Mrs. Tinkham.

"That's me," said Alfred.

"Just think of sitting at the same table with the famous Alfred Eaton," said Donald. "My goodness, what a story to tell my grandchildren."

"Oh, you two," said Martha. But she was particularly delighted by Victoria's enjoyment of their little game.

"Tinker and I eat at the same table three times a day," said Alfred.

"I thought as much," said Mrs. Tinkham.

"Do some more," said Victoria.

"I can't think of any more," said Alfred.

"Oh, don't be modest, Mr. Eaton. Tell us about your exploits on the Knox varsity crew," said Donald.

"Oh, that!" said Alfred. "You tell them."

"Oh, I'm sure they'd rather hear it from you."

"Well, all right. Shall I tell it the way it really was?"

"Yes, I didn't know you had a crew," said Martha.

"Oh, wait'll you hear," said Donald.

"Our shell is an old flat-bottom boat about this long. Five feet. And our lake is the dam, not much bigger than this tent. And one night last winter I said when I went to college I was going out for the crew, and somebody else said why did I think I could make the crew, and I guess I talked too big, so a bunch of hoodlums pounced on me and tied me up and took me down to the dam and put me in the boat, and then gave it a shove."

"Heavens. That was for boasting," said Martha.

"Oh, sure."

"And what happened, tell us?" said Martha.

"It's all right, Mrs. Eaton, he wasn't drowned," said Donald.

"No thanks to certain hoodlums," said Alfred. "The boat drifted to the breast of the dam and they all kept yelling, 'Row, Princeton, row!' Row! with my hands tied. 'Stroke, Eaton! Stroke!' Then bang! the boat hit the dam, the breast of the dam, and out I went. Oh, was that water cold!"

"How did you get out, with your hands tied? You couldn't swim," said Martha.

"I just stood up. The water was only up to my shoulders."

"And he's never boasted since," said Donald.

"Were you a boaster, Alfred?" said Martha.

"Well, I was that night," said Alfred.

"Anybody that boasted," said Donald. "Boasting lesson."

"Did you ever boast?" said his mother.

"Oh, no," said Alfred.

"No, I never boasted," said Donald.

"That's boasting now, boy. I'll see you tonight," said Alfred.

"I take it back!" said Donald.

"I won't let you take it back unless you tell about *your* lesson," said Alfred.

"Yes, that's only fair," said Mrs. Tinkham.

"All right," said Donald. "Which time?"

"They had to give you two lessons?" said his mother.

"I only deserved one. Some people don't know the difference between boasting and plain, ordinary facts."

"Oh, my," said Alfred. "I'll remember that."

"Just plain statement of fact," said Donald.

"That's true, Alfred. Sometimes what sounds like boasting isn't at all," said Martha.

"There you are, Eaton," said Donald. "Thank you, Mrs. Eaton."

"Don't think you're going to get out of telling about your lesson," said Alfred.

But at that point a nearby mother asked Martha to pass the mustard, a request that also involved introductions all around and exchanges of observations on the weather, the events of the morning and the events to come, and instead of a unit of five persons they became a group of seven, then ten, and they never got back to Donald's story. Luncheon was followed by an hour during which the mothers and the young ladies were shown the boys' rooms, then a baseball game between Oranges and Blacks (who were known as Lemons and Niggers by their respective opponents). One of the Main Line mothers offered Martha and Victoria a lift to the Norristown railroad station; the invitation was accepted, thus cutting short the mothers' and Victoria's stay at the headmaster's tea, but enabling them to make better train connections. It was also a more comfortable ride in the Pierce-Arrow phaeton than in the chartered horse-drawn omnibus that the school was providing.

There were only seconds left to Victoria and Alfred for their goodbyes. "I had a very good time, Alfred."

"I had the best time I ever had," said Alfred.

"So did I," said Victoria. "Everything was just right. And I love the medal."

"Do you love the person that won the medal?"

"I'll tell you when I get in the car."

"How can you?"

"You watch and see," said Victoria.

"Goodbye, dear," said Martha. She kissed Alfred. "We had a lovely time, lovely. Thank you ever so much."

They got in the automobile, Victoria in the middle between the two women. The chauffeur closed the door, went around to the other side, got in, took his place behind the wheel. "All right, Walter," said his mistress. The gears meshed.

The car was moving, and Alfred raised his hand in general farewell, but kept his eyes on Victoria, watching for the promised sign. He walked alongside the moving car until he saw what he wanted to see: she took the medal in its case out of her purse and held it in the palm of her hand, and nodded, twice, three times, with an unmistakable meaning. He smiled

89

and nodded, and the car picked up speed. He slapped the rear fender and they were gone.

For Alfred that was the termination of his life at Knox, the good day ending the career as he wanted it to end and as he wanted to remember it. The remaining few weeks were crowded with cramming and examinations, nights that were too warm for sound sleep, days that were full of confusions. Commencement he was sure would bring no surprises: he was expecting no miracle to raise him to the top of his class in studies, and none that would create new friendships or antagonisms; and in sport he had no reason to hope that he would get beyond the semi-finals in the tennis singles or above five feet in the high jump. In four years he had done better than passing in all his subjects, in his relations with his schoolmates he was liked more than he was disliked, and he had been a regular on the varsity football team for two seasons, with two letters to show for it. He had not made his letter in track and field. His football playing had been something he made himself do as his participation in school spirit. He hated the drudgery of practice and especially he hated the scrimmages, the coaches' insisting on simulating game conditions when no score was being kept. The team played three "outside" games a year, against other schools, and they had not won or tied against either. But at game time Alfred invariably kept up his hopes if only to stifle his fears, and when the game began, after the first scrimmage and the shock of the first bumping of bodies (and sometimes the first hidden punch by an opponent), he would forget all the world that was not on the field. He learned the great truth that football is not a gentleman's game; it could be played by gentlemen, but not only gentlemen went to gentlemen's schools and played on gentlemen's schools' teams. And as a result he also learned to protect himself and not to rely on the protection of the rules. If a man punched you, you then punched him every chance you got. If you saw a man twisting your quarterback's ankle, you kicked that man and you told your teammates what you had seen. If you saw a teammate walking on an opponent's hand, you wished you hadn't seen it and you stayed out of it when your teammate got his just deserts.

It was a school rule that every boy had to go out for two sports, and boys who did not make any team were compelled to do calisthenics, out of doors during the fall and the spring, indoors in the winter months. Alfred regarded basketball as a nervous sport, a constant hysteria, and as a football and high-jump man he was excused from it. He chose the high jump because it looked easy and he was convinced in advance that he had the makings of a high jumper. But he was taken on only one trip with the track and field squad, and that only in the hope that as a second or third he might win some points in the dual meet. He won no points. He was not fast enough for the sprints, and he had no stomach for the longer distances. A more conscientious coach might have cut him from the squad, but Alfred reported every afternoon and stayed out of the way, and so was allowed to remain. His only interest in baseball was in watching it. He was uncertain as to the activities at Princeton that would bring him to the attention of the better clubs, but he was positive that in his case they would not be athletics.

The confusions of the final days before commencement were manifold: he was leaving a way of life that he had known for four years, one that had been generally satisfactory, in which notwithstanding rules and regulations and the restrictions of communal living, he had been able to make his own decisions and control his own efforts; at the very same time he was trying to think in terms of the new life that would begin in the fall, with new freedoms, new friends, a thousand strangers, and standards that were strange. He had never seen Princeton, a result of another of his father's unfulfilled promises. Then there was the tension of examinations, made no easier by a sudden spell of hot weather that seemed to make the pages of textbooks stick to the fingers and to each other. There were no screens on the dormitory windows and the insects large and small made the boys uncomfortable. The dining hall was so hot that many boys had no appetite for anything but iced tea. The water-closets stank worse than usual, and the hot and cold water pressures in the shower-room were more unmanageable than ever, so that a slight turn of the hot valve-wheel would bring forth steam, and a full turn of the cold-water wheel would produce a trickle. It was a trying time for everyone, and a boy in Two was shipped home for striking Mr. Deland and breaking his glasses.

In the midst of it all Alfred had one reliable, dependable source of pleasure and comfort: the knowledge that he was in love with Victoria and would see her soon. He had never told anyone about Victoria; there had been no one to tell, which was itself revealing of his self-sufficiency at the school. He had had to introduce her on Spring Day, but the boys were so completely ignorant of her place in his life that they looked at her with interest in her comeliness but without curiosity, then or later. The exception was Tinkham, who said: "Was that your one and only?"

"I wouldn't say that."

"No, you wouldn't say it, but actions speak louder than words."

"What actions?"

"Not exactly actions, I guess. I just knew it."

"There's no law against thinking, boy."

"Well, she's pretty. And nice, too. She didn't say much, but that's the kind of a girl I'd like to marry."

"So would I."

"Don't play-act with me, boy." said Tinkham. "You're going to."

"A lot can happen between now and when I get out of Princeton."

Alfred had not yet reached the stage at which he could consider the possibility of leaving Princeton to marry. He still accepted the fact of Princeton as in grammar school he had accepted the fact of Knox. The grand plan of your life was still ordered by your father and mother. After four years you got a degree, then you got a job or studied for a profession, and then you became engaged. Alfred never had earned any money, but the earning of money was neither expected of him nor would it have been sanctioned, and he consequently had no sense of futility or embarrassment on the subject. At certain intervals his allowance was raised, and it was increased by fairly regular gifts from his grandparents. In the fall he would have his first checking account at a bank, and until then his financial problems would be to keep within his mailed allowance or to write for more when he went over it. In the fall he was to be given a large sum—he did not know how much—to establish the checking account, and from it he would be required to pay his bills. At eighteen he knew the prices of his suits and shoes and haberdashery, but he did not know the amount of a good day's wages, the value of a house in any section of Port Johnson, or the cost of food. He only knew that he would be supported by his parents until he began earning a living some four years hence, and since that was to be the case, marriage was to be the romantic realization of a romance, but no more than a topic of wishful conversation until that time. No matter how much they might be in love, Victoria herself would not expect him to consider marriage as a possibility until he was through with college. Any other thinking was foolish, and any other course of behavior was reckless.

And yet in spite of believing that all those things were right he was disturbed by the very equanimity that his beliefs would require. Anything he had felt for Victoria four or five or six years earlier might as well have been felt for another person by another person. He kept his present love a secret from his schoolmates, but he could not keep it secret from himself. This Victoria had breasts, high and firm, and a waist that went in and hips that went out. He knew about himself. He had not yet touched a grown girl where her legs met, but from the Cuban photographs that were circulated through the school he had learned all that he could learn vicariously. Eventually

92

he would do with Victoria the thing that a man and a woman do, but how was he to avoid frightening her long before that time came? A girl, he had often heard, could not always control herself. Then what if the same thing happened to her that had happened to him on Spring Day? What if it happened to both of them at the same time? Knowing what he knew, and knowing what eventually they would do, could he count on his sense of decency to prevent a happening that he did not really want to prevent, that he secretly wanted to happen and that in some of his thoughts he even planned to happen? It was women, not girls, who lost control of themselves, but a girl's body was the same as a woman's and he remembered now that he had been able to believe that his mother, a woman, had lost control of herself. It could happen to a young girl, and it could happen to a young girl who loved you.

Here was love, with its sweetness and comfort, just beginning but already creating a problem that had to be fought as he had had to fight against the ghost of a brother who died, a father who despised him, the habit of the secret sin, the temptation to cheat in exams, the impulse to run off the field before the kick-off. But this was a problem affecting love, and love was a special way of thinking and feeling that could be fulfilled in the act of passion but that would and did exist without it. He loved this Victoria as he had not loved the other Victoria and as he had not loved Norma Budd, but he loved this Victoria in a part of the way he had loved Norma Budd and in a part of the way he had loved the other Victoria. Victoria *was* the lovely girl whose quiet sweetness had first made him love her, but now she was also and equally a source of desire such as Norma Budd alone had ever been. He was eighteen years old, and his conscience was young and strong, but his youth and his strength were not helping him now, when he was feeling both helpless and old. He was at the top of his age, which happened to be eighteen. At the top of eighteen one can be old, with nothing but youth to look back upon and nothing but aging in the future to look ahead to, and the enormity of eighteen years behind him was beginning to have serious meaning to him. In Port Johnson there were boys of eighteen who had knocked up girls; other boys who had caught the clap; other boys who had run away and joined the Navy; other boys who supported their families; other boys who already had tuberculosis because they had started work too soon. He corrected himself: those things made them no longer boys; they were men; and all those things were things he could do, and now he saw for the first time that no matter how young he was kept by the conventions of family and school—his dependence on his family for money, the artificialities of the treatment of freshmen at college—he was as old as the youngest officers in the British army, who were leading men into battle and themselves meeting death at an age when he was just getting ready to enter college. He had no desire to become a soldier. He sided with the British because the English were more like him than the Germans were, and the Germans' recent use of poison gas established him firmly as anti-German. But it was a European war and not ours. Nevertheless the young subalterns or sub-leftenants or whatever they called themselves were the final proof: if you were eighteen you could fight and die fighting, as well as love and make love and earn your living and do everything a man could do except vote, and voting was more of a nuisance than not. He might get a little taller, and he would fill out, and he certainly expected to learn a lot more, but in those confused last days at Knox he was not bothered by regret at leaving. He only wanted to hurry away so that he could properly consider himself a young man.

Alfred's father came to commencement, along with Martha and the girls, driven in the Packard by George Fry. Samuel Eaton was polite to everyone, jovial with some. Alfred and his classmates were seated on a raised platform, facing the families and friends and members of the other three classes. The ceremonies took place on the lawn, in the sunlight. There was an invocation by an assistant rector of a reasonably fashionable Main Line church, followed by the salutatory, the awarding of prizes, and the valedictory.

From his chair Alfred could see his family without difficulty. They were in the first row. After the valedictory the diplomas were handed out in alphabetical order. Alfred was fourth and, as had been rehearsed, he rose when the name of the boy two ahead of him was called. His own name was called, he took a few steps, accepted his diploma, thanked Mr. McCready, and returned to his chair.

After he was seated he looked toward his family, and saw that his father's seat was vacant, and then he saw his father, already off the lawn and disappearing among the parked cars.

Alfred got the story from Sally: "First he said to Mother, 'Billy would have been twenty-one,' and Mother said yes. He didn't say anything more till you got up to get your diploma, then I heard him say, 'I'm sorry, but I've got to leave.' And left. I'm sorry, Alfred. You know I am."

"Yes, I know you are, Sal."

"Mother's upset and trying not to show it."

"Why did he have to come? I hoped he wouldn't. He always made excuses before. But no, he had to be here because he couldn't have spoiled it if he'd stayed home."

94

"No, Alfred. He wanted to be nice. Honestly he did."

"It isn't in him to be nice."

"But you be nice for Mother's sake."

"For yours, too. I like you, Sal."

The conversation was taking place in the crowd. Martha had "gone to look for Father," and Constance was talking to another fourteen-year-old girl. In about ten minutes Martha appeared.

"Father's all right. Just a slight attack of indigestion. He's waiting in the car. How soon will you be ready, Alfred?"

"For what?"

"To go. I don't think we ought to stay around. George said your valises are strapped on the back of the car, so all we have to do is say goodbye to Mr. and Mrs. McCready."

"I'm going home by train."

"Oh," said Martha. "By train?"

"Yes, Mother. I'd much rather."

"Well, this is your day, so if you—"

"Oh, yes. This is my big day."

"Alfred, please, dear. He couldn't help it," said Martha.

"Mother, I'll say goodbye to the McCreadys. You go on. And will you ask Grandfather Johnson if it's all right for me to stay there tonight?"

"Oh, he'd be—"

"I have a date to see Victoria after dinner."

"Oh, well now that's nice."

"Yes. Goodbye, Mother. I'll see you tomorrow. Goodbye, Sal. Constance." He kissed them all and they left, obviously relieved that the ride home was not going to be as bad as it could have been.

Alfred walked from the Port Johnson station to his grandfather's house. His grandfather, now seventy, was feeble in body after two strokes, and had had the small sittingroom on the first floor changed into a bedroom. At Martha's insistence he employed a trained nurse, a Miss Flood, who had little enough to do but whose presence was reassuring to Martha.

"Well, m' boy, congratulations. Let me see your diploma."

Alfred unrolled the document, and the old man held it out in front of him. "Don't need my specs for what I'm looking for. Yes, it's there. Raymond Alfred Eaton. Who did that?"

"I did. If you mean the Raymond. They asked us for our full names, and I gave them mine."

"Well, that pleases me. I'm sorry about what happened."

"Oh, you heard about it, Grandfather?"

"I guess when you get old and useless and stay in one place all the time—I know I hear more gossip than I used to. Yes, I heard all about it."

"How did you find out so soon?"

"If you thought a minute you could guess."

"George Fry."

"Was it? I'm not saying. Your father can't help himself. You must realize by this time that your father and I never hit it off. No love lost there, on either side. However, you're old enough to know now that every man has his limitations, and with your father it was this way: he only had enough love in him for one woman, your mother, and one child, your brother. Everything else is the mill. Mind you, I'm not saying he's a smart business man, because he's not. He's getting rich now because he's in the richest war business there is. But his limitations. The reason why I objected to your mother marrying him was he had no imagination whatsoever. A young fellow ought to have imagination, and I hope you have it. Without it you get old too quick. Your father was old when he was thirty-five. Only room enough in his imagination for one woman and one child, and the rest was the business. No imagination there either. He had a chance to buy another mill. They were in financial difficulties. I said grab it, grab it while you can. But no imagination. You couldn't buy that mill today for fifteen million dollars. Next year it'll be worth—I don't know. Did I buy any stock in it? Is that what you're thinking? Yes, I did, or I wouldn't have advised your father to buy it. Oh, my. Here's my baby food. Isn't that a great feast to look forward to all afternoon? Do I get any ice cream tonight?"

"Not tonight, Mr. Johnson," said Miss Flood.

"Then give me some more turnips. I have to eat something, and I know you're not going to give me any more chicken."

"You can have more chicken," said Miss Flood.

"Is your steak the way you want it?" said the old man.

"Yes sir. It looks fine."

"Miss Flood, would it be against the law if you dipped a piece of bread in that steak juice and gave it to me?"

"Oh, I guess a small piece would be all right," said Miss Flood.

"You eat and I'll talk, Alfred, Raymond-Alfred. It's a pleasure to see you go after that steak."

"It's a good steak."

"Look at those teeth. I have to give your father credit for them. Samuel Eaton has as fine a set of teeth as I ever saw. But he doesn't have any *imagination*. The mind wanders when you get old, Alfred."

"When you're young, too. Exams."

"That's different. The young mind *should* wander, all the things there are to see, think about. Victoria Dockwiler, there's a girl for a lucky young fellow. She comes in to see me every so often. Her parents put her up to it, I know that, but once she's here she's good company. *You* find her good company, I gather."

"You bet I do."

"Don't do anything foolish, though. Finish your education."

"I'm going to."

"When you graduate from Princeton do you know what I'm going to do?"

"I'm not even there yet, Grandfather."

"I'm going to make you a present of a trip around the world. Be just about the right time. The war'll be over and you'll be able to visit Europe. But even if it isn't, you can go every place but Europe, and you can save Europe for later. The war'll be over in two years. The English aren't going to give in. The Germans are beating them now, but we're going to have to help them, the English, and then it'll be all over but the shouting. I don't mean we're going to get in it. Oh, no. We can't do that, we mustn't do that. But we'll help them every other way. Money. Food. Ammunition. Then when it's all over we're going to have to help them all get back on their feet again. France. Belgium. Italy. And what does that mean? It means a lot of business for this country. I'd be willing to help the German people get back on their feet if they got rid of old Kaiser Bill, but they'd have to do that first. Now that's the opposite of what I said about your father. Kaiser Bill. There was too *much* imagination. Too much imagination, too much power, not enough to do with his time. Putting on fancy uniforms, sitting there on a horse, reviewing his troops. Gets to thinking, with those troops why not rule the world? Do you want to know why we have to stay out of it? I'll tell you. It's because that's a family fight over there. The Kaiser is a cousin of the Czar of Russia, and the Czar of Russia is a cousin of King George. Don't ever mix in a family fight or they'll all turn on you. All those people are related. I just hope Woodrow Wilson doesn't find out he's related."

"Is he?"

"Not that I know of, but we're all descended from the Battle of Hastings, or so I'm told, and I don't trust Wilson. Maybe I shouldn't say that to a Princeton man."

"I won't be a Princeton man till September."

"You've been a Princeton man from the day you were born. You never had any say in the matter. Well, I got nothing against Princeton. I'd rather have seen you go to Lehigh or Haverford. We don't have to go to New Jersey to find a good college, but a man likes his son to go where he went. I had no trouble in that respect, but in 1915 everybody wants to send their son to college. Jonas Rothermel is sending his son to college."

"Which one is Jonas?"

"Gas Company. Sent two daughters to Normal, now the son's going to college."

"Tom. I know Tom."

"Well, he's a bright, willing youngster and he ought to be given his chance. But I'll give you a little private piece of information. Jonas was so anxious to educate those children, for twenty years or more he never had more than a couple pieces of bread and cheese for his lunch. Starved himself. Last year he fell down the cellar and broke his leg. No wonder he broke his leg, what he ate. That meant doctor bills. Finally one day he came to me and wanted to borrow a thousand dollars. A thousand dollars! Why? Because he didn't want to take any money out of his savings account. Then he told me the whole story, so I said to him I wouldn't lend him a thousand dollars but I'd pay all his doctor bills and put in a good word for him at the Gas Company, meaning they'd pay him for all the time he took out on account of his leg. Which they did. He was worth it, but they didn't have to, you know. He was out for three months and could have lost his job. It isn't every place that would keep a man on salary for three months. But I fixed that for him. But why wouldn't I lend him a thousand dollars, he wanted to know? Because he was a bad investment, I told him, and a thousand-dollar loan would make him a worse one. If I lent him a thousand dollars he'd only eat *one* piece of bread a day, and pretty soon he'd break his leg again, starving himself to pay back the loan. A very bad investment. Then why would I take care of the doctor bills? Because a man that thought so much of his family was entitled to some consideration. This is a family town, and I'd rather give a family man a hundred dollars than give the same amount to some charity."

"Oh, you *gave* him the money for the doctor bills?"

"Yes. I didn't let him have the money. I paid the bills myself. The doctor. Drug store. I just asked them what he owed and sent them a cheque. Why are you so surprised?"

"I thought you loaned him the money for the doctor."

"You don't understand. I wouldn't *lend* him money. Jonas Rothermel isn't a man I'd *lend* money to."

"How much did you finally give him?"

"Oh, it came to a little over eight hundred dollars. I paid his salary—"

"I thought you said the Gas Company paid his salary."

"*I* paid his salary, through the Gas Company. I'm a principal stockholder in the Gas Company, but I wouldn't ask the other stockholders to pay a man's salary under those circumstances. That was my affair. And it's good business. Jonas Rothermel thinks the Gas Company is just great."

"I think *you* are."

"Now, now."

"I do, though."

"I just wish you wouldn't be so surprised. I've often helped people that I thought deserved it. And some of them didn't, as it turned out. But when you think a man deserves it, you help him. Just as long as you don't put it on a business basis. You remember that, because when I pass on you're going to have to know what to do with your money. You're eighteen now, and not a boy any more, and I'm glad you came here this evening. Families. They're this town. Families. Help families. If a man hasn't got a family, let him go somewhere else for help. Every time you help a family, you do something for the whole town. But every time you help a man that hasn't bothered to start a family, you're only helping one man. You're going to have to think about this, Alfred. Three more years you'll be twenty-one, and you get quite a respectable sum then."

"I do? Who from?"

"From me. A trust fund. It isn't a million or anything like that, but it's enough so you'll get used to the idea of having it. I'm doing the same thing for your sisters when they're twenty-one. But you'll get yours first, and maybe you can show them how to spend it. Later on you'll all three get more, but from twenty-one to twenty-five you'll have enough to practice with."

"This all comes as a surprise to me."

"Well, it ought to. Your father doesn't know about it, neither does your mother. And you can be sure your sisters don't. Now, who're you going to tell?"

Alfred considered. "I don't think I'll tell anybody."

"That's the best thing you could have said. *Don't* tell anybody. That's what I hoped you'd say, but I didn't want to put the words in your mouth. Never let anybody know how much money you have. They'll all want to know, but it's none of their darn business. Those that have more will think you have more, those that have less will think you have less. That's a good position to be in."

"Well, thank you, Grandfather. I don't know what else to say, except that I'm surprised."

"That's all there is to say, and I say you're welcome. I've kept an eye on you for many years. I don't want to say too much, but you could have turned out a lot differently. I didn't know how to help you without looking like I was interfering, so I didn't help you and I don't guess anybody else did, much. Therefore you can take all the credit yourself. You changed from a nice, agreeable little boy, into a young man that I have confidence in. And you did it yourself."

"Thank you."

"As far as I can see, as far as I can *tell,* you only have to watch out for one thing."

"What's that?"

"The opposite sex."

"The opposite sex? Why do you say that?"

"I wish I *hadn't* said it. But since I did, I'll tell you what I mean. Anybody can see that you're going to be a good-looking man, and you're decent. But that's a combination that the wrong kind of woman can raise the dickens with."

"They won't with me."

"I guess you're thinking of Victoria. She's part of the combination. A good-looking young man, decent, and caring for a nice girl. That's the combination. And later, you'll have quite a lot of money. You see what I mean?"

"Now I see, yes. But I'm not worried about it."

"I'm not worried about it either, but you have to watch out. It's in your blood. Not on you father's side. I'll say that for him, if he was ever untrue to your mother I never heard of it. But I had a brother, your Great-Uncle Isaac, two years older than I. He went away to the Civil War and was wounded at the Battle of Antietam. They had to take off his right leg. I'll never forget when he came home, with that stick of wood where his leg should have been. 'All right,' he said. 'Stare at me! I know what I look like.' You know how old he was then? One year older than you are now. He took to drink. Then he married a farm girl, a nice respectable girl, and for a while there he didn't touch liquor. But that only lasted a matter of months before he was a real drunkard. He had some woman in a bad house down on River Street, and that's where he lived. We stopped giving him any money because we thought that would bring him to his senses, but when he had no more money the woman had no use for him and for several weeks he was sleeping in a livery stable that used to be down there on Second Street near Montgomery. Finally one night he fell into the Canal, and whether he fell or did it on purpose we never found out, he was just as dead either way."

"I never knew any of this."

"No. That's not the way you're liable to hear about your Great-Uncle Isaac, but that's the way it was. The Canal boatmen, they were a rough lot, and there was some little talk that Isaac quarreled with one of them, but I never believed that. I always believed that he took his own life while under the influence. Naturally you never heard any of this, because our family aren't proud of it, and as far as other people are concerned, a lot of people in this town would rather stay in my good graces than not."

"Is that all, Grandfather?"

100

"All I want to say now."

"Well, you blame it on the woman. I blame it on liquor and losing his leg in the war."

"Sure you do. But did you ever stop to think about this: some men drink and go home. Other men drink and stay away from home because they want to be with that kind of woman. My brother was the latter. There's some hope for the drinker that goes home, but not for the one that wants to be with women *and* the booze. And you see what makes the difference there? The woman."

"Oh," said Alfred.

"That's a danger signal, Alfred. When you don't want to go home. When you'd rather stay in a saloon. That's when you ought to stop and consider. What's wrong with home? Or what's wrong with me? If you don't, that's when the woman enters into it. What are you smiling at, boy?"

"How you know so much."

"How I know so much. I have to pass on every loan of five hundred dollars and over, that's how I know so much. The bank does a lot of four-hundred-dollar business since that got around. They know. They know, all right. When a man comes to the bank for a thousand dollars it's like the Catholics going to confession. They're going to have to tell me all their sins, granted that I don't know them already. I don't want to hear a man telling me how good he is, how honest he is. I want to know why he's in trouble, if he's in trouble, and I always ask him what he thinks can go wrong. I make him tell me that before I let him have a cent of the bank's money. And once they get over their surprise you wouldn't believe it, how willing men are to *prove* to me that I almost made a bad loan. I can't ask a man to bring his wife to the bank, but nine times out of ten I can tell without her coming in. If everything else seems in good order, nine times out of ten so is the man's home life. And when I reserve decision, one of the first things I do, I take the receiver off the hook and I telephone, first the grocery man. Second, the dry-goods store. Third, the millinery store."

"Millinery store, Mr. Johnson? Are you going to buy a new bonnet?" said Miss Flood, bustling in.

"You're interrupting me, Miss Flood."

"I am, that's my intention. It's time for our visitor to say goodnight, as it's time for you to get ready for bed."

"At this hour?" said Mr. Johnson.

"Now, now, now, now, now. We heard the clock strike eight, didn't we? And what's it going to strike in a few minutes? Eight-thirty. We're over an hour past our regular time, so's it is."

"Oh, you're going to catch it, Alfred. I'm sorry."

"I'm not sorry, though, Grandfather. I had a good time."

101

"Well, I'm sure I did," said Mr. Johnson.

"You're staying the night, Mr. Eaton, I understand. If you want to go to the kitchen when you come home, there's some brownies in the cake-box. But say goodnight now so you won't have to say goodnight later."

"What if I'm awake and hear him?" said the old man.

"You won't be awake, so you won't hear him. You'll be dead to the world."

"I'll be that soon enough," said the old man.

"I didn't mean it that way, Mr. Johnson. That's just an expression."

"If my light's still on, come in, Alfred. She's usually asleep at ten o'clock." The old man laughed quietly.

"I'm nothing of the kind."

"Goodnight, Grandfather," said Alfred.

He went out into the last of the daylight and walked the short distance to the Dockwilers'. In the front room at the right he could see Victor Dockwiler reading the newspaper and smoking a cigar. The front door was open, the screendoor was in place. Alfred rang the doorbell, and he could see Victor Dockwiler's reactions to the sound: putting down the paper, taking off his glasses and resting the cigar in the ash tray, and starting to get to his feet, then stopping when Victoria, from upstairs, called: "I'll go, Father." Then Victor Dockwiler put on his glasses and took up the newspaper again. He found his place in the paper, and reached out for his cigar. He was a nice man, Mr. Dockwiler, but it was hard to believe he fully appreciated Victoria.

Alfred heard Victoria on the stairs, then saw her, beginning with her shoes, her skirt, her waist, shoulders, her face. The hall light was burning and she had her hand on the door before she could recognize Alfred, but when she did her expression changed from the calm and dignity she had maintained on her way down the stairs to the brightest smile he had ever seen. She opened the door and came outside.

"Hello, Alfred. Welcome home."

"Hello, Victoria."

They shook hands and she let him hold on to her hand, while gently leading him to the wicker chairs around the porch table. "I'd rather sit out here, wouldn't you?"

"Much rather," he said.

"The other side, you can hear every word from the front room where Father is. These chairs aren't as comfortable, but this is more private."

They made conversation until ten o'clock struck through the house and Victor Dockwiler came to the doorway.

"Alfred?"

"Yes sir."

102

"Welcome home. Congratulations. I hear you did very well." He came out to greet Alfred.

"Oh, nothing special, sir."

"Well, no special trouble, either, so you have that to be thankful for. And your mother and father have, too. Not always the case, I'm afraid. Well, you'll see that Victoria gets to bed at eleven, won't you?"

"Yes sir."

"Goodnight," said Mr. Dockwiler. "Goodnight, my dear."

"Goodnight, Father." She kissed him on the cheek and he left. He turned out the lights in the front room and the hall, but then immediately turned the hall light on again.

"Victoria?"

"What?"

"Now we can sit on the swing?"

"No."

"I thought you'd let me kiss you tonight."

"I'm going to, but we mustn't sit on the swing. Come here." She stood near the edge of the porch. He went to her and put his arms around her and kissed her mouth. She freely allowed their bodies to come together while their mouths were pressed against each other. Then she began to breathe more deeply. Three times she breathed that way and he drew his head away and saw that her eyes were closed and she continued to take those deep breaths until he was afraid she had fainted. She opened her eyes, not all the way, and there was a sleepiness and a distant smile in them that he had never seen before in anyone's eyes, and that in Victoria's eyes made her momentarily unrecognizable. And this, he knew, was what he had so often heard about girls losing control of themselves. In one second he could touch her anywhere and she would not stop him, and if he did touch her there would be no stopping at touching. But he knew that if he spoke, no matter what he said, the mood would vanish.

"I love you," he said.

"Oh," she said, and she sounded as though she had just been awakened. "Oh, dear. Let's sit down, I must get my breath."

"Our first kiss," he said.

"Yes," she said.

"Can't we sit on the swing? I hate to be so far away from you."

"It's absolutely forbidden. Mother said if she ever catches me sitting on the swing with a boy, she won't allow any more boys to come see me."

"Boys? What boys? Do boys come and see you?"

"Why, yes. Boys that you know. Of course they do. How do you think I get to the dances?"

"Oh, dancing school."

"Yes, I started evening classes this year."

"You never told me that, Victoria."

"But why should I?"

"You know, I should have known that."

"Why?"

"Your father, I wondered why he was so—he wasn't a bit surprised to have me come here tonight."

"Well, why should he be? They want me to go to the dances with boys, and have them come here, just as long as one boy doesn't start coming too often."

"Oh, well that's something to be thankful for. But tell me the truth. Do you love me?"

"Yes."

"Do you love me as much as I love you?"

"I don't know how much that is."

"It's as much as I can love anybody."

"I love you as much as I love anybody. But . . ."

"But what?"

"Well, that's not saying I can't go to dances with other boys, or have them here. Mother absolutely forbids that. I'm not allowed to see any boy twice in succession."

"I can't see you tomorrow night?"

"No, not unless I see someone else in between."

"You mean go on a picnic with someone else."

"I guess so. Even then I'm not sure. I don't think they'd like me to see you two nights in succession, but I'll ask them if you want me to."

"Of course I want you to."

"But don't be surprised if they say no."

"Hell, I didn't know it was going to be like this."

"But Alfred, I'm only sixteen, and they don't want me to go out alone till I'm eighteen. I couldn't go to the movie show with you unless another girl and boy went along with us. Your mother won't let Sally go out alone either."

"But Sally—well, she's sixteen too, I guess."

"All the mothers have the same rules. What one girl does, all the others have to do. And some mothers wouldn't allow you to be here alone with me, in my own house and with my father and mother here. If you think my mother's strict."

"Do you know what that means?"

"What?"

"Well, you're going away in August, and I'm going to college in September. That means during July I won't be able to see you more than fifteen times. Every other night."

"Not even that much. No matter how many other boys I see, Mother won't allow me to see you more than twice a week. I'm sure of that."

"Do you want to see me more than twice a week?"

"Yes."

"Twice a week! Hell, Victoria, how many weeks are there till August? Six? I can only see you twelve times before you go away?"

"Is that how many it is?"

"What can I *do*?"

"Nothing that I know of."

"You don't seem too upset about it."

"What would be the use? They could forbid me to see you at all."

"Would you let them do that?"

"I'd have to. What else could I do?"

"I don't know. I don't know a damn thing."

"I never heard you swear before."

"If you knew what I was thinking you wouldn't call that swearing."

"I don't mind your swearing."

"Victoria."

"What?"

"Have you ever kissed anyone else?"

She did not answer him.

"Have you?"

"No."

"You have, haven't you?"

"What if I have?"

"Then you have."

"I didn't say so, but what if I have?"

"What if you have? Oh, nothing. Nothing at all, just that you *don't* love me, and you don't give a damn whether you see me twice a week or seven times or any time. Is that right?"

"Not if you talk to me that way. No gentleman would talk to me that way."

"I want to know who kissed you."

"Nobody kissed me, that's who kissed me, but you can go home right this minute, because I don't have to stand for your nasty insinuations, and I won't."

"Nasty insinuations. You practically admitted it."

"Goodnight, and thank you for a very *un*pleasant evening." She left him, went inside, and closed the front door, and the hall light was extinguished.

The light was on in his grandfather's room, but there was still too much of anger in his misery, and he could not direct his steps toward the room of the lonely old man. He went to his own room and undressed and got into bed without hope of sleep. The evening had begun so well; to the anticipation of seeing Victoria his grandfather had added a new feeling of strength and confidence with the news of the trust fund. In

105

three years he would be independent and could do anything that his dependence on his father now prevented. In a matter of minutes he had been able to accustom himself to the idea of independence, quite as positively as if the money had been given him then and there. The prospect of financial independence was unexpected but it was essential or at least highly desirable to the new phase of life he now was entering. It had come at precisely the right time: it had not come while he was still at Knox, and therefore did not belong in the Knox part of his life; it had come as the first recognition to his new status, young man and no longer boy. He had gone to Victoria's house with the private knowledge that in three years he would be able to ask her to set a date for their marriage. He had come away without dignity, with a prospect of a dismal summer, and heartsick from her casual bruises to his love. There was no *worst* among the things that had happened to him, but one of the worst was the confusion of doubt and jealousy. He did not believe her claim that nobody had kissed her, and he had not even succeeded in identifying the boys who he was sure had been allowed to go as far with her as he had gone. She would never know what he had done for her by speaking at the right, unselfish moment, and the only doubt that even in his misery he did not encourage was the suspicion that other boys had not stopped where he had stopped. At Knox the boys had pooled their experiences with girls, nice girls, and even allowing for boasting lies, some of the accounts had been too explicit and too well corroborated to be entirely invention. There was a girl known to most of the Philadelphia boys and whose family had sent her to school in Switzerland because of the extreme liberties she permitted the boys she knew and a butler in her own house. There was a girl in Fort Penn. There was a girl in Reading. There was a girl, it seemed, in every town but Port Johnson, and for his inability to contribute to the pool Alfred was first marked as a prude, then as a fellow who knew a lot that he wasn't telling. In spite of his jealousy he was not yet so despairing that he was ready to believe that there was indeed "a girl" in Port Johnson and that she was the girl he loved.

Thus Alfred Eaton in the early summer of 1915, eagerly abandoning the conditions of boy, and hurt and confused in his earliest moments in the new condition of man.

It was the new custom in Port Johnson to have a Young People's party late in June. It took place at the Idle Hour Tennis Club at the far eastern end of town, and was in the nature of a get-together for the members' children who were home from college and boarding-school, many of whom would be leaving shortly for the seashore and the mountains. The invitation list was by no means confined to young people who had been away at school. For one reason or another—and not always financial—a goodly number of East Montgomery Street parents kept their children at Port Johnson High School for two years, and a smaller number, who were influenced by finances, had their children in the high school the full four years. But among the high school representatives at the party there were only those whose families were members of the Idle Hour (which had playing and non-playing classes of membership) and a painfully few boys and girls who were going on to college in the fall. In that category was Tom Rothermel, who had frequently delivered groceries and soft drinks to the Idle Hour kitchen, but never had been asked to sit on the porch or slide across the dance floor. Nor had he been asked to play tennis, a game which he did not know how to score; or to take a shower bath, a rite which he never had observed since his own cleanliness was maintained by the use of a galvanized iron washtub and Fels-Naphtha soap.

Two weeks before the night of the party Tom came home from his steadiest, daily job at the drug store and was greeted suspiciously by his mother: "You got a letter."

"Where is it?"

"It's from the Idle Hour Tennis Club. What do you want getting letters from them?"

"Let me open it and I'll see. Where is it?"

"Mister Thomas Rothermel."

"Mom, I got letters to Mister before. That's because I'm class president. Give me the letter."

She drew up her skirt and took the letter out of a pocket in her petticoat. He studied the envelope, then opened it with a table knife. "Holy smokes," he said.

"What does it say?" said his mother. "Who's it from?"

" 'The Idle Hour Tennis Club requests the pleasure of—' that's printed '—Mr. Thomas Rothermel's—' that's written by hand '—company at a dance. June 24, 1915. Subscription one dollar. Refreshments. R. S. V. P.' "

"Oh, they want you to pay," said Elsie Rothermel.

"You can't get in for nothing."

"Who is S. R. P. V.?"

"R. S. V. P. Uh, French. It means—now wait'll I think. Repondez s'il vous plait."

"Shit."

"No, you ought to be proud I knew it. It means, please answer, please reply. Repondez means answer, or reply. If you please. Answer if you please. R. S. V. P."

"A nerve to ask you for money."

"I don't pay unless I go," he said. "I'm going. I can get the night off. That's a Thursday night."

"Going? No you aint. Here's Pop."

Jonas Rothermel limped in and hung up his hat, coat and vest. "Going?"

"I got an invitation to a dance."

"You don't know how to dance."

"What if I don't?"

"Well, if you can't dance, what do you want to go to a dance for? An atheist don't go to church. Whose dance? You mean the school dance?"

"Here. Read it," said Tom.

"Get me my glasses out of my vest pocket," said Jonas.

"He wants to spend a dollar to—"

"Keep quiet till I read the thing."

"Here," said Tom, handing him his glasses.

Jonas mumbled the words of the invitation. "Whose initials at the bottom? Van Peltz? Only, Van Peltz's name is Peter."

"He don't know no more than me," said Elsie. "It's French."

"It's English. It's R. S. V. P.," said Jonas.

"It stands for French, Pop. It means repondez s'il vous plait. Answer if you please."

"Oh, now I know. I heard about that. Who sent this?"

"The tennis club."

"Who do you know at the tennis club?"

"The same ones you do," said Tom.

"Were they ever in this house?"

"No."

"Then why do they want you at their dance? One dollar. Refreshments. What are they giving you for a dollar? You can eat here and save a dollar. They never invited Jean and Eudora."

"You won't let me go?"

"No."

"I'm going anyway."

Elsie got up and slapped her son's face.

"Cut that out, Mom. You cut that out."

Jean Rothermel entered the kitchen. "What's the matter here?"

"This snot-nose got fresh," said Elsie.

"Don't call him that," said Jean.

"I got an invitation to a dance and they think it's a crime because it costs a dollar."

"You wait here a minute," said Jean. She went out and came back quickly, carrying her purse. "Here's the dollar. You go to the dance. That's *my* dollar and I'm giving it to him to go to the dance. He's the first one in this family that ever got invited to that club, and *he's going*, you understand?"

"What do you know about it?" said her mother.

"I know all about it. So would you if you read the paper, instead of looking at the pictures in those old magazines. He's the first one of us that's going to amount to something, and stop thinking you're doing him the favor, sending him to college. It's yourselves you're thinking of. *I know.* Let somebody have some pleasure out of life. Here's another dollar, Tom. You want to have some money in your pocket."

"Where did you get that money?" said her father.

"I saved it, and I have more."

"Then start paying me back for your education."

"Start? Start? What do I keep out of what I earn? Eight dollars a month! If I knew that was the way it was going to be I never would have gone away to Normal."

"Then get yourself a husband," said her mother.

"How? Get a job on a farmer wagon, the way you did? You're not spending *your* money to send this boy to college. He earned the money, and more. I'm going to see he gets some pleasure out of life. All he did was work since he was five years old, and now you begrudge him a dollar. The brightest student in High and all you gave him for graduation was a suit of clothes. A suit of clothes, with money he earned!"

"You shut your big mouth," said her mother.

"You be careful or I'll move out, and so will Eudora. Then you'll have to get off your big fat behind and not leave all the housework for us."

"What?" said Jonas.

"That's what I said," said Jean. "We teach school all day and then come home and scrub and clean and make the beds before you get home. Ask her. See what she says."

"I'll slap you in the face," said Elsie Rothermel.

"Not me, because I'll slap you back."

"Uh-uh. Mind there," said Jonas Rothermel.

"She's crazy. She got her monthlies," said Elsie.

"You're wrong, and I'm not crazy, but it's a wonder I'm not. And maybe I will be, maybe I will." Jean suddenly began to cry and left the room, followed by her brother.

"Get supper," said Jonas Rothermel.

"Why didn't—"

"*Get supper!*" he repeated.

The Idle Hour clubhouse was a one-story structure resting on piles that were hidden by lattice-work, with an entrance at the west, a long porch at the east, ladies' and gentlemen's locker-rooms at the south, and a kitchen at the north. The single principal room could be used for dancing or for large card parties. The clubhouse had been put up as inexpensively as possible, with the thought that some day the land would be sold for residential plots, after the club itself had attracted prospective buyers to the neighborhood. There were four lawn tennis courts, enclosed with chicken-wire, fairly well drained and reasonably free of pebbles. The walls inside were unfinished and the roof timbering was exposed, but in spite of its wooden simplicity it was the headquarters of Port Johnson society. By 1915 nearly all the people were in it who were ever going to be in it, with the exception of a few relatives of members and the rare newcomers to town who came properly connected and recommended. It was Port Johnson's only society club. The men had not yet organized their own refuge, and the ladies were content to meet for auction bridge and charitable endeavors at each other's houses. It was not unusual for an entire year to pass without the admissions committee's having any work to do. In the words of one committee lady, "Nobody's going to be blackballed. Nobody like that will ever get this far."

Two mothers were sitting at a card table just inside the entrance when Tom Rothermel arrived at eight-fifteen, alone, and in his graduation suit and with three dollars in his pocket, the extra dollar a contribution by his sister Eudora. He recognized one of the ladies, who said: "Good evening, our first customer."

"Good evening, Mrs. Van Peltz."

"Tom Rothermel. Mr. Thomas Rothermel. If you'll give me the large sum of one dollar I'll place a check-mark beside your name. Thang-*kew*. There we are. Oh, would you like to know where to put your hat? All the way down to the end of the room and there you'll find a rack, and you can put it just anywhere you please."

"Thank you, ma'am," said Tom.

His shoes sounded heavy on the cornmeal-spread floor. He hung his hat on the back of the rack and stood for a while, admiring the decorations, which consisted of red, white and blue streamers extended from the rafter in the center of the room, and as many college and school pennants and banners as could be borrowed. At the other end of the room the members of the three-piece orchestra, wearing tailcoats, black waistcoats and white ties, were sitting in readiness, forcing conversation among themselves, running a finger between neck and collar, fingering arpeggios but not playing, taking deep breaths and staring as one man at the club entrance. Tom joined them.

"Hello, Rothermel," said the pianist.

"Hello, Tom," said the violinist.

"Hyuh," said the cellist.

"Hello, fellows," said Tom.

"Want a job?" said the pianist.

"What doing?" said Tom.

"I don't know," said the pianist.

"You here for the dance?" said the violinist.

"Uh-huh," said Tom.

"Where's your girl?"

"I don't have one."

"Well, there's always a couple extra girls at these affairs," said the violinist.

"Not always," said the cellist. "I seen a lot of times when they had more fellows than girls."

"No, mostly the girls outnumber the fellows," said the pianist.

"I played at more of these affairs than any other man in town, and it's my contention there's usually more fellows."

"For the older ones, yes. That I'll grant you. The older ones, they usually have more fellows. But if you take and think back to last year this time, the girls outnumbered them," said the violinist.

"That's my impression," said the pianist.

"Why do you keep arguing with me? Did you ever see a woman come without an escort to the Charity Ball?" said the cellist.

"I don't know," said the pianist.

"But the Charity Ball isn't tonight," said the violinist.

"That's what I'm saying. I play at all these affairs, and there aint any doubt about it, the fellows outnumber the women."

"Well, it won't make much difference to me. I don't dance," said Tom.

"Then what are you here for? You *have* a job," said the pianist.

"No, I paid," said Tom.

"Paid a dollar just to be here?" said the violinist.

"He paid a dollar to hear us make sweet music," said the cellist. "That and the refreshments. But take my advice and don't drink too much of that fruit punch."

"Why?" said Tom.

"It'll give you the diarrhea of the blow-hole," said the cellist. "Stick with us, we got a half a case of beer on ice."

"Thanks, but I don't drink beer."

"All right. Drink fruit punch."

"Give me your *A* again, will you?" said the violinist.

The pianist tapped his *A*. The musicians continued with their nervous small-talk and silences, and Tom remained with them, discovering after a bit that he too was watching the door for the arrival of guests.

"Well, I make it twenty-nine," said the pianist, with watch in hand.

"Twenty-nine and a half," said the violinist.

"Well, they hired us to play music. I'm ready," said the cellist. "You ready?"

"All right. Lively now. Uh one, uh two," said the violinist, and at almost exactly eight-thirty they began to play the Castle Walk to an empty dance floor. But twenty minutes later all the young people had arrived, most of them on foot, a few by motor, and Tom saw that he was the only male not wearing white pants. Even the youngest boys, still in knickerbockers, wore white duck.

He stood, then sat, with the musicians until the eleven o'clock intermission. He waved to and was waved to by high school friends but he stayed with the musicians as though they were a dugout and the dance floor No Man's Land. They invited him to go out for a beer, but he declined. He was alone then, but not for long.

"Hello, Tom," said Alfred Eaton.

"Hello, Alfred."

"Do you think it'd be all right if we sat in these chairs, till they come back?" said Alfred.

"I guess so," said Tom. "Here, have my chair."

"You know my sister, Sally, and Victoria Dockwiler, and Peter."

"Pleased to meet you," said Tom.

"Keep your seat," said Alfred. "It's the girls that want to sit. You having a good time?"

"Pretty good. Yeah, pretty good," said Tom.

"Did you get any refreshments?" said Alfred.

"I'm gonna wait."

"That's a good idea if there's anything left. I hear you're going to Lehigh."

"I was but I changed. I'm going up to State."

"Oh, I heard Lehigh."

"I was going there, but I guess I just changed."

"Oh, I think we play Lehigh. I'm not sure, but I think we do. I don't know whether we play State or not. Peltzer, do we play State?"

"I don't know. Sometimes we do, sometimes we don't. It depends."

"Depends on what?" said Sally.

"On whether we do or whether we don't," said Van Peltz. Victoria laughed. "Peter, you're so funny."

"As funny as a crutch," said Alfred. "You didn't drag a frau, huh, Tom?"

"No, I came by myself."

"Then we can't trade dances, but let's see your card."

"What card?" said Tom. "I don't have a card."

"Oh," said Alfred. "Oh, I see."

"I don't dance."

"Don't you even waltz?" said Victoria.

"Nothing."

112

"Well, there are a lot here that think they can dance but can't," said Alfred.

"I've seen you a lot of times," said Victoria to Tom.

"I've seen you, too."

"Isn't that astonishing, in this great big city?" said Van Peltz. "Think of it. In this great metropolis known as Port Johnson. Crowded streets. Thousands of people, hurrying to and fro."

"Peter, stop," said Victoria.

"He's a great humorist. I'm sure he'll be the editor of the *Tiger*," said Alfred.

"Don't think so. Don't think I'll have the time. Too many social obligations and all that sort of thing, doncha know, old top?"

"He sounds just like an Englishman," said Victoria.

"Not any Englishman I ever heard," said Alfred.

"Ah, methinks I discern the musicians on yonder horizon. Wouldst care to trip the light fantastic, Countess Dockwiler? We have it anyway, so thou hast no choice."

"Who have you got this with, Sal?"

"Walter."

"I have it with Betty. Well, so long, Tom."

"Goodbye," said Sally.

"Goodbye," said Tom. "So long, Alfred."

The musicians returned, and Tom casually made his way to the clothes-rack, got his hat, and went home.

In the kitchen he opened a bottle of homemade root beer and was drinking it when Jean came in in her bathrobe and with a cap on her hair.

"Did you have a good time?" she said.

"Sure, and I didn't need the other two dollars. Here."

"No, keep it," said Jean. "Did you, you know, get along all right with them?"

"Sure. Intermission I was with Alfred and Sally Eaton."

"Alfred and Sally *Eaton*."

"Victoria Dockwiler. And Peter Van Peltz."

"Oh, the *real* ones. Were they nice to you? No looking down their snoots?"

"They were nice. We all talked."

"Who were you with before that?"

"Oh, some fellows."

"Were there a lot there from High?"

"About twelve or thirteen, I guess."

"Did they all see you?"

"Sure. Those that I saw, maybe some I didn't see."

"Did they see you with the Eatons and Victoria and Van Peltz?"

"I guess they did. I'm pretty sure."

"I wish I knew how to dance, I'd teach you. You didn't dance any, did you?"

"No."

"Then what did you do?"

"I—hung around."

She looked at him for a long moment.

"What?" he said.

She smiled gently. "You don't have it in you to lie to me, do you?"

"Oh, well," he said. "They all knew one another and I didn't. But I had a good time. I saw them."

"Some day," she said.

"No."

"Yes, some day. When you get away from here. When you get to State you join one of those frats. I'll pay for it. You can pay me when you get out."

"They have to invite you first. Anyway, I don't know if I want to join one. What would they want with me?"

"You don't know, but I do, and they will. Which did you like best? Sally Eaton or the Dockwiler girl?"

"Like? Sally Eaton. But the Dockwiler girl is the prettiest. She's *pretty*."

"She's a beauty. But you liked Sally Eaton better."

"Oh, you can't help liking her," said Tom.

"Well, there's twelve o'clock. Goodnight."

"Goodnight."

At twelve o'clock the music stopped, but at twelve-thirty there were still some young people at the Idle Hour Tennis Club, trying to prolong the evening, trying to put off the moment when the young men would have to restore the girls to their parents. Only the youngest were being picked up by fathers and chauffeurs. The others were walking home. The Eatons, Alfred and Sally, were spending the night at their grandfather's house.

They left the clubhouse together, Alfred with Victoria, Sally with Peter Van Peltz. There was a moon, but it was dark under the trees, and out that far on Montgomery Street the sidewalks had not been bricked. Sally and Peter Van Peltz led the way. Alfred put his arm around Victoria, but she freed herself.

"*Now* when is our next date?" said Alfred.

"Is that the way to ask for one?"

"All right, when can I see you again?"

"I'm not sure. Tuesday, probably."

"Tuesday? Friday, Saturday, Sunday, Monday, Tuesday. Your mother can't count tonight as a date. We weren't alone."

"But it's seeing you."

"Seeing me? You saw less of me than practically anybody

else at the dance. I had three dances with you, and I was never alone with you. I'm not even alone with you now."

"Well, you're at the Idle Hour every afternoon, I'll see you *there*."

"Victoria, you know perfectly well what I mean."

"Yes, I do. You want to sit on the porch and criticize everything I do and accuse me of things."

"I apologized for that a hundred times. You don't realize. Don't you love me, Victoria? I thought you did. You said you did."

"I did. But that was before you began accusing me."

"Is that another way of saying you don't love me?"

"Well, if you want to know the truth, I don't feel the same way about you as I did. Suddenly you've begun acting as if you owned me. And I don't want anybody to own me. I won't let anybody own me, you or anyone else."

"Then is this the end for us?"

"I don't know, Alfred. I just think we ought to stop seeing each other for a while."

"How long?"

"I don't know."

"You mean, no date next Tuesday."

"That's only five or six days away. I don't think we ought to see each other all next week."

"Do you love someone else?"

"There you *go*. If I don't love you, I have to love someone else. Well, I don't. I don't have to love anybody. You boys all want to get serious, and own me."

"Boys. Plural."

"There you go again. Why can't you be like Peter? Listen to Sally, laughing, having a good time. I don't love Peter, and I don't expect him to love me, but I like to be with him. At least he doesn't try to own me. All he does is make me laugh. *You* don't make me laugh. Kissing, that's what you want."

"I want to kiss you because I love you."

They were silent, and now could hear Peter saying: "Are you game?"

"No," said Sally.

"Oh, come on."

"No, Peter, positively no."

"What does he want you to do, Sally?" said Victoria.

"Ask him," said Sally.

"If they said yes, would you?" said Peter.

"They won't say yes, they have more sense," said Sally.

"Ask us, Peter. Or ask me," said Victoria.

Peter and Sally stopped and waited for the others to catch up with them. "Are you two game to go for a ride in Harry's car?"

"Your brother Harry?" said Alfred. "That new car? Can you drive it?"

"Of course I can drive it. I drove it this afternoon."

"But with him in the car. Are you allowed to drive it by yourself?" said Alfred.

"Of course not."

"Then count me out," said Alfred. "Anyway, a Stutz. You'll wake the whole neighborhood getting it started."

"No I won't," said Peter. "I won't turn on the garage lights. If they hear the motor they'll think it's some other car, as long as the garage lights aren't lit. Will you go, Vic?"

"She certainly will not," said Alfred.

"Sally, will you come?" said Victoria.

"No, she won't, and that's final," said Alfred.

"I didn't ask you, I asked Sally," said Victoria.

"We can't, Victoria, really we can't."

"What's the matter with you three? Mother and Dad's room is on the other side of the house—" said Peter.

"Where's Harry?" said Alfred.

"He's spending the night in Philadelphia. We can go for a ride and nobody'll ever know it."

"I *love* that car," said Victoria.

"Then you and I go," said Peter.

"I won't let you," said Alfred.

"Who are you to stop me?"

"I won't stop you, I'll stop *him*," said Alfred.

"Oh, now come, Alfred. You're not giving orders, not to Vic and I. If you want to fight, I'll fight you. You've been a wet blanket all evening."

"Don't fight him, Peter. I'll go with you and he can't stop me," said Victoria.

"Don't you fight, Alfred," said Sally. "Let them go, both of them."

Victoria stepped quickly in front of Peter, and suddenly they ran from the Eatons.

Alfred and Sally were still seven blocks away from their grandfather's house. They walked on in silence for about four blocks.

"Here they come," said Sally.

The red roadster, brand new, picked up the light from the street lamp at every intersection. Victoria was holding her skirts down. The car had no windshield or doors and was proceeding slowly until Peter saw the Eatons. He sounded the Klaxon, which now had a particularly contemptuous tone, and then accelerated the car.

"Don't look at them," said Sally.

"I won't," said Alfred. "I'll have a talk with Mr. Peter Van Peltz tomorrow, don't think I won't."

He did not have his talk with Peter.

At five o'clock in the morning a farmer discovered the Stutz and, a minute or so later, the bodies of Peter Van Peltz and Victoria Dockwiler. Apparently Peter had tried to turn the car around at Five Points without slackening his speed, and struck a stone abutment. Victoria lay in the ditch, her neck broken. Peter's body lay on the road, death being caused by a fractured skull and hemorrhaging. The radiator and headlights were smashed, and the engine block was moved back some inches, but the car was not a total loss.

ALL SUNDAY afternoon, the 27th, men and women and boys stood and looked at the damage to the stone abutment at Five Points. The Sabbath-day stroll out Montgomery Street was a Port Johnson custom, but the citizens usually walked out as far as Sixteenth Street, crossed over, and came back on the other side. At Sixteenth, Montgomery Street narrowed into a country road, without sidewalks and now, as always after a late spring, in bad repair. But the citizens, all with the same idea, and often without discussion, pressed on to Five Points with little regard for the rough going, the hard, dry ruts, and the distance. And all but the earliest arrivals were a little surprised to see that so many other citizens, including many farm people in *their* Sunday best, were there ahead of them.

A new arrival would join the group that stood a superstitiously respectful distance from the abutment, and always there was one man—although not always the same man—who was providing an account of the accident that would have done credit to an expert eyewitness. "Them tracks was where he put on his brakes already. But too much speed he had, like such a pazzenger train making up time. *Boom!* he goes, into this here now abutment they call it. Miss Dockwiler flies out into the ditch yet and gets the neck broken. Him, the young fellow Van Peltz, they say he got held in by the steering-wheel and the hand-brake and the gear-lever and the auto rolled over and fractured his skull."

"Did you see them?" someone would ask.

"No, but I was told. Norman Leinsdorfer told me."

"Norman Leinsdorfer? Who is that?"

"Norman Leinsdorfer? Norman is Pud Leinsdorfer that found the accident's brother."

"What did they do with the auto?"

"She got towed in town with a team."

"What for make was she?"

"Such a Shtootz. Brand new. Two thousand dollars yet, some say three."

The white crepe was hanging on the Dockwiler door and the citizens on their way back from the viewing of the scene of the accident delicately tried to keep from staring at the house, and many succeeded. The Van Peltz residence was not on Montgomery Street and therefore presented no such problem.

No one in the town had not heard about the accident, and many had read about it in the *Beacon*, a smaller number in the Philadelphia *North American* and the *Press*, in which the vehicle was described as a high-powered racing car. Peter Van Peltz and Victoria Dockwiler were called the most popular members of the Port Johnson young social set, he an heir, she an heiress; he handsome, she beautiful. The time of the accident was left unstated in all the newspapers, although one of the Philadelphia papers reported that the young couple were returning home after a ball. A few long distance telephone calls by the right people to the right people ended the Philadelphia newspaper coverage of the accident.* The *Beacon* published the times and places of the respective funerals, which were private, and the only other journalistic record of the accident is contained in an editorial in the New York *Herald*, deploring the tragedy but absolving the automobile, and mentioning no names.

The town might not have been so saddened by one death, even if it had been the death of a young and pretty girl. But Peter and Victoria were too young for scandal, not old enough for severe censure. They *had* been beautiful and handsome, as the anonymous rewrite men had made the newspaper readers imagine them to be. And the broken body of a very young girl, brought to that condition through a young impulse that she shared with a boy who was not yet a man, was in the minds and almost in the vision of men and women who knew her hardly at all. Among their friends, their contemporaries, it was a foregone conclusion *ex post facto* that Peter would have received some punishment for taking his brother's car; it therefore became outrageous punishment that his life and Victoria's were also ended by God, and for a few days the young people who had known Peter and Victoria maintained a resentful reserve toward their own parents that they themselves did not understand and that their parents attributed to sorrow. But these young were still young enough to regard the mature as the enemy, who still had the power to punish as well as to sustain. It made no difference to the unaware young

---

* It is perhaps worthy of note that no more Stutzes were ever purchased in Port Johnson.

that for those same few days their fathers and mothers thought them more precious than ever before. Fathers looked at daughters, mothers looked at sons, with unspoken love, and then turned with gratitude to the fathers and mothers of Peter and Victoria. And it was as well that they did turn with something of the kindly nature of gratitude. There was one man who needed all they could give.

Victor Dockwiler had always been such a tolerant man that his virtues were not admired. He spoke well of his fellow man, or he held his tongue. He was generous with his money and his time, and he never refused to grant a favor that was in his power to give. His niceness was so constant that there was no contrast, so that many another man, who did fewer kindnesses than Victor Dockwiler, was more greatly admired for the few. He had inherited stock in one of the breweries and as vice-president was given some dignity, some authority, and no serious responsibility. His principal selfish expenditures were on fishing tackle and guns and dogs for his four or five yearly trips to the Poconos. And all the poetry that he could ever feel was hidden in his love for his daughter.

When the new motor ambulance brought Victoria home from Five Points Stephanie Dockwiler answered the doorbell. The ambulance driver had recognized Victoria and the easily dominated intern agreed to the driver's insistence that she be taken home and not to the hospital.

Stephanie Dockwiler stared at the intern in his whites. "She's dead?"

"Yes ma'am, I'm very sorry to say," said the intern.

"We've been waiting up for her. My husband just came home from the police station."

They heard Victor Dockwiler calling, "Who is it? Is that the chief?"

"Oh, God, you tell him. Please, I can't tell him."

"You want me to tell him, ma'am?" said the intern.

"You, yes you. *Please?*"

Victor Dockwiler came to the door. "You're a doctor?"

"Yes sir. I'm afraid I have some very bad news for you, sir."

"Where is she?" said Victor Dockwiler. "She's in there, she's not at the hospital? Then she—*God*, man, then she must be *dead!*"

"Yes sir."

"Did you hear that?" said Victor to his wife

"Yes, dear."

The intern turned to the driver. "Look here, we've got to take the body to the hospital. That's the rule. Do you want to come along with us, Mr. Dockwiler?"

"You're not going to take her to the hospital."

"We have to, sir."

"Never. Bring her in here."

"I'm sorry, sir," said the intern.

Victor left them, coming back a moment later with a double-barreled shotgun. "I know what they'll do to her there, and they're not going to. Carry her inside."

"Victor," said Stephanie.

"Don't talk to me now, Steffie."

"This is a very serious matter, Mr. Dockwiler," said the intern, but he and the driver opened the ambulance doors and pulled out the stretcher and carried Victoria into the hall.

"Now go," said Victor Dockwiler.

"Let them take her upstairs to her room," said his wife.

"All right."

"Will you, please?" said Steffie.

"I'll wait down here," said Victor.

"No, I want you to stay with me."

"Why, Steffie? Are you afraid?"

"Yes."

"What are you afraid of?"

"I don't know, but please put the gun away."

"All right," said Victor Dockwiler. He put the gun back in the glass-doored closet, and the men carried Victoria to her room.

"You can have me arrested if you like," said Victor Dockwiler.

"I have to report it," said the intern. "I shouldn't have come here."

"I'm glad you did, though," said Victor Dockwiler.

"They'll come and take her away," said the intern.

"Not while I have a gun."

"Please tell us what happened before you go," said Steffie.

"Tell my wife in the hall, don't tell me."

Steffie hesitated, then went out with the men, closing the door. When she came back her husband was sitting beside the bed. He got up and rolled the counterpane back over Victoria's body in its party dress and covered her bruised face and twisted head. Steffie knelt on the floor and put her head in her husband's lap.

"I'm going to kill Alfred Eaton, then go to the police."

"She wasn't with Alfred," said Steffie. "She was with Peter, and he's dead too."

"Oh, there's nobody to kill for this," said Victor Dockwiler.

"No," said Steffie. "You could kill me, and then yourself."

"I could never kill you, Steffie. No matter what you did."

"No."

Charlie Sampson, Port Johnson's leading undertaker, had had too much experience to make the same mistake the young intern had made. As soon as word came to him that there had been a fatal accident involving a Van Peltz he hitched up his pair of blacks to the dead-wagon and drove out to Five Points. "Van Peltz? We do all their work. I'll go right out," he told his informant, the patrolman on night duty at the police station. At an even trot the blacks arrived at Five Points a quarter of an hour before the ambulance. The farmer who had discovered the accident was talking to the state trooper who had ridden out from the constabulary sub-station in town. The farmer and the state trooper had lifted Victoria's body out of the ditch and placed it beside Peter, and the young dead lay covered by the trooper's black rubber cape.

"I'm Charlie Sampson, I do all the Van Peltz's work."

"You got here in a hurry," said the trooper.

"That's what I'm supposed to do, mister," said Charlie, who was accustomed to jokes and rebuffs. He lifted the cape. "Occipital fracture."

"Keep your hands off till the doctor gets here," said the trooper.

"Whatever you say. Young lady's neck broke. That anybody can tell."

"All the same, wait for the doctor," said the trooper.

"Just look at that brand-new car. They won't get much for that. Still, I don't know. The raddiator's all bunged up. The headlights. She don't look as bad as you'd think. I can give you their names, if you want."

"All right," said the trooper.

The ambulance arrived, and after a conference Peter's body was lifted into the dead-wagon, Victoria's into the ambulance. "The borough uses my place for a morgue," said Charlie.

"We aint in the borough," said the trooper.

"Township," said the farmer.

"The same difference," said Charlie. "I get all the township and county work too. Pierce, you leave her off at my place."

"No," said the intern. "I understand both bodies have to go to the hospital."

"What for?" said Charlie. "You're not gonna do anything for them. They're as dead as they'll ever be, and you agreed, you said I was to take the one body and you the other."

"I only agreed that you would *transport* the boy's body. I didn't say to your place," said the intern. "The hospital was called, and they're the hospital's responsibility."

"Pierce, tell him he's wrong," said Sampson to the ambulance driver.

"Not me," said Pierce Wagner. "I don't have no say. But if it was my daughter I wouldn't want her either place, hospital *or* undertaking parlor. I'd want her home."

"State Policeman, you represent the law. Tell them."

"I say quit fighting over them. One take the one body and

121

the other take the other. Just tell me where so I can put it in my report," said the trooper.

"There'll be trouble over this," said Sampson.

"Well, I know *two* that won't make any trouble," said the trooper. "So go on, get them back to town. I'm disgusted."

"Look here, Officer," said the intern.

"Don't look-here me. You and the rest of you, give me a hand, get this automobile right side up. Come on, now. One, two—*heave*. Try it again, and all together. One—two—heave. Watch her there now. All right. Now let's push her over to the side of the road, out of the way. You, what's your name? Wagner? When you get in town you telephone my sub-station, find out if they want this automobile towed in."

"Do you want to ride in with me?" said the intern.

"I can't leave my horse, and somebody has to keep an eye on this automobile."

In the Van Peltz house there was no less sadness than in the Dockwilers', where Stephanie and Victor Dockwiler delayed the practical decisions. In the Van Peltz house there was a presence that was not to be thought of as a human form, as the body of Victoria Dockwiler was a human form, but as a breeze through the rooms that could not be inhaled, or a sound that could not be heard, a smell that eluded the sense of smell. It was the presence of guilt, that Henry Van Peltz and Maude Van Peltz had to acknowledge because it was insistent, undeniable, real, and because they were the only ones who were eligible to acknowledge it. They assumed it because they were the makers of their son and it was their son's guilt.

It was nine o'clock in the morning and the Van Peltzes had been told all there was to be told, really all that anyone would ever know that was not conjecture. No one would ever know whether Victoria had asked Peter to turn back, or to go faster. No one would ever know if Peter had called out to her, "I'm sorry," or in that last second had tried to shout a warning. It could be believed that Victoria never saw her party dress all dirty and torn and that she felt no more after the impact shot her body into the ditch. But for what remained of their lives Henry and Maude Van Peltz would have to have some doubt that death had been so quick with Peter.

Henry and Maude Van Peltz were sitting in the morning-room, the only room in Port Johnson that was given that name. They kept looking at each other and looking away, as a man and a woman will do who are sharing a grief and trying not to seem too ready with comfort, one for the other.

"You did telephone Harry," said Maude.

"Yes."

122

"And you spoke to *him*," said Maude.

"Yes, dear."

"It's too bad we had to tell him over the telephone. I know just how he's going to feel—that it was his car—that he should have driven it to Philadelphia. I *don't* want Harry to think of it that way. Don't let him, will you?"

"No, of course not."

"He wanted that car so much, Harry. And he deserved it."

"Yes, he did. He worked hard for it."

"Yes, it isn't easy to be the kind of boy Harry is and pass all your subjects."

"What kind of boy do you mean, dear?"

"Oh, you know, dear. Harry likes to have a good time. Not studiously inclined. Light your pipe."

"In here?"

"Yes."

"Well, if you don't mind, I will. You sure you don't mind?"

"I want you to."

He put a match to the filled pipe he had been holding. "What about you? Can I get you some more coffee?"

"Ring for it, we'll both have some."

He tugged at the bell-pull and presently Maude told the nervous maid to bring the coffee.

"I've been wondering if it isn't my place to go over and see the Dockwilers."

"Yes, I've been wondering that too. I came to the conclusion that you ought to wait."

"Yes, I agree with you. I came to the same conclusion, but I wasn't sure whether I was right or not. Of course I'm going to have to go some time."

"I know, but it's too soon."

"But some time this morning? I mustn't put it off too long."

"No, we can't put it off too long. It's got to be this morning."

"You're not going, Maude."

"Oh, I have to. Just as much as you do. I must see Stephanie."

"They may not want to see us."

"They won't want to see us, but Victor's a gentleman and he'll know why we came."

"Tell *me* why."

"You *know* why," said Maude.

"Because we want to take the blame?"

"Yes. Because we *have* to take the blame. Henry?"

"Yes?"

"If we take the blame, if we're there and they can hate us—"

"Then they won't hate Peter so much."

"I can't imagine anyone hating Peter, but yes, that's the reason. It isn't going to be very easy to live in Port Johnson any more. Nobody's going to remember that Peter died too. They're only going to remember Victoria."

"You may be right. We'll see."

The coffee was brought in.

"The hardest thing to believe—oh, it's all impossible to believe. But the oddest thing—Peter wasn't very fond of Victoria. Did you know that?"

"No," said Henry Van Peltz.

"He much preferred Sally Eaton. I wonder why it wasn't Sally that went along with him. They were together when I left the club, all four of them. Victoria, Sally, Alfred, and Peter."

"I have no idea. Sally is more sensible, maybe he asked her and she wouldn't go."

"Well, that would have been *too* much for Martha. Her older son dying that time, and then Sally."

"I'd forgotten about Martha's other son. Billy?"

"Yes," she said. "Billy."

"Aren't you going to have any coffee?"

"I don't think I will. I've changed my mind."

"Does my pipe bother you?"

"It isn't your pipe. It's everything."

"Don't you want to lie down?"

She smiled. "I'm not tired. I had a good night's sleep."

The maid reappeared. "It's Mrs. Eaton, ma'am, wishing to speak on the telephone but not to disturb you."

"It's started," said Maude Van Peltz to her husband. "Thank you, Theresa, I'll speak to Mrs. Eaton."

The Dockwilers' maid was startled to see Mr. and Mrs. Van Peltz at the door.

"We would like to see Mr. and Mrs. Dockwiler," said Henry Van Peltz.

"Come right in, suh. Rest your hat, please, I'll tell them, but I don't know."

The Van Peltzes waited in the front room. "Don't stand," said Henry to his wife. "Save your strength."

In a few minutes Victor Dockwiler entered the room. "Good morning, Maude. Henry."

It was not the custom to shake hands at every meeting, but Henry Van Peltz extended his hand, and it was not accepted. But when Maude Van Peltz went to him and kissed him, Victor Dockwiler bowed his head. "What is there to say, Victor?" she said.

"Nothing, I guess. Steffie's in her room. I didn't tell her you were here."

"Is she awake? The doctor hasn't given her any sedative?"

124

"She hasn't seen the doctor."

"Then I'll go on upstairs," said Maude. She left the men.

"Sit down, Henry."

"Thanks, I'd like to."

"I had a drink of whiskey a while ago. Would you like one?"

"Well—yes."

Victor poured two thimblefuls of whiskey and drank his immediately. Henry Van Peltz drank half of his and held the glass in his two hands, turning it around and around.

"Have you made your arrangements for the funeral?" said Henry Van Peltz.

"Monday morning, eleven o'clock. A service here. And strictly private."

"Nobody but family?"

"Nobody but family."

"Ours will be Monday afternoon, two-thirty. We've invited a very few friends," said Henry Van Peltz. "Not our friends so much as Peter's. Don't you think some of Victoria's friends—"

"No. We don't want any fuss."

"No, I agree with you on that, but her friends—"

"It was a friend that . . ."

"Go ahead, say it, Victor, if it'll make you feel any better. It was a friend that drove the car. My son. Our son."

"Henry, I can't be as polite about this as you can. If Peter hadn't been killed in the accident, I'd have killed him. When I first heard about it I thought Victoria was with Alfred Eaton, and I was ready to go and shoot him."

Henry Van Peltz put his glass on the table. "Two young people are dead, Victor, not one. You and I'd better not talk any more."

"Oh, I don't mind talking."

"But I do," said Henry Van Peltz. He got up and went to the window and stood with his back to Victor Dockwiler.

"Why did you come to this town, anyway?" said Victor.

"As a punishment. As a matter of fact that's exactly what it was. I was sent here to run my uncle's silk mill instead of to a larger one in New Jersey. But I don't think they meant to punish me as much as I have been. Now why don't you shut up if you can't behave yourself? I'll gladly leave this house the minute my wife is ready. Meanwhile, there's nothing keeping you here."

"Not a God damn thing," said Victor, and left the room.

Henry Van Peltz stood at the window until Maude spoke to him. There were vestiges of tears in her eyes, but she was smiling. "I'm glad we came," she said. *"Steffie* was glad we came. She sent you her love, and she has no bitterness. She was as much a comfort to me as I was to her, or as I tried to be. I never really knew Steffie before, and I love her, Henry. Where is Victor?"

"He asked to be excused."

"Poor man."

It was evening at the Samuel Eaton residence in the country. Samuel Eaton entered the sittingroom. "You heard the awful news?" said his wife.

"Peter Van Peltz and Victoria? Yes."

"Will you go upstairs and speak to Alfred? Please?"

"What about?"

"*What about?* You cold, unfeeling fool!"

Sunday afternoon. The callers at the Dockwiler house now came in a frame of mind that was different from that of the Friday and Saturday callers. The earlier visitors were responding to a shock that had occurred within themselves, and their conversation was accompanied by half turns of the head, as though they were looking over the shoulder at the scene at Five Points (which not a few of them had inspected). On Sunday afternoon and early evening the visitors, although they might have been considered tardy, were in reality closer to Victor and Steffie Dockwiler, not in degree of friendship or sympathy, but because they sat *with* Victor and Steffie and with them were looking together into the future, the immediate future and the business of the burial, and the blank future that was to be lived in the eternal absence of the dead girl.

The Sunday afternoon callers at the Dockwilers' included relatives from other towns and cities, and "working people" who had no other time off, and a few Port Johnson people who had been away and come back especially to attend the funerals. Victor Dockwiler had made a change in the plans for Victoria's funeral; he yielded to the gentle pressure and let it be known that those who thought they were her closer friends would be admitted to the house on Monday. He made sure not to invite anyone, but when they asked if they might come, he replied that he thought it would be all right.

The Dockwilers (and the Van Peltzes as well) had a surprise visitor on Sunday afternoon. She was Norma Budd. "Mind you, we were on a cruise, on Long Island Sound. We left City Island shortly after lunch on Friday. Saturday morning we had engine trouble—I say 'we.' The yacht belongs to friends of Father's that we've known a long time. But Saturday morning something happened to the motor and the owner thought it best to put in at New London, and we did, and we all went to the Griswold, you know, the hotel, and had lunch, and I just *happened* to buy the Philadelphia paper. I always do when I'm away. And that's how I found out."

"You were nice to come all that way," said Steffie.

"Oh, without a moment's hesitation. Victoria was my favorite among the younger girls, and I could see a wonderful future for her. Everyone could. I wasn't the only one. So pretty, so sweet."

"Thank you," said Steffie. "Where are your mother and father now, Norma?"

"They're still in London," said Norma.

"Oh, in New London," said Steffie.

"No. London, England. I sent them a cablegram, but I don't think they'll get it till tomorrow. When they're in England they go away every weekend. But you'll hear from them, I know. I must go now."

"Where are you staying?" said Victor.

"Oh, I feel embarrassed about that, but I invited myself to stay at the Eatons'. Our house is closed till September."

"I wish we could have offered you a room here," said Steffie.

"Oh, I'm not embarrassed. Well, yes, I was, a little. But I'm not now. Goodbye, Mrs. Dockwiler. Mr. Dockwiler."

They went to the door with her.

"Think of her coming all that way," said Steffie.

"A nice girl, a good heart," said Victor.

"And stunning-looking. But no husband. And Norma's close to twenty-five if she isn't that already."

"Always on the go," said Victor.

"Well, there's nobody for her here in Port Johnson."

"Or in New York or Philadelphia."

"I wouldn't be too sure about that. I'll bet there's a married man."

"Norma? She's not that kind," said Victor.

"Depends on what you mean by 'that kind.' Norma's no different than most of us. If she fell in love with a man she'd be any kind he wanted her to be. I was just lucky that *you* were *your* kind." She took his hand.

The conversation at the Eatons' supper table was kept going by Samuel Eaton and Norma Budd, with some assistance from Martha and very little from Alfred, Sally or Constance, but Martha's contribution late in the meal was the most welcome to Alfred and Norma.

"Norma, you know how to drive a Packard, don't you?"

"Oh, I can drive them all. Why?"

"Then after supper you and Alfred take the Packard. You both want to talk and you won't have much chance with us here."

"I'd love it, if Alfred would."

"I would," said Alfred Eaton.

"Then that's settled. Go while there's still daylight. Don't you think so, Sam?"

"I have no objection," said Samuel Eaton. Martha's suggestion had been her own, without any consultation with him, but to raise an objection would have involved the admission that he had not been consulted, and such an admission was not of a kind that Samuel Eaton habitually made, not in front of his entire family and a pretty outsider. "But don't be gone too long. I want to hear more about England."

"I have Mother's latest letter upstairs. I'll get it," said Norma.

She excused herself, returning with the letter, and left with Alfred.

"I don't have to drive. You drive if you'd rather," she said.

"All right. Where shall we go?"

"It doesn't make any difference, as long as the roads are good."

"We'll have to stay on the main roads then," said Alfred. Most citizens who owned automobiles preferred not to be on the road in the evening. No garages stayed open, and if a car broke down it was sure to be there for the night. Tire trouble, from horseshoe nails and blowouts, frequently occurred in triplicate, necessitating the use of the customary two spare tires, then abandonment of the car.

They drove for a few miles, but when Norma saw that Alfred was unable or unwilling to drive and talk, she made a suggestion: "Why not go back to your place and just drive in the driveway and stop there? They can't see us from the house, and I'm sure nobody will be out for a stroll."

"That's a good idea," said Alfred.

They nosed the car into the Eatons' driveway and Alfred turned off the motor. "I hope it starts again. It gets balky sometimes," he said.

"Well, we haven't far to walk. Have you started smoking?"

"A pipe. Do you smoke?"

"I've been dying for a cigarette all day. I have some." She took out a small white enameled case and they lit cigarettes. "Now from the beginning," she said.

"From the beginning," he said. "First, before I tell you anything, you're not going to like me when I've finished. I don't like myself. And when I've finished you won't either. I'm responsible for Victoria and Peter being killed."

"By that you mean you've *taken* the responsibility. That doesn't mean that I'm going to agree with you, but go on."

Alfred then related in detail and in good chronological order the unfortunate events on the Dockwiler porch, the strained relations at the dance, and the scene on the way home after the dance. He talked almost steadily for an hour, during which they smoked all the cigarettes and did not notice the passing of the daylight. "And so I guess that's the whole story," he said.

"Well, now you know what tragedy is, Alfred," said Norma.

"Yes, that's what it is, isn't it?" he said. "That's exactly the right word for it."

"It's a tragedy because it was all so unnecessary, and such a waste. There were any number of times when she could have said something or you could have said something, or something could have happened, and now instead of sitting here with me, you'd be with her."

"Oh, Norma."

"That brings it too close. I shouldn't have said that. But what's the good of the whole thing if you can't get some good out of it? I didn't say that very well, but do you know what I mean?"

"I think so. Try to learn something from it?"

"Well, yes. Yes. Any unhappiness should teach us something. At least there's something to be learned, if we know how to learn it. If we can see it. I'm not a very good one to talk. I don't seem to learn from unhappiness. But you may be luckier than I am. I know you have more sense."

"I don't think I have any sense."

"Oh, yes you have," she said. "For instance, you must have noticed I haven't said anything about you not taking any blame."

"I noticed it, yes."

"I'm not going to say you don't have to take some blame. You were at fault. Therefore, you contributed to what happened. Where you were at fault was in not understanding more about Victoria, or girls, but especially Victoria. Ever since she was this high I can remember thinking that some day she was going to stop being the quiet, pretty little girl. Those eyes, even when she was ten, or even eight, I knew she would grow up to be a *femme fatale*. Forgive me for saying that, that just came out. But if Vicky had gone on living—no. I won't say that."

"She wouldn't have married me? Is that what you were going to say?"

"She might have married you. If a man loves a woman she has a hard time rejecting him, even if she doesn't want him very much. A woman, after all, if a man loves her, she can't just dismiss him and say he's a fool. I'm not being personal now, I'm telling you things you ought to know. You see, Alfred, a girl like Victoria, a girl that's pretty and popular, she's going to find out that no matter how many boys want to dance with her, or kiss her, there aren't very many of them

129

that really love her. Sometimes the most popular girl isn't loved by anyone. I imagine you never knew that."

"No, I didn't."

"It's true, you have my word for it. Look at me. I'm twenty-five. Haven't you wondered why I haven't got married?"

"No, I just thought you never wanted to."

"Never wanted to! Well, I didn't want to marry the men who might have proposed, or did propose. But why hasn't one of the right ones proposed?"

"I don't know. You haven't encouraged them enough, I'd say."

"Partly that. I've always made such an effort to be popular that the nice ones—I don't know."

"Well, you've never fallen in love."

She was silent until her silence made him turn. "Do you really think I've never fallen in love, Alfred?"

"Yes, I think so."

"I hope you're right. Maybe you have some instinct that tells you that. Is that what it is?"

"I don't know what it is, but I've never thought you were in love with anyone."

"Do you know why you think that? Tell me what makes you think it."

"I'll have to put it in my own words, but it's something about the way you look. You don't look as though you were loving somebody. You look as though you didn't have anyone on your mind."

"No, the last part isn't true. I've had somebody on my mind. You haven't seen any difference in me in the last three years?"

"No, I don't think so."

"And yet for three years I've thought I was deeply in love. But it didn't show? It didn't make me look as though I were in love?"

"Not to me."

"I couldn't have married him anyway, he's married already. But I've always thought I loved him, and maybe I do."

"I don't think you do, or you wouldn't have any doubt. I was suspicious and jealous of Victoria, but I never had any doubt about *my* side of it."

"Have I shocked you?"

"Why? Because you thought you were in love with a man that was married?" He laughed. "I guess it shocks me, but it isn't the first time, and the other time was much worse. The—lady was married, too. That was a shock. Maybe I never got over it."

"I see."

"No you don't," he said.

"But I do. It was your mother, wasn't it?"

"It was Mother. How did you know? Does everybody know?"

"No. I made a guess. Only a guess. Word of honor."

"How did you guess?"

"Well, you're not a gossip, so it must have been something you discovered yourself. And in the second place, you wouldn't have cared very much if it had been anyone else."

"That's very clever, and correct."

"You learn to be clever about some things when you're having a secret affair."

"Mother's is past and gone."

"Yes, because the man died, didn't he?"

"If I'm right, yes. Have you guessed that too?"

"I think so, but I wouldn't want to say somebody else and be wrong. How did it make you feel about your mother?"

"At the time, pretty badly. But after a while I began to think of her as a human being and not just my mother. After all, you know, I can easily understand how she could fall out of love with my father."

"But remember this, she loves your father."

"I guess she does."

"Did she ever suspect that you knew?"

"Never. And never will, if I can help it."

"Don't be surprised if some day she tells you."

"Not Mother."

"She may want to help you some time."

"No. I may not be very bright about some things, but I know my own family. And myself. I've discovered something about myself. At school, mostly, but outside of school, too. I'm a person that with the exception of you, people don't go out of their way to help me. They like me to help them, and I do when I can, but they all seem to think I don't *need* help. A fellow at school. 'Eaton, you're the coldest fish I ever knew,' he said. But I'm not a cold fish. I'm anything but. But I guess that's what Victoria thought, too. Peter was fun, I wasn't. Peter made her laugh. I don't think I ever made her laugh."

"But you did one thing."

"What?"

"One thing that Peter couldn't do."

"What?"

"When you kissed her she didn't want to stop there."

"I said that. I'm not sure of it."

"It's true."

"But it didn't make her love me."

"She did in her way. She didn't love you as much as you loved her, but I think I know why."

131

"Why?"

"She knew that even if you did love her, you'd always hold back some of yourself."

"But I wouldn't, and I didn't."

"Alfred, that's the one thing you have to be careful of. You, Alfred Eaton. You always have held back some of yourself, and maybe you always will."

"Then I *am* a cold fish, and that's a pretty picture."

"But you're not. But you've never really *needed* anyone."

"I've needed you."

"Yes."

"For years."

"And I wonder why. I've always liked you, and loved you, not in a husband-wife way, but something different. You know, as long as we live we'll be something to each other, won't we?"

"Yes."

"Do you want anything from me now?"

"Yes."

"I wanted to give to you, that's why I'm here. It's time, isn't it?"

"Yes."

"Do you know why I went upstairs and got that letter?"

"Why?"

"To take off my corset." She undid her shirtwaist.

"Have you ever done the whole thing?" she said.

"No."

"Then kiss me. I want you so, I'll always want you. Let's kiss for a long, long time."

He kissed her until she pressed his head down to her breasts. "I love that," she said. "Whenever you want me I want you. I feel you. Oh, yes, I do."

"I *love* you," he said.

"I love *you*, I love *you*. Don't go away from me just yet. Please stay."

"You're lovely, Norma, lovely."

"I'm happy. I know I'm wrong, but I'm happy."

"I am, too."

"But not wrong. Don't ever be afraid to take what's given to you. That *would* be wrong. What's the date?"

"The 27th of June, 1915. Why?"

"Well, don't you want to remember it? It's the day I first became your mistress."

"Is that what you are?"

"Yes. Mistress and friend. Friend before, but mistress and friend from now on."

"I'm not your master."

"No, but I'm your mistress."

"I can't support you."

"Not all mistresses are supported by their gentlemen, dear boy. Rest assured of that. Often quite the opposite, in fact."

"Well, what do you call me?"

"You're my lover."

"I like that much better."

"So do I. Will you be my lover in New York next winter?"

"Before that, I hope."

"Not much before, I'm afraid. But next winter for sure. Are you happy now, Alfred?"

"Yes, I am."

"So am I. This isn't really wrong, you know. It only becomes wrong when one other person knows about it. One other person. If I tell someone, or you tell someone. Then the world knows, and the world can be hurt and the world can get nasty. But for the time being we've only got to watch out for one person."

"Who's that?"

"Your mother. And that's why when we go in the house, I want you to have your arm around my shoulder."

"What?"

"Yes. If we do that, she'll be misled. She'll be surprised, but she'll say to herself, 'They wouldn't dare, not if there was any more to it.' But if we pretend nothing, she'll look for things. Which reminds me. Are you all closed up in front?"

"Gosh, no, I'm not."

"Well, we mustn't pretend *too* much."

The Budd family were accidental residents of Port Johnson, and by their comings and goings and the somewhat complicated origins of Devrow and Marian Budd, the high style in which they lived, and their aloofness from all but a few Port Johnson families, they had created an impression, first, of elusiveness, and second, of near-mystery that most Port Johnson citizens found distasteful, a distaste that often took the form of respectful hostility. There were a few families—the Johnsons, the Eatons, the Millers, the Van Peltzes, the Dockwilers among them—who were not mystified by the Budds, since to those families there was no mystery. Marian Siddenham was an orphan at two and had been brought up by maternal grandparents in Philadelphia. She had been rescued from the seaside hotel fire in which her father and mother were killed, although the rescue had not entailed any heroism. She was simply wheeled off the porch of the hotel in her perambulator; her mother and father were trapped while taking a post-luncheon nap in their room, forgotten by the hotel staff and other guests. Marian's grandparents gave her everything they could, which was ample. She was not only an orphan, but an orphan who was entitled to a little extra because of the dramatic circumstances that had made her an orphan. In the natural course of the social life of Philadelphia and Baltimore she met and fell in love with Devrow Budd and they were married.

Devrow Budd was not the man Marian's grandparents would have picked. He had left the University of Virginia in his second year, under circumstances that were never explained to Marian's grandparents, who were, after all, Philadelphians and not Baltimoreans or Virginians. But it was too late for the grandparents to start denying the girl her wishes, and with the consolation that it could have been worse they gave her a big wedding and an iron-bound trust fund. Marian also came into a large house and three hundred acres in and adjoining Port Johnson, this from a paternal uncle named George Siddenham whom she never had seen, who never had seen her. The establishment suited Devrow Budd and they went there to live. The fact that they had no friends in Port Johnson made the establishment even more attractive to Devrow Budd, since it was his intention to live as a country gentleman and it was easier to lord it over people one didn't know. The unconfirmed rumor that Devrow Budd had left Charlottesville over something to do with gambling was given substance by his choice of business activity after his marriage. He was, and frankly admitted to being, a speculator, and he lived like a successful one, which indeed a great deal of the time he was. He found that the remoteness of his country place, as he called it, in an obscure town in Pennsylvania, became by its remoteness and obscurity a character asset: other business men seemed to feel that a fellow who claimed Port Johnson as his home town must be a sound man underneath it all. Some of the land was sacrificed when Devrow Budd made bad guesses in the stock market, but he did not allow those setbacks to affect the rather grand scale on which he and his family lived.

In a few years of marriage he expanded from the tall thin bridegroom to a tall, imposing husband, and he was one of those few fortunate men to whom portliness was becoming. He wore clothes well and his stoutness and his large black moustache complemented each other. He was the only man in Port Johnson to possess a monocle. In Port Johnson and Philadelphia he left the eyeglass at home, but when dining out in New York he always employed it while studying menus, and menus were always studied by Devrow Budd. His breakfast alone would have warded off starvation for two or three days; to Devrow Budd it was only what a man had to have to carry him through to lunch. As a trencherman he was conforming to the custom of the day among financiers, who had greater confidence in a man with a good appetite.

As a fine figure of a man Devrow Budd enjoyed success and variety with women. He did not complain of the lasting shyness of the girl he married, but he reserved the right to enjoy himself with other women, so long as they were not the wives or mistresses of men who could do him financial harm. He had no subsidized mistress of his own and he spent no great sums in cash or for trinkets on those who insisted on something tangible. But among his New York acquaintances he was reputed to possess exceptional phallic equipment, a reputation which his men friends' jokes helped to spread, with the inevitable result that their women friends had to satisfy their curiosity.

In Port Johnson Henry Van Peltz was the only man whose company he sought when he felt the need of male company. He had misjudged Samuel Eaton. He had thought Samuel Eaton was a man whose tastes were similar to his own, and he was sharply disappointed when Eaton had declined an extremely cautiously worded invitation to a very small party in Philadelphia. Devrow Budd did not like to be wrong about a man, and he never again quite trusted Samuel Eaton. Henry Van Peltz had not been a disappointment; Devrow Budd had not imagined Henry to be a man who might be interested in a very small party in Philadelphia; but Henry was unmistakably a gentleman and Devrow Budd considered Henry his social equal, although somewhat lacking in masculine vigor. As to the Port Johnson women, none of them had the style or the promise of evil or the eagerness to yield that so many New York women had to offer, and consequently Devrow Budd gave Port Johnson women no cause to gossip, and Marian Budd was always glad to have him home and to herself.

She guessed he was not faithful to her, but she knew none of the other women and was equally sure she knew what kind of women they were. They were the beautiful women of restaurants, always dining with men who obviously were not their husbands and almost always dining with one man alone. Marian Budd had never spoken to one of those women and had not forced herself to imagine Devrow naked with one of them naked and responding to the excitement she sometimes felt with Devrow. If he used them, it was because of an appetite he had that he could not help. Marian could not eat as much food or drink as much wine as Devrow ate and drank, and if he had to use those other women, it was because he was different from her in that respect as well. The big body that got into bed with her was so unlike her own that it was certain to have extra needs that had not been revealed to her.

She could put both of her feet in one of his shoes; he could hold her at arm's length with her feet not touching the floor; she could not span one of his biceps with two hands; he could exhaust her with his love-making, so that he was not ready when she was already spent, and his final charge into her was often an act of cruelty that she knew was unintentional and that she endured because it was his way. He was a god.

The children that came to her—Norma, and three years later, Jack—were hers only until they were drawn to him, and then their unquestioning admiration of his physical magnificence became as fixed as her own. They compared him with George Washington. Later they began to look at the town as he looked at it, as houses and shops that derived their relative importance from the degree of usefulness they achieved in the comfort of Devrow Budd. Neither the girl nor the boy had friends whose company was preferable to their father's, but Norma was a naturally friendly child and a smiler, while Jack was contentious and sardonic. He was a year older than Billy Eaton and the two families thought the two boys were suitable playmates, but Jack was always Billy's last choice in team games, and arrangements for the two to play together were invariably conducted by parents or nurses and not by the principals. The four-year difference in age between Jack and Alfred Eaton was so enormous that they were almost strangers, but Norma at seven was permitted to hold the infant Alfred in her arms and she continued to think of him as her baby until she was able to think of him as a little-boy friend.

As she grew older Norma's feeling toward the town underwent a slow, steady change, which in reality was no more than the difference between having her own opinions of the people and accepting her father's. She found out for herself, as Alfred Eaton later found out for himself, that the merchants and clerks invited small tyrannies by being obsequious, but as she became accustomed to them and to their obsequiousness she, and they, began to know each other, and the better they knew each other, she and they, the less frequently the acquaintance was delayed by the clerks' over-respectful treatment of her. And there came the time when she could go into a Lower Montgomery Street store with the comfortable feeling that they were not going to treat her in the old way, a way which she was acute enough to realize they resented, although it was their own fault and not hers. *Then* she became aware that they *liked* her and her trips to the stores became fun.

There was of course no special day that ended the old way and commenced the new. There was only a special year—her fifteenth. For two years she had been waiting for her mother to recognize the physical changes that were taking place in her figure, and to offer some enlightenment on the subject of menstruation. The enlightenment never was offered, and Marian Budd thus lost forever an opportunity to improve her relationship with Norma. Formally, and routinely, the relationship was that of loving mother and daughter. In deeper actuality it was a great deal less. Her mother was often irritable and absent-minded and sometimes without reason would burst into tears and then *find* some reason to blame the tears on Norma or Jack, who might be temporarily blameless. Always at such times Norma's mother would say, "If your father were here you wouldn't be so naughty," completely ignoring the fact that their father hardly ever disciplined them. The children did not fail to notice that such outbursts were followed by acts of kindness and tokens of generosity, and Jack was so conscious of the sequence that he once told Norma that the way to get something was to wait till Mother had one of her "cries." But Norma only wished that she could do without the cries, even if it meant doing without the generosity. And at thirteen Norma suspected her mother of being a hypocrite, who did not show that side of her nature when Father was at home. She often wanted to say, "If Father were here *you* wouldn't be so naughty," but it remained one of the unsaid truths. Norma noticed things long before she learned to look for reasons for them.

Her cheerfulness with non-family people was, then, a genuine expression of a genuine liking for them. She could count on a smile returned for a smile given and a warmth of greeting in anticipation of her own friendliness. And it became her public way, available to stewards in steamships as well as to the peerage and relatives of the peerage whom she saw in her travels abroad. To some of the girls she met at school in Philadelphia and New York it was a tiresome way and an exercise of face muscles and display of good teeth by an obvious social climber, but the judgments of schoolgirls on other schoolgirls are not even final for the girls who pass the judgments, and in Norma's case they were unsound at the beginning. There was only one social climber in the Devrow Budd family, and he was so convinced of his unassailability that it was society's money and not its invitations that he schemed for. A small Baltimore legend had it that a nineteenth-century ancestor had adopted the name Devrow because he had difficulty in spelling Devereux, but Devrow Budd's ready answer to that was to point out that Virginia had Leighs as well as Lees and that old Devereux-Devrow, nothwithstanding his near-illiteracy, had been in a position to manumit many more slaves than most of his highly educated critics had owned. And as to the Budds, they had *always* been wealthy, down to the second generation preceding Devrow's, when Devrow's paternal grandfather invested heavily in a race track—summer resort that he hoped would be attractive to the Southerners who had patronized Saratoga. The Southerners stayed home or resumed their visits to the Springs, and in three years the weeds were growing in the infield and the bats were nesting in the hotel. It was a grand failure, which Devrow's father, Baxter Budd, used as his reason for staying out of business and spending most of his time at the Maryland Club. Baxter's wife, a medium-artistocratic Baltimore girl, supported the family through loans from her father, who was in insurance, and who met her modest demands until Devrow's departure from The University. At that point the grandfather put the Baxter Budds on an allowance that was too small to permit Devrow to follow in his father's footsteps, and Devrow was forced to marry or find a job.

The nearest recognized hunt to the Siddenham place was more than twenty miles away, and Devrow Budd altered his original intention to establish a stud farm. It was a fortunate decision, not only because the climate was not ideal, but because Devrow and Marian were away so much and knew so little about the breeding of horses that they would have been placing in the hands of a capable superintendent a strong temptation to steal everything portable or negotiable. They bought a couple of park hacks (which would have foundered if their only exercise had consisted of the rides Marian and Devrow gave them) and a succession of ponies for the children; a pair of good chunks for farm use, and a pair of fine harness horses. It was almost as though they had been born to be the ideal prospective purchasers of the early automobiles.

Devrow Budd got into the stock market with a minimum of subtlety. He bought lunch in Philadelphia for a stockbroker, a Baltimore friend, and at the cigars he said: "I want to take a flyer in the stock market. What's a good thing?" He rejected the first cautious offerings and made it clear that he was eager to speculate. The broker then told him about a cement company stock. Devrow bought a thousand dollars' worth of the stock on margin, and in two weeks made nearly ten thousand, took his extraordinary profit, and settled down to his life work. Raymond Johnson disapproved of Devrow Budd, as might be expected of a man who consciously represented conservatism, and yet in the many years of their acquaintanceship Raymond Johnson never gave Devrow Budd sufficient credit for his timidity or for his greed. For Devrow Budd was not an all-out gambler; he was only a man who liked a sure thing at good odds, and thus in his fashion was as conservative as Raymond Johnson. There was some irony in the fact that Devrow Budd in his timidity risked relatively small sums in the hope of extraordinarily large returns, but because he spent a lot of money on his own pleasure he was regarded as prodigal;

while Raymond Johnson, investing the same sums in enterprises that would only pay small returns, was considered to be the better business man. It was also a fact that through the years Devrow Budd lent money to men rather like himself, and invariably got his money back, while Raymond Johnson allowed for the loss of money on between five and eight percent of the loans he made to men who were not of the gambling stripe.

It would have enraged Devrow Budd to be told that the big men found him useful, because Devrow Budd could not ever consider himself usable. Nevertheless the big men found him useful. Some of the very characteristics that made him unacceptable to the big men as a partner or an equal were in his favor when they chose to use him—to his profit as well as to their own. They knew that he was timid, and not a genuine gambler; they knew he was arrogant; they knew he was greedy; they knew he wore a monocle and had a stomach for food and a taste for wine and a lust for women, a condescension toward his equals and a respect for his superiors, and they correctly surmised that he would obey orders. He was, therefore, an ideal choice to represent them on business missions to London. The Englishmen in the City recognized him for an American the moment he opened his mouth to speak, but he made no effort to simulate an English accent or to pretend to be anything but an American, except in his clothes and in a manner that Englishmen thought belonged to Englishmen alone, but that was just as genuinely Devrow Budd's as it was of the most supercilious member of White's Club. It was impossible for an Englishman to snub him or patronize him, largely because the only kind of Englishman whose snub he might recognize was too secure to snub anyone. Devrow Budd had the gift of looking away from an Englishman who was trying to snub him so that the Englishman found himself talking to thin air. And a snubbed Englishman is an ineffectual one, since he has always believed that the snub is an indigenous art. Then, too, in the matter of size Devrow Budd was imposing, and it was difficult for an Englishman to believe that a man who occupied a large suite at Claridge's was no more than a messenger boy. And the firms and syndicates whose messages Devrow Budd carried back and forth were as impressive in London as in Wall Street.

When the war broke out a syndicate sent Devrow Budd to London once again, and when he remained in spite of the Zeppelin raids of the next winter and in spite of his being fifty-one years old, even the Londoners who had learned to dislike him conceded that he was to some extent in it with them and was therefore not altogether a bad fellow. Marian joined a group of American ladies who rolled bandages and made up parcels for the British expeditionary forces and otherwise prejudiced their official neutrality. Devrow Budd's espousal of the British cause went so far as to inspire him to urge his son Jack to join up with the Canadians or the Royal Flying Corps, but Jack was not yet ready to become a belligerent and he remained in the apartment in New York which he shared with Norma.

On the morning of Victoria Dockwiler's funeral Alfred Eaton awoke to such disgust that it seemed to have been prepared for him through the night. Somewhere on the next floor below Norma Budd was up, or getting up, or taking her bath and on terms of intimacy with herself that included something of him that he had wanted to have belong to Victoria. He tried to shut out of his mind the re-felt grotesqueness of the act that had taken possession of him, the loss of what he had given, and to reject the overwhelming pleasure he had taken. He tried to invent a plausible excuse for staying away from the funeral and for avoiding Norma, the one as much as the other. And there was a light knock on his door.

"Alfred?" It was Sally.

"I'm awake," he said.

"Don't go back to sleep," she said.

"I won't, I'm awake," he said.

"It's half past seven, and you really haven't much time, Mother says," said his sister.

"I *said* . . ."

"All right."

Sally had been nowhere in his thoughts, she was seldom in his thoughts, but now she became someone he wanted to talk to.

"Sal?"

"What?"

"Come on in."

She entered the room. "I *knew* you weren't up. Lordy, look at your whiskers. You have a beard."

"Of course I have a beard."

"Do you have to shave every day?"

"Every other, nearly every. Hell, I've *been* shaving ever since I went to Knox."

"Is it as rough as it looks? Let me touch it." She passed her hand over his chin. "It *is* rough. Heavens, you with a beard."

"Why *not?*"

"Oh, no reason why not, it's just strange. It's really all over your face, isn't it? Like a man's."

"No, like a woman's. Mrs. Taylor's."

"No, Mrs. Taylor lets hers grow. She looks like one of those Chinese mandarins, if you've seen her lately."

"Is everybody downstairs?"

"They're all just finishing breakfast. I was sent up to waken you."

"Is Norma down?"

"Everybody's down, except you. What did you want me for?"

"Oh, I guess I just wanted you to wake me up."

"You mean if I talked to you you wouldn't go back to sleep?"

"Uh-huh."

"I wish we didn't have to go to this funeral."

"Funer*als*."

"No, I'm not going to Peter's. Mother thinks it doesn't look quite right for girls my age."

"I don't follow that. Victoria was old enough to get killed, to die. And you were *with* Peter."

"I didn't decide it, Mother did. She said if you go that'll be enough. I'd go if it was up to me."

"Were you very *very* fond of Peter?"

"I guess I was. I kissed him."

"You did?"

"Yes."

"You mean—not just once? You often did?"

"Yes."

"Then you must have been in love with him."

"Half."

"Did you ever tell him you were?"

"Why?"

"If you don't want to tell me, all right."

"I'd tell you, but I don't know why you want to know. Yes, I used to write it to him, more than I told him."

"I can never think of you as being as old as Victoria."

"A little older. I'm not a child any more, Alfred. There are a lot of things I know more about than you think I do."

"Such as?"

"Oh, love, for instance. Alfred?"

"What?"

"Now I don't want you to get cross at me."

"I won't."

"Do you promise?"

"All right," he said. "What?"

"Norma's too old for you."

"Too old for what, for heaven's sake? I'm not going to marry her."

"Now you promised you wouldn't get cross."

"All right. Anything else?"

"Yes."

"What?"

Sally looked away from him. "I don't think Norma knows

141

it, but I think she's in love with you. Now wait a minute."

"She's just a friend."

"Not any more. That was when you were younger. You know you could marry somebody seven years older than you are. And have children."

"I know that. You're not telling me anything new. But where are you finding out all these things?"

"Do you really want to know?"

"Yes."

"He's dead."

"You mean Peter."

"Yes."

"And he got the idea that Norma was in love with me?"

"No, I did. But he agreed with me."

"How did Peter know anything about Norma?"

"I don't know."

"What *did* he know?"

"I don't know. Listen, you'd better get dressed."

"Come on, you're holding back something."

"I can't tell you anything that Peter told me."

"I'm your brother, you can tell me."

"No, I can't."

"Then I think it's rotten of you—"

"I think it's rotten of you to try to force me to." She left his room.

The services at the Dockwiler house were brief in point of time, but Alfred was not conscious of time. It was a gathering of people, all of whom he had known all his life, and all now being seen for the first time in a new status, that of their relationship to Victoria, hers to them. There was his father, far removed from her because to him she was no more than the daughter of friends and a playmate of his own daughter. There was Victoria's mother, hidden in hat and veil and thus imaginably the only person in the room who was in communication with the girl who was hidden in the casket. There were the other older people, who were more used to death and who could listen to the words of the minister while gazing about the room. And there were the faces of Alfred's friends and Victoria's, more baffled than sorrowful. There was the clergyman, conducting a ceremony but seeming more to be speaking privately to someone alive who was inside that silver-mounted cabinetwork, as though no matter what he said, it could only be understood by her, and further that what he was saying was stern and initiational. Toward the end of the ceremony Alfred turned and looked at Norma Budd, who was standing beside him, and he saw the regular rise and fall of the bosom he had so recently kissed and he was filled with desire for her that was even stronger for the knowledge that she was wholly unaware of his inspection. She was his now, and for his more leisurely possessing. Her placidity and the occasional outlines of her figure under her dress stimulated him even more than a kiss might have done, and then she turned her eyes, but not her head, and faintly smiled and he knew that she was with him too; thinking of him and not of anyone else and lying to the world until the world could be forgotten.

She amazed him. They left the Dockwiler house together; the Eatons, of whom there were five, and Norma, and George Fry. They drove out to the Eaton house and sat down to lunch, and throughout it all she chatted in her usual fashion, so that at lunch it seemed not at all remarkable when she said: "Mr. Eaton, *could* I borrow the car to go and see if everything's all right at our house?"

"I don't see why not. Of course," said Samuel Eaton.

"Alfred? Will you go with me? Would you mind?"

"Of course not."

They drove to the Budd house, and on the way she spoke only once. "There won't be anybody there. It's locked, but I have the key."

All the furniture was covered against dust. He followed her to her parents' room, and she opened a window. "You go in there, Father's dressing-room. I'll only be a minute." He undressed and lay on the bed, which was stripped down to the mattress pad. Nothing he had ever known before came to mind to relieve his ignorance of this moment before she made her appearance, and then she walked in, wearing her high-heeled slippers and a short pearl necklace and a kimono of cold blue. "Shades are too high," she said, and lowered them, then she faced him and suddenly dropped her kimono.

"Are you pleased?" she said.

"You're beautiful."

"This way I am," she said.

She lay down beside him and the love-making began. She instructed him with her hands, breathing evenly and calmly and putting him off by turning her body slightly away from him until his fury was greater than her sensuality, and then she matched him in violence. He stored up in his memory every sight and movement and touch, and that much was not over when it was over. He was proud to share it with her, even though it meant knowing a new person, someone he had never known in someone he had always known. He was proud because she had chosen him for the sharing. As long as he lived, (and he knew it), this time—not the evening before, not any other time to come—would always be somewhere in his senses. Not even with her would it ever be like that again.

They lay side by side, and once he started to speak, but before he could, she put her hand over his mouth. "Hunh-uh," she muttered. After a while she sat up, leaned down and kissed him, and suddenly was gone. He heard the water running, waited, then went to her father's dressing-room and put on his clothes, and when he came out she was straightening the room, lowering the windows, dressed for the street, her gloves on. Just as they were about to leave the room she stopped and stood in front of him and looked up at him and kissed him.

"I have so many things to say," he said.

"Have you? Or questions to ask?"

"Both."

"But more questions than things to say."

"Well, maybe."

"Who was my first?"

"Yes."

"My second?"

"Yes."

"Then how many?"

"Yes."

"You haven't learned anything about jealousy, have you?"

"Oh. No, I guess not."

"That was cruel, but I had to say it to you. You could spoil this right now with jealousy, those questions. Don't let's spoil this, shall we?"

"All right."

"Some time I'll tell you all the things you want to know. But when you're more sophisticated. You can tell me you love me, if you want to."

"I do love you. I always will."

"And I love you," she said. "But I think we're going to have to stop seeing each other, publicly, that is. This was all right. I had a reason for coming back to Port Johnson, a good excuse. I won't have any more, and people are going to begin to talk. No protests? No objections?"

"No. Because you're right."

"I've decided not to go to Peter's funeral. I'll drop you there and come back for you. Or better, I'll go to your grandfather's and wait there."

"Why aren't you going to Peter's funeral?"

"Alfred, you mustn't ask me for explanations of things I do. Please don't get in that habit. I *hope* I never ask you. The only way we can have anything is if we both realize—me as much as you—that what we have now is as much as we can ever have. It can't be public, we can't get married. We're both going to have to marry other people, and I'm not

144

going to tell my husband about you. Not about you. I'll always lie about you."

"Why?"

"Why? Don't you know why? I'm a woman, and you're a man, but I'm years older than you are and I'm ashamed, that's why. At least I'd be ashamed if anyone knew. You know, we're never going to be friends again, not after today. We could have been after last night, but not after today. Last night doesn't even count any more."

"It really doesn't, does it?"

"Those boys at Princeton are going to seem awfully young to you."

"I know."

"They will be, too. And you ought to be like them, but I wouldn't let you alone. Now I know that today was just as sure and—a word with a *v* in it—"

"Inevitable."

"Inevitable, thanks. All that time, when I used to send you postcards and little presents. Have you still got your fountain pen?"

"Sure, of course I have."

"Give me a present some time. Not expensive. But some time when you're feeling *pretty* flush, and you see something that you think I ought to have . . ."

"All right. I will."

"Something small, that I can carry with me without attracting attention. Something I can carry in my purse."

"All right. I'd like to."

"I think I'll let you out at your grandfather's and then you can walk to the Van Peltzes'. If I let you out at their house it'll look strange if I don't go in. Here we are."

"That's one of the questions I want to ask you."

"That may be one of the questions I won't answer. Remember what I said about explanations. I'll be back here in about an hour. I have a few things I want to buy downtown."

"All right."

"Alfred."

"What?"

"Don't look at me like a lover. Remember, you're Alfred Eaton and I'm your older friend Norma Budd."

"I know."

She drove away. She was cool and pleasant and efficient, and for a moment he felt himself to be part of her efficiency, and he did not like it.

On a hot September day he arrived in Princeton to begin the signing of the many papers that would place him on the rolls of the University and in the books of laundries and magazines and lunchrooms. From his class at Knox there were two other freshmen, Sterling Calthorp from Philadelphia, and Malcolm Reeder from Fort Penn. There had been others in his class at Knox for whom Princeton was the first choice, but they had been deficient in the scholastic requirements. From Port Johnson there were Theodore Miller, a graduate of Hotchkiss; Chandler Householder, from The Hill, and Guy Stroud, also from The Hill. The boys from The Hill and Hotchkiss, and Red Calthorp from Knox had all visited Princeton at least once before, and Guy Stroud had played football against some boys who were sure to be on the Princeton varsity. Mike Reeder and Alfred Eaton were seeing Princeton for the first time, but the fact no more made for a common bond than did the common home town or prep school with the others. It was convenient and slightly reassuring to see a familiar face and stop to chat in the midst of those brigades of strangers, but none of the boys was committing himself to a close or permanent association. Alfred never had seen so many foreign cars, which were kicking up the dust of Nassau Street for a day or two, and then would be back again for the big games. He tried to remember the faces of undergraduates he saw in the automobiles, but faces without names were impossible to remember, and faces with names were hard enough. He discovered that all conversations with strangers opened with the question, "Where did you prep?" which led to an exchange that in his case was repeated almost word for word with every stranger.

"Where did you prep?"

"Knox," Alfred would say.

"Oh, you're a transfer?"

"No."

"But isn't Knox a college out west somewhere?"

"Yes, but I went to a prep school by that name."

"There's a girls' school—"

"Not that one, either. That's in upstate New York. The place I went to is in Pennsylvania. It's new."

"It must be. The school of hard Knox, eh?"

"That's what all the *new* boys called it. Where did you go?"

Wherever the boy had gone, Alfred would pretend to have difficulty placing it. "Groton? I always pronounced that Gorton. St. Mark's? That's in Garden City, isn't it?" He could be as snooty as he chose with another freshman; freshmen could not keep you out of a club.

If a boy said, "What does your father do?" Alfred would reply, "He's in the steel business."

"Oh, a steel magnate?"

And if the boy was being fresh, Alfred would say, "Exactly."

He thought he had seen all types at Knox, but Princeton offered not only all the types and some new ones, but refinements and deviations from all the types. When classes began he learned something non-scholastic that he had not learned at Knox: it was impossible to tell anything about a boy from his conduct in class. At Knox, under close discipline and living with the teachers, the boys were more in awe of the teachers and so anxious to please that they were often guilty of sycophancy. At Princeton the boy was being given some of the trust and respect that were essential to the appearances of an egalitarian relationship. The relationship never was achieved in four years, since the instructor always had the power to flunk a student, but the student was encouraged to think of himself as a man more manly than the boy he had been, with the result that he tried not nearly so hard to butter up the teacher. In that simple difference between prep school and college, that the University offered learning but did not force its acceptance, and only rarely could be misled by the ass-kissers, lay at least the possibility of enjoying the new freedom. And he noticed, or he thought he noticed, that the other fellows felt the same way, although without putting the same reasons on it. They went to classes and lectures and were instructed or entertained or bored or baffled, but with no deliberate intent to advance themselves through charm exerted on the teacher.

There were, to be sure, many other differences from the prep school life. In prep school when a master addressed the students as "Men—" the students knew they were not men and they squirmed under his insincerity. At Princeton Alfred knew he was a man and, privately, more of a man than anyone he met in his first few weeks, including Guy Stroud, the burly candidate for the freshman team. By slow degrees he began to realize that his classmates did not doubt that he could have been a transfer from Knox College of Galesburg, Illinois. They were ready to accept as fact his admission that he had already gone through one freshman year. He was only months older than his class average, but after two classmates had told him they thought he was twenty or twenty-one, he had evidence that the summer had given him maturity. A girl he loved had been killed, and another girl, a woman, had shown him that he was desirable to a woman and could please her. He was sure that none of the other brand-new men of the freshman class had had such a combination of maturing experiences. And while it did not make him more of a man than his classmates, there was the fact that he, as well as they, had removed themselves from prep school intellectual

147

grade by passing the entrance requirements for Princeton.*
What he did not realize, and had not been able to realize all
summer, was that so long as he was so concerned with the
proofs that he was a man, he would remain partly a boy. He
would be a man, but the time was not yet.

There was some proof of that in his discovery that he was
lonesome. It was not homesickness; he had never even been
homesick at Knox. In truth, he was lonesome for Knox, where
he had spent most of four years and established himself with
himself and his schoolmates. Here at Princeton he was nobody,
as all his classmates were nobody, most of them lonesome
or homesick, nearly all of them being careful of the impression
they were making, and all of them, admittedly or not, under
self-induced pressure from the existence of the upper classes.
It was lonesomeness as much as any other factor that brought
freshmen together in friendships that might last weeks, might
last out the year, or through the club invitations, through college, throughout life. Alfred Eaton would not have been so
lonesome if he had not had the advantage of prep school.
Now he was starting all over again, with the difference that
he had not had a bad time at Knox and had good memories
of it. To be made a nobody again, and in a place where he
wanted not to be a nobody, made his first weeks at Princeton
unhappy ones, and he was grateful for the routines of attending classes, eating meals, going to the movies. He got little
mail, since he never had been much of a letter-writer at Knox.
A brief note from Norma, in which she only said she would
let him know the date of her return to New York; duty notes
from his sisters, and two letters from his mother. The remainder of his mail was commercial in one form or another.
It took three weeks for classes to become routine, in that
on certain days of the week he automatically sent himself to
the certain classes for those days. When he was thus settled
in the classroom routine he at least became less alone of
himself and part of a group, which was some improvement.
He was thankful to be rooming alone. If you were going to
be lonesome it was better to be lonesome by yourself than to

* Alfred Eaton as a member of the Class of 1915 had had to pass
examinations in Xenophon's *Anabasis,* Homer's *Iliad,* and Greek grammar and composition; Caesar, Cicero, and Virgil; general reading of
selections from the Old Testament, Shakespeare, Bunyan, *The Spectator,*
Franklin, Hawthorne, Macaulay, Dickens, Dryden, Wordsworth, Cowper,
Byron, Arnold, and Tennyson, and "careful" reading of selections from
Shakespeare, Milton, Burke and Carlyle; algebra, through quadratics
and the binomial theorem, and plane geometry, solid geometry and
trigonometry; and two years of French. He entered Princeton without
a condition, but also without distinction.

have to pretend that you were not. As it turned out he had another reason to be thankful.

The weather stayed warm and until he was actually ready for bed he left his door open. One night in his third week a freshman he had seen but whose name he did not know tapped on the open door.

"Come in," said Alfred Eaton.

"Thanks. My name is Porter. Are you busy?"

"Not so you could notice it," said Alfred Eaton. "Sit down, have a cigarette."

"Thanks, I will. Omars? That's what I smoke, too. I don't want to butt in, but I was told to look you up. I'm from New York."

"I could tell that," said Alfred.

"You could?"

"You talk like a New Yorker. Who told you to look me up?"

"Miss Budd. Norma Budd? She went to school with my older sister."

"Oh, when did you see her?"

"Miss Budd? Well, I haven't seen her for over a year, but she wrote to my sister and my sister wrote to me. What are you smiling at?"

"Do you want to know the truth?"

"Of course."

"I'm from Pennsylvania and we never drop our r's, and I like to hear a New Yorker talk."

"Well, thanks. And I like to talk, but Christ, I've almost forgotten how. I know a lot of fellows here, but my best friends went to Yale or Harvard."

"Where did you prep?"

"Groton. Where did you?"

"Knox. It's a new school in Pennsylvania."

"Any of your fellows here?"

"Two others. Red Calthorp and Mike Reeder. And there are three others from my home town. Chan Householder, Teddy Miller, and Guy Stroud."

"I think I know Miller, if it's the same Miller. He's a tennis player?"

"Yes. Hotchkiss."

"And Stroud. He's built like a brick shit-house, a cinch to make the varsity next year. Are you going to stay here?"

"At Princeton? Sure. Aren't you?"

"If I had my own way I wouldn't. I went to a God damn strict school, but I thought when I got to college I could enjoy myself. Not so. These sophomores are a bunch of shits, and the others, the juniors and seniors—my word! Hoity-toity, lords of creation. Or maybe you don't agree with me."

"You took the words right out of my mouth, but I'm going to stay. I have to stay till I'm twenty-one."

"Same here, although I don't know what's to stop us if we suddenly decided to join the Royal Flying Corps."

"I don't want to do that."

"I've thought of it."

"Seriously?"

"Well, I've considered it. But I wouldn't know how to go about it."

"And it might be just as bad in a different way."

"It might be. Although we'd be officers, and not just God damn freshmen. What do you think about these clubs?"

"What about them?"

"Which one are you going to join? I'm slated for Ivy."

"How do you know?"

"How do I know? I have two uncles in it."

"So was my father, but I'm not counting on that."

"I am. I know you're not supposed to talk about it, but what the hell, I'm not going to let them think they're doing me a great favor. It's the other way around. I'll pay *them* dues, they're not going to pay me. And if they don't like me, they're not going to like me anyway, whether I talk about their club or not."

"Well, it's a long way off."

"I know it is, but everybody's as worried as if it was next week. I'll let my uncles do the worrying, and they will. Believe me. Your father went to Princeton. What does he do?"

"He's in the steel business."

"Bethlehem? United States? One of those?"

"No, it's his own company. Eaton Iron & Steel."

"And he went to Princeton, and was in Ivy? You have no more worries. That is, if you *want* to go Ivy."

"Maybe I won't want to when the time comes. Right now it's the only one I know anything about, and that's very little."

"Your old gent didn't talk about it all the time? He must be a remarkable man. My uncles—oh, well. Do you feel like going up to that quick-and-dirty on Nassau Street and having some delicious shredded wheat?"

"Yes, I'd like to."

"Delicious shredded wheat. I hope I never have to say that when I've had a flock of Bronxes."

"What are Bronxes?"

"You come to New York with me and you'll find out."

In the lexicon of college freshmen there is no such word as captivated; nevertheless Alfred Eaton was captivated by Alexander Thornton Porter, who never used the Alexander when he could avoid it, but was known as Lex. His directness, it later developed, was a part of him that had been thwarted by the mass cautiousness of the freshman class, and neither he nor Alfred Eaton ever understood why it came out on their first meeting. The fact that it was Alfred who was given the first look at it at Princeton made Alfred, for whatever the reason, seem to Porter to be the first classmate he wanted to be friends with, and so it was. Alfred, always in the past slow to make friends, tried to be tentative with his new acquaintance, but Lex Porter was completely lacking in guile, completely forthright, courageous, independent, and full of self-confidence. He was profane and apparently outspoken at all times, but Alfred was to discover that Porter did not always give expression to everything that was in his mind. He had his reticences and he respected them in others.

Alfred never had been taken over by anyone as he soon was by Porter. Porter would tell him when and where they were to play tennis, lead him for long walks and set the pace, invite him to the movies. Soon Alfred forgot his lonesomeness and did not even have to plan his day; Porter could be relied upon to do that for him. There was another side to Porter which was not so strange and not in the least contradictory of the rest of him. One evening they were cutting across the campus on their way home from the lunchroom. "Excuse *me*," said Porter. "I want to see that fellow."

Alfred followed a few steps behind and heard the conversation.

"Hey, there," said Porter. "Sophomore!"

The fellow halted. "What do *you* want?"

"You were one of those smart guys that tied me up last night, weren't you?"

"What if I was?" said the sophomore.

"You were the one that said, 'Tie the son of a bitch up good and tight,' weren't you?"

"What if I did?"

"Do you want to call me a son of a bitch now?"

"Yes, you son of a bitch," said the sophomore. He backed away to assume a fighting stance, but Porter was too fast, hooked him in the ribs with his left fist, upper-cut him with his right. The sophomore fell and Porter fell on top of him and they rolled over twice. Alfred pulled Porter to his feet and the punching was resumed until the sophomore's lips and chin were covered with blood, whereupon Alfred pushed has way between the young men. "That's enough, Porter. He's licked."

"Who the hell are you to say I'm licked?" said the sophomore.

"Take a look at yourself in the mirror," said Alfred.

"Do you want some more?" said Porter.

"There won't always be two of you," said the sophomore.

"There aren't now," said Alfred. "But you're not going to have any teeth left."

"He'd look better without any teeth," said Porter.

"Come on, Lex."

"I'll see the two of you again."

"My name is Eaton, E, a, t, o, n. I live down the hall from Porter."

"Oh, I'll find you."

"You do that, whenever you're able to," said Alfred.

The friends continued their walk back to the dormitory. "I better put some iodine on this knuckle. I hit him as hard as I ever hit anybody in my life."

"You sure did."

"I don't know whether he called me a son of a bitch or not, last night. But there were four of them, and I noticed that he was the one that was sneaking little punches at me. The others just tried to hold my arms and legs, but he was hitting me with his fist. They'll be coming to see *you* now."

"Most likely."

"They will. There'll be four of them, and when they do come, be sure and crack one of them right on the chin. Don't let all of them get off scot-free. Inflict some damage."

"What did they do with you?"

"Last night? Nothing. Tied me up, and when my roommate came in he untied me. It was nothing, except for that horse-cock sneaking in his punches. But the next time it'll be something fancy. I'm sorry you got into it."

"That's all right," said Alfred.

"Just pick out one of them and give him a good crack on the chin."

"If I can," said Alfred.

Lex Porter nodded. "Yes, they may surprise you," he said. "They may wait a couple of days so that they *will* surprise you, but we know they're coming. That much we can be damn sure of."

They parted, and Alfred went to bed and was at last asleep when the sophomores came. One of them was sitting on his belly, and one of them was shining a flashlight in his eyes. Alfred swung his arms ineffectually and they quickly bound him with clothesline and dumped him out of bed.

"March," one of them said.

"Gag him," said another.

Alfred then yelled at the top of his voice: "Freshmen! Freshmen! Nineteen-nineteen!"

"I told you to gag him."

He struggled and tried to make sounds, but in his bare feet his kicking was not dangerous, and they stuffed one hand-

152

kerchief in his mouth and tied another about his head. With a third they blindfolded him.

"Over to the Junction," someone said.

"Shut up, now he knows where he's going."

"All right, we'll take him some place else."

They conferred in whispers and then pushed him out of his room, out of the dormitory, and after walking several minutes, into the back seat of an automobile.

This was not being done in fun.. There was no laughter, there were no jokes. They hated him and he hated them, and he was as frightened of the new thing that was going on inside him as he was of their grim silence and the threat to his safety. It was now past loss of freedom and dignity, and he had no way of knowing what he himself might do. It was cold now, and they were in an open car, with a valve-in-head motor and probably a Buick by the sound of it. It had a tappet knock on hills, and the driver frequently changed gears. They made numerous turns, which he was sure they were making to confuse him. After about half an hour one of them said: "Here. Let's stop here."

The car was stopped.

"All right, you. Get out."

They pulled him out of the car.

"Don't try to walk around—"

"Stay where you are, or you'll fall in the river."

"Come on, let's go."

They got back in the car and drove away. He lowered himself to the ground. He moved his feet until he deduced that he was lying on grass and on roadway. He noticed that close by a dog was barking, and then he recalled that he had also noticed it when they pulled him out of the car. Now the dog was growling and nearer to him. Alfred made sounds that he meant to be pacifying but it continued to growl, then the dog ran away and resumed its barking somewhere in the distance.

The cold was now universal and cruel and his feet felt dead. He rolled on his back from right to left to try to keep some warmth and he found that the pebbles in the road, though they hurt his back, seemed to sting the circulation and keep it going.

He bethought himself of the dog. The dog surely meant a farm, and the farm surely was on this road. He decided to try to move his body along the road until he came to the place where he guessed the dog had returned home. Alfred did not know what time it was, within hours, but it was better to try something than to lie there and freeze.

He began to move himself, stretching his feet out and pull-

153

ing himself forward in caterpillar fashion, putting his feet
down at the end of every forward movement to test the
terrain. He continued this for he knew not how long—ten
minutes, half an hour—and then he heard the dog again, with
its deep-throated bark sometimes nearer, sometimes farther
away. Then he heard men's voices, footsteps, and at last a
man's voice, and a lamp shone through the blindfold.

"Who are you?" said the man.

"He's blindfolded," said a younger man. "And his mouth."

"Holy Christ," said the older man. "He's all trussed up.
Loosen him. I'll keep the gun on him. Can you hear me, you?"

Alfred nodded.

"Stay in the light of the lamp, I got a shotgun here."

"We both got shotguns," said the young man.

"Untie him, Dewey."

The younger man did so, and Alfred, as soon as the bonds
and handkerchiefs were taken off, fainted.

When he came to he was in a bed, in a room lighted by a
kerosene lamp on a marble-top table. A woman in a blue
flannel bathrobe was sitting in a chair, yawning and holding
her arms across her chest.

"Are you awake? I think he's awake," she said.

"Are you awake, mister?" said a boy of fourteen or fifteen.
He stood up, and with a single-barrel shotgun in his hand came
over to the bed.

"Thanks," said Alfred.

"Who are you?" said the woman.

"Alfred Eaton."

"Where are you from?"

"Port Johnson."

"Port Johnson?" The woman looked at her son.

"You're from over at the college, aint you?"

"Oh, yes. Princeton?" said Alfred. "Yes."

"My husband went for the doctor," said the woman.

"What were they doing? Initiating you?" said the boy.

"Initiating? You could of died. They could of killed you.
You ought to see your back."

Alfred now realized that he was wearing a flannel night-
shirt and underneath it he could feel some sort of dressings.

"Take some of this, it'll do you good," said the woman.
She held out a large tablespoon. "It's milk toast." She fed
him several spoonfuls and he thanked her.

"There's Pop with the bay," said the boy.

"And that'll be the doctor in the auto."

Presently the farmer and the doctor appeared. The doctor
was a moustached man, needing a shave and wearing a buttoned muffler instead of collar and necktie. The farmer and

his wife and son left the room while the doctor questioned Alfred and tested and examined him. "What happened to you?"

Alfred told him the latter events of the night, ending with the question: "Where am I?"

"Hopewell Township. These good people are named Leeds. Abraham Leeds and his wife and kid. If you're like most of the students over at the college, your father and mother are well fixed. Am I right?"

"Yes."

"Well, if you don't get pneumonia and die, you can thank these people for saving your life. Do you know what it is out? It's thirty-eight degrees, Fahrenheit. I guess you don't want me to report this to the constable?"

"No sir. Wouldn't do any good anyhow, I don't know who brought me here. I never saw their faces."

"You'd better stay in bed here till tomorrow. I'll be in some time late this afternoon and have a look at you, but I guess you'll survive. You're young and healthy. But you wouldn't have been so healthy if it wasn't for Abraham Leeds."

"I have to get some clothes."

"Well, I'll get you your clothes. I have to go to Princeton some time today."

"I'd be very much obliged if you'd look up a friend of mine named Porter. He'll pack a bag for you."

"All right. But you stay in bed. You'll be more comfortable if you lie on your side. Your back is like raw meat. Do you know how to take your temperature?"

"No sir."

"Well, never mind. I'll be in toward evening. If you have a high temperature I'm going to make you stay here tomorrow too, but I think you can go back tomorrow some time. Report to the infirmary and they can telephone me at my office in Hopewell. My name is Doctor Torrance. They know me over there."

"Did Mrs. Leeds take care of me?"

"She can do anything, that woman. Oh, did she see your bare little ass? Yes. How do you think you got in that night-shirt?"

"What do you think I ought to give them?"

"Whatever you think your life is worth. Well, if you have a hundred dollars you don't know what to do with. I'll send you a bill, but they never would. That has to come from you, voluntarily."

The next afternoon Lex Porter came out in a taxi and took Alfred back to the dormitory. The University proctors had begun a quiet investigation of his absence, which ended with Dr. Torrance's report. Alfred was notified to appear at the

Dean's office. "We don't like this kind of hazing at Princeton," said the Dean. "So don't feel compelled to withhold any information. Have you got any information?"

"No sir."

"None at all? Voices? No names? They didn't address each other by name? Even first names will be a help."

"No sir."

"If you *heard* the voices again would you recognize them?"

"No sir."

"You realize that you're not protecting gentlemen? Those men were thugs, and we'd like to find out who they are and get rid of them. They put the whole sophomore class under a cloud, and the whole University. You know, Eaton, I'll find out who they are."

"When you do, sir, let me know, too."

"That's *just* my point. We don't want your private vengeance, either. Good afternoon."

The campus gossip credited Alfred with a refusal to divulge the names of the men who had kidnapped him, and many sophomores as well as upperclassmen went out of their way to say hello to him. One immediate effect was disgust on the part of influential sophomores with the unidentified thugs, and Lex Porter suffered no reprisal for his personal attack on a member of that class. That sophomore paid a call on Alfred.

"My name is Bonfield, I guess you remember me," he said.

"I remember you," said Alfred.

"I want you to know I had nothing to do with what happened to you."

"You weren't one of them, I know that," said Alfred.

"And I had nothing to do with it."

"Didn't you?"

"No. Don't you believe me?"

"That was just coincidence? Picking me out so soon?"

"I don't know."

"Yes you do," said Alfred. "You told them what happened to you, and they came down and got me."

"If that's the way you feel about it."

"That's the way I feel about it. But you don't have to worry about me, Bonfield."

"No?"

"No. Somebody else has got *your* number. Close the door on your way out."

"Close it yourself."

"Oh, one thing more. The five of you won't be able to keep your secret. Five is too many."

Bonfield left, and when Alfred told Lex Porter of the visit, Porter laughed. "You know what let's do?"

"What?"

156

"Let's put the gipsy curse on him, give him the evil eye. Every time we see him, don't say anything to him, just stare at him. He'll go out of his mind. And of course watch who he goes around with. I think I've guessed three of them. One of them is his roommate and the other two I've seen him with. I give them the gipsy stare whenever I see them. They don't know what to expect. Let them think we know more than we do. Psychology. Mysteries of the Orient. The Black Hand." Lex made the gesture of passing his forefinger across his Adam's apple. "I'm going to try to stay in this place at least till I get a crack at those four."

"Why bother?"

"Christ, you only got in it because you were there when I beat up on Bonfield. I'll tell you what I'd like to do. I'd like to find out pretty damn positively the name of just one, or maybe two. Then next summer, when we're miles away from this place, go pay him a visit. We'd get it out of him. Two against one isn't as bad as four against one. In fact I'd be only too happy to do it alone."

A few days later Alfred received a communication by mail; the name, address and message printed in carefully childish letters. It read:

One of the 4 who took you on your recent automobile ride is Lanchester, '18. More later. (signed) '19

He showed the communication to Lex. "Lanchester, eh? He wasn't one of my suspects. But he rooms next to Bonfield. Well, we're making progress. Maybe our secret service agent will save us a lot of trouble."

"You don't like one of these letters any more than I do."

"Naturally. At least I wouldn't like the fellow that wrote it. But there it is, written, telling us what we want to know. And it's quite fair, you know."

"What is?" said Alfred.

"The letter. It's anonymous. Well, so was the automobile ride anonymous. We call that irony, old boy. Irony."

"Lex, I've made a decision."

"What's that?"

"I'm not going to do anything about this whole God damn thing. If I ever found out who did it, that's different. But I'm not going to try."

"It isn't as easy as that. You'll see," said Lex Porter.

Then (and many times in later years) Lex Porter had stumbled into wisdom. It was not easy for Alfred to dismiss the kidnapping or to wish it away and out of the memory of the college. Other matters of general interest and of more personal enjoyment or concern—football games, dances, examinations

—removed the kidnapping from its leading position as a topic of conversation, but it remained in the mind of the college, and through it Alfred was to learn another unpleasant truth that applied in his present world no less than in the world he had not yet entered: he learned that a man who gets the world's sympathy, freely accorded, can soon become in the world's eyes a nuisance. No matter how much his misfortune may have entitled him to sympathy, the world starts to take it away before he has fully recovered from his misfortune and while he may still be counting on it. Alfred was not aware that he had accepted the indignation of the college, which was a kind of sympathy, until he noticed that some of the men who had spoken to him on the campus began to ignore him. Their indignation, their sympathy, lasted only so far, but no farther. Not only was it not to be traded on; it was not to continue, and the campus attitude was to forget the whole thing, which was precisely what Alfred said he wanted, but now was being given no choice. He was not yet wise enough to know that it would take some spectacular achievement to make the college forget that it had once given him its full sympathy, and thus restore him to full stature as a man and not the crippled object of pity that he was for a few days. The pitied figure remains pitiful, becomes even more pitiful unless he becomes whole and strong again, superior to pity. True pity is so spontaneous, and the world is so extravagant with it at the moment, that a moment later the world is ashamed and embarrassed by its extravagance, and the object of the pity becomes suspect. Was the falsely accused bank cashier absolutely honest? Did the raped girl offer total resistance? Didn't the woman know she was marrying a drunkard? Didn't the little newsboy ever short-change anyone? And why did the sophomores happen to pick on Alfred Eaton? What kind of a guy was he? Who knew anything about him? Where was he from? Why single him out? It was too much to learn at eighteen, but Alfred was going to have to perform some noteworthy act, or to prove by consistently acceptable behavior that he could live down his blameless participation in a scandal that provoked community pity. But at least he was under no compulsion to live down the flashing reputation that goes with being a hero.

In his ignorance of his standing in the college community he tried only to live his life with a minimum of discomfort to himself and of inconvenience to others. His major concern was to keep his marks at or slightly above the gentleman's C, which would lead to his only ambition, which was the earning of his A. B. In so doing, all unawares, and without planned intent, he was setting the public character of himself that would be what Princeton saw and, in many instances, all his Princeton acquaintances would have to remember. The quick division in a freshman class was between athletes and non-athletes, and particularly between those who did and those who did not go out for football. Alfred had immediately classified himself among the non-football players, and with no prep school reputation as an athlete in other sports, he was not automatically expected to try for the harriers, autumn track and field, or any future sports activity. He was not, then, considered to be one of the class athletes. It usually took a little longer for freshmen to decide the off-campus social status of their classmates, and in most cases they relied for guidance on the man's prep school background and on the known social standing of his family. But Alfred had come from a small town in non-Philadelphia Pennsylvania, and he had gone to a small, new, and rather dubious prep school. Ordinarily he would have been thereby dismissed as one of the possibilities for social leadership in the class. But several factors caused his classmates to withhold judgment on his social standing. There was the fact that his father was a member of Ivy, which almost invariably carried with it some social prestige. There was the fact that Alfred had a well-bred look about him and was obviously not suffering financial strain. But in the eyes of his classmates Alfred Eaton's most valuable social asset was his friendship with Lex Porter. It mystified the freshmen, the sophomores, and the juniors, and especially the sophomores and juniors, who would be in college when the time came for invitations to the clubs. Porter had not yet expressed to anyone else the thoughts he had uttered to Alfred on the subject of Princeton and its clubs, but he had *the manner*. He was afraid of no one, in awe of no one, and his independence was not a quality of protest but the expression of an attitude that had been bred into him, the result of having enough money behind him and of having no cousins who were not socially secure. He gave the impression (which did not make him popular) that Princeton was on trial, and that Princeton's position in that respect could be taken by whatever individual he was speaking to at any given moment. He was not a snob, but there was no one from Dr. Hibben to the most penny-wise scholarship student whom he would not snub. It was therefore a matter for perplexity when he chose Alfred Eaton to be his friend: who *was* Eaton? Where had he known Porter? Why had Porter picked *him*?

The principals remained unaware of the small mystery they caused. They were comfortable in the new friendship, which became an essential in each of their lives. The growing paradox was that Alfred, the more reserved of the two, came to count on the friendship more than Lex, who had had no reservations in creating the friendship. And the next phase was when Alfred, warming and relaxing in the friendship, discovered that Lex needed and insisted upon solitude as most men do companionship. It was, in fact, companionship rather than friendship that Lex needed, and when a realization of the distinction came to Alfred he had made his most important progress toward understanding Lex. Lex, on the other hand, understood no one, but Alfred learned that too, and in the continually close observation of the vagaries of his friend, Alfred was acquiring some useful information about himself. It is not the same as learning, but it is the first step.

On an afternoon in late October the new companions were walking across the campus when Lex said: "My mother would like you to come for dinner next Sunday. Will you come?"

"Sunday?"

"At one-thirty. We always have dinner at one-thirty on Sunday."

"Sure, thanks, I'd like to. Shall I write her a note?"

"Don't have to. It'll be just you and my mother, my sister, and my two uncles."

"And your father."

"He won't be there," said Lex. "My father and mother are divorced."

"Oh, I'm sorry to hear that."

"It's nothing new. They've been divorced for five or six years."

"That's funny, that I never knew that."

"No it isn't. For all I know, your father and mother may be divorced too. No, I know they're not, from things you've said. But I've never *asked* you about them, and you've never asked *me*."

"That's true."

The Porters lived in a house in East Forty-ninth Street, as severely anonymous on the outside as a thousand similar houses in its neighborhood, but Alfred was sure he spotted it while still more than a block away: in front of it were parked a Rolls-Royce brougham and a Crane-Simplex phaeton with a victoria top. Lex never had mentioned either car, but Alfred had fabricated some impressions of the uncles. His guess was correct; the house was the Porters'.

A butler in silver-buttoned, tailed livery admitted him. "Mr. Eaton? If you'll follow me, sir." They ascended a brief curved staircase. "Mr. Eaton, madam."

The woman who came to greet Alfred was no younger than his own mother, but she retained more youth in her manner and in her action, the quick way she came toward him and the directness of her greeting. He was conscious of diamonds and pearls and of a dress that could be worn only inside the house, but all details were lost on him. "Mr. Eaton, I'm so glad and complimented that you came."

"How do you do?" said Alfred.

"I don't think you've met anyone, except the gentleman on my right."

"Hello, Alfred."

"Hello, Lex."

They shook hands, and it was the first time in their acquaintance that they had done so.

"This is my sister."

"How do you do?" said Alfred.

"How do you do?" said the sister.

"My Uncle Fritz, and my Uncle Alec."

"Thornton," said the Uncle Fritz. "Frederick Thornton is my name. Alexander Thornton is my brother's. We all run to such regal names in this family, Christian names, that is, that I like to get it all straight. My sister, Lex's mother, is Victoria. His sister, my niece, she's Elizabeth. I'm Frederick the Great, my brother is Alexander the Great, and Lex is another Alexander the Great."

"Well, I guess I belong in there. The King of Belgium."

"Oh, yes. Alfred. King of the Belgians, my boy. King of the Belgians. They're very touchy about that, I don't exactly know why. He isn't King of Belgium, he's King of the Belgians."

"Very, very interesting, Fritz. Very interesting, I'm sure," said Mrs. Porter.

"Yes, very," said the Uncle Alec. "Especially because I seem to be the only one in this room that knows the Belgian king's name. It's *Albert,* not *Alfred.*"

"*Is it? Are you sure?*" said Uncle Fritz.

"Quite sure."

"Come on, Uncle Alec. Alfred wouldn't make a mistake like that. It's his name," said Lex.

"I might. In fact, I guess I'm wrong," said Alfred. "I am wrong. It *is* Albert."

"Well, then damn it all, there must be some Alfred that was a king. Hurry up, Alec. Think of one," said Uncle Fritz.

"Alfred the Great. Ninth century," said Uncle Alec.

"What nationality?" said Uncle Fritz.

"Not Danish, you may be sure. He defeated them. He was English."

"Oh, yes. I think I—" said Uncle Fritz.

"Don't fake, now. You boys'll be reading about him," said Alec Thornton.

"Very likely," said Victoria Porter. "But Mr. Eaton isn't here for that. He's here to get *away* from that."

"I promised him a Bronx," said Lex.

"Well, I'll keep your promise for you," said Fritz Thornton. He left the room, and Alfred took a chair near Elizabeth Porter.

"*Where* is your good friend Norma *Budd?* Have you heard anything from her?"

"I don't really know. I had a note from her, but that was over a month ago."

"She's very fond of you."

"Is that Norma Budd you're talking about?" said Mrs. Porter.

"Yes it is," said Alfred.

"Well, I rang her up yesterday and I spoke to her brother. She's coming back in a week or two. I wanted to ask her to come today. I thought it would be nice if you weren't too out-numbered by Porters and Thorntons, but unfortunately . . ."

"I don't mind that a bit," said Alfred.

"Well, it's nice of you to say so," said Mrs. Porter. "And I am glad you could make it, very pleased."

"Here we are," said Fritz Thornton, handing Alfred the cocktail. "You see if that isn't the best Bronx you ever tasted."

"It's my first, so it will be."

"Oh, now you shouldn't have said that. You should have tasted it and rolled your eyes and said it was the best you ever drank. And it would have been. You're not going to get any-where at all if you don't learn to lie politely." Fritz Thornton had the family directness but his special manifestation of it was to say what was in his mind in a tone of frivolousness that caused him and what he said not to be taken seriously. "Well, let's drink to our birthday boy. Alexander Thornton Porter, on this your eighteenth birthday, I'm sure you have nothing of moment to say, so I suggest you sit in silence as we drink your health, and then if you care to, you may say thank-you. You already have your present from me, I know that your tight-fisted Uncle Alec intends to make some small gesture, and I'm sure your mother and your sister have done something in the haberdashery line that you wouldn't be found dead wearing."

"I'll keep quiet till I see the size of your cheque," said Lex.

They all drank, and Victoria Porter said: "I owe Mr. Eaton an explanation. Lex made me promise not to tell you it was his birthday. He didn't want you to feel that you *had* to come or that you *had* to buy him a present."

"Well, thank you. As you see, I came, but I don't know if I'd have bought him anything even if I had known it was his birthday. I've never bought a present for anyone outside my— well, I've never bought a present for another boy. But I'm so glad to be here that this might have been the exception."

There was a brief silence; they were touched, and Alfred was

162

embarrassed that his graceless speech had even for a moment affected this outwardly casual family.

"All right, make the exception tomorrow," said Lex. "I'll tell you what I want."

The butler entered and announced that *luncheon* was served.

"It's been Sunday dinner ever since he first came with us, but he won't say the word dinner as long as it's daylight," said Elizabeth to Alfred.

Fritz Thornton drove his nephew and Alfred to the new Pennsylvania Station in his Crane-Simplex. He offered the wheel to Alfred, who declined with thanks but sat beside Thornton on the front seat while Lex sat in the back and quite unnecessarily urged his uncle on to greater speed.

"I'll be down to see you in a couple of weeks," said Thornton.

"That'll be fine, Uncle Fritz. Drop me a line, care of Tiger Inn."

"I can still stop payment on that cheque, you know. Good-bye, Mr. Eaton. I never got a chance to talk to you about your father, but when you write to him, tell him you saw me."

"Thank you, I will," said Alfred.

"Oh, now don't tell him I sent my regards. He wouldn't believe that. Just tell him you met me, and then hold your ears for the big explosion."

"Yes sir, I'll do that."

The companions found seats together on the train and passed sections of the New York *Tribune* to each other, their substitute for conversation while postponing the inevitable conversation about the Porter-Thornton family gathering. It was postponed until after supper and Lex's visit to Alfred's room.

"Well, you made a hit with that crowd today. I could tell."

"I'm glad I did. How could you tell?"

"By the way they behaved. First my mother liked you right off the bat, and the others took their cue from her. If she hadn't liked you they'd have been formal, polite. You can't say they were *that*."

"No, they made me feel right at home."

"Christ, no! That isn't what they were doing. *They* were feeling at home. They weren't trying to make *you* feel that way."

"But that's the effect it had."

"Oh, sure. Just as long as you see the difference. I like them best when they're not trying to make someone feel at home. Today, for instance. Then they're themselves. Uncle Fritz bubbling over, Uncle Alec bringing him up short. You never heard about the famous Thornton brothers? Didn't your father ever say anything about them?"

"No."

"They're famous for—well, as a team, like a vaudeville team. Uncle Alec has never been married, but Uncle Fritz was. They say it didn't last because his wife broke up the team. I mean that. I've heard my mother say it. People said that Fritz and Alec Thornton had more fun *acting* together, and Fritz's wife didn't fit in. Of course there were other reasons. Fritz is very fond of the ladies, Follies girls. He most likely dumped us at the station and then hurried off to take a Follies girl for a spin in the country. And Alec went calling. Uncle Alec's a great one for calling on people. You ought to see him. You didn't see his silk hat and walking stick. You did see the spats. Every Sunday he goes calling. Not haphazardly. He plans who he's going to call on so that they're not too far apart. Three calls, say one on Fortieth Street, then the next on Forty-ninth, and the next on Fifty-something. He walks from one house to the other, and his car follows him, in case it rains or his corn hurts him. Once a week he goes to the opera."

"What does he do for a living?"

"Nothing. Not a thing."

"What about your Uncle Fritz?"

"He does nothing either. But Uncle Alec is much more respectable, and people don't realize he does nothing. He's on boards. He goes to board meetings. The bank, and the copper company, and a lot of charity boards. Uncle Fritz is on the bank board and the copper one, but no charity boards that I know of. He's a *sportsman*. Uncle Alec is—I don't know what you'd call him exactly. You must know people like that."

"I don't, though. Where I come from everybody has a job," said Alfred. "Except the old men, the retired ones."

"Listen, Uncle Fritz and Uncle Alec, they keep busy. But not in business. Uncle Fritz, he plays tennis. Not lawn tennis. Tennis. It's court tennis, but he never calls it court tennis. Just tennis. He's out to win the championship. He never will, and he's getting on, but that's his ambition. That and the best three-year-old in the country. He might have that some time, because you can buy yearlings every year and one of them could turn out well." He paused for a moment. "You see, my uncles do a lot of work that their friends haven't got time for. That's what my mother says, and she's right. Uncle Alec and Uncle Fritz put up the money and spend their time on things that aren't business, but they do some good, and Uncle Fritz, for instance, well, he belongs to a lot of clubs. His friends belong to them, but Uncle Fritz does the dirty work. He's on the house committees and so on, and it's a kind of a charity. If he didn't do the dirty work, some of those clubs would go to pot, and a lot of men would miss them."

"You like your uncles. I thought you didn't."

164

"I certainly do. What made you think I didn't?"

"Something you said, I guess."

"I never—oh, I know what it was."

"Joining Ivy."

"I know what it was. I said I'd let them do the worrying. I will, too."

"But I gathered they forced you to come to Princeton and you wanted to go some place else."

"They did. They made me come here, but not in preference to some place else. I didn't want to go anywhere. I thought college was a lot of shit and I still think so. I wanted to travel for four years."

"I don't blame you."

"Not on the big liners and the fancy hotels. I wanted to go by tramp steamer. The Orient. Africa. What am I going to get out of college? Not a damn thing. At least if I'd had my own way I'd have learned to speak Chinese and see a lot of different people. Instead of that I'm at Princeton and even here my uncles want me to join a club that's exactly like the clubs I'll join when I get older. That makes me sore at them, but I like them. I like them a damned sight better than I do my father." He looked at Alfred. "I'm sorry, Eaton. You don't think a fellow ought to speak that way about his father."

Alfred laughed.

"What?" said Lex.

Alfred laughed again. "If you only knew," he said.

"What?"

"How I feel about my father. There's nothing you could say about your father that I couldn't say worse about mine."

"Oh, I don't know about that. How much did your father steal from your mother? Where is your father now? Was your father nasty to your mother before he flew the coop? I'll bet not."

"My father is right at home."

"That's what I thought."

"It wasn't what he did to my mother. It was what he did to me."

"How, to you? Or would you rather not talk about it?"

"I never have talked about it. I guess I don't want to very much. I'll tell you the cause of it. I had a brother that died. Older than I was."

"I knew that, or at least my Uncle Fritz said you couldn't be in my class because he remembered your father had a son that was too old to be a freshman. He'd never heard about you, but he knew your father had a son that would be twenty-one or -two."

"Three years older. When he died he was fourteen and I was

165

eleven. God knows my father never paid much attention to me, but when Billy died I think he began to hate me. As though I'd killed my brother."

"Did he die in an accident?"

"Spinal meningitis."

"I've heard of it."

"That's all," said Alfred. "If I tell you any more I'll sound as though I felt sorry for myself. Like some character in Charles Dickens. I did, but I don't any more. I guess I got over it."

"How did you get over it? You don't like your father."

"No, I don't. But when I was in prep school I used to pretend he was dead. That's a terrible thing to say, but it's true. Then on vacations—well, I guess when I was about fifteen or sixteen I suddenly realized that if we ever had a fight I could probably lick him. We never did, though."

"Well, that's not so bad. I knew a couple of guys at Groton that couldn't stand the sight of their fathers, and one of them had the same experience you had, except that the brother that died was a kid brother, and the one I knew *was* partly to blame. The kid got drowned in a lake and they weren't supposed to be swimming."

"Well, whatever way it happens it's a son of a bitch of a thing to go through life with."

"Yes," said Lex. He went to the window, opened it, and tapped his pipe. "This is getting a good cake in it . . . Didn't you ever hear about me?"

"Before I came here? No."

"Or since? About my father? You weren't just being a gentleman?"

"Only what you told me tonight, and the time you said your mother and father were divorced."

"You don't know the New York crowd. A lot of them know, I'm sure. My father did the opposite of your father. Yours didn't pay any attention to you. Mine tried to kidnap me. When he and my mother had their falling-out. I was on my way home from school, another kid and I, and my father suddenly appeared out of nowhere and grabbed hold of me and started to pull me into a carriage. Just then my Uncle Fritz, *he* appeared out of nowhere, but I found out later he was watching me all the time, every day, but this day when my father grabbed me, Uncle Fritz cracked him square on the chin and knocked him ass over tincups and got me away."

"How old were you?"

"I guess about thirteen, twelve. Not very old. I was still going to school in town."

"Well, at least he wanted you, your father."

"He wanted me, but what for? To get some more money out of my mother. He didn't give a damn about me. He had some woman that was his mistress and they invented this scheme to kidnap me and take me abroad with them. Hadn't been for my uncle I'd be living in Europe this minute. Or, no. No, I'd have run away. He had the nerve to take me to lunch with her one time, while he was still married to my mother. He took me to Brooks Brothers and then to a hotel and she joined us, accidentally on purpose. I didn't know what a mistress was, but I knew there was something fishy when he tried to make me promise not to say anything to my mother about the lunch."

"Did you say anything?"

"No, but I wouldn't promise not to, and I'll bet he was on the anxious bench."

"Had you ever liked him before the trouble with your mother?"

Lex looked at the empty pipe. "Had I ever liked him before that? Well, the answer is, if I had, I stopped."

"And he *had* liked you, hadn't he?"

"I don't know. Well, time to hit the hay." He rose and left.

Elizabeth Porter's information was correct; a note from Norma Budd arrived less than two weeks after Alfred's visit to the Porters.

> I am here in my new apartment and anxious to see you once again. I shall reserve a room for you at the Biltmore next Saturday and if convenient for you we can have dinner *à deux* and see a show. If inconvenient perhaps you will write but otherwise I shall expect you Saturday. Ever, Norma.

Alfred considered various lies to tell Lex Porter but eventually he decided to tell the literal if not the whole truth: that he was going to New York, planned to have dinner and go to the theater with Norma Budd, and was stopping at the Biltmore. Even that much was more elaborate than was necessary; Norma Budd was a friend and contemporary of Lex's sister Elizabeth, and therefore to Lex too old to be of interest. Alfred dutifully checked in at the Biltmore, took a bath, put on a clean shirt and collar and rode in a taxicab to the large new apartment house on Park Avenue. He was passed along by three liveried men—doorman, hall porter, and elevator operator—before reaching the tenth floor, and there a maid answered the doorbell.

Norma stood up to greet him. She shook hands with him. "I'm so glad to see you, Alfred. Jack will be sorry to've missed you, but he had to go away at the last minute. Will you have a glass of sherry?"

"Yes, thanks, I will."

"I'll have one, too. Jane, we'll have our sherry in here."

The maid departed and for the moment Norma's manner changed. "Hello, darling," she said. "All that was for the benefit of the maid."

"I was wondering."

"I can't have any talk, and she's new. You're a friend of Jack's more than mine. First, the schedule for tonight. I got tickets for the Hippodrome. I hope you haven't seen it."

"I haven't."

"It's called *Hip, Hip, Hooray*. I thought you'd like it better than some of the shows, although I tried to get tickets for *Chin Chin*. We'll have dinner here. The cook and the maid will be gone by the time we get back from the theater."

"I was wondering about that, too."

"Oh, we'll be alone, eventually. But you're my young brother's friend until later. You have so many things to tell me, I want to hear all about Princeton, and how are your mother and father, and the girls, Sally and Constance."

They dined and went to the theater. He tried to hold her hand, but she squeezed his hand, patted the back of it, and withdrew her hand. The show put no strain on the intellect except for the problem of the swimming chorus and their disappearance. "I think they go down the steps into the pool and then swim underwater till they're somewhere offstage. That's what I've been told," said Norma. It was a splendid show and they came out into Sixth Avenue in good spirits.

"Shall we walk? You might as well say yes, I don't see an empty taxi," said Norma.

She took his arm and they walked close together until they reached Park Avenue, where she drew away from him. She continued to be a friend of her young brother's friend until they closed the apartment door behind them, and then she put her purse on a foyer table and kissed him generously.

"I'll be with you in a minute. There's a little room there, if you want to wash up."

She rejoined him in five minutes. "They've gone home. I made sure. Would you like some ginger ale, or anything else?"

"Some ginger ale would be fine."

"How do you feel about drinking?"

"I suppose I'll take it up. I haven't wanted to so far, but there's quite a bit of it at Princeton."

"Yes, I know. Well, you'll drink like a gentleman, more than I can say about my brother." She brought the ginger ale and some small sandwiches.

"This is better than nothing, but it's still far from perfect," she said. "I have to be very careful. I *can't* have any talk, so I have to have Jack live here with me. An unmarried girl in New York—this is my family's apartment, and I live with my brother, and there are the two servants and all those people

168

that go with the apartment building, but I wish I could have a place of my own. I'm sure Jack has a place of his own. He hasn't told me so, but I'm sure he has. Everything is so much easier for a man."

"This is so big, it doesn't seem like an apartment. More like your own house."

"Who are your friends at Princeton? The Porter boy. Who else?"

"Mostly him. Why?"

"Well, there's such a thing as your sharing a *pied à terre*. I don't suppose you could afford that on your allowance."

"Not yet, not alone, and I don't know anyone but Lex that I'd ask—"

"Heavens, not him. Elizabeth's brother? One slip and my reputation would be ruined forever."

"I'll have my own money when I'm twenty-one."

"Ah, you're sweet. Are you counting on us to be together three more years?"

"Of course I am. Aren't you?"

"It's a long time. We can hope. You may not like me. I may get in your way. You'll meet a girl, you'll fall in love."

"I'm in love with you . . . You're so—what? Depressed?"

"Yes, I guess I'm depressed."

"Why?"

She looked at him. "It would take some men hours or days to see that I'm depressed, and you saw it right away. *When* did you see it?"

"Before we went out, then I thought you were all right, but then when we got back here."

"Are you as quick to notice those things with other people, or just me?"

"I don't notice much about other people. I don't make friends easily, and maybe that's a sign that I don't care much for people as a rule."

"No, that isn't what it's a sign of, Alfred. You like people, but you don't count on them for very much. You're so different from me. I like people, and I show it, and I get hurt by them. But we do count on each other, you and I. This isn't love, you and I, the kind that ends in marriage, but if I didn't have you to count on, to love, I don't know what I'd do."

"What?"

"I've had a very bad summer."

"I don't even know where you've been."

"That wouldn't make any difference. The places don't matter. I've been to Maine, Long Island, New Jersey, the mountains. The places are all places that were built to make people happy, enjoy life. But I didn't enjoy life at any of them."

"You're in love, aren't you?"

"Oh, yes."

"Then what am I, Norma?"

"What are you?"

"I'm not a kid any more."

"No, you're not a kid."

"Then what am I? You really love someone else."

"You're someone that I love that doesn't hurt me."

"What does that mean? Do you think you can't hurt *me?*"

"I don't want you to be hurt by me. I want to give you happiness, in return for what you give me."

"All right, what's that?"

"What do you give me?"

"Yes."

"Confidence."

"Confidence?"

"Confidence in myself, that you love me. Because you love me. That I can count on you, that I can come back to you and be loved by you. Am I wrong?"

"I don't know."

"There's nothing else for us. If there were, do you think I'd ever let anyone else—get the power to hurt me? If we were going to be together the rest of our lives, do you think I'd ever so much as look at anyone else? Haven't I always loved you, since you were a little boy? Haven't you always loved me? Then can't you see that we have our own kind of love, regardless of other people? You loved Victoria, and I understood that. I'm sure you still love her and always will, but you love me too. We don't have to let loving someone else spoil our loving each other."

"I see."

"A long time ago you kissed me. You didn't love Victoria any the less. But you wanted to kiss me, and you wanted me. And you've had me, and nothing takes away from that. I think that as long as I live, whenever you want me I'll go to you. And happily. But the sadness is in the fact that we'll never be any more than what we are. People who love each other but will always be apart, and trying to love someone else until some day we will. But even then, Alfred, I'll love you and you'll love me. Your mother, your sisters, Victoria, the girl you marry—and me. How can I know that? I know that because it's already happened to me. I'm terribly old for twenty-five. And I'll always be too old for you. But not to love you."

"I guess that's all true," he said.

"And there's more to it," she said.

"What?"

"Do you want to undress me? But not in here."

He followed her to the bedroom.

170

"You first," she said. "You have so many buttons and things."

"Do you want me to undress in front of you?"

"Yes. You hide yourselves in such unbecoming clothes."

"What else is there to wear?"

"Oh—a cloak, like a monk."

"It would save time."

"Don't hurry. I'm pretending we're married."

"I want to hurry."

"Don't throw your things on the floor. You mustn't be all rumpled up when you leave here. I wish you could stay all night. I'd love to sleep all night with you."

"So do I."

"Alfred."

"What?"

"You have the smallest behind I've ever seen."

"Have I?"

"And the flattest tummy. Don't drink a lot of beer at Princeton, please?"

"All right."

"Now me," she said.

He did not speak until, between them, they had taken off her clothes. "You're beautiful. You are."

"I feel beautiful. And happy. And belonging to you. And you to me."

"Don't be sad, Norma. We do love each other."

"How could I be sad now?"

They made love again the next afternoon, after the servants had left at three o'clock. He asked her to accompany him to the Pennsylvania Station, but she refused.

"What are you going to do the rest of the day?" he said.

"Read. Have you ever read Rupert Brooke?"

"No, but I've heard of him."

"He just died, you know."

"I know."

"I met him."

"You met him? Where?"

"In London. A friend of Father's had us for tea and he was there. He's only a couple of years older than I am. *Was.*"

"He's very popular at Princeton just now."

"I've never read him, but I'll think of you. Do you know why?" She smiled.

"Why?"

"The poem is called 'The Great Lover.' "

"Thank you."

"You're welcome," she said. "Promise me you won't run away and join the British army?"

"I promise. I wasn't even thinking of it."

"But your friend Lex Porter is. His family are worried."

171

"He doesn't talk so much about it any more, but he did when I first knew him."

"Well, don't let him convert you."

"I won't."

"You're my love."

"You're my love. What else are you going to do besides read Rupert Brooke?"

"I'm going out for the evening."

"Oh. Where?"

"You wouldn't know them. People I visited in Maine."

"That made you unhappy. Those people?"

"Yes."

"Oh, God."

"I have to do something."

"What time is he calling for you?"

"Seven o'clock."

"And then it'll be the same with him as it was with me."

"No, not any more."

"I don't believe you."

"It's over. Honestly it is. He knows it's over."

"Then he must be stupid. I could tell him that he can have you any time he wants to."

"Not true, Alfred. Not true. You don't know."

"He's a God damn fool if he doesn't take you right into the bedroom."

"Don't say those things."

"I'll say them and repeat them."

"Then please go."

"Gladly."

He went out and waited for the elevator. She did not follow him.

A note from Norma to Alfred four days later:

We are both going to be invited to Mrs. Porter's a week from Sunday. I am going to regret—so don't let that prevent you from accepting. I do not wish to see you for a long, long time. You were horrid to me. You hurt me. N.

Alfred saw Norma from a distance at the Yale game; only briefly, and she did not see him. She was in a foursome who were hurrying down the hill to the new Palmer Stadium, obviously having had lunch at one of the clubs. The men were older, in their thirties or even in their forties, and as they approached the Stadium they veered to the left and the Yale side. One of the men, the man Alfred first saw with Norma, wore a long raccoon coat; the other wore a greatcoat and motoring gauntlets. They were talking amiably among themselves, and Alfred saw the men and the girls change partners, so that he was unable to determine which man was for Norma, which for the other girl (who appeared to be older than Norma). In Alfred's mind there was no doubt that *one* of the men was the one who possessed the power to hurt her, but to the same degree there was no doubt that she was enjoying herself and suffering nothing. Yale, which had not been favored, won the game 13-7, thanks largely to Coach Shevlin and his Minnesota shift, a tricky bit of business that Shevlin had introduced at New Haven when he was brought in toward the end of the season. But the advantages of the new technique went largely unobserved by Alfred, who tried throughout the game to pick out the foursome on the opposite side of the field. The campus and the team had been so confident of winning that the defeat put the undergraduates in a mood that somewhat corresponded to the mood that Alfred suffered for his own reason.

"I didn't know you cared so much about football," said Lex.

"What makes you say that?"

"You'd think you lost your last friend. It's only a football game. We'll win sometimes, and sometimes we'll lose."

"That's the first time you've ever said 'we.' You're getting patriotic yourself."

"Where are your family going to be?"

"At Mrs. Tompkins', on Library Place. All but my father. He'll be at Ivy."

"With my uncles," said Lex. "Do you still want me to go with you?"

"Yes, I haven't said anything different, have I?"

"No, but you're as sore as a boil, and I know good and damn well it isn't this football game. What is it?"

"It's not you."

"I was pretty sure of that. If you were as sore as that at me we'd have had a fist-fight. Cheer up. 'I should worry, I should fret, I should marry a suffragette.' "

"Oh, balls, Porter."

"Balls to you, Eaton. Double balls, triple balls, quadruple balls."

"Well, quintuple balls to you."

"I was going to say that but I couldn't think of that word. Quintuple. Didn't know how to pronounce it, either. You're so bright. Now try to be bright and cheerful, not for me, but for your family and Old Lady Tompkins. Who *is* Old Lady Tompkins?"

"Oh, she lives here. She's some friend of my mother's. She's the one whose house I go to for a steak dinner about once a month."

The Eaton car, with George Fry behind the wheel, was at the curb in front of Mrs. Tompkins' house. Alfred shook hands with George Fry and introduced him to Lex. "Are you cold? Why don't you go inside and warm yourself by the kitchen stove?" said Alfred.

"I want to get an early start and I hoped they'd see me out here and that would remind them."

"Is my father here yet?"

"Got here just a minute ago. A gentleman with a Crane-Simplex fetched him and drove away. Tell them it's getting dark, Alfred. I don't like to drive these strange roads at night."

"Neither does Alfred," said Lex. "He got lost on one of them, didn't you?" He roared with laughter.

"I did," said Alfred, and laughed, somewhat less heartily.

"Everything all right at Princeton, Alfred?" said George Fry.

"Fine, thanks, George. You?"

"Oh, about the same, about the same. Will I see you at Thanksgiving then?"

"No. Christmas. I'm going to New York for Thanksgiving. This rude gentleman's family have invited me."

"He's not a rude gentleman at all. I take him to be a fine-looking, nice-mannered lad."

"Thank you," said Lex.

"Very lucky to have him for a friend, Alfred, if I'm any judge," said George. "That's on short acquaintance, but I aint very often wrong."

"Oh, he's all right," said Alfred.

"Well, I'll say so long till Christmas, then, and hurry them up in there if you can. A horse'll find his own way home, but I don't relish getting out and looking at road signs every five miles."

By good fortune Samuel Eaton was seated beside Mrs. Tompkins as Alfred and Lex entered the Tompkins library. She was a woman he respected and whose opinion of him mattered to him, and he was therefore agreeably stimulated by her and his desire to keep himself in good standing with her. He put his cup and saucer on a table and rose to his feet, shook hands with Alfred, and said to Lex: "I just left your uncle a moment ago, your Uncle Frederick."

"Uncle Fritz. So I was told."

The greetings and introductions were completed and Alfred and Lex seated themselves to the right and left of Martha Eaton. "It's so nice to see you after hearing so much about you from Alfred."

"And I can say exactly the same thing to you, Mrs. Eaton."

"From New York City, aren't you?"

"Yes, I am."

"We don't get to New York very much. Philadelphia's so close, only about an hour by train, and when the roads get

174

better I hope we won't have to rely so much on the train."

"Why don't you get them to improve the roads to New York, then you could go there instead of Philadelphia."

"Oh, I don't know. Philadelphia's city enough for me."

"Is Philadelphia a city? I suppose it is."

"Indeed it is, I believe it's the second largest in the Union."

"I was joking. I don't know anything about Philadelphia."

Samuel Eaton's voice now carried an announcement: "I don't like to put an end to this delightful visit, but we have a long way to go."

"I wish you could stay," said Mrs. Tompkins.

"Oh, Daisy, it was so nice of you to have us, but I'm afraid Sam is right."

"Where do you go to school?" said Lex to Sally.

"I still go to school in Port Johnson."

"I guess Alfred told me that, but I wasn't interested before."

"Are you interested now?" said Sally.

"Well, not hysterically, but more than I *was.*"

"Isn't that dear of you? I'm so glad I met with your approval. Heavens, it would have spoiled my whole trip if I hadn't. The great Lex Porter."

"Correct, sit down."

"I'm not standing up, I don't stand up for gentlemen, not even Princeton freshmen."

"You will learn to, my girl."

"Sally dear," said Martha Eaton. "We're ready."

They all went out to the curb for the leavetaking. Daisy Tompkins stood with the young men and waved to the Eatons. "Would you boys like to come in and finish the sandwiches?"

They thanked her but declined, and walked to Stockton Street and on to Nassau Street, which was lively with cars and noisy Yale partisans, and from there to Lex's room.

"Well, now I've met *your* family. Has your sister got a heavy beau?"

"Sally?"

"I should hope so, the other's a bit young for me."

"I don't know."

"Well, I'll write and ask her. Your father's on the bossy side, isn't he?"

"I told you he was. He's used to giving orders."

"And having them obeyed."

"Well, he can fire almost anybody that disobeys."

"But not my Uncle Fritz."

"Why do you say that?"

"They had a disagreement. Not today, a long time ago. Uncle Fritz wouldn't tell me what caused it, but it ended in fisticuffs. It's too bad our two fathers couldn't have been the ones to fight."

"I don't see that it makes the slightest difference."

"I guess not. Although it might have. I don't think your sister would like me if our two fathers had fought. Girls are very loyal to their fathers."

"Is your sister loyal to your father?"

"Oh—you must never criticize my father, or she'll jump down your throat. I know she doesn't like him, but that wouldn't make any difference if you criticized him. You're not supposed to know what he was."

"Well, you're not supposed to know what my father was. And is. Except today . . ."

"What, today?"

"He isn't young any more. His neck, his skin, the back of his neck looked old. Not that he's young. He's well over fifty. Fifty-three, I think. But today I really noticed a big difference in him."

"Then I won't say any more."

"No, don't. I don't like him any better, but I don't feel so much like fighting him."

"I wonder what my old man looks like now. He's about the same age. And I'll bet Paris isn't very comfortable right now. Especially for somebody that loved his comfort as much as he did."

"Would you like to see him?"

"No. Let's go get something to eat, if we can get in any place."

"Let's wait a while. We might run into somebody I don't want to see."

"Some particular person?"

"Yes."

"All right. Would you like to shoot some pool?"

"I'd rather stay here. We could play some cards."

"All right. I'll get out the deck. Or would you really rather be alone?"

"No. Do you know how to play two-handed rummy?"

"Sure," said Lex.

If there had been anyone in the world to talk to, it would have been Lex Porter. But their friendship, or companionship, had instituted its own formalities, which the members of the companionship observed and would continue to observe until the formalities disappeared, which might be never, which might be instantaneously in certain unpredictable circumstances. The conveniences of the friendship, or companionship, were its limitations. Beyond those conveniences they were not yet ready to go, if they ever would be. With the two companions the last confidences, the ultimate ones, would be in matters pertaining to women, the same confidences that be-

176

tween two other, and different, men are often among the very earliest. It was easy enough to make a guess as to Lex Porter's attitude toward women; the obvious guess would have been that he was vigorous and irresponsible. But something warned Alfred not to accept the obvious guess; to have been wrong, and moreover to have acted upon the wrong guess, would have been (he was sure) disastrous to the companionship. He suspected that Lex respected his own reserve in the matter; he respected Lex's reserve, partly as it represented ideally gentlemanly behavior, but more deeply as it showed Lex to be a man who had a specific secret or operated under a personal code that in either case he wanted to keep under cover. In his own case Alfred was simply keeping a secret, a secret that was the more secret because it was not his alone to break and because the breaking of it could do irreparable harm to someone else; and this was all less difficult for Alfred than it might have been for someone else who had not lived so much of his life within himself. Alfred had been ready all his life to abandon the prep school manners of thought and action that he never quite had assumed, and he had been ready most of his life to assume the mature manners of thought and action that ideally were assumed when he became a member of a university. It seemed to him now that he had always been impatient to get out of boyhood and to take on the methods and appearance of manhood, and to reject the immaturity and unhappiness of the early years, down to the final tragedy of it as symbolized and factualized by the stupid useless killing of Victoria. He had been encouraging in himself the hope that that final, stupid, useless killing would be the end of his own immaturity and an end to the immaturity of life itself in its handling of him. He had been well, pretty well, on the way to a positive belief that the bad years had come to their bad end. But now he could not avoid or dismiss from his thinking the resemblance between his guilt in the death of Victoria and his guilt in the hurt he had given Norma. Of her hurt he was convinced beyond self-effacing doubts of modesty. He had delivered a blow to the kindest person he had ever known, and he had battered her as surely as Victoria had been broken in the ditch. In this his very inexperience of love-making was potent; he had not had enough experience of love-making to make him doubt the truth of her passion, to suspect himself of confusing artfulness with love, induced pleasure with free expression. At night he would forgive himself for his part in Victoria's death—but then he would dream about her, and always the dream would be some form of her going away from him without love. In the dream she would have no malice or anger against him, but neither was there any of the warmth that she once had shown him; and always she would go away. And when he came awake he would feel abandoned and alone. His dreams of Norma were erotic, but when he awoke from them he felt a cold disgust with himself, not for the actions of his dream but a wakeful castigation of himself in judgment on the evidence.

There was no one to talk to, and he dimly saw that it was just as well. The temptation often came, to ask Lex Porter to hear it all out. But what he realized, although dimly now, was that it would be better to keep the guilt and sorrow intact and his own. He was partially aware that he had lost something— he knew not what—by telling Lex as much as he had told him about his relations with his father. He was determined not to lose whatever that was by confiding in anyone about Norma. Sorrow was nothing new to Alfred Eaton, but sharing it was. And there was no doubt in his mind that his self-respect, as well as his pride, was safer if he kept secret the intimate aspects of his relationship with Norma. Rather defiantly, as much to her as to himself, he promised that no one would know about it through him. His father's purposeful neglect had made Alfred live within himself through the first eighteen years of his life; now Alfred was beginning to live within himself as a result of his own decision, and not as a result of an exterior force. What that meant was that the habit was the same, but for a different reason. He would always be a man who would always be alone, more alone than all men are alone, and it would become apparent to him that he could always find a reason for so being: to be alone was his personal condition, a fact which he would not recognize until many years had passed, but which he identified now as the unhappiness that was caused by the end of his affair with Norma and his bad conduct that caused its end. Luckily for him—as for anyone at the age of eighteen—he had not the power to see or the wisdom to understand that there already existed that personal condition, as much a part of his soul as the color of his eyes was a characteristic of his physical self.

Before going home for Christmas holidays he wrote her a note, the final result of a dozen tries of varying lengths:

> I ask you to forgive me. I want to see you, either before I go home or in Port Johnson, preferably both. All my love. Alfred.

There was no answer to the note, and on the day before he left Princeton he telephoned her apartment. "Miss Norma is in Palm Beach, Florida. I don't expect her back before the end of January. Do you wish her address there, sir?"

He thanked the maid; no, he did not wish Miss Norma's address. He was sure his letter had been forwarded, read, and tossed in the wastebasket.

During the holidays he was conscious of his new prestige as a college man and of the extra cachet of Princeton college man. As a freshman from Port Johnson, Pennsylvania, he was not yet on the lists for the debutante parties in Philadelphia and New York, but after first declining, he changed his mind and accepted Lex Porter's invitation to spend part of the holiday in New York. The prestige he enjoyed in Port Johnson was satisfactory for the first few days, but it was not something he had earned, he had come by it too easily, almost by purchase, and the town was too full of Christmas without Victoria and Montgomery Street to remind him of Norma. Before he left he paid an afternoon call on his grandfather.

"I came to thank you for my Christmas present."

"Yes, and to say goodbye. I hear you're off to New York City, so you'll have good use for the present. Well, we can't think of you as a boy any more. You're a man, all a man's powers, none of his responsibilities. Lobster palaces."

"Lobster palaces?" said Alfred. "Is that what you said?"

"Taxicabs, and cabarets. Cabriolets and cabbages and all the rest of it. Wars and rumors of wars. Airships and airplanes and air rifles and heiresses and son-and-heirs. Putting on airs. Everybody putting on airs. The Czar of Russia at war with his cousin the Kÿ—zar of Germany. I lost the sight of the *one* eye. Have to have the paper read to me. Well, are you learning anything over at Princeton?"

"A little, I guess."

"A little bit of knowledge is a dangerous thing. But I don't know. What's the use of learning it all? Next year they're going to change it all. All be changed. Pancho Villa. Pancho *Villain*. The Germans are behind him. Where does he get those machine guns? The Germans. Then watch out. Send Teddy. Destroy Pancho Villain before the Germans conquer Mexico. Teddy is the man. Teddy and the Rough Riders. They can lick Pancho Villain. But don't you go with him. You might get killed. Sunstroke. But Teddy's used to those climates. Well, here she is, my Red Cross nurse. You've got to go now, Raymond. Give your grandfather a kiss."

Alfred leaned down and kissed the old man. The old man smiled. "If you ever want any money, just send for it. Enjoy life. Don't miss anything."

"I'll try not to. Goodbye, Grandfather."

The old man nodded and forgot him.

The nurse tapped her right temple, and Alfred wanted to strike her. "He can't stay on the one subject for long," she said.

"Well, next year they're going to change it all," said Alfred. "What?"

"Nothing," said Alfred, and left.

179

On a day during his visit to the Porters Alfred was taken to lunch by Fritz Thornton. Lex was having a long session with the dentist and was not present. Alfred went to the selected club, was told he was expected, and mounted the stairs to a small bar. Thornton introduced him to a group of older men, asked him if he would have a drink, and then took him to the diningroom and a table for two.

"I daresay this is breakfast for you, is it not?" said Thornton.

"Yes sir, except for a cup of coffee."

"Then why don't you have the Spanish omelet? You can't go wrong on that. Sometimes the food here is as good as any club in town, but at the moment we're having a little trouble in the kitchen, breaking in a new chef. I'm going to try him out on something else, but you have the omelet, just to be on the safe side."

The waiter took their order and Thornton rested his elbows on the arms of his chair and folded his hands. Alfred found himself copying the position, and felt himself being examined as to the part of his hair, the closeness of his shave, the knot of his necktie. "Lex treating you right? Meeting a lot of pretty girls?"

"Plenty of them. I've never seen so many."

Thornton nodded vigorously. "It's a good year for them. I've noticed that myself. If I had a daughter on the market this year I'd be a bit worried. Competition, very stiff. Say, you didn't want any soup, did you? I'm terribly sorry."

"No thanks."

"Or oysters or anything like that?"

"No sir. It's breakfast for me."

"That's what I thought. Well, now. You're from Port Johnson."

"Yes sir."

"And of course I've known your father a good many years. But I want to ask you about someone there. This isn't prying, you understand, but I would very much like to have your opinion of Devrow Budd. I understand you know the family quite well?"

"Yes sir, all my life."

"Well, what kind of a fellow is Budd? I don't believe in beating about the bush. I want to know what you *think* of him. Is he a good fellow? If you uh, well, if you were a member here would you put him up? Or what kind of a letter would you write for him? I want you to be absolutely frank with me, and it won't go beyond this napkin, rest assured."

"Well, of course he's my father's age."

"I don't care anything about that. You have a good head on your shoulders, and the hell with how much older he is.

You're what? Twenty? Around there somewhere?"

"Eighteen."

"Gave you a few extra years, but that's all right. I don't apologize for that. If you were a female I'd have to, but I don't think men ever mind being taken for older than they are, unless they're God damn stage actors, and I don't consider them much in any event. Although I have had some fun with one or two. However, you impress me as a young man with good judgment, and I can tell you your friend Lex, my nephew, the sky's the limit when he starts talking about you, and I'll take his word any old time."

"I'm glad to hear that."

"Well, it isn't any horse-shit. It's the truth. But now let me hear what *you* think of Devrow *Budd*."

"Well, he's very colorful."

"Mm-hmm."

"There's no one else like him in Port Johnson."

"I shouldn't think so."

"Everybody works in Port Johnson."

"You'll never find *me* living there, but go ahead."

"Well, that's it. Mr. Budd is the only man in town that lives that way. Some others don't work very hard, but he doesn't work at all."

"In Port Johnson. He works. I don't like to disillusion you, but he does work. He's not entirely a man of leisure."

"Well, I always heard he was in the stock market, and in London."

"Exactly. Now what I'm getting at is, do you disapprove of him because he doesn't work, or would you disapprove of him anyway?"

"Did I say I disapproved of him?"

"You didn't have to. I'll put it to you this way, and you can tell me if I'm right or wrong. You don't like him, do you?"

"Am I under oath?"

"Well, you make me sound like the grand inquisitor, but yes. Under oath."

"I don't like him."

"Why?"

"I never gave it much thought. I never gave it any thought."

"But you have no *reason* to dislike him."

"If you mean, did he ever do anything to me—"

"Not only to you. To anyone."

"No sir."

The waiter served the food and they suspended the conversation, then resumed it.

"Now then, it's only fair to you to tell you *why* I've been so inquisitorial. Or inquisitive. I may have put you in an awkward position, now I'll put myself in one. Fair exchange is no

181

robbery, as they say. You see, Eaton, I know all about Devrow Budd in a business way, how he makes his money, his rating and so forth and so on. But I wanted to get your opinion because we knew all about how he was in New York and London, but not a damn thing about what anybody thought about him in his home town."

"It isn't his home town, Mr. Thornton. He comes from Baltimore."

"Well, his legal residence. Where he hangs his hat, so to speak. At one time I thought of writing to your father, but your father and I haven't been cozy pals, and for all I knew he might have been cozy pals with Devrow Budd."

"I see."

"No, you don't see. But I'll tell you, and you will. I'm interested in a firm that are thinking of engaging Devrow Budd to execute some assignments overseas. These jobs, they require —well, let me start again. The work isn't all transacted in business offices or in business hours. And while we know Budd's capabilities, we like to know all we can, every possible bit of information."

"Well, don't go by what I say."

"Put your mind at peace on that score. What you told me about Budd is unfavorable, of course. But it isn't going to keep us from giving him the job."

"Then I don't understand why you asked me."

"Because you'd tell me the truth. Don't think you're the only one that didn't give him good marks. But we like to know everything, good and bad, and then we decide whether the man is going to be good for us or bad for us. We hire men that I wouldn't bring to this club on a bet, but we know what we're getting. Now I can say that I talked with a young man who's known Budd all his life and doesn't like him."

"That isn't worth much."

"Isn't it? What if we got nothing but flowery, flattering reports on him? We wouldn't hire him. Not for this job. If he was a teetotaler, we wouldn't hire him, and if he dressed badly, we wouldn't hire him. And if he had so little personality that he was practically inhuman, we'd look elsewhere. We don't want a namby-pamby for this job. And I guess you know as well as I do that Devrow Budd is no namby-pamby."

"I don't know, but I'd guess he wasn't. He looks—sophisticated."

"To say the least. You'd never expect to see him wearing long gaiters and an apron, like the vicar."

Alfred smiled. "No."

"I've only met him two or three times. I didn't like him either. Haven't met his wife, although I understand she's entirely different. Quiet. A lady. But it's a damned shame about the daughter."

"She's a friend of mine."

"I know. That's why I say it. If you had an older sister that was carrying on an open affair with a married man, you'd try to do something about it. Lex would, if Elizabeth were in the same position. I understand the daughter is an extremely attractive young woman. But my Lord, she has really tossed her cap over the windmill. And I gather the brother is just no help at all. Elizabeth is very fond of her, they're the same age, and my sister has tried to get her to come to her house, but she's always busy, always going away somewhere. And everybody knows who with. Damned shame, damned shame. Well, there's nothing *we* can do about it. And even if we tried it would probably be resented. You never know which way a woman's going to jump, and I suppose that's part of their attraction."

"I don't know," said Alfred.

"Very wise. Take it from an old hand, we *never* know about women. Now how would you like a demi-tasse? Or some dessert, if you like?"

"A demi-tasse would be fine."

"Cigar? We have a medium panatela here's nice and mild after lunch."

"No thanks."

"I told Lex you boys could have my car any afternoon until Saturday. Shall I send around for it?"

"Thanks very much, but I think I'll walk back to Mrs. Porter's."

"And have a nap, I'll bet."

"Very likely."

"Appreciate your frankness about Devrow Budd. I hope it wasn't too much of an imposition. But frankly, I go on the theory that if you start giving a young fellow responsibility— well, he responds to it. Fellows your age are commanding troops in France, and I'm in favor of giving you boys all the responsibility you can handle. Of course I'm also in favor of the old motto, all work and no play, et cetera, especially for the young. And don't you let Sam Eaton try to tell you he didn't have a good time in college days. He settled down, and I didn't, but don't you let him bamboozle you. He raised his share of hell, too."

Fritz Thornton thought he might stay around a little while longer and pick up a game of auction bridge, and Alfred left him.

At Mrs. Porter's the butler let him in and he was on his way to his room when he encountered Elizabeth Porter. "Oh, hello, Alfred. Back from lunch?"

"Hello, Miss Porter. Yes, I had lunch with your uncle."

"I guess poor Lex is still having his tusks drilled."

"I guess so. I just came in."

"Let's sit down and have a cigarette," said Elizabeth.

"All right, let's."

They moved into the small front room.

"Lex isn't having a cavity filled," said Alfred.

"What is he having?"

"Well, he *is* having a cavity filled, but he's having something more. You and Mrs. Porter didn't see him this morning."

"A fight?"

"No. Hockey. This tooth." Alfred tapped one of his canines.

"Oh, dear. He won't have any teeth left."

"He won't need them, playing hockey," said Alfred.

"He'll need them later on, when he wants to smile at a girl."

"He doesn't seem to care much about them."

"That's where you're wrong. He's very fond of your sister."

"He likes her, but that's as far as it goes."

"Well, that's as far as it *should* go at eighteen. You both have plenty of time for romance later on. I didn't fall in love until I was twenty-four. Last year. I don't think you know your own mind much before that."

"Oh, some people do."

"Very few. They think they're in love, but they're not. Then they marry too early. Most of the girls that came out my year are married and have children. I don't expect to get married till after the war's over."

"I didn't know you were engaged."

"Not officially. My fiancé is with the British, and we agreed that it was a mistake to marry when everything was topsy-turvy."

"I don't see how you could do that if you were in love."

"On the contrary, I don't see how you could do anything else. I'm sure I wouldn't want him to be worried about a wife at home, and he didn't want me to be worried about his safety abroad."

"I wouldn't look at it that way."

"Most people don't, but we do. I don't believe in snatching your little moment of happiness. I think it's better for him to feel that I'm sure he'll come back safe and sound. I think it gives him assurance. People who succumb to the war hysteria, and the uniform—they're not building for the future."

"They're not as optimistic as you are."

"They're not as optimistic about their love, to my way of thinking. Girls who fall in love too easily deserve the unhappiness they get. And they always get it. I know one—well, let's talk about something else. But I hope for your sake that you won't think of love before you're out of college a few years."

He stood up. "I wish I knew you better."

"Thank you. I wonder why."

"To talk to."

"You used to talk a lot with Norma Budd, didn't you?"

"Quite a lot."

"We're as different as day and night, Norma and I. I *like* Norma. But if you and she had this conversation I'm sure she'd say the exact opposite to everything I've said."

"Oh, I'm sure of that, too."

"I see. Then you don't mind if I don't agree with you."

"I don't mind a bit."

"I hope you don't take offense at this, but you're an unusual boy."

"The only thing I take offense to is that I'm not a boy."

"On the contrary—and you won't like this at all—but you are one of the youngest boys I've ever met."

"No I'm not."

"But you are, and I like it. And you always will be."

"Me? Everybody thinks I'm at least two years older than I am."

"Well, I don't. It isn't a question of years, either. It's something about you that when you're *fifty,* I hope it's still there. And don't ask me what it is."

"But I do ask you what it is."

"You won't like me."

"But I'd like to know."

"It's your innocence."

"There you *are* wrong."

"Not by what *I* mean by innocence. This may save your manly pride. Do you know who else I think is innocent?"

"Lex."

"Not at all. Uncle Fritz. My Uncle Fritz Thornton. Not Uncle Alec, or Lex. But you and Uncle Fritz. Now puzzle over that."

"Puzzle is right. Well, time for Baby's nap."

"Sleep peacefully, if you can."

"I always do. The sleep of the innocent."

He got no sleep. He lay on the bed and tried to feel important and responsible by recalling his conversation with Fritz Thornton, but it had been followed too soon by the conversation with Elizabeth Porter, which in spite of her tardy apologetic comparison of him with her uncle made him feel that he was not out of Knox. She was right and incisive and truthful, and she had seen the raw innocence in which he believed but which no one else saw. But he had been wanting so much to feel securely older that he had forgotten about his innocence and that it was there to be seen by someone as astute (and at the same time as wrong) as Elizabeth

Porter. But no matter how mature he might seem to the uncle and how young and innocent to the niece, niece and uncle seemed to have failed completely to consider the possibility of the kind of relationship he had had with Norma Budd. Their failure pleased him; it reminded him once again of the fact that no one knows everything about anyone, and that ignorance of one fact can make anyone's judgment completely wrong, and that therefore no one really knows anything about you, since they can't possibly know everything. Apart from the reasoning, more immediately mundane, was the realization that Norma had been as careful of their secret as he had been, and for that he was grateful.

For he was now in the midst of preparations for one of the most maturing experiences of his life: he was about to desert a friend; a friend in need of even the silent, long-distance help he could give, a friend who had loved him and trusted him, and whom he had loved. There would be no public knowledge of the desertion, perhaps not even knowledge of it by the deserted friend. But *he* would know it and carry the knowledge with him, shamefully but firmly, and somehow she would know it too. He was not going to do anything that was not precisely what she had asked him to do. He would keep the secret of their affair, which was what she had asked him to do. He would say and do what was expected of him if their relationship had been what everyone assumed it to be: an innocent friendship between a young woman and a much younger young man.

He had already begun. At lunch with Fritz Thornton he had made the weak gesture of reminding Thornton that Norma was his friend, but he had made it so weakly that instead of its acting as a word of caution to Thornton, it had only made Alfred seem like the loyal friend he was not. Alfred Eaton was going through the experience of running away from trouble, and it was a delicious experience because it was completely evil and contrary to all the good things he believed in, and all the accusation and trial and guilt would be inside himself. And already he knew that for the rest of his life he would mark this time as his first real sin. Now he was beginning to know the meaning of sin, of calculated evil, and the sin with which he was beginning was one of the worst.

He lay on the bed and stared at the Porter ceiling and saw not the stippled wallpaper, but himself unreflected and invisible; a man capable of cowardice and treachery, planned and undiscoverable, and stimulated by his own surrender to an evil force of his own creation. All that had happened to him in the past now seemed like minor infractions, unworthy of a feeling of guilt. But now he was fuller of living than he had ever been before knowing that he could so carefully, so cruelly

186

walk away from someone who needed in one heart, in all the world, one heart, in which love for her was kept alive. He shut his eyes and he could see her face, her lips closed, a face as still as a photograph. *"No!"* he said. And it was done.

RAYMOND JOHNSON and Jonas Rothermel died within a week of each other in the late winter of 1915-'16. They were buried with a minimum of fuss and ceremony, Johnson because he had so desired, and Rothermel because neither his family nor the community were impelled to make a display of the pathetic little sorrow that his departure occasioned. It could be fairly, though incompletely, stated that what the two deaths finally came down to was that Raymond Johnson had occupied a position in the community that he had made for himself and that was uniquely his own, and could belong to no one else; while Jonas Rothermel's death created a job vacancy that would soon be filled. But the deaths, or, more accurately, the lives of the two men were there for study by any citizen who cared to take the trouble. Both men had worked hard all their lives, one quite as hard as the other; and they had worked hard at making money, in Johnson's case, and to make money, in Rothermel's. Johnson, who had inherited money, would have had to have an excuse not to make more; Rothermel, born poor, had the ready-made excuse that he lacked education, and he soon turned the excuse into a crusade against the next generation: the next generation of the advantaged educated were not going to be able to use their advantage over his representatives, his children. And the little man who went half-starved had at least lived to see two of his children not only educated but educators, and the third child a student in whom the town was already taking some pride. To that extent Jonas Rothermel died with a sense of fulfillment not achieved by Raymond Johnson, whose only child had married an uninspired, unimaginative man, because of which Johnson had had to postpone by one generation his vicarious participation in the world that followed his own. His death came before there was much to see: the grandson Alfred was tall, healthy, sensitive, unexpectedly humorous and with a charm that might and might not outlast his youth. The granddaughters were yet undeveloped; Sally giving hints of a quiet charm and eventual beauty; Constance promising early prettiness and an unsubstantial *joie de vivre* that was like her mother's at the same age. It was the grandson that Raymond Johnson wanted to see solidly and safely matured, and he died without seeing anything but signs of characteristics and qualities that could operate against the boy's happiness as well as in its favor. Raymond Johnson knew (as Norma Budd alone had also suspected) that Alfred could never depend on his father or his mother, for critical help or sympathetic understanding, whenever and whatever was needed. His own position as grandfather limited his participation; he could only be friendly and kind and loving, but never critical to any influential degree or in any basic problem. Thus Raymond Johnson passed out of the world with his own moderate tragedy; while Jonas Rothermel, having the satisfactions that Raymond Johnson sought, died poor because he had not got rich. But it was not within either man's personal philosophy to realize that the only satisfaction in death is that of the suicide, who picks his own time, but is able to pick it only because he is giving up nothing in exchange for a hope.

The son of Jonas Rothermel and the grandson of Raymond Johnson did not meet during the week of the funerals. They did, however, meet on paper, in that they were benefited under Raymond Johnson's will. Raymond Johnson forgave Jonas Rothermel's debt, and Alfred Eaton, in addition to a trust fund already established, stood to inherit a third of the principal that was left to Martha J. Eaton in trust and of which she would enjoy the income during her lifetime. The trust fund for Alfred had originally been established with $100,000, but war conditions and interest had already brought it closer to $200,000 while Alfred was still two years short of coming into possession. The gross estate was approximately $3,000,000, which for the moment at least made Alfred feel that he was a millionaire, and the brother of two millionairesses. But until he reached twenty-one he had no more financial independence than Tom Rothermel. His checking account at the bank in Princeton was there at the whim and the pleasure of his father. And he had seen enough of wealth outside Port Johnson, at Princeton and in New York, to be firmly aware of his comparative position among the wealthy. He had begun to use the Thornton brothers as a measure of wealth. Alec Thornton owned a house and land at Purchase, New York, and a house in town; Fritz Thornton owned a house in town and another on Long Island, with land sufficient for the boats and the horses he raced and hunted, and money enough left over to pay for the court tennis house he was building. Alfred had not seen any of the Thornton houses, but he guessed that the most optimistic income from a million dollars would not pay for the upkeep of Fritz Thornton's sporting establishment, or the more formal establishment of Alec Thornton, of which Alfred only knew that there was a pipe organ as well as a collection of paintings by unidentified

Old Masters, a greenhouse two hundred feet long, and the word Hall in the name of the place. And even they, the Thornton brothers, spoke of their *rich* friends. It amused Alfred to have Lex borrow a dollar from him. It amused him even more to be reminded that Lex had not been given a checking account. And when he considered the social system of Port Johnson it amused him to realize that he had a nodding acquaintance with a member of the junior class whose father could write a cheque to buy Port Johnson and everything in it, including Eaton Iron & Steel and both breweries. But that young man's father was a household name, one of the American synonyms for steel. It was people like the Thorntons who impressed him the most and made him for the first time realize that it is a big country: where there could be so many people of wealth he never had heard of and whose source of wealth he could not name; the owners of the steam yachts and the racing stables and the anonymous marble and limestone houses of Fifth Avenue. He was familiar enough with the names of the Schwabs and the Carnegies and the Fricks and the Rockefellers, the Morgans, Bakers and Harrimans, but he was discovering that there were hundreds of Thorntons, families who lived in the style appropriate to the famous wealthy, but seemed to use their names to hide their wealth rather than reveal it. He knew that Tom Rothermel would consider him a rich boy; he wondered what Tom Rothermel would think if he told him about the Thorntons. But then, thinking about Tom Rothermel, and Port Johnson, he recalled a carriage ride with his grandfather, in 1905 or thereabouts. They had stopped for root beer at the farmers' hotel in Eckburg or Stone Fence, one of the villages near Port Johnson.

"Hello, there," his grandfather called out. "Hello, there. Anybody inside there?"

The saloon door was open—it was summer—and a bearded man appeared. "What?" he said.

"Bring us a couple of glasses of your root beer, please," said Raymond Johnson.

"Bring it? I aint no servant. Come in and drink it or go thirsty," said the bearded man.

"Well, if we have to, I guess we have to," said Raymond Johnson. He tied the horses to the long pipe-rail and Alfred followed him into the bar. The bearded man was engaged in some polishing activity behind the bar. He looked up in his own good time.

"Two root beers, please," said Johnson.

The man put two home-brew bottles on the bar, opened them, poured the root beer into beer shells. "Ten," he said, and put out his cupped palm.

The grandfather paid him and he and Alfred drank the

cold, foaming drinks. When they finished and were about to leave, Raymond Johnson said: "Are you Schlichter?"

"If it's any of your business."

"My name is Raymond Johnson."

"That's nothin' to me."

"I didn't think so. But look at the bottom of your mortgage. Enjoyed the root beer. Come on, Alfred."

They drove away. "Politeness never hurt anybody. It's good in business just as much as in the home. That man was rude to us, but he just learned a lesson."

"He did? How?"

"Well, he didn't know who I was, but he owes our bank money. A lot of them don't know who I am, don't even recognize me when they see me. But he shouldn't be rude to me just because he doesn't know me. I frightened him a little and I did it on purpose. Hereafter he'll be politer and that's good for his business and ours. Money is often where you least expect it, Alfred. Remember that."

Alfred remembered it now, ten years later, eleven years later, but he had had to find it out in his own way. He tried to remember other words of wisdom and pieces of advice his grandfather had given him through the years but nothing came of his concentration. His own experience would have to confirm the disremembered counsel. He would miss his grandfather, he knew, but not for his words of wisdom; rather for his reliable kindness, friendliness, and uncritical love.

So many things had just been new to Alfred that he barely noticed what was old and final and the last for other people. In the weeks after his grandfather's death he noticed the seniors, for whom college was now newly old, and he heard more and more talk among other men, not seniors, about not returning to college but going off to fight for the British and the French, and among them college was newly old. Then later, when the alumni were coming back for their reunions, he caught among them the repeated sense of an ending that was not yet but was near. The man whom his grandfather called Pancho Villain and now another confused man named Carranza were actually defying our army in Mexico, and the older brothers of quite a few Princeton students were in uniform and under arms, thousands of miles from home. And to them college, still fairly new to Alfred, was old. Boots and spurs and leather puttees were on view in the show-windows of Chestnut Street and Fifth Avenue, and the men's clothing store advertisements now regularly contained a line or two announcing their officers' uniform departments. No single day passed in which Alfred did not hear, or utter, some statement that derived from war news. No one was saying it very loud, but the feeling during that spring and summer was that we were occupying ourselves with a small, private war in Mexico while half-heartedly hoping to stay out of the big one in Europe. The more conventional thing to say was that we were preparing an army against the day when we might be dragged into the European fight. But there existed the small, secret hope that we could confine our belligerency in a belligerent world to a bandit-chase on our own continent. The hope existed in much the same way that a desperately ill infant exists, fed by an eye-dropper, and making the parents exaggerate every tiny sign of progress. But the Europeans had been fighting for two full bloody, muddy years, sending men against artillery and decimating a generation; putting ships on the sea that contained the submersibles; and meanwhile money was expensive and becoming more so as the cost of the war pyramided. We were not in it, and there was not much we could say to the British and French officers who were sent here to talk ever so informally and unofficially at the gentlemen's clubs and the ladies' at-homes. There was not much we could say, and very little we wanted to say to the personable young men in horizon blue and well-cut khaki, who came ostensibly to look at the foundries and the nitrate plants, but whose greatest effectiveness was in making themselves agreeable to strangers on trains, clerks in the stores, small boys on the street, the reverend Protestant and Catholic clergy, the easily flattered newspaper publishers, the discreet senators who could ignore the German vote, and the impressionable wives of the men who commanded our finance and industry. The 1916 Mexican Border campaign was the nearest thing we ever had to a gentlemen's war; the semi-private and wholly private National Guard units were made up of the American scions; the Kappa Alpha's from Williams and the Psi U's from Cornell, the Delta Psi's from Penn and the Dekes from Lafayette, the Chi Phi's from Franklin & Marshall and the A. T. O.'s from Virginia. There were not many mothers who protested in song that they didn't raise their boys to be soldiers after they had met the French version of an Alpha Delt from St. Cyr or the English version of the Phi Gam from Sandhurst. Moreover, the Plattsburg camps had semi-militarized an older group of Dekes and Ivy Club men, and often the presence of one man from a county (who was, to be sure, usually a man of wealth and position) made the county aware of Plattsburg, military training, the desirability of preparedness, and, inevitably, the cause of the Allies. (No one went to Plattsburg or Texas with the notion that he might one day replace a wounded Uhlan.) We wanted to hope that we could stay out of the European war, but the Germans were making the hope impossible and almost everything else was making the hope a cause for embarrassment, if not for shame. And as a nation

191

we had become too big to stay out of big wars. It was not merely that our commercial involvements would eventually compel us to take sides; the brutal fact was that the big United States of America was ready to declare itself a great power in the only contest that men are born knowing. The skirmish against Spain and the earlier mutual slaughter of Northerners and Southerners had not established us among the great powers, and our peaceful pursuits were only successful, not glorious. No one man wanted to get hurt by a bayonet or blown apart by powder, and he singly therefore wanted to hope to stay out of the European war; but when he thought away from himself and the petty penalties and thought for the United States of America, he became a member of power thinking, great-power thinking, and multiplied by millions he became an insistent volunteer, restrained only by Wilson's purposeful delays until Wilson decided it was no longer right or expedient to maintain non-belligerency. As a nation we were in it because we could not stay out of it, and we could not stay out of it because we were only a nation of men. We set out to prove that we were a big power, but in all the world we were the only country that did not know we were one already.

Throughout that year 1916 and the first quarter of 1917 Alfred Eaton, like so many of his contemporaries, pondered his position and postponed a conclusion: slowly but with increasing strength his sympathies went with the Allies so that, for instance, by mid-summer his support of the Allies transcended his support of the Philadelphia Athletics (who had not won the pennant in 1915 and were on the way to losing it again that year). He had a side, if he chose to fight for it; and on the other hand he could stay out of it and do so with dignity, no adverse comments on his courage, and the official approval of his government, his university, and his family. And indeed the Allies no longer encouraged the slapdash enlistments of the adventurous: they wanted, and needed, the nation's full and official support; they did not want the individual volunteers who so quickly became casualties, with a consequent dubious effect on the martial spirit. (There was also the undeniable fact that the adventurous American did not take easily to military discipline, the English accent, the French language, the body lice, the tedium between excitements, the noise, the silences, and all the differences between war as he had imagined it and as it really was.)

For the first time in many years Alfred found that he was thinking about his brother: what would Billy have done? He probably would have gone to the Mexican Border with the Port Johnson company of the Pennsylvania National Guard. But what might he have done a year ago? Would he have joined up with the British? Some of the things he remembered about his brother almost convinced him that Billy would have quit college and gone overseas; but whenever he was about to decide that that was what Billy would have done, he had a final doubt: the athlete would have wanted to go, but in all other respects Billy had been so conventional, and enlisting with the British was so unconventional, that he might very easily have stayed home. Eight years had passed since Billy's death, and Alfred was astonished to find how little he knew about his brother, and how completely unfeeling toward him he had become. He understood now the fullest meaning of the remark, "He might as well be dead." How long it had been since anyone at home had mentioned Billy's name! And the silence was not a deliberate thing, a delicate handling of Samuel Eaton's feelings. It was nothing more than the acceptance of his no longer being alive, and the easy transition from acceptance to forgetting. Now, continuing the transition, it was easy for Alfred to pass from forgetting to remembering to wondering and, finally, to another kind of acceptance, the acceptance that was almost an embrace. It was not at all impossible that if they both had lived, if both were alive today, they could have reached an understanding between themselves that would have been sufficient for a tolerant relationship. Yes, he told himself, that was quite true; and a part of that truth was a new conviction that they would have been closer to each other than Billy would have been to their father.

It was fascinating to discover, too, that the many new and positive things in his life had crowded out his resentment against Billy, which was his own version of his father's resentment against *him*. It was as fascinating as a mathematical problem, made clear on the blackboard by an instructor, for Alfred saw that the one equaled the other, one resentment fairly matched the other resentment; but now that his own resentment was become non-existent by reason of so many more immediate and lively occurrences and relationships in his life, it did not follow that there was any change in his father's attitude. His father was left with the resentment and probably nothing else, certainly nothing more than he had had for the past eight years since Billy's death. It was somewhere in his thinking that for the first time in his life Alfred felt the faint beginnings of pity for his father. He was a long way off from forgiveness, but now forgiveness was possible, now that pity was not only possible but recognizable.

There was too much to forgive for forgiveness to be a consideration as yet. Forgiveness involved not only the generous act of the mind and heart: it involved also a complete denial of what he had suffered under his father, a denial which would also have implied a denial of his sense of injustice, which was the same thing as his sense of justice. The injustice

193

of his father's treatment of him—neglect, contempt, boorishness, cruelty—had been so great and real that it had served Alfred as the bad example of what injustice could mean in the lives of other human beings. To deny the fact of his father's injustice would have been to create false doubt of his own opposition to all that was represented by such injustice; cruelty, coldness, and selfishness (for he vaguely realized that his father's resentful sorrow was a continual act of selfishness).

This new and minute pity was the second part of two essential parts of an understanding of his father. The other part, which was five years old, had been the realization that he had come into possession of the courage to stand up to Samuel Eaton. For five years he had not been afraid of his father; now his father was quite appreciably losing the power to hurt him. But in reaching this position one thing had been lost: not now, and not ever again, would he love his father. He could love the absent Billy as sort of legendary older brother who continued to contribute to the legend by whatever contributions Alfred provided; but Samuel Eaton had finally destroyed Alfred's love for him, and done so not merely by his cruelty but even more thoroughly by the unconscious process of becoming ineffectual. Alfred's kind of pity was not the kind of pity that can create love; it was the kind that is inextricably connected with contempt. But in any event, Alfred would never again be vulnerable to damage by his father, and when he finally reached the willingness to grant complete forgiveness, he would also have reached that state in which forgiveness of his father was a mere intellectual formality.

In the autumn of 1916, his life was filled with other matters, present and reminiscential, that were affairs of the emotions. The belligerent state of the world was so universal that it had less personal application than such other matters as the total disappearance of Norma Budd; the unsatisfied revenge upon the former sophomores who had abused him; the coming social test in the club elections; the rare but still recurring dreams about Victoria Dockwiler; the laying aside of the hated designation of freshman; a girl from Philadelphia; the flattering satisfaction of the approval of Fritz Thornton; a surprising nomination for class president, which eventually went to someone else but gave him a new estimate of his standing among his classmates; the letter from Sally in mid-November.

Sally Eaton was at Miss Titherington's in Bryn Mawr, a school that derived some of its prestige from the nearness of the women's college but was acquiring an increasingly good reputation as each year more of its graduates were accepted for the college. Sally was now seventeen and only mildly enthusiastic about preparing for higher education, but agreeing with her mother that it would be nice if she could prove that she could

194

go to college if she wanted to. Alfred knew very little about his sister that was not to be known from a surface examination. There was a mutual admiration that neither party cared to demonstrate but that both felt was reliable. Their conversations together were almost telegrammatical and not uncritical in content, but they managed to avoid the roughness that a brother and sister inflict upon each other in a friendly relationship.

Sally's note, her briefest to date, read:

Please make arrangements to go home for Thanksgiving. It is vital that you do instead of proving yourself irresistible to the N. Y. debutantes. I am serious—never more so in my *vie*. Love.

He replied immediately, telling her that it was indeed his intention to make himself irresistible to the N. Y. debutantes, and asking her why she was so obscure and mysterious. She answered his note as follows:

I think you are a pig not to do as I ask. I don't ask you many favors and the only reason I am being mysterious is because I have to be. I repeat, this is serious and more vital than all the deb parties in N. Y.

A telegram from Alfred to his sister:

Let me know full details otherwise plans remain same.

A special delivery letter from Sally to Alfred:

I am not able to send you a telegram any time I please. This is a girls' school. Very strict. I still cannot tell you any more, but will say this is a family matter. I am serious.

A telegram from Alfred to Sally:

Will plan to go home for Thanksgiving Day but leave for Newyork following afternoon.

He went to a party on Thanksgiving Eve, stayed in New York that night, and took a morning train to Philadelphia which made connections with a late-morning to Port Johnson. George Fry met him at the station. They shook hands, but George made no conversational effort. "Miss Sally's waiting in the car," he said.

"George, is there anything wrong?" said Alfred.

"Wrong? Who with?"

"There is, isn't there?"

"Don't ask me. I'm just the coachman. Hostler. Shofer. Whatever I am."

"All right, be disagreeable."

The side curtains were up in the rear of the car, and there was a partitioning curtain between the front seats and the rear. Sally was sitting in a corner of the back seat, largely hidden by the old buffalo robe.

"It isn't *that* cold," he said, and kissed her.

"Don't start off by criticizing me, before I have a chance to thank you."

"What's preying on your mind?"

"Wait a minute," she said, and leaned forward. "George, drive towards home but don't go in till I tell you," and then, to Alfred: "I want to talk to you before we get there."

"Everything's all right with me. I want to know what the matter is with you."

"It isn't me. It's Mother."

"Oh."

"I think she ought to see a doctor, but I don't dare tell her that. I'll try to tell the whole thing, just let me tell it my own way and don't interrupt me. When I've finished you can ask questions, but just let me tell it as it comes to me, even if I seem to jump around. Are you agreeable to that?"

"I don't care how I find out, just so I do find out."

"Very well. Last summer when you were visiting your friend Lex Porter you remember I went up to Eaglesmere with the Conways for a month. Then they invited me to stay an extra week and so I wrote to Mother and asked for permission. Oh, and Constance was in Cape May with the O'Briens, you know, from Fort Penn. That's important because in other words all three of us were away. You in the Adirondacks, Constance at Cape May, and I was at Eaglesmere. All three away. Well, I wrote to Mother a little over a week before I was originally supposed to come home. That would give her time to write and give me permission to stay the extra week, or else say I couldn't stay. Well, I got no answer, yes or no. No answer at all. I mailed the letter myself, so I knew it hadn't gone astray, and I put a stamp on it because I remember putting an extra penny stamp on because it was such a long letter. It had a two-cent stamp and a penny stamp. Well, when it got to be time for the end of the original invitation, and no answer from Mother, I said to Mrs. Conway I guess Mother was cross because I hadn't written much before, and that was her way of telling me to come home. But Mrs. Conway said no, it wasn't like Mother to do a thing like that, and she probably was away somewhere with Father, so why didn't I stay till I heard from her? Well, that's what happened. I did stay at the Conways' and then in the middle of the extra week I got a note from Mother saying it was all right. Not a word about why she hadn't answered my letter, and the postmark was dated early that week. In other words, she had been away, but she didn't tell me where or even that she had been. Well, I stayed the rest of the week and then Mr. Conway brought me home because he had to go to Philadelphia and we drove.

"I thought Mother looked perfectly all right when I got home, but the same evening I asked her why she hadn't answered my letter before. I said it put me in an embarrassing position with Mrs. Conway, and some mothers would have just let me go home when I was supposed to. Well, we had a terrible fight about it, and I don't often fight with Mother."

"Where was Father during all this?" said Alfred.

"Please, Alfred. You promised. And we had this fight and she accused me of being a busybody and snooping and all sorts of terrible things like that and then in the same breath she sent me to bed as though I were still ten years old. One minute accusing me of things a child wouldn't think of, and the next minute treating me like a ten-year-old. I did go to bed and I cried, because I'd never seen her like that before. She wasn't a bit like our Mother. She was more like—well, I don't know who, but somebody in a stage play. I didn't know what to do. I mean, it was late at night and if I could have gone somewhere I would have, just for the night but anything to get away from home, I was so upset.

"Well, I finally stopped crying and I went to the bathroom and washed my face and dabbed myself with eau de cologne and went back to bed and started to read a book, just to get my mind off things and hope I'd fall asleep.

"Now I want to prepare you for a shock. There'll be more, but this is the first one. I know you have courage and all those good qualities, but now I'm coming to the bad part and it's only fair to warn you. And please don't, *please* don't say I'm exaggerating or anything like that, not till I've finished. Every word is true, every syllable, and more.

"I was in bed, trying to concentrate on my book, and I heard someone come in the driveway and I knew it was Father, putting the little car away. Then I heard his footsteps crunching on the driveway, coming back to the house, and the front door, and then upstairs to their room. I guess she told him I was home, but I don't know, but I could hear them talking without recognizing any of the words. You know, all the windows open. Then they began talking louder and very angrily. And I heard him say, 'You don't love me, and you never did.' Those were his exact words, and then *she* said, 'You never said a truer word.' This was at the top of their voices. Then there was more that I couldn't make out, and then I heard him leave the house —this was after midnight, remember—and go out and get the little car and drive away.

"I stayed awake the rest of the night, or most of it, thinking she'd come to my room, or wondering whether I ought to go to

197

her, but I didn't go because, well, I couldn't. I didn't think she'd want me. So I stayed in bed and waited, but he never came back all night, and the next morning I went down about nine-thirty and had breakfast and while I was still at the breakfast table Mother came in and said she was sorry she had spoken to me that way the night before, but she was tired and over-wrought. I don't even know what overwrought means, but that's what she said, and I said it was all right and I was glad she didn't think those things of me. But now she had a perfect right to think those things, not that I told her that, but I was a sort of a busybody, and I did say, 'What happened to Father?' 'Father?' she said. 'Yes,' I said. 'Where did he go after he left?' 'Oh, you must be mistaken. Father hasn't been here. He's in Pittsburgh.' In Pittsburgh! 'But I'm sure I heard him come home last night,' I said. 'No, you had a dream. That's my fault,' she said. Well, I wondered whether she wasn't right. Maybe I *had* had a dream. But just then Nellie came in and said, 'Will Mr. Eaton have his breakfast in his room?' And Mother looked at me and then at her and said, 'But he isn't here,' and Nellie said, 'Oh, excuse me, ma'am, I thought I heard him come in last night.' And Mother said no, that either Nellie and I were both dreaming or we'd had a prowler, but Father was still in Pittsburgh on business. 'Go look in the stable,' she said. 'The big car's there, but the Mercer won't be there because Mr. Eaton took it with him and left it in Phila-delphia.' Nellie didn't dare look at me and I didn't dare look at her, because we both knew she wasn't telling the truth.

"The rest of the day she didn't say anything at all about Father, just asked me about the Conways and my visit to them, but not a word about my letter or why she hadn't answered it sooner or anything. Father came home late that afternoon. I wasn't there when he got home, so I don't know what they said to each other, but they both pretended that he had just got home from Pittsburgh and after dinner he took some business papers with him and said he had a lot of work to do. I know what you're going to ask. How were they to each other? Just as though nothing had happened. And I might have believed about the dream but I know Nellie didn't have the same dream, and then he made a slip. He said to me, 'Constance is having a fine time at Cape May. I saw Dr. O'Brien at the Union League yesterday and he said she's probably going to win the girls' singles.' *That* was the day he was supposed to be still in Pitts-burgh, but he forgot, and I didn't say anything.

"And that's all I have time to tell you about that part of it. The next thing was worse, but it's shorter. In September she took me to Philadelphia to buy some clothes for school, and we were spending the night at the Bellevue. We did our shop-ping and we had dinner in that room at the end of the lobby

198

and while we were having dinner a man came over to the table and said, 'Mrs. Eaton? Do you remember me? So-and-So and we met at So-and-So's? Is Mr. Eaton with you?' She said no, and introduced me, and then when he left she was furious. 'Very ungentlemanly to be so persistent,' she said. 'I didn't know him from Adam,' she said. But I didn't believe her. She knew him, and he knew her, and I think what made her angry was that he came to our table."

"Is that all?" said Alfred.

"No it isn't all. I was considering whether to tell you the rest. But I have to. We went to our room and I guess it was about nine o'clock and we were ready for bed and the telephone rang. Mother answered it and I heard her say, 'Miss Eaton? Are you sure you want Miss Eaton?' and then said, 'It's for you.' I took the phone and this man's voice said, 'This is Charles Frolick. I just had the pleasure of meeting you downstairs. Wouldn't you like to see something of the town? You and I?' I did the first thing that came into my mind. Hung up. 'They wanted somebody else with the same name as ours,' I said. And suddenly Mother burst into tears. I won't try to tell you all she said. Bad mother. Didn't deserve such lovely children. Made a mess of her life. Then she stopped, just as suddenly as she started. She took the receiver off the hook and asked to be connected with Mr. Frolick. Mr. Frolick, mind you. She knew who had called me. Then she said into the phone: 'Charles, this is Martha. I'm saying this very calmly. Don't you ever do that again. Don't ever speak to my daughter again. That's all.' She put the receiver back on the hook and told me that if he ever spoke to me or tried to see me, to let her know instantly. Then she said, 'Think the worst things you can about me, because they're true. I can't blame anybody but myself.' 'Didn't you ever love Father?' I said. 'Yes, and I always tried to even after I knew I was in love with someone else, not Charles Frolick,' she said. Then she asked me not to tell you or Constance and said she hoped I'd be happier in life than she was, and thanked me and so on, about my being very young to learn these things. She was calm, very nice, but after we went to bed and she finally got to sleep I had to wake her up several times because she was having such awful nightmares. And now only one more thing to tell you."

"What's that?"

"This." She handed him a folded envelope and he took out the notepaper and read: "Dear Sally: You were quite naughty to tell your mother it was I who telephoned at the Bellevue that evening. If you expect to become a woman of the world you must learn to be discreet. I shall, however, forgive you if you will drop in for tea and a chat during your Thanksgiving or Christmas vacation. You are a most interesting young lady as one could observe through watching you as I did. Sincerely yours, Charles Frolick."

"Did you notice the date? Then do. That was when I first wrote and asked you to come home for Thanksgiving."

"I see. Describe him for me."

"Well, I only saw him once. He's older, not as old as Father but not young. Middle-aged, I guess you'd call him. Not as tall as you are, but heavier. Dark hair and a dark moustache."

"Can I keep this? It has his address and I want to have tea and a chat with him. Or at least a chat."

"That's what I was hoping," she said. "I never hated anybody before, but I hate him."

"Yes, he's a hateful customer," said Alfred.

"I wish Mother knew you as well as I do. But she's afraid you'd be ashamed of her. She'd die if she thought I told you all this. But she didn't know about you and Norma."

"Norma Budd? What about Norma? Do you know the last time I saw her? Over a year ago. I don't even know where she is."

"Is that the truth?"

"No, just about a year. But I don't know where she is, I haven't heard from her."

"Oh, I thought you often saw her in New York."

"Not since before last Christmas and we went to the theater. Norma isn't interested in me, and I'm not interested in her, if it comes down to that. She was nice to me when I was a kid, but she goes around with men twice my age. I know, because I've seen her with them."

"Oh. I was wrong. I'm sorry. And I ought to apologize to Norma for what I was thinking."

"Well, all right, if you ever catch up with her."

"I'm glad, really, because I like Norma, but I don't like her for you. She was too old for Harry Van Peltz, and he's older than you are."

"You were going to tell me something about Harry and her one time. What was it?"

"Oh, I guess it's all right to tell you. Peter told me, poor Peter. Poor Victoria. Do you still love Victoria, Alfred?"

"I always will."

"But you'll be able to love someone else."

"Yes. But you were talking—"

"Peter told me that Harry and Norma did other things besides just kissing."

"Well, I doubt it, but if they did, it was their own business, not that I'm saying anything against Peter."

"Or me?"

"Well, it would be against you, wouldn't it? I think you were just wrong, or Peter was. Exaggerating."

"I believe Peter," said Sally.

Alfred looked at his sister. "You were in love with him, weren't you?"

"I loved him so much that I couldn't even tell him. I still do. That's why I can't be in love with Lex."

"Lex Porter? Why would you be in love with Lex? You've only seen him about three times. Last year at the Yale game, here last spring, and the time in New York."

"I didn't say I should be or wanted to be. I said I couldn't be."

"Oh. Then it's Lex that wants you to be?"

"He says he does."

"Then he does. But the son of a gun would never tell *me*."

"Good for him."

"You bet, good for him. The son of a gun," he said. "Well, here we are at our vast palatial estate. You know, Sal, I used to think we were rich. We weren't *supposed* to think that. Vulgar. But I thought it. I don't any more, not since I've seen some of those places around New York. Lex Porter's Uncle Fritz, he's building a house on his place. Not to live in, mind you. Just to play court tennis in. Two hundred thousand dollars. Tell you later."

Martha Eaton came out to greet them. She was trying to hide her anxiety, but she was unsuccessful, while Sally and Alfred were completely successful in pretending they had not been discussing her. They knew they were successful because her anxiety disappeared after their first study of their faces. "Welcome home to the prodigal son," she said.

"I hope you didn't kill a calf. I want turkey, not liver. We get enough leather-and-bacon at college," said Alfred. To his astonishment his father came out.

"Hello, Father."

"Hello, Alfred. Put on a little weight, haven't you?" It was, for Samuel Eaton, a cordial greeting.

"Yes, some. One eighty-five. You haven't lost any."

"I don't get enough exercise."

"Your father's at his desk morning, noon and night."

"At noon?" said Alfred. He patted his own middle. "He doesn't look as though he missed lunch."

"Now, now," said Martha. "But we're all going to have a delicious big turkey as soon as you wash up."

"Where's Constance?" said Alfred.

"There's Constance," said Sally.

Alfred looked at his younger sister, now standing in the doorway. "Why, she's pretty."

201

"You've never said that about me," said Sally.

"I don't know that it's very complimentary the way he said it about me. Like as if it was impossible. Hello, Society Boy." Constance presented her cheek for his kiss.

He took her hand and kissed the back of it. "In high society we only do this."

"Oh, stop it, Alfred. Give me a kiss."

"Both of you stop it and come in out of the cold," said Martha. Her self-confidence was returning and she gave Sally a rewarding smile.

"I thought of getting tickets for the Penn-Cornell game," said Samuel.

"But I persuaded him not to. Then we wouldn't have seen anything of you, and·do you care who wins the Penn-Cornell game?"

"No, just as long as it's Cornell," said Alfred.

"Oh, now, you have a lot of friends at Penn," said Martha. "All those boys at Knox. Didn't most of them go to Penn?"

"Those that couldn't go to Princeton," said Alfred.

"You *are* Society Boy. I've met some charming boys from Penn," said Constance. "St. Anthony's is just as good as anything they have at Princeton."

"St. Anthony's is all right," said Samuel Eaton.

"All right? I prefer them to the Ivy Club crowd," said Constance.

"Crowd? Who do you know in Ivy?" said Alfred. "And where did you meet them?"

"There was a swarm of them at Cape May last summer—"

"A swarm of them?" said Alfred.

"And I had the *great* pleasure of beating one of them in the mixed doubles. *My* partner was from St. Anthony's. Seven-five, six-one. If you don't believe me I'll show you the cup."

"I've seen it," said Alfred. "You could use it for an eyecup."

"That was for girls' singles. You haven't seen my mixed-doubles cup because it wasn't here when you went back to school. And I have another cup you never even—"

"Constance has been playing very well, but now let's give Alfred a chance to go upstairs," said Martha.

"Would you be interested in a cocktail?" said Samuel Eaton.

"Why, yes," said Martha.

"I meant Alfred."

"Sure."

"Any special preference?" said Samuel Eaton.

"Yes, a Manhattan."

"I'm glad to see you don't go in for some of those fancy ladies' drinks."

"Fancy ladies, Father?" said Sally.

"You stop that. I don't like that one bit. It wasn't funny," said Samuel Eaton.

"What did she say?" said Constance. "I missed it."

"You don't miss much," said Samuel Eaton. "Now you remember, Sally. No more of that kind of talk."

"I *only* said something very mild, Father. Not really risqué."

"That's what you call very mild."

Alfred returned from his bathroom visit and noticed immediately that the drinks had not been served and that the moment he entered the room his mother rose and took a cocktail glass and held it out. His father made the cocktails slowly and slowly poured Martha's drink. "Am I not to have a full-sized one?" she said.

Her husband filled her glass so that she had to bend down to take the first sips, rather than risk spilling the drink by raising her glass.

"When can I start having cocktails?" said Constance.

"Never, if I can help it," said her father.

"That's not fair. When was Mother allowed to? Mother, how old were you when—"

"About forty-two," said Samuel Eaton.

"Forty-three, to be exact," said Martha. "I never drank cocktails until two years ago."

"Yes, *just* two years ago," said her husband.

"Well, I'm not going to wait that long," said Constance.

"No, I guess it doesn't make much difference *when* you *start*," said Samuel Eaton.

"What your Father means is when you stop is what's important. Isn't that right, dear?"

"That's exactly right, dear. Exactly right. Knowing when to stop is very important, not only about cocktails, but damn near everything else in this life."

"But how about when to start?" said Constance.

"Some things should never start. Let's go in, shall we?" said Samuel Eaton.

"I haven't quite finished?" said Martha, in a semi-questioning tone.

"All right, we'll wait. Alfred? A heel-tap?"

"Thanks, yes."

The heel-tap for Alfred finished off the contents of the shaker, Samuel Eaton placed his own empty glass on the table and stood waiting and watching while Martha finished her drink. There was not much to finish, but she drank it thirstily, and then set down the glass and rose to her feet in a simultaneous action. It was a nervously decisive action, as though she, and not her husband, had been the one who had been impatient to go in to dinner, and the others had been

203

holding her up. But there was also something about her performance that brought to Alfred's mind the word forlorn.

There was a party that night at the Idle Hour Club. Alfred took the Mercer, did his duty dances, and came home. He was home well before midnight, but his father and mother apparently had gone to bed. He made himself a turkey sandwich and was eating it and drinking a glass of milk when his mother pushed open the swinging door of the butler's pantry.

"Oh, good, you found it. Oh, no, you didn't," she said. "I made some sandwiches for you. They're in the bottom of the icebox, wrapped in waxed paper. Oh, well."

"Why don't you have one?"

"Oh, no. No thanks." She held her bathrobe close to her body and frankly yawned without putting her hand to her mouth. Her eyes were cloudy and she was focusing weakly. "I wanted to talk to you, but—" she interrupted herself with a wide open yawn. "Excuse *me*. I was asleep."

"I'm tired, too."

"You must be. You must have had to get up very early. And we don't really rest on trains. I don't believe in Darwin."

"What?"

"Arthur Darwin? *Charles* Darwin. I don't believe we can be descended from monkeys. I could never get any real sleep except in a bed. I couldn't sleep on the ground, or in a tree. I wonder if I ought to have a sip of some beer. There's some out in the old icebox on the back porch. Would you like some beer?"

"Not on top of this milk."

"No, I guess not. It's too late for anything else. Your father locks up the wine and liquor. On account of George Fry, of course. We haven't spoken to George, but there's been some whiskey disappeared, and we're sure it wasn't Nellie or Josephine. Of course it would be so easy for anyone to just walk in and help themselves. We've had those men repairing the driveway and last month, the tree surgeons. And delivery men. Wouldn't you like a bottle of beer, Alfred?"

"I'll get it."

He went out and brought in a bottle of beer, opened it and poured a full glass. She drank three sizable gulps and then put down the glass without releasing her grip on it. "It isn't very satisfactory, but it's better than nothing. I could have fixed you a nice hot toddy if your father hadn't locked up everything."

"I'll sleep without it."

"I know. It's wonderful to be young. Well, sleep as late as you like. When are you leaving? I wish you weren't going back to New York tomorrow. I never see you any more, dear." She reached over and put her hand on his cheek. "Alfred. Nice, kind Alfred. You know what it's like, don't you?"

"Yes, I guess I do."

"I'm sorry."

"There's nothing to be sorry for, Mother."

"I was never much help. But maybe you had to learn early. Maybe you wouldn't have turned out so well. I don't know. A lot I don't know. I never had much brains to speak of."

"Don't you want to finish your beer?"

"No, I don't want to finish my beer. I hate beer. I hate the smell of it. I'd hate to tell you what it reminds me of. Those brewery horses, they used to stop in the middle of the street and out would come that long—" She stopped and stared at him. "Did I say that? Did I just say something awful?"

"No, not awful."

"But I did say it. What's happened to me? I used to be nice. But I don't even remember what made me change."

"That's all right, Mother."

"What's all right?"

"You are. Don't be hard on yourself. I know a lot more than you think I do, and you're still my mother."

"I don't know what could change that. I *had* you. I was five hours in labor having you, so I know that much. I know I'm your mother. But what was the other thing you said? You know something else?"

"For years and years."

"You're not *old* enough to know anything for years and years, Alfred. You've only been alive nineteen years. Weeks and weeks. Or months and months. But not years and years. You haven't lived that long. Don't be superior, Alfred. Not with me. I'm your mother. I was five hours in labor having you. And I was nine hours with Billy. Or maybe it was the other way around. No. Five with you, and nine with Billy."

"Let's go to bed, shall we? I'm dead tired."

"So am I. Would you like some brandy?"

"It's all locked up, isn't it?"

"Except."

"Except what?"

"He forgot."

"What did he forget?"

"The sideboard. Come with me, I'll show you."

He followed her to the diningroom and she went to the sideboard and picked up a cut-glass decanter.

"Empty," he said.

She nodded. "I thought I left some, but I guess I drank it all up."

"Tonight?"

"Oh, sure. There wasn't much. This much." She held up forefinger over thumb, separated by two inches. "I would have saved some if I'd known you'd want it."

"I didn't really want any."

"You'd think he'd leave one bottle out for you. What if you'd brought home some friends?"

"Oh, well, I didn't, so it's all right."

"Give me your arm and we'll retire dignified, Mrs. Samuel Eaton and her handsome son Raymond Alfred Eaton, named after Raymond Johnson of Port Johnson, Pennsylvania. He loved you."

"I loved him." They began the ascent of the stairs.

"He loved *me*, too."

"So do I."

"Even when I'm like this?"

"Of course."

"Are you sure?"

"Yes."

"Because I'm like this an awful lot of the time. But I used to be nice. I was nice for a long time."

"You still are."

"No, don't say that. I like to remember when I was nice, and if you say that, then I was no different then than I am now. And I *was* different. I was nice."

She opened her door and they could hear the heavy, open-mouthed breathing of the husband and father; each breath taking a long time from the beginning of inspiration to the end of expiration, and followed by a momentary silence as though the sleeping man were gathering strength for the next effort. "Listen," she said.

They stood silent for a few seconds.

"Don't you notice anything?" she said.

"What?"

"Sadness."

Alfred listened again. "By God, you're right," he said.

"Forgive him, Alfred."

Alfred nodded.

She kissed her son, patted his cheek, and went in and closed the door.

The son mounted the steps to his room and lay on his bed and wept in pity; something he had never done before, something he had never really known before.

They all saw him off at the train the next day: his father and mother, his sister Sally, his sister Constance, and George Fry. He was $50 richer from his father, $50 richer from his mother, and the money would come in handy in New York. But he had not been concerned about money, and so the extra $100 had not relieved a pressure. But a pressure had been created during his brief visit, a strange one because it had come new at the age of nineteen, had not existed in all those years. Yet it was not unpleasant in spite of its strangeness: for the first time, because of the revelations of the past twenty-four hours and to no small degree because of the sight of his parents and sisters and George on the station platform, Alfred Eaton appreciated the strength of family feeling.

In Philadelphia he checked his kitbag at Broad Street Station and took a taxicab to the address in Frolick's letter to Sally. It was a brick house in South Twenty-first Street. The brass hardware was polished, the marble stoop was scrubbed, the windows were clean. He rang the doorbell and almost instantaneously the door was opened by a man of forty or more, wearing an expertly cut brown suit, brown necktie, and a starched collar that was not so tall as the prevailing mode. He had a dark brown moustache, small and recently trimmed, and oiled-down dark brown hair. "What can I do for you?" he said.

"Are you Mr. Frolick?"

"I am, but if you're from the University, I've taken all the ads I'm going to. Sorry."

"I'm not from the University, at least not Penn, but I want to talk to you."

"I was just putting on my coat. What do you want?"

"May I come in?"

"No," said Frolick.

"Well, I'll come in anyway," said Alfred, and pushed the door hard and quickly.

"What the hell do you—"

"I'm going to give you a beating. Like this." Alfred punched the man in the stomach and as he bent forward, struck him with a left hook to the right ear.

"You son of a bitch," said the man, and fought back. They fought in the space between the front door and the foot of the stairs, entirely in the hall. The man fought back with some skill, but he was soon winded by the pace of the blows, and Alfred, in better condition and with the advantage of twenty years, seeing that the man was out of breath, changed from pummeling tactics to boxing. He punched the man's nose and mouth until they bled together, and opened a cut over the man's left eye.

"I quit," said the man, and retreated and sat down on one of the lower steps. "Who the hell are you? What did I ever do to you?"

"My name is Eaton, E, a, t, o, n. If you ever speak or write to any member of my family again, I'll kill you." He went over and slapped the man's face back and forth. "And I may do this again just for luck, you scurvy son of a bitch."

"And if you ever come here again, I'll shoot you."

"Just for that, how's this?" Alfred slapped him again until he went to sleep. In the hall mirror Alfred saw that he had been cut on the cheek, probably by Frolick's diamond ring. Knuckles on his right hand were bruised and one was beginning to swell. He straightened his collar and tie and went out and after a long wait got a taxicab on Market Street.

"You a University boy?" said the driver.

"Yep. How did you know?"

"I could tell that, easy. You been celebrating?"

"Yep."

"What frat are you in?"

"Frat? Oh, I go to Yale."

"Yale, uh?"

"Good old Yale," said Alfred.

"The honest truth, I'm not much for these Penn lads. If there'd of been two of you I never would of stopped."

"But you'd have stopped for two Yale men, wouldn't you?"

"If I could of told the difference, maybe."

"Always stop for a Yale man. We're all gentlemen there, you know."

"You're feelin' pretty good."

"My dear good fellow, I never felt better in my life."

In his exhilaration he gave the man a seventy-cent tip, and he wished he could go immediately and report the episode to his new girl; but it was not a story he could tell her, and oddly enough, although she was a Philadelphia girl, at the moment she was in New York. He was even doubtful about telling Lex Porter. He could have told him if Sally alone had been involved, but secretly he had always felt that his mother was a little *nicer* than Mrs. Porter, who, innocent victim or not, had been mixed up in divorce; and he wantd to continue to have everyone else think his mother lived a quiet, unreproachful life in an uninteresting Pennsylvania town. He was sure that the beating he had given Frolick would keep the fellow away from the Eaton women, and that if Frolick should try to seek revenge it would be upon him and not through his mother or sister.

In Broad Street Station he looked at his watch and compared it with the station clocks: the whole business of Frolick, the ride out to his house, the fight, the ride back, had taken less than an hour. He bought a ticket on the Pullman car, boarded the train and went directly to the washroom to change his blood-spattered collar and shirt and necktie. He now realized for the first time that he had not followed his own original plan of attack on Frolick; he had fought the fight without removing his topcoat. There was some blood on the coat, but his suit was spotless. It had been his intention to carry his topcoat over his arm, regardless of the weather (which turned out fair). But in the excitement of anticipation of this first fight of its kind he had forgotten the details of preparation. With a younger man, equally matched, the topcoat could have made a difference in freedom of movement and his wind. It could have been a costly oversight. And now, sitting in the Pullman chair, he realized something else: that from the time of the ride with Sally until this second of seating himself in the railway car, he never once had considered the possibility of losing the fight, of receiving a beating instead of administering it. Once again a new experience; totally unlike football or the fist-fights of prep school; a murderous fury that disregarded the instinct of self-preservation and the intellectual exercise of caution. And now he began to feel sick, and was sick in the Pullman toilet. When he came out of the toilet the porter was all understanding: "Young gentleman took too much plum pudding, I reckon. We stand out on the platform and get the cool fresh air. Be good as new by Trenton."

The plum pudding and the Pullman washroom provided the explanation for his color and the scratch on his cheek, which he told Lex had been caused by his shaving on the train.

"A likely story, I don't *think*," said Lex. "You were in a fight. Who'd you fight with? Your father?"

"Not this time," said Alfred. "Some day I'll tell you. It's too long now."

"Too embarrassing, you mean."

"That, too."

"We'll put a piece of sticking plaster on the cut. I'll introduce you as my friend from Heidelberg."

"No, not Heidelberg. Not *this* year, thank you."

He saw the blond, blond, blond girl from Philadelphia (who was not really his girl) every chance he got. Her name was Clemmie Shreve and her skin was whiter than anyone's. When someone was speaking to her she held her mouth partly open and she moved her lips as though she were in chorus with the speaker, and her eyes so blue moved from the speaker's eyes to his mouth, but not missing anything else: she was a beauty and knew it as a boy would know that he played good tennis, as fun and a social asset but not in itself a guarantee of social success. She was trying to be liked by the other girls, but after the startled pleasure of a first look at her beauty they decided singly but as though by agreement to call her a pretty little thing and concede nothing else in her favor. She was the prettiest girl in New York, and she came from Philadelphia. She was born with all the little wisdoms: a slope-chinned young man behind thick lenses and wearing his uncle's tails came away from a dance with her with a memory, not knowing that her beauty had made him *be* a charming boy and that she had recognized the transformation. It was her debutante year and even without the advice of her mother she would have avoided a firm alliance with any of the young men who were ready to announce their engagement or elope, or hang themselves. But she had shown a willingness to be with Alfred alone: a soda at Brennan's when she was supposed to be shopping; a soda at Acker's on her way home from a music lesson; a single football game, an early breakfast on a Far Hills house party. There had been no talk of love, and no reason for her special favors to him, but he knew that she liked something in him that she did not find in anyone else, and for whatever it was he was patiently grateful. There were juniors and seniors who were reconciled to less.

The frequent mention of her name had indicated to Lex Porter that his friend was among the smitten, and Alfred had told him of his small progresses. "I know she likes me, but I don't know why," said Alfred.

"Do you have to know why? If it's any help to you, I know why she doesn't like me."

"Doesn't she?"

"No. She said to me, 'Don't you ever hold still?' I wasn't moving a muscle, and said so. 'I know,' she said, 'but you're ready to spring.'"

"*Were* you ready to spring?"

"Well, she's a God damn pretty girl. I've sprung at some that weren't half as pretty. So there's a helpful hint if it's any good to you."

"Thanks, buddy. Incidentally, damn smart of her to know you *were* ready to spring."

"Say, I never thought of that," said Lex. "And damn smart of *you* to know it was smart of *her*. Maybe that's what you've got to offer. Headwork, boy. Headwork."

"You go after the kangaroos. That's the law of natural selection."

He danced with Clementine Shreve that night. "My hand shook when I thought of you," he said, explaining the adhesive plaster.

"But Alfred, you shave every day, don't you? And you've never cut yourself before."

"This was to be a special occasion. I wanted to know when I could see you during Christmas."

"I'm arranging that. It'll be as often as I can. Is that all right?"

"It has to be, I guess."

"One afternoon, all by ourselves. That is, between lunch and tea. I promise that. Is that all right?"

"Fine. Fine."

210

"And you'll go to all the Philadelphia parties, won't you? I can see you then."

"I'll go to whatever ones you're going to. Will you send me a list?"

"I'll send you a list, and the day we'll be alone. Oh, it's Mr. Saltonstall, from Boston. Goodbye, Alfred. Well, Mr. Saltonstall . . ."

"My name is Codman, if that's all right with you. That's Saltonstall dipping."

She winked at Alfred, and whirled away with Codman.

During the Thanksgiving-to-Christmas doldrums, which occurred as usual in spite of the increasing consciousness of the war, Alfred had a letter from Tom Rothermel:

Dear Alfred:

I am writing to you to request a favor from you. If, however, you are not willing to grant same, please do not think I shall hold a "grudge" against you as it is a business matter. I was hoping to see you last summer, but you were away while I was home; and I was away while you were at home. You no doubt will recall that in Mr. Johnson's will the unpaid portion of a debt owed to him by my father, Mr. Jonas B. Rothermel, was forgiven. The amount of money owed to Mr. Johnson's estate would have been $600.00.

You will no doubt be of the opinion that I could have taken this matter up with your father, Mr. Samuel Eaton, or perhaps your mother, Mrs. Eaton, but I do not believe that your father knows me from Adam, although your mother often passes the time of day, addressing me by name. Therefore, I wish to "sound you out" in order to enlist your support. If not, let us both forget the matter.

To put it in a nut-shell I wish to borrow a sum of money in order to assist with my education at Penn State. Like you, I am a sophomore in the School of the Liberal Arts. Thanks to the kind generosity of Mr. Johnson, I was able to enter State College in Autumn 1915 with sufficient funds to more than cover the necessary expenses of a four-year course leading to an A. B. That was in addition to the money saved by my father during his lifetime. As you no doubt have been informed, my father also saved sufficient funds to pay for the education of my sisters. They are graduates of Normal, down in West Chester, teaching in the Port Johnson public schools. They have also contributed toward my education.

Unfortunately, following the death of my father, the late Jonas B. Rothermel, my mother contracted an illness, which has eaten up a large portion of the sum set aside for my education. I am therefore compelled to seek the loan of funds, or else leave college in order to earn money to enable me to return at some future date. My mother was forced to undergo an operation for gall stones, removing 154 stones and she is still under doctor's care. My two sisters have been supporting her and paying the doctor bills, but I have also felt it my duty to use some of my college money. It is now at such a low ebb that if I do not succeed in securing a loan, I shall be unable to return to State after Xmas.

With your kind permission I shall show you what my expenses amount to for one year. Incidental fee, 1st semester, $18.00; second semester, $17.00. Gym and medical fee, 1st semester, $5.00; 2nd semester, $5.00. Library fee, 1st semester, $1.50; 2nd semester, $1.50. Damage deposit covering both semesters, $1.00. Board, $3 per week for 36 weeks. Room rent, $45 per 36 weeks. Furniture for room, $16. Uniform for military drill (without shoes) $12. This comes to $230.00 but does not include railroad fares to and from State College, Pa., to Port Johnson, Pa., It also does not include entertainment, smoking (pipe tobacco; pipe was given to me for h. s. graduation present); fraternity dues, subscriptions, etc., which I have tried to curtail but come to close to $75, including laundry.

I am a member of Phi Delta Delta, which you no doubt never heard of as it is a local, although we have petitioned a certain national. Our house is one of the smaller ones here at State, but has the advantage of fraternity life without entailing large expense. We were chartered four years ago, therefore do not have wealthy alumni as most of our alumni have not begun to earn big money yet. Many fellows in my position refuse to join a fraternity, but I do not regret it. Much to my surprise, I pay less rent in a boarding-house with a roommate although I sleep in a dormitory with 16 fraternity brothers, but you get used to it.

Perhaps you are wondering why I am writing to you? It is because I intend to write to your father for a loan. As he is older and has not been to college in many years, I wish to get you acquainted with the finances here, hoping you will corroborate my figures when I write to Mr. Eaton. One disadvantage of State is very little opportunity for jobs up here for students who wish to work their way through. However, we do not pay tuition at State, so that is an advantage.

I would not like to give up my education and have enjoyed nearly every minute of my stay here and if I have to quit and get a job I shall always have very pleasant memories upon which to look back. But I must act quickly or else notify the college that I am unable to return after Xmas. I am going to tell your father that I will do any work summers at the mill to repay the loan or any other method he suggests. I apologize for such a long letter, but I wished to give you all the data in case your father requests same. If he will loan me $150 for the rest of this year (till June) and $150 a year junior and senior years, I can manage to stay for my degree.

I wish to thank you for your kindness in reading my letter. I will ask permission to call upon your father during Xmas. In closing, best regards,

Yours sincerely,
Tom Rothermel

Alfred read the letter while Lex Porter was in his room. "Do you think Princeton is expensive?" he said.

"It's too damn expensive. Why?" said Lex.

"Read this, then you'll *know* it's expensive."

"All of it? You want me to read all of it?" said Lex.

"Yes, read the whole thing."

Lex read the letter, writen in ink on Phi Delta Delta stationery, which was thin and cheap so that the handwriting was almost as heavy on one side as the other. It was slow reading, and at the end of it Lex said: "Who is this guy?"

"From my home town. A friend of mine. I've never known Tom to have less than two jobs, and he's been working since he was—I don't know—six or seven."

"What are you going to do?"

"I think I'll send him some money. I don't want him to ask my father for anything. He might turn him down."

"How much are you going to send him?"

"Well, I got a hundred dollars I wasn't expecting at Thanksgiving, and I'll get a wad at Christmas. I think I'll send him a hundred and fifty. He's a good egg."

"You know, I've never given anybody anything in my life? I haven't. Nobody ever asked me for anything, and this is the first year I ever had a checking account."

"I know."

"Well, I'd like to give this fellow something. Just to see what it feels like. Is that O. K.?"

"I don't know how it's going to feel to you, but I have a pretty good idea how it'll feel to him."

"It's a hell of a note, you know. Money being spent on me and I don't give a shit about college, but this guy, it's the biggest thing in his life."

"All right. Take down his name and address and send him a cheque."

"Oh, no. I'll give it to you and you include it in your cheque."

"No sir. You don't know Tom. This is a loan, a business proposition. Whatever you send him, he'll pay you back. I know that, and that's the only way he'd take it. Maybe you won't get it back for three or four years, but I know Tom."

"I'd rather *give* him something."

"So would I, but we can't."

"O. K."

Alfred's note:

Dear Tom: I am glad you wrote me as my father has been spending a lot of time away on business and might not get your letter. If it's agreeable to you, I would like to lend you $150 to carry you through this year, and you may repay it when you are able. I would also like to tell you that when I

213

reach 21 in 1918 I will come into some money from my grandfather through a trust fund. I will be glad to lend you $150 during your junior year and the same amount in senior year, which you may also repay when you are able. My grandfather would have preferred to give you this money, but I know you would prefer it as a loan. I therefore inclose check for $150 and will send you check for junior year next September. If you would like to increase the amount of the loan please let me know. I hope this reaches you in plenty of time.

As ever,
Alfred Eaton

Lex's note to Tom Rothermel:

Dear Mr. Rothermel:
I enclose check for $100. Read your letter to Alfred Eaton. He is the best guy I ever knew and you are lucky to have him for a friend & so am I. Pay this back when you can. Take as long as you like.

Yrs truly,
A. Thornton Porter

A note from Tom Rothermel to Alfred:

Dear Alfred:
I have started ten letters to you but tore them all up. I thought I could never express how much I thank you for your assistance, but I was re-reading Mr. Porter's letter and I guess you didn't see it before, so I am sending it to you because it expresses my sentiments. I guess they don't come any better than you, but Mr. Porter must be a close second. Please accept my sincere thanks. I hope to do so at Xmas in person.

Yours sincerely,
Tom Rothermel

From Tom Rothermel to Lex Porter:

Dear Mr. Porter:
To say that I was surprised by your generosity is putting it mildly. My first idea was to return your check but on second thought I considered it in the spirit in which it was given, namely, generosity coupled with you being a friend of Alfred, therefore feeling friendly toward another friend of his.
Thanks to you both I shall remain a student at Penn State for the full four year course which has a great meaning to my family and myself as my father and sisters worked hard to contribute to my education only to have my mother contract an illness which forced her to undergo an operation for gall stones.
I shall make every effort to repay the *loan* at the earliest possible date. In the meantime I remain,

Yours gratefully,
Thomas P. Rothermel

It is quite impossible to be orderly about the future. A few days before going home for Christmas, Alfred, who liked to be orderly and was indeed more orderly than most of his contemporaries, planned his vacation with some care. The easiest to plan were the events for which invitations had been accepted or regretted. That was bookkeeping of an elementary kind. Somewhat more complicated were the arrangements by which he hoped to get more time alone with Clemmie Shreve, and there were details to work out in connection with the two-day visit of Lex Porter to Port Johnson, which was on the schedule by Lex's request and quite transparently had something to do with Sally Eaton. It was also going to be necessary to see Tom Rothermel and to see at least a little of other, closer friends, if only to put the quietus on the talk that he was deserting Port Johnson for New York. Alfred had heard such talk from his sisters, and he admitted the truth in it, for after Princeton, New York, and the kind of living the Porters and Thorntons had opened up to him, Port Johnson offered little excitement or fun. The more serious truth was that he could not go to a Port Johnson party without first noticing the absence of Victoria Dockwiler and Peter Van Peltz. He always got over their absence, but before getting over it he had first to feel it, and regardless of the knowledge beforehand, he was always unprepared for the quick sense of loss. In a curious way that he vaguely but as yet only vaguely understood, the sense of loss was provided by the absence of Victoria and Peter jointly. They had begun to merge as a symbol comprising two units. They were two persons of beauty, never to be anything but beautiful, never to be seen again by the eye but never to be totally invisible, whether in the bright light of a ballroom or the pitch dark of his bedroom under the roof. Their presence *in absentia* was a serious truth, and yet it was not a problem since he did not consider it to be a problem. To Alfred Eaton at that stage of his growth a problem was a situation in which a solution, however drastic or simple or impossible, was implied. Since there was, he felt, no solution to the reappearances of Victoria and Peter, he was facing not a problem but a recurrent condition. As defense against the recurrences he avoided those other conditions, such as social gatherings, where the recurrences would most likely come, and the grander life as represented by Lex Porter's family made for a convenient avoidance of the troublous occasions of the now placid faces of Victoria and Peter. He was chilled by their unity and fearful of their placid faces, because one of his soul's secrets was not merely the loss by death of a girl he loved, but the loss of her love for him and his love for her through the new love she had created with Peter, which Peter could share and he could not. Always Peter was with her, she was beside Peter, and the calm of their faces was mutually of such precise degree that Alfred was sure that no earthly ecstasy could help him and anyone else attain it. Dreams asleep could not be helped, but he could stay away from the Idle Hour, and he did so.

But during this vacation, he had some reason to believe, his father would improvise some opportunity to talk about his future as it related to the mill. Alfred's relationship with the people of the town thereby became a factor in his vacation plans: he had no desire to take over from his father, but who else was there? There was no one. The easy solution, Alfred knew, was to sell the mill now, when it was making huge profits, but if that also meant his father's relinquishing control it would be the end of his father's life in the two meanings of the term. The only acceptable substitute for his own indispensable self, in the view of Samuel Eaton, was his son. Alfred could hear the arguments in advance. He knew the arguments, he knew his reluctance, and he knew that the only answer he could give was the positive one. It made no difference whether he agreed out of a sense of duty, or because of flattery, or the promise of power—the result would be the same. He had no inclination to study medicine, to play the violin, to paint pictures, or to preach the gospel. He had no honorable reason to refuse except the most honorable one of all: that with his almost lack of interest in the mill he might very easily ruin it. But his father would not consider that an argument. Alfred would go into the business, have his ups and downs, and in twenty-five years pass it on to *his* sons. Alfred played with a scene in which he would suggest that one of the girls might marry a Lehigh man, but in the scene his father said: "I don't want a metallurgist, I don't want an engineer. I *hire* those men. I want someone to run the whole God damn show, and I mean you." And so he would go home for Christmas vacation and be polite to Port Johnson citizens, and agree to go into the mill after college or after the war. And so the orderliness of that much of his life would be maintained without regard for his own wishes in that matter or in the larger matter of what to do with his chance on earth.

But even more disturbing was his share of the responsibility of "doing something about" his mother. So far he had done nothing (other than to give Frolick a beating). He had written her a few chatty letters, trying to pretend that he attached no significance to her behavior in the kitchen. He had been unable to correspond freely with Sally, since her outgoing and incoming letters were subject to faculty scrutiny. He was minutely reassured by the fact that George Fry had not written him; he had a hunch that if things had worsened, George Fry would have communicated with him or, in extreme circumstances, come to Princeton. Alfred, who had been looking eagerly for developments and signs of developments that confirmed his maturing, now saw that he had all but become the head of the family, what with the defense of his mother's and sister's honor, the impending assumption of control of the family business and placing himself in the position of decision-maker and keeper of secrets. Men of fifty-four dropped dead; there was really not so much that separated his present status from the real thing. In the final days before college closed he directed his thoughts more and more to the sheer pleasure of Clemmie Shreve. But it is quite impossible to be orderly about the future.

At noon of the day before college was to close Alfred was in his room, making a final selection of the suits and haberdashery that he would take home, while waiting for Lex Porter to come and join him for lunch. Lex entered the room, closed the door behind him, and stood with his back to the door.

"We haven't got all day, bud," said Alfred.

"You never read the New York papers, do you?"

"Hardly ever, why?"

"I've got some bad news. It's pretty *bad,* Alfred. If you want me to I'll wait out in the hall."

"No, what is it?"

"Here," said Lex, handing him the newspaper.

Alfred took it and read aloud:

"Society tragedy. Police Find 2 Dead of Bullet Wounds from Same Pistol. The bodies of two socially prominent persons found dead of pistol wounds were identified yesterday as Miss Norma Budd, about 23, of London, England, and Joseph W. Waterford, 36, insurance broker and former Yale football star. Death was caused by bullets from the same .32 caliber revolver, under circumstances leading police to announce that Mr. Waterford fired the shot which killed Miss Budd and then turned the weapon on himself, taking his own life. The bodies, fully clothed, were found in the studio apartment of Karl Koenig, portrait artist, a friend and college classmate of the dead man.

"According to police, Mr. Koenig had last seen the couple on Tuesday afternoon when they called on him at the West 10th Street studio. The artist left for Boston later on the same afternoon, returning shortly after noon yesterday. He frequently had allowed Mr. Waterford to occupy the studio during his absence. When he returned yesterday he found the door locked and bolted and at his request the door was broken open by the janitor using an ax.

"The bodies lay on the large bed in Mr. Koenig's sleeping quarters. Mr. Waterford's left arm encircled the young woman's neck and was clasped in her left hand. They lay facing each other, a blanket drawn up to their shoulders. There was a bullet hole in her left temple and another in

Waterford's right temple. His right hand clasped a .32 caliber revolver. An empty bottle smelling of whiskey was found in the studio. An orchid was pinned to Miss Budd's grey squirrel coat.

"Miss Budd is the daughter of Mr. and Mrs. Devrow Budd, of London, England. Mr. Budd is said to represent American business interests abroad. He maintains a large country estate at Port Johnson, a suburb of Philadelphia. The young woman attended fashionable schools in Philadelphia and New York and was prominent in Red Cross activities here and in Palm Beach, Fla. She recently has made her home with an uncle in this city, but police have been unable to reach him.

"Mr. Waterford was a member of the Yale football team in 1902 and 1903 and has been an outstanding polo player in Connecticut and Long Island. He was married and the father of three children, who, in addition to his parents and two brothers, survive."

"I'm sorry, boy. I know she was a great friend of yours."

"I wasn't a great friend of hers, though. If I had been, maybe this wouldn't have happened."

"You couldn't have stopped that, Alfred."

Alfred looked at the newspaper. "They didn't say any more than they had to, did they?"

"Well, I guess the Waterfords have a lot of pull."

"Somebody has. Somebody must have. Wait till the scandal sheets get hold of it."

"They have. I read one, but I didn't bring it with me. I threw it away."

"Lex."

"What?"

"I wonder where she is?" Alfred could not say "her body."

"I don't know. But the paper I tore up said they found her brother, the one they call her uncle in this paper."

"He's no good. I think I ought to go to New York."

"All right. I'll go with you."

"You don't have to."

"She was a friend of my sister's, and Uncle Fritz and Uncle Alec are pretty good when there's trouble around."

"Mr. Budd worked for your uncles. Did you know that?"

"No, I didn't, but if that's the case they'll take care of everything. You know, he'll get the British embassy to notify her family and find out what they want done. It all has to be in code now, I imagine. Censorship. Uncle Fritz is very good at cutting that red tape."

"Lex, I don't think I feel like any lunch."

"You want to be alone, don't you?"

"For a while. All right?"

"I'll be back in an hour or so. I'll telephone Uncle Fritz and see what he knows." Lex went out, but before closing the door he said: "Would you like me to bring you anything?"

"No thanks."

Alfred re-read the newspaper and put it down and looked out the window and saw nothing but what there was to see: the hard ground, some of it dug up for trench warfare exercises; the leafless trees; the young men in civilian clothing and some in the uniform of the officers' training units; the corners of dormitories; the tops of towers; the groundkeeper's wagon. There was not a woman in sight and not a man in this little world of men who had known Norma Budd, who had felt anything with her. He noticed a man with a Krag slung from his shoulder; an older, Regular Army man, a sergeant, who was probably on his way to teach some younger men to shoot. It took some skill to shoot, it even took a rather special skill to shoot a girl in the left temple and then shoot yourself in the right temple. It took an awful kind of guts to hold on to her that way while you were moving the .32 from her head to your own, you could only do it quickly. You could never stop to think about it. And you could only do any of it, and all of it, if you loved her so desperately that you were left with no other choice. You had to love someone beyond the power to resist death, and almost nobody loves that way. But that fellow in the raccoon coat that he had seen her coming down the hill with, down that hill a couple of hundred yards from here—that Yale guy with his wife and kids and father and mother and two brothers, and his polo friends and his football friends, and the people he sold insurance to—he got rid of it all, which had been his life (not so much different from Samuel Eaton's life), because if his life wasn't going to be with Norma Budd, it wasn't going to be at all. And *she* wasn't going to be around for someone else, for someone like a despicably ungrateful schoolboy named Alfred Eaton.

He looked at his face in the mirror. "Father was right, right all along. You're a prick," he said.

He lay on the bed, wide awake, not even tired, and remembered when he had deserted her. "There's something wrong with me," he said. "Something was left out." In a little while some tears came, but he knew they were for himself.

He was not used to such confusion as now came over him, and the confusion brought with it fears that became terror. For no reason that he could explain to himself, his thoughts turned to Charles Frolick and the beating he had given him. Charles Frolick was in no way connected with Norma Budd, but he almost expected Frolick to come in the room and accuse him of some connection with the murder and suicide. And as soon as the reasonable workings of his mind convinced him that Frolick was not going to appear, his terror began to stir again, this time with thoughts of the night he had been manhandled by the sophomores. His innocence in that episode made no difference: violence had been done, the score had not been settled, and those men were still his enemies. His innocence was no more to be considered than the sure knowledge that the juvenile thugs had no connection with Norma Budd. Then when common sense had argued away any relationship between the new tragedy and his own frightful experience on the Hopewell road, memories of Victoria and Peter came back. Not now as the calm-faced lovers who floated in eternity, but as a girl he had loved and a boy who had been his friend, and who had gone from live to dead because he had been stupid and possessive. And here there was a connection: he had before him a New York newspaper with the evidence of the power to damage that was in his stupidity and possessiveness. In his present mood he could see only that in failing Norma he had made it possible for her to become more and more deeply involved with Waterford, with the final, inevitable, eternal result. And throughout all three phases of his self-blame—his guilt in the Frolick episode; his desire for revenge in the Hopewell incident; his clear responsibility for what had happened to Victoria and Peter—he had an expectation of punishment that was so strong as to be a need; and the very real, present-moment scandal that had reached its climax with two revolver shots that could almost be heard by anyone who read the newspapers, might be the occasion by which punishment could at last be dealt. Hence his fear, his fears, and his terror, made worse by his inability to release some of it in an expression of his guilt and alarm to another living person.

For he was not risking Lex's contempt by confiding in him. Their relations with girls had remained a closed subject, which made for an incompleteness of their pool of information on each other, but gave to the friendship a dignity that both partners to the friendship, each independent in his own way, had always found desirable in all human relationships. A sudden revealing, which would have to be complete, would be as distasteful to Lex as it would be desperate and painful to Alfred, and nothing but momentary release would be gained, while the institution of the friendship would be lost. Alfred actually took some comfort in Lex's approval of his course of behavior, even though Lex would never know he had approved or the cause of his approval. It was the only comfort he was able to enjoy in that present mood.

Then a curious change occurred as a result of some new information.

Lex came back from lunch, obviously alive with news. "I talked to my uncle on the telephone, Uncle Fritz. He sent you a message. He said he knew you'd want to *do* something. Well, it won't be necessary. Miss Budd had an aunt and uncle living in Washington, D. C., and they've taken charge. They're arranging for the burial and everything else. My uncle talked to her, the aunt, and she said she and her husband would take the body to some place in the South, everything strictly private, nobody to know where the funeral was to be. Understandable. So it's all out of your hands. They don't *want* anybody."

"How do they know Norma wouldn't have wanted anybody?"

"Well, under the circumstances."

"Oh, sure."

"The one I feel sorry for now is the man's wife. What's his name? Waterman? Waterford? Mrs. Waterford. Think how she must feel."

"She'll get plenty of sympathy from everybody."

"That won't bring him back."

"Who the hell wants him back? If he was tired of living, all right, let him blow his God damn brains out. But he didn't have to kill *her*."

"Be fair, Alfred. They did it together. She must have agreed. It says so in the paper."

"I'll tell you what else it says in the paper. Read that about the bottle of whiskey."

"You think he got her drunk first."

"I don't think it, I know it. I have as much right to think that as you have to think she agreed to it. She didn't shoot herself. He shot her. But filled her full of liquor first. You'll never convince me otherwise."

"Well, maybe. I don't want to argue with you, Alfred. He killed her, there's no doubt about that, and she was a friend of yours, so naturally I'm sorry. But I can feel sorry for his wife, too. That's a hell of a fix to be in, especially with kids."

"She should have divorced him, then maybe it wouldn't have happened."

"I don't agree with you. I think it was going to happen and it happened. Nothing anybody did was going to stop it."

"If I could have seen her—"

"No. And the fact remains that you didn't see her. It wasn't intended to be that way. Let's go for a walk. It's starting to snow and the walk'll do us good."

"If we don't talk."

"All right, we won't talk. Brisk walk. No conversation."

"If I start to talk, don't let me."

"If you start to talk, I'll start to run, and you won't be able to talk."

They put on sweaters and raincoats and walked to Kingston and back, and stopped at the lunchroom and had bacon-buns and hot chocolate. They had had no conversation that went deeper than observations on the weather and the slippery going.

"Alfred?"

"What?"

"I only want to say one thing. Don't let this, what happened to Miss Budd, don't let it ruin your vacation. I have a hunch it may be our last, so let's cut loose and have a good time. Next Christmas we may be in the trenches. And just to show you my heart's in the right place, I'll pay for the buns. Lend me a dollar."

"What for? I paid for them."

"But I want to pay you back."

"Mail me a cheque."

They went back to their separate rooms and for a while Alfred took pleasure in gratitude toward his friend and his efforts to distract him. But the distraction passed and there occurred a change from the earlier terror to a depression that remained with him long past the weeks of vacation: the unpredictable action of the unknown aunt and uncle had shut him out of even the last dead moments Norma would have on earth, and once again—too often for his own years on earth—he was carrying the unforgiveness of someone who had lost the power to forgive, who had left him for someone else and left him with no one. But at least (he told himself) he could take himself out of the life of Clemmie Shreve before he did her any harm. He did so, without so much as writing her a note, and merely by staying away from Philadelphia.

It was an honorable gesture and a mature one, or the result of mature reflection. The two girls to whom he had meant something, who had meant the most to him, had been killed; one in an accident that occurred only minutes away from his actual presence and in which he could soberly and without melodrama admit to having had an influencing part. It was harder to relate Norma's murder to himself, but for that reason, just as hard to claim total innocence. In the one case he had been quite directly responsible; in the other, his responsibility was indirect and remote, but spiritually real. And if he had wanted to, he could not deny that he had been unlucky for the two girls he had loved, the only two.

He was not in love with Clemmie Shreve, but she would be easy to love, with her startling blond beauty, her lively blue eyes, and the high-breasted promise of exquisite pleasure when —as he knew they were going to—they exchanged the first of many kisses. She was a virgin, of that he was sure, and he had no expectation of a relationship that would go beyond the long kiss and the close embrace. Even that much, or little, was more than she was accustomed to giving, for the Princeton gossip had not included her among the New York-Philadelphia girls who were easy to pet. But Alfred knew she liked him, was possibly ready to love him, and he had been ready to love her.

Now, quickly, he wanted to protect her from the bad luck he had brought the others, and he resolved to let her forget him. There had actually been no words between them that could not have passed between her and someone else—a promise to be alone during the Christmas holidays. In honesty he knew she intended to make the special effort to see him alone, but she had not committed herself further in so many words, and therefore neither had he.

He stayed away from Philadelphia and did not see Clemmie during the holidays, and when he got back to Princeton he felt that the holidays had been a complete waste, during which he had taken many more drinks than ever before and had gone without seeing the only girl he had wanted to see. But he had stuck to his resolution. He had denied himself the pleasure of seeing her, and he had protected her from the bad luck he brought. In that frame of mind he was succeeding in doing some penance for his past stupidities, and then one afternoon he had an encounter which had an effect as lasting as anything he had ever experienced.

Sterling Calthorp, his Knox and Princeton classmate, was a Philadelphian whom Alfred was glad to see when they met away from Princeton, but glad enough to forget on campus. They spoke from habit, with a total lack of cordiality and animosity, with no curiosity or interest in each other beyond that which had been created by the happenstance of their parents' sending them to the same schools at the same time. Red Calthorp's friends were all Philadelphians and would be all his life, and Port Johnson was not part of Philadelphia.

Alfred was sitting in the lunchroom late one afternoon and Calthorp, carrying a hot chocolate and bacon-bun, seated himself at the table. "I didn't see you at any of the dances," he said.

"I didn't go to any, not in Philadelphia."

"You were missed."

"I'll bet."

"You were, though."

"Well, if I'd known that I'd have managed to put in an appearance."

"I didn't know you were making time with Clemmie Shreve."

"I didn't either."

"No? Then it was just her line. You never know with Clemmie. I've gone to parties where she was all my life, but this Christmas I guess she must have discovered that you and I went to school together, and here. How long have *you* known her?"

"About four or five months."

"Oh, well."

"What does that mean, 'Oh, well'?"

"Then you don't really know Clemmie. She's got a line. Nice to everybody. I guess she has to be."

"Why?"

"Well, like a couple hundred other girls, or a couple thousand. She's looking for a husband. Only she's looking harder than most. If Clemmie doesn't get one this year it won't be Mrs. Shreve's fault. They've been saving up for I guess eighteen years. It doesn't mean much at home, but she may lasso some New York millionaire."

"Why would she have to lasso one? With her looks?"

"Hell, I like Clemmie. But I know damn well anybody that marries her has to marry her father and mother too. They're perfectly nice people, but one jump ahead of the sheriff. Mrs. Shreve's father was an army captain and he didn't have any money, and Mr. Shreve spends most of his time playing Sniff. That's a game. Dominoes. He did have a job, but he was thrown from a horse and hurt his back. And I guess he couldn't sit at a desk any more. More comfortable chairs at the Philadelphia Club. Oh, he's all right. But everybody knows that it's up to Clemmie."

"You keep saying you like her, but it doesn't sound that way to me."

"Hell, I do like her. I even feel sorry for her. If she had any money she'd be the most popular girl in Philadelphia. But everybody knows she has to marry a millionaire and what is it they say? Pull their chestnuts out of the fire. It's a damn shame. They didn't have to make this big splurge for her. If she'd just come out quietly a lot of guys would want to marry her. But when Old Lady Shreve showed her hand, that was the warning. Come with your checkbooks, boys. I wouldn't say a word against Clemmie, but Mr. and Mrs., that's another matter altogether. And scooting her off to New York every chance they get. That's always a bad sign."

"What if some Philadelphia guy fell in love with her?"

"How could he? Her mother spoiled that. Everybody *knows* what Mrs. Shreve wants, and you either accept that or they won't give their consent."

"What if Clemmie and some Philadelphia guy fell in love and eloped?"

"Well, now you're not talking sense. Clemmie wouldn't elope. She knows what she has to do."

"Oh, then she's part of it."

"Part of it? She's the whole show. Clemmie doesn't hate money, you know. She doesn't want to be poor."

"How do you know?"

"How do I know? Because a lot of guys that haven't got

224

much money have fallen hard for Clemmie, but Clemmie never fell for them."

"Has she ever fallen for anybody?"

"Not that I know of."

"Why don't *you* marry her?"

"Listen, you think you're kidding me, Alfred, but I would if she didn't have that mother and father."

"Why don't you just tell them to go to hell?"

"Because Clemmie would tell me to go to hell first. Oh, Clemmie's no fool. She knows she's going to end up with some New Yorker or somebody like that. We all like Clemmie. Pretty, and good-natured. But don't let's get serious, boys. Let's see those gilt-edged securities."

"So that's Clemmie."

"Well, in a way I don't blame them. The guy that marries her's going to get his money's worth. Wouldn't you like to wake up with that face across the pillow?"

"Yes, I would."

"Well, then tell your old man to buy the Bethlehem Steel Company and you'll have a chance. But not the Eaton Company. That's not big enough for Mrs. Shreve."

"Oh, she's aiming really high."

"All the way, boy. All the way. And it won't have to be old money. She'll take new money, as long as there's enough of it."

"Ours isn't very old but it isn't very much either."

"Then you can't have Clemmie. However, some mothers aren't so particular, or so hard up. Don't despair. Be somebody on that pillow some morning, even if she isn't as pretty as La Shreve." He looked far away. "That *would* be nice, wouldn't it?"

They walked across the campus together and Alfred left him and continued on to his room. He tried to study, but Calthorp's final remark in the lunchroom was too strongly evocative of his own pictures of Clemmie and he wrote her a letter, full of desire, and tore it up. There was something almost as strong as desire that he wanted to express to Clemmie. He wanted her to know that he had not stayed away from Philadelphia because of anything he had heard about her. He wanted to tell her that he loved her now in spite of what he had just heard about her. He wanted her to know that in spite of what he had heard, he did not doubt her sincerity with him. But most of all he wanted to say that he had not deserted her. But when he came to put that thought on paper he failed. It was not possible to put it on paper without telling her why he would not desert her. He could not tell her a little without telling her everything, and he could not even hint to Clemmie or to anyone that he was capable of what he had already committed: the Judas act. He would have to tell her all about Norma in language that was strong enough to make her realize that the crime was enormous and not to be dismissed as anything less. But he could not write the words that laid him open, and so he wrote none. But out of the experience came the fixed knowledge that a wholly decent act could have an effect as cruel as any cruelty. He had tried to protect Clemmie from his injurious influence, and in so doing he had accidentally told her that he had discovered she was a fortune-hunter. He did not know that that was what she believed, but she was subtle and intelligent and vulnerable, and it was what she could be expected to believe.

He waited a week or so, and wrote her:

Dear Clemmie:
    I never got to Philadelphia during the Christmas holidays, as all my plans were changed at the last minute. Is there any chance that we might have dinner together or otherwise meet very soon? I look forward to seeing you.

                                    Sincerely,
                                    Alfred Eaton

In a week or so he got his answer:

Dear Alfred:
    I am off to Florida this afternoon and while I am away there will be an announcement of my engagement. I am going to marry John P. Hennessey, Yale '12, of Hartford, Connecticut, after Easter. The wedding will be in Philadelphia, of course, and I hope you can come and wish us happiness. If not, perhaps you will come see us sometime in New York, after we have finished building our house.
    Best of luck at Princeton.

                                    Sincerely,
                                    Clementine Shreve

The hardest thing to believe (in spite of Red Calthorp's report) was that Clemmie Shreve was actually contemplating marriage. Alfred re-read her note; was rebuffed, snubbed, patronized by it as no doubt he was intended to be. But now he found it difficult to rearrange her status and thus in a sense reconstruct *her*. It was difficult because he understood now that however poignantly and tenderly he might have felt for her there had been in his feeling for her none of the hope or concern for their permanent future that had existed in his feeling for Victoria or for Norma. When he had been most deeply in love with Victoria he had often been afraid and ashamed of the part that he was convinced Norma would always play in his life. He was reluctantly sure in those days that he would always have a relationship with Norma that he would not regard as disloyal to Victoria, but that Victoria, if she suspected, would quite properly consider unfaithfulness. And conversely, he could never love Norma in the full and lasting way that he loved Victoria. Now they both were out of the land of the living and could not touch or be touched and as persons could not figure in his life, but even in death they still more really affected his love than Clemmie had. (And he marveled at how quickly he could put Clemmie in the past.) Her beauty was exciting, her friendliness was glowing, the luxury of her body and the promise of its visual and tactile pleasures and the confiding release of her restraints—all were more than most men ever get, too good for the faceless Mr. Hennessey of Yale, and would have been enough for Alfred if he had not loved Victoria and Norma. The worst he felt now was chagrin, an embarrassment within himself that would be known only by himself, brought on by her note and that patronizing line: "Best of luck at Princeton." Almost immediately Alfred was able to perceive that while he had been attracted to Clemmie and she to him, the relationship never would have been deep and lasting, and he knew why: Clemmie was a part of the world of cut-glass chandeliers, Markel's orchestra, satin evening dresses, long white gloves, pearly teeth, radiant smiles and half-promises of gayety continuing; the white and sparkling world that would still be photographed by Bachrach when she became Mr. Hennessey's bride; but all so cool and ordered and dry, so different from the world personified in his permanent recollection of Norma and the startling circles about the nipples of her breasts and the compelling dark tuft at the bottom of her belly. Before he had seen Norma naked he had been able to imagine Victoria naked, naked of clothing and stripped of restraints, but in the midst of his desirings for Clemmie he had often been disturbed by the brightness that she moved in and of which she herself was the brightest part.

Clemmie's note did produce some small chagrin, but to his astonishment, considering the recentness of his anguish over Norma, he suddenly found that he was regarding her note as a *laissez-passer*. It was not until much later that he realized that he had had all he could stand. For a while at least he could be free to wander and to feel nothing, and in this he was considerably impelled by the rapidly developing crisis-upon-crisis at home and abroad.

EVERYBODY KNEW that when Eaton's whistle blew it was not just another summons to the next shift, and not just another call to the members of the Port Johnson fire department. Men who belonged to the fire companies would smile at each other and say, "Fire's out, Jim," and Jim would say, "Yah, fire's out, Harry," and point his thumb over his shoulder even though he happened not to be pointing toward the east. It was going to be a fine November day and Lower Montgomery Street was more crowded with people than it had been since the Six-County Firemen's Convention, more crowded with citizens of the borough than it had been since Company K had entrained for Camp Hancock, Georgia, only a little more than a year ago. A young fellow in olive drab, with two gold chevrons on his left cuff and one gold chevron on his right cuff, was hoisted to the shoulders of some older men in overalls. They put him down gently when he convinced them that it was not modesty but the pain in his leg that bothered him. He spared their feelings by taking dollops of their pint bottles of whiskey. They then lifted a young marine to the sky, first making sure he had no injury, and disregarding his protesting, "I wasn't over, I didn't do anything."

"You got a medal, you got a medal," they shouted.

"Hey, gyrene, tell them what the medal's for," shouted the soldier.

"You tell them, soldier," shouted the marine.

"He shot the Navy in the ass," shouted the soldier. "He's a sharp-shooter."

A small boy pushed through the crowd making flatulent noises with a battered, short-belled cavalry bugle, and other boys clapped saucepan lids together like cymbals and some few had tin horns left over from Hallowe'en and another had a hand Klaxon that he had stripped from a truck. Women carrying pots and pans beat on them with wooden spoons and three or four of the more decorous shook dinner bells in the faces of their friends. A boy in a campaign hat pointed a Daisy air rifle at anyone at all and said "Bang, bang," and down in the railway yards a party of section hands were industriously exploding signal torpedoes by running a hand-car over them. As the morning grew lighter the noise rose and fell, and sometimes in the quieter moments there would be the sound of a school bell, a church bell from the outer wards of the borough and even from the nearby villages. It was a good war to be over. Most of these people had German blood,

228

some of them no other; many of them spoke Pennsylvania
Dutch and some of them could speak nothing else; and there
had been days when the Port Johnson casualty list could have
been posted in a Bavarian town without strangeness to the
names: Hochgertel, Lechleitner, Schwab, Eisenhauer, Eisen-
acher, Fritzinger, Laubenstein, Gudebrod, Lichtenwalner,
Schmidt, Rothermel, Wildermuth, Vomrath, Stumpff. It had
been a little worse for those families than for their neighbors
whose names would not be found in that Bavarian town.

It was still dark when Samuel Eaton stirred in his bed and
forced himself to remember that it was a special day. He put
on a bathrobe and went to Martha's room as he had promised
to do. "You must be sure and wake me," she had said. He had
looked at her dubiously. "I mean it. I'm going to bed in just
a little while." But now even before he could make out her
features by the hall light he knew she would not get out of
bed, not now and not for hours. She had gone to bed without
raising a window, and the smell of her gin was heavy, heavier
this morning than usual, and as he put on a table lamp he saw
a large splotch on the carpet and the gin bottle almost empty
where it had rolled after spilling. He opened two windows, as
much to air the room before the undeceived Nellie appeared
as to lessen Martha's headache. He picked up the bottle, put
out the light, and went to his room and dressed.

Nellie had got his breakfast. "Good morning, sir," she said.

"Good morning."

"Poached or boiled this morning?"

"Boiled."

"Sir?"

"Boiled, please. Soft-boiled."

"I was going to ask you something."

"All right."

"Is the war over now?" she said. "I thought I heard a racket.
Shooting-crackers or the like."

"It'll be over in an hour or so. Six o'clock. That's because
of the difference in time between here and Europe."

"It wonders me why the forners can't have the same time
like we do. Surely they don't have to go to such extremes to
be different than the rest of us."

"I'll explain it to you sometime."

"Well, I wish you would. Them as tried have never succeeded."

"I will. Now could I have my eggs, please, Nellie? I want
to be early this morning."

She brought in the eggs and watched him slash off the tops.
"Then I take it Mr. Alfred'll be home any minute?"

"I doubt it. We have two million soldiers over there, you
know, and we have to bring them home."

"Couldn't you use your influence? You manufactured all them supplies for them."

"I also got very well paid for doing so. No, I couldn't use any so-called influence. But I should think the kind of service he was in, he might be one of the first out. If the war's really over we won't have to worry about submarines."

"*If* the war's really over. Is there the least doubt of that?"

"No, not much, but some. An armistice—look it up in my dictionary. It's on my desk."

"Don't you have the slightest idea where he is?"

"Only that he's on a transport."

"Maybe they'll let him get off it next time in port, do you think?"

"I hope so, Nellie. I hope so."

"And so do I. What a terrible ordeal for a young man twenty-one years of age, there in the black of the night, looking to the right and left, never knowin' will the next moment be his last with one of them frightful torpedoes. And all them soldiers asleep in their staterooms, depending on Alfred to shoot the dirty no-good Huns. A terrible, terrible ordeal, not to mention the responsibility of it. It took a lot of bravery, and I'm proud indeed. I hope he was able to get some use out of the muffler I knitted him. Well, St. Anthony seen to it he got my letters at least."

"Yes, and thank you, Nellie. Now I'm off."

"Will you be home for dinner, if anyone should ask?" The question, in this form, had become routine for Nellie; it was so much more respectful than to ask Mr. Eaton if he thought Mrs. Eaton planned to spend the day in bed and would therefore be incapable of ordering dinner, in which case Josephine would plan the meal without her help.

"As it looks now, I don't think I will," he said. His reply meant that Nellie must confer with Mrs. Eaton from time to time during the day, until her decision was forthcoming. It also could mean that Mrs. Eaton might be getting up some time later in the day, feeling fine, in which case she might telephone Mr. Eaton and let him know that he was expected.

George was standing beside the Mercer. "Good morning, sir."

"Good morning. I won't need you today."

"Then could I hop a ride in with you?"

"How will you get back? I didn't mean you could have the day off."

"Oh."

"Mrs. Eaton might need you."

"Yes sir."

"Or was there some particular reason . . . ?"

"The Armistice. I was gonna celebrate it."

"For how many days?"

"Just the one. I'll be on the job at six in the morning."

"Well, all right. Get in."

"Thank you, sir."

They got in, Samuel Eaton taking the wheel. "Where shall I let you off? I don't know of any saloons open at this hour."

"They will be today. A man won't have any trouble getting a drink today."

"No, I suppose not."

"I'll go to the mill with you, if that's all right."

"It's more than all right. It means I won't have to go downtown. Why do you want to go to the mill? To borrow some money?"

"No sir."

"Then why?"

"Do you want to know why?"

"I'm asking you."

"I want to blow the whistle."

"You want to blow the whistle? The big whistle?"

"Yes sir. I don't ask you many favors, but I'd appreciate it if you'd let me blow the whistle, maybe for just as long as it takes to count up to three. Fast. One, two, three."

"Why?"

"I promised your son when he went away, I said, 'Alfred, the day this war's over I'm gonna blow the whistle for you.' "

"You took a lot for granted, doesn't it seem to you?"

"Yes sir, that I did."

"You were that sure that Alfred was coming back. What if he'd been torpedoed? Would you still want to blow it?"

"No. It didn't mean that. It meant I was sure he was coming back."

"But what if he hadn't?"

"I got rid of that thought the minute it came."

"How? I wish I could have that easily."

"Prayed."

"Prayed? You prayed? You're no more a praying man than I am."

"I didn't use to be."

"But you became one? When did *you* hit the sawdust trail?"

"That's Billy Sunday. I didn't. I'm something else."

"What?"

"A Catholic."

"You a Catholic? Did I hear you correctly? When did that happen?"

"I received my first Communion a year ago August."

"Will wonders never cease? How did all that happen?"

"Well, it wasn't all of a sudden."

"But how did it happen? What made you want to? What gave you the idea in the first place?"

"Two decent women."

"Two *decent* women. I always knew you had plenty of experience with the other kind. In fact, I didn't know you knew any decent women."

"I didn't either, but they were here all the time. And right under my nose."

"Two of them. Not one? I suppose that means you didn't fall in love with one of them."

"There was only ever the one decent woman in my life, Mr. Eaton."

"Your wife."

"And you know how long ago that was. Close on to forty years she's dead. From then on I bought a woman when I had to, the way a man does or start acting strangely."

"Yes, and then you saw these decent women and they made a Catholic out of you. How did they do it?"

"It wasn't only that. I began thinking a lot about getting old. I had a good job, I liked the work and I was treated fairly, and I saved most of my wages that I didn't throw away on a spree. But what was I, I asked myself. A human being, but who did I do most of my talking to? To the horses. I did more talking to horses in my life than I did to people. And every so often I'd go with a whore, get pig drunk and go with a whore, and come back to work and worry was I going to pull up with a clap? Then having to take care of me clap and afraid it'd be found out and you'd sack me."

"And I would have."

"I know that, and you'd have been right. But I had a few you never knew about. I had my last clap over six years ago, but it leaves a bad effect and the last one I went to an honest doctor."

"That was when you had that hernia."

"Yes sir. He told me to say I had the hernia."

"Well, you didn't fool me entirely. But go on with the Catholic religion."

"Yes. Well, I used to say to myself a man with his two eyes and his brains and able to think better than an animal, read and write and do sums, but he might as well be off living in the woods, and only the one life to live. And that got me thinking. I always did a lot of thinking, but not along those lines. I was getting older, that's what it was. And then I said to myself one day, Josephine and Nellie, do they have it so much better than me?"

"Oh, they were the two decent women?"

"Josephine and Nellie. They didn't have it so much better

232

than me. But pretty soon I wondered about that. They had their work, like I had mine, but how many hundred times did I drive them in to their church for the confession and Sunday for the Mass? Nobody in God's world was making them get up early on Sunday morning or stand in line Saturdays for confession. But they did it.

"Well, then I began asking them a few questions about it, and they thought I was trying to insult their religion, but when they got over that, well, I had a talk with the priest and pretty soon I started taking instructions and finally I was baptized and received my first Holy Communion and was confirmed. And now when I take them in to church, I go in with them. I'm one of them."

"I can't believe it. And I never knew a thing about it."

"You're away half the time the last couple years."

"True, but it's amazing that I didn't find out somehow. And what's it like being a Catholic? You're going to get drunk today, aren't you?"

"I'll have a few."

"I don't want to pry into your personal life, but what about River Street?"

"I don't get the temptation as much."

"Is that because you're older or is the Catholic religion doing that for you?"

"A little of both, I guess."

"But you tell your sins to this man, the priest?"

"I don't think of him as a man."

"Well, I would. I remember going to an artist's studio one time and there was a woman there, naked as a foal, and the artist tried to tell me he didn't think of her as a woman. Not me. A naked woman is—but you're not supposed to think those things. That's another thing I don't understand. Oh, well, that's the least of my worries."

"I don't know. There's a lot of men in your class are devout Catholics."

"Who?"

"Charles M. Schwab."

"Oh, I thought you meant my college class. I don't remember whether there were any in my college class. I suppose there must have been. But I did know about Mr. Schwab, at least I heard it somewhere. But don't try to convert me, George."

"No sir, I won't.

"You a Catholic. I wonder if my wife ever suspected that."

"Yes sir, she knows it."

"Oh. Do the children know it?"

"Miss Sally and Miss Constance."

"But not my son?"

"No sir."

"But you prayed for him, isn't that what you said?"

"Yes sir. Every day."

Samuel Eaton was silent, then: "Thank you, George."

"You're welcome, sir."

"I've never prayed. I said prayers, but I never prayed. I never put much stock in it, but all the same I'm glad there was somebody to pray for my son."

"There was three of us, right in your own household."

"You and Josephine and Nellie."

"Yes sir."

"What if there was something in it? I don't mean to be rude, but you don't really *know* any more than I do."

"Yes I do."

"No you don't, George, but suppose it turned out that you were right. Then that would mean it was your prayers, yours and Nellie's and Josephine's, and not his own family's that, uh, protected him. Wouldn't that be, uh, ironic?"

"Erronic is a word I'm not familiar with, but Mrs. Eaton prayed."

"Did she really?" He was silent again. Then: "Hear that noise? That sounds like railroad torpedoes."

"Very likely, sir."

"I'll bet they raise merry hell in this town today."

"Not only here. Everywhere."

"Yes, I guess so. I would myself, but I guess I'm past that age."

"You have a better right than most of them. You had a son in it."

"Yes."

"And by the will of God you're gonna have him back."

"Yes."

"Well, Mr. Eaton?"

"What?"

"You're getting another chance now."

"Don't overstep, George. Don't preach to me."

"No sir."

"Now when we get to the mill I'll take you over and give orders that at six o'clock, you're to blow the whistle. Nobody else but you."

"Where will you be, sir?"

"I will be in my office."

"Why? Because you remember twenty-four years ago, the last time you blew that whistle? Man to man, is that why?"

"You have my permission to blow the whistle, because you prayed for my son."

"Yes, and I'll hold you to that as a man of your word. But

234

after that I don't want to work for you any more, Mr. Eaton."

"No, I shouldn't think you would. When would you like to leave?"

"As soon as you get another man."

"I think it would be better if you left today. I'll have your cheque ready for you tomorrow morning."

"Yes sir, and a reference."

"You can be sure of that."

"I didn't have the slightest doubt. No servant of yours ever got but the fairest treatment."

"As long as he remained a servant."

"Exactly, sir, as long as it was a servant."

"Yes. Well, here we are, and now we won't have any more time for your sarcastic remarks, will we?"

"No sir, and anyway, they'd be wasted."

"Wasted, and probably a sin on your soul. Don't forget *that*, George."

The company had more than doubled in size and tripled and quadrupled its tonnage since the morning of August 21, 1894, when Samuel Eaton had signaled the birth of his first-born son, but the whistle still was mounted on the roof of the 18-inch mill, and sounded by the pull-cord from the old shack of the night watchman. The plant office was now a square two-story brick building and there was a corrugated-iron-roofed garage with room for six cars across the way from the office building. Samuel Eaton drove the Mercer to the garage (where it was washed and polished daily as though George Fry's washing and polishing were not enough). The two men got out of the car.

"Follow me, Mr. Fry," said Samuel Eaton.

"Yes sir."

"Oh, you don't have to 'sir' me any more."

"I don't work for you any more, but it's your steel mill. You give the orders."

"And you're afraid I might change my mind about the whistle?"

"No sir, not a bit. That was a promise. But you're entitled to 'sir' on your property."

"Thank you, Mr. Fry. That doesn't bother you, when I call you *Mister* Fry?"

"No sir, I guess I'm entitled to that."

They entered the watchman's office and a man in a blue uniform, unbuttoned at the collar, stood up and leaned on a thick cane. "Good morning, sir."

"Good morning, Nunemacher. You know George Fry."

"Sure, I know George."

"Well, at six o'clock we're going to blow the whistle. You

235

can blow it all morning, for all I care, but I want this man to be the first one to get a whack at it. Six o'clock, Fry blows the whistle. Is that understood?"

"Yes sir."

"Thank you, sir," said George Fry.

Samuel Eaton made no reply. He left and went back to the office.

The watchman looked at his watch, the Seth Thomas clock on the wall, and at George Fry. "You got about twelve minutes, eleven and a half. How did he happen to pick you?"

"He didn't pick me. I asked him."

"Why?"

"I wanted to. Why?"

"Well, I got my eldest over there with Company K and I blow this God damn bull-horn every morning, but the time I want to blow it, *you* get the privilege."

"Then you blow it. I only asked him to blow it, I didn't ask him to blow it first."

"Aah, it's his orders."

"What if it is? Can he tell who pulls the rope, you or me?"

"Well, you know him and his orders."

"I ought to, but I don't have to worry about him any more. I just quit working for him."

"*You* quit?"

"I did. Do you know anybody wants a good hostler, sober and reliable?"

"I aint sure about the sober, George, some of the times I seen you. What did you quit for if you don't have other work?"

"A matter between him and I."

"Over thirty years you must of been with him."

"Forty, counting when I was with his father."

"And you just quit. And you don't get no pension either, do you?"

"I guess I would of if I'da stayed on. This way I don't."

"Well, I guess you got some put by."

"Oh, I won't starve, not right away."

"It was a good job, George. You're sure you done right to quit? Jobs is gonna be scarce, you know. I hear they're gonna lay off four hundred here by the end of the week, and then when the young fellows come home from the Army they're gonna want work right away. This fellow's all business, but a man that was with him as long as you, if you talked to him in the right way he'd let you come back."

"The trouble is I don't want to talk to him in the right way. I quit, Floyd, I didn't get the sack. Although I was only one jump ahead of him, I guess. It was more of a man-to-man kind of an argument."

"Then you don't have a chance. I'm sorry to say it, but you

236

don't, George. There was never a man that stood up to that fellow that was on the payroll the next day. My old man, that had this job before me, he used to say Sam Eaton was all right as long as you did your work and just answered his questions. 'Don't you tell him anything first,' my old man said. 'Just answer his questions.' I said to my old man, 'Well now what if there was a fire in the mill? Would you wait till he asked you about it?' 'That depends,' my old man said. 'If there was a fire and he wasn't there, I'd put it out and I'd get a lot of questions later. If there was a fire and he *was* there, he'd say "What the hell's going on?" and I'd have an answer.' That's Sam Eaton. Well, George. You sure you don't mind?"

"You go ahead, Floyd."

"We got a few more minutes," said Floyd Nunemacher. "I wonder. You know what I wonder? I wonder are they shooting right now, down to the last minute. We sit waiting to blow a whistle. Do you think our boys are shooting at the enemy and the enemy's shooting at them. What if—no."

"I know what you're thinking. I'm gonna pray. 'Hail Mary, full of grace, the Lord is with thee, blessed art though amongst women and blessed is the fruit of thy womb, Jesus.' "

"Catholic, George? Don't pray for *Carl* with a Catholic prayer. Where did you learn to pray Catholic?"

"I am one. I turned Catholic over a year ago."

"Is that what you and him had the fight about?"

"No, you couldn't say it was that."

"Four minutes. It's the same God. The Lord's Prayer. Will you say that with me? 'Our Father, which art in heaven—' "

" 'Who art in heaven—' "

" 'Which art in heaven, hallowed be Thy name. Thy kingdom come, Thy will be done, on earth as it is in heaven. Give us this day our daily bread—' "

" 'And forgive us our trespasses as we forgive—' "

" 'Our debtors. And lead us not into temptation, but deliver us from evil—' "

" 'Amen.' "

" 'For Thine is the kingdom, and the power, and the glory, for ever and ever, Amen.' "

"It's time, Floyd!"

Floyd Nunemacher reached up with both hands and pulled the blackened cord, and the shanty office shook with the announcement of Peace.

To the celebrators in Lower Montgomery Street the first blast of the Eaton's whistle came as a shock, very brief, and followed by exchanges of grins. The whistle made it official for Port Johnson. There were those in the crowd who believed that Eaton's had received word direct from Washington, if not from Foch's railway carriage. The first blast, which lasted more than thirty seconds, was followed by a second and shorter one (long enough for George Fry to utter the letters in Alfred Eaton's name) and by others of varying lengths. Word got around that there was free beer, good beer, and not the weak wartime stuff, being dispensed at both breweries, and men and women formed two parades to march on the supplies of lager. The rumors turned out to be half-correct; there was free beer, but only for brewery workers and their families, and the men and women counter-marched to the borough saloons, disappointed but admitting that the saloon-keepers had to make a living. The war, and Eaton's, had brought a lot of strangers to Port Johnson, and among them were single men who liked whiskey and loose women, which resulted in the establishment of new saloons and whore-houses, with an inevitable effect on the character of the town. For more than a year the streets that paralleled the railroad tracks had been the playground of the fast-spending men with the high wartime wages, and the area was as tough as any in Philadelphia or in the coal-mining towns to the north. There were four prospering whore-houses for whites, one for Negroes, and one for Portuguese, as well as numerous boarding-houses where the landlady and her "daughters" competed unfairly with the professional madams who did not offer board and room. The homicide rate of the borough was greater than it had ever been since records were kept; in one year, 1918, there had been more fatal shootings and stabbings—nine—than in all of the ten years preceding. Often the men went to work in striped silk shirts and cloth-top shoes and driving large second-hand cars from the salesrooms in North Broad Street, Philadelphia. The pool-hustlers and pimps came and stayed long enough to make a wad, and usually left before they aroused suspicion as draft-dodgers. Police graft was now overlooked: the borough councilmen originated and insisted upon the segregation of the whore-houses and dives, and the police enforced the extra-legal decision, which kept the rowdies out of the respectable districts of the town. The police were called only when a disturbance became too much for the bouncer to handle, and arrests were made, fines collected, brief lock-up sentences imposed, and the madam would add a little extra to the policeman's customary stipend. The graft was not legal, but the extra pay was earned and no one was dissatisfied, not even the churchgoing councilmen, who did not officially know about the graft but did officially know about the scarcity of labor and the desirability of keeping the rougher element in one section of their own. There were men who spent a whole year in Port Johnson without ever having seen any of the town east of Third Street.

238

In those early morning hours almost nothing occurred to warrant police action under the liberal interpretations of the law that obtained for this occasion. Martin Updegrove, the chief burgess, and Joe Brophy, the chief of the borough police, went on an inspection tour of the Lower Montgomery Street area and saw numerous small incidents that would have been frowned on any other day, but Brophy looked the other way. "This here's a respectable crowd, Burgess. If somebody did anything serious the crowd would put a stop to it before it got anywhere. And anyway, they're mostly good-natured. I seen a couple things. A fellow back there had his hand on a woman's ass, but I didn't notice her complaining, and these here people, you won't find much of that, what we call morals offenses. Later in the day, I guess, you'll have some fornicatin', but as long as they keep out of sight that's their business. Down by the tracks we don't care what happens as long as they don't start shooting and slashing. I won't have that. But fist-fights and the like of that, let them knock one another's brains out. I hear they're gonna lay off six hundred at Eaton's, and if they do, that whole crowd'll clear out inside of a week."

"Where did you hear that about Eaton's?"

"Now where was it I did hear it? This morning somebody said it. Was it at headquarters now, or was it on me rounds? Somebody said they heard Eaton's was laying off five, six hundred men because the minute the war was over, all government contracts ended. Frank or Harry or somebody. Might of been Lou. I don't remember truthfully. It stands to reason, though. You don't make war munitions if you don't have a war. *It was Frank.* He said he heard it on good authority, Eaton's was gonna keep on the maintenance men, but the last heat was gonna be pulled tonight and then start cooling out."

"I hope our people saved some money."

"Well, we don't care about them others as long as they got enough to leave town. And even if they don't I'm gonna stop the first string of empties and *assist* them out of town."

"Some of our people saved, I know."

"Oh, our own people, yes. The family men, sure."

"Looking at them, I wonder if they realize."

"What's that, Burgess?"

"Well, we're in for some bad times, Joe. When the boys come home from the Army, they're gonna want work. Thirty dollars a month isn't much money."

"Or thirty-three, the ones that went overseas. I wrote to my young lad, I said maybe nine hundred a year don't look like much, but I'd put in an application anyway and he could start as an ordinary policeman the way I did and if he done his work right he'd be eligible for the pension by the time he was fifty years old."

"Mm-hmm. If Eaton's is closing we're going to have to cut down on the force, you know that, Joe?"

"Oh, I *told* him that. I said if they close down Eaton's we were gonna have to cut down on the *force*. We get rid of the last five or six men we took on, or seven. And that way Vince won't be an *extra* man. We won't have no trouble making room for Vincent, and he'll start a lot cheaper than the ones we're getting rid of. The last five we took on are getting a thousand a year and uniform."

"I know. Have you spoken to anyone else about this?"

"Only the other councilmen. But nobody outside. They said they'd all be willing if you would. I said, 'Listen here, the burgess knows Vincent even better than you do.' High school graduate, corporal in the Army. A lot of men would be overjoyed to hire Vincent, but he had his heart set on being a policeman like his Dad. You know, he'll be the third Brophy on the force. Me, and my Dad, and now Vincent. Oh, yes, I wish my old Dad was alive to see it. Remember my old Dad, Burgess?"

"Oh, yes. Everybody remembers old Mr. Brophy."

"He was a great old Dad, was he. Those boatmen on the Canal, there was a ruffian crew for you and I busted more than one knuckle on them myself, but my old Dad, old Jerry Brophy, may his soul rest in peace, he had nerves of steel and the muscles to go with it. No boatman that ever made trouble in this town ever forgot it, and never come back for more. And wouldn't he of been proud to be here today and see his grandson a corporal in the Army, one of the lads of the 28th Division. Maybe not as proud as I am, but proud just the same. Yes sir. Well, Burgess, I think we got everything well in hand, so if you don't want me for anything else, I better be on my rounds. And forgive a proud father for ringing the praises of his son, but this one day I guess you'll understand it. Maybe I'll even stop in and say a little prayer of thanksgiving."

"So long, Joe," said Updegrove. "See you at eleven."

"So long, Burgess," said Brophy. "Eleven o'clock sharp I'll be there."

The hour of eleven had been designated by the chief burgess as a suitable, appropriate time for a gathering of borough officials, prominent business men, the clergy, representatives of patriotic organizations, and war casualties already home. The chosen place was around the new flagpole in front of the borough hall, where there was a large signboard on which was painted a list, as nearly complete as could be, of the names of the Port Johnson men and women in the Army, Navy, and Marine Corps, and the two men who had gone to serve with the American Red Cross and the Y. M. C. A. There was no

240

way to announce the ceremony in such a short time as there would have been twenty years later when Port Johnson had its own radio station, but the Port Johnson Silver Cornet Band had been notified and its music would attract the citizens.

At ten-thirty the members of the band, most of them in uniform but a few wearing only jacket and cap above their work pants, took their places at one side of the flagpole and began playing a medley of recent and old tunes: "Where Do We Go from Here, Boys?"; "The Old Grey Mare"; "Over There"; "Keep the Home Fires Burning"; "K-K-K-Katy"; "The Battle Hymn of the Republic"; "Tenting Tonight"; "Oui, Oui, Marie"; "Oh, How I Hate to Get Up in the Morning"; "The Rose of No Man's Land"; and a reprise of "Over There," after which the short concert was temporarily halted to make way for oratory.

It was, as Chief Brophy had said, a good-natured crowd. It was, in fact, unique for Port Johnson as all the other crowds in all the other towns of the nation were unique: it was happy and gay, universally friendly, but unlike any of the usual celebrating crowds—New Year's Eve, firemen's conventions, alumni reunions, family picnics—it was always ready to change from gayety to an unforced solemnity. In the eighteen-year-old century the country had not had the opportunity for such celebration, and it is even doubtful if such a celebration had occurred in the nation's history; too much sadness and bitterness remained in 1865, the belligerents continued to kill each other after the Christmas Eve treaty of 1814, and the peace of 1782 was celebrated by a people not yet united, many of whom had fought to be free of one king but were determined to live as subjects of another. But on that morning in 1918 the citizens joined together in victory and release, united by joy and grateful enough to be willing to listen to words of prayer and earnest considerations of the sterner ideals. They dropped their heads when told to do so, they were respectful to the other fellow's preacher, they applauded the names of Wilson and Pershing and Foch (pronounced Fotch, Foash, Foatch and Foke) and laughed with scorn but without the recent loathing at the mentions of Kaiser Bill. The term, the Iron Division, had of course a double special local meaning, since it not only applied to the 28th but to the principal industry, and Samuel Eaton, standing on the steps of the borough hall with the other prominent citizens, looked pleased, although most of the crowd knew that his son was a lieutenant in the Navy. He was not called upon to speak, not through oversight or because the chief burgess failed to appreciate Samuel Eaton's standing in the community, but because he had declined the honor in advance.

With the playing of "America" the formal ceremonies were

241

concluded and the band then broke into a brisk "Old Grey Mare" and marched away, followed, and in some cases preceded, by members of the crowd in the first parade of the day in which all the paraders were going in the same direction. The important gentlemen who had been selected to stand on the borough hall steps were invited to the mayor's office where beer was being served and whiskey could be had. The important gentlemen had become acquainted, in cases where they had not been friends earlier, through their work on Liberty Loan and Red Cross drives. The occasion was for some of them the last opportunity to address Samuel Eaton as Sam and Henry Van Peltz as Henry, and they knew it. There in the chief burgess's office the war was suddenly over; the music was gone, the party had ended; the boat had docked; school was not out, it was starting tomorrow. The pharmacist was a druggist again, and no longer the chairman of the Business Men's Committee for the Fourth Liberty Loan; the hardware store man was no longer chairman of the Business Men's Division of the Red Cross; the clothing store merchant was no longer co-chairman of the Inter-Denominational Council of the War Chest; the president of Eaton's Iron & Steel was no longer general chairman of Port Johnson Community League. There were those who wanted to stay and drink beer, wishing to hold on to the familiarity of the past two years, but there were also the others who wanted to end the association. Samuel Eaton had not even taken off his overcoat.

"Sam?" said the chief burgess.

"Yes, Martin?"

"Could I have a word with you?" This was a phrasing that Martin Updegrove had unconsciously picked up in his meetings with Samuel Eaton.

"Yes, yes. Of course."

"Well, I heard you intended to lay off six hundred men. How much truth is there to it?"

"Now where did you hear that? Oh, excuse me. Henry?" Samuel Eaton waved a finger at Henry Van Peltz and elbowed his way to him.

"Yes, Sam?" said Henry.

"Let's get the hell out of here. Can you?"

"I was thinking the same thing. Let's go over to the club."

Henry Van Peltz, who had succeeded to the general managership of the family-owned silk mill, was more courtly than Samuel Eaton and was often said to have the best manners in Port Johnson. He made his way to the door, speaking to everyone present and calling him by name. Samuel Eaton's method was totally unlike Van Peltz's: it almost seemed as though Samuel Eaton was not so much taking leave of the gathering as adjourning it.

The two men left and walked to the Port Johnson Club, a new institution in an old house—the Raymond Johnson Mansion on Montgomery Street. Port Johnson had always got along without the usual gentlemen's club, but after the death of Raymond Johnson in 1916 the house, somewhat afflicted by the name The Mansion, attracted no suitable purchasers, and when one woman offered to buy it and turn it into a boarding-house, Samuel Eaton easily persuaded Martha to make it available for a club, and Henry Van Peltz was easily persuaded to assume the task of organizing. It followed the usual course of the American gentlemen's club: the charter members were the usual graduates of Yale, Princeton, Penn, Lafayette, Lehigh, Penn State, Franklin & Marshall, Haverford, Ursinus, Albright, and Lebanon Valley. They were predominantly Protestant, with a small mixture of Catholics who got in in spite of being Catholics. There were no Jews; there were, in fact, only two Jewish families in the borough. The initiation fee was $25—charter membership $100—and annual dues of $25. The club was immediately popular, not only as a male refuge but as a happy answer to the threat of the boarding-house. The first, and so far the only president of the Port Johnson Club was Samuel Eaton, elected by acclamation. He had contemplated declining for rather obvious reasons, but they were not as strong as his sense of history and the satisfaction of going down in the books as the club's first president. His name was already on the lacquered pine board in the downstairs hall for 1916-17, 1917-18, and 1918-19. You couldn't miss it. And in the booklet containing the roster it was gratifying to see *Eaton, Samuel, 1916 (Charter)* and *Eaton, Alfred, 1918*. It would have been nice to have had *Eaton, William, 1916 (Charter)*; Billy could have just made it. The whole property had gone for $18,000, including all but a few pieces of furniture and rugs that Martha wanted, and the price was so small and the terms so easy that Samuel Eaton had in mind a plan to persuade Martha to relieve the club of financial obligation in memory of her father. But all in good time, and not so soon that she might recall that her father never had seen the need of a club in the town, and never had joined one in his life.

Samuel Eaton and Henry Van Peltz went from the coatroom to the lounge, ordered their whiskey and water, crossed their legs, and rested their hands on their waistcoats.

"Glad to get away from that crowd, aren't you? All that noise and confusion," said Henry.

"Damn glad," said Samuel Eaton. "Thank you, William. William, did everybody show up today?"

243

"Yes sir, everybody showed up, sho enough, but I don't know exactly how many we still have on the premises by nightfall, Mist' Eaton, sir. *If* the's *any*."

"Well, I guess we have to look the other way, today," said Samuel Eaton.

"Afred so, sir, I'm afred so." He nodded and left.

"How's all this going to affect you?" said Samuel Eaton.

"Well, in one way, the same as it's going to you. I drink to our sons, to Alfred and to Harry. Thank God," said Henry Van Peltz.

"I drink to that," said Samuel Eaton, and did so. "And now, Henry, a drink to our other sons, who would have been there with their brothers. To Peter and Billy."

"Yes," said Henry Van Peltz. They drank.

"Did you ever think of what they might have been if they'd lived? In the war, that is. You remember Billy, don't you?"

"Of course. Of course I remember Billy."

"I think he would have been in the marines. I don't know much about the marines. To tell you the truth I hardly ever heard of them before this war. But everything I heard about them, Billy seemed to be their kind of person. Peter—do you know what I see Peter as?"

"No."

"An aviator. With Eddie Rickenbacker, or Lufbery or one of those squadrons. The Lafayette Escadrille. Raoul Lufbery."

"Yes, I think Peter would have liked flying. Harry likes it, but he hasn't much to say for the aeroplanes they've been getting. Italian planes. But he likes flying. Who knows? If Peter hadn't been killed in that Stutz he might have lived a few more years and been killed in a defective Italian aeroplane. Then I'd be sitting here—well, I wouldn't *be* sitting here. I'd be home with Maude, glad that one of our boys was coming home but consoling her because the other one wasn't. And that isn't the way to spend today. I'm not religious, not one bit, but today I feel like thanking God for letting Harry come through. I'd almost rather not think about Peter today."

"I think of Billy every day of my life."

"I know that. But today is Alfred's day, Sam. Harry's day and Alfred's day. We've both lost sons in peacetime, let's be thankful that our other sons survived war. And maybe if you do it'll help you get over Billy."

"I don't want to get over Billy."

"But you have to, Sam. Billy's been dead ten years, or almost."

"Ten years this year."

"And he was only a boy when he died. Now you have a son a grown man, an officer in the Navy, I'm told very well liked at Princeton, and no doubt about his being liked here at home.

244

Good-looking boy, a gentleman. I say you're damn lucky."

"I know all about Alfred."

"No, I don't think you do. You were so grief-stricken over Billy that Alfred grew up right past you, so to speak."

"A man can feel badly over one son without ignoring the other."

"He can, but have you?"

"What kind of question is that? Of course I have. I hesitate to say this, Henry, but you seem to have got over Peter's death without any trouble at all."

"Then I'm glad you think so, because that's what I would like you to think. Not you, as Sam Eaton. But people. I don't want the whole nosy God damn world feeling sorry for me, and more to the point, I didn't want Maude to suffer any more than she had to, and she would have if I'd brooded over Peter."

"That almost sounds as if you think Martha's unhappy because I brooded over Billy. Well, if so, kindly leave Martha out of it."

"Sam, we know each other too well for this kind of talk. We don't have to pretend that Martha is her old self, but I haven't said I blamed you."

"Martha didn't start to drink, to excess, till a couple of years ago, so it had nothing to do with Billy or how I felt about him. She's probably going through change of life, and when it's over she'll be all right again."

"I think so. Let's have another drink."

"That suits me," said Samuel Eaton. He tapped the bell and nodded to William, who understood the nod. "I started to ask you how this is going to affect you. Are you going to lay off any men?"

"We sure are."

"How many?"

"At least ten."

"Ten?"

"Ten men—and a hundred girls."

"Oh, that's right. You employ mostly women. Well, I have to talk to our lawyers and the government lawyers, but I know what they're going to say. They're going to say, 'Mr. Eaton, as of today, any wages you pay are out of your own pocket.' I think that's the way our contracts read. Doesn't take long for the bad news to travel, either. Martin Updegrove asked me if I was going to lay off men. I didn't answer him, but the rumor's around. All my men want to go out and get drunk today, but I guess they're working so they won't be the first to get the sack. I don't even know if we can start the three-to-eleven shift today. Almost positive we won't start the night shift. Well, we'll just close down and live off our fat. Next year I don't want to be in business. Next year we can all lock up and

245

go fishing, the way I see it. At least in my business."

"Well, luckily for me, I don't decide those things. I get my orders from the main office."

Samuel Eaton tapped himself on the chest. "I'm the villain in this town. I'm the son of a bitch that's going to take the bread out of the babies' mouths. If there's no milk in the women's teats, it's my fault. Not a single one said thank-you when I raised wages voluntarily, but wait till you hear them next year. *Next week!* Thank you, William."

"Thank you, William," said Henry Van Peltz.

"Well, if I didn't have a thick hide I'd have been out of this business years ago."

"Sam, I don't consider myself on the same plane as you when it comes to business, because I'm not. I give orders that don't originate in my brain, and I'm the first one to admit I wouldn't have the job I have if my father hadn't married my mother. I have to admit it. Everybody knows it. But since they made me general manager here I've tried to earn my salary, tried to make a business man of myself. And when you say you had to have a thick hide, I say that goes for every business man. And the more responsibility you have, the thicker your hide has to be."

"I guess mine was thick to begin with," said Samuel Eaton. "What are you aiming at?"

"In this conversation? Oh, nowhere, I guess. I guess I just didn't want you to think you're the only man with a thick hide. In the last fifteen or twenty years mine has gotten thicker, too."

"Thicker than it was, maybe, but not thick. All I've ever been was a puddler, an ironmonger. Fifty-six years of age, and I've made some money and lost some. Right now I'm ahead of the game, but not because I'm a clever business man. I'm not. The man that built this house, Mr. Johnson, he once accused me of having no imagination and I don't know but that he was right. Now he could size up a property, big or little, and tell what it was worth and what could be gotten out of it. He had that kind of imagination, and he was a clever business man. But he never gave me any credit for knowing anything about my business. But I do, Henry. Unfortunately for other people it's the only thing I do know. I can walk through my place and I see everything that's going on. I don't do things the way Charlie Schwab does. He has his way, and I have mine. He'll stop and talk to the men and they love him. I don't do things that way. I walk through my place and I go back to my office. But if I go through it again in an hour, I'll know what's been done in that hour. Or what hasn't been done. I know how many 'I' beams there were in the lower yards, and by God I know if the kid threading bolts has been on the job or out loafing in the crapper. And I like that part of the work. I'd rather be the general superintendent than the chairman of the board. Except for the money. But I pay a man a salary to do the work I like while I sit at a desk and try to run a profitable operation, doing the work that old Mr. Johnson would have liked. I'd like nothing better than to take charge of the blooming-mill for a week, and boss the open hearth, run one of the traveling cranes. But I can't. If I got up in the cab of one of the cranes my men would think I was trying to be Charlie Schwab. They all know I can run one, they all know I can run a drill press or back-up for a riveter. But if I went down in the mill and did any of those things they'd think I was crazy, and I'll tell you what else they'd think. They'd think the work was so easy that they'd get careless. Did you ever see a man get his arm caught in the blooming-mill? Or *hear* him? I did. I got a couple of one-armed men on the payroll from that kind of an accident. And could I ever tell them that it happened through carelessness? Their own God damn carelessness? Huh. They'd lynch me. They wouldn't lynch Charlie Schwab, but they'd cook me on the slag heap. I inherited *my* job, and it doesn't make any difference to them that my father made me work in every mill and shop and storeroom and shanty on the property. I wear a collar and tie, and I don't bring my lunch in a pail. But I love it, although pretty soon I'm going to have to start carrying a revolver again. Today is Monday? By Thursday I'll start getting threatening letters again. By Christmas I'll get one or two every day. That reminds me, I must remember to put a night watchman on at the farm. In fact, one for day and one at night. I guess I didn't tell you, George Fry quit this morning."

"George Fry quit? Oh, he'll be back."

"Oh, no he won't. I'll have something to say about that."

"Well, now, did he quit or did you fire him?"

"He quit. But I hope *he* doesn't think he's coming back. It's between him and me, by the way, so don't let that affect you if he comes to you for a job. It didn't have anything to do with his work."

"What happened, if it's any of my affair?"

"Oh—let's just say that George expressed a more or less typical, a more or less general opinion of me. In a matter that was none of his God damn business, or anybody else's, for that matter."

"I see."

"Well, maybe you do, Henry. I don't know."

"Did he threaten you?"

"Did George threaten me? Oh, no. He got a little fresh, he overstepped, but George wouldn't threaten me. Why?"

"Oh, I thought you may have had that in mind when you said you were going to start carrying a revolver."

"No, no. The revolver, and the watchmen, they're to be on the safe side in case one of those crank letters materializes. No, it had nothing to do with George. Besides, George has got religious in his declining years. Turned Catholic."

"He has? Since when?"

"I guess about a year ago, I think he said."

Henry Van Peltz looked at his friend. "Sam, I think you ought to be careful."

"About George Fry?"

"Yes, about George Fry."

"To tell you the truth, Henry, I don't think he's all there. He's harmless, but I can't have him around any more after the way he spoke to me this morning. And he quit, I didn't fire him."

"That isn't going to make much difference. I agree with you that you wouldn't find it pleasant to have him around if he got fresh, but don't get careless. George is going to be sore as hell at you for letting him go, and he may want to take it out on you some way."

"Henry, is this psychology or something?"

"Yes. Psychology. It's a very interesting subject."

"Sure. I use psychology all the time. Well, not all the time. But you can't use it on everybody."

"Yes you can, or a psychologist can. In any case, I think you ought to watch out for George Fry. As you say, he may not be all there."

"But harmless."

"Have you ever felt like killing anybody?"

"Have I!"

"But you're all there. George isn't, and he may feel like killing you."

"I wish I didn't have any more to worry about than the danger I'm in from George Fry."

"You may not be in any danger, and I certainly don't want you to worry. But don't—get—careless."

Here William extended to Samuel Eaton a pewter salver on which lay a folded piece of paper. Sam took it and read it and thanked William, dismissing him. "Now that was one of your rules, Henry."

"It's a good rule. I didn't make it up. Any good club, when there's a message for a member, the servant hands it to him folded."

"Well, it's all right in Philadelphia, or New York. Those fellows, there are always some of them that are carrying on sub-rosa with this woman or that one—"

"Who sometimes happens to be the wife of another member."

"But not in Port Johnson."

"Not very likely, but there's always a first time."

"Henry, you're too sophisticated. You should have lived in New York. Or Paris."

"Probably."

"Mind you, I think most of the things you do for this club are a good idea. We're not the Elks, so let's be as much like the good clubs as we can. But one or two things *are* a little fancy. Anyway, this message is from my mistress. Martha wants me to call her. Excuse me?"

Samuel Eaton went to one of the telephone booths and called Martha.

"Sam, isn't it wonderful?"

"Isn't what wonderful?"

"Peace! The Armistice!"

"Yes, of course. It's great. Is that what you called me about?"

"Of course, dear. Just think, we'll have Alfred home in no time. We will, won't we?"

"Very soon, I should think."

"Oh, I'm so happy."

"Well, just don't get too happy."

"Oh, I'm all right. Who are you with?"

"Henry. Henry Van Peltz."

"Oh, isn't that nice. Tell him I'm so glad for him and Maude. I think I'll just telephone Maude."

"That would be nice. Yes, why don't you?"

"I feel like stretching out my arms and saying how glad I am for everybody. Are all the people marching and parading? I have a notion to come in and join the celebration."

"Most of it's over, now, Martha."

"But is it *all* over? I could have George bring me in and we could meet you."

"There really isn't anything to see now. A few intoxicated people on Lower Montgomery, but I think most people have gone home."

"Oh, that's too bad. This is a day they ought to celebrate all day."

"I imagine they are, at home."

"Then, Sam, why don't you come home? Bring Henry. Bring Henry and Maude. It isn't much fun here, with just the servants. I gave them each a glass of champagne."

"Oh."

"Oh, I only had one glass, Sam. When I say I gave them each a glass, I meant I only had one glass and gave the rest to them. That's what I meant to say."

"Well—if you'd like to call Maude, go ahead. And I'll wait till you let me know. Will you call right back? I'll wait here beside the phone."

In a few minutes she called him again. "Maude isn't home. The maid said she went across the street to the Nagles, and I didn't want to call her there. Intruding. Would you like to bring Henry home for lunch?"

"Well, we are just about to order it here, and I have a lot to do this afternoon."

"All right. Goodbye."

Among the many hundreds of celebrationists there were only a few who spoke to George Fry by name as he made himself a member of the crowd in Lower Montgomery Street. He had not been in many crowds in his lifetime; his work had always been of a nature that kept him by himself, for most of the years among horses, and in the recent years with the horses and motor cars. Some, if not many of the people who did speak to him had literally never been on the same level with him: they were the citizens who knew him as the Eatons' coachman, sitting in a carriage and waiting for some member of the family, or as the Eatons' chauffeur, but always the height of the carriage or the automobile above the citizens on the sidewalk. Some of those people had never seen George Fry standing up, and to them his face was familiar enough after so many years, but the face and torso belonged in a vehicle and in livery, and the man who alone and on foot was being jostled along by the crowd was almost a stranger to them. To them it was like suddenly coming upon their clergyman, a familiar figure in the pulpit on Sunday, in a baseball uniform; different height, different garb, different surroundings. Hardly any women in the crowd recognized George Fry. He would have been recognized by the ladies who were friends of the Eatons and by their servants, but few of either were in the crowd. Most of the few who did recognize him were women and girls who worked in the stores patronized by the Eatons. The whores whom he had patronized were staying out of this crowd, partly because Brophy's men had ordered them to, partly because business had commenced early that day.

George Fry liked being in this crowd, this good-natured crowd that now, as the morning changed over to afternoon, was slightly thinning out, walking arm-in-arm in pairs and fours and sixes, and stopping to be amused by any little divertive behavior—a dancing couple, a man playing a banjo, a girl child in a homemade Red Cross nurse uniform, a trio of men with a half-barrel of beer in a wheelbarrow, a couple of Negroes playing mouth-organ and bones, a small boy waving an American flag and a tricolor. Church bells had been ringing off and on all morning, so that the ringing of the Angelus had failed to remind the citizens that it was dinner-time, and for the same reason the noon whistle at Eaton's had been ignored.

But hunger itself did what the usual signals had not done, and some of the citizens were leaving the crowd to go home to eat. Others, very festive, decided to eat at one or another of the downtown restaurants, but in every case there was a line waiting their turn, even at the lunchroom in the Reading Railway station.

The thought of food was the first reminder to George Fry of his new status. In more than thirty years he had seldom been required to arrange for his own meals. At the farm and on trips with the Eatons his meals had been provided for him and all he had to do was eat them; and when he was on a drunk he cared nothing about eating. But now, sober and alone, and unable to get into a restaurant, he felt the first shock of the separation from the old life and its habits. Immediately, too, he began to wonder what he would do for a bed that night. He was determined not to return to the farm except to get his clothing and a few belongings. And he had heard often enough that there was not a bed available in a boarding-house in the borough; indeed, some men at the mill occupied beds in shifts; a man's bed would be slept in while he was at work. Food; a place to sleep; and now he realized that he had no friends. To live in the same place more than thirty years, to bid people the time of day, know their names and faces, be known to them; but he could not think of a time when a man or woman had asked him into his house, invited him to share a meal. There was not a home in which he was welcome. Among all these laughing, smiling, happy, friendly men and women there was not one to whom he could say, "Will you give me a bed for the night?"

His hunger was a problem easily solved. He bought half a loaf of bread at the bakery and asked them to slice it for him; at the meat market he bought some sliced ham and bologna, and at the drug store he bought a pint bottle of ginger ale to wash it all down. He took his food and drink to the railway station where he was sure he could sit down while eating and would not be subject to the stares of the Lower Montgomery Street celebrators. After he finished he bought a cigar, and tried to put away the thought of the coming night by enjoying the sights at the station. But the prospects were disagreeable.

He was decently dressed in his black suit and overcoat and brown fedora. His collar and cuffs were clean and his shave was lasting him well. His shoes were polished and only slightly smudged from his mingling with the crowd. But he had only three or four dollars in his pocket. The rest of his money was in his savings account, and he could not draw it out under two weeks' notice. In the morning he would have whatever money Samuel Eaton decided to give him, but until then he had to be careful. They would welcome him in the whore-houses; he had always been generous; but he was as determined to stay away from them as he was to shun the Eaton farm. Josephine and Nellie would help him out: they both kept some cash hidden somewhere in the house; but there again, it was the farm.

It was not that he had been softened by the easy living on the farm. He rose every morning at five, or earlier if necessary, and no work on the farm was too hard for him to do, even now. The Eatons continued to keep two saddle horses that would also go in harness, and George Fry took care of them and exercised them daily, which was not back-breaking labor but was not clerk's work either. He could clean and repair the tack, which kept his hands in good condition; his shoulders and arms got good exercise with the pitch-fork and broom and shovel; and his legs were supple (which he pronounced soople). And his work with the automobiles was almost entirely physical, since he understood very little of what went on under the hood. For a man his age, which he often had a hard time remembering, as birthdays meant little to him, he was in fine shape, and he was not afraid of the physical discomfort involved in sleeping elsewhere than in his cot at the Eatons' stable. The stationmaster, whom he had known long but not well, probably would give him permission to stretch out on one of the station benches for the night. And there were other places like that in the town—hotel lobbies, livery stables, the harness shop, the blacksmith shop—where he would have a roof over his head through the night. But he could fancy them all wanting to ask him questions, even if they didn't come out with them, and he did not want them *looking* questions at him and wondering why he was not sleeping where he had always slept. And he knew his people: as the Eatons' coachman, a steady man with a steady job, he derived a certain standing commensurate with the Eatons' standing; as George Fry, a man without work, he was a lone man whom they had not got to know very well. Most of them would take a chance on him, but he did not want that favor. He wanted favors from no one. He was George Fry who had that day quit the best job of its kind in Port Johnson because he was independent. There was no one in the town, his world, to whom he could say that he would not work for a man who worshipped a long-dead boy more than he admired a son who had been spared from death many times in a war.

In this new habit that he was forming, this practice that his church called the examination of conscience, he asked himself why he had not quit before. For many of his years with Samuel Eaton he had hated the man, even before the older boy died, but especially afterward, for what Eaton had done to the younger son. He had sometimes wondered whether Eaton had knowledge that the younger boy was not his son, but Eaton could not have sanely thought so. The boy was a refinement of the father, getting from the Johnson blood a thinner nose, a cleaner chin-line; but the shape of the head was a duplicate of the father's and the set and color of the eyes were the same. And in order to give belief to the suspicion, George Fry had had to consider the mother's disposition and opportunity for going with an-other man, and on both counts he had had to judge her inno-cent. In recent years she had taken to the bottle, but in the years when she might have made the child that turned out to be Alfred, she was bedazzled by Samuel Eaton and by no one else. The Miller fellow who shot himself, he had seen Miller staring at her with nothing short of love in his eyes, but George Fry could almost take his oath personally that they had never been alone together long enough to commit adultery. Even if she had not been so bedazzled by Eaton, even if she had been willing to get down on the floor for Miller, there would not have been time before a servant or someone in the family walked in on them. In those days the only man with the opportunity was George Fry himself, and in those days he had wanted her so much that if he had believed her guilty with someone besides Miller, he would have thrown her on his cot and taken his pleasure of her even if he went to prison for it. But a man knew. You could wrongly suspect an innocent woman, but when it was a guilty woman, a man knew. In those old days of twenty years ago, Martha Eaton was faithful to Samuel Eaton, no matter what she may have done later that she did in drink or made her take to drink.

And now George Fry, deliberately separated from the Eaton family, was beginning to understand why he had not quit be-fore: the lust he had felt for Martha had turned to love for her and wanting to be at least that near to her—sitting beside her in the runabout, giving her a hand-up when she rode, seeing her day after day—as long as he could. And he loved the son because he loved her, continued to love the son for no reason other than that he had learned to love him. And it was easy to hate Samuel Eaton because he was stupid and because his stupidity made him cruel. And the love for Martha that had begun as lust turned into pity and protection of her when the years took the lust out of his love for her, and—he knew—she began to give herself to someone else, somebody in Philadel-phia. When the great suspicion came that she was meeting a man in Philadelphia, George Fry wanted her no more. And he wanted not to want her, for he had learned that to want her was a sin, and to want to want her was a mortal sin. In his new life the only one of the Eatons that he could find room for was the boy. There was a sin somewhere in what he felt against Samuel Eaton, and there could be venial sin in what was left

253

of the old lustful thoughts of Martha, but his feeling for Alfred was the nearest thing in his own life to the experience of loving his fellow man.

He heard a voice, and realized with embarrassment that he had fallen asleep. "George? George? Wake up, George. Are you taking Number 7? She's getting ready to pull out."

The speaker was Dory Boxmiller, the railway policeman.

"No, no. Hyuh, Dory. No I'm not taking Number 7. I guess I fell asleep."

"All dolled up, I thought maybe you was going to the city. A lot are."

"No, not me."

"You didn't have one too many, George?"

"No, I didn't have none at all."

"Because if you did, come back in our office and sleep her off there. Here it don't look good, you know, all dolled up and like you was drunk. We got a sofa back there."

"I appreciate that, Dory. But I guess I just needed a couple minutes."

"More than a couple minutes, George. You're lucky your missus didn't see you."

"My missus?"

"Eaton. She's taking Number 7. She come in and bought her ticket and I seen you and I stood in front of you to keep her from getting a look at you."

"Taking this train?"

"She can't see you from here, she's in the chair car on the hind end. Don't worry."

"How did she get here? Was he with her?"

"Eaton? No. I don't know how she got here, but she's on that train pulling out now. Pulling out near ten minutes behind time, too. Some God damn fool's gonna get ground into hamburger. They been walking on that right of way all day and we got coalies and freights goin' through that don't make a stop. I'll be back in a couple of minutes, George."

"All right, Dory," said George Fry.

He had never expected that the time would come when he could apply the popular saying, nothing to do and all day to do it. Now it was that and more: something he wished he could do, but no way to do it. What was there he could do for Martha Eaton? Was there anything anybody could do for Martha Eaton? Anybody could do for anybody? People tried; Dory Boxmiller had just tried, and that had made George Fry feel good for a minute. But he had been led to believe, or had led himself to believe, that he would be a better man when a time like this came, and he was not a better man. There was nothing he could do and no zealous wish to do anything. He stood up and straightened his necktie and overcoat and hat, and

254

without even consenting to it he was on his way to River Street; for company, yes; for a place to spend the night, yes; for lust, no. Most of all to return to one part of the only life he had ever known. And he secretly knew that in the morning he would go to see Samuel Eaton and try to return to the rest of that life.

He rang the doorbell of the River Street house and the mistress of the establishment opened the door a few inches. "We're closed. Come back tonight . . . *It's George! George Fry. You* can come in. My goodness." She opened the door wide, closed it quickly after him and led him to the parlor where four or five men were sitting around a table, drinking whiskey. "You better come out in the kitchen with me, Georgie."

She put a bottle on the kitchen table. "The long-lost stranger," she said. "You shouldn't of stayed away so long. You had me thinking maybe one of my girls gave you a dose. Then I thought maybe you married a rich widow."

"I'm not as young as I was."

"Listen, George, once you start doin' without it, a man in his fifties they say he can get used to doin' without it and then when the spirit is willing the flesh is weak. I got all new girls since you were in last. And after the parade broke up it's been like Saturday night. You're lookin' good."

"I feel all right, Em."

"Wuddia think about this? We beat those dirty Huns finally."

"Yes, we finally beat them. Here's to you, Em."

"Have a smile, Georgie." She raised her glass. "I got a new young Southern girl. Oh, she's white. She come very highly recommended from a friend of mine runs a place in Baltimore, Maryland. You'll see her. A good worker and I hope you get to like her. That is, if you don't stay away so long this time. She says she's twenty-one and I believe her. Twenty-three at the most. I had to raise my prices, but you never complained."

"I won't be able to pay you till tomorrow."

"Oh, are you broke?"

"I don't have any with me."

"Well, you're not gonna get attended to and then stay away for a couple of years I hope. Expenses are murderous, George, and a good worker like this Southern kid, she can practically name her own price."

"What *is* her price?"

"She gets ten dollars and up, George. That is, *I* do. But I might as well tell you, she makes a lot extra on tips because she likes to please."

"Ten dollars!"

"Listen, George, there was men working out at your boss's, they wanted to *marry* her. I tell you, she's the star attraction. They bring her presents. Maybe you'd rather go up with one of the other girls in their early thirties."

"I was gonna stay all night.

"Without no money, George?"

"I can give you an I. O. U."

"How would I collect that? I'll take a bank cheque on a town bank."

"I don't have that kind of an account, Em."

"Well, I never turn a man away that aint drunk, but you object to ten dollars for the best little hooker I ever had, and you want to stay all night and give me an I. O. U. And I guess you wanted to drink my booze and have a little light collation. Be reasonable, George."

"I got my watch and chain I could leave with you."

"Listen, I got enough watches up in my room to start a jewelry store. Rifkin can run his jewelry store and I'll run this place. You can go up with one of my girls in their early thirties and I'll trust you for five dollars, but that's all. You owe me four bits already for the drinks, but I won't charge you."

"Tomorrow I'll pay you double what I owe you."

"Tomorrow I may be in jail. I don't fear Brophy, but it'd be just like them state cops to raid me tonight. Anyway, how do I know you only come here because your were broke. I don't have no way of knowing whether you been going to my competitors the last couple years. Not that I call them competition, the kind of places they run."

"I never went any place else."

"Now I wonder. I wonder."

"How much would it cost me to stay all night?"

"Who with?"

"This Southern one."

"I knew you had the money. Fifty dollars in advance. But you don't get her till after eleven o'clock. She'll be busy right up till then."

"It's too much money, Em. That's what I used to get a month till the war started."

"Well, take it or leave it. You'll be keeping her away from the other customers and she'd make that much. And some of them don't want anybody else. And fifty dollars I'm making you a price."

He shook his head. "That's almost three weeks' work for me."

"And how do I know you won't abuse her? If it's two years since you had a piece, you don't know what you're liable to do, and this is a good kid. No sir, fifty dollars in advance. That includes the girl and the room and supper and a few drinks. I'm losing on it, so take it or leave it, George."

He shook his head. "I'd have to go around and try to get the loan of the money and I never borrowed a nickel from any son of a bitch in this town. No, I'm too old to beg for money to go to bed with some whore."

"You don't use that word in my place and you know it. Anyway, you been begging me for the last ten minutes. You can have one of the other girls and I'll trust you for the five-spot, but that's as much as I can do."

"No, thanks just the same."

He started to get up and a young girl entered the kitchen from the backstairs door. She was wearing a silk kimono and smoking a cigarette.

"Hello, mister," she said.

"Is this her?" said George Fry.

"That's my darling," said Em. "Come here, darling."

The girl went to Em and sat on her lap, and Em stroked her hair and made waves of it with her fingers. The girl put her arm around Em's neck and looked expressionlessly at George Fry.

"Who's he?" said the girl.

"Oh, he used to be one of our regulars."

"Not since I come here, though," said the girl.

"No, dear," said Em. "Stand up, dear, and give him a free look. Open your kimono."

"I don't want to," said the girl. "I don't like him." She made *him* a two-syllable word.

"Oh, now, George is all right. Gettin' a little tight-fisted, though."

"It wouldn't do him a bit of good even if he wasn't. I wouldn't go up with him for a hundred dollars."

"Why wouldn't you? What's wrong with me?"

"I don't trust you, that's why. Em, if you make me go up with him I'll move up the street, I swear I will."

"You're not gonna have to go up with him, darling. But you got him wrong. He don't make trouble for anybody. I know George a long time."

"I can't he'p that. Don't you look at me, old man. You stop lookin' at me like that." She put her hand to the collar of her kimono and closed it to her chin.

"I guess we were wastin' our time talkin'," said Em.

"I guess so," said George Fry. "Before I go, why don't you like me?"

"Like you? Mister, I hate you. You look evil."

Em laughed. "She gets funny spells, this little kiddo. But don't go away mad, George."

"What's a man *supposed* to do?" said George Fry, and turned and left them.

He pushed his way angrily through the men on River Street until he reached Lower Montgomery. It was still day-light, not yet five o'clock, but the lights were bright in the shop windows. He turned up Montgomery Street until he came to Rifkin's jewelry store. There was no other customer in the store, as Rifkin came from the partitioned rear section.

"Good evening," said Rifkin. "Yes sir?"

George Fry placed his watch and chain on the showcase. "What'll you give me for the watch and chain? Till tomorrow."

"Oh, I'm not in that business. We don't buy, we sell. Don't you happen to be Mr. Eaton's driver?"

"Yes. I want to get some money on my watch, till tomorrow."

Rifkin took a loupe out of his pocket and examined the watch. "It's a nice mechanism, needs a cleaning. Are you financially embarrassed, is that what's troubling you? Short of ready cash? You live out at Mr. Eaton's farm, am I right?"

"Yes. I only want the money till tomorrow."

"I see. Financially embarrassed and would like to pledge the watch and chain. Well, we don't make it our policy, but I might be able to help out an employe of Mr. Samuel Eaton. What amount of cash did you have in mind?"

"Fifty dollars."

"Fifty dollars. Well, now I wouldn't be able to sell it for fifty dollars, you know that, my dear sir. It didn't cost you that new. Or whoever presented you with it. Therefore if you forgot to come in tomorrow or the next day or the day after that I'd have to take a loss. I couldn't go over ten dollars, and then I'd be going against our policy. Is ten dollars any use to you?"

"All right. Ten."

"I'll make you out a receipt. I don't have the regular pawn ticket, because we're not in that business. This is what you might call an accommodation. Nice watch. Shouldn't leave it go so long without a cleaning. There you are. And here is five and five is ten dollars. And you'll stop in for it tomorrow or would you like to leave it here and I'll give it a good cleaning. Two dollars."

"All right, Thanks."

"Come in again."

Thirteen, almost fourteen dollars. It would buy all the whiskey he needed and a cheap woman, and whatever happened to him after that he did not care.

It was a day on which millions of Americans, forsaking their usual habits of proper behavior, were saying they did not care; saying it, or illustrating it without saying it. For much the most of them it would be only a temporary thing, without serious consquences, without lasting effects. But it was one of those few days in our history in which all the living shared a participation, that would be remembered by all; and in the future recollections of the day each man, each woman, and almost all boys and girls would be able to recall the day totally and more accurately than he could most of his personal holidays or days of personal disaster.

To J. R. Weinkoop it was, as he kept saying, certainly a day he would never forget. He wanted to be nice, he wanted to join in the fun, he wanted everybody to have a good time. He had a son in the 103d Engineers, 28th Division, and the Armistice almost certainly meant that his son would be coming home. But J. R. Weinkoop had passed most of his life under discipline that in its way was as strict as the Army's, and as he often reminded himself, he too was working for the government, since the government had taken over the railroads. As conductor of Number 7 he had been encouraged to think of himself as part of the gigantic effort to win the war and he had put into his work even more of the conscientiousness and pride that, with some help from seniority, had got him his regular run on one of the Company's best trains. As is so often the case, he looked more like a bank president than he did a sea captain, but a lot like both and for good reason since his job carried with it the dignity associated with the one job and the special learning required of the other. He ran a taut train but a happy train.

But on today's run the public had just about exhausted his patience. Beginning at Gibbsville, which was the end of the passenger line, the passengers had shown they did not care how many rules and regulations were violated. He had left Gibbsville at 2:25, fifteen minutes late, because some grown men who should have known better wanted to ride on what they called the cow-catcher. They were removed by the railway police. Then there were dozens of people who rode the train only as far as Swedish Haven, the first station stop after Gibbsville, and had good-naturedly refused to pay their fares and announced they were going to ride home free on Number 8. J. R. Weinkoop's train had four coaches and a Pullman car and the money the Company—or the government—lost by the passengers' refusal to pay fares was more than it had lost in J. R. Weinkoop's entire career. Hardly any of the passengers had bought a ticket and those few had represented the legitimate traveling passengers. The others were joy-riding deadheads, and until this day nobody deadheaded on a J. R. Weinkoop train unless he was on Company business.

They were not vandalistic people, but they were causing damage in the coaches, burning the velour in the coaches, blocking up the toilets and twice breaking windows. At Gibbsville there had not been a legitimate passenger in the Pullman, but the chairs had been taken over by some deadheads. J. R. Weinkoop handled that outrage by announcing that he would not move his train until they got out of the Pullman, and when they moved to the coaches he had Arthur Woodruff, the porter, lock the doors. It was bad enough to have destruction in the coaches, but the Pullman upholstery and linen and mother-of-pearl inlaid paneling and frosted glass ceiling lamps and Brussels carpet runner would have cost a pretty penny to replace.

At Port Johnson station J. R. Weinkoop and Arthur Woodruff recognized Mrs. Samuel Eaton and she was whisked into the Pullman. She knew J. R. Weinkoop as Mr. Weinkoop and Arthur Woodruff as Arthur, and she seemed to them like someone from the past, orderly history of Number 7. She had never failed to give Arthur a quarter at the end of a trip, which would have made her memorable among passengers who usually gave him a dime or nothing; and she always asked about Mrs. Weinkoop, whom she never had seen and never was likely to see, and always reported to J. R. Weinkoop that her own three children were well. It was by no means the first time that she had had the Pullman car all to herself, but on this day there was something reassuring about having the only passenger turn out to be this particular lady. But the train had hardly pulled out of Port Johnson yards before she went to the ladies' room, remaining there for the better part of a half hour, and when she came out and went to her chair, or to a chair which was not hers, Arthur Woodruff knew that her swaying was not being caused by the motion of the car. She was either very sick or very drunk, and when he went to investigate, by a solicitous adjustment of the carpeted stool at her feet, he got a whiff of drinking-liquor that relieved him of doubt.

She quickly fell asleep. He knew she was asleep by the fact that she ceased her repeated humming of the first six notes of "Keep the Home Fires Burning." She began to snore in a manner that caused her lips to vibrate, and when a bend of the tracks threw her out of her chair and onto the floor, she lay there. Arthur Woodruff was reasonably sure she had not been hurt, but the possibility of injury was a serious matter and not his responsibility. He summoned J. R. Weinkoop.

Together they put her back in her chair without her waking, and at the next station the train was delayed by J. R. Weinkoop while he composed a discreet telegram to the stationmaster at the Reading Terminal in Philadelphia:

CONFIDENTIAL AND URGENT HAVE WIFE OF PROMINENT MAN ABOARD MY TRAIN SHE IS UNCONSCIOUS MAY BE FROM DRINK BUT ALSO FELL IN PULLMAN NUMBER 65 PLEASE MEET NUMBER 7 WITH NURSE AND STRETCHER (SIGNED) J R WEINKOOP CONDUCTOR

The telegram was dispatched over the Company wire and at the next station J. R. Weinkoop was handed a telegram addressed to him:

BY ORDER DIVISION SUPERINTENDENT TELEGRAPH WOMANS
NAME (SIGNED) D D JONES STATIONMASTER

J. R. Weinkoop telegraphed the name and boarded his train, the matter now technically out of his hands, but as he went about the performance of his duties he had unconsciously the distinction of being one of the few citizens who were going through the day less with jubilation than with pity and disgust. The Iron Hat himself, the division superintendent, was on the platform at the Reading Terminal.

"Hyuh, Weinkoop. Where is she? Did she recover consciousness?"

"No sir. I'll take you to her."

"We're going to wait till all the passengers are off the platform. This is the Company doctor. He'll examine her in the car first, then we can decide what to do with her. All right, Doc."

Arthur Woodruff, unbearably nervous in the presence of the Iron Hat, told the doctor all he knew, and the doctor made his examination.

"She's dead drunk," said the doctor. "I'll say something else in my report, but that's what it is. Everything. Malnutrition. She's in a bad way. She ought to be in a hospital."

"I want to get rid of her. I don't want her on Company property. Why the hell didn't she take the Pennsy?" said the Iron Hat.

"I don't think it made any difference to her whether she took the Pennsy or the Reading or the Lehigh Valley," said the doctor.

"Well it does to us. Weinkoop, you write a special report, confidential, and let me see it before you sign it. You, too, Doc. I want to see your report before you sign it. I'll get the porter's from the Pullman fellows."

"In the meantime, she ought to be in a hospital. I'm going to say that in my report."

"I don't mind that. That'll prove she was drunk before she ever got on Company property. There's nothing wrong with her that happened since she bought her ticket, is there?"

"Not unless you count what she drank on the train."

"I don't count it. I tell you what, if she goes to a hospital, Doc, you go with her and you be sure and get it straight with the hospital people, we're not taking any responsibility. This is a courtesy to her husband, a friend of the Company's but that's all. Put her in a private room and keep her there till Mr. Eaton can get here. I'll get the hospital superintendent on the phone, but in the meanwhile don't let some God damn underling make you sign a lot of papers."

"I know how to take care of underlings in a hospital," said the doctor.

"All right, I'm glad you do. I'll leave it all up to you. Weinkoop, get to work on your report and bring it to me. You go back on Number 10? That'll give you plenty of time."

The Iron Hat turned and walked down the platform to the passenger gate. It was opened for him by an anonymous trainman and he walked through. In a few steps he saw a man he knew. "Hyuh, there, Frolick, what are you doing on Company property? Looking for a piece of tail as usual?"

"As usual."

"I thought so. Well, you won't find any here."

"Nobody left on that train?"

"Nobody left but the crew. Come on I'll buy you a cup of coffee. There was a lot of nooky on that train but they're all down on Market Street by this time."

"Well, then I'll go down on Market Street too. Thanks for the invitation. So long."

"So long." The Iron Hat watched his friend until he was out of sight, and a thought came to him: Frolick and Mrs. Eaton? No. Frolick didn't know women like Samuel Eaton's wife. But a woman who got drunk on a train might know a man like Frolick. Well, that was what railway detectives were for. Information was protection, and Samuel Eaton had often made things hot for the Company, taking things all the way to the top, and then the top passed the heat back to the Iron Hat. Information was protection.

Doris Muhlenberg received the call when the Iron Hat telephoned Samuel Eaton. She was quite irritable, for her, having been deprived of her own share of the Armistice celebration, and having been snapped at by the secretaries of other men who had worked all afternoon.

"Mr. Eaton is here, yes, but I'm sorry you can't speak to him. He's very busy."

"Listen to me, miss, I don't know whether you recognized my name, but I'm the division superintendent of the Reading and this is important. And what's more, it's personal. So you be a good little lady and connect me with your boss."

She got up, for the fiftieth or hundredth time that day, and entered Samuel Eaton's private office. "Now it's the division superintendent on the Reading. He says it's personal."

"Oh, all right," said Samuel Eaton. He picked up the receiver. "Hello."

"Mr. Eaton, I got some bad news for you."

"Well, that's different from usual. Usually I have bad news for you. But my secretary says it's personal."

"Can anybody hear me, overhear me?"

"You're safe. What is it?"

"It's about Mrs. Eaton. Your wife. Do you know where she is?"

"Yes, she's at our farm."

"No she isn't. She's in the Jefferson Hospital."

"You're crazy. It must be someone else."

"Now I'm not used to being called crazy, Mr. Eaton. I have as many men under me as you have under you, even if I don't make as much money. More men, if it comes to that. So I'm not used to being called crazy, and what's more I'm doing you a favor."

"All right, you're not crazy. Now what is this about my wife and the Jefferson Hospital?"

"We took her off Number 7 at the Terminal, and I hate to tell a man this, but she was intoxicated. In fact she was so intoxicated that we met her with a doctor and put her in an ambulance."

"How did you happen to do that?"

"The conductor on Number 7—"

"That's Weinkoop, isn't it?"

"J. R. Weinkoop, a thirty-year man and one of the best. He saw what condition she was in and he wired ahead, luckily for all concerned. The doctor examined Mrs. Eaton and said she had advanced alcoholism and malnutrition, I think those were his words."

"Was she alone?"

"Yes, she was alone, but we got her in a private room with a trained nurse. She fell off her chair in the Pullman car, but she wasn't hurt. No injury of any kind whatsoever from the fall. It was a case of intoxication pure and simple. She even had some liquor with her on the train."

"Have you spoken to her?"

"Nobody has. Unless by this time maybe the nurse has. She's safe where she is, but I presumed you'd want to know."

"Thank you very much for your kindness. Looking at my watch, I can't get anything before Number 11 on the Reading. And there's nothing on the Pennsy before ten-twenty."

"I can make up a special and put it at your disposal, the only thing is you'll have to wait for a locomotive to come down from Reading. That'll cost you the price of thirty fares, Mr. Eaton."

"Thank you very much, but I think I'd do better to drive in by automobile. Less fuss. Who knows about this?"

"Well, we did what we could, but the train crew know, the Pullman porter, the doctor. The hospital people. And me."

263

"Can I rely on you to handle the crew?"

"You can rely on J. R. Weinkoop. But it's liable to get out anyway. You know, one man tells his wife, and she tells some other woman. But I don't have any Port Johnson men on that Number 7 crew, so maybe it won't get out."

"Good. Well, I have my car here and I'll start in about a quarter of an hour. How is she signed in at the hospital?"

"That's where we took care of you, Mr. Eaton. She's there as Doctor Williams's patient. Room 502. There aint gonna be any newspaper reporters finding her name registered."

"Congratulations. And thanks. I've had to go over your head once or twice to complain, but this time I'm going to see to it that you get some praise."

"You better not, Mr. Eaton. You'd have to tell them why you wanted them to praise me."

"Well, that's quite true. But I can say a good word for you in some other connection. Doctor Williams's patient. Room 502. Thank you."

"Just remember, Mr. Eaton. Last summer, I wasn't trying to put you out of business. I just didn't have the cars."

"Oh, that's all forgotten," said Samuel Eaton.

"In a pig's ass it is," said the Iron Hat, but not before he had hung up.

Samuel Eaton stopped at Doris Muhlenberg's desk. "I have to go to Philadelphia right away."

"Is there something wrong?"

"Well—yes. I'll be at the Bellevue-Stratford overnight. Back some time tomorrow. No, I won't be at the Bellevue. I'll be at the Racquet Club, but you're not to tell anybody, no matter who it is. You can go home whenever you want to."

"I hope it's nothing serious."

"Well, it's serious enough to—I'll tell you about it when I get back."

A letter from Sally Eaton, now a sophomore at Bryn Mawr College, to her brother Alfred:

Dearest Alfredo:

If you got my letter written on the night of Nov. 11 you know how overjoyed I was that you will be coming home safe & sound, but I must start by warning you that this is not written in the same mood. Father has asked me to write you so that you will be forewarned and prepared for a shock upon your return. To make a l. s. s., Mother had a very bad relapse on Armistice Day—took the train to Phila.—extremely intoxicated—had to be taken to the hospital—now in a private hospital near Swarthmore. I have a dreadful fear that she was on her way to meet that awful person C. F. but cannot prove it and Father has no inkling of it, so do not mention it to him. She had seemed to be improving. Came to see me here and was at her very best—charming, well-dressed etc.—made a big hit with my friends, many of whom were seeing her for the first time. But Armistice Day was too much for her, dear knows why or how. I suggest you come to B. M. before going home, so that we can discuss the problem. Constance knows. Father and I thought it best to tell her lest there be a slip somehow, somewhere. I hope the Navy discharges you before Xmas, altho it is extremely unlikely that Mother will get home. However, we can hope and pray, altho I feel a hypocrite to mention praying. Nevertheless, I prayed for you, with splendid results, and perhaps it will be effective for our poor, sweet Mother.

All my love,
Sally

They had all longed for the ending of the war and the return to peace. For two years they had been so absorbed in the simplicity of war—the common cause against the common enemy—that they had given no thought to the complexities of peace.

SALLY EATON had chosen a high-backed chair on the Peacock Alley of the Bellevue. By leaning forward and looking to her left she could see anyone who entered from Walnut Street, and by looking to her right she could see the registration desk and above it the wall clocks that gave the time in various distant cities. She was looking at those clocks when she heard his voice.

"Hello, kid."

She jumped to her feet and threw her arms around her brother and kissed him, departing entirely from the warm but dignified procedure she had planned.

"Alfred! Oh, my big handsome brother." She drew away from him. "I thought you'd be in your uniform."

"Not a chance."

"Where is it? When did you arrive? Why are you wearing a suit? I *like* it. But I thought you'd—"

"No. I became a free man at League Island this morning, and then I went to Jacob Reed's and bought a suit, shirt, tie, and then I got these shoes at Steigerwalt's."

"Aren't you going to wear your uniform home?"

"I am not."

"Where did you leave everything?"

"At the Racquet Club. You look well."

"I look *well?* Is that all you can say? I at least said you were handsome."

"All right. You're pretty."

"Not pretty, but I guess that'll have to do. *You* look *older.*"

"Yes. I've been through hell. It ages one."

"Oh, stop, Alfred. But was it bad sometimes?"

"No. The weather was bad sometimes. Cold, and rough, but I can easily see why a man would want to make it a career. I enjoyed it, frankly."

"But the danger."

"Oh, it was there. We saw two submarines, or periscopes, to be accurate. We think we got one of them, and we're not sure of the other. So there was that much danger. I'm sorry, Sal, but the Army fellows and a few marines, they're the ones that had to be brave. *We* had to keep awake, that was the most difficult thing for us. Where do you want me to take you to lunch? Here?"

"No. The Arcadia."

"Is this passé?"

"No, but the Arcadia is more chic. And you'll see lots of pretty girls there."

"Friends of yours? You're not luring me there to meet Bryn Mawr, are you? I want to meet Bryn Mawr all right, but not today."

"No, this isn't a trick. I can't promise you we won't see any, but I haven't planned it."

It was a short walk to the Arcadia, which was below the street level. They ordered oysters, the last of the season, to be followed by lobster Newburg and potatoes Julienne. Until the lobster was served they chatted, as though by agreement, about where he had been and what he did during a typical day. But when the captain and the waiter left them alone Alfred said: "What about home? Where is Mother?"

"Mother is home. You'd never suspect there was anything wrong until you noticed that she has a nurse. Miss Trimingham. I don't know her very well, I've only seen her a few times. But Mother seems to like her, and she's gentle."

"Father. How is he behaving?"

"Extremely well. He's kind and considerate—"

"For him."

"No, not just for him. Really kind and considerate."

"Then he doesn't know anything about Frolick."

"Oh, Lord, no. Mother is supposed to be recovering from a nervous breakdown."

"Well, I guess that's what it is, isn't it?"

"Well, yes, it is."

"Have you found out any more about Frolick?"

"I'm sorry I mentioned him, Alfred. When I wrote that time I was acting on impulse. Suspicion. I didn't know why else she'd want to go to Philadelphia that day. But I'm sure she hasn't seen or heard from him, so I'm sorry I mentioned him."

"A damn good thing for him, I can tell you. Has he ever bothered you?"

"Never."

"Then I guess he learned his lesson. I went to see him. I never told you that, but I did. I beat him up."

"You did? You mean literally beat him up with your fists?"

"Yes. Two years ago Thanksgiving. It's the only way to handle a son of a bitch like him."

"I guess it is."

"I'd be very glad to do it again, too, so if you have any reason to suspect him, just tell me. What about Constance?"

"Constance—Constance has blossomed out."

"And?"

"She thinks she's in love. Convinced of it. A young man from Villanova."

"Where does he go to school?"

"That's what I mean. Villanova College, not the town."

"How did she ever meet him? Where's he from?"

"He's from Gibbsville, or a little town near there. She met him on the Paoli Local."

"He picked her up?"

"Oh, she has some story that she fell and turned her ankle and he helped her get back to school."

"Have you seen him? What's his name?"

"No, I haven't laid eyes on him. His name is John Murphy."

"It is? That's a coincidence. I had a seaman second class named John J. Murphy with me during most of the war. *He* was all right, although not the type for Constance."

"This one I gather is tall and has wavy hair and he's a very good baseball player."

"They all are, the Irish. Well, is he someone we must worry about?"

"I can't truthfully say no. She doesn't get much chance to see him. I have a feeling that it's more on her side than on his."

"It may wear off. We'll see. Have you heard anything from Lex?"

"One letter a year ago."

"I saw him in London at Christmastime. He's thinking of going to Oxford."

"Lex?"

"Thinking about it. That's as far as it'll get. There's some arrangement that Oxford will accept a certain number of American officers, and he thought he might do it. But he won't. He got the Croix de Guerre with palm, did you know that?

And he may get the D. S. C. The Distinguished Service Cross. He wouldn't tell me what for. *There* was somebody you should have seen in uniform. Boots and Sam Browne belt all polished up, uniform made by an English tailor. Swagger stick. And a moustache."

"Lex has a moustache? Awful."

"No, it wasn't. He made me feel like a bus conductor."

"Are you going back to Princeton?"

"No, not the way I feel now. It'd be worse than going back to Knox after a year and a half in college. Much worse. I may change my mind, but I doubt it. I don't know what I want to do, that's the trouble. But right now there's nothing I want to do that I'll need a degree for, and the only reason to go back to Princeton would be so I could tack A.B. after my name."

"Have you got a girl?"

"Nope. No girl. I did something different. Instead of having one in every port, I had several in one port, New York."

"What kind?"

"*All* kinds, and you may draw your own conclusions. What about you?"

"The question I've been dreading. Well, I'm sure Father will tell you, so I might as well. I have a beau."

"Good. Who?"

"Harry Van Peltz." She looked at him appealingly.

"I think I can guess what Father says."

"I don't care what Father says. What do you say?"

"Well, I know more about you than Father does. Father didn't know that you were in love with Peter. That's the first thing that comes to my mind. Are you in love with Harry, or still in love with Peter?"

"I love Harry."

"Are you going to marry him?"

"I would, but I don't think he'll wait till I finish college."

"Is college that important to you?"

"No, but being sure is. I have two more years after this year. I've told him that I'd be secretly engaged to him till then, but he doesn't think that would work. You understand what he means by that."

"Yes, I understand."

"He's twenty-six."

"I thought he was older than that."

"No, he's twenty-six. He loves me, I believe that, but he says he can't promise me that he'd wait two and a half more years."

"That's putting it up to you, isn't it?"

"Yes."

"Well, I'm not going to advise you on that, Sal. I say no. But I know how Harry feels, and at least he's honest."

"But if I can wait, why can't he?"

"Listen, I'm on your side, but I couldn't wait either."

"Wouldn't you have waited for Vicky?"

He hesitated. "I might have waited for Vicky, but I never would for anyone else. After Vicky was killed I learned very fast."

"About sex?"

"Yes."

"Is there so much to learn?"

"Yes, there's the difference between having had it and not having had it. I knew all about it or thought I did at Knox, but the experience is what makes the difference. And I guess Harry's had that."

"I don't know why you say you guess. Of course he has."

"Yes, I'm sure he has. But it hasn't kept him from falling in love with you."

"No, but it's keeping him from marrying me, from waiting."

"Well, Sal, you both know where you stand. There's one thing you ought to realize."

"What's that?"

"You're not *sure* you love Harry."

"Yes I am."

"No you're not. You're using college as an excuse while you make up your mind. You said yourself you want to be sure. In my opinion you're not sure now. You better stay in college, and you better hold on to your chastity."

"I could slap you for that."

He laughed. "Harry should have fallen in love with Constance."

"I didn't laugh at you when you were in love."

He stopped laughing. "No, that's right. You didn't. You know who did, though."

"Nobody did."

"Yes, I think Victoria was laughing at me in that Stutz Bearcat. God, that was a long time ago, wasn't it? I wasn't laughing at you, Sal. I just don't want you to make any mistakes, and I guess I don't want to take the responsibility for what you do. Whatever you do, I'll back you up. I can always take care of the old man."

"Thank you. I didn't mean to get cross."

"That's all right. What else is there I ought to know. How's your tennis?"

"Fair. I'm the singles champion at the Idle Hour."

"That's hardly news."

"No, but now I'm *women's* champion. Over eighteen. And Harry and I are going in the mixed doubles together."

"You ought to win. I've decided that for a year I'm not going to do anything but eat and sleep and play tennis. Now that the old man has given me a membership in the Racquet Club I'm going to learn to play court tennis. Then I'll be able to play with Lex's Uncle Fritz. For the first week I'm going to have breakfast in bed, not because I like to, but when Nellie brings the tray in I'm going to eat and then fall right back on the pillow and go back to sleep. I'm going to get some perfumed bath salts and eau de cologne. I'm going to take an apartment and go in for riotous living."

"Where are you going to take the apartment?"

"I don't know yet. Maybe here, maybe New York."

"I can't see you going in for riotous living."

"Why not?"

"It isn't like you."

"Oh, no?"

"No. I've known some boys that seemed dissipated just by lighting a cigar, but it wouldn't make any difference what you did, you'd still be—"

"What?"

"Dignified, I guess. Does that irritate you?"

"I think you've got me mixed up with Mr. Van Peltz, Harry's father, that is. I know the kind of fellow you mean, that has a cigar and looks like someone trying to be a rake. But I have no intention of appearing to be dissipated. I'm not even going to *be* dissipated. But I'm going to have one hell of a good time, and if I can still look dignified, so much the better. Nobody my age ought to look dissipated. You don't like a young man to look that way, do you?"

"Well, I don't know. I just thought of a boy I know that goes to Penn. He's very wild and he's dissipated-looking, and all my friends disapprove of him heartily, but they all talk about him all the time and always have the latest sleuth on him."

"The what?"

"Sleuth. Gossip. They'd all go out with him if they had the chance, but they say he's carrying on an affair with a married woman."

"Would you go out with him?"

"I might. Once. To see what he's really like."

"Wouldn't Harry object?"

"If he knew, he would. But if I ever went out with the boy I'm talking about I'd certainly never tell Harry. Or anyone else."

"You'd better watch your step."

"You'd better watch *your* step. Every girl you go out with is going to want to marry you, but this boy doesn't want to marry anybody. In fact, they say he has a child in Conshohocken. Or Manayunk. I don't know where, but—why are you looking at me that way?"

"You know, I hardly know you any more. All these things you're telling me."

"I don't know why you should be surprised. It's more or less in the blood, isn't it?"

"No, it isn't. You mean Mother."

"Naturally."

"Are you going to let that be an excuse for the mistakes you make?"

"So far I haven't needed any excuses."

"Well, I'm glad to hear that. But if you have an excuse all prepared, you may need it sooner than you think, and it isn't a very good one. Don't you know why Mother—what happened to her?"

"I'd like to hear your theory."

"I can give it to you in one word: Father."

"I knew that's what you'd say. But I don't think that's enough, I don't think it's the whole reason. If it was, why did she wait so long?"

"Because in Port Johnson it's impossible for a respectable married woman to have an affair. In those days, when we were small children, a lady didn't even go to Philadelphia by herself. It just wasn't done. Why, Mother wouldn't even go in to Port Johnson without George."

"Not to change the subject, but George isn't with us any more."

"He died?"

"No."

"Then what do you mean he isn't with us any more?"

"He stopped working for us. He quit."

"George quit? George never quit, not of his own accord. What happened?"

"I thought the same way you did, I didn't think he up-and-quit, but apparently that's what happened. I asked Mother, and I asked Josephine and Nellie. Using great discretion, of course. I couldn't be disloyal to Father, but I had my doubts, too, so I was very discreet. But apparently George decided on Armistice Day that he didn't want to work for us any more and told Father so."

"Go on."

"And that's all. He went on a brannigan, as Nellie put it. A drunk. A spree. He was arrested and put in jail, and Father sent money to pay his fine. Oh, and there was apparently some fuss about his pay. He went out to the mill to get his salary, and this part I learned from Mother. After he got out of jail he went out to the mill and went to see Mr. Halcomb in the paymaster's office and Mr. Halcomb told him that he was to get two weeks' pay, whatever that amounted to, but the extra money that Father was giving him, six months' pay I think it was, he could only get that one week at a time. Father knew that if he got it all at once he'd spend it in a few days and then have nothing."

"If that's what he wanted to do with it, that was *his* business, not Father's."

"I don't agree with you. This is one time when I agree with Father. It was entirely up to Father whether he got any extra money or not, especially since George resigned and wasn't fired. Father didn't *have* to give him anything."

"Six months' pay was damn little for all those years."

"Well, all the more reason for seeing that he didn't spend it on River Street in a week and then have nothing. No, Father was right."

"That's Bryn Mawr talking."

"No, it's me. Or maybe it is Bryn Mawr, too, but I don't see that any good would come of—"

"All right, next question. What's happened to George? Has he got another job?"

"I don't know. I'm not sure. When I was home for Christmas I tried to find out about him and somebody told me that he spent most of his time at the blacksmith shop."

"At the mill?"

"No, Mr. Colligan's, the horseshoer."

"Oh, yes, of course," said Alfred. "But I gather you didn't see him."

"No. Mr. Colligan said he was usually there, but he hadn't seen him for a day or two. I didn't want to *ask* Mr. Colligan whether George had a job there. I didn't want to seem like Miss Butinsky."

"Sometimes I don't understand the female mind. You went to Colligan's, but then you wouldn't ask him what you went there to find out."

"The female mind is every bit as good as the male mind, in some cases much better. But there's also such a thing as delicacy. I *inquired* for George, and when he wasn't there, I saw no reason to display any curiosity to Mr. Colligan. If I'd seen George, I'd have asked him whether he had a job, but I didn't feel that it was any of Mr. Colligan's business to know that I was interested in whether George was working or not. That would have made me feel like a social worker, and then you'd have some right to make disparaging remarks about Bryn Mawr, because those are the kind of Bryn Mawr girls that I have no desire to be. And rest assured won't be. You Princeton boys, you have what Professor Leuba calls an inferiority complex."

"You tell Professor Lurber that we have no inferiority at Princeton. Only degrees of superiority."

"I'm sure he'd be delighted to hear that. It tells so much about Princeton, so much more than you have any idea. So you're not going back, going back, going back, going back?"

"No. No. No. No. No. I'm going home and see the fond parents for a few days, and then I'm going to New York—"

"For some riotous living."

"For some riotous living, with Lieutenant Porter and other disreputable acquaintances of mine, and after that, who knows?"

"When you get home, I might as well warn you in advance, Father is going to be sweet as 'lasses candy. Do you know why?"

"I think I can guess, but you tell me why."

"He's going to give you all the time in the world, but he's going to want you to say that eventually you'll take over the mill."

"Then he's doomed to bitter disappointment. I have a thousand reasons, such as not being qualified to run a thing that size. But the reason that makes the most sense as far as I'm concerned, I personally, is that you can't run the mill from New York City or Philadelphia. You have to live in Port Johnson, and I *am not* going to live in Port *Johnson*. I have no desire to king it in Port Johnson, or to run the mill better than Father has, and certainly not to run it worse than he has. I've had my own money for almost a year now and I can live anywhere in the world till I make up my mind what I want to do. In the Navy I met fellows from all over the country, damn nice fellows from California and Texas and Minnesota, and older fellows, some that want me to come out and work with them. 'Guarantee you I'll make you a millionaire inside of ten years, Eaton. Maybe less'n that.' There was one fellow I got to be friends with and he used to try to persuade me to come home with him as soon as the war was over, and when I said I couldn't he said if I ever changed my mind I'd always be welcome, always have a good job. 'Just ask anybody in South-Central Texas for Jack Tom Smith.'"

"Smith?" said Sally.

"Jack Tom Smith. I found out later that Jack Tom will inherit twenty-five million dollars when he's twenty-five years old."

"Where did he ever get that much money?"

"Oil."

"Oil?"

"At first I thought he was just a harmless prevaricator, and he amused me. But then one day in London he asked me if I'd mind stopping in at Barker's with him. Well, Barker's makes special bodies for Rolls-Royces. *They* knew him. He

273

wanted to make sure that he was high on their waiting-list for after the war, not with one Rolls-Royce, but two. He had letters to Sir This and Lord That, but he never used them. 'Ah sure don't need an Englishman to tell me how to spend mah money,' he used to say. 'And Ah sure don't want to marry a gal that's gonna present me with a big bill for gettin' her little old teeth fixed, and these English gals sure aint spendin' their own money on dentists.' He was right, too. In fact, he was no fool whatever way you looked at him. His father took a correspondence school course in civil engineering and then he took another course in banking. And Jack Tom had a degree in geology, one of the Texas colleges."

"You never would have met anyone like him at Princeton."

"Ah, there you're wrong. He went to some military school in Missouri and he tried to get in Princeton, but couldn't. We have an engineering course at Princeton, don't forget."

"Why on earth did he want to go to Princeton?"

"Because his father's best friend went there. Degrees of superiority. No inferiority, see? I'm going to visit Jack Tom. But I'm not going to live in Texas. I'm pretty sure it'll be New York for me."

"You had a *good time* in the war, didn't you?"

"I don't know, I guess I did. It was so different from anything I expected to be doing at my age. Standing a watch, when you really couldn't see your hand in front of your face. And the feeling at dawn that everything's been washed and scrubbed during the night, and then you remember what you're there for and you hope you won't do anything wrong if you have to do anything. And you're tired half the time and the rest of the time you're more awake than you've ever been in your life and you think you're never going to need rest again, but by God you do, and when you do it's usually the wrong time, and you'd give your soul, your mother, anything, if you could only shut your eyes and take one deep breath and sleep, sleep, sleep. And then your watch is over and you lie down and you think you're never going to get to sleep. Your underwear is wrinkled, your blanket, the ship is creaking—and then a complete blank and somebody is shaking you and you've been asleep for three hours. Of course sometimes you dream. You wake up every five or ten minutes, not knowing where you are, and it takes such an effort for you to get your bearings that you're almost fully awake, so that it's harder to get back to sleep. I always promised myself that on my next leave I'd stay in bed around the clock, but I never did. They'd have had to chloroform me. I'd take a bath and feel refreshed as soon as I got to my room, and then I'd decide to go out for a few drinks. But then I'd fall asleep in the God damn chair, with one sock in my hand. Wake up stiff and with the beginning of a head cold. Still it was better than the Army. When you go to sleep in a ship there's only one thing that's going to hurt you, and at least you're in a sort of bed. But in a dugout—the mud, the rats, a raiding party, a night bombardment, gas. If you want to know what the war was like, ask somebody that was in the infantry . . . Yes, I guess I had a good time. I had some good time-zz, plural. And I met a lot of different kinds of fellows, some good, some bad, some I'll never see again, some I'd like to see again. I knew that no German was going to run a bayonet into my belly, the one way I did *not* want to die. The only things that could happen to me were if we got torpedoed or in an action with their deck gun, I might get shot. Or we might get sunk and have to go over the side. You don't last long in the North Atlantic. Five minutes at the most in the winter-time. I don't know, Sal. I've only been out of uniform a few hours. Ask me a year from now. Maybe by that time I'll be feeling sorry for those Germans we think we sank. But I'll tell you one thing, I don't feel sorry for them now. I hope they're feeding the fishes, and I suppose this man wants me to pay the check."

The presentation of the check put an end to the intimacy of their conversation, and they were momentarily silent while Alfred waited for his change. They smiled at each other, liking each other in the new relationship that growth and absence had brought about.

"Are you going to vote? I understand women are going to be able to next fall."

"I beg your pardon, I'm not yet old enough to vote."

"Well, when you *are* old enough?"

"I don't know. They tell us it's our duty at college, but I don't see it that way at all. I think it's entirely up to the individual, depending on whether you want to or don't. But I wouldn't admit that to some of my friends. They'd hoot at me for being a mid-Victorian. Well, in some ways I suppose I am. In other ways, not. I've never been able to get interested in politics. Government."

"That's the trouble with the whole damn thing. Women will vote the way their husbands tell them to, because they don't know any better. Or they'll vote just the opposite way because they don't like their husbands."

"Well, now when you say things like that you make me want to be a typical Bryn Mawr woman, *your* typical Bryn Mawr woman. I've had just as good an education as you've had, right this minute, and really I know girls, attractive girls, that have much more brains than some men that have been out of college for years."

"I'll bet I wouldn't think they were attractive."

"I'll bet you would. Are you leaving a dollar tip?"

"Yes."

"Father never does, when he takes me to lunch. Fifty cents is the most he ever tips at lunch, and sometimes not that."

"We got good service, and we're almost the last ones here. I always used to tip exactly ten percent and I never used to look at a waiter. But in the Navy I learned to look at everybody and try to separate the sheep from the goats."

"I wish we could go on talking."

"Well, we have the rest of our lives, when you're not busy with Harry, and dissipated young roués from Penn."

"And you're not engaged in riotous living."

"I don't like that word *engaged*. That is the farthest thing from my mind."

"Where to now?"

"Over to the Racquet Club, 16th Street, pick up my gear, and then take the 4:35 home."

"I'll walk with you as far as Wanamaker's."

On Chestnut Street he saluted a lieutenant commander, who grinned. "I wonder how long it'll take me to get out of that habit," said Alfred.

"I like it."

"To tell you the truth, so do I. Now that I don't *have* to."

Alfred took his seat in the Pullman and the man in the chair immediately forward looked at him and said: "Did I understand the porter to call you Mr. *Eaton?*"

"Yes sir," said Alfred.

"Then am I right in guessing that you're Samuel Eaton's son?"

"Yes, I am."

"I know your father. My firm has had some business dealings with him. My name is Chapin. I'm from Gibbsville. How is your father?"

"Well, sir, I don't really know. I haven't seen him for over a year."

"Oh, you're just getting home from the Army?"

"The Navy."

"Well, welcome home, Mr. Eaton." Chapin put out his hand.

"Thank you, sir."

"I never knew your father had a son old enough to be in the Navy. Of course I don't know him awfully well. I'm a partner in a law firm up in Gibbsville and we represent the steel mill, and we've had occasion to meet for dinner a few times. Trying to hold our own with the big companies, you know. I suppose you'll be the third generation of Eatons in the steel business."

"I doubt it."

"Oh, headed elsewhere? Well, I've never encountered any law that required a son to go into his father's business. And the way things are beginning to look, the steel business is in for a lot of labor trouble, so I hear. And after the Navy I suppose you'd like to take it easy for a while."

"Yes sir, that's exactly what I'm going to do."

"Wasn't your grandfather a Johnson of Port Johnson?"

"Yes, he was. I think it was named after his father."

"That's what I thought. I'm a lot older than you, but my grandfather and your Grandfather Johnson also had business dealings. Your grandfather and mine had some money in a coal mine, if I'm not mistaken. They lost money, through no fault of their own. Couldn't pump the water out or something of the sort, and had to abandon it. Well, I know you'd like to be alone with your own thoughts, just getting home, so I'll go back to my paper, but I'm awfully glad to have seen you and I hope you find everything the way you'd like it to be. Good luck, and please remember me to your father. Joseph Chapin. Gibbsville."

"Thank you, sir. It was a pleasure to meet you," said Alfred, and was alone with his thoughts. A total stranger, a man of whose existence he had not been aware fifteen minutes ago, had put into words the source of his misgivings: *I hope you find everything the way you'd like it to be.* He knew he was not going to find everything the way he would like it to be; but he was not even sure what he wanted.

At Port Johnson he spoke a polite goodbye to Chapin, to the porter, and to the conductor. He was not met at the station; he had not sent word of his arrival time. A young girl looked at him, then, recognizing him, smiled and said, "Hello, Alfred Eaton," and then giggled in a way that revealed that she never had spoken to him before. Whoever she was, he would probably see her again in a few days, and from that small encounter he knew that after a token resistance she would lie on a blanket for him near some country road. She would be a bore on the way home, but she would go on meeting him on the sly, giving him all that she was withholding from the churchgoing young man whom she called her fella. Then one night she would talk about love, and he would know the time had come to stop seeing her, and she would telephone him at the farm, and she would be angry and tearful and lie about her condition, and finally she would give up and the churchgoing young man would suddenly discover that he was able to get his hand beyond her garter and would marry her prematurely because he wanted to get the rest. Alfred saw all of this in the few moments required to get his luggage and hire a taxicab.

The taxi was a Vim and one of a fleet of three at the station, and that was new. The driver was a stranger, a young man with a cigarette stuck in the corner of his mouth and a boil on the back of his neck, resentful of having for a fare a man who was no older than himself and determined not to be mistaken for a country boy. "Jake, hey, Jake," he yelled at another taxi driver. "I got a pazzenchuh for otta-tahn." His Pennsylvania Dutch accent almost made the passenger for out-of-town burst out laughing. He drove the little car, which was sturdy but not fast, with a total disregard for the transmission and the tires. "Ach, such a Goddam fuck-up."

"What did you say?" said Alfred.

"Such a Goddam fuck-up, I said."

"Oh. Well, now the next block turn left."

"I know how to get there."

"I know how you're going, and I know a better way. Just do as I tell you."

The driver obeyed the cool voice of command, but he took every bump at as much speed as he could get out of the Vim, and he continued to call it a Goddam fuck-up all the way to the house.

"Aren't you supposed to get out and help me with my bags?" said Alfred.

"Who said so?"

"Never mind. How much do I owe you?"

"Three dollars."

"Yeah, who said so?"

"I said so. Three dollars."

"You wait here till I go in and telephone."

"Telephone who?"

"The taxi company. I want to find out when they raised their prices."

"Two dollars."

"Here's one dollar. Now beat it, you prick, or I'll pull you out of that cab and bust your nose for you. Go on, scat!"

The man drove away, punishing the car all the way down the driveway.

"Alfred, Alfred! Oh, my Alfred, it's you! It's you-you-you-you."

Alfred's back was turned toward the house, he was watching the departing taxicab, when his mother's joyful cries broke the evening quiet. He turned and saw her, trotting toward him with short, silly steps, hampered by the tea gown of crepe de Chine and the looseness of the mules she was wearing. In the instant of recognition he was aware of the remarkableness of recognizing her, of finding in her face the little that remained of what he had been remembering; and in the same instant he was thinking irritably that she could

278

have made more rapid progress by walking than by her little trotting steps. And then when she was hardly more than arm's length away from him one of the mules dropped from her foot and she fell with a small cry of pain as the sole of her foot came down on a pebble. He jumped forward and caught her before her face hit the ground, but there had been enough of collapse for her knees to strike the stones.

"Oh, forgive me," she said. "Look at me, how horrible, how nasty." She looked downward and lifted her skirt to examine her knees, which were dirtied and bruised and now began to show blood in several places. "Why didn't you let me know? I wouldn't have been so excited, and awkward. Oh, but you're home." He kissed her tightly closed mouth and knew she was holding her breath, but the odor of alcohol was unmistakable.

"Hello, Mother," he said.

She laughed. "Hello, Mother. Is that all, after all these months and months?"

"No, there's a lot more," he said.

"Oh, I'm sure there is. I wasn't taunting you, dear. Let me take your arm and you assist your wounded mother back inside. Leave your things exactly where they are, it's not going to rain, and the servants will be fighting for the privilege. You leave the bags there and help me in and we must do something about these nasty little wounds of mine. Oh, how you used to hate to have me wash the dirt out of your bruises."

She was as voluble as one whose speech had been pent up for weeks and had now been granted brief permission to talk.

"I'm the only one home, but I'll have you to myself, at least for a little while. You saw Sally, I'm sure, but did you see Constance?"

"Sal, but not Constance."

"No, Constance spends every minute with her Catholic. Oh, not that she wouldn't want to see you. Sally is so matter-of-fact. Devoted, but she *looks* at me. If Sally'd been prettier, just a tiny bit prettier, pretty girls don't look at people that way, do they? But she has her own life now. Have you had your dinner? I'm sure you haven't."

"No, I'll have it with you."

"Oh, dear. You really don't know, do you? I have *my* dinner on a *tray*, in my *room*. I had my chop and my junket hours ago. An hour ago. I was sitting in my room, and when I heard the voices I knew it couldn't be your father. Then I looked out and saw you. Port Johnson is getting so important, real taxicabs like Philadelphia, not just jitneys any more. Your father's in Reading. He's having dinner with some men at the Wyomissing Club. He doesn't expect you till tomorrow, and I don't know whether he plans to spend the night in Reading or come home late tonight. He has the car and Walter, so he could be planning to drive home tonight. Walter's a very good driver."

She was studying him, then she spoke. "Oho, you're not surprised."

"Should I be?"

"When I said Walter. Then I guess Sally told you about George. Well, then I don't have to."

"Well, as I said before, there's a lot to be talked about."

"George has been getting stranger and stranger—*had* been, I should say. It didn't surprise me. It just isn't good for a man to live the way George did all those years. Whatever you do, don't stay single too long. Marry before you're, well, I don't know what age, but before you become a settled bachelor. And you could, you know. You could become a settled bachelor. I know you like girls, I can tell that, but even as a little boy, even when you were so in love with Vicky, I used to notice certain tendencies."

"What kind of tendencies, Mother?"

"Content to be alone. But nobody is, really, you know. And it's a good thing to have your children while you're still quite young, before you're so much older than they are that you have no common ground."

"I'll remember that. But at least you're getting me married."

"What do you mean by that?"

"Well, I'm glad you're not going to try to get me to go back to college."

"Oh, heavens. You could never go back there now, could you? Could you go back to that life now?"

"No."

"I didn't think so. Take a good long rest and then decide what you want to do."

"Such as going into the mill?"

"Well, you're not thinking of doing that—at least—you're *not,* are you? I don't want to say the wrong thing."

"No, I'm not going into the mill."

"I didn't think so, but for a moment—"

"Why don't you want me to?"

"I didn't say I didn't want you to. But I know *you* never wanted to. Your father will want you to, he wants you to already. I think he takes it for granted that you will. But I know better. Just as long as you make it clear to him that I had nothing to do with your decision."

"I'll make that clear, all right."

"You have a good excuse. The mill is only on part-time now, you know. And there's going to be a steel strike, all over. Your father's laughing at them. He says that if they strike they'll do him a favor. It'll save him the trouble of laying off the men that he's kept on. And very few of them saved their money when they were getting wartime wages and all that overtime. They'll have their strike and then when they come back to work we'll pay them what we want to, because they just won't have any money left and they'll have to take what's offered them. If they strike, your father says he's going to go to Alaska and hunt bear, and might even go to Africa for a lion."

"Well, it might be a good idea to get pretty far away in case the men get hungry. Where will *you* go?"

"I don't know. I guess I'd stay here. I never thought of that."

"Apparently Father didn't either."

"Oh, I'd be safe, if that's what you mean."

"If there's a long strike, you'll have to leave, too. But we'll talk about that some other time."

"All right, dear. How was the war?"

"How was the war? Okay. We won it."

"Oh, Alfred, stop. You're joking with me."

"I know I am, Mother. But don't you think I could have dinner? Some fatted calf?"

"The servants are waiting to come in, I know. Would you like something to drink?"

"Yes, I'd like some whiskey, if you have it."

"If we have it? Oh, there's no secrecy any more. They don't try to stop me any more. It only takes a little to—you know. And then I usually go to sleep. If I'm not asleep by a certain hour, the nurse puts me to sleep. I have a trained nurse, but I guess Sally told you all that. You understand, don't you, Alfred?"

"I guess so."

"You thought it would do me more good to let me talk than fuss over my scratches, didn't you? I know that, Alfred. You're a man now, you couldn't think of going back to college. I have a few things to tell you. Not many, but a few. Please don't go away till we've had two or three good talks, and I'm going to give you a present so that you can do whatever you want to for a year. I've never been certified, you know."

"Certified? For what?"

"Oh, my—condition. I still have the income from Grandfather Johnson's trust fund. You and the girls will get the principal, so I couldn't touch that anyway. But quite a lot of income has piled up, thanks to your father. He's been very good about that. He's paid all my bills, and I haven't had to spend anything, hardly. I'll write you a cheque right this minute."

"No, please don't, Mother. I wish you wouldn't."

"I want to. It's something I want to do. Please let me do it this way, nicely, because I might as well tell you, I'll have the bank deposit it to your account tomorrow, but this way it'll be nicer."

"All right."

She stood up and her legs hurt and hurt worse when she took a step, but she went to the secretary and wrote out a cheque and brought it back to him. "With love, Alfred," she said.

"Thank you, Mother."

"Aren't you going to look at it?"

He looked at the cheque. "Twenty thousand dollars?" he said.

"It's enough, isn't it?"

"It's enough for four or five years."

"Or for one very good year, or two pretty good ones. Or for that matter, six months, foolishly. Whatever you decide. You can start with a whole new wardrobe. But don't buy a car. Your father's buying you a car. Do things you wouldn't ordinarily do, use your imagination."

"Imagination. That sounds like Grandfather."

"Well, it was his money. You liked Grandfather."

"I loved him."

"Yes, so did I." She glanced about the room. "And he loved me."

"Oh, well—*yes*," said Alfred. He put extra enthusiasm into it; he had lied to her about her scratches; he had *not* deliberately made her go on talking; he had quickly forgotten the bruises. And he was afraid that he did not love her as he wanted to love her. He loved her, but it was no more than a state of love, a continuing habit and of dwindling intensity. For quite a while he had been loving her as he loved the American flag; he loved her because he did not *not* love her. But now there were things to dislike, to pity: the lack of muscular control, the foolish effort to hold her alcoholic breath, the weeping-weary weakness of the eyes, the semi-exposed veins in her cheekbones and in the curl of her nostrils, the missing upper second molar, the thinning hair that she kept combing with her fingers. From far back in the past he recalled her saying of some forgotten woman: "She let herself go." He was ashamed to be able to look at her this way, to see the imperfections in detail and to allow the total of them to form this new picture of the human being who had given him life and love. But love? Had she given him love? Yes, as much as she had been capable of allotting him among her other loves and hatreds; and she loved him now, at this moment, because he was here, and that was more than he could say of his feeling for her. She and his father had surely long passed the end of their physical pleasure in each other, and he wondered whether that much of her skin that was covered by clothing remained smooth and white for her lover in Philadelphia, or had she made herself so artful in love-making that she made love in the dark and held him with tricks. Alfred knew that it was some measure of his love for his mother, or lack of it, that he was able to imagine her pleasing a lover; he did not yet know, and for some time would not know, that he had begun a new relationship with her.

"What are you remembering about Grandfather?" she said. And that was what she attributed his silence to.

"I beg your pardon. Oh, I wasn't thinking any one thing. Talks we had, I guess. He'd be a good person for me to talk to now, wouldn't he? About my future."

"I knew you were miles away, or I should say years away. Yes, his advice would be good"—she laughed—"even if you didn't take it."

"Well, I guess it's that way with most good advice."

"He would never advise you about women. Girls."

"Yes, he would. He did. Stay away from them."

"Well, that's advice you'd never take. One thing I know about you, there'll always be women. Of that I'm positive, I'm like a fortune-teller in that. I can look into your future and positively see you always with a woman. There'll never be a woman very far from you."

"I'm not that kind at all, Mother."

"I didn't mean *that kind*. But there are some men, and you're one of them, Alfred."

"You've got me wrong."

"No, I haven't. You'll see. Alfred, I have no illusions about you right this minute. But I don't mind." She patted the back of his hand. "It's part of life, dear."

"You've got me all wrong."

"Oh, no. No I haven't. But that's all I want to say. Let's first have the women in to welcome—why didn't you wear your uniform?" She tugged at the bell-pull. "Oh, I can't get used to the—this doesn't work any more. Here, I'll show you. Underneath, see? A button. All electric now. Upstairs, little telephones. Little square telephones, all connected with the kitchen and the stable."

"We had them before I went away."

"Oh, did we? But not before you went to Princeton."

"Yes, I think we did."

"No, not before you went to Princeton, Alfred. Well, here we are. Josephine and Nellie."

The women bumped into each other in their progress toward Alfred. Josephine won, shook his hand, and then impulsively kissed him. Nellie did not kiss him, but on an impulse he

283

kissed her and the reserve she had been maintaining was broken and she burst into tears.

"Stop, Nellie, for the Lord's sake," said Josephine.

"I can't help it," said Nellie. She held his hand in both of hers, unable to let go until he gently withdrew it.

"Well, you two look fine," he said. "Josephine, turn around."

"I *will* not."

"You don't have to. It's getting bigger, I'm telling you it's getting bigger."

"It is not."

"She don't have her corsets on," said Nellie.

"Shut your mouth, for the Lord's sake," said Josephine. "Now did you ever in your life hear such filthy talk, Mrs. Eaton? I don't know which of them is the worst."

"It wasn't filthy talk," said Nellie. "I was only explaining for you."

"Did I ask you to explain for me?"

"Well, she did you a favor," said Alfred. "At least it, uh, it wasn't—"

"Never mind, never mind," said Josephine. "You didn't let us know. Tomorrow we're ready for you. But with the Mister away, tonight I don't have only some lamb chops. I did bake a nice apple pie. You'll have to fill up on that. I'll serve it hot with a pitcher of cream and that'll hold you over."

"I brought you some presents from London."

"You didn't have to spend your money on us, all we are is thankful you're home."

"Well, I'm glad to be home and back with you two."

"Any time it's ready," said Martha, dismissing them.

"It'll be twenty minutes, ma'am."

"All right, Josephine, and Nellie, will you bring the whiskey, and some water, Alfred?"

"Yes, please, and some ice. The English don't believe in ice, and I do. And they believe in soda, and I don't."

"I suppose they drink to keep warm as much as anything," said Martha.

"I don't. I drink to feel good and at peace with the world. And it does the trick."

"Oh, and this is Miss Trimingham. Miss Trimingham, my son Alfred."

Miss Trimingham, obviously having been drawn by the extra voices in the room, inclined her head in a dignified nod. She was well in her thirties, a powerfully built woman with a masculine face that reminded Alfred of a Regular Army sergeant he had known on a convoy. She wore a starchy uniform and her nursing-school cap and a nurse's badge in her collar, and a Canadian military device over her heart.

"Good evening, sir. May I welcome you home, too?"

284

"Thank you."

"Miss Trimingham lost her brother with the—the . . . ?"

"The Pats, ma'am. The Princess Pats,". said the nurse. "I'm sure Leftenant Eaton—"

"Oh, yes indeed. Everybody knows about the Pats," said Alfred. "I hope you're not here to take my mother off to bed."

"Well, it *is* time, you know."

"I'm going to let you two decide my fate between you," said Martha.

Here Nellie appeared with the whiskey, set it down and departed. Trimingham looked at the bottle so expressionlessly that she might have been trying to ignore a cobra. Quickly Alfred poured himself, and only himself, a half water and half rye. "I'm sure it's against your rules to drink on duty, so I didn't offer you one, Miss Trimingham."

"On duty or off duty, it's all one to me where that's concerned," said the nurse. Alfred could see that she was somewhat relieved that he had not poured a drink for his mother, but he saw that the nurse watched Martha for indications of an active thirst.

"Alfred, Miss Trimingham doesn't mind if you give me a touch of whiskey."

"I don't mind, but if you don't really want it, what's the use of taking it, Mrs. Eaton? You've been pretty good these past four or five days. We haven't had any of the bad nightmares."

"We'll have one tonight if we don't stop talking about it," said Martha. "I think I'll have a nip. All the drinks I've had for no reason, I think I ought to have one when I have a good reason. To welcome my son home again, safe and sound."

"What will you have, Mother?"

"What you're having."

"I'll get a tumbler," said Trimingham, leaving.

"I could murder her in cold blood," said Martha. "But my common sense tells me she's very good for the job. She's almost made me hate liquor as much as she does and, I don't know, maybe that makes me cut down some. Maybe. I don't know."

"What I can't understand is that you can talk about it as though it were happening to someone else. If you can do that, I should think you'd be able to stop it entirely."

"Maybe I could. But why should I?" She spoke the words as though she were asking a reasonable question, but with a lingering ring to her question that made it not a question but a declaration of resignation, and as though all the possible answers would be arguments against her stopping.

She was given her drink and she raised it to toast her son,

took a sip, and drank no more of it until Nellie announced Alfred's dinner. She took the tumbler with her while she sat at the table with Alfred, and even though she drank no more, she became noticeably intoxicated. Trimingham had waited for them in the front room and was standing when they returned to it.

"Will you say goodnight, now, Mrs. Eaton?"

"That's an order, you know, Alfred. I have to go, and I have to leave you alone. The little car's in the garage if you feel like seeing anyone in town. Or there are some records that the girls bought at Easter-time, if you want to play the Victrola."

"Thanks. I think I'll read the paper for a little while and then go to bed."

"It isn't much, your first night home."

"There's plenty of time, and I'm pretty tired. I was up at five-forty-five this morning." He suddenly yawned. "You see? I may not even read the paper."

"Your old room is all ready for you. I imagine Nellie put out a pair of your father's pajamas for you. I don't think he'll be home tonight, so you get a good night's sleep." She kissed him and started to leave. "Ugh." She grunted. "It wasn't kissing you did that. It was my darned knees."

"Did she fall again?" said Trimingham.

"Yes, she skinned her knees."

"Goodnight, sir," said Trimingham.

"Goodnight. Goodnight, Mother."

"Sleep as late as you like, and I'll see you at lunch." She made another start to leave, then boldly went to the table, picked up her tumbler and drank the whiskey and water without stopping. Then without a word to Alfred or the nurse, defiantly but unsteadily and highly pleased with herself, she walked out of the room.

Alfred sat there for a while, soon becoming accustomed to the quiet, of which the ticking of the glass-boxed clock on the mantel was a fixed part. Without the familiar ticking of that clock—a wedding present to his mother and father— he would have been listening for less familiar interruptions of the silence; but the ticking was there, as it had been for almost thirty years, during all his absences, and now in a small way he discovered that he hated it, as though it were some household god, self-righteous and disciplined and superior to all those who lived in this house, with their pleasures and their sins, and their unworthy sufferings and their trivialities of conversation. He had no thought of it as a measurer of time, but only as a symbol of contemptuous respectability, and when it struck the hour of nine it still did not cease to be a symbol, nor did the hands on the face of the clock make it a timepiece. The steady ticking, the steadiness of the ticking, gave it this other character. And then oddly it was striking again and the little hand was at ten, and he realized that he had been asleep. When he came awake he had no animosity for the clock, no recollection of his earlier thoughts of it. He went to the switches and found that the same old lamps went out at his touch, and with an enormous effort he climbed the stairs and took off his clothes and brushed his father's pajamas to the floor and dropped into the bed. When he awoke it was a few minutes before four o'clock by the radium hands of his wristwatch. His body seemed to be waiting for sounds and sensations that did not come, and after a few moments his intelligence told his body that the sounds and sensations would not be coming ever again. He was home, and now he could turn over and go back to sleep. And so it was.

He slept without much change in position until nearly noon. He shaved and took a shower in the tub. He found some Princeton clothes in his closet, but his socks, his shoes, his shirts, his suits did not fit him. He put on some B. V. D.'s and old white flannels, which did fit him, and a pair of sneakers that were not too uncomfortable without socks, and a Brooks shirt that he left open at the collar.

He went directly to the kitchen and ordered his breakfast: oatmeal, ham and eggs, toast and coffee. He had a cup of coffee at the kitchen table while Josephine was preparing the meal.

"How did you sleep? Did you sleep all right?" said Josephine.

"I slept fine. How did you sleep?"

"How did I sleep? My goodness, I don't know. The same as usual. I never heard anybody ask me that before. I always sleep the same. I get into my bed and say my beads, but I very seldom ever finish them before I'm sound. And I always wake up about the same time, summer or winter. Ten of six, five of six. Even this war time. The saving daylight time, I got used to it. But I aint a chicken. *They* didn't get used to it."

"I think you're quite a chicken, Josephine."

"Oh, shut up. And don't you pass remarks like that last night. I could of slapped you one, Alfred Eaton. Remarks like that in front of your mother."

"I see you've got them on this morning."

"Now you shut up. It's none of your business whether I have them on or I don't have them on. It's none of your business. You oughta have more respect. I'm not one of those French women."

"What French women?"

"Oh, I know you. All right, go on in and sit down at the table."

"Where's Nellie?"

"Doing her upstairs. Oh, you're to call up your father on the telephone, if you're down before twelve noon. If you don't, he's coming home for lunch. But he wants you to call him up if you're up before noon."

"Is Mother down yet?"

"She's never down mornings any more," said Josephine. She spoke with no more embarrassment for her mistress than would have been caused by Martha's suffering from a broken leg. Alfred began to realize that his mother's disintegration had become so much a part of the life at the farm that he alone was not accustomed to it; his father and his sisters were reconciled to it, the servants were reconciled to it; and so much so that they had already assumed that he, like his father and his sisters, had grown accustomed to it with the passage of time and in spite of his absence from the scene.

"I want to ask you about George," said Alfred.

"Oh, him. Poor George. That's a long story. I guess they wrote you about it in letters."

"Well, I know he quit and so forth. Has he turned into a bum?"

"George would never be a real bum, but pretty near, I guess. I hear about him every so often. He hangs out at the blacksmith shop in town."

"Where does he live?"

"Where does he sleep nights? I don't like to think. They let him sleep at the livery stable during the winter, but I don't know that he has a room regular anywhere. This place and that place, I guess."

"Doesn't your priest try to do something for him?"

"He did, Father McGroarty, but it was no use. As quick as he turned Catholic, he fell away. I heard tell he gave Father a tongue-lashing right out on Montgomery Street and they put him in the lockup. Father wouldn't prosecute, but they gave George three days for drunk and disorderly. There's some people had enough of George when he acted that way towards Father and I guess it was a good thing for George they locked him up that time. A priest, you know, his hands are consecrated, and—"

"George didn't hit him, did he?"

"No, but it's almost as bad. Me and Nellie told them, the ones that were for giving George a thrashing, we said George was never a Catholic long enough to learn some things. Respect for the holy priesthood, like. If you're gonna go looking for George he won't be hard to find, but don't be disappointed if he don't want to see you. He's bitter, bitter about everything, everybody. But still and all I can't help feeling sorry for him, poor man. Nellie feels different, although she won't admit it. Sometimes Nellie's too devout for her own good. I wonder sometimes did Nellie think George turned Catholic so's to marry her?"

"Well, that wouldn't have been such a bad idea, would it?"

"Not for Nellie, but for George. They'd of been much worse off. Nellie's you might say an old maid, and there'd of been trouble when George wanted his rights, and the Church says if he wants his rights, she's supposed to let him. That's what the Church says, in plain black and white."

"What does the Church say if the woman wants *her* rights?"

"Her what? The woman? What kind of a woman are you talking about? You're worse than I thought, even. You must of consorted with the dregs of humanity, to get such ideas."

"Come on, now, Josephine. Don't you belie—"

"Shut up, shut up, I tell you. I'll have no more of that kind of talk in my kitchen. Go on in and sit down and eat your ham and eggs, and stop scandalizing me with your pagan talk. Pagan, that's what you talk like. Not just a poor, ignorant heathen. It was the Navy where you got such ideas. Always when a young fellow goes to sea, they lose all their respect for women."

"That's because they don't get it as often as the"—he held his arms to protect his head and laughed at her as she tried to beat his ears—"the soldiers."

"Wait on yourself, you scoundrel. I wouldn't wait on anybody that says such things. And here it is the morning, a fine time I must say, to be thinking such thoughts. Here, here's your oatmeal. Take it in yourself."

"My eggs are going to get cold."

"They'll keep warm under the dish-cover."

"Oh, good morning, Nellie. Just in time to give me my breakfast. Now you won't have to bother, Josephine."

"Good morning," said Nellie.

"*You,*" said Josephine to Alfred.

"What's going on?" said Nellie.

"Not fit to repeat, the things he's been saying."

"You don't want me to repeat everything *you* said, do you?" said Alfred, and went to the diningroom.

"Your mother says for you to stop in her room after you had your breakfast. And your father wants you to call him on the telephone if you're up before noontime. He's coming home for lunch, so you better do that before you go upstairs. The man that owns the taxicab company called up and said he apologized. He said you'd know what he meant. Harry Van Peltz wants to know if you would like to play tennis this afternoon. He'll be at the Port Johnson Club for lunch and after that the Idle Hour all afternoon. A newspaper reporter for *The Pilot* wants to talk to you about some kind of a write-up and he wanted to know did you have a picture of yourself in your uniform. His name is Baker. And you had a long distance telephone from New York City, but I was told not to waken you. Those are all the messages for you. No, one I didn't write down. Your sister Constance left word and asked you to call her on the telephone this evening between six and seven, at the school. What do you want done with your uniforms?"

"Have them cleaned and pressed, and then bury them."

"You better not do that," said the humorless Nellie. "They have a lot of affairs in town and the service men all wear their uniforms. It's Memorial Day soon."

"Luckily I won't *be* here, Nellie, so I won't have that to worry about. Besides, a naval officer's uniform makes you look like a musician in Sousa's Band."

"Not with your medals."

"One ribbon. I haven't got the medal yet, just the ribbon. And it isn't for bravery, Nellie. It's just for being there. We all got them. Most of the fellows from town will have at least three ribbons, for the Mexican Border, and France, and Army of Occupation, and I'd look pretty cheap with just one. And I can think of a couple of fellows that'll have *five* ribbons. The Distinguished Service Cross, and the French Croix de Guerre. You remember Mr. Porter? He'll be covered with them."

"I think he's who telephoned you from New York."

"I'm almost sure it was." He heard a car in the driveway. "That's Mr. Eaton. Home early on account of you."

"Touching," said Alfred.

"Wud you say?" said Nellie.

"Nothing," said Alfred.

He heard the heavy front door open and close and he felt like a nervous and unskilled actor: he wanted his father to discover him with a forkful of food on the way to his mouth, which would sufficiently explain without words why he had not telephoned. He had no fear of his father; what could his father do to him? But why was he nervous, and why was what he was feeling so much like fear?

Nellie went out to the hall and Alfred heard her say: "He's in the diningroom, sir."

"Is Mr. Alfred down yet?" he heard his father say.

"In the diningroom, sir, having his breakfast," said Nellie, louder. It was the first time Alfred had the slightest knowledge that his father was growing deaf.

"Oh, fine. Fine, Nellie." Samuel Eaton, growing deaf late in life, adjusted by speaking louder and did not have the gentle voice of the long-time hard of hearing. He entered the dining-room and paused. "There you are. Welcome home, my boy."

Alfred put down the fork with the morsel of ham and got to his feet. "Hello, Father." He reached out his hand and his father came and grasped it and put his left hand on Alfred's right shoulder, an advanced greeting form that he never had employed before. "Home at last. A day early, too, weren't you? I'm sorry I wasn't here last night, but I had to see some men in Reading. A business dinner at the Wyomissing Club, and then I spent the night out at a fellow's house. I could just as easily have come home if I'd known you were here. Sit down, finish your breakfast. Nellie, bring me a cup and saucer. I'll have a cup of coffee with Mr. Alfred. Well, how did it feel to sleep in your old bed? Your mother wanted to buy a new mattress, but I said no, it wouldn't be like coming home."

"I slept well. In fact I just came down a little while ago. How are you, Father?"

"Well, just the way I look, I suppose. A few pounds over-weight, short of breath when I try to do too much. And I seem to be getting deaf, although I have no trouble hearing you. All those years at the mill, with all that racket. I never thought it was a racket, but I guess it was. It was music to my ears. A quiet mill is the sound *I* don't like. But I guess I'm all right for a man fifty-seven, considering the way I worked my ass off during the war. However, the way things look, I'm going to have a chance to rest. We all are, in our business. Big contracts of course were canceled five or six months ago, but now those ridiculous sons of bitches are going to strike. And let them. They'll stay out till there's nothing but gas in their bellies and their kids start dying off from lack of food, and then they'll come back for whatever we want to pay them."

"Well, then what do you care?"

"I care because I'm against strikes. Any son of a bitch that goes out on strike against me, I paid as good wages as any-body in the whole industry, I kept men on when it cost me money because with a steel mill you have a lot of second and third generation men, sons and grandsons on the payroll. My men know that they were doing made-work just so I didn't have to lay them off till the last minute. Well, if they want to strike against me, I don't owe them a thing. But we'll have plenty of time to talk about that later on. You've aged."

"Have I?"

"Yes, you have. For the first time in your life you've begun to show some resemblance to your Grandfather Eaton, and you can take that as a compliment."

"I do."

"Well, you ought to. And you've matured, too, I imagine. I mean, handling men, and self-control, your general outlook."

"I'm not so sure about that."

"That's all right. If you came home and said, 'All right, I'm ready to go to work. Give me a job with a lot of responsibility,' I'd say go on back to Princeton, because I'd know you hadn't matured at all but *thought* you had. I suppose you are going back to Princeton, by the way?"

"No."

"No? Do you feel that you've had enough education? Or are you thinking of going some place else for special training?"

"I'm not going anywhere. I don't know about the education. Oh, I know I haven't had enough. But the idea of Princeton doesn't appeal to me at all. It'd be like going back to Knox after two years at Princeton."

"Well, I can see how that would be. Still there are a lot of service men going back to finish, so I wouldn't let that deter you. Think of all the fellows in your class that are in the same position, and I understand a lot of them are going back for their degrees."

"I'm afraid I've had all Princeton has to offer."

"You're wrong there. What you mean is, you're not going to get any more out of it, which isn't the same thing."

"All right, you put it better than I did."

"It's nice to have a degree. I've never regretted having a degree. But there are a lot better things to do than go back there and twiddle your thumbs and drink beer for two years. You'd be better off traveling, seeing something of the country."

"That's one of the things I had in mind."

"You had? Good. I can give you letters to the best people in all the important cities in the country, and I imagine you know quite a few people yourself. I sort of wish I'd sent you to a bigger school than Knox, but it's too late to have any regrets about that now. Confidentially, I think Knox is on its last legs."

"It is?"

"Yep. Mac McCready lost four or five masters during the war, some went in the Army, and the others grabbed the chance to go to better-known schools. He came to me for some money and I gave him some, not as much as he asked for, and he frankly admitted he was having serious difficulties. In fact, it wouldn't surprise me if he didn't open up in the fall. So now I guess you belong to an exclusive club that isn't going to take in any new members."

"Oh, I used my Racquet Club membership yesterday. Thanks for that."

"It's the best club for a young fellow in Philadelphia. When you get older I'd like to see you in the Philadelphia Club, but that's a long way off, and you'd make a mistake to be put up there too soon."

"If I join another club it'll be in New York."

"Which one?"

"Racquet and Tennis."

"What makes you think you'd make it? We have no New York connections."

"Lex Porter's uncle would put me up."

"I'd go easy on that. Join the Princeton Club if you have to belong to one in New York. Later on you can join something like the Union League. But you won't need any New York club for a while."

"I might."

"I don't see why. It's just an expense, and you won't get anything out of it. A Philadelphia club is different. We go there a lot, and you have a great many friends there. But New York, even I don't go there very often."

"I expect to spend the next year there."

"You expect to spend the next year there? I thought you said you were going to travel."

"That, too. But my home base will be New York."

"The hell it will."

"The hell it won't."

His father was silent. He gazed at Alfred and turned away, making an effort to control his temper, then he stood up. "I guess you won't want any lunch so soon after your breakfast. Tell them in the kitchen I'm not staying."

"Don't you want to hear anything about my plans?"

"I'm in no hurry to. I realize now you're not going to do what I hoped you'd do, and you've thought it all out without discussing it with me."

"I'd be glad to discuss it with you."

"You don't want to discuss anything. You want to tell me I can go to hell and take the mill with me. You've been wanting to tell me that all your life, and now because you have a few dollars from your mother's father, this seems like a good time to do it. All right, if—"

"What I wanted to do all my life is be friends with you."

"—that's what you want. *Be friends with me?* Listen to me, young fellow. I'm fifty-seven years old and I haven't got a friend for every ten years of my life. I was hoping we'd be friends, too, but first you were going to have to show me you were the kind of man I'd *want* to be friends with. The job in the mill was going to be yours because the mill would be yours, and I hoped the friendship would come out of that."

"Well, I'm sorry you feel that way about it."

"Why do you think I kept the mill going? Money? I could

have sold the mill any time in the last four years and made barrels of it. But I didn't want it to get out of our hands. You don't have to tell me. You never intended to go in the mill. Well, I just got finished telling you what I think of anybody that goes on strike against me." He walked out of the room and came back immediately.

"I bought you a car," said Samuel Eaton. "They're bringing it here this afternoon. You might as well keep it. I bought it because you had a good record in the war. But keep it because it's the last thing I'll ever buy you."

"I don't want it, thanks."

"You might as well take it, because it'll just sit there and rust if you don't."

"All right, I'll take it, on those conditions. That it's the last thing you'll ever buy me, and it'd rust if I didn't take it. We hated rust in the Navy."

"Uh-huh. I'm glad you learned *something* in the Navy."

"Well, you're not *very* glad, Father. What you *hoped* I'd learn, in the Navy or some place, was that sooner or later I was going to have to go in the mill, because that was what you wanted me to do. You had nothing but contempt for me for twenty-one years, but then I was supposed to jump at the chance of a job in the mill. Not because I gave a damn about the mill, regardless of anything else I wanted to do, but because I happened to be named Eaton, and your son, and it was what you wanted. What if I'd wanted to be a doctor?"

"Well, you're not going to be. You're not even going back to—"

"I know I'm not, but you didn't know that till just now. You never asked me what I wanted to be. A minister. A lawyer. You walked all over me all my life, and then you expect me to take your job. And that's another thing. Suppose I took a job in the mill? Suppose you made me superintendent, president? Would I be the superintendent, or the president, or the boss of the oil shanty? In a pig's ass I would. I'll tell you what else I learned in the Navy. You give a man a job and you make him responsible for it. If he does it wrong, he gets punished, but while he's doing it you let him do it. And I realized in the Navy that even if I went into the mill to please you, I'd never have any responsibility. I'd be a sort of a lackey for you. As long as you lived, I'd be nothing but a figurehead. All those years you were sore at me because Billy died. You never made any attempt to let me take his place, you never made the—"

He did not finish the utterance; Samuel left the room and the house, and in that minute Alfred knew that henceforth and forever their relationship was to be unencumbered, at least on his part, by any vestige of dutiful love or of active hatred. They were like two business men who had had a falling-out, and—again on his part—his feeling was of relief. He had not been able to love his father, and he did not like to hate him. He thought back and realized that in his profane language to his father he had been revealing an attitude that he had not yet consciously taken, but that had been his attitude from the moment Samuel Eaton had entered the room— and for months before. On some watch in the North Atlantic, looking out at the sea, or staring into the darkness, he had separated himself from his father; today's conversation only happened to take place today instead of at some later date.

And it was the real reason he had come home, to have this conversation, or at least to achieve the separation that was the principal result of this conversation. His mother was dead. The woman upstairs who had offered and re-offered her body to that pig in Philadelphia, and who soaked her soul in alcohol— she had managed to separate herself from his father, too, but from everyone else as well. The only life left to her was a regimen of self-destruction, watching out for moments of so-briety and conscience and anaesthetizing them at the first sign of them. She was gone. He doubted that there was anything she did to the pig in Philadelphia that made her interesting to Frolick. Alfred had learned that a drunken woman takes no imaginative part in love-making, no more than the cheapest whore. But whatever Frolick did to her was interesting to Frolick, and because he wanted it she was flattered and com-placent and self-deceived, felt desired and desirable when she in truth was less than a partner and not more than an instrument.

Alfred's own love for his mother had proceeded from in-stinct to the acceptance and then, as he grew, the conscious recognition of her prettiness, her kindness, her sweetness—and something he took a long time to identify as sadness. The sad-ness was the last characteristic he recognized, but when recognition was made, he had begun to understand her as a whole person and not merely the dainty being in satins and laces who was a sometime refuge from the harshness and finished worsted of his father. But with the understanding of her did not come only sympathy; even before the Frolick affair he had been noticing weaknesses where before under-standing there had been neither weaknesses nor strength. Between the time of instinctive love and the time of the be-ginning of understanding, weakness and strength were charac-teristics that did not pertain to the person who was his mother. She walked through life with a smell of cologne, gave the gentle commands that caused him to be fed and bathed and bedded and, occasionally, punished, and exhibited no strength or no weakness because her commands were sufficient and not challenged. To discover that she could weep and call a man "darling" who was not his father was possibly not so dramatically important to Alfred as the long, interrupted, recurring, growing realization that what he had discovered had not happened just that day, but that it had been happening all those years that preceded the discovery, and would continue to be part of her always. It was not so much disillusionment, since he could not condemn her for looking away from his father for love when he himself was looking everywhere; it was a difficulty, the difficulty of changing all his known facts and experience to make room for the effects of the new discovery, which was that his mother was subject to influences more mysterious than the household ailments that made you sniffle and sneeze, or go to the dentist, or have ointments rubbed into you.

Thus the discovery of the Frolick catastrophe was less a shock than it might have been to another woman's son. The consideration in regard to Frolick was largely pride, family pride, recognition of the extent of his mother's weakness and vulnerability, and contempt for Frolick himself, personally and as an outsider. He now contemplated another visit to Mr. Frolick, in which he would beat him more thoroughly and severely. And even as he made fists he knew that his mother had deprived him of that pleasure: if he had given her up as dead, he had no right to deny her the illusions that she got from Frolick.

And after all, how did he know that she was still seeing Frolick? She had been in a sanitarium, she now had a nurse —the opportunity to be with Frolick was almost non-existent. And yet he knew that the woman upstairs was continuing the affair with Frolick in her mind, and needed only opportunity to continue it in his bed. He wondered how much his father really knew.

Alfred had been sitting alone in the diningroom for many minutes. The servants must have been at their usual practice of eavesdropping, for they had not come in after Samuel Eaton departed. The practice was looked upon like sanctioned poaching on an English estate, and members of the family raised their voices at their peril, especially after Samuel Eaton began to lose his hearing. Alfred was glad that they had been listening (if they had been listening) if as a result they had given him these moments to himself. He had a life to plan, and it was going to start sooner than he had anticipated.

Back in his room he opened the bureau drawer in which Nellie had stowed the small parcels that were his gifts to the remarkably few persons who counted in his life: his father and mother, his sisters, George, Josephine and Nellie, Lex Porter, his mother, and his Uncle Fritz. For his father, a pair of worked-gold cuff links from Carpentier; for his mother, an amethyst pin from Cartier; for his sisters, gold pencils from Asprey; for Josephine and Nellie, silver rosary beads from a shop in Cobh; for George, a pocket-knife with many blades and tools, from a shop in the Burlington Arcade; for Lex Porter, a silver cigarette lighter from Dunhill's; for Mrs. Porter, a box of Liberty squares; for Fritz Thornton, a stock pin in the shape of a hunting crop from a shop near Asprey's. The presents were wrapped for travel, but he could identify each by marks he had made, and altogether they had taken up less space than a large box of cigars. They weren't much beside the new automobile he was getting from his father, nor costly to a man who had just been given twenty thousand dollars. But what made them small as he looked at them was what they represented in terms of persons who counted in his life, and what was conspicuously missing was a present for any girl who was not his sister. He had bought each present especially for each person, always with some affection, even love, and with the thought of buying for each person and the thought of giving it, handing it, to each person, as he made the purchase. Momentarily, in Paris, there had been forgiveness for his father, love and nothing but uncritical tolerance for his mother, love and humorousness for his sisters, affection and humorousness for Nellie and Josephine, affection and—he suddenly remembered—an odd and surprising pity for George, respect and affection for Lex's mother, admiration and a desire for approval for Fritz Thornton, and love and tentative embarrassment for Lex. He could remember conversations and palaver that went with each purchase, even in those purchases in shops of which he could not remember the name, and when the recollections had taken him back to those scenes briefly, he returned as quickly to his room, this bureau drawer, and the great fact that he was home, where he had wanted so much to be at the time when those purchases had made a sort of tangible connection with this present moment, this present fact. But he had not believed then, at the time of any of the purchases, that he would reach this moment without having bought something for someone, a girl, for whom he would feel only love, and not love and something else, or affection and something else, or admiration and something else, but love itself alone.

There had been a rather quiet English girl whom he had been told to look up in London. She had a small and pretty face, with a short straight nose, dimples, and round cheeks. They went to a restaurant of her choosing and he drank most of a bottle of wine and several cognacs, and in the taxi to her apartment he put his hand all the way to the top of her legs under her skirt. "Don't do that, please," she said. He told her he was sorry, and moved away from her, and did not expect to see her beyond the door of her flat. But she walked in and left the door open, with no other signal for him to follow.

Still without turning around she said, "There, if you'd like a drink," and went to the bedroom, which was behind glassed doors. When she came back he was still standing, and she was wearing a negligee. "Do you want to wash? Through there. And you can hang your things in the wardrobe." In bed she let him make love, which he did with awareness of the recent rebuff, but when his passion had reached a point that would have been dangerous for her, she lay back and opened her legs for him. She turned her face away and closed her eyes and was no help to him. But then she opened her eyes and forgot whomever she was remembering and he saw a smile in her eyes that had not been there all evening and that was separate from the character he had known. She was frankly looking at a stranger with whom she was enjoying herself and she made a big circle with her hips, repeated it, and then, afraid to lose him, went back and forth until there was a great outcry from him and she clung to his back until in a few more seconds her hands dropped and she again closed her eyes.

He watched her for a little while, then said: "Are you asleep, Betty?"

She shook her head, without opening her eyes. "That was lovely." Then she opened her eyes. "Did you find it so, my dear?"

"Yes."

"I know you did."

"I'm glad you did."

"I don't always, you know," she said.

She could have meant various things with the statement, but she chose to think that she meant no more than that she did not always find it so lovely.

"When does your train leave?"

"Five after six."

"This morning?" she said.

"This morning. Can I stay here till five?"

"Of course, darling. Sleep now, and I'll wake you—oh, before five. A half hour before five, do you think?"

"That would be fine."

She was already making love to him when he awoke, and he made love to her with confidence and strength, although at the beginning he was not altogether free of sleep, and not much caring who she was.

"I'll get you some tea," she said presently.

"Don't bother, I'll be all right."

298

"Oh, I can sleep a few hours more. Besides, I want to."

He kissed her when he was leaving, and in the taxi he thought kindly of her as the perfect, undemanding girl. He saw her again, months later. "I wasn't sure you'd see me again," he said.

"Why not?"

"Well—I met a fellow who gave me your name and phone number."

"Yes?"

"It wasn't the same fellow that gave it to me the first time."

"No?"

"Well, to be candid, don't I owe you some money for the first time?"

"Yes, you do. But I didn't ask you for it the first time, did I?"

"No, but you didn't have much time."

"Yes, I'm what you found out I am. But what on earth did you think I was? Surely you didn't think nice little English girls go nipping off to bed first crack out of the box."

"I guess I thought I was a real Don Juan. And I don't know *what* you thought I was. A cheap skate, for one thing."

"No, I don't think so. Do you want to pay me now for the first time? Five pounds, please."

"Hmm. Five pounds."

"That's why you thought I was a nice little English girl. I'm expensive. And that's why I'm expensive."

"So I was told, but I was told it varies."

"For the queer ones I get quite a bit more, Alfred. And for the old ones, quite a bit more than that."

"Do we have to be so cold-blooded about it?"

"I have to, but you're quite right, we needn't discuss it any further. Unless you, now that you know I'm for sale, if you have any fancy notions, nothing shocks me. I have a friend, a very beautiful girl, if you'd like that."

"I might."

"Tonight? I could ring her up and see if she's busy," said Betty. "What would you say to twenty pounds? I have to ask because she'll want to know."

"That's a hundred dollars. All right."

"I'll be back in two shakes."

They were in the restaurant of their first meeting. She returned and said, "No luck. I have another friend, if that's what you'd like, but this other one isn't nearly so pretty. Her figger leaves a lot to be desired. I know a *boy*. He was in here a minute ago?"

"No thanks."

"I didn't think so. Well, just me?"

"Just you."

"Do you ever smoke?"

"I'm sorry," he said, and held out a package of Lucky Strikes.

"I didn't mean cigarettes. Have you ever smoked? Opium?"

"No, never."

"Like to some time? For the experience?"

"I don't think so, thanks. Do you?"

"I have."

"And gave it up? I thought once you started you couldn't give it up."

"That's not true, you know."

"Betty, do you mind if I ask you a personal question?"

"A personal question. Well, of course I don't promise to answer. Try me."

"How old are you?"

"That *is* personal, isn't it? Very well, I'm twenty."

"Twenty."

"No, I'm twenty-three. Do I look twenty-three?"

"No, you don't."

"I never worry, that's why. What's going to be is going to be. I learned that philosophy of life when I was very small. My Dad walked out on my mother when I was ten. Wasn't really my father. My real father is quite something in the City. My mother worked and slaved to send me to school and dress me nicely, then she took sick and died and I went to live with an aunt. Shortly after that a gentleman she knew took quite a fancy to me and, well, he came to our rescue, financially speaking. He took us to Switzerland, France, Italy, all over. We were very nearly stranded in Italy at the beginning of the war, but we managed to get home. Now follow me. Dad left Mum, Mum died. I went to live with Auntie. In less than one year's time Uncle Fred—not really my uncle, of course—appeared on the scene. Nearly stranded in Italy, but on the homeward journey, I met X, a major. He took a fancy to me, asked Auntie if he might come to call. She refused, but we'd hardly left the ship at Plymouth when Uncle Fred had heart failure. Passed away without providing for us, so Auntie invited X to come to tea, and there we were on our feet again. Every time I've had a misfortune, something good turned up. Consequently I never worry."

"What happened to X?"

"There again. He was a hypocrite and we had to give him his walking papers. But a barrister friend of his came to our rescue, financially speaking, and through him I met some young chaps like yourself and since then I've never *had* to worry."

"Have you ever been in love?"

"Of course, my dear boy. Madly. But never for very long.

I could only be in love with a young chap, but the trouble with them is jealousy, and I won't have that. At the very first sign of jealousy I say, 'Thank you very much, nice to have known you.' You might fall in love with me, Alfred, and I'd like that. But beware the green-eyed monster."

"Well, I guess you can't afford it."

"Exactly. *You* see that, why can't—well, two of them from the peerage. I like you, Alfred, and don't you ever call yourself a cheap skate, ever again."

A young man in civilian clothes stopped at the table. "Hello, Betty."

"Hello, Charles."

"Well, aren't you going to introduce me to the leftenant?"

"No, I've already inquired and he isn't at all interested," said Betty.

"Don't be so sure. He might be another time," said Charles, moving along.

"That's what we don't like about the boys. Charles is the boy, if you'd wanted a boy."

"I gathered that."

"They're really in competition with us, but they have a lot of advantages. They don't get into trouble with the police. And if they take a fancy to a man they'll do anything to undermine us. And some men do prefer boys. You heard me offer to engage Charles, but he'd never offer to engage me. Not that I'd ever be dependent on the Charleses. He doesn't worry me." Under the table she rubbed his thigh slowly. "How are you feeling, darling? Shall we go over to the flat? Just you and I?"

"I'm ready."

"Yes, you are, aren't you? Very much so, aren't you, dear?"

Inevitably the more days he was out at sea, the closer he came to letting his desire for her get confused with love. He was at first shocked and a little disgusted to discover that he could see in her a facial resemblance to Victoria, if Victoria had gone on living. Moreover he was for a time distressed by the thought that the memory of Victoria was still liable to cause him pain. Betty in practice should more closely have reminded him of Norma Budd, but that was not the case. He knew how much larger Norma's breasts had been than Betty's, how much shorter her legs, how much thicker her fuzz. But the roundness of Vicky's face, or rather of her cheeks, and her quietness that was like the early quietness of Betty; and the calmness of their eyes, which had been disturbed when he first aroused Betty and had angered Victoria—these points of resemblance became almost interchangeable when there were months between assignations with Betty. But each time he saw her again, all resemblance immediately disappeared. And so did the near-love for Betty, and Victoria became uniquely Victoria again, physically unlike Betty, and unlike her in that Betty was sure of herself, cold-minded, clever, and incomplete. He now had some doubt that if he had gone to bed with Betty before he went to bed with Norma, he would have fallen in love with Norma. With Norma he had experienced the exquisite pleasure of beholding a woman's body gladly shown and happily given, and experienced it for the first time. From Betty, after several visits, he had learned all that he was ever likely to learn about the uses to which a woman might put her body for the pleasure of a man or a woman. Before Betty he had been simple and rather innocent; with Betty he became a pupil, because it delighted Betty to be the first to show him things that were not new to her or her friends. Sometimes he left Betty's flat with the feeling that he was being corrupted, but the feeling lasted no longer than the realization that it could not be corruption when Betty had no sense of evil and no desire to do him harm. She was, as it were, tutoring him in pleasure as she knew it. With the Betty experience behind him he sometimes believed that the affair with Norma could never have become love. There had been no thought of love with the other women he went to bed with after Betty.

There was no present for a girl in his bureau drawer, no symbol of simple love. He wondered whether at twenty-two he could ever fall in love again. Betty had been so unmarked by her life that he had not suspected her of being a whore, and that could happen again, if indeed it did not happen that there was no woman who would be free from his suspicions. He remembered a petty officer who often went about muttering, apropos of nothing at all, "All women are whores." It had been funny at first in its pointlessness, then monotonous, then a bore, and Alfred had ordered him to stop saying it.

He looked down at the presents: "My mother isn't a whore, my sisters aren't whores. Josephine and Nellie. Mrs. Porter." But as he argued for their virtue he thought of his mother and Frolick; the trend of Sally's thinking; Constance and her Catholic; Nellie and his boyhood experience with her; Mrs. Porter and her divorce. Was Josephine to be the last surviving representative of virtue? It was funny, and it may have been just in time. Something funny brought sense into his thinking, proportion and perspective: for a year he had been looking at women, at girls, and wondering how much like Betty they all were, instead of facing the most obvious fact that what made Betty unique was how different she was from most girls. For anyone so American as Alfred it was still not easy to believe that a girl with a non-Cockney English accent could be such a complete whore. It was a valuable lesson, at the price of a few hundred dollars and some provincial illusions.

He knew that his mother was waiting for him to come down

302

to her room, but he was not yet ready to talk to her. In his present mood he felt he owed her nothing more than politeness as the representative of what she had been but had stopped being. Here, now, on his first day home, with the freedom he had been looking forward to, he saw that the freedom consisted principally of being free from his mother and free from his father, and being free of them was not what he had wanted. Secretly he had hoped to come home to a mother who was sound in body and mind and even a little more interesting and mature, his kind of mature, after her experience with Frolick; he had hoped, secretly, to come home to a father who did not see the world exclusively from his desk at the mill, a man mellowed by the success of the mill and the money he had made. But he had come home to nothing different but only a little worse. They had not really changed, they were only the same a little older. And here he was learning through his father and mother a great truth that would be applicable to everyone else that had not been in the war. The mud-and-bayonet men would feel it more intensely, but to some degree all men who had been in uniform, under discipline, undergoing inconvenience, hardship and pain, treated like schoolchildren even in the matter of rewards—ice cream, cigarettes, chocolate, medals, small amounts of money, vacations measured by the hour or the day—were wanting or were going to want things to be different, and the first things were their people, and the difference was that they should be the same but better. And it was too much to ask. The people they came home to had not been subject to pain, seldom to hardship, and only a little oftener to inconvenience. They had not been told what to wear, they had had to eat sugar and bread of a different color from what they had been accustomed to, and they slept in their same beds; they had not had to learn to walk thirty inches at a step, raise their hands respectfully to strangers or to men they hated, or to live in fear of prison or death if they fell asleep at the wrong time. The people at home had gone on living and therefore grown gradually older; the men who had gone away had been set back into a kind of life that at best was standardized at a typical age of fifteen, and at worst meant that their balls would be shot off. Already in towns and neighborhoods of the country the men who had been away were forming clubs and associations (well in advance of the expansion of the American Legion), apparently with no more profound reason than the national urge to join something. But in truth it was more profound, though unexpressed: it was an instinct to take refuge among other men who had shared a more or less common experience, and who were now sharing (without recognizing it) the new experience of not understanding and not being understood, a bewilderment they could not classify, a want that they could not possibly state. In their little clubs and associations they played pool, drank whiskey and beer, shot crap, organized baseball teams, went on roughhousing picnics, and never talked about the war except to tell stories about women, latrines, or other crap games. Such refuges did not last, but while they did they had no trouble getting the members out for meeting nights. And the people who had stayed at home saw in the clubs only the crap games and the beer, bad habits that had been learned in the service. (*"We have to take into consideration that even the clean-living American soldier boy was exposed to temptation, but thank God most of them . . ."*) The uniform had served its purpose, to set the military apart from the civilian; it had served it only too well, and permanently. Later, when months had passed, Alfred was to say: "I never had to ask a man whether he'd been in the service. I could always tell, and without looking at his discharge button."

The freedom he had not wanted and the hopes he was abandoning left him with a desire to leave Port Johnson and anxious to see Lex. Lex, impulsive and unpredictable, the son of divorced parents, was still a part of a house and a family that provided a refuge more reliable than he had ever known at home. He would stay around for a few days for appearances' sake, but he knew that when he left Port Johnson he would not be in a hurry to return. He loved and would protect Sally and Constance; he owed his mother and father nothing. He could almost see that his mother was in her way as selfish as his father, and that even her over-generous gift of money was a whim that had cost her only the effort of a minor decision and the scratching of her signature on paper. Except literally, it had not cost her money; she was and always would be well taken care of, and no sacrifice was entailed. He had owed his father exactly what he had paid him: the opportunity to establish a relationship based on mutual respect; and his father had rejected him.

He went to his mother's room. As he entered the room through the open door she was holding up her hand, not to ward off something, but to catch the right light with her fingernails. She had a silver-mounted buffer in the right hand. "Good morning, dear," she said.

He kissed her cheek and sat in a chintz-covered easy chair that was too small for him. "Don't you remember that chair? That was in Sally's room."

"I don't remember it. I guess I never noticed her furniture very much."

"It was always a favorite of mine. It *was* mine, you know, and I gave it to Sally, but she said she didn't want it. I thought she'd want to take it to school with her, but she didn't. I hardly

304

ever sit in it, but I like it there. I had a cat, you know. Did I write you that?"

"Yes."

"But one day I saw him killing a bird, and I just couldn't have him in the house again, at least in my room. I told Nellie to give him away that very afternoon. Oh, it was awful. I watched him, standing there poised, then creeping up, then waiting for just the right moment. And then—flash! Down there on the front lawn, you see down there where the azalea bushes are? That's where it was. He was a beautiful specimen, but I just couldn't have had him in my room again. What made me think of him was he always sat in that chair. Why don't you sit on the ladderback? You'd be more comfortable."

"All right."

"I take it you and your father didn't get off to a good start."

"No, we didn't."

"I was afraid that would happen. I knew as soon as he left like that. He didn't even give Walter a chance to finish his lunch. But you must give him time."

"I've given him fifty-seven years. Or twenty-two years. He's had fifty-seven, though."

"Is what you're trying to say that he'll never change?"

"I guess that's what I meant."

"Well, I can't deny that. All the same, if you gave him time he might get used to your ways."

"I don't think I have that much time, and neither has he. It'd take at least a hundred years, Mother."

"No, now there you're wrong, Alfred. I admit it won't happen in a week or two, but if you gave him time to get used to you, and learn that you're independent, too, you could get along together. I've been thinking about you, dear. You mustn't get too independent. Independence is fine, but don't cut yourself off from everybody. I know you like the Porters, and they must like you a great deal. But don't cut off your own flesh and blood."

"I sound like a butcher."

"That was just an expression, a figure of speech, and you know it. Don't make *me* cross with you. I'll do anything to avoid a quarrel, and you won't win anything. Quarrels never do win anything anyway."

"Big ones do, we won the war."

"Oh, did we? According to the headlines, even the Allies are fighting among themselves."

"You're very clever this morning, aren't you?"

"I've never been clever, but you don't have to be clever to see that people are still fighting all over the world. Armistice—" She stopped speaking and quickly looked out the window.

"What's the matter? Another cat after a bird?"

She slowly turned and looked at him. "There's something you have to guard against."

"What's that?"

"I can't do it for you, you have to do it yourself."

"But what?"

"I don't think I'm going to live very long. Forty-eight isn't old, but it can be, and I think I ought to tell you this. You've had a lot of sadness for someone as young as you are, and you've always had a lot of sweetness. But you must guard against cruelty. I think you could be very cruel, Alfred. I don't mean the way some boys are. Billy was cruel, in a way that you never were, but it isn't surprising when it comes from someone like Billy, or your father. But it is when it comes from someone you don't expect, and that makes it worse. I hope you'll meet a nice girl and marry her, but I hope she isn't a weakling, because you'll take advantage of her."

"That's a nice portrait you're painting."

"Oh, you wouldn't beat her or anything like that. But you can be so cold that it's worse than beating somebody. It's our fault, your father's and mine. Your father was a rough, masculine man and he'd lose his temper something awful, but when it was over it was over."

"Oh, come on, Mother."

"I know I'm losing you."

"Well, you're not doing anything to hold on to me, not with this conversation. And you're wrong. You may be right about me, but you're wrong about Father, sore at everybody since 1908, when the apple of his eye got sick and died. That's eleven years. Do you call that being over when it's over? An eleven-year grudge against the human race. Stop making excuses for him. And I could say a lot of other things, too, but I won't."

"About me?"

"Consider the subject closed."

"My dear boy, that isn't politeness. That's rudeness. I know that you've found out about me, and not only about drinking. Don't you think I *know* that you beat a man in Philadelphia? I know that. I'm not what you think your mother ought to be, and I'm sorry if it embarrasses you, but I'm not going to make any excuses."

"That sounds like someone I knew in London. She said she never worried."

"Oh, I did worry. I don't much any more, but I did. Your coldness, Alfred. I could feel it last night, your very first look at me, down in the driveway. What am I? A hopeless drunkard, but they'd rather have me a hopeless drunkard than the other thing, an unfaithful wife. The drinking makes a good cover-up for the other. 'It wouldn't have happened if she hadn't been a drinker.' Oh, no. Blame it all on whiskey and gin. Little do they know, little do any of you know."

He could not think of anything to say, and she seemed to be thinking of what to say next. But to his astonishment in a few moments she picked up the silver buffer and began to stroke it across her nails, calmly, and as though he were not present.

He left her then, for there *was* nothing to say. He could put away for the future the things she had said to him, but to argue with her now, or even to try to talk with her, would be futile. It would be like trying to conduct a conversation with a professor of higher mathematics on the professor's terms; the words as words would be understood, but the thinking behind them would make the words unintelligible.

He passed Trimingham in the hall. He said, "Good afternoon," and went on a few steps. She called to him: "Mr. Eaton, in future it might be better if you spoke to me first, before going in."

"Oh, you heard?"

"No sir, but I can see you didn't have a very pleasant few minutes. I usually know when she'll be at her best, and I can spare you the other times."

"This was one of the other times. Thank you, Miss Trimingham."

"Very good, sir."

He would not have been surprised if she had clicked her heels and saluted, but for the first time he liked her. It did not make him like her the less that she relieved him of responsibility; in her care his mother would be protected as well as anyone could protect her, and right now he wanted to be relieved of all responsibility toward his mother, his father, to some extent his sisters. It had rained awfully hard for this picnic: coming home had been a total failure.

He went downstairs to use the telephone. He had no desire to talk about or avoid talking about Sally with Harry Van Peltz, and he had no desire to have Harry beat him badly at tennis. He accordingly called the club and left a polite message for Harry, without having conversation with him. He finished the call, and was sitting at the telephone, when Nellie appeared. "Your new auto is here," she said.

"My new auto? What new auto?"

"The present from your father. The man has it out in the stable-yard."

He went to the stable-yard and it was there: a battle-ship grey Marmon. It had a cloverleaf body—the front seats

307

divided and room for two in the rear—and wire wheels, and on both doors the letters A. E., inch-high in black with a narrow orange border. The leather upholstery was covered with tan canvas, removable, and on the left-side running board there was a large drum-shapped searchlight.

"Good afternoon, Mr. Eaton," said the man. "My name is Sinzer. How do you like your new car?"

"Are you sure it's mine?"

"Got your initials on it. Yes sir, it's all yours, and your father made sure you got a good one. We don't make anything *but* good cars, but I drove this one from the factory myself. I'm a factory man."

"Where is the factory?"

"Indianapolis, Indiana. But don't ask me how long it took. I didn't try to break any records. I broke it in the way you should break in a fine car, and I spent all day yesterday with her, and now she's all ready to drive."

"I can drive it any speed I want to?"

"Well, I don't recommend that till you get another thousand miles on your spiddometer. If you wanted to, if you had a good stretch of road, you could get her up to eighty-five, ninety miles an hour. But you wouldn't have as good a car five years from now as if you kept her under forty for another thousand miles. Are you experienced around cars, Mr. Eaton?"

"Not very."

"Well, here's a manual that you ought to keep with you in the pocket, and I wouldn't let any but Marmon dealers work on the motor. Shall we go for a spin?"

The purity of the body lines and the seeming fragility of the wire wheels had him unprepared for the immediate feel of tremendous power and heaviness of handling.

"It's not a ladies' car, Mr. Eaton. Although we sell them our share. It's a man's car. You'll get used to it, but in the beginning you want to go into your turns not too fast. Don't go into these sharp turns on country roads too fast, or you're liable to be picking yourself out of a ditch, and we wouldn't want that to happen."

"No," said Alfred, absorbed in this new experience.

"You handle a car better than most. Were you a horseback rider?"

"Rode all my life."

"The two go together," said Sinzer. "Not always, but as a rule. They don't ask too much of the horse or the car. I never rode anything but a brewery horse in Indianapolis, but I can always tell by how a man drives a car if he was a good horseback rider."

They drove for half an hour, stopping and starting, and on the better roads taking the car up to forty m. p. h. And then suddenly the car was his, and he found that he loved it as he had never loved any other thing. It was his, but equally he was *its*. It would be a long time before he could ever go away from it without taking one look back at it. Now, while it was taking a unique possession of him, he had no thought of how much it had cost, and no regret that it had been a gift from his father. The lines of the Marmon were female, unembellished round all over except for the tiny sharp point under the radiator cap, but Alfred Eaton was not one to call a car *she,* and for the present he was unaware of any resemblance to the body of a woman. In a half-hour's time he had gained something to love, and *anything* to love was the supplying of a need.

"You like this car. I can see that," said Sinzer.

Alfred did not bother to reply.

"Well, if you wouldn't mind driving me back to the hotel I'll let you enjoy her all to yourself. I'll fix you up with a couple of cards. My own card, at the factory. And here's who to get in touch with in Philly."

By the time he had returned to the farm Alfred had made up his mind about his immediate future. He telephoned Lex Porter in New York. Mr. Porter, the maid said, was at Mr. Thornton's for the weekend; Glen Cove, Long Island, six-five, was the number. After two more attempts he heard Lex's voice.

"Who is this?" said Lex.

"This is an old friend of yours from Pennsylvania."

"Well, God damn you. You son of a bitch. You hire a car and get right out here. I've been trying to get you all day."

"I don't have to hire a car. Wait till you see what I have."

"Where are you?"

"At home."

"At home, Port Johnson?"

"Yes. Ask your uncle if it would be all right if I—"

"Listen, he's been prodding me. He's having a house party and you've got to come. How long'll it take you?"

"I don't know. I've never driven to New York from here. And I have a new car."

"What did you get?"

"A Marmon. Wait till you see it."

"Nice, huh?"

"It's the—I can't describe it, Lex."

"Well, bring it here and you won't have to. Now you get started right away and I'll tell Uncle Fritz you're coming."

"What clothes will I need? I haven't any."

"Well, you used to have that Norfolk suit with knicker-bockers. Tennis clothes. And your Tuck."

"None of those things fit me."

"Then the hell with it, wear your uniform."

"No, I won't wear my uniform. I've taken that off for good."

"Listen, just get here. Uncle Fritz'll fix you up with all you'll need. He'll explain that you're a hick from Pennsylvania. But get started right away. There's a party tonight that I wouldn't want you to miss. Markel's orchestra, two hundred beautiful Long Island virgins. Pre-war champagne. And you know who the guest of honor is."

"You."

"None other than. Tonight I can do no wrong, unless of course I get pissy-assed drunk and start taking the little girls upstairs. There's one I think might go without too much persuasion, but I'll put a brand on her before you get here. When will you start?"

"In five minutes."

"That's the way I like to hear you talk. Oh, everything all right down there? Your family? Will you remember me to them, and Sally and the younger one—Constance?"

"Right. Thanks. I'll be there—eight, nine, I can't say for sure, but I'll be there."

"And don't worry about clothes. Oh, what do you weigh, and how tall are you?"

"About one eighty-five, and six-foot-one."

"What size collar?"

"Fifteen and a half."

"Shoes? I'm writing this down."

"Ten."

"Jesus, you've got big feet. All right. I'll have everything. Alfred?"

"What?"

"How was it?"

"How was what?"

"Getting home."

"I'll tell you when I see you."

"Yeah. Same here. Well, snap out of it, Admiral."

Alfred went to his room and packed a small bag. On the way downstairs he stopped in his mother's room, leaving the bag in the hallway. She looked at him in his new suit and said, "You're going to show off your new car. It is a beauty, isn't it?" She spoke with no rancor.

"I am. In fact, I'm going to show it to Lex Porter."

"Oh, you're leaving us."

Trimingham left the room and his mother turned her face away.

"Yes, Mother."

"You don't know when you'll be back."

"No, I don't."

"When you come back I'd like to go for a ride in your new car. Will you take me?"

"Of course. I could take you for a ride now."

"No, not now. Not today. You're doing a—it's better for you to clear out now. Sensible. I've been thinking, and the Porters are like a second family to you. But just remember, they're not. You're disappointed in your father and I, all of us. Nothing very nice, very good, happened while you were away, and you didn't come back to very much. But go away for a while and then when you come back again maybe you won't be expecting so much. Of course when you come back again things may be much worse, I don't know. I don't know why they should be any better. Maybe they'll be a *lot* worse. Who knows? And who knows? You may be disappointed in the Porters."

"Well, I'm glad you warned me. Maybe that'll keep me from expecting too much from them."

"You didn't think of that, though, did you?"

"No, I hadn't."

"Everybody can disappoint you, you know, if you happen to catch them at the wrong time. That includes you, too, Alfred. Haven't you ever disappointed anybody?"

"Yes, I have."

"When they needed you, counted on you?"

"Yes. I said yes."

"Have you been conscious of it lately?"

"No, I don't think so."

"So disappointed yourself that you never stopped to think that perhaps you disappointed a few people, such as your father."

"Oh, *well.* You knew I wasn't going to do what he wanted me to do."

"But *he* didn't. That's why he was disappointed. And when he's disappointed he gets angry."

"Did I disappoint *you,* too? I suppose I did."

"Yes, you did."

"How?"

"It would take too long. But it wasn't a big disappointment. It wasn't a *little* disappointment. But it wasn't a shock to me. I don't expect anything else but disappointments. Are you going to speak to your father before you leave?"

"I'm going to phone him and thank him for the car."

"Why?"

"*Why?* Common politeness."

"Write him a note and leave it here for him. And don't say anything you don't mean. Just tell him you like it, and thank him, and you're going away. No matter what you say

311

now, he's not going to like it, so you're better off writing him a note than calling him up on the telephone. Enjoy yourself, and remember us to the Porters."

She put up her cheek to be kissed, to spare him the awkwardness of leaving without making the gesture, but it was plain that she did not take any pleasure in the kiss nor suffer any pain at his departure. He spoke to no one else on his way to the car and as he drove away and left the farm behind him to his new joy in the car was added, for a little while, a sense of sinful pleasure as though he were stealing the car. It had been given to him unconditionally, without strings, but the gift was giving the giver none of the pleasure of giving, and the enjoyment of the car was his alone.

He lost his way four times between Port Johnson and the Fritz Thornton country place, and the drive took him six hours, what with the self-imposed speed limit of forty m. p. h., and the need to slow down in the towns and cities of Pennsylvania and New Jersey. At the main gate of Fritz Thornton's establishment a stout man in a policeman's uniform halted him. "Name, sir?"

"R. A. Eaton," said Alfred, automatically. "Mr. Eaton."

"Just a minute, sir." The special partolman obviously was suspicious of Alfred's business suit, and consulted a typewritten sheet. "Can I have that name again?" This time he did not add *sir*.

"Eaton. E, a, t, o, n."

"I don't have no Eaton on this list. Whose house is it you're looking for?"

"Mr. Thornton's. Mr. Frederick Thornton."

"Does Mr. Thornton know you?"

"You have a phone in that lodge, haven't you?"

"I have a phone, yes."

"Well, then use it. Call Mr. Thornton and tell him I'm down at his gate and being detained by a fresh cop."

"Now that kind of talk won't get you there any quicker, and if he don't know you, it'll get you something you aint looking for," said the cop. "Just a minute." The cop walked over to a just-arrived car containing two young couples in evening clothes. He passed them through, and then, taking his deliberate time, entered the porter's lodge. He came out presently and stood in front of the Marmon and wrote down the license number, then sauntered around to the left side of the car. "You can go in."

"I always could have, but I wanted to see you make a prick of yourself."

"Young fellow, I'm only here temporary, but I live near here and I used to be on the County Police. I'll tell my friends to keep an eye out for a Marmon with a Pennsylvania license. I'll tell them the driver don't like cops."

"You scare the shit out of me, you do," said Alfred. He drove on, and at the house a chauffeur in livery and puttees took the Marmon to the garage, while a footman took his kitbag, and led the way to a bedroom on the second story.

"Are you a regular member of the staff?" said Alfred.

"No sir, I'm not. But I have my instructions. I'll draw you a bath, and as you see, your clothes are all laid out. Have you had your dinner, sir?"

"No, I haven't."

"They didn't wait dinner for you, but if you'd like a steak, you can have it on a tray. And what do you wish to drink before dinner?"

"A Martini cocktail. When did they start dinner?"

"About an hour ago, perhaps a few minutes over. Some that are only invited for the dancing have begun to arrive."

"What course are they at?"

"That I can't say, but I'll find out when I go downstairs. Your steak medium rare, sir?"

"Medium rare. And that's all I want. No soup or salad or dessert. Steak, and coffee, and by all means——"

"The Martini cocktail. You're familiar with this house, sir? That button's for the pantry, that one's for the maid. But I'm afraid you wouldn't get any response tonight."

"What's your name?"

"John, sir. It happens to be my family name, not my first name."

"All right, John. Thank you."

"Very good, sir."

Lying in the tub Alfred could hear through the open window some recognizable snatches of "Hindustan," but the orchestra must have been stationed on the far side of the house, for he found himself singing a fourth chorus of "Hindustan" to an accompaniment of an orchestra which had switched to "Oh! Frenchy." He cooled off the water in the tub and got out feeling none of the fatigue that had been partly the cause of his irritation with the cop at the gate. He sat in the trousers and waistcoat of his borrowed Tuxedo (there was no name inside the inner pocket of the jacket to show whom it belonged to) and was pleased that a soft shirt with button-down collar had been provided. The shoes were dull calf pumps and could have been made to his order. In a few minutes John appeared with the food and drink and in a few more minutes Alfred was ready to go to the party.

There were French windows in all the rooms of the first floor, and they had been generally opened for air in the warm night. The members of the dinner party were still at table, with a few gaps made by couples who had got up to dance. The rugs in the hall and the two largest rooms had been taken up and the furniture removed to make room for the dancing, and a bar, already busy, tended by three men, occupied space in the smaller of the dancing rooms. In the time it had taken Alfred to bathe and eat, the party had increased in size, more than doubled by the simultaneous arrivals of new guests from other dinner parties. Pretending to be searching for someone, Alfred wandered about. He recognized a few girls but only a very few of the young men; it was a Yale and Harvard party that greatly outnumbered the Princeton men, and as an alumnus of an unknown prep school called Knox, and a citizen of a Pennsylvania town called Port Johnson, Alfred had no common background with most of the young men. A few of them were still wearing uniforms—those who had been commissioned officers. There were several in Navy summer whites and aviation greens and Marine Corps blues, and here and there an American in a British officer's tunic. But the new uniform was the popular one: dinner jacket with soft white shirt, the Brooks classic, with the innovators deviating to the extent of tucking their black ties under the shirt collars. Almost every young man thus attired wore a gold watch chain from which depended a collegiate charm, and the majority parted their hair in the middle. Some of them, but not many, wore fraternity pins on their waistcoats. It was a young party, with the parents disincluded from the usual debutante party list, and Alfred did not see a tailcoat wherever he went. From one of the terraces he could see a gathering of black-putteed chauffeurs smoking their pipes in the moonlight. It was 1919, and a good many of the young virgins went to such parties under the remote chaperonage of the Murphys and the Harrys and the Perkinses who drove the family Pierce. The girls wore what their mothers—and sometimes their fathers—told them to wear, or did not wear what they were told not to wear. Five or six of the young ladies wore bandeaux low on their foreheads that gave promise of immunity to a young man who wanted to be a bit forward. It was the beginning of the brief era of "the vamp," in which the young lady could match the conversational efforts of the young man who had "a line." The cut-in dance was firmly established.

Alfred took another turn about the house and had a look at the Thornton-Porter dinner party. It appeared that they were giving toasts, so he rejoined the dancing people. He cut in on the handsomest couple in the room. The young man, darkly handsome and a few years older, smiled at Alfred and at the girl, and left her with Alfred. The girl was not altogether pleased at the cut-in.

314

"I thought I might as well start at the top," said Alfred.

"Did you?"

"This is my first dance on American soil since—over a year ago. And you're the prettiest girl at this party."

"Thank you for the compliment. Who are you?"

"My name is Alfred Eaton, but that wouldn't mean anything to you."

"Yes it would, if you're related to Francis Eaton."

"Who is she?"

"He."

"Then I'm not related to him, if I didn't even know he was a he. Where is he from?"

"Providence, Rhode Island."

"No relation that I know of. What's your name?"

"Mary St. John."

"Now that's a nice, respectable name."

"Well, I must say—respectable? Of course it's respectable. Really, what a thing to say."

"Am I the first person to call it respectable?"

"You're the first person that ever raised the question."

"Well, then I'm glad I thought it was respectable instead of the opposite."

"Are you trying to annoy me, Mr. Eaton? If so, you're succeeding."

"I'm not, not a bit. Didn't I pick you as the first girl I wanted to dance with?"

"How do you happen to be at this party? To change the subject."

"Mr. Markel is my mother's brother. I always go to parties where he plays. I tell him if the people like the music."

"I've been to a hundred parties where he played, and I've never seen you before."

"I don't usually come to the New York ones. Philadelphia, Baltimore, Wilmington. That's where I usually work."

"Do you play a musical instrument?"

"Oh, I play them all. I'm best on the xylophone, but we didn't bring it tonight."

"So you'll be playing something else, I suppose."

"The glockenspiel."

"Oh, yes, of course. Don't you get out of breath playing the glockenspiel?"

"I did at first, but you learn breath control, like the trudgen in swimming."

"That's funny. I thought the glockenspiel was something you played with a little hammer, *like* the xylophone."

"Well, maybe it is. I'll have to ask Uncle Michael."

"You do that. I'd like you to play at my party."

"Oh, I don't think I'll be there."

"Couldn't you try?"

"No, I'd like to, but as I said, I hardly ever get to New York."

"I know you did. But I'm from Wilmington. I know why you're here. You went to Princeton with Lex Porter."

"That's the one and only reason. How did you know?"

"Just a clever guess. You had Princeton written all over you as soon as I saw you."

"And you don't like Princeton. Do you like your host?"

"That's different. I knew him before he went to Princeton."

"What do you like? Yale? Harvard?"

"Boston Tech."

"Why?"

"Because my father went there. And then I like Yale, and then I like Harvard, and then I like Penn, and then I like Leland Stanford."

"Leland Stanford?"

"And a few others. And *then* I like Princeton. But quite a few others."

"What comes after Princeton in your estimation?"

"Oh, let me think. After Princeton? No place, I guess."

"Where is your education being pursued? Notice I say pursued."

"In New York."

"Any place in particular? Fordham? Columbia?"

"Just a girls' school. You wouldn't be interested."

"No, but I'm getting up a list of places not to send my daughter to."

"Oh, I see. Well, we'd be awfully glad if you didn't send her to—never mind. I don't think she could get in anyway."

"Well, there we are. Intermission. Weren't we disagreeable, though?"

"Yes, and it was so *easy*."

"Would you like to go upstairs and cry, or anything?"

"No. I won't even mind if you just walk away and disappear into thin air. I have a lot of friends here."

"Now, now, Miss St. John. I think you're exaggerating. A lot of friends?"

"Well, let's see how many friends *you* have in this group."

"Goodnight, Miss St. John."

"Goodnight, Mr. Eaton."

He left her at the edge of a group of young people and went to have another look at the Thornton dinner party. The tables had been vacated, and the dinningroom doors were being closed. "Where will I find Mr. Porter?" he asked a waiter.

"Mr. Porter, sir? Oh, Mr. *Porter*. I last saw him with Mr.

316

Thornton and the other gentlemen. I believe they went to the billiard-room, sir."

"All right, then I'll go to the billiard-room," said Alfred. He whispered to the waiter. "I'm a pool shark. Maybe I can win some money, huh?"

"Yes sir," said the waiter.

Alfred went to the basement. A rumble of male voices was coming from the billiard-room, but one voice hailed him the moment he stood in the doorway! "Eaton! Alfred!" Lex pushed his way through the gathering and grabbed his hand. Lex called back, "Uncle Fritz, look who's here." He hit Alfred a paralyzing punch on the right bicep. "How's your muscle, God damn you. When did you get here? Have you had a drink?"

Fritz Thornton came to welcome Alfred. "Alfred, I'm so glad to see you. This party wouldn't have been complete without you. We didn't even know you were in the country till Lex decided to give it one more try and telephone you. You've sprouted out."

"Yes sir, I guess I have," said Alfred. "It's nice to be here."

"There's a man called John I told to look out for you," said Fritz Thornton.

"He took very good care of me, sir."

"First-rate. Would you like some champagne, or something else?"

"I'd rather have a whiskey and water."

"You can have anything you please, and I'll get it myself. You mean, of course, Scotch whiskey."

"Yes sir."

"You stay right where you are, don't move, and I'll be with you in a second." Thornton went to get the drink, and Alfred looked at Lex, who had been studying him. They smiled at each other.

"Well, God damn it," said Lex, gently.

"Yep," said Alfred.

They said nothing more until Thornton hurried over with the drink, and carrying two other highballs for himself and Lex. "Boys," he said, with an implication of a question coming.

"Yes sir?" said Lex.

Thornton raised his glass. "I hoped for this moment, the three of us together like this, as much as I hoped for victory. God bless you." He drank his drink bottoms-up, then tossed the glass on the flagstone floor. He put a hand on Lex's shoulder, the other hand on Alfred's shoulder. "I'm a little overcome, but I'll be all right."

"To you, sir," said Alfred.

"Bottoms up," said Lex.

They drank, and smashed their glasses.

During the ceremonial the others in the room had become aware of its being a special moment, and Lex's and Alfred's glasses were smashed in the midst of a gradual but rapid silence.

Fritz Thornton turned and addressed the roomful. "Gentlemen, this is our very good friend, Lex's *best* friend and, in spite of the difference in our ages, a good friend of mine—Alfred Eaton. Some of you know him, some of you don't, but come and say hello to him. In every way but legally, he's a member of this family."

Alfred found himself the center of an impromptu reception, with Lex introducing him to the young men who were strangers. For the first time he had been made to feel that someone was glad he was home. For the first time he was glad he had come home.

The orchestra packed up their instruments at five minutes past four; the last of the guests went through the main gate at a quarter of six, according to the night watchman's check. "Boys, I'm going to bed," said Fritz Thornton. "It's not that I'm not in condition. To the contrary. I'm in such good condition that I'm not up to making a night of it any more. I have a lunch date at Piping Rock, but I'm not at all sure I'll get there. You sleep as late as you like. Alfred—glad you're back. We all are. Hope you're going to stay with us for a good, long visit."

"Thank you, sir. I may take you up on that."

"First-rate. Well, goodnight, and good morning."

They were sitting in Lex's bedroom, their jackets over their arms, their ties undone. "I ought to be drunk, but I'm not. How are you?" said Lex.

"Just about right, I don't want another drink, but I'm glad I had that last one. At peace with the world."

"He's a great guy. He did this whole thing himself. All he asked me was to tell him what day, and the rest—the invitation list, orchestra, he did himself. Did you get your souvenir of the occasion?"

"No."

"Well, you will. I know there was one ordered for you. Silver cigarette case with your name on it and the date. I guess he has yours tucked away somewhere. It's the same as this." Lex tossed him a silver case, curved and of hammered silver.

"It was a good party."

"Did you get any poon-tang?" said Lex.

"No."

"No, neither did I. I didn't really expect any. I don't think

318

anybody got any. I don't know these girls. They say they were fucking like minks during the war, some of them, but I couldn't spot which ones tonight."

"I thought you had one all sewed up."

"So did I, but I couldn't even get her to go for a walk. I guess I misjudged her."

"Who is Mary St. John?"

"Yes, I saw you gave her a rush. Why, her old man is with the du Pont factory in Wilmington, Delaware. You never knew her before?"

"No, never saw her before tonight."

"I heard she was secretly engaged to—that dark-haired fellow she was with tonight? Jim Roper. He's a pretty good fellow, known him all my life. But he may not be rich enough for her. She has plenty of money, but they like to marry money, too, and Jim's father is a minister. No du Pont money there."

"Well, I wasn't thinking of marrying her."

"Well, you better, because you can forget about anything else. The way I heard it, she likes Jim, and he's certainly gone on her, and he's a handsome dog, but he wants to be a doctor. She won't wait forever. Why do you like her?"

"I don't know. We didn't hit it off very well."

"No, she's sarcastic. She knows she's good-looking, and she's young, very young. Seventeen, I think. She's coming out next Christmas. My advice is to forget about her. You're not rich enough for her, and if you have any other plans, I don't think she ever had a real twitch in her twat. Jim's lucky if he gets a maidenly little goodnight kiss."

"Well, I'm not as nice a fellow as he is."

"All right, maybe you're the one she's been saving it for. But I know her too well. She's just a society girl. You know, there wasn't a single one there tonight that appealed to me."

"You're too particular."

"Yeah. I don't like ladies."

"That's news to me. What do you like? Tarts?"

"Well, I like them better than ladies."

"When did that start?"

"Don't be like my mother. Don't blame the war."

"Your mother wasn't here tonight. Neither was your sister Elizabeth."

"They weren't invited. Or at least they weren't welcome. They could have come, but they knew better. Mother went visiting some friends in New Jersey, and I don't know where Elizabeth is. I never do know. And care less. I feel sorry for her, her fiancé got it, or did you know that?"

"No."

"He was with the British, you know. He got it last August

with the Fourth Army. She didn't hear about it till a month or so after it happened. His family didn't bother to tell her, I guess because he never told them about her. When she finally did hear it it was in a roundabout way, and I understand she took it hard. Mother said she took it very hard."

"I know why," said Alfred.

"Why?"

"At least I can guess. She told me she didn't believe in wartime marriages and wartime love affairs."

"I see. That explains it, I guess. She was sorry when it was too late. Well, that's one of the reasons why I don't like ladies. Now she's full of regret. She's pure, but she's full of regret. And her purity was no consolation when she heard the guy was killed, or since."

"What does she do with herself?"

"Interferes with other people's lives. She has mine all mapped out for me. Very disappointed I decided not to go to Oxford. Now she wants me to go back to college and get a degree and then settle down with one of those nice girls you saw tonight."

"What are you going to do?"

"I haven't the slightest idea, but none of that," said Lex. "Are you going back?"

"No."

"Well, maybe we can plan something together. The first thing is to get away from home and mother."

"I've done that."

"So soon? What about your father?"

"Him, too."

"You didn't lose any time. I've been farting around for over a month, seeing the wrong kind of people, never getting up before noon, terrible disappointment to my mother and my sister. Can't understand why I don't want to graduate with my class and resume a normal life. What is a normal life? If it's what they plan for me, they have a long wait ahead. And this town is full of guys in the same predicament. You go to a club and at twelve noon there are guys like you and me lined up three deep. All they want is to drink in peace and be left alone and not have their God damn families dictate their lives for them. You see the same guys late at night at the Pre Cat, and there's getting to be a kind of army of them. Us, I should say. I'm one. Most of us know we're going to get jobs eventually and settle down, but except for the guys that were married before they left, or publicly engaged, we want a little time to ourselves, and settle down when we're ready, not when other people are ready. I don't want to be a bum the rest of my life, but it looks good now."

"Have you thought about staying in the Army?"

320

"I've heard about the Kosciusko Squadron and the French Foreign Legion, and I know a fellow that left last week to be a general in a South American revolution. But can you see me signing up for five years with the French, *as a private?* Not me. From force of habit I still start lacing up my boots when I get up in the morning."

"I still want to salute when I see two and a half stripes."

"I'm a civilian, forever more. Is there anything you'd like to do tomorrow, or when we get up?"

"Yes."

"What?"

"Have breakfast."

"That's the way I feel about it. We're going to a dinner party tonight, but I can even get out of that if you don't feel like it. Do you want to play tennis this afternoon?"

"Do you?"

"That depends entirely on how I feel when I've had my breakfast. If you want to play golf we can go over to Piping Rock, or if you'd like to get some Long Island Sound air in your lungs we can go for a sail. You're a fucking admiral, maybe you'd like to do that. As far as that goes, I could give you a ride in an aeroplane."

"Not today."

"All right, if you don't trust me. Can I get you anything? Glass of milk? Something to read?"

"No thanks."

"Well, sleep as long as you can. Ring for your breakfast whenever you like. If you know what you're going to want to eat, write it down and I'll see that your order is carried out with neatness and dispatch. Otherwise, goodnight."

"I'll decide when I wake up. Goodnight, boy."

"I'm glad you're here. Goodnight."

ALFRED EATON's marriage to Mary St. John was inevitable or the courtship would not have survived the frequent breakings-off, the doubts and recriminations and separations, as well as the very first meeting. Lex Porter's warning, that Mary St. John was the daughter of wealth who would marry only wealth, was based on misinformation and was only half accurate, but for several months it kept Alfred from thinking thoughts of marriage and influenced his attitude toward Mary and his treatment of her. In those early months, while he was falling in love with her without any awareness that that was happening, he conceded to himself that he was in the midst of

321

a "strong infatuation." Increasingly she was becoming the girl most often in his thoughts, with whom he wanted to share more and more of the big and little experiences, from a passionate kiss to a cartoon in *Life;* but Lex's warning, given innocently enough, precluded any consideration of marriage while it did not in any degree rule out seduction. A marriage to a rich girl, he told himself, would not work, somewhere, sometime in the future, he told himself, he would find a girl who had been given the benefits of money but did not possess or stand to inherit a fortune, and he would marry such a girl. In actual fact his knowledge of marriages was not vast, but he believed that in cases where the wife had the greater money, the husband lost authority; a wife with independent means could be independent in other ways if not in all ways. The Devrow Budds provided his favorite case in point—a weak enough case considering that Devrow Budd had not seemed to lose authority in his own house—and another case was that of his own father and mother, wherein the husband made more than enough money for both, but the wife could feel free to behave as she pleased without threat of financial pressure. Lex Porter's father and mother had had trouble over money, and Alfred, in his soliloquies, would say, ". . . and lots of other cases."

Since Mary St. John was not marriageable she became— indeed, from the first moment always had been—a girl to be seduced, if possible, but without deep or permanent involvement. With this kind of self-imposed restraint Alfred conducted his pursuit of her, and one of the consequences of his noncommittal approach was her refusal to be even slightly romantic. Once she said to him: "Why do you dance with me? Why do you ever want to see me? We're always sarcastic with each other, and we usually finish up having a spat. If you don't like me, stay away from me. I'm sure I won't *perish* of un*happiness.*"

They were seldom alone together in the first months, and then never for as long as an hour. He danced with her and played tennis with her during the Long Island season, then on a cruise with Fritz Thornton and Lex Porter he found out that she was visiting a friend on Mount Desert. It was the first time he had been able to see her without Jim Roper somewhere nearby.

"Where's Jim Roper?" said Alfred.

"He's taking a course at Columbia. He's coming up over Labor Day. I *should* say *down,* I suppose."

"How long are you staying here?"

"Well, obviously till after Labor Day."

"Then back to Wilmington?"

"For a while, yes."

322

"I live not very far from there, you know."

"I didn't know. Where?"

"Port Johnson."

"Where's that? That sounds like New Jersey. Or Maryland."

"Pennsylvania."

"It's funny. I never knew where you lived. I never even thought of you having a family."

"Oh, I have, though. But I never go near them. I send the old woman money for the children, but—"

"Oh, there you go again."

"It may be true, for all you know."

"It may be, but I doubt it. You're too selfish to have children."

"Don't tell me you don't know how people *have* children. It has damn little to do with unselfishness."

"I know how people have children, but mostly when they have them they're not quite as selfish as I think you are."

"I'm the soul of generosity. To prove it I'd like to have children with you."

"And then send me money, I suppose."

"No. Just have the children."

She was silent, and he waited for her to make an angry reply, but instead she blushed, from confusion or modesty or anger he could not be certain. They were sitting on the deck of Fritz Thornton's yawl, and they were alone in the boat, having rowed out to inspect it.

Presently she spoke: "You'd be an awful father."

"No, I wouldn't," he said. He spoke vehemently and without humor. She turned and looked in his face.

"I shouldn't have said that," she said. "I'm sorry. I don't know you, Alfred, and that *was* a nasty thing to say." Then, as though it were required as part of her apology, she gently put her arms about him and they kissed. They drew away and looked at each other and then she closed her eyes and let him kiss her with more meaning, and without taking her lips away she slowly lay back on the deck and he put his leg between her legs, but when he began to unbutton her blouse she sat up.

"Let's go back," she said.

"Do you insist?"

"I don't want to stay."

"Do you mean that?"

"Yes, I mean it."

"All right."

"I'm going to marry Jim Roper, that's why."

"I'd heard that. So it's true?"

"Yes."

"Well, he'll make a good father."

323

"Let's forget about that, will you, Alfred?"

"I'm not sore. I mean it. Jim *will* make a good father."

Not so much to him as to herself she said: "I've never let him kiss me that way."

"You ought to. He wants to."

"Not Jim. You don't know Jim. Jim idealizes me. You could never do that. You would have gone as far as you could, wouldn't you?"

"Yes."

"Without thinking of what could happen to me."

"I was like Jim once."

"Why didn't you stay that way?"

"Oh, maybe I'll tell you sometime. The girl was killed. It's a long story."

"I know you better now, Alfred. But I'm going to marry Jim Roper."

"Why do you repeat that?"

"Because I'm not going to let you kiss me that way again, and I don't want you to be angry if I refuse. So don't try to get me off alone somewhere. I knew you were going to try to kiss me today." She smiled, and was beautiful. "But I didn't know I was going to kiss you. Let's go now. This minute?"

On his first visit to Wilmington he knew immediately that Lex's report of Mary's wealth was exaggerated. The St. John house was as large as but less imposing than the Raymond Johnson Mansion. It shared an irregular block with three other residences, just off the Chester highway, but closer to the business district than the landed properties of the very rich in Greenville. The excuse of his call on Mary was that he had been duck-hunting on the Eastern Shore and was passing through. An excuse was needed. Mary's mother was polite, but no more, and made frequent opportunities to mention Jim Roper's name during the serving of tea and watercress sandwiches. Alfred had expected to be questioned carefully about his own background, but Mrs. St. John fooled him there. It was plain to see that she was avoiding even the appearance of cordiality, and sought no information that would encourage a personal relationship or a repetition of this visit. "This," she said to her husband when Mr. St. John appeared, "is Mr. Eaton, a friend of Jim's."

St. John was a rather round-shouldered, quietly well-dressed man, who wore pince-nez spectacles with small lenses, a blue and white polka dot bow-tie, and a Tau Beta Pi key on his watch chain. His tan kid oxfords were polished and he had on black silk socks with a thin white stripe. He was half business man, half professor, to someone meeting him for the first time.

"Ah. What brings you to Wilmington, Mr. Eaton?"

"I've been to Chestertown—"

324

"Ah. Any luck?"

"Yes sir. I got a few. Could I offer you a pair?"

"Please don't," said Mrs. St. John. "I don't like to look at them, much less to eat them."

St. John smiled and took a cup of tea. "How is Jim?"

"Well, I'm afraid I haven't seen Jim since early summer."

"But you do know him. You did say that," said Mrs. St. John. "I had the distinct impression that you were a close friend of his."

"No, not close. Not at all close. I'd be going under false pretenses—I really know Mary better."

"Oh, well now I—not a friend of Jim's? Isn't that strange?"

"No, Mother, it isn't *strange*. Jim and I both met Mr. Eaton at the same time. Last spring."

"Well, then he's really a friend of yours, more than Jim's."

"Yes, dear, I gathered that," said St. John. "On your way north, I take it, Mr. Eaton?"

"Not very far. Port Johnson, Pennsylvania."

"Oh, yes. The steel mill. You're that Eaton? We have other Eaton friends in Providence. But I know your family's mill. What do you think of that strike?"

"I'm not in the mill, but my father doesn't like it."

"I'm sure he doesn't. Nobody does."

"No sir. Well, I'm afraid I'll have to get on my way."

"My husband will see you to the door."

"Nonsense, Mother. I will."

"Very well. Goodbye, Mr. Eaton." Mrs. St. John did not offer her hand.

In the vestibule Mary was embarrassed for her mother, but tried not to admit it. "Your mother is not very encouraging," said Alfred.

"In what way?" said Mary.

"If I wanted to call again."

"She's very fond of Jim. And I could see what was going through my father's mind, too."

"What?"

" 'What does this young man do, that he can go duck-shooting in the middle of the week, and doesn't work in his father's mill?' My father's not terribly rich, but he's proud of earning it all himself, whatever he does have."

"I've never earned a cent, except my Navy pay."

"Well, maybe you're rich. You seem to be, the way you live."

"I'm not. I'm spending a big present I got last spring. It's going pretty fast, faster than I expected. Next year I'll have to go to work. What do you want for a wedding present?"

"I haven't come out yet, let alone announce my engagement."

"I know, but it's all cut and dried, and I'd like to give you something nice while I still have some money. I'll have Bailey, Banks & Biddle put it aside."

"You don't think I'm going to marry Jim, but you're wrong."

"You won't if I can help it."

"You can't help it, so don't try." She looked at him in puzzlement. "Do you want to marry me?"

"I do now," said Alfred. "I didn't before."

"Why now?"

"Well, I thought you were rolling in du Pont money. You're not, are you?"

"What we have is du Pont money, but no, we're not rolling in it."

"Then yes, I do want to marry you."

"*Mary!* I said *Mary!*" Mrs. St. John called out.

"Goodbye, Alfred. Come to my party in December."

"Oh, I'll be sure to do that."

Mary looked at him in alarm. "Don't kiss me!" she said.

"All right, but I'm going to write to you. And I have friends in Wilmington, you know."

"Go, hurry, before she calls again."

The breaking of Mary's unannounced engagement was signified by Jim Roper's non-appearance at her coming-out party, an event which took place in the unhappiest circumstances. "They're nothing and nobody. The mother is a drunkard and other things besides, the father is a noisy, *nouveau-riche* war profiteer," said Mrs. St. John of the Eaton family.

"How do you know? You haven't met either of them, Mother."

"I have my sources of information and I've made it a point to inquire. As to the young man himself, he's never done a day's work in his life, he couldn't finish college, and he's putting on a great show of being a young gentleman of leisure in New York and Philadelphia, but when he was still in prep school he was having an affair, *an affair,* with an older woman who was later *murdered.* But you still want to have him at your party. If he were a gentleman, he'd stay away and stop the tongues wagging. I don't want him, and your father doesn't want him, and that's all there is to it. Why, I didn't even know his name was on the invitation list."

"His name is on all the lists."

"I meant ours."

"All right. I'll ask him not to come."

"Well, I should think you would. I should certainly think you would."

In November, a month before Mary's party, and on the day of the previous conversation, Mary obediently disinvited

Alfred, and when she had posted the letter, as soon as the iron slot-cover of the mail-box banged shut, she allied herself to Alfred Eaton. Her letter had not been disloyal to her parents or over-apologetic or even deeply regretful. It stated simply that her family did not want him to come, that they did not approve of him and things they had heard, and that she was therefore withdrawing the invitation. For such an insulting message it was remarkably unemotional, but having posted it, she walked home and went to her room and after two hours composed a letter to Jim Roper, unbeknownst to her family.

Dear Jim [it began]: I have written you two long letters and tore them up because one of them was too cold and the other was too much the opposite. This is my third attempt and knowing you, how honest you are, I do not wish to be anything but honest with you. Therefore, this is to tell you that after many days and nights of serious consideration, I have decided that it would be best for both of us if we ended the understanding we have had since last April. I have not told Mother and Daddy that I have made this decision as it would not meet with their approval, because they are fond of you and have always taken it for granted that I was not interested in anyone but you, which met with their approval. The time has come, however, much as I regret doing so, and if we had announced our engagement I would return your ring and announce that our engagement was broken but since we did not announce our engagement and luckily you did not buy a ring, our "understanding" is over.

Yes, there is someone else, whom I will not say. I do not know whether I am in love with this other person or not, but as long as I have any such feeling toward someone else it would not be fair to either of us if I pretended to still be in love with you. I shall always care for you as a dear friend and hope this will not hurt you or cause you as much sorrow as it does me to write this. I hope you will forgive me if you think I am fickle but I am not, as you would know if you could read my thoughts. Please do not write me or come to see me, it would only make matters worse and difficult for both of us. You will quickly forget and find a much nicer girl who will appreciate your many good qualities and I close with good wishes for a splendid career and true happiness with someone you love.

Sincerely,
Mary

She did not then write to Alfred. She waited until he wrote and asked her to meet him in Philadelphia. They met for lunch at an oyster-and-chop house, unfashionable with their mutual friends, and she commenced by asking him how much of her mother's charges was true. They were together all afternoon, driving about in the Marmon over the country roads of southeastern Pennsylvania and Delaware. Now and then he would stop the car and light a cigarette—Mary did not smoke—and tell and retell the story of Victoria Dockwiler and Norma Budd, withholding details that he was afraid might shock her, but making a franker confession than he had ever made before, even to himself. "You *want* to know all this, don't you?"

"I want to know everything about you," she said. This question-and-answer came first at about three o'clock, and then again a couple of hours later. On the second occasion he said: "I know there's some reason, besides what your mother said about us. What is the reason?"

"I've broken off with Jim Roper," she said.

"Why?"

"On account of you."

"Why on account of me?"

"I don't know. I'm not sure."

"You're not sure that you love me."

"I'm not at all sure that I love you, but I am sure I don't love Jim. You have no obligations, I did this all myself. But when I saw how much I was thinking about you, I knew I had to break off with Jim."

"You may want to go back to Jim, Mary. There are other things, that your mother doesn't know."

"Things having to do with girls."

"Yes."

"Well, I guess I always suspected that. Some boys, you know it right away, instinctively, I guess. And I knew it about you. And yet, all this you told me this afternoon, it isn't you, Alfred."

"I don't know who else it is."

"I think the real you was the boy that was in love with the girl—what was her name—Victoria. But I don't say that she was in love with you. I don't think that would have lasted."

"I've wondered about that myself."

"But except for her you've never been in love."

"Until now."

"Let's not say it. I don't want to say it yet, and I don't want you to till you're sure . . . Isn't it strange that a girl doesn't have to have as much experience as a man?"

"What made you say that?"

"It just came into my head. I don't know why I said it now. Yes I do."

"Why?"

"Well, what we've been talking about is sex."

"Yes."

"I've never had any—sex. And you've had a lot. But it doesn't seem to make any difference. I'm not jealous of the others. Do you think Jim ever had any sex?"

"I'd doubt it."

328

"But I always wondered about it with Jim."

"Don't you with me?"

"Not the same way. I can't explain. Jim and I never talked about it, and when he kissed me it was nice, but I didn't have to be afraid. And yet I *thought* of it all the time. I *can't* explain. I didn't want Jim to go too far, but it was like something in the air, a heavy perfume, the calm before the storm, but never any storm. I didn't like it. Good Lord, now I've said it. I didn't like it with Jim. Do you know, I think if I'd let Jim really kiss me he'd have been much worse than you."

Alfred laughed, for the first time that day. "You don't know very much about me in that respect."

"Yes I do. On the boat last summer. You could have—I couldn't have stopped you."

"You did, though."

"No, you stopped yourself. I'm glad you did. I want it to be perfect."

"I hope it will be. Am I ever going to see you again?"

"Why not?"

"Everything's against it."

"I won't be able to see you alone for a while, not till after Christmas. And if I see you with other people it'll get back to Mother. She always has to know who I was with every minute. What are you going to do?"

"What am I going to do?"

"Yes. Are you going to get a job? If so, where?"

"Do you think I ought to get a job?"

"Yes, I do. I know you won't be welcome at my house till you do. Alfred?"

"Yes, Mary?"

"Nothing."

"What were you going to say?"

"I never really thought I was going to marry Jim. Please get a job."

"And settle down?"

"Yes."

"With you?"

"You're nasty to make me say it. Yes, with me. We won't be engaged, we won't even have an understanding, but it will be a *kind* of an understanding. You'd have to give up more than I would. Women. But I never expect to have any other man, anyway."

"*Do* you love me, Mary?"

"Yes, I do. I love you. I've said two things this afternoon. I didn't like Jim, and I love you. I loved you the first time I met you, and then I loved you again on the boat, and I love you now. But now that I've said it to you I can admit it to myself. And I know you love me. I know it better than you do. Alfred, you're not going to be in love with anybody else, not for a long time."

"I know that."

"There's a car coming. Wait till it passes."

The car passed them and he leaned across the little aisle between them and kissed her. Trust and apprehension were in her eyes. "You know I'm all yours," she said.

"Yes, but I won't always be so respectful."

"Yes you will. Because I am all yours. Yours, Alfred."

"That kind of handcuffs me, doesn't it?"

"You do, yourself. I've said I'm yours, and I am, and you believe me."

"You don't want anything more till we get married."

"No. But I would. If my father and mother won't let me marry you . . . but they will, eventually."

It was easy for them to meet in Philadelphia and New York, much easier in New York where Alfred and Lex maintained a bachelor apartment overlooking Gramercy Park. Their servant was Tom Burfort, who had quit the Pullman service because of a hernia, the long absences away from home, the drafty cars, the inadequate sleep, the bad tips, messy women, the white conductors, and the real reason, which was that he liked to drink. He was cranky and disapproving of the life the two young men led, but at the same time he was skilled in cooking and valeting and looked so respectable that he sometimes acted as a restraining influence on Lex's and Alfred's guests, and even on Lex and Alfred themselves. Except for the toting of whiskey, which he alternately denied and admitted, he was a highly moral man, honest to the penny, and vigilant against overcharging by tradesmen. He was paid $15 a week and carfare, or $15.60 a week.

The apartment, consisting of a livingroom, diningroom, kitchen, two bedrooms and one large and one small bathroom, was furnished completely with articles from storage warehouses, the property of Lex's uncles and his mother. Elizabeth Porter called it very *fin de siècle*, but it was extremely comfortable, and the location had become sufficiently unfashionable to provide remoteness while still only ten minutes from the Grand Central Terminal, less than that to the Princeton Club, a little more to the Racquet & Tennis Club, and seldom more than fifteen minutes by taxicab from Times Square. Across the park at the clubhouse of The Players there was a convenient hack-stand occupied by worldly drivers, and not far to the south and west there were many young women who had come to New York to write or paint and to live their own lives, which last to some extent they did in the apartment on Gramercy Park East. But the principal advantage of the

330

apartment was that the building was owned by a friend of Fritz Thornton's.

From late August of that year to the day in November and the scene on the Wilmington road, the details of Alfred's life would have been characterized by Sally Eaton as riotous living. On Sunday afternoons he and Lex would entertain at cocktails, men and women of ages between twenty and thirty-five, married and unmarried or about to be unmarried, but all coming from Society, born into it or married into it. They all knew each other, quite a few were related to each other, and the New Yorkers among them were usually continuing a second-generation friendship. ("It's Port Johnson all over again," Alfred once said.) They were generally friendly enough and relaxed, with a common fondness for Lex and an automatic acceptance of Alfred, some because they had met him before, and the others because of his friendship with Lex. They were forming or reviving smallish dancing groups that met four or five times during the winter ("Let's steer clear of *them*," said Lex) and their conversation was chiefly of sport, Wall Street, weddings, engagements, new apartments, the theater, and lightly-touched-upon scandal. The women wore expensive clothes and re-set family diamonds and re-strung family pearls, and the men wore white starched collars and derbies. No one got too drunk and they had all gone uptown by seven-thirty. Such parties were Lex's idea. "I can stand them once a week. Matter of fact I like most of them. And it pleases Mother to know I'm seeing them." But between Sundays there was almost always a girl in one of the bedrooms, and often a girl in each. They came from the Village and they came from Broadway. They would glare at each other when their origins were not the same, each girl knowing what the other was there for and both unable to assert their superiority with a haughty exit. Neither of the young men always went to bed with the girl he had brought to the apartment, and they did not always stay with the same girl all night. In the morning, dressed, the girls would be friendlier toward one another and sometimes they would leave together, bound together by shared guilt and an amiable, mutual distrust. The Ziegfeld girl and the cubist would part at the hack-stand while four stories above them Tom Burfort grunted at the lipstick on the coffee cups.

After breakfast, Lex once said: "You know, we got to cut this out."

"Cut what out?"

"This screwing."

"Why?"

"Well, I don't know why. But we've been awfully damn lucky."

"You mean a dose?"

"Or knock them up."

"All right, Father, when are you going to cut it out?"

Lex made a funny face. "A week from Tuesday."

"Two weeks from Tuesday."

"All right, two weeks from Tuesday. No, after Thanksgiving."

"After Christmas."

"Easter?"

"Fourth of July. Next Labor Day."

"What do we tell our wives when we get married?"

"Frig 'em young, treat 'em rough, and tell 'em nothing. That's the old motto, isn't it?"

"That's the old motto, all right, sure."

"The modern girl doesn't expect her husband to be the soul of purity."

"What does the modern husband expect his wife to be? I'd like you to make yourself scarce Friday afternoon. I'm having a visitor, young lady you've met at several of our Sunday at-homes. She's coming on condition I get rid of you and Tom."

"All right. Tom and I'll go to the Metropolitan Museum. As a matter of fact, I won't be here Friday. I'm driving down to Wilmington."

"Mary St. John?"

"Yes."

"Are you falling for her?"

"I like her."

"You haven't seen her since last summer."

"Yes I have. A couple of times. I've been to her house once. It isn't a very big house, by the way."

"It isn't? Why do you say that?"

"They're not what might be called enormously wealthy."

"That's not what I heard. I heard her father is one of the prime movers and shakers at the du Pont factory."

"Oh, they're not poor, but take it from me, they're not rolling in money."

Lex studied him. "Then I was wrong about her?"

"That much. They're not filthy rich."

"Then maybe I was all wrong about her. If I was, I apologize."

"You don't have to apologize. You were misinformed."

"I must have been. I wouldn't say anything against a girl you liked."

"I know that."

"You *have* fallen for her."

"Not exactly. I don't know. You see, Lex, I'm not very good luck to girls that I like."

332

"Horse-shit. You've said that before, and it always was horse-shit."

"No, it isn't. There's a reason for it. My dear mother told me the reason. I'm selfish. Cold, and selfish."

"She'd have a hell of a hard time proving you were cold. And I know you're not selfish. I'm more selfish than you are, much more. You worry about people, and I never do. They can all take care of themselves. Or go screw themselves. Alfred, are you in love with Mary St. John?"

"The answer is no, but I could be."

"You're on the way?"

"I guess that's it."

"Is this little whore-house we have here, is this keeping you from falling in love with her?"

"It's not this little whore-house. It's me."

"Yes, I guess it is, or you wouldn't have had that neat little piece of tail here last night. She was the bee's knees. But if you —you know what I want to say. If I fell in love with some-body, I don't think this atmosphere is conducive to the real thing. We never thought it *would* be. You know, a funny thing, I'll tell you quite candidly. I had an idea that you were hoping you could persuade Mary St. John to come here, and not on Sunday afternoon. That's how far wrong I was. I could have told you that you never would get her here, but that wouldn't have kept you from trying. At least if I'd been right. Last summer, on the boat, I thought—well, never mind. It shows how wrong we can be, even the great Porter, expert in human psychology."

After that the apartment, the arrangement, was not a suc-cess. Alfred stopped bringing new girls to the apartment, and those he brought he brought less often. Moreover, he became self-conscious about bringing any; Lex said nothing, but Alfred felt that when he brought a girl to the apartment, Lex did not approve.

"Out with it, Lex," he said one day. "You don't like me bringing girls here. You think I'm being unfaithful to Mary."

"I haven't said anything, have I?"

"You don't have to. Mary and I haven't had any serious talks."

"All right, boy. I'll be honest. You're not giving it much of a chance. You come back here after seeing Mary, and for a couple of days you're in love with her. But then from force of habit the first time you get rooty you call up Arnette or Judith, one of those sure pieces of tail. That's what I call not giving it much of a chance. I think you ought to do one thing or the other."

"Don't rush me, big boy."

"Well, you started the conversation."

"Naturally. I got pretty damn tired of those pious looks of yours. Now I know that you're a puritan. Maybe a bit of a hypocrite."

"Oh, come off it, boy. A hypocrite, me? I'm not in love with anybody, and I'm not kidding anybody. You're half-kidding Mary, if not more than half."

"There's only one thing for me to do, that's obvious. Move out."

"You don't have to do that."

"Wouldn't you, if you were me?"

"Well, when we get to the point where we're calling each other hypocrites maybe you should."

"Yes, I think so."

"Stay till the end of the month, till you find some place."

"I'll stay till the end of the week. If I stayed till the end of the month I might offend your sense of morality."

"Well, all right. Suit yourself. As far as my sense of morality, balls to that remark. I just don't think you behave that way with a girl like Mary St. John."

"I was under the impression you didn't like Mary."

"Like her or don't like her, you don't string her along, any more than these dolls we have here night after night. When they come here they know they're going to get screwed, and that's the end of it. If they don't like that, they don't come here. Most of them like it. If Mary had ever shown up here I'd have known that that was the arrangement between you two. But she never has shown up, so that leads me to believe you're stringing her along, and Mary isn't that kind of a girl. As I said before, you're not giving it much of a chance, or Mary, or yourself."

"You're so considerate."

"Sarcasm, but somebody has to tell you. Listen, Alfred, let's stop bickering like a couple of prep school boys. Why don't you go home for a while, back to Port Johnson, and see Mary every chance you can get. Then decide whether you're in love with her, and she's in love with you. If so, fine. If not, at least you'll know it, and then you can come back here and between the two of us we can fuck every doll from here to Bridgeport. Leave your things here, use the apartment any time you come to New York, and I won't look around for another roommate. You pay, oh, one week's rent a month and Tom's salary for one week a month."

"I don't know. Maybe that's a good idea. It *is* a good idea. I'm not sure about living at home, but I can get a room at the Racquet Club."

"They have no rooms."

334

"Philadelphia Racquet Club. Much better equipped than 370 Park."

"Great. If anything comes of it, I want to be the best man."

"You would be anyway."

"Well, I should hope so. But this way I'll stand there like a smug son of a bitch saying to myself, 'I brought them together, the little dears.'"

"Yes, you're smug enough to think just that."

"Oh, now don't be hard on old Lex."

Alfred took a room at the Racquet Club, explaining to his mother (who asked for no explanation) that he was thinking of taking a job in Philadelphia. The mill had been struck in September, and Samuel Eaton had almost immediately made good on his threat to wild life in Georgia, Maryland, Mexico, and Pennsylvania. From time to time a crate would arrive from a distant taxidermist's, and Sally and Constance were sent postcards, but neither Martha nor Alfred heard from him in any way. Then, early in December, the strike was ended, to the satisfaction of the mill-owners, and Samuel Eaton returned to Port Johnson.

"Well, I hear you're looking for a job in Philadelphia," he said to Alfred at dinner on his second night home.

"I've talked to several men."

"Anybody I know? I know a lot of fellows in Philadelphia."

"You may know some of them." Alfred was lying; he had at that time spoken to no one about a job.

"*May?* Didn't they recognize your name?"

"One gentleman thought I might be from Providence, Rhode Island."

"Well, if you want to go back far enough, you are. Three, four generations. But what line of work are you interested in? It must be the glove business, or chinaware, if they didn't recognize your name in Philadelphia. It wasn't banking, railroading, any of the heavy industries."

"I'm afraid they don't automatically come to attention and say, 'Eaton of Port Johnson.' Look in the New York telephone directory some time. It's full of Eatons. Two Samuel Eatons and one Alfred Eaton."

"The hell with New York, I'm talking about Philadelphia."

"It's just as bad in Philadelphia, Father."

"Then God knows what kind of a job you're looking for, and you're not going to tell me. All right."

"I've just been looking around."

"Loking around what? Arch Street? Market Street? You're living at the Racquet Club, your mother tells me."

"Yes, I've taken a room there."

"Well, at least you're not living with some woman, unless you're using the club as a cover-up."

"Nope. Not living with any woman."

"What do you do when you're not entertaining offers to go to work?"

"Oh, see my friends. I play court tennis every day, almost every day."

"You play court tennis. Do you know how to score?"

"Yes."

"Where did you learn that?"

"Mr. Thornton has a court and I've played a lot there, and the New York Racquet Club."

"You're in there?"

"I'm up."

"Uh-huh. Tell me, just as a matter of curiosity, don't you ever get tired of doing nothing?"

"I haven't yet."

"Didn't being in the Navy make you want to do something?"

"It made me want to get out the first chance I got."

"All right, you've been out six months."

"So I have."

"And in that time you haven't wanted to start making a life for yourself."

"I have a life. All for myself."

"That's true, by God."

"Didn't you have a good time doing nothing?"

"Doing nothing? Oh, you mean hunting? I had the best time in my life, it took years off me. But I wouldn't call it doing nothing, sleeping on the ground, getting up at four o'clock in the morning, riding horseback. I shot a mountain lion in Mexico. Next year I'm going to Alaska and get a bear."

"What for?"

"That's the kind of a question I could expect from you."

"I think I got about thirty Germans during the war."

"With one shot from a .30 caliber rifle?"

"No, with eight ash-cans, depth charges. Of course I can't be as sure as you are."

"Well, if I had missed, I wouldn't be here."

"Well, they're two different things."

"So they are. But if you weren't doing nothing, I wasn't doing nothing. So that's a stalemate."

"Well, I wasn't trying to take anything away from your war record, and you know damn well I wasn't. But the war's over now, and it's time we all got back to business. We beat those bastards that called the strike on us, just as we beat them ten years ago and we'll beat them again in 1929."

"You won't always beat them."

"What?"

"You won't. I don't know much about it, but the coal miners finally won."

"No they didn't, that's where you're wrong. Only the hard coal . . . Are you a Socialist?"

"Not a bit. But if the men that do the work want to have a union why shouldn't they have it?"

"Because the next step after that is when they start telling us how to run our business, and the next step after *that*, my friend, is taking over the business. And if they take over the right businesses, just a few but important ones, then they'll run the whole economy, and people like you won't have Marmons and play court tennis."

"Well, I wouldn't like that very much, I will admit."

"Then don't make foolish statements like, 'Why shouldn't they have a union?' That means either you're on their side, or you don't know what you're talking about. But with ideas like that, maybe you'd *better* stay out of the mill."

"I never had any other intention. See how right I was? If I'd taken that job you'd have had to fire me, your own son. Think how embarrassing that would have been."

"It wouldn't have embarrassed me, not for a second. I'd have kicked your ass out of there so quick . . ."

"No, just fired me. No kicking. Nobody kicks my ass, Father."

"Maybe not, but I'd have tried, and who knows? I might have succeeded. This hunting trip I've been on, I found out that I was still in pretty good condition, for a man my age."

"Well, that's good, then you won't miss me at the mill."

"No, I won't miss you, Alfred. No more than you'd miss me if I keeled over tomorrow. You finished?"

"Yes sir."

"Then let's have our coffee in the front room. I want to talk to you about some other matters."

Alfred rose and allowed his father to lead the way into the front room. He sat down and his father remained standing, causing Alfred to wish he too had remained standing, since it seemed to give Samuel Eaton an advantage before a word was said. "Cigar?"

"No thanks," said Alfred.

"Care for something to drink? I'll get it."

"No thanks."

Samuel Eaton rubbed his back under his coat. "I have several matters I want to talk about, out of earshot of those busybodies in the kitchen. They listen to everything we say, and while I trust them both, Josephine and Nellie, I haven't had this new fellow with me, Walter, long enough to have full confidence in him."

"Well, that's too bad. Of course it could have been averted."

337

Samuel Eaton looked down at him angrily. "Yes, it could have. If George Fry hadn't quit his job. That's another thing I want to discuss with you, but not now."

"Why not now? Let's get that over with. You know I've been sending him money."

"All right, if you insist. Yes, I knew you were sending him money. I know how much. Ten dollars a week. He only needs about a dollar a week, where he is. Pipe tobacco."

"Where he is?"

"I knew you didn't know that. He's in the county jail, serving six months to a year."

"What for? I didn't know that."

"Naturally you didn't. You went looking for him, but he hid away from you out of shame. Then you found out where to send him money, and you sent it. Very laudable. Disloyal to me, of course, but a little thing like that wouldn't matter to you, would it?"

"I had some obligation to George. I don't apologize for sending him money after all those years of being nice to me."

"Well, nice sentiment. Very pretty. And you get off cheap. Ten dollars a week and no responsibility. You haven't even laid eyes on him."

"I plead guilty. What's he in jail for?"

"The charge they put him in for is habitual drunkenness. That was the charge they sentenced him on."

"In other words, there was something else, worse."

"Yes."

"What?"

"Indecent exposure. I got them to drop that charge. *I* did, not you."

"What did he do?"

"He stood in front of a whore-house on River Street and took out his private parts."

Alfred laughed. "He must have been drunk."

"It wasn't funny. It was no joke, drunk or sober. Women and children could see him from the train, it was broad daylight, and he didn't just open his pants. The law says if you make a lewd gesture by touching yourself in a suggestive way, that makes it a more serious charge, and he was touching himself all right."

"No, it isn't funny."

"I heard about it and I got him a lawyer. We arranged to let him plead guilty to the drunkenness charge and get him out of the way for a while, away from the booze. But from what I've heard, he's going to have to serve his full sentence, a year. And when he gets out he's going to take that money you've been sending him and he'll be back in prison in a week, if not in the insane asylum. The warden thinks he has softening of

338

the brain. He said he's seen a lot of cases like that. He says it probably comes from syphilis."

"They could find that out quickly enough."

"I don't doubt that for a minute, but the county jail isn't a private sanitarium. If they took the venereal cases out of the jail they'd just about empty the place."

"Well, why don't they? They could—"

"So they could run around infecting innocent people?"

"You didn't let me finish. They could put them in the county hospital."

"There's no room for them, and besides, they have to serve their sentences first. Well, that's your friend George, just in case you want to call on him. Visiting days, Thursdays and Sundays."

"I'll go to see him, Sunday."

"If you do, don't come back here. There are a lot of innocent women in this household." Samuel Eaton sat down. "At least there are some."

Alfred waited, sure that he knew the next direction the conversation would take.

"I don't know how to start this," said Samuel Eaton. "Start at the beginning, start at the beginning. But how do I know what the beginning was? How much does a man know? How much do you know that I don't know. And how much do you know that I don't give you credit for?"

Alfred still waited. His father moved his lips, shaping words but not uttering them. Then he leaned forward and said: "Did you ever hear of a man named Frolick?"

"Yes sir."

"In what connection did you hear of him?"

"I'd rather you'd put that question some other way, Father?"

"Will you tell me the truth if I do?"

Alfred though a moment. "I won't lie to you. I may not answer all your questions."

"Did you ever meet this fellow?"

"Not exactly meet him. I saw him once."

"Did you beat him up?"

"Yes sir, I did."

"Thank God!" Samuel Eaton lost his aggressiveness. He bent forward with his hands clasped together, staring at the floor, the figures in the rug, the caps of his shoes—nothing. "You're a lot of things I never gave you credit for, and a man my age can't change in a few weeks or a few months. I can admit that I was wrong for twenty-two years, but that doesn't make anything right. What do I do when I admit that I was wrong? I only say what was the truth, that white wasn't black all that time, that black wasn't white. It doesn't cost me very much to admit that. It doesn't take away what I felt all those

339

years, and what I still feel, regardless of what I know in my brain. I had the wrong facts, and they weren't facts, but I thought of them as facts. They were what I felt, and that was the only fact I went by. Why can't I like you, even now, this minute? I'm closer to you now, this minute, than I've ever been to any of my children. Yes, including Billy. Including Billy. You'll know sometime, when you have children of your own. One of them—one of them is in here, as if you had tits. He shines, his voice is music, you love him as if he never lived in his mother's body. That was Billy to me, long before he died, and when he died there was nobody that understood what happened to me. I don't blame them now. They couldn't understand, because they never knew what I felt while he was alive. But I didn't care whether they understood me or not, and sometimes when they'd try to understand, I'd hate them, because they had no right to understand. They'd never known what I felt while he was alive. They thought they did, but they didn't. And if they didn't know that, they had no right to try to know how I felt when God did something to me that—I didn't stop believing in God. I believed in Him more than I ever did, but as an enemy. And you were living, you were alive. A deliberate thing that God did to me. If you hadn't been alive, maybe your mother and I would have had another son, in another year or two, or five, and I could have believed that the new son would be as much to me as Billy was. I could have believed that, if you hadn't been playing out in the yard and kissing me goodnight and all those things a child does. But with you here, I didn't want another son, or anybody in my life—you, your sisters, or your mother."

He stopped, and the sudden silence was like a shot breaking a real silence. Then he went on, lower and more slowly: "That's why your mother took to Frolick, and before Frolick, one other man. It isn't bad to tell you that there was another man before Frolick. Once you knew about Frolick, you knew that those things can happen. Now you know why they can happen. It isn't because your mother is immoral. It's because I never even told her I didn't love her any more. She had to find that out for herself, and I guess she knew it before I did."

Again he paused, but this time Alfred knew his father would continue unassisted. He soon did so: "And yet," said Samuel Eaton. "If I had it to do all over again, even knowing how badly it turned out for everybody, myself included, those fourteen years—it was a wonderful thing to love someone that much. Always in your thoughts, always planning for him, and I can feel his arms around my neck this minute."

Here he broke with a loud cry from the bottom of his soul and he put his hands on the top of his head, to shut out a vision or to hide his foolish, anguished face. Alfred stood up and could only think to put a folded handkerchief on his father's knee.

"Don't go," said Samuel Eaton.

"Don't go? What do you think I am?" said Alfred. He went out and put on a topcoat and walked to the garage. The cold engine of the Marmon spat and roared as he primed it until it settled into its distinctive heavy hum. The night was clear, and he had left the top folded in the boot and he was not wearing a hat. He drove wherever the roads took him, by-passing towns and people and man-made light, but mysteriously comforted by the lights on the dashboard. He could not yet begin to enjoy the victory that he recognized his father's outburst to be: a surrender to a need which now Alfred alone could fill. He had long since grown superior to any fear of his father, but resentment had always stayed, and tonight the resentment was revived by Samuel Eaton's eagerness to acquire a warm something for a cold nothing but cold truth. There were things in his father's confession that Alfred would forget tonight but remember all his life, but on this journey in the clear and freezing night he fought against pity and his father's communicable tears until more than an hour had passed and he was on unfamiliar roads, with signposts pointing the way to strange villages.

He drove for a while along a riverside road at the bottom of a steep mountain, then out of the gap and over some rolling hills until in the distance at the top of a high plateau he saw a patch of light that began to attract him. He passed through two sleeping villages before he came close enough to realize that the light was emanating from a large private house where, judging by the motor traffic, a grand party was getting under way. He came to a pair of posts that he judged to be the foot of the driveway, and followed a Lincoln phaeton up the frosted path. The Lincoln came to a stop at the porch steps of what unmistakably was a country club, and three girls and two young men in coonskin coats got out and went inside. Alfred drove to the parking area and found a place for his car that was out of the range of the brightness from the clubhouse. He waited until the Lincoln was parked and its driver, a short young man in a long coonskin, got out and started for the clubhouse, then suddenly halted and uncorked a quart bottle and took a swig from it. On an impulse Alfred hurried to the young man. "Could you spare one of those?"

"A drink or a quart?" said the young man.

"Oh, just a drink."

"Do I know you?"

"No, never saw me before in your life."

"Here, but don't get over-anxious," said the young man, handing him the bottle. "You're not going to get in without a Tuck," the young man said while Alfred was drinking.

"Thanks very much. Then I guess I won't get in."

"Where are you from? Haven't I seen you some place before?"

"You may have."

"Are you visiting somebody?"

"Just on the way through."

"I know. You have that grey Marmon."

"Yes."

"Take my advice, don't try to crash this party. We're getting a little sore at you Reading people dropping in whenever you feel like it. And this isn't a club dance. It's an engagement party. Dinner dance, place-cards, the whole shooting-match."

"Why, I wouldn't think of trying to crash your party. But when I say your bottle . . ."

"Where did you go to college?"

"Princeton."

"I should have known. I—should—have—known."

"Where did *you* go?"

"The Montessori School for Backward Children. So long, Princeton boy."

"Thanks for the drink. By the way, what's the name of this place?"

"The Lantenengo Country Club. If you can spell it, you can have it."

"Thanks again for the drink," said Alfred. He watched the short young man in his ridiculously too-large coat until he closed the clubhouse door behind him, then he went up to the porch and walked around to the far side where he would not be seen by arriving guests. Two large tables and a smaller one had been set, and waiters were standing against the wall. The orchestra was playing a waltz, but no one was dancing. Just inside the dancing room, which obviously served as a lounge at other times, an older man and an older woman—husband and wife—and a girl in her twenties—their daughter—were shaking hands with the elaborateness of people who saw each other constantly without shaking hands, but now were practicing their party manners. The girl, tall, lovely and blond, was happy and nervous. The guests would go down the little reception line and then form their own groups on the dance floor. Where Alfred stood there was a strong wind whistling past him, regularly changing tone as it blew past the great stone pillars that supported the porch roof. The noisy wind and the snugly closed French windows—most of them with draperies half closed—made it impossible for him to hear any voices or more than a hint of the music. He watched the progressing party for fully ten minutes, and he began to have a sense of an aloneness that was not unpleasant because along with it he believed that only his own good manners kept him from becoming a member of the party, and looking at the people without hearing their words, he realized that it was the happiest gathering he had ever seen. He saw four fellows whose faces he remembered from Princeton and another who had been a couple of classes behind him at Knox and another whom he recognized from dances in New York or Philadelphia. Their names did not come to him and did not matter. He had never seen any of the girls before tonight, but he was sure he could place most of them: the most popular, the best dancers, the less pretty who relied on conversation and tennis, the quickly passionate, the poor relations, and four, maybe five, girls who could have gone to any dance in the United States and caused a stir in the stag line: the very dark and unsmiling girl; the startling blonde who was like Clemmie Shreve; the blue-and-white girl who was probably called Tiny; the round-shouldered girl with the wide-apart eyes and too-large mouth who spent the most money on clothes; and the classic beauty who would be mysterious anywhere but here, where she was known and liked, but whose flawlessness of face and body caused her elsewhere to be admired without being lusted for. Alfred's appreciation of the party was suddenly ended by a man's voice: "Come on in or you'll freeze."

Alfred turned and saw a young man in a Tuck. "I wasn't invited," said Alfred.

"I can see that, but this is the coldest place in the county. Second coldest. The coldest is the top of Broad Mountain. Come on in and get warm."

"I don't think I'd better, thanks."

"You look all right. Why not? Don't you know anybody here?"

"Yes, as a matter of fact I do."

"Your girl is here, that's why you're here. Keeping an eye on your girl."

"Wrong. My girl is miles from here."

"Then may I ask what the hell you're doing, standing here in this arctic wind, watching a party that you have no interest in?"

"As a mater of fact, I was driving by and I saw the lights and I was curious."

"You did? You know, I've often felt like doing that, but I never have. Come on back to the locker-room and I'll give you a shot of whiskey. My name is English. I go to Lafayette."

"My name is Eaton. I went to Princeton, didn't finish."

"Where are you from, Eaton?"

343

"Port Johnson."

"Your family own that steel mill, I've often seen it from the train."

"Yes."

"Well, I'm getting cold, even if you're not."

"What are *you* doing out here?"

"Well, I guess you'd understand this. I came out to look at the stars. I like to look at the stars on a cold night. But enough is plenty. Let's go."

"Thanks very much, but I think I'll be on my way."

"Well, if you change your mind. If not, so long, Eaton."

"So long, English. Thanks for the invitation."

"More than welcome."

English walked briskly to the end of the porch and disappeared in the darkness, but a minute later he appeared on the dance floor with a girl, the first girl Alfred had seen before. Alfred could see that they were talking about him, as English looked toward Alfred's window, frowned, but could not see Alfred. The girl was speaking with animation and likewise looked toward the window several times and seemed to be telling English to do something, for English left her and walked rapidly toward the French door. Alfred retreated into the darkness as English shaded his eyes, Indian fashion, and peered through the glass, but could not see Alfred. Alfred had recognized the girl and now remembered where he had seen her—at the Arcadia restaurant. She was one of the Bryn Mawr girls Sally had noticed. He now had no desire to have a conversation with a friend of Sally's, and he made his way to the parked Marmon and headed for home.

He was on a main road that would take him directly to Port Johnson and he wanted to get home. He sneezed a couple of times and his hair was stiffened by the freezing air, and he knew he was in for one of his infrequent colds. But he reckoned that he would be home in less than two hours, in the warm kitchen with a hot cup of tea. He had the road almost entirely to himself and he drove fast. He had paid a visit to another world, in which no one knew or cared about his problems. He was not so stupid as to believe that those people had no problems of their own, but he had watched he knew not how many men and women having a good time, men and women not too much unlike himself, and he could have been one of them and been watched by someone else and believed by the someone else to be having a good time like the others. He had never thought of himself in just that way; as a young man who could be, to an onlooker, an anonymous member of an enjoyable party. For the first time in his life he could almost see himself from a distance and as one of a group, and the momentary sacrifice of his individuality was less disconcerting than the notion of belonging to a happy crowd was comforting. He was far from ready to give up his individuality; he was sure he would not do so; but there was something to be said for the pleasure of belonging to a group, especially after a lifetime of going it alone. And then he remembered with excitement that out of his calculating self he had altogether naturally referred to "his girl." When the English fellow made reference to "your girl," it had immediately and unqualifiedly summoned up the image and the name of Mary St. John, and somewhere there was a good conection between that fact and the not unpleasant notion of belonging to a crowd. All his other girls had been related to his individuality; Mary St. John had made him want to belong, with her, to the world of happy people. As he drove toward home he wished that his mother could know what he was thinking. He could never give utterance to his thoughts, but if she could know them she would be less insistent in her charge of selfishness.

Mary St. John was his girl, and he was going to marry her.

Their engagement period was a time of hazard followed by hazard, partings without finality but reconciliations without passion. But passion had been proscribed early in their romance, and the absence of it, or the complete control of it, had made the romance, for Alfred, unique in his relationships with the opposite sex, and thus contributed to the substantiality of his love. He had now, at twenty-two, participated in erotic experience to a degree that was unusual among young men of his acquaintance. From Norma Budd he had learned to believe that only lack of opportunity kept some girls who were ladies from going to bed with a man, and it was important education because it contradicted successfully the accepted belief that a girl who was a lady simply did not go to bed with a man to whom she was not married. Thus educated, he was able to look at all young ladies and at least wonder. His other important experience was, of course, with the casual depravity of Betty, whom he never entirely considered a whore, although she never pretended to be anything else. He vaguely understood that whatever Betty did was mechanical and not truly passionate of the kind of passion he hoped to share with Mary. He had not known Betty very long before he was able to see men and women through her eyes, the quick estimate of their weakness and vulnerability, and the price her knowledge would bring. She even knew about him: that it was all new, exciting, wartime, on foreign soil, and wild oats. Already, in a year's time, Betty was in the past. Betty had gone into the past on the day he resumed wearing civilian clothes, just as London itself returned to its status of a city he had not seen in peacetime, a creation of Dickens and Doyle. But it was Betty

345

as a person who was in the past, and their shared experiences remained as part of his attitude toward women, which was now functioning practically in his attitude toward Mary: Mary was Mary, and after marriage she would discover from him, with him, the pleasures of love as he had learned them from Norma. If there was more to Mary's love-making than he now suspected, his experience with Betty had prepared him against the shock of innovation on the part of a girl who at this stage would not even allow a kiss to make them forget their agreement.

Their agreement was not one of the hazards of their engagement period, except insofar as it detracted from the intensity of their reconciliations. It was obvious that there would be trouble with her family as soon as they learned she had broken with Jim Roper. Mrs. St. John correctly guessed the reason immediately. "I never heard of such a thing," she said. "A girl using her coming-out party *to break her engagement!* What shall we do with her?"

"Don't ask me," said her husband.

"I will so ask you. Whatever's done I want you to back me to the limit."

"Father will back you, you can be sure of that," said Mary.

"Yes, and *you* may be sure of it, too, young lady," said Eugene St. John.

"I'm so sure of it that I'm willing to call off the whole party. Give the money to charity. Do what you please. It isn't my party any more. But there's one thing, I won't re-invite Jim, and after it's over I'm going to see Alfred Eaton. I've humiliated him enough, and I'm going to make up for it."

"A man who has this much influence over you—" said Mrs. St. John.

"Jim Roper had *no* influence over me, and I wouldn't want to marry that kind of a man." Mary carefully did not glance at her father.

"The party will go on as scheduled," said Eugene St. John. "I shall have a talk with Mr. Eaton after Christmas."

"Alfred, or his father?"

"I meant the young man, but you've given me an idea."

"I forbid you to speak to his father," said Mary.

"This is the first time you've ever *forbidden* me to do anything, and I'll tell you right now, it had better be the last, because for that bit of rudeness I'm going to make a point of seeing his father before I see *him.*"

"I apologize, Father, if only you won't see his father."

"I do not accept a conditional apology. This is what comes of letting you persuade us not to send you to school in Lausanne," said Eugene St. John. This was a subtle charge of ingratitude: St. John knew that his daughter knew he had sided with her against her mother's plan to send Mary to school in Switzerland.

"I apologize, unconditionally, Father. I don't want to be rude, I didn't mean to be, but it's my life."

"Your life! And look what you're making of it," said Mrs. St. John.

Mrs. St. John held her husband to his angry threat to speak to Samuel Eaton, and an appointment was arranged after Christmas. They met at the Racquet Club on Samuel Eaton's insistence. "My son has a room here, you know," said Samuel Eaton.

"No, I didn't know. If I'd known that I think I'd have preferred to meet some place else."

"I don't see that it makes the slightest difference, Mr. St. John. Naturally I'll have to tell him we've met. And we might want to send for him, if he's in town." Samuel Eaton disliked the other man on sight, the practical man against the theorist. They had clam juice and oysters on the half-shell at the oyster bar and then sat at a table for two.

"You're with the du Pont corporation. I have a few friends in your organization."

"Probably as many as I have, Mr. Eaton. I'm in research and we're rather clannish. We shouldn't be, but it always seems to work out that way. I of course have met your Mr. Hackenschmidt."

"You know Henry, do you? Well, just don't try to steal him away from us. It's hard to hold on to a good chemist these days, with you big fellows prowling around."

"We've never been able to sign a man who didn't want to come, Mr. Eaton. But you and I have a quite different matter to discuss."

"Very different, although not entirely. I don't want to lose a good chemist, and I gather you don't want to lose your good daughter."

"My good daughter, Mr. Eaton."

"I understand perfectly. I have two daughters of my own, so I appreciate your position as a father. Also, I know my son, and I can understand why a father would be concerned. Alfred had a fine record in the Navy, but when he got out he was like so many others, he didn't want to go back and finish college. Princeton. I took my degree at Princeton, and I wanted him to, but he has some money of his own—not a multi-millionaire, by any means, but he's independent of me, now and in the future. He never wanted to go in the mill with me, and I understand that, too. But frankly, till he fell in love with your daughter—Ann?"

"Mary."

"Till then he never showed any signs of wanting to settle

down. He has a lot of New York friends. He's joining the New York Racquet Club, which I don't approve of for a young man in his circumstances, and he even had an apartment in New York with a friend of his. Attractive boy named Porter, good family, but we're Pennsylvanians and on his mother's side Alfred goes back to the time of William Penn. Not your Main Line crowd, but good, reliable stock, and I want to see my son amount to something in this neck of the woods, not New York. The best thing in New York is the Pennsylvania Railroad pointed this way. You don't agree with me, naturally, because you people have close ties with New York, but that's the way I feel. But then, as I say, Alfred fell in love with your daughter, and for the first time in his life he began to show some interest in getting a job and making something of himself, and I'll tell you quite frankly, the girl that can do that, although I haven't had the pleasure of meeting her personally, she has my approval. She has my approval, and I wouldn't do a thing to stand in their way. Well, there you are, Mr. St. John. That's my speech."

"Well, it's very eloquent, and quite complimentary to my daughter, who by the way is an only child, and therefore very close to my wife and me."

"Alfred and I were never very close."

"What I have to tell you, in my little speech, is that Mrs. St. John and I are quite alarmed by the serious turn events have taken. Our daughter Mary had one suitor, I suppose you'd call him, a fine young man who's studying medicine but won't be practicing for five years or more, therefore not in any position to get married very soon. But Mary has broken off with this young man and announced to us, my wife and me, that she cares about nobody but your son. Mary is eighteen, just turned eighteen, Mr. Eaton, a debutante this year. Your son is a man of the world, experienced far beyond most young men his age, and yet at the same time only beginning to show signs of readiness to assume real responsibility."

"He has to start sometime."

"And with somebody. But not with our daughter. Under no circumstances would we permit an engagement to be announced for at least three more years, and during that time I want Mary to travel, to see something of the world, to meet other young men—"

"And forget about Alfred Eaton. Hell, you want to break it off and you want me to cooperate with you. Mr. St. John, you're wasting your time. I appreciate your feeling for your daughter and I'm having somewhat the same problem with mine, both of them, but I think it'd be a good thing if Alfred married your daughter—"

348

"A good thing for whom?"

"For Alfred, but also for your daughter, and—"

"Now just a minute, Mr. Eaton. Just one minute. Isn't it true—I was hoping we could avoid this—but isn't it true that your son was mixed up in the Norma Budd scandal? Wasn't he at one time engaged to a girl named Shreve here in Philadelphia? Wasn't that apartment he had in New York a continual wild party? And isn't it true that Mrs. Eaton gave him fifty thousand dollars to squander as he pleased?"

"What else do you know, Mr. St. John?"

"More, but that's enough to make us have some misgivings about Alfred Eaton as a prospective son-in-law. In fact, nothing but misgivings."

"If you paid a detective agency for your information, you got more than your money's worth. For instance, my wife gave him twenty thousand dollars. That's one of your facts exaggerated two hundred and fifty percent. I never heard of Alfred's being engaged to anybody. I don't even know anybody named Shreve except a Boston jewelry store. Norma Budd was murdered and if my son was mixed up in it, so was everybody we know in Port Johnson, because the Budd family were friends of ours, and Norma Budd used to bring Alfred toy soldiers from England. If all your misinformation is on a par with what you've told me, God help the research department of the du Pont corporation. I'd advise people to steer clear of Wilmington if they value their safety."

"Be careful, Mr. Eaton. There *is* other information, and none of it came from a detective agency. Some of it's fairly common knowledge right in this club. Good day, sir." Eugene St. John left.

Samuel Eaton beckoned to his waiter. "The gentleman won't be back. Will you take his dishes away, please?"

"He didn't hardly eat anything, sir. Was he taken sick? We had a gentleman get hold of a bad oyster last week."

"That's it. He's getting hold of a bad oyster."

"Getting hold of one, sir?"

"No, he's got one."

"You're talking in riddles, sir. I guess I'm not quick-witted enough for you."

"Oh, I'm quick-witted, for a fact. Find out if my son is in the club."

"That I can answer you and the answer is no, he is not. He ate his breakfast at nine o'clock and ordered his machine ready for ha' past ten. That I know because it was from me he got his breakfast and me I give the order to concerning his machine."

"All of which leads you to believe he's not in the club this minute?"

"No sir. What leads me to believe that is I saw him drive away on Sydenham Street at about twenty to twelve when I got back from the drug store getting the laudanum for my sore tooth. I been miserable with this tooth for three days and I don't understand why I don't conquer my fears of the dentist and have it drawn. It isn't as if I cared about the tooth."

"Have the damn thing out and I'll pay for it."

"Against the club rules, sir."

"There's no rule that says I can't treat you to a tooth extraction, is there?"

"They'd say it come under the head of tips and gratuities."

"I'll take it up with Mr. Stotesbury."

"He isn't president any more, sir. Mr. Packard."

"All right, I'll take it up with Mr. Packard."

"I'd rather you didn't, thanks just the same. It isn't the money. I have the money. It's the losing one more tooth of the few I got left in my head."

"Ah, yes. And you wouldn't want it to affect your power of speech."

"Well, I didn't think of that. One tooth? I lost one tooth before this and it had no effect on my power of speech."

"You didn't notice it made it harder for you to talk?"

"No sir. Oh, a little till I got used to it."

"But that didn't take long?"

"No sir, two or three days at the most."

"A remarkable recovery."

"Well, I don't know. It shouldn't take long to get over having one tooth out. Now what can I do for you, sir?"

"*Now* you can take my dishes *and* the other gentleman's dishes. And you can bring me a chocolate éclair."

"Oh, I'd hate to eat a chocolate éclair with this tooth aching the way it is."

"Then I'll just eat it myself, Philip." Samuel Eaton began to laugh. "Don't you even bring an extra fork."

"Mr. Eaton, sometimes you puzzle me. It isn't my place to say it, but a few minutes ago I'd of said you were fighting mad, but now you're cracking jokes and laughing, having a jolly old time. I guess a person has to be natured that way. When I'm miserable, the whole world knows it."

"Now you're going to make me miserable if you don't bring me that chocolate éclair."

Samuel Eaton did not like to be seen alone and killing time at the Racquet Club and he left shortly after he finished his meal. During the war he had been compelled to open an office in Philadelphia, but with the termination of government contracts he had reduced the staff to one woman who took care of the forwarding of mail, and he had not set foot in the office since the calling of the strike in September. He decided to walk from the club to the office, which was in a building on Chestnut Street near Fourth. The wind was from the east and steady and strong and cold as it often is in January in Philadelphia, and a couple of times he was forced to turn his face away and even to walk backwards. When he reached the office he had tears in his eyes and he was short of breath. The entrance door was locked and he let himself in with his key, and sat at his desk without taking off his overcoat. "I don't feel so good," he said to himself. A few minutes later Miss Spannuth returned from her leisurely lunch, and as soon as she saw the boss she called the doctor. Her own dear father had had several strokes, and she was familiar with the signs.

On the second day following Samuel Eaton's stroke Eugene St. John was having breakfast alone with his daughter. There was a continuing coolness between the father and daughter, but it always lessened when the mother was not present. "Mary, I've been to see Mr. Eaton. My next step is to have a talk with the young man himself."

"You've seen his father? When did you see him?"

"The day before yesterday. It was very unpleasant."

"It must have been. More for him than for you."

"I wouldn't say so."

"Well, I would. He's in the hospital, and you're not."

"He's in the hospital? When did he go to the hospital?"

"After lunch the day before yesterday. You had a quarrel with him."

"Yes, we exchanged some very angry words, but when I left him—I'm sorry to hear this."

"Are you?"

"Of course I am. Deeply sorry. What is the latest news on him?"

"The latest? I don't know. Alfred called me up last night. He said he didn't know when he'd be able to see me, his father was in the hospital with a stroke. He'd had it in his office after lunch. Alfred was coming down here today and he called to explain why he wouldn't be able to." She spoke with quiet defiance. "So I told him I'd go to Philadelphia. I hope you or Mother don't try to stop me, because if you do it's going to be very embarrassing for both of you."

"I don't think your mother would try to stop you in a case like this, and I'm not going to."

"Mother will try. If she does, Father, you keep her from interfering, because as soon as I hear from Alfred I'm going to Philadelphia and I'm going to stay as long as he wants me to."

"Where are you going to stay?"

"I'm going to stay with Priscilla Langley."

"All right. You have my permission. I'll attend to matters with your mother. This doesn't alter things, but it's a perfectly natural and commendable impulse, for you to want to be with Alfred now."

"It doesn't alter things, you say. It alters them a great deal. It alters them so much that I may not come back. If Alfred needs me, I'll marry him."

"He needs you, of that I'm sure, but the last thing he needs now is the extra added responsibility of a wife."

"A wife doesn't have to be a responsibility. A wife can share some of the responsibility."

"That's true, but you'd be a responsibility nevertheless. No, don't go to Philadelphia in that frame of mind. I'll give you my permission to go and stay a week, if necessary."

"Don't try to put any time limit on it, Father. You don't seem to realize—"

"Mary, I'm entirely sympathetic to your feelings. I do realize that you want to be with Alfred, but there are other things to consider. He has to take charge now. His mother, two sisters, and he's going to have to act as his father's representative in business matters. Do you know the name of his father's doctor?"

"No."

Eugene St. John pinched the clamps of his spectacles and held the glasses away from his face, a characteristic gesture when he was making a decision. "I'll go to Philadelphia with you."

"No! Please don't."

"Let me tell you something, Mary. If I go now, I can be of some help, and later on, if you do marry Alfred Eaton, we'll be much closer than if I could have helped him and didn't."

"Who is we?"

"You and I, but it could also mean Alfred and I. Mr. Eaton, Samuel Eaton, is a man who ran his business himself and didn't take other men into his confidence, including his son. Consequently Alfred is going to need that kind of help, and I can give it to him."

"Do you give up?"

"Yes, I give up. I know you're going to marry him. I can see you love him. And this thing that's happened to his father, it may remove some of our objections."

"Can I tell him that you don't object to my marrying him?"

"No. That wouldn't be true. I give up in the face of your determination, but that doesn't remove all the objections. But this, uh, mishap puts him at the head of a family, at least temporarily, and he'll realize overnight that there's a lot more to life than duck-shooting and high-powered automobiles. And a lot more to love than the romantic side of it."

"I realize it."

"Yes, you've begun to. Eighteen." He smiled. "Do you remember when you got that napkin ring?"

"No."

"I do. I don't remember whether your mother said it or I said it. Maybe both of us. 'She isn't a baby any more.' And now suddenly you're rushing off to a man you love. You make me feel very old, Mary."

"You make me feel sad."

"But at the same time happy."

"Yes, I guess it's happy. It isn't un-happy."

"When I came down to breakfast I didn't even expect to see you."

"I almost waited till you left the house."

"Don't ever avoid me. Let's never come to that. Well, I've missed one trolley and I don't want to miss the next. As soon as you hear from Alfred will you telephone me at the office? And for the time being we won't say anything to your mother. I'll have a long talk with her this evening. One thing more. Mr. Eaton may live for years."

Eugene and Mary St. John and Alfred Eaton met at a Childs near the hospital. It was in the middle of the afternoon. "Have you had any lunch?" said St. John.

"No sir, I haven't."

"Have some buckwheat cakes with me. Some buckwheat cakes and sausage."

They ordered their food and a chicken sandwich for Mary. "What is the report on your father?"

"He can go home in two weeks. He could go sooner, but they'd like to keep him here that long to be sure."

"Is that going to be such a good idea, with your mother an invalid too?"

"You know what kind of an invalid my mother is, Mr. St. John."

"Yes, I do. But what does your doctor say? A man who's had a stroke needs rest. Quiet. Will he get that at home? Alfred, we have to talk facts, and you *can* talk to me. I hope Mary's given you that much confidence in me."

"It isn't easy to forget everything overnight."

"I'm here because Mary loves you and I love Mary."

"My father wants to go home and go back to work. One doctor says he might as well, the other says he should have complete rest and not to try to do anything for six months."

"Are things in good shape at the mill?"

"They're in pretty good shape. Everything was shut down

during the strike and my father hasn't been in any great hurry to get any big contracts. He's sore at the men and he says they can wait till *he's* ready now."

"You have a good man in charge?"

"Two good men, the office man and the plant man. The only thing I'm worried about is they won't want to stay on forever if my father doesn't have the mill operating on peacetime capacity this spring."

"You haven't changed your mind?"

"I'll never take a job in the mill."

"Can I help you in any way?"

"Yes sir. You can give your consent to my marrying your daughter."

"Would you do that if you were in my position? If you were Mary's father?"

"I can't think of myself as Mary's father and I'm not going to try, especially to make a point for you. Mary and I want to get married and live in New York. I have plenty of money for both of us and I can get a job."

"Get the job first."

"No. I don't want to take a job and then quit as soon as Mary and I get married. I may want to go into business for myself, or with a partner."

"Any special business?"

"Yes, but I'm not at liberty to say what it is. We'll have good financial backing—"

"And no experience."

"Nobody has a hell of a lot of experience in the business we have in mind."

"A speculation?"

"That's what I think all business is, including du Pont, Mr. St. John."

"Experience and judgment and skilled men remove the speculative element to a great extent, Alfred. Don't think of us as just a gunpowder mill, dependent on war contracts. You're going to be surprised at some of the businesses du Pont's in before long."

"They sound speculative to me."

"Oh, they are, they will be. But we think we know what we're doing, and we can afford to let research minimize the speculative danger. With us, you know, research isn't just playing with pots and pans. It's an investment, and we look at it that way. We'll always get our money back. But another firm might just go broke, with nothing to show for their research but a big bill at Eimer & Amend's."

"Who are they?" said Mary.

"Laboratory equipment," said her father. "Flasks. Retorts. Test tubes."

"All you have to worry about is my ability to support Mary. I can do that."

"How, may I ask?"

"Money I inherited from my grandfather, not my Grandfather Eaton, therefore not Eaton's Iron & Steel. Also money that will be coming to me from him, and eventually from my mother."

"The whole business amounting to how much, would you say?"

"I don't know how much, altogether. Maybe a half a million."

"That's a great deal of money, and at five percent a considerable income. Twenty-five thousand a year. But if you make a few bad investments the twenty-five thousand could vanish very quickly and I understand you to say you do intend to invest some of this money in your own business, about which very little is known. Now, Alfred, this may sound like a strange thing to say, but Mary's future might be safer if you just went on being a gentleman of leisure. Then at least the twenty-five thousand would be constant."

"My argument against that is that a gentleman of leisure ought not to get married. I don't think they make good husbands. Not the few I've seen."

"I'm glad to hear you say that. We haven't even had a soldier in our family in almost a hundred and fifty years. We've all been preachers and scholars and scientists. On my wife's side it's been different. Southerners. The gentry, of course."

"My family are all iron foundrymen on one side and farmers on the other, no gentry that I know of."

St. John addressed his daughter: "Well, Mary, I wasn't much help, was I? You were right."

"But you wanted to be, and I appreciate that, Mr. St. John," said Alfred.

"Well, I hope so. I hope you don't think of me as a tyrant."

"No, I never did," said Alfred.

"That's good, and I'm glad we've had this talk, because now that you know me a little better, we can discuss things without animosity. Am I correct?"

"Yes sir."

"Very well. With that in mind will you give me your word that you and Mary will not rush off and get married? We don't necessarily want a big church wedding, and all those fancy trimmings. But I want you to promise me that you'll wait till the present crisis is over and you can get married in a decent, orderly manner."

"What do you say, Mary?" said Alfred.

"I say all right as long as you and Mother stop opposing us." Mary was speaking to her father.

"Then I say all right, too," said Alfred. "It's not going to make any difference to my father, whether we get married today, or six months from now."

"Oh, I don't know about that. Your father when I talked to him was very much in favor of the marriage."

"He was?" said Alfred.

"He thought it would be a good way to get you to settle down."

"Oh."

"Don't be too severe on your father. For instance, he made it quite clear at the very beginning of our meeting, he said of course I understood that he was going to tell you that we had our discussion. In other words, nothing was to be done in an underhanded way, and he wanted to make sure I understood that."

"Oh, he's too blunt to be underhanded," said Alfred.

"It isn't only that. People don't always behave the way you expect them to. Life itself—just consider this, Alfred, and you, too, Mary. Less than one week ago I was firmly opposed to this marriage. Today, I am not only reconciled to it, but I'm secretly in favor of it. Why? What brought about this change? Well, now consider it. I went to Philadelphia to try to persuade your father to oppose it as strongly as we did. What happened? First, I find that for his own reasons he's opposing me, not you, although you and he I gather have never hit it off very well. Then something absolutely unpredictable happens, and automatically your life is drastically changed for you. In a few hours' time you change from an irresponsible young man to the active head of a family, and that removes a lot of the objections we had to you as a prospective son-in-law. Life is full of those ironies. A man that you don't like very much has an unfortunate accident, and through it you get what you want. But a week ago you never would have thought that it was your own father who was going to be responsible for this change in *my* attitude. Do you see how all these things are interrelated and yet completely unpredictable? We all would like to keep our lives very simple because it would be easier that way, but people's lives won't behave according to plan. Not our own plans. But there must be a plan. I have a hard time believing in a formal religion, but there is a master plan. Otherwise it couldn't get so complicated and at the same time appear so simple."

"It goes back to a fight I was in at Princeton. That's how I got to be friends with Lex Porter, and through him, met Mary. Or, if my father hadn't given me a new car I might not have driven to Long Island that night. If I hadn't had the car I wouldn't have taken the train. So there's my father again. Or, if it hadn't been for an automobile accident at home, I'd probably have had a Stutz instead of a Marmon, and the man that drove a new Stutz from Indiana wouldn't have arrived the same day that the man did with the Marmon, and I wouldn't have met Mary. And if I hadn't been so—" He stopped himself: he was thinking of his quarrel with Victoria Dockwiler and her ride in the Stutz. "Too many if's."

"Yes, there are a lot of them, and it doesn't do to think too much about them. It makes you nervous about what you do next," said St. John.

"Then don't start putting if's in our way, Father. The only thing Alfred and I can be sure of is that we love each other. The if's come from you and Mother."

"The if's come from not being as sure of ourselves as we were when we were younger."

"This morning Father said I make him feel old," said Mary.

"Sometimes you make me feel old," said Alfred.

"Oh, but you are old, and Father isn't. Father's *older*, but you're *old*."

"Not too old for you, I hope."

"No. I'm pretty old, too."

"Well, we better hurry up and get married before it's too late," said Alfred.

"There's still a little time," said Eugene St. John, but not sternly. He was watching them together and liking what he saw. He placed his knife and fork precisely in position on the empty plate. "You'll be at Priscilla's?"

"I'll be at Priscilla's."

"After your father's had some rest we must arrange for our families to meet. Now I must go home and tackle my wife. Tackle? *That's* an unfortunate word. Well, goodbye, my dear. Goodbye, Alfred."

Samuel Eaton went home in two weeks, accompanied by a male nurse and Edmund Barlow from the mill, and driven by Walter in the curtained Packard. At the farm the greetings were kept to a minimum by Alfred, who had instructed Josephine and Nellie to confine themselves to a simple "Welcome home, sir." Samuel Eaton took the stairs slowly and went to his wife's room and kissed her forehead.

"You look very well," he said.

"So do you. Are you tired?"

"Holy hell, Martha. What from? This dry nurse I have tried to make me stop on every step. Walter drove twenty miles an hour most of the way, and everybody's opening doors for me as if I couldn't open a door. I'm not a delicate flower.

I'm a big man who's had a stroke. I'm not going to try to run the hundred, but I can still open an automobile door and flush my own toilet. He does everything but take my cock out for me. I'm going to keep him another week and then I'm going to let him go."

"Would you like a cup of tea?"

"Yes, I'll join you in a cup of tea. And I'd like some cinnamon toast."

Martha gave the order to Trimingham and they were alone again.

"What do you think of this news about Alfred?" he said.

"Good, I suppose. He'll be home this evening. He's in New York seeing about that business he wants to go into with Lex Porter."

"Yes, that mysterious business. Are you going to put any money in it? I suppose that's a foolish question."

"I will if he wants me to. Aren't you?"

"A little. Not much. Whatever they invest now they'll lose. Neither one of them knows anything about business. I'm going to let him have five thousand dollars."

"Is that all?"

"That's all, and the only reason I'm letting him have that is because that's about what it would have cost him to finish college. You know what they want to do, don't you?"

"No."

"They want to build aeroplanes."

"Who wants to buy aeroplanes?"

"Nobody. The Army will sell you all the second-hand ones you want. Do you remember the Johnson Special?"

"No. What was that?"

"It was an automobile they were going to manufacture at the old carriage works."

"Yes, I do remember. Father put some money in it."

"And said I didn't have any imagination because I *didn't* put any money in it. I had enough imagination to see where the money would go. They never even finished two cars. They built one car and that was the end of the Johnson Special."

"Father didn't think it was a very good investment. He just thought the town ought to help."

"The town helped. Over two hundred thousand dollars was lost in that foolishness, but no money of mine. The same thing's going to happen to Alfred and Lex Porter. But the Porters have a lot of rich friends and relatives. Thank you, Miss Trimingham. How are you feeling these days? Your patient looks well."

"Thank you, sir. I'm well, thank you," said Trimingham. She left immediately.

"Didn't ask how *I* felt," said Samuel Eaton.

"An oversight," said Martha.

"Only you know damn well it wasn't," said her husband. "Well, we're a fine pair, you and I. Me fifty-eight and you forty-nine, and both of us with our own nurses. I've decided to sell the mill."

"What? Sam, are you serious?"

"I wouldn't joke about a thing like that."

"When did you decide that?"

"I decided that while I was lying on a bed in the hospital, having people treat me like a dead man. The idea first came to me during the strike when a couple of Jews from New York made me an offer. The offer was so low that when Barlow mentioned their price I almost didn't answer his telegram. I was in Wyoming at the time. Then I didn't think much about it till I got this stroke, and I'd lie there and wonder what I was going to do when I got out. And that's when I decided."

"Why?"

"Well, this thing scared me. I admit it. I don't want to alarm you, but the doctors think I had one before. In other words, this is my second, not my first. Well, I can go on living for another fifteen, twenty years, but not working as hard as I have the past four or five or six years, and I'd have to work pretty hard to get the mill going the way it ought to. And what for? For my grandchildren? If Alfred had a son tomorrow I'd still be close to ninety by the time the boy was ready to take over, and even then I have no guarantee that he won't want to be an aeroplane manufacturer —or a court tennis player. As to the girls, it's even less likely that their children will want to go in the mill."

"Yes."

"So I've decided to look around for a buyer. If it isn't going to stay in the family I'd like to see Bethlehem take it over. Or U. S. I don't care, just as long as they don't try to buy it cheap and turn it into a junk-yard. I'd like to see a sign over it. 'Bethlehem Steel Company, Eaton Branch.' When I croak it won't matter what they call it. Charley Schwab's Mule Yard, for all I care. But while I'm alive I'd like some recognition of all the years I put in it. It's all I ever did."

"Everybody knows it's yours."

"They'll soon forget . . . My father always used to like a cup of tea."

"It's very refreshing in the afternoon. I have a cup almost every day."

"Do you?"

"Almost every day. Of course I have my supper so early that I don't take anything else. Toast, I mean."

"How have you been while I was away?"

"In the hospital? Oh, there isn't much change in me, Sam. Don't look for any, then you won't be disappointed. I can go a day or two without anything, but the amount I take is so small, really it isn't worth giving it up."

"It might if you gave it up for six months or a year, I don't care what anybody says. You could be yourself again."

"I am myself. That's what you don't see. I've been as much myself these past ten years as I was the ten years before."

"I'll never be convinced of that. You're doing what you want to do, sure. But that isn't the same thing as being your real self. I did some more thinking in the hospital."

"You must have."

"I did. Part of your—trouble—is my fault."

She smiled. "Well, I'm not going to deny that, Sam."

"I neglected you for the mill."

"Oh, well now that's a new one. I always thought you blamed it on Billy's death."

"Yes, but that was the cause of it. The effect was for me to put all my energy into the mill."

"Oh, I see. Well, I knew that."

"Martha, you never asked me about other women."

"No, I never did."

"Didn't you care enough if I had other women?"

Her eyes were troubled. "This conversation—I don't want to talk about these things, Sam."

"I'm not going to accuse you of anything."

"But that's what you're doing. You know what I was, you know what I did. Bringing it up again is the same as accusing me again, and what can I say? Deny what I've admitted? I wanted to be loved, and someone loved me—and died. And the other was—it wasn't love, Sam. It was like the drinking."

"I know all that," he said. "But what I asked you was, didn't you care if I had other women?"

"I cared. Yes, I cared."

"But not very much."

"As a man you had to have your satisfaction with a woman. You didn't want me any more. There had to be somebody."

"There wasn't, though. Only when I needed a woman for my health, two or three times a year. Sometimes not even that. Once I went for almost two years."

"I didn't know a man could go that long."

"I did."

"Why do you want me to know all this now?" she asked. "I've never asked you for any explanations."

"Because when I was in the hospital, with a stroke, nurses and doctors, the smell of the hospital—I wanted you. I've never wanted any other woman."

"Well, I guess that's the saddest thing of all, isn't it?"

"It doesn't have to be."

"Then *that's* the saddest thing, Sam. It does have to be."

"We could make another try."

"No we couldn't."

"But we could, Martha. That's one of the reasons I decided to sell the mill. To have more time with you."

"Now that you're ready, now that you've had a scare . . . I shouldn't have said that. But I haven't been anything but your housekeeper for ever so many years, and lately not even that. What do you want to do, Sam? Move your bed back into my room? Hope we can be sweet to each other again? I've said things to other people that I couldn't say to you again, Sam. And meant them, because whenever I said them I was getting that much farther away from you, and I *wanted* to be away from you. I wanted to leave you long ago, you know that. And I left you. I was here, but I might as well not have been, except for the children. And maybe it would have been better for the children in the long run. They know what their mother is. At least Alfred and Sally do. Constance, too, most likely by this time."

"I never asked you to stay for the children."

"You never even asked me to leave. It would have been better if you'd been old-fashioned and sent me away with my memories of my dead lover."

"Martha! Anyway, he wasn't dead then."

"Then you should have sent me away and maybe he'd have followed me."

"Not him. He never gave anything up for you."

"Except his life," she said.

She looked out at the azalea bushes, eyes dry, mouth set, calm. "He never asked me to leave, either. I would have, with him. His way. All this would have been over so long ago."

Samuel Eaton stood up. "I see there's no use."

"If he had asked me I'd have gone. His way, too. Then all this would have been over long ago. It wasn't very trusting of him. I'd have gone. A few seconds in the heart, the brain. What was he sparing me? A few seconds? What for? He wasn't very trusting, not very kind to leave me with all this. *Miss Trimingham?*"

Trimingham appeared in the hall doorway. "Yes, ma'am?"

"That bluejay's after that robin's nest again."

Trimingham went to the window and clapped her hands. "I'm afraid we were too late this time," said Trimingham.

361

"Oh, dear," said Martha. "Those poor robins. I see the most awful things from this window. Walter shot a chicken-hawk last week. Did he tell you?"

"Did he tell me? No," said Samuel Eaton.

"He didn't want to worry you. Yes, it spread from here to here, three feet at least."

"Closer to four feet, I believe, ma'am."

"Yes, it was. If you'd like to have a look at it I think he has it tacked up on the stable-door."

"I don't particularly want to see it," said Samuel Eaton.

"But we have all those animals you sent from Mexico. I thought you'd like to see it."

"Well, I'll have a look at it some other time."

"Oh, I didn't mean for you to go out there now. You ought to lie down and rest a while."

"All right, I guess I will," said Samuel Eaton.

"Alfred will be home this evening and we'll hear all the news about his factory. And Miss St. John. Do you have a tendency to call her Victoria? I do."

"No, I don't," said Samuel Eaton.

"I do. I always have to stop myself. Don't always succeed, either."

"When he gets home will you tell him I'm in my room, please?"

Samuel Eaton's nurse, who seemed determined to show that he could be a valet, helped him off with his clothes and into pajamas and bathrobe, and Samuel Eaton did not spurn his help. He was weary and resisting fear. He had spoken the truth to Martha: in the hospital he had allowed himself to entertain a desire for her that he had been successfully denying for years, but that, when it came to him in the hospital, was so right that he had substituted it for all the reasons he had given himself to conquer any desire for her in the recent past. The substitution had been so quick that he had made it without thinking about forgiving her. It was enough for him that he could want her again, and had thought that that would be enough for her. It had not been enough for her; he was as much out of her life as though he had been the guilty one, not she. And now he took only some small comfort in being able to recall that at least he had not been humble. And he found an excuse for her rejection of him: she was crazy.

In the past when her mind and her speech had wandered, he had blamed her drinking, to which he had also attributed the strangely perceptive flashes of wit she sometimes displayed. In the first half of their marriage she had been occasionally humorous, almost frivolous, funny without any depth. She had often made little jokes that he could laugh at. But at some stage—which he later placed at the time of her love affair with Allan Miller—her humor had become what he called sarcastic and even cruel. And when she began to drink heavily and, as she thought, secretly, the drinking explained it, rather than the affair with Miller. He had never wanted to attribute any change in her to the affair with Miller. His hatred of Miller had been so fierce that he refused to concede that the affair had had that much, that deep, an effect on Martha. In spite of the evidence, he maintained a disbelief in a sharing of bodily intimacies by Martha and Allan Miller. In his thoughts, and in the angry conversations with Martha, he used the term *go to bed with*, but he fought against its meanings; the causing of erection, the caresses, the gripping of the hard flesh, and the wild motions that he knew her to be capable of in her little hips as she made Miller give to her and as she took from Miller. Almost never had he yielded to the obtrusiveness of that picture of her with Miller. With Frolick, there was no other picture. With Frolick she had made herself animal and cheap. All the caprices Samuel Eaton had memorized through her faithful years, which delighted him in the experiencing but made her seem childishly evil in retrospect—all that, but no more, she gave to Frolick. When he thought of her and Frolick there was no insistently recurring, obtrusive pictures of intimacies: there was no other picture. He could imagine her walking around naked, in her bare feet, in Frolick's apartment, but he would not admit graphically that Allan Miller had touched the nipple of her breast.

His pictures of the two affairs were made easy by the respective circumstances of the rendezvous between Martha and Miller, and Martha and Frolick. "Where did you meet him? Where did you go?" he had demanded.

"I won't tell you."

He had held her shoulders and shaken her until she gave up. "In the carriage-house."

"Here? Where the servants could see you? Where George could see you? Was he in on it?"

"Father's carriage-house. In the hayloft."

It had been so easy; with no coachman living in, with the Millers living so close to Raymond Johnson's house that Allan's presence in the neighborhood, Martha's presence in the neighborhood, caused no suspicion.

When? When the coachman went home in the early evening, when her father would go to bed early, when she would spend the night at her father's house.

How would Miller know when to meet her? When she would lower the shade of one of the windows in her old room in her father's house. That was the sign that she would be in the carriage-house within the hour. If Miller could be there, he would be; if not, she would not wait. "You always made the sign?"

"Yes."

"Where else did you meet him?"

"Nowhere else."

"You're lying to me."

"Once in Philadelphia, at a hotel."

"The Bellevue. You were with him in the Bellevue."

"No, the Adelphia."

"Did you spend the night?"

"No."

"Where else?"

"The boat-house," she said. "Down at the river."

"His boat-house?"

"Yes."

"I knew it. That's when I first got suspicious. I saw you on the river road that day, and you told me you'd been out to Eckburg. Stupid lie, stupid liars."

"Yes."

"You could be with him, and be with me the same night. Couldn't you?"

"I don't know."

"You do know. You know all right. Couldn't you?" He slapped her face.

"Yes."

"And were, often. Two men in the same day. What did you think of yourself?"

"I don't know."

"Did you think you were any better than a whore on River Street?"

"I'm not proud of myself."

"Not proud of herself! she says. How could you look at the children?"

"That's why I stopped."

"That's why you *stopped,* after how long?"

"Two years, three years."

"Endangering their reputation for three years, *then* you stopped. Who's protecting their reputation now?"

"You are. And I will."

"You will, you say. Isn't it a little late for that now?"

"Allan is dead, no one will ever know now, if you don't tell them."

"Do you know what makes me laugh? Your father, so proud of you, so sure that I was never good enough for you. And all that time you were fucking a weakling, right on your dear father's property. Go away from me. I don't want to look at you. Your conceited little father, and your dead, cowardly lover. Your heroes."

364

"I have no heroes. Only some people I love. *You* were my *hero*."

"Get out of here!"

Then the years of her quiet drinking and her frequent drunkenness, the house that often seemed full of hate until the imperceptible change in his feeling toward her when he became aware that what she had done to him had ceased to have the power to cause shame and pain, and he gave all his love to his dead son and all his strength to the mill. And when what had been imperceptible became acknowledgeable truth he found he was having with her a friendship that he could not have had with a housekeeper and a cool independence he could not have had with a friend; an appreciation of her management of an orderly, quite charming house, and a woman to whom he could confide all the secrets of the mill without extracting promises or providing background. He seldom went into her bedroom, she never entered his, and they both carefully avoided a meeting of the eyes, afraid they might not find the nothing that was always there, but that still would not be good to see. His need for a woman was always strong when it occurred, but less and less frequent, and always satisfied by one of the women of New York whom he could take to dinner at Mouquin's and the Club de Vingt, and whom he would pay a couple of hundred dollars not so much for the one night as to keep her available for the next time, and keep her from the tackiness and promiscuity that went with the women who took less money. They had all been divorced, all been kept by rich men, some of them had sons at distant military schools, none of them had live-in maids or trusted women friends, and their only foolish extravagance was a young lover who would be banished at the first sign that he was over-curious about the men who paid the bills and who might be susceptible to blackmail. The end of the association with a Samuel Eaton was usually pleasant: "I'm getting married to a wonderful chap . . . Don't send me a present, but you can send me a money-order if you feel like it." They made it possible, those women, for Samuel Eaton to go home at night without any fear of love or the passion of desperation, the overwhelming surge in the night that might lead to rape and even to suicide. The inconvenient momentary excitement was not complicated by the overwhelming demand for immediate satisfaction lest it be the last ever. New York was only a hundred and forty miles away, and a telegram would alert Consuelo or Blanche or Georgia. Rape of Martha was unthinkable, since her drinking and its resulting ill health had brought her to a state of fragility that made any violence as distasteful to Samuel Eaton as it would have been to her. In a way that was oddly intellectual for

Samuel Eaton, his affairs with the Blanches, Georgias and Consuelos prepared him for an understanding, although not a sanction, of Martha's affair with Frolick; he continued to profess the double standard; but a woman like Martha could have only one reason for going with a man like Frolick, and it was the same reason that Samuel Eaton had gone with the women of New York.

He had found out about Frolick early in the affair. As a small courtesy, and not because Samuel Eaton insisted on it, Martha had got into the habit of telling Samuel Eaton that she would be going to Philadelphia on certain days, on certain trains, but without volunteering additional information. When he began to suspect that her trips were not for the purpose of shopping—confirmed by the fact that the monthly bills did not show any purchases on the days of her trips—Samuel Eaton, having taken an earlier train, waited for her to arrive at the Reading Terminal or Broad Street Station, and followed her to restaurants and her meetings with the same man on successive trips, and then he followed her several times in taxicabs, to the same address, which was Frolick's house. It was not difficult for Samuel Eaton to find out the name of the owner of the house: he asked his Philadelphia attorney to ascertain the ownership of all the property in the square, with a possible view to real estate investment, and in twenty-four hours he had Frolick's name. After that it was remarkable how often he saw Frolick, on the sidewalks in the old and newer business districts, in hotel diningrooms, and once even in the same elevator of an office building. Frolick did not know Samuel Eaton by sight, but Samuel Eaton collected many items of information on Frolick, principally the fact that Martha was far from the only woman in his life, and that none of Samuel Eaton's business acquaintances thought very highly of Charles Frolick. On two occasions—once on South Broad Street, another time as he walked across City Hall Plaza—Samuel Eaton had had to turn away quickly so that he would not be recognized by Charles Frolick's companion: Devrow Budd. It was hardly a surprise that Devrow Budd would be a friend of a man like Frolick, but Samuel Eaton preferred to remain a total stranger to Frolick. It gave him, he felt, a certain advantage. (It was, although Samuel Eaton did not know it, a permanent advantage: Charles Frolick was an extremely near-sighted man whose vanity prevented him from wearing glasses except for reading.)

Samuel Eaton regarded Martha as the victim of her desires, ruled by what he secretly described as an itch that affects women until it controls them from the first menstruation to the menopause, with some women affected more than others rather than some women affected less than others. The proof that Martha had been affected worse than most was the fact that she had had an affair with Allan Miller. Her desires, this itch, had completely got the better of her later, when she sought excitement with a man like Frolick. Only a woman, not a man, would let that side of her get the better of her so completely, and with such weak and unsavory men as Allan Miller and Charles Frolick; the weak Miller, who blew his brains out on a petulant impulse; and the roué Frolick, who deserted his mistress when he could have helped her. Samuel Eaton never knew that Frolick had actually been at the Reading Terminal on Armistice Day, 1918, but he knew positively, because he had seen to it, that Frolick never had communicated with Martha after she was taken to the hospital that day. It was a case of desertion; Frolick had not even attempted to speak to Martha or to see her. Only a woman, never a man, could have made such miserable choices—and Samuel Eaton never wondered why he had chosen Martha, or she had chosen him.

He fell asleep and when he opened his eyes Alfred was standing in the room. "Welcome home."

"Oh. Oh, hello, Alfred. Oh, it must be after seven. Well, aren't you going to shake hands with me?"

"Sure."

They shook hands.

"Oh, Lord. My mouth feels like a garbage pail. Tell that fellow I'd like some mouth-wash. His name is Wardle."

"I'll get it."

"Bring a basin and I can slosh it out in here."

Alfred brought the mouth-wash and his father rinsed his mouth out noisily.

"Would you like company for dinner?" said Alfred.

"What company?"

"Just me. Mother's had hers."

"I know. Why, yes, I'd like that, if you don't mind. You can tell me about your trip to New York. When are you going to open your factory?"

"When we get the money, and the land and so forth."

"Well, put me down for five thousand dollars. It isn't a hell of a lot, but it's my limit."

"It's five thousand more than I expected from you."

"Well, as I told your mother, I'd have given you that much to finish your education. Consider this part of your education, because that's what it will be."

"Maybe. Fortunately everybody doesn't feel the same way about it."

"Lex Porter's uncle?"

"Both uncles, and some friends of theirs."

"What are you going to contribute, Alfred?"

"You mean invest?"

"No, I mean contribute."

"That's what I said to Lex."

"Well, what did he say?"

"I'll be the manager. He doesn't want to have anything to do with that side of it. He wants to work with the designer and the engineering experts, and fly the planes."

"You have no business experience."

"We don't expect any business for a couple of years. Meanwhile, I'll be learning."

"Oh. Now that seems sensible. I was under the impression you fellows thought you'd be manufacturing these machines in a few months, and cleaning up next year."

"No. We're not deceiving ourselves. All we know is that aviation is the coming industry in this country. In ten years everybody's going to want aeroplanes."

"Personally I'd rather have some Dodge Brothers, common or preferred."

"Who wouldn't? That's a sure thing, for those who like sure things, and I like sure things, too. But we're hoping to *be* Dodges. They've only been going since 1915, five years. We're allowing ten years."

"You're joking, I hope."

"Yes, but not about aviation. Last year that Navy plane flew the Atlantic Ocean, the NC-4."

"Are you planning to fly the Atlantic Ocean?"

"No, but it can be done, that's been proven. No, Father, the way we see it, the distances in this country are so great that the aeroplane is bound to be popular. Speed. That's the whole secret of transportation. Steamship, locomotive, aeroplane."

"When you have come down, where will you land? Cornfields?"

"That's the weak point. Not enough places to land."

"Who's going to buy your machines?"

"Well, suppose you owned a ranch in Wyoming. Wouldn't it be a good idea for you to have a plane?"

"I wouldn't have a plane if you gave it to me."

"If you had a ranch, one of those hundred-thousand-acre places, you could cover more ground in a day than you can now in a week. You could go from one end of the ranch to another in a day, and be home that night."

"What for?

"To inspect your property."

"You don't know much about ranching. You send a cowhand out on the range and you don't expect to see him for a month. He keeps an eye on the cattle, fixes the fences, puts in the salt licks. Why go to the expense of inspecting my property?"

"Suppose a steer has a broken leg?"

"You shoot him and butcher him."

"Suppose a cowboy has a broken leg? Do you shoot him, too?"

"That's an accident that doesn't happen once in a thousand times. I wouldn't buy an aeroplane to go looking for cowboys with broken legs. What else is your machine good for?"

"Mail."

"Mail?"

"They have it already between Washington and Philadelphia and New York, and some places in the West. There's going to be more and more of that, and we're going to build the planes for it. And there's a lot of private flying that you don't know about. Long Island. New Jersey. Connecticut. And out in the western states there's a lot of it. I understand California is very enthusiastic."

"Well, if there's so much of it you better hurry up and open your factory before some other fellows beat you to it. By the way, I had a nice bunch of flowers from Miss St. John."

"I know."

"No, you don't know. These came yesterday, the second time she sent me flowers. Do you know that I've never been sent flowers before in my whole life? Oh, your mother and your sisters had Battle send some to the hospital, but they're members of the family. I'm talking about outsiders. I've been sent cigars, whiskey, calendars, but never flowers. I want to meet this girl."

"When?"

"Any time. The sooner the better."

"How would tomorrow suit you?"

"That would suit me fine."

"I'll drive down and bring her here tomorrow afternoon."

"Not too late in the afternoon. I'm not thinking of myself, but your mother. Late in the afternoon her mind begins to wander and she's liable to say things that would worry your girl. I can call her your girl, can't I?"

"I don't know why not. She is my girl."

Samuel Eaton studied his son.

"Is my tie crooked?" said Alfred.

"I was just thinking, things may turn out all right for you. No, your tie isn't crooked."

"Well, they seem to be all right now," said Alfred.

"I hope they are. I hope they are."

"Thanks, Father. That's the first time I ever got any flowers from you." Alfred laughed.

"You're a snotty son of a bitch, aren't you?"

"Yes sir, I guess I am. And it's no accident."

"I hope I don't croak too soon. I'd like to see what you're like in about ten years from now."

"Well, if you take care of yourself you'll be here longer than that. But you know what they said at the hospital. You *have* to take care of yourself."

"Do you know my chief interest in life right now?"

"No."

"Your son. You'll have a son, and when you do I'm going to make damn sure he likes me. You wouldn't put anything in the way of that, would you? No, of course you wouldn't."

"Of course not. Not as long as you didn't try to run his life."

"You want to do that yourself."

"That's just what I don't want to do. I want him to run his own life. Are you ready to eat? I'm going downstairs now and telephone Mary and I'll tell them to send up our dinner."

"What's the matter with that telephone over there?" said Samuel Eaton.

"What a question," said Alfred.

He brought Mary to the farm the next afternoon. It was a day for the top to be down, to take advantage of the premature spring weather. As far as possible they rehearsed the two interviews with Martha and with Samuel Eaton, which Alfred was keeping separate to minimize the strain on all concerned. It turned out that there was no awkwardness in either case. They spent about five minutes with Martha, a little longer with Samuel Eaton, concluding the latter interview with Alfred's announcement that he wanted to show Mary about the place.

"All this belongs to your family?" she said, after they had walked a little while.

"All of it, and more. What you think is ours, and also the farms to the north, the east, and the south. They're not very big, but they're ours. All told, about two hundred and fifty acres. My father tried to buy the farm across the road, but it's owned by a stubborn Dutchman who said he didn't want to sell but would buy our place. That was all my father wanted to know. He just wanted to be sure that the Dutchman wasn't going to sell to someone else . . . That's the old pig-pen that I used to pretend was my fort. After we got rid of the pigs. Box-stalls for the ponies. That's my sister's horse. Get over, boy, get over. I don't even know his name. He's new since the war, or since I went away. What's your name, boy?"

"Danny Boy. It says here," said Mary.

"I didn't notice that. So it does." He patted the gelding.

"Do you want to pat him?"

"No thanks."

"Are you afraid of horses?"

"My shoes."

"Excuse me." He closed the door of the box-stall and they continued their tour. "Do you want a ride on the elevator?"

"Elevator?"

"That's an elevator. We used to run the carriages on that flooring, and then pull those ropes. Only I see there aren't any ropes, so I withdraw the offer. That was my grandfather's pride and joy, that elevator. The only one around here. My Grandfather Eaton, that is. In that room is where I smoked my first cigar."

"How old were you?"

"I think I was about ten."

"I hope it cured you of cigars."

"It did. Harness pegs. Closets for the best harness. Saddle pegs. Those iron loops in the ceiling, they used to hold ropes with hooks on the end and we'd hang the harness on the hooks when we cleaned it."

"We?"

"George Fry and I. That was fun, making a nice thick lather, getting all dirty and usually catching cold."

"Who was George Fry?"

"My best friend. As a matter of fact, he was the coachman, then chauffeur."

"Where is he now?"

"In the county hospital, insane. I'll tell you all about him sometime. Would you like to see the greenhouse?"

"Yes, everything."

"Nothing growing there now. My mother used to raise flowers, but she hasn't done that for years . . . It's hot in here, isn't it? Look at all those flower pots. I had no idea there were so many till I see them empty. I wonder how long it's been since those windows were washed. Nothing here, let's take a look at the tennis court."

"All it needs is a little rolling and some tape."

"This is a good court, very well drained. A French drain, I think it's called. My sisters play, Sally particularly. Very good backhand for a girl."

"I'll have you know I have a very good backhand."

"It isn't as good as Sally's, not what I've seen of it."

"It's much better than when you saw it. That was early last summer. I improved enormously by the end of the summer."

"I'd still bet on Sally."

"You're not very polite about my tennis."

"You swim better than Sally. Does that make it even?"

"No. Because I swim better than almost anybody, and that includes you."

"If you like to think so, you go ahead and think so. Women are hollow, that's why they can swim, but you really can't swim better than I can, Mary. Don't fool yourself."

"Women are hollow? They aren't any hollower than men."

"But they are. Unless they're pregnant."

"Oh."

"This would be a good place for me to kiss you."

"Can they see us from the house?"

"No."

They kissed warmly and held together close.

"Oh, darling," she said.

"Yes."

"Oh, so close."

He lifted her skirt and drew his hand up between her legs.

"Touch me," she said.

"And you touch me."

"No, I'm afraid. Touch me just a little bit, just for a minute. Now stop. Don't hold me."

"I don't want to let you go."

"I don't want you to. But we have to. Darling, please move away from me and I'll be all right. That was dear, and sweet. And I'm not cross with you." They separated by a few steps and he stood facing her. "That's what we have to watch out for."

"I shouldn't have," he said.

"I'm glad you did, though. It seems all right here, on your place. Doesn't it?"

"Yes."

"Now you've touched me. Nobody else ever has."

"They haven't?"

"Not really. By forcing themselves, by being stronger, but not with me letting them. Let's go where people *can* see us, away from temptation?" She smiled and they kissed again. "Now I'll never let you go. I don't mean this minute. But I mean for the rest of our lives. Come on, let's walk. Oh, I must look a wreck. Do I look a wreck? You do, so I must even more so. Let me fix your tie. All right. Here, hold my bag while I put on some powder. My *nose*, Alfred! Why didn't you *tell* me it was shining like a lighthouse."

"I like your nose to shine, and it wasn't shining."

"Are we going back to your house?"

"I'd like you to meet Josephine and Nellie. The cook and the maid. They've been with us for four hundred years. They'd be hurt if I didn't take you to see them. I'm sure they're sulking in the kitchen this minute."

Josephine and Nellie were sitting at the kitchen table in complete silence, their heads held high, their hands folded on the table, and unmistakably resentful. They stood up when Mary and Alfred entered from the porch door.

"Good afternoon," said Josephine.

"Good afternoon," said Nellie.

"This is Miss St. John. All right, now you've seen her, good-bye." He pretended to leave.

"Alfred! Don't go," said Mary, alarmed.

"Oh, he thinks he's so smart," said Josephine. "I'm pleased 'o make your acquaintance, ma'am."

"Pleased to meet you," said Nellie.

"A beautiful day for this time of year, don't you find it so?"

"It is beautiful, isn't it?" said Mary.

"Now you say something, Nellie," said Alfred.

"What?" said Nellie.

"It's your turn to say something. Then Josephine, then you, Mary."

"Oh, dear me, don't some people think they're clever and they're not clever one bit, not a single iota," said Josephine. "I admire your hat, Miss St. John. Is it the very latest? I took notice to it when you come in."

"Thank you. It is new," said Mary. "The first time I've worn it."

"Well, it'll be Easter before you know it. Oh, how this winter trickled away, but I'm not one bit sorry," said Josephine.

"It was unusually severe, wasn't it?" said Mary.

"Terrible severe," said Nellie. "One of the severest we've had."

"Oh, the blizzard of '88 was much worse, and you were no chicken then," said Alfred. "Come on, Mary. They've seen you."

"Do stay and have a cup of tea, Miss St. John, if you don't mind sitting down in the kitchen," said Josephine.

"I'd love to, but I've got to drive back to Wilmington."

"Oh, my. All the way back to Wilmington, Delaware. Well, bundle up and don't take cold. It was a great pleasure to have this little minute with you, and I trust we'll be having the pleasure soon again in the near future," said Josephine. She addressed Alfred: "Will *you* be home for dinner? I guess not."

"You guessed correctly, my dear. However, I will be home for breakfast tomorrow, and I would like some scrapple."

"You can't have any scrapple. Nobody in this house eats it any more, and it's too late to call the meat market."

"Then I would like some fried mush and molasses, and I don't want Karo, I want molasses."

"When did I ever give you Karo? I always give you molasses."

"I didn't say *you* gave me Karo. I'm just hinting to Miss St. John. She's going to have to know all these things before long."

"Poor dear, is all I can say," said Josephine.

The custom of getting acquainted with each other's family, and the families with the families, and the friends with the friends, was observed within the limitations created by the illnesses of the parents of the bridegroom-to-be. Mrs. St. John was able to take advantage of the situation: Mary's fiancé became a young man who was crippled by his parents' disabilities and it is always an advantage for the mother of the bride to be able to call some attention to the groom's short-comings. The groom's family are thereby prevented from taking a superior attitude. "I don't think Alfred's father *or* his mother will be able to get to the wedding," she said more than once. "It *will* seem strange. But weddings *are* for brides." And for brides' mothers, and this one was especially so, since the groom's sisters were bridesmaids, and consequently not a single Eaton was there to occupy the prominence of the first pew on the groom's side of the church. Over on the left side of the church there were St. Johns in quantity and a fair number of males whose first name was St. John, and as many Rowlands as St. Johns—Rowland having been Mrs. St. John's maiden name, and a convenient first name or middle name as well.

The pre-wedding entertaining was neither extensive nor lavish. It was naturally subdued not only by the Eatons' absence but by the fact that Eugene St. John and his wife were not blood relations of the du Pont clan. Business association made them subject to du Pont and other Wilmingtonian scrutiny. As a member of the corporate du Pont organization, Eugene St. John knew, without being told, that his daughter's wedding expenditures would be carefully estimated by most of the local mothers and fathers present or invited, and placed in comparison with recent du Pont wedding expenditures. For that reason the inclusion of the Eaton sisters made for a slight awkwardness, since it added two attendants to the bridal party, which was already quite large enough for a St. John wedding. There were eight bridesmaids, eight ushers, a maid of honor, and a best man. Mrs. St. John had forestalled some of the criticism by emphasizing the absence of the groom's parents and the need to include the Eaton girls, but her husband said he still wished they could have kept it down to six bridesmaids, or better, four. To her intimates Mrs. St. John would whisper: "But the Eaton girls didn't really count, if you want to know the truth. If Mary'd been marrying someone else they wouldn't even have been invited." Her explanation and confidential comment were completely satisfactory to Wilmington society, and no one seriously accused Eugene St. John of putting on an unseemly splurge.

As the Princeton son of a Princeton man, Alfred was not a totally unidentified stranger in Wilmington. "You know a great many more people than I did when I came here," said Eugene St. John.

"Well, they don't think I'm a Choctaw Indian. That's as far as I'll go."

"Oh, you'll like them as time goes by."

"I don't dislike them now. I'm just not overawed by them."

"I wouldn't say that if I were you. They consider any generality as unfavorable to the family."

"I'll remember that till Saturday," said Alfred. "I won't say anything at all about the du Pont family."

"That's been my rule. Of course I live here, and I know them as individuals."

"Oh, they are individuals?"

"Are they not! Alfred, have you even been to Martha's Vineyard?"

"Twice, not for very long," said Alfred. "Why?"

"Oh, I was just thinking, there's a family named Bethancourt on the Vineyard. I think there are more Bethancourts than there are Smiths. My point is, *they're* all individuals. Why shouldn't the du Ponts be?"

"Ah, come on, Mr. St. John. You know the answer to that. How many Bethancourt millionaires are there? How many railroads do *they* own?"

"Let's quietly drop the subject. But can I swear you to secrecy?"

"Yes."

"I'm glad Mary's marrying you. I've been happy here, they've been decent to me. But I'm glad you don't have to learn to pronounce N, e, w, a, r, k."

"Newark?"

"New-ark. Newark is in New Jersey. And you know who Irenee du Pont married, of course?"

"No."

"Irenee du Pont married Irene du Pont."

"Oh, that's nothing. At home Francis Schumacher married Frances Schumacher."

"Yes, but how many railroads do *they* own?" said St. John.

For the few days preceding the ceremony Alfred felt that Eugene St. John was making an effort to get close to him, in a way that was different from the polite effort of bride's father toward son-in-law. On the morning of the ceremony Alfred had final confirmation of his intuition. He was in his room at the hotel, playing rummy with Lex, when St. John appeared.

Lex and Alfred were in their B. V. D.'s. "I wish I were as comfortable as you look," said St. John.

"Wait till I get something on," said Alfred.

"I don't want you to do that, but Lex, will you give us a minute or two together, would you mind?"

Lex went to the bedroom and closed the door.

"Go on, put your pants on, Alfred. A man's at a disadvantage."

Alfred put on trousers and shirt and returned to the parlor.

"I came to see you," St. John began, "because when a father is as pleased and as happy about his only daughter as I am, I don't think he ought to let that thought go unexpressed."

"Jesus, Mr. St. John," said Alfred.

"I wasn't going to express it. We seldom do say the things that are in our hearts. But this *is* my only daughter, that I've watched grow, been in my thoughts more than I suppose most children are—well, maybe not. Maybe I just think so. But this is something a man can say only once in a lifetime, and some, the truth is, never are that lucky that they can say it with any meaning. So I want you to know, my boy, I'm happy for her, confident in and grateful to you. 'Who giveth this woman?' I do, Alfred, and now God damn it you look the other way because I can't help it, I'm going to cry."

He turned away and looked out the window. "You don't have to say anything."

"I can't," said Alfred.

"I know," said St. John. He resumed speaking without facing Alfred. "I'm sorry your father and mother can't be here today, not for Mary or not for ourselves, but for you." Now he turned around again. "But I want you to feel, Alfred, that if another man can take a father's place . . . Look at me, Alfred."

"Yes sir."

"You trust me, don't you?"

"Implicitly."

"I know you do. Then I've got to tell you."

"What?"

"Your father died an hour ago."

"He's dead?"

"An hour ago, in his room. I'm the only one that knows. Your mother telephoned me, asked to speak to me personally, and told me not to say anything to anyone, above all you. So I came to see you—I was coming anyway, I was in my car when I was called to the telephone. And I was going to say only what I had intended to say, how happy I am that Mary is marrying you. But I couldn't leave this room."

"Have you told Mary? You haven't told Mary."

"No one. Your mother didn't want anyone to know till after

the reception. Now I've thought this over, and you and Mary can be married ahead of time and we can call off the church and the reception."

"I wouldn't do that to Mary, Mr. St. John."

"I know you wouldn't, but I had to let you say that. That was your decision, and I knew that's what it would be. I'm very sorry about your father."

"Well, he was consistent," said Alfred.

"How do you mean?"

"I couldn't explain it to you."

"Well—here in my pocket, I had this in my pocket when I was called to the telephone. It's a private present from me to you." St. John handed Alfred a box. "Open it. I want you to see what it says."

Alfred opened the box, in which lay a Vacheron et Constantin watch.

"In the back," said St. John.

" 'Raymond Alfred Eaton—with paternal affection—Eugene St. John—May 20, 1920.' "

"I know you always wear a wrist-watch," said St. John.

"Because I've never had anything as beautiful as this. Thank you. And thank you for the inscription."

"More prophetic than I realized at the time."

Alfred put out his hand, and St. John took it. "And accurate. I don't mean the watch. If I had one for you I'd express the same thought."

"What you've given me is ever so much more. When your daughter is old enough you'll know what I mean."

"I have a watch that my grandfather gave me. I'd like to give it to you."

"I'll take it, on condition I can leave it to you in my will."

"All right." Alfred sat down, holding the Vacheron in both hands.

"You want to be alone. You have every right to be. Are you going to tell Lex about your father?"

"No sir, I'm not. I'm not going to tell anyone but Mary, and not even her till we've left Wilmington."

"When would you like me to tell your sisters?"

"They'll have to know, won't they? Can *you* tell them, after Mary and I've gone? I would like you to tell them yourself, even before you tell Mrs. St. John."

"Alfred, I'm not going to tell Mrs. St. John till after I've told your sisters, I promise you. I understand your reasons."

"I'd just rather have them hear it from you."

"I understand your reasons, and I respect your delicacy. And now—I'll see you shortly." He put his arm around Alfred's shoulder and gripped him tight. "I'm pleased, I'm proud of you."

"Thank you, sir."

St. John went to the door, and had his hand on the knob. "I had one thought. I don't know where you're going on your wedding trip. That's your and Mary's secret. But it's possible that you could be hundreds of miles from here, maybe out at sea, by midnight."

"Yes?"

"And out of touch with everybody. A couple on their wedding trip? Nobody knows where they are?"

"Yes, I think I know what you mean."

"Well, just that you'd have a very good excuse for not going to the funeral."

"I have a better excuse than that, Mr. St. John, but I'm going."

St. John nodded. "You're not a boy. You're a man. Goodbye, son."

Alone, Alfred kept looking at the closed door, which was not a symbol of the man who had just gone through it nor of anything else. It was an inanimate object that was as unstimulating as the shockless news that an hour ago life had ended for his father. His only complete thought on hearing the news was that his father had been consistent; a quick history of his father's relationship with him was contained in Samuel Eaton's inability to be present at his wedding and then his refusal even to be on this earth when the wedding was being solemnized. It was the right and consistent moment for Samuel Eaton to die, a last protest against Alfred's going on living all those years. Samuel Eaton had not taken his own life by a suicidal act, but he had removed himself by his unwillingness to live. It was not foolishness to think these things; Alfred was on a plane of understanding with his father, in which the news of his death, even though it came through Eugene St. John and Martha Eaton (and whoever may have informed Martha Eaton), came to him from his father like a direct message. It was as though his father had said it was not enough to be absent from the wedding; it had to be complete: "I will not even be alive on your big day." He did not accuse his distant dead father of the petty wish to spoil the party aspect of the wedding; it was simpler and bigger than that. He simply did not want to be alive at the moment of the climax of Alfred's personal history. He would never doubt that his father had died deliberately.

"I heard him go. Is there something wrong?" Lex's voice brought Alfred back to the small realities.

"He was very sentimental. He wanted to give me this." Alfred was glad that he had the watch and its presentation to justify his vagueness.

"Say, this is a beauty. My uncle has one something like it.

The old boy must like you, to shell out a thou—whatever this cost."

"A thousand dollars?"

"Close to it."

"Have you got the ring?"

"Sure I have the ring. I have it pinned inside my waistcoat pocket with a safety pin," said Lex. "We have almost four hours. I thought you weren't going to get nervous. What would you like to do? Play some more cards?"

"I'd like to go get Mary and drive away somewhere and skip the whole thing. You marry one of the bridesmaids."

"All right. I'll marry Sally. Although Constance was quite a revelation to me."

"If you're not sure I'd rather have you marry one of the others."

"It'd be nice if I could marry both. How would that look in tomorrow's paper? 'Miss Sally Eaton and Miss Constance Eaton, daughters of Mr. and Mrs. Samuel Eaton, Port Johnson, P A, were married to Mr. Alexander Porter in Wilmington, Delaware, yesterday. It was the social event of the season.' It would be, all right. 'The happy threesome, or happy couple and their husband, departed after the ceremony for a wedding trip in Bermuda.'"

" 'Mr. and Mrs. Porter and Mrs. Porter plan to make their home in Constantinople, where Mr. Porter is an official of the Turkish government. He prepared at Groton School.' It'd be nice if you could have old Peabody marry you."

"Oh, the Rector has to marry all his old boys. That's the only thing standing in the way. If he were here today, if you'd gone to a proper school instead of that jerkwater place you did go to, why old Peabo would be here today, ready to say the magic words."

" 'I pronounce you man and wives.' "

They dropped the joke and Lex began whistling with his tongue on the roof of his mouth. "No more cards?"

"I don't feel like it."

"Well, if we were a little younger we could drop water bombs down on the Wilmingtonians. My sister and I used to do that. What time is lunch?"

"You're supposed to know that. One o'clock. That's just across the way at the Wilmington Club."

"I'm in two more weddings this spring. One in Boston, and the other one in Glen Cove. Emmanuel, and St. John's Lattingtown."

"Emmanuel sounds like a synagogue."

"Well, you can bet your sweet ass it isn't, and St. John's isn't Catholic, in case that was worrying you."

"I never worry."

"No, you have me to do your worrying for you."

"Boy, if I did, then I *would* be worried."

"Well, what *are* you worrying about? You've got some kind of a fig up your ass, ever since old St. John was here."

"I told you, he was very sentimental."

"If you want to know what I think, he was damn inconsiderate to come here and be sentimental now."

"No, don't razz him. He's all right."

"Do you know they have a theater in this hotel?"

"What made you think of that?"

"I saw a billboard and it had an actress's name that I know. I guess she's playing here. Maybe she's staying here, too. She may be lonesome late tonight."

"What are you doing tomorrow?"

"Well, there's a big lunch at somebody's house, and then I guess we're all supposed to scatter to the four winds. I'm going to drive Sally and Constance back to school."

"Oh, you are?"

"That was what we'd planned. Why?"

"And then what?"

"Well, I drop them at school, then I was going to go back to New York by way of Port Johnson. See your family on the way and tell them everything went off according to schedule."

"Lex?"

"What?"

"I've been keeping something back."

"Oh, hell I know that. I've just been waiting to see how long it would take to get it out of you."

"You like my sisters, don't you? I mean as a friend."

"You know that without asking. There's something wrong at home."

"Yes. My father died, a little over an hour ago."

"I'm sorry to hear that, Alfred. Is that what St. John told you?"

"Yes. My sisters don't know it. My mother called Mr. St. John and asked him not to say anything till after the reception."

"Heart attack?"

"I guess so. Now nobody knows but you and I and Mr. St. John. He's going to tell my sisters, after Mary and I get away. Mary doesn't know, either, and I'm not going to tell her till the whole thing's over and we're out of town."

"No, you mustn't tell Mary. It's too bad you have to tell her at all."

"It'll be all right when we're alone, but I don't want anything to spoil today for her."

"Naturally," said Lex. "Then what you want me to do is take the girls back to Port Johnson tonight."

"Would you mind?"

"Listen, that's what I'm here for. How is your mother?"

"I don't know. I haven't spoken to her, because I'm not supposed to know about my father."

"I take it back about St. John. He had to tell you. You're no kid. What about Monday, are you still sailing Monday?"

"No. I'm going to cancel our passage. We're not going to have much of a wedding trip, two nights in New York, but I'll make it up to Mary later."

"Sure you will. Well, now what else can I do?"

"I've been thinking. I'll make out a list of names and who they are, such as Ed Barlow at the mill, he's probably at the farm this minute, taking charge, but names like that. Will you stay at the farm till I get there?"

"Of course I will. Don't you want Uncle Fritz to help out, too? He's very efficient, and after all, he's one of your ushers. He's downstairs now, I'm sure, getting all dolled up. Or else he's over at the Wilmington Club having a pick-me-up."

"I've thought it over, and I'd rather not ask him."

"Well, you know how he feels about you. He insisted on being an usher, and you didn't really *have* to ask him."

"This is different. If you're there, I'll feel all right. Your uncle doesn't really know my family, and he's never been to Port Johnson. *You* know."

"You leave it all up to me," said Lex. He studied his friend. "You know, Alfred, it must be worse for you and me than it is for a guy that really loved his father. If my old man dies I expect to read about it in the paper, but I won't feel anything. Is that the way you are now?"

"A few years ago I would have felt relief. Now I don't even feel that. I'm a little sore at him, that's all. Because—the only one he's really spoiled it for is Mary. Even if she doesn't know it this afternoon, still it's a cloud over the day that's supposed to be the happiest day of a girl's life."

"But she knows all about you and your father. It isn't as if you were made unhappy on your wedding day. A great sorrow and so forth."

"I'm still sore at him."

The telephone rang and Alfred answered it. "Alfred, this is Fritz Thornton. You gentlemen better get over here *toute de suite*. The oldest living usher's dying for a drink, and the man's here to tie your ascots."

"We'll be right over." Alfred hung up. "Your uncle. He said the fellow's there to tie the ascots. I guess we'd better go."

Lex put out his hand. "Well, boy, this is the last chance, I guess. All the happiness in the world to both of you. A wonderful girl, and the best guy *I* ever knew."

"I'll say exactly the same thing when your turn comes."

"Fair enough," said Lex. "Have you got your ascot?"

"I'm not even going to take it out of the box. We can go that far without a tie."

"I don't think Mrs. St. John would like it, but I'm game."

"Mrs. St. John doesn't like a lot of things about today. And she's going to like a lot less before the day is over. Can you just imagine what she's going to say when she finds out my old man died? Why, I could almost like him for that."

The wedding went off according to schedule and as rehearsed. The weather was warm, as it is likely to be in Delaware late in May, and Sage Rimmington, a bridesmaid who had been born and brought up in Delaware, fainted in the bridesmaids' car on the way from the St. John residence to the church, but was revived by the smelling salts that in their cutglass bottle were standard equipment in that model limousine. A fox terrier belonging to a wedding guest found its way to the church and marched up the middle aisle until Donald Tinkham, one of Alfred's ushers, picked it up and carried it out to the street. Zilph du Pont, the only bridesmaid who was taller than Mary St. John, tore off the heel of her right shoe getting out of the second limousine and had to go through the entire ceremony pretending nothing was wrong. James McCready, now without a school, told an usher he was a friend of the bride's in order to be seated on the du Pont side of the church and thereby missed being seated in the pew with Charles M. Schwab, whom he never did recognize. Rowland Culpeper, a second cousin of Mary's mother, let out a loud, double sneeze as the clergyman was uttering the crucial let-him-come-forth warning, to the unanimous amusement of the assemblage. Cynthia Grosscup, whom Mary had picked because there was no way out of it, refused to walk out as briskly as the other couples preceding her and thus divided the exiting wedding party into two parts. One McCallen, chauffeur to James Arthur Hinchcliff of 23 Wall Street, flooded the carburetor of the Hinchcliff Rolls-Royce, causing the Hinchcliffs to accept a lift to the country club in Donald Tinkham's Dodge phaeton, and to sit down heavily on the tire pump which lay on the back seat.

Alfred was well aware that on the next day the men and women who had been guests at the wedding and reception would be recalling, with varying degrees of accuracy, his every expression, his every word, and that they would be wondering how much Mary had known. With the next day in mind he was carefully blank as to expression and dull as to speech.

"Don't *worry*, darling. It only happens once in a lifetime," said Mary, when they started the dancing.

"I can see why."

382

"It'll all be over in two hours and we'll be by ourselves."

"Thank God."

"Yes, thank God. But remember, nobody pays any attention to the groom."

He suddenly kissed her and the hundreds of men and women spontaneously applauded, and from that moment on the reception was a success, and even Mary's mother knew it when Eugene St. John and Alfred changed partners.

"You always ought to wear a cutaway, Alfred. Very becoming. Isn't my little girl a vision, honest and truly?"

"She's all of that and more, Mrs. St. John."

"She spoke up so bravely and courageously, I could hear every syllable. I couldn't always hear you, my dear, but—"

"I said everything I was supposed to say. The minister heard me."

"Harry Kinsolving. He married us, think of it. I've known Harry since I was a little girl. I'da sooner you been married by a justice of the peace if you couldn't get Harry to tie the knot today. That's an expression he uses. Always speaks of it as tying the knot."

"Well, I hope he tied a good one today."

"Why of course he did. There can't be any doubt about *that,* can there?"

"Not in my mind."

"In the heart's where it matters, Alfred."

"And in my heart."

"That's what I wanted to hear. Just you be good to my little girl. I can look around this room right now and see a lot of boys that envy you. Wilmington's gonna miss her, and I don't know what ever I'm gonna do without her. *Having a good time, dear?* Your sister Constance. She's cute. Vivacious, isn't she? Lots of *pep,* the young people say nowadays. You just dance me over to the side now, Alfred." They moved to the edge of the floor. "Beautiful dancer, your new husband," said Mrs. St. John to Mary.

"He's a beautiful everything."

"Oh, now, you don't call a man beautiful. I'm sure no man likes to be called beautiful."

"I do. By Mary."

"You should be calling *her* beautiful, 'cause that's what she is."

"Mary, you're beautiful."

"But say it as if you meant it," said Mrs. St. John.

"I will, later," said Alfred. He knew that the word later would annoy Mrs. St. John, but now there was nothing she could do about that.

Cynthia Grosscup caught Mary's bouquet, knocking off an

older woman's glasses in the effort. When the happy couple were ready to leave, Lex drove the Marmon to the front door of the clubhouse and turned it over to Alfred. The bride and groom, pelted with rice, proceeded quickly out the club driveway and were soon lost in the traffic of the highway.

"Now we can be ourselves," said Mary. "How long will it take us to get to New York?"

"Three or four hours, I guess."

"I wish we weren't going to stay at the Vanderbilt."

"We don't have to stay at the Vanderbilt. I can cancel the reservations and we can go some place else."

"I've stayed there so often with Mother and Daddy."

"Then we'll go some place else."

"Can we? And not one where you've stayed?"

"Not one where I've stayed with another girl?"

"That's what I was thinking. I didn't want to say it."

"Darling, we don't even have to stay in New York. We can stay in Trenton, or Newark. Noork, not New-ark."

"No, I'd like to go to New York, but let's go to another hotel."

"The Waldorf-Astoria. The Astor. The McAlpin."

"Let's go to the Astor."

"All right," said Alfred.

"What are you thinking?" said Mary.

"I was going to stop about a mile back there," said Alfred.

"Where we had our first long talk?"

"Yes."

"Why didn't you?"

"Do you want to go back?"

"No, but what decided you not to stop?"

"I'm in a hurry to be alone with you, in the new life, in a room in a hotel together. Nothing like we've ever been before."

"I liked what we were before."

"So did I, or we wouldn't be here. But I want everything, and you must too, or *you* wouldn't be here."

"But I don't want to talk about it. I want to save everything till we're alone and—and—it's too late to turn back. I don't want to turn back, honestly I don't. But until then I always could, couldn't I?"

"Yes."

"I love you, I want to be in bed with you with all my clothes off and you with all your clothes off. But I guess I want to pretend to be a shy bride. I'm not though. I haven't really thought about anything else for weeks. That day at your house —it's a good thing we got married, a good thing I knew we were going to get married, because you started something. You

384

could have had me any time, all the way, any time since that day. Oh, Alfred, I want you so."

"We're going to stop in Trenton if you don't change the subject. Here." He took her hand and directed it to his erection.

"All right," she said. "Let's talk about—the League of Nations. Do all those people in the League of Nations—no, I'm not going to talk at all. Open up the windshield and maybe the air will purify my thoughts. You loosen your side and I'll loosen this side ... There ... Now you screw your side and I'll screw—I know that word, Alfred. I *know* what it *means*."

"Will you please shut up?"

"Ah, he's embarrassed. My husband is embarrassed, my little innocent husband."

"If you don't stop that we're going to roll into a ditch."

"And would you roll right on top of me?"

"Mary! God damn it. Shall we stop in Trenton?"

"Shall we? No, I'll be good. Let's wait till New York."

She settled in her seat and for a while they said nothing, and then when they came to Trenton he smiled and looked over at her, but she was asleep. He was grateful for her nap. The suddenness of the very words, "roll into a ditch," had postponed the image of Victoria Dockwiler that came inevitably when the sound of the words summoned a meaning from out of the past. He loved Mary, seeing her asleep, but the name Victoria Dockwiler, polysyllabic and half-euphonious, was still a call to misery that had been with him too long to be got rid of through another, present, vital love. The living, sleeping girl who was his wife, and already sharing his life, had put everyone else out of her life. The decent thing was to put everyone else out of his. And now, as he thought these things, he decided not to tell Mary about his father. It could wait till morning; the night as well as the day belonged to Mary.

The car and their luggage and the bellboy's signals to the room clerk made smooth their registration at the Astor and they were given a room on the Times Square side. The noise and the electrical advertising spectaculars made Wilmington and the wedding seem long ago and far away. The bellboy left them and Mary took off her hat and the jacket of her suit. "I forgot to look when you registered. Did you say Mr. and Mrs., or Alfred Eaton and wife?"

"Good form, my dear. Good form. Very bad form to say, 'and wife.' After all, an old Knox School-Princeton boy. I very carefully wrote Mr. and Mrs. Alfred Eaton, Port Johnson, Pennsylvania."

"But I'm not Port Johnson, Pennsylvania."

"I couldn't say Wilmington. Shall I have them send up something to eat? Are you hungry?"

"You're so blasé about this."

"Not if you knew the truth."

"What *is* the truth?"

"That I love you, and I want you more than anything in the world." He held her close to him.

"There's too much light in here," she said. "I'm going to take a bath. I want to unpack, and then take a bath. Why don't you unpack your things?"

"All right, and I'll take a bath, too."

The unpacking was their first intimacy, the separate appearances in bathrobes the next. "Twin beds," she said. "I hadn't thought of that." She stood in the semi-darkness, with only the light from the bathroom for illumination of the bedroom, and looked frowningly at the twin beds, and it was obvious she was disappointed. Suddenly she flung open her bathrobe. "Here I am, Alfred. Am I what you wanted?"

"God, yes. You're beautiful."

She dropped the bathrobe on the floor and stood bare for him to touch her. Then they sat on the edge of one of the beds and she let her curiosity guide her eyes and fingers, and finally she lay back with her head on the pillow and one hand at the back of her neck and watched his every touch and caress, apparently unaware that the deeper and more rapid rise and fall of her breasts was telling him, at least, that her calm sensuality was deceiving her.

Then: "Alfred!"

"Yes, darling."

"I *want* you."

"I know."

"Must I wait? What must I wait for? Can't you put it in me?"

"Yes, and I will."

He entered her easily and slowly, and he was unprepared for the immediate change that occurred, the change from the sensuality of enjoyment of his making love to the ferocity of her embrace and the demand to achieve her climax. The completeness of it was new to her, and as he looked down and kissed her lips gently he saw worry that was almost fear in her eyes.

"You're my love, you're my wife."

"Oh, such joy, but I'm afraid. Am I supposed to feel like that? I lost myself, Alfred. I'm still lost. Feel my heart."

"Feel mine."

"Tell me you'll never go away from me. Oh, my dear. Is that right? It's not—unusual? My whole life is changed, Alfred.

386

Me. Let me look at you, now. I see. That's what happens to you."

"Yes."

"But how does it?"

"Oh—I see you and want you, and the blood rushes there, and the nervous system, and it gets bigger."

"And now can I call it mine?"

"Me? Sure."

"And it isn't unusual for me to feel so completely, so drowned, my finger tips, my face."

"It's the way I want you to feel."

"Passionate, yes. But that much? Darling?"

"What?"

"Will you hand me my hand mirror? On the bureau?"

He brought it to her and she looked at herself. "I expected some lines or something. I don't see anything, except my eyes aren't the same."

"You can't expect them to be. You're a full-fledged woman now."

"Will everybody be able to tell that?"

"No."

"I will. I'll be able to tell. I could tell you now, all my friends that are virgins and those that are not. Oh, dear, I don't think Sage is a virgin. Can you tell?"

"I can only guess."

"Do you think Sage is a virgin?"

"Sage Rimmington? I've never studied her that closely. I might have if I'd been interested but I wasn't interested. But you're not supposed to be a virgin. You're Mrs. Alfred Eaton."

"I never asked you."

"What?"

"Was it as wonderful for you?"

"The most wonderful moment of my life."

"And we can go anywhere in the world and do this. Think of it. We don't have to care where we are, as long as we're together and can go to bed."

"We don't even have to go to bed."

"But I wouldn't like it any other way."

"You'll see."

"It wouldn't have been as perfect on the boat last summer. Or in Port Johnson."

"No, it wouldn't."

"That's the most wonderful thing, that it is so perfect. It isn't always perfect, I know that. Some girls never get any pleasure from it. But they haven't got you for a husband. I'm glad you had a *little* experience. Think of how worried we'd have been if this happened to both of us for the first time.

387

Think how worried I was, and then if you'd been the same way."

"But you're not worried any more? You shouldn't be."

"I'm not afraid any more. Yes, I am, a little afraid. I don't see how I could ever feel that way again."

"You will, though, and without the fear. After a while you'll know you're going to feel that way."

"I don't think so. I was feeling wonderful, then I felt very differently. I thought it was enough to be kissing and touching each other. I knew what else you did, but you wouldn't have had to, until something happened to me and I was like . . ." She did not finish.

"But that's what it is, Mary. And yet different every time. Don't think about it too much. Let's go to sleep."

"I'm too wide awake. You go to sleep and I'll watch over you, to see that the hostile Indians don't come after you. That's what I was like. An Indian. I wonder if I have any Indian blood."

"You might. Pocahontas. Your mother's side."

"I'm going to open the window. I'll put a sheet over you. It's cooler in New York. Would you like something when you wake up?"

"Yes."

"What?"

"You."

"You mean what we just did? Again? You must get some sleep."

"Yes."

"When you wake up come over to my bed. You're almost asleep now. Go to sleep, I'll guard you." She kissed him and he slept, deeply and with no bad dreams.

THE LAND they picked was about thirty miles out from the General Sherman equestrian. The tract, roughly rectangular in shape, was three-quarters of a mile long by half a mile wide, approximately 240 acres. The main axis ran almost due north and south, to take advantage of the prevailing southwest wind. The quoted price was $350 an acre but sold as a unit the price became $85,000, plus 20 percent for the realtor's commission and expenses, and the land thus cost them $102,000 before the outlays for conditioning the surface, plowing and seeding, grading, building an access road of cinder, digging a 250-foot well, and bringing in the electric power and telephone lines, so that they ultimately put $121,100 into the property. They spent $10,300 of that money in converting potato patches into a factory site-landing field, but at least the Nassau Aeronautical Corporation, although it did not own a shack or anything to put in it, was a landowner, and half a dozen Long Island potato farmers took their new cash to Florida to try their luck at growing oranges.

The Nassau Aeronautical Corporation got its name from two sources: it was a compliment to the county, and an appropriate tribute to the university in New Jersey, which was the alma mater of the founders and their principal backers—Alfred Eaton, Lex Porter, and the Thornton brothers. The name was Fritz Thornton's suggestion; alone together Lex and Alfred had discussed other names, such as the Kiwi Aeroplane Company, in honor of the non-flying bird of Australia; the Josephine Flying Machine Company; the Porter & Eaton Buggy Works; the Flying Potato Bug Company; the Long Island Undertaking & Embalming Company; the Pré Catelan Manufacturing Company, in honor of the Thirty-ninth Street cabaret; the Bottoms Up Corporation, and Tailspins, Incorporated. But these titles were not discussed in from of Fritz Thornton. "Levity is not Uncle Fritz's long suit," said Lex. "If he ever thought we were going into it as a big joke we'd never get the money. It's strange, but Uncle Alex has more of a sense of humor than Uncle Fritz."

The Thornton brothers, Fritz and Alex, furnished the capital in the amount of $500,000. "We could get more, we could get a lot more, if I spoke to some friends of mine," said Fritz. "There's a great deal of money lying around loose, boys. War profits. I'm a war profiteer, so's my brother. We'd resent it strongly if anyone called us that, but what else are we? And I can't think of a better thing to do with some of the profits than get you two started in business. Bu that's *my* money, mine and my brother's. I would never ask a friend to put money in this venture. It's risky, we all know that, and if a friend of mine lost money in this corporation, I'd feel almost duty bound to reimburse him, and that really isn't good business, assuming I could *afford* to reimburse him. Let's keep it in the family for the time being, and later on, a couple of years from now, if we want some outside capital and our prospects are better than they are now, we'll be able to get fresh money without any trouble. But for the time being, let's do all our financing ourselves, and let's keep the whole thing on a modest scale. A half a million may not seem like a modest scale, but you're going to find that by the time you've bought your land, put up a few buildings, and got yourselves the equipment you'll need, and saddled yourselves with a payroll—that half a million is going to look smaller and smaller."

In the preliminary talks that took place before Alfred's

marriage and after it, the policies of the Nassau Aeronautical Corporation were established, for good or ill, sink or swim. The purpose of the company was to build a small aeroplane of up-to-the-minute design and highest quality workmanship, built to sell to men who could afford Rolls-Royce automobiles. The financial criterion for the potential buyers was symbolized by the Rolls-Royce for the obvious reason that the Rolls-Royce owner would not be concerned about the price of the aeroplane if he knew he was getting what he wanted. But there was a secondary consideration, introduced by Fritz Thornton: by appealing to the Rolls-Royce market the Nassau Aeronautical Corporation minimized the hazard of bad debts; and a third consideration, introduced by Lex, was that a man who owned one or more Rolls-Royces was quite likely to possess better-than-average mechanical knowledge, and his purchase of an N. A. C. aeroplane would be a testimonial to the quality of the aeroplane. A Rolls-Royce owner either knew motors well or not at all, and they expected to make no sales to men who were ignorant of engines. The policy, then, was to produce a "quality" aeroplane, which would not compete for sales with the Signal Corps—Air Corps surplus aircraft that were on the market, nor with the "assembled" aeroplanes that would be produced by manufacturers who were aiming at a larger market. The term "assembled" was one they borrowed from the automobile industry, and described the hundreds of automobiles of which the Johnson Special had been one, built by manufacturers who did not build their own motors, but bought the motors from Continental and other motor-builders of the time. An "assembled" car was already beginning to be less well thought of than a car produced by a manufacturer who built his own chassis, motor, and body, and the term was becoming slightly opprobrious, despite the fact that there were some good assembled cars, usually distinguished for body design. And despite the opprobrium, an assembled aeroplane was precisely what the Nassau Aeronautical Corporation planned to build.

In line with the policy to produce a high-quality aeroplane, and at the suggestion of Fritz Thornton, they adopted a sub-policy: to erect a first-rate plant and equip it with the best available machinery, tools, and facilities. "When I stop at a garage and see they haven't even bothered to put flooring over the ground, I buy my gasoline and go," said Fritz. "And I often suspect that the gasoline's been watered. I don't subscribe to that theory that some of those ramshackle garages have first-rate mechanics. If they were first-rate they'd have better jobs. You boys want your employees to be proud of their plant. You'll get better work that way. When I go through a stable for the first time I look to see whether the feed pails and water buckets are turned upside down or left sitting there to rot. I look at the tack, I look at the bits, to see if they've been cleaned immediately after they've been used. If the grooms are lazy and slipshod, that's the fault of the trainer, and if the trainer's careless about such things, he'll be careless about other things and I won't buy one of his horses. When you boys have built your factory, don't forget to buy some brooms, and see to it that they're used."

"I hope you don't expect them to find any horse-shit in our plant," said Lex.

"Now, now, Lex. Now, now."

"Sorry, Uncle Fritz. Only fooling," said Lex, but to Alfred he said: "Pegasus. We forgot Pegasus."

"What *about* Pegasus?" said Fritz Thornton.

"Oh, we were discussing names for the company."

"You couldn't find a better name than the one you have. It means something, and it has dignity. Dignity's very important in business."

"Well, that's Alfred's *métier*. Alfred, you're going to have a big laundry bill, two starched collars a day. I expect to be in overalls most of the time."

"I pictured you in a leather coat, and boots and breeches," said Alfred. "The dashing pilot."

"Later, when I have something to fly. Meanwhile, overalls."

"This is all very humorous, Lex, but I hope it doesn't go any deeper than kidding Alfred and me."

"Have no fears. After all, this whole thing was my dream. I'll be serious when the time comes."

"Get into the habit, it's a good thing to get into the habit," said Fritz Thornton.

When they were alone Lex said to Alfred: "My uncle is building another tennis court. This time it happens to be our factory, but it's the same difference."

"He's looking ahead," said Alfred. "If we're a failure, at least we'll have some good buildings and improved land to re-sell."

"I know that, but I wish that instead of putting so much money into a show-place factory, he'd spend a little less now and let us have the cash to spend on building an aeroplane. You wait and see, we're going to have rose bushes and an American flag and all that stuff. I know the architect, Ken Englander. He did my uncle's tennis court."

"Well, the tennis court *is* a little bit like a hangar," said Alfred.

"So it is, but Englander wouldn't know how to build a log cabin. He's built some log cabins—in the Adirondacks, for millionaires, and I've been to them. But he couldn't build one for Abraham Lincoln. And he couldn't build the kind of plant we ought to have to start with."

"Well, it's your uncle's money," said Alfred. "What I'm just a little worried about is when does it stop being his money and start being ours?"

"Yes. I wish he'd go abroad. Maybe we can get him to go abroad. We don't want this to turn into a sort of hobby for him. I'm going to have to impress it on him that we want to do this ourselves."

"Good. That's what I've been wanting to say, but it had to come from you first. After a certain point, we want to make our own mistakes."

"Well, maybe that certain point is now."

They had not credited Fritz Thornton with sufficient intelligence and sensitivity. Before they could plan their strategy he summoned them to his office. "I don't know what you boys have been thinking," said Fritz Thornton. "I don't know whether you've been disturbed by my interest, or maybe you'd call it interference. Or maybe you've been counting on me to pilot you through these dangerous shoals. But in any case, whether you've been annoyed, or counting on me too much, from now on my brother and I are going to pursue a policy of hands-off. If you want to ask anything, all right. But my brother and I've had several conversations and we've decided that from now on you're going to have to get along without our help, or interference, whichever you're pleased to call it.

"I have here a blueprint, metaphorically speaking. It isn't an actual blueprint, as you can see. It's a plan of our financial structure, the financial structure of the Nassau Aeronautical Corporation.

"Alfred, I have you down for $35,000 worth of common stock. Lex, the same. Your designer, Lawrence B. Von Elm, $3,000. Mr. Edmund Barlow, of Eaton Iron & Steel, $1,000. Miss Mary M. McIlhenny, my secretary, $1,000. And my brother and I, $12,500 apiece or $25,000. That comes to a total of $100,000, or a thousand shares at a hundred dollars a share.

"Now then, I will hold a mortgage on the plant for $200,000. I will also purchase $100,000 worth of ten-year debentures, which will give you that much operating cash. A debenture is something like a bond, but it isn't a bond. In this case it is money I lend the corporation, unsecured. I already have a $200,000 mortgage, which of course *is* secured, but these debentures are a technical term for saying I have put up $100,000 without getting stock or bonds in return. I am lending you money without acquiring any more controlling interest than I have in my $12,500 worth of stock.

"You understand, of course, that my brother and I are in effect giving you each $35,000. We are also in actuality giving Mr. Von Elm $3,000, and the same is true of Mr. Barlow's

392

stock and Miss McIlhenny's stock. We are doing this because we want Mr. Barlow to look out for Alfred's interests, which he would be doing anyway because of his position at the Eaton Iron & Steel mill, and because he is an executor of Mr. Samuel Eaton's estate.

"I think you ought to know, Alfred, that your father-in-law, Mr. Eugene St. John, for whom by the way I have the highest admiration, came to me several weeks ago and wanted to invest a rather large sum in the corporation. He did that because he wanted to show his confidence in you, and he asked me at the time not to say anything to you, but I am taking the liberty of violating his confidence in me, his confiding in me, I should say—because I think as a young husband you ought to know that your father-in-law approves of you. Ahem. I declined his offer because I thought you would prefer to have this whole thing on your side of the family, meaning Porter and Thornton and Eaton, since as you know we regard you as one of our family. I promised him that later on, if and when we go looking for fresh capital, he will be one of the very first we go to. But I liked his making the offer, and I liked the way he did it."

"Very complimentary, and thank you for telling me," said Alfred.

"You're very welcome," said Fritz Thornton. "Now we come to the officers. If there is no objection, the officers of the corporation are as follows: president and treasurer, Alfred Eaton; vice-president, Lex Porter; secretary, my lawyer and my brother's lawyer, Mr. Charles C. McDonald, of Pickett, McKinstry, Livingston, Chase and McDonald. And assistant-secretary and treasurer, who will have the power to sign corporation cheques, the accountant, Mr. Joseph W. Stauffer. Those are the officers. The directors will be you, Alfred, Lex, Charley McDonald, my brother, and myself. Desirable to have an odd number, and that's why my brother will be on our board.

"As you readily see, Alfred, the officers and directors are predominantly Thorntonian and Porterian, but I think we overcome that to some extent by having you president and treasurer."

"I still think Lex ought to be president and I vice-president."

"We've gone over that before, and you're overruled," said Lex. "I don't want to be president."

"It's the fair way to do it, Alfred," said Fritz Thornton. "You're doing Lex and all of us a favor. The corporation was Lex's idea, but it never would have got beyond the idea stage if we hadn't been able to count on you. He'd never have gone in with a stranger. No, don't think we're handing you anything on a silver platter. There'll be times when you'll wish we hadn't done you this so-called favor. I frankly wouldn't have gone into it without you. Lex knows that. So there we are, and there you are, on your own, gentlemen. I will now take you over to 60 Pine Street and offer you some steamed clams. Later on, when you're big aeronautical magnates, you may want to be members there, so I might as well introduce you to a few fellows."

"Uncle Fritz prides himself in never being more than ten blocks from one of his clubs."

"That's a slight exaggeration. Between here and the Princeton Club is much more than ten blocks, and I have nothing in between."

"Why, Uncle Fritz, yes you have."

Thornton gave his nephew a stern, over-the-eyeglasses look. "I suppose you're referring—Lex is referring to a very informal club that you could hardly call a club. Is that what you're referring to, Lex?"

"The Boys Club. Yes."

"You can tell by the name of it that it's very informal, Alfred. It's nothing more than a flat, third story of a house in East Twenty-fifth Street."

"Of all your clubs, it's my favorite," said Lex.

"You're not even supposed to know it exists, let alone talk about it, but since you've mentioned it I'll have to explain to Alfred what it is. A few of us, twenty-five fellows including myself, wanted to have a place where we could go that wouldn't be one of the general run of clubs. I'm a bachelor, of course, but most of the other fellows are married and one of the conditions—I shouldn't be telling this to a newly married man—but one of the conditions is that none of the wives should be told that this place exists. We have a secret telephone number. We have a kitchen where we can scramble eggs and brew coffee, if we like. A refrigerator. Do all our own cooking and serve our own drinks. We have a colored woman comes in every afternoon to dust and put things in order—"

"Make the beds."

"There's a room with two beds, cots, really. But don't get the wrong idea about *that*."

"No, don't get the wrong idea about that, Alfred," said Lex. "Don't let my uncle fool you into thinking—"

"Now, now, now, Lex. No more of that, please."

"You were going to tell him all about it."

"The cots were put in in case a member imbibed too freely. And we've had some all-night poker games. If the cots have been used for other purposes, I officially don't know about it. I'm a bachelor, and I never have that problem. If I want to entertain a lady I can always have her to my house. Or, there are always the hotels. And by the way, always go to the first-class hotels, always take a suite, and never register as Mr. and

394

Mrs. unless, of course, you happen to be with your wife. But a first-class hotel will never embarrass you if you take a suite. On the other hand, never have a woman in your room when you've only registered for yourself. Hotels are first of all interested in making money, and they don't like to be cheated out of the double rate. I have all this information from a fellow in the hotel business, but I suppose I'm not telling you anything new, you two. I'm sure there are a lot of things *you* could tell *me*."

"Not many," said Lex.

"Hmm. I gather that your apartment on Gramercy Park is a howling success. That's all I'll say about *that*, Mr. Porter."

"There won't be as much howling from now on. I expect to come home every night, carrying my lunch pail, and drop off to sleep like an innocent babe."

"*With* an innocent babe, is more like it," said Fritz Thornton. "But I hope you mean that. If you're determined to work, if you get off to a good start, this venture will have a positive effect on the rest of your lives. There will be discouragement, difficulties, even differences between the two of you, but I'm banking on your enthusiasm and good common sense. Just remember that every day you're going to learn something that will be of value to you in later life, even the mistakes. Or especially the mistakes. As you both know, I happen to think that the day of the aeroplane is a long ways off, but last year when those Navy fellows got all the way to the Azores—well, I may be wrong. I've taken losses before when I've been wrong. This time I stand to take a profit by being wrong, and that's never an unpleasant prospect. I know Joe Stauffer is a good accountant, he hasn't long to go before he's a C. P. A. And I like what I've seen of your Mr. Von Elm. A trifle eccentric, perhaps, but heavens, the things I hear about this fellow Steinmetz, and Henry Ford himself. And we've had two terms of an eccentric in the White House and we still managed to win the greatest war in history. He graduated before I entered Princeton, but I've met him half a dozen times. Sarcastic, arrogant—and a hypocrite, you know. People voted for him thinking he was a stiff-necked Presbyterian, but he was anything *but*. However, the poor son of a bitch is paying for his mistakes today, and no use maligning him any more than we have to."

"No, just malign him a little bit for luck," said Lex.

His uncle shook his head. "Lex, I hope I'm wrong, but sometimes I think you're deliberately trying my patience. It's really time you got to work. Alfred, you've got to watch out for this fellow."

"He's pretty frisky sometimes, but I know when to use a tight rein."

"Tight reins are passé. Hereafter it's throttles."

"All right, Pegasus," said Alfred.

The partners had agreed that neither would sign up a man whom the other strongly objected to—"could not stand the sight of"—and Alfred nearly invoked the terms of the agreement on his first meeting with Lawrence B. Von Elm, who was Lex's choice for head designer. Lex had known Joe Stauffer through Fritz Thornton and had no objection to him, and Alfred accepted him on Thornton's recommendation. But Von Elm had almost seemed determined to make a bad impression on Alfred Eaton, and as a consequence the Nassau Aeronautical Corporation nearly missed signing a very good workman. Lex had already had several interviews with Von Elm and was enthusiastic about the man and his qualifications, and all that remained before final arrangements was Alfred's approval.

The two men met at the Princeton Club without Lex in attendance, and the first word that came into Alfred's mind as the club servant escorted Von Elm to Alfred's chair was "dowdy." Von Elm wore a double-breasted brown suit with slashed pockets and high peaked lapels, a striped shirt and detachable soft collar, and high laced shoes that were as pointed as his lapels. Across his waistcoat was a watch-chain fashioned of small gold bars, from which hung the Tau Beta Pi key, and pinned under the upper left-hand pocket was the badge of a Greek letter fraternity which consisted largely of seed pearls. The man himself was fairly tall and bony, about five feet ten in his rubber-heeled shoes, but weighing no more than a hundred and forty pounds, fully clothed. He had a mop of brown hair brushed back in a pompadour, an irregular bony nose and a bony chin that would have been all right except for a neglected dental malocclusion, which caused the chin to recede.

Alfred rose to greet him, and although Alfred extended his hand, it was not taken. "Shall we have a drink?" said Alfred.

"I don't drink," said Von Elm.

"Well, then, shall we go downstairs and have a bite to eat?"

"I ate on the train coming over, but you go ahead."

"I will, if you don't mind. I'm hungry. We can talk while I eat."

Nothing more was said until Alfred had ordered his liver and bacon whereupon Von Elm passed a small piece of paper across the table.

"Those are my expenses. My railroad fare and lunch on the train. I like to eat on trains. I don't often get the chance to. The rest, I have it down there. I phoned here to make sure you were here, or they'd most likely keep me out of an exclusive club like this. Five cents. Two cents for the paper. I get the paper delivered at home, but I left before it was delivered. Cross it out if you don't think I'm entitled to it."

"Do you want the money now?"

"Might as well, I guess."

Alfred put down his fork and counted out $7.77 and put it on the table in front of Von Elm, who added it without touching it, and then put it in a snap purse.

"I guess Porter told you all about me," said Von Elm.

"Not all, I don't think."

"All right. I was born in Greensburg, P A, fourteen October eighteen-and-ninety-six, and attended grade school till we moved to Pittsburgh. Graduated Fifth Avenue High School. Attended Penn State, graduated second in class—English pulled me down or I'd have been first—with a B. S. in M. E. Do you want to know what I studied?"

"Anything you want to tell me," said Alfred.

"Well, Kinematic Drafting, Drafting and Machine Design, General Machine Design, Kinematics of Machinery, using Barr's *Kinematics* and Mechanics of Machinery, using Barr and Kimball's *Elements of Machine Design.* Also, Elementary Mechanics, using Church's *Mechanics of Engineering.* Engineering Materials, using Johnson's *Materials of Construction.* Testing Materials, using both Johnson and Church, and that of course included the testing of wood under various conditions in which they may be subjected to stress."

"I see."

"I haven't finished."

"Well, maybe we'd better skip over the textbooks. I wouldn't recognize any of the names. I didn't go very far in college."

"As you prefer. When the war came I enlisted in the Navy, not to ride on boats, but I wanted to get in on the work they were doing at M. I. T., and I did. I was commissioned ensign in February nineteen-and-eighteen, and I finished up as lieutenant junior grade in December the same year. You will want to know what I've done since then. Nothing. They thought I had T. B., but they were wrong. I didn't. But my parents made me stay with an aunt who lives in Hazleton, P A, because that's near White Haven, supposed to be good for people who have T. B. My father is a conductor on the Pennsylvania Railroad and he spent a lot of money on my education, but I saved a little money in the Navy, and my mother supplied the rest so I could loaf for over a year."

"But I understand you didn't loaf."

"Well, I wasn't earning any money. All going out, nothing coming in. I call that loafing."

"Oh, do you?"

"Yes, what do *you* call it?"

"In your case I wouldn't have called it loafing. My partner

397

tells me you were actually working like hell on some aeroplane designs."

"I couldn't even sell them to *Popular Mechanics*," said Von Elm. "I'm not trying to give you the impression that I was a poor boy. We always had enough to eat and a nice place to live, and my father's always been very well thought of. But after you've been given a college education your parents have a right to expect you to earn your own living and spend their money on themselves, and all the time I was in Hazleton that bothered me."

"You're very conscientious."

"Yes, I am," he said with finality. "I'm never going to take another cent from my parents. Well, I won't have to. You're going to pay me $100 a week and that's a lot of money. I'll save half of it. And you're going to give me stock, $3,000 worth that I can't sell to anybody but the corporation. I'm rich, or will be as soon as we start work. When do we start work?"

"When do you go on the payroll? The first of October."

"Then I'm to consider myself hired, or do you want to ask me some more questions?"

"I'll probably think of some more questions after you leave, but I'll say yes, you can consider yourself hired."

"Will you write me a letter to that effect? I'd like to have something in writing. Then I'll write you and you'll have something in writing, just an agreement on my part not to take another job. I'll have to let the other people know."

"Oh, there were some other people?"

"Mr. Eaton, I don't think you realize! I have four other offers waiting for me to let them know."

"Well, good for you."

"Crimmy, yes. I could have gone to work any time, but I've been waiting for the job with the best prospects, not just the pay, but what I want to do. I could go with the Ford Motor Company, but they wouldn't let me do anything on my own. It's all Mr. Stout out there. I'm going with you for two reasons. First, I'll start as head designer and I can work out my own plans without interference."

"And what's the second?"

For the first time Von Elm smiled. "It has partly to do with you."

"Me?"

"Do you remember lending a fellow some money about four years ago?"

"I lent quite a few fellows some money."

"Tom Rothermel."

"Oh, sure. Do you know Tom?"

"He's a fraternity brother of mine. He's a good kid."

"I see. You're coming with us because I lent Tom some money?"

"No, not exactly. It wasn't you lending him the money. It was Porter giving money to a young fellow he never even saw. When I answered Porter's ad I remembered right away where I knew that name from. It wasn't only the money, but the way he did it. And it wasn't only the uh, generosity. What's a few dollars to a fellow like Porter? But the impulse, that's it. The impulse. A fellow that would do that, he's not going to sit around trying to make up his mind if I have a good idea. He'll either say yes or no, right away, and most likely yes."

"You're pretty good at analyzing people."

"Better than you think. I have to go now. Have to buy my mother a present. Where would be a good place to buy her something?"

"That depends. Lord & Taylor's are near here. B. Altman. Franklin Simon. All those stores are just a few blocks from here. Or R. H. Macy, on your way to the train. Or Tiffany's is right near here, Thirty-, uh, -seventh Street I think it is."

"That'll have to wait till five years from now, when I pick out a wife. I'll write you my letter tonight when I get home."

"I'll write ours this afternoon, but you won't get it for a couple of days till after I've shown it to our lawyer. You understand that, of course. I can't be as impulsive as my partner."

"I guess that's what they call a dig, but I guess I deserve it. So long, Eaton."

"So long."

Alfred was not pleased with himself over the handling of the interview. He had almost immediately decided to oppose the hiring of Von Elm; then when Von Elm asked when he would go on the payroll, Alfred found himself committing the firm, and as he thought back over the interview he did not know which instinct to trust. Later in the afternoon he expressed his uneasiness to Lex in a detailed report of the meeting. "Before I knew it, I had him signed."

Lex laughed. "That happened to me, too. Of course I saw him oftener than you did, but I practically signed him up the first time I talked to him. Or he talked to me. You don't expect a guy that looks like him to hit you like a tornado. It's a good thing he's honest. He'd make a good salesman for crooked stock."

"I guess I expected more humility."

"None. One of the times I saw him he brought over some sketches, and I damn near ended up calling him sir. 'Now Porter, how familiar are you with the work of Charles L. Lawrance, that's L, a, w, r, *a*, n, c, e.' I said I was afraid the name meant very little to me. 'Well, he's one of your competitors and he's an expert on air-cooled engines. Find out all you can about Lawrance and what he's doing.' He practically ordered me to start taking a course in draftsmanship, and when I told him I was already doing that he slapped me on the shoulder and said, 'Good work, good work.' We don't have to like this fellow, Alfred. Mary wouldn't be able to stand him, and Mr. Gould won't be playing tennis with him. But he's what we want. In fact, he's so much what we want that I'm in favor of giving him more stock."

"Let's wait. And don't forget, we're what he wants, too. He may be good, I suppose he is, but you can be damn sure the Ford company didn't offer him $100 a week. That's a hell of a lot of money for an unproven genius."

"Unproven genius. That's pretty good, Alfred."

"Oh, as Al Jolson says, I have my moments. Are you going to be able to see Englander today?"

"Yes."

"Do you know what the main building is going to cost us, according to Englander?"

"No idea."

"Forty thousand dollars."

"Does that include the rose bushes?"

"No, nor the flagpole. It's too late, now, but I have my doubts about Englander. Not about his ability. As far I can see, he's a good architect. But I wish he didn't know that Thornton money was behind this. For instance, we're going to use stoves to heat the building, which is okay, but when I asked him about it he said, 'Well, if they don't work out next winter we can put in a furnace and heating lines in the spring.' Jesus, Lex, I know we're going to make changes as we go along. Some day we're going to have to expand. Your uncle took those options on the land that borders ours. But I'd like to be able to say the building costs us so-much and forget about it for a couple of years anyway. Then we'd know pretty closely how much money *you* can spend. Englander seems to think, 'Oh, well, there's plenty more where that came from.' I have to watch him."

"I enjoy this, seeing you the business man."

"I must get it from my grandfather."

"Not your father?"

Alfred shook his head. "No, my father was a production man. My grandfather, on my mother's side, was a business man. I don't think my father was a very good business man. At least my grandfather never thought so."

Lex was silent.

"What?" said Alfred.

"I wish I hadn't gone to Princeton. I wish I hadn't gone to Groton."

"Why, you *had* to go to Groton. No place else."

"I know what you mean. But I wish instead of there I'd have gone to public high school and Cornell, or M. I. T., or one of those places. If I'd gone to a high school I'd have taken manual training and courses like that, and then studied engineering at college. But nobody in my family ever thought anything about it, the fact that *I* was the one that fixed the doorbell, not the butler. Or that I used to when I was a kid get five Meccano sets and fill the playroom with my inventions. Rube Goldberg inventions, but I loved it. Another boy and I that lived across the street from us had a telegraph wire from his house to mine, and then the cops made us take it down. I learned the old Morse code before they changed it. I don't know whether I'd have been any good, but my family just took it for granted that I'd go to Groton School and Princeton and nobody ever paid any attention to what I liked. I didn't even pay much attention to it myself, because when the boy across the street moved away I didn't have anyone else to build things with. Uncle Alex *sort of* encouraged me. At least he was the one that gave me the Meccanos. But he was always shy and interested in art, and Uncle Fritz was the one that I spent the most time with. Taught me to swim and play tennis and ride, shoot, had me take boxing lessons. I guess Uncle Alex is a fairy, and Uncle Fritz didn't want me spending too much time with him. Afraid I might turn out the same way."

"I guess he doesn't worry about that any more."

"No, but I sure did waste a lot of time practicing my half volley, when I could have been learning something about stresses. This Von Elm makes me feel like an ignoramus."

"Yes, but when he makes his pile he won't know how to enjoy it. He'll *never* be able to go to the net."

"Maybe he'll never want to."

"No sir, you're absolutely wrong. In six months from now Von Elm will be getting his clothes from Brooks Brothers, and five years from now he's going to want to get in the Racquet Club. I think I know Mr. Von Elm. You look at his clothes. They're awful, but they're not awful where he comes from. I'm sure he thinks he's a snappy dresser. He cares about those things. And his remark about the exclusive Princeton Club. If he was one of those real geniuses he wouldn't give a damn about whether the Princeton Club was exclusive—or the Princeton Club. And liking to eat in Pullman diners. Oh, he may be very good at his work, but I'll bet you he misses the things that you had and to some extent

I had. I hope he's good. We need him. But I'll make you a small bet that in six months he's going to hint around to meet your family."

"He already has. 'I'd like to meet your folks,' he said."

"What did you tell him?"

"What could I? I took him to the house and introduced him to Mother. He didn't see much of her because she left the room immediately. Took for granted that the only reason I'd bring *him* to the house would be to talk business. Then Elizabeth came in and I introduced him to *her*. Oh, and did he get horny for her? That's the only way to describe it. Staring at her legs and trying to get a little peek every time she crossed them, and trying to stand up close to her. My sister! She was the one that described him as horny."

"I'm surprised she knows the word."

"Elizabeth? She knows *all* the words—and what they mean. Elizabeth has some books in her room that she had to get through a doctor. Stuff so raw that—well, anyhow. Von Elm. 'That was quite a specimen,' she said. She didn't like him any better than you did, and you don't often agree with Elizabeth."

"No."

"Well, I don't *like* him myself. I probably dislike everything about him with the exception of the thing we want him for, and it may be a good thing all around. If he wants to call me Porter, I guess that's all right. When he starts calling me Lex, I'll just go on calling him Von Elm till he gets the hint. We'll excuse a lot to get a good man, and I'm convinced he's good. He knows more about what makes aeroplanes fly than anybody our age I've ever met, and he has ideas how to make them fly better. Well, with my ideas and experience, and his ideas and theory, we ought to be in the air a year from now with a ship that will get off the ground quickly, maneuver well without being too sensitive and lose a wing or go into a spin with an amateur at the stick, and land not too fast. And as soon as that ship is in the air we'll start working on the refinements."

"Ugh. Shudder."

"Why shudder?" said Lex. "You're not going to fly it unless you want to."

"Cost is what I was thinking about. Why don't you set an objective, this ideal plane, and then freeze the design while we go out and try to sell a few?"

Lex looked at him angrily. "We'll never do that! Never! Freeze the design? If we sell an aeroplane in, say, November, 1921, and another one in December, 1921, the December one may be so different that you wouldn't recognize it as coming from the same maker."

"Oh, listen, boy, that isn't the way to do business. You and I have to have some heart-to-heart talks about manufacturing,

I can see that. Granted that we're going to build a quality aeroplane, let's not think we're going to build custom-made aeroplanes. I don't care how much we charge for the aeroplane, we're not going to start making money till we can produce it in some quantity, even if it is a small quantity. We ought to build next November's aeroplane and manufacture it, produce it, till we have, say, fifty sold. A year later we manufacture the new model, with all those refinements you speak of. We don't sit around waiting for some guy to come and ask us to build a special ship for him. We make fifty and sell them. I should think that would be exactly what you'd want to do. If we sell fifty of the November 1921 model, we'll be established in business, which is what I want, but more than that, there'll be fifty men flying that model and giving us reports on it good and bad. That way we may lose some money, or even make a little, but all the time learning how good or bad our aeroplane is, and not learning at our expense, or on the drawing-board. Lex, you're not going to be able to do as much testing on Long Island as fifty guys all over the country, I don't care how much time you spend in the air."

"Jesus H. Christ! Are we going to build Dodges? I thought we were going to build a fine aeroplane."

"I hope we are, but not one by one. If we do it the way you seem to think we ought to, every aeroplane we make is going to cost more than the last one. We'll never make a profit on a basic design. And what's wrong with building Dodges? If we could build a thousand fine aeroplanes and sell them, I wouldn't object."

"You mean have a 1921 model, and a 1922 model, and a 1923 model?"

"Well, I won't go that far. But not a November model and then a December model, and a first-two-weeks-in-January model and a second-two-weeks-in-January model. It'll take a year to find out how really good or bad a model is."

"Or one flight."

"I don't agree with you. An aeroplane that will crack up in one flight—I don't expect you and Von Elm to ask me to sell that kind of an aeroplane."

"Thank you," said Lex, sarcastically.

"Oh, you're more than welcome. I'm glad we got on this subject now. If you and Von Elm want to run an experimental station and aren't interested in selling the aeroplane, you don't need somebody to run the business end. All you need is an inexhaustible bank account, and there aint no such animal. If I'm correct in my understanding of what you and apparently Von Elm want to do, your uncles' half a million won't last us a year. And believe me, old boy, I don't relish the prospect of sitting in an office just to say no to you guys when you want to spend some more money. We have to spend money, sure. But I'd like to be able to see a time when we begin making some. It doesn't have to be next year—it couldn't be—or the year after. But the way you and Von Elm are looking at it now, the time when we begin to make money will be never. And it's just as well I'm finding that out now. And I mean now, this afternoon, before we see Englander. I'm not going to authorize spending $40,000 of your uncles' money—and that's only a drop in the bucket—if you and Von Elm are never going into *business*."

"It's my uncles' money that's worrying you."

"It is indeed. But it's also running a business as though it were the Navy or the Army, where they spend money that isn't theirs, and all they have to do to get more is ask for it. Well, I'd never ask anybody for another nickel if I knew in my heart that we were never going to show a profit. Incidentally, I notice that whenever I mention Von Elm you don't deny that he feels the same way as you do."

"We're in agreement."

"Well, in that case, Lex, I better go home and tell the old lady her old man's out of a job. But first of all I'll have to cancel our appointment with Englander."

"You're not sore at me, I hope."

"No, I'm not sore at you. I'd have been God *damn* sore if I found this out a year from now. This way, all I have to do is transfer my stock back to your Uncle Fritz."

"You do that and it means the end of the Nassau Undertaking & Embalming Corporation."

"Not necessarily. You ought to be able to find another president-and-treasurer."

"Necessarily, yes, necessarily. You're doing exactly what my uncle wanted you to do, and if you're not there to do it, he'll withdraw. I don't say he'll withdraw his money. He wouldn't do that. But there'll never be any more. If I know him he'll give me your stock and his own and have nothing more to do with the corporation."

"Well, that may be what you want."

"You know better than that."

"I didn't mean that you wanted to ease me out. I only meant that it would be more desirable from your standpoint to have a sort of aeronautical laboratory instead of a business. Hell, you might be able to get contracts to *do* experimental work and that would be fun for yōu *and* for Mr. Von Elm. A lot of big companies do that, and you may be starting a new industry. But that isn't what I went in on. I went in on a manufacturing enterprise, and I guess you didn't. The manufacturing side of it was something you never paid much attention to."

404

"You're a production man like your father and a business man like your grandfather. See, the two *can* be combined."

"If that's sarcasm, I can be sarcastic, too. You're still playing with those Meccano sets."

"Oh, go fuck yourself."

"Oh, go play with your fucking doorbells. Do you know what your trouble is? That boy that lived across the street, the telegrapher—he's back again under the name of Lawrence B. Von Elm. I'd better go before we start punching."

"Maybe you had, because I sure feel like punching this minute," said Lex. "Where are you going from here?"

"To the phone and cancel our date with Englander, unless you'd rather. Or maybe you'd like to keep the appointment. It's your firm, and your uncles' money. Then I'm going home."

"I'll keep the appointment with Englander."

"All right, good luck. Do you want to be there when I talk to your uncle? I can't just write him a letter, and I'd much rather have your present when I tell him why I'm resigning."

"You don't have to be quite so open and above-board. I don't think you're going to malign me."

"I might malign you. You're not Woodrow Wilson."

"Neither are you, but you think you are."

"Oh, all right. I'll go see your uncle right away."

"At this hour he will be at the Racquet Club, East Court," said Lex, elaborately looking at his wrist-watch.

Alfred left Lex at their office, a half-furnished single room in a brick building in Forty-second Street near Third Avenue, and another reminder of the help they had been getting from the Thorntons: the building, once a private residence, had been converted into store and offices while the owners, the Thornton brothers, still waited for the favorable price that had not been offered after the opening of Grand Central Terminal ten years ago. Alfred was not "sore" at Lex; he would not admit to that to Lex; he was angry and fed up but he would not even to himself admit that it was such a childish thing as being "sore." The truth was that no other ready word described it. He was sore. Already Von Elm and Lex obviously had been excluding him from policy discussions, and apparently Lex himself had long been planning in his own mind independently of Alfred, relegating him to a desk in a corner of a plant that was not even built, and to the thankless role of bookkeeper. In his anger as he walked to the Racquet Club he thought of the plans they had made together: Alfred was to learn to fly an aeroplane; Lex was to be present in all business transactions and keep acquainted step-by-step with all of Alfred's decisions, expenditures, and economies. Ideally either partner would be able to take over in the event of accident or illness to the other. Plainly, Alfred had been kept in the dark while Lex and Von Elm played with their Meccano set.

Quietly and unobserved he stepped into the *dedans* and watched the match between Fritz Thornton and a neat little man with close-cropped grey hair and a thin moustache. The marker, a shiny-faced young Irishman, called out, "Chase better than a yard," and Fritz Thornton, who was serving, had his work cut out for him. The chase was played off and Fritz Thornton won and his concentration relaxed. He frowned and peered into the *dedans* where Alfred was half hidden by the protective ropes. "Is that you, Alfred?" he said.

"Yes sir."

"I thought it was you, but this fellow had me hopping. Mr. Warren, Mr. Eaton."

Alfred went out and shook hands with Fritz Thornton's opponent. "Howdia do," said Warren. "Do you play this noble game?"

"I've started to," said Alfred.

"So have I, by the look of things today. Or maybe I've finished. Fritz, you never used to beat me. Now you've beaten me the last four times we've played, and when that happens it's time I gave up the God damn game. How do you play against this fellow, Mr. Eaton?"

"Oh—he beats me all hollow. I don't even know how to score yet."

"You *must* learn to score," said Warren. "You young fellows that are just starting, you all say, 'Oh, let the marker do the scoring.' But you *mustn't*. It isn't all that difficult, and scoring affects your strategy, you know. This game is all strategy and a good wrist."

"Well, I don't think I'll ever be very good," said Alfred.

"Alfred's a better than average lawn tennis player," said Fritz Thornton. "Usually beats me in straight sets."

"Oh, lawn tennis has so little to do with this game, they ought to change the name of lawn tennis to something else. They never should have stolen our name." Warren looked up at the wall clock. "Fritz, I'm terribly sorry, but I'm going to have to take my shower and run along."

"Play tomorrow? Same time?"

"No, I'm going back to Boston tonight. I'll write you a note when I'm coming to New York again. Have some doubles? You get Pierre and someone else. Goodbye, Mr. Eaton. Sorry to rush."

"Anything in particular you want to see me about, Alfred?"

"Yes there is."

"Wait for me downstairs. You might order me a dry Martini cocktail. I won't be long, but you get us a table on the Fifty-third Street end, where we won't be bothered. Is Lex coming?"

"No sir."

"I see," said Fritz Thornton. "Well, give me ten minutes."

It was longer than ten minutes and it was an additional three minutes from the moment Fritz Thornton entered the bar, paused on his way to greet and be greeted, and seated himself at their table. "No matter what they want to say about this club, they do serve a man-sized Martini cocktail. I understand they do at the University Club, too, but I never go to their bar. Fellow I don't care to run into, there morning, noon and night. Wanted to name me co-respondent. Would have had one hell of a time narrowing it down to me, I'll tell you . . . Hello, Ben. Don't sit down, Ben. We want to talk. Mush along now, like a good boy . . . How did you like Jack Warren?"

"I guess he's a typical Bostonian," said Alfred. "I liked him, what I saw of him."

"Oh, he's all that. Porcellian Club, and a fine all-around athlete. A little more height and some beef on him he'd have been one of the great athletes of our day. He's sixty-five or -six years old."

"He doesn't look forty."

"Oh, he looks forty. But he doesn't look *fifty*. But whatever his age, he was with the French army for four years. Croix de Guerre with two palms and up for the Medaille Militaire. No, he's not a *typical* Bostonian, but I don't know what that is. They're all the same till you begin to know a little bit about them, then I couldn't imagine a group of men more individualistic than they are. Has so much money, some of the finest paintings—he's really a friend of my brother's. I'm only a friend of his for games. *And* food. *And* wine. Likes good food and a great judge of wines, a little partial to Bordeaux. He has a mistress here in town."

"At sixty-five?"

"Oh, he had a little French bastard at sixty, the story goes. The wife of a man very well situated in the Ministry of Munitions. Young woman, late twenties, early thirties. Husband in his late forties, never thought old Jack had anything left. But Jack got his end in, as they say. Everybody in Paris knew about it, but the Frenchman stayed married to her because if he kicked her out that would be an admission that he was cuckolded by a little American runt. But everybody knew about it. I heard all about it here when it happened. My brother keeps up a voluminous correspondence with friends in Paris. I must say it amused Alex. Did me, too."

He tapped the bell on the table. "The Martini cocktail was not invented to quench a man's thirst, was it? I had a bottle of ginger ale while I was dressing, but I'm still thirsty." The waiter did not come to their table, but at Fritz Thornton's nod went to the bar for more drinks, which took place without an interruption of Fritz Thornton's monologue, and which Alfred was reluctant to break into. "Jack Warren is one of those Bostonians who love their town, but have to get away. Some of them can satisfy that need by coming to New York two or three times a year. Jack, of course, comes a little oftener. They come down here and see some different faces, but not *too* different, mind you. The men they see in New York usually turn out to be Harvard men and members of the same final clubs, or they're men the Bostonians have met through sailing, or buying pictures. The women they see— well, either the wives of their men friends, or the kind of women we have in New York and just no place else in the United States. Mistresses, semi-mistresses. I suppose there must be some in Chicago, San Francisco, but I doubt it. I shouldn't think there'd be much of a market for them. They're not strumpets, and they're certainly not ladies. But—well, they *are* strumpets, really. I just don't want to call them that, because they are good company. I don't think there'd be much of a market for them in Chicago and such places because the kind of women those men would like you'd never for a second wonder about their status. Of course I don't really know, never having been to San Francisco, and the few times I've been to Chicago I've been overwhelmed by their respectability. It's quite a sad thing to send a Chicagoan East to school and then yank him back to Chicago. He's never the same after that. He's stopped being an honest, genuine Chicagoan, and God knows he hasn't become an Easterner. If they could have their own Groton out there in Illinois—no, it still wouldn't work out. They'd still want to be like us, and they never are. Of course they all came from the East originally, but it only takes one generation or at most two for them to lose their Eastern-ness, to coin a phrase. No country can have more than one metropolis, and in this country we're it. Your town and Boston each have their own special quality and characteristics—"

"My town being Philadelphia? I'm not a Philadelphian, you know."

"I consider you one, without the family encumbrances. All the advantages of a Philadelphia background and none of the cousins and uncles."

"I'm going to have to correct that impression."

"Some other time. Let me go on about New York and the rest of the country. There's one thing that embarrasses me more than any other about this country, including New York

City, and that's to see my countrymen—it isn't only the women—accepting any and every half-assed Englishman that comes along. I've seen some really worthwhile Americans bow and scrape to an English title without any curiosity about the man bearing the title. And I've seen Englishmen without a title arrive here with one or two letters and *presto!* invited everywhere. They may be the dullest bastards, or fortune-hunters, or even crooks, but the fact of their being English is enough for some of our people. And I sometimes wonder if there isn't a similar, uh, phenomenon in our West in relation to New Yorkers. The world may be moving westward, but we all seem to be looking back over our shoulders at what was older and possibly better. I say better, because I'm willing to admit that a first-rate Englishman is as good a man as there is on the face of the earth. But I haven't met many first-rate ones. You've been to London. Did you meet many really first-rate Englishmen?"

"Not a one, but I didn't meet many of the others, either."

"Well, of course the first-rate ones were off fighting the war when you were there. Oh, I'll give you an amusing situation. Have you ever been on a large house party where there were two Englishmen who didn't know each other? About ten years ago I was in Newport, a house guest. Same party were two Englishmen, both about the same age, both upper-class. But one of them was slightly higher upper-class than the other and they both knew it right off the bat and it spoiled the party for both of them. Suspicious of each other. Eying each other while pretending not to. Jealous of each other. Contradicting each other, very politely of course, but you know how an Englishman can ask a question in the politest language but call you a liar by his tone. That's what they were doing before the party ended. Two Americans wouldn't behave that way at an English house party. Of course we're English by ancestry, but it takes just about the same length of time for a man to lose his Englishness as it does an Easterner to lose his Eastern-ness. The second generation English-American becomes an Easterner, the Easterner becomes a Chicagoan, the Chicagoan I suppose becomes a Californian, and I don't know what happens after that and I'm not going to be around long enough to care."

"I expect to do a lot of business with Westerners," said Alfred. Then, remembering his mission, he added: "Or I did."

"Do you mind if I smoke one of your cigarettes? I don't often indulge and the only time I carry them is when I'm going to be out with a lady."

"Have one," said Alfred. "Fatimas."

Fritz Thornton applied the match to the cigarette and waved the match long after the flame had gone out. "I'm very sorry about what's happened," he said.

"Do you know what's happened?"

"I do. Lex got me on the telephone as soon as you left the office. I ordered him to follow you here. That's why I asked you if he'd come with you. Well, he's not here. I want you to tell me your side of it."

"You've heard it all from Lex."

"No, Lex was angry, but at the same time leaning over backwards to be fair. I hoped he'd come with you. That's why I've been prattling away about Jack Warren and the English, to give him time to get here. But he's obviously not coming. Never very good at taking orders from me or anyone else. I'm surprised he got through the war without being court-martialed. Well, I'll stop talking."

Alfred took almost an hour to tell his story, with his digressions and side comments. Through it all Fritz Thornton was understanding of Alfred's discomfort and on that score made his only interruption: "He's my nephew, but I haven't been saying I consider you a member of this family without its meaning something. So don't spare the horses."

When Alfred finished he flipped his hands open and said, "There it is. Any more, I'd just repeat myself."

"I see. Well, first let me thank you for the story, and the way you conducted yourself with Lex, and all the other things I ought to thank you for. And you can be sure I'll tell my brother that you came through as I said you would. I also admire you for standing up to Lex. It would have been much easier to coast along. But I feel much better that you didn't, and I'm glad you realized that you never have to take any horse-shit from Lex. And for your own benefit, you've proved to yourself that you don't have to take it from anyone if you don't take it from your best friend. That knowledge is as good as money in the bank, Alfred."

"Lex must have known that."

"You've been closer to Lex than anyone else he's ever been friends with, but you don't know him as well as I do, at least in some ways. Lex is the most completely self-centered boy I've ever known, and he's not above trying to see how much he can get away with. Now I have to ask you, is this a break that can't be repaired? In other words, do you feel that there's no possible hope of your ever working with Lex?"

"I wouldn't say no possible hope."

"That's all I'm going to ask you now. That, and to ask you not to resign until after I've talked to Lex. You were wrong about one thing, Alfred, or Lex was. I *would* withdraw my financial support. With only Lex and this Von Elm fellow in it, I'd vote the corporation out of business tomorrow. I have plenty of money, and so has my brother, but generosity is one thing and damn foolishness is damn foolishness. If you and Lex can't reconcile your differences, then the corporation will have to find someone who will follow exactly the same policies that you quarreled over, and if Lex won't conform to that, the corporation will cease to exist. Are you going home for dinner?"

"Yes."

"Take my car. I'm going to be here all evening. David can drive you home and be back before I'm ready to leave. And I may telephone you later this evening. That is, I may *if* I may?"

Alfred had anticipated no family partisanship from Fritz Thornton, and none had been displayed. Thornton, in fact, left no doubt as to his position in the dispute: he was all with Alfred, not only as indicated by his final remarks, but throughout Alfred's recital as indicated by sympathetic, approving nods and "I see's" and "Go on, Alfred's." At the same time there never was the slightest doubt in Alfred's mind that he was up against the Thornton-Porter family alliance, regardless of how completely sympathetic and fair Fritz Thornton was showing himself to be. Alfred would not have had it any other way, but coming away from Fritz Thornton, leaving the club that Fritz Thornton had eased him into, driving away in Fritz Thornton's Brewster town car, he already had the conviction that he was proceeding and had proceeded from one phase of his relationship with the Porters and Thorntons and into another. Regardless of the outcome of the present dispute, there was already a change in his own attitude toward the family alliance collectively and individually, but instead of a sentimental regret Alfred felt a faintly insubordinate relief. For a long time he had hardly made a move without considering the Porters and Thorntons—Lex Porter and Fritz Thornton—and it was high time a change occurred. They were not his family, he was not theirs, and there could not be the give and take, the rough give and take, that exists in a genuine family relationship. Too much of the relationship was governed by fondness that was not love, and politeness that controlled protest. The first test of the relationship was now taking place and whatever the result, Alfred was sure the relationship would never be the same.

(Nor was it.)

The beautiful little car moved at its luxuriously moderate pace through the streets of Queens, from the factories to the low-income two-family dwellings to the tree-lined suburban streets and finally (and Alfred thought he could almost hear the Brewster sigh with relief) to the beginnings of the North

411

Shore concentration of splendor and ease and of men who owned the money and lent the money, and spent the money oftener than not with intelligence, taste, imagination and good sense. "Almost there, sir," said David into the speaking tube.

"Almost there, David," said Alfred. David had a last name but Alfred had never heard it and did not miss it any more than he missed a further description of the Brewster, which some called a town car and others a landaulet and others a brougham. David was David, the Brewster was the Brewster. David with his gauntlets and puttees and high-collared tunic was a much sought after chauffeur, not because he was a pretty man or even an exceptionally good mechanic, but because on the box of the Brewster he became an ornament as significant as the less readily discernible crest and motto on the tonneau doors. The people who offered David higher wages to leave Fritz Thornton had thereby automatically lost David forever: they had broken one of the rules, and David lived by the rules. Rules covered every situation conceivable in David's life: the rules of the Roman Catholic church, to which he belonged, and the two sets of rules of etiquette to be followed by employer and employed. Fritz Thornton minded his own business and did not stick his nose in matters that did not concern him; he did not ask David to keep unreasonable hours; he permitted David to buy gasoline for the town and country garages from the dealer of David's preference; he gave David's two sons second choice after the butler on his old suits and shoes; and through Miss McIlhenny he sent birthday cheques to David and all members of his immediate family. Fritz Thornton never visited David's apartment over the garage without being invited (as he was every Christmas to see the *crèche* and the tree). And Fritz Thornton never asked David to have a drink with him. No matter how tiddly Fritz Thornton might get he never forgot that if David wanted a drink he would have it where and when he wanted it and not at the whim or insistence of the boss.

There were no potentially awkward subtleties in the kind of relationship enjoyed by Fritz Thornton and David as there were between Fritz Thornton and a Chicagoan, as there were between Fritz Thornton and Alfred. Reflecting on this, Alfred put down for future consideration a plan to adopt a set of rules that would govern his relationship with business associates and acquaintances and that would be patterned on the David–Fritz Thornton arrangement. The important thing was to define the business relationship at the very beginning so that politeness would not lead to a confusing social-business relationship and from that to a friendship. Friendship had started him with Lex and Fritz Thornton and had become confused by the business aspects, which was the same thing

412

in reverse. It was almost impossible in the United States to keep the two lives separate, but Alfred was going to have a try at it.

The trip to the country did not mean overtime for David, so Alfred did not offer him a tip for the ride. His thanks took the form of a few polite words. He got out of the car and stood near David, who was gently closing the car door. "Well, that was a nice ride, David."

"A little breath of fresh air, sir. How do you like living in the little house? It has one advantage, it's as cool a house as you'll find, big or little."

"It is cool."

"And easy to heat in the wintertime. Well, I might as well go up and say hello to my Missus, now I'm here. Goodnight, Mr. Eaton."

"Goodnight and thank you, David."

Easy to heat in the winter? It would not be a problem. The house was the porter's lodge on Fritz Thornton's place, for which Alfred paid $50 a month rent. It was a one-story building of cut stone, somewhat ecclesiastical in appearance and containing a sittingroom, bedroom, kitchen and bath. The white plastered walls were relieved by sporting prints, and the furniture, all of it Fritz Thornton's, was heavily oaken. The rent was not low for the size of the house, but with it went electricity, gas and telephone, and the services of a maid from the main house. It was a temporary measure until Mary and Alfred could make more permanent plans, subject to Alfred's hours at the plant and the desirability of being closer to it. Since the corporation property consisted only of some former potato fields with stakes driven in it, Alfred's days were spent in New York, and as a rule he took the Long Island train to Locust Valley and was met by Mary in the Marmon. This evening she was not meeting the train.

She heard the motor and came out as David was putting it in gear. "Good evening, David," she said.

"Good evening, ma'am," said David. "I put the new bulbs in your headlights."

"I noticed you did. Thank you."

"Goodnight, then," said David, and drove away.

"Good evening, my husband."

"Good evening, my wife."

He kissed her and held her with one arm about her waist. "Are you tired?" she said.

"A little."

"Who did you have the cocktails with?"

"Fritz. Let's go inside. Did you play tennis?"

They went in and he took off his blue flannel coat and vest. "No, we went sailing. Marjorie won't go with any other girl but me. Well, Tom won't *let* her go with any other girl is the real truth. She wanted to go sailing, said we could play tennis any old time."

"Excuse me," he said, and visited the bathroom. When he came out she handed him a mint julep. "I killed a mosquito in there that was as big as a de Havilland bomber."

"I suppose that's an aeroplane. Did Fritz have anything interesting to report?"

"Well, no, but I have."

"Yes, I knew that. What?"

"I am resigning as president and treasurer of the Nassau Aeronautical Corporation."

"Lex? You and Lex had a spat?"

"Yes." He then told her the story, but at less length than his recital to Fritz Thornton. "I guess I've been afraid of that all along. Lex doesn't care about business. He should, but he doesn't."

"He would if it affected him more. I don't like to say this about your best friend, but Lex is selfish."

"Well, we all are. And I knew that about him. Selfishness and independence, they're the same thing. I liked it when I called it independence. I don't like it now. Well, what the hell. Let's go and live in a hotel for a while, till I get a job, and then take an apartment in New York?"

She shook her head. "I don't think this is final. I think you're going to win out."

"I don't want to *win* out. I just want to *get* out," he said. "Thank God for you. Thank God I married you."

"Yes, thank God. Why?"

"If I weren't married to you I probably wouldn't have taken the stand I did. But I have you and a real life to live now. It's you and me now, and not just me and the Porters and Thorntons."

"I thought of you all day." She got up and sat beside him on the davenport. She took his hand. "You know where you come around that point in Manhasset Bay?"

"I think I know where you mean."

"I don't know what it was, but without any warning at all I felt as though I were blushing all the way from my toes to my head, I wanted you so much. No warning. We hadn't been talking about sex, or our husbands, but I wanted you any way and every way. Do you know what I did? I put my hand in the water, up past my wrist. I was sure if Marjorie looked at me she'd be able to tell what I was thinking. I'd hate that. I want you to know, but I don't want anyone else to know what a hot number I really am."

"Are you a hot number?" he said, smiling.

"Don't you think I am?"

414

"A hot number is something different. A hot number is hot for anybody and everybody. You're not that."

"But I'm a hot number with you, and when I'm not with you but thinking about you. About this." She touched him. "I'm not going to have to wait till later tonight, am I? I haven't a stitch on under this dress. Do you want to see?"

"Yes."

She stood up and unbuttoned the dress. "See? Isn't all this nice?" She put her hand across her breasts and down her belly. He reached out to her but she stepped back. "Oh, no you don't. Put out the lights and lock the screendoor. Then nobody'll come calling, but there's enough light so that we can see each other."

When they finished their love-making she lay with her head on his arm and took puffs from his cigarette. "Do you know what Tom and Marjorie do?"

"No. What?"

"They get in the tub together."

"They do? How do you know?"

"Well, I certainly didn't hear it from Tom. Marjorie told me. Have you ever done that?"

"No."

"Really, haven't you?"

"Well, not exactly. How did Marjorie happen to tell you that?"

"Oh, she hardly talks about anything else. I know she's trying to find out what we do, but I pretend I'm terribly innocent. But *she's* not."

"No, I never thought she was."

"You know they went around the world on their wedding trip, and every place they went they went and watched the sex shows. Have you done that?"

"Yes."

"Did you have a girl with you?"

"Yes."

"And then got so excited—"

"Sure. Naturally."

"Where was that? In London?"

"And in New York."

"I didn't know they had them in New York."

"If you know where."

"Will you take me to one some time?"

"You wouldn't like it."

"Why wouldn't I?"

"I just don't think you would."

"Do you know what else Tom and Marjorie do?"

"What?"

"This is a deep secret. Tom lets other men do it to Marjorie. As long as he's there."

"That isn't as much of a secret as they think. I can tell you one guy that did that we both know."

"Who?"

"Lex."

"Lex had an affair with Marjorie?"

"I don't know if you'd call it an affair, but he screwed her with Tom in the room. But why would she tell you all this?"

"Oh, I know why."

"Why?"

"Not today, but Monday when I saw her, they'd had two people down for the weekend. She wouldn't tell me exactly what they did, but Tom and the girl slept together and Marjorie and the man, and there was more to it than that."

"I'll just bet there was."

"Then she said they weren't having anyone down this weekend, but why didn't you and I come over and spend Saturday night."

"What did you say to that?"

"I said we couldn't. She asked me again today. She said Tom told her to ask me."

"Persistent bastards, aren't they? I guess the time has come to drop them. We don't have to see them."

"No, but Marjorie's very sweet except for that. It's Tom, not Marjorie."

"Who's in bed with the other guy? That's Marjorie, isn't it?"

"Yes."

"Well, there's your answer. Can you imagine me letting another man get in bed with you?"

"No."

"But would you if I asked you to?"

"No."

"But Marjorie does, quite willingly. And incidentally she doesn't always wait till Tom's around. It isn't only for Tom's pleasure. Marjorie started with her brother, if you want to know the whole story. He committed suicide when he was seventeen. He hanged himself at prep school. Tom was her brother's best friend. I got all this from Lex, who's known all of them since he was one year old. The brother was two years younger than Marjorie, and so is Tom. She seduced her own brother and the kid finally hanged himself. When I had that apartment with Lex, Marjorie used to come down there at least twice a week."

"Have you ever?"

"Yes, God damn it, I have, and I'm ashamed of it. And now she thinks she can get you to be one of her playmates."

"Well, she has another think coming now. But I wish you'd told me that before."

"I didn't even want to tell you now. I never liked her. She used to parade around without any clothes on in front of—well, me, and if I had a girl there. This one night I came home and she was there, and Lex was dead drunk. I don't want to tell you all those things I did. If you ask me, I'll tell you the truth, but I don't like to volunteer the information."

"She's seen you this way. She must think I'm an awful fool. Did you do our things with her?"

"I told you, I didn't even like her. She came in my room and—hell, Mary, it was all over in no time."

"I told you when we were first married that I didn't mind. But I do mind. Then it wasn't—I didn't know who they were. But when it was somebody I was sailing with this very afternoon . . ."

"It happened a year ago, and I wasn't in love with you then. No, that's not true. I was in love with you, but I hadn't told you I was, and you were Jim Roper's girl at the time. Listen, Mary, if I'd wanted to go to bed with Marjorie again, I had plenty of opportunities. Let's stay away from them. They're bad news, and I've had enough bad news for one day. Are you thirsty? I am."

"First give me a kiss."

He took her in his arms and kissed her and, lightly at first, caressed her with the tips of his fingers, but soon they were making calm, expectant love, wordlessly, and when he went inside her it was slow and deep-thrusting until it suited her to vary the motion and surprise him into the climax that she followed with her own.

He slept then and when he awoke it was to the smell of coffee. She was in the kitchen, whistling "Tell Me Why Nights Are Lonesome."

"Mary?"

"Yes m'dear? You awake?"

"What time is it?"

"Twelve minutes past eleven. I'm making you some scrambled eggs."

"Did Fritz telephone?"

"Yes, and I told him you were asleep. He'll call you in the morning."

"He must have thought I was taking it very calmly."

"That's what I wanted him to think." She came out of the kitchen and bent down and kissed him. "I love you, Alfred Eaton. We won't take any s, h, i, t—I hate that word—from any Thorntons or Porters or anyone else. Come and have your scrambled eggs and I'm making a lot of toast to fill you up. Wash the sleep out of your eyes and put on your

417

pajamas and I'll be ready by the time you are."

"Ready for what?"

"Ready for anything you are."

"For the time being, scrambled eggs." They smiled at each other, and she continued to smile after they stopped looking at each other.

"Why the big grin?" he said.

"I'm just happy. I'm glad we started out living in a place like this. You know, like the song, 'Just a Love Nest.' " She watched him eating his supper.

"Aren't you having any supper?"

"I'm not hungry. I had a glass of milk before you woke up, and I never have a very big appetite in warm weather. It was a hundred in Wilmington today."

"Wilmington's the South."

"Listen, the North Shore isn't the North Pole. Oh, my, a witticism."

"You must have been talking to your mother. How are they?"

"Well, not very comfortable in that heat."

"They have the electric fans. I'd never seen one of those big fans in a private house before. They look like aeroplane propellers."

"I was hoping you wouldn't think of aeroplanes the rest of tonight."

"Did you have a conversation with Fritz?"

"Only that he would call you in the morning, and the usual polite how-are-you's. He said not to disturb you, and I said I wouldn't think of it."

"I don't know that you should have said that."

"I wasn't rude. He laughed."

"Are you with me on this?"

"I surely am. But you forget something. I knew Lex and his family before you did, so please don't try to tell me how to talk to Fritz."

"I never remember that."

"At one time Fritz wanted to marry my mother——before she married Daddy, of course. And it must have been a temptation, with all that money and Mother's family quite poor from the War. But Daddy just swept her off her feet. Imagine Daddy sweeping anybody off their feet? But he did. He took her away from Fritz Thornton right under his very nose."

"So you were almost his daughter, and Lex's cousin. Well, I still could have married you."

"Honey, I doubt it. Most of the nice things about me I get from Daddy, and I wouldn't have had them if my father'd been Fritz Thornton. Oh, I know what my good qualities are.

When I was at Miss Hebb's I had to write a composition on Character and I thought and thought and then decided to write about my own character. That was the first time I ever thought much about character and I got so immersed in the subject that ever since then I've thought about it a lot."

"Then how did you happen to marry me?"

"I almost didn't. Not because your character was bad, but because it was too good."

"Me? My character too good?"

"You don't know that about yourself, but it's true. Jim Roper was supposed to have a fine character, but I never really thought so. I wouldn't like to be married to Jim Roper, especially now that I know what I know." She fell silent.

"What's preying on your mind?" he said.

"As sure as I'm sitting here, if Marjorie'd asked Jim and me to spend Saturday night, he'd have gone."

"In fairness to Jim, you don't know that."

"As sure as I'm sitting here. It's just the kind of thing that used to give me the creeps about Jim. I never knew what it was, but I told you how he used to make me feel."

"Well, maybe."

"This is fun, isn't it? It is to me, to be able to talk about all these things with a man. Could Marjorie and her brother have had a baby?"

"With two heads or something awful."

"Is that what happens when a brother and sister screw?"

"So I'm told."

"There was supposed to be one of those in Wilmington. It was when I was about fifteen and just beginning to find out about such things. This woman that lived on Franklin Street, the girls at Miss Hebb's used to point her out to me and say she had a baby with two heads. That meant she'd been screwing with her brother?"

"It could have."

"She moved away. But they have to really screw, don't they? Because I knew some sisters and brothers that did other things."

"They'd have to screw. That's the only way you can have a baby that I know of."

"No, honey. You can have a baby if just a single drop of the man gets in you. That's supposed to be a positive fact, and why petting parties are dangerous."

"That always seemed pretty far-fetched to me. It may be possible, and I suppose it is, but I never heard of a real case of it. And it certainly seems like a damn shame to get knocked up without getting screwed, doesn't it?"

"I know I wouldn't like it."

"Well, we won't let it happen, shall we?"

"I don't guess we will. Now you embarrass me."

"Why?"

"Calling attention to how much we do it. Almost every night since we've been married, and sometimes twice and three times, except when I couldn't."

"Well, that's usually five days when we don't at all. Almost a week out of every four weeks."

"You'll get tired of me."

"I'll never get tired of you. You are a woman of infinite variety. Shakespeare."

"Who was?"

"I think it was Cleopatra."

"I'll thank you not to compare me with her. Wasn't she supposed to be touched by the tarbrush?"

"Sunburned from riding on those barges. I wasn't comparing you with her. Just explaining why I'd never get tired of you. Plus the fact that I love you."

"That's what I like to hear."

"I like to say it. I love you. I like to hear it, too."

"It's a wonder everybody on the place didn't hear it tonight."

"You didn't say that very loud."

"No, but what I did say. You know."

"I love to hear you say it."

"You know what's awful is I love to say it. Would you like some more coffee?"

"No thanks. There goes the Brewster."

"How do you know?"

"I know the sound. It's easy to tell all the cars on this place."

"I can only tell by the horns."

"Don't you recognize the little hum that the Brewster has? But don't start learning them now. He's getting rid of the Simplex and buying a Rolls. Although that's going to make small difference to us."

"Honey?"

"What?"

"You don't want to give it up, do you?"

"No."

"Then don't. You won't have to. You showed them you have spunk. They'll come around."

"Nobody ever had as good a wife as you."

"Nobody was ever so crazy about her husband as I am."

Within twenty-four hours the dispute was ironed out to the limited satisfaction of all concerned and the Nassau Aeronautical Corporation was back on the track. It was Lex who said they were back on the track, Fritz Thornton who mentioned the limited satisfaction, and Alfred who said it was ironed out. Nothing, of course, was permanently settled, and that was Lawrence Von Elm's comment.

THE BIG FIRE at the Eaton Iron & Steel mill occurred in the summer of 1921 and about a month after the mill had closed down for an "indefinite period." A few maintenance men—four working the twelve-hour day shift and three the twelve-hour night shift—and an office staff of ten, including book-keepers and stenographers, remained on full pay, but men who owned their own tools had been advised to take them home, and the other workmen had been given little hope that the mill would soon re-open. The orders that had been obtained while Samuel Eaton lived were kept on the books and filled, but thereafter no new orders had been granted and none had been sought. By the spring of 1921 it was obvious to most men in the industry that the market for steel and iron products was almost non-existent and as usual reflected, if it did not foretell, conditions in the nation as a whole. In the formal reorganization that followed Samuel Eaton's death, Alfred Eaton had been elected president and chairman of the board, but the mill was being run by a one-man regency consisting of Ed Barlow, who knew the company better than any man alive. No one knew as well as Ed Barlow that the three-shift activity during the war had forced the postponement of repairs and replacements, and that Eaton's was going to have to try to raise as much as a million dollars to restore the mill to its pre-war status, but no one knew as well as Ed Barlow that the money would be hard to get. The obvious sources of money—the banks and insurance companies—were restricted by law from providing the kind of money the mill needed on the kind of terms Barlow considered proper and fair. But there were other factors that influenced Barlow in his decision to close down. He knew, for instance, that Eaton's was considered in the industry to be a one-man operation, and the one man was dead. He also knew that even if some new money became interested—although that in itself was rather fantastic in the present economic situation—an expert valuation of the property would discourage or frighten the potential investors, and he was unwilling to risk having the plant on record as a dubious investment.

In my opinion [he wrote Alfred], it would be much more desirable if we closed down tight and did not re-open until conditions improve all over the country. Should that happen, as it is bound to do, we will have a better chance of borrowing the necessary new money, or in my opinion we may also receive offers to buy Eaton's lock, stock and barrel. I am not getting any younger. In fact, I told your late father that I intended to retire next year. I will stay on until the end of next year, should you so desire. However, I cannot promise any more than that and in any case I would not undertake to remain in charge should we resume full-scale production. It is a job for a younger man. I am aware that you have no desire to take the helm and I therefore, looking into the future, urge you to consider seriously any and all suitable offers for the purchase of the mill. Meanwhile, I have cut the office staff down to a minimum, put seven men on maintenance (watchmen more than actual maintenance) and hope thereby to eat up as little of our surplus as possible. If conditions improve in two years (my guess) you should be able to sell at a fair price. As of now you would not get a fair price and it is more desirable to continue with the skeleton staff and pay our taxes than sell now in the present market. Your mother and sisters are well taken care of under your father's will as you recall. Likewise, your mother and sisters are comfortably fixed through your Grandfather Johnson. Therefore your position is not as bad as it looks. However, as a lifetime friend of your family I take the liberty to state that in my opinion this is not the opportune moment to risk capital in an aeroplane company, in case you were considering so doing, although I am sure the Messrs. Thornton have all they need without going to you for more. (I looked them up in Dun & Bradstreet's a year ago.) Before closing would also add that when laying off the laboratory and draughting-room men I advised them to seriously consider looking for work away from Port Johnson as I did not expect the mill to reopen inside of a year. I trust you approve of my frankness to them as we owed it to them for faithful service at lower pay than we gave men in the yards and shops during the War. I do not know what is going to happen to Port Johnson. The men used up their savings in their reckless strike in 1919 and we never went back to full-time after the Armistice. There are more and more men with nothing to do but "hold up the building" on Montgomery St. That is what they say when you see them leaning against a building. The Lutherans and the Catholics have started to take up a collection among the Montgomery St. merchants to open soup kitchens. Both bakeries have promised to donate all their stale bread, etc. But you would not think there was any trouble if you walked into the saloons. They are just as crowded as ever despite the new law and being laid off. Likewise I have been informed that certain men in town are selling "hooch" and finding many buyers. You are lucky to be young and able to seek your fortune out of town.

The men who were "holding up the building" on Montgomery Street soon acquired the faraway look of men who are accustomed to work, want to work, and are deprived of the opportunity by circumstances that they do not understand beyond the local, immediate, simple fact that they are not needed. At first the older men, as in previous periods of unemployment, made the repairs to their houses that they had put off: replacing tar paper, re-laying brick walks, cleaning chimneys, but further postponing repairs or improvements, such as painting and paperhanging, that would involve the expenditure of cash. Soon the children's music lessons were stopped and their visits to the dentist and the younger ones allowed to run barefoot. The rare wife who could not sew was expected to trade some service with the wife who could. It was summer when the lay-off was begun and fuel was not needed for heat, but the wiser heads were again picking coal against the distant winter days. And many a wife first looked it, and then said it: "What did you get out of that strike? What have we got to show for your three months of sitting home?" And the man would go off and drink the new, ether-smelling, varnish-tasting, more expensive beer, spending cash and getting strangely drunk but not exhilarated by it. Then for days they would stand in front of the store-windows on Montgomery Street, jumping out of the way like guilty children when the owner would come out with his crank to raise the awning. And there would be the cops shooing the men away from the building line and ordering them to stand at the curb, and some merchants who even objected to that because the men who chewed tobacco would spatter the sidewalk with their spittle. They had nothing to read, they had no credit at the poolrooms, their lives had depended on work, work for money and work to occupy ten of their sixteen waking hours. Now they huddled together on the curbstones, discussing the automobiles they could not hope to own, laughing seldom, and often standing silent for long periods with a common desire to avoid the mental effort to sustain conversation. They knew what they were in for; it had been like this only a little more than a year ago; but now they were not by their idleness fighting for something. They were not making a sacrifice in defiance of Sam Eaton and Eaton's. The men who had hated and continued to hate Sam Eaton got only perfunctory agreement from the men who hated nobody, and they soon became bores: what was the good of hating a man that was dead a year, and what was the good of thinking back to the strike that had gained nothing and cost three months' wages? They would begin lining up along Montgomery Street before the stores opened for business, as though there had to be that much regularity in their lives. They would walk home at noon for whatever the wives had rationed out for them, then they would go back to their places on the curbstone until time for supper. There were no jobs, there was no work. The men who had been laid off before Eaton's closed down were the lucky ones; they had taken all the little jobs that paid children's wages.

And inside the stores the merchants sat on their stools and leaned against their counters, pulling at their lower lips and wondering how long they could stay in business, what story to tell the landlord, what argument to give to the bank. And every sunny afternoon they would wonder how long before it would be dangerous to go out with the awning crank and disturb those bewildered, unhappy men. And the first of the merchants to go was Theodore Dykeman, the florist. For two weeks he had not taken in a cent except for four two-dollar funeral sprays, and when he was informed that this year's high school class had voted against boutonnieres and bouquets—on which his total net profit would have been $6.20—he went down-cellar and cut his throat with his pocket knife. He bled to death on the duckboard, and was discovered by Patrolman Vincent Brophy, who noticed that Dykeman's awning was down, the front door open, and no lights on in the shop at 9:05 P.M. There were four one-dollar bills, a quarter, five nickels, and five dimes in the cash drawer. The business had been established in 1894, and in twenty-seven years Theodore Dykeman had delivered flowers to every wedding and funeral in Port Johnson, every high school commencement, every First Communion, and every Charity Ball. For old times' sake Charlie Sampson embalmed Dykeman, gave him a nice casket, supplied the hearse and two carriages, and did not send the widow a bill. (Charlie took some photographs of the deceased before and after the embalming to show other members of the profession how skillfully he had employed the collar, but the widow had not permitted a viewing.)

For a few days the sidewalk in front of Dykeman's was deserted by the men, but after the flowers had been removed and a sign, offering the fixtures for sale, put in the window, the place once again attracted the men and some even began sitting on the three stone steps that led to the entrance. In a few short weeks the location which once had been visited chiefly by women and girls became as terrifying to them as the poolroom on Lower Montgomery Street. The front and back doors were padlocked, but that did not keep the men from going down the areaway and using the backyard privy, and for the time being the property as real estate was totally undesirable. "That's what's going to happen to all of us," said one storekeeper.

In the Port Johnson scheme of things there was a class distinction which was unconsciously revealed by a speech mannerism of the Montgomery Street merchants and their families. Of a man who was a draughtsman they would say, "He's a draughtsman at Eaton's." But of other workmen, men who wore overalls, they would say, "He works at Eaton's." Socially, a draughtsman, a laboratory assistant, and a few book-keepers were the equal of merchants, but a traveling-crane operator who was twice as well paid did not expect the same treatment. And now the men who had not customarily worn neckties to work were not even dignified by the word work. Instead of being men who worked at Eaton's they were being referred to as "that bunch from Eaton's" and "those bums from Eaton's." The merchants and the Eaton's men were staring at the future like a farmer staring at a blackening sky before he has had time to get the wheat in. And it made for no common cause that the merchants were going to suffer with the men, from the same disaster and at the same time. Nor did it unify merchants and other merchants, Eaton's men and other Eaton's men. The men stood together on the curbstone, and the merchants complained together, but adversity did not create harmony or loyalty. If two men had been invited to fight for one job at Eaton's, they would have fought. If two merchants had been able to bid for all of a certain supply contract at Eaton's, they would not have shared the contract and divided the profit.

The merchants were better off in one respect: at least for the present they had their stores to go to, they had something to do. They had salesmen to see, even though they gave the salesmen no fall orders; they had the store to open in the morning and close in the evening, the chores to do, and the dignity of a desk and a chair and mail to read and letters to sign, and from their desks most of them could look out at the clusters of able-bodied men who were losing their pride and virility in helpless idleness. "They just stand there," said one merchant. "They'll watch the sparrows going after the horse-shit and they don't do anything and they don't learn anything. If the horses stopped coming to Montgomery Street, so would the sparrows. You'd think they'd get away somewhere and try to find some work, but no, they're dumber than sparrows. I have to stay here and mind the store. If I was one of them I'd hop a freight and go out West. Even if I didn't find work I'd be better off than just standing on a man's curbstone."

Thus the mood of the merchants when the fire broke out at Eaton's. It started in the template shop at the lower end of the yards, a small building that was cleaner than the others because of the nature of the work usually done there. And for that reason, because it was so clean and free of grease- and oil-soaked lumber, it was often ignored or given only a perfunctory inspection by the watchmen on their rounds. But the stacks of uncut boards and cardboard from which the templates were made were highly inflammable kindling for the timbers of the shop, and the fire jumped quickly to the nearby

425

oil shanty. The walls and flooring of the oil shanty contained the soaking of years, and after the structure was ignited it was only a matter of seconds before the flooring and walls were aflame. There was still some daylight, and the flaming oil shanty did not light up the sky as it might have done an hour later, and the first knowledge the watchmen had of the fire was the rapid series of explosions of kerosene and oil drums, which tore off the shanty roof and spread the fire to the Bridge & Structural shop. Corrugated iron covered the outside walls and roofs of most of the buildings at Eaton's, but they had been placed on frameworks of lumber, and wood, always oil-and grease-soaked, was used for flooring, machinery supports, ties for the narrow-gauge railway and a hundred other uses. The Bridge Shop, as it was called, was a spacious building, with a roof high enough to accommodate numerous hoists and cranes. From a dozen small fires there grew a large, continuous fire, guided, as it were, by the two narrow-gauge railways that ran from one end of the shop to the other.

The three watchmen on duty got as close as they dared to the oil shanty, from which the flames now shot high in the air. "Go on back and blow the whistle," said one of the watchmen.

"We don't have no whistle. We aint got no steam," said the other.

On this night, the Eaton's whistle that had sounded the alarm for all of Port Johnson's fires, for the starting of work, for the changing of shifts, for the time of day, and even for the birth of a baby—was silent. It had been silent since the closing-down of the mill.

"Then phone the hose company, for Christ's sake," said the first watchman.

The fires burned and spread without human resistance for the better part of an hour before the apparatus arrived. Without Eaton's whistle Port Johnson was dependent on the bell in the borough hall cupola for fire alarms, and the bell had a limited range. There were only five men aboard the American-LaFrance combination as it arrived, followed by the Garford hook-and-ladder truck with a driver, a tiller-man and two firemen. Atherton Fenstermacher, the new fire chief, brought four more men in his red Ford chemical-chief's car, and he was met by Ed Barlow.

"The Bridge Shop is gone, Athie. Don't pay any attention to the Bridge Shop."

"Well, what shall we try to save, Ed?"

"Try to save from here north. There isn't much to burn south of the Bridge Shop, mostly yards there. A couple of shanties. But north of the template shop is where the valuable

426

equipment is. Try to keep it out of the 18-inch mill. If it gets in there it'll ruin equipment and it could burn for days. The Bridge Shop's going to burn for days but let it. But if this thing gets to the 18-inch mill the heat's liable to make those girders buckle and down'll come four 50-ton cranes worth a lot of money, and liable to kill a lot of people. And another thing, if it gets to the 18-inch mill, that isn't so far from the laboratory and there's no telling what would happen then. I don't know much about those chemicals they have there, but I wouldn't want to be responsible."

"How did it start? Do you know, Ed?"

"I don't know, and I don't guess we ever will."

"It looks fishy to me. Don't it to you?"

"I couldn't say, Athie."

"Well, see you later. But if you hear anything, let me know. There's a lot of soreheads in town."

There were a lot of soreheads who stood and watched as the firemen poured water and chemicals on the burning template shop and oil shanty. They worked all night, and saved the 18-inch mill. They got help from the hose companies at Eatontown, Eckburg and other nearby places, and Norristown and Reading. They poured water on the roof and walls of the Bridge Shop and it came off as live steam. They watered down a row of dwellings east of the mill property and the occupying families stayed on the alert through the night. At eight o'clock in the morning Atherton Fenstermacher said to Ed Barlow: "Ed, you better go home and get some sleep."

"Somebody has to be here."

"There'll be men here all day and tomorrow too, by the look of it. But look at that sun. Today's gonna be a piss-cutter, and you're entitled to a rest."

"So are you, Athie."

"I'll hang around for another hour and then go. Ed, you know George Fry."

"George Fry that drove for Sam? Sure I know George."

"He didn't have no job here, did he?"

"Job? The last I heard George was in the crazy house," said Barlow. "No, he hasn't set foot here for over a year."

"There you're wrong. He set foot here last night. We found him in the template shop. What's left of him."

"In the template shop? Do you think he started it?"

"Well, we'll never find out by asking him. When we got the fire out in the template shop two fellows went in and the stink—it was awful, Ed. Then they found George, under a workbench. All his clothes burnt off him, but they recognized him by one side of his face where he laid on it. It was George,

427

all right. I had a look at him myself. And there was an empty pint there."

"Good heavens! He certainly didn't do it on purpose."

"No, I don't think so either. But I wonder how he got in. Your gates are all locked, aint they?"

"All but one. The standard gauge track, the Pennsy spur at the south end that comes into the lower yards. They left that gate unlocked for the yard engine. He could easily have come in there. George knows his way around the mill as well as I do, and three men aren't enough to keep a close watch on every square foot of it. I guess the poor man's been sleeping in the template shop."

"Well, he's never gonna wake up from this one. But I guess he done one good thing."

"What was that?"

"Well, a lot of people were ready to say this was arson, and blame the men that got laid off."

"It's too soon for that, Athie."

"I don't know. It don't take long to build up a grudge when you don't have nothing to do, Ed. You better lock that gate and keep it locked."

"Yes. After the horse is stolen, as the old saying goes."

"Go on home, now, Ed. You got insurance men and the coroner and all them the next couple days. You're gonna be a busy man."

"That never hurt anybody. Ask the men that used to be here."

An early edition of the Philadelphia *Evening Bulletin* was lying, folded at the story of the fire, on the chair facing Martha when Ed Barlow was announced.

"I've been reading all about the fire," said Martha, removing the newspaper and giving him the sign to seat himself.

"Then there isn't much for me to tell you. The *Bulletin* article has most of the facts."

"What on earth was George Fry doing, sleeping in the template shop? You didn't stop his money, did you?"

"No. I was sure Sam would have wanted him to keep getting it," said Barlow. "But I'm afraid George used all his money for liquor."

"I hope he was drunk last night. Think of dying that way."

"It's a possibility that he died without waking up. The smoke could have asphyxiated him in his sleep."

"Let's hope so. What happens now, Ed?"

"Well, you're all right. That's what I came to tell you."

"I never thought I wouldn't be. Why would I not be?"

"I thought you might be worried about money. The fire doesn't affect your present income. As to your future income,

428

it may add to it, although not for several years. The mill will get some insurance when the loss is adjusted. That will make it possible for us to rebuild and put money into equipment, if we want to. I'm not sure we're going to want to."

"I know. We may want to wait and sell. Alfred explained all that, weeks ago, months ago, whenever it was. But how is the fire going to add to my income?"

"Well, this is way in the future and complicated, but you can see how we're better off with three or four hundred thousand dollars cash than with the buildings and equipment that were lost. Some of that equipment was thirty years old, and the buildings weren't much, and a buyer would take all that into consideration. Of course we're going to have to spend some money tearing down what's left of the buildings and so forth, but even that may be covered in the insurance policy, I haven't looked. I'm going to do that tonight."

"That will give the men some work to do."

"Not too hasty, Martha. I don't know how that's going to be handled, and anyway it'd only be a couple weeks' work for twenty or thirty men. It isn't going to have much effect on conditions in town."

"But you still haven't told me how my income would go up."

"I only said it *may* add to it. It depends on how we can distribute that cash if we sell the mill. You're the principal stockholder, so you'd get the most. You own thirty—"

"I know. I own thirty percent, and the children twenty percent each, and you ten. I hope someone buys it soon, and changes the name right away. I hate to think of the men blaming Eaton's."

"It won't be soon. You can be glad your father took care of you."

"And Sam. Don't forget, Sam always gave me stocks and bonds besides the mill stock."

"Yes, that's true. Are the girls here?"

"No, they're still out in Wyoming. Will you write to them if I give you their address? I'll give it to you before you leave. Have you spoken to Alfred?"

"No, but I sent him a telegram. I couldn't reach him by phone. Do you know where he is?"

"I haven't the faintest idea if he isn't at home."

"He's in Texas, visiting somebody named Jack Tom Smith. That's where I sent the telegram."

"Did you talk to his wife?"

"She's in Wilmington with her folks. I didn't want to call her there."

"In Wilmington. She could at least have brought the baby here."

"Oh, I only think she went there a day or so ago, from what I gathered."

"Don't worry about it. You have enough on your shoulders without worrying about us. Any more than you do worry about us. And what about you in all this? Are you all right, Ed?"

He smiled one of his rare smiles. "Martha, I've been saving money since I graduated from High. I'll tell you something about myself. Do you know that I've saved something, even if it was only one dollar, every week of my life since I graduated. Even if it was only one dollar, I put something in the bank every week. Then at the end of the year I withdrew half and bought securities. And I never bought one cent's worth of mill stock. Sam gave me some every Christmas till I owned ten percent, and then he stopped. After that at Christmas he gave me money. He said ten percent was the limit anybody outside the family would ever own. I missed a lot of things, I guess, but now I don't have any worries about my old age."

"Well, that's fine."

"But thanks for asking me. It shows an interest."

"Score one for Sam. I used to wonder whether he was treating you properly, but I never dared ask him."

"Sam Eaton was the finest man I ever knew."

"What?"

"I said Sam Eaton was the finest man I ever knew."

"Did he ever know you thought that?"

"Not by me telling him. A man doesn't tell that to another man. But he must have known I thought very highly of him."

"But the finest man you ever knew."

"*Yes* ma'am. If I could have been anyone else in this world I'd rather have been Sam Eaton than anybody."

"I never knew you felt that way about Sam."

"Well, what else did you think, Martha? You must have thought so, being his wife. I only knew him at the mill and when we had to go away on trips together. But I had over thirty-five years with Sam Eaton and every minute was a pleasure. He could be firm and sometimes fly off the handle, but he was always honest with you and fair and if you did your work and treated him right, he treated you right. Never mean. Never nasty. Never took advantage of his position to get more out of you than he was paying you for. Never spied on you. Never did any of those things a lot of other employers do. I know it's over a year since he passed on, but there's never a day but that I miss him like he was one of my own family. And if Sam Eaton was alive today, the mill wouldn't be closed down. The men did him a bad turn when they went out on strike and they don't deserve much consideration, but he'd have kept the mill open. We'd be on part-time, but he'd have got some new business. The day Sam Eaton passed on, this town went to pot, if you'll excuse the expression."

"You really believe all that?"

"I wouldn't say it if I didn't believe it. I don't talk just for the sake of talking, Martha. You know that. And it shouldn't surprise you. He was your husband and you were his wife and no two people ever had a happier union than you two, except when Billy died. I know you were both grief-stricken after that. But it brought you closer together. That, and when you got sick."

"I'm tired now, Ed. You have to go. Come back Thursday or Friday."

"I apologize, Martha," said Barlow, rising. "I didn't mean to get you all upset, but I just got thinking about Sam."

"All right, all right."

"Aren't you feeling well? Shall I send the nurse in?"

"Yes, yes. Just leave me alone, Ed. I'm sorry."

He went out and presently Trimingham came in. "Mr. Barlow said you wanted me."

"I don't want you. He's wrong about that and he's wrong about a lot of things. Go away."

"Now we're not going to have any more of that, Mrs. Eaton. I was in the middle of having my supper and he rushed in as if you'd had a serious attack and it just isn't fair."

"Go finish your supper."

Trimingham studied her. "Did he tell you something about the mill? Have you lost all your money?"

"I have more money than ever."

"Are you sure that's the truth?"

"There'll always be enough to pay you, so don't let that worry you. It's all you care about anyway. Go on, go on, go on, go on, go on. I'll throw something at you."

Trimingham sighed. "You're all right. Just another one of your naughty tantrums. Why don't you get ready for your tub? I'll run it for you and you can soak while I finish my supper."

"I don't want a bath."

"No, what you really want is a good spanking. That's what I'd prescribe for you when you get like this."

"Stop talking to me as though I were a child."

"I do talk to you as though you were a child because that's what you are. A spoiled, disagreeable child. Now I want you undressed by the time I've run your tub, and you're going to stay there till I come back from my supper."

"I don't want it too hot. If it's too hot I won't get in. I'll take the stopper out."

"Oh, shush."

"All right, just for that I won't let you see the baby."

"Now what? What baby are you talking about?"

"Rowland. My grandson, Rowland Eaton."

"They're bringing the baby here? Or is this just something you made up."

"He's in Wilmington and naturally his mother is bringing him here."

"Did Mr. Barlow tell you so?"

"No. I know it."

"Oh, Lord. Get undressed, will you please?"

Trimingham could never explain it to herself satisfactorily, but while Martha was taking her tub and she was finishing her supper the telephone rang: Mrs. Alfred Eaton calling from Wilmington. The mystery to Trimingham was how Martha Eaton knew that young Mrs. Eaton was in Wilmington and would telephone; Trimingham or Nellie or Josephine intercepted all calls for Martha, and Trimingham herself steamed open the little mail that came for Martha, and Trimingham believed that Martha had not discussed Mary Eaton and the baby with Barlow. Barlow, she knew, was not on terms of intimacy with Martha. She was a nurse, and had a somewhat skeptical mind, but as she told Josephine, crazy people sometimes have a sixth sense about some things. They sometimes understand things that mystify normal people. It came under the head of compensation, like blind people developing a more acute sense of hearing.

The simple, and accurate explanation was that the St. Johns read about the fire in the Wilmington paper, and Mary telephoned as a routine duty. Nellie answered the ring, "Eaton residence," she said.

"Is this Josephine?"

"Do you want to speak to Josephine?"

"Nellie? This is Mrs. Eaton. Is everything all right?"

"Everything's all right here, about the same as usual, ma'am." Nellie enjoyed her momentary importance and the curiosity shown by Trimingham and Josephine.

"Well, I thought I'd drive up tomorrow and see Mrs. Eaton, and bring the baby. Would that be all right? That is, if the weather stays like this. About two o'clock, I'll be there."

"That will be fine, ma'am. I know it will. Thank you, ma'am. Goodbye."

Nellie, for the first time in her life the representative of the household, said nothing to the other women, but hurried upstairs to present the news intact to Martha. Martha was lying in the tub. The bathroom doors were closed, but the keys had been taken away a long time ago, and at Nellie's knock Martha told her to come in. It embarrassed Nellie to see Martha in her nakedness, but it embarrassed Martha not at all. "I could be a young girl, couldn't I, Nellie?" she said.

"Yes, ma'am."

"My bust is quite nice for someone's had four children. But they never did get very big. Remember?"

Nellie was blunt. "Mrs. Alfred is coming tomorrow and bringing the little fellow."

Martha sat up and held a washrag over her breasts. "Are you telling me the truth? If you're lying to me I'll do something dreadful to you. I warn you, Nellie."

"On the Blessed Virgin Mary, if I'm lying may I die without the priest. I just got finished talking to her on the phone. Not five minutes ago she rang up and said she was coming. Two o'clock in the afternoon if the weather keeps up."

"Why doesn't she come for lunch? Hand me the towel. I must call her up."

"You don't have to. She's coming. Will I help dry you off?"

"I can dry myself. I want someone to go to the drug store and get half a dozen anti-colic nipples and six baby bottles. I think they're six-ounce bottles and they have marks on the side. Oh, what else will we need? Milk. Heat some milk and then put it in the icebox. Have we still got that alcohol lamp we used to have?"

"It's probably in the kitchen closet, but we have the gas stove in now and we don't need it any more. And it's *tomorrow*, ma'am, not this evening. Two o'clock tomorrow afternoon. If you get all excited tonight you won't look your best tomorrow."

"I have to look my best," said Martha.

She was spared some of the agony of waiting next day when Mary, in a Hudson limousine and accompanied by a youngish nurse, arrived fifteen minutes early. She got out of the car and the nurse handed her the baby.

"Yoo-hoo? Yoo-hoo, Mary? Rowland? Yoo-hoo?"

Mary looked up at the second-story window and saw Martha, moving just her fingers in greeting through the screen. "Hello, Mrs. Eaton. Here we are."

"Come right, right up. Don't stop on the way, come right up."

Trimingham led Mary to the second floor. Martha was standing in the middle of the room. "*Let* me hold him, *let* me look at him. Excuse me, hello, Mary. Welcome, thrice welcome. *May* I hold him?"

"Of course," said Mary.

"Sit down, first, ma'am," said Trimingham.

"All right. Just give him to me, let me look at this beautiful child, this beautiful, beautiful *child.*"

"Afraid he's not much for beauty, but he's a darling."

"He is darling and he's beautiful. Your eyes, Mary. There's no question about that. Your eyes. But look at that chin. His grandfather. Sam Eaton's chin. He has a jaw. Babies never have jaws at his age, but this one has. They're not supposed to know anything at this age, and yet look at him staring at me. 'Who is this woman? She's someone I ought to know. She isn't some stranger, even though I've never seen her before.' There it is, there it is! That smile. Oh, God."

"You'd better give him back to his mother, ma'am," said Trimingham.

In the transfer the baby began to cry.

"Can't I hold him just a little longer?"

"Later on, ma'am," said Trimingham.

"I brought some milk along with me. Do you think his nurse could have it heated? It's time for his two o'clock feeding and then he can have a nap. Miss Trimingham, will you take him downstairs and tell my nurse? Her name is Miss Macdougall."

"Is that all I'm going to see him?" said Martha.

"Oh, no. After his nap," said Mary.

"You be careful now, Miss Trimingham."

"Don't you worry, I've handled a thousand babies."

"But not this one," said Martha.

Trimingham left with the infant.

"Could I use your bathroom?" said Mary.

"Of course, and would you like a cup of tea? Or coffee? The coffee's all ready. And do you want to tell your man to go back and have some lunch, or lemonade? You and I might have some lemonade, on a day like this."

"I'll tell him," said Mary. She called out the window: "Frank? Wouldn't you like to go back to the kitchen and have some lemonade?"

"Yes ma'am," said the chauffeur.

"You look so fresh and cool," said Martha.

"I'll feel fresher in a minute," said Mary. "And then I'll have some lemonade if I may."

Nellie brought the cut-glass pitcher and tumblers but was not given time to converse with Mary. "Run along, Nellie. You can see her when she leaves. We don't want to be disturbed."

"Do you mind if I smoke a cigarette?" said Mary.

"I'd be a terrible hypocrite if I objected to that," said Martha, not so much to Mary as to herself. "Now I feel that I am a grandmother, now that I've seen him and held him close. Your mother and father must be in seventh heaven to have him in the house with you."

"They are, but I'm very strict with them," said Mary.

"I didn't know you had a nurse for him."

"The nurse is for me. Rowland was quite a lot of trouble."

"But I didn't know that, Mary."

"I know you didn't. Alfred didn't want you to know, and the only reason I'm telling you now is because I don't want you to think we were selfish, not to bring the baby here sooner. They kept me in the hospital for an extra two weeks."

"But you must be all right now, or Alfred wouldn't have gone so far away."

"I am, but I still get tired easily. And I don't want to drop the baby on the floor."

"Heavens, no."

"The next time I'm going to have a Caesarean, if there is a next time."

"There will be, and it will be fine. I just know it."

"Your flowers are lovely."

"We've had a very good year with everything. I have a new man, an Italian. You've never seen our greenhouse close to, have you?"

"Oh, yes. The first time I was here."

"Oh, but this new man has it filled, filled. He's done a lot of transplanting. Pays no attention to what I say, but the results are worth it. He speaks hardly any English and I don't know any Italian."

"Yes, I've been to the greenhouse. That was the day I was really sure I loved Alfred."

"What in the world is he doing in Texas? *Texas,* that's just over the border from Mexico, and somehow Mexico seems farther away than Russia."

"It's a business trip. He has a friend there he met in the Navy named Jack Tom Smith. Alfred wants to buy out the Thorntons and Lex Porter. This is a deep secret, but I can tell you."

"It hasn't been going well?"

"Swimmingly for a while, after their first row. Jack Tom is coming North in September for the polo matches, but Alfred wanted to see him before that. He's immensely rich and he loves Alfred. If Alfred can't buy out the Thorntons and Lex, I'm afraid he's going to resign. The whole trouble is Larry Von Elm. He's turned Lex against Alfred and the two of them run up bills and Alfred has to find the money to pay the bills without going to Fritz Thornton. He knows Fritz Thornton would be on his side, like he was a year ago, but Alfred doesn't want to be a tattle-tale."

"He never was. He always kept his troubles to himself. Too much so."

"I know. But he said the only thing to do is raise the necessary money and then go to Fritz Thornton again and say either the corporation is run on a business-like basis or he'll get out."

"Then why does he want the money?"

"To buy out the Thorntons. If he has control, Lex will have

435

to do as he says, and so will Larry Von Elm. The way it is now, Alfred can't help feeling that it's Lex's money in a way, and it is. But he isn't very hopeful. Oh, he's sure he can get Jack Tom to pledge the money, but he doubts whether Lex would like working under Alfred as the real head of the corporation."

"I have loads of money"

"But Alfred won't take any of it. It's too risky. And people aren't risking their money these days. Alfred's been to see a dozen men and they all have the same story. No money to invest. Then he suddenly bethought himself of Jack Tom Smith."

"Jack Tom Smith. What an awkward name. Why do those Southerners have to have double first names? It's bad enough for a girl, but a man! Jack Tom. It sounds like an old colored rag-picker."

"Picking up thousand-dollar bills, from what I understand," said Mary. "Not all Southern ladies have double first names. My mother didn't, and she was a Virginian."

"I know that, Mary, and I didn't mean any offense or I wouldn't have said it."

"Perfectly all right," said Mary, in a tone that was self-contradictory.

"You mustn't let things I say upset you, Mary. You have no idea what it is to sit here day after day with no one to talk to but a woman who wouldn't be here if she wasn't paid well. You lose touch when you don't see people. You lose the knack of talking to them. I don't want to take advantage of being—an invalid. But you know all about me, Alfred told you. And you don't know how grateful to you I am for bringing the baby here. It's wonderful to see that baby. It was wonderful to know about him, that he was on the way. And all the time you were carrying him, it gave me some excuse to go on living. I haven't had much excuse, you know. Nobody needs me. The girls go their own way, and thank God they have it in them to, because I haven't been much help. And Alfred didn't need me. He needed you, even before he ever knew you. I never thought Alfred would marry young, and I never thought I'd see an Eaton grandchild. But now I have, and it's wonderful to. A grandchild isn't your own, but you get something from having a grandchild that you don't get from your own children. What is it, I wonder? I know, but I can't put it into words. It's—suddenly there are three generations of you. You yourself, and your child, and his child. And it makes you think. I never would have gotten into so much trouble if I'd known I was going to have a grandchild. Oh, I knew I was going to have grandchildren, everybody does if they live long enough. But I didn't know how I was going to feel. And now I can't say how I feel. I just go gab, gab, gab. But now I want to know what Rowland's going to be like, and being his grandmother I can think about that without having the work and responsibilities of raising him. That's it. You're so busy raising your children and so much a part of their lives that you don't really give much thought to their future . . . I don't want to embarrass you—"

"You don't embarrass me," said Mary.

"Wait till I tell you. I don't want to even ask you to come to see me, because that must be—that takes an effort. But I hope, I sincerely hope, that if the time ever comes when you want to talk to somebody, that you want to talk to somebody other than your mother, just remember me. There's one good thing about my awful life, Mary. I've had the experience."

"Why do you say that? What experience?"

"Oh, Mary, we know. Do I have to say it in so many words? I knew the first day you looked at me, Alfred had told you about me. Alfred is so honorable that he'd feel he had to tell you that his mother had been an unfaithful wife. Well, I was. Of course I was."

"I know. I'm not pretending I didn't know that part of it. But why are you saying all this now?"

"For the future. If I'd had anyone to talk to—well, things probably would have turned out the same way. But maybe, just maybe having someone to talk to would have—no, maybe not. No, I suppose not. My first love affair was so different from my second. I was thinking that the second one could have been prevented. But I guess not. No, I don't think so."

"Is what you mean that I might want to have a love affair? That's simply never going to happen. And I must say, Mrs. Eaton, I can't say I like your thinking it might happen."

"It's because I don't want it to happen," said Martha.

"No, I don't believe you. You think it *is* going to happen. I don't say you want it to happen, but you're convinced it will. In fact, listening to you, I got the feeling that you thought it had happened or was happening now."

"No, Mary, I don't think it has happened or is now. But when I married Alfred's father I didn't even know it ever happened. And not many years later it happened to me. That's what I meant by the experience. Because when it happened, Mary, the man was just as innocent, or ignorant, as I was. He had never been in love with anyone but his wife. It's people like us, innocent, ignorant people, that it does happen to. A friendship, and he's nice when you need someone, and before you know it you can't stand to be separated. And with married people it isn't like a boy and a girl who aren't married. With married people there's only one ending."

"No there isn't. There are two endings. You put a stop to it, as I did. I *did, too*."

"Then you were lucky, and strong."

"Whether I was lucky or strong, I put a stop to it before it ended the way you think it has to. And I always will. And I expect Alfred to do the same thing."

"Then you're both lucky, and both strong. And very lucky to have each other. Does he know about the danger?"

"Of course. We don't see so many people. And it wasn't Lex Porter, so don't imagine things there."

"I'm glad you put a stop to it, and grateful. Glad for you and grateful for Alfred. You're right. I did think it was Lex Porter."

"Well, it wasn't."

"Lex could be a heart-breaker."

"Not my heart. Lex only appeals to a certain ty—" Mary changed her speech: "I don't think of Lex that way."

"He only appeals to a certain type of woman," said Martha. She smiled. "I guess he does. And I guess I have nothing to worry about."

"I wasn't classifying you with Lex's girls, Mrs. Eaton."

"Why not?"

"Can't we talk about something else?"

"Yes. That's the trouble with not seeing people. You lose the knack. When someone comes to see me it's an event in my life, and I forget that *they're* seeing people and making polite conversation all the time. I haven't people any more. I have servants, and whatever birds and animals I can look out at. Some women like to read, but I doze off. I'd like to meet Mr. Galsworthy, John Galsworthy, the English author. He would have been on my side. And I read a book by a woman, Edith Wharton. But most writers have a tendency to gloss over things. Oh, well, most people do, too. I think about the lives of the people I've known, some of them pretty interesting, but nobody'd ever put them in a book, because everybody has that tendency to gloss over things. Nobody'd ever put George Fry's life into a book. Just a coachman, finally burned to death in a fire. And yet it was an unusual life, if you knew the facts about George and didn't want to gloss over certain things. My Miss Trimingham would rather read what she's reading now. *The Sheik*. Have you read *The Sheik*, Mary?"

"Yes."

"Did you like it? I haven't read it. I wouldn't even know about it if Miss Trimingham hadn't tucked it behind a pillow out of my sight. Was it naughty?"

"Well, parts of it, I guess. It never really *tells* anything in so many words. I guess they wouldn't be allowed to sell it if they did. But it never could have happened, at least I didn't believe it. It was written by a woman. The author is really a woman. Uses initials instead of her first name."

"Ethel M. Dell."

"No, it's almost that, a name very much like that. Hull. E. Something Hull."

"Hull, yes. That's it."

"A woman would never write about sex. Everybody'd think she was writing about herself."

"No, we're not supposed to know about it, even in 1921."

"I know. Since I've been married to Alfred he's told me some things, but I heard them when I was fifteen. We talked about it, but outwardly we pretended we didn't know about it."

"The men make us do that. They all want to marry a virgin, and then when they get the virgin they turn right around and want her to be Cleopatra."

"Cleopatra? Why do you say Cleopatra?"

"Oh, because I always think of her as very naughty. My father used to have a picture of Marc Anthony and Cleopatra in his den. It was considered very risqué, especially for my father, but it wasn't really. She didn't have anything on above the waist, but everybody had statues that showed a lot more. Women, of course. Not men. If the statue showed a man, he always had something on. Leaves, or those things the Indians wear."

"It's a strange conversation to have with your husband's mother."

"Not any more. Not since you've been giving your baby a bath. My thoughts about Alfred go back to when I used to give him his bath."

"I don't think I understand that."

"Don't you? I guess I didn't make it clear. I often have thoughts that I'd have difficulty expressing. Out of practice. All I meant was, Alfred to me is more baby than man. If you and I talked about naked men, we'd think of them as men, even if we were talking about my son and your husband. But now that you have a baby of your own, you can see how I could only think of my son as a baby, naked, not as a man. I've never known Alfred naked as a man. And you have. Do I shock you?"

"Maybe you might if I understood you better, but I don't."

"Well, just as well," said Martha. "Tell me about your mother and father. Have they been in Wilmington all summer? The heat must be even worse there than it has been here."

"Mother's been away twice for a week at a time, but my father's been there most of the time. He likes to take his

439

vacation in September, in Canada. He and some other men have a place where they go fishing and gunning."

"They're very kind. They call me up on the telephone every once in a while. I'd like to have them here, but I know if I asked them they'd feel they had to come, and when they got here there wouldn't be anything for them to do. I couldn't entertain for them. The only time I've had people my age in the house was when my husband died. And you were really the hostess then. What a burden for a brand-new bride! I often think of that and how wonderful you were."

"It wasn't hard. The people were all so nice, so considerate."

"Do you know who sing your praises? Nellie and Josephine. After that ordeal they said, 'Never worry about Mr. Alfred. He has a real lady and a real woman.' I don't do their brogue very well, but that's what they said."

"I'm devoted to them."

"Well, they've been staunch and true to this family. I wish the girls were here."

"I meant to ask you about them. How are they?"

"Well, I get a long letter from one of them every week. They've been on pack trips, and of course they've had to learn to ride western style and Constance says she's come to prefer it. Not Sally, though. She still prefers the English saddle. They've met a lot of new people. They've visited another ranch that's owned by an Englishman, an English lord, or will be. Their letters are interesting to read if you've never been out there. I'll give them to you to read on the way home, but will you return them, because I'm saving them?"

"I'd love to read them, and I'll send them back tomorrow morning. Give them my love when you write to them."

"Oh, and it's so nice to have something to write about, this visit from you and Rowland. Can't you imagine the clucking and cooing that's going on down in the kitchen right now?"

"Yes, I can."

"Now you must take care of yourself, Mary. Don't overdo. I've given birth to four children and I know from experience that it isn't only having the baby that's exhausting. It's afterwards that you have to be careful and not overtax your strength. Men *never* realize that."

"Alfred does. The doctor told him."

"I'd love to see Alfred with his son."

Mary laughed. "He tries not to be a typical father, and the more he tries the more he's like the one in the funny papers."

"Yes," said Martha. "His father was like that with Billy . . . Mary, I know you want to go now, and much as I'd love to have you stay, I don't want to keep you. It was a great

440

kindness, sweet of you to come all that way when you haven't been feeling well. Come often if you can, but as often as you like. Say goodbye to me now and would you send the baby up for just one more look?"

"Of course." Mary rose and put out her hand, then changed her mind and bent down and kissed Martha's cheek.

"I will never do anything to hurt you, Mary."

"Of course you won't."

"Please remember that, because sometimes I say things that come out differently than the way I intended them to." She relaxed her grip on Mary's hand and the girl smiled and left.

In a few minutes Miss Macdougall, accompanied by Trimingham, brought the baby to the room. Martha was sitting in her chair and did not turn when they entered. "Here's the wee one to say goodbye," said Miss Macdougall. She held the child in front of Martha and Martha looked at him and nodded.

"Thank you," she said.

The nurses looked at each other and Trimingham by a quick motion of her head signaled the other to leave. At the sound of the Hudson starter Martha stood at her window and waved, but Mary and her baby and the nurse were already in the car and did not see her. Martha returned to her chair and picked up a fan.

"This was hand-painted," she said. "When I was little I had one that folded. It came from Japan, and it was made of ivory. I think this one came from China. The Japanese ones are prettier, but this one's better to have on a warm day."

"You get more air with that kind," said Trimingham.

Martha tapped the fan with her fingers. "It has almost the same sound as a drum, hasn't it?"

"Yes."

"Mr. Barlow's coming tomorrow or the next day."

"So I believe."

"What time is it?"

Trimingham looked at her Army wrist-watch. "Ten till three."

"Is that all? We still have most of the afternoon left."

"Yes, it seems later than that."

"If I look at that sprinkler too long it makes me dizzy."

"It has that effect on me sometimes."

"Your watch must be slow, there goes three o'clock."

"I know. This watch, you see it isn't only a wrist-watch. You can take it out of this leather thing and use it for a pocket watch, but then it runs fast. I guess it wasn't even meant to be a wrist-watch but somebody thought up this strap."

"How much does a real wrist-watch cost?"

"Well, I saw one for twelve-fifty, in the window. And they

441

go on up to as high as fifty, in this kind of a watch."

"Pick one out for twelve-fifty and charge it to me."

"You mean as a present?"

"Well, I wasn't going to take it out of your pay."

"Well, thank you. Thank you very kindly. Then I can give this one to my nephew. Such a fine lad."

"Today let's not talk about your nephew."

"I do go on about him, I know. But he's all I have. At least the only one I have any use for. The others just use me, to borrow money and never pay it back."

"They almost called him St. John Eaton. I'm glad they didn't. It might have been all right when he grew up, but Rowland is better for a young boy."

"Much better."

"I never really liked the name Alfred. Raymond was good enough for his grandfather. I should have insisted, no matter what Sam said. The finest man in Port Johnson."

"That's what I've always heard. They still speak very highly of him."

"We're not talking about the same person."

"Your father."

"No. My husband."

"Oh, I thought you were talking about your father. Well, Mr. Eaton *was* a fine man."

"Oh, dry up, Trimingham."

"Have a care, now. By rights you ought to be taking your afternoon nap. I only let you stay up because you were good today, but now you're getting just as bad as ever."

Martha stood up and looked at Trimingham and began to laugh. "You're lucky."

"Am I?"

"Yes. Just think if I were your nurse. Oh, I'd be so awful to you."

"You're bad enough as it is," said Trimingham.

"I know. Poor woman. Poor Trimingham. I never have a kind word for you, do I?"

"I don't expect it. I have my duties and that's what I'm paid for."

Alfred came to Port Johnson as quickly as he could, but that was four days later. He went to the mill from the station, taken there by Ed Barlow, who would not have been able to comprehend the confusion created by the pleasant news that Jack Tom was willing to advance the money necessary to buy out the Thorntons and Lex, and, on the other hand, the bad news of the fire, which so far Alfred could regard only as bad news. It was disturbing to have the great good news followed so closely by the bad. The good news was so good and so great that he had not had time to digest it, to revel in it. If he had had the bad news alone, that, too, should have been thought over, appraised, regretted, until it had run its course. He had gained something and lost something within a twenty-four-hour period, and the one followed the other too quickly. He was therefore uncommunicative on the ride out to the mill.

Ed stopped his car at the south end of the property, to show the damage at a distance.

"I can't believe it," said Alfred. "It reminds me of someone who's had his front teeth knocked out. No more Bridge Shop."

"No more Bridge Shop, template shop, oil shanty, yard-crew shack, watchmen's hut, loading platforms in the lower yards, the crapper."

"Where was the dinkey? I hope that was saved."

"Which dinkey? We had three. Well, we still have all three. They're boarded up and white-leaded in the engine-house up at the north end."

"We had three? I guess you must have added two during the war. The old one, Number 2, I used to love to ride on that when I was a kid."

"I remember. We could always tell when you were taking a ride, ringing the bell and blowing the whistle."

"Francis Xavier O'Day was the engineer. Always gave me a piece of cake from his lunch-pail. I used to consider it a privilege to be allowed to throw the switches."

"Frank O'Day never minded that, I'm sure."

"And the big whistle didn't blow the night of the fire."

"No. We had the steam. The insurance company makes us keep up enough steam in a small auxiliary to give us pressure for the fire hydrants. But I gave orders to disconnect the whistle when we closed down."

"Then there's no fire whistle in Port Johnson at all?"

"None. They might as well get used to it now. They're going to have to sometime, Alfred. The first good offer we get, we're going to have to sell."

"I wish we didn't have to. I wouldn't have said that two weeks ago, but seeing the hole in the scenery, where the Bridge Shop used to be, I get sentimental."

"I'm having some pictures taken of all that's left. You'll want to show your grandchildren. We don't have a picture of the Bridge Shop. Only the main office."

"I'm just beginning to realize, Eaton's Iron & Steel is a thing of the past."

"A thing of the past. To be cold-blooded about it, financially we might have been better off if the whole shooting-match burned down."

"Well, let's go have a closer look."

Most of the men in the clean-up crews recognized Alfred and nodded to him, but with neither affection nor hostility. "They're glad to get the work," said Barlow. "We hired them back on seniority and those with families. They're all either ten-year men or younger men with three children or more. That seemed the only fair way. It didn't satisfy everybody, but it was the best we could do. They all get the same money, thirty cents an hour. I put them on a six-hour shift to spread the work around a little bit, but some of them put up a howl. Some that were hired wanted to v rk ten hours and hog it all. 'Take it or leave it,' I told ther 'There're plenty of men will work four hours just to make a little cash.' "

"And here's the old template shop. Not a wall standing. Where did they find George Fry?"

"About here. The way I pieced it together, George must have been using the lower shelf of one of those big work-benches for a place to sleep. It was like a Pullman sleeper, only not as comfortable."

"I just spent three nights in them, they're not so comfortable. But more comfortable than a workbench. Did George have a funeral?"

"The Catholic Father said George was a Catholic. I never knew that. They had a service for him. He had a nice funeral, a pretty good turn-out. The two women that work for your mother, and I went representing the mill. Some of the men that hang around the livery stable. The mill paid for it. It'll come to under two hundred dollars."

"A man was burned to death right there." Alfred shook his head. "But I don't feel anything. I thought I would. I did on the train, but I don't now. George was my best friend."

"You get used to the experience the older you get. I buried all but two of my classmates from High. Only three of us left out of eleven in our class, and one of them's ready to go any day now. Not counting your father, I've been a pallbearer five times in the last year and a half. Counting your father—six. Then I sat with the family, so you wouldn't call that a pall-bearer. And being on the degree team I go to all lodge funerals."

They spent an hour at the scene of the fire and another hour in the office until Walter came to take Alfred to the farm. He had supper with his mother and she retired for the night immediately. They exchanged bits of information and it was not until he went downstairs to read the evening paper that he realized that he had enjoyed every minute of their conversation. She listened, she did not interrupt, she did not convey that impression that she was laughing at him from the superiority of her disordered mind, and when it was time for her to go to bed she put up her cheek to be kissed as of old. But not as of old, not at all as of old. She could easily have been Elsie Ferguson, playing a charming invalid, and he a young admirer worshipping from afar. He had been afraid of this meeting, with its potentialities for emotional outbursts, especially on the subject of Mary's visit. But she paid routine compliments to Mary and the baby and let it go at that. She was not his mother of old; she was, for this meeting at least, normal, settled, and strong. Perhaps, he told himself, she was often like this. But he knew that she was not. This was new, and she was new.

He saw her in the morning, before leaving for Wilmington. "I hope you'll come again very soon," she said. "And I'd love to see Mary and the baby, but I suppose there's not much chance of that before Christmas. If you go to Wilmington for Christmas, try to get up for a day."

And then he had left, knowing this woman less well than he had ever known her before; less well than he had ever known anyone.

He often says that this was the time that he could have made a decision that would have altered the course of his life. Sometimes he speaks of it as the last chance he had to go back to Pennsylvania, stay there, raise a family there. He had spent most of his life in Pennsylvania and it was the only place he really knew. He had roots there. When his son was born he realized for the first time that roots meant something to him. He began to take secret pride in the accomplishments of his family. He had always been proud of his grandfather, but now he also began to feel some pride in his father. He could not love his father. That would have been asking the impossible. But when he saw what had happened to the mill he says he felt the way most people were supposed to feel over the destruction at Louvain. The destruction at the mill seemed to him like a desecration of a man's life work, and he was almost tempted to change his mind and give up the aviation business and take charge of the mill. He knew next to nothing about how the mill should be run, but he could count on Ed Barlow, and he would have time to learn a lot until business conditions improved and the mill went back into production again. He was also encouraged by the improvement in his mother's health. He did not count on it to last, but at least he had seen her take hold of herself instead of letting go when she had a legitimate opportunity. If she could do that unassisted, there was no telling how much more she might improve if he brought Mary and the

445

baby to live somewhere in Port Johnson—not at the farm, but somewhere in that direction. He says that when he went back to New York, armed with Jack Tom Smith's promise of financial support, he felt that his battle had been won. He could go to the Thorntons and offer to buy them out, and they would not have any very good reasons to refuse. If they agreed, he could then lay down the law to Lex and Von Elm and if they opposed him, he could get out. He had no intention of continuing the corporation without Lex, but Lex would have to decide whether he wanted to go on with him or without him. Jack Tom Smith's promise of money gave him the opportunity to have a showdown with the Thorntons and Lex. If they resisted his efforts to run the company properly, he could resign with dignity, having offered to buy out the company. It was not like it had been the first time. The first time he quit it was more in a fit of pique and not very dignified. He was getting out of something that he had not put anything into. In fact, it was even worse than that. He appeared to be ungrateful and dictatorial. But now he had the money behind him and he was on equal terms with the Thorntons and Lex. That was what made him feel that the battle was won, no matter how they reacted or how it turned out.

He sometimes says that although he was only twenty-four at the time, he had gone through almost everything a man experiences in his lifetime and that everything else that happened later was repetition. The only thing that he did not have at twenty-four was the perspective that you get from more years of experience, but he had to be reminded that it was not true that everything that happened after that was repetition. He would often reply by saying that basically the situations were the same and therefore repetitious, but then he would be told that the results were not always the same and also they involved different people and therefore the experiences were totally different since no two people are ever the same. Sometimes he would agree to that, but sometimes he would argue.

Looking back he would often take pride in the extent of his maturity at twenty-four. Not many young men had had as many important experiences as he had had, he would say, and he admitted that it gave him a sense of superiority to be able to say that. What were they? And his answers were almost always the same, namely, that he had been in love twice before he was twenty and both times the girls had been killed, which was an experience many men go through life without having had once. He had been in the war and in some danger, although not much, and he had had responsibility in the Navy at an age when he should have been going to proms. And he had had a lot of business experience in a year and a half. But he would be told that the one thing that gave him his sense of superiority more than anything else was his experiences with women. He was inclined to dismiss that experience, but it was true. He would change the subject, but the next thing he would talk about was having had a son at twenty-four. He says that he was young to be a father, although he was not the first in his class at Princeton to be a father. He was only comparing his experience with other rich boys and not with boys of the middle class and the poor; there were thousands of boys whose parents were not rich, who had had every experience he had had at twenty-four. But he said, "Well, they never played court tennis and they never rode in a private car. That's experience, too, don't forget." Well, he had never starved. To this he would say, "And damn few people you ever heard of starved either."

He says he is not sure just what decided him against going back to live in Port Johnson but there were several reasons. The real reason was that he was not a second-rater. He could have been the leading citizen of Port Johnson without much competition, but it would have been avoiding life and rather cowardly. Port Johnson was not good enough for him. He had to live in the big world, compete with the big people. He practically said that himself. He said he did not take pride in beating Harry Van Peltz at tennis. He wanted to beat the first man on the Princeton varsity. It was the same with other things he wanted to do. All through his life he has been one of those men who gravitate toward the top by instinct, and I suppose that is one of the reasons why I love him. It is very complimentary to a woman to know that she is loved by a man who has a touch of greatness.

THE HOUSE at Jagger's Cove was too big for the young Eaton family and their staff of two, and the $150 monthly rent was more than Alfred wanted to pay, but it had its advantages and the primary one was that Mary wanted to live there. It was a two-story structure, a center unit to which an east and a west wing had been added, with a porch facing north that ran the length of the north elevation for the view of the Sound. The halls and rooms were high-ceilinged and there was a widow's walk. The house belonged to friends and contemporaries of Eugene St. John's who were taking two of their remaining years for a leisurely trip around the world, and Alfred and Mary were in effect paying-caretakers. The owners provided the necessary two gardeners, one of whom lived in a cottage on the place, but the owners wanted a reliable, socially acceptable couple who would appreciate the contents of the

447

house, and the modest rental carried with it one condition: that the Eatons must live there the year 'round. It was as cool a spot as there was on the North Shore during the months when coolness is not easily found on the North Shore, but the location and the airy, spacious halls and rooms created a costly heating problem in cold weather, and Alfred, who had never had to pay a coal bill, learned why there were so many rich people back in Gibbsville, Pennsylvania. He learned to operate a furnace—although that was supposedly the head gardener's duty—and he learned to refrain from remarking that the apparatus was big enough to run the *Vaterland*—now the *Leviathan* and now berthed at Hoboken. He learned that any such criticism of the place annoyed Mary, who had visited the house as a child and as a girl in her teens, and regarded any slighting comment as ingratitude. "If we're ever offered Otto Kahn's place for $15 a month, don't take it," said Alfred. "We can go broke on that kind of a bargain." But Jagger's Cove was only six miles from the Nassau Aeronautical Corporation plant and not more than ten miles from most of their friends' houses. They were less than a mile from the Long Island Rail Road station and the village of Jagger's Cove, where the merchants astutely charged them summer prices all year 'round. "This is good training for when I make my first million," said Alfred. "Every young married couple ought to start out like this. It gives the man the proper incentive."

"Your sarcasm is wasted on me, because that's exactly what I believe."

"But it isn't as though we hadn't seen some big houses before. You grew up with du Ponts, and I've been to the mansions of the rich. In fact, my grandfather's house was once known as The Mansion. Although God knows it was nothing to compare with this."

"Well, just get to work and make your million dollars," said Mary. There was confidence, and no sarcasm, in the way she said it, and he had lost his point to a compliment. But it was unusual for her to be unresentful during such conversations, and during her pregnancy he refrained from criticism of their bargain—her bargain—and in time he became reconciled to the expense. She protested when he bought a second-hand Indian motorcycle-and-sidecar. "You're pretending we're poor, and we're not. You're making people think I'm extravagant and you know I'm not."

"I know you're not. But there's hardly room in the garage for the Marmon. They have five cars up on blocks and they had to move them closer together to make room for our car. Tight squeeze, too. I got the motorcycle because I want the guys at the plant to know I'm economizing. Good example for them. And anyway, I've always wanted a motorcycle."

"That's what it comes down to. You've always wanted one."

"But it's an economy, too, Mary. I get about seven miles to the gallon with the Marmon. I get almost ten times that with the Indian."

"Pow-wow-wow-wow, you and your Indian."

"You'd like it if you'd go for a ride in it."

"I'd lose the baby, too."

"Oh. I'm sorry."

Any mention of the baby, before or after its birth, instantly had such a magical effect on Alfred that she ceased to take pleasure in watching his response. It was like throwing a stick for a dog to retrieve; the response was so predictable, he would chase the stick when none had been thrown, and the performance became tiresome. It was, finally, the healthful aspects of the place for mother and child that made the Jagger's Cove house acceptable to Alfred.

After the baby was born Mary's own pleasure in the child had been detracted from by the enormity of Alfred's love for it. The love had been anticipated, but the seriousness and completeness of it made her feel that she was being overlooked, by-passed, unappreciated, ignored, in spite of his gentleness and solicitude and tenderness. His concern for her during her postpartum hemorrhaging was genuine and unqualified, and made more touching to her by his helplessness while wanting to help. But she saw in his love for the baby an emotion that she could not share because Alfred could not share it, a love that was more nearly intellectual than—in spite of its depth— passionate. It was a love that by the nature of the man who held it and the child who was the object of it could never reach a climax. Passion and the practices of passion had been exquisitely pleasurable to her, as to Alfred, but from the most ecstatic love-making a man turned to sleep, and this love, she knew, was not subject to the vicissitudes of the expression of love. It was an even and an eternal thing, inexhaustible and indestructable beyond self-destruction, invulnerable to lethal attack by the man who held the love for the man-to-be who was the object of it. It was not that Mary did not understand this love; she understood it only too well. And in her depressions she could not help wanting what was impossible to have, what her husband could not even give. It was no comfort to contemplate what she had, that was freely given. There was no reasonableness in wanting what she wanted, thus no hope that she could be satisfied without it. And so, as though to pay for a successful birth of her first child, she was left to think the thoughts that even in their minutest form had the power to eat away the love that existed between Alfred and her.

Concurrently, her own love for her child was not affected by Alfred's love for it. It was deep and true and passionate, and good-humored, and besides all the other things, the baby was fun. She was not aware of any destructive force within herself, and she had confidence in her physical recovery, and she therefore was free to enjoy the day-by-day growth of the baby and to take pleasure in the exercise of her newly developed power to observe the minutiae that indicated its progress in life. She saw things that no one else saw; a single new eyelash, the disappearance of a wrinkle, the enlarging of a nostril. Out of her womb the baby was more truly the whole of her life than he had been as an insistent heavy presence inside her. She bore no resentment toward the baby for his father's love of him; it was the love itself she resented. And a woman could not complain of her husband's love for their child when it had done nothing to lessen his love of her. There was no reasonableness in wanting what she wanted, thus no hope that she could be satisfied without it.

They had curtailed their social activities after the early months of Mary's pregnancy. A woman's pregnancy was not discussed in her presence if it was mixed company—and the company was seldom mixed. It was, in fact, an indicator of the closeness of a friendship for a husband to invite a male friend to dinner and bridge with his pregnant wife, but even then the subject was embarrassing, although the wife might be great with child. The whole process of love-making and reproduction was so new and fascinating to Mary that she escaped most of the gestative boredom, and visits from her mother, visits to Wilmington, and the running of the household occupied much of her waking hours. And while the baby remained in her womb she was maternally protective toward Alfred, who was dissatisfied with the state of affairs at the plant. He told her everything, day to day, and she became interested through the accumulation and possession of his information, rather than through an original interest. Alfred confided in her, and in no one else, that the armistice between him on one side and Lex and Von Elm on the other was ended in three months, at which point Lex and Von Elm on their own ordered two Wright engines. Alfred's first knowledge of the order was the presence of the crated engines in the plant yard. He went looking for Lex, but Lex was not in the draughting-room office he shared with Von Elm, and Alfred ignored Von Elm. About an hour later Lex appeared in Alfred's office.

"You were looking for me. I guess I know why," said Lex.

"Well, I saw those crates and I knew they weren't perambulators."

"That's just the trouble, Alfred. Perambulators are more on your mind that aeroplanes these days."

"There's room in my mind for both. What are they going to cost?"

"A thousand dollars apiece. The Navy's ordered a hundred of them from Wright and we heard about it, so we got these two. We could never have got them for that price if the Navy hadn't given Wright the big order."

"We're in the business, so we're going to need engines. I don't object to spending the money for essentials, and engines are essentials. But I don't like you going over my head. How do *you* like it?"

"I don't. I didn't like doing it, but I didn't want to have an argument over it, so I went ahead. I never know how you're going to take it when we want to spend some money."

"Try me," said Alfred. "I'm not objecting now."

"No, but just before we ordered the engines you'd just given us hell for ordering a hundred gallons of dope."

"Fifty gallons was more than enough. It didn't take anywhere near fifty gallons to paint those wings and fuselage, so why tie up cash? I've *saved* enough money around here to pay for those engines. Do you realize that? But if you and The Genius had your way, we'd have a stockroom filled up with stuff we're not going to need for at least two years, if ever. And all representing cash tied up. The only way I can make you understand what I'm doing is to hammer away. Now you can understand what I do by saving here and there, because you can see those engines and you know how much they cost. Let me give you an examination. I'll get out some data for you. Here it is. Take the machine shop. How much does a lathe cost?"

"Search me."

"Seven hundred dollars. A shaper, how much?"

"I don't know."

"Six-fifty. The air compressor system? A thousand. We have a lathe, a miller, a shaper, a power hack saw, two drill presses, a grinder, a forge, the air compressor system, the line shaft and pulleys, the vises and small tools and chucks, and two chain hoists. It adds up to eight thousand fifty dollars in the machine shop. Take this office, this room and the outer office. It doesn't look like J. P. Morgan & Company, but we spent twenty-four hundred on furniture and equipment."

"I know things cost money."

"But you don't know how much, and you don't know that they would have cost more if I hadn't paid cash in some cases, and in other cases bought second-hand. If I let you and The Genius have a free hand you'd order from catalogs, everything new. Your uncle wanted everything new, too, but he didn't know the difference when I bought some things second-hand. There are some items in here that are better second-hand. A workman can't complain that a machine hasn't been broken in. Do you know what our annual payroll is?"

"No."

"Over $50,000. That's a figure you can understand. And believe me, I can too, because it's something I can't fool around with. But just remember, Lex, we got those engines for nothing because I do the shitty job."

Lex rarely apologized to anyone for anything, but the conversation temporarily had the effect of censure, and it pleased Alfred that it had been accomplished with facts and figures and a minimum of personalities.

The relationship with Von Elm had been permanently damaged in the first dispute between Alfred and Lex, and communication between Alfred and Von Elm existed almost entirely through Lex. There was little occasion for more direct contact, since Von Elm worked with and under Lex. Alfred and Von Elm hated each other soundly and comfortably, once they had passed beyond the stage of compulsory, tentative politeness. Alfred's motorcycle irritated Von Elm because it was rather dashing and at the same time an economy that Von Elm—loving money that was his own—could not carry off. Von Elm had bought himself a Brooks-type suit at Nat Luxenberg's, but he still wore the pointed high shoes and the fedora hat with the bow at the back. The hostility between Alfred and Von Elm disposed of any social relations after working hours, but Lex had been a disappointment to Von Elm on that score. Once, and only once, Lex invited Von Elm to his uncle's for a swim, and when Von Elm replied that he could not swim, Lex made no other offers to introduce Von Elm to the territory of the rich and elegant. Von Elm lived in a boarding-house in Huntington and drove to work in his Dodge roadster. He was hardly a half hour's drive from the power and the glory of the North Shore, but he was still as far away from it as Greensburg had been from Sewickley. On Sunday afternoons he would drive slowly along the narrow, winding roads of Nassau County, seeing nothing of the great estates except the protective shrubbery and French fences and the mighty names on the little black or green signs. The simplicity of the signs amused him—all but the sign at Jagger's Cove reading A. Eaton. It would be a pleasure some day to kick that one over.

Since Mary had neither curiosity nor social ambitions to disturb her, her residence on Long Island was not attended by the nervousness of the newcomer. There was not much difference between taking up residence there on a permanent basis and the frequent visits in the past, and what difference there was was favorable to her enjoyment of her status as mistress of the house at Jagger's Cove. The only disturbance during the months of her pregnancy was the reappearance of Jim Roper, now a full-fledged medical student at Columbia. Alfred and Mary saw him at a wedding and she invited him for Sunday

452

lunch. "I had to do something," she said, on the way home. "He knows I know he's going to be here tomorrow. He knows I've invited the Broomes, and he's staying with them. I couldn't say, 'We're having your host and hostess tomorrow, but don't *you* come.' "

"I'm not blaming you. You had to invite him. He didn't have to accept."

"Well, he's the only ghost in my past, and heaven knows he isn't much of a one. Although I declare he looks like one."

The Broomes already knew the Jagger's Cove place, but Jim Roper did not, and he accepted immediately Mary's casual offer to show him around. Later that afternoon, when they were alone, Alfred asked Mary what she and Roper had talked about. "He didn't have his, wuddia-call-it, stethoscope with him, so I guess he wasn't clinical."

"He still loves me."

"Why are you so frank about it?"

"Because, honey, I give you credit for knowing he did. You wouldn't have believed me if I'd said we talked about the landscaping."

"No, I wouldn't, not after seeing the cow-eyed looks he was giving you today, and yesterday. Are you planning to elope with him?"

"He didn't go *that* far, but he allowed as how if you ever whupped me or didn't treat me kindly, he'd always be there, ready and waiting, open arms."

"You're making a joke of it, but he didn't mean it as a joke and you didn't take it as one. Did you let him kiss you? Did he try?"

"No, neither."

"Is that all you talked about?"

"I told him he ought to get out and play tennis or something. He said he played a little, they have courts where he is, but he didn't play often enough to get a real tan."

"Very solicitous of you. I suppose you told him he wasn't getting enough to eat—"

"I couldn't after the lunch he ate."

"—that's what I was going to say. Herr Doktor Roper had all kinds of an appetite today. I suppose he hasn't got a girl to make him forget you."

"I asked him that. He hasn't."

"You really went into it, didn't you?"

"Well, why shouldn't I? We were engaged, don't forget, and he's never done anything to you. I like him, and I always will like him. You can't expect me to stop liking all my men friends, any more than I expect you to your women friends. Most of them I knew years before I ever met you. So let's not talk about it any more."

All she said was true, and it was not the truth. She was not reporting the bitterness and intensity in Jim Roper's words, nor the moment in their stroll when he stepped several paces away from her and said: "I can't even bear to touch your hand, you carrying his baby. You never gave me the chance to show you that I'm a man. Now when I stay with a girl I pretend it's you. I've had a dozen girls since you gave me the gate, but they've all been you, Mary. And that's the way it'll be. Some night in bed he'll turn into me."

"That's horrid! That's a filthy horrid thing to say!"

"Only half of what I've been wanting to say for two years. Does your doctor say you can still go to bed with him? Then think of me, tonight."

"If I think of you it'll be with loathing, now or ever."

"That'll be even better. Maybe you'll get to loathe him and that's what I want. You made a fool of me, Mary. Did you think I was going to be the litle gentleman about it? I've taken enough from all you bastards that had everything. I went to a good school because my father was a clergyman and they gave him a special rate. I had to wait on table in college and miss half the fun because I had to keep up my marks for my scholarship. And I'll owe money for five years after I get my degree. But it would have been worth it if I could have had you. But no, a rich bastard with a big car came along, and I got the gate."

"I didn't know you had to work in college."

"I was ashamed to tell you. You knew I didn't have any money, but I wasn't going to admit I waited on tables, serving meals to some of the bastards that you know."

"They've never mentioned it."

"Oh, no. Of course not. Wouldn't think of embarrassing good old Jim."

"Still, it was nice of them not to mention it."

"Oh, the hell with them and how nice they are. But they took my girl. You were *my* girl. I had them all licked till Eaton came along. If you expect me to be the little gentleman about it, you've got another think coming."

"Jim, don't feel this way. I'm sorry. But I found out that I loved Alfred and I didn't really love you. It wasn't money. He isn't very rich, like Lex."

"*He* had a big grey Marmon and *I* couldn't afford the carfare to Wilmington. He could be everywhere that I couldn't be, and even your father, that I thought was my friend—he turned against me."

"Nobody turned against you."

"All right, then I turned against *them*. He isn't rich? Look at this place. You have to be rich to be a guest here."

"That's practically what we are."

454

"Ha. Mirthless laughter, mirthless laughter."

"He's a wonderful husband, and he works as hard as you do."

"And he's the boss. President of a company at his age. Did he work his way up to that?"

"Let's go back, and don't come here any more, Jim. It doesn't do you any good and it worries me. If you wanted to make me feel awful, you've succeeded. And you couldn't say these things to anybody you ever really loved, so I wasn't your girl."

"You're my girl even with his kid floating around inside you."

"At least try to be a gentleman. They can see us now."

In the lovely autumn at the start of their second year at Jagger's Cove Mary and Alfred began to settle into the enjoyment of a marriage. There had ceased to be the frenetic concern over the ability to have a child and the having of the child. The child was there, he was healthy even in his illnesses, and he gave them joy. Alfred was learning and Mary was learning that to go to sleep without making love was not a cause to take offense. Without prejudice to their love they had begun to renew their interest in the world outside themselves and in so doing had taken on an individuality that was stronger and more assured than either had had before marriage. They were now a man and woman who were a husband and a wife, a wife with a husband, a husband with a wife, in the community of mankind, of the United States of America, of polite society, of Jagger's Cove, Long Island. They had achieved nothing unusual, but they had achieved it irrevocably and as a husband and as a wife they had each forsaken the solitary incompleteness of the unmarried state. They had learned and would never stop learning the greatest joy of parenthood, which was the instinctive thinking of the child's well-being before one's own, and the joy of the consciousness of that thinking. Their own youth was only comparative; they were infinitely older than the child but in his helplessness they retained the special privilege of communication through dependence, without language but in the one case by means of an angry or a happy trust, and in the other a devoted curiosity and a practical comprehension.

On Saturday afternoons and Sundays they would play lawn tennis at one or another of the indoor courts of the very rich, or golf as guests at Piping Rock. Mary was so secure in her human motherhood that she asked for, and Alfred gave her, a collie bitch, six weeks old and young enough to grow up with the baby without jealousy. She called the puppy Prima because it was their first dog, and because a Donna was in the pedigree. Through that fall and winter and spring they were busy with small things, with their lives and their life together, with their popularity in society, with their deliberate prolongation of the practices of passion, with an unself-conscious contemplation of their tranquillity. The greater worries were, for those three seasons, subdued and postponed by the day-to-day routines of their happy life. The danger in Mary's fear of Alfred's love of the baby was unreal against the realness of the pleasure he gave her and took with her. And she was totally unaware of any danger that might be attributable to Jim Roper's assault on her subconscious mind. Her casual small lusts for other men were scarcely more than self-assuring responsiveness, provoked by her detecting similar covert lusts of her women friends for Alfred. She was no longer a defenseless virgin, unequal to the competition of other women. At a dance she would sometimes look about the room and know that she could not only match her beauty of face and figure with any other woman's but could attract any desirable man by the serene self-confidence she had gained with Alfred. She knew from her debutante days that some of the young women described her as "cold as marble," and she knew that some of them had not bothered to change the description. But some of their menfolk had changed the description without, for sure, knowing why. "Whatever young Eaton is getting," they would say among themselves, "I'd like to have some of it, hot, cold, or lukewarm."

Among the women there was no doubt about Alfred Eaton. It was only a question of time, they said—and in their cynical judgment of a man whom they did not know very well they were not conscious of the harsh judgment they were passing upon themselves. The trouble was to come, they implied, with one of their own number, and not stopping at one. But until Alfred selected one and one selected Alfred, they were all as guilty as they were innocent; all inadvertently comparing their set to a herd of mares awaiting their turn with the stud. Too many of them remarked that it was only a question of time; the prediction was made so often that the identity of the speaker and present company changed over and over again and the speaker and present company became the absent and available ones. Tuesday's good woman and virtuous sisters became part of Wednesday's good woman's potential adulteresses.

And yet they were not especially and particularly cruel to Alfred. It was only that he was new. They had seen it happen before; it was happening now, and as soon as Alfred had made their prediction come true, there would be someone else to take his place as the watched one. They were shrewd, and they needed no legal evidence as satisfactory proof. The watched one always gave himself away and in so doing he only confirmed their suspicions about the woman; the woman was always designated a little before the fact. She was suspected because the man had shown one extra courtesy, one extra effort to be in her company; and her availability, the degree of her availability, was known to those of her sisters who had knowledge of her discontent at home, her stupidity, her nymphomania, her boredom, her curiosity, or her present admiration of or common interest with or even love for the man.

The presence of love was a cause for worry among the sisterhood. Individually they would aid and abet an affair that did not go beyond clandestine meetings for the pleasures of the body. But an affair that began as or became love, and threatened two marriages, was not to be encouraged. No one thought of mentioning the "sanctity" of a marriage. The marriages had been sanctified at no higher altitude than St. John's Lattingtown. But no one not immediately concerned wanted divorce. The serious pressure was always saved for arguments against divorcing, by the friends and contemporaries of the principal parties, then by the next older generation. And an adulterous man and woman who obstinately divorced their wife and husband and went on to a marriage of their own were held in low esteem. They had violated good order. Even in the least scandalous of such developments the love-stricken pair had momentarily exposed the special small world to the attention of the outside world, and the high hedges and French fences that hid the big houses from the view of Lawrence Von Elm were only small evidences of the smaller world's passion for privacy. But it must not be thought that good order was the vocation of the women. It originated with and was enforced by the men.

The fathers and the grandfathers, the uncles and great-uncles were the hardest sophisticates in the world, and peculiarly American. They had had their money long enough—even when it was no more than a single generation—to discover that it would buy anything that the Englishman had, whether it was a servant or an elephant's tusks or a thousand grouse or a soft-rolled lapel or a Shakespeare folio, and there was no title under duke that would tempt them to change citizenship, since all other titles were by their very nature restrictive, and these men resisted all restrictions they had not themselves made. They were sentimentally attached to the English, often through lineage and most often by the Englishman's commercial sense; they easily acquired English habits and tastes. But they regarded the Englishman's system of recognition and reward as undesirably immature and even slightly cheap. The title, the medal, the order, the sash, the velvet, the ermine, the buckle, the sword—they had all been copied and adopted by the undertakers and dentists and insurance agents and railway conductors who belonged to the more flamboyant Masonic side-shows. The reward for accomplishment was more power, and as the power increased so did the desire for and desirability of privacy. Underwood and no one else took their picture and it was expected to satisfy the public curiosity for at least ten years. Blythe and Marcosson were permitted to convey the public statements of these men, but other journalists and less thoroughly processed methods were given no consideration. Some of them were affable men, some kindly, a few humorous, and they were all subject to the heartache and the thousand natural shocks that flesh is heir to, but they demanded obedience in all matters pertaining to their work, and since privacy was essential to their methods, the demand for privacy easily extended over matters not directly connected with their work. It was expected that the habit of obedience would be cultivated by all those who could not meet these men on precisely equal terms. At the moment there was no one living who alone and unaided could put these men in the secondary position. A gardener was more likely to take a firm, opposite stand than a United States senator or a Knight Commander of the Bath, but the gardener had earned that privilege. A man who allowed an illicit love to jeopardize his marriage and thereby to disturb good order forfeited what privileges he had and was likely to obtain. A similar punishment awaited the cuckolded husband who took his nasty discovery into the courts. He, too, had violated good order. One effect of this uncompromising attitude toward divorce and scandal was that it ironically gave a sense of security to wives who contemplated or were indulging in extra-marital affairs. This effect was unknown to the keepers of good order, who were more likely to attribute adultery to the idleness and shallowness of the women than to the protection they enjoyed under the system of good order. A man on his way up suffered his wife's infidelity rather than take public action that he knew would end his career. And the women knew it and made use of the knowledge. This unsuspected immoral effect of an apparently highly moral prohibition might have been truly laughable had the keepers of good order established their rules as a moral code. But in reality, and although some of the keepers of good order were religious and sternly moral men, the purpose of good order and its enforcement was to keep the public in ignorance of the personal lives of these men and their families. No publicity was better than any publicity, a rule which applied even in the matter of public benefactions. The library or the hospital or the museum might bear the donor's name—or, more likely, his deceased mother's name—but he remained as nearly anonymous as practical in the circumstances. A scandal attaching to a friend's name was unthinkable, and punishment awaited the disobedient. The women, therefore, while secretly enjoying security under the system, helped to maintain it for a less selfish reason. They knew that a man's career could be ruined by divorce, and they protected their women friends as long as they were able. The women's version of the code made for a practical loyalty that was at least as sound as a sentimental one, less subject to caprices of small envies and jealousies and not always dependent on close friendship. But if the system controlled the divorce rate, it also made a minor misdemeanor of infidelity.

Neither Mary nor Alfred was a blood relation of the families which maintained good order, and their financial connection was so remote that it was unimportant. Mary's father had gone as high in the du Pont company as he could hope to go, and the total fortune of the Eaton family would have been exhausted if it had had to cover the living expenses of any of a dozen North Shore families for a couple of years. But Mary had friends of long standing on the North Shore, and Alfred had been taken up, in the current phrase, by Fritz Thornton, who, while not a business figure of the first rank, was a very rich man who was prominent in most of the right sports. As such he commanded more respect than if he had devoted his time and money to high finance. In sport he was one of a few; in Wall Street he would have been one of many. He worked as hard at his games and his clubs as other men worked to make money, with the result that in the matters on which he was expert, the men who had more money sought his advice. He was, moreover, safely conservative in his attitude toward outsiders, and his approval of Alfred Eaton was as good as a letter of unlimited social credit. If Fritz Thornton liked the boy, the boy must be first-rate.

The boy who became the man had made a good marriage and was off to a good start in business by proving he wanted to work. He was good-looking, good at lawn tennis, a promising court tennis player, a good swimmer, drank but had never been seen drunk, had some sort of a way with the women, and at the same time had a reserved something in his manner that signified good breeding and not merely a middle-class unfamiliarity with his new surroundings. He was said to be an extremely good influence on young Porter, and the older women considered him charming, charming. Bit by bit Alfred's reputation was being assembled and his name had come up in houses he had not yet entered. He was new, but he had made a good impression, especially on families which had no sons. But the favorable impression needed the dramatic touch to have a lasting effect, and it was provided in February of the young Eatons' second year on the North Shore.

The MacHardie estate main entrance was just under a mile from Fritz Thornton's and at any time but the dead of winter the lawns and the big house and the pond were hidden from view. But the hedges and other foliage were denuded except for burlap on this sub-freezing Sunday afternoon. There had been snow for two days and the roads were cleared for passage but only at low speed as Alfred and Mary made their way to Fritz Thornton's tennis court. It was just before three o'clock and they were going to be slightly late for their tennis date, but the drifts and icy road forced Alfred to drive in second gear. "Look at that little boy," said Mary. "His little ears are going to fall off. But he's a good little skater. *Alfred! Stop the car! He's going through the ice!* Oh, God! Alfred."

"Where? Where?"

"The pond, the pond, the pond. On the left."

A woman in a heavy dark-blue cape was screaming, "Sandy! Sandy!" But she stood as though frozen at the edge of the pond.

Alfred moved the car through the gateposts, got out and ran to the pond. It was plain to see where the child had gone through, but the child himself was somewhere under the ice. Alfred dropped his overcoat on the snow and took off his jacket, waistcoat and shoes and walked slowly on the ice until it gave way and he went under. He found the child immediately and brought him up and still holding him in his arms, walked in the shallow pond until he was able to hand him to the nurse.

"Alfred, you're bleeding," said Mary.

"Never mind me, let's start working on the kid."

"I know how, I know how," said the nurse, now somewhat composed. She lay the boy on his belly and began lifting him in the rhythm of artificial respiration.

"Will you help her, Mary? I'll go telephone for a doctor."

"I want to help you. Your neck, your throat is cut. Alfred, please?"

"I'll be all right. You help her."

He got into the Marmon and drove to the main house. A butler, whom Alfred could see through side windows, made his annoyed way to the door, putting on his tailcoat as he walked. He stared at Alfred, wet and bedraggled and bloody, and started to close the door in his face, but Alfred pushed his body against the door and spilled the butler.

"Where's your phone? I have to have a doctor. Little boy fell in the pond."

"Little boy? Sandy? Master Sandy?"

"Yes, now get to the phone, you damned fool, and call the doctor. Better yet, call an ambulance, tell them to bring a pulmotor."

"You, sir? What have you done to yourself?"

"Get to the God damned telephone, will you?"

Alfred opened his eyes some time later and saw Mary, a man identifiable by his stethoscope hanging about his neck, and another man in a Donegal tweed suit and wearing a wing collar, all standing near the bed. The green velvet window draperies had been drawn and Mary was in the tennis dress she had worn under her beaver coat.

"Hello," said Alfred.

"How do you feel?"

"I feel all right, I guess."

"Take a sip of this," said Mary, coming to the bed.

"What is it?"

"Steer-o. Bouillon."

"Oh," said Alfred. "Is the boy all right?"

"The boy is alive, thanks to you, sir. My name is MacHardie, James MacHardie. I'm the boy's grandfather."

"Is he all right?"

"He'll *be* all right," said the doctor. "Try not to move around, Mr. Eaton. I've had to take twelve stitches in your neck. Apparently cut yourself on a jagged piece of ice bringing the little fellow out of the dam. A nasty cut, but it could have been much, much worse, an inch or two to the right."

"Did you call Lex? Tell him we weren't coming?" said Alfred.

Mary laughed and then began to cry. "Lex is downstairs. I'm terribly sorry."

"Perfectly natural reaction, I'd say," said MacHardie. "Your wife has been very brave, Mr. Eaton, and—well, very brave."

"She always is." Alfred took her hand. "I'm sorry I didn't recognize you, Mr. MacHardie. I'm in a fog, I guess."

"Think nothing of it, my dear sir. Your friends are downstairs. My friend Fritz Thornton, and his nephew, Lex Porter."

"I have a son of my own. Is your grandson all right?"

"He's alive, and he's asleep. Naturally we have to consider the possibility of pneumonia, am I not correct, Doctor Blane?"

"We have to, yes, Mr. MacHardie."

Alfred shivered uncontrollably. "Do I have to consider that possibility? I can't bed down in Mr. MacHardie's house. Is there any whiskey?"

"You can have a drop of whiskey, I suppose," said the doctor.

"You can have everything here you'd have in the hospital," said MacHardie. "I don't think we ought to move him, do you, Doctor Blane?"

"No, he'll be better off here for a day or two."

"Would you like some more bouillon?" said Mary.

"I like—sleep," said Alfred, and dozed off.

Alfred remained at MacHardie's house for three days. Mary was given a room connecting with his through a bathroom. They were driven to Jagger's Cove in MacHardie's Daimler, and in every room in the house there were dozens of hothouse

461

roses. At the end of the week there was a large package from Tiffany's. When they had removed the wrapping Mary said: "Heavens! I've *seen* this. I've *seen* this, Alfred. I saw it when I went to exchange wedding presents. I know what it cost."

"Twelve stitches."

"Twelve stitches, yes. And—six thousand dollars."

"A tea service, isn't it?"

"Not *a* tea service. It belonged to some very famous person. Let's see the card."

Alfred handed her the card, a calling card of Mr. James Duncan MacHardie, with the *Mr.* crossed out and written at the top: "Profoundly grateful."

"Five hundred dollars a stitch," said Alfred.

"It belonged to Thomas Jefferson or Benjamin Franklin. Mother would know. She remarked on it when we were in the store."

"I did all the work and you get all the hardware."

"You're getting something, but I'm not supposed to tell you."

"What? Some cream and sugar to go with the set?"

"Never mind. And act surprised when we go there to dinner."

"I'll act surprised when we get invited."

"We have been and I've accepted. Next Friday. Alfred, you're a wonder. I saved a little boy from drowning once, at Rehoboth Beach. I was twelve years old and I got a five-pound box of Page & Shaw's. *You* saved James D. MacHardie's grandson."

"I used to like those Page & Shaw jordan almonds, all covered with white sugar stuff."

"Is your mind all right?"

"My mind's all right, all right. I don't mind his giving us a present, but I don't like going there for dinner. I wish you hadn't accepted. I wish you'd told him—anything."

"He didn't invite us. His daughter did. She wants to thank you and you can't refuse her that."

"Oh, the old boy isn't going to be there?"

"I didn't say that, honey. But his daughter's the hostess."

"I wish they'd let it go at giving us a present. You can't stretch out undying gratitude through a whole evening," said Alfred.

He need not have worried. They were admitted by the butler, their coats were taken by a footman and maid, and they were led to the library, a cheerful room in spite of the massiveness of the furniture and the gold-and-leather formality of the sets of books. Logs were burning in the fireplace, there was a globe large enough for a general staff, silver paper cutters and framed photographs of Booth Tarkington and Mark Twain among other photographs of royalty, Republican government notables and family. There were also some framed handwritten letters which Alfred did not have a chance to read before MacHardie's daughter briskly entered the room. "How nice of you to come, Mrs. Eaton, Mr. Eaton. I'm Jean Duffy, Sandy's very grateful mother. And this is my husband." While speaking she pushed a wall button, a maid appeared in the doorway, and Mrs. Duffy nodded, all without interrupting her talk. "My husband and I wanted to thank you alone—"

"And we do," said Duffy.

"And we do, but we also wanted Sandy to meet the gentleman who saved his life, and as a very special treat for him, I think he's on his way downstairs at this very moment. At least if my arrangements are working out. Yes. Here we are. Sandy dear, this is Mr. and Mrs. Eaton. Mrs. Eaton, this is our boy, and Mr. Eaton, you *have* met before."

The boy, in pajamas and bathrobe, took Mary's hand and bowed over it, but when he shook hands with Alfred he stared up at him in adoration. He was about six years old, thin and with light brown hair.

"I'm glad to see you're all dry, Sandy," said Alfred.

The boy laughed. "All dry, yes. That's *good*. I'm glad to see you're all dry, too."

"Well?" said the boy's father.

"Oh. Thank you very much for fishing me out of the pond," said the boy.

"And?" said his father.

"And—and. Oh, yes. And it's a good thing I wasn't any smaller or—or—or you would have had to throw me back."

"Very good. Very—*good*," said his mother.

"Very good, son," said Duffy. "And now skedaddle. Kiss for Mother, kiss for me, and up up up up."

"But Daddy, we all forgot," said the boy.

"What did we forget?" said Duffy.

"Mr. Eating. I hope your neck is better," said the boy.

"Thank you, Sandy. It's much better. I still have the bandage. Do you want to see it? Well, I guess I can't open my shirt to show you, but it's right here, and much better."

"You remembered and we forgot," said Mrs. Duffy. "You have much better manners than your mother and father. But now off you go, and go right to sleep, please. This is very late for you."

The boy again bowed to Mary and took Alfred's hand. "Will you go for a swim with me in Grandpa's pool sometime?"

"Almost any time you say," said Alfred.

"And *I* say, no more delays. Goodnight, darling," said Mrs. Duffy.

The boy departed. "Now I'm sure you're ready for your

cocktail. You were very sweet to him, Mr. Eaton, and he's been looking forward to this meeting as much as we have."

"And that's saying a lot," said Duffy. He was a portly man, forty years old, with thinning hair parted in the middle. He wore a white waistcoat with his dinner jacket and had the look of good food and Turkish baths, but also of powerful arms and shoulders and coldly appraising blue eyes. His teeth were white, even, and small for his face as it was now but probably not out of proportion before he had begun to take on weight. He wore the ribbon of the Military Order in his satin lapel. Alfred judged him to be a good boxer and a punishing one. His wife, who was probably thirty-five, wore a black lace dress, firmly corseted underneath, and she had large full breasts that squeezed together almost to her throat. Her jewelry was a double strand of pearls, a ring of rubies and diamonds on her right hand, and a plain gold wedding ring and one-carat diamond in a Tiffany setting. Together the Duffys presented a picture of opulence with obvious inferences of frequent sexual contests, tending toward slappings and laughter.

"Creighton, dear, you and Mrs. Eaton lead the way?"

James MacHardie and the other guests were waiting in another room, all white and gold even to the concert grand piano, which stood in the far corner with a concert harp, and white and gold music stands. All the smaller chairs were matching, all the larger chairs matched, and the two sofas were a pair. The room had a crystal chandelier and after the shaded lamps of the library the light of this room was a glare, and the six persons seemed lost. The butler was serving Martini cocktails and sherry from a small glass mixer and a small silver-leafed decanter.

"Mrs. Ripley, Lady Sevringham. Mrs. Pearson, Mr. Thornton, Lord Sevringham, and my father. Mr. and Mrs. Eaton. I think that does it."

"Mrs. Eaton, you come and sit beside me, won't you?"

"She has you at dinner, Father. No."

"Don't be bossy, now, Jean. Mrs. Eaton and I dined together for three nights straight and we still had a lot to talk about, didn't we, Mrs. Eaton?"

"I had a very good time, speaking for myself."

"Sit down, now, and tell me, how is Master Rowland Eaton, and have you any news of our mutual friends in Wilmington?"

Alfred took a seat beside Lady Sevringham, a fiftyish woman who smiled at him until he was more or less settled and continued to smile until he thought she was not going to speak. Then, abruptly, she did speak. "Mm. Tell me, Mr. Eaton, what do *you* think of the chain drive?"

"The chain drive? The chain drive."

"Precisely. The chain drive. We've been discussing it. I say it's a nuisance, dangerous, inconvenient, ugly, and on the way out."

"I agree with you."

"You agree with me. Now you see, this young man agrees with me, and all young Americans are expert mechanicians."

"All but me," said Alfred. "But I agree with you."

"Oh, now you mustn't be over-modest. You do know cars, don't you? What do you drive?"

"A Marmon."

"A Marmon. Now let me see. Marmon. Yes, I know that one. Now *it* hasn't a chain drive, has it?"

"No."

"No, of course not. Now let me ask you something else. Where is O-re-gon?"

"Oregon? It's in the Northwest."

"On the Pacific Ocean, isn't it?"

"Yes."

"And therefore at least three thousand miles from the Long Island, wouldn't you say?"

"Easily. Closer to four thousand."

"Then will you please tell Sevringham, my husband, the gentleman who's trying to talk to your *pretty* little wife but has an ear cocked to our conversation—will you please tell him that he simply cannot take the sleeping-car and expect to be in Portland next morning?"

"Portland, Maine, he can," said Alfred.

"Portland, Maine? The State of Maine? I know Maine. It's just below Canada. But there are two Portlands in the States?"

"More than that, I think."

"But why? When you have a new country like this you have a splendid opportunity to start from scratch with all new names. No duplication whatever. Why are there two Portlands?"

"Oh, we have some worse ones than that, Lady Sevringham."

"You have? How worse?"

"Well, you've heard of California?"

"Of course. I have a friend there."

"And you've heard of Indiana?"

"Yes, I think so. Yes, yes. Indiana. India-*napp*-polis."

"And Pennsylvania?"

"Of course. Philadelphia is in Pennsylvania. I know a dozen people there. The Pennsylvania Railway takes you to Philadelphia."

"Right. Well, there's a California in Pennsylvania, and an Indiana in Pennsylvania."

"A state within a state? *Two* states within a state? How could there be? I'm sure there's a perfectly reasonable explanation, but spare me it, please. This is my first visit to the States and I'd so looked forward to it, but you know, I'm quite discouraged. You make it so difficult for us, you Americans. I *like* New York. Filthy dirty, but it has a vitality. Philadelphia, with all those Welsh names, I was quite touched. My mother was born in Wales. But why do you, for instance, call a place the Polo Ground and they've never had anything but baseball there?"

"I never saw an elephant in Piccadilly Circus."

"No, I daresay. You know London, then?"

"During the war."

"I don't think I'd have come to America if I'd judged you on what I saw of you then. You must confess you were—shall we say—you got out of hand."

"Some of us did, I'll admit. I know I did."

"But I'd known one before the war, perfectly charming and later I admired him because he stayed right on through the air raids. Shared them with us, so to speak. I wonder if you'd know him. Man called Budd. Devrow Budd. Completely American, but understood our ways."

"I know him very well."

"You do? Now did his wife shoot someone? I never met his wife, but there was some story that she went back to the States and shot her lover. I'm not scandalmongering. After all, you say you knew Devrow very well, you must have known that he was very fond of the ladies and made no bones about it. What did happen?"

"His daughter was murdered, then the man shot himself."

"His daughter it was. There was a daughter, I knew that. He was terribly fond of her, but quite concerned about her, and I gather not without reason. Devrow told me she was having a, well, surely not an affair, but a strong attachment for a boy much younger than she was. And so the boy shot her and then killed himself, did he?"

"No, he did not. That's not the way it was at all."

"It wasn't? Where did you know them?"

"We came from the same town."

"Oh. Were you related to them? I'm sorry if I've hit on a tender spot.

"I wasn't related to them."

"I'm a fool, but not entirely a fool. You were the boy, weren't you? I *am* sorry. I'd do anything to take back everything I've said, but I can't do that." She put her hand on his arm.

"Yes, I was the boy."

"Will you share a secret with me? I was his mistress," she said. "I offer you that secret as a token of my regret. I would never, never hurt anyone through his love. Do you forgive me?"

"Yes, I do."

"Dinner—is served," intoned the butler.

"Will you ring me up? We're stopping at the Waldorf-Astoria Hotel. I must talk to you."

"No. I don't want to be rude, but there's nothing to talk about."

"I see," said Lady Sevringham.

The seating arrangement kept Alfred and Lady Sevringham together. James MacHardie sat at the head of the table, and Jean Duffy faced him at the opposite end. On MacHardie's right were Mary Eaton, Lord Sevringham, Mrs. Ripley, and Fritz Thornton, in that order. Alfred sat on Jean Duffy's right, and to the right of him were Lady Sevringham, Creighton Duffy, and Mrs. Pearson. Mrs. Ripley was—Alfred guessed—the widow of Standish W. Ripley, the former Ambassador to the Court of St. James's, and Mrs. Pearson was the wife of Ray Pearson, a friend of Fritz Thornton's whose quick identification was that he had been on Walter Camp's All-America while at Harvard and was otherwise known to the North Shore as an insatiable satyr, who made no discrimination in regard to race, color, or social-economic status. At least in the minutes Mary and Alfred had been in the MacHardie house no one had inquired for Ray Pearson or his whereabouts. The fact was that Frances Pearson was not likely to know and had long since ceased to care. Alfred had met her before in Fritz Thornton's company, and was as convinced that they had had an affair as he was now that the affair was ended.

They were served Cape Cods on the half shell, potage Mongole, filet mignon, Brussels sprouts, French peas bonne femme, chef's salad, cherries Jubilee, and petits fours. There was a red wine with the meat and champagne with dessert. The dinner was served by two footmen, assisted in the clearing-away by two maids, while the butler stood behind and to the right of MacHardie.

Jean Duffy addressed herself to Alfred through the oysters and soup and he talked without imparting any secrets but without letup until she dropped him for Fritz Thornton.

"And now you're back to me," said Lady Sevringham, as the table was turned.

"Yes," said Alfred.

"Afraid I wasn't very communicative with Mr. Duffy, but of course it's my own fault. I was thinking of you and my own guilty conscience. I'm much too direct, and I haven't yet learned that this is a small world. I've never been anywhere, you know. We see always the same people, and they see us.

That's the size of it. I've never been to India, or South Africa. I've been to Italy and to France and nowhere else. My husband's away a good deal and I like the country. When he's home we go up to London to brush out the cobwebs, but I'm always ready to leave London after three or four days. Although I confess I was quite taken by Monte *Carlo*. I discovered that I loved to gamble. For that reason I never went back. One never knows what secret weaknesses one has. Not secret. Undeveloped. Undiscovered. But why am I telling you all this? I'll tell you why, if you haven't guessed. I had no idea that you and I might know anyone in common, therefore I felt free to prattle on as I did. All unawares, I was opening up an old wound of yours, and now I find that I've opened up an old one of my own."

"I'm sorry," said Alfred.

She paused. "Yes, I suppose you are. Sorry for me, of course?"

"Yes, that's what I meant."

"Yes, I knew that. You've known sorrow, and I think more than was brought about by Devrow's daughter. Well, so have I. And that's what I wanted to tell you when you came to see me. Since you don't care to see me, and I can't say I blame you, I must take advantage of these few moments to correct your impression of me. I can't have you, if ever you think of me or hear my name, you must not think of me as a heartless, gossippy woman. I could have convinced you of that if you'd let me talk to you about Devrow Budd. I was in love with him, and heaven help me, I'm not sure but that I still am. To me it was the most mysterious experience of my life, but it happened. I'd been married for ten years, eleven, twelve. Thoroughly domesticated and content, and when my husband brought this man to our house, I was my usual self. I gave the same nice party, with the same nice people, and that night— this is important—I was visited by my husband and we had a good thing. Our usual, Friday-night custom. Devrow Budd was not in my mind. The Saturday was—another Saturday. Shooting, or golf. Someone's house for dinner. Then Sunday. Devrow was called back to London and I knew that my husband had something to do so I offered to drive Devrow to the train and did so, in my little car. I felt quite sure he had business on his mind, because he seemed so preoccupied all the way to the station. We had something like ten minutes to wait for the train, and in those few minutes he stripped away all my complacency just as a few weeks later he stripped off my clothes. 'It's getting late, you know,' he said to me. 'I know,' I said. 'Past five.' 'Past *thirty*-five.' he said. 'How can you do it? How can you go on living at the bottom of a well?

468

You're almost blind now, and in a few years it'll be too late. Did Sevringham sleep with you Friday night? Yes. And he will next Friday night, and he did last Friday. Did he bother to look at you? Did he find any new delights in you, or you in him? Is that all you're to get, and all you're going to give?' I was astounded. Was this the way Americans behaved? Until then he'd been a gentleman, everything as right and proper as Sevringham himself. 'I have a flat, and I'm on the telephone,' he said. 'I promise you none of the noble things, but I'll take you off the green-grocer's shelf and at least make you feel like a great whore.' "

She took a deep breath. "Oh, when I think of how I felt at that moment. Degraded. Murderously angry. But I had no resources, my life had left me with none. Morally I had no muscles, no sinew. Nothing to fall back on such as a sense of humor. No experience to warn me that I was just possibly not the very first woman he'd treated so. Well, he did make me feel like a great whore, but a great one, Mr. Eaton. He never made the slightest mention of marriage and divorce and a permanent status. For three years I went to his flat whenever we thought it was safe to do so, and not a soul the wiser. Then one day I had to change my plans at the last minute and that did it. He discovered that he was in love with me. When he told me that—I hope you can understand this—he became another husband. Is that too simple? It's the way it was. *And* I had to drop him. He became insistent, jealous, demanding, and insofar as scandal was concerned, dangerous. I told poor Sevringham that we couldn't have Devrow any more, that he was drinking too much."

"And what did you tell Budd?"

"That I had another lover. It was the only thing he could understand."

"Did you? I mean had you?"

"Not then. Later, briefly. But the other man meant less than nothing to me, only served to show me that I was in love with Devrow. Not *really* in love, longing for him, his childishness, ingenuousness I believe is the word. I have no excuses and no very good explanation. Sex, to be sure. But I need more than that. It was his simplicity. I was the complex one. He only wanted his own way. He was a terribly simple, sweet man, and I don't expect you to understand that for a second. Only another woman would understand that. Was his daughter like that?"

"I never knew it until this minute, but she was exactly like that."

"Then don't be afraid to love her, Mr. Eaton. It can't harm that lovely creature you're married to. We all have secret

469

things. I said weaknesses, but they don't have to be either weaknesses or strengths. You're not a Roman Catholic, by any chance?"

"Lord, no."

"Well, I was until I ceased to be something on the greengrocer's shelf. Sevringham is still, but very tolerant about my losing it. I was damned if I'd confess to a priest that I had sinned. It seemed to me very ungrateful and hypocritical to Devrow Budd. I was—well, I see I must leave you. Lovely dinner. Au vwah."

"Thank you."

"Thank you? What for? Oh, the girl. You're welcome."

Mary on her way out, stopped beside him. "What did you two talk about?"

"England. London. American ways and so forth."

"That's exactly what *we* talked about, Lord Sevringham and I. She's awfully attractive."

"She thinks you are, too. And you are, I'll give you that."

"Gentlemen, I think the billiard-room for us," said MacHardie. "Creighton, good fellow, would you lead the way?"

Fritz Thornton linked his arm with Alfred's. "How's the temperature at the plant?"

"The temperature? Oh. Why, I'd say it was above freezing, but not warm."

"Not warm. That's too bad. Shall I continue to stay out of it?"

"I don't want *you* to catch our cold."

"I appreciate that. Good boy. I'm afraid the third party was the germ-carrier there."

"Well, it isn't hopeless."

Thornton patted Alfred on the shoulder. "If it gets to be, let me know."

There was a large oaken tavern table at one end of the billiard-room and a dozen stout chairs around it. "That was a damned good dinner, Jim," said Lord Sevringham. "And I couldn't help noticing that Duffy and Jean and my good wife consumed every morsel of the filly. Devoured it like a crew of starving Protestants. Nor do I recall choking on it myself. Duffy, does he do this to you all the time, insidious Presbyterian trying to undermine our holy religion? By God, Jim, I'm going to have some Benedictine and let the good monks wash away my sin. Better have some, too, Duffy. I knew damn well it was Friday and I never hesitated. Pitched right in and ate every damned, sinful scrap of it. And to make matters worse, it's Lent. MacHardie, you're a scoundrel. Thornton, what do you say to that? Is he a scoundrel?"

"Known to be," said Thornton.

"There you are, Mr. Eaton. Take warning. I gather you

aren't very well acquainted with our host, but you see what we think of him that know him well. Thirty years, man and boy, I've been observing his ways and never have I detected any sign of a change for the better. With those appropriate courtesies disposed of, I shall have one of those Havanas and in all likelihood doze off before I get the damned thing lit. Jim, your good health." He raised his glass of Benedictine and took a sip.

"Jerry, you're incorrigible," said MacHardie. He obviously liked and was accustomed to Sevringham's fun, which was not obsequiousness in disguise but Sevringham's own method of treating an important American financier. MacHardie, a widower who seldom entertained younger people, was also grateful to Sevringham for the light touch that this phase of the dinner party required. He was a conscientious host rather than an adept one and he now turned to Fritz Thornton. "Fritz, what is this I hear about you?"

"Well, I don't know, but for heaven's sake, what kind of a question is that? Everybody's waiting for you to accuse me of almost any crime in the books. I am, too."

MacHardie smiled, pleased that his question had accidentally provided Thornton with a humorous response. "Nothing criminal, although you do seem uneasy. No, I wanted to ask you to tell all of us here about your new boat."

"Oh, well that's safe ground. But first, please don't speak of it as my boat. It's a syndicate, Jim. You know perfectly well that I couldn't swing that alone."

"I don't know that, but go on."

"Well, I'm in it with five other fellows. It's still only in the talking stage and that may be as far as it ever gets. But even if that's all that comes of it, we've had some fun. We meet for dinner once a week and I let the others do the talking because they know more about it than I do, and then somehow it always turns into a game of poker."

"Oh-ho, well, haven't you managed to make your share out of the poker games?"

"Not quite. I'll admit I could contribute a dinghy thus far and we're playing—that is to say, meeting—again next Tuesday. But this is 'way in the future. Two years at least before we ever got a boat in the water. I was roped in on it, as I always am when someone has a splendid idea but needs some dilettantish idler to take the wheel. I know this much: when I die, if they put down all the committees I've been on, from charities, to monuments to generals I never heard of, my survivors are going to say, 'Why, poor old Thornton worked himself to death, and we've always thought he was nothing but a lazy bum.' Yes, Jerry, I know what bum means in England. They'd call me that even if they knew what it meant.

Already have, more than likely. My friend Alfred Eaton will bear me out, won't you, Alfred? I told him many times when he was younger, get a job, any job, and you'll have a good excuse."

"Fritz, you'd be lost without your committees and the rest of it," said MacHardie.

"Of course I would. Now. *Now* when they form a committee and I'm not on it, I begin to wonder. But you must admit it's a hell of a way for a man to go through life, and with nothing to show for it but a few silver trays and an umbrella. Yes, one committee gave me an umbrella. Not a walking stick. Not a sword-cane. An umbrella. I've never known why, and I've been afraid to ask."

Wall Street and Throgmorton Street were carefully kept out of the men's conversation, as were women, politics and all other topics that would call for complete and mutual trust or that could be mentioned on Monday as having been discussed at James D. MacHardie's house. Nothing was said that was worth repeating to a speculator or a politician or *Town Topics.* And yet in the presence of such impenetrable discretion Alfred sensed the practice of power, and if MacHardie or Sevringham had said anything memorable about the New York, New Haven & Hartford, Alfred would have been disillusioned. He had never been on such terms of familiarity and informality with a man of MacHardie's standing in the financial community, and MacHardie had behaved in a manner true to form—until, that is, the gentlemen rose to join the ladies.

MacHardie looked at his watch, allowed the man speaking to finish what he was saying, and then laid both hands on the tavern table and leaned forward. "Gentlemen, if no one else wishes to pay a call in the little room in the corner, I suggest we . . ." He did not complete the sentence. They all rose, but Alfred felt that he was being held back by MacHardie's smile and he waited while the others moved toward the stairs, leaving Alfred and MacHardie somewhat alone. In a quiet tone, not a whisper but inaudible to the others, MacHardie said: "I wonder if you could have lunch with me at my office, next Wednesday at twelve-fifteen? Just say your name to the man at the door. May I count on you?"

"Yes sir, thank you."

"Good."

"What do you think he wants? Is that all he said? It sounds like an order, a command," said Mary.

"It is."

They were in bed, reporting to each other all details of the party. "Oh, I can hardly wait to tell Mother. *And* Daddy."

472

"If you say a word to anybody I'll divorce you. He's going to offer me a job. He wouldn't waste his time otherwise. At least he wouldn't have me make the trip to Wall Street. He's too considerate for that. It's a job. But what, I don't know."

"Whatever it is, take it," said Mary. "This shows how clever Mother is."

"How clever is she?"

"Well, not clever, but she does know people. When I told her that it was James D. MacHardie's grandson you saved, she said, 'That's his only grandson and there'll be no limit to how grateful he'll be.' And she was big enough to admit something too."

"What was she big enough to admit?"

"That I was right about you and she was wrong about Jim."

"Jim MacHardie?"

"Jim Roper, you silly. Jim Roper never would have been playing tennis on a Sunday afternoon in February. He'd be studying his lessons."

"As far as that goes, I should have been, too. Studying how much we spent that week at the N. A. C."

"Well, you weren't, so luck was with you. And luck is half the battle. That was the trouble with Jim Roper. He's an unlucky person and I despise him."

"You don't despise him."

"Don't I? I'd never do this to Jim Roper."

"I hope not."

"I never did. But I like doing it to you. You like me to do this to you?"

"You know I do."

"Yes, you do like it, don't you?"

"You can see I do."

"Yes, I can see you do. You wouldn't want me to be anyone else, would you? That Lady Sevringham. She was flirting with you."

"No."

"Or Mrs. Duffy, with those big, big things of hers?"

"No. Nobody but you."

"I don't *want* you to think about anyone else."

"I won't."

"Put out the light, will you, honey?"

"Anything you say."

"Don't talk any more. Let's just don't talk but make love in the dark."

The things that were different about what she said and did this night he put down to her excitement over his coming meeting with James D. MacHardie. He considered himself extremely wise and knowing to realize she was seeing him with new respect and that this fresh reappraisal of him made her want to be especially pleasing to him. But it was unusual for her to be asleep when he came back to bed after opening the windows and having a look at the baby. She was asleep, far on her own side of the bed, breathing regularly, and soon he too was asleep.

There was a number but no name-plate at the entrance to MacHardie & Company, a fact which humorists of the financial district attributed not to modesty but to frugality. "Think of the money that Scotchman saves on metal polish," they said. And: "After all, one of those brass signs is only good for fifty or sixty years, and then you have to get a new one." And: "Old Jamie's afraid the Salvation Army will find out where he is and come around for some of those suits."

The uniformed guard just inside the revolving door spoke to Alfred before he could ask for directions. The man, tall and white-haired and clean-shaven, touched his cap in a semi-military salute and said: "Mr. Eaton, sir?"

"Yes."

"Across this room into the hall at the far end, and it's the fourth door on your left. Room marked *eight*, sir. Room 8."

Alfred knocked on the door of Room 8 and it was opened by a manservant in a sort of livery: black business suit, black shoes, wing collar and starched white bow tie, a costume which required only a change of necktie to transform the man from servant to another anonymous bookkeeper. "Good afternoon, sir. May I take your hat and coat? I'll just hang them on this clothestree where they'll be in plain sight when you wish to leave. Sherry and a biscuit, sir?"

"No, thank you."

He had scarcely selected a chair in this pictureless but comfortable room when James D. MacHardie entered. Immediately Alfred saw a man who was totally unlike the worried grandfather and uneasy host. His gait was heavier and firmer, his shoulders were squarer, his hands hung at his sides, and the barest nod sent the manservant out of his room.

"Good afternoon, Mr. Eaton. Quite cool coming in this morning, wasn't it? If you'll keep that chair, I'll take this one and the table will be here. You don't take anything before lunch?"

"No sir."

"Here's our table. Are you going to be comfortable?"

"Yes sir."

They faced each other across the table, the servant served their consommé vermicelli, and retreated to a corner while they drank it, which MacHardie did in three gulps, between lines of conversation.

"A great pleasure to have you and your charming wife

Friday evening. She's a very agreeable conversationalist. A touch of the Southern accent I find easy on the ears, and she has wit. She has an original way of expressing herself. I've met Mr. St. John on two occasions. And your son was named Rowland after his maternal grandmother's family. I hadn't realized that before." He leaned over to his left and made a motion to start turning his head, which was all that was necessary as a signal for the servant to remove the soup cups and serve the next course.

"I have a glass of milk with my lunch," said MacHardie, implying a question.

"Yes, I'd like a glass of milk."

Liver and bacon, string beans, boiled potatoes, and milk were served.

"Twenty minutes, Simmons."

"Very good, sir," said Simmons, and departed.

MacHardie picked up his knife and fork, Continental fashion, and commenced his meal and his statement. "We have here, have had in recent years, a training course that we don't call a training course. In the first place, a man who works for us is making, or trying to make money for us, and if he has to tell his friends he's taking a training course it does his dignity no good, and it doesn't give our outside connections much confidence in him. It is not the Harvard School of Business Administration or the Wharton School of Commerce & Finance. There is no prescribed curriculum of textbooks, although we do recommend certain reading if our young men haven't had it. I say young men. The term may be misleading. We haven't made a practice of offering this course to recent undergraduates. Most of the men have been past twenty-five and in two cases, past thirty. You are twenty-five?"

"Soon."

"We are a private bank and a house of issue. Are you familiar with those terms?"

"As a house of issue you sell stock?"

"That's all it is. We will look at a given property and supply its banking needs, and in some cases, but not all, we will also arrange for the sale of stock in this given property. However, we do not sell stock in a concern for which we do not also supply the banking facilities.

"Our greatest success in our *not*-so-called training course has been in sending young men out to investigate properties, considering their reports, and acting on them to the best of our ability. We do not by any means rely entirely on the young men's reports, but we have been known to do so. Sometimes with successful results, sometimes not.

"The young men to whom we offer this opportunity, and it is an opportunity, have almost invariably had some business

475

experience other than in the general field of banking and securities. In fact, I may say we prefer young men who have not been dealing in stocks and bonds and so forth, and have had no experience in a bank. We can get such men, that is, men who have had that experience, but we don't want them. We'd rather have a man who's run a small grocery store, or a fruit cannery. Too many men come down here and get into banks and brokerage houses and never do learn what those pieces of paper actually represent.

"We do not expect any young man to come here at a financial sacrifice. Consequently there is no fixed salary for those who participate in this training course of ours. A man is given in any case a salary he can live on, because almost immediately he is given considerable responsibility.

"We have never had a refusal, but before I actually offer you a job with us, are you interested?"

"I'm interested, and I'm honored."

"Thank you. Naturally you came to my attention through a heroic act, and you thereby earned my personal gratitude. But all that served to do was to call attention to you. We are not in the habit of hiring men who qualify as life guards and nothing more, and I would never allow my personal gratitude to influence me in a matter that would involve this firm. I have eight partners. But in your case, having met you and been favorably impressed by intangibles that had nothing to do with your expertness as a swimmer, I made inquiries, and I am now in possession of a set of facts concerning you that I daresay is as complete as any ever compiled. These include transcripts of your marks at the Knox School and Princeton, your Navy record, your health report—we have a participating interest in an insurance company—your credit rating, and such out-of-the-ordinary facts as the time you were beaten up at Princeton, your close relationship with your maternal grandfather, and various extremely private matters concerning your family. We are, or our agents are, quite thorough, Mr. Eaton. We are also careful. But at the same time, with a limited opportunity to get to know you, I have been most strongly influenced by my own, call them hunches, although I detest that word for what it means down in this part of the city. Now, is there anything you would like to know about us?"

"Yes sir. Are all the men who took the training course still with MacHardie & Company?"

"Twenty-eight men have taken it. One did not come back with us after the war. He renounced us for the fleshpots of Paris. He was a good man, too, but he wanted to write music, so he's better off where he is. One left us to go into his father-in-law's business, a large going concern in the prairie states.

One is on sick leave and I'm sorry to say has tuberculosis and he may not be back. And two of them did not live up to our expectations, possibly through no fault of their own but because we made errors in judgment. The others are still with us, some as long as ten years. The men who have been here ten years have made enough money to retire. By that I mean, each of them is worth a sum fairly well up in six figures. Neither one has a million."

"Why not?"

MacHardie smiled. "You all have that goal of a million, haven't you?"

"No sir. I want much more than that."

"How much more?"

"Well, sir, not to be impertinent, but as much as you have. I don't want to stop at what my father had."

"Let me ask you a question. What would you do if you had five million today?"

"Today? I'd wait till you offered me a job, and then I'd take it."

"That is the right answer. Because there's no limit to what you can earn here, within reason. You certainly should have five million by the time you're fifty."

"I will no matter where I go. I want to have five million by the time I'm forty."

"Fifteen years? That's $340,000 a year."

"I don't look at it that way, Mr. MacHardie. It might be impossible for me to make $340,000 a year every year, but it won't be impossible for me to make two million in one year and half a million for six years."

"How is this money to be made? Speculation?"

"Naturally. That's how all money is made, all big money. A company that pays big returns on a small investment is speculative or it wouldn't pay the big returns."

"There is such a thing as information, Mr. Eaton."

"That would be my job, wouldn't it?"

"There is also such a thing as misinformation, and loss."

"Loss would account for the nine years that I didn't make much."

"Another question. Are you imagining that you make all this money as a partner in this firm?"

"I'm imagining it for the moment, yes sir."

"Will you explain to me why your present partnership is unsatisfactory?"

"I could give you a lot of explanations, and some of them you already know."

"I still want to hear your explanation."

"Well, it finally comes down to this: I want to make money,

477

and my principal associates at the plant just want to spend it."

"So I am told," said MacHardie. "Well, sir, how long will it take you to arrange your affairs?"

"Three months."

"You've given it thought."

"Naturally. Two months to arrange things at the plant, and one month with my father's estate."

"Do you take coffee with your dessert?"

"Yes, please. A large coffee with sugar and cream."

"You will be hearing from Mr. Connifer. Mr. John T. Connifer. He is office manager and the man in charge of personnel. He'll arrange the details. I'll be abroad on the first of June and in any case your work won't be directly with me, but you'll find that I'm easily accessible. I have one of those roll-top desks you passed on the way in. I'm pleased that you're going to be with us, and I trust you'll never have cause for regret. Misgivings once in a while, but not regret. This is the finest establishment of its kind in the United States of America, and we mean to keep it that way. Those words will have some meaning to you after you've been here a while. Good day, Mr. Eaton." He did not wait for dessert or coffee, but then he had not said he would.

Simmons not only was accustomed to such behavior; he was accustomed to explaining it. He came in with his watch in hand. "Mr. MacHardie never waits."

"I understood him to say twenty minutes," said Alfred.

"Oh, he said twenty minutes. But that was only if he didn't finish before that. If your conversation lasted twenty minutes, I was to come in and that would remind him that the twenty minutes was up. He always does that. Sometimes fifteen minutes, sometimes half an hour. He won't take a ticker in here, but he doesn't like to be away from it very long during trading hours. Remarkable man for his age."

"What is his age?"

"I don't rightly know, sir. But I've been here twenty-two years and he looked the same the first day I started." Simmons finished serving the coffee and cabinet pudding, and stood with his hands behind his back. "May I ask, sir, are you going to be with us?"

"Yes I am."

"Then may I be the first to welcome you, sir? I usually am. In our training course, Mr. Eaton?"

"Yes."

"Very good. And I trust I shall be here to wait on you the next time you have lunch in here."

"Are you quitting?"

"Oh, no. No sir. Very few ever quits MacHardie & Company. But I'm not getting any younger and five years isn't a long way off at my age."

"Oh. Five years before I have lunch in here again?"

"Five years minimum, sir. It's a bit like the Army in some respects. Promotion is slow, you know, sir? A year or two don't mean very much in a firm like MacHardie & Company. But I warrant you, the next time you do have lunch in here, this room'll be exactly the way you see it now. Oh, I like it. It gives you a real feeling of something permanent. Out there, the same gentlemen at the same desks, conducting their business nice and quiet, never raising their voices like in some other firms down here."

"Which desk is Mr. Connifer's?"

"Oh, not one of the big ones. Those are the partners'. The nine big desks are for the partners. Mr. Connifer will never be a partner. Mr. Connifer *never* had his lunch in here, if you see what I mean, sir. There may be two young men doing the same work for a while at the beginning, but everybody knows which one of them may some day be a partner and which one won't. If a young man starts out by lunching with Mr. *Connifer,* we all know he's never going to be a partner."

Alfred finished his lunch and Simmons helped him on with his coat and said goodbye. The smile and the crispness of manner of the white-haired man at the street door revealed to Alfred that the word had got around, inexplicably, as it so often does in Wall Street and in the most secure prisons. "Good day, Mr. Eaton," he said. Good day, and not goodbye.

The next order of business was a consultation with Fritz Thornton. Alfred took the East Side subway to Grand Central, changed to a local to Fifty-first Street, and walked to the Racquet Club. There was only a slight chance that Fritz Thornton would not be there, and at the door Alfred confirmed his guess. He waited in the lounge until Fritz came out of the diningroom, accompanied, somewhat to his dismay, by Jack Warren, of Boston.

Warren remembered him and then excused himself with a word to Thornton that he would see him again at four o'clock.

"Did you want to talk to me about something special? If so, we can go to the bar and I'll build a fence around us," said Thornton. "I'm free until four o'clock, as you heard."

They went to Thornton's favorite table. "What will you have? I'm going to have a bottle of Apollinaris water."

"So will I."

"With a slice of lemon. I prefer it that way. Before I forget, a pleasant coincidence. Jack Warren inquired for you less than ten minutes ago."

"That's good to hear."

"All right, Alfred. You may fire when ready."

"Well, I just have to start with a big long *well.* I have a lot to say."

"May I make one guess, and then I won't interrupt you again. You are getting out of the Nassau Aeronautical Corporation?"

"Yes."

"I'm not surprised. Now go ahead."

"Well—another *well.* You remember our last long talk, when I offered to buy up all the stock in the corporation? I told you I'd been to see this fellow in Texas, and he agreed to put up the money. I told you why I was doing it. I felt that with outside money that I had dug up, I would be in a better position to exercise my authority than I was as long as Lex and Von Elm knew the money came from you and your brother."

"I remember."

"You said then that you understood completely why I was doing it, and you appreciated the fact that I hadn't done anything underhanded."

"Of course."

"To repeat what I said then, I did what I did because I thought it was for the good of the corporation collectively, and in the long run, better for Lex and Von Elm and me individually, and also relieved you of any feeling of responsibility. And then you said to me privately, you didn't want to be relieved of the responsibility, *and* that you thought that by offering to buy up all the stock, by doing that, I would achieve the desired effect, namely, to prove to Lex and Von Elm that I *could* buy it up, that I wanted to buy it up, and was in a position where I didn't have to feel that Lex had you on his side in any difference of opinion. And even if he did have you on his side, I did not depend on you, and therefore wasn't made to feel that I was outnumbered, or there on sufferance, or any of those things. Somebody besides a member of Lex's family had enough confidence in me to be willing to back me for a hell of a lot of money.

"Now then, Lex flared up when I offered to buy up the stock, but then when he calmed down he realized that what I was really doing was to prove that I was at least as interested in making a go of it as anyone else, and possibly even a little more so."

"Which was true. You weren't using your uncles' money, and Lex was."

"But he calmed down and as you predicted, for a while he tried to be more economical and not go on as though we, or *you,* had unlimited resources. But that was too good to last, and before long we were back at the same old problem. Just as bad as ever. And when you suspected that and faced me with it, you made the suggestion that I fire Von Elm, which I had the authority to do. Well, I said I wouldn't do that, that I would give it till Christmas.

"I guess you wondered why I didn't say anything at Christmas, because you must have known that things hadn't gotten any better. They'd gotten worse. But oddly enough, they'd gotten worse for a reason that was good. I'm not trying to be What's-His-Name, the paradox guy, Chesterton. I wouldn't know how to make a paradox any more than I'd know how to make a parachute. I'd rather read W. O. McGeehan than Chesterton anyhow. But what I mean by this paradoxical business is that I discovered something good, that is, favorable to the firm, that was not bad for my position. I found out that Von Elm, no matter how much of a prick I think he is, or how careless he can be with other people's money—he's a good designer. How did I find that out? I found it out by accident.

"I knew God damn well, and I know God damn well, that we will never make any real money by trying to make aeroplanes for the people who buy Rolls-Royces. Do you know how many Rolls-Royces there are in this country? Twenty-seven hundred. That's all. I took the trouble to find that out. In a country of over 105,000,000 population, only twenty-seven hundred want to or can buy Rolls-Royces, and I agree with you that that's a pretty good way to judge our market. Let's say there are three thousand people who might even be slightly interested in buying a good, small aeroplane. Not enough. Lex always accuses me of wanting to make flivvers or Dodges, but I think it's a financial fact that you have to stop somewhere and build one model and stick to it for a while. Mass produce, even on a small scale. But we've had all this out before, and I know you're more inclined to agree with Lex.

"But as president of the corporation I wanted to find out if there could be a market for a good aeroplane in quantity. So I wrote a letter to a friend of my father's and through him I went to Washington and spent three days talking to guys in naval aviation. I knew I wouldn't be able to talk their language very well, so I took some designs along with me, some drawings and blueprints. I didn't tell Lex or Von Elm. I did this entirely on my own.

"Well, one officer wanted to throw me out of his office for wasting his time, but he was the only one. The others were like a bunch of kids on a farm, seeing their first electric train. One officer even said, 'Do you by any chance have a man named Von Elm working for you?' He'd recognized some Von Elm touches.

"Well, Christ, I thought, this is the best news since the Armistice, and I began rubbing my hands and counting the shekels. 'Can I count on you fellows for a big order?' I said. 'We'll be in production next year.' I made it 1923 because I wanted to give us a chance to get a few ships in the air before offering one to the Navy.

"They all shook their heads. Not a chance. Congress wouldn't give them the money, and even if Congress did, the battlewagon men in the Navy were still sore as hell about buying a hundred engines from Wright. They liked that about as much as they liked old Daniels trying to make them drink grape juice.

" 'All right,' I said. 'We'll give you one. We'll sell you one for a dollar.' Anything to get the Navy interested. But they wouldn't even take one as a gift. And anyway, all I had was drawings. I didn't have an aeroplane. Then I asked one nice guy, an officer, how about the Army? I said I was pretty sure I could get to see General Mitchell. But he said to lay off Mitchell. Mitchell wrote a book, *Our Air Force* it was called, and was making himself unpopular all over. In fact, I don't think this officer liked Mitchell very much himself. So I never bothered to go see Mitchell or anyone else in the Army. I came home with my tail between my legs, because I not only couldn't get any business, but I'd found out that this shit Von Elm was really pretty good.

"Mr. Thornton, that was the blow that killed father. I knew then that as far as the N. A. C. was concerned, my days were numbered. If it came to a real showdown, you'd have to fire me, or I'd have to quit. So I went on marking time, trying to decide what to do and how to do it, and then three Sundays ago on my way to your house to play tennis, I happened to hear a woman scream, and I guess you know the rest as well as I do."

"In other words, Alfred, you're going with MacHardie & Company."

"Yes."

"Well, let me be one of the first to congratulate you."

"As a matter of fact, you're the first. And so far, the only one. I had lunch with him today, and I came here hoping to find you. I haven't even called up Mary."

"When does all this take effect?"

"I told Mr. MacHardie I needed two months to arrange things at the N. A. C., and then I ought to spend another month with my father's estate, things at the mill, insurance, and so forth. I start the first of June, I guess."

"Do you want me to break the news to Lex?"

"God, no. No thanks. That will have to be done with a
482

bottle of whiskey on the table and maybe some eight-ounce gloves nearby. But I owe him that."

"Yes, I think you do. I was just thinking about the eight-ounce gloves part of it. I hope there's none of that."

"I'll take my licking like a little man."

"I just hope Lex does—a different kind of licking."

"Yes, so do I."

"He may not, you know."

"I know only too well."

"I have an uneasy feeling that I was the one who rushed you two into this and you at least were too polite to say no."

"I have a feeling that most of the good things that Mr. MacHardie knows about me came from you."

"I won't deny that we had several conversations. But you made it on your own. He's been looking for someone like you, and you owe me nothing. He owes me something, but you don't. At the moment I have only one piece of advice for you."

"What's that?"

"Watch out for Duffy, his son-in-law. He's a smart Mick and he likes to pretend he'd rather be a partner in Mortimer & Miller than in MacHardie & Company, but I happen to know he's never been offered anything by his father-in-law and I happen to know he's boiling inside. He'll never need money. He's done well, and his wife will inherit, besides the money her father settles on her every five years. But he thinks the old gentleman has snubbed him because he's a Catholic and made his wife join that church, and the child is being brought up a Catholic. That isn't the real reason Jim MacHardie doesn't want him in the firm. Don Shanley's a Catholic and he's a MacHardie partner, and Jerry Sevringham is a good friend. But there's a difference between a Catholic and a Mick, and Duffy is a Mick. Sharp, shrewd, brilliant, dresses well, good manners and all that. But when I meet an Irishman and I get that instinctive feeling that I can't trust him, I know he's a Mick. I've had it with grooms and I've had to fire them. Other grooms, I have one that's been with me for thirty years. Charlie McDonald is one of my best friends, and Charlie didn't have as good an upbringing as Duffy. Duffy's family had a place on Long Island long before he ever married Mac-Hardie's daughter. I can't say any more than that I just don't trust him. I suppose it's a good thing I can classify them as Micks and just Irishmen.

"The only other piece of advice is that everything you do at MacHardie & Company is made a part of your record. Five or ten years from now you'd be surprised to find out that they know you stayed in Chicago one day longer than necessary, or you had a margin account for two weeks because you had a hot tip. They'll know if you've had trouble at home, and they'll also know that you won a handicap tournament at Piping Rock. It'll all be down on paper. They're famous for it. One of the partners said to me one time, 'If I had to know where I was on a certain night ten years ago, I'd find out at the office.' He was only half-joking. Don't get into any scandal, don't get to be known as a drinker. And stay out of the newspapers unless you happen to get on the sporting pages with other men like yourself. And if I were you, I wouldn't come here so often. Don't resign. But don't make a regular habit of this place."

"I thought this place was the best."

"It is, of its kind. But if you're here every day, or three or four times a week regularly, they naturally wonder how you can spare the time, and they also wonder why you do. Next year I'll put you up at a smaller club, an older crowd. You won't get in before you're thirty on account of the waiting-list. The people at MacHardie's approve of this place, and they highly approve of your being a member. It's what a young man should do. But James D. MacHardie doesn't expect his embryonic partners to have time for the Racquet & Tennis Club life. Above all, never be found at the bar here at three o'clock in the afternoon. That could finish you. I've always regretted that I was never tapped for MacHardie & Company, and I'd like to see you make good in my stead."

"I'd rather be you than any other man I know."

"Thank you, Alfred, but that isn't as true as it was two or three years ago, and it'll become less true as you get older. But God! I wish I had your life for the next forty years. I'm certainly tired of mine."

Alfred remained silent.

"That's imposing on you. I shouldn't have done that. A statement like that makes you feel you have to make a reply, and there is no reply . . . This stuff aids the digestion, but it does nothing for the soul. Shall we try some of that so-called Gordon's gin? I'm certainly not going to toast your new career in Apollinaris."

"Can we put it off till some other time? It's just that I'd rather not have a drink now."

"Are you rushing off?"

"No, I'm staying a little while longer."

"Oh? Well, good. Good."

Alfred smiled. "You know, I know you better than I used to."

"Well of course you do, dear boy."

"I'm not as easily fooled as I used to be."

"Now what's behind that remark?"

"I think you know. You have a very clever way of steering the conversation in the direction you want it to go. Or at least away from something you don't want to talk about."

Thornton smiled. "You've caught wise, have you?"

"It took me long enough."

"All right, what was I steering away from this time?"

"What I wanted to talk about, and you knew I wanted to talk about."

"In all probability. The stock?"

"Yes."

"I'd like you to keep it. It may be worthless in a year, and you couldn't sell it for much now. On the other hand, I wish you'd keep it because you've only been taking $50 a week for your salary. If this little corporation should ever amount to anything you've more than earned your share. Call it half business and half sentiment, if you like."

"Mostly sentiment."

"Your stock isn't worth its face value, you'll agree there. Nowhere near. It would make the bookkeeping much easier if you just kept what you have. And technically, you can't sell it to anyone but me or my brother or Lex, and naturally if we refuse to buy, you're left holding it. On the other hand, there's no more stock for sale at this time, so you can't buy any and I wouldn't accept payment for what you hold. Therefore, Alfred, you remain a stockholder willy-nilly."

Alfred laughed. "You've worked that out very neatly."

"I think so. Lord knows, in years to come you may want to have your stock certificate as a souvenir of your first business venture, and the way it looks now, that and the experience will be all you'll have to show for it. I am extremely pessimistic about the future of the Nassau Aeronautical Corporation, and that isn't mere politeness because you're leaving. What you found out about Von Elm is precisely true, the good and the bad. I did some inquiring on my own, and that's why I never came to your support as you probably thought I should have. I found out he was good, or promising, and if I'd supported you and tied a tincan to his tail, I would have been doing you a disservice. Von Elm is going to be somebody, and I'm glad you're not going to have it on your record that you failed to appreciate him. You'll make mistakes, Alfred, but oddly enough, the mistakes that are remembered in business are not always business mistakes. Oftener than not they're mistakes in personal judgment, judgment of other men. As I see it, twenty years from now Von Elm is going to have it on his record that he couldn't get along with you, a very easy man to get along with. I'd much rather have it that way than vice versa."

"You win. It's easy to lose to you. I never really lose by it."

Thornton bowed. "Would you like to wait around for Jack Warren? He's a very good connection to have in State Street,

485

although Devonshire Street is where he has his office."

"I imagine it'll be a long time before I need any high connections."

"Never hurts, but I suppose you'd like to get home and tell Mary the news. By the way, how's your neck?"

"Practically healed."

"That's where the chicken got the ax, so bear that in mind, Alfred. But I know that this is one of the most important days in your life, and you know you have my hearty good wishes and my promise to be of any assistance at any time."

"I know that if I know anything at all."

THE MAIN OFFICE of the Buffalo, Fort Penn & Trenton was in Fort Penn, a fact which in certain other circumstances might have hurt the pride of citizens of Buffalo; but while the millionaires of Delaware Avenue were as proud of their city and as sensitive to a profitable operation as citizens anywhere, they were also quite aware that they had allowed the old Buffalo & Fort Penn to slip away from them almost unnoticed, and when they eventually realized that James D. MacHardie had been quietly putting together the Buffalo, Fort Penn & Trenton, it was far too late to do anything about it. The old Buffalo & Fort Penn had become, or very nearly become, one of the joke railroads of which Americans are so fond. As the initials on the cars of the Delaware, Lackawanna & Western were said to mean Delay, Linger & Wait, the Buffalo & Fort Penn initials on its rolling stock stood for Bad For Passengers, a title that was not altogether inaccurate. Most of the standard American jokes about poor railroad service applied to the Buffalo & Fort Penn; its equipment, its right of way, its personnel, and its methods. When the announcement came that James D. MacHardie had effected a merger of the Buffalo & Fort Penn with an almost mysteriously unknown New Jersey railroad, Buffalonians uttered the hope that the newly organized system would put up a new station, not necessarily so elaborate as some then a-building, but a substitute for the crumbling eyesore that had served the traveling public so many years. The prayer went unanswered, the station got worse than ever, and the line itself was not regarded as a credit to Buffalo. Fort Penn could have the main office, and the only regrets were mild, lingering ones on the part of a few gentlemen at the Saturn Club who had not known of James D. MacHardie's interest until it was too late. They could take some consolation from the knowledge that gentlemen just like them at the Fort Penn Club had been no smarter, nor was there any jubilation in the Trenton Club.

It was obvious from the beginning of the Buffalo, Fort Penn & Trenton that the new owners had no intention of losing money for the sake of prestige. The passenger trains fulfilled the requirements of the system's franchises, but no more. A Fort Penn millionaire might have his new Pierce-Arrow shipped from Buffalo via the B. F.-P. & T., but on a journey between the two cities he would unhesitatingly take the Pennsy, which would deliver him at his destination on time and reasonably clean. The B. F.-P. & T. liked to carry coal, iron ore, iron and steel products and, least of all, mixed freight, and the merger had been arranged so that the line could pick up business in the anthracite region of Eastern Pennsylvania and the growing industrial area from Trenton westward to Fort Penn. Most of the business in coal was dependent on the line's arrangements with the large and small independent coal operators, since the Pennsylvania and the Reading, the Lehighs and the Delawares had extremely friendly ties with the largest mining corporations. It had not been so long since the mining and railroading operations had been separated by the government, one of the rare instances of government interference to have the tacit approval of James D. MacHardie.

But it was not to the main office in Fort Penn that Alfred Eaton was sent in the autumn of 1927. MacHardie & Company received daily reports from Fort Penn, voluminous ones by mail for the less urgent reports, by leased telephone and telegraph wires for the questions needing ready answers. On an October morning he was told by his secretary that Mr. Hasbrouck would like to see him.

"Ah, hello there, Alfred," said Hasbrouck.

"Good morning, Mr. Hasbrouck," said Alfred. He seated himself comfortably, facing Hasbrouck, who as a partner rated one of the nine roll-top desks.

"Alfred, you come from Pennsylvania. Port Johnson, I believe."

"Born and raised there, yes sir. Mother and father born and raised there."

"And your mother still lives there, if I'm not mistaken."

"Still lives there, and so does one of my sisters."

"I knew most of these things, of course. No use pretending I don't. But there are some things about your Pennsylvania background that I don't know about."

"Thank God," said Alfred.

Hasbrouck, who enjoyed a mildly naughty joke, chuckled. "I don't think I'd like them to dig down too deep in Englewood, either. That's where I spent my young manhood, and—well, the less said about some things the better, eh?"

"Check."

"Check and double-check," said Hasbrouck. "What do you know about Lantenengo County?"

"Lantenengo County? Coal. One word, and I've used up all my information, I'm sorry to say."

"It isn't very far from your town. You must have friends there."

"None. I've never been there. No, that's wrong. I was there once for about an hour. I'm afraid I'm not much help on Lantenengo County. In fact, I'm not even sure what the principal town is. Is it Gibbsville? Gibbsville belongs up there somewhere."

"Gibbsville is the county seat."

"I knew some fellows from Gibbsville in prep school and college, but they were never particular friends of mine, and I've completely lost touch with them. And I've never been to Gibbsville. I've only been to a country club somewhere near there, and it was at night. There was a dance, but I didn't go to it, and I never even got inside the club. I'm sorry, Mr. Hasbrouck."

"Everything you say is music to my ears."

"Oh."

"Exactly."

"Like the Louisiana sulphur proposition?"

"Ex*act*ly. The fewer people who know you, the better from our point of view."

"What are we after?"

"First, information. Second—as always, the second depends on the first. This has to do with Buffalo, Fort Penn & Trenton, which, as you know, is one of our investments. At the moment we don't go into Lantenengo County, but that doesn't say we never will. Nor am I implying that we intend to. But within twenty-five miles of Gibbsville there are eighteen independent coal companies, aside from the illegal bootleg coal operations. These eighteen have no connection with the big fellows, the Reading, or the L. C. & N."

"What's that?"

"Lehigh Coal & Navigation."

"Oh, yes. Shows how little I know about it."

"You recognized the name, if not the initials. Now we may be overlooking something worthwhile there. They've had a bad strike in the anthracite coal industry and they lost a considerable amount of their domestic market to oil. Nevertheless we haven't given up on coal or on coal mining or on coal-carrying. Coal is still our big source of revenue on the B. F.-P. & T., and they're still mining it in Lantenengo County. You don't have to concern yourself with how we'll get in there if we want to. That's for us to worry about. But if there's a big future there in the independent operations—and there may be—we want

488

our share of that business."

"You're bucking the Pennsylvania and the Reading. I know that much. Their coal trains used to rumble through my home town, night and day, eighty-car trains. I know because I used to count them."

"Well, that's quite true. The Reading gets the Coal & Iron Company business, naturally. The Pennsylvania—well, the Susquehanna Collieries Company, Mr. Hanna's outfit. We know that, and I'm glad you do because you have some perspective on it. But we'd like you to go down there, or over there, or whatever you choose to say, and spend a couple of months looking around. You know how to sell a bond?"

"Yes. You say, 'Would you like to buy a bond, mister?' and you either sell it or you don't."

"Except that in this case, you won't be in a hurry to leave the office if you *don't* sell a bond. You will be there as a new man for Rowley & Cruickshank, opening up new territory. That will give you an excuse to be chatty and friendly. All new bond salesmen are chatty and friendly and all small-town bankers like to chat, except when they're half expecting a surprise visit from the bank examiners."

"Do I get the four dollars if I sell a bond? I have a wife and two children, you know."

"Is it four dollars? I thought it was five. Whatever it is, yes, you can keep the commission. Rowley & Cruickshank will supply you with a small car and their various lists. It's getting a little late for golf, but take your sticks with you. However, you are not to confine yourself to bankers. Rowley's will give you the names of business men, priests, dear old ladies, lawyers —all sorts of people. I wouldn't waste too much time on the dear old ladies, but a priest knows as well as anyone in the town if a mine is in good shape. Doctors the same. Are people paying their bills? It's almost wide open down there so have a good look at the saloons."

"That part is always a pleasure."

"Yes. You see, if the owners are letting the mines go to pot, that's important for us to know. The state has strict mining laws, but I understand they're not being rigidly enforced, and the bootleg operations are under no supervision at all."

"What are these bootleg operations? I don't understand that."

"It's stealing, and it's getting to be an industry. When a big operation shuts down, the miners sink their own shafts and take the coal and sell it by the bucketful."

"Why don't the owners stop them?"

"They don't dare. Bloodshed. There's going to be some trouble, because some of the miners are stealing it by the truckload and carting it away to Philadelphia, Reading, probably your home town."

"They won't get rich in my home town. Since our mill shut down there aren't many people who can afford coal."

"Well, you'll learn about bootleg coal mining, Alfred. We have a lot of figures on tonnages—legitimate, legal tonnages —and all the rest of the figures. But we would like you to find out the kind of thing that doesn't show up on Department of Labor reports and statistics. And who knows, you may come across something like that splendid sulphur proposition. I may as well tell you, Mr. MacHardie is taking a personal interest in this trip of yours."

"Well, I'll do my best."

"We know that. You always do."

"Will I be able to come home on weekends?"

"I'm afraid not. Not for the first month. I imagine that when you get there you'll find that you get a lot of your best information on Saturdays and Sundays. Are you a churchman?"

"I was christened but I don't think I was ever confirmed. I'm an Easter Episcopalian. Not much help there, I'm afraid."

"Well, we can't have everything. You might spend this afternoon over at Rowley & Cruickshank's and I suggest you leave here next Sunday."

"Oh, my wife is going to love that. Our second Sunday in the new apartment and she's asked some people in for five-thirty."

"All in the name of MacHardie & Company," said Hasbrouck, with an attempt at levity, but without yielding. "I had to give up a month at Fishers this past summer while Mr. MacHardie was abroad. But it's worth it. I've never made any sacrifice for the firm that I didn't feel amply repaid, and not always the money consideration."

"I'm not complaining, but my wife will."

"They often do," said Hasbrouck. "Now there are one or two men who could be helpful to you, who don't fall into any of the classifications I've already mentioned. One is a politician named Slattery. He lives in Gibbsville. As a general rule we stay away from politicians, but this fellow is safe. We've tried him out on any number of things and found him reliable. You can go to him if you're stuck for anything, but don't go to him if you don't have to. We always prefer to have them come to us, and we'd rather not have him know you're there. At least in your true identity. It's quite likely that you'll run across him, but on the other hand you may not. But if necessary you can tell him who you really are."

"It shouldn't be necessary."

"No, it shouldn't. But we have him there in case it is. Mike

Slattery. A Republican, by the way. Don't be misled by the name. In Lantenengo County the Democrats don't elect. The other fellow is a man we've had our eye on for some time. In the deepest confidence, if we ever decide to go into the mining of coal in that section, this man is the one we'd like to take charge. His name is Ralph Benziger. R. W. Benziger. He is general superintendent of the Mountain City Coal Company, the largest of the independents in that section. I would like you to go and see him and I'll have Rowley's give you a letter to him."

"Ralph W. Benziger, or Benzinger?"

"Benziger, without the second *n*. Benziger. Now in this case, under no circumstances must you let him know who you are. The letter will simply say that you are a new man with Rowley & Cruickshank, and any small courtesies, et cetera. Perfectly logical, because Benziger has a small account at Rowley's, and Rowley's have done some business with Mountain City. If he's aware that there is any connection between Rowley's and MacHardie & Company, well, it's no secret. Everybody knows that there's *some* connection, everybody that takes the trouble to find out such things.

"Benziger—I don't want to prejudice you—but he's one of the nicest fellows I ever met. I met him in Philadelphia two years ago and then again last year. He didn't know it, but the meetings were not accidental. He has no idea that he was being looked over, and I'm the only partner who's seen him. He's never seen Mr. MacHardie, and he's never been in this office. He probably knows that I'm a partner in MacHardie & Company, but I'm not even sure of that. He is not a rich man. He may be worth three to four hundred thousand, most of it in Mountain City. He works like a mule, but with a great deal more intelligence. He's the old-style mining engineer. High school education, engineering corps, self-taught, even studied a little chemistry at the I. C. S. The men in the mines trust him because he's shown in the past that he'll put on a pair of rubber boots and a miner's cap and go inside if necessary. He's not afraid to dirty his hands, they say. He's had less labor trouble than almost any general superintendent, but he'll stand up to the union officials whenever the local superintendent can't handle a dispute. Now we know these things about Benziger, but we want to know all we can, and this is the second most important part of your trip. He's in his early fifties, but I'd like you to get to know him if you can. He will probably invite you to dinner at his house, and if he does, I leave the rest to you. This will never be as big as the Louisiana sulphur proposition, but it's the first one you won't have any help on. This is all yours. Stay two months at least, more if you feel it's necessary. After that you'll have

491

a week to dictate your report, and then Mr. MacHardie wants you to lunch with him. *In the little room.* Good luck."

Mary received the news without enthusiasm but without displeasure. "And you're not to come home at all for the first month. Of course they mean by that that they hope you don't ever come home."

"I'll come home the end of the first month, you can be sure of that."

"And of course I'm forbidden to go there."

"Not forbidden."

"Enough said. All right. Every year they seem to send you on longer trips."

"This isn't very far. About two hundred miles, I'd say."

"I wasn't talking about distance."

"And I was in Louisiana longer than a month."

"But there I was allowed to come down and see you. The trouble with these companies, they're all run by old men. It isn't good for young couples to be separated for such long spells. What's more, I got the curse today, so that takes care of that till you get home. No fond farewell on Sunday morning."

"Well, God damn it, that's my luck."

"Your luck? It's my luck, too. That's what I mean about old men. And you won't even be here Sunday afternoon? I've invited thirty people. Will you call up Forty-two West Forty-nine and order the liquor?"

"Let's go there for dinner tomorrow night and order it then."

"All right."

"Let's play some golf on Saturday. I have to go out and pick up my clubs anyway."

"Are you taking them with you to Pennsylvania?"

"Hasbrouck suggested it."

"And your Tuck, too?"

"I guess I'd better, to be on the safe side."

"I thought you were going to bury yourself with a lot of coal miners. Doesn't sound much like that to me."

"They have a country club there. I've seen it."

"Oh, good-*ee*. And I sit here with two small children, one of them teething. It isn't fair, you know."

"Alex is teething? A fever usually goes with that, doesn't it? I didn't know he'd started teething."

"How would you? You're never home long enough."

"Oh, come on, Mary."

"If you're going to be playing golf and going to country club parties, I'm not going to just sit here."

"You don't have to just sit here."

"I mean if somebody asks me to go to the theater."

"*Go* to the theater."

"What if it's somebody you don't know?"

"That's different."

"That's what *you'll* be doing."

"I don't want you having dates with guys I don't know. If Lex or somebody wants to take you to the theater, okay. But not a stranger."

"Lex—all he wants to do is sit in a speakeasy. What if it's somebody you do know and don't like?"

"For instance?"

"Jim Roper?"

"No. What made you think of him?"

"He's coming Sunday afternoon."

"How did that happen?"

"I saw him on the street and I invited him."

"I'm glad I'm not going to be here."

"Maybe it's just as well you're not, if that's your attitude."

"That's my attitude, all right. I'll tell you what else is my attitude. You're not going out with Jim Roper. That's final."

"Final? Don't be too sure."

"I'm not at all sure, but you'd better be."

"This is 1927."

"Yes, and you haven't learned much if you think I'm going to let you go out with that prick. I don't care if it's nineteen *forty*-seven."

"He's not a prick. You have friends that I think are worse pricks than Jim Roper."

"They don't happen to be in love with you and screwing some nurse on the side. Not that that would be very easy. Screwing a nurse on the side."

"Oh, you're so witty."

"I am sometimes. Sometimes I surprise myself. If you'll excuse me, now, I'm going in and have a look at the baby, and congratulate him on having such a witty father. And, of course, beautiful, pleasant-dispositioned mother."

"Oh, go piss."

"On the way, dear. On the way. Thanks for reminding me."

Roper was not again mentioned and Alfred took off for Pennsylvania. He was halfway to Phillipsburg before a slight fear grew up in the midst of the homesickness and eagerness for the new assignment that occupied his thoughts on the dull ride across New Jersey. He happened to look at his watch, saw that it was past six o'clock, and imagined the apartment, crowded with thirty guests and noisy with the sounds of Mary's cocktail party. He knew who had been invited; all of them friendly, some of them decorative—and

493

Jim Roper, serious with the dignity of his new degree, resentful of the others' money, confident of his attraction for the women, and free to pick his moments with Mary.

Two hours later Alfred was in Gibbsville. He had a drink of whiskey in his room at the John Gibb Hotel, then went down to the diningroom, which had just closed. He walked along the main street until he saw a crowded Greek restaurant. He sat at the counter and ate half a dozen fried oysters and some French fried potatoes. The people in the restaurant were loud and rather drunken, and from their conversations Alfred finally learned that most of them were celebrating the victory of the Gibbsville football team over the Providence Steamrollers. A girl left her table and walked around the counter and tickled Alfred's ear.

"You're that Providence left end, I know you."

"Nope. Sorry."

"You played awful dirty. You should have been kicked out of the game."

"I was."

"No you weren't, but you should have. But you're cute. Come on over and sit with us. We have a quart."

"No thanks. I'm in training."

"For what? I'll bet you're married."

"Right the first time."

"Well, so am I. Do you see that poor unsophisticated piece of humanity over there with the glasses? That's who I'm supposed to be married to. Come on, I want to introduce you. Wud you say your name was?"

"I'm sorry, little friend, but I have to get going."

"You got a car?"

"Why?"

"Meet us at the Stage Coach. We're all going to the Stage Coach. You go to the Stage Coach and I'll meet you in the bar. I don't promise anything but I'll bet you won't be sorry. I won't promise, mind you, but if I like a person. Here." She took his hand and crushed it to her breasts.

"I hate to say no to a lady, but I've got to beat it."

"Wuddia mean you got to beat it?"

"Just that. I got to be on my way."

"Oh, you do. Well, fuck you, Buckley."

"Goodnight, my dear." He left a quarter on the counter and laid down the exact change at the cashier's desk and returned to the hotel. The girl had not been bad-looking. Still in her twenties, with a tight round figure and resistance in her breasts. The man she had pointed out as her husband had never looked at her when she left the table. Momentarily Alfred was pleased that she had picked him out, and the

494

promise that she had insisted was not a promise was exciting. But alone in his room he felt relief to have escaped not only the girl, but the attachment and its possible effect on his assignment. He looked at his watch, then put in a telephone call to Mary. He heard the maid tell the operator that Mrs. Eaton was not expected back before midnight, and he canceled the call. He read *The Saturday Evening Post* and *The Literary Digest* and went to sleep with the light on.

He paid six calls on banks during the next day's business hours and at three o'clock in the afternoon he had nothing to do. He had made no sales, but in each case he had asked if he could stop in again in a week or two, and the prospective customers all gave their consent, with the admonition that Thursday, Friday and Saturday were bad; payrolls, store business, and so on. It began to appear—and he was learning —that a salesman's worst enemy is time; too little of it, and too much of it. In a week, at the present rate, he would have visited all the banks on his list. He would have established his new identity. He remembered that any stranger in Port Johnson had been a marked man, and it was important to have the curious know who he was. He decided to cover the county banks in the first week and worry about the rest of the assignment later. At six o'clock he telephoned Mary.

"I called you last night," he said.

"We went to Michel's."

"How was the party?"

"Very nice. A lot of people brought presents. They all loved the apartment."

"Who did you have dinner with?"

"There were seven of us. Peg and Bill, Edith and Joe, and Lex and Jim Roper and I."

"Jim Roper managed to horn in?"

"He didn't horn in. He came along."

"Who brought you home?"

"Jim did."

"What time?"

"I think it was about twelve-thirty, might have been a little later."

"Did you ask him to come up?"

"Yes."

"Why are you making me ask a question for every step of the way?"

"Because I don't want to make it easy for you."

"You're not. How late did he stay?"

"Not late. About an hour."

"Possibly two o'clock. Did he make a pass at you?"

"No."

"Naturally I believe that. Are you seeing him again?"

"Probably. Yes. He's going to be at Peg and Bill's on Friday. I'm going there for dinner."

"And he'll undoubtedly bring you home."

"Possibly. I don't know."

"You know what you're doing, don't you?"

"I always know what I'm doing. Do you know what you're doing?"

"Never mind me for the moment. You're showing this son of a bitch that as soon as I leave town, you're ready to go out with him."

"I'm not showing him anything at all. But I'm showing you that I don't intend to stay cooped up in this apartment while you play golf and go to country club parties and call it business."

"Well, now I'll tell you something. I hereby forbid you to have Jim Roper in the house."

"I suppose you can do that."

"I can do it, and I've done it. The next step is to tell him. If you force me to, I will. So make up your mind. Stop having him in the house or I'll come back to New York and tell him myself. He'll have a hell of a time explaining a shiner to his doctor friends."

"Yes, you'd do that, I guess. Very well, I won't have him in the apartment. Is that all?"

"No. Let me speak to Rowland."

"Before you do, I have something to say."

"I'll be delighted to listen."

"Just this. You're making a big thing out of nothing."

"I don't happen to believe that. You're my wife and I'm not going to let this fellow walk in and do to our marriage the same thing that's happened to others we know about. I'm not *making* a big thing. It *is* a big thing that's happening now."

"I'll call Rowland."

In a moment the boy's voice came over the wire. "Hello, Daddy. This is Rowland."

"Hello, boy."

"Where are you?"

"I'm in Gibbsville, Pennsylvania."

"Is Grandmother Eaton there with you?"

"No, she's quite a distance away from here."

"Is Aunt Sally there?"

"No, she's in Port Johnson."

"Is Aunt Constance there?"

"No, she's with Grandmother."

"Are you all alone?"

"Yes. All alone. Very much so."

"What did you say?"

"I said very much so. How are you? What did you do today?"

"You ask me too many questions."

"You're your mother's son."

"What?"

"I said how are you?"

"Fine. How are you?"

"Fine, thank you. How is your brother?"

"He vomited, Daddy. Alex vomited on his dress. And yesterday he did duty when a lady was holding him."

"He'll have to learn better than that. Too bad he didn't do it on one of the gentlemen."

"What?"

"I said too bad."

"Yes, too bad. Too bad. I have to go now. I'm listening to the radio. Goodbye, Daddy. Sleep tight, don't let the bedbugs bite."

"Is your mother there?"

He could hear the disconnect signal, and he hung up, but not without the suspicion that Mary had heard his last question to the boy.

The roads were not too well marked and in his week of calling on bankers he lost his way several times, but he completed that part of his assignment on Wednesday afternoon, and thus was left with half the week open. Mary did not telephone him, and he was tempted to disobey Hasbrouck's order and go back to New York, which he could almost certainly have done without Hasbrouck's knowledge. But he was determined to make a good showing on this assignment and in truth it was of more importance to him than the quarrel with Mary. He could not in fairness characterize her as a quarrelsome girl; she took pride in her house and her children and in her husband, and in her pride she was justified. The kids were inevitably called "Mennen's food babies" and for reasons that were probably not unrelated to favorable comments about Alfred in Wall Street, as well as the photogenic quality of the children and their mother, they had been photographed for the Sunday rotogravure section of the *Herald Tribune*: "Mrs. Alfred Eaton, Long Island young matron, and her interesting children, Rowland (left) and Alexander. Mrs. Eaton is the former Miss Mary St. John, of Wilmington, Del." She had been asked to pose for a Pond's advertisement, and on Alfred's insistence had refused. She had by-passed the activities of the Junior League and she was highly selective in allowing her name to be used on lists of patronesses. She had, in other words, elected to subordinate her own social career to the business career of her husband, a decision which was quite likely to be more rewarding in the future but prevented her from joining in the more obvious and immediate gayety of the larger young married set. On such matters she sometimes did quarrel with Alfred. "What harm can that do?" she would ask. "None, but let's stay out of the papers," he would reply. He discovered that her mother had subscribed to the *Herald Tribune* for the society news and went through it every day for mention of Mary and Alfred. "Tell your mother we'll be in Personal Intelligence every day—after I'm made a partner." Their other quarrels were not atypical for their life and the time. He would object to her deep décolletage for a fancy dress party; she would complain about his falling asleep at the bridge table; he would complain about a lack of the stiff collars he wore to work; she would object to his readiness to break any engagement for the firm. But as their marriage grew older he had noticed that no matter how trivial the cause of the quarrel, while it lasted she stayed in a fury, using words and combinations of words that he did not know she knew although she had learned them from him), and sometimes striking out at him with her fists. Then one evening in the midst of a quarrel he threw her on the bed and she lay there looking up at him with what he at first thought was hatred growing out of the quarrel, but almost immediately realized was something besides that. She was breathing deeply from the exertions of the quarrel, but then she slowly drew up her nightgown, all without taking her eyes off him, and for the first time he understood that there was a strong, direct connection between her angers and desire. He took her with almost no preliminary love-making, and later she asked him to forgive her for her bad temper, paid him compliments, spoke of love. Lovemaking did not become a means of settling all quarrels between them, but he now possessed the secret knowledge (which they never discussed between them) that if a quarrel led to love-making, or was followed by it, she retained no resentment; and he possessed the corollary knowledge that resentment remained if he did not make love to her while the heat of the quarrel lasted. In the latter event her resentment could continue for days, as it was doing now.

But there was a difference in this quarrel. It was a double quarrel. It had begun with the announcement of his trip, it had not been dissolved in love-making, and in her resentment she had defied him, and he suddenly thought of Victoria Dockwiler. For a moment it was an alarming thought, as nearly all thoughts of Victoria Dockwiler were either alarming or saddening or sweet, but now he minimized his fears and dismissed them by summoning up the dissimilar facts of his last quarrel with Victoria and his present quarrel with Mary. There was really hardly anything that the two quarrels had in common, he told himself. This quarrel would just have to work itself out, and it was one time when he would not yield, nor would he placate her with words of love.

Now that decision was made, and he gained strength from it. He could turn now to an undistracted consideration of the work at hand. He got out his lists and read the names of Hasbrouck's dear old ladies and priests and professional men, and they seemed on paper to be such an unattracting lot that he got out the letter to R. W. Benziger. On an impulse he telephoned the Mountain City Coal Company office, which he knew to be about fifteen miles away, and by merely asking to speak to Mr. Benziger he was put through to him.

He introduced himself in his role as Rowley & Cruickshank salesman, and asked for an appointment the next day. "Oh, I'm very sorry, Mr. Eaton, but if you want to see me it'll have to be before supper. I'm going away tomorrow and I won't be back till a week from Sunday."

"Oh, I'm sorry," said Alfred. "I must have caught you at your busiest."

There was a laugh. "I don't know when I'm at my busiest. But why don't you come over anyway? We could talk for ten or fifteen minutes, get acquainted."

"Unfortunately I'm in Gibbsville."

"Hmm. Got a car?"

"Yes."

"Well, you can be here in half an hour if you think it's worthwhile. I'm not going to buy anything, but I know how it is to break in a new territory. Come on up, if you feel like it."

"I'll be there in half an hour."

"Watch out about ten miles up the mountain. There was a big slide there early this morning. Must be about thirty tons of rock there."

It was dark when he got to the Mountain City office and the town was at least ten degrees colder than Gibbsville. Every bulb in the building was burning and the brightness (and possibly the advance information on Benziger) made the place seem cheerful. It was the end of the day for the office staff and Alfred arrived simultaneously with a party of men carrying lunch cans and transit, rod, tape-spools and other surveying equipment. All but one of the men were young, wore Army breeches and hob-nailed boots and they were all dirty-faced. Vaguely they reminded him of a group of junior officers from his Navy days. They were tired and ready for a bath, but they joked among themselves and made easy conversation with the girls of the office. Merely to see them was to feel very far removed from Hasbrouck's list of dear old ladies and dear

499

old men, and the thought abruptly brought him back to his purpose.

Benziger's office had a temporary look about it, in spite of the heavy furniture and enlarged photographs of collieries and tipples, first-aid teams and mule yards. The paperweights were lumps of sculped polished anthracite and a varnished spragger, and there were calendars and foot-rules bearing the names of firms that supplied the Mountain City Coal Company with dynamite, cable, dualin caps, electric locomotives and such. The only personal touches were Benziger's hat and coat, hanging from a wooden clothes-tree, and a Bachrach photograph of his wife, daughter, and son.

"Have a cigar," said Benziger, after the exchange of greetings. He took a walnut humidor out of a drawer and offered it to Alfred. "This is the only thing I have to keep out of sight here. I could leave a ten-dollar bill on my desk and nobody'd put a finger on it. But not a box of cigars. How long you been here, Mr. Eaton?"

"Since Sunday night."

"Drive?"

"Yes, I did."

"Came by way of Easton, I suppose, and that way?"

"Yes." Alfred felt the not unfriendly study he was undergoing.

"First time in the region?"

"First time, although I was born in Port Johnson."

"Oh. One of that family. Of course. Was that your father? Samuel Eaton?"

"Yes it was."

"We had some dealings with your father's mill, a long time ago. I met him only the one time. From then on everything went through our purchasing agent. Well, it's always nice to do business with the second generation, but I'm not in the market for any bonds just now. Excuse me, just one minute please. *Ethel!*"

His secretary opened the door.

"You might as well go home. I'll be here at seven, but you don't have to come in till eight."

"I might as well be here at seven. Goodnight." She closed the door.

"I can't *ask* a good secretary to be here at seven o'clock in the morning, but she knows darn well I'll need her. Uh, what are you doing for supper? At home they always give me a steak the night before I go off on a trip. You won't get as good a steak at the John Gibb."

"If that's an invitation, you've sold me."

"Sure it's an invitation," said Benziger. He picked up the telephone receiver. "Five one one, please . . . Natalie? Dad.

500

Tell Mother I'm bringing a guest for dinner. Be there in fifteen minutes . . . There we are, Mr. Eaton. See how easy it is? That was my daughter. I forgot to ask her whether she's going to be home. There she is in that picture, with Mrs. Benziger and my son. My son's a lawyer in Wilkes-Barre, graduate of Lafayette and the Harvard Law School. Just starting out. Daughter Natalie went to Miss Baldwin's but didn't go on to college. Where did you go, Mr. Eaton?"

"Princeton, for two years only."

"Quit to go in the Army, I suppose."

"Navy. Then I never went back."

"No interest in making steel?"

"None whatever."

"Well, Ralph was the same way. He's been inside. I had him working on the engineering corps, summers, and I even had him what we call muckin' in a drift, the lowest job in the mines. But he never cared anything for mining, and his grandfather, Mrs. Benziger's father, was a very well-known judge in Wilkes-Barre, so we're hoping he'll follow in his footsteps. You have your car? I'll ride along with you and show you the way. I'll send my driver home."

They put on their hats and coats and went out. A man in a cloth cap was sitting asleep at the wheel of a black Cadillac phaeton.

"I don't think I'll wake him up," said Benziger. "He's been up since half past four this morning, and he'll know I've gone home when he wakes up."

"Did you get up at half past four, too?"

"No, I got up at five. Sharp left. He comes to the house and puts the coffee on and we have a cup of coffee. Then today, for instance, we drove to Scranton and had our breakfast and I transacted my business and we got back here around noon. Then I had to go to Gibbsville for bank meeting, and back here at four. So he's gotten about a two-hour nap. Straight ahead. The only trouble is, some of the school kids know about him and how he takes naps, and they sneak up and blow the horn, and I've had to give him merry hell for the language he uses to those kids. He'll sleep there now for another hour. He can sleep anywhere, anytime. You talk about your colored gentry in the South, that fellow—well, he drove a motorcycle in France during the war. Dispatch-rider. He's been driving for me now for eight years last August, and he can still tell me stories. G. Dewey Hollingsworth, better known as Dewey. Knows more about the V-type eight-cylinder engine than the man that invented it. Now left. That car is a little over a year old. Do you have any idea what the mileage on it is? You can take a look at the speedometer. Fifty-four thousand miles. I couldn't do that if I didn't have a man like

Dewey. I'm *glad* you stopped by, Mr. Eaton. I hope you'll do it often, whenever you're in the region. Now if you'll just pull up at the white house with the iron fence, on your right."

They got out of the car, and a dog growled. Alfred could not see the animal.

"Rupert. Quiet, boy," said Benziger. "Now we're all right." Benziger opened the gate and a handsome German shepherd came into sight. "He can be very embarrassing at times, but my wife and daughter are here alone a good deal at night. And the cook, but she's a woman, too. I keep a .38 in my bureau drawer, and Natalie knows how to use it, but I don't think she ever would. And we have to fire men in our business, and if one of them ever got drunk on this boilo they drink nowadays—new whiskey, still hot—he might come looking for me and I wouldn't be here. We live closer to the basic instincts than you might think. Down there, you can't see it now under this poor light, but at the end of this street last winter they found a man frozen to death. You don't think of this part of the country being cold, but we have readings of fifteen, eighteen, twenty below. And you get off a road less than a mile from this house and you're in scrub oak that all looks the same, and even people that were born here have been frozen to death. They start home a little drunk. In the summer, they fall down an air shaft. Get bitten by a rattlesnake. Drown in a dam. Not as bad as it used to be, but payday we still have a shooting or a knifing about once a month, a little oftener. And yet I have to say I love it. I wouldn't live anywhere else if you paid me. When these mountains around here are covered with laurel, or even snow, there's something so beautiful about them, and to me, knowing them from the inside, having spent so many years in the coal-black insides of these mountains, with just a carbide lamp that only makes you realize the darkness of it, and the danger, always there, gas that you can't smell but that can kill you, and the coal above you and on all sides of you that can crush you. And the people. The men, their women. The Irish faces, especially of the old Irish men. The old ones, not the young. Dignity. Wisdom. Sorrow, and pride. Not much time left to them, and not much to show for working like niggers all their lives. But have a look at their skin sometime. Go to a saloon and look at them. You know miners are the cleanest laborers there are. They scrub every evening and every Saturday they shave. You'll see an old man in his seventies or eighties and he'll have the skin of a young girl but with a light in it that isn't a greasy shine. And the Polacks. The schwakies. I go to one of our collieries in the early morning, before they get the coal dust on their faces, and they get in the cage, line up to get in the cage, and I look at their faces and I can almost see them back on the steppes of Russia, not working in the mines, but riding horses with their swords swinging around and the reins in their teeth. Cossacks. Men who fight with knives. Wild men. Oh, well. Let's go in. I always stand out here for a minute or two when I get home. Just that minute or so between my work and my home. It's a habit I have. But I'm not always so talkative. I usually only have Rupert to talk to, but he ought to understand me. He isn't far from being a wolf."

The door was then opened by the most beautiful girl Alfred had ever seen.

"Hello, Dad."

"Natalie, this is Mr. Eaton."

"How do you do? Come right in," she said. She swung the door wide and held out her hand.

"How do you do, Miss Benziger."

They shook hands and she kissed her father. "*Dad?* Like the side of a match-box."

"Can't think why. I shaved at five o'clock this morning. Growing boy, it ought to last me a week."

"Well, it won't. Let me take your hat and coat, Mr. Eaton. We have a place for them under the stairs, usually. But we're having new shelves built. Did you hear that, Dad?"

"I heard it. They're not finished yet?"

"They didn't show up today, not once all day. So I'll take Mr. Eaton's things." She left them and Benziger led the way to a small room on the left.

"This was intended to be a sort of a den, but as you see, it's as much office as den. Wash up in there and I'll be downstairs in a minute."

Alfred was alone for a moment when he came out of the lavatory. The room was overcrowded with souvenirs of Benziger's past life and articles for his present ease. There were framed acknowledgments to his Red Cross and Liberty Loan activities in the war, a mounted bass, a mounted trout, the head of a deer, a cabinet containing four shotguns and a leather fishing-rod case, and everywhere framed photographs; family snapshots and posed cabinet-size pictures of men. A presentation cigar humidor and a large silver cigarette box that needed polish. A desk with two small filing cabinets. Two telephones. A black leather sofa and three tufted leather chairs. A carpeted footstool and stacks of trade journals, a bookcase containing technical volumes and textbooks and a 1922 *Who's Who in America*. On the desk were the day's Philadelphia and New York morning newspapers, still in their wrappings. Alfred turned when he heard her step.

"I'd never seen a coal mine before last Monday. Is this

503

one of your mines?" He indicated a photograph he had been looking at.

"It certainly is. That's Number 4. Dad wanted to name it the Natalie, after me, of course. But not seriously. There's a Natalie company that we have nothing to do with. But Number 4 is the biggest our company has. This one is Number 1, which of course is the oldest, but Number 4 is our pride and joy. When that was built it was the most electrified colliery in the world. This is my favorite room in the whole house. I always used to come in here to do my homework."

"Especially your arithmetic?"

"Why do you say that?"

"So you could get your father to help you."

"No, I was good in arithmetic. But he helped me with everything else. He'll be here in a second and you can have a drink."

"I'm in no hurry for one."

"Here's Mother. Mother, this is Mr. Eaton."

"Good evening, Mr. Eaton. It's very nice of you to come."

"It's very kind of you to have me. And Mr. Benziger to invite me. This is the first house I've been in since I got here, and you and Miss Benziger are the first Lantenengo County ladies I've ever met."

"Yes, but how long have you been here?" said Natalie.

"Since Monday, but I've had a lot of free time."

"Do you know anybody around here?" said Natalie.

"Until now, no. I know I went to school with some Gibbsville fellows, but I don't know their names."

"Where did you go?" said Natalie.

"To prep school, a place called Knox, now defunct."

"I can't help you. Did you go to college?"

"Princeton, for two years, before you were aware of Princeton."

"I'm twenty-two, and I've been aware of Princeton for seven years."

"No, you haven't, Natalie. At fifteen?"

"I was aware of it. Ralph talked enough about it, although not complimentary-ly. Complimen-tarily. Ralph is my brother, and he went to Lafayette."

"Well, what's everybody standing for? Natalie, you know where I keep the liquor," said Benziger. "Introductions all taken care of, let's see what we've got here. Mr. Eaton, the choice is gin and whiskey. The whiskey is pre-war, and the gin is made by one of our men in the lab. If you're going to be around this section I'll have to give you some names of bootleggers. And if you like beer, there's some good beer to be had, but not everywhere. A lot of it is etherized and some of it is just slop."

504

"You sound like an old toper," said Mrs. Benziger.

"Well, if I hadn't married such a strict Methodist that's what I'd be. Let's have whiskey, shall we? Natalie? Grace? Mr. Eaton?"

"I'd like gin," said Natalie.

"So would I," said Mrs. Benziger.

"I'll have whiskey. I wouldn't pass up a drink of pre-war." The drinks were served in shot-glasses with water chasers in tumblers.

"Welcome to our fair city, welcome to our house," said Benziger.

They each had two drinks, and when they finished them Mrs. Benziger said: "Let's have dinner, now. No more drinking, and I don't want our steak ruined."

At dinner the conversation was autobiographical, biographical, and anecdotal and after dinner the men were left alone in the den while the women sat in the livingroom and knitted. At nine-thirty Mrs. Benziger came in to say goodnight and Natalie followed her into the room. "I might as well say goodnight, too," said Natalie.

"Keep Mr. Eaton company for a minute," said Benziger. He left with his wife.

"Mother has a heart condition," said Natalie. "She never stays up later than ten."

"What do you do with your time? Or have you a heart condition, too?"

"No, I have no particular heart condition of either kind. I play bridge, go to the movies, the usual. Dances at the club."

"Will you go to the movies with me sometime?"

"No."

"Because I'm married?"

"You guessed it. None of my friends would think of going to the movies with a married man."

"I haven't asked your friends."

"I'm telling you what their answer will be."

"Would you go to the movies with me in—Philadelphia?"

"No."

"Why? Again because I'm married?"

"Yes. I think that you probably have a very nice wife, an attractive wife. There's no percentage for me in playing around with a married man. I never have, and I never intend to."

"Are you angry because I asked you?"

"No. I consider it a compliment."

"I hope you do, because you're the first girl I ever asked to go out with me since I've been married. That's six years. But I have something more to say."

"Maybe you'd better not say it."

"I'll say it. I hope to go on seeing you for the rest of my life."

"I was right. You shouldn't have said it."

"Maybe, but you know I mean it. You knew the minute I looked at you, didn't you?"

"I don't want to encourage this conversation."

"In two hours—in two minutes—my whole life has been changed, just by seeing you. You don't want me to disturb you. I want to disturb you. Not to make you unhappy, or uncomfortable, but to convince you of this one thing."

"Don't say it, please."

"I love you."

"You still shouldn't have said it. I could have thought it and you could have let me think it, but you shouldn't have said it."

"I'm going to be here for two months. Even if I don't ever say it again, or get the chance to, I have said it and it's true."

"I think I'd better go away."

"You're not going to give it a chance?"

"Give what a chance? What *has* a chance? You have a wife and two children."

"And a very important job and a future that's practically guaranteed."

"That's more than most people get out of life." She looked up at him. "It's more than I have, and what you're doing now is spoiling any chance I have of getting it."

"Yes, you're right. I hadn't looked at it that way. Before your father comes back, will you meet me sometime, to talk? Will you phone me at the hotel?"

"No. I know that if we stop it now it won't get worse."

"Then you felt it too?"

"Of course I did. This doesn't happen to just one person."

"I'd have loved you if it hadn't happened to you."

"How old are you?"

"I'm thirty."

"And you don't know the first thing about love . . . *And then we stayed in Paris for three weeks and then we went to London for a week. Is Mother all right?"*

"Oh, yes," said Benziger. "Few things I wanted to tell her. I won't be seeing her in the morning. Dewey's coming for me at five minutes of seven."

"Well, I'll wander along, Mr. Benziger."

"Now wait. Natalie's having some people in for dinner on Saturday and Mrs. Benziger and I think it'd be nice if you came, too!"

"They had a pow-wow to decide whether it was all right to invite a married man. Yes, Dad?"

"Well, something on that order. This isn't New York, and I'm sure Mr. Eaton realizes it. You know how small towns

506

are. But a dinner party in our own house, with Mother here, that changes the complexion of it. And I'm sure it's all right with the real hostess, Natalie?"

"Yes, of course," said Natalie.

"Fine. Good. You understand why Natalie didn't invite you herself."

"Oh, I was brought up in a small town."

"But it's so much closer to Philadelphia than we are, we tend to think of towns down that way as part of the city."

"Well, we never did. Do the men dress on Saturday?"

"No. It isn't a big party. It's really only two tables of bridge."

"Then I'm excess baggage. Let me have a rain check for Saturday and invite me some other time.'"

"Dad, I think that *would* be better. We keep the scores individually for the whole season, so I'm afraid Mr. Eaton wouldn't have much fun just talking to dummy."

"Well, you two work that out yourselves. But Mrs. Benziger and I hope you'll come here for dinner, if not this Saturday, some other time. Natalie, will you lock up? Goodnight, Mr. Eaton."

"Thank you for everything, you and Mrs. Benziger, and have a good trip."

"Oh, yes. I always have a good trip. When I go to Pittsburgh I always feel that I'm getting the Middle Western point of view. Goodnight."

His failure to kiss his daughter indicated that he expected to see her momentarily upstairs, and Alfred put on his coat and went to the door. She went out to the porch with him, and let out the dog.

"Innocent, aren't they?" said Natalie. "The last thing they'd ever want to do is throw us together, but they almost did."

"You're bucking fate, Natalie. That's dangerous."

"Not as dangerous as some things. Goodnight, Mr. Eaton."

He clasped her hand for a moment, but she shook her head slowly. "I wouldn't have minded kissing you if you hadn't said what you said. I would have liked it, a casual kiss from an attractive man. But now it would be misinterpreted."

"I can wait forever."

"That's what it's going to be."

"I'll stay till the dog comes back."

She whistled, one long low note and one short high note, and the dog, out of the darkness, was upon them in seconds.

"That's my answer?" said Alfred, laughing.

"That's your answer." She opened the door and she and the dog went inside and he heard the bolt being shot. As he slammed the door of his car the porch light went out.

The car did not start easily, and he soon became conscious

of the cold. His topcoat was light, his gloves were thin. The car was a Chevrolet business coupé, unheated, and he drove with the disturbing knowledge that there was water and not alcohol in the radiator. But he enjoyed the ride and when he got to the hotel he had a cup of coffee in the coffee shop, which was decorated in a simulation of the interior of a mine, and he was thankful for the warmth of his room and for his solitude.

He had decided for his own future guidance to make a daily written report to himself, which two months hence he would use in preparing his report to the firm. He got out his notebook and wrote "R. W. B." at the top of the page.

From the beginning everything he wrote, and the unwritten thinking that produced his impressionistic notes, proved the inadequacy of Hasbrouck's information on Ralph Benziger. Nowhere would Hasbrouck have considered it valuable to have a record of most of what Alfred had observed about Benziger. Benziger had the eye of the poet without the poet's constricted tongue, but what was Hasbrouck's picture of Benziger? A hard-working man who had the good will of the people who worked for him. If there was more, it was only more of the same, and the sameness could have been repeated for a thousand, ten thousand, men who employed labor. Hasbrouck's information was inaccurate because of its incompleteness, but Hasbrouck could not be expected to know that. Hasbrouck was a snob, the worst kind of Wall Street snob, who would excuse his failure to appreciate a man like Benziger, on the ground that it was undesirable in a business relationship to take the time and trouble to understand any more about him than that he was efficient, industrious, sober, and honest. The cold truth was that Hasbrouck did not *want* to understand a man like Benziger, who had no Harvard or Yale background (Hasbrouck considered Princeton an institution which some of his prep school friends attended because of family ties, but was at least a member of the Big Two-and-a-Half). Hasbrouck would describe as virtues some of MacHardie's characteristics that in Benziger he would dismiss as ordinary. Hasbrouck could never get Benziger to open up as he had tonight in his nearly lyrical description of his mountains and his people. Benziger would know in two minutes that Hasbrouck would never see the faces of the men lined up at a shaft but only that they represented certain items on the time-sheets that had to compare favorably with the tonnage figures. But Alfred had found out that Benziger was a man who knew what he was doing and why he was doing it, and he had found out because Benziger, in the same two minutes it would have taken him to judge Hasbrouck, had judged Alfred and opened up to him. It was a complimentary judgment, to be sure, but it resulted in a more accurate picture of Benziger than Hasbrouck would ever get, and therefore was even more valuable for its results than any set of facts respectfully submitted to Hasbrouck.

Alfred was pleased by the compliment, but he was equally pleased by this additional confirmation of his own judgment of Hasbrouck, whom he did not like. Whenever he was called to Hasbrouck's desk he would come away with the conviction that of all nine desks, Hasbrouck's was most likely to become his own. Whether Hasbrouck suspected him of such ambitions he could not tell. Hasbrouck was always so precise in his praise and so careful not to patronize him that he gave Alfred no reason to complain or resent. He did not underestimate Hasbrouck, who worked hard, was shrewd in his work, and was respected and even feared in and out of the firm. It was said of him that he "would cut your throat while you thought he was tying an ascot for you, and he'd tie a damn good ascot, too." But he was an arithmetician, not a mathematician; he was a snob, and he lacked what old Raymond Johnson liked to see in a business man—imagination. Both characteristics would work against him in an appraisal of R. W. Benziger, the business at hand, as the lack of imagination had somewhat worked against him in the Louisiana sulphur proposition . . .

It had been one of Alfred's first important assignments, and one in which he was expected to function as a student in the MacHardie training course that was not a training course. He went along as a clerk, messenger, and in a perfectly self-respecting way as valet to Hasbrouck. As he left New York he was totally ignorant of the uses of sulphur and he arrived in New Orleans with only a sketchy, general idea of its value. In the next few weeks he absorbed more information, but still only what he could pick up from Hasbrouck and the local men whom he was able to chat with when Hasbrouck was not giving him clerical and messenger chores. He was amused by the fact that the oil industry had to go to a lot of trouble to remove the sulphur from crude oil, and then put sulphur back in, a fact which he learned was also true of steel and the manufacture of certain kinds of steel, and which explained the carloads of sulphur he remembered lying at the north end of his father's mill. The usefulness of sulphur in the oil and steel industries was what concerned MacHardie & Company, since the firm was the heaviest stockholder in Cullingworth Steel and Ziegler Oil, the latter an East Texas company which was being used to justify Hasbrouck's presence in Louisiana.

They had been in the state about two weeks, and one night after dining alone, Alfred was sitting in the hotel lobby. A thin, carelessly dressed man with an untrimmed moustache took the chair beside him.

"Cigar?" said the man.

"Smoking, thanks," said Alfred.

"How would you like to make yourself a nice piece of change?"

"How would I go about doing that?" said Alfred.

"Well, it would cost you money, all things do in the long run, all things that a man can buy. A woman like that there, she wouldn't have to pay money."

"I noticed her. She a friend of yours?"

"No sir, she is not. I'm past the age where I get in the saddle any more, but I still look, from habit. Clutch that little bottom of hers and hang on, twenty years ago."

"Well, somebody's going to be hanging on tonight. She just made a pick-up."

"Well, let's hope he don't wake up with a bead on it some morning next week. The bead that won't shake off. Oh, that old bead. At least I don't have that to worry about no more. You never caught it."

"Nope."

"Just luck, if I may take the liberty of sizing you up right."

"That's all it was. Luck."

"Don't go low-ratin' luck, mister. This may be your lucky night."

"You never can tell."

"'She may be thin and look all in, but you never can tell. No sir, you never can. But you can make a nice piece o' change if you believe in luck."

"I can?"

"Provided you believe it was lucky you saw old Jack Rawlings tonight."

"Jack Rawlings being you?"

"None other."

"Yes, I do believe I was lucky, Mr. Rawlings. But now I think my luck is about to run out, because I'm headed for bed. Up early, you know."

"Hasbrouck works you pretty hard, does he?"

"Yes, but how did you know that? Not that it's any secret," said Alfred.

"I've lived in this hotel ever since it opened, and I always take a look at the registry every morning."

"One of the owners?"

"Not any more. Used to own a few shares, but they bought me out a while back. Not that you have to answer me if you aren't so inclined, but are you down here to buy up some oil properties?"

"You said if I wasn't so inclined—"

510

"You didn't have to answer me. Well, you can't shoot a man for asking. Just curiosity, an old man sticking his nose in where it don't belong. But when I see a partner of James D. MacHardie in town, well I knowed right away it was something bigger'n crabbing. Only two things in Louisiana big enough to interest James D. MacHardie, and I already asked you about the one. If I asked you about the other I'd get the same answer."

"What is the other, Mr. Rawlings?"

"It wouldn't be sulphur, would it?"

"Well, I'm off to bed, sir. Goodnight."

"Pretty good. You're smarter'n I took you for."

Hasbrouck went out to dinner every night, and Alfred would chat with Rawlings in the lobby. He reported that the old man had identified Hasbrouck, but Hasbrouck seemed unconcerned and accepted the recognition as his due. One evening when Rawlings did not show up Alfred inquired for him and the next evening Rawlings mentioned the fact. "If I was to just die in my sleep nobody'd miss me. That is, I thought so, but I'm reliably informed you asked after my health last evening."

"Yes, I did. I'm glad to see you're all right again."

"Thank you, sir. I stood in water and muck all my life and now I'm paying for it with the rheumatism."

"Have you lived here all your life?"

"In Louisiana? No, but a big piece of it. Last year I went pretty near broke when the sulphur ran out in Calcasieu Parish, and this year my rheumatism bothers me. Next year it'll be something else and the year after that all my worries'll be over. But it was right nice of you to ask after me."

"Well, I enjoy our evenings together."

"I don't mind telling you I do too, sir. I'll be sorry to see you go."

"So will I, although I have to admit it's only because of our chats. My wife is coming down next week for a few days. You'll have to meet her."

"I can give her a good report on her husband."

"She knows I behave. I don't want to misbehave, that's why."

"Mr. Eaton, that first offer I made you to make a little money for yourself?"

"Yes."

"You wouldn't of made any money. I was hoping to get rid of some land I own. There's no oil underneath it. But I know where there is some. Have you got $25,000, or could you lay your hands on it?"

"Mr. Rawlings, I don't want to buy anything."

"Yes you do. You're out to make money, that's why you're with James D. MacHardie."

"I'd rather remember you as a pleasant gentleman I spent

some pleasant evenings with. I don't want to think of you as a man who took me for a sucker, so let's steer clear of business and tell me about the old days."

"Oh, I've made some deals that don't make me proud of myself in my old age, but I'd never cheat a young fellow that's been nice to me. Have you got $25,000?"

"Yes, I have."

"Then I tell you what to do with it. Your Hasbrouck man, he's fixing to buy up the St. Bovard Parish Sulphur Company. You don't have to say yes or no. I know it. Likewise he's buying the Beau Reve property, Number Twelve. I know. Both those deals have been shaken hands on and ready to sign. But next door to the Beau Reve is a thousand acres of swamp, that's all it is and nobody's interested in it. They had surveyors on it, they sold options on it, they had geologists give their opinions. Nothing there but trap-lines now. Well, Mr. Eaton, you can option that land for $25,000, twenty-five dollars an acre. You do it."

"I'm just a clerk, Mr. Rawlings."

"You're a clerk with $25.000, though. Hasbrouck won't buy it and I don't care what Hasbrouck does. You option it for yourself and that lovely wife and son of yours that you showed me the pictures of. And then you tell James D. MacHardie to go plumb to hell."

"Why do you want to sell it?"

"That's a natural question. I can't sell it because I don't own it. I don't own a single muskrat on it."

"But you have $25,000."

"I have a little more than that, but I don't have any wife or young ones to leave my money to, and I'm too full of the rheumatism to get any pleasure out of work. I'm an old man living alone in a hotel, that's all I am, waiting for somebody to claim the body, and that's going to be an undertaker I hired three years ago. Here they don't even put you in the ground, so I'm getting cremated and my ashes sprinkled on Lake Pontchartrain, if the undertaker remembers to take the trouble."

"Well, at least you can laugh at it. If I did want to take an option on this land who would I talk to?"

"I'll write down their names for you. And my lawyer, a man named Xavier O'Ryan. Let him do the buying for you."

At lunch the next day Alfred told Hasbrouck the old man's story and Hasbrouck seemed to enjoy Alfred's naïveté. "Naturally we're not interested," said Hasbrouck. "But you seem to be."

"I don't know whether I am or not, Mr. Hasbrouck."

"Well, can you afford to pay $25,000 more for your education?"

"No, but would you have any objection if I did? Would the firm object?"

"Not if you made sure the firm was kept entirely out of it. Sometimes the best thing that can happen to a young chap is to lose money early in his career. However, I must warn you that if you do decide to do it, it goes down on your record at the office. Your work has been satisfactory and I'm going to say so in my report, but I'm also obliged to report this, too. *If* you do it. Just as I will report that you *didn't* do it if you follow *my* advice. The St. Bovard and Beau Reve are investments. The other land is worthless—unless, of course, you're planning to go into the fur business. I understand the trappers make a good living, some years. But you'd have to go a lot deeper than the Frasch process goes if you expect to get any sulphur out of that land, and as to oil . . ."

Hasbrouck's smiling superiority became so infuriating that Alfred could answer it only by taking the old man's advice in defiance of Hasbrouck. He went to his room and telephoned Ed Barlow in Port Johnson, instructing him to telegraph $20,000 that same afternoon. The Postal Telegraph notice was in Alfred's mail-box when he returned to the hotel before dinner, and he immediately paid a call on Xavier O'Ryan. O'Ryan, a short man with thick black eyebrows and a shock of white hair, was not surprised to see him, and said so.

"You realize, Mr. Eaton, this-yuh aint a speculation. It's a gaimble, a gaimble pure and simple," said O'Ryan. "Otherwise I'd sure be in it, and I'm not."

"I realize it."

"But you're doing it because you like Jack Rawlings."

"I guess that's what it comes down to."

"Ve' well, sir. I foresee no difficulties. Your money order will be deposited when the bank opens in the morning, and this is your personal cheque for the remainder. Am I to understand that I'm to have the honor of acting for you in a legal capacity after you go North? There'll be such matters as taxes, collecting rents and so on. The one won't balance the other, you know that."

It was obvious that Rawlings had instructed O'Ryan to treat Alfred with every consideration, and back at the hotel Alfred waited for Rawlings in anticipation of the pleasure the transaction would give the old man. But Rawlings did not appear that night, and the next morning the elevator boy told him why. Rawlings had died during the night.

Hasbrouck permitted Alfred to go to the funeral in the small Episcopal church. The service was attended by a sizable group of men of substance, Negroes of the elevator boy—bellboy class, and a few elderly women who had survived the rigors of their past. O'Ryan spoke to him after the service. "I just wanted to tell you, since there's no money changed hands yet, and Jack passing away, you don't have to go through with the deail. I mean to say, he's past taking offense if you druther not."

"I'll go through with it, as planned, Mr. O'Ryan."

O'Ryan looked at him. "He was right about you. He said you were a gentleman," said O'Ryan, and Alfred knew that he had a new friend.

About three months after their work in Louisiana was completed Hasbrouck sent for Alfred. "I'm not going to beat about the bush," said Hasbrouck. "How much do you want for your options on that Louisiana land?"

"I don't know. You must know something I don't know."

"We do. Mr. MacHardie should be handling this himself, but I have a sneaking suspicion he wants me to eat crow, and I'm prepared to do that. I was wrong, and you were right. There's oil. How much, we don't yet know. Now you can raise the money to finance additional investigation yourself, if you like. Or you can sell us your options at a considerable profit and we'll develop the property if there's anything there."

"*If* there's anything there?"

"There's oil there, but we don't know that it's one of the great pools, or just one of those freaks. And I have been asked to tell you that your decision in no way affects your job here. That's up to you."

"Will you give me some time to think about it?"

"Take a week, if you like. Go down to Louisiana and find out what you can. This firm will be here when you get back."

"I didn't mean a week. I meant a couple of minutes," said Alfred. He watched Hasbrouck's effort to retain his composure, turning a long gold pencil over and over, running his fingers down the pencil to the bottom, then up-ending it and starting again at the top. Hasbrouck had well-manicured hands and his cuffs were starched, and hands and cuffs became symbols of the man in the present situation: whatever was going on inside him, he was not showing it. He had spoken of eating crow, but he had displayed no humility or even respect, and yet Alfred sensed that if he gave an answer that was unsatisfactory to the firm, Hasbrouck would resign. Months might pass, but only to enable Hasbrouck, and indirectly the firm itself, to save face.

"All right, Mr. Hasbrouck," said Alfred. "I've decided. I'll sell the options for $250,000 and one condition."

"What is the condition?"

"That the first well you bring in be called the Jack Rawlings."

"Now let's understand each other. You sell us the options— us will be a company we'll form, of course—for $250,000. That ends your participation in the deal?"

514

"Yes. That, and the naming of the first well."

"That's satisfactory. Congratulations. I think you showed great good sense. You didn't ask for too much money, you didn't gamble $250,000, which is what you'd have been doing, you know. And you did nothing, I may say, to jeopardize your position with the firm. I'll tell you now that you made a very good guess. If you had asked for more than three hundred thousand, you wouldn't have got it. And regardless of our good intentions and our sincerity, I don't think you'd have been very happy here. Now tell me, please, why did you decide to risk $25,000 of your own money for those options? Do you know why?"

"I think I do. The old man trusted me, and he was a human being. I had no reason to trust him, but he trusted me. I'm almost sure to lose by it sometime, but I'd rather lose by it than hurt somebody who did trust me. Hard to explain."

"Well, we'll see that his name is perpetuated, or at least that's what we hope."

"Now I'd like to ask a question if I may. How do you know there's oil on that property?"

"You may ask, but I'm not at liberty to tell you. I *am* at liberty to tell you one thing you may have overlooked. If you'll read your contract with the firm, re-read it, you'll notice that there's a clause in it that covers just such situations as this. Technically, under your contract, you *had* to sell us that property, and we didn't have to pay you a cent more than $25,000."

"I knew that, Mr. Hasbrouck."

"Oh, you did, did you?" For the first time there was some respect in Hasbrouck's smile, and that much respect remained there permanently.

. . . Alfred finished his notes on R. W. Benziger and put them in a folder. He was amused by the workings of his own conscience: the complimentary jottings about Benziger had made up for the deception he was practicing. And yet he was sure that if Benziger ever discovered that he was not actually a bond salesman for Rowley & Cruickshank, it was a deception that Benziger would forgive. And he realized that Benziger's forgiveness, Benziger's approval, had in a few hours become as important to him as the approval he had never got from his father but had been given by his grandfather, Fritz Thornton, Lex, and even Jack Rawlings. It was strange, he remarked to himself, that he had not automatically included James D. MacHardie in that list, but then not so strange; James D. MacHardie was scarcely more of a human being than J. P. Morgan & Company, the Pennsylvania Railroad, the Pennsylvania Company for Insuring Lives and Granting Annuities, the Philadelphia Contributorship for the Insurance of Houses for Loss by Fire, the Girard Trust Company, E. I. du Pont de Nemours, or any other business organization which had been a name to Alfred since he first learned to read. Often months would go by without his seeing James D. MacHardie, and even when he saw him it was no more than that; MacHardie in his wing collar and slightly squared derby hat, marching splendidly alone on the Axminster runner with his silver-mounted cane, on his way to his car; carefully looking downward and forward a few paces but speaking to no one (except the white-haired guard at the door) and fully confident that no one would get in his way. Alfred did not resent the augustness of MacHardie, but neither did he yield up any affection for the senior partner. But his feeling for R. W. Benziger was already that of warmth and eagerness for Benziger's approval —a feeling he was beginning to recognize as traceable to the lack of it in his relationship with his father.

And now he saw that in the list of men whose approval he sought he had not included the name of Eugene St. John, and he thought about the omission for a long time. Yesterday, and at any time in the past five years that he had made such a list, he would have had Mr. St. John's name among the first. Now he had not thought of him at all, and he knew what that meant, not in reference to St. John, but as it implied the state of his relationship with Mary. He knew then that the things he had said to Natalie were true. He knew more than that; he knew that nothing he had ever felt for any other woman would help him now. The easy comparisons were with Victoria and Mary, but Victoria had become a romantic wound, and Mary was an accomplishment, a capture, and then in their marriage privately a sharer of passion and affection, publicly an adjunct in the life he had chosen to lead. There was not a minute's worth of future for him and Natalie; in this October night, alone in a hotel room, he would not argue with the realities or his conscience, the proper loyalties, the responsibilities to his sons, the responsibilities to the career he was so firmly building. He conceded all the arguments but one: he had seen Natalie, he had met her, and what he had said he had had to say because to leave it unsaid was a concession not to those other arguments, but to self-doubt and insincerity. He had been faithful to Mary in word and in deed, and he was reconciled to the continuation of their relationship as it stood, and if it stood. But whatever might happen, he had not treated what he felt for Natalie with the disrespect of polite conversation or silence. If he never saw her again, the good had been done. She would know for the rest of her long life that the sight of her had once created love, that it was a love that dispelled doubt before it arose, that it had been declared, and that it would go on.

He was not ready to go away with her tonight; that was his first concession to the realities. But if this were to be his last night on earth, he would spend it with her. And always it would be that way, whatever happened, whatever did not happen. It was almost a fact now that he could not live with her, but he wanted to be with her at the end of his life.

And now the telephone rang. "Hello," he said.

"You got home all right," she said.

"I was thinking about you this very second. Have you a telephone in your room?"

"No, I came downstairs. I'm in that little room. I went to bed but I couldn't sleep. Can you hear me all right? I don't dare speak louder."

"You've thought about what I said."

"Yes, that's why I called you. I wanted to tell you—I'm glad you said it."

"So am I. I wouldn't want to die without having said it."

"I know. I'm writing you a letter. Goodnight—my love."

She hung up, and he turned out his light and lay there, hearing an occasional automobile and with some regularity the starting and stopping of the trolley cars and on every half-hour the bell of the court-house clock. He wanted to stay awake and retain a consciousness of this tranquillity, these last moments before there was passion in their love and the rest of the world came back into their lives.

In the morning he awoke refreshed and cheerful without immediately knowing why, but he soon remembered. It was a good idea to keep busy and after breakfast he paid three calls on two business men and a doctor who were on the Rowley & Cruickshank list. After lunch he drove to the country club and was surprised to see a large number of automobiles in the parking area, but on his way to the golf shop he saw the reason: ten tables of ladies' bridge.

"My name is Eaton. Mr. Benziger is giving me a guest card but I know it hasn't arrived. Is it all right if I hit a few?"

"R. W. Benziger? Sure. I'll get you a match if you can wait till three o'clock. You paying your own greens fees or is Mr. Benziger?"

"I'm paying them myself."

"Three dollars a day. Caddy fee, if you want a caddy, two bits for nine holes, for second-class caddies, and thirty-five cents for first-class. But you won't get any kind till after three, school leaves out then. You'll want a locker. I'll take you over and meet Otto and he'll take care of you."

Alfred changed to knickers and sweater and returned to the golf shop.

"Just put your name and address and home club in this book

517

and when Mr. Benziger's card comes I'll sign you in officially. You weren't expecting Mr. Benziger?"

"He went to Pittsburgh today."

"I know," said the pro.

"Just testing me out?"

"Well, it's nothing against you, and don't hold it against me. The only trouble we have is like two years ago a nice-looking fellow said he was a friend of one of our members. Member happened to be in Europe at the time, and this stranger, he had a Packard car and he looked all right. But he hung around here for a week and finally he took over $800 from one member and four hundred from another and around four hundred from another. He'd been playing this course in the middle forties but boy, when he started bearing down he came in with a 68 for the eighteen, that's when he got the eight hundred, and in the low seventies the other two times. The best eighteen I ever put together was a 67 and I play this course every day it don't snow. After that the greens committee tightened up on guest cards."

"Well, I don't want to get you in any trouble."

"That's all right. You knew Mr. Benziger was gonna be in Pittsburgh."

"And you could call Mrs. Benziger. I had dinner there last night."

"No, that's all right. But no matter whose guest you are, I advise you, don't you be the one to offer to play for any important money. They'll call the state cops. Mr. English will be here at three o'clock, if you want to wait for him. He has an automobile agency and he can play any time he feels like it. About your age, maybe a little younger. Plays a nice game when he's on his game, but he can go haywire worse than anybody I ever saw. There he is now. Hey, Mr. English, I was just talking about you."

The newcomer nodded to Alfred. "Yeah," he said to the pro. "I'll bet you were. Is my mashie-niblick ready?"

"No. I said I'd have it ready for Saturday."

"Well, I was hoping you'd have it today. Is Mickey going to be here this afternoon?"

"If he isn't kept after school."

"Then how about Smiley?"

"Smiley ought to be here. Uh, make you acquainted with Mr. Eaton. Mr. Eaton, this is Mr. English."

"Glad to know you," said English.

"Glad to know you," said Alfred.

English hesitated. "Haven't we met before? Are you from anywhere around here?"

"Originally from Port Johnson."

518

"No, unless I met you here. Your family used to own the steel mill down there?"

"Yes," said Alfred. "I've been here once before, for about five minutes one night. Oh, a long time ago."

"Maybe I met you then, or maybe I'm all wrong."

"I didn't meet anybody then. Oh, now wait a minute. Did you go to Lehigh?"

"I most certainly did not. But *now* I remember. You went to Princeton. Right? You drove a Marmon. A grey Marmon with the top down?"

"That's me. We stood up there on the porch and watched the people dancing."

"Freezing our balls off, as I remember. What are you doing in these parts? Are you going to live here?"

"No. Trying to sell some bonds."

"Where's your stiff collar?"

"I didn't wear it today."

"You'll be drummed out of the regiment if they ever hear about it. Have you got a match all set? If not, I'm playing alone and I'd be glad if you'd join me."

They played nine holes before dark and in the locker-room English supplied the gin for their ginger-ale highballs, and signed the chit for the ginger ale. "I have to scat," said English. "Having dinner at my mother-in-law's. But I'll call you at the hotel next week and maybe we can think up something to do."

At the hotel there was a special-delivery letter in his box.

Dear Man:

I have to call you that because I do not know your first name. I wonder what it is? I have gone through all the names I could think of, starting with Abner and ending with Zebulon. I hope it's neither because I am not fond of either name. I don't know anyone named Abner and Zebulon is a name I only remember from geography—Pike's Peak. But what difference does it make? My father and my brother are both named Ralph and yet it is not a name I would choose. Is your name Ulysses? Percival? Malcolm? Those are other names I do not like, and yet if it turns out that one of those is your name, I shall begin to like it immediately because it is your name.

After you left our house I locked up all around and then climbed the stairs to say goodnight to my mother and father. They said complimentary things about you (which they would not have said had they known the gist of our conversation in the den). They asked me my opinion and I, too, joined in the chorus of praise, but I was not sincere. If I had expressed the disapproval I felt, they might have wondered why, and it would have been impossible to tell them since I did not know

519

why myself. Then I took a bath and tumbled into bed, but not to sleep. I soon realized the reason for my sleeplessness. I was still startled by what you said, but soon I realized that I was believing your words and that was even more startling. That was when I called you up. I guess I wanted you to reassure me, or perhaps I merely wanted to hear your voice. Nothing like this has ever happened to me. I have been in and out of love several times, of course, and was half engaged last summer but it collapsed because the boy had no intention of settling down. He was from Pittsburgh and had never worked a day in his life. His idea of matrimony was to take a world cruise for a year, after which we would live in Sewickley (near Pittsburgh) and Southampton and also have an apartment in New York. I could not help but compare him with my father and picture our marriage ten years from now and realized that marriage to him was impossible, much as I liked him. I do not wish to masquerade under false pretenses. I enjoy a good time. But he lived in another world, totally different from mine or from the kind of world I want to live in. And yet if you were to ask me what kind of world I prefer, I should have difficulty in answering.

Why do I ramble on like this? Is it because I do not want to say goodnight to you? This will be a long night for me but a happy one. I could not say this over the phone, but I can say it now. I love you, too. My mind is in a whirl and I cannot say (write) the other things that I should say, such as to tell you that we must not see each other again and all the other sensible things that have always meant so much to me and still do. I have never kissed a married man and of course I have not kissed you, and yet I wanted to so much that it might have been better if I had. If I had kissed you and let you kiss me, perhaps I would be able to say now that "he just wanted to kiss me." Then I would be able to forget you as easily as I have some boys I kissed. As things are, I shall never forget you. Whether or not we ever see each other again, some day when I am fifty and perhaps a grandmother, I shall always remember that one night in October 1927 I met a handsome man who told me he loved me and I believed him without even knowing his first name.

Dear Man, please stay away. But that is not my heart speaking, it is my brain and common sense. Wouldn't it be better to keep what we have this minute instead of the pain and sorrow that we will cause not only to ourselves but to those who love us? But it is not for you to decide, it is for me. What that will be I cannot tell. Tonight I love you, but tomorrow I may love you more. If I mail this you will know which way I have decided. If I had to decide now there would be no doubt.

Natalie

He tried to visualize her as she had been during the writing of the letter. He re-read it many times, wholly and in parts, to try to reconstruct the thinking that resulted in the written sentences. He wondered how long it had taken her to write the letter, and at what hour of the morning she had taken it to the post office. It was a special delivery, but instead of a special stamp the envelope had five two-cent stamps, and the postmark told him only that it had been canceled before eleven o'clock in the morning. Where was she now? He was surprised to find himself in an unreasonably angry mood, as though he were imprisoned in his hotel room and she the belle of some forbidden ball. Yes, it had come to that. She was as far away as the telephone—but so was he. And the girl who had written that letter would call when she could.

He went to a movie because one of the stars in it was Greta Garbo, but it was an unfortunate choice in the circumstances of his new romance. The title was *Flesh and the Devil,* but the story was still *Anna Karenina,* and Alfred was not receptive to the idea of the tragic aspects of illicit love. He knew what they were, he had been thinking about them, he did not need to be told. He did not stay to see the beginning. He was making his daily report when the telephone rang.

"Hello," he said.

"What *is* your first name?" she said.

"Abner, and my middle name is Malcolm. How are you? Where are you? I loved your letter, and I love you."

"I love you, and I guess I'll never have a letter to love."

"You may. Where are you?"

"Home. Mother's gone to bed, but I can't talk long. Please tell me your first name?"

"My real first name is Raymond, but I never use it. The name I use is my middle name, Alfred. Hardly anybody knows about the Raymond."

"May I call you Raymond? It would be appropriate."

"Why?"

"I'll use your secret name for our secret love affair. Have you ever had a special delivery addressed to just Mr. Eaton? On blue stationery?"

"No, I haven't."

"What did you do today? Work?"

"And played golf at your club with a fellow named English."

"Julian. He's nice. I could tell *him* that I love you. But I'm not going to, never fear. Did you mention my name at all?"

"No."

"I'm glad you didn't, because he and his wife are coming here Saturday. The club might be a good place for me to—no. No. Let me think. There's a road about a half a mile south, south of the club driveway. I could meet you on that road at three o'clock tomorrow, for a little while. It's the only road on your right going south. I must say goodnight. Goodnight, Raymond."

He found the road easily. It was narrow and unimproved, and a farmer driving a team of mules hitched to a manure-spattered wagon stared at him, nodded and said, "Hyuh," and passed on. Then Alfred saw a Chrysler roadster in his rear-view mirror. Natalie was driving it. She went past him, turned around and came back and parked on the other side of the road.

"Hardly anybody knows my car down this way," she said. She got in his car and for a moment sat with her hands in her lap, and then he took her in his arms and they had their first kiss. Her response to the kiss was whole and trusting, with both arms around his neck, with no hand held back to fend off his hand.

"Yes," she said. "If I had any doubt, I haven't now. Is everything else going to be perfect, too? No, of course not. We know that, don't we, Raymond?"

"The nicest thing is that you trust me."

"I do, and you must trust me. Why do I say that? Because—you're married. I'm a virgin. But it isn't only that I trust you. You must believe me when I tell you why we can't have necking parties. You're not used to stopping, and I've never had the other. And I don't want to. Do you know why?"

"Yes. My wife."

She nodded. "Not that I'm worried about her finding out. But I don't want to be the one that you're unfaithful with."

"You mean you don't want to be the first one I'm unfaithful with?"

"No, that *isn't* what I mean. I'll go the limit with you. I believe in that for us, some day. But not as long as she's faithful to you. I would never, never while she's faithful to you."

"I might want you enough to lie to you."

"Not to me."

"No, not to you."

"This is the beginning of our troubles, isn't it?"

"Yes, if you put it that way."

"It is. I know. You want me, and if I ever wanted anybody I want you. Oh, how silly to say that. I do want you. But you said you knew you loved me as soon as you saw me."

"It happened in seconds."

"Then understand this. You loved me because of what I'm saying now. You knew that I would feel that way about your marriage. It shows, Raymond. Not that you can always tell whether a girl is a virgin or not. But the very second you loved me, you knew all the good and bad things you have to expect."

"Very wise."

"Very much in love. Thinking of nothing else. I'll tell you something about *your*self."

"What?"

522

"I'll tell you several things, and I only know them because I love you. Let me think . . . First, something happened to you when you were quite young. Something sad. So sad that for a long while you were more unhappy than happy."

"Right."

"I have to think of something else now . . . You're quite accustomed to being alone. More than most people are. You don't depend on other people as much as most people do. Maybe that has something to do with the first guess."

"Yes and no, but you're right."

"I'll try one more guess. And I'm not doing this to be clever. I couldn't do it with anyone else. Let me think. Yes. You like my father. Not just like, because everybody likes him. But you like my father better than—better than he gave you any reason to."

"Absolutely correct."

"Do you know why?"

"I could give you reasons, but they'd all be reasons, if you know what I mean. Reasons are like excuses, sometimes. I like your father as much as any man I've ever known, and I don't really care what the reasons are."

"I'm very glad, because then you'll understand about me and the way I feel about him. I know the nasty stuff, the sex stuff. Incest, and fixations. That isn't why I like my father. Sex is one of the reasons I love *you*, Raymond. I know that. But I like my father because there isn't any of that in my feeling for him, and there is in my love for you. I'll always love my father, but no girl can completely love her father the way I—yes, the way some day I'm going to love you."

"Some day. You think there will be some day?"

"Yes. And there again I trust you. A less honorable man, but in love the way we are, might drive his wife to being unfaithful to him. You won't."

"No."

"No. If I were married, Raymond, and just met you, I'd love you just as much, more than I loved my husband. But I'd never be unfaithful to him while he was faithful to me. I hope that girl is as good to me as I am to her."

"She wouldn't be."

"No, I guess not. A wife has more on her side. What are you thinking?"

"I can't say it. It's something I believe, but don't know, and I can't say it to you till I know."

"Oh, Raymond. You think she's unfaithful to you?"

"No. I honestly don't."

"I won't ask you any more. But I'm glad she hasn't been. And now what happens to us is really up to her, isn't it?"

He nodded. "And remember. You trust me."

"There'll never be any doubt about that."

"What's next for us?"

"Oh—I'm going away. We can't just talk about our love. If I stayed home, some night all our good intentions would be swept away and I'd begin to hate your wife and children, and you would too. We'd still love each other, I know, but we might even get to hate our love. Is that possible, all that?"

"Yes."

"I'm going to be in a wedding in St. Louis the week after next but I'm going to leave before that. I can visit a girl in Pittsburgh—"

"That boy?"

"Oh, he isn't there. He's at Oxford. Oxford got him on the rebound, and you can imagine what he's learning there. No, this is a girl I went to school with. Then I can go to Chicago for a few days."

"I'll still be here when you get back from St. Louis."

"I won't be back before Christmas. You'll be gone then."

"Probably."

"Is there some club where I can write to you?"

"Racquet Club, 370 Park. Where can I write to you?"

"Nowhere."

"Is this goodbye?"

"I can wait forever, too. Remember saying that? You don't know that about me, Raymond. I can wait forever, and I will." She took his hand and pressed it against her bosom, kissed it, and quickly got out of the car.

She was gone. She was gone into their indefinite future, of which five minutes now was its enormous and infinitesimal part, as much as the whole time would be, and as little as five minutes. He gave her the five minutes to get away so that he would not catch up with her in his car. As he approached the country club driveway he thought of stopping for a drink and some human companionship, but he dismissed the notion. He did not want a drink, and the kind of human companionship he wanted now was possible only with Lex— the companionship of silences in the midst of confidences unexchanged. For the present he felt as though there had been passion spent without the previous ecstasy; something finished but not completed; and a loss of dignity that was like that which follows a sudden, hard fall. For the first time in his thirty years he cared about nothing in the future, and was alone with a refrigerated love that was like a meat that had been frozen and packed in Chicago, for consumption God knew when, and that might spoil before it could give sustenance to anyone.

She was gone, and she was going away from him, and she could do that. She was young, twenty-two, she would only have to enter a room or a city and life would start up around her beauty so that the time would pass for her and she would be stimulated and restimulated by the effect of her own personality. She had wisdom, but she knew nothing. He did not want to doubt her love, and did not doubt it, but he thought of a line from a novel he had read a year ago, a short novel by a Princeton man named F. Scott Fitzgerald: "There're things between Daisy and me that you'll never know, things that neither of us can ever forget." What was there between him and Natalie to never forget? A kiss? A hand clutched to her bosom? Or would this love that was new and that had yet surprised her so little become old enough and strong enough to last? And not only to last; it was not something he wanted only to last, to be contemplated privately after the ball. What did she know? What could she know in her virginal state, without having shared the ultimate ecstasy, without having a regret that she had not shared it first with him? A virgin belonged to no one but was possible to every man living. And then, having reached the lowest point in his miserable meditations, he called himself a liar. Where had he left all the facts of their love, so undeniable and convincing and more real than all facts outside their love? He gave a deep sigh, and committed himself to whatever their love would bring.

There was no word from Mary that night, but she telephoned him before nine o'clock in the morning. "Did you phone me last night?" she said.

"Obviously if I had, you wouldn't have been there."

"That depends on what time you'd called. I got home late, it was after three."

"No, I didn't phone you."

"You didn't care enough to. Is that it?"

"Oh, I don't know. Is that the way it looks to you?"

"How else could it look? Are you having a good time?"

"Well, now what the hell difference does that make to you? You made your decision Monday, before I even met anybody here. I've had dinner here alone every night but one, and that was Wednesday. I had dinner with R. W. Benziger and family at his house. I've played golf once with a fellow named English. That's my hell-raising so far, but I'm not telling you this to show what a good boy I am. I just want you to know that this is not New York. I'm going to play golf this afternoon, and tomorrow I think I'll go to the football game."

"Football game? You don't go to football games on Sunday."

"Here you do."

"Are we going to the Princeton-Yale game?"

"No. I have to stay here."

"Is it all right if I go?"

"Oh, boy. You'll be sitting on the Yale side, I take it."

"Yes."

"Then why ask me if it's all right? You don't give a damn about my permission, and I'm certainly not going to give my approval. Your friend wouldn't have asked you if you hadn't told him I was going to be away then. Got any other little excursions planned before you get written up in Cholly Knickerbocker's column?"

"I'm not going to call you again till you decide to be polite."

"I'd like to speak to Rowland."

"They've gone to the Zoo."

"Then as far as I can make out, the main purpose of this call was to announce that you're going to the Yale game with your friend."

"Well, I said I'd let him know tonight."

Alfred realized that that was a slip and he could sense her alarm. "Then you let him know tonight, dear. And don't you call me any more till I decide to be polite. I'll be calling tomorrow to speak to Rowland, but you don't have to be polite to me. I know there's a limit to what you can endure, cooped up there in that apartment. So long, kid."

She lay on the bed, smoking a cigarette, with a sheet covering her from the waist down. He came in, drying himself with a large Turkish towel, and sat on the edge of the bed.

She sat up. "What are these marks on your back?" she said.

"Scratches and tincture of iodine."

"Scratches?"

"You did it, last night."

"I did?"

"Yes. Are you sorry?"

"I'm not sorry for last night. But I don't like to scratch you up like that. You shouldn't be so—"

"I shouldn't be so what?"

"I'm trying to think of a word. You shouldn't prolong it."

"Shouldn't I? I thought you liked that."

"I do. Do you ever think of the time we wasted?"

"Not any more."

"I guess I don't either. We had to try other people first. Shall I tell you something?"

"What?"

"When we were going together I used to get this strange feeling about you."

"Well, I'm a strange man."

"You are?"

"Yes. I know it now, I didn't then. Oh, I guess I did know it then. But luckily you're a strange woman."

526

"By strange do you mean queer?"

"Not in the usual sense of the word."

"Because I'd never let another woman touch me."

"Don't say never."

"Some have tried."

"I'll bet they have."

"Why would you bet they have?"

"Because the kind of woman that would try, would know that there's something there."

"Yes, I think you're right. Yes, they always thought I knew more than I did. One of them got really angry. Called me a hypocrite. She said I was leading her on, and I just thought she wanted me for her husband. But she was a bad girl. She had an affair with her own brother and he killed himself."

"Oh, sure. I know them. Stay away from them."

"I did, finally."

"They're what you might call sexual blackmailers. They use people to get other people, if you know what I mean."

"How are you strange? Do you want to tell me?"

"I'll let you find out."

"Are you queer, in the usual sense of the word?"

"Don't ask any more questions, Mary. I'll let you find out."

"Do you love me?"

"I adore you. I don't think I can love anybody. But that's all right. You don't love me, and I don't ask you to. The kind of love that you mean, I don't believe in it. It's really much more flattering to have someone adore you, the way I do you. Sensation is what really counts, you know. The other junk was thought up by the State. Kings. The Church. Isn't it much more intelligent for us to be like this, you wanting me, me wanting you, instead of prattling on about how much we love each other? And swearing to love each other forever? When the sensation dies, I want you to find someone else. *I* will."

"You are strange."

"Of course. That's what brought you here Sunday night, last night, tonight. It's what you used to feel when we were kids. Isn't it so much more intelligent to be together like this, talking sensibly and thrilling to sensation than chattering about our devotion, forever and ever? Look at you. With some men it would have been all over by this time. You're just beginning to feel deeply and I haven't even put a finger on you. I'm sure you secretly think I'm rather evil."

"A little, yes."

"Only because you're still remembering what you learned outside this room. But after a while, weeks or months, you'll think the same way I do."

"I wonder."

"Naturally you wonder, dear. It's all so new to you. You wait till I've taught you a few things about the nervous system. I'm going to read something to you." He stood up.

"No, don't. Just make love to me."

"All right."

She was home before midnight, bringing with her two books, a translation from the Hindustani and another from the German, the first illustrated with line drawings. She was wondering how to break off the affair with Roper, and continued for several days to seek an excuse that would not make him contemptuous of her, but she had already been unfaithful to Alfred, not only a casual once but deliberately and willingly twice again, and after her half-hearted attempts to find a way out of the affair she began to visit Roper's apartment almost every afternoon that he was free. Her mother, in New York for the day, remarked on how well she looked, vaguely allowing the inference that a rest from Alfred's demands might be responsible. Mary encouraged her mother to think what she pleased, so long as it was an idea that satisfied its own curiosity.

The unsatisfactory state of his marriage and of his love had a salutary effect on Alfred's work. In the next two weeks he and Mary made no attempt at cordiality in their telephone calls, and without an outright declaration on either side, it was understood that Mary was having an affair with Roper. In those two weeks he accomplished what he had set out to do; he had information that was sufficient for his report, and he was trying to decide whether to wait the full month or go back to New York when the decision was made for him.

He was dining, as always, alone in the hotel, with the morning's *Herald Tribune* folded on his table. A man stopped at the table, then moved on a couple of steps to get a better look at his face. "Alfred Eaton, I was sure it was you. I was positive. It's Tom Rothermel."

"Well, by God."

They shook hands and Rothermel took a chair.

"What are you doing here?" said Alfred.

"I belong here, but what are you? Is James D. MacHardie coming into the coal regions?"

Immediately Alfred was on his guard. "Oh, I'm not here for James D. MacHardie. I'm in the bond business, with Rowley & Cruickshank."

"Oh, the last I heard you were with James D. MacHardie. Now I can't tell my friends I know a MacHardie partner."

"Partner? Jesus, Tom, you promoted me awful fast. What do you do here?"

528

"With the Power & Light Company. I've been with them ever since I got out of State."

"Married and all that?"

"No, still batching it. You know the old saying, why keep a cow when milk is so cheap? Not that I have anything against it for some guys, but not me. But you're all settled down I understand. Two young ones?"

"Two sons."

"Well. Your mother and sisters all well?"

"Fine, thanks."

"And how is Porter, your friend? Didn't you start up an aviation company with him?"

"It didn't last."

"Well, you gave Larry Von Elm his start. He's going great guns, I hear."

"Yes, so I hear."

"I guess aviation will be the new thing now, since Lindbergh."

"Looks that way. But I've had all the manufacturing experience I'll ever want. I'd rather sell bonds."

"A capitalist."

"Hmm?"

"Nothing."

"You said capitalist, didn't you?"

"Well, yes, I did. That's what you are, aren't you?"

"Yes, aren't you?"

"Well, I'm working for them."

"The way you say it, you sound as if you didn't like it."

"Well, if you were still working for MacHardie & Company I wouldn't admit it, but I think the capitalistic system stinks."

"You? You used to be the smartest capitalist in Port Johnson."

"Sure, and I saw my father starve to death, and now I'm working for a big public utility company and I see enough there to know it stinks."

"Well, I'm afraid it's here to stay."

"You may change your mind about that."

"Say, you've got it pretty bad, Tom."

"Well, you just take a look around this part of the state. You'll see enough to make you wonder, anyway."

"Why I'd have thought you'd approve of things around here. I've only been here a short time, but I've found out it's a solid union country."

"Unions run by Irish Catholics. They're not going to change anything."

"I was under the impression they had. In fact, I've been

given to understand that they damn near wrecked the coal business, that strike they had two years ago."

"You've been talking to the operators."

"Other people, too."

"Not the people they tried to starve into submission. Those people don't buy bonds. This place is through, and the reason why it's through is because the operators tried to break the union, and while they were doing it, they lost their market."

"I've heard some of that, put in a different way."

"I'm giving you the facts. But hell, I don't expect you to see it any other way. Your father was Samuel Eaton, and he was no friend of organized labor."

"No, he certainly wasn't. So here we are, on opposite sides of the fence. But you're working for a public utility. You ought to be working for a union."

"Well, maybe I am. I don't expect to last long where I am. They've started to look at me funny. Company spies everywhere."

"What's your opinion of R. W. Benziger?"

"Benziger? He's the worst enemy labor has around here. He soft-soaps them and they fall for it. Mountain City is supposed to be a model company but the men would be a darn sight better off if Benziger cracked their skulls and maybe beat a little daylight into them. That's the trouble with the men. A few pennies, a few safety precautions, then they go back to work."

"What do you want them to do? Take over?"

"That will come."

"Tom, I don't recognize you any more."

"No. Your kind of people think I ought to stay Tom Rothermel, the errand boy. Child labor. Working three hours before school and five hours after. That was my eight-hour day when I was twelve years old."

"So you think this section is through."

"I know it is. It'll take a little time."

"Before the miners take over the mines?"

"That's only the local problem. As soon as your father stopped making profits he closed down and threw a thousand men out of work."

"The whole steel business was shot to hell then."

"You mean a few Wall Street men stopped making big profits. If things were run right a few men wouldn't be able to deprive the working-man of a living."

"Oh, well, you just want socialism."

"That's all."

"Instead of Samuel Eaton running things, you'd rather have Tom Rothermel."

"Much rather."

"Well, are you getting anywhere?"

"Laugh at me if you want to, Alfred."

"I don't want to laugh at you, but I think your ideas are pretty damned foolish. What I don't see is why you aren't more interested in getting rich. When you were a kid you made money every chance you got, and I remember my grandfather saying you'd be a rich man."

"I am a rich man, for me. I've made money in the stock market. You think that's inconsistent. Well, it isn't. If I have brains enough to make money out of you people, why shouldn't I? But I want more than money. I don't want a God damn yacht, polo ponies. I can skip all that stuff."

"I think you want the same thing James D. MacHardie wants. He's had several yachts. No polo ponies, but several yachts. But you make the mistake of thinking that was all he wanted. It wasn't. He wants power, and he has it. You want it too. If you think he's bad, you're just as bad as he is."

"What do *you* want?"

"Now I want a piece of cherry pie. Ten years from now, when you and I are forty, I want to have $3,000,000 tucked away so I can forget about it. Twenty years from now I'd like to be one of the four or five biggest capitalists in Wall Street. And you'll be one of the biggest union men. Unless of course you start to make really big money in the market. I wish I knew how much you've made for yourself."

"I'll tell you. At four o'clock this afternoon, a little over $38,000."

"You're a margin player, of course."

"How else would I get up to $38,000? And I've made some selling short, too, you know. When they fire me at the P. & L. I can tell them to kiss my ass."

"Why don't you tell them to kiss your ass anyway, and quit?"

"Why should I? They're paying me two hundred a month, and I'm learning all about how a big public utility is run. I'm not husky enough to fight the company police. When I get in the labor movement I'll have something besides a pair of fists to offer."

"Can I sell you some nice safe bonds?"

"Oh, no. No bonds for me, thank you. No money, and no fun. How much are you worth, Alfred?"

"Tom, that's exactly none of your God damn business."

"I just don't understand why you're selling bonds. A guy that was with James D. MacHardie. You inherited money from your old man and your grandfather, and I understand your wife has plenty."

"I'm like you. Learning all about Wall Street. And I meet a lot of interesting people."

"Yeah. R. W. Benziger."

"I think he's a swell guy. Well, Tom, would you like to go and drink some beer?"

"Where? At the Gibbsville Club?"

"No, I haven't been there. I've been going to an old-fashioned saloon. One block north and turn to your right."

"Murphy's. No thanks. I have a date with a telephone operator, gets off at ten o'clock."

"Does she believe in free love?"

"It hasn't cost me anything so far. The price of a condrum. She does it because she likes it. I give her a little hump about once a week. I sneak her into my room and as long as we don't make too much noise the landlady doesn't mind. She has to be out of there by twelve o'clock, but that's all right. I take her home in my car, sometimes I give her another little hump on the way home, but it's getting pretty cold for that now. I have this little Ford coop, but it's cold here at night."

"Stop talking about it. I don't give a damn about your tail."

"I guess you get yours from the country club crowd."

"Nope."

"Well, you wouldn't say so even if you did."

"You're right. I wouldn't."

Rothermel stood up with Alfred. "All I told you tonight is private, isn't it?"

"Oh, sure. As you said before, they probably know all about you anyway," said Alfred. "Company spies. By the way, what were you doing here tonight? This is a sort of a capitalist hotel, isn't it?"

"Oh, I like to put on the dog now and then," said Rothermel. "I'm on the committee for the Penn State dance at Christmas. We got a free meal out of the hotel tonight, the members of the committee. Honest graft. If you're gonna be here Christmas that's the night to get laid. We all rent rooms."

"Sorry I won't be here. So long, Tom."

"So long, Alfred. Funny world, huh?"

"Pretty funny."

Instead of going to the old-fashioned saloon Alfred went to his room and wrote a note to Hasbrouck.

My work here is completed and I am firmly convinced that my further presence in the neighborhood would serve no useful purpose. Therefore I am checking out of the hotel in the morning and shall spend the weekend at my mother's house in Port Johnson, arriving in the office Monday morning. My report should be ready before the end of next week.

To himself he said: "If anybody ever asks me if I've been to Gibbsville, I can always say I have. It is a town consisting of one hotel room, situated about halfway between Mountain

532

City, where I first saw the love of my life, and a nameless country road where I first kissed her."

Martha was not surprised to see him, not because she had knowledge of his whereabouts, but because nothing surprised her any more. She was fifty-six now, old for her age because of the fragility that was caused by her sedentary manner of living, and young for her age in that all she seemed to need was the light touch of a magic hand to smooth out the skin and she would be forty again. In her eyes were suspicion and humor and cynicism and skepticism, and the humor was not a characteristic of its own but a part of the suspicion, cynicism and skepticism. She had her own language now, a combination of sensible speech and incoherent wanderings, as though she were speaking 1927 American English with lapses into the dialect of Chaucer. He was not there to see her. He had gone there because it was a place, the only place, in which he was answerable to no one in any way. He owned the house; his father had left it to him, no doubt in the belief that Martha was unfit to take the responsibility of it and that the girls wouldn't live there long. There was a new maid to do the work that Nellie and Josephine could no longer do, and Miss Trimingham had grown into the woodwork with the older servants. It was a house of silences that were broken only by familiar sounds at predictable moments, a Wallace Nutting house that when viewed from the road appeared to be ready for occupancy at any time a new owner chose to move in. The windowpanes glistened and there was often smoke from the chimneys, but the women who lived in the house had done all they could to give it life when once again they had seen to its cleanliness. Almost no man ever entered the front door. Sally, now twenty-eight and married to Harry Van Peltz, would bring her son and daughter to pay duty calls on their grandmother, but Harry stayed away whenever he could. Constance, now twenty-six, spoke of the house as "home" but it was no more than a convenience, a place to which she could escape from Philadelphia weekends while her married lover put in his appearance at The Rabbit parties and golf at Gulph Mills.

His sisters came to the house separately while Alfred was there. "Is there anything wrong between you and Mary?" said Sally.

"Yes."

"Permanently wrong?"

"I'll be able to tell you better next week, if I decide to tell you."

"Oh, then it's not you. It's Mary. That's surprising. I always thought you'd be the one."

"You're jumping at conclusions."

"Still, she's a damn good-looking girl. And you're away a lot. That's the trouble with New York."

"What's the trouble with New York? My being away a lot?"

"No. I meant that in New York if a husband *is* away a lot, there are thousands of other men."

In his conversation with Constance he took the offensive. "Constance, when are you going to start making some sense out of your life?"

"What is your interest in the matter? My honor? The family name? Or the chaps at your clobb, old deah?"

"All those, *and* I always liked you."

"Then keep your aquiline nose out of my affairs. Or my affair, singular number."

"What if you got pregnant?"

"It might interest you to know that I've *been* pregnant, so we've crossed that bridge."

"Has he ever talked about getting married?"

"You know who it is, of course."

"I think so," said Alfred. "John Coddington."

"Yes. And therefore you must know that John isn't going to push his wife down a well, and he's not going to ask her for a divorce."

"How nice for him."

"That would be a real dig if it weren't for the fact that he's as much in love with me as I am with him. You're no rose, Alfred. Why are you preaching? Has James D. MacHardie gone to your head?"

"Yes."

"That explains a lot, even if you did mean it sarcastically."

"What does it explain?"

"Well, let me ask you a question. Is your married life so perfect that you can pass judgment on everybody else?"

"No."

"Are you and Mary perfectly happy?"

"At the moment, no."

"All right, you asked me about marriage. I'll ask you about divorce. Are you thinking about getting a divorce?"

"Come to the point."

"That *is* my point."

"I know you. There's something else."

"Then *you* come to the point."

"All right. Mary is seeing another guy."

"I'll tell you something else. Mary is *being seen* with another guy. She was seen by me at the Princeton-Yale game, sitting on the Yale side about four rows in front of me."

"Did you speak to her?"

"No, but I was somewhat grateful to her. At least she gave Philadelphia something else to talk about besides John and me.

534

And I want to warn you, Alfred. This is meant kindly. The man she was with wanted everybody to see him. He stood up every chance he got and waved to friends of his, and just generally showing her off. And there were a lot of them she knew. Is he an old beau?"

"Yes."

"It looked that way to me, as though they just didn't care who knew it. That made me sore. I know where she spent that weekend, because I was invited to the same place, and you have my word for it, that particular host and hostess don't go around checking who's sleeping where."

"Would you mind telling me where?"

"Englewood. People named Cash. Joe and Peggy Cash. I'm tattling, but I can assure you it's an open secret now. The Cashes can put up—let me think—I've been there when they've had eight house guests."

"Why did they invite you if they knew Mary was coming?"

"Oh, the Cashes don't invite the girls. They invite the men and the men bring whoever they please. John invited me, but I don't like the Cashes. You see, John doesn't know Mary. But he knows her friend, Mr. Roper?"

"Doctor Roper."

"And when Roper began making a show of himself John said he was one of the people on the Cashes' party."

"Well, don't feel sorry that you told me. We haven't been pretending much lately."

"I'm not sorry I told you. But I'm sorry it happened to you. Haven't you got anybody?"

"Not really."

"You love somebody besides Mary?"

"Yes, but it isn't going to work out."

"Does Mary know it?"

"Nobody knows it. There's nothing to know."

"You? Platonic love?"

"One kiss."

"That's even worse than Platonic, from what I've learned about you. I know somebody who still has a yen for you. Do you remember Clemmie Shreve?"

"Sure, but I didn't have an affair with her."

"I know, and she's had a long time to regret it. She told me so herself. Don't take it from Mary, Alfred, and don't start mooning over this other girl. If she won't sleep with you, forget her. You can have Clemmie tomorrow night if you want to. I mean that literally. She's in Philadelphia, and a very unhappy girl."

"Clemmie and I are a thing of the past, and we never were very much. What happened with her and her husband?"

"He turned into an awful drunkard."

"Maybe Clemmie drove him to it."

"Maybe she did. I'm not suggesting that you marry her, but I just thought that you'd want to see her. She hasn't lost her looks, and I know for a fact that she still likes you. You have nothing to lose," said Constance; then added, "now."

He was not, then, astounded when Clemmie Shreve Hennessey turned up for dinner the next evening. She drove out from Philadelphia in her own car, a red Packard roadster with six wire wheels and a Lalique mascot on the radiator. She was wearing a blue tweed suit and a Basque beret and a blue polka-dot scarf. She was not the picture of tragedy and through dinner she chatted like the Clemmie of old, substituting the names of winter and summer resorts for the colleges she had once talked about. Then Constance said: "Goodnight, you two, and good luck," and left them.

"You didn't want me to come," said Clemmie.

"To tell you the truth, no," said Alfred. "But it's good to see you, now that you're here. You're so damn pretty."

"I'd better not lose that, because it seems to be all I have. What's the matter with me, anyway? I know I'm not brilliant, but neither was John Hennessey. Did you ever meet Dorothy Parker?"

"No."

"Unfortunately John did. He met all those literary people. You know, the Hotel Algonquin Round Table? He met them all, I think through somebody he went to Yale with, and now he thinks he's one of them. I'll bet *they* don't. I *know* they don't. He and Heywood Broun talk about baseball all the time and one night when we sat down with Broun and Dorothy Parker I heard Dorothy say, 'The Spalding Guide.' John thought it was funny. Then he and Broun talked, talked, talked about old first-basemen. John never heard anything Dorothy said, but when we got home he told me I was a stupid blonde, and why couldn't I enter into the conversation instead of just sitting there."

"So you left him."

"He left me! He has a girl friend that writes about fashions but her office is in the same office as *Vanity Fair*. That makes her one of the intelligentsia."

"You're not unhappy, are you?"

"Not to lose him. But he goes around saying I haven't got a brain in my head, and he didn't marry me for my brains. I didn't marry him for his, either."

"Why did you marry him?"

"Because he was good-looking, had money, was tapped for Death's Head at Yale, and was older than you and the other boys I saw. And I thought sex. Ugh. Sex. He'd get drunk and couldn't do anything and then blame me for being cold.

536

And when he wasn't drunk it was always so quick that he was quite right, I *was* cold. I went to see a doctor and the doctor said I was all right, and told me to have my husband come and see him. But I knew that would be a waste of breath. John thinks he's a real virile, hairy-chested man. Well, I then proceeded to have an affair with the doctor, lasting about a month or two, but he was too much sex. He gave me Hindu books and German books and—I think he must be trying to write a book himself, that doctor. I *like* sex, Alfred. I'm a healthy, normal woman. But ·I certainly didn't want to make a career of it. He wanted me to write down every sex thought I had. Keep a sort of diary. And I told him I couldn't, or wouldn't do that, so he gave me up as a bad job, although actually I gave him up."

"You must have had some experience in between."

"I did. A writer. He was quite nice, but in love with someone else, and whenever she'd raise her skirt just a little bit he'd go running back to her. But at least he was nice to me. If he thought I was stupid, at least he didn't say so, and he didn't try to get me to furnish him with material for a book. I'm not so sure that Constance hasn't got the right idea."

"Except that one of these days she'll find herself forty years old and Coddington settling down like any good Chestnut Hill guy, and she'll be out in the cold."

"Well, fourteen years of being in love with a man? Is that the worst thing that could happen to a woman? It's inconvenient at times, but unless you want to have children I can think of worse ways to spend your life. The trouble with me is that I'll keep looking for a husband or somebody like John Coddington and before I'm forty I'll have slept with so many men I won't remember them all. And I'd hate that. You know, Alfred, when I was young and so popular, there were really only two boys I liked. One was you, and the other was that friend of yours, Lex Porter. But you had your mind on someone else, and Lex—I said to him one time, 'You always seem to be ready to pounce on me, even when you're sitting still.' "

"Lex is still unattached."

"But maybe I wouldn't like him now. Maybe he wouldn't like me. Look at us, you and me. We're almost like brother and sister."

"That's news to me."

"I said almost. Nothing would please Constance more than if I came tripping into your room in the dead of night, but don't worry. I won't. I don't even know where it is."

"It's the floor above you, turn right at the top of the stairs." She smiled. "Very chivalrous of you, but you have a family."

"Things are not what they seem, Clemmie."

"Oh, I'm sorry to hear that. Serious?"

"I should think Constance would have hinted as much."

"She wouldn't have had me here if everything was going smoothly, that's true. But I thought she was trying to do me a favor. Do you want me, Alfred?"

"Of course I do."

"Because I want you. I need you. I'm low. If I come to your room will you make me feel popular again? You used to make me feel attractive, and desirable. I haven't felt that way lately."

"You're as attractive and as desirable as you ever were. In some ways more so."

"It may be quite late. Will you just let me stay with you for a little while?"

"Stay all night. The servants go to the Mass on Sunday morning. The only person you have to watch out for is that battle-ax Miss Trimingham. She gives Mother her bath about nine o'clock."

"Oh, I wouldn't stay that long."

It was some time between midnight and two o'clock—the single strikes of the clock were lost as he dozed off—and he became conscious of her. She was standing beside his bed and in the light of his reading lamp he saw her, barefoot and in a blue silk dressing-gown. She smiled and dropped the dressing-gown and got into his bed. They never spoke, but she kept smiling while he made love to her and she was ready for him at every moment. She continued to smile and was full of thoughts after the intensity was gone.

"What?" he said.

"What am I thinking?"

"Yes."

"That I've been needing this for years. With you. It was so nice. It couldn't have been this way with anyone else. We owed this to each other for a long time, Alfred. What are *you* thinking?"

"Almost exactly the same thing."

"I knew everything about you but this. I'm awfully happy. It isn't love, but it's so friendly. I wanted you to feel good, and you wanted me to."

"And did you?"

"Did, and do. You haven't for a long time, either, have you?"

"At least a month."

"This is the way affairs start."

"Usually."

"No, not what you mean. But you and I could have an affair that was just between us. When you needed somebody, or when I needed somebody. We wouldn't have to go out together and be talked about. Nobody'd ever see us together . . . Of course it would never work out that way. But tonight

538

it has. I'm going to lie to Constance, and you do too. Shall we never tell anybody, anybody in the world?"

"All right."

"Can I stay here till daylight? I'd like to go to sleep with your arms around me. I promise I'll wake up."

"I'll promise you that. The chickens will see to that."

"Then it's all right?"

"How much do you weigh? Eighty-five?"

"A hundred and five. Why? I'm so small? You never saw me with my shoes off. Not to mention. No, you're not too heavy, if that was what was worrying you. Let's go to sleep."

They slept for a while and he awoke with renewed desire and curiosity. In the beginning he made love to her while she was half asleep but this time it was longer and more sophisticated, the love-making of highly experienced and adept persons, in contrast with the earlier consummation that had been postponed from their youth. She got out of bed and kissed him good-morning. "We may have to do this a lot," she said, and left him. As to Alfred, he had an odd wish to tell everyone he knew that he had slept with Clemmie Shreve and that it had been wonderful.

She was gone before he appeared for breakfast.

"I'm not very good as a procurer," said Constance.

"Well, you did your best," said Alfred.

"Didn't you even try?"

"What was the use? I told you Clemmie and I were a thing of the past. It's a mistake to try to arrange people's lives for them."

He took the early afternoon train to Philadelphia and was back in New York before the usual Sunday-night supper hour of seven-thirty, and a few minutes ahead of Mary.

"Oh, you're back," she said. She put her gloves and handbag on the foyer table and began taking off her hat and coat. He was sitting in the livingroom. He did not rise, and she did not go to him. "Have you seen the boys?"

"Yes, for a minute."

"I'll be back in a minute," she said.

When she returned to the livingroom she sat down and lit a cigarette. "Are you back for good now, or is this just a visit?"

"For good."

"You finished up sooner than you expected."

"Yes, and sooner than you expected too, probably."

"Yes, sooner than you'd led me to expect. Have you had your supper?"

"It can wait."

"To be sure." The only sign of any uneasiness was her rapid smoking.

"Now that I'm back you're going to have to start behaving yourself."

"Did you say start?"

"You heard me. From now on I will use the guest-room. You can move my things in there tomorrow."

"Mother's coming to New York this week."

"Mother can go to a hotel or sleep in the room with you. Any explanation you want to give her is okay with me. This marriage, as a marriage, is all washed up, but that doesn't mean you're going to be allowed to do as you damn please. You've had your fling. The next one, you and I talk to our lawyers."

"Oh, you have it all figured out."

"No, not all, but that much. I could divorce you now in New York State."

"But Mr. MacHardie wouldn't like that."

"Mr. MacHardie wouldn't like it, that's correct. But there's somebody else that wouldn't like it. Doctor Roper. I don't know exactly what the medical associations do in cases like this, but I'm sure they don't give one of their members a gold medal for sleeping with patients. Before you interrupt—I didn't say *you* were a patient. I just happen to know about a woman who was a patient, and I'm sure her husband would be delighted to name Roper."

"Oh, blackmail."

"Pressure. All I have to do is follow suit, because I have all the winning cards. If I named Roper and this other guy named Roper he'd be through. You're a clever girl, you can see that. As a matter-of fact, of course, you're not so damned clever. I could subpoena everybody that spent the night at the Cashes' party. And I would. And wouldn't that make a beautiful story in the tabloids? You think I wouldn't? Well, I'll tell you why I would. You flaunted your affair publicly. That isn't the same thing as having an affair when you were desperately in love and made every effort to keep it secret. Just stop to think of how many people already know that you slept with Roper, in Englewood, New Jersey. So it isn't as though I were the one to bring it out in public. You've already done that. Hasbrouck, at the office, comes from Englewood. I didn't find out from him, but I'll be curious to see what he says or doesn't say tomorrow. No, they don't like divorces at MacHardie & Company, but I don't particularly like having my wife thumb her nose at me and think she can get away with it. You see, you overestimated my dependence on MacHardie & Company. I've had other offers for more money, so let's have it understood now that your next fling will be your last. At least as my wife."

She hesitated before answering, apparently going over all his points. "What are *your* plans?" she said.

"I've told you my plans."

"No, I know you. You'll have an affair with somebody. You have to."

"I deny that."

"Go ahead and deny it if you like, but you'll get some woman to sleep with you. While that's going on, what am I supposed to do? Enter a convent?"

"I will not say anything that smacks of collusion, collusive adultery. I deny that I will have a mistress, and I refuse to condone your having a lover. Another lover, since you've already had one."

"Listen, I'm not afraid to say things out. Nobody's listening, and we're not in court—"

"Yet."

"But I'll tell you this, Alfred Eaton. The minute I find out you're sleeping with another woman, I'm going to have myself a lover, and you can sue me to hell and gone. I'll bet you slept with somebody the minute you found out I had."

"I deny that."

"Deny it, but I don't believe you."

"I repeat, I deny it."

"I just wish I knew what big-mouth told you about the Cashes'."

"I'll give you a hint. It was somebody who wasn't there but knows everybody who was there. That just about leaves 120,-000,000 people."

"All right, you win. Temporarily. But, oh, you better watch your step. You better be able to explain every minute of your time."

"I foresee no difficulty."

"Talk like a lawyer if you want to, but you'll slip, if you haven't already."

"I've been living at a very respectable, small-town hotel, and I spent the last couple of nights at my mother's. And I expect to be here every night till I'm sent away again, and that won't be till spring. Of course if you're going to keep tabs on me, I'll have to be very vigilant about you, dear heart."

The telephone rang. "I'm sure it's for you," said Alfred, "I'll be listening to every word."

She answered the ring but the call was for Alfred, and it was Hasbrouck. "I'm going to be uptown all day tomorrow," he said. "Why don't you take the day off and meet me for lunch at one o'clock at the Astor?"

"Did you say the Astor?"

"Yes, and plan to be with me for at least an hour if you can."

Hasbrouck had something on his mind.

They met a few minutes before one o'clock and after they ordered their food Hasbrouck began to reveal how much he had on his mind. "Alfred, I'm so much older than you that I know you'll permit me to exercise certain prerogatives that go with my age." Such was his preamble, but he continued without waiting for Alfred's granting of the prerogatives.

"Are you having trouble at home?"

"Yes sir."

"Very well, we can go on. I know what it is, but I had to be sure you would admit it. The firm is very paternalistic in the best sense of the word, about the promising younger men, and you're perfectly well able to see for yourself that you are highly thought of. It's almost a sure thing that we're going to take your advice, whatever it may be, on this latest job of yours. The next job will be bigger, with more responsibility, and the one after that will be still bigger. You know where you're headed, everybody in the financial district knows.

"Now this trouble you're having at home, it was very distressing because of its possible effect on you. Not altogether unselfish on our part, but more so than you might think. When you're one of the family—and you're considered just that—we back you up, we cover up for you, we do a lot of things that show that our confidence in you doesn't end with the business relationship. So when we heard about this, uh, domestic infelicity we knew we might have to do something about it. I don't like to talk about these things in the office, so I arranged to spend the day away from there. I changed a dentist appointment, seeing the man from Peal shoes, my tailor, and so forth and so on. But the most important thing was seeing you."

It took Hasbrouck half an hour to state all the facts: after hearing about Mary at the Cash party, and incidentally learning the names of all others present, Hasbrouck had made sure that Mary's affair was an open secret, "more open than secret." He had then gone to Wilmington and had an "informal" conversation with Eugene St. John, asking him to take no action at the time, but extracting from him a promise to speak to Mary if necessary or advisable or desirable. "And that is where the matter stands," said Hasbrouck.

"Well, Mr. Hasbrouck, thank you very much, and I hereby resign from MacHardie & Company. I'll finish my report on the Buffalo, Fort Penn & Trenton matter, and I'll leave when I've handed it in."

"Let me hear your reason for wanting to resign."

"Well, there is only one. I think it's none of the firm's damn business what my wife does."

Hasbrouck smiled. "Never underestimate James D. MacHardie."

"I never would. I never have."

"Mr. MacHardie predicted this, and almost gave me your

542

very words. He said you would probably tell me to go to hell."

"It just came out differently, Mr. Hasbrouck. I'm surprised that Mr. St. John didn't tell you to go to hell."

"Mr. St. John is older and less impetuous, and he realizes that what was good for your interest is also good for his daughter's."

"He's also intimidated by du Pont."

"Not for one minute. There you're wrong."

"You thought he might be. That's why you went to him."

"Mr. MacHardie anticipated that, too. There was no intimidation for the very good reason that there could be none. The du Pont people aren't afraid of us. They do business with the people across the street."

"Then I certainly don't understand why Mr. St. John didn't tell you to go to hell."

"Well, he didn't because he's fond of you, and if there's anything he or I or anyone else can do to save your marriage, he's for it. For instance, I didn't tell him the name of the man involved, but he guessed it. Mr. St. John said he was always afraid his daughter was going to marry that man, and he was so delighted when she married you instead, so relieved."

"Mr. St. John is a fine man. I'm sorry he had to know anything about this."

"Eventually he was bound to, Alfred. Knowing it now may help to stave off any drastic action on your part. That is, if you would like him to have a talk with his daughter."

"I don't. I don't see any future for the marriage, but at this moment we are not going to get a divorce."

"I'm glad to hear that, no matter what else you do. But I've failed? The resignation still stands?"

"It still stands, Mr. Hasbrouck."

"In that case, will you have lunch with Mr. MacHardie on Wednesday?"

"Of course."

Nothing much mattered between the lunch with Hasbrouck and the appointment with MacHardie, not even the new relationship with Mary. It was too soon for any real test of that. Alfred waited upon MacHardie, who bustled in, said, "One-thirty," to Simmons, and with a nod of his head indicated the wheeled table with its covered dishes. "I ordered for both of us. Cheese omelette. We don't want to be interrupted." He placed his finger tips on the edge of the table and sat looking at them until he heard the click of the door closing behind Simmons, and then looked up and faced Alfred.

"Mr. Hasbrouck feels that somehow he's failed. I don't think he failed. I don't know what else he could have done, and I don't know what else you could have done. Under the circumstances. You not only have a future with this firm. You have a past. You've worked hard and well, and successfully. You've given up your own pleasures and pastimes to remain here until three and four o'clock in the morning. You are thirty years old, too old to start with another firm, but with five good, sound, basic years put in here. You can't afford to throw that away. What do you say to that, young man?"

"With all due respect, sir, I say that I can afford to do as I please."

"And I say, with all due respect, that you can afford nothing of the kind. It isn't money that counts now. It's time. In ten years you will be forty, and you know how we do things here. In ten years you'll be told whether you get one of the roll-top desks, or become—let's be truthful—one of our working pensioners. You know what I mean by that—the men who have jobs here, but can never hope to become partners. If you leave us, you will be giving all the other men at your next place of business a five-year advantage. Can you, or any man, take a five-year chunk of his life and hand it to his rivals on a silver platter? No. You cannot.

"There's more to it than that, too. It isn't only the matter of five years. It's five years of good association, earned respect, increasing responsibility and pleasant experience. It would take you two years to learn the ropes elsewhere. Here you know everybody that you have to know, and we know you. Who is Miss Loughran? Miss Loughran is Mr. Hasbrouck's secretary. Who is Miss Bumble-bee? I don't know, you don't know. Miss Bumble-bee is the secretary to a junior partner in some other firm. Who is Mrs. Kelly? Mrs. Kelly is our trained nurse. Who is Mrs. Penwiper? I don't know. Mrs. Penwiper is the woman in the supply room of some other firm. Two years wasted while you're finding out who Mrs. Penwiper and Miss Bumble-bee are. Do you know what thirty is? It's the beginning of middle age. Thirty to fifty. From fifty on you have no right or reason to expect to live another day. Between forty and fifty are the years when you may properly expect to reap the benefits of your ability and experience. In our previous conversation I believe you said you wanted to have five million by the time you're forty. I said you'd have it by the time you're fifty. According to *your* calculations, your average would have to be $340,000 a year. Obviously you haven't maintained that average. Do you think you can maintain it, and more, by going elsewhere and handing over a seven-year advantage? Or, in the light of recent events, have you decided to settle for considerably less than *four* million?"

"In the light of recent events in the stock market I could still have the five million at forty."

"Or lose your shirt. I thought you had that gambling instinct of yours under control."

544

"It's under control, but it hasn't disappeared."

"So, as I see it, you plan to leave here and become a speculator."

"I might do that," said Alfred. "It was one of the possibilities I've been considering."

"No. You wouldn't like that. Not any more. It's too late for that."

"Why?"

"Because you might enjoy a few big speculative profits, but it would soon become very unsatisfactory. Since you've been with this firm you've learned to enjoy the satisfaction of working for your money. Studying a proposition, really learning something about it, and basing your decisions on judgment, considered opinion. Oh, that's the real pleasure of business. The other stuff is nonsense, foolishness. What it comes down to is cutting for high card. If I thought you were nothing but a gambler I could arrange to have you introduced to a Greek gentleman who would cut you high card for $500,000 this afternoon. Now then, shall I pick up that telephone over there and arrange the introduction?"

"I wouldn't cut him for five hundred thousand."

"Why not? You have it."

"Yes, I have it. But I can't afford to lose it."

"You might win."

"My theory is that the percentage is against the aggressor in gambling."

"And you're quite right. It is. But I have just proved to you that you are not a gambler. The gambling instinct, yes. But not a gambler. And incidentally, neither is the Greek gentleman. I've watched him in Palm Beach. He has an overdeveloped gambling instinct, and he would cut you high card for $500,000. But that would be less of a gamble for him than for you. Gaming, not gambling, is his business, his profession, if I may use that word. He would win from you in a poker game or a dice game, because gaming is his business, and he would win for the same reason that you would win against my grandson. He would also win from me, in the extremely unlikely event that I might play poker with him. But if he came down *here* with a million dollars, and I had a million dollars, which one of us would go broke first and which one of us would make another million? I think you'd agree that I had the better chance."

"Naturally."

"Naturally. There, that's the word. Naturally. Here I'm in my element, he is not. There are very few gamblers, Eaton. Male, that is. I'm not even sure that I've ever seen one, not a single one. On the other hand, I have known of several members of the opposite sex whom I considered gamblers. Is it

545

possible that your present difficulty is due to the female gambling instinct?"

"I've never thought of that, so I don't know."

"A great risk has been taken. A marriage, possible loss of children, certainly the hazard of scandal. A lot to lose there. Everything a woman holds dear. Gambled on what? Not on the chance of discovery, but on the chance of your accepting the situation."

"That was a foregone conclusion, how I would react to the situation."

"Ah, therefore the greater gamble. But I'm a very incompetent judge of women. I made one decision and it was perfect and therefore I'm not qualified to sit in judgment in a case that involves anything less than perfection. But I believe that divorce is a damnable thing. It violates good order, and it's a constant threat to good order."

"How do you feel about infidelity, Mr. MacHardie?"

"Haven't I expressed myself on that? Didn't you just hear me use the phrase, good order?"

"Well, don't you believe that infidelity is grounds for divorce? Flagrant infidelity?"

"There are no grounds for divorce, Eaton. But if you want my personal theology, infidelity is the lesser sin. I would do anything in my power to prevent a divorce."

"Including condoning infidelity?"

"I consider your word *condone* disrespectful. I condone none of it. The problem of infidelity is between husband and wife. The problem of divorce concerns the whole of civilization. I have a Roman Catholic son-in-law, whom you've met. He would like to convert me, not entirely for spiritual reasons, I'm afraid. There's no chance of that whatsoever, but he and I, or his Church and I, agree on the matter of divorce. In fact, I don't believe in their annulment system. Marriage is an institution based on what? Love? Not always. Lust? Sometimes, but not always. The raising of children? No, not always. Marriage is first of all an exchange of vows. A contract, Eaton. To me the sanctity of marriage means the sanctity of the vows, the promises, the contract, the given word. I expect every man to honor my word, because *I* honor it. A business contract is only something that the lawyers write so that we'll know what is agreed to, what is covered. The real contract shouldn't even require signatures. It is the given word that matters. 'I will do what it says in this instrument.' That's all that should be necessary. I, James MacHardie, or I, Alfred Eaton. It was all your father needed, it was all your grandfather needed. Your present unhappiness is a part of life. Whether you leave this firm or stay, my duty to myself and to a man who has worked for me is to demand that he honor *all* his contracts. *All* of them. You found out when you came here that we always honor our word, even if it means taking a loss. This is the first opportunity you've had to put yourself to our test."

"You don't always insist on observing the letter of a contract."

"You're harking back to the Louisiana proposition?"

"Yes."

"You earned that money. But as I'm sure Hasbrouck made clear, if you'd been greedy you'd have got nothing. You passed that test, and I hope you pass this one."

"I didn't know that I was taking a test."

"You know it now, and I'm not giving it to you. You don't even have to look in the back of the book for the answers. Your resignation has not been put through. There is not even an office memorandum on it. So if you decide the right way, there won't be anything to tear up, and only Hasbrouck and I the wiser. Before I leave you, in one word what is your report on the Buffalo, Fort Penn & Trenton proposition?"

"No."

"Oh, my. I was afraid that's what it would be. I wanted to have that man Benziger working for us. He's my kind of man. I wish I'd known him thirty years ago."

"I didn't know you knew him."

"Eaton, I know what he had for breakfast last Thursday. I've never seen him, but he could be Quasimodo and I'd still like his looks. You liked him?"

"As much as any man I've ever known."

"Well, I guess we can't have everything. I look forward to your report. Tell me all you can about Benziger. In these days it gives me pleasure just to read about a man like Benziger."

"Yes sir."

The old man rose and Alfred started to get to his feet, but MacHardie pressed a hand on his shoulder. "Keep your seat, son. You've had a bad time."

"Not really so bad, I guess," said Alfred.

ALFRED DID NOT go back to work after his luncheon with James D. MacHardie. Instead he left the building and went for a walk in a direction he never had taken during his years in the financial district, and by allowing himself to be swept into the current of foot and vehicular traffic, he boarded the Staten Island ferry, went out on deck, and discovered that he had been living in a seaport.

He saw vessels of foreign registry under flags he could not

547

identify and he watched one ship which he estimated to be of three- or four-thousand tonnage proceeding slowly into the East River. It was a freighter, a tramp, either improperly loaded or in trouble with a bad list to starboard. Alfred prided himself on his eyesight, but so badly peeled was the ship's paint that the best he could do toward reading the name on the bow was *ALGEBRA,* and he was reasonably certain no ship was named *Algebra.* There were men at work on the deck of the *Algebra,* but there was one man in a knitted peacap, heavy black sweater and blue jeans, who leaned against the port rail, looking down at the water, and never looking anywhere else. He had no curiosity about New York harbor or the Staten Island ferry or the work that was going on about him or, apparently, the nearness of Brooklyn and the waterfront entertainments. The able-bodied seaman never raised his head, but to Alfred his attitude was disgust, dejection, discouragement, and defeat. The ferryboat headed toward St. George and began to pick up speed. Like anyone else who has ever been to sea for a short time, Alfred had often in moments of surfeit thought of escaping to the life that was unfortunately represented by the seaman at the rail of the *Algebra.* But now the seaman also represented something else: the long way Alfred had to go before despondency.

He got off the boat at St. George and strolled around the plaza until the next ferryboat, which he boarded. Now and in spite of the stiff, cold breeze, he stood forward of the upper-deck cabin and for twenty minutes gazed at the skyline of lower New York, becoming, in his way, and not altogether consciously, the antithesis of the seaman on the *Algebra.* This was the first time since Alfred had become a part of the financial district that he had seen the towers from the bay, and he knew he could not now separate himself from that life. He actually turned his head, to tell someone, anyone, that in among those buildings was the desk where he worked. But he was alone in the breeze that came from the direction of the buildings and that perversely seemed to be pulling him back to them. He was not going to give up all that for a wife who rather despised the work he had come to love, and who would henceforth hate it because she hated him.

He returned to the office and, against custom and regulations, walked straight to Hasbrouck's desk. Fortunately for protocol, Hasbrouck was alone. He looked up at Alfred, still in his overcoat and carrying his hat. "Oh, Eaton?"

"I just wanted to tell you—I'm staying."

"Good man. Glad to hear it," said Hasbrouck, and Alfred felt as much as heard the sincerity in his voice.

From that day forward ambiguity and distractions were no part of the career of Alfred Eaton. He was not and would not be ready to renounce the pleasurable responsibilities of fatherhood and a few friendships, but as the new arrangement with Mary took on the permanence of days and nights and months, it became to both of them a fixed habit, less unendurable than in the beginning they had thought it would be. The necessary intimacies were conducted on a system of politeness that by tacit agreement was not violated through extreme rudeness any more than by forced demonstration of non-existent affection. In discussions of problems relating to the children, the household, money, and their social engagements they were factual and fair, blank of expression, and careful now not to meet the other's eye and reveal the known but politely hidden animosity each held for the other. The double threats of surveillance were not carried out, and soon were forgotten in the self-imposed strictness of their outside behavior. There was no talk of divorce, and while Mary did not know it—because Alfred had not told her so—she was actually free to take a lover so long as it remained secret. Since there was no tenderness between them, they were safe from the revelations and discoveries that might be caused by diminished tenderness.

Their marriage arrangement told on their faces, in the set of their jaws, and the beginnings of lines above the eyes and down from their nostrils to their chins. But as this occurred, Alfred and Mary became—in their public visage—more and more austere, conventional. The gossip concerning Mary and Roper had been passed around among their friends, but all that winter no one had seen them together, and by spring their friends altogether quick and ready to recall the gossip, did so in a statistical manner rather than a lubricious: Mary had had an affair, yes, and she was therefore no one to be haughty, but it had only been a whirl. Alfred had been perfectly splendid about it. No reprisals, complete understanding. There were even a few (who had not heard the details of the Englewood weekend) who remained doubtful that Mary had actually gone to bed with Jim Roper. That kind of theory, however, was not accepted among the women who had begun to appreciate the many skills of Jim Roper. The more cynical women, who did not waste much time in seeking kindly attitudes, were convinced only that Alfred had laid down the law to Mary, and Mary—perhaps a little tired of Roper anyway—had conformed, and the marriage had lapsed into one of many like it, in which the husband or the wife had broken the contract in public but—for whatever the reason— legal action was not taken. Frequently an odd, defensive sort of dignity was acquired by the women in such marriages; it was dignity of manner, part arrogance and part defenselessness, and the experience was common enough so that a woman in such circumstances could look about her at a party, in a restaurant, and recognize the characteristic manner even among women she did not know. It was a manner they could not hide from one another, and a woman who saw it in another woman was immediately vigilant for signs that the second woman was interesting herself in the observer's husband. Among the men there were few who retained the recognizable innocence of total fidelity, and the most cynical of the women had little interest in a man who was so incurious about her sex. For that reason Alfred became to them something of an enigma. He was only just past thirty, handsome, maturing in manner and appearance, and being talked about as one of the men to watch in the financial district. He had weathered his first marital squall and come out of it unquestionably the dominant figure in his marriage. This he accidentally achieved by making no reprisals and by staying out of the divorce court; the cuckolded husband who became a vindictive garter-snapper was regarded as a bad loser and a second-rate lecher, who was not in it for fun or sport but only to make a belated effort to assert himself. Alfred, it was believed, had risen supremely above Mary's misconduct and in so doing had kept himself above minor temptations and petty revenge. The women who made it their business to be informed on such matters and to create opinions of the principals were, in that winter of 1927-1928, unsure of Alfred Eaton. He had baffled them once before, early in his marriage, by remaining faithful to Mary in the face of many Long Island temptations and in spite of his own youth and previous record. (The Gramercy Park apartment with Lex Porter was moderately notorious at the time and well remembered in the present.) And there was always "something" about Alfred Eaton that was comforting to the gossips: they were sure he had never really been faithful to Mary and was not now being so, but for lack of any proof to the contrary they were unable to pin anything on him, a fact which would make eventual discovery more amusing than otherwise. They did not trust him, because so far they had had to trust him. The gossips also somewhat lost interest in Mary; her next affair, whenever and with whomever, would be less dramatic, since Alfred had shown no disposition to make a public fuss. The interest now was in Alfred. Mary was beautiful, it was true, but her beauty alone could not sustain interest in her doings. Her father was a respectable, respected man who had something to do with the du Pont company in Delaware, but whatever the job was, it was still only a job. Her mother was a Virginian, perfectly respectable, but important only in the eyes of other Virginians. The St. John connections obviously had been good enough to get Mary invited to the New York parties, but the reminiscent judgment on Mary was that she had been very lucky to get as far as she had. And yet although Alfred's social qualifications were almost precisely the same as Mary's—small town in Pennsylvania, obscure prep school, two years at Princeton, good looks, and the backing of the Thorntons and Porters— he had turned his own luck into a promising future that was less and less the future and more and more the present. The men said he had ability. The older men were now speaking to him and having no trouble remembering his name.

Thus was Mary receding, with the help of gossips and gossip repeated. Thus, too, was Alfred's career observed and advanced, undamaged by gossip because he had had the good sense to take good advice. There was even a bit of men's gossip concerning Alfred: that he would be a MacHardie partner by the time he was thirty-five.

That was the year in which work and the firm became almost obsessive with Alfred, almost like the religion he never had had. The subway ride to the office was too slow for him, where in other years it had been a chance to look at the newspaper. He was taken into a lunch club after three years of waiting, and he seldom used it. He stayed downtown until the last minute before a dinner engagement, and he frequently said goodnight to his sons over the telephone instead of in their room. He saw midtown New York so little that a large new office building on Fifth Avenue made him say: "When did that happen?" It was only when he was very tired, too tired to sleep, that he would admit that he knew what was missing.

In a casual way he had formed with Lex the habit of lunching on Saturday. The habit had become a custom, subject to last-minute change by either man, but it was the only non-business engagement Alfred tried hard to keep. They would meet at the club, drink two Martini cocktails, and have their lunch in the diningroom. From week to week there was always enough of each man's news to keep the luncheon conversation going, and after lunch they would play backgammon, stopping at five o'clock or, as sometimes happened, when Lex would say: "You better go home and get some sleep. You've been yawning all afternoon."

The friendship had been resumed virtually undamaged by the collapse of the Nassau Aeronautical Corporation and had reverted to its early, undergraduate relationship, in which deep confidences were not exchanged. They were now friends because neither wanted anyone else to be so close to him; it was sufficient, satisfactory, and required no stimulation.

On one of those Saturdays there were two letters waiting for Alfred. One, postmarked Philadelphia, was in handwriting he did not immediately recognize. The other was in hand-

551

writing he had seen only once but would never forget, and was postmarked Mountain City, Pa. "Is Mr. Porter in the club?" he asked the club servant.

"In the bar, Mr. Eaton. In the bar, expecting you."

Alfred opened the strange letter first, before going upstairs, and was forever grateful that he did.

Dear Alfred:

    I hope this reaches you in time. I am desperately worried that it will not & in that case the damage may be done. Please, please, please, when you see Lex do not tell him anything about you and I. I have never heard this about you, but men do talk and what happened in Port Johnson was so casual that if you two got to talking you might tell Lex, never thinking the harm that might be done. Believe me, Alfred, I would give anything to take back that night. Not that I have any regrets because it was you but I have suddenly fallen in love with Lex and he with me & I know you often meet him for lunch, practicly every Sat. I gather that you have not said anything so far but please please please never say anything about me. You have always been very dear to me even when we did not see each other for all those years and I appeal to your friendship and kindness to say nothing to Lex. I am going out of my mind with uncertainity. Could you phone me when you receive this (number below) or at least send me a telegram saying all is well, unsigned, and I will know and be forever grateful. Anxiously,

Clemmie

He went to the booth and telephoned the telegram, happy to do it with the knowledge of the other letter in his pocket. He then joined Lex.

They were well along with their lunch and had come to a silence that was not altogether accidental—Alfred and Lex each for his own reason waiting for the silence—when Lex said abruptly: "What would you think if I got married?"

"What would I think? I think you ought to. But I don't think you ought to just because I think so, or you think so, or you're past thirty. You sound as if you'd made up your mind."

"Just about."

"Do I know the girl?"

"You used to, five or six hundred years ago."

"Are you going to be coy? Where did I know her?"

"Princeton. Philadelphia. Oh, I'll tell you who it is. It's Clemmie Shreve."

"Clemmie Shreve? Good news, but isn't she married? Don't tell me she got rid of that Mick she was married to."

"Getting rid of him. She left him last year."

"Well, I know you're getting one of the prettiest girls I ever saw. At least she was then. Is she still as pretty?"

"Every bit. Will you be the best man?"

"You're damn right I will. As soon as she accepts you."

"I think she will. This is the first time in my life I've ever been in love. She says it's the first time she's been."

"That's not very complimentary to me. I used to think she liked me."

"She still does, but not that way. She told me that you and she never stopped talking long enough to fall in love. Then she married Hennessey."

"Do you know why I talked so much then? Clemmie was so pretty I couldn't believe it, and I was nervous. I remember her in a white dress—I guess all the other girls were in white dresses, too, but she was like a princess. Is she in town?"

"She's living with her family, in Philadelphia."

"When are you getting married?"

"Some time this summer."

"Did she have any children?"

"No children."

"What are you going to do? Are you going to get a job or anything like that?"

"I'm going to buy a ranch and get the hell out of this fucking shambles. Everywhere I go I hear about you, and I know I'd be no damn good downtown, but you've had a tougher time than I have and you came through. Maybe I can, with Clemmie."

"When did all this happen?"

"Not too long ago. I was over in Philadelphia for a tournament, two days, and I saw Clemmie at one of the parties. They had a lot of parties for us. And I've been seeing her ever since."

"Did you see my sister Constance at any of the parties?"

"No, I didn't. Why?"

"I just thought you might have."

"I know all about that, Alfred."

"Oh, do you?"

"Yes. Don't forget, I went through it with Elizabeth. Elizabeth finally saw the light of day, and so will Constance. It isn't the way it used to be. We don't have to go around shooting guys that sleep with our sisters. Our sisters might want to shoot us if we did."

"Is this under the hat, between you and Clemmie?"

"Yes, for the time being."

"Well, it's the best news in I don't know when, for both of you. And for me. I won't have to worry about you any more."

"Why the hell would you ever worry about me?"

"I don't know, you just didn't seem to be having a very good time."

"I wasn't. But I'm all right now. I know where there's a ranch for sale in Wyoming. I'm going to build a landing field and put up a couple of small hangars. I'll buy a tractor and a snow plow and add another month to the season. When the dude season ends, guys can fly in for the hunting. It snows early out there. It's also a good way to get out if Clemmie gets bored and wants to go to Denver or some such place. She says she'll never get bored, it's the East that bores her, but she hasn't tried it yet. Maybe I can get you to come out and visit us next year. I'm sure Mr. MacHardie owns some mines out that way."

"He does, in Montana."

"Well, you can charter one of those Ford tri-motor jobs and drop in on us."

"You sound as if you were leaving tomorrow."

"I wish to Christ I was. So damn many things can go wrong."

"Not if I can help it."

"I know, but this is something where you can't help. Nobody can. I'll believe it when I have the ring on her finger and we're on our way. Do you mind if we skip the backgammon this afternoon? I'm going to take the four o'clock to Philadelphia."

"No, I have a lot to do. Letters and things."

"Have you any message for Clemmie?"

"I could make some joke, but I don't want to. Just tell her I'm glad for the two of you, and there are no two people I'd rather see happy."

"Thanks."

"As far as good wishes are concerned, you can write your own ticket and I'll sign it. You know that."

"Yes I do. And I wish things were better for you. Are they any better?"

"They're no worse. They'll never be any better."

He accompanied Lex to the coatroom and to the door, then went upstairs again and chose a corner where he would not be disturbed and slowly opened Natalie's letter:

Do you remember my first and only letter to you, that I had to address as Mr. Eaton because I did not know your first name? This is something like that, not that I no longer know your name, but that I do not know where you are or even that you are alive. But I do know that. I could not swear to it in a court of law, where they might ask me for proof. Nor do I know it by hearsay, which they do not accept in court. But I know you are alive, living your life, going to your office, seeing your friends, catching cold (did you have a cold this winter? I'm glad you didn't see me in January when I had my annual snuffles), doing all the things that a busy man does in New York. But my instinct that tells me you are very much

554

alive does not seem to work geographically. In other words, I do not know where you are. Perhaps you are sunning yourself in the south of France—Palm Beach—the Hawaiian Islands, and if you are, heaven only knows when you will see this letter.

You told me that I could write to you at the Racquet Club and you gave me the address at the time but I neglected to write it down, so I had to go over to Daddy's office where they have a N. Y. telephone book and pretend to be looking up the address of Franklin Simon's. The girl at the switchboard, whom I have known most of my life, said, "Nat, would you like me to get the number for you?" And I, without thinking, said "370 Park Avenue." She laughed and so did I, but later on I realized how careless of me. I was actually nervous because I was so close to you. All I had to do was give the number and in a few minutes I might be able to hear your voice (not really—it was about 11 o'clock in the morning and I doubt that you would be at a club at that hour of the day). I went home in a slight daze, thinking about it. It was the first time thinking about you had had that effect on me, so no matter where you are, you are not really so far away if the thought of hearing your voice can do that to me.

Come to the point of the letter, Natalie. All right, said she, I will. I am going to be in New York for a week beginning next Monday, which as I write is the *second week in April* (shall I also say 1928?). I will be chaperoned, or at least accompanied, by another girl, Caroline English. You met her husband when you were here. We will be staying at the Hotel Chatham. Her husband is coming to New York on Wednesday and we are going to the theater on Wednesday, Thursday & Friday nights, but have not bought tickets for Monday or Tuesday. We will be busy shopping every day, including lunch, but I will keep the late afternoons free in the hope that you will get this letter in time and we can see each other. I could also have dinner with you Monday or Tuesday night, although I would not like to go to the theater. Caroline is not the nosy type, but if I had dinner with you it would mean leaving her alone at the hotel and I don't think that would be the nicest thing I ever did, so if you and I have dinner either of those nights I would want to be back at the hotel around nine o'clock. We should be at the Chatham at three o'clock Monday afternoon. If you can leave a message please use the name of Mr. Raymond. There is no point in using your real name, either for you or for me.

I have had a winter full of doubts and yet a lot of little doubts do not seem to amount to as much as the one belief. The time has come for me to know what to believe, if anything.

Natalie

It was a nervous but sensible letter, which had to be written at some time, and had to be written by her, since she was the one who had made the separation and at whose pleasure the silence could be broken. Accidentally (as he believed) or by design, she had expressed some of their closeness without

555

compromising herself or him, but there was no denying the underlying urgency of her need to see him again.

The message he left at the hotel was as simple as he could make it: "I will be at Charlot's, a speakeasy at 77 West 49th Street, at five-thirty Monday afternoon. Love, Raymond."

Charlot's was a handy place, handy in the sense of convenience and in the sense that it had attracted a clientele that could afford the prices but was not society nor show-business figures. Few men went there with their wives. By custom it had become a rendezvous for the unfaithful, and by unspoken common consent the patrons kept quiet about what they saw and heard in Charlot's, or even that they had been there. Alfred knew that he was taking a chance on being recognized, but the motto of the patrons was, "You saw me, but I saw you." The wives of men like Alfred Eaton never went there at all until they had otherwise made public their extra-marital affairs, and by that time they did not need Charlot's. There were rumors that a few favored patrons could avail themselves of the bedroom behind Charlot's second-story office, but of that Alfred had no certain knowledge.

Charlot was always a surprise to persons seeing him for the first time, who usually expected to meet a man who would look like Enrico Caruso in his Pagliacci costume, clown hat, pompons, bass drum and all. Instead they were greeted by a hardfaced Marseillais in short coat and striped trousers or, in the evening, high wing collar with butterfly tie, white waistcoat and Croix de Guerre ribbon in his lapel. An item of the Charlot legend was that he had killed a man with his hands, and playful women patrons often tried to discover whether he carried a revolver. He did not, but some of the women paid for their curiosity by visits to the room behind the office, partly because he misinterpreted their pawing and partly because he was actually very attractive to them, and no less so after the first visit to the upstairs room. The afternoon women, as he called them, the women who came to lunch and sat drinking stingers until cocktail time, were a profitable nuisance.

It was dark in the front room when Natalie was led in by Charlot's nephew, and momentarily she did not see Alfred. He rose from the table and went to her and took her hand and guided her to the banquette.

"What shall I have?" she said. "I haven't been to many speakeasies."

"Long drink or short drink?"

"Long, I think. I won't want more than one. Could I have something very mild? I don't really want anything."

"Rhine wine and seltzer."

"All right."

She took off her gloves and put them with her purse on one

556

of the chairs. She looked at him and smiled. "How long will he take?"

"The waiter? Two minutes. Three minutes."

"Then quick!" She put her arms around him and kissed him. "Hold me close."

It was her kiss, not his, and when she stopped she said: "That makes it real. The only real thing this winter. And it isn't winter any more, it's spring. Does that give you some idea of what my winter's been like?"

"No, and yes."

"Well, it's what I wanted to do all winter. At any given moment, whether I happened to be thinking about you or not, I was ready to kiss you."

"That can be a very bad state to be in."

"For a man, too?"

"Yes."

"Are we both saying the same thing?"

"I guess we are."

The drinks were served and they were alone. "Will you kiss me now?" she said.

He kissed her and put his hand on her breast. Without taking her mouth away from his she unbuttoned the jacket of her suit and he discovered that she was wearing a dickey, not a blouse, and then put his hand down into her brassière until he was able to cup her breast in the curving palm of his hand.

"If we could close that door—but I guess we can't," she said.

"No, there'll be people here any minute," he said.

"Thank God you've got some sense," she said.

"I won't much longer."

"No, we'd better stop," she said, and sat back and rearranged her clothes. She took a handkerchief from her purse and touched it to her tongue and removed the lipstick from his mouth and chin.

"That came first, before any talk," she said. "I wondered. I was wondering. But now I don't wonder any more. A whole winter swept away, as if it never happened. When are we going to do all our talking, when all I want to do is kiss you and be kissed by you," she went on. "Are you still with your wife?"

"In name only, as the old saying goes."

"Then you must have another girl."

"Strangely enough, I have not."

"You?"

"I've proved it was possible. It isn't easy, but it's possible."

"But it wasn't even necessary. You had no reason to be faithful to me, if that's what you were being."

"I was, and I wasn't. I wish I could say that I was being

faithful to you, but that wouldn't be the absolute truth. Part of it was disgust, I guess, and part of it was just not making the effort. It isn't hard to get someone to sleep with you, but the arrangements get complicated."

"That's what prevented me, once. It's even more complicated in Mountain City, as you can imagine. And I have my father and mother to think of. I wonder if my father would understand what I feel now."

"What *do* you feel now?"

"I've shown you as well as I can. I'm in love with a married man, and I've never been in love before. I know what can happen to me—what's probably going to happen to me—but I don't care. My eyes are open, I'm no child—"

"You are a child, though, when you say it that way."

"I realized that as soon as I said it. It's what children say, isn't it? But you're no child, and what we just felt, there was nothing childlike about that. All man and all woman. I've never actually gone the limit with a man, but I'll never feel more—erotic, I guess—than I just have. *As* erotic, but I couldn't feel more."

"Oh, yes you will."

"I don't care for that word. It reminds me of a thing a girl had at boarding-school. It was gold, and she wore it on a charm bracelet with her father's fraternity key and a lot of things. It was just a little gold Buddha, but if you tilted it a certain way it became a—not a phallic symbol. Not a symbol at all. Just phallic. I could never look at that girl without looking to see if she was wearing her bracelet, and yet I hated it when she'd show it to me. I didn't want to be like her."

"Well, you're not."

"No, I'm not. But I wish that girl and her nasty little Buddha didn't have to intrude on my thoughts now."

"It's not so hard to understand why."

"No. Is there some place we could go this minute?"

He looked at his watch. "A friend of mine. I'll give him a call." He went to the booth and telephoned Lex at his apartment and at the club. He did not answer at the apartment and was not in the clubhouse. Alfred returned to her, shaking his head.

"We could go to a hotel," he said.

"No, not a hotel. I'd be afraid. There might be only one chance in a million that a friend of my father's would see us, but I'd be afraid for that one chance. Can we keep trying your friend?"

"You're going to have dinner with me, aren't you?"

"If you want me to. I want to get back to the Chatham at nine-thirty at the latest."

558

"The next time you come to New York I'll have an apartment of our own."

"You shouldn't go to that expense."

"I've never had so much money in all my life."

"Neither have I. I'll go halves with you. I'd like to."

He smiled. "Do you know, I'd like you to. As a matter of fact, I could sub-let my friend's apartment. He's getting married."

"That would save a lot of complications."

"It certainly would."

"But about my coming to New York. I have to live at home, you know."

"Yes."

"And two or three times a year is the most I've ever been here. That's a complication. Some girls, a lot of girls, can get jobs here, but I can't. If I did, my mother would have to have a nurse living in."

"She would if you got married."

"Yes, but that's different. We're a very close family, and I wouldn't leave home just to take a job in New York. My mother has one of those heart conditions that she might live for twenty years, or she might die tomorrow."

"But they surely don't expect you to spend the next twenty years in Mountain City."

"Oh, they'd like me to get married, but otherwise they expect me to live at home."

"As a virgin."

"Of course. My father and mother would never believe that I, their Natalie, could want a man to touch her bare breast. And as for cold-bloodedly discussing a love-nest—that's just fantastic. My mother always knocks before she comes in my room, in case I happen to have no clothes on. I've never seen my mother or my father naked."

"Have you ever seen any grown man naked?"

"Of course. Hundreds of times. Tall ones, small ones, fat ones, thin ones, hairy ones, hairless ones. I've seen more naked men than I have girls. They go swimming in a dam not far from our house. During the summer that's where a lot of them take their baths. They take soap and towels and they don't care who sees them. If a woman comes along they even—well."

"What?"

"They show off. They shout at her and wave, you know."

"Did they ever do that to you?"

"Me especially. The boss's daughter. 'Hey, Natalie, look what I got for you.'"

"What do you do in a case like that?"

"Pretend they don't exist. I'm a frontier girl. I've seen

559

people do what I've never done myself. If you go for a walk on Sunday afternoon, one time I saw four men waiting to get at one girl."

"How old were you?"

"Twenty."

"Did you stay and watch them?"

"I couldn't leave. I was terrified they'd see me, and I was fascinated."

"Were you excited, or disgusted?"

"Excited. Then when I got home, disgusted with myself. I had no right to watch those people. The girl was making money, and the men were all single—I knew them—and couldn't afford to get married, and that was their way. Every Sunday afternoon when we sit on our porch after dinner you'll see young couples headed for the bushes, the boy carrying a blanket. My mother and father always just look the other way, or go on reading their newspaper. Oh, I've seen worse things than that, at least I think it's worse. It's horrible when a girl has to sell herself to make money, but an old man who corrupts children. They finally caught him, though. But then what happens to those children?"

"I remember a talk I had with your father."

"About the mountains, and the people?"

"Yes."

"I know. Maybe he's never seen what I've seen. Maybe he just doesn't want to see what I see. But I have seen it and I can't pretend I haven't. I don't know whether I'm worse off or better off. I know this much, that when I want you as much as I do, I know what I'm wanting. I know what you will do and what I will do, because I've seen it done. It hasn't repelled me, so I don't think it's done me any harm. The girl at school repelled me. But never you, or the thought of you and me."

"But you wouldn't want me if I were still getting along with my wife."

"I always wanted you. But I wouldn't be the first you were unfaithful with. She did it, and according to my beliefs, that set you free. Well, I'm glad she did. I couldn't go through life without you. You know that by the way I kissed you. And I don't think I could go through another winter without somebody. Or summer. Or spring. I almost succumbed last winter, but I couldn't go through with it. At the last minute I knew I'd have to tell you, and I knew you wouldn't like that."

"I would have hated it. But I'd have had to try to be modern about it."

"It was going to be a modern affair. The man was even older than you are, and married, too. 'Why shouldn't I?' I said. But I didn't."

"Where was that?"

"On a train. Coming up from Pinehurst. The man was a rotter—doesn't that sound mid-Victorian?—and I knew it, but I was at that low point where I'd given up on you. Then when I realized that you were the real reason why I wouldn't become the Madonna of the Sleeping Cars, my low point was passed. And here I am. And that, dear children, is how I met your father. Oh, God—what's that I'm saying? Children?"

"You know, you're talking awful big, Natalie. You're talking awful fast, too."

"Am I?"

"I don't think you're ready to make the supreme sacrifice."

"I don't like to be laughed at."

"No, but you're as nervous as a witch and you're trying to convince yourself that you're ready to lead a life of sin. You're not."

"I'm twenty-three."

"Sure, and you've seen people screwing on the mountain."

"You didn't have to say that."

"I said it deliberately."

"To see if it'd shock me."

"Yes, and it did."

"Yes, it did. You don't want me. Is that it? I don't believe that."

"I don't want you to believe it."

"Then what do you want?"

"You. You know, when I saw you back in Mountain City, I had a hard time believing you were only twenty-two, or -three—"

"I was twenty-two then. I've had a birthday since."

"Well, whatever you were. You seemed much older, or at least much more mature. You had real poise, and no matter how much experience you'd had, or didn't have, you were much more of a woman then than you are now. I think it's being in a speakeasy, in New York. It's like the first time I ever went to Paris. There was that wonderful city, and all I could think of was that I wanted to see a peep-show."

"I haven't the slightest desire to see a peep-show, I assure you."

"Well, there wouldn't be much of a novelty in it for you, would there?"

"I'm sorry, but I've got to leave."

"Sit down and stop being twenty-two years old. Maybe when I get through talking to you you'll never be young again, but I have a few things I have to say."

"Then say them quickly, please, because I've had enough."

"All right. First, I love you. My winter has been work, love of my children, and a relationship with my wife that's about as bad as it can get and will never get any better. I now no longer care what she does, just as long as she doesn't make a spectacle of herself or a fool of me. It isn't only wounded pride. It's that, but that's not all it is. It's all those years I was married to her, sleeping with her, having children with her, all spoiled because the guy she finally stepped out with was the guy she was engaged to when I met her. In other words, she'd always loved him and should have married him, but he had no money and was going to medical school and— what the hell? I might as well say it—I was a better marriage for her than he would have been. So I buried myself in work, and I enjoy it, I like my work. But I have to have love, loving somebody or being loved, preferably both, and when I allowed myself to think of love, I thought of you. I'll always think of you. It took me thirty years, but I just don't see anyone else in my life. But I don't want to mean no more to you than a casual affair in New York City, like Bonwit-Teller's and going to the new plays.

"I spent most of my boyhood and my teens as a very lonely kid. Then I had a lot of girls, and then when I married Mary I thought the loneliness was over forever, and especially when my first son was born. A family. But the loneliness all came back, uh—there's a word for it—retroactively, when I discovered that Mary had always been in love with this other guy. It wasn't wounded pride, it was her spoiling those good years, or what I'd thought were good years. As though I'd been Mr. Stradivarius and spent six years making a violin and some son of a bitch jumped on it and smashed it. And laughed at me while doing it. It's not a very good comparison. I have the kids. But I have to love a woman, not two little boys. And I did, and I do. You.

"I was an old little boy and an old young man, and I'm older now than thirty-one. I prefer the company of older men and at least half the time I think like them. I've always gotten along well with older men, and that fits in with my work. As to women, I've always been able to help myself to them. Immodest, but true. What's the use of kidding myself about that or anything else? This past winter I lived like a monk by choice. Why? Because I loved you and I was sure you still loved me. I don't know how much longer I would have gone on, but I did go on this far without anybody, waiting for you.

"You probably want to say, 'Well, what do you want?' You know damn well what I want. The impossible. But for a few years I want you to be my girl, for as long as you want to be, till you decide to get married. After that I expect you to be faithful to your husband, but loving me as I'll always love you. Your friends and your family will wonder why you don't get married, and you may wonder why I don't get a divorce. Well, if you wait long enough I probably will get a divorce, but not unless Mary asks for it, and I don't think she will. The doctor's not going to marry her, and I don't think she's going to ask me for a divorce until something awfully good comes along. Maybe not then.

"I haven't given you any very good reason why you should accept what I offer. But there isn't any. It's just something you do because you want to, and for no other reason. That's why this is such a serious matter, and not just an adventure in New York."

"It's serious, all right."

Two other couples had come in and taken tables. "Would you like to go some place else for dinner?" he said.

"I think I'd like to go back and have dinner with Caroline."

He paid the bill and they went out in the twilight. "It's only about two blocks to the hotel," he said. "Shall we walk?"

"Yes, let's walk."

She took his arm and they did not speak until Fifth Avenue. "You're right. I guess I'll never be young again."

"It doesn't mean we can never laugh again."

"I don't feel much like laughing now, though. You didn't paint a very bright picture of my life for the next indefinite years."

"I couldn't," he said. "Now we go down Fifth and turn east at Forty-eighth and in half a block I may never see you again."

"Do you really think that, Raymond?"

"I don't know."

She looked straight ahead as they walked in step. "I'm not leaving you. I'll never leave you," she said. When he said nothing she turned her head and looked up at him. He was smiling, but there were tears in his eyes.

"I haven't done that since I was seventeen years old," he said. "Then it was disappointment."

"Who disappointed you? I'll kill her."

"You can't. It was a he, my father, and he's dead."

They said no more until they reached the hotel. He took off his hat and shook hands with her. "Will you telephone your friend tomorrow?" she said.

"Yes."

"And let's meet there, not at the speakeasy. You'll leave word here?"

"Yes."

She kissed him. "I feel like a bride," she said, and left him.

It was a few minutes past six when she appeared at Lex's apartment. He opened the hall door and they embraced and went into the livingroom. "Ah, the Deke house," she said, waving her hand at the furniture and the shelves of loving cups.

"Is that what it reminds you of? The Deke house where?"

"At Lafayette. Or it could be St. Anthony at Penn, or Zeta Psi at Yale."

"Why can't you mention Princeton?"

"Cottage is the only one I've been to there."

"Wrong frat."

"What were you?"

"Orchard. There's my picture, and there's our host. His name is Lex Porter. Two weeks later we were both making the world safe for democracy, but that's how we looked then."

"Say, you were pretty. I didn't know they wore knickers that long ago."

"They did at Princeton. We were always a little ahead of the rest, naturally. There's a fellow that came from near you, Gibbsville. His name was Ogden and he was killed in the war."

"He has a brother, Froggy. Very belligerent. Lost his arm."

"That's what he gets for being belligerent."

"I never knew this one, but they all say he was very nice. He was younger than Froggy. Here's your name on a cup. Tennis."

"Court tennis."

"That's the game that nobody knows how to score?"

"That's what they say about it. Took me about a year. Not really. It isn't that tough."

"This of course is his mother. Who's the English girl?"

"She's not English. It's his sister. She does look English, though, doesn't she?"

"Oh, and here you are in uniform. Oh, so serious, my love is."

"Well, of course. I had to get all those doughboys over to France."

"And is this Mr. Porter again? Look at the medals. How vulgar."

"He earned them. And he has one more that isn't in the picture, the D. S. C."

"And he's getting married? I don't think I'd like to be married to him. He looks moody and I'll bet he has a ferocious temper."

"He has a temper, but he's all right."

"Groton. You didn't go to Groton, did you?"

"No. Porter did. I went to Knox."

"Oh, yes. Oh, and now who are all these?" She stopped. "This is your wife. It's not a very good picture of her, is it?"

"No."

564

"Here's a girl I know, but I don't know her name."

"I'll tell you her name. It's Constance Eaton. She's my younger sister. Where did you know her?"

"She's your sister? You don't look a bit alike."

"Not very much. Where did you know her?"

"Oh, I've seen her at different places. She was in Pinehurst while I was there. Your wife is very beautiful."

"I won't deny that. Did you like my sister, what you saw of her?"

"I didn't really get to know her. As I say, I didn't even know her name. She's attractive."

"Natalie."

"What?"

"Don't hedge. My sister was with a guy named Coddington. It's no secret."

"Yes, and I didn't like Coddington. He was a rotter."

"Did he come up on the train with you?"

"Rotter gave it away, didn't it?"

"Yes. And I think you felt sorry for my sister, am I right?"

"Yes."

"Well, don't. Her mind is made up. I forgot about these pictures. I've seen them so many times I never even look at them. I promise you that no one will ever feel sorry for you. At least not for those reasons, or any reason that I can prevent."

"Let's sit down."

"And have a good talk?"

"No, I'm not worried about people feeling sorry for me. But your sister's getting a dirty deal from Coddington."

"She tells me to mind my own business."

"I guess that's what I'd tell my brother, too. Promise me that if I ever go away with you you won't refuse to introduce me to people. Your sister would sit there while he was out riding with another girl, and she just isn't the kind of a girl you do that to."

"Maybe it's a good break for her."

"Not the way he's doing it. She's not through, but he is."

"And you're worried about the similarities between them and us."

"It's depressing."

"On both of us. Shall I fix you a drink?"

"No, but you have one if you like. Or let me get it. What would you like?"

"Scotch and soda. It's all in that cabinet."

She fixed his drink and brought it to him. "Are you tired?"

"Yes, as a matter of fact, I am. I went back to the office and worked last night."

"Till how late?"

"It was about one o'clock when I got home."

"Do you often do that?"

"Fairly often. I don't mind working, but seven-thirty comes awfully early some mornings."

"Is that when you get up?"

"As a rule I do."

"Why don't you go in and lie down?"

"Why don't you come in and lie down with me?"

"I'll let you get a nap, then I will."

"I'd love to doze off for about fifteen minutes. Would that be very unromantic?"

"I think it would be very cozy."

"So do I."

"Where does he keep his pajamas, Mr. Porter? I'll turn down the bed for you."

She found pajamas and turned down the bed and took Alfred by the hand and led him into the bedroom, kissed his cheek, and left him.

He fell asleep and when he opened his eyes he was in darkness. Her voice came to him: "Are you awake?"

"Yes, where are you?"

Before he had a chance to repeat the question she said: "Now I'm in bed, with you, at last."

They put their arms around each other and stayed close for a while. "What are you wearing?" he said.

"The top of his pajamas."

"You don't have to," he said.

"Neither do you."

They tossed the pajamas on the floor and were close again. "If I begin to hurt you, don't let me."

"You won't. You could never hurt me."

"But I am hurting you now."

"A little, but don't stop. I won't let you stop." Then she shrieked: "Darling! Love!"

It was soon over. "Are you going to bleed?"

"No," she said.

"Does it hurt?"

"It hurts a little, but only a little, and I don't notice it, honestly I don't. I'm so happy with you, so wonderful to give, to be part of you. I didn't have to be so noisy, though, did I?"

"You weren't."

"Thank God it was you and never anybody else."

"Thank God," he said. "I'm glad it was nobody else."

"Remember what I said last night? I do, I feel like a bride."

"And I feel like a groom."

"I went to the doctor a year ago."

566

"For the Pittsburgh guy?"

"Yes. I wouldn't have married him without having an affair first. Wasn't that smart of me?"

"You're a darn smart girl."

"You have no idea. We're not going to have a baby, either."

"Oh, that smart?"

"Sure. But some day I *am* going to have a baby with you. When we finally part, and I'll go to Spain with my little nameless child and I'll be the American lady who always wears a veil."

"Natalie, for God's sake."

"As soon as I see you getting tired of me."

"You'll be too old to have a baby when that happens. And I'll be too old to give you one."

"You said exactly the right thing. I feel better now. You really do love me."

"I really do."

"Because I really love you, Lieutenant."

"Why lieutenant?"

"I don't know. I guess because the last time I saw your face was in that picture. Shall we turn on the light?"

"Yes."

He snapped the lamp switch and she sat up.

"Oh, my God," he said. "You *are* beautiful."

"I'm glad you think so."

"Michelangelo would think so. Anybody would think so, not just me. Let me see the rest of you."

She lay full-length with her arms stiff against her sides, her eyes following his gaze. "All right?" she said.

He smiled and scratched his head. "Perfection," he said. "How is your disposition?"

"Even, except when my jealousy is aroused."

"Have you ever been jealous?"

"No, but I expect to be. You stand up. Turn around. Keep turning. Perfection. How is your disposition?"

"Rotten, but not now."

"You have a very good disposition. And I like your manners. You must have been very well brought up."

"A constant stream of governesses and tutors, not to mention a fencing instructor and a member of the Household Cavalry who taught me to bow."

"Bow for me."

"A pleasure, mum," he said, bowing with one hand at his side and the other over his belly.

"Come here a second," she said. "What's this?" She reached up and touched the scar on his neck.

"That's my million-dollar scar, my James D. MacHardie introduction."

She touched it gently with her finger tips and then drew his head down so that she could kiss the scar. "A man shouldn't be too perfect," she said. "Do you know James D. Mac-Hardie?"

"Know him? I work for him."

"I thought you worked for somebody named Crowley."

"Oh, Lord, so you did." He lay beside her with her head on his arm and told her the story of the Duffy child and of his masquerade as a bond salesman.

"We wondered why you never came back. I thought it was because you were trying to stay away from me, but I couldn't tell that to my father. You're just a big liar, aren't you?"

"A prevaricator in the pay of big business."

"Well, we have to have spies, too. We have them, the union has them, and even James D. MacHardie. He knows about my father. That would really please Daddy."

"Well, let's deny him that pleasure for a while. I'll tell you anything and everything, but a lot of things you'll have to keep to yourself."

"Won't I, though?"

"I'm making all the demands on you, you're not making any on me."

"Well, as your sister would say, that's none of your business if I'm doing what I want to do. What can you offer me to persuade me to be your girl? Nothing. It's something I have to do of my own free will or not at all. I couldn't be bought, you know that. The boy from Pittsburgh had all the money in the world, but he never got this far. And I wouldn't marry him, either. I couldn't be had for money, Raymond. Only love. And my idea of love is to be your girl.

"Raymond, my dear, there's something else. My family. They wouldn't want me to marry you. They'd be horrified to know what I *am* going to do, but they'd be just as horrified if you left your wife and children to marry me. Either way from their point of view it's hopeless. But from my point of view at least I have you, you're my—what? What are you? Lover. But that sounds like something in a French play. Do you have to be anything? Do I have to have a name for what you are? You must never call me your mistress."

"I never would. Not only out of respect to you, but it sounds so phony for a guy from Port Johnson, P A, to have a mistress."

"There isn't much of Port Johnson left in you."

"There's a lot more than you think, and getting to be a lot more the older I get. James D. MacHardie is only my grandfather multiplied by a hundred. Eugene Grace is only my father multiplied by ten. I'm speaking in terms of money."

"Yes, I know what you meant."

"If they hung my grandfather's portrait in the MacHardie board room he wouldn't look out of place. My grandfather made thousand-dollar decisions, and Mr. MacHardie makes decisions in the millions, but the same thinking goes into both decisions. I'm not nearly as awed by the Wall Street big shots as I was five years ago. There's a hell of a lot more paper work preceding a $15,000,000 investment, but the decision is finally, Do they get the money or don't they, whether it's a railroad or a hardware store on Lower Montgomery Street. The big difference is in getting accustomed to saying $2,000,000 without catching your breath, realizing that it's real money but at the same time considering it as a figure among a lot of figures . . . *This* is a figure that could turn the tide of history."

"I'm glad you like it."

"You must be proud of it."

"Yes, I am."

He snapped out the light and took her hand. "Come with me," he said. She got out of the bed and he led her to the window and parted the draperies. "New York, this is what you're missing." She put her arm about his waist and they stood at the window, looking out at the lights and the shapes of the buildings. "I'm proud of you," he said. He closed the draperies and they lay down again together.

"You're so quiet. Didn't you like me to do that?"

"Yes, I liked it."

He turned on the light. "But there was something wrong," he said.

"No, not wrong. I'm just beginning to know you and getting some idea of what we'll be like together. Tell me you love me?"

"I love you, more than it was ever possible for me to love anyone."

"That's the way I love you. No way to compare it with anyone else because it couldn't *be* with anyone else."

"What I knew the first time I saw you was like knowing the title of a book. The title was This Is the Girl I Love, and that was all I knew. It was enough for that moment, but now there's more and more."

"Yes," she said.

"You're so quiet," he said.

"I know."

"Are you happy?"

"I'm resigned to happiness."

"Yes, that's better."

"I've found my place. It's with you. Peacefully now, and passionately in a little while when you feel like it."

"I'm beginning to feel like it."

"I know you are, without even touching you I knew it.

You wouldn't love me as much if I didn't have a nice body, would you?"

"No. It wouldn't be you without the nice body."

"Did you know that?"

"I knew it without thinking about it. The eyes first, then the mouth, the nose, the forehead, the hair, the chin, in just about that order I saw you. The body was inevitable. And yet I didn't look to see if the rest was good. And that's unusual for me."

"I'm sure it is. I know how you'd look at a woman, but I was glad you didn't look that way at me."

"It was all unintentional."

"Raymond."

"What?"

"Whatever gives you pleasure gives me pleasure. We're wanting each other more and more, little by little. Oh, dear, I love you. I must kiss you."

"I want you to."

Later she sat in her slip and shoes and stockings, watching him as he dressed. He turned once and saw that she was smiling.

"All right, what?"

"Why am I smiling?"

"Yes."

"A man's little vanities," she said. "Getting the knot to sit just right under your collar."

"This tie has seen its best days. I had to retie it so the knot wouldn't come at the wrong place."

"It was all right yesterday."

"It wasn't the same tie. One like it. I have a dozen like it. I try to rotate them but sometimes when I'm in a hurry I grab the wrong one. This one's going to be rotated into the Salvation Army."

"Now your watch-chain. Why do you put it through the buttonhole. Afraid of pickpockets?"

"No. If you want to know the God's honest truth, I started doing that when I went to work for MacHardie & Company. Mr. MacHardie does that and we almost all copy him. The only ones who don't are Phi Beta Kappas and members of the Porcellian Club."

"My father wears his watch-chain up top."

"Two weeks in Wall Street and he'd bring it down."

"May I see your cuff links?"

He showed them to her. "Absolutely plain, not even your initials."

"They belonged to my grandfather."

"Let me see your watch."

"That was given to me by Mr. St. John, Mary's father.

570

I'll stop carrying it if you want me to."

"That would be pretty small of me."

"I don't carry anything she gave me. My cigarette lighter was a birthday present from Lex's uncle. My billfold was from my mother. My gold toothpick was from Marie Antoinette."

"Have you really got a gold toothpick?"

"Of course. Now what did I do with it? It was somewhere around here."

"You're pulling my leg."

"Stroking it gently on the way to the top."

"Do you want to?"

"It wouldn't be very successful."

"I was wondering."

"Are you all right?"

"Mm-hmm." She nodded. "Are you going down to your office again tonight?"

"Yes."

"Sometime I wish you'd take me down there and show me where you work."

"You could come down tonight."

"Not tonight. After you've fed me I'm going back to the hotel . . . I haven't figured out a way yet that you can write to me."

"Well, we'll figure out some way."

"It has to be within the next hour."

"Why?"

"Because I won't see you again. You knew that."

"This is our last time together?"

"Till I come to New York again. I'm going to be in a wedding in Hartford, the second week in June."

"But can't I phone you?"

"In Mountain City? No. I could phone you. This is one of the complications. Would you mind if I took Caroline English into my confidence? I trust her."

"Could I write to you in care of her? He seemed like a nice enough guy, but you know him better than I do."

"They're the only ones I *would* trust." She wrote the English address on the night-table pad. "But you can't ever phone me. You mustn't, ever. But that raises another point. If I ever have to, can I phone you at your office?"

"Any time. If you say it's a personal call you won't have to give your name. But can't I see you again before you leave?"

"I'll try to see you Thursday afternoon. If I can, shall we meet here?"

"Yes."

"It's the only time I'll have free."

"And now the conventional world descends upon us, in all its stifling grandeur, in all its musty redolence."

"What's that from?"

"That's from right here." He tapped his forehead.

"But you mustn't be unhappy. Think what we've had. I can live on this for a year, if necessary. We must start getting used to our life."

"I know, and I will," he said. "Let me kiss your breasts just once."

She took down her straps and drew back her shoulders and he kissed her. "No more now," she said. "I'll come Thursday, for sure. I need you as much as you need me, never forget that, my love."

"I'll never forget anything about you."

"And remember that the only things that keep us apart are the things we know about. That we know about now, here, tonight. I know a little bit now what it's going to be like. I don't want to go out with Joe Ginyan tomorrow night and Thursday night and Friday night."

"Who is Joe Ginyan?"

"That's just a name for nobody in particular. Not a real person. Actually I'm going out with three different men and none of them will mean anything to me. But I'll always be going out with somebody. That's my other life apart from you. In a way, like your job. You can't be jealous and neither can I. It will ruin us if we are. When we meet we must meet for love, with love, for each other, for the lovely pleasure of staying together. Are you going to get that apartment?"

"Yes."

"In June I want to stay all night with you, maybe two nights, maybe even two nights on my way to Hartford and two on the way back. But even then I'll have to leave you again and it will always be that way, my love. And those are the years we have ahead of us. We take what we get until there's nothing for us to take."

"Or everything."

"No, you can't hope for that, and you mustn't let me. I'll be your girl, but I don't think I'll ever be your wife. But don't be jealous and don't ask for more than you know we can have. I'm strong, but the wrong kind of hope could destroy me, and it could destroy me in a year. We have to face the god-awful facts."

"How do you know as much as you do?"

She looked away, wearily. "Oh, darling, I don't know very much. All of a sudden those nights are more than I can bear. Leave me for five minutes. I mean it. Please. Then I'll be all right."

He went to the livingroom. In about five minutes she came out, dressed for the street, and smiling at him to reassure him. "I've been told that the female is apt to do that when she's

572

happy," she said. "And I am happy, and God knows I'm female. As proof, I think I'm getting the curse."

"Are you sure that's what it is?"

"Quite sure. I haven't got it yet, but I know the signs. No, it isn't losing my technical virginity. Certain cramps and a tendency toward tears. I think you'd better take me to the hotel and I'll go to bed with a hot-water bottle."

"All right."

"I'm afraid Thursday will be cinnamon toast and tea, but I want to see you. We might as well get used to that, too. We've really lost very little time, when you think of it."

They got into a taxi and he put his arm around her and she sank down and held his hand. "Will you open the windows, please?"

"You feeling strange?"

"No, it's just that the last passenger must have been smoking a cigar with the windows closed. I'll be all right. The air feels good."

"How would it be if I sent you a bottle of brandy?"

"All right. I think that'd be fine."

"Have you got other things? Scotch? Gin?"

"Julian will get all that tomorrow, but if I could have some brandy tonight."

He kept the taxi after she got out and he stopped at Charlot's and had the brandy sent to her. He had dinner at Childs and went home and to bed, to sleep the sleep of the loving and loved. In the morning he telephoned her from the office and was answered by Mrs. English. "Is this the gentleman she saw last night?"

"Yes."

"I didn't want to mention your name, Mr. Eaton. She's still sleeping and if it isn't urgent, I hate to wake her."

"Please don't. But you will tell her I called?"

"She'll be pleased. And thank you for the brandy. I had some of it, too."

"I'm glad you did. I wanted to send some other stuff."

"I know, thank you. I needn't tell you this, Mr. Eaton, but we love Natalie."

"I love Natalie, Mrs. English."

"And she's never loved anyone before. My husband thinks you're a swell guy and he doesn't say that about everybody."

"I'm very glad to hear that. Thank you."

"It's not an idle compliment. I hope you go on being a swell guy."

"I'll try. I'm sure we understand each other."

"I may be less sure of that than you. I just wanted to be sure you understood that Natalie is our favorite person, and the favorite person of a lot of people. Goodbye, Mr. Eaton."

He did not like Mrs. English.

When he was in middle age and would look back on his life, Alfred learned to distrust his memory. He could recall incidents with near-completeness and accuracy, but the dangers of imbalance and wrong emphasis were encountered whenever he tried to chapterize a period or a phase. His personal history suffered from the same weaknesses as the larger histories of a nation or a century or an era. The Civil War began at Sumter but it did not begin at Sumter; the middle years of Raymond Alfred Eaton began with Natalie Benziger but did not begin with Natalie Benziger. As personal historian he began those years with Natalie because he had to begin them somewhere; they were the Natalie years, just as England had had her Elizabethan and Queen Anne and Victorian and Second Elizabeth years; but they were the only block of years to which he gave the name of a woman. The Natalie Years, the Years with Natalie. No Victoria Years, no Mary St. John Years. "My first love," yes; "My marriage," yes, but unnamed for the girl he had first loved or the woman who was his wife.

One day, that may have been a whole season, she stopped being his girl and became the woman in his life, the personification of the word and conversely the symbol of the sex, and the only woman in his life. The transition did not take a second or a year or the three years, since something that was one thing became something else by a process that was not to be measured by the measures of time. But one day (that may have been a whole season) she was what she had not been before, and he never knew (and it did not matter) exactly when he became aware of the difference in himself that was also the difference in her status in his life. It was sometime in the spring of 1931 that he became aware of the difference, and so he could say that three years had passed between the consummation of their love and the passing into the second phase of their attachment. They were a long three years of hard facts in his work, in his relationship with his wife and his growing sons, and in his formation of a public character and a public face. Photographs of himself, taken during those three years, more closely resembled the face he had at fifty than the face he had at twenty-five. At thirty-four his features were set; at twenty-four they had had most of the early flexibility, and could have stretched or contracted into any of a number of faces as the man himself could still have changed and, as it turned out, did change into the man of thirty-four, who was so like the man of fifty and beyond. The indeterminate face of youth, and youth, were gone at thirty-four, and the woman of this man was Natalie.

Their separations—almost always for months at a time—

were more difficult for him than for her, although he had his work and she only waited. "What do you *do?*" he would say, although he knew what the obvious answer would be: she played golf, and was good at it; she played bridge, and was very good at it. She marched up the aisle with her marriageable friends and she bought silver porringers for their firstborn, and she allowed herself to be amused at being left out of the more serious discussions of her friends among the officially deflowered. One year would pass, and another, and she would notice that friends who had been close to her were by degrees becoming farther away as she stayed out of the community of the married. Caroline English alone, who alone knew the degree of her relationship with Alfred, was her friend. "What do I do? Why, I sit and knit and wait to see you," she once replied, and it was the literal truth. They were together as often as it could be arranged, sometimes in their apartment in West Thirteenth Street; sometimes when he had to go to Boston and she would drive him there in her undistinctive Buick coupé. They had a week in Chicago in the spring of 1930, and many single nights in Philadelphia, always reasonably explained to her family and always in conjunction with business trips of his own. Their worst times were at Christmas, and the worst of all during the Christmas of 1930, when Julian English committed suicide by asphyxiating himself with the carbon monoxide fumes of his automobile; killing, by killing himself, the spirit of gayety for the holiday season and of her set, and frightening her with her first doubts of romantic love. She went to Caroline because she had known that Caroline had left Julian in protest against a scene he caused at the club dance, and she was the only one who knew that Caroline was determined to separate herself permanently from the only man she loved.

"You ought not to be here. You ought to be in New York," said Caroline.

"Why?"

"You've asked the right person why. Because no matter what they do, we have no right to desert them. Desert your family, Natalie. Go live in New York. What am I now? What shall I ever be? I'm a girl who had good and just cause to walk out on her husband, and now for the rest of my life I can sit here with my good and just cause." She held out her hands as though the good and just cause lay in them. "He was nice, and God help me he was nice to me." It was the only time Natalie saw her weep. "I loved him, I loved him."

Of all the people Natalie knew, Caroline was the last she would have expected to reconfirm her in the life she had chosen. But when she tried to reach Alfred on the telephone his secretary would only say that he was out of town for the holidays. Her father and mother were gentle and kind, aware of her fondness for Julian English and her love of Caroline. They could not be blamed for confusing grief with panic. "I'm going to New York next week," she said.

"Yes. It'd be a good idea for you to get away," said her father.

"Take someone with you. I'll give you the trip as an extra Christmas present. I only wish you could take Caroline with you."

"I don't want to take Caroline. I don't want to take anybody."

"I don't think she ought to take Caroline, Mother," said her father.

"I just want to be away for a few days."

"You do what you like, daughter. We understand," said her father.

Alfred was shocked by English's suicide, but he could not tell the strangely unhappy girl that part of his shock was in being astonished that English had ever felt anything so deeply that he would see death as the only answer. "I don't think I could ever commit suicide," he said.

"Why?"

"Bcause I had some reason to when I was a kid, and it never occurred to me. The worst thing that could happen to me now would be if you died. Then the rest of my life would be empty, but I'd live it. I might do things that would endanger my life. I might become a drinker and give up that way. But I'd go on, just as Mrs. English is going to go on. If English was in all that trouble, he couldn't *wait* to kill himself. He had to have relief, Natalie, and there was only one way in God's world to get it. I've heard of animals caught in a trap that chewed their own leg off to get free. Then of course they bled to death. But English wasn't an animal. He was a highly intelligent human being, and he used his intelligence to do the job thoroughly, once and for all."

"He wasn't a friend of yours, that's why you can talk about him so cold-bloodedly."

"I am not cold-blooded. But maybe I have more capacity to endure things than English had. But that's far from being cold-blooded. I'll tell you something that may also convince you that I *am* cold-blooded. I saw a man kill himself about a month ago."

"Where?"

"I was in a fellow's office on Broad Street, and I happened to be standing at the window, looking toward Broadway. It was about ten o'clock in the morning, and I saw a man, pretty high up in one of the Broadway buildings, climbing out on the ledge. He looked to his right and then to his left and then sort of leaned forward and looked down. Then he looked up at the sky and jumped. From where I was standing I could only see him falling about three stories and then one of the other buildings got in the way, cut off my view."

"What did you do that was cold-blooded?"

"I did exactly nothing. I never said a word to the fellow I was calling on. We went about our business and I went back to my office. Later I bought the noon editions and it was there. It was somebody I didn't know. And yet it's just possible that I was the very last person to see him alive. Not very likely, but possible. That was the only thing that connected me with the poor son of a bitch. Even if I wasn't the only one, I was one of the few to see the poor bastard jump off. I felt as though I were intruding on his privacy, but he obviously wasn't worried about privacy."

"Why is that cold-blooded?"

"Well, I thought you might think it was. Not saying anything to the man I was calling on. Not having any feelings about the man who jumped, except that I felt I shouldn't have been looking."

"Both those things are part of good manners."

"Well, I knew English, and liked him, but I'm not deeply affected by his death. Only by its effect on you."

"Then I guess I'll go home tomorrow. I was going to stay in New York, get a job, to be near you."

"I wouldn't let you. What would it be like, being in the same town all the time and not being able to see each other every day? This way at least we can blame the distance."

"I feel better now. I don't ask this often, but can you stay all night?"

"Yes. The market's in such an erratic condition that I stayed downtown all one night last week, quite innocently."

"Are you going broke?"

"No. I'm back about where I was a year ago. I did lose a hell of a pile, as you know, but I've been pretty lucky. I wish I could help your father. I hear things once in a while, and I often wish I could let him in on them."

"He has his salary, and he'll have his pension. When he was wiped out he said—"

"I remember. 'I'm still ahead of the game even if I'm not ahead of the stock market.' How's your mother?"

"She doesn't look well, but she hasn't for a long time. No better, and I guess no worse. How is your mother?"

"I think she's better than she's been in years, and she'll be sixty this year. She gave me hell, when we were all there at Christmas."

"What about?"

"Mary. She said, 'It's none of my business, but I think

you're neglecting Mary,' and I said, 'You're right, it's none of your business, so keep the hell out of it.' "

"Do you talk to her that way?"

"It's the only way I can talk to her. She says things to get a rise out of me, and when she does she's pleased with herself. It's that or cold politeness, and we tried that and balls to it. She still goes off on a tangent in the middle of a conversation, but most of the time she's pretty good. She asked me if I had a mistress and I told her everybody in Wall Street had a mistress, and some had two. I said I was working up to two and might make it this year."

"Over my dead body."

"She's really on Mary's side, you know."

"Because she had lovers herself."

"Of course. And now she's got me confused with my old man. I'm sure nobody's told her anything, but she has some hunch about Mary and she thinks Mary's like her, and I'm like my father. Well, maybe she's right."

"She *is* right. Don't you see that?"

"Well, maybe. I'm not like him, but there are certain parallels, except my father never had a Natalie."

"How do you know that?"

"I don't, but I'd stake my life on it. I think my father had whores."

"Do you ever want whores?"

"No. Listen, I'm the most faithful guy in New York City. Or anywhere. Can't you tell that?"

"Yes, but you still might want whores."

"What for?"

"Well, some of the things you've told me about, and I'm just me."

"Is there anything I can think of that you wouldn't do?"

"Not as long as it's just you and I."

"We've been sleeping together for three years and all you have to do is stand there in that doorway without any clothes on and I'm like a sex-starved schoolboy."

"Let's prove it."

"No, let's go over to Benito's and have some spaghetti first."

"That doesn't sound much like a sex-starved schoolboy."

"Did you ever see a schoolboy that wasn't hungry? Come on, the sooner we have our dinner the sooner we'll be back home to our true purpose in life."

"Which is?"

"If I say it, you'll say it, and if you say it I'll get rooty and we'll miss dinner and I'll get a headache, and tomorrow I'll lose $650,000,000 for poor old Mr. MacHardie."

"Well, balls to poor old Mr. MacHardie. I'll be ready in a minute."

"You are the most wonderful God damn dame that ever lived and don't you let them tell you different, hear? And I don't only say that because you have such a beautiful ass."

"Mm, I just revel in your pretty compliments."

"Think nothing of it, kid. I'll tell you something else, too, while I'm up."

"Some more dainty compliments?"

"No. I love you every minute of the day and night and I always will and I think I always have."

"I know," she said.

Benito's, a basement speakeasy less than a block from their apartment, was closed. Alfred stood at the door and rang the bell until the patrolman on post, whom Alfred recognized by sight but did not know by name, paused in his leisurely walk.

"Closed," he said to Alfred.

"Why? Did you raid it?"

"Oh, no. Death in the family," said the cop.

"Who died?"

"Nicolena's mother, over in Staten Island. They be closed till tomorrow. She was an old lady over eighty years of age."

"Sorry to hear it. Thanks," said Alfred.

"That's all right," said the cop, moving on.

Alfred looked at Natalie. "Now where?"

"You're asking me where? Heavens. I guess any of these places is a speakeasy."

"I'm sure of it, but they're not going to let us in just because we're customers of Benito's. I guess we'll have to go uptown."

"Why don't we just go to a regular restaurant? There's a Childs over on Fifth Avenue, and Lüchow's on Fourteenth Street."

"There's a place I always wanted to try. Cavanagh's. Steaks and chops."

"All right, let's go there. Where is it?"

"It's somewhere on Twenty-third. We'll get a taxi."

They were driven to Cavanagh's, which was crowded, but the captain had one table for them in the rear. He led them to it and they seated themselves. "I suppose it would be foolish to ask if we could have a drink."

"I don't know about that, but it'd be foolish to expect to get one."

"That's what I thought."

"Well, then you thought right. There's no more roast beef if it was roast beef you wanted." He took the two menus and crossed off the item. "There's a couple of nice steaks left."

"How did they stay nice in such disagreeable surroundings?" said Natalie.

"Lady, if you don't like the surroundings—"

He did not finish.

579

"Jerry, are you taking good care of these people? They're friends of mine. Only the best. Hello, Alfred."

"Oh, hello, Creighton," said Alfred, rising. "Miss Benziger, this is Mr. Duffy. Will you sit down. I can't offer you a drink."

"You can *now*," said the captain. "If you'da told me you were a friend of Mr. Duffy."

"I didn't want to tell you anything," said Alfred.

"All right. What will you have?" said the captain.

They ordered drinks, including a brandy for Duffy.

"What brings you to an Irish saloon? Next you'll be joining the New York A. C."

"Oh, I'd heard it was a good place for steaks and chops, and we happened to be in the neighborhood."

"Did you have trouble with Jerry? You mustn't mind him. Most of the people here are old customers, and they don't need any new ones. I used to come here with my father, as a kid."

"Is Jean with you?"

"No. I have dinner here once a week with some fellows. The same ones for almost fifteen years. Once a week except during the summer. And I saw you come in and I decided to come over and say hello."

"I'm glad you did."

"This man saved my son's life," said Duffy.

"How is he, by the way?"

"Well, you knew I have him in Buckley School. But you knew that."

"Yes. I'm going to send my boys there, too. Then where is he going?"

"Canterbury. His mother wants to send him to Groton, but I don't think they take Duffys at Groton, even if their grandfather does happen to be who he is."

"Well, what do you care whether he goes to Groton or not? Canterbury's a good school."

"I *don't*, but his mother does." He tossed off his brandy. "I better get back to my table. They're on politics and I can't afford to miss anything. Nice to have seen you, Miss Benziger. Goodnight, Alfred."

"Remember me to Jean."

"And me to Mary," said Duffy, and left.

Alfred reached under the table and squeezed Natalie's hand. "We are now public property," he said.

"I gather he's Mr. MacHardie's son-in-law."

"He wouldn't have missed this for the world. It's not going to do him any good. He knows that, but now he knows something about me that he didn't know before."

"I guess he'd never think we were just friends. No, not with those beady eyes."

"I would never attempt to lie to Duffy. I'd only make a fool of myself. Oh, he's a hell of a lawyer and he makes a lot of money, and *would* make a lot of money regardless of who his wife is."

"And he hates you."

"Really hates me, and he knows I know it. Well, why shouldn't he? I pulled his kid out of the water, and *he* should have. And I'm with MacHardie & Company and he isn't. And why? *Because* I pulled his kid out of the water. The worst thing about it is that he can't officially hate me. All his life he has to thank me. But it's nice to know that I have a girl friend. He wouldn't have missed that for anything."

"Most people don't get my name the first time they hear it. But he did."

"You bet he did. When he goes home tonight he'll look you up in the Social Register and the Locater and the phone book. I'll bet he even looks you up in the Port Johnson phone book tomorrow."

"Well, considering that he won't find me in any of those . . ."

"Right now I'm sure he's trying to figure out some way to find out who you are."

"Oh, why don't you go over and tell him?" she said, impatiently.

"What?"

"Well, if we're public property."

"Are you sore?"

"Yes, I am."

"This had to happen sometime."

"We were going to be found out, sure. But you talk about me as if I weren't even here. Girl friend. Public property. The two of you ignoring me as though I were on a chain, behind a veil. Well, I'm not on a chain."

He kept silent.

"And I'm not your mistress."

"No, you're not," he said. "And you're not on a chain. If you ever start feeling that you *are* on a chain . . ."

"What?"

"Break it."

"Is that what you'd do?"

"Yes. I wouldn't see you one minute beyond the time I want to see you. I've never felt that I was held by a chain. But if you do, you're wrong. There's only one thing that holds you to me, me to you. Make sure of that, Natalie. Maybe you're *not* sure of it."

"Maybe I'm not."

"Then there it is. Suddenly we're nothing."

"If that's the way you want it to be."

"The way *I* want it to be? You're the one that's not sure."

"You want to break the chain."

"Oh, now stop arguing like a woman. Even if we're going to have a fight at least observe the rules."

"What rules? Have you a set of rules for quarrels with your mistresses?"

"I have no rules, no mistresses. God damn it, you really don't fight fair. You've said six things that weren't true."

"What six things have I said that weren't true? Just name them."

"That I had a set of rules, that I had mistresses, that I wanted to break the chain. None true."

"That's three. You said six," she said. "I thought only women exaggerated."

"I didn't even say you exaggerated. I said stop arguing like a woman. You take everything I say and twist it out of all recognition."

"The trouble is you don't recognize what you say when it's repeated to you."

"Not by the time you get finished with it. Listen, if you don't love me, say so, but for God's sake stop this God damn—" He made a sweeping hand gesture and knocked a stem glass to the floor. The water spilled on her lap. The table waiter and the captain came and began mopping up, and the people at the nearby tables stared at Alfred and Natalie.

"Change the tablecloth," said the captain, Jerry.

"Hold your horses, I will, I will, I will. Did the little lady get all soaked?"

"I'm all right, thanks," said Natalie.

"Stand up a minute, you wouldn't want to be sitting in a puddle of water," said the waiter.

"How did it happen?" said Jerry.

"How do you think it happened? It jumped up and bit me," said Alfred.

"That's what I thought," said Jerry. "I accidentally give you one of our jumping glasses."

"But not one of the biters," said the waiter. "The biters are real dangerous. There now, little lady, you're all dry and you can sit comfortable."

"Be getting her another glass of water."

"It wasn't hers, it was his."

"All right, give him hers and get a fresh one for her."

"First give me a chance to pick up the broken glass," said the waiter.

"What are you, worried that somebody'd come around in their bare feet?" said Jerry.

"Some around here hasn't been wearing shoes too long."

"And there's some won't be wearing their waiter's uniform if I hear any more of their lip."

"Now, now, now, there, Jerry. Don't be threatening."

The waiter and the captain had become the principal figures in the scene, even to the real principals, who were momentarily silenced by the exchange between Jerry and the waiter. When they were alone again Alfred said: "I'm sorry I spilled the water on you."

"I had it coming to me," she said.

"Are we at peace?"

"Yes, and I'm damn uncomfortable."

"We almost had our first real knock-down and drag-out."

"We had the knock-down. We didn't have the drag-out."

"Oh, the glass. Yes." He reached over and touched her hand. "But we came too close. We said things we shouldn't say."

"Don't you know that we're going to say worse things? That we're going to come much closer? When we *could* walk out on each other we never even thought about it. But now that we can't bear to be without each other—you see what I mean?"

"I see what you mean, but why should that be so?"

"Because I'm a woman."

"And you don't like the way we have to live?"

"Do you like it? No. Do you like it for me? No."

"Will you marry me?"

"If we're still in love after you get what you want. I would certainly not marry you and risk your not getting that. If I married you and you lost out on your partnership you'd hate me."

He said nothing.

"Let's have some dinner," she said. "And let's not try to settle everything tonight. We've always had these problems, and we're going to go on having them."

They ordered their food and ate in silence, but they had often had meals without much conversation and it was not until they were having their coffee that he realized that on this occasion there was a reason for her silence. "That Duffy man—he'd never have any reason to know my father, would he?"

"Almost none, that I can think of. It's not impossible."

"I wish it were impossible. A man who looks at you like that and sees everything, another thing he does is tell everything. He could look at my father in a way that would tell my father that this man knows something. Those beady eyes look right through you, but you can also look right through them. He knew immediately that I'm sleeping with you, but *I* knew that he *knew* it. Ugh. I don't like that man. He's so clean, and so dirty. I didn't even like the way he spoke my name."

IN THE CITY OF NEW YORK in the month of November in the year 1929 there were 119 persons who committed suicide. That was only six more persons than had committed suicide in January of that year, and the total for the year was 1,313. But in the year 1932 the total number of suicides was 1,609, the greatest number in the City's history, and the high point of a steady climb.

In 1930 there were 1,471 suicides.

In 1931 there were 1,582 suicides.

In 1932 there were 1,609 suicides.

In 1933 there were 1,378 suicides.

In 1934 there were 1,236 suicides.

The annual rate for the City corresponded almost exactly to the annual rate for the nation.

In the country as a whole there were only sixty-seven more business failures in 1929 than there had been in 1928, when there had been 23,842.

But in 1930 there were 26,355 business failures.

In 1931 there were 28,285 business failures.

In 1932 there were 31,822 business failures.

In 1933 there were 20,307 business failures.

In 1934 there were 12,185 business failures.

And in 1932 at the age of thirty-five, Alfred Eaton became a partner in MacHardie & Company, the youngest in age and in the service of the firm in its history. There was no formal announcement of his elevation; that would be done with the simple listing of his name among the partners in the firm's statement in the advertising columns of the financial pages of the *Times,* the *Herald Tribune,* and the *Sun.* But the occasion did not pass unnoticed, in spite of the fact that it was so unsurprising that not a few men in the financial district remarked that they thought he had been elected a year or two earlier. For the first few days at his new desk his telephone was busy with congratulatory messages, and in the first few weeks he was invited to fill out a questionnaire for *Who's Who in America* (which he ignored), to sit on the board of a hospital (which he declined), to chair the annual giving of his class at Princeton (which he declined), to become a trustee of his sons' school (which he accepted), to visit a vineyard in France so that he could begin to stock a cellar in anticipation of Repeal (which he ignored), to join The Pilgrims and the English Speaking Union (which he politely declined), to call on the man from Peal's at the Murray Hill Hotel (which he

584

did), to inspect some extremely desirable shore-front properties in Connecticut, Rhode Island, Massachusetts and Maine (which he ignored), to join the Aeademy of Political Science (which he declined), and to contribute to fifty-five alert organizations which never had solicited him before. The *Alumni Weekly* printed the news in Alfred's class notes: "No announcement so far but we have it on the best authority that *Alf Eaton* has been made a partner in MacHardie & Co. Well, that's the one bright spot in the Wall St. news. Congratulations, Alf." No one had ever called him Alf, and the man who wrote the item was no more than a name to him, but it produced a quantity of mail that cast doubt on Princeton's reputation as a rich man's college. He lent one man $1,000, five men $500 each, and two men $100 apiece. He sent a cheque for $300 to Mr. Deland, his old schoolmaster at Knox, who was living with a sister in Lancaster, Pennsylvania, and tutoring a few students at Franklin & Marshall College. Another cheque went to Charlie Fentriss, his classmate at Knox, who needed $250 for his son's tonsillectomy. He replied to all the personal requests but one: Carter Lanchester's. Somehow Lanchester over the years had managed to convince himself that Alfred would remember the most frightening night of his life as a college-boys' prank. He was not sure that he would not have helped Lanchester if he had *heard* Lanchester was in trouble, but the letter from Lanchester was so crawling and yet so arrogant that he wrote several bitter replies, tore them up, and closed all books on Lanchester.

He had one caller at the office.

The engraved card read: *Mr. Devrow Budd.* Written in ink was the message: "Could I have a moment with you while I am in the neighborhood? D. B."

"Send him in, please," said Alfred.

"Well, sir, he's not in the best of shape, I think I ought to tell you that beforehand," said the guard.

"It's okay, thanks. I know him."

Devrow Budd appeared in the partners' room, smilingly at his ease and approving of all that he saw. He had a black topcoat folded over one arm and in the other hand he carried both walking stick and Lock bowler. He wore a blue double-breasted suit and a starched collar and black-and-white small-figured tie. Very adeptly he shifted his hat and stick to shake hands with Alfred. "Alfred, this is good of you to spare me a moment." He sat down and placed his hat and coat on his lap and put both hands on the crook of his stick. He looked to right and left. "They've kept everything as it used to be. I'm glad to see that. In a changing world, you know. And even to see your face in these surroundings, that's a link with the past, too, if you see what I'm driving at. Look at old

585

Percy Hasbrouck over there. He wouldn't remember me, I'm afraid, but I used to know Percy in years gone by."

"Don't you want to say hello to him?"

"No, no, no thanks, Alfred. It must be twenty years since I've sat down to a bird and a bottle with Percy. Both of us lost touch. One does. One does. I, uh, read about you, the usual circumspect little line in the *Journal,* and I meant to drop you a line, but I decided since I was coming down this way . . . That was over a month ago. I haven't been, uh, I've been living at a small hotel, Alfred, but I go to the Public Library every day. I've been thinking about writing a book, you know. Sort of my memoirs. I've known them all, you know. Kings. Prime ministers. Four dukes. Cabinet ministers. And of course the lighter side, from Maxine Elliott to Max Beerbohm, right down to the newer people. Noel Coward. Bea Lillie. Charming Gertie Lawrence. I go to the Library most every day. Trouble was I never kept a diary and I'm a bit rusty on dates, but several publishers are interested and they've promised me quite a respectable advance royalty as soon as I've whipped my notes into shape. Rather give it to Scribner's than some of these new johnnies, but Nelson Doubleday's a gentleman, too. Well, it'll go to the highest bidder."

"Well, I'm glad to hear it. You certainly have a lot of memories to draw on, haven't you?"

"Yes. Yes, I have." He stopped speaking, and while waiting for him to go on Alfred saw the inverted cuffs held together by the kind of safety pin that came in the back of neckties, which meant that the last of Budd's cuff links were in hock; the cracked uppers of his shoes; the nap gone from the fabric of the suit; the absence of rings on his fingers where he formerly had worn two; the hole in the heel of his cotton sock; the large eruption on his right temple; the gaps where teeth had been.

"Could I have a glass of water, please?" said Budd.

Alfred poured him a drink from the carafe and Budd sipped it but not without dribbling some on his chin. "I thought the walk would do me good, but I must be out of shape."

"You walked all the way downtown?"

"But I used to play thirty-six holes before tea. Do you suppose there's a glass of milk to be had? There used to be a kitchen somewhere in this office. If I could have a glass of milk with an egg in it."

"Mr. Budd, did you have any breakfast?"

"I never take—no, I didn't. What's the use of pretending to a boy I've known so long?"

"Did you have any dinner last night?"

"Oh, yes. Vegetable soup and bread."

586

"Did you walk down because you didn't have subway fare?"

"Must you ask me these questions, Alfred? I have the fare, but if I spent it I'd have to do without my vegetable soup tomorrow night."

"As bad as that, Mr. Budd? What do you live on?"

"I have ten dollars a week. Six dollars for my room, and the rest goes for luxuries. Cheap joke, isn't it?"

"Where does the ten dollars a week come from?"

"I'm a bond-holder, Alfred. A bloated bond-holder. I have an income of about $600 a year. I'm sixty-eight, you know, and that's all I've been able to hold on to. At sixty-eight I'm often tempted to sell one of my bonds and live decently for a month, but I'm afraid of the consequences. I can barely subsist on what I have now, and we Budds are a long-lived family."

"I gather that Mrs. Budd is not alive."

"Oh, she passed on eight or nine years ago."

"Forgive me. Let's go have some lunch."

"Could we go to the Down Town? The D. T. A.? I imagine you're a member."

"Would you like that?"

"I'd like that very much."

"Then that's where we'll go."

"But don't let me get carried away by the menu. An oyster stew."

They walked slowly to Pine Street, but once inside the clubhouse Budd responded to the atmosphere. He recognized some men he had known and his spirit and dignity came back as he ate the soup.

"What sort of a place do you live in?" said Alfred.

"It's not so bad, really. I have a tiny room with running water, hot and cold. I share a bath with five or six other men but I have my bath in the morning and if the truth be told, some of my fellow-inmates use the tub hardly at all. Six dollars a week. No women, but that isn't the hardship to me it would have been in days gone by."

"Where is Jack?"

"My son Jack? I haven't the faintest idea. He must be forty. No. He's thirty-nine, al*most* forty. I haven't heard a word from Jack since before his mother passed on. I sent him three thousand dollars in care of a bank in Hong Kong, China. He never even wrote and thanked me. He was in Paris right after the war, and I gather he got into some trouble with the Polish army. Money. He persuaded them to let him have some *cash*, to buy aeroplanes for the Kosciusko Squadron. Wouldn't you think they'd know better?"

"I'd have thought so. Europeans."

"Ah, but there's something international about a really clever crook. And Jack had that American look that's very disarming. We all look like Boy Scouts—or scoutmasters—and the Europeans aren't as suspicious of us as they are of each other. I didn't want to see my only son killed, so I prevailed upon a general I knew to have Jack spend the war at G. H. Q., and I feel sure he made himself indispensable to all the generals when they wanted to relax in Paris. He wasn't in Tours very much of the time. Always had some liaison work in Paris. What kind of liaison, I didn't inquire."

"Well, the generals need their relaxation, too."

"I wouldn't question that for a minute. What's the use of being a general?"

"What did you have in mind when you came downtown?"

"Your generosity, Alfred. If I only had a little money besides my six hundred a year. I don't need much more than I have. My appetite isn't what it used to be and I haven't got the teeth to chew a thick steak. But this is all I've got to wear, my only suit, my last pair of shoes. I haven't even got a pair of cuff links left, and sometimes I'd almost give up my vegetable soup for a good cigar. If I had fifty cents a day more than I have, I'd have coffee and doughnuts for breakfast, ten cents. I could have something in my belly at lunch, that makes thirty. I could have some cigarettes and once in a while a cigar. That would come to about $14 a month, call it fifteen. I'd like to get a decent ready-made suit and a pair of ready-made shoes, and I need some linen. I have it all written down here if you'd like to see it. Sixty-three dollars for a suit, $15 for a pair of shoes, $9 for half a dozen pairs of socks, $12 for some underwear, $7 for a soft hat. That comes to $106, plus $180 for my extra food and comforts, is $286. That's so close to $300 that I call it $300. Next year I wouldn't need that much. I'd save on the clothes. But what I would like to ask you, Alfred. Could you give me three hundred a year for the next, say, five years? It would have to be a gift, because I never can pay you back, but if I were sure I had that much, could count on it, I'd have really all that I need for the rest of my life. I don't think I'll last more than five years. As a matter of fact I *could* repay you. I could make a will leaving you my capital. I never thought of that till now, I've been so careful not to touch my capital that I almost forgot that it is capital. I have about $15,000 in good bonds. I'll make a will leaving it all to you."

"In that case my so-called generosity doesn't enter into it, Mr. Budd. Why don't you borrow $15,000 from me, interest free."

"I could do that, couldn't I? And leave you my bonds. Would you do that, Alfred?"

"Sure I would."

"With that money I could live at a club. Three thousand a year. But what if I go on living?"

"Save some. Don't spend the whole three thousand. Spend two and save one. You'll still be living well on your own money, and you'd rather do that than take money from me, wouldn't you?"

"I'm taking six hundred a year interest from you."

"Let's pretend that doesn't exist."

The old man's eyes sparkled. "Could I have the money soon?"

"You can have it today. I'll open an account for you. You'll be able to write a cheque this afternoon."

"I don't think I'll live in a club. I think I'll live in one of those Allerton Houses. But I'll rejoin one of my old clubs so I can go there every day. That'll be nice, to live in one place and have another place to go to every day. I hate the Public Library. They aren't my sort of people. I used to belong to three or four clubs here, and I shouldn't have much trouble getting back in. Oh, Alfred, you don't know what you've done for me. I came down here to ask for pennies and now I feel like a prince. I'm going to take a taxi, when I go back uptown. I know why you're doing this for me."

"I'm not doing very much."

"Norma always used to bring you little presents from England. Poor Norma. Kindness itself, and look what happened to her. It seems so many years ago, doesn't it?"

"Yes, it does. And it was. It was seventeen years ago, Mr. Budd."

"Twenty-five years old. I wasn't thinking of Norma when I came down to see you, but now of course that's why you're helping me."

"I'd have done anything for Norma, Mr. Budd."

"I wish you'd been born a few years earlier. I think there was real love there, Alfred, even if she was older than you. That happens, you know. Something like it happened to me, when I was a young fellow in Baltimore. The lady is still alive, nearly eighty years old, and I'm sure she hasn't thought of me in years, but the fact is she was the first woman I ever went to bed with. Now here I am, an old fart of sixty-eight, with nothing to be proud of in all those years. And I guess she's a great-grandmother, husband dead these many years. I wonder what she'd say if I went and called on her. I wonder if she ever gave me a thought. But she was a real woman. For one whole summer I used to sneak up the kitchen stairs to her room, every night her husband was away. Then I went back to school and she'd never give me a second look. I guess she got somebody else, but there was never any scandal. I didn't love her. I've only been in love once in my life, and I regret to say that came quite late in life. In other words, I'm afraid it wasn't Norma's mother. But this woman in Baltimore, now close to eighty years old—oh, hell. You young fellows today, I don't know what you think, and you don't care what we think. I know that I once thought of shooting myself, but it never entered my mind to shoot the woman I was in love with. Would it yours?"

"Neither. I'd never shoot myself and I'd certainly never shoot the woman I love."

The old man looked at him steadily for a moment. "I could ask you a question, but I won't. Instead of that I'll give you the benefit of my experience. No, I can't even do that. I won't interfere in your life after the botch I made of my own."

The old man was being too tactful to suggest that Alfred was not in love with his wife, and Alfred respected his tact and avoided confidences. Their conversation turned to the men and women they had known in Port Johnson, a common ground of reminiscence and a skillful reminder to Alfred that they went back a long time together.

"I'm so tempted to ask you to buy me a cigar, but I'm afraid that in my present condition I might disgrace you. A cigar should follow a heavy meal, and my old belly's got out of the habit. Oh, but do you remember how I used to eat? A real trencherman, Lord Sevringham used to call me. You never hear an American use that word, but that's what Sevringham called me. Sevringham by the way was a friend of your senior partner, James D. MacHardie. I don't suppose you've ever met him."

"As a matter of fact, yes. Once, at dinner, and then several times at the office."

"Did you meet Lady Sevringham?"

"Yes, I did. I sat next to her at dinner."

"Well, you must have enjoyed that. She has a very keen mind."

"She was very interesting and very charming. I liked her enormously."

"Yes. Yes. I knew them both quite well, you know. Very dear friends of mine. He turned down Chancellor of the Exchequer, you know."

"No, I didn't know."

"Well, he did. He had public reasons, of course, but the real reason was that he knew it would mean neglecting her. That's the real reason. Seems odd, doesn't it, that a man who's just been dickering for an extra fifty cents a day could know these things about the great and famous, but I *did* know the Sevringhams. Upon my word, I knew them all. And I didn't have to kiss any English arses. I haven't got a timepiece on me, Alfred, but isn't it getting late for you?"

"Well, we ought to go back and arrange for your account. It can all be done in less than an hour, if you wouldn't mind waiting in the reception room."

They walked back to the office, pausing once when the old man lost his balance by misjudging the tap of his cane on the sidewalk. "A stick wasn't meant to be worn in these crowds," he said.

Alfred put him in the reception room, a small room containing a pair of vis-à-vis writing desks, six straight-back chairs, a sofa, a crystal vase with a dozen mixed red and white carnations, and a screen in front of a lavatory door. As a further concession to femininity there were two copies of *Vanity Fair* and four of *The New Yorker,* and scattered about were six identical imitation jade ash-trays.

"It shouldn't take me more than half an hour," said Alfred. "That's a lavatory, if you feel the need."

"I'll be quite comfortable, Alfred, thank you," said the old man.

Alfred, back at his own desk, sent for a young man in the legal department and explained what he wanted done. He then had the assistant treasurer prepare the cheque and other papers for the old man's account, and while waiting for the men to complete their assignments he returned the telephone calls that had come in during his absence. He was on the telephone when the guard appeared at his desk, and he knew from the guard's distressed expression that Devrow Budd's account would never be active. He finished with his conversation and hung up the receiver.

"I'm sorry, Mr. Eaton, but the elderly gentleman, he looks to me as if he passed away."

Alfred got up. "Have you sent for the doctor?"

"We have, and the ambulance from Beekman Street, but our nurse says it's all over."

Alfred and the guard proceeded to the reception room, and the MacHardie physician was getting up off his knees and removing his stethoscope.

"No signs?" said Alfred.

"None. Who was he?"

"A friend of mine," said Alfred. "Heart attack?"

"Yes. He went like that," said the doctor, snapping his fingers. "A friend of yours, Mr. Eaton?"

"Yes. Why do you say it that way?"

"But you hadn't seen him for a long time," said the doctor.

"No, why?"

"I didn't think so. This poor old fellow hasn't been eating

too well. Frankly, I don't see how he had the strength to cross the street."

"You can tell that?"

"So can you," said the doctor. He reached down and pulled up the old man's trouser leg. "Take a look." He raised the old man's coat sleeve.

"Good God," said Alfred.

"At his age you can't afford to go that hungry. I don't know if it's any consolation to you, Mr. Eaton, but I doubt very much if he'd have gotten well even if you put him in a hospital."

"Do you know what he did today, on those poor old legs? He *walked* from *Forty-third* Street."

"Not on those legs, Mr. Eaton. On the human spirit. I still say he couldn't walk across the street on those legs."

"You're right, Doctor."

"You have all the data I'll need for the death certificate?"

"Yes, and I'm going to see that he gets a nice obituary."

The nice obituaries were as nice as they could be, but they did not fail to mention in the leads that Mr. Budd was the father of Norma Budd, who was shot to death in a suicide pact that shocked society in 1915. "Surviving," said the newspapers, "is his son John Budd, of Hong Kong, China."

With good help from Harry Van Peltz, Alfred saw to it that the old families of Port Johnson rallied 'round for the funeral, and Devrow Budd was buried in the plot with his wife. At the farm, after the funeral, Alfred said to his mother: "I never even knew that Mrs. Budd had died. Did you go to her funeral?"

"There was no funeral," said Martha Eaton. "She died all alone in a hotel in New York, and Devrow shipped her body back here. But he didn't come."

"He didn't? Why?"

"She didn't want him. She left detailed instructions with her lawyer. No funeral, no ceremony, nobody even the family to see her buried. I suppose it was her way of telling him what she thought of him. Of course she left him what money she had, and I guess that was part of telling him what she thought of him."

"But I can't understand why *you* never told *me*."

"I don't know. Maybe I was having one of my spells."

"Did the girls know? Sally and Constance?"

"I don't suppose they did, at the time."

"All right, Mother. *Why* didn't you tell me?"

"Because I didn't want to, that's why. If Marian Siddenham, Mrs. Budd, didn't want a fuss, that was the way she wanted it. You would have made some kind of a fuss, on account of Norma."

592

"To the extent of sending flowers, that's all."

"That wouldn't have been all, and anyway she didn't want flowers. Marian wanted to slip out of this life unnoticed, and maybe find some peace elsewhere, if she believed in that. Well, now they're all off your conscience, Alfred."

"What a lousy thing to say," said Alfred.

"Yes, isn't it? But I couldn't resist saying it."

"No. And you *tried* so hard."

"I tried *so* hard, and it just forced itself out." She smiled at him. "I'm a dreadful woman."

He laughed. "No, Mother. You're a card."

She, too, laughed. "All right, I'm a card," she said. "Are we going to be favored by your presence tonight?"

"I'm afraid not, Mother-of-mine. I'm spending the night in Philadelphia."

"All those offices keep open all night, I hear."

"Oh, not all of them. Some of them haven't even been open in the daytime lately. But you're all right, aren't you?"

"Yes, I don't see how you do it, when everybody else is losing all their money."

"Oh, you've lost some. Don't think you haven't. But not as much as some people."

"Well, you go right on taking good care of what I have, because you know where it's going when I die."

"Why don't you change your will and cut me out? I mean it. Leave it to Sal and Constance."

"Because it's easier to do what your grandfather and your father did. You and the girls get the principal that your father and your grandfather left. And whatever I have of my own, there won't be much income from it but the principal might come in handy for your children and Sally's children. I've thought it all out, it's settled, and please don't make me spend any more time with lawyers. I just keep bobbing my head, yes, yes, yes, and don't understand a word they say. Do you?"

"Of course I do."

"You never studied law."

"Yes I did. You see, you didn't know that."

"When did you study law?"

"I took night courses at the Fordham Law School when I first went to work for Mr. MacHardie. I didn't take the bar examinations, but I took courses for two years."

"I don't even know where Fordham is."

"It has a beautiful, vine-covered campus in the Woolworth Building."

"You're talking nonsense."

"Partly. But I did take some law courses."

"How noble of you."

"I had no choice in the matter."

"How is Mary?"

"Mary is fine. Sent you her love."

"Not very warming, the way you say it."

"Well, what do you want me to do? Play a balcony scene? Opera? I could sing it for you, if you'd like. The boys also sent their love."

"Thank you."

"Is there anything you want?"

"No, I guess not. Not anything that could be bought, and that's what you meant, isn't it?"

"That's what I meant, but you don't have to limit me to that. What else is there?"

"You could find a man for Constance."

"Oh, no you don't."

"Well, that's the only thing I want."

"Have you any friends that need help?"

"If they do, they don't tell me. It's years since anyone asked me for anything. I give when I know, but they don't ask me. When people stop asking you for things you can consider yourself retired. Dead might be a better word for it."

"Well, by that line of reasoning I'm very much alive, at the moment."

"How nice. And you're generous? Yes, you'd be generous."

"Why would you doubt that? You've always been generous, and so was the old man. So I come by it honestly."

"And not forgetting your Grandfather Johnson. Well, you're off to Philadelphia and so endeth another of your quick visits. Give my love to Mary and the boys, and tell Mary that any time she wants to go away on a trip, she can always bring the boys here. They don't always have to go to Wilmington. City children love the country and this is still country. If they'd come oftener, I'd buy a pony, but I won't attempt to bribe them with it. Give your old mother a peck on the cheek and be on your way."

He laughed and kissed her on the cheek.

"Just be careful," she said. "Mary will take only just so much, you know."

"You and Mary should be great friends."

He signed in for his room at the Racquet Club and spent the night with Natalie at the Ritz-Carlton. (After the death of Julian English his wife Caroline had lived for a while in New York, thus making communication between Natalie and Alfred more difficult, but Caroline was back in Gibbsville, and able to transmit messages to Natalie.) They had an early breakfast in Natalie's room to enable Alfred to catch the New York train.

"I always mean to buy you a razor, but I always forget."

"I can shave on the train," he said.

"Why is it your beard shows more than a dark-haired man's? I guess it's the light."

"I guess so."

"I know you're miles away, but I have to bring up a painful subject."

"What?"

"Finances."

"Do you need money?"

"Not exactly. But my father has cut my allowance in exactly half. I'm going to have to renege on my share of Thirteenth Street."

"That's not reneging. I always wanted to pay that."

"But I always wanted to pay half. It was more fun that way. But I can't go on paying it, I'm sorry."

"I'm not. I want to pay it, it isn't much."

"It's a lot for me, now. I borrowed money from Caroline to come here. I borrowed fifty dollars from her, because I have about eight dollars in my checking account."

"God damn it, Natalie, why do you let youself get so low? You could have come to me. That's what I'm for."

"Oh, no it isn't. I always paid my share of our expenses. Not really. But I paid half of Thirteenth Street, and all my travel expenses when I wasn't traveling with you. Now I just can't do it any more, because I haven't got the money. Strange how I sound like a middle-class housewife, whining over money."

"Ride over to New York with me and we can talk about it on the train," he said. Then: "No, better not. I'm sure to run into some Philadelphia guys."

"Then you'll have to miss your train because the time has come, the time has come."

"Why couldn't we have talked about all this last night?"

"Because you were in no mood to."

"All right."

"I'm taking a job."

"You are? Where?"

"I have my choice of a job in the Court House, in Gibbsville. It's a political job. Or, I can have a job in Mountain City, as clerk in the company store. The Mountain City job pays better, but the county job will let me have more time off. I know my father doesn't want me to take the job in the company store, because it ought to go to someone else who really needs the money, but I can have it if I want it. But the political job he doesn't mind so much. He's contributed enough over the years, and he's never asked for that kind of a favor."

"What would it be?"

"The simplest kind of clerical work. Copying names out of one book into another, in the office of the Clerk of the Courts.

It pays eleven hundred a year, with a month's vacation and ten days' sick leave. Hours, nine to four, one hour off for lunch. I've just about decided to take it. I can go on seeing you as much as I do now, except that I wouldn't be able to take time off in the middle of the week, and I'd always have to let them know when I wasn't coming in."

"You'd have your commuting expenses, lunches, probably a political assessment of ten percent."

"I know. It won't be eleven hundred clear, but I think I'll take it anyway. It'll be something to do, and I need that."

"Now we're getting to the point."

"Yes. I'm getting closer to thirty and I've never had a real job. I didn't go to college or even secretarial school, and nobody knows when this depression is going to end. I ought to be able to earn my own living, but I have nothing to offer. If I take the county job I'm going to business college and learn shorthand and typewriting. An hour a day after work."

"I can't help feeling that you've been doing a lot of thinking behind my back."

"Well, I have, obviously."

"And even getting ready to give me the air."

"No, but getting ready for the time when you might have to give it to me."

"That, I keep telling you, will never happen."

"What if you were wiped out in the stock market?"

He smiled. "Then you and I could get married the next day, or as soon as I got a divorce. But that isn't likely to happen. This is a depression, not a collapse. Do you hear that elevator? Do you hear those automobile horns? When there's a collapse you won't hear them. Some men are making money now, and I'm one of them. I'm only making back what I lost, but I am making some. I'm not worried about money, but now I am worried about you and me. A minute ago you said you were talking like a housewife. Now you're talking like a woman who expects to be a widow."

"All right, if you put it that way."

"You won't marry me."

"You couldn't take the children away from Mary, she's bringing them up as they should be. And I wouldn't marry you and take you away from them. That wouldn't last."

"Of course I could get you a job in New York, but I know your answer to that. Your mother."

"And even if something happened to Mother—"

"You wouldn't leave your father."

"There's only one way I can leave him, that would please him."

"To get married?"

"Yes. So you see, I might as well take a job and take some

courses so I might be able to get a better job. I can't think of anybody who'd like to hire the second or third best lady golfer in the Lantenengo Country Club. Or the fourth or fifth best bridge player."

"I can think of several model agencies that would hire the most beautiful girl I've ever known."

"You're not as critical as they'd be. Thank you, though. Especially at breakfast."

"The most beautiful shape."

"I love hearing these things, but I couldn't be a model. They want younger faces, and I'd never show them my shape. I keep that for you. I'm a little vain about my shape, but the real pleasure is the pleasure it gives you, still, after all this time and all those times. I still have a long way to go to sleep with you oftener than anyone else has."

"I shall do my utmost to see that you achieve that laudable ambition. But I need help from you, and the way you've been talking this morning—Christ, I had a feeling we were through as of today."

"As far as wanting you is concerned, we'll never be through. But it's a fact that seeing you is going to be more complicated."

"Natalie, what if some nice, eligible guy asked you to marry him?"

She examined the Ritz-Carlton's grapefruit spoon. "A year ago I wouldn't have taken two seconds in answering you. Today, I have to say I don't know."

"At that rate, if a nice, eligible guy asks you a year from now, you'll probably say yes."

"If the nice, eligible guy lived some place where I'd never see you, and if he'd marry me with the understanding that I'm committed to loving you . . ."

"You could sleep with him?"

"Yes, I could sleep with him. If I didn't see you for a long time, a very long time, I'd sleep with a man just for the physical part. You know what I am, what I'm like. I couldn't turn that off now. No more than you could."

"Never mind me."

"Well, then never mind me, either. I learned about myself through you. No, I learned to feel with you, and to have that need. But now I have it so strongly that—yes, I'd sleep with a man just for sex. Not just any man."

"No. A nice guy. And you'd probably fall in love with him."

"Well, if I did, that would solve all my problems."

"You're telling me an awful lot without meaning to."

"I realize that. Everything I say is more than I mean to say. What would you call it?"

"Discontent."

She nodded. "And uncertainty. A woman who isn't married at thirty—and that's not so far away for me—she's on the shelf. And if she's not hopelessly unattractive, men wonder about her and while they may want to sleep with her, they're cagey about wanting to marry her. If she's a widow, or divorced, it's different. But if she's never been married—oh, hell."

"I'd like to end this conversation, Natalie. Not because I want to catch my train. I've missed that. But we seem to go from discouragement to discouragement. We're very close to saying very final things."

"Yes."

"We may have lost something already."

"The trouble is we've never really had the chance to live together. The week on Mr. Thornton's boat was the most we ever had, and the week in Chicago, and that was such heaven that it wasn't real. All the other times have been so short. Two or three days."

"What is this leading to?"

"Nowhere, I guess. I happened to think of it and I said it."

"I'll tell you what it is. It's further evidence of your discontent. Are you trying to break it off?"

"No. But I knew when I came to Philadelphia that this was going to be the last time I'd be able to come at a moment's notice. Dinner together, sleep together, and off you go in the morning, to your orderly life. While I go back to Mountain City and wait for the next time you can see me."

"The more you say, the plainer my duty becomes. My duty to you. What I owe to you. Your great common sense is telling you that it's time you made a new start. Why don't you say it, Natalie?"

"Because if I do, the minute you leave this room I'll feel that my life is over."

"Although your great common sense will tell you that it isn't."

"Are you trying to force me to say it's over?"

"I guess maybe I am."

"All right, then. I'll say it."

He had not expected the effect her words would have on him. It was like a blow in the stomach, literally so, and he fell back from it. There was physical pain as well as the clarity of his look into a future without her. And she understood both reactions and began to weep. He made no attempt to console her. She sat with her hands covering her face and weeping freely as he had never seen her do before, and he in his turn realized that her weeping was not only for them and their love, but a final ending to the lonely, worrisome nights in Mountain City.

He rose and put his hand on her shoulder. "I love you. I'll always love you."

She took his hand and kissed it, and nodded. It was a moment of rare understanding, both of them seeing their life and its hopelessness without an effort on the part of either of them to take the other's mind off the omnipresent and inevitable facts. She was young in her weeping, never having learned to shed womanly tears. She was as young now as the first night he had seen her, and the happiness they had had had left her unprepared for the misery of this moment.

"Natalie, my love, I love you so." He drew his hand out of her grasp, and he left her with her hands still covering her unforgettable face.

On the train he was unable to reconstruct precisely the sentences and speeches, reversing and proceeding, that had led up to her final, actually unstated conclusion. "All right, then. I'll say it," she had said, but what she said was all in implication and never in spoken words. What was it they had said? She had said: "Are you trying to make me say it's over?" That was almost it. And he had answered: "Yes, I guess I am." And she had said: "All right, then. I'll say it."

He looked out at the New Jersey countryside, ready through habit for the first of the several glimpses of the towering heights of the Princeton graduate school. He had not been back there many times, and today Princeton was no more to him than a stony symbol of the youth he would never feel again. He wanted to hurry past Princeton and what it symbolized, and he was pleased that the train did not stop at the junction. He wanted to hurry back to the world of things and men, away from the life of the emotions and women; to a world where he was winning, away from a life in which he had always lost.

Not immediately, but in a few days, Mary commented on a difference in him. He came home one evening and made himself a highball and was sipping it while reading the newspaper. "This is the night we're going out with the Colliers," she said.

"Oh, Christ. That thing at the Waldorf?"

"We can get out of it," said Mary.

"Not at the last minute. I'm sorry. I forgot all about it."

"I reminded you at breakfast."

"I know you did. It's my fault. White tie, too, isn't it?"

"Yes, but I can think up an excuse."

"God knows I'd like to pass it up, but we've turned down how many invitations of theirs? And they don't mean any harm."

"This would be the third."

"I'll finish my drink and get changed."

"You'd even have time for a nap. This is going to be a late party, you know. We won't sit down to dinner before nine-thirty, if then. Finish your drink and I'll wake you at nine."

"All right. I'll do that."

"Have you anything you want to unload? At least I can listen."

"No, but thanks."

"Oh, well if it's *that* kind of trouble."

"*That* kind of trouble?"

"You'll usually talk if it's business, even when you know I don't understand half of it. But whatever it is that's eating you, Alfred, you ought to talk to somebody about it and get it out of your system. When is Lex getting back?"

"He's not getting back."

"Well, that's too bad. Then I suggest that you take a few weeks off. Frankly, you look like hell, and you don't seem to be getting enough sleep."

"How would you know that?"

"I see you at breakfast, don't I? The last few days I've wanted to tell you to go back to bed, but I know that'd be no use."

"No."

"I don't know anything about your girl, or your girls, if it's more than one, although my guess is that right now it's only one. But I just hope she understood that we weren't getting a divorce, and if she did, then she has no right to complain. If she didn't know, if you let her think we might get a divorce, then I have no sympathy for you. But knowing women, she probably kept hoping you'd ask me for a divorce and now she's making it tough for you because you won't. I'll go through with a divorce, but not before Alex is ready to go to college, and there aren't many women who'll wait that long."

"All of a sudden you seem to be the one that's making all the decisions about a divorce."

"No, but obviously you're not as innocent as you were a few years back. You haven't turned into a fairy, so obviously you must have had some women."

"Very shrewd deduction, but still nothing proved."

"Would I really have so much trouble if I started out to get proof?"

"I think you'd have a hell of a lot of trouble."

"No. And this is a piece of information that came my way without my looking for it. Didn't you spend a week on Mr. Thornton's boat last summer?"

"That's news to me."

"News, but you don't deny it. It's just news that I know

600

you did, Alfred. Don't quibble. You did. The *Thor* is too easily recognized. You should have chartered something smaller and not as well known. My volunteer spy spotted you through the binoculars, couldn't pick out any Thorntons or Porters, but did see a woman, one unchaperoned woman. I lied for you. I said the woman was your sister, and you and she were sailing the boat to Mount Desert and meeting Mr. Thornton there. I don't give a damn, Alfred. But don't insult the little intelligence I have, and don't be a hypocrite."

"I admit nothing."

"I said I don't give a damn. If I did, I could have gotten reports from the paid hands of the *Thor,* but I didn't. Listen, for God's sake, I'm not admitting anything, either. But I give you credit for guessing that I've had some sex. There, if you want to use that against me, you're welcome to it. But I'm not afraid to admit that much. I won't admit any more, but I'm more honest than you are. I've often thought that you and I could have a very pleasant relationship if you weren't such a God damn hypocrite."

"What kind of a pleasant relationship?"

"Whatever we liked, including sex. I've seen you look at me. There's no love between us, but if you didn't have to put on this act of the aggrieved husband, we could have the same relationship that a lot of our friends have. How many of our married friends are still in love with each other?"

"Not many, I guess."

"Sometimes when I've gone in to say goodnight to you, you'd give anything to have me stay, and I go back to my room and think what a God damn fool you are. And for what? Because you were being faithful to your mistress, whoever she was? She has no rights, she's a mistress, sleeping with a married man."

"That's one way to look at it, of course. Unfortunately it doesn't change what happened when you decided to become Jim Roper's mistress."

"Oh, Jim Roper. That fool. Does that still bother you?"

"Call it that. I was in love with you and trusted you."

"Well, I shouldn't have had the affair with Jim, but I did, and I should have known that you'd take it to heart, but I didn't hurt you out of meanness. I just fell for Jim, and then got over it."

"But I didn't."

"Well, did you gain anything by being spiteful?"

"No, I guess you never do. But whatever you and I had was gone forever."

"No. Only the love. And that would have gone in time."

"Mary, I don't think I ever asked you this. Do you believe in love?"

601

"If I did I don't any more, not the kind that you believed in."

"Were you ever in love with me, the way I believed in?"

"I've often wondered. Truthfully, I guess not. Now that I know so much more about sex, I think it was sex."

"Have you ever been in love with *any*body, as I understand love?"

"I think it was always sex."

"We certainly were an odd couple to get married."

"Why?"

"Because with me it's always been love."

"Every affair you've ever had?"

"I think so. Love, or looking for it."

"There couldn't be that much love, and anyway, the kind of love you talk about, it's only supposed to come once. Twice at the most."

"I didn't say I always got it, but I always wanted it."

"Oh, well. A little bit of love is fine. We all have that. Except Jim Roper."

"Now why bring that son of a bitch into it?"

"Because he's the complete opposite of you."

"Then he must be the exact same as you."

"I hope not. I wouldn't want to be exactly like him. Oh, I know what love is. You can have it for your children, your parents. And Jim Roper doesn't have it for anybody. But I don't have it the way you have. Is that why you're having trouble now? Is that why you're not getting your sleep and eating like a sparrow?"

"Yes."

"Honey, I wish I could help you. I mean that."

"I know you do, and I thank you."

"Did you lie to her? Did she think you were going to go out and get a divorce for her?"

"We faced the facts."

"Then you see it's your kind of love that's got you both in trouble. But I guess you can't help that. Is it all over?"

"It looks that way."

"Go on in and get your nap. I'll wake you at nine o'clock."

"Thanks, Mary."

"You're welcome," she said. He stood up and as he was passing her chair she reached out her hand. "Isn't it better to be friends, Alfred?"

"It *is* better, Mary."

He undressed and lay down, admiring of her friendliness and her ability to see things so clearly, even though her way of seeing them was not his way. Her candid willingness to resume or commence a marital relationship of sorts was neither disturbing nor inviting, and at the moment he was more interested in sleep. She had made it easy to sleep by showing a concern for his health and comfort; the other offer was so practical and cold-blooded that he did not feel that he had been singled out for attention. It was as though she had thought of several men whom she would pass upon to share her passion, and had decided on him because he was the most convenient. And yet she had been kindly and friendly, and for the first time in years he felt kindly and friendly toward her, and feeling so he fell into a deep sleep.

The street sounds had changed when he came awake, brought back to consciousness by a succession of attacks on his senses: the differences in the outdoor sounds, the light from his desk lamp, the odor of coffee, and the presence of Mary holding cup and saucer and waiting for him to become fully awake. She was wearing a Japanese dressing-gown. "It's a quarter past nine," she said. "I brought you some coffee."

"Oh, thanks," he said.

"I phoned the Colliers. I said we'd be a little bit late, but that's all right. So will everybody."

He sat up in bed and drank the black coffee. "Jesus, I slept as though I'd been hit with a hammer. I must have needed that."

"You look better."

"How about you?"

"I'm all ready except my dress and shoes. I put the studs in your shirt and the buttons in your vest. Are you going to take a shower?"

"Yes."

"Then call me when you've finished your shower and I'll finish dressing."

She left him, and he knew she got out of the room because he was naked under the bedclothes. Together they said good-night to their sons, and in the taxi he said: "You're very chic tonight."

"Am I? Thank you."

He could not tell whether her abruptness was due to a reconsideration of her earlier friendliness, or her usual pre-party manner. When Mary went to a big party she was at it long before the party began. Every large party excited her, at least in its early stages, and would continue to do so until she lost her individuality in it and became one of the crowd, at which point the party ended for her as prematurely as the excitement of it had begun. A condition that made a party desirable was the number of men and women who would be seeing her beauty and chic for the first time, and the Waldorf dinner-dance would be crowded with people new to her and to whom she was new. Alfred made no attempt to find out the reason for her abrupt response to his compliment.

This was a dinner-dance for the benefit of a hospital, a home, or a fund that had not suffered extinction during the early years of the Great Depression. There were dozens of cocktail parties in upstairs rooms and there was no pretense of concealment of the champagne and whiskey at the large tables. Among the two thousand men and women present there probably were not five hundred who could instantly supply the name of the benefited charity, but it had served a useful community purpose: people with money were spending a little of it without embarrassment or shame, and men could joke freely in this company about the threat of revolution that to many of them was very real—and would be real again in the morning when they read the reports of their labor experts in the field. But tonight it was the great Emil Coleman playing a perfect society-beat tune called "You're an Old Smoothie," and the proletarians could go to hell.

Alfred and Mary knew their host and hostess and no one else at the Colliers' table for twenty. Alfred dutifully danced with five of the women, all older than he, and between dances drank one, or, with luck, two Scotch highballs. Mary left the table with a man named Newton Orchid, who controlled Films Par Excellence, according to Collier. She was gone more than an hour and when they returned Orchid was not looking at her. He held her chair for her, and then without making excuses to anyone, departed, leaving her with vacant chairs on both sides. On an impulse not unconnected with the highballs and champagne he had drunk, Alfred left the woman beside him and sat in one of the chairs at Mary's side.

"If you start wearing a diamond necklace, I'll know where you got it from," he said.

"Take me home," she said.

"What for? I thought you were having a merry old time."

"Be nice, Alfred. I was nice to you."

"All right."

They said goodnight to their hostess and since it was the easiest way to get out of the room, they danced through the crowd.

"Did you have trouble with the movie magnate?"

"I don't want to talk about him."

"I'll give him a punch in the nose if you want me to, but why did you go away with him?"

"I can take care of myself."

"All right, then I won't punch him in the nose. Do you want to go home, or do you want to go to a speakeasy?"

"If you want to go to a speakeasy, all right, but don't let's go on my account. But if you want to get tight, I'll sit with you."

"What makes you think I want to get tight?"

"You're off to a pretty good start, aren't you?"

"Fair. Fair. The next six or seven drinks should tell the story."

"If you're planning to get *that* tight, maybe you'd better take me home first."

In the taxi he gave the driver their address, and until they reached the apartment house he was undecided between leaving her and going upstairs. He decided to go upstairs.

She went back to the boys' room and he poured himself a highball. It was more than half finished before she returned, wearing mules and the Japanese dressing-gown. She sat wearily on the sofa.

"Can I get you anything before I go to bed?"

"Nothing I can think of, thanks. Sit and talk a while."

"I'm tired. I'll stay for five minutes."

"Well, five minutes is better than nothing."

"It may not be, in my present mood."

"Is Mr. Orchid responsible?"

"Oh, if it hadn't been Orchid it would have been someone else. He happened to be pretty disgusting, but that was my fault for leaving with him."

"Where did you go?"

"To his apartment. His company has an apartment in the Towers."

"Did he try to rape you?"

"People don't rape people, Alfred."

"Well, then, he made passes at you."

"And how."

"But what did you expect him to do? I hold no brief for him, but if a good-looking girl walks out in full view of her husband, and goes to a guy's apartment—what the hell?"

"I decided it was better all around to have him make passes at me in his apartment than under the table. He was feeling me up, somebody used to say at school."

"Why was it better all around?"

"When I said no in his apartment, he knew I meant no. But just pushing his hand away didn't stop him at the table. 'Am I not good enough for you, Mrs. Eaton? I assure you, ladies in your social class are no strangers to me,' he said. 'I could show you a picture in yesterday's society page of *The New York Times,* a lady who was stripped naked in this very apartment last night.' 'Well,' I said, 'I don't read *The New York Times* but I'm certainly going to get a copy of yesterday's paper.' 'No need to do that, I have it here.' And he handed me the paper and there was a picture of our hostess. He may have been telling the truth, or he may have been lying. But what's to prevent him from saying he had me stripped naked in his apartment? That's why I asked you to take me home. I suddenly couldn't stand any of those people. Who is Orchid? Have you ever heard of him?"

"Sure. I've heard of him."

"Then he probably did sleep with all those movie stars he told me about?"

"Well, he has the opportunity."

"Would I be interested to know that this one does this and that one does that, and this one is queer for that? He had their pictures in big silver frames. Did I know that this one had a baby by that one? This one took dope? That one was a fairy? I don't know how much of it's true, but I should think he'd want to keep it quiet instead of blabbing it to a stranger. Oh, I know he thought it would put me in the right frame of mind. Which one was his wife?"

"The one that sat there with her hands on the table, staring around looking like a fortune-teller at a carnival. You know how they sit there waiting for a sucker?"

"I know which one she was."

"Was that jewelry real?"

"The necklace was, I saw it in Cartier's before Christmas. And the rings looked real. 'Have no fear that my wife might surprise us in a compromising position, Mrs. Eaton. Mrs. Orchid and I occupy an apartment on upper Park Avenue and she never comes here,' he said. 'And she takes a very liberal attitude, because she's three years my senior.' I wonder if some lady of my social class is there now. When I finally convinced him that I wasn't going to play, he was in a great hurry to get back."

"I imagine there were a lot of sure things there tonight."

"Probably. He asked me about you."

"Oh, he did, did he?"

"He wanted to know if you'd remember him in case he called up and invited you for luncheon. He said luncheon."

"Did you tell him you'd make sure I'd remember him?"

"Well, he wanted to be sure that I didn't take this personally, and he thought it might be an excellent idea if I told you that he and I had been trying to win a Cadillac at one of those wheels. You know, where they sell chances?"

"You didn't win one, did you?"

She laughed. "No, but I took a chance, didn't I?"

He did not laugh. "Do you take many chances like that?"

She became serious again. "No. Not as many as you do, probably. My reputation is all shot, yours isn't. So you have everything to lose, and I haven't. But answering your ques-

606

tion, no, I don't take many chances. Well, I must retire to my couch." She stood up. "You ought to go to bed, too, Alfred. You're all sobered up, and you have to get up early."

"I'll finish my drink."

"All right, but don't sit here and brood over what's happened to you, whatever it is."

"I won't."

"You were very nice tonight, Alfred. It does you good to have things go against you once in a while. You've had it too easy for a long time."

"Do you think so?"

"Yes, and so would you if you compared your life with a lot of others."

"I guess so."

"Goodnight."

"Goodnight, Mary. You were nice, too."

He was not looking at her, but he was aware that she rushed from the room, and her footsteps in the hall told him how fast she had gone to her bedroom and distinctly closed the door. He drank the watery mixture that was left in his glass, turned out the lights and went to his own room and undressed. He put a fresh blade in his razor and arranged the clothes he would wear in the morning, putting off going to bed as long as he could. But it could not be put off forever, and he lay down and turned out the light and gave himself up to his love of Natalie, pitied his love, and struggled against this new, imminent, almost irresistible dependence on Mary.

Once a year each MacHardie partner and his wife were invited to James MacHardie's house for a weekend, which commenced with lunch on Saturday and lasted until early supper on Sunday. MacHardie never invited two partners on the same weekend; he fancied that he got another aspect of his men by this separation from office associations. The parties were not informal; the country atmosphere was only a matter of geography and unpolluted air, and the daytime clothes. And since MacHardie engaged in no sporting activity, his guests were not inclined to take advantage of the nearby golf courses, the three tennis courts in the neighborhood, the lawn tennis courts, the available stables, the waters of Long Island Sound, the skeet layouts or even the croquet pitches. Surrounded by the most expensive concentration of sporting facilities in the United States, the MacHardie weekend guests took naps and read on Saturday afternoon, ate the equivalent of state dinners on Saturday night, conversed politely after dinner, and went to bed early. On Sunday morning breakfast was served in the guests' bedrooms, and at one-thirty on Sunday afternoon MacHardie was host to twenty or thirty men and women in addition to his house guests. The extra guests who were free to go would leave shortly after three o'clock, and the house guests, who had done nothing but sleep and eat since Saturday lunch, retired again for naps and reading until the early supper and the subsequent contest with the traffic leading to the Queensborough Bridge. An indication of the mutual trust existing between any two MacHardie partners was their willingness to comment on a MacHardie weekend, but only a summons from Mr. Hoover himself took precedence over the old man's invitation, and there were not many North Shore people who would send regrets for the dinners and luncheons.

It was Alfred and Mary's turn, as it happened, on the weekend after the party at the Waldorf, which had taken place on a Thursday night. All day Friday, at the office, Alfred knew that he was facing a crisis in his marriage and in his relationship with Natalie. Natalie had not written him, she had not telephoned, and her silence could mean only that their relationship stood as they had left it on their last meeting. It was the way she wanted it, whether or not it was what she wanted. He was sure as ever that she loved him, sure that she knew he loved her, but she was letting time pass and extend the separation, so that now every day that passed made the separation an older and a more permanent condition, taking on the character of an institution they had created and were letting grow. The almost accidental manner of the separation, which would have made it possible and easy for them to go together again in the beginning of the separation, was now a minor and negligible factor against the increasing size and strength of the separation as a fact. Time was hurrying by, and every day she did not end the separation made it bigger and lessened their potential ability to deal with it. The separation was so patently the right thing for her that she alone could decide to end it. It was time and past time for her to arrange her life to the exclusion of him, and the only right thing for him to do was to make the arranging less difficult for her than it would be if he tried to communicate with her.

A broken love was, finally, his own business and his own sorrow, and he discovered that he was so convinced that Natalie intended to conform to her decision that he himself was preparing to retire into a way of life he had known as a much younger man, with the difference that now he could accept sorrow as part of life itself and not only the peculiar condition of a young man named Alfred Eaton. The nation had taken some severe blows, the only system he believed in had been attacked by mysterious forces within itself, Devrow Budd had starved to death in an Anderson & Shepard suit, his sister Constance was being treated like a cheap whore, a decent man named Benziger was facing a worrisome old age, and boys he had seen playing polo were now men wanting to borrow sums they would once have spent on a Whippy saddle. He looked back on the years with Natalie and even that happiness had been paid for at the time with petty inconveniences and the lies of caution, strain on her and the sacrifice of years of her life and her young womanhood that were gone with the passing of every second. That first sight of her real face after every separation, those first moments alone, and even the leavetakings that had no finality—all and more had made the strains and inconveniences and sacrifices negligible and easy, but the demands their love had made upon her had been costly, damaging, and inevitably enfeebling to her love and very nearly ruinous to her. Less so to him, who had lived with early sorrow as a natural state, and to whom the years with Natalie were a gift from God. He had had those years and they were still enjoyably his to remember as on the other hand they might to Natalie seem lost. A young girl who had not been trained in sorrow had been able to enjoy the only love she had ever known, but the love had been clandestine and without hope, and the truth of its hopelessness had finally been impressed on her.

It was out of deep love of Natalie that he found the reasons to justify her renunciation, in all likelihood reasons that she had not discovered and would not accept. At home in Mountain City she was, he was sure, reproaching herself for her disloyalty to their love. But before any peace could come to her she would suffer somehow, and self-protectively her suffering would come to an earlier end if the reproaches were directed against herself and no one else, since there were limits to the punishments she could inflict upon herself, and thus a kind of peace would come to her and she would begin to make ready for the next stage of her life.

But already he had come to know something about his own future: a miserable peace might come to him, too, but he could not weep. That release had been denied him. Night after night his longing for Natalie—her deep voice, her smiling eyes—had been so intense that in the next second he expected to weep. But his need of her was deeper and more universal than one that could be expressed and purged with the falling of tears. What was left to him and what had been taken away were one and the same; the future was all memories, the past was all memories, the present was never. True, there would be days to come, food to be eaten, air to be breathed, and his sons would grow, his hair would grow, and he would express himself into the bodies of women; and he would match his wits with men and keep silent for a passage of music and smile on recognizing a friend and hate the men who were his enemies; there would be chagrin and laughter and surprise and fright. Nothing would really change. But she would be absent from everything, and he would only be there.

On Saturday night at MacHardie's he had gone to bed and was reading about salmon fishing in an English magazine. As was customary at MacHardie's, he had a room of his own, and shared a bath with Mary. She had already said goodnight to him and he had heard the water plunging into the deep tub. He did not notice that the water had stopped, nor even that he had not been reading the article on salmon. He was between awake and asleep but with his eyes open, and Mary came in. She was wearing her Japanese dressing-gown and she sat on the edge of his bed.

"What did you say your name was?" she said.

"My name. My name is Alfred Eaton."

"My name is Mary Smith," she said. She lay down beside him, with her elbow bent and her head propped in her hand. "What would happen if I put my hand down here?"

"Why don't you try it and see?"

"I think I will. Oh, something is happening. I think I'll have to investigate more thoroughly. I have to take these heavy clothes off. Do you mind?"

"Not at all."

"These other things of mine, do you think I ought to take them off, too?"

"Yes, I think you'd be more comfortable."

"There isn't much, just this," she said. "See how easy it is? I said to myself at dinner, 'I'd like to do this to that man, that terribly attractive Mr. Eaton.'"

"You're very good at it," he said.

In fact she had not needed to play Mary Smith. In the minutes that followed she was not Mary St. John or Mary Eaton, but someone new and different, and when finally she lay back in contentment it was she who returned to reality. "As always, you were wonderful," she said.

"So were you."

"Oh, I suspect there isn't much difference for men, but there is for women. At least there is for me."

"There is for men, too."

"You stayed away from me for five years, and maybe you would have still if I hadn't seduced you."

"I doubt that."

"Why couldn't we—not start over again, but start with a new beginning?"

"I guess we have."

"No, not necessarily. Have you thought of having any more children?"

610

"No, not lately."

"Whenever I go to see Dr. MacDowell he always says it's a pity I don't have another child."

"I don't want to be unkind, but I'm surprised you haven't."

"I had one abortion, but I would like to have another baby by you. But I won't unless you want to. I'd promise not to cheat on you, and I'm a very good mother, you know."

"I know you are. But I don't understand why you want to have another baby."

"Women either want them or don't want them, and I'm one of those that do. I'd like to have five or six."

"Thank you, no."

"Well, I wish you'd think about it. One, anyway. Can I stay here tonight?"

"Of course."

"I wouldn't want to have a baby by you if I didn't think we have a chance."

"A chance of what?"

"A new beginning. I'm ready for one, and I think you are. I'm fond of you, especially the last few days, and you've been nicer to me, too. Alfred?"

"What?"

"I need you."

"You do? Why?"

"You protect me. No one else ever thought I needed that, but I do."

"Protect you from what?"

"Howling winds, thunder and lightning. I've missed all that. I don't want to go back to Jagger's Cove, but I want a man and not just a lover. And you really always did protect me, even while I was bad and you hated me. Shall we try it, Alfred?"

"It'll never be the same, you know that."

"No, I fixed that, but I'm sure we could make a go of it if you wanted to a little bit."

"Well, we can try."

"I'd like to have a daughter. You'd be very good with a daughter, especially when she got older. You'd be fifty-three when she came out. She'd be very proud of you, dancing with her." She went to sleep presently, and he stayed awake, wanting to call out a last farewell to Natalie, and thinking of a daughter and the only name he would want to give her but never could.

The bookkeeping balances of life and death had a mild fascination for Alfred as they have for nearly everyone, but when his daughter was born in the spring of 1933 he was too full of love for the child to pause and record the new life as against the death of Devrow Budd. It would take many years for him to notice the connections between the appearance of Devrow Budd at the MacHardie office and the birth of his daughter: Devrow Budd's fatal collapse, his burial in Port Johnson, the morning with Natalie at the Ritz-Carlton, the separate then mutual need that brought him together again with Mary, and the monkey-faced little creature who was too preoccupied with the sudden release from the confining darkness of her mother's womb to open her eyes on the bright world around her. The humor of her imperiousness made her father laugh; she was like an aging, helpless dowager queen, screeching orders that were unintelligible and with no power to enforce her demands—no power but the ultimate one of her total helplessness and her father's and mother's willingness to oblige.

More than a million little girls were born in the nation that year, and those born in the first half of the year had been conceived in a time of much despair, but were born in a time of new hope. Baby Eaton Female White, as she was temporarily called at the hospital, was born in auspicious circumstances that were local as well as national; there was pleasure and even some rejoicing among her parents' acquaintances when it became known that Mary Eaton was having a baby. It was not so much an announcement of a vital statistic as it was a proclamation of a true reconciliation. It was good news to their friends on both sides, and hopeful news to contemporaries with troubles of their own that were similar to the never-forgotten troubles of the Eatons. After the brief announcement in the *Herald Tribune* Mary especially was astonished at the number of telegrams and notes that were sent her from women she knew only slightly, and some women fell in love with Alfred because he had forgiven Mary the same offense for which they still lacked forgiveness.

Both families were so delighted by the birth of the baby that they unconsciously revealed their concern over the marriage. The St. Johns, who had arrived in New York on the morning of the day Mary went to the hospital, were so anxious to please Alfred that they were not offended by his rather tardy announcement of the birth, which occurred at six o'clock on that evening. It was nine o'clock before Alfred telephoned the St. Johns. He telephoned his mother shortly after seven, as much to hear her comment as to give her the news. She obliged with an unorthodox comment.

"A girl?" said Martha Eaton. "I was so sure you had nothing but boys in you, you're so superior toward women. Well, I'm glad. Give Mary my love, of course, and of course congratulations to you. What will Rowland and Alex think of it?"

"Rowland was hoping for a sister, and Alex didn't care

what it was. It'd be too young for him to play with even if it was a boy. Which reminds me, I have to call Rowland. I'm not sure they'll let him come to the phone, but I'm going to try."

"I'd insist."

"I know you would. Well, will you pass the word on to Sally and Constance?"

"I'll tell Sally. I haven't the faintest idea where Constance is. I think she's in Virginia, but I don't know where."

"Call the governor of Virginia. He ought to know, too, Mother. Mary's mother belongs to the *leading* F. F. V."

"Now I've never heard *that* before."

"No, but I have. Goodnight, madam."

He was allowed to speak to Rowland, now a third-former at Groton School. "Did Mother come through it all right?" said the boy.

"I keep forgetting you know about these things. Yes, she was in labor less than three hours."

"Swell. I'm going to send her a telegram."

"That's a very good idea."

"If I could borrow two dollars out of next month's allowance I'd like to send her some flowers. What kind of flowers can you get for two dollars?"

"If she got flowers from you it wouldn't make any difference what they were. I'll telegraph you the two dollars tonight, and I'm very glad you thought of it. How's everything else?"

"Fine. What are you going to call the baby?"

"We haven't decided. Have you any suggestions?"

"Yes, but it's the name of a girl I know."

"Well, what's the name? We might consider it."

"Barry."

"I mean her first name."

"That *is* her first name."

"Oh, a family name. Well, that's out, I'm afraid."

"Why don't you just call her Mary? Is Mother too modest?"

"She says it's too commonplace."

"Well, the good old names are often the best, Father. Barry is a pretty name, but it wouldn't be right for everybody. How about Martha, for Grandmother Eaton? Or Sally? Or Constance. They're all good substantial names."

"Well, I'll tell your mother you're in favor of the simple names."

"Swell. Well, it's been nice talking to you, and give my love to Mother and my sister. Goodnight, Father."

"Goodnight, son. And give my regards to the Rector."

When the baby was two days old Alfred said to Mary: "We still haven't got a name for the *jeune fille.*"

613

"I have one, if you don't object. I've had it for a long time but I thought it might be bad luck to say it."

"Well, good. What is it?"

"I would like to christen her Eugenie, after my father and not after those hats a couple of years ago, or the empress. I would like to christen her Eugenie, but call her Jean. Here, see, it has a nice look about it when you write it. Eugenie Eaton. And Jean is a pretty name."

"All right, that's what it'll be. Any middle name?"

"Oh, I guess Rowland."

"She'll go through life with most people not knowing her real name. Well, my first name is Raymond, and nobody ever called me that."

"What's the matter? You look as though you just remembered something important. Did you forget to do something?"

"Yes," he said. "Something at the office."

"Well, I'm rather glad you're forgetting things, to tell you the truth. You're so efficient most of the time, I like to see you in a daze. You didn't really want this baby, but I did. And now that she's here, I think you're glad."

"I am glad. Glad isn't the word for it."

"I wanted *this* baby. You know that. I wanted to have the boys, too. But then I—it's so hard to explain. *Then* I wanted to have children. *This time* I wanted this baby, this little girl. And I wanted you to want her, too, and now you do. Alfred, you've been very good to me, and I'm grateful to you."

"I'm just as grateful to you. You were the one that had the baby, and we never would have had it if you hadn't been sensible, I guess is the word."

"If I hadn't had such hot pants for you, if you want to be really honest about it. I had, I admit it. I had a feeling you wouldn't go to bed with me at home, but at Mr. MacHardie's it was a different atmosphere, and I was determined to seduce you."

"Well, you didn't meet with any maidenly resistance."

"If I had I'd have left you. I would have been so ashamed that I couldn't have faced you again, if you hadn't slept with me that night."

The nurse came in to give her a bath and he left for the office. In the subway, alone among strangers, he wanted to tell Natalie about the baby, as he had many times in the year just past wanted to tell her many things about himself. But the year was not a long enough time; he knew nothing whatever about Natalie's life during that year, but he knew that at the slightest sign from her the year would vanish and they would be farther away than yesterday. There were always small accidents to weaken his confidence in the new marriage with Mary—Rowland's wanting to name the baby after his own girl; the remark that "nobody ever called me Raymond." Some day it might come to pass that he had put enough time between them, but that day was not yet.

THERE FOLLOWED a decade in Alfred's life that began with the birth of his daughter, ended with the death of a son, and was personated by a man for whom he had no respect or regard yet did not hate; but always in thinking about those ten years Alfred would see the pudgy, well-barbered face of Creighton Duffy. To the rest of the Western world (and to Alfred, too) those years were inextricably identified with the faces of the common man gone mad and the aristocrat assiduously making history; but Hitler and Roosevelt were everybody's symbols; Alfred's was Creighton Duffy, who took out his hatred of the aristocracy in his support of the defecting aristocrat, and his contempt for the common man in his work toward the destruction of the housepainter. It did not take long for James D. MacHardie and his like to become suspicious of Roosevelt; most of them had been suspicious from the beginning and their suspicion soon became distrust. Consequently the gossip-loving financial community greeted with sardonic glee the published reports that Creighton Duffy, son-in-law of the arch-conservative James D. MacHardie, was spending more and more time in Washington and less and less time at his desk at Mortimer & Miller. Officially, Mac-Hardie would not comment on Duffy's action; unofficially, he stated that Duffy was free to do as he pleased, since he was a member of the law firm of Mortimer & Miller and—he was quite emphatic about this—*in no way* connected with the firm of MacHardie & Company. Privately, with only members of the firm present, the old man said: "My son-in-law must have known long ago that I had no intention of inviting him to become a partner. He certainly knew it when he married my daughter, because one of the things that made me rather like Creighton was his candor. He said to me at the time, 'Mr. MacHardie, I know it's not going to do me any harm to have people know who my wife's father is, but I promise you I'll never try to take advantage of that.' I will tell you gentlemen that I never turned him down. I never even considered him. But of course I never knew what went on in *his* mind." When he finished speaking he looked across the table at Don Shanley, the Catholic partner, who knew something was expected of him and did not need to be prodded.

"Creighton Duffy was right," said Shanley. "It never did him any harm to be the senior partner's son-in-law. But by the same token I don't see why it should do us any great harm to have him where he is. He never asked us for anything and we don't intend to ask him for anything, but now that the circumstances are somewhat reversed, let's just sit back and see what happens. If there's any prestige—or perhaps implied influence would be a better term— why, I'm perfectly willing to let it come to us. There are other firms down here who are trying to decide how to get a man where Duffy is without compromising themselves. We already have our man." The partners smiled approvingly at Shanley's estimate of the situation.

"Don?"

"Yes, Alfred."

"You're not for one second implying that Duffy's going to be of any practical help to us?" said Alfred.

"Not for one second, not in this room. But this world is full of people with over-active, imaginative minds. They're going to supply their own interpretations," said Shanley.

"I just wanted to be sure we weren't counting on Duffy for anything. Because I'd hate to be the one to ask him for it."

"Now more than ever nobody's going to ask him for a thing," said James MacHardie, sternly. "You don't have to wear kid gloves out of respect for me, Alfred."

"All right, sir, then I'll take them off," said Alfred, quickly pantomiming the action. "I think Creighton Duffy would hurt us in any way he could. For the time being it isn't directed against this firm. Only against the whole banking community. But if he got us down there before the Senate Banking Committee he'd drop more than a midget in our laps."

"Let him," said MacHardie. "Our friend across the street came out of that with great dignity. I'm proud of him."

"I know. But in our case it wouldn't be a midget. It would be more like a bombshell, or a basket of rotten eggs," said Alfred.

"I think he'll bide his time," said MacHardie. "If he has any, uh, vindictive purpose he'd be very foolish to spring it on us so soon."

"There I agree with you, sir. And it's the one thing that keeps him from going after us now. However, without putting on my kid gloves again, I would like to say that except for the midget on Mr. Morgan's lap it has been pretty dull stuff. The papers are trying to make something of it, but you don't hear much about it uptown. Therefore, if I were Duffy, or

Pecora, I'd have you down there like a flash. The newspapers would go to town on that story, you and your son-in-law at opposite sides of the table."

"But you're not Duffy, and he's not you. If he were, he'd be sitting where you are," said the old man.

"Thank you," said Alfred. He enjoyed these meetings; from the beginning of his partnership he had been encouraged to speak up and to pay no attention to his juniority. The old man had said to him: "You served your apprenticeship outside of this room. When you come in here you're on the same footing with Hasbrouck or Shanley or any of them. Don't waste time. This isn't the United States Senate and it isn't Yale. We're all seniors, and you're not a freshman." Thus reassured, Alfred did always speak up and his experiences in the partners' meetings had a desirable effect on his self-confidence in his intercourse with other men in Wall Street. Frederick Cross, the fox-hunting Connecticut partner, expressed it in his own way: "You don't have to take any horse-shit from anybody." William Zabriskie Kingsley, the High Church and Society for the Prevention of Cruelty to Children member, said: "We've needed young blood. New vigor, my boy." Guy Titterton, the rails, steamship and yachting partner, said: "Half of us are hard of hearing and won't admit it, so don't mumble. And if you've got any new stories, don't be afraid of shocking Billy Kingsley. He won't tell them to more than one fellow at a time, but he has plenty of them—all old." Percy Hasbrouck had no suggestions, nor had Stephen Van Ingen, who was manager of the London office, nor John Miller, who kept an old-fashioned ear trumpet in one of the partners' room closets and was studying lip reading with a graduate of Gallaudet. With such company Alfred usually entered the meetings a young man and came out a little bit older but stimulated.

Duffy became appositionally known as the maverick Wall Street lawyer (*Time,* the weekly news magazine) and news stories out of the Washington bureaus unfailingly mentioned his family connection with James D. MacHardie; and when Jean MacHardie Duffy bought a house in Washington and began entertaining for the new administration, Duffy had a brand-new career for himself. The most reactionary Republican senators and former Cabinet officers could have no objection to dining at the table of James D. MacHardie's daughter while getting a good look at the young men who arrived on nearly every train with their plans for rewriting the Constitution. Creighton Duffy was a $75,000-a-year lawyer who had given up the money which, thanks to his wife, he did not need. His wife, who in marrying Duffy had given up much of whatever social position she could claim as Mac-

Hardie's daughter, now became an important hostess in the city where everything was happening. The President would greet her as an old friend (which she was not) and ask politely after her father (whom he knew only by reputation). The gentlemen from the embassies and legations, who were more accustomed than the simple Americans to situations like that of James MacHardie and Creighton Duffy, would sit at her table and speak French with her, eat her good food and drink her good wines, and try to make a proper estimate of the real position of her husband. Some cultivation of Duffy was indicated, but how much of it should be done by the top man and how much by one of the attachés was yet a question. There was no question in Duffy's mind; he had privately turned down an ambassadorship to one of the Lowland nations and he therefore considered himself slightly above ambassadorial rank. As a Papal knight and still a MacHardie son-in-law he was useful to the party in calming the fears of the Roman Catholics and Democratic conservatives whom he saw on his many trips with and without Jim Farley in the campaign for 1936, which was already well under way. There was never the slightest doubt about Farley's Catholicism, but Farley was echoing some of the philosophy that Stuart Chase had called The New Deal, and there were many men who wholly trusted Farley's word but were dubious about his judgment. For some of these the mere physical presence of Creighton Duffy was enough to assuage their doubts and allay their fears, and they even thought of him as their ambassador to Farley. He was rather like Farley in appearance; younger, obviously a college product, not quite so tall as Farley, but like Farley a man who had always enjoyed good living and practiced it even better than Farley, since he had an apparently limitless capacity for alcohol, which Farley did not touch. Together they restored confidence among the men who were beginning to hear reports concerning the radicalism of the young lawyers and economists who were getting the jobs in the federal government. And over and over the truth of Don Shanley's observation *in camera* was being demonstrated: over-active, imaginative minds simply refused to believe that the man who was married to James D. MacHardie's daughter would remain in a government that was socialistic.

Among the young men who were getting the jobs in the federal government was Alfred Eaton's old friend Tom Rothermel, who fitted in nicely in the early studies of the electrical power phase of the Tennessee Valley Authority. Alfred had again lost touch with Tom, but upon hearing from Sally Van Peltz that Tom Rothermel was "something important in one of the government agencies" Alfred half-seriously wondered how Tom would get along with Creighton Duffy, if they ever met. The presence of the two men in the new government typified to Alfred the diverse attractions of the administration. Duffy, he was convinced, was in it for personal prestige, willing enough to punish individual members of the financial community, but not so willing completely to sacrifice the system. But Tom Rothermel was a zealot, an educated errand-boy with an errand-boy's psychology, willing enough to avenge his early poverty but neither willing to stop there nor eager for the personal power of high office. Tom was bloodthirsty but not ambitious; Duffy was in favor of change for the sake of Duffy, but presumably intelligent enough to foresee that in an absolute change he would be sacrificed along with the system, and in a drastic, overnight change, he would be shot as quickly as James D. MacHardie and even against the same wall. Whenever he thought of Tom and Duffy Alfred would imagine them together, the two irreconcilables under the same banner. By a typically simple device of fate he brought about the imagined meeting.

"Alfred, I'd like you to go to Washington and see Templeton Avirett," said James MacHardie. Templeton Avirett was the senior partner in the Washington firm representing Mac-Hardie & Company.

"Oh? What for?"

"On business," said MacHardie. The old man chuckled. "I really don't know what business, but we can think of something. He gets a good retainer so we can have first call on his services. I'd like you to go there and spend a week. Naturally nobody would think of asking you what business you and Templeton were discussing, but it's perfectly logical for you to be there, for you to be together. I'd like you to take Mary with you, if that's not inconvenient for her, and I'd like you to stay at the Aviretts' house. They'll have people in for dinner, and they'll see that you and Mary are invited out. I want one of your old-time reports. I can't rely on the newspapers, they're either prejudiced for or against, and those other reports we get regularly, those letters, I'm afraid they tell us what they think we'd *like* to read. We pay $200 a year for one of those letters and I could write it here without leaving the office. So could you."

"Any particular line of inquiry?"

"Yes. Who is running that show. What do they intend doing if they win the next election, which I'm afraid is what's going to happen."

"Yes, I've been saying that all along. He's not a four-year president, he's an eight-year man."

"Please God it stops there!" said the old man.

"If I'm invited to the Duffys' shall I go?"

"Oh, most certainly. And I have one other suggestion, one only. Templeton has a great many friends among Army and Navy people. See them. They have the best intelligence service in Washington, and nobody ever thinks of that, it's so obvious. But they have. They won't tell you very much, but what they'll tell you will be reliable, and I don't think they like Mr. Roosevelt very much, in spite of his fondness for the Navy. You were in the Navy."

"U. S. N. R. F., not the regular Navy."

"Well, use your own judgment about that. I hope you enjoy yourself, although that's not my principal reason for asking you to go."

"I'll enjoy myself."

Templeton Avirett was always one of the first names mentioned when Virginians were guessing the membership of The Seven, the University of Virginia secret society whose roster never was made public. But behind the excessive courtliness and under the full head of white hair was a first-rate legal mind and skillful barrister, something of a Shakespearean scholar, a man who corresponded in Latin with a Georgetown Jesuit whom he seldom spoke to even on the telephone, and author of a privately printed book on contract bridge. He was a man who was born with a lot of brains and used them. He never had run for public office and twice when it had been the South's turn to fill a Supreme Court vacancy he had declined with more than polite regret: he would not run the risk of reviving the scandalous suicide of his wild younger brother, who in 1889 had tried to hold up a Lynchburg bank and turned his pistol on himself when the paying teller resisted the holdup with gun fire. Templeton Avirett's distaste for personal publicity was not the least of his good points in the eyes of James MacHardie, and Avirett, who never had had any genuine affection for MacHardie, became warmly sympathetic (although not outspokenly so) upon the arrival of Creighton Duffy on the Washington scene. He was also opposed to Roosevelt from the moment of his nomination, and was thankful that as an unfranchised resident of the District he was not compelled to choose between Roosevelt and the Republican electors. "He's not a lawyer, although he claims to be, and while he may be an aristocrat, he's no gentleman," said Avirett. "My yard-boy Oscar is no aristocrat either, but he *is* a gentleman. Al Smith is a gentleman. A gentleman is a man who is completely at home with other gentlemen, and this particular Roosevelt is not at home with anybody. He has to be the center of attraction, and that may be one of the marks of the aristocrat but I've already conceded that he is that." This opinion found its way back to the White House and undoubtedly contributed to the President's attitude toward the Washington cliff-dwellers, which was hostile.

Mary Eaton's Rowland blood made her automatically acceptable to the Aviretts, and as a MacHardie partner on a mission Alfred Eaton's blood did not matter. The week was planned so that Alfred could have lunch every day with the men Avirett selected; he would remain with Alfred until the coffee was served, and then leave him with the other men. Lunch was at the Metropolitan or the Cosmos club, and dinner, except for the Duffys', was always at the Aviretts' old house in Rhode Island Avenue. The days were boring enough for Mary. "I've met two cousins I never knew I had, and they didn't know each other. And my Southern accent's coming back."

"Coming back? It's never been very far away, honey pie."

"That's pronounced pah, short and quick. Not py-ee, the way you pronounce it. Anybody'd know you were a Yankee."

"You slobbered a bibful, and I get more Yankee every day I'm here. Well, Fat Ass, tonight's the big night."

"Why're you calling me Fat Ass? You must be thinking of Jean Duffy."

"I am. Big Fat Ass Jean Duffy and Big Prick Creighton Duffy."

"Do you know that for a fact?"

"About Duffy? No. He is, I don't know that he has. They remind me of a saying we used to have at Knox School for Boys. What's the height of desperation? Answer: two fat bellies and a small prick. Do you want to know the height of uselessness? Men's tits. Did you ever read the Cat's Revenge, by Claude Balls? Did you ever read The Passionate Russian, by E. Nawder Titzoff? Or The Passionate Lover, by E. Roder Haggard? I wish I could remember some of the others."

" 'E. Nawder—' oh, I get it. And what was the other? E. Roder Haggard. Oh, yes. He rode her haggard. Did you make them up?"

"Lord, no. They were in circulation in every prep school in the East, I guess. I'd like to try them on Templeton Avirett, but I guess I won't."

"Let me try them on Mrs. Avirett first."

"No, let me try them on Mrs. Avirett. That way we'll never get invited back again. Not that we were invited this time. I'll be very glad to get home, and I'm sure you will. As a matter of fact it's been interesting for me. Are you as a comparatively young mother prepared to face the fact that your first-born is likely to be cannon fodder?"

"You mean there's going to be a war?"

"Not for a while, but it's coming. The seeds are being planted."

"I don't believe it."

"I haven't made up my mind whether I do or not."

"Who'd start a war?"

"Who started the last one?"

"The Germans invaded Belgium."

"They did, but that isn't what started it. Did you ever hear of Sarajevo? No. Well, that's where they poured the gasoline on the fire. War in five years, that's what I've been hearing this week, and by the way, that's not to be repeated."

"I'm sure no one I know wants to hear it. But we'd get into it? They could draft Rowland?"

"How could we stay out of it? England is going to get into any war there is in Europe, and we'll get into any war England's in, like it or not. I *don't*, but they're not going to ask me what I like. Rowland will be just ripe for it, and he'll want to go anyway. That really fine, nice, attractive boy."

"You sound as though they were going to start tomorrow."

"No, I don't mean to, but I know a lot more than I did a week ago, and for the first time it hit me that my kid is probably going to have to fight a war. It made me wish I'd done more than I did in the last war."

"You were so funny a minute ago, and now you sound like the voice of doom."

"Well, they all say five years at the earliest, so don't let it upset you."

"Who is they?"

"They is, or are, two colonels, a general, two captains, and two Navy captains and two lieutenant commanders. Oh, and a guy in the Army Air Corps Reserve, a great admirer of my old chum Lawrence B. Von Elm. Do you remember Lawrence B.? At the Nassau Aeronautical Corporation?"

"Not very well."

"Big shot now, you know. Has his own firm. Designing consultant. Lawrence B. Von Elm Associates, Forty-second and Fifth. Do you think I'd have time for a nap before dinner? Would my wife wake me at six o'clock?"

"Yes, your wife would. What your wife is wondering is, you've taken a nap before dinner every day we've been here, but you never take one at home. You ought to."

"No, down here I've been on a sort of a vacation and I let myself get lazy, that's all. Call me at six, huh?"

"Coffee?"

"Too much trouble. You might ask them for a Coke."

Alfred had been counting on the Duffy dinner as an opportunity to meet the New Dealers with, in the current phrase, their hair down. But he had not been in the Duffy house ten

622

minutes before he began to realize that Creighton Duffy had outsmarted him. There were five other male guests, and four of them were members of the New York Racquet Club; the fifth was a seedy Virginian who hunted the fox and sold spavined horses to Middleburg Yankees. In its way it was a coldly calculated snub that Alfred was forced to admire, since he had not credited Duffy with such shrewdness. "I think you'll know everybody that's coming tonight," Duffy had said on the arrival of the Eatons—and indeed Alfred did know everybody with the exception of the Virginia horse-trader. It was almost as though Duffy had said to him: "If you think you're going to just walk into *my* club, guess again." There was a great deal of drinking, but out of polite consideration for their host, the Racquet Club men refrained from all political reference, and Alfred did not even get to observe Duffy under attack. It was also—and Alfred was not sure that this was intentional—an indication of where Alfred stood in Duffy's estimation: he was a MacHardie partner, but still only a Racquet Club boy. The evening was a total loss, so far as an intelligence report was concerned, and the Eatons gave themselves up to a party that might just as well have taken place in New York in 1928. But Alfred would never again underestimate the bland, baby-skinned Duffy.

They took the one o'clock back to New York the next afternoon. Alfred had arranged to be met at Penn Station by a man named O'Flynn, a former private chauffeur who was in the limousine rental business. O'Flynn was waiting for them at the top of the train-shed stairway, and after greeting them he marshaled the two porters with the Eatons' luggage and accompanied Mary to the limousine while Alfred was in a telephone booth in conversation with the office. He spoke to his secretary and to Percy Hasbrouck and to MacHardie's secretary, and, this chore completed, was on his way to join Mary in the Thirty-first Street motor entrance—The Pit, as the taxi drivers called it.

He saw O'Flynn's limousine and then saw Mary, who was conversing with a woman in a mink coat and a hat that was almost a beret but was not a beret. From their gestures and the movements of their heads it was apparent that the two women were discussing their luggage, and Mary, whose face Alfred could see, was amused by the conversation. Then she looked up and saw Alfred and smiled and said something to the woman in the mink coat, and the woman had not fully turned her head when Alfred knew that the face would be the one he would see as long as his mind would let him see.

She turned fully and faced him, and the steps he took toward her were endless but uncounted. Her mouth was softly set in the first stage of a formal smile, but her eyes were looking past his face and over his shoulder. Walking toward her and taking off his hat were actions that were controlled by the subtler forces of habit as was also his greeting to her: "Why, Natalie, how nice to see you. Do you know my wife? Mary, this is Natalie Benziger."

"We're *getting* to know each other. I tried to make off with Miss Benziger's suitcase."

All three looked down on the platform at the identical Vuitton bags.

"Hello, Alfred. I think we must have come in on the same train. I got on at Philadelphia, and I noticed there was a bag like mine."

"And I guess the Pullman porter must have put my bag with Miss Benziger's."

"It's Mrs. Eustace now, by the way," said Natalie.

"George Eustace?" said Alfred.

"His brother, Ben. I think you know him," said Natalie.

"Of course. When did that happen? I never got any word of it. You missed out on a wedding present."

"Well, I didn't give you one."

"But Ben did."

"It happened just about a year ago. Very quietly."

"Let's continue the reunion in the car. We can give you a lift after trying to steal your bag, can't we?" said Mary.

"I'd love it. I'm staying at the Ritz."

"At the Ritz," said Alfred. "I've stayed at the Philadelphia Ritz, but never this one. Will you get in first, Mary, then Natalie, then me. We can stop the car on the Forty-sixth Street side."

Once under way Mary resumed the conversation. "Now where did you two know each other? In Philadelphia?"

They both said "No" simultaneously, and Alfred said, "You go ahead."

"You spoke first."

"Same story. I tried to sell Natalie's father some bonds, about six years ago, I guess it was. Mountain City, P A. How is your father?"

"My father died two weeks before I was married, and two months after Mother died."

"Good heavens, you had a lot of courage to go on with the wedding, but some people believe it's bad luck to change a wedding day," said Mary.

"I'd had all the bad luck I could ever have that year."

"I wish I'd known about your father. I never knew a man I liked better. You really should have told me."

"Not really," said Natalie.

"Alfred's father died the day we were married. I didn't know about it until the next day," said Mary.

"I would have come back," said Alfred.

"But I didn't want you to," said Natalie.

"Is your husband the Ben Eustace that I knew? He played football at Penn?"

"Yes," said Natalie.

"Yes, there were two brothers, Ben and George. They both played on the same team."

"Yes, and I know what you're going to say, but you're too polite to say it," said Natalie. " 'Either Ben was very bright or George was very stupid,' because they were both in the same class."

"Well—that *is* what they used to say," said Mary. "But you married the bright one."

"What does Ben do now?" said Alfred.

"He's in the coal business. Not mining, like my father, but that was how I met Ben."

The words mattered so little, even when they could be put together to form double meanings. She had told him all he needed to know: that she had gone through her private hell without coming to him for comfort or help, and that she had married a man who was as different from him as any man she could find—Ben Eustace, black-haired, black-browed, built like a Jersey bull; unsubtle, unclever and almost inevitably protective and grateful.

The car stopped at the side door of the hotel and he got out to assist her. She tried to keep away from him, but she could not refuse to shake hands, and he took her hand and said: "It won't work."

"It seems to be working for you. I hear you have a daughter to prove it."

"You're responsible for that daughter."

"Well, then you may be responsible for my having one, because now I'm going to try. *Yes, I love you.* Now please let go."

He got back in the car.

"So there she is," said Mary.

He turned and saw that it would be useless to lie. "Yes, there she is."

"You could take her away from Ben Eustace."

"I'm not going to try."

"If I could believe that . . . but I can't."

"I think we ought to have another baby."

"You're not always going to be able to postpone her by having a baby. And I don't want you to leave me when you're forty. I have a life, too, Alfred."

"Yes. With me. And mine is with you."

"What a bad bargain you make that seem."

"It hasn't been so bad, has it?"

"No. And you haven't tried to see her and she hasn't tried to see you. I believe that."

"Then nothing has changed."

"Oh, how wrong you are! This girl came up to me and said, 'I'm afraid you're going away with the wrong suitcase,' and I turned and saw a face that was so beautiful it startled me. You know me. I like *men*. But I wanted her to go on talking, just to watch her eyes, so calm while she's listening to you, and then animated while she's speaking to you. I actually wanted to keep her there so you could see her, too."

"Well, you had to meet her sometime, especially since she married Ben Eustace. Our paths would cross."

"Ben Eustace. She's ruined *his* life."

"Ruined it? How?"

"What will there be for him after she leaves him? Look what she's done to you."

"Haven't I been all right for the past year?"

"It's the next year I'm thinking of, and the years after that."

"The only difference now is that you've seen her."

"Seen her, yes, and liked her, and can understand why you were like an old man when she left you or you left her, whichever it was. And there's one thing about this that you being a man could never understand."

"What?"

She put her hand on her chest. "It's about me. I have a face that people like to look at, and a figure, too. 'The beautiful Mrs. Alfred Eaton.' Oh, Washington was wonderful for my ego. Those foreigners. And this is nothing new to me, it goes back to the year I came out, and even before that. But no man appreciates a woman's beauty as much as another beautiful woman. Before I'd call another woman beautiful she'd have to be twice as beautiful as one that you'd think was. And when she's that beautiful, I don't hate her. The ones I have no use for are the pretty ones or the sexy ones. You know, it's no accident that you often see two or three beautiful women having lunch together. You've never thought about that, I'm sure, but men are so ignorant about beautiful women. We're either jealous of each other or we're Lesbians. That's how men simplify everything. Two good-looking men can be friends without being jealous or fairies, but did I ever accuse you of jealousy of Lex, or of being his sweetheart?"

"No."

"I'm not a bit jealous of your affair with her," she said, after a silent moment. "I think you were lucky."

"Do you?"

"Yes, because she loved you. And still does. She has something I haven't got. Niceness. And that's probably the love that

I can't make myself believe in. But I have something she hasn't got."

"What?"

"Honesty. And strength of character. And guts. She has no guts. But she's beautiful, she's really beautiful. And if you want her, I won't stand in the way."

"Let me have that in plain language. You mean you'd give me a divorce?"

"Why, yes, if you were fool enough to want to marry her."

"I don't get this. I thought you said you liked her."

"I'm honest and I've got strength of character, and I have guts. But if you start having an affair with her again, I'll have affairs, too. Only, I'll be the one to suffer. I'm not afraid to suffer, mind you. But I don't want to. I don't want the children to hear gossip about me, and they will if I have affairs. I had my life get a new start last year and it was all right until you saw this girl again, but it isn't all right now. I'd give you a divorce because I don't want to have affairs. I want to get married again."

"Oh. Have you got anybody in mind?"

"No. But I have to find someone while I'm still young enough to make him willing to marry me with three children. The ideal man would be a widower with some children of his own."

"Well, Mary, I'm glad you're ready for any contingency, and I'm sincerely glad you think so straight. But maybe you can follow this with your straight thinking. You can't hold it against me that I fell in love with Natalie Benziger, since you don't believe in love. But I am not going to try to see Natalie, therefore, I am going to go on being your husband on the same terms as before. Meaning, the great pleasure of sleeping with you. Our friendly relationship. The children. The pleasant times we have together. And whatever protection I give you and the great help you give me. It sounds cold-blooded, but they're your terms. I see no happiness for anybody in our getting a divorce, but I do see a lot of unhappiness and an enormous amount of inconvenience."

"All right, Alfred. If you want to try. But if you have an affair with her, and don't warn me first, I'll be nasty."

"That's fair enough."

"I'm dying to have lunch with her, now that I know she's the one."

"Don't do it. If you do, all bets are off."

He could not understand how she could not know now that he was lying. She had sensed immediately that Natalie was "the one," but throughout the later conversation she listened and talked with no suspicion, not even when he made her repeat that she would give him a divorce. She believed his tinny, lying statements of his intention not to see Natalie, as she seemed also to believe in his desire to continue their marriage. He could find only one reason for her gullibility: she had so convinced herself of the non-existence of love in herself that she could not fully comprehend its effect on others. She had been acute and perceptive in the car, and had seen through his and Natalie's efforts to fake a casual friendship; but in all probability what she had sensed was the strong mutual physical attraction between him and Natalie, and since she was actually proud of her simplification of such attraction as nothing more than sex, she had been unable to recognize the stronger attraction, which was love.

They had a joyful reunion with the children and a pleasant dinner *à deux,* and until it was time to retire they kept busy with their accumulated correspondence and telephone messages and their household and social problems. She kissed him goodnight and went to their room and was asleep when he lay down in his bed. No more had been said about Natalie Eustace or their marriage, and in Mary's favor he noted gratefully that she apparently did not intend to worry the question. They did not make love; after the drinking at the Duffy party they had let themselves go in love-making in their ante-bellum room at the Aviretts', and perhaps that very knowledge had made Mary secure in spite of her quick recognition of Natalie as the girl who had been Alfred's mistress.

Alfred went to the office early the next morning, a Saturday, knowing that James MacHardie would not be in but with work to catch up on—and a telephone at his side in the event he could invent a device for speaking to Natalie. But his ingenuity failed him and he went uptown at two o'clock and joined the drinkers at the Racquet Club bar. A Yale football game was being broadcast and the radio was the focal point of the room, and he managed to keep from becoming a member of any single group. His only reason for going to the Racquet Club was to avoid going home, since he had given up the Saturday custom of lunching there. He was leaning with his back against the bar, with a tall light Scotch and soda in his hand, and having said hello to his friends and acquaintances without joining any of them, and after several casual sweeping glances at the rather crowded room he had about decided to go home. Then he looked about the room just as casually, but more slowly, and at a table at the north end of the room, sitting with three other men, he saw Ben Eustace. Carefully now, not to attract the slightest attention by a sudden action, he put his glass on the bar and sauntered out to a telephone booth. He had to give his name to the club switchboard operator, but since he had no way of knowing how long Ben Eustace would be in the club, he decided against going outside to telephone. "Mrs. Eustace, please," he said to the Ritz-Carlton operator.

Natalie's voice was friendly and expectant as she said "Hello."

"Natalie, can you talk?"

For a moment she was silent.

"It's Raymond," he said.

"I know that."

"I'm at the Racquet Club. I saw Ben, he didn't see me. Can you talk?"

"I can, but I don't want to."

"I have to see you."

"No. At least you're not going to. What you said yesterday —you're wrong. It *can* work. There's only one person to stop it from working, and that's you. But even so, I'm not going to see you. You can make yourself unhappy, you can make me unhappy, and the two of us can make Ben and your wife unhappy, but I'm not going to see you."

"You've made up your mind? You've thought about this?"

"A great deal, even before I saw you yesterday. It had to happen, and when it did, I was ready. Now I'm just testing out whether I meant it or not, and I do."

"Does this mean you're never going to see me?"

"I'm never going to see you alone."

"Of course you know what that means."

"Oh, sure. It means I'm afraid to. But I know that."

"That isn't what I was going to say. I was going to say that we won't be able to deceive Ben and Mary forever. Some day they'll both find out that we love each other and always have. And that's going to make them unhappy and bitter. They're going to look back on the years that we deceived them and they're not going to remember anything good about those years. And you and I will be together for the rest of *our* lives, but they won't have anybody . . . Did you hear me?"

"Yes, I heard you. And I agree with you. But I'm not going to see you. My only hope for myself and for Ben is that I'll get over being in love with you. Ben knows about you. I told him."

"Mary guessed about you. When I got back in the car yesterday she said, 'So there she is.' "

"You'd never told her before?"

"No. She knew there'd been someone, but she didn't know it was you until she saw us together, and then she guessed."

"It was nice of you not to tell her. That way we had a few minutes of being friends. She's beautiful, and I liked her, too. But we're talking too long. Ben's going to telephone me as soon as that football game is over."

"All right, Natalie. I love you."

"I love you. It's sad, but it's nice."

"Yes."

"My dear?"

"Yes."

"Stay away from Ben. Don't let him see you. He's a bad drunk and you're on his mind, after yesterday."

"In that case he shouldn't have come here. He's not a member, and I am. If there's any trouble here, he started it."

"Please?"

"Wait a minute. Will he do anything to you if he sees me?"

"Never. He's almost too gentle with me. But he might fight with you, and whether he fights you or not, he'll go on a bender. But he won't hurt me. Only himself. Please don't let him see you."

"All right. I guess that's asking little enough."

"It is, considering what we have that he'll never have. And knows it. Before I hang up, I have a piece of news for you."

"What?"

"They've torn down Thirteenth Street. It isn't there any more."

"How do you know?"

"I went down there this morning, just to have a look."

"I can live on that for five more years. Goodbye."

"Goodbye."

He left the club and went home.

Whenever possible, the MacHardie partners dined together on Monday night, the dinner hostship rotating among the various partners and the dinner being actually served in their New York places of residence. The wives were present for the meal itself, after which they would retire while the partners conferred in an atmosphere of brandy and cigars and orderly conviviality. The dinner was provided by a catering service and paid for by the firm, as much to eliminate the possibility of a hospitality competition among the wives as to place any unusual burden on their staffs. The night's hostess was thus freed of all cares except that of seating her guests differently from the arrangement at the previous dinner, although James MacHardie was always seated on his hostess's right. The gentlemen wore black tie and there was some effort to maintain the illusion of a social occasion, but if the gentlemen could not wholeheartedly deceive themselves, the dinners at least—in the words of Percy Hasbrouck—helped to keep the ladies on their toes, by which he did not feel it necessary to explain that he meant that the ladies were expected to show precisely the proper interest in the firm's affairs, while yet giving no evidence of turning into Hettie Greens. A wife could know the meaning of the term short-selling, but she was not encouraged to study the more recondite financial operations.

Beulah Hasbrouck was the hostess for the Monday following Alfred Eaton's Washington trip, which guaranteed a minimum of frivolity at table and no lingering over dessert. She was a humorless, well-bred woman who was so much like her husband in so many respects that she could have been his sister and, given the choice after the first week of their marriage, would have preferred that relationship. Instead they had coldly hated each other for forty years, produced no offspring, and were generally looked upon as models of respectability, which indeed they were. In the third year of their marriage she had asked him if he would not as a gentleman give up his monthly forcible entries into her body, and as a gentleman he complied. Her life thereafter was made happy or unhappy by the success or lack of it achieved by her handling of her hackney ponies in Madison Square Garden. (She refused to show at Devon because her brother had divorced his wife, a Philadelphian, and she would not give the Philadelphians such an obvious opportunity for revenge.)

At two minutes past nine she rose and led the ladies to her large, Louis XV bedroom and its large, Louis XV–Crane Company 1910 bathroom, and Percy Hasbrouck as host addressed his partners. He spoke without rising from his chair, but he had the manner of a moderator. "As we all know, at least I think we all know, Alfred spent last week in that new hotbed of socialism on the Potomac, now ruled by the gentleman who should never have been allowed to leave his modest little farm on the Hudson. I haven't had the opportunity to buttonhole Alfred, and so I'm just as eager to hear what he has to say as the rest of you. Alfred, the floor is yours."

"The floor. That's what I almost hit last Thursday at the Duffys'. We dined there that night, and I have to start by reporting that I found out absolutely nothing. Kid gloves, wasn't it, you said I didn't have to wear in discussing Creighton Duffy, Mr. MacHardie? Well, I want to tell you that that's a smart cookie. Naturally I'd hoped and we'd all hoped that he'd have some of his new pals for dinner. But no. Four guys I knew from seeing them at my club in New York, and a broken-down Virginia horse-trader. Duffy's a clever bastard and all I got out of that evening was half a skinful. The guys he had for dinner were if anything more conservative than I am, and it was Duffy's way of telling us off, in case we thought we were going to learn anything with any help from him.

"That was our last night in Washington, and when I saw what he'd done, while I ordinarily don't drink much on the job, I felt like getting slightly plastered because of some of the other things I learned on my trip.

631

"Templeton Avirett arranged for me to have four lunch meetings with men he thought would be helpful, and the most informative men I talked to were in the Army and the Navy. As you said, Mr. MacHardie, they're the ones to see, if they'll talk. I saw a general, two colonels and two captains, and two Navy captains and two lieutenant commanders, in addition to a fellow in the Army Air Corps Reserve. I didn't see them all together, and not all of them were in universal agreement with each other, and I won't attempt to tell you what each one of them told me or we'd be here till Friday. But to start the ball rolling with a big generalization, the consensus, and this is the majority consensus, is that we'll be at war in five years."

"We? The United States?" said W. Z. Kingsley.

"Excuse me, Billy, but let's hold our questions till after Alfred's finished," said James MacHardie.

"But that's such a shocking statement," said Kingsley.

"As much to me as to you," said Alfred. "I have one son who'd be just ripe for it. First, let's take up Mussolini. Il Duce. Every time his name is mentioned someone always says something about how he's getting the Italian trains to run on time. Well, that may be one of the smartest pieces of propaganda anyone ever pulled, because it makes us think he's only interested in improving Italy for the Italians, shooting a few thousand *paisanos* now and then to keep in practice, but instilling efficiency and uniting the country so that it'll become a first-class power, which God knows it hasn't been under old Victor Emmanuel. It's no news to anyone in this room that Mussolini would like to have some Yankee dollars, and if he can prove that he's cut out most of the waste and corruption, and united the Italian people, he'll have a much easier time of it. That's the way our thoughts go when we keep hearing about those punctual trains.

"But the British navy isn't thinking about those trains. Do you know what else Benito's been doing and is doing right now while we think about his trains? Old Lantern-Jaw has been building submarines. He already has enough submarines so that he could walk across the Mediterranean from Naples to Africa without getting his feet wet, and he's building more every day. And believe me, gentlemen, the Admiralty doesn't like it a bit.

"The British as I understand it gave up some land to him in East Africa seven or eight years ago and then some more in Egypt and Libya. But that didn't satisfy him, and the question is, how soon is he going to ask for more, where is it going to be, and what can the British do about it?

"Our Navy men think the British are going to give up more territory because Mussolini has this submarine program so well under way that the British fleet is in serious danger this

632

minute. The British aren't ready for war. Steve Van Ingen's reports convince us of that. But sooner or later, sometime the British are going to have to stop backing away, and when they do—*bang!*

"This guy is nuts, and one of our fellows told me he has syphilis, but that doesn't improve the situation. If Il Duce does have syphilis, and is crazy, bang-bang could start any old time. Quite a few people have taken a shot at him—more than we've read or heard about. But either he's bullet-proof or the would-be assassins have been neglecting their target practice.

"Now let's skip from Rome to Berlin. I must preface these remarks by saying that the men I talked to were all West Pointers, professional Army officers, and don't you go by their rank. The colonels should be generals, and the captains should be colonels, but Army promotion is slower than ever now, a fact which we may have cause to regret. And the same thing is true of the Navy officers I talked to. They all should be flag officers, but we've been economizing. The only military information I got from a non-West Pointer or Annapolis man was from a reserve officer, but he's very close to the West Point men, even though as a civilian he makes four or five times as much money as they do. We can thank the good Lord that they don't like money as much as he does. I don't know why they stay, unless it's because the Army or the Navy is their religion. The reason I'm saying this about the professionals, and especially the Army, is that I've had some difficulty with the Army officers' attitude toward Hitler.

"These men rather like von Hindenburg and they don't like the way Hitler is using Old Von. They say he laughs at the old boy behind his back and just uses him for political reasons. However, it's too early to make any real predictions about Hitler. What I think about him isn't worth much because I don't know much, and I'm not a German. I have to say that because as far as I'm concerned, he's as crazy as Mussolini, although in a different way. But if I go by the facts, such facts as we have, that everybody has, he's offering something that a lot of Germans seem to like, and I repeat, I'm not a German, so I have a hard time judging him. But having said that, I'll pass on to you gentlemen the scraps I could pick up from the officers I saw.

"For the immediate future, they don't think Hitler will last. Most of the professional German officers consider Hitler a cheap, common upstart. He's accomplishing some of the things the German officers would like to see accomplished, namely, political things like getting the German people in a frame of mind to thumb their noses at us. They—the German officers—also know that Hitler fully intends to re-arm Germany, and to that extent they're cooperating with him. The

British of course know that, too. In fact, I guess they know it better than we do. But one of the colonels that speaks German and has a German name told me that when Hitler has accomplished their purpose, the German officers will give him the boot or just quietly put a bullet in his skull. One thing is sure, the German officer class doesn't intend to take orders from this guy, who isn't even a real German and never got higher than corporal in the war.

"However, I have to reiterate, my sources of information were men who are professional soldiers, most of whom saw action against the Germans in '17 and '18, but still look at things from the point of view of the professional soldier and officer. And I guess they're pretty much the same the world over. They may be on different teams, but after the game is over they like to get together and compare notes on how one touchdown got scored and why another play failed. I was in the Navy and I never met any captured German officers, but my best friend flew in the last war and he's often told me about the treatment of our officers that were captured, and German officers that we captured. All members of the same club. Therefore, gentlemen, I have to warn you against swallowing whole everything I was told.

"But one thing is certain. If and when Hitler re-arms Germany and gets away with it, and the German officers begin to run things, they are going to have another go at Europe. The same thing over again, except that England is going to have a chance to stay out. England will be invited to sit still while Germany takes over Belgium, Holland, Denmark, Austria, Czechoslovakia, Hungary, Yugoslavia, and Poland."

"Good heavens," said W. Z. Kingsley.

"You left out France," said Shanley.

"It's up to England to keep France out of it. The Germans will stay out of France on condition the French listen to the English. That's going to be the Germans' bargaining point with both Britain *and* France."

"Well, the French aren't going to listen," said Shanley.

"Gentlemen," said James MacHardie.

"I've almost finished, and those are questions I was going to answer anyway. If you think of your map of Europe—"

"I can get one in a second," said Percy Hasbrouck.

"I don't need it, thanks, Percy. All those countries I mentioned touch on Germany or Russia, and Poland touches on both. The Germans' argument, not only to the English but to us, the United States, is going to be that they will be doing us a favor. Sooner or later, the big test is going to be between Communist Russia and all the countries to the west of it. And that includes Italy, of course. One more piece of information, Germany expects no trouble with Mussolini. Mussolini will play ball with the Germans, or if he doesn't they'll give him a spanking and send him to bed. And I understand he spends a lot of time in bed. Hitler, by the way, doesn't. He has no use for women, or not much. However, Mussolini makes up for it. Just a note I threw in to show you one difference between the two men. The importance of Italy to the Germans is the threat to the British Mediterranean fleet, with those submarines. It's just possible, you see, that the British may have a war on their hands regardless, and that will be a great advantage to the Germans when they offer Britain the chance to stay out on condition they keep the French out.

"I could go on at great length because what I've been telling you is the result of, oh, I guess about sixteen hours' conversation with the men in Washington. This is only a summary. But no matter how I rearrange the pieces, I always come back to believing what those men agree upon, namely, that there will be war in Europe inside of five years, that Great Britain is somehow going to get into it, and if they do, we do."

"Alfred, I congratulate you," said MacHardie. "An excellent summary, no matter how unpleasant it may be in its implications. It's quite true that we make money in wartime, but the older I get the more I'm convinced that we don't make as much as our dollars say we do. The dollars lose in value, and governments gain in power over the individual. Taxes rise and stay risen. Whenever a government in time of war or other disaster, or emergency, takes away some of the private rights of the citizens, they never give back any of the important things. We gave up sugar and meat during the last war, and we got them back, but the income tax is here to stay, and I'm only afraid that the gentleman now in the White House has just begun to take away other freedoms in the guise of meeting an emergency. Thank you, Alfred, and I know you're going to be bombarded with questions, so I'll just shut up and listen."

"Thank you, sir," said Alfred.

"Alfred," said Guy Titterton, "suppose the Germans do start something. Is Ramsay MacDonald going to sit idly by?"

"I have no idea, Guy. His name was never mentioned. But you've spent a lot of time in England, and you know how they do things. MacDonald was prime minister, then Baldwin came and went, and now MacDonald's in again. I suggest we write to Steve Van Ingen and get his opinion on that. If the British don't like what MacDonald does, maybe they'll put Baldwin back in."

"Baldwin would be my man," said Kingsley. "I think it's a great handicap for a man to be illegitimate, in spite of Alexander Hamilton."

"Yes," said Frederick Cross. "If somebody calls you a bastard, what can you do? Nothing, if you are."

"Who's a bastard? I don't want to miss that," said John Miller, who was relying on his lip-reading.

"Alexander Hamilton, and Ramsay MacDonald," said Percy Hasbrouck.

"Oh, dear," said Miller. "How did we get on that subject? I must have missed something. James, I'd like to suggest that Alfred be requested to dictate a memorandum that we can all see."

"That's been arranged, John," said MacHardie. "Alfred promised to do that some day this week."

"Well, in that case, Jim," said Hasbrouck, "may I suggest that we ought to wait until Alfred does that before we pummel him with questions. Our questions now won't be as intelligent as they would be after reading his memorandum. We could all read the memorandum over the weekend and ask our questions next Monday night. Where are we next Monday?"

"My house," said Cross. "And everybody's going to be sick as dogs. Just had it painted from top to bottom, and the hell of it is, didn't need it. Whenever Ruth can't think of anything better to do she sends for the painters."

"Well, then, gentlemen, shall we join the ladies?" said Hasbrouck.

"I'll be in in just a minute," said Shanley. "I want to talk to Alfred."

"Well, now don't keep him too long, Don. He's a favorite with the ladies."

"Well, Mary's a favorite with the men, too," said Shanley. "We won't be long."

Hasbrouck did not like to be left out of anything, but he knew that Shanley admired Alfred and sometimes acted as his advisor, and almost invariably supported him in affairs of the firm.

"I'm going away tomorrow," said Shanley, when he and Alfred were alone. "So I won't have a chance to see you at the office. Tell me what you know about a man named Rothermel. I know he's about your age and comes from your home town."

"Tom? Tom was a hard-working kid. Father worked for the Gas Company."

"The Gas Company? In utilities that far back?"

"Tom wasn't. His father was."

"But he has that much of a connection, eh?" said Shanley.

"Yes. His father saved every cent he could to educate Tom and his sisters, and I guess starved himself doing it. Where did you run across him?"

"I haven't. But I hear he's one of the bright young men in

636

the government's electric power program. Is he a communist?"

"He may be headed that way. It's six years since I last saw him and he was working for the power and light company in Gibbsville, Pennsylvania, and expecting to be fired any minute. For his radical ideas. At the same time, however, he was making money in the market. Very good at math, apparently, but he may have been wiped out since then. Very bitter."

"Then he's right where he belongs, with that combination. He's a sort of rate-schedule expert and they've got him in this Tennessee Valley Authority. And you know what that's going to do to us."

"Tom Rothermel is a—what do you call it?—foeman worthy of our steel. I've thought about him. He isn't like Duffy. Duffy is out to advance his own career. Tom is sore at the whole system. You know, Tom was a happy kid. He had two or three jobs at a time when he was ten years old. Older people respected him, and he was popular among people his own age. I liked him, my sister liked him, and he wasn't sore at anybody. But he went up to State—State College—and I used to see him at vacation-time, and I remember thinking that every time he came home from college Tom seemed to be a little more—I don't know exactly what to say. A combination of self-assured and independent, and less the bright, happy kid that everybody liked. I used to think that that was part of growing up. We all change. But I've since thought that there was more to it than that. Tom didn't change. I think he was changed, passive voice. Whether it was a teacher at State, or coming up against the fraternity system—he made a fraternity, but not a very good one—and finding out that the cruel outside world was even crueler than Port Johnson, P A, I don't know. Why the interest in Tom? Is he a big shot?"

"Not yet. But he's one of those that could be. His name keeps coming up, all out of proportion to the job he holds. A lot of young men have jobs in this administration that bear no relation to the work they're doing. A man may have a job in the Regional Studies Department of the Tennessee Valley Authority. The director's office is in Knoxville, but the man lives in Washington. We don't know what he really does and we don't want to ask too many questions. But we may happen to know that three or four nights a week he meets men from the Economics and Statistics Branch of Interior. What are they cooking up? We'd give a lot to know. And if a man's good, we might offer him a job."

"My hunch is you're not going to get anywhere with Tom, not that way."

"I suppose not, and we're certainly not interested in hiring a man who'd probably use a job with us to supply information to another bright young assistant attorney general. Sure, we operate within the law, but those people have every intention of changing the laws. Eventually, they hope to put us out of business—speaking now as a director of two gas and electric companies."

"Oh, I understand. Well, is there anything you'd like me to do?"

"Can you think of anything?"

"Yes, I can go back to Washington and see Tom and ask him if he'd like a job with one of those companies. He'll say no, but I may learn something."

"I hate to ask you to go to Washington on such an errand."

"I can go down in the morning and be back the same day."

"Good. I'll talk to you some more next week," said Shanley.

A couple of weeks later Alfred had his meeting with Tom Rothermel. They met for lunch at the New Willard, and Alfred knew immediately that they had nothing to say to each other. Tom had put on considerable weight, and the slight, neat young man was as completely buried in this stout double-chinned man as the pleasant boy and youth was indiscernible in this ostentatiously bored, hostile cynic. "I only have a half an hour, Alfred," he said.

"Is that all they give you?" said Alfred.

"It's all I take."

Alfred then made haste to state his proposition, which was rejected before Tom heard any of the details, and rejected so peremptorily that Tom seemed to feel some guilt about the very offer. "I didn't know I was important enough to get an offer straight from a MacHardie partner, but I guess I am."

"The last time I saw you you were interested in making money," said Alfred. "You have the qualifications and experience, so don't consider this as having any sinister implications."

"No? Then why didn't they send Shanley? Shanley's the man in your outfit that I'd be dealing with."

"I know you, Shanley doesn't. That should be obvious."

"I never go by the obvious when I'm dealing with big business."

"Well, Tom, as of this minute you're not dealing with big business, at least as much of it as I represent. Let's eat our lunch like two hungry men and try to get through it without any more unpleasantness."

The next morning Tom Rothermel was asked to have lunch with Creighton Duffy, a man he had never met.

A letter from Alfred Eaton to Lex Porter, dated June 2, 1934:

Dear Two-Gun:
    This is the first social correspondence I have attempted in X months, whenever I last wrote you, which I am afraid was in the previous calendar year. That is, if you do not include

638

letters of condolence in social correspondence. In that department I have been very busy, and I have also had to do some traveling when a note would not suffice. I have made four trips to Port Johnson since January, beginning with my brother-in-law, Harry Van Peltz, husband of my sister Sally. Harry dropped dead on Sydenham Street, Philadelphia, just outside the entrance to the Racquet Club where he had been playing (and lost) a squash racquets match. If it makes you feel any better, he was 42, which is five years older than we are but still fairly young. I don't think you ever met Harry except at his and Sally's wedding but he was a damned nice guy who was quite wild in his younger days but settled down after he and Sal were married and they had a good life together. I'm sure Clemmie must have known him from deb parties. It was quite a shock to Sal but she is kept busy with the three kids. Mother would like them to move out to the farm with her but Sal has not yet made up her mind, although she has put her house on the market. My other funereal visits to Port Johnson were for a maid who had been with us for 26 years—Nellie, perhaps you remember her. She died of cancer in the Port Johnson Hospital. Also the man who ran the mill when my father wasn't there—Ed Barlow, who honestly believed my father was the greatest man in the U. S. And Mrs. Victor Dockwiler, the mother of the first girl I ever fell in love with (the girl who was killed in a motor accident in 1915—you heard me speak of her many times). There will be one more funeral in the very near future. Mary's mother has cancer. Doesn't know it, but she is not going to last out the summer. On that lugubrious note let us turn to other things.

Notice I said other things. I cannot say more cheerful when I look at the state of the world, whether it is our world or the whole God damn universe, however I shall try to find some cheerful items to report. I hope you consider my typing an improvement over my chicken-scratching and therefore a cheerful note. Mary gave me a portable for Xmas and I am getting to like it in spite of the resistance it puts up the moment I take the lid off. We went up to your old school for the Groton-St. Mark's baseball game and were pleased that a promising young left-fielder named Rowland Eaton went two for four, a double and a single. Unfortunately St. Mark's had hired a bunch of Irish ringers from Holy Cross and won the game by the narrow margin of 9 to 2. But as you can readily see, it was close all the way. Young Eaton has had several offers from the Yankees and A's but would like to finish his education first which should be in about 16 years from now. Actually he is doing pretty well and is headed for Harvard. Your namesake Alexander Porter Eaton is going through a succession of illnesses, all of a minor nature but they come one right after another before he gets a chance to recover and I worry about him. My daughter, whom you have yet to see and is still a little too young for you anyway, is fat and round and is said to look like me unless the viewer happens to be her maternal grandparents.

I had lunch downtown with your Uncle Fritz one day last winter and he seems to be taking the passing of years better than anyone I know, considering that he must be 70 or over. He can certainly get as mad at F. D. R. as men half his age, and that is mostly what we talked about. In fact it's what everybody talks about. Speaking of Fritz Thornton, a ghost from the past has reentered my life in the shape of Larry Von Elm. As you probably know, he has his own firm, consulting designers for several of the big aircraft manufacturers. We are interested in one or two aviation companies and, indirectly, an airline, therefore it was bound to happen that Larry would cross my path. Gone are the days of the Walk-Over shoes and Kuppenheimer suits. I would say Tripler and Frank Bros. nowadays. The tin-rim glasses have been supplanted by tortoise shell and the neckties are greatly subdued. He talks about "21" and El Morocco and his 48-foot cabin cruiser with Kermath engines, which he was able to pick up cheap for $10,000 two years ago. Luckily in my dealings with him I do not have to exercise any control over his expenditures but I wonder whether he is so free and loose with his own money now that he has a payroll to meet. He spends it on himself, obviously, but I'll bet his draughtsmen have to account for every yard of blueprint. He is getting a divorce from his first wife, whom he married when she was a stenographer and he was working for Curtiss after the N. A. C. broke up. I have never met his wife but I did meet Number 2-to-be and she is quite something. She is a babe from Stamford who is about 30 and was married twice before and I had often seen her in El Morocco before I met her with Von Elm. Not that I get to Morocco very often but every time I've been there she was there, rubbing it up with the night club set. She may be just what he always wanted but I don't see her spending much time visiting her new in-laws in Pittsburgh.

(Later)

Some day I'll finish this letter. It is now Sept. 20 and a whole summer has passed. To bring you up to date, I heard Von Elm married his babe. He has traded in his boat for a bigger & better one. I hope you and Clemmie had a good summer and I gather you did. I saw the Calthorps one night a week or so ago and they said you and Clemmie have without a doubt the best ranch in Wyoming as far as clientele is concerned. They said they would never think of going anywhere else. I pass this on to you because Sterling is not given to exaggerated praise and would not say it if he didn't mean it.

Mary's mother died in August. They kept her full of morphine but it was pretty bad at the end and Mr. St. John is a wreck. He has been given an extended leave of absence by the du Ponts but he wants to sell the house, retire, and live in England. I don't think I told you last winter that we bought a house about a mile from your Uncle Fritz's place on Meeting House Road. It was the old Ashbel Berry property. I am sure you must have been there. I bought ten acres and the house and garage. The Berry family are holding on to the remaining 20 acres and have promised me protection on three sides. It would make you weep bitter tears to know what I paid for it but I will admit that I got house, garage and land for much less than the house cost to build. We can run it with two servants and a gardener, exclusive of the nurse for the baby, otherwise I would not have touched it. I have made the painful discovery that my son can beat me at both golf and tennis. I did not take a set from him all summer and toward the end of the summer *he* was giving *me* strokes whenever we played golf, instead of the other way. He has the same coordination you have—or had. I don't know whether you still have it. I can beat him at court tennis. I took him over to your uncle's court whenever I could talk him into it but he says court tennis will ruin his stroking and serve and he tries to get out of playing. My only hope is to practice my golf shots on an indoor range this winter and pin his ears back next summer, but I'll never be able to take him at lawn tennis again. The wind and the legs—Oh, those legs!—have begun to go. Jean and Alex got through the summer without anything worse than measles, thank God. I suppose you and Clemmie are hard as rock, bronzed by the sun and looking like Vikings. I heard you also had Ben Eustace and his wife as paying guests when the Calthorps were there, so you and Clemmie must have been brought up to date on Philadelphia news.

If I am ever going to get this off I'd better stop now and will do just that. My love to Clemmie and a swift kick in the blue jeans to you.

As ever,
Alfred

A letter from Lex Porter to Alfred, dated October 12, 1934:

Dear Horse Cock:

The last of our paying guests have now departed and we are bedding down for the winter. It was a profitable summer, financially speaking, but we were not sorry to see them go. It was fine while the kids were here in July and the first two weeks in August but your friend Mr. Ben Eustace stayed on after the Calthorps left and made such a damn nuisance of himself that we were strongly tempted to give him his money back and kick him the hell out and would have if we had not felt sorry for her. He is a 24 karat shitheel and nobody understands why she puts up with him. I do not wish to pry into your personal affairs but is it possible that Natalie was at one time enamored of you? You don't have to answer that by Western Union but I will tell you why I asked. One night after supper Eustace and Natalie were in our cabin having a few drinks and Eustace went over to my gun cabinet and began admiring my small arsenal. He picked up the Purdey and examined it enviously and I said you had given it to me last Christmas. "How do you know that son of a bitch?" he asked. "Take it easy," I replied. "He happens to be my best friend." Then he said I had very strange taste in friends or words to that effect. I replied that it was still a free country and we could still pick our friends.

He didn't say any more then, but later in the evening, after he had put down about ten more drinks he began harping on you. Natalie was helping Clemmie with the dishes the first time he mentioned you (or I mentioned you), consequently when he began talking about you it was all new to them. He commenced by announcing that he couldn't go anywhere without hearing about that s. o. b. Eaton. I told him to lay off again but he said I had said it was a free country and he didn't know why he couldn't call an s. o. b. an s. o. b. if he felt like it. "Well, I do," said Clemmie. "Alfred happens to be one of our best friends." "Oh, you too?" said Eustace.

I didn't like the way he said it at all and I interrupted. "Just a minute there, boy. Don't say anything you'd be sorry for," or some such mild remark. All this time Natalie said nothing but I could easily see she was on the verge of tears, so I told Eustace it would be a good idea to turn in and get some sleep. He was strongly tempted to swing at me but Natalie said to him: "Come on," and he left obediently. He apologized the next day, without mentioning your name, but the next time he had a snootful it was the same as before. The odd thing was that Natalie could always stop him, and Clemmie had the theory that he was afraid of Natalie. That is, afraid she would walk out on him. But that did not keep him from trying to make you sound like the worst bastard that ever lived. Then one night very late Natalie came to our cabin and asked if we had seen Eustace but we hadn't, so I got out the kerosene lamp and went looking for him. I finally found him in a gully, sound asleep and I was tempted to leave him there for the night but that happens to be the headquarters of several families of timber rattlesnakes so I woke him up and took him back to his cabin, saw he had no bones broken, and let him collapse on the floor and Natalie spent the night in our cabin. They stayed three more days and the rest of the time he behaved himself and didn't drink anything. But you can be sure that if he wants to come back here next summer we are going to be all filled up. I will also see to it that the other ranches are warned because that fellow means trouble for someone. We have to look the other way when some of the dudes are doing their drinking and screwing as long as they don't get out of hand, but Eustace is nothing but a pest and I predict that some day there will be trouble. I don't think he will ever harm Natalie, but she is the only one who has any control over him. He will say anything at all when he gets drunk and he said some other things that I have not put down on paper. But I would advise you to steer clear of him. You are Public Enemy No. 1 to all husbands, according to Eustace.

I am sending this care of the R. & T. Club so it won't be opened by mistake at home. We may come East for Xmas and then again we may not, but I will give you plenty of warning if we do. The next best thing if you and Mary can't come out would be to send Rowland here next summer, and I will see that he never touches a golf club (we haven't any) and you may be able to beat him. I will even give him a job so that you won't have to shell out any dough, except train fare. Clemmie sends love to you both and as far as Mary is concerned, so do I.

As ever,
Lex

And so went the days and the seasons for Alfred Eaton in the years that he could not know were an approximation of peace and could not know were an approximation of happiness. Contrariwise, he was aware of the incompleteness of the peace and the incompleteness of the happiness, and no day in its passing was like any other day that had passed or was yet to come. The pleasures were small, and so were the irritations; the one pain was not great; the triumphs were not great. His health was good. Any random day in October was vastly different from any random day in the succeeding July, and that was a fact at the time, just as it was equally truly a fact that when the Julys and Octobers and Aprils became all only parts of the whole of that period, the period itself became no more than a succession of days that were identical; but to reach that perspective time was necessary, the distance of time and the hardening and corruption of existence were necessary to make the felt and observed facts of each day and of many days into a personal glacial squeeze. One fact did not make a lie of another fact; each was true in its time. One day was breakfast, subway ride, work at office, lunch at club, work at office, evening paper, evening meal, sleep; the woman and her conversation and the orange juice at breakfast; the smells and jostlings of the strangers in the subway; the misunderstandings and appreciations at the office; the friendly and the distracted and scarred and nervous at lunch; the daydreaming and the hints of weariness at the office again; the vicarious living in the evening paper; the ease or the petulance at the evening meal; the mystery of sleep that came or did not. And always the degrees of intimacy and involvement with the many human beings that made each day different, and varied from day to day. Today was not Tuesday, it was Wednesday, because on Wednesday you saw *him* and on Tuesday you did *that*. And a little girl grew and a little boy grew, and a woman got older and a man aged, and a tooth came out and a muscle ached and a man did not get his money and a waiter fell dead, and thunder slapped and a bell rang and paper crinkled and an elevated train abraded the track and a flying machine fanned the air, and a letter came and a sweetness was tasted and a taxi was found and a piss was postponed and a door would not close and a party hung up and a lion escaped and a woman's oil brought joy and the approximation of peace and the approximation of happiness. And then that day was gone to join the others to await the squeeze of time, but one day passed was already a day in the past and petrifying before the final pressure. The dead waiter was a fish a million years old.

Alfred Eaton had many interests and involvements. He knew many people and some of them were interests because of who they were and what they were to him—his children, his wife, the woman he loved, his mother, his friend, his sisters. To be his interests they needed no more than to be who they were and what they were. Then there were those of the next but lesser intensity—Fritz Thornton, Alexander Thornton, Josephine the cook, Shanley and, latterly, Kingsley. Then James MacHardie in a position of his own, unacquisitive of affection and unacquiring of it, but admirable in his mentality and respectable in his principles. Then the first-name acquaintances and the last-name friends and nickname friends, the recognized nameless, the business associates, the servants of friends, the cousins of acquaintances, the sons of watchmen, the maitres d'hotel, the doctors' receptionists, the part-time chauffeurs, the reverend clergy, the assistant caddymasters, the hat salesman, the man who cut his hair and the man who taught his son history. And those were only some of the living who took part in his existence and shared the hours of his life and whom he honored, respected, approved, tolerated, forgave, rewarded, saw, spoke to, liked. There was the bootblack whom he knew only because he was a bootblack, but Alfred's consideration of him was consideration of him as a man and not merely as a softly humming Italian who used Meltonian cream. There was the gardener's son who acted as marker at Fritz Thornton's tennis court, but he was very soon the freshman at St. John's–Brooklyn as much as a boy who had learned the rich man's game. There was the Italian whom he had met at Fordham Law School and whom he saw almost every time he walked a block of Wall Street: "Hello, Alfredo"—"Hyuh, Alfredo." Never more than those words and the exchange of smiles over all the small coincidence of the same first name.

And there were the others. Those he could not like, those he had learned not to trust, those who did not want to be known, the suspicious, the angry, the markedly cruel, the loud, the mean, the dirty, the self-pitying, the swift. The Percy Hasbroucks, the Creighton Duffys, the Tom Rothermels, the Beulah Hasbroucks, the Ben Eustaces, the captain at "21," the traffic cop in Astor Place, the trainman on the Long Island, the septuagenarian brothers at the Racquet Club, the retired opera singer, the head gardener at Fritz Thornton's place, the

644

Morgan partner, the pediatrician's locum tenens, the taxi driver in Port Johnson, the nuns at Belmont Park, the insufferable butler to Alexander Thornton, the Cashes of Englewood, the vice-president of Rowley & Cruickshank, the cousin of Guy Titterton, the President of the United States.

On any random day he would share some of his life with a goodly number of the rich and the poor, guests and hosts, the distant and the close, the warm and the cold, the cruel and the kind, the handsome and the ugly, the above and the below, the truth-tellers and the liars, the helpful and the enemy. All of them, and the day, were his present existence until the day itself was stacked away, pushed further into the past, joined by another day and many more days, with their special people for each day. Then all—days and people—becoming a solid block of his time on earth that was later to be seen as a period of living with an approximation of peace and an approximation of happiness, the small pains and discomforts having been endured and forgotten.

Such a period of living began for Alfred sometime in 1934 (a date could not be put upon it). It lasted five years, a longer space of time than that decided upon by statesmen as a fair trial of a man's right to remain President, and longer than that decided upon by pedagogues as the normal maximum in which a man might become a bachelor of arts. For Alfred Eaton it was a period in which he lived well inside the extremes of ecstasy and of misery; a period in which, according to the scheme of things, he was allowed to get his breath, to be nourished, to make ready for whatever tests the later years might, and inevitably must, present. The pleasures of the period were repeated or at least foreseeable, even the pleasure of watching his daughter grow out of babyhood into a child who wanted to ask questions more than she wanted to be admired, a characteristic that had been true of her brother Rowland. There was that joy and the joy of watching the younger son leaving behind the illnesses that had attacked him in childhood, a joy that was repetitive because all children have illnesses. And the joy Rowland gave his father was foreseeable; it had never been in doubt. Alfred and his elder son had arrived at the boy's eighteenth birthday with their mutual respect intact, a condition achieved through the maintenance of reasonable discipline and no violations of the boy's reticence. Their quarrels had been over matters which were decided by the father, and from which there was no appeal; such matters as the denied right to own an automobile until the boy had completed freshman year at Harvard; the denied right to risk malaria by taking a trip to the Brazilian jungle; the father's insistence on four weeks' summer work as a messenger at Rowley & Cruickshank, regardless of its interference with the long vacation; the father's refusal to serve cocktails at the son's seventeenth birthday party.

In all these matters the boy had his mother's unuttered support, and knew it, but Alfred's decisions held, and the relaxing of some rules on the boy's eighteenth birthday was thus pleasurable to give and to receive. "You can drink if you have the money to pay for it," Alfred told him. "You won't be able to afford much of a wine cellar out of your freshman allowance, but I don't think you have the makings of a lush, or of a sponger, so that's no problem. I'll give you a Ford, a Chevrolet or a Plymouth as soon as I get your marks at the end of freshman year. As to summer work, I advise you to go into R. O. T. C., which I believe requires six weeks at camp. If you don't, you still work downtown for four weeks. I'll buy you a dinner jacket and tails at Roger Kent and I won't take it out of your allowance, but if you want to spend more than that, you have to make up the difference. I think you'd be foolish. If you go out for the freshman crew your clothes won't fit you a year from now, but I have something here for you that you won't outgrow." He handed his son a complete set of evening studs, buttons and links, for both black and white tie. "Good goods. Came from Tiffany's. Should last you the rest of your life."

"Good Lord, Pop. What did these set you back?"

"That's a vulgar question, and don't call me Pop. You'll get an idea how much they cost when you try to hock them, as I suppose you will. They cost plenty, but you deserve them."

"Thanks. I mean for the remark about deserving, and of course thanks for the studs and stuff."

"You're welcome. And by the way, there are no restrictions about hocking them. I don't give things with strings attached. They're yours."

"I'll never hock these."

"I hope you never have to. Your mother has a present for you."

Mary handed him a package wrapped in tissue paper and a crimson ribbon, which he quickly opened. "A wallet. Just what I need. Have a look at my old one." Mary's present was a pigskin wallet with gold clips and the boy's name stamped inside. "Got my name in it."

"Keep looking. You won't embarrass me," said Mary.

"Well, I can tell by the feel of it—" He spread the wallet and took out the money. "It looks like a hundred dollars. Ten tens?"

"I don't know," said Alfred. "Your mother gave it to you, I didn't."

"Ma, it is. A hundred bucks. Thanks, honestly."

"You're very welcome, dear. As your father said, you deserve it."

"And thanks for that, too."

"You also have cheques from Grandmother Eaton and Grandfather St. John."

"Listen, I feel like taking you two to the Stork Club. I wish I could, but I didn't know I was going to be so rich."

"And you *have* a *date*," said Mary.

The boy was already dressed for his date in the uniform of the day—tweed jacket, flannel slacks, Groton baseball tie. He stood up, raising the glass of champagne at his side. "To my mother and father. Tops in any league." He drank the wine, kissed his mother and grasped his father's hand, then quickly went out, leaving the studs on the table.

They heard the front door closing, then, from the hall, his voice calling out: "Ma, will you put my studs in my top drawer?" And then the front door was closed again.

"I was never that young," said Alfred.

"At his age you'd never been happy. He's never been anything else, and it's mostly due to you."

"I'd like to think so, but far from it. You did it."

"You're wrong, Alfred. You learned your lesson from your own father. That's why both boys are happy. You didn't spoil Rowland, and you didn't neglect Alex."

"I hate to sound like an old patriarch at forty-two, but by Christ I think it's been pretty good."

"Especially when you consider what it could have been."

"Well, I wasn't going to say that."

"But you thought it," said Mary.

"In any case, we've got a good boy. Really a good man. You can really begin to see what he's going to be like as a man."

"Let's not hurry it, please. I don't even like it much when people say, 'Oh, Mrs. Eaton, don't tell me you have a son old enough to graduate from Groton.'"

Rowland's birthday was not the precise point at which the period of peace and happiness ended; and it must not be inferred that Alfred was aware it was ending even when it did end. It was not so much that the peaceful period was ending as that a new period was beginning, and he did not at the time know it was beginning any more than he knew he was in a peaceful period while he was living it. It merely seemed to be life as it is lived, and it was many years before he could see those five years as a period and to characterize them as approximately peaceful, approximately happy.

Talk of war—transatlantic war—was unavoidable in the latter half of that five-year period. European news, none of it good, took up half the front pages of the newspapers and shared air time with the commercial announcements on the

647

radio. A new form of semi-celebrity came into being: the man who worked in a European office of an American broadcasting company and was given the official governmental announcements to read. There was not a first-rate journalist among them, but emphatic repetition of their names, before and after their nightly readings of the propaganda, made their names familiar to the American public and particularly to American book publishers. Soon those men—some of whom had not even covered a strawberry festival for their home-town newspapers, who knew neither the language nor the geography of countries from which they broadcast, and whose acquaintance in government was limited to the bureaucrats who handed them their "communiqués"—were the nominal authors of books on politics, military strategy, the psychology of ancient races, the unhappy childhood of Adolf Hitler, the intractability of Stanley Baldwin, the courage of Henri Pétain, the appetites of Edda Ciano, and the impenetrability of the Maginot Line. The books sold rapidly and the errors in them were quickly forgotten. The public interest in European developments was so great that some of the broadcasting companies sent their staff announcers abroad to read the communiqués. Most of the Americans who had had journalistic experience abroad were from three to six thousand miles west of Paris, holding forth on the lecture platforms of Orchestra Hall, Shrine auditoriums, Junior League clubhouses, the Academy of Music, university theaters, and tents. Money was again plentiful and the best men's club in every city in the country offered a good dinner and a sizable fee for off-the-record lectures by men who had spent a couple of years copying down the names of the latest arrivals at the Hotel George Cinq.

"Do you remember when you said it'd be five years till we got in a war?" said Don Shanley one August day.

"After I came back from Washington that time," said Alfred.

"I don't think you're going to be right, but you're not going to be far wrong," said Shanley. "I just hope and pray we don't get in it before we get someone else in the White House."

"Not a chance, Don," said Alfred. "I was only a freshman, but I can remember that 'Don't swap horses in midstream' line. And this guy is a hell of a lot more popular than Wilson ever was."

"Don't tell me *you're* falling for it?"

"I don't suppose I'd be around here very long if I did, but no, I'm not falling for it."

"Now wait a second. You're going to be around here as long as you want to be. Don't ever say things like that. You know where you're headed for."

"I know where I'm headed if you have any say in the matter."

"I think you're going to be surprised at how little opposition you'll encounter. But to get back to Roosevelt, you seemed to want to say some more."

"Well, perhaps I do, and since it may come up, I'll tell you what's on my mind. He's going to run again, and he's going to win. We all hear a lot of dinner-table talk for Wendell Willkie, but *I'm* not going to support Willkie. In fact, Don, I'm not going to support any Republican candidate. I've thought about it and thought about it, I read these God damn books and everything in the *Times* and the *Tribune*, and I listen to the radio. I have no faith in anything I read or hear except when they've told us a fact, something that's already happened. Every fact points to war, has been pointing to war for ten years, and I don't mean because it's ten years since the stock market went blooey. Actually longer than ten years, back to the Versailles Treaty. A year ago we found out what the Germans thought of that, and if I were a German I'd have felt the same way. If my country had lost a war I'd honor the peace treaty only until I was strong enough to say the hell with it, and that's what Hitler had to play on with the German people. He played on it for all it was worth and got the Germans thinking big again, plus the fact that he's the greatest rabble-rouser that I've ever heard of.

"I went to a guy's house for dinner last week. He has a regular-size movie projector and shows feature pictures and sometimes newsreels. Whenever I've been there and seen pictures of Hitler making speeches I get him to re-run the shots of the people. Don't let anybody kid you that they're not for Hitler. Morrie Goldblatt says those pictures are fake, the crowds are terrified of the Storm Troopers. Well, we've heard different, and I've studied those faces carefully, and Morrie's absolutely wrong. The German people are going to do what Hitler wants them to do because it's what *they* want to do. And I don't know whether Morrie is trying to influence me or just going in for some wishful thinking, but the only people in Germany, aside from the Jews and some Catholics, who don't like Hitler are the *older* officers. And—"

"Do you know that, or is it a guess?"

"Well, you've heard it in this office, but I've also heard it—confidentially, from Mary's father. He's living in England, but he travels on the Continent, gets to see the I. G. Farben boys, the Opel crowd. And they make no bones about it. They're all for Hitler. And here's the thing to remember. The older German officers are against Hitler, but they're not against what he's done so far, and they're not going to stop a war. They're only going to postpone it. Then when they fight, if Germany is successful, they'll give Hitler a bellyful of Mausers and take over. But there's one guy they're not fooling. Two guys. One of them is Hitler himself, and the other is the fat guy, Goering, who knows all about officer-psychology because he *is* one.

"Where does all this leave Roosevelt and me? I'm glad you asked me. You didn't, but you're ready to. Do you know who Roosevelt's trying to get to come to Washington? Lovett. Do you know who else? Forrestal."

"Forrestal doesn't surprise me, but I'd like to make you a small bet on Lovett."

"I won't take your money. It's no longer a question of how you feel about Roosevelt. I hardly know Lovett, but if Roosevelt asked *me* to go to Washington—"

"Has he?" said Shanley.

"We'll come to that. I'd go. I don't like Roosevelt. I think he's a phony, although I suspect that some of that phony in him is phony, too. I mean I think he has something more on the ball than the big smile and 'Mah frands.' He knows how a government operates. He's been in it before, when he was Daniels' shadow, and he's been in it now for seven God-forsaken years.

"All right, Don. I'm coming to it. In one word. Efficiency. In another word, inefficiency. Hitler is not going to invite us to a small war, black tie, R. S. V. P. We're going to be in it quick, and soon, and no matter how much I despise most of the people in the government, I would hate like hell to start fighting a war while an old government was getting out and a new one was coming in."

" 'Don't swap horses in midstream.' "

"Sure. Same old argument. But a war will be run from Washington, and we could lose a battlewagon because a new Secretary of the Navy doesn't know where Swanson left the key to the men's room."

"Well, you haven't convinced me, but I'm a good twenty years older than you are. I'm set in my ways."

"I'm getting to be," said Alfred. "I thought I *was.*"

"Ah, back to the question you were going to come to."

"Kind of hoped you'd ask me that. I've been sounded out, very tentatively."

"By the great man?"

"Oh, Lord, no. A fellow named Von Elm that I was in business with before I came here."

"Lawrence B. Von Elm Associates?"

"That's the guy. Staunch Republican, by the way. I couldn't have been more surprised if Creighton Duffy'd asked me."

"I rather think Creighton was consulted, don't you?"

"It'd be very strange if he wasn't," said Alfred. "In fact, so strange as to be unbelievable, and therefore why did I get asked? I haven't said anything to Mr. MacHardie yet, but I'm telling you because I think some partner should know. In other words, I am not keeping it from members of the firm *as* members of the firm. You have my permission to say I've told you about it, if one of the other partners should ask you."

"Just what am I to say, Alfred?"

"That Von Elm sounded me out. He wanted to know if my feelings about the Big Boy were so strong that under no circumstances would I take a job with the government. He made no concrete offer. I gather that quite a few men have been asked the same question in the same tentative sort of way. No job offered, but either Hopkins or Roosevelt himself—or both—are trying to weed out the men who hate Roosevelt so deeply that they wouldn't raise a hand to help him. My answer was, 'Without prejudicing my attitude toward Roosevelt and his administration, I would take a job if I thought the job was going to be useful to the country, and I felt I was suited for the job.' Naturally I made it clear to Von Elm that if some smart prick tried to make political capital out of my taking a job, I'd not only resign immediately, but I'd give a statement to the press that would make every Republican think twice before having anything to do with the administration."

"Next move is up to them," said Shanley. "But you're realistic enough to know that the minute you take a job in the government, the mere mention of your name is political capital?"

"I'm afraid that's true, to a certain extent. But when the shooting starts there's only going to be one party and that's the Roosevelt party, and that's going to be the case until the shooting stops. Roosevelt will be king, dictator, whatever you want to call it, and I'm afraid, Don, that I believe that's the way it should be."

"Oh, you do? You believe that?"

"I do. In a shooting war, the only thing the Republican party can do is try to protect individual peacetime rights. By that I mean that Taft and the others, they'll have to do what the king says, but every time there's some legislation that takes away individual peacetime rights, they'll have to fight to make certain that it's understood that we get those rights back at the end of the war."

"Some job."

"Yes, but there we have a slight advantage. Suppose the Democrats want a law that says every civilian has to give up his car for the duration? The Republicans say okay, but it

651

has to be written in there that it's only for the duration. Then the Democrats say, 'Well, we don't want to write that in.' Immediately we have them. They've shown that they're taking advantage of a war to get legislation they couldn't get otherwise."

"You've thought this out, haven't you? Maybe you ought to go into politics."

"Don, 'way back in 1903, when I was six years old, I fell into a manure pit and had to climb out without any help. That was as deep in politics as I ever want to get." He smiled. "Of course I don't mind playing a little office politics, but that's different."

"May I say a very cautious word to you?"

"You ought to know by this time that you can say anything you please."

"Office politics can be very dirty too."

"Now I wonder what you mean by that," said Alfred.

"Let's just call it a general observation."

"Oh, I'll even forget it was you that said it. I'll even forget you said a while ago I'd be surprised at how little opposition I'd encounter."

"I said you'd be surprised, because I think you're expecting more than you'll get. But don't expect *none*. Anyway, it's a long ways off. We hope. When John Miller died—well, I was sorry to see him go, but I was awfully damn glad it wasn't James Duncan MacHardie."

"So was I."

They were lunching together at the Down Town Association as was their custom when, as on this day, they were the only partners in the office. MacHardie was taking the day off at home, Hasbrouck and Titterton were cruising aboard Titterton's sloop, Kingsley was at Bar Harbor, Cross was playing golf at the National. Van Ingen, presumably, was at the office in London, since it was a Wednesday and the weekend had not begun. They had finished their food and were sipping their iced tea, comfortable with each other and for the moment silent.

A tall man in a blue flannel suit and bold-striped tie stopped at their table and looked at them as though inspecting them.

"Well, Charley," said Shanley. "Did you never learn that it was rude to stare? Sit down and have a drink, or go stare at someone else."

"Hello, Mr. Lippincott," said Alfred.

Lippincott was a senior partner in a brokerage house, a prankster and self-consciously eccentric. "You two fascinate me," he said, continuing to inspect them and refusing to sit down. "Such composure."

"It's too hot to get excited," said Shanley.

"Even over the Russians?" said Lippincott.

"What have they done? Walk out on that conference?" said Shanley.

"Ah-ha, it wasn't composure at all. It was blissful ignorance," said Lippincott.

"Of what?" said Shanley.

"Oh, my. You *don't* know. Well, I'll test your composure. The Russians and the Germans have just signed a non-aggression treaty."

"They can't have," said Alfred. "The Russians were having a conference with the *British and French. Those* three are the ones that are signing a treaty."

"Charley, you're slipping. You used to do better," said Shanley.

"Oh, well, this isn't the first time we brokers have had to teach you bankers the facts of life. Go have a look at the ticker," said Lippincott, and marched jauntily away.

"Do you suppose he's telling the truth?" said Alfred.

"I have a feeling he is, this time."

"The bastards," said Alfred.

"Which ones?"

"All of them," said Alfred. He stood up, but remained where he stood.

"What are you going to do?"

"I'm going to call my son and tell him he can have a car. I want him to have all the fun he can, now."

Shanley looked up at him and nodded. "You're unfortunately right," he said.

Civilization, which has been defined as a state of social culture characterized by relative progress in the arts, science, and statecraft, has been dependent for its existence on the communication of words. The words were spoken, sung, stamped on the skin of a goat, pressed on the pulp of a tree, speeded along guiding wires, flung into the air. Among the innumerable purposes to which the communication of words was put was the exchange of promises on how, and sometimes when, one civilized nation might or might not attempt to destroy or subdue another civilized nation. But always at the same time that such promises were being kept, the words communicated by one civilized nation also unintentionally conveyed warnings to other nations that the first nation was about to attempt to destroy a second if the second did not make the first attempt. Thus words, the communication of words, contained some declaration of intention. Two civilized nations were able to communicate their points of difference, and neither could ever complain that it was ignorant of the other's worldly wishes. A civilized Czechoslo-

653

vakian, a cultured Dane could not protest that he did not know what Hitler wanted. He had known for years, known through the communication of words that had been pressed on the pulp of a tree, speeded along guiding wires, flung into the charged air. But the version of civilization known as western had been repudiated by the rulers of Russia, and the statesmen of Japan had never adopted the western version, and the words of the rulers of Russia and the statesmen of Japan were not communicated with any sense of responsibility or respect for the good opinion of the western-civilized. The ruler and statesmen of Germany felt not much more responsibility or respect, but they were living in the western world and they acted in the western fashion. It was not inconsistent for the Russian statesmen to announce partnership with Hitler while pretending to arrange for friendship with the nations he had chosen to be his victims. Nor was it inconsistent for the statesmen of Japan to have diplomatic conversations with the American statesmen at the very moment that Japanese aircraft were on their way to destroy the Americans' Pacific fleet. The Russians and the Japanese were under no obligation to behave consistently with the rules of the western-civilized, and their treachery was not so judged at home. The western-civilized had allowed themselves to be deceived by the Russian and Japanese somewhat western taste in suits and hats, a mistake as foolish as it would have been to believe that the common use of the French language implied diplomatic accord.

The attack on Pearl Harbor was successful partly because it was not only a tactical surprise, but because in the communication of words there had been no declaration of intent such as had been conveyed to the civilized Czech or the cultured Dane. The grocer in Watertown, Maine, did not know what the Japanese wanted, and so his equally ignorant son was sealed up in the U. S. S. *Arizona*. The father suffered and the son died because of their inability to detect any warning in the words of the Japanese.

But as a nation we had been getting ready for war, and only the overt act was a surprise. Britain had been in it for more than two years; the French, the Dutch, the Belgians, the Norwegians, the Danes, the Poles had been out of it almost as long. The Germans had turned on their strange Russian allies six months before the Japanese bombed Pearl Harbor and two months after the Russians signed neutrality agreements with the Japanese allies of the Germans. (The ten-year agreement between the Nazis and the Russians lasted slightly less than two years.) For more than a year Alfred Eaton and his elder son had been carrying draft cards, for a year and a half the British had been in possession of fifty American destroyers, and for one month the Russians had been richer by one billion American lend-lease dollars. The boy whom Alfred Eaton had fished out of James MacHardie's icy pond was already a naval aviation pilot in Florida, and Sterling Calthorp's son had been killed by the live ammunition during the Louisiana maneuvers. There was, at the time, no power on earth that could stop the slaughter before it became greater, and the Japanese, by the geographical nature of their attack, made it impossible to argue that the war was primarily the business of the eastern states. Cleveland was suddenly the same distance from Pearl Harbor as from Paris; Honolulu was only as far from Tokyo as Fort Worth was from Honolulu. A man could walk across the Bering Strait, and Seward, Alaska, was only about as far from Helena, Montana, as Helena was from Miami, and that was no longer far enough. It almost seemed as though the Japanese had planned to lose a war for the pleasure of one quick victory.

On the Sunday afternoon that the news from Pearl Harbor was broadcast, Alfred was at his desk in the small room he called his study, trying to dispose of the correspondence that had to be done by hand. Alex and another boy had gone to a movie; Jean and Mamselle had gone for a walk; Mary had gone down to the Vanderbilt to have lunch with her father, who had taken a suite of rooms in the hotel while deciding where to live. Alfred and Mary had quarreled about that. "Let your father come here."

"The children crawl all over him."

"He ought to be damn glad they do."

"He isn't, though. I'll be back about six."

"Six?"

"Six or six-thirty. I'm going to stop in at Sage's on the way uptown."

He looked at her contemptuously and then left the room. There were no new words for Sage Rimmington; they had all been said in attack and defense. For years all that Alfred had known about her was that she had fainted at Mary's wedding and that she was an orphan who was being brought up by an aunt and uncle. He had suspected she was a Lesbian, but the arguments against his suspicion were numerous: in 1939, upon coming into the final and largest chunk of her father's estate, she had moved to New York and bought a house on Sutton Place South and become a hostess to a group of second-billing movie actors and actresses, theater people from respectable out-of-town families, clever imitators of Cole Porter, alumni of the Yale Lit, ugly old actresses with long memories for scandals, a young Episcopal clergyman, two fashion photographers, and an assortment of fashion models. Her guests, who called her Say-gee, came and went all Sunday afternoon and evening. There was always someone playing the piano, usually well, and the conversation was almost entirely gossip of the theater world. The medical profession was represented nearly every Sunday by Dr. Jim Roper, and at eight or nine o'clock in the evening, when the others had gone, he stayed. But until the first appearance of Jim Roper there had always been one man who stayed, although by no means always the same man. A burly movie actor of the second magnitude was still believed to have the strongest claim on Sage's attentions, in spite of Roper, and she was known to have given a first-ten tennis player a Buick convertible sedan. She was generous and sympathetic to the male and female homosexuals who largely comprised her Sunday at-homes, and out of gratitude or some deeper understanding of her they refrained from commenting on her weakness for men. The tennis-player was a bisexual, the burly movie actor was a transvestite, and Roper's practice was almost entirely among Broadway, literary, and idle private-income people, to whom his name was a password. The guests' behavior at Sage's parties was physically irreproachable; the men pretended to be gentlemen, the girls were ladylike. They all had money and most of them had a good earning capacity. The men dressed according to the standards set by the articles in the theater programs, and the women—except for the ugly old actresses—were a weekly fashion show. They loved Sage and they loved her parties, because she was enormously rich and socially secure, and at her parties they could feel that they were very close to being the real-life representatives of Mr. Coward's comedies. But when a friend would say, "Say-gee dear, can I bring Noel next Sunday?" she would reply, "Please don't. I couldn't bear it if I didn't like him, and I just mightn't, you know." It was the only possible, acceptable reason for her refusal, barring the less obvious one that she was afraid Coward might not appear.

Mary Eaton had brought Alfred to Sage's twice; once to a dinner party at which he had known everyone present, and once to an early Rimmington at-home, at which he had known no one and wanted to go home after the first five minutes. He had never gone again, but he knew the character of the Sunday parties had not changed. Sage had come to New York with some slight thought that she could condescend to the Eatons, since Mary St. John had been fractionally below her in the Wilmington social scheme and Alfred Eaton was just somebody from a place she was likely to call Fort Jackson. But in a few months in New York she learned that Alfred Eaton and, because of him, Mary were in the position to condescend, and she made efforts to have the Eatons at later dinner parties, but finally gave up when Mary told her it was no use. The effect on Sage was to make her hate Alfred Eaton and to ply Mary with invitations and small gifts. Mary, satisfied that Sage appreciated their relative positions in New York, began to use Sage as a convenience, sure of a welcome on Sunday afternoon, equally sure that Sage could be depended upon for larger favors if they became necessary. In time they became necessary.

During the approximately peaceful, approximately happy period of Alfred's life the Eatons had encountered Jim Roper seldom and by accident. If it was unavoidable, the men would exchange nods, but as a rule they did not speak, and Mary, sharing happiness and peace with Alfred, was polite but not so polite as to annoy Alfred. They never mentioned Roper by name. He ceased to be a factor in their present, and they proceeded on the assumption that he could be of less importance in their past.

But it was almost inevitable that he would turn up at one of Sage Rimmington's Sundays, which Mary dropped in on about once a month. At first she was known, behind her back, as the mystery woman. She came alone, went home alone, attached herself to no one in particular, and her beauty and her clothes and her appearance in their lives only at Sage's made her a candidate for the title among the Sunday regulars. They were not really mystified; they knew who Alfred Eaton was and they knew Sage had been a girlhood friend. The only genuinely mystifying question was why she ever came at all. One day in May one of the fashion models followed her into Sage's bedroom and kissed her like a man, saying, "I just had to, you're so lovely."

"Save it," Mary said.

"You'll forgive me?" said the model. "I did have to know."

"Yes, I'll forgive you, and now you know. And you can tell the others."

"I wouldn't dream of it. They don't even know it about me."

"*I* did."

"You felt it?"

"I saw it," said Mary.

"Because if you felt it, maybe I didn't make a mistake."

"Well, get rid of that idea. You made a mistake. Just—not —interested."

"Mrs. Eaton, I'm sorry, but I don't believe you."

"You don't look as if you could take a very hard slap, but you're going to get it if you ever make another pass at me. And you realize, of course, one word to Sage and you'd never be invited back here again."

"Oh, there you're so wrong."

"Would you like me to call Sage in this minute?"

"No, of course not. I hate scenes."

"You'd get one."

"I dare you to come to my apartment sometime."

"What will you do, dearie? Play soft music and fill me with Pernod?"

"If that's what you'd like. But I'm more sure of myself than you are of yourself."

"I've never met anyone as sure of herself as you are."

"And *not*—without *reason*."

"Well, I've got to piddle and you'll excuse me if I lock the door," said Mary.

When Mary returned to the large room with the view of the river she joined Sage. "Mary, I hope you don't mind my asking you this, but did Tee make a pass at you?"

"Tee? Is that her name?"

"Did she? I'm not going to do anything, unless you want me to, but I want to see if I'm right."

"Nothing very serious. She tried to kiss me," said Mary. "On the mouth."

"I like that afterthought," said Sage. "She has it bad for you. I've watched her. Was today the first time?"

"And the last."

"I hope it's the last. I can refuse to have her again. She's the only one that's ever been—bold. They're fun, you know. All of them. I like them. They're as different from Wilmington —well, I don't have to tell you."

"They're pretty different from New York, too, the New York that I spend most of my time with. Oh, they amuse me, too. The little boys are terribly witty, much funnier than the girls, except old Mrs. Cannaby . . . Wait a second. Just came in. Is that who I think it is?"

"Yes," said Sage.

"I'm leaving."

"I think you're making a mistake."

"I made that particular mistake, and I have no intention of making it again."

"Well, he's seen you, so you have to wait and say hello . . . Hello, Jim."

"Sage, my dear. And Mary!"

"Aren't you surprised, though?" said Mary.

"I didn't fool you for a second," said Roper.

"No, and neither have you, Sage. You two can get me into trouble."

"You *are* in trouble," said Roper.

She left, but for two weeks she puzzled over the possible meanings of Roper's remark, and so on the second Sunday she appeared at Sage's. Roper was there, and she sat with him.

"Have you figured it out?"

"Figured what out?"

658

"My little germ for thought, 'You are in trouble.' "

"How could I be in trouble?"

"With three handsome, healthy children and a devoted husband, and plenty of money and a place in society? Now how *could* you be in trouble?"

"Yes. How could I?"

"Well, there's only one of those things that you never can be sure of."

"I'm sure of all of them, and I'm sure you're a son of a bitch who's trying to make trouble."

"Mary, it's—let me see—this is '39. It's seven years since you and I gave each other such exquisite pleasure, and I've been nice. I haven't bothered you. But I still adore you, and you know damn well you have moments when nobody else will do for you, just as nobody else will do for me. You're thirty-eight now, aren't you? You're at the height of your powers, you still have the bloom of youth, but you have so much more. If you're waiting to be asked, I hereby ask you. Three o'clock Tuesday afternoon?"

"You're not very complimentary. I haven't been wasting on the vine, or whatever the saying is."

"Oh, that I can see. And I'm sure you get propositioned all the time. But you must have a curiosity about yourself. You used to, and I know you still have. And I encourage curiosity."

"Well, Jim, why don't you go over and encourage it in Tee?"

"Tee? Not very interesting. Caught gonorrhea from one of your polo players and had a hysterectomy. Soured on men, turned to women. Turned to you, I'd guess. She get anywhere?"

"About as far as you're getting, Jim."

"Oh." He was genuinely rebuffed. "Pardon me. I thought you were just about ready. Well, if you need an excuse, I have one for you any time you change your mind."

"Oh, cut out the elaboration. Are you trying to tell me Alfred's been sleeping with another woman?"

"You get nothing from me without giving something in return. Neither reassurance nor confirmation. But if this makes you any happier with Mr. Alfred Eaton, I'll be very much surprised."

"Go sit with the boys."

"I'm going to, but don't be high-handed with *me,* Mary. My timing may have been wrong, but I know you."

In two weeks she confirmed the suspicions created by Roper. Unexplained gaps of hours in two days of those two weeks, and Alfred's remark, "I have to go to Washington, and I'm not sure where I'll be staying. I couldn't get a room at the

Mayflower," so strengthened her suspicions that she charged him with being unfaithful. He admitted that he had resumed the affair with Natalie Eustace.

"When did it start again?"

"About two weeks ago," said Alfred. "I'm really sorry."

"That's a yellow-livered remark. 'Sorry.' Sorry I found out?"

"Sorry you found out."

"You shouldn't be. Now you won't have to go to so much trouble."

"What are *you* going to do?"

"What do you *think* I'm going to do? Have you any objections?"

"None that would do any good."

"That's fine, because there *are* none that would do any good." She got up and went to the telephone and gave a number.

"Who are you calling?"

"Listen and find out," she said. "Hello, Jim? Would you like to take me to dinner tomorrow night? . . . No, I'll meet you at your place. Goodbye."

"Just like that," said Alfred.

"Mm-hmm. Just like that, Alfred. And I know just how you feel. It's awful to be found out, and guilty, and all that business."

"Yes it is. I never knew how awful."

"Of course you didn't."

Alfred did not come home for dinner the next night, and she met Roper at his apartment, had a drink there, and they went to the Montparnasse, had dinner, and danced. "Will you answer me one question truthfully?"

"Truthfully or not at all," he said. "The answer is, if it's the natural question, Ben Eustace is a patient of mine."

"Does he know about his wife?"

"Not positively, and neither did I, but it was a good guess, wasn't it?"

"It was a very good guess."

He looked at his watch. "Let's go back to my little house by the side of the road and be a friend to man. Are you pleased to be back? Are you relaxed and curious?"

"Fairly," she said.

They went back to his apartment and when they opened the door a very tall young man who looked like an oarsman put down a magazine and rose. He was in his shirtsleeves and no necktie.

"Look what I have for you, Mary."

"For me?" she said.

The young man grinned.

"Kenneth, this is Mrs. Eaton."

The young man continued to grin and she looked from one to the other. "Well, why not?" she said.

She never saw Kenneth again, but from time to time there were others like him, almost all having the same grin, all young and proficient and obedient to Roper. As with Kenneth, there was never the same one twice and occasionally there would be a lengthy hiatus between them. "They have to be just right, and I have to be careful that you're not to get emotionally involved with any of them," said Roper. "I reserve that for myself. You're so adorable, Mary. So agreeable. If we were two other people I'd say I love you because you're so wicked."

"Jim, what's the matter with *you?* It was you I came back to."

"Oh, Mary, I could go on at great length about that, but to put it most simply, I've gone completely the other way."

"You have? You're having an affair with Sage, aren't you?"

"No. Not what you mean by an affair. But I help her. We talk. She won't give in to what's troubling her, and that's why it's troubling her. So she has these men of hers, and when she hasn't got them she and I talk, talk, endlessly for hours. She adores you, you know."

"No use. I just don't like women, that way."

"Oh, I know what you like."

"You should," said Mary. "Am I a nymphomaniac?"

"Don't use terms like nymphomaniac, and abnormal. When those words began getting popular they did a great deal of harm. They made everything too simple, on the one hand, and they were awfully inaccurate, on the other. You don't know. I've had women of thirty come to me to cure them of nymphomania, and it turns out that they've had sexual relations with three men in thirty years. Then I've had an actress, forty-five. She has slept with over a hundred men. You might call her a nymphomaniac, but I know what a lot of men call her. A lousy lay. And it's obviously true. She's an exhibitionist—another of those sweeping terms, but applicable to her. I'm almost sure that if she could walk down Fifth Avenue naked about twice a year, she'd never go to bed with any man."

"Jim, who is your boy friend?"

"You could put me on the rack and I'd never tell you that."

"Do you know who I think it is?"

"Whoever you say, it'll be wrong."

"I don't think he's really your boy friend. I don't think he ever has been."

"Who do you have in mind?"

"My husband."

He nodded. "Yes."

"Do you get a sort of revenge when I'm in bed with one of those young men?"

"Yes. And when I cause trouble. He's always treated me like dirt, you know. Always. But I adore you, Mary. Always have. You know that, don't you?"

"Yes, I think you do. But don't worry, Jim. I hate him, too, and I get my revenge at the same time you do."

"You must try to control that hatred. You might go back to him."

"You're afraid I love him? Even if I did, I fixed that forever the day I telephoned you, with him standing there listening."

"Mary, I do love you."

"You mustn't say that, Jim. We mustn't believe in it. Say adore, but don't say love."

"Now the pupil is teaching the master."

"I like the irony of it. He thinks I'm sleeping with *you*."

"It would be a hundred times worse if he knew the facts."

"No it wouldn't. The facts would be so awful to Alfred that he could put me completely out of his mind."

"Why did we ever have to meet that bastard?"

"Oh, you know. Fate, and that sort of thing. But here we are. Have you ever thought of marrying me? I mean since we've grown up. Say ten years from now?"

"You mustn't count on me, Mary. Do you hear? You mustn't. You're not like a patient. I have files on my patients, case histories, and another doctor could be guided by them, if anything happened to me. But I haven't written down what I know about you, and you'd be in a mess without me. So don't count on me."

"Are you going to die?"

"When I'm ready."

"That sounds like suicide."

"Well, that's what it will be."

She was silent for a moment. "You're terribly depressed tonight."

He half smiled. "I gave up a major secret. I'm used to hearing them, not giving them. I haven't been analyzed, you know, not since I did my post-graduate work. Except by you. And you're pretty good." He smiled again. "You're a lovely, lovely human being, Mary, and if it's any consolation to you, Mrs. Eustace is having a very bad time."

In that spring of 1939 Natalie Eustace said to her husband: "Do you want me to try to get a house for August?"

"Why, sure."

"Where?"

"Anywhere you like," said Ben Eustace.

"Anywhere I like. You make it sound so easy, and it *is* easy for *you*. All you have to do is tell me to find a place where we'll be welcome, where they'll *have* us, and that we can afford. It's getting harder every year, you know, and I'm not talking about the expense."

"What are you talking about?"

"Why do you make me put it into words? You know. We've never been able to go to the same place two summers in succession."

"Eustace the leper."

"Not the leper."

"All right. Eustace the lush."

Natalie found a house in Quogue, which she hoped was far enough removed from Southampton to make it inconvenient for him to congregate with his Southampton friends. The distance was not great—ten or eleven miles—but the Quogue social life consisted largely of the Saturday night dance at the Field Club and one large cocktail party every weekend, and except for the club dance, night life did not exist. Canoe Place Inn, seven miles away, was the nearest temptation, and Ben had been ejected from it during their one summer in Southampton. She was cautiously looking forward to Quogue, but they never got there. On a Friday afternoon in May, Ben, drunker than usual, fell on the steep stairs between the basement and the main floor of the Racquet Club and broke his right arm above the wrist. The accident to his arm was followed by his suspension from the club, and too many members agreed that it was about time.

"Ben, this would be a good time for you to do something about your drinking," said Natalie.

"I have. I haven't had a drink in a week," he said, waving his splinted, bandaged arm.

He was lying and she knew it, but she went on. "I don't mean only the wagon."

"The Keeley Cure?"

"No. A psychiatrist."

"Fat chance."

"Then you're not going to do anything?"

"I'll go on the wagon."

"You mean you're not going to do anything? Because I know you're not on the wagon now. You've drunk at least ten bottles of beer so far today, and you have a whiskey bottle behind the sofa. I don't ask you to go to a doctor in Philadelphia, if that will embarrass you. But if I get the name of one in New York will you go to him?"

663

"No."

"I said I'd never leave you, Ben. But I'm going to go back on my word. I've had about all I can stand."

He capitulated, and she obtained the names of four New York doctors. She went to see them, and the first three would not take the case. The fourth was Jim Roper, who took the case with the understanding that Natalie would be available for supplemental examination, and she agreed. Ben went to see Roper three times in the first two weeks, got off the train drunk after the second and third visits, and told Natalie that he was not going back again.

"You haven't given it a chance," she said.

"Oh, yes, I have. He's found out all he wanted to know."

"Impossible, in two weeks."

"Two hours was all he needed. *Two words.* Sex life. Hell's kitchen! Don't you think I knew that?"

"Does he want to see me? I told him I'd go if it would help."

"There's nothing wrong with you, except that you can't stand to have me in bed with you. All he'll ask you is are you sleeping with Eaton? Or do you plan to? By the way, are you?"

"No, Ben, I'm not."

"But do you plan to, sometime. Life wouldn't be worth living if you thought you were never going to again, would it? You think about him every day, don't you? Does your thing twitch when you see his name in *Time?* Come on, Natalie, wouldn't you honestly like to cut out this God damn dutiful-wife horse-shit and jump in the hay with Mr. Alfred Eaton?"

She did not speak, and for the first time in their marriage he struck her. He hit her cheek with the hairy back of his thick left hand.

"Oh, Christ, I'm sorry," he said, immediately.

She looked at him steadily and unforgivingly. "Do you want the answer to your question?"

"No."

"You've earned it. The answer is yes, but I'm not going to."

"I deserve it."

"Yes, you do."

"But if you don't, I'll go on the wagon."

"No trades, Ben."

A few days later her telephone rang. "Natalie?"

"Hello, Raymond," she said.

"Are you all right? You recognized my voice. You still recognize it."

"Of course. Yes, I'm all right. Why?"

"After five years."

"Of course. Why did you call me?"

664

"I'm here in Philadelphia."

"You're here often, aren't you?"

"Fairly. I heard that Ben's been suspended from the Racquet Club."

"But that isn't why you called me."

"Yes it is. If that happened to him, things could be difficult for you. Are they?"

"I never expected them to be easy. I made two decisions, one led to the other, and I've stuck by both of them."

"You're not answering my question."

"I haven't learned my lesson. Men like to have their questions answered promptly, don't they?"

"That's double talk, or thinking out loud. Natalie, are you all right?"

"Yes, I'm all right."

"Do you still love me?"

"Oh, dear. Yes, I still love you. I *said* I would."

"Would you like to see me?"

"I can't."

"That isn't what I asked you. I said would you like to?"

"More than anything in the world."

"Then will you see me?"

"No. I've got accustomed to not doing what I'd like to do, if that's what you were going to say next."

"That's exactly what I was going to say next. What do you do every day?"

"Good Lord, why did you ask me that?"

"I don't want to hang up."

"You don't really want to know what I do every day. If you're not careful, I'll tell you, and *that* would be a dull recital. Why did you call me today?"

"Because this is the first time I ever worried about you, I mean as far as Ben's concerned."

"I don't get that."

"Well, I heard that no matter how drunk he got, you could always make him behave. But this suspension is a pretty public thing, and when I heard it I wondered whether you could still control him."

"I'm not as good at it as I was."

"Oh. Are you afraid of him? You can answer that truthfully."

"Am I afraid of him? Maybe I am, a little bit."

"Have you thought of leaving him?"

"Twice, lately. But I won't."

"I think you *are* afraid of him, and if you are, you ought to leave him."

"If I get too afraid of him, I will."

"Now we're getting somewhere. Has he ever struck you?"

"Once."

"How long ago?"

"Three days ago. He hit me once, then he was sorry. Now let me ask a question. Have you got a girl?"

"No."

"Is that something new?"

"I haven't had a girl since you sent me on my way, right here in Philadelphia, about two squares from where I am now."

"I'm glad. I don't mind Mary. She's your wife. But I wouldn't like your calling up if you had a girl. You and I could never be old friends, and I'd hate it if you tried to be. I was your girl, and I couldn't stand it if you tried to be an old pal. Not with what I remember."

"I do mind Ben, even if he is your husband. I'd mind anybody. Have you ever been unfaithful to Ben?"

"Yes."

"Who with?"

"Sterling Calthorp."

"You shouldn't have."

"Why?"

"I don't know, but I wish you hadn't."

"Well, I was."

"When?"

"Last year."

"Where did you meet him?"

"You mean where was I introduced to him, or where did I go to bed with him?"

"The latter."

"Here."

"In your apartment?"

"Yes."

"Then I'll never—" He halted.

She laughed. "You'll never what? You'll never go to bed with me here? Is that what you were going to say?"

"Yes, God damn it, that is what I was going to say."

She laughed again. "You're wonderful! The first time we've spoken in five years, and we're lovers again. Haven't even seen each other. Oh, that's wonderful."

"Well, at least I furnished you with something to laugh at."

"Don't be cross, darling. It *is* funny, and you know it."

"I guess it is. But I wish you didn't have to go and have an affair with Sterling Calthorp."

"That's just what I did, too. I went and had an affair with him, and that was that. It was simple, physical need with a man who'd been a friend of yours."

"Did you tell him about us?"

"I didn't tell him anything. I picked him, among all the

men I've met in Philadelphia, and I flirted with him, and I think he was just as amazed when he found that he was having an affair with me, as he was when I told him it was over. I think the whole experience did me a world of good. Made me understand the man's point of view."

"God damn it, stop saying those things. Sterling Calthorp, for God's sakes. First City Troop. Fish-House. Ivy Club."

"A gangster sent me flowers once. Do you think I should have picked him instead?"

"What gangster?"

"Oh, I don't remember his name. He was somebody Ben knew in Atlantic City. Ben said he owned a lot of whore-houses. Do you think he wanted me for himself, or the convention business?"

"I don't believe any of this talk."

"I don't either. I'll probably wake up in a minute and be disappointed that you didn't really call me at all. Is this you?"

"It's me, all right, but is this *you*, Natalie?"

"It's both of us."

"I'm coming over here again next Wednesday and I'll be at the Warwick. Five o'clock?"

"If I can."

"What would stop you?"

"This time I'm married, too, don't forget."

"Will you try?"

"You may not like me, Raymond. I've changed a lot."

"*You* may not like *me*. I'm just the same."

She appeared a week later in his room at the Warwick wearing a black hat of varnished straw and a blue linen dress with a narrow white leather belt and black pumps, and she had on a necklace of small pearls. She went to a chair and sat down, taking off her short white gauntlets and placing them on top of a small black envelope purse. She did not kiss him. She crossed her legs and allowed him to light her cigarette.

"You never used to smoke," he said.

"I did, and then I stopped for a long time, but then I took it up again. Now I smoke quite a lot."

"As you see, I'm having a Tom Collins. I didn't order anything for you."

"I don't want anything."

"Iced tea?"

"I don't believe so, thanks."

He sat sideways on the straight desk-chair and looked at her, but she looked at the toe of her shoe, the end of her cigarette. For a little while the only sound either of them made was her forceful blowing of the cigarette smoke out of her mouth.

"Well, say something," she said.

"No, let's get used to each other."

"That may never happen. Again. I'm jittery."

"You needn't be."

"I am, all the same."

"Well, so am I, for that matter."

"Your position is different from mine. I didn't want to get out of the elevator. I didn't want to ring your doorbell. Now I'm here and I can only think of the one thing I'm here for, but I don't even know whether you want that."

"Well, I do, but I'm not going to press it."

"If it's all you want, I will."

"First, would you mind taking off your hat? It's a nice hat, but it's very forbidding."

She took off her hat and with her right hand patted her hair, with her left hand held the hat.

"Give me that hat," he said.

She held it out for him and he got up and took it and put it on the desk. "You look sixty-five years younger," he said. "That hat's too old for you anyway."

"It's the only one I have this spring. It goes with almost everything."

"It doesn't go with you."

"Oh, yes it does. The hat *is* me. I told you I'd changed a lot."

"You've gotten a little thinner."

"I've gotten a little thicker, if you must know. I'm six pounds heavier than- the last time you saw me."

"I don't see it."

"I'm sitting on most of it."

"Oh, well I hardly had a good look at you from that angle."

"I'm also an inch larger up top."

"I have no objection to that. Did you ever get pregnant?"

"No. I tried to with Ben, and I tried very hard not to with—"

"I'd rather you didn't mention his name," he said.

"All right. It's nothing. It never was anything except what I said it was."

"Nevertheless you shared something that I can't stand to think of your sharing."

"If you want to talk about it, I will, but if you don't want to talk about it, don't talk about it at all. If it meant any more than what it meant at the time, I wouldn't be here. I'd had four years of a man who fumbled and made himself unhappy and me unhappy, after those years of perfection with you. I didn't expect perfection with Sterling, because I didn't love him, but at least I—"

668

"All right. Would you mind please not going on?"

"I just want to get it clear in your mind. And don't forget, you were having the same thing with Mary," she said. He made no reply and they were silent. "I wish we didn't have that bed staring us in the face. Why didn't you get a suite?"

"They didn't have one. I tried," he said. "There's a war on in Europe. A lot of you Philadelphians are getting rich again."

"I hear nothing but how rich *you're* getting," she said. "Is it true?"

"It's pretty true."

"Then I wish you'd give some of it to Constance."

"My sister?"

"Yes."

"Money won't help Constance, and she has quite a bit. But why do you say that?"

"Because the Philadelphia talk is that John Coddington would marry her if he had enough money."

"John Coddington has no intention of marrying Constance, and never did have. Instead of being ashamed of himself he's been using that excuse for years. Of course I suppose I'm in no position to criticize Coddington."

"You wouldn't be if I'd told the whole world that I wanted to marry you and you refused. That's what Constance does."

"If Constance needed more money, she'd ask me for it, but as a matter of fact she lives well within her income. I wasn't changing the subject."

"Oh, your conscience is clear. You asked me to marry you, and I wouldn't. Maybe I never will."

He smiled. "Do you realize that that's the first thing you've said that's like old times together? Now at least you imply that we're back where we used to be."

"I wasn't thinking when I said it."

"Yes you were. You weren't calculating, but you were thinking. Ever since you've been in this room you've been self-conscious and restrained. But when you said maybe you never will marry me, you were talking naturally. You know there's never been anyone for either one of us but each other. And there never will be."

"Oh, *I* knew that while *you* were trying to forget it."

"Well, you're right. I did try to forget it. And you were good. You helped. That day I called you at the hotel, all you had to do was weaken a little bit, and I'd have given up everything."

"Yes, and where would we be today? I've often thought that some people were meant to be in love but never married. Is that us? I guess it is . . . I'm relaxed now, Raymond.

669

I'm not fighting you any more. I'm going to take off my dress because I don't want to get it all wrinkled. You know how linen is."

"Yes, I do."

She hung her dress in the closet and stood facing him in her slip.

"I think I notice the one inch at the top, but I don't notice the other six pounds," he said.

"Well, it isn't all in one place, and I've still got my girdle on underneath the slip."

"Well, let's see how effective it is."

She removed the girdle and put it on a chair, but kept the slip on. "Do you see the difference?"

"I can't seem to take my eyes off a dark shadow in front."

"I'll bet I can make you," she said, and quickly took down the straps of the slip and brassière. "No, now stay where you are. I'm entitled to a strip tease, too."

"I haven't got as many attractions to offer." He took off his clothes and then they stood naked and embraced. They were standing close, eagerly rediscovering places on each other, when there was a click at the door and immediately the door was swung open.

Two men, total strangers, entered the room. The shorter and older man stood inside the door, and the other took a succession of flashlight pictures with a speed Graflex. Alfred made a rush for him but the shorter man jumped in front of his companion, who continued to take pictures. The shorter man got a hammer lock on Alfred's left arm and while Alfred was breaking the hold the shorter man said, "Get some more of her. Get the muff."

"I got plenty of her."

"Well, then let's get the hell outa here. That's what we want," said the shorter man. He hammered a blow at the base of Alfred's neck and Alfred fell, and the men ran out of the room.

Natalie got down on the floor and put Alfred's head to her breasts and held him in her arms. He was unconscious for two or three minutes, and when he opened his eyes she kissed him.

The grogginess left him and he sat up. "A hell of a lot of help I was," he said.

"He was a gorilla, an ape," she said.

"Who do you suppose sent them?"

"I can think of two people, can't you?"

"I imagine we'll soon find out," he said. "I'd better go home with you tonight."

"I honestly don't think it was Ben. Lie down."

670

"I'm all right. I really am. My neck is sore, but I have a great desire to make love to you."

"You're a remarkable man."

"I guess it's the instinct for something or other, or maybe it's just you."

"Let's do it quickly, as though it were our last. Can you? Yes, you can. Oh, my darling darling."

After a few minutes she lighted cigarettes for both of them. "It wasn't Ben. I know that."

"I don't see how it could have been Mary, either. She can't read my mind."

"The reason I'm sure it wasn't Ben is that I threatened to leave him. He knows I still love you. I told him so. But he's sure we haven't seen each other. He's been home every night, he knows I've been home with him every night, and he'd really rather have me sleep with you than leave him."

"But they wanted your picture. Do you remember what they said?"

"I'll never forget it. 'Get some more of her. Get the muff.' Did they mean get my middle in the picture, or is that the way they'd refer to any lady caught naked with her naked gentleman friend?"

"You're very brave, but I think they meant you, Natalie B. Eustace, housewife. And that leads me to believe that it may have been Mary after all. She knows I'd do anything to suppress those pictures."

"Darling, it wasn't Mary, either. I don't think she'd do it."

"Why?"

"I can't give you a reason. I just don't think she would."

"Well, it's one or the other. And now that my brain is beginning to function again, why haven't we had a call from the management? The hotel people. This has nothing to do with the police, *or* the hotel. No one knew I was going to meet you, that you were coming here. When I telephoned you last week I was in an office, on a trip that I hadn't even planned a whole day ahead. No wire-tapping, in other words, unless of course Ben had that done on your phone."

"Out of the question. He doesn't want to, and he'd rather spend the money on liquor."

"However, if for some reason I was being watched all the time, and followed to Philadelphia today, it's quite possible that whoever was following me—the little gorilla—would have a photographer ready in case what happened did happen, namely, that an unknown housewife came to my room. They know who I am, obviously, and now they have a picture of you. I hope they come out well, I'd like to buy a dozen and keep one in my wallet."

"You cad."

"Not at all. Lover of the form divine."

"But why would they say, 'Get some more of her ... That's what we want'?"

"I guess I really don't know. I could just as easily argue that all they wanted was a picture of you without any clothes on, in a room in a hotel. To hurt *you*. How do you get along with Ben's family?"

"They think I'm Florence Nightingale. Always telling me I'm the best thing ever happened to Ben. Oh, they'd rather have me taking care of Ben than do it themselves."

"It could be some business chicanery. Contrary to everything you hear these days, Big Business is not always the model of propriety. I've heard rumors that once in a great while a business firm has been suspected of naughty deeds. As a matter of fact, there's a union leader who hates another union leader and he happens to have some photographs of the man he hates in the act of a sexual perversion with a lady. Whenever the second guy gets out of hand, the first reaches in his pocket and pretends to be bringing out one of those photographs, and the second guy shuts up."

"But we didn't happen to be committing any perversion, darling."

"No, but we were dressed for it."

"I'm glad I haven't got any children."

"What made you think of that?"

"I just suddenly thought of what my father would think and my mother would think, if they ever saw one of those pictures of me. But they're safe. And I have no children."

"Well, of course, I *have*. But I think these pictures are never going to be seen by children. They want to get at me through you, whoever they are. Well, let them try. Are you afraid?"

"Of what? If it's Ben, who would have anything to do with a man who'd stoop to that? If it's Mary, she wants a divorce and I'd marry you tonight if *Mary* sued for the divorce."

"What if it's neither one?"

"Well, then they can threaten to show the pictures to Ben and you can tell them to go ahead, because then Ben would feel he had to divorce me, and we could find another place on Thirteenth Street. I don't think Ben and I are going to last very long anyway. I want to be your girl again."

"You never really stopped."

"No, not really. I always thought of myself as your girl," she said. "Can I be somebody's girl at thirty-four?"

"In this case, yes. You're a little old to start being somebody's girl, but you started being my girl a long time ago. Therefore you retain the title, girl."

She was not listening. "I don't think we ought to go down in the same elevator, but I wish you'd go home with me. Not go inside, but stand at the corner and watch the middle window. There are three windows, and it's the second floor. If I'm all right, I'll go to the window and wave from right to left, right to left. Like this. If I don't think I'm going to be all right, I'll wave in a circle. And if I don't wave at all in five minutes, I guess you'd better come and pick up the remains."

He walked a dozen paces behind her out Walnut Street to the house in which they had a flat. In a few minutes he saw her wave from right to left, and he then returned to the hotel.

That was in late May. They ascertained almost immediately that neither Mary nor Ben Eustace had employed the private detective and photographer, but that mystery receded with Mary's accusation and Alfred's admission, and her own resumption of the affair with Roper, a couple of weeks after the Warwick incident.

"She would have found out, she would have guessed anyway," said Alfred. "It's a long while since I went two weeks without sleeping with her."

"You haven't slept with her?"

"No. But that's not saying I wouldn't have."

"How did she find out?"

"I told her."

"No, but how did she know enough to ask you? Do you see any connection between that and the photographer?"

He sat straight up and looked at her. "Of course I do! Why didn't I think of it before? The psychiatrist that Ben went to in New York. Was his name Roper?"

"Yes, Dr. James Roper, he has an office—"

"Oh, hell," said Alfred. "How did you happen to pick him?"

"He was fourth on the list we had. The others didn't want to take the case because they said there were plenty of good men in Philadelphia, and they didn't *care* when I told them that Ben didn't want to go to a doctor at home. One of them said to me, 'Mrs. Eustace, from what you tell me your husband's drinking is public knowledge. It's not going to be *worse* to have it known that he's trying to do something about it.' And that was just about what the other two said, and the last name on the list was Dr. Roper. He asked me quite a few questions about my sex life with Ben, and he said he remembered Ben as a football player, and he'd take the case on condition I'd agree to cooperate. Which meant that I'd see him every so often and supply him with facts when he thought Ben was lying. Naturally I agreed, because Ben is a terrible liar when he's on the defensive."

"You told me you only saw Roper once."

"Only once, but don't forget he only saw Ben three times and then Ben wouldn't go again."

"Why did he stop?"

673

"Well, he said Dr. Roper wanted to know things that were none of his business, like names of people, and Ben said he refused to give any names. I don't believe him. I think he told Dr. Roper your name, and then lied to me about it because he was afraid I'd raise the devil."

"That's what happened. Well, I'll tell you all about Mr. Roper. I can't call him Doctor."

When he had finished she said: "I know who he is. You told me about him when we first knew each other, in Mountain City, but you didn't tell me his name, and even if you had I wouldn't have remembered it."

"Well, now I suppose the next thing is to find out what he plans to do with those pictures."

They learned soon enough. A large, glossy print of Alfred and Natalie, nude and embracing, and facing the camera with startled expressions, arrived at the office of James D. Mac-Hardie & Company. It was addressed to Alfred, marked Personal & Confidential, and sealed with red wax. The return address of the heavy Manila envelope was Jim Roper's and included his name. On a plain piece of paper, clipped to the photograph, was typed: "You asked for this."

"In other words," said Alfred to Natalie, "we don't know what he's going to do with them exactly. Obviously he sent it to the office as a warning that the next time he might send one without sealing wax or marked Personal, and my secretary would open it. If you could see my secretary you'd be able to imagine her reaction. A dead faint."

"But what does he want?"

"He wants no interference with his affair with Mary. But he wants more than that, because he knew I wouldn't make any trouble. How could I?"

"I wonder if Mary's seen the pictures?"

"I wonder, too. Maybe not. Maybe he's saving them to get her steamed up against me, in case she ever cooled on him. He could also hold them in reserve for Ben's edification. Well, that's how we looked, my dear."

She studied the photograph. "It's explicit enough."

"Well, it doesn't look as if I were trying to take a cinder out of your eye."

"I've often heard of pictures like these. I never dreamed I'd ever pose for one. Even with my mouth open and my eyes popping, I'm still very recognizable."

"You don't care, do you? Of course you do, but are you afraid?"

"No, I'm not afraid."

"I could go to Roper and offer to buy the negative, but I honestly think it'd be a waste of time. He doesn't want money. He wants to make trouble. And he can."

"What would happen if Mr. MacHardie got one?"

"I'd resign. And now that you bring it up, that's what I'm going to do."

The next day he wrote out his resignation, entirely by hand, and asked to see MacHardie alone in one of the private offices. Such requests were seldom made and never refused.

"What is it, Alfred?" said the old man.

Alfred placed the resignation in front of MacHardie, who read it—it was only three lines, and contained no reason for the action—and placed it in front of him. "I see. Now tell me why."

"I'm afraid it's very simple. About three weeks ago, in Philadelphia, I was entertaining a lady in my room in the hotel. A man, obviously a private detective, and accompanied by a photographer, burst into the room and got some photographs of the lady and me."

"You and the lady, I should hazard a guess, were not having a polite cup of tea."

"We were stark naked and at least one picture shows us in each other's arms. I've seen that one. I haven't seen the others."

"Who sent these people? Your wife?"

"No, sir. And neither did the lady's husband. The pictures were ordered by a doctor who was once half-engaged to my wife, and has always been in love with her. This guy is unscrupulous, I'm sure he doesn't want money, and he did have an affair with my wife since we've been married."

"Oh, yes. I did hear about that some years back. The same fellow, eh?"

"And he's having an affair with my wife right now."

"Well, Alfred, we'll have to do a little thinking." The old man slowly picked up the resignation letter and began tearing it lengthwise and crosswise as he spoke. "I don't know what we were rated at at the opening of business this morning, but every God damned cent of it is there to fight this thing." It was the first profanity Alfred had ever heard the old man utter. "This vile creature doesn't want money, but money's no good if it can't be used to exterminate him, and it can be. Let's give him twenty-four hours to hand over his pictures and the negative, and forty-eight hours to leave New York City."

"No sir."

"Why not?" said MacHardie. "I refuse to accept your resignation, therefore you're still a member of this firm. If every man resigned that's been found in adultery, this firm wouldn't have the present membership."

"I want you to believe me, sir, I don't want this firm to appear in this thing in any way, directly or indirectly."

"Then why did you feel you had to resign? You didn't want

us to be defiled. Well, that would be for us to appear quite directly, although defensively. If we don't do something about this creature, he's going to do something about you, and everybody knows where you put your hat every day. Right on top of your desk at MacHardie & Company. And that's where it's going to remain."

"Thank you, sir. But I'm willing to take the risk if you are—"

"What risk? What risk precisely?"

"The risk involved in waiting. This man is now having an affair with my wife. If anything drastic is done now, in all probability she'd divorce me and marry him. But if we wait, if I wait, she'll lose interest in him and get rid of him herself. Then she can do as she pleases without getting any sympathy for him. If anything is done now, all the sympathy will be on their side. If we wait, and she doesn't marry him, he'll have nothing."

"Eventually, of course, you and your wife are going to get a divorce. I know that, and I also know that the reason you haven't is your respect for my beliefs. I therefore have a responsibility in this matter. All I ever said about divorce I still believe to be true, but from this moment on I release you from any such obligation to this firm or to me personally. I do so because I don't want you to be handicapped in fighting this thing in your own way. But I want you to fight it, and with every cent we have and every ounce of influence. I hate divorce, but I have no words for what I think of the blackmailer. And if the lady is who I think it is, I hope that some day you'll be truly happy with her."

"What?"

"Oh, Alfred. What do you think I am? A dried-up, unobservant old man? Well, I am dried-up and old, but don't you ever forget that you never would have met this lady if you hadn't been sent on a job for this firm. Heaven knows I had no such intention, but we did inadvertently serve the cause of —well—of what?"

"Of love, Mr. MacHardie."

The old man nodded. "I was going to say romance, but if it's love, so much the better. I *believe* in *love*. Love was very easy for me to understand. Know why?" He leaned forward, and half whispered. "Because I didn't even try . . . Put a match to that damned silly nonsense, will you please? Now if you'll excuse me?" Alfred put a match to the torn-up resignation as the old man rose and left.

In July Natalie Benziger Eustace left Ben and took a small apartment in East Fifty-fifth Street in a block where there were still some trees. Ben obtained a leave of absence from the family firm and went to live with his mother in the fieldstone house in the Whitemarsh Valley. Before the summer was over he was said to be down to two drinks before dinner and nothing after. Single-handed he rebuilt the stone fence surrounding his mother's place, and stocked the cellar with more than enough firewood to last the winter. Unfortunately he died of a heart attack in the press box of Franklin Stadium, where he had gone to watch the Penn-Cornell game. Death was not pronounced in time for an announcement between the halves, but the *Evening Bulletin* carried a one-column box on the front page. In an early edition he was referred to as a former star halfback, but this was later corrected to his true position of guard. Flags were raised and lowered to half-staff at Weightman Hall, Delta Psi, and the Racquet Club.

Some excerpted correspondence between Alfred Eaton and others:

Dec. 12, 1941

Dear Pop:

. . . therefore, with my knowledge of cars and good coordination, I intend to put in for Navy Aviation. It is fortunate that I have completed sophomore year as I understand that is one of the requirements. I should prefer to be a fighter pilot but naturally I shall fly whatever they give me. Ironically enough, a guy I know who just got his wings in Florida advised me against even mentioning that I have logged 28 hours in Aeroncas and Cubs. He informed me that the Navy considers that in much the same manner that a college coach considers prep school football—in other words, forget it. The stuff they are flying in the Navy is so hot that flying a Cub is like flying an Autogyro. I will tell Ma when I see you both about 10 days hence . . .

Jan. 10, 1942

Dear Alfred:

. . . I have also written to Jim Forrestal but it is too soon for an answer. However, he was always very friendly when I saw him in N. Y. and he might help me get into this thing they are doing at Quonsett, R. I. Where the hell is Quonsett? If you happen to run into Forrestal in Washington will you put in a good word for me and remind him that this is the very same Porter who although armed with only a .45, single-handed, frightened Richthoffen and his Heinies out of the air in '17 and '18. I was known as The Scourge.

I would appreciate it if you would go see Uncle Fritz if you get a chance. He is up at the Presbyterian Hospital with uremia poisoning and Uncle Alex is afraid they may have to amputate Fritz' leg. I know he would like to see you. (They have not told him about leg.) Several other matters to discuss with you when we meet again, which will be in the near future . . .

677

Brother dear—

Your wayward sister wishes to warn you that she has given your name as a reference to the Red Cross. As B. Lillie says, I am madly keen to entertain the troops and I hope to go far enough away so that an old hag of forty (me, dearest!) will be as welcome as Hedy LaMarr. Other than that I have little news for you that you would wish to hear. I have been up to see Mother the past two week-ends and was also there on Pearl Harbor day. She is taking the war as a personal insult and goes around saying, "that son of a bitch Hitler" and "that son of a bitch Tojo." She has the radio turned on all day . . . I hear wonderful things about you but I also hear some disquieting things and I trust only the former are true, but I always told you to mind your own business so now it is your turn to tell me the same, but I can't help but think how obtuse I must be to have only recently heard about something that has been going on for a couple of years. 'Nuff said. I am on your side, or will be if you give me a good recommendation to the Red Cross. Did you know that the Dockwiler house has been turned into apartments and has been rented by some army doctors from Valley Forge Hospital for their wives? Sal's house (Van Peltz palatial mansion) is also apartments but of course Sal sold that long ago . . .

Dear Mother:

I'm afraid it will be impossible for me to do anything about getting you extra gasoline. That is a matter that is entirely up to your local board and even if I could intervene for you I would not. The Packard always used too much gas and my only suggestion to you is that you try to find a much smaller car and try to get along on the gas you will be allowed for it and the Packard. Even that is violating the letter and the spirit of gas-rationing but I see no other solution to the problem of getting. Josephine to Mass every Sunday. I am quite sure that she will not burn in hell if she fails to attend Mass and even if she does it should be no serious discomfort to her if I am correct in my recollection of the temperature she liked to maintain in "her kitchen." Perhaps you could call her priest for his advice. At least he could write her an excuse to present to St. Peter when her time comes . . . Yes, it looks like a long war, but I have not yet begun to worry about Alex and the draft. I make no predictions about the duration, but I won't start to worry about Alex until he is out of Groton, and he still has five years to go after this year. Rowland has not yet heard from the Navy but he should be getting the word soon. So far the only effect the war has on Eugenie has been a good one, at least in my opinion; the children at her school have not been able to get their messy little hands on any bubble gum . . .

Mary has enrolled with an organization called the Grey Ladies and is giving a great deal of her time to it. In answer to your question, no, she is not going through change of life. Isn't forty a little early for that? She is, of course, older than when you saw her a year ago and whatever was upsetting her that day may have been something entirely unrelated to the menopause, and since I did not happen to be present I don't know what caused you to believe that she was not her normal self. I, too, have moments when you would not recognize me for the happy, carefree, fun-loving little tyke I used to be, that you remember with such affection.

Let me know if there is anything I can do for you that does not involve gas-rationing, etc . . .

March 10, 1942

Dear Jim:

I hate to bother the Secretary of the Navy, but my kid Rowland, whom you have played tennis with, is very anxious to get in the Navy aviation program . . .

11 March 1942

Dear Eaton:

I have written a letter about Rowland to BuPers.

Regards,
JVF

April 28th, 1942

Dear Mr. Eaton:

Most likely you will glance at the signature of this letter and ask yourself, "Who is Sadie Warren?" But before tossing this into the nearest wastebasket, may I re-introduce myself? I use the word re-introduce correctly, as I have met you twice even though I can hardly expect you to recall the first time. That was at Groton commencement nearly three years ago at the graduation exercises for the class of 1939. Your son Rowland and my brother Francis T. Warren were classmates both at Groton and Harvard—still are, in fact. You would remember Frank better than you would me, since he has visited you in New York and on Long Island. The next time I met you I had the pleasure of having lunch with you and Rowland at the Ritz Hotel in Boston, in 1939. You had just given Rowland a new Ford convertible and after lunch all three of us drove out to Dedham, where I live but you did not stop in since you wanted to return to Boston in time to catch the New York train. If you have "hung on" this far perhaps I may take this opportunity to tell you more about myself. I was born at West Chop, Martha's Vineyard, on the twentieth of August, 1921. My father, who died in 1925, was the late John Curtis Warren, of Dedham, and my mother was Sarah Warren, a distant cousin of my father's. My brother, Francis Tudor Warren, is my only other close relative, although I have numerous cousins. I attended the Winsor School and came out two years ago. My father was in the class of 1919 at Harvard and a member of Porcellian. My mother attended Miss Winsor's and Bryn Mawr.

I am writing to you because in spite of our brief acquaintance, you immediately impressed me as having an unusually sympathetic understanding of the "younger generation" and all its faults and problems. Rowland has told me many times that you possess an excellent sense of humor and understanding without becoming "one of the boys." My brother, Frank, also agrees with him. If I did not have my "woman's intuition" to give me confidence, I could not write this letter.

I am in love with Rowland and I know that he loves me. When he received word from the Navy that he was to report at Squantum he asked me to marry him and I said I would, thinking he meant right away. But I soon discovered that he wanted to be engaged to me, then get married after the war. I would wait forever for him, but he is opposed to our getting married because so many things could happen, as he put it. I asked him to be specific and he replied that a war is a war and men get killed or badly wounded and he would not want me to risk becoming a widow, possibly with a child, or tied to a man who was crippled for life. It was asking too much, he said. But it was not asking at all! He had not asked me my feelings in the matter, only that I would marry him after the war was over. I want to marry him as soon as possible and told him quite brutally that if he thought he was going to be killed in the war, at least we could have that much happiness that could never be taken away from us. I want to be with him wherever he goes until he is sent overseas and I hope that when he leaves I will have a baby on the way.

I could not write this to anyone or even say it if I did not know that Rowland and I are in love as two people seldom are. We have been in love for over a year and if it had not been for the war we would have gotten married as soon as he finished Harvard, but now because of a misguided sense of "what's right" he wants to postpone it not only for a year but for the length of time the war will last! It is not a question of my being faithful to him or him to me. I *know* that neither of us could ever care for anyone else.

Therefore I am appealing to you to do what you can to convince Rowland that the only thing that matters to me is to be his wife. I have just realized that I have been taking for granted that you would see things as I do, but I am correct, am I not? Isn't it better for him as well as for me? As his father you will want to do what is best for him, but surely you will understand that it is only his principles that is making him put off the marriage that he wants every bit as much as I do. Incidently, my mother and brother both think Rowland is the right man for me to marry "when the time comes."

I know how much Rowland respects your judgment and therefore you are the one person I feel I can turn to.

Yours sincerely,
Sarah Warren ("Sadie")

29 April 1942

My dear, dear Sadie:

Thank you sincerely, deeply, and often for your letter, which I hasten to reply to in order to put your mind at ease. I am with you 1,000 percent and I am so happy for my lucky, obstinate, high-principled son. I believe there is some Navy regulation regarding his getting married immediately, but all the weight of whatever influence I wield is going to be exerted to propel him to the altar with a splendid, honest, warm and, if I may say so, extremely pretty girl named Sadie Warren. As a prospective father-in-law to that fine girl, I send my affectionate regards and my promise to help convince a young man that love must never be postponed for war.

Again, affectionately,
Alfred Eaton

May 19, 1942

Dear Alfred:

Could you drop in at my office sometime in the next few days? You need not make an appointment but telephone Miss McCarthy that you are coming and she will fit you in. I am at the hospital Monday, Wednesday and Friday, and at the office Tuesday, Thursday and Saturday before noon.

Best regards,
Don
Donald P. Tinkham, M. D.

26 May 1942

Dear Alfred:

I wrote you a week ago but apparently my letter has gone astray. Could you drop in at my office in the next day or two? You need not make an appointment but telephone Miss McCarthy that you are coming and she will fit you in. I am at the hospital Monday, Wednesday and Friday, and at the office Tuesday, Thursday and Saturday before noon.

Best regards,
Don
Donald P. Tinkham, M. D.

26 May 1942

Dear Alfred:

The President is most anxious to have you reconsider your decision as you outlined it to me in your letter of the 24th. He will not, of course, stand in the way, but I can personally assure you that you will be much more valuable to the country by serving along the lines we have discussed. I felt exactly as you did after Pearl Harbor, but we both might as well face the fact we are too old for combat and therefore must make our contribution to the war effort where we will be most useful. There are hundreds, if not thousands, of lieutenant commanders who are qualified to perform the work for which you are at present qualified, assuming you would get sea duty within a year's time. On the other hand, as a civilian working along the lines we have discussed, you would be making a unique contribution which, while possibly less glamorous than a billet on a carrier or a DD, would provide you with the quiet satisfaction of work well done, plus the knowledge that you will be doing something you and few others are equipped for.

I saw Jimmy Forrestal last week. He is doing a whale of a job and he is not in uniform, either.

Please remember me to Mary, and with best regards to your good self,

> Sincerely,
> Creighton
> Creighton Duffy,
> Special Assistant to the President

Everything was happening too fast in that first year of the war; too fast, and incompletely. There were always things being left unsaid, other things left half-done; haste, where there was no need for it; delay, with the war used as an excuse for it. Alfred could remember the delays and the waste in the previous war, and he recognized the inevitability of them in any war. But he marveled at the inefficiency in that first year of the new war as much as he admired the accomplishment. Somehow new ships were going down the ways, soon to be loaded with trained men and generally reliable equipment, and from Baltimore to Glendale, including Wichita, there were new things in the air, remarkable for their bigness—the B-19 —or their weird shape—the Black Widow. The popular new words were ersatz and logistical, near antonyms that never got coupled together but were useful just the same in expressing criticism of the shoddy and the efficient, and yet not so contrary as the angriest two critics of the war effort—the communist wailing for "the second front" and the other, the conservative hater of Roosevelt growling at everything the man did, unselectively, and blaming him for a war that could with equal justice have been blamed on Bismarck's mother. A man named Eli Basse wrote, and a great comedian named Joe E. Lewis sang, a bit of minstrelsy that was true of the time: "You can't get the merchandise—It's tough to get the stuff."

And yet the ships went down the ways, and the Garand rifle fired, and the Black Widows went into their steep climbs, and fragile teachers of classical Greek were learning how to subdue the bullies of the Third Reich and pale little Polish priests were learning how to control the shrouds of parachutes, and young Americans who had never set foot on Manhattan Island were on their way to French Africa, while other young Americans were on their way home from Guadalcanal. The New York Junior League bought a Navy sword for the proper cutting of hastily baked wedding cakes, and little boys in Central Park tried hard to pretend that they did not know where the ack-ack guns were hidden.

Natalie was within walking distance of the job she had taken after leaving Ben Eustace, and she was likewise within walking distance of Grand Central and her work with the Travelers Aid Society. The apartment in Fifty-fifth Street was only a little more than four blocks from the Fifty-first Street subway station, and Alfred often let himself in to wait for Natalie, and almost always he would be asleep in a chair when she arrived. On an evening in May of that first year of American participation in the war he was lying on the bedspread, his shoes off, his coat hanging on the back of a chair. He opened his eyes upon hearing her key in the lock.

"I'm awake," he said.

"Oh, I can always tell," she said, laughing.

"How are you? Did you sell a lot of maternity dresses today?"

"What made you ask that, for heaven's sake?"

"On the way uptown I read something about the birth rate. The whole country's knocked up."

"You'll be glad to hear *I'm* not."

"I'm never glad to hear that except for your sake."

"And yours."

"Well, yes, I guess and mine."

"I'm going to have to turn the light on."

"Kiss your aging lover first."

"You're not my lover, you're my love." She kissed him but she did not lie down with him, although he ran his hand from her shoulder to the back of her knee and up again under her skirt. "Not today. I told you."

"I don't know," he said. "You better not waste these. You know what Lord Droolingtool said to the butler. 'The hell with her ladyship, I'm going to sneak this one up to London.'"

"I've always liked that story, because if you were Lord Droolingtool I'd be the lucky lady in London. Alliteration. But what's all this *old* talk? I haven't heard that for at least a month."

"I'll tell you at dinner. I guess I better wash my face if we're going to get anything to eat."

They went to Enrico's, down the street. Enrico shook his head slowly, partly chiding them, partly sad, but more chiding than sad. "I kept your table until half past eight, Mr. Eaton. But I think in fifteen minutes I have a nice table for you. For Madame, *four* packages of Philip Morrises. *Four*. I give them to you before you leave. I take your order for Scotch, Mr. Eaton. If you ask at the bar, Johnny must say no. Everybody want Scotch tonight, everybody come in want Scotch, even my ladies who never ask for Scotch. Tonight they want Scotch. But I held out one bottle for Mr. Eaton. And Mrs. Eustace? A very dry Martini?"

"Don't throw him and order Scotch," said Alfred.

"How could I, after he's saved me four packs of Philip Morrises? Thank you, Enrico. Thank you very much."

"Always a pleasure, Mrs. Eustace. Ah, this war. Coupons, points, black markets. Oh, yes, Mrs. Eustace. The nylons? I have them for sure next week."

"Oh, how wonderful."

"Oh, yes. Thank you."

They waited at the bar, and when they got their nice table— not their usual nice table, but a nice table—she said: "All right. Now you can tell me why your bones are creaking."

"Well, the Commander-in-Chief, that is to say, Creighton Duffy, has told me that I'm too God damn old for a commission. I brought his letter, if you'd like to see it."

She read the letter. "I'd say on the whole, very complimentary. Must I restrain my curiosity, or can you tell me what the job is?"

"It's big. I won't tell you here."

"Okay," she said. "Well, you're going to take it, aren't you? You always said you would. You might as well, you've been doing a lot of work for them."

"But I've never taken a job. Two reasons. I wanted to go back in the Navy and get sea duty. He has it all wrong, probably deliberately. I didn't want to get on a carrier or a destroyer. I wanted to get on something smaller, a corvette or something like that. Hell, I've had over twenty years' experience with small boats, thanks to Fritz Thornton, and there are any number of things I could do. It's no secret that we have— well, thousands of men in England and Ireland, and what are they there for? Well, before there's an invasion we're going to be landing guys everywhere, from small boats and submarines. Thank you, no, on the submarines, but small boats, yes. This was my last chance, Natalie, and now it's gone. That's why I bellyache about being forty-five. I can do anything Lex can do. No, I can't, but damn near."

"But he's not going to be on a small boat."

"No, he'll be on a carrier, and he'll be damn good. The D. S. C. is the same as the Navy Cross, and they'll respect him."

"You said there were two reasons why you've never taken a job. What's the other?"

"Those pictures we posed for. What if Bertie McCormick got hold of those?"

"Who is Bertie McCormick?"

"Colonel Robert R. The Chicago *Tribune*."

"He couldn't print them."

"Well, I didn't exactly mean him, or that he could print them. I was just using his name as one of the F. D. R.-haters that turn on anybody that takes a big job in the government. I'd have to be confirmed by the Senate, you know. Well, you don't know, but I would. And I can see some of the boys in the cloakroom passing those pictures around."

"Are you afraid for me?"

"Naturally, but not entirely."

"Because I think everybody must know by this time that I'm your girl, everybody that it would mean anything to. Enrico knows. Mary knows. All Philadelphia knows. So it's no longer a question of protecting me, dear."

"Not quite everybody knows."

"Your children."

"My children, your friends in Mountain City and Gibbsville. Most people in Port Johnson. Your brother. And quite a few people in New York, more than you realize. Older people. The kind you just don't repeat gossip to, like one or two of the partners. But I'm quite sure Creighton Duffy knows. I even had a crazy hunch that he was the one responsible for the pictures. But he knows about us all right, and I'm hesitant about putting myself in a spot where I'd have to knuckle under to him. Creighton Duffy to me represents the whole Washington setup. Maybe that's giving him more importance than he deserves, but it's the way I feel.

"Here is this son of a bitch starting out his letter by saying that 'the President is most anxious,' et cetera. In other words, Frank and I had one of our chats. Duff the Guff, would be a good Roosevelt nickname for him. If I take the job, I'll always be known as one of Duffy's boys."

"No you won't."

"Why would I be the exception? Anybody that Duffy has dealt with gets to be known as one of Duffy's boys, the same way as Harry Hopkins's boys are. Oh, I guess I'll go. The next move is for Duffy to have me see Roosevelt and Roosevelt turns on the charm and says, 'Alfred, I hope you're not going back to New York *this time*.' Polite, but insistent. And he's the President of the United States. I wouldn't have the strength of character to resist that, you know I wouldn't."

"If you wanted to resist it, you could. But you don't really want to. I hope they do that. I hope they fix it so that you have to go to work right away, that day, and in two weeks you'll be so busy you'll forget about your misgivings."

"You're entirely right, as you usually are."

"About you."

"Well, about most things. Speaking of which, I've had a long letter from Rowland. Would you like to read it here, or wait till we get back to the flat?"

"I'd rather wait. Are you spending the night?"

"If I may."

"You always say that."

"I think I *should* always say it."

"No, you never should. It always sets us back a little, at least temporarily. As though you had to have my permission, as though there might be someone else going to be there. We're too close for those little courtesies. Those courtesies are really suspicions. I don't want anyone else, and I never will and I take that for granted, and you should too."

"I can't do it. As long as Enrico looks at you as though he'd give everything to put those nylons on you himself. As long as that man at the bar stops talking just to admire you. As long as Sterling Calthorp tries to get you to marry him. Have you heard from him again?"

"He telephoned at the shop today. I told him all over again, I wasn't going to see him."

"That was the affair that didn't mean anything to either one of you."

"Well, it still doesn't to me. You've got to believe that, and you do, really."

"You told me when I first knew you that I didn't know anything about love. *You* don't know anything about *men*. No man that ever lived really believed that he couldn't go back and sleep with any woman he ever slept with."

"I hope you realize what you're saying."

"Oh, *I* believe that, too."

"What about Lex's wife?"

"What about her?"

"Do you believe you could sleep with her again?"

"It's a lousy thing to say, but you happened to pick one that I think I could sleep with any time. The wisest thing Lex ever did was to retire to that ranch."

"Yes, and even that wasn't good enough."

"Why? Did Ben sleep with her?"

"No, but Sterling did. Just once. But he did."

"If Lex ever knew that, he'd kill her."

"And he'd be killing the right one, if there ever is a right one. She's always touching men, sitting on their laps. Sterling volunteered to drive to the town and get the mail, and at the last minute she said she'd go with him. When she knew no one else would. All the way in she made a pass at him till just before they reached town, and he stopped the car, and they performed right there in broad daylight. She's the only girl I ever knew that was always in season, as my mother used to say."

"And Lex is going to the Pacific. How convenient for her."

"Very. But not for you."

"I wouldn't anyway. If not for you, for Lex."

"But watch her. Maybe she's never told Lex about you but

she might. If she got a lech for you and you didn't respond, I think she'd tell Lex about you."

"Yes, I guess she would. Without telling him when. Not that that would make any difference to Lex. He'd hate me worse than anybody else."

"And she'd know that. I'd almost say, 'Sleep with her,' but even if you did, that wouldn't make it any better. Then she'd have two things to tell Lex. Once before he married her, once after. And she's a real threat, because I'm sure Lex will want you to take her out and he'll be offended if you don't."

"If I do, you'll be there. We'll both take her out. Take her to '21,' the theater, and dump her at her hotel. Or Mrs. Porter's."

"Yes, that's a good idea. Illicit love has its uses after all, hasn't it?"

"It has many. But let's call it illicit marriage. If ever two people were husband and wife, you and I are. Christ, I tell you everything, things I've never told anyone else. I show you my Top Secret letters. Even letters from my children."

"Am I ever going to see that boy?"

It was always a sensitive point for them. "Yes, of course. But everything has to be right. He's very damn fond of Mary, and I'd like you to meet him first without me. I'd like him to meet you, and like you, and then maybe I could tell him what you are to me."

"We had almost this identical conversation just about a year ago, almost word for word."

"Yes, but there's a difference now. Now he's in love himself."

"The girl would like me. I'm not sure Rowland would."

"The girl *is* you, really, in many ways."

"I'm very pessimistic. I don't think I'll ever meet Rowland. But let's go home and read his letter."

"All right."

Enrico, as they were leaving, handed her a paper sack. "*Six*, Mrs. Eustace. Six, not four. And I have the nylons next week, for sure."

"How lovely, Enrico. Thank you so much," she said.

Out in the street she said, "How much did you give him?"

"I gave him ten bucks."

"But you're not supposed to give him anything."

"I'll be damned if you'll *take* anything from him. And don't worry, I didn't have to hold a gun to his head."

"You're jealous, aren't you? How nice," she said. "How comforting, how reassuring, to have your man jealous." She took his arm. "How comforting, how reassuring, how young." She spoke in the rhythm of their steps. "How dear, how sweet."

"How now/brown cow," he said.

She was happy. "I love you," she said, squeezing his arm.

"And I/love you," he said, in the same meter as before. They marched in step in the blackout, under the trees of Fifty-fifth Street, along the concrete path to the aged brownstone house that was the place where they could be together.

"Our illicit cottage," he said.

"Mm-hmm. I finally found a laundry that doesn't starch your shirts."

"The one I told you about?"

"The one you told me about hasn't been there for two years. The whole building's gone. You don't realize what a problem that's been, ever since we've had this flat."

"I realize it's been a problem as soon as I button my collar."

"Finding a laundry, I mean. They don't give a darn whether I give them my business or not. I have to admit, this isn't a laundry, either. It's a maid in that big house across the street. She charges fifty cents a shirt, by the way. So you're going to have to raise my house money."

"A white market in shirt-washing."

"I've still never seen anyone go in or leave that house. I think you're wrong. I don't think anyone lives there but the servants."

"Eisenhuth. I didn't say they live there. I said they own it. They live up the Hudson somewhere and come to town for the Ring operas. I don't even know whether they're doing Wagner any more. Are they?"

"You know better than to ask me a question about opera. Let me see Rowland's letter."

"I'm going to take a bath," he said. "Don't let me fall asleep in the tub."

She frowned. "Are you still tired, after your nap?"

"Pretty," he said. "Duffy might be right, you know."

"I'm a better judge of that than he is."

"Thank you, my dear, if you mean what I think you mean."

"What else could I mean?" she said. She smiled, but she watched him until he disappeared into the bathroom, then she put on her reading glasses and opened Rowland's letter:

Dear Pop:
I humbly apologize for not having written ere this but I have not had a moment to call my own since I came to Squantum. They really give it to you here. This is an E Base, so called because E does not mean the Navy E for efficient or expert but stands for Eliminated. Until I finish up here (one way or the other) I am a Naval Aviation Cadet. I wear a Marine enlisted man's uniform but a black necktie and a cadet's cap. We spend most of our time in "yellow perils" and when I have completed 10 hrs dual in the back seat I will be okay for solo

in an N3N or an N2S. While getting dual my instructor talks to me through the gosport, a pair of tubes connected to my helmet and converging at a mouthpiece that the instructor holds. There are 14 other guys in my platoon, two from my class, two from Dartmouth and the others from Holy Cross etc. I am platoon leader. We all eat and sleep and drill together and take ground school together. After solo I will do formation flying and basic aerobatics in the yellow peril, then be sent to either Jax, Pensacola or Corpus (Christi). Then I learn to fly instrument under a hood in an SNJ. That is as much as I can tell you from the scuttlebutt. There is a lot to be done before I become a Naval Aviator.

I appreciate what you have done regarding Sadie. I had to give my word that I would not get married until after I get my commission. I know that some of the guys pay no attention to that but I do not have a very high opinion of them either as prospective Naval Aviators or as prospective husbands. I never told you much about Sadie because it was the kind of thing I thought we should keep to ourselves until we were both sure. She is the only girl I ever loved or ever will, but so many things can go wrong in peacetime, let alone since Pearl Harbor. She told me you phoned her and had a long talk and now that she understands a little better I am no longer in fear of losing her. Before that she thought that I was inventing the excuse about the Navy's rule against marriage, but she should have known me better than that. However, she is a girl and they are sometimes difficult. It is tough on her and in fact tough on both of us but in this case I think the Navy is right. Some of the guys argue that it is bad morale to have to worry about your girl if you are not married to her, but my reaction is that a girl who is going to cheat is not going to be prevented by having a minister say the magic words. This does not apply to Sadie (or to me either) as neither of us has any lack of trust in the other. I have had a few experiences, enough to convince me that I love Sadie and want to spend the rest of my life with her, but it will be quite a while before we can get married, after I finish the above plus a couple of months advanced carrier training. But I am sure we can still be married earlier than we had planned, which was after graduation from Harvard, so if she looks at it that way it is not so bad. I hope you will tell her that in your own way.

I have written some of this to Mother so you can exchange letters and between you get all the news I have had time to write. With many thanks for all the many things you have done in the past and present,

Love,
Rowland

She put the letter back in its envelope and tucked it in Alfred's inside coat pocket. She opened the bathroom door, which was ajar, and she saw that his eyelids were drooping as he lay in the tub. In a soft voice so as not to startle him, she said, "I hope you didn't use all the hot water."

"Hot water? What?"

"You've been in there long enough."

"Okay. Okay," he said. "You know, I was just about ready to take a very wet nap."

"Just about ready." She got a large towel and wrapped it around him. He made no move but stood on the bath mat enveloped in the towel, and she dried him off and gently pushed him into the bedroom, got him into pajamas, and led him to the bed. He lay down, and before she was in the tub he was in a deep sleep. She finished her bath, her teeth, her hair, and turned out the lights, opened the windows, and got in beside him. "Goodnight," she whispered, but got no answer.

"It's worth it," she said, half aloud, partly to herself, partly to the sky over Mountain City, Pennsylvania, and partly to Natalie Benziger, age seventeen, and Natalie Benziger's notions and plans. "He's worth it," she said. He loved her.

The first sound she heard in the morning was the slow, careful rustling of the newspaper, which he was reading at the chair near the window. He was clad in his shorts, socks and shoes, and his hair was brushed. "Good morning," she said. "What time is it?"

"Good morning, my dear. It lacks twenty minutes of the hour of eight." He put down the paper and brought her a cup of the bad wartime coffee, which she took almost half cream to disguise the disagreeable taste. He kissed her. "You had a good sleep."

"I always sleep better when you're here," she said.

"*I* always sleep better when I'm here."

"Are you going to be here tonight?"

"No. Tonight we're dining with an Englishman, a nice old guy named Lord Sevringham. His wife was killed in the blitz. She was a lovely woman. He's over here on some mission and he particularly asked to have me tonight. I guess I won't see you before Monday. What are you going to do?"

"You can't stay Monday night. Caroline English will be here. She couldn't get a reservation at any of the hotels."

"I can always fix that. You know that."

"I know, but not for Caroline."

"I do it for all your other friends. She doesn't have to be stuffy about it."

"Yes, but my other friends don't know that it's through you I get them rooms. Caroline does."

"If that's the way it is, she's being more inconsiderate by staying here. She knows I can't stay here if she does."

"She'll get over it."

"How little I care."

"I do, though. She's been a good friend."

"Okay. Then will I see you Tuesday?"

"Yes. Unless Caroline decides to stay over another day. I'll call you at the office, or leave word at the Racquet Club."

"Wednesday I'm going to Washington. Not to see Duffy. I'll be back Thursday afternoon, late." He had begun to put his clothes on. "Good laundress. She knows how to do shirts."

"I meant to ask you this before—are you definitely going to East Hampton again?"

"Oh, and I meant to tell you. Yes. When is your vacation?"

"The last two weeks in July."

"Maybe we can go somewhere. At least for one week."

"No, let's just stay right here."

"No, let's go to Atlantic City for the whole two weeks. You ought to get out of New York, get some sun. We can swim every day, play some golf. Sleep. Wouldn't you like to do that?"

"I'd love it, but *can* you?"

"Why not? I'd only be away from East Hampton over one weekend, and God knows the only thing I like about East Hampton is its inconvenience. There, do I look the real executive type? Every God damn junkman now calls himself a steel executive."

"You look fine."

"I feel better. I was dead last night." He sat on the edge of the bed, and took her hand. "You know, you could have these clothes offa me so quick. You're possibly one of the most attractive women I ever met."

"I'm out of circulation at the moment, but I'll be all right Tuesday. Do you really think I'm attractive?"

"*I* think so. I don't know what anybody else thinks, but *I* have a sort of perverse admiration for you. Perverted, too."

"That's nice. It's always nice to hear, even when a girl is thirty-seven. I have some degenerate thoughts about you, every once in a while."

"Tell me about them."

"Oh, I'd be embarrassed. As a matter of fact, I *would* be embarrassed."

"Then don't say a word. But let me have a small look at these round objects and send me out into the morning air, full of pure thoughts and a determination to succeed."

"What do you want to succeed at that you haven't?"

He became slightly more serious. "To make you happy, and to keep you happy."

"You do pretty well, Raymond." She put her hands on his cheeks and drew his head to her bosom. "They're very sore today."

"I'll leave you. Do you want me to fix the alarm so you get an extra half hour's sleep?"

"No thanks. I'll get up as soon as you leave."

"Goodbye."

"I'm sorry about Caroline. I'll shoosh her out Tuesday. Goodbye."

"Just remember, girl. Things are tough all over. We're not the only ones," he said, and left her.

All day—it was a Friday—he considered, and postponed, the conversation he must have with James MacHardie. MacHardie would be at the dinner for Lord Sevringham, but the conversation was too important to the firm to be made a fractional part of another occasion. At the same time it would not look well on, say, Monday, to have been in MacHardie's company on Friday evening without having had the conversation. It would then have become a case of holding out on MacHardie, and MacHardie would have good reason to regard that as a breach of faith. At one-thirty he asked for a conference with MacHardie.

"He's leaving early this afternoon, Mr. Eaton," said MacHardie's secretary. "Could it be postponed?"

"It could be, but I don't think it ought to be."

"Very well. Two o'clock?" said the secretary. "I'll shift his other appointments around."

"Thank you," said Alfred, glad now he had not left it the other way.

The old man entered the conference room and seated himself with his hands folded on top of the table. "What is it today, Alfred?" Alfred could not be sure that there was not a hint of rebuke in the old man's tone, but he overlooked the suspicion.

"I know you're leaving early, sir, but I didn't want you to go without mentioning that I've had a letter from your son-in-law. Would you care to read it?"

"Can't you summarize it for me?" said the old man. "He's a lawyer and he loves to write letters. Or is there something in the letter you'd like me to see?"

"Yes, there is. The first five words."

MacHardie took the letter: " 'The President is most anxious.' " He looked at Alfred. "It's almost unnecessary to read the rest, isn't it?"

"Yes it is."

"Well, are you going to take it?"

"Not without discussing it thoroughly with you, sir."

"Oh, no you don't. I wouldn't utter a syllable that would influence this decision. This one is entirely up to you. Thank you for the courtesy of keeping me informed, but I can't and mustn't advise you in any way." The old man stood up. "However, I may say I'm not sorry you asked to see me. I knew about this. My daughter told me."

"I would have been in a hell of a spot if I hadn't let you know, wouldn't I?"

MacHardie halted on his way to the door. "Let's say that I'd have been disappointed. See you this evening? And of course I say nothing to the other partners until you've made your decision."

"If you don't mind."

"Don't mind a bit. They don't always tell you what they tell me, either." The old man smiled and went back to his desk.

The breach between Mary Eaton and Alfred had not widened in three years; it had only deepened. The distance between them had been established the moment Mary telephoned Jim Roper in Alfred's presence; it was sufficient and, they both knew, permanent. Mary then had not had time to think it out, but she could not more effectively have made the break more contemptuously and irreparable than she had by the more or less impulsive act of arranging a rendezvous with her old lover while her husband sat in his own guilt. It was a passionately angry act, but it had been done so cold-bloodedly—and this she could not know, nor, for a while, did Alfred—that she was unconsciously abandoning her womanliness. She had, in effect, pierced his scrotum, made him ineffectual by renouncing her femininity. This time there would be no stifling of desire through pride; there would be no desire, and she had left him no pride. If she had hung up the telephone and he then had murdered her, they might have been reunited in passion of a sort, but uxoricide had been bred out of Alfred Eaton two generations back. His father had not murdered his mother.

From the beginning of their second break Mary and Alfred knew where they stood. Their experience of the earlier break had been, in a manner of speaking, valuable, but with the significant difference now that there was no deception. (Or at least so Alfred thought.) During the first long hostility he had had reason enough to suspect that Mary was sleeping with other men than Roper, but he did not know and he did not ask. Now he knew that Roper was her lover, and she knew that Natalie was his mistress. There had been pain for him in the other hostility; there was none now; because she had left him at least temporarily with no pride, he felt only an annoying but painless irritation, a moderate anger, and, with the restoration of his pride through the satisfactory relationship with Natalie, the beginning of a sense of superiority and contempt for Mary and Roper. The peculiar nature of Mary's second relationship with Roper was unknown to Alfred and entirely unsuspected by him, and in a natural revival of his self-respect he had come to regard Mary's affair with Roper as rather uninteresting and, to him, convenient.

It was no longer necessary to lie to Mary as to his comings and goings and absences. He would "be home on Tuesday and Wednesday but not Thursday." He was not compelled to mention Natalie by name and reciprocally Mary did not mention Roper. Without specific agreement they had come to an understanding regarding Roper in the matter of his appearance in their apartment: Roper could call for Mary when Alfred was not there. Appearance publicly with Roper was potentially a point of dispute, but Mary solved it by her own wishes: she was fully aware that a public appearance with Roper would revive the gossip that had been harmful to her during the earlier breach, and she was also increasingly aware of Roper's reputation as a physician whose practice was the contemporary version of the "society doctor" of the preceding period. He was seen too often in fashionable restaurants, reviewed too many quasi-medical books in the Sunday newspapers, and had become a familiar face at the play-openings on Broadway. His professional contemporaries observed a deadly, ethical silence upon mention of his name, but in other circles he was called Jimmy Roper more frequently than Doctor. In fact, one small indication of a young actress's burgeoning success was the intimacy she could imply in her reading of Jimmy Roper's name; it proved that she had vacated Little West Twelfth Street and was settling down in Turtle Bay. But Mary wanted no such career and indeed was more than content in her position as Mrs. Alfred Eaton. At Sage Rimmington's Sunday afternoons Mary was made to feel like a patroness of that certain small world, and she had gradually maneuvered her relationship with Roper so that there and elsewhere he was regarded as her attendant, her admiring companion, but subject to her wishes and not she to his. This was true likewise in the more intimate spheres of their relationship: she had come to realize that Jim Roper's love for her was special but real. He had lost all power to dominate her through superior knowledge and sophistication, and irrespective of the degree to which the present woman was his own creation, he loved her. He had been conscious of the shift in their relationship, but his love for her was greater than his amused resentment, and soon the resentment did not exist. They quarreled twice when she used his apartment for rendezvous without telling him beforehand, but reason prevailed when she told him on the one occasion that the young man was being inducted the next day, and on the other, that the young man—the same one—was being shipped out to foreign places. And on both occasions she had said she was sure that the young man would not have understood the presence of a third party: he was the Princeton son of some friends in

Wilmington, and secretly in love with her. In truth he was neither the Princeton son of Wilmington friends nor in love with her nor off to the wars, but was the young man who followed Kenneth in the succession of lovers provided by Roper. His occupation was taking parties on guided tours of Radio City, and he lived with a middle-aged friend who had an antique shop in Third Avenue, who had made him swear never to see Jimmy Roper again. He was a stupid young man who had used basketball to get him through four years of an obscure Indiana college and continued to use his body to get him the small luxuries and pleasures that were the limit of his ambitions. He could barely read and write, and he would stand for minutes at a time, clenching his teeth and examining them close up in the mirror, or studying his arms and chest and legs for imperfections of complexion. Mary met him about once a month at Sage's apartment, but he was too simple a mind to be invited to the Sunday parties. She gave him small sums, never more than fifty dollars, to purchase the items of haberdashery that he asked for instead of candy. He had remarkable neural and muscular control, and that was all she asked of him. His name was Royal West and he did not like it when she called him Whirlaway, but he was good-natured and agreed with her that the nickname was quite complimentary, all things considered.

He served, unknowingly, another useful purpose: he helped Mary to become independent of Jim Roper, enabling her to have a lover of her own choosing at times of her own choosing and not Roper's time and choosing. She became secretly convinced at one point that Roper was trying to dominate her by rationing her assignations with the young men he procured for her. Since that was true, Roper was mystified and misled and made a new estimate of her demands and of his own power over her; his single power over her was weakened by her diminishing demands, he thought, and while thus confused he yielded up his authority, never to regain it.

Mary proceeded from her late thirties into her forties with a proper claim on the impactive words stunning and striking, which were frequently applied to her beauty. She had taken good care of herself. She drank little, she did not need tobacco, and flesh meat was the constant item in her diet. She had not yet lost a tooth. She soaped herself all over at least once a day and cold-creamed her face every night. Her hair was naturally oily and she had a shampoo every week. She could wear red, deep blue, and black, and her dresses were cut so simply that one could be taken out of the closet after four years or more and needed only the alteration for the prevailing skirt-length, an economy which was also applicable to her suits. Her extravagances were lingerie and shoes. Her feet were long, and she had all her shoes made to order. Upon being made a partner in MacHardie & Company Alfred had given her a sable coat costing $16,000, the price of the Rolls-Royce he wanted but did not buy. She had not wanted the sables, but she never regretted the gift, sentimentally or practically.

Mary was a fraction over five feet seven inches tall and after Eugenie was born her weight settled at just under 130. It needed no watching. She remained high-breasted after the children and the pregnancy which she had aborted. But her superb figure was only a supporting feature of her beauty.

There was no trace of young girl in the beauty of Mary Eaton at forty; no lingering, borrowed quality. Her body was the completed version of which the young girl's had been the formative; her face was now set in the form for which it would be most memorable, as a President's face, an actress's face, an athlete's face, even an author's face reaches its most memorable stage. And in Mary's face there was a woman and not a girl. The question was often asked: "What do you suppose Mary Eaton is thinking about?" At a table in a restaurant, as a listener at a party while someone else had the floor, at the swimming pool at the club, on any of the occasions when conversation did not require her participation she would sit erect with her chin up and her rather thin, well-formed lips together, and her thoughts no one knew where. But she was never surprised or startled by a remark suddenly addressed to her. She had been listening, following the conversation, and proved it by her words. "I've seen her at a dinner party with the same expression that I've seen on her face when I've been riding on the same bus with her," Elizabeth Porter once said to a friend. "She never reads on the bus. She's always remembering something, or maybe it's planning something, but it's more like remembering than planning. I've never given her credit for having a great brain, but that mind is working all the time." All minds are working all the time, but Elizabeth's remark was a sample of the impression Mary's beauty made: the very placidity of her expression was so unusual, in a face that seemed to be made for animation—smiles, raising of the eyebrows, movement of the lips, flashing of the teeth, and even tears—that people who saw her supplied their own explanations for her calmness. The near-perfection of her features was meant to be used, and when it was not used, people looked for a reason, an excuse, a motive. If the features had been less subtly formed—the lips a bit thicker, the nostrils a little more curved, the eyes larger or smaller—it would have been classified as a sensual face and easily forgotten. But there was no extra flesh on the basic lines, and cerebration was the handiest explanation. People have always preferred the handy explanation.

In one sense, of course, the handy explanation was correct, if superficial. Mary's private sensuality was not unplanned or impulsive. In the beginning of her marriage she had learned through her impulses and Alfred's, then in the first affair with Roper she had developed her conscious sensuality, and finally she had found in Royal West a human machine that could be used in her well-thought-out experiments in pleasure. He was a far from ideal companion; his stupidity and cheapness and small vulgarities made him a bore, but he was totally uninhibited and apparently had always been so. As a boy of fourteen in his small Indiana town he had heard the grown men make jokes about his sexual apparatus, and one of his schoolteachers, a woman of thirty-five, lost her job when the other children talked too much about her appetite for him. There were always girls and young women telephoning him at the poolroom and walking slowly past his house in the warm summer evenings. He was an only child, his father had been a victim of the 1918 influenza epidemic while at an Army camp, and his mother supported him and herself with a job in the grocery store and the extra money she made as mistress to a middle-aged widower who lived in the house next door. From the time he was five years old until he went away to college ten miles distant Royal knew that when there was a certain knock on the kitchen door, he was to stay in the parlor and his mother, dropping whatever she was doing, would take the man to her room and stay there for an hour or less. He was ten years old before he actually saw the man in his house, but he had always known who it was, and what his mother was doing. He noticed early that only after the man's visit was he given pennies for candy, a nickel for a Rocket, a quarter for a pitcher's glove, a dime for a bat. He also noticed that his mother and the man never said more than how-do when they met on the street, and when Royal was older and at college he had the reputation for being high-hat, which some of the co-eds attributed to his basketball write-ups but others attributed to their own generosity.

Mary encouraged his reminiscences in detail. She had long since come to think of herself as a New Yorker and it fascinated her to be told that in the country of the sycamores and the Wabash the young men knew that the weaknesses of a church organist and a paperhanger and a hotel man's daughter and a schoolteacher could be turned to financial advantage, that a football coach could be a pederast and a lady lawyer a Lesbian. "Why did you decide to come to New York?" she once asked him.

"Hell, there wasn't no future in that town," he replied. "I didn't have a car till I was twenty."

"But you could have, couldn't you?"

"'Cause talk. 'Where does Royal West get the money to buy a car?' They'd have figured it out who it was put up the money, and like that schoolteacher, they'd of got fired."

"Then how *did* you get one, finally?"

"Told them I was gonna transfer to Michigan State. I didn't have no offer from Michigan State, but they collected a thousand bucks from the alumni and I bought a second-hand Hudson convertible. I sold it for $300 when I came to New York. A loss, but it didn't cost me anything to start with. Blue. Light blue, with a radio and white-walls. An air horn on it this long. Twins. Give a blast with that horn and every cow in the county thought the bull was loose. But you don't need a car in New York. Everybody I know has a car. I guess you have one with a shofer. I wouldn't be a shofer and take that shit."

"What shit?"

"Gettin' out in the middle of the street and almost get hit by a taxi to open the door for some old lady. Old ladies. Do I ever hate them?"

"A lot of them are very rich."

"Money. I'd no more get in bed with one of them old ladies than if they offered me any amount of money."

"Some of them don't want you to go to bed with them. They'd just like to have you around."

"Did you ever get a whiff of their breath? With all that money you'd think they'd spend some of it on a mouth wash. That's one thing I gotta say for you. You're the cleanest woman I ever saw."

"Thanks."

"I am, too. When I don't have anything else to do, I just as soon go in and take a shower."

"I've noticed that. Did you ever read Freud?"

"What was that?"

"An Austrian. Psychoanalysis."

"I heard the name. Would that be in psychology?"

"Yes, indeed."

"That's where I heard the name. I think that was a two-thirty and we had to be in the gym at three. I *passed* it, though. Sigma. Wasn't that his name?"

"Very close. Sigmund."

"I was a Sigma Nu. We were all Sigma Nus on the basket-ball team except the manager. They always gave that to the Kappa Sigs. It didn't make no difference if he was a lousy manager. Kappa Sig always got basketball manager while I was there. Maybe it's different now. It'd be funny if all the players went Kappa Sig and the manager was a Sigma Nu. But I don't think that'll happen. How are you, honey? You want a little lovin'? I think you do. I think you want Royal to give you a little lovin'."

"I do."

On occasion she had seen him from a bus, from her car, walking on Fifth or Madison Avenue, usually hatless but in the clothes he loved, which were English-influenced. He did not wear his hair in the thick, long fashion of Englishmen of his age, but it was not that so much as his gait that made it impossible to confuse him with an Englishman. He was six feet three and a half, which is not uncommon in England, but he still walked like a basketball player, slightly pigeon-toed, which few Englishmen are, and with his hands opened ready to take a pass and begin to dribble, ready to pivot or to shoot. It had become his natural walk and only funny because not many basketball players wore Sulka ties.

The affair with Royal West had begun in 1940 and continued in sporadic fashion until the spring of 1942, at which time, by the accident of residing in a district composed in large measure of office buildings, stores, and hotels, Royal was re-classified. The Local Board was having difficulty filling its quota and Royal was drafted. "I could of told them I was a homo, but I didn't want to tell them that," said Royal.

"No," said Mary.

"They asked me, though. They asked me did I like girls and I knew what they were aiming at, but I wouldn't give them the satisfaction. I said, 'What do *you* think?' The one doctor was sure I was, but I wasn't gonna give him the satisfaction, so tomorrow I'm a soldier, and I guess that's the end of us, Mary. The end of you and I. You'll get somebody else, a woman built like you and all that. Something personal I always wanted to ask you but I never did."

"Ask."

"What kind of a guy is your husband? Is he an old jerk or what?"

"Not so old. He'll soon be forty-five."

"Forty-five. What was he, weak or something? Impotent?"

"No. He had another girl."

"Boy, *she* must be something, to give you up for her."

"Am I something, Royal?"

"Mary, you're a society woman and all that, but now don't take this the wrong way, but all the other dames I ever went with, they were a bunch of knotholes. You were tops, baby."

"So were you, Royal."

"Yeah. Well, I'm better hung than most guys and I got this
699

big physique, you know. But when I start thinking of some of the times we had. Well, what the hell, we had a good time, didn't we, honey?"

"Yes we did, and I'm sorry I didn't have a chance to buy you a going-away present. Will you buy yourself one? Here's, let me see, I'll need two dollars. Here's a hundred and sixteen dollars. Buy something you'd like."

"All right, thanks, Mary. It's no use saying I'll write to you, because I'd rather hit myself over the head with a hammer in preference to writing a letter. But I wish you good luck and I hope you find a horny young 4-F. Well, good luck, Mary. How about kissing me goodbye?"

"I want to very much."

They kissed each other and he drew away and looked at her. "Sentimental, huh, Mary?"

"Mm-hmm. Good luck to you, Royal."

"All the good luck I want is to get the hell out of this fuckin' army the first chance I get. So long, Mary. Keep your knees together. Fat chance of that, eh, Mary?"

She smiled and he left. He was a thing of the past as soon as he closed the door. He had never opposed her in anything that mattered, he had never said anything that sharply displeased or exhilarated her, and she had never been afraid to lose him. She had never given him anything of herself, never surrendered anything, never been wooed or won. He was a faceless contrivance that made an essential contribution to her own pleasure, but it was all her own pleasure, and his successor might have a different name, eyes perhaps of a different color, but would be a different man only in what he was of himself and not in his place in the life of Mary Eaton. She was already planning what the new man would be, and when she found one to fit her requirements she would arrange for his place in her life.

Alfred had so completely removed himself from Mary's emotional life that he gave as little thought as possible to the details of it. Although he did not believe that she confined herself to an affair with Roper, it suited him to act as though that were the case. If he had known the extent of her erotic activity he would have found it impossible to believe what he saw of her as mistress of the household and mother to the children. Their apartment was an entire floor in a building in Seventy-second Street, staffed by a man who was chauffeur-butler and his wife who was cook; a chambermaid-waitress, and a nurse for Eugenie. Thomas Humber, the butler, was in his middle fifties, with a good record except for two years' drunkenness in his early forties. At forty-five he had married his present wife, the cook, and she had helped him back to total abstinence. He was grateful to Alfred for the manner

700

in which Alfred had given him the chance to regain his self-respect: "There'll always be liquor here and you'll be exposed to it every day of your life," Alfred had told him. "But that's not my problem, Thomas. It's yours. And the only time I'll ever mention the subject again is if I have to fire you. Is that a satisfactory arrangement?" It had been entirely satisfactory because it was cold, impersonal, and not in the least patronizing or meddlesome. But gratitude to one side, Thomas's first loyalty was to Mary, whom he thoroughly understood without knowing any of the facts of her extra-marital life. Whatever she was doing, he and his wife Celia agreed, she was doing it away from the house, and man who had come up in the world—meaning Alfred—had probably been hard on a lot of people including his wife. Thomas did not like rich men any the more for the fact that his own skills and abilities made him depend on them for his living. He had lied for too many of them, helped too many of them to bed, overheard too many of their conversations about their friends and their friends' wives. As a result of the Humbers' sympathetic feeling toward Mary, she ran the household with almost no mistakes that they could prevent, and after they had learned what she liked and what Alfred liked, the Humbers quietly took over. Mary was thereby left with the dignity of her authority but without the need to exercise it, and with more time for the two younger children.

In his final years at Groton Rowland grew more conscious of his father's place in the world, and at Harvard his attitude toward his mother was a result of an advancing development of that consciousness combined with a somewhat condescending view of women from which not even Sadie Warren was immune. Mary had no reason to doubt that Rowland loved her or that he loved Sadie, but his masculinity was expressed in a courtesy that was not truly respectful and a kind of protectiveness that was short of but close to contempt. He was the logical product of Samuel Eaton, the grandfather he had never known, and of the manliness tradition of Groton, Harvard and Boston. He was comfortable in that tradition, in spite of being the first generation of his line to come under its influence. Soon after Mary saw how he was turning out she adjusted her relationship with him; he was her son and entitled to his small demands on her time, her convenience, her generosity and her support, but he could not—and did not—expect spontaneous affection or steady warmth. Her love for him became precisely as traditional and conventional as he seemed to want it to be, and she devoted herself to her younger son and her daughter.

She made several mistakes in her relationship with Alex, but the boy realized that they were good mistakes. At day school in New York she tried to have him excused from boxing which was the sport most strongly emphasized at the school, and from which the boys were excused only at the express, signed request of a family physician. It was a year-long and not a seasonal sport, and every boy in every class took part in it. For Alex it was something to be endured, but more preferably endured than to be excused from it. She had never interfered while Rowland was at the school, and her opposition to the compulsory boxing embarrassed Alex. She also made efforts to be overtly affectionate to compensate for Alfred's offhand manner with the boy, but she had not learned that in such matters no one can substitute for anyone else. Alex knew what she was doing and loved her for the good intent but rebuffed her for her failure to understand its inevitable failure; he loved her for herself, but he could not also love her as proxy for his father. The boy had early wisdom. He was sensitive to the change in the relationship between Mary and Alfred, and he knew that Mary hoped to have him on her side, but he could not disguise his eager acceptance of any scraps of affection Alfred tossed him, yet he could be complacent about the reliable, continuing love that his mother transmitted. It was easy to pardon his father's casualness because Alfred always behaved fairly toward him. It was not so easy to be unsuspicious of his mother's motives.

He was a slender, almost frail boy, with a gentle charm and a misleading air of innocence that made his Brooks shirts and tweed jackets seem to dissolve into cassock and surplice. But he was protected by a genuine sophistication that directed him to books which in turn contributed to his early intellectual maturity. He laughed with Daumier and Hogarth at an age when his friends were preoccupied with Gravel Gertie and Superman. He subscribed to a correspondence-school course in cartooning and gave it up because it was too slow for his native gift. His vocabulary was extensive, although his pronunciations were not always accurate. His marks at school were low; seldom near the top, yet never down to failure, a fact which Alfred attributed to the boy's heterogenerous interests, which also included the building of model airplanes, the Philadelphia Phillies, Lana Turner, Woody Herman, Eddie Anderson as Rochester, Vera Vague, the New York Rangers, Stanley Woodward, and Henry Armstrong. Except for his admiration for Lana Turner's palpable attractions he mystified his mother, not only in the subjects of his interests but in his seemingly retarded concupiscence. She would look at him and remember the period of ardor with his father which had made the child that was now this passionless boy, and she would theorize that so much passion had been spent in love-making that none of it had carried down to him.

But she knew she was wrong; he always lingered when she had as guest a woman acquaintance who had large breasts or deep décolletage displaying medium ones, and there were the usual other evidences that he pursued women in his dreams. Nevertheless the boy's look of innocence was persistently baffling to her, as baffling as everything about his brother had been obvious.

The daughter Eugenie was the youngest human being in the apartment building (as Alfred and Mary were the youngest couple). The building was a cooperative, and the owners of the apartments were slightly more unified than apartment-dwellers in non-cooperative buildings. They could block the sale of an apartment to an undesirable, and they had in common various legal, real estate, operational and social problems, so that while there was no compulsion to fraternize or to be neighborly, bows or nods were usually exchanged in the elevators when an apartment owner recognized another apartment owner, somewhat in the same manner as independent farmers who used the same narrow road. They were all, however, free to speak to Eugenie Eaton without the fear that she would misinterpret cordiality for an invitation to tea, or even an invitation to invite to tea. "Mummy," she said one day, "what is enchanting?"

"Enchanting? Well, it means charming. Very charming." Mary looked at her penetratingly. "If you're enchanted, you're under a spell. Why?"

"Like a witch?"

"Not necessarily. It's a nice spell."

"Oh. Do you think I'm enchanting?"

"I do, most of the time."

"Mrs. Farley on the eleventh floor thinks I am. She said I was an enchanting child. I heard her."

"That's very nice of Mrs. Farley to think so, but little girls sometimes hear very nice things about themselves and then they stop being as nice as they were. Older people are sometimes too complimentary to little girls."

"But they *mean* it."

"They mean it, of course. But then the little girls must try to live up to the compliments. The compliment isn't worth much if it makes the little girl conceited. Of course an enchanting little girl never becomes conceited. As soon as she does she stops being enchanting."

"Were you ever enchanting?"

"No, I don't think so. At least nobody called me that in my presence."

"Were you ever adorable?"

"Uh—yes."

"So was I. Mr. Farley said I was adorable."

"Well, Mr. and Mrs. Farley are very friendly, kindly people, and they like little girls."

"*All* little girls?"

"I imagine so."

"How do you know?"

"How do I know? Why—they say very nice things about you, and they don't really know you except in the elevator, so they must like little girls or they wouldn't notice them."

"Oh."

"Your father and I think you're enchanting and adorable—"

"But you have to, because you're my mother and father."

"I hadn't finished. We think you're all those nice things, but we say it because we know you so well. Don't pay too much attention to compliments from people who don't really know you. A lady can be beautiful but still not very nice. But when you get to know her well you may find out that she's nice, too, as well as beautiful. *Or,* you may find out that she's only beautiful and not nice at all."

"But I like compliments."

"Everybody does, but the best ones are those that you earn, and not what people say about how you look. And I think we've talked enough on that subject."

"Mummy."

"What, dear?"

"Do you like Frank Sinatra?"

"I don't know Frank Sinatra."

"But do you like his singing?"

"Not very much."

"Oh, you're as bad as Alex. Alex says he sounds like a lost calf, and he does not."

"But he does to Alex. What does he sound like to you?"

"Nothing. He sounds like Frank Sinatra."

"I like Al Jolson."

"Oh, *Mummy!*"

"Your father likes Bing Crosby."

"He imitates Frank Sinatra!"

"No, I think if anything it's the other way. Anyway, I like Charles Trenet."

"Rowland says they all stink."

"A word I have asked you not to use."

"I didn't use it. Rowland did. I was just saying what he said. Who is your favorite girl singer?"

"You are."

"Oh, Mummy, that's not an answer."

"Well, Ethel Merman, I guess. Who's yours?"

"Frances Langford. Who's your favorite orchestra—if you say Woody Herman I'll be cross."

"My favorite orchestra? Emil Coleman. Or Mr. Markel.

Michael, I think. Michael Markel."

"They must be new."

"I'm afraid not. Mr. Markel played for my wedding, and Mr. Coleman played for that dance we had in the country. Remember?"

"Yes, but I couldn't hear very well. Just bump-bump-bump. I couldn't hear what they were playing."

"Your day will come, my dear. In 1951."

"Nineteen fifty-one? Ten years from now? That's more years than I am now."

"You have no idea how soon that'll be, how quickly you'll be eighteen. Married. I was only one year more than eighteen when I got married. Heavens, this makes it seem so close."

"I'm not going to get married till I'm twenty-one."

"Why?"

"Because Alex told me we all get our own money when we're twenty-one, and then I won't have to ask my husband when I want to buy something."

"It won't matter if your husband is generous."

"Is Father generous?"

"Very. He's never refused me a penny."

"*I* wouldn't refuse anybody a *penny,* if they asked me."

"Just an expression."

"I know, Mummy. I was joking."

"Well, you know me and jokes. I'm very slow. Now you scoot. I've got to go down to Aunt Sage's for a little while."

When school closed in the following spring Mary took the children to East Hampton and gave herself up to the sun while the unknown man who would take the place of Royal West was following the course of his life that would lead him to her. She swam with the children twice a day, walked a great deal to save gasoline, had lunch at the Maidstone Club to save food-rationing points, played gin rummy and read some books. She followed this simple regimen as strictly as did the wives whose husbands were in uniform, although among those women a certain amount of envy was inevitable since they all believed that when Alfred came down for the weekends she could sleep with him, the routine connubial pleasure that the war was denying them and that thus was no longer routine. Mary was therefore not quite one of the sisterhood in wartime fidelity and chastity. Nor did she join the disturbed ones among them whose feeling of unavoidable neglect made them drink too much and in several cases to lapse into Lesbian attachments, the technically faithful wives who reverted to the emotional practices of boarding-school days. The relationship between Mary and Alfred had reached a point of impersonal yet intimate comment, and she was not without a sense of the irony in their situation in that summer of 1942. "If you wanted to," she told him, "you could run wild down here. All these sex-starved women."

"I'll bet they're all watching each other like hawks."

"You can be sure they are. And they're all so jealous of me. Have you ever noticed them at the station? They see you get off the train, and they're all thinking, 'Huh, that damned Mary Eaton. Probably be in bed with Alfred the minute she gets him home. And he'll be back again in a week or two.' "

"Well, do you suppose I'd be helping the war effort if I told them the truth? In most cases down here it'd be a real effort as far as I'm concerned."

"I don't know. Some of the women are very attractive. And any number of young girls."

"Well, if you hear of any emergency cases," said Alfred. "Unfortunately I think they'd have remorse and insist on confessing the next time the husband had leave."

"What about you? Wouldn't you have remorse and do some confessing yourself? I don't think Mrs. Eustace would see it as patriotism."

"And Mrs. Eustace would be quite right, as she so often is. Naturally I don't think you're telling me all this with any insidious intent."

"Alfred, I couldn't care less, one way or the other."

"Well, you've just about stated the case for both of us, haven't you?"

"I suppose so. But in case you do feel the strong patriotic urge, we're going to have a visitor next weekend."

"I won't be here, but who?"

"Oh, that's too bad, because I think she was rather counting on you. And your patriotism."

"Who?"

"Clemmie Shreve Hennessey Porter. She's invited herself down."

"Aside from the fact that she happens to be married to my best friend, what makes you think Clemmie would be unfaithful to Lex?"

"Oh, you forget. I have my source of information."

"I did forget. I wonder how much he's been the source of information about you? But that was before she married Lex."

"How did you know that?"

"Why, I don't know. I just knew it."

"Why, Alfred Eaton! You had an affair with Clemmie Shreve! You couldn't possibly have known that unless she told you, and she'd only tell you if you had an affair with her. I know Clemmie."

"She did tell me. But I didn't have an affair with her."

"Of course you did. Why deny it?"

"Don't be a damn fool. I haven't seen her since she married Lex. I don't think she's been East."

"All right, then it was before she married Lex. If I really put my mind to it I could figure out when."

"You'd still be wrong."

"Well, all I have to do is ask her."

"And what do you think she'd say?"

"If she knew I didn't give a damn she'd probably tell me the truth. Well, you sanctimonious so-and-so. Screwed the wife of your best friend. Heavens to Betsy, are there no scruples left in this world? Oh, I can't tell you how much this amuses me. I can account for most of your time. Was it when she was married to Hennessey? Was it that far back? It couldn't have lasted very long. But that's going to give me something to occupy my mind. Unless, of course, you want to save me the trouble. I wouldn't tell Lex. I just want to know, for curiosity's sake. Come on, Alfred, when did you sleep with Clemmie?"

"On the thirtieth of February nineteen-two."

"All right, then I'll have to figure it out for myself. At least until next weekend."

"I forbid you to mention the subject to Clemmie. It will only upset her to know that you even think we had an affair."

"You *forbid* me? We don't use that word. That's like one of those words the children don't use, such as lousy or stink. You and I have stopped forbidding each other to do anything."

"All right. I can't forbid you. But every once in a while you still have to ask me for a favor. Next time you want a favor, save your breath."

"Unfortunately I'm going to want a favor quite soon. All right, I won't say anything to Clemmie. But now I know you had an affair with her."

"You don't know anything of the kind. What's the favor you're going to want?"

"This is a good time to ask it, isn't it? Well, can you get Sage Rimmington a seat on the plane for Los Angeles next Tuesday?"

"A pleasure, if it's one-way."

"That's all it is. She wants to go out there for a couple of months. She's sure she can get back, but she's having trouble getting out on short notice. She just heard yesterday that her movie actor is going in the Army."

"I don't know anything about her movie actor. I didn't know she had one, although nothing surprises me about her. But I can't promise you that she won't get bumped in Wichita or Fort Worth."

"That's not your fault, if she is . . . You and Clemmie.

707

Of course what I don't understand is how you didn't happen to marry her years and years ago. She was a girl of yours, wasn't she?"

"She was a girl of everybody's, but I wasn't important enough for her."

"Ah, then it was after you became important. That puts it in more recent times. When do you think you became important, Alfred?"

"Oh, I have been for many years, many years. But you were the first one to recognize it. You knew this kid was a comer."

"As a matter of fact I did. At least I was that much smarter than Clemmie. She had all the sophomores panting after her, but I got Mr. Alfred Eaton. I mean that. I never doubted for a minute that you were going to be a big shot."

"Yes you did. You and your family were all convinced that I was a bum. A playboy."

"Well, you were. But Daddy and I knew you were better than that. We don't have to get sentimental about it. I just knew that you had better stuff in you than the other boys I knew."

"Is that why you married me, dear?"

"No, dear. I married you because I believed in something that doesn't exist."

"Jesus, what a way to go through life!"

"Is your way any better?"

"For me it is. Maybe not for you. But that's such a basic difference that there's no point in arguing about it."

"No, there isn't. You and Mrs. Eustace can go right on kidding yourselves and—"

"And you can go right on believing in nothing."

"At least I don't have to pretty it all up, the way you do. She married a drunken pig on the rebound from your pretty nonsense, and the drunken pig drank himself to death because he was so miserable. He believed in what you believe in. Your sister Constance. What has it got her? And this girl that wants to marry Rowland? Why doesn't she just sleep with him instead of all this to-do about marriage?"

"Maybe she has."

"Maybe she wants to. But Rowland is such a little prig that he doesn't want that."

"I seem to remember that you didn't want it, either."

"No, because my mother and father had filled me with the same nonsense. If I'd known enough to have an affair with you we might have saved ourselves a lot of headaches. At least you'd have been better off, you wanted to have an affair. I shouldn't have stopped you that day on Mr. Thornton's boat."

"This is all fine second-guessing."

"Sure it's second-guessing, but that doesn't make it any less the truth."

"All this is the kind of bullshit you get from Jim Roper. You used to think he was queer, and I still think so. I think he's a fairy."

"As a matter of fact, he is. But you'd never guess who he likes."

"Sure I can."

"Who?"

"Lex."

"Lex Porter? Why him?"

"Because he's a man, and not very bright, but handsome."

"Well, you're wrong."

"Okay. But I've just found out something quite by accident."

"What? I think I know. But what?"

"The great doctor isn't your boy friend any more."

"Aren't you clever, though? I knew that's what you were thinking. But if he isn't, who is?"

"Oh, hell. It's a big country. I imagine it's somebody in the Army or Navy. I don't think it's anybody down here."

"As a matter of fact, I haven't got a boy friend."

"But you're looking."

"I'm just like you in that respect, Alfred. I'm human."

"Well, at least I can congratulate you on getting rid of Jim Roper."

"I don't want your congratulations. Jim Roper is my best friend and the only man who ever loved me."

"That's where you're wrong, but you go on thinking that. It makes it much easier for both of us."

"Jim Roper loved me and loves me in a way that you will never understand. Unselfishly. He loves me as much now as he did before he gave in to being a fairy. He gets nothing from me, he asks for nothing, not even kindness. He's blind-loyal to me. That's why he had those men take those pictures."

"You knew about the pictures?"

"Sure I knew about them. It gave me a very strange feeling to see how my husband looked making love to another woman. Jim did that for me, in case you ever got nasty. Mrs. Eustace has quite a figure. Even better than I thought. I wish I'd saved them. No I don't, not really."

"Oh, you had them?"

"No, I never had them, but I saw them."

"Well, why did you say you wish you'd saved them, if you didn't have them?"

"I made Jim destroy them."

"The hell you did."

"Yes I did. He sent you one, I know that. But I made him destroy the rest, the negative, too. In my presence."

"Why did you do that?"

"For only one reason. Because I knew you didn't have detectives following me. After those men took those pictures I was sure you'd try to do the same thing to me, but when you didn't, I made Jim burn the pictures and the negative."

"Well, that was damn nice of you. Thank you."

"You're welcome. Oh, *I* don't hate you, *or* her. I wasn't a bit jealous when I saw the pictures of you together. I've seen a lot of dirty pictures, at least quite a lot, and I don't remember looking at the faces of the people. But there you were, and there she was, and if anything I was embarrassed for you. Two people I knew, in a very embarrassing situation."

"Then I owe you another favor."

"Not really. As I said before, I made Jim burn the pictures because you hadn't tried to get some of me. And you could have. You knew that. I had nothing to do with taking the pictures of you and your very shapely lady friend. But I didn't tell Jim to burn them till I was sure what you were going to do. Well, you were more of a gentleman than Jim was, but then you are anyway. And I like to think I'm a lady, at least most of the time."

"Well, I guess you are."

"Most of the time."

"I imagine there are some prints left."

"The detectives may have some. They said not, but yes, I imagine they kept some, especially of her. A figure like that and a quite lovely face. Quite a pin-up. The one that shows you both together doesn't show much of her, just that she's naked, but none of the details. But the one of her alone was a very excited, angry woman, showing everything, front view."

"Tell me, do they know her name?"

"Yes. Jim had both of you followed and her phone was tapped. He told me he spent about a thousand dollars for detectives."

"Did you reimburse him?"

"I was going to, then I decided not to. I told him it would teach him a lesson not to interfere where I didn't want him to."

"Why have you waited so long to tell me all this?"

"I wasn't going to tell you at all. I just happened to think of it in connection with Jim and his blind loyalty to me, and I let it slip."

"Why weren't you going to tell me? What you did makes you look awful damn good in my eyes."

"All I want from you, Alfred, is politeness. Respect in front

710

of the children. And of course, to keep on being married to you till Jean comes out, and you want that, too, so I'm not really asking for anything. Otherwise, I don't really care how I look in your eyes, or how you look in mine."

"I know," said Alfred. "Would you like me to tell you what annoys me most about you?"

"You're *going* to tell me, aren't you?"

"Yes. It's the way you have of—just when I have you ticketed as a real, 24-karat bitch, you do something nice or generous."

"Well, as I said before, it doesn't make any difference to me how you ticket me. If it makes you feel better to have me a 24-karat bitch, don't change it. My opinion of you doesn't vary a great deal. Most of the time I ticket you as a 24-karat prick, since we're going in for name-calling."

"Nothing personal."

"Certainly not. I'm a bitch, and you're a prick. Nothing personal, though."

"Certainly not."

"But at least I know I'm a bitch. You don't know that you're a prick."

"Now there you are wrong. I know that better than anyone else in the world. I'm sincere about this. I live in constant fear that the world will find out what a prick I am. I don't give much of a damn for your good opinion, either, so I can admit this to you, Mary. I've often despised myself for years at a time. That's true. I spent years, uh, castigating myself. I behaved like a prick, and a darling little girl got killed in an automobile accident. I behaved like a prick and a hell of a swell girl got murdered. I think I should have been more helpful to Constance, but I didn't know how to be. And every time I visit Mother I can feel her looking right through me and saying what a jerk I am. And a lot of other things. I never got up to the hospital when they amputated Fritz Thornton's leg, so he died without ever hearing from me how much I owed to him. I don't and won't admit that I've been a prick where you were concerned. You put the kibosh on this marriage. But I can't hold my head very high where Natalie Eustace is concerned."

"Oh, you know that, do you?"

"Do I know it? Of course I know it. I don't talk about it, not even to her. But I'm not giving her much of a life."

"But luckily she believes in the same nonsense you believe in."

"Luckily. Luckily for me. And luckily for both of us, we know it isn't nonsense. That's where I feel sorry for you, Mary. We believe in what you call this nonsense, and it's for keeps. You're not going to have that later on, when there

711

won't *be* anything else. If you believed in praying, which I know you don't, you ought to start praying that you'll learn to fall in love. How to tell your friends from the apes."

"Thanks."

"Oh, hell, it has nothing to do with your beauty. But your beauty has no effect on me, has it? And yet I'm a very susceptible guy. If I didn't know you, if I were just down here for a weekend and meeting you for the first time, and we had a dozen Marts together, I can conceive of our ending up in the hay together. But I do know you, and so we'll never end up in the hay together."

"Of that you may be very sure, my friend. But now how do you tell your friends from the apes? A dozen Martinis and an attractive woman, and that's all it needs for you to be unfaithful to Mrs. Eustace, the girl you love so well. You're being honest for a change, you're making exactly my point. As long as you don't drink those Martinis, you're safe in your own hypocritical niche. It can't be much if it only takes liquor to make you forget it."

"My intention was only to show you that I think you are a beautiful woman, but that your beauty has no effect on me because I don't *like* you."

"I wonder how long it would take me to disprove that, with or without Martinis. If you didn't see Mrs. Eustace for three or four months, or anyone else. I could still seduce you, Alfred."

"It wouldn't be you, old girl. It'd be your body. I admired you at the beach today. There isn't a better shape on the South Shore of Long Island, and you're practically an ad for suntan oil. None of that escapes me quite yet. And if I'd gotten back in the Navy and been away for months, well, to use a nautical expression, not very complimentary, any port in a storm. But then I'd have been reverting to apehood, my dear, and you'd know it after the first lay. It wouldn't be you, and as a matter of fact, it wouldn't be me. It'd be a male pawing the ground for a female, and absolutely nothing more. The nonsense that you don't believe in is what makes the difference, and as a nice guy to a woman he once loved, I hope you find that out. If you don't, the years ahead are going to be very tough. And very lonely."

"The only time I've ever been lonely was when you were in the next room and not sleeping with me, a long time ago. But that'll never happen again."

"Probably not. Until your looks begin to go."

"Then I'll buy me a Pomeranian. Or maybe an Argentinian."

"How about an Argentinian Pomeranian?"

"Thanks. Anything but a Pennsylvanian. I've had one of those."

"Yes you have, off and on, among others."

"Oh, you're so smart, Alfred. What shall I tell Clemmie Shreve Hennessey Porter when you don't appear next week-end?"

"Tell her I'm in Washington."

"Will you be, or is that naïve?"

"I'll be in Washington some time this week."

"Oh, I made an interesting discovery the other day. Mrs. Eustace is in the phone book."

"She has been for quite a while."

"But I never thought to look her up before. Now I know where you go, and the funny part is I've often walked through that block."

"Well, just as long as you keep on walking. You know the old joke. First guy says to second guy, 'I passed your house yesterday,' and the second guy says, 'Thanks a lot.'"

"You're a riot, Alfred. Just no two ways about it."

"A riot of fun. Good-natured. Loved by young and old alike."

"Phil Barry said to tell you he's going in on the early train, if you want company."

"I have to go in tonight, tell Phil. If I wait till morning I won't get to the office before ten o'clock."

"Well, I'll get supper while you change."

"Where are the Humbers?"

"I told them they could go to the movies."

"Will you call me a taxi, please? They know you."

"We have plenty of gas. I can take you to the station."

"Save it, but thanks for the offer. If you'll excuse me, I'll get out of these old threads and into my zoot suit. Where's Alex?"

"At the movies."

"Can Jean have supper with us?"

"She's had hers hours ago, but she can sit with us if you like."

"I do like. Will you tell Alex that I don't mind his wearing my Peal shoes, even if they are a little too big for him. But I do insist on putting the trees back in. Twice this weekend he's borrowed shoes of mine and put them back without the trees. If he does that again he's going to damn well have to wear his own shoes and give up coupons. Those shoes have lasted ten or fifteen years because I took care of them."

"Or Thomas did."

"We didn't always have Thomas. And that's why I've been able to give you my coupons. And tell Alex he's to stay off the beach after dark or the Coast Guard'll plug him with a .45."

"He never goes to the beach after dark."

"That's all you know about it, little Mother. He and another boy and two girls were necking there last night and they were sent home. But those Coast Guard fellows carry Tommy guns, and one burst would do it. I'm not kidding."

"Who told you all this?"

"Nugent, the cop. What other instructions did I have on my mind? Oh, yes. Tell him he ought to know better than to wear my Racquet Club ties. I don't wear his God damn Groton tie."

"Although you wish you could."

"No, if I'd gone to a good school it would have been St. Paul's. That's where dear old Daddy went, it's where Brother William was going, but Knox was good enough for little Alfred. What else? Nothing else, I guess." He yawned. "God, I get sleepy down here."

"You stayed in the water too long."

"I guess so," he said. "I wanted to talk to you about Washington, but we haven't time now."

"Are you going to take the job?"

"Yes," he said. "But don't say anything to anybody."

"I won't."

"Not that I think the Germans are going to surrender when they hear it, but I'm not supposed to make the announcement."

"Well, I couldn't say much about it because I don't know much. I don't even know what your title will be."

"Assistant Secretary of the Navy in Charge of Utter Confusion."

"When will it be announced?"

"Well, I go to Washington this week, I probably have six minutes with the Great White Father, shake hands all around, 'Glad to have you aboard,' and the announcement will come a day or two later."

His prediction was substantially correct, although he was given ten minutes instead of six with the President, during which Mr. Roosevelt spoke good-humoredly about shanghaiing Alfred away from MacHardie & Company, and referred inevitably to the fact that the post to be held by Alfred was one that he himself had held under Josephus Daniels, and that therefore there was no telling where it might lead to, even for a Republican like Alfred.

The trip to Atlantic City was canceled. He returned to

714

New York for what he and Natalie knew would be their last weekend together for an unpredictable time.

"When do you actually start work?" she said, in the apartment on the Friday evening.

"I'll be sworn in on Monday and I start right away."

"Where are you going to live?"

"At the Wardman Park. You'll like it."

"Am I ever going to see it?"

"Of course you are."

"Isn't Mary going to move to Washington?"

"She is not. She's not even going to be there when I'm sworn in. It's customary, and she knows it, but I'm not going to ask her to be there, and she's certainly not going to invite herself. If you can't be there, I don't want anybody."

"What about your sons?"

"Rowland couldn't come. I wouldn't want him to interrupt his training. And I can't very well have Alex without inviting Mary. Darling, it comes down to this. I couldn't look at a picture of myself surrounded by my happy family. The whole thing would be so damned phony that I'd start out by hating the job. I expect to hate it soon enough, but there's no use starting by hating it."

"Don't do this to spare my feelings," said Natalie.

"Why not? It's your feelings I care about, and you wouldn't be you if you didn't deep down resent it if you saw my picture in the paper with Mary. You wouldn't like it."

"No, but I wouldn't be upset."

"Well, she's not going to be there. If anybody down there asks any questions I'm going to say I look upon the job as a job and not a social occasion. And that'll be no more than the truth."

"What do you do about your real job?"

"I'm glad you call it my real job. Well, I've resigned as a full partner and I've become a limited partner. I don't withdraw capital, but I cease to be active in the business. I've got rid of securities in corporations that I'm likely to do business with for the Navy. That's going to mean quite a tax rap in some cases, but there's no way out of it. The other guys in my spot had to do it, too, and it's better that way. Then no jerk senator can ask me how I happen to own stock in Grumman when the Navy's buying fighter planes from them. This way I can look him straight in the eye and say, 'Senator, go piss up a rope.' Actually I don't expect any trouble for a while. They confirmed my appointment so quickly that for the first time in my life I feel respectable and uninteresting."

"If Mary hadn't burned those pictures you wouldn't be

feeling so smug. Do you think I ought to write her a thank-you letter?"

"By all means. It's the custom, whenever a wife burns pictures of her husband and his girl. Page 355, Emily Post. On page 356 it tells how Mary should answer: 'Dear Mrs. Eustace: Thank you for your note. I hated to destroy the pictures—' "

" 'They were such excellent likenesses.' "

" 'They were such excellent likenesses. But you must promise to send me proofs of your next set. Your appendix scar showed up very well and I trust, and I trust—' Well, you finish it."

"Well, she did destroy them. I can't take that away from her."

"Nobody can take anything away from Mary that she wants. Except me. And I guess she didn't want me very much."

"Well, *really!*"

"Well, what's wrong with that? Fifteen years ago Mary and I were all through, and I met you and fell smack-bang in love with you. The hypothetical question is whether I would have fallen in love with you if Mary and I had been happy. But the actual fact is, I did fall in love with you, so the hell with the hypothetical question. I'm a great man for the facts."

"When you talk like this you ought to be smoking a cigar and have your hands folded on a big pot belly."

"Would you mind if I had a pot belly?"

"Not really."

"I hope you never get one."

"Would you stop loving me if I did?"

"Completely hypothetical. You never will. As far as I'm concerned, you're just right."

"Thank you."

He was stretched out on a sofa, sans shoes, sans necktie, and she was knitting in an easy chair.

" 'In our little den of iniquity.' Do you remember that song?" he said.

"Oh, sure. Vivienne Segal. What was that thing about the glass ceiling? Was that supposed to be a mirror?"

"Yes."

"I see. I always meant to ask you that. Did you ever have a mirror on the ceiling?"

"No, but I knew a girl in London in the first war, and she had mirrors everywhere *but* the ceiling."

"I should think it'd be very distracting?"

"Well, it was. But she was all distractions, that girl. I wonder what ever happened to her. The way she was going, I don't imagine she lasted very long."

716

Natalie put down her knitting and took off her glasses. "I'm glad you had all that, but *I* wouldn't have liked it. It makes sex an end in itself, and it isn't. It hasn't been with us. It hasn't been what's kept us together."

"Never kept us very far apart," he said, laughing.

"No, but it never meant very much to me except with you."

"I'd have preferred to have you say it never meant *any*thing to you except with me."

She put her glasses on again and resumed her knitting. "Well, that's almost true."

"You never got anything out of it with Ben."

"Never."

"But you did with Mr. Calthorp?"

"Yes. Not always. But a few times. Enough so that I knew it could happen with someone besides you. But with him it was an end to itself, and I didn't like that, so that's why I stopped." She took off her glasses again. "I could see that if it went on with Sterling, then there'd be someone else after him, then someone else. I didn't like that prospect. By the time I was forty-five I'd have had affairs with twenty or thirty men. I wasn't meant to have affairs with twenty or thirty men, and yet that's the way I was headed if I'd had a new affair every year or so."

"I wonder how many American women have slept with ten men by the time they're, say, forty-five. Just among the women of the higher social and economic brackets."

"More of them than among the lower brackets, I'd say. I imagine that every woman that's been divorced has had intercourse with at least three men in her life. Two husbands, and one other, and most likely two others. I've had three."

"My mother had three, that I know of."

"My mother had one, and I'm sure of that. One man in her whole life. But think of the women who've had two unhappy marriages, and think of those who experimented before marriage. Girls who let boys go the limit, as we used to say, and had two or three or four affairs before their first marriage. There was a lot more of that than parents realize. And there was another category. The girls who were virgins when they got married, but weren't really in love with their husbands. They're the ones that would increase the average. I knew girls who really thought nothing much of laying a man once and never again. Necking that didn't stop at necking. One time I was at a party in Gibbsville and I went out to the kitchen to get some ice, and there was a girl I knew having an affair standing up. Later on she asked me not to say anything about seeing her necking So-and-So. She wasn't necking. Her skirt was up and he was inside her. He didn't even see me. I don't suppose she'd count that as an affair."

"I'll bet he did."

"I don't know. But if he did, he was right. Awful little man. I hated to dance with him. His favorite word was jazz, and he was always making jokes about it. Double-entendre. 'Uh-uh, here's Natalie. Watch your language,' he used to say, but then he'd dance with me and say things about jazzing on the floor. And he had another word. Kazoo. He was always talking about his kazoo."

"Did he goose girls and whistle?"

"Yes. Did you know him?"

"The type, only too well."

She put her knitting in a basket and her glasses in a Florentine leather case. "Are you tired?"

"Pleasantly. Do I look tired?"

"A little. What would you like? A drink?"

"Nope."

"How would you like some ice cream?"

"Have you got some ice cream?"

"Yes. Chocolate and vanilla."

"I'd like some chocolate ice cream. But first give me a kiss."

She sat on the sofa's edge and they smiled at each other. He started to speak and she put her hand over his lips.

"Don't say it," she said.

"How do you know what I was going to say?"

"Wasn't it something about—Washington?"

"Yes."

She nodded. "I knew it," she said. "Let's pretend there is no such place till Sunday night." She bent down and kissed him, lightly on the lips and on the cheeks, and ran her fingers across his eyelids so that he closed them. She sat with him for a while and then slowly eased herself up from the sofa and got a blanket and covered him with it. He slept for an hour and a little more, and when he opened his eyes she was ready for his look, ready because she knew his breathing so well; but she was not ready for what she saw: love, yes, but helplessness and even fear. "Did you have a bad dream?"

"I don't know. Yes." The helplessness and fear went out of his eyes as he became more awake, and he sat up. "How long was I asleep?"

She looked at the clock. "A little over an hour."

He put his feet on the floor and leaned forward with his elbows on his thighs. "It wasn't a dream. I don't think I saw anybody, but it was like the news ticker. No, it wasn't, either. It was like a news ticker but I didn't see any words. I heard words. I wasn't going to see you any more. Somebody was saying that. It was you . . . Oh, I know what it was. This was going to be our last time together for a long while. We were talking about that, weren't we?"

718

"We agreed not to talk about it. That's why you dreamt it."

"I guess that's what it was. It's funny, I often dream sounds."

"Do you want to go to bed now?"

"No, let's have some coffee. Do I smell coffee? You were going to give me some ice cream."

"I've made some coffee. Do you still want the ice cream?"

"No thanks. Just the coffee. Think I'll wash my face."

"Yes, and I'll get the coffee."

Presently he had coffee and smoked a cigarette. "Are you sorry we didn't get to Atlantic City?"

"No, this is much better."

"I think so, but it isn't much for you."

"Atlantic City wouldn't have been very good. A lot of Gibbsville people still go there. Not friends of mine, but they'd know me because I was my father's daughter."

"I wonder if your father would forgive me for what I've done to you."

"No, he wouldn't. But I could make him understand that I'm happy."

"I wanted his approval."

"He'd never approve of this, but he'd accept it for me, because it's what I want. But I don't think he'd speak to you. That'd be how he'd show his disapproval. Is that too complicated?"

"No, I get it."

"But he'd be much better about this than about my being married to Ben Eustace. He never said anything. Remember he died two weeks before I married Ben. But he didn't like the marriage. I knew that. He didn't understand it. Oh, he liked Ben. But I always had the feeling that when I told him I was going to marry Ben, he felt that Ben had done something underhanded, taken advantage of my father's hospitality."

"I know. You told me."

"Don't be afraid of anything, my dear."

"What am I afraid of?"

"I don't know, but if it's about me, don't be. Don't have bad dreams about me. You're as much to me as I am to you. Don't forget, I'm not a good age to start having children, and my father's dead. So it's all you. It always has been, always will be. I'm saying all this over again because I know what Washington's going to be. It's going to be bad for both of us. Harder for us to see each other, and I imagine especially hard for you."

"Why for me?"

"Because from everything I've heard, nobody really trusts anybody there, and you've gotten so used to trusting me."

"Would you take a job there?"

"No. In two weeks everybody'd know why I was there, and that wouldn't be good at all. Even I, working in a dress shop in New York, I hear Washington gossip and I hate it. It's somehow so much more vicious than New York gossip. In New York it's just a man and a woman. In Washington it's not only the man, but it's the job he holds. And the woman. If it were Washington we could never go to Enrico's. When I go there I'm never going to let any third person see us together. And you'll never be able to make hotel reservations for me. What shall we use for the Racquet Club in Washington?"

"I don't know. The Metropolitan Club, I guess. I'm not a member, but I guess I can wangle it. That's called a message-drop, in international intrigue."

"A message-drop."

"Not a sheep drop, or a teardrop. I'll get old Templeton Avirett to put me up for the Metropolitan Club. He carries a lot of weight in Washington. I suppose they'd call him ante-bellum now. And he is a kind of auntie. Not really. Just a stuffed shirt." He smiled at her. "You're right. I'm not going to be able to pop out with whatever I feel like saying, the way I do with you. I've gotten into the habit of saving things to tell you."

"I know. I love it."

They talked for a while longer and then they decided to go for a walk in the brown-out. "This would be a good night for a bombing," he said. "I just don't understand why the Germans don't come over with a few eggs. Of course nothing would do more for the war effort. They'd actually be doing us a favor if they bombed New York, and they know that. And yet the temptation must be almost irresistible. We couldn't stop them."

"We couldn't?"

"No. They'd get through. I'm sure the only thing that prevents them from coming over is the psychological factor. But if I were in command of the Luftwaffe I'd argue that the psychological factor works both ways. Can you imagine the panic in this town? It would be as good as winning a battle. Communications loused up, transportation snafued. People quitting their jobs to move some place in Ohio. And the sabotage that could go on during the panic. With a couple of .22 rifles they could sabotage the transformers out on the Jersey meadows and no trains would get through to Penn Station. A man dressed as a railroader could walk right through Grand Central to the tracks, underneath where we are this minute, and raise such hell that it'd be a week before trains would be in Grand Central again. And look what happened to the *Normandie* last winter. Maybe it was an accident, and maybe it wasn't but the same thing could happen deliberately to the *Queen Mary* . . . Next week I won't be able to talk like this. Not even to you. I might accidentally give you some information that I got through my job."

"And I'd tell a German spy?"

"Yes. You might. You might not know that it was information, and you certainly wouldn't know that it was a spy. But in a war of this size all sorts of facts become important. I'll give you an illustration. If you worked in the Kotex factory and you happened to find out that a rather large consignment of the product was being put on a ship to Brazil, what would you think?"

"I suppose you want me to think that the Brazilians were neglecting their women or something like that."

"That would probably be a sound deduction. But if the same information got to Berlin it would mean something quite different. It would mean that we were going to land troops in Africa."

"Why?"

"Because Brazil is one of our stops on the way to Africa. Kotex would mean, to a German, Army nurses. Army nurses on their way to Africa? Why nurses? You see?"

"I do now."

"If you worked in a rubber factory in Akron, Ohio, and suddenly there was a high priority on a certain size of bicycle tire."

"Bicycle troops."

"*Paratroopers.* There's a folding bike that paratroopers use and it needs a special-size tire. But here's the worst kind of leak. A couple of weeks ago two young girls, friends of Rowland's, married, moved to San Francisco. Both girls are married to j. g.'s, and both j. g.'s are on different DE's, DE's are destroyer escorts. What that means is that at least two, and therefore probably more, destroyer escorts are being taken off the North Atlantic run and sent to the Pacific. Naturally the Japs have plenty of spies watching everything that goes through the canal, but we're not doing anything to make it harder for them. The boys talk too much, the girls talk too much and move to San Francisco. Every time the Germans buy a ball bearing in Sweden, we find out about it, and the Germans know we do. The Germans know we have agents in Lisbon, and probably know who most of them are. But we're a gabby lot. The British don't like to tell us a thing, and neither do the Russians. Incidentally, everything I've told you is common knowledge, and yet I won't talk like this after tomorrow night."

"Tomorrow night. Then Sunday and you go away."

"Yes. It's probably an unpatriotic thing to say, but it's the first time the war's been brought home to me, personally."

"The second, isn't it? When Rowland joined the Navy?"

"Not even then. I didn't feel quite this way. I didn't feel that *I* was in the damned thing. Now I do. It's a little like the first time I shipped out during the first war. I didn't know what was ahead of me, and I don't now. Shall we go home?"

"Yes, let's."

IN THE QUESTIONNAIRE that Alfred had filled out upon agreeing to work for the government there was a space for his nickname(s). The space was greater than he needed for his answer: "None." He had never been Al, Alf, Alfie, Freddie, or Fritz; not Spike, Bud, Whitey, Slim, or Duke. But not long after Alfred took his oath of office someone in the late afternoon crowd at the National Press Club bar called him Speedy Eaton, the new AsSecNav, and while the name did not achieve wide circulation, it stuck. No matter how exalted a man's position and his title, he had a nickname, even if it was no more imaginative than Tom for Thomas, and the nickname was always used when the man was not present. To refer to a five-star general or a Cabinet official as General or Secretary was considered to be an admission of unfamiliarity, and in a city of contacts unfamiliarity had no place. It was quite true that no one who knew Forrestal ever called him anything but Jim, and no one at all called George Catlett Marshall anything but General, but every day at the Press Club bar and in the groups at the Mayflower, Forrestal was called Jimmy and Marshall was Georgie, in their absence and by men and women who were strangers to both men.

Alfred's nickname stuck because it was apt, and it was used for the most part disparagingly. On his own, Alfred refused to grant interviews, but when it was pointed out to him that he might as well consent and get the nuisance over with, he agreed to a meeting with the press at which he said nothing worth repeating, and all too obviously indicated that the sooner the ladies and gentlemen took themselves elsewhere, the happier he would be.

"Mr. Secretary, does your taking a job in Washington imply any change in your attitude toward the administration?"

"I consider that a political question," said Alfred.

"Well, sir, it is."

"The whole subject of politics is out," said Alfred.

722

"But may I ask," said another reporter, "whether your taking this job means you may at some future time become active in politics?"

"Now *you* heard what I just told that other gentleman. My answer is the same to you as it was to him."

"Well, then, Mr. Secretary, can we infer that your attitude toward the administration has *not* changed?" said the second reporter.

"You can infer what you damn well please, but you're not going to get me to talk politics," said Alfred.

"Is Mr. Knox an old friend of yours?"

"I've known the Secretary for several years. I could hardly call him an old friend. His home base is Chicago, and mine's been New York for the past twenty years."

"Would you care to tell us what your special activity will be in this job?" said a third reporter.

"I'll do what I'm told."

"Even if some of the things you're told may run counter to your beliefs as a Wall Street man?"

"Oh, come on, now. Aren't you trying to say, 'Even if you don't agree with Mr. Roosevelt'?"

"I'm trying *not* to say that," said the reporter.

There was mild, general laughter.

"Well, at least you're candid," said Alfred.

"Mr. Eaton, if I may ask a non-political question?" said a woman reporter.

"You may indeed."

"You are married and have three children. A son in the Navy, another son at Groton, where of course the President went to school—"

"So did Colonel McCormick, for that matter," said Alfred, provoking some more mild laughter.

"So he did. And one daughter. You make your home in New York City and have a place on Long Island."

"That is correct."

"Is Mrs. Eaton planning to live in Washington while you're here? So many of the people I imagine are friends of yours have taken houses in Georgetown."

"No, we don't plan to set up another establishment in Washington, if that's what you mean. I'm living at a hotel."

"Yes. The Wardman Park," said the woman. "But Mrs. Eaton doesn't plan to take up residence here?"

"No."

"She will visit you at the Wardman Park."

"Naturally, I hope so. Although not on any permanent basis. My daughter is quite young, nine years old, and Mrs. Eaton doesn't want to take her out of school."

"Would you like to tell us something about Mrs. Eaton?"

"That's all on those biographies you were given."

"She was a Miss Mary St. John, of Wilmington, Delaware, but aside from that and her schooling it doesn't say much about her. Who was her father?"

"Eugene St. John. A research man. Her mother was a Miss Rowland, a Virginian by birth."

"Oh. Did her father work for the du Pont corporation?"

"He did, but he's retired and now lives in New York."

"Is Mrs. Eaton going to be in Washington soon?" said the woman.

"Quite possibly, but I wouldn't count on her for an interview, if I were you."

"Well, I'll at least try," said the woman.

"Mr. Eaton, weren't you at one time in business with Larry Von Elm?" said a fourth reporter.

"Not exactly. A friend and I were partners in a very small aviation factory on Long Island, over twenty years ago. Mr. Von Elm was our head designer. He was given some stock, but he wasn't a principal stockholder by any means, and all he really got out of it was his salary. The company was liquidated after two years."

"Why did the company fail?"

"It didn't fail, except in the sense that we failed to produce. We simply shut down. But it was a very closely held corporation and nobody lost any money except my partner and I and a few of our relatives. We paid off a hundred cents on the dollar.'

"What did you think of Larry Von Elm?"

"A brilliant designer. Perhaps way ahead of his time."

"Have you seen the E-1-F?"

"I have, but I didn't know you came out with questions like that in a press conference, identifying aircraft."

"The E-1-F is no secret, Mr. Secretary."

"Oh, but I beg your pardon. It is *top* secret, and will continue to be until the enemy captures one and has had a chance to study it. Which I hope won't be for a long time. But indiscriminate conversation and newspaper references to our aircraft is something I'm against."

"Are you in favor of stricter censorship of the press?" said the man who had been asking the political questions.

"Quite frankly, yes, I am."

"Even when it can be used to cover up blunders?"

"What do you mean by blunders?" said Alfred.

"Botches. Waste of money on inefficient aircraft, for instance."

"Yes. I'd be in favor of censoring our mistakes. Why should we spend millions of dollars on an experiment and then have it reported to the enemy that the experiment is a failure? That may be negative information, but it's information nonetheless. It tells something to the enemy, and I don't want to tell them a damn thing."

"Don't you thing the American people ought to know when money is being wasted?"

"War itself is a waste, my dear sir. Or, to put it another, more accurate way, war is wasteful. In a war, waste is inevitable and war is destructive. I think the American people want to know that most of us, most of the time, are doing the best we can to win this war, to end it successfully and as soon as possible. I don't think the people kid themselves that winning a war is cheap, and I think most of them would rather not hear about blunders."

"But then wouldn't you censor news of defeats, military losses?"

"We weren't talking about that, but no, I wouldn't censor that kind of bad news except when and where it might help the enemy tactically or strategically. And that's being taken care of. I'm afraid this isn't a very popular attitude with you gentlemen, but I'm being completely frank about it."

"Then you think freedom of the press should be suspended during wartime?"

"Isn't that what I've been saying? We all give up various freedoms during wartime. The press has no special right to be an exception. And the responsible press doesn't expect it. On that happy note, if there are no more questions, ladies and gentlemen . . . ?"

"I have one more question, please, if you don't mind," said the political-minded reporter.

"Okay."

"Would you call yourself a Creighton Duffy man?"

"No, but I imagine you would," said Alfred. "Now let's get on with the other war, shall we? Thank you, and good afternoon."

Thereafter, whenever it became necessary to refer to him in print, Alfred was called the Princeton–Racquet Club–Wall Street banker. The newspapers that were most hostile to Roosevelt made the point that Alfred was one of the misguided souls who had gone to Washington with patriotic motives but were actually being used by Roosevelt for "window-dressing" and a spurious show of bi-partisanship. In this, of course, he was not alone, but at his first press conference he had so thoroughly alienated the reporters that some of them made faces as they walked past his door on the second deck of the Navy Building. His detractors said he was going nowhere in a hurry, that he seemed to think nothing had been done about the war until his own appearance on the Washington scene, that he was arrogant, and that he had charm.

725

Charm, even as dispensed at the White House, was beginning to be a handicap because the reporters of the pro-Roosevelt persuasion had begun to realize belatedly that it had been exerted upon them to mislead them and to keep them disciplined, and they had become suspicious of its appearance elsewhere than in the White House. The reporters recognized arrogance when they saw it; so many of them had come to regard themselves as little Lippmanns and waxing Kents that they forgot it was their jobs and not their own personalities that made them welcome, or tolerated, in the offices of the mighty. It would have been almost as easy for Alfred to have been pleasant with them, but he had sensed immediately that they were challenging him to be ingratiating, and that he would not take. His long indoctrination at MacHardie & Company had fixed his position in relation to the press, and when he recognized their challenge he responded to it with insolence of his own, made no less damaging by the fact that he had come to Washington as a successful man and by his refusal to see himself as a timid candidate for their good will. The damage was permanent, but he was so relieved to have the conference ended that he gave no thought to any future relations with the press, good or bad.

He had come out of that first experience with his self-respect intact and possibly a little inflated, but he was already the loser, although it would be months before he saw his mistake. He had gained by the interview, but where he had gained was precisely where he would lose in the future: he had gained the information that he had somehow become associated in the Washington mind with Larry Von Elm, and he had learned that he was, as he had expected, at least nominally a Creighton Duffy man. Alfred had said nothing to anyone that would lead to those conclusions, so it therefore was fairly obvious that Von Elm had been talking about some association with him, and Duffy likewise had been talking. They were older hands at the Washington game, and they had established early claims on Alfred Eaton, who was an attractive newcomer in a sub-Cabinet job. It did them no harm to establish such claims; they could be abandoned if Alfred did not pan out. But Alfred had not seen that while a press conference may be an ordeal, the members of the press are sources of information. He despised and feared gossip, but gossip expressed in the form of press conference questions was often informative. A reporter's question was frequently the first hint of a development that had been kept from the man most concerned, and now Alfred had lost this source of information, speculation, warning, and preparedness.

The E-1-F was a fighter plane. It had been designed in Larry

Von Elm's office and was a Von Elm effort from the ground up. The secrecy with which Alfred had attempted to surround it was not only of a routinely military character: the Navy had provided the money for the design in accordance with a policy under which separate and independent aviation companies were building almost identical airplanes. Von Elm was given the money and told to go ahead with his design so that the Navy could become less dependent on Grumman for its fighter planes. The plan was to perfect the design while the new Sierra Aircraft Corporation was proceeding with its work on its somewhat unfortunately named Broncho engine. The E-1-F was never accepted by the Navy and actually it had never been officially anything but the E-1-FX. The E-1-F question asked by the reporter at the unfortunate press conference may and may not have been related to the other question regarding blunders and botches, and the possibility of such relationship occurred to Alfred, but in his inexperience and ignorance (and in his relief) he did not know how to go about correlating the questions, and instead of acting on his curiosity, he made the mistake of letting the matter end there. Obviously the first reporter had been talking with someone who knew something about the E-1-F, but it was not obvious that the second reporter's remarks about censoring inefficiency were supported by any information that should have been secret. The E-1-F as such had not turned out well, and no one knew that better than Larry Von Elm, but whether Von Elm was conducting a personal propaganda campaign, or merely being indiscreet with friendly reporters, Alfred owed it to the Navy and to himself to find out. He did not find out.

He was aware of his usefulness as window-dressing and as a symbol of bi-partisanship. The subject had been discussed during his conversations with Creighton Duffy, as frankly by Duffy as by Alfred. "We know what you're thinking," Duffy had said. "We've had to solve the same problem with other fellows like yourself. The Boss is no fool, you know. He knows that most business men hate his guts, most of the men in the big law firms, and practically all members of the financial community. But he doesn't expect you to come down here and start campaigning for a fourth term. He wants men like you in the government because you have the industrial and the financial know-how, and it's our American know-how that's finally going to beat the Germans."

"And the Japs, I trust."

"Of course the Japs. Alfred, this man is a great American, he really is. The other day he had a Navy captain in the executive office to pin a Navy Cross on him. He had the citation in front of him, but somehow or other he already knew every-

727

thing that was in it. I don't see how he does it, but he does. Anyhow, he congratulated the officer and the officer's wife, and then when they left he said to me, 'That man is a very active America Firster, but he's one of the finest officers in the Navy. I wish I could make him see things our way, but I guess I never shall.' Then he went on with his work. But it takes a big man to do that, to be able to submerge his own personal feelings and honor a man that he knows hates his guts. There's not a day goes by but that something like that happens. Remember, he has very few friends left among the class of people he grew up with, and yet it's that type man that he's relying on to provide what you might call the sinews of war. And I'm glad to be able to say that there are a lot of men like yourself that whether or not they like him personally, they're beginning to grudgingly concede that he's a dedicated man. Aren't you secretly glad that Willkie isn't there instead of F. D. R.?"

"Nothing secret about it. I never liked Willkie. I voted for him, but that was because I'd never vote for a Democrat."

Duffy smiled. "Watch out, Alfred, you may find yourself voting for this man two years from now."

"You wouldn't like to make a very large bet on that, would you, Creighton?"

"No, I guess not. You'll vote for the little man on the wedding cake, just because he's a Republican."

"After what you fellows have been doing these past ten years, that's a good enough reason to vote for anybody."

"Bertie McCormick?"

"That's not a decision I'll ever have to make. He has no more chance of the nomination than I have. And that leads me to the one thing we haven't really discussed."

"I know what you're going to say."

"But will you let me say it, so there'll be no misunderstanding? I've mentioned this to you before, but I want to say it again. I want to say it for myself, although I'm sure the other fellows have said it for themselves and it's old hat by now. I am not going to be used for any political purpose. I don't even want to be used as a Republican example of the bi-partisan administration. If Frank Knox wants to be known as a bi-partisan, that's fine. He was a candidate for vice-president, he was a Rough Rider with Theodore Roosevelt, he's a newspaper publisher. A lot of things I never have been. I never hope to be as great an American as Frank Knox is. But I am me. It may not be much, but I'm me and not somebody else, with my own few principles and beliefs and quite possibly my own defective character. But I have to stand or fall on that, Creighton, and I want to remain as independent as possible, subject to orders from on high, but I'll kick like a mule at the first sign that I'm being used to further the career of Mr. Roosevelt or his party, and at the second sign I'll be on the Congressional on my way back to Wall Street. Is that perfectly clear?"

"Of course. We knew those were your terms."

"This goes for small things, too. By that I mean I'm not going to be gracious about posing for pictures with Mrs. Roosevelt and labor leaders."

"You won't be asked to."

"I just might. I might be representing the Secretary at the dedication of a new plant—"

"Oh, I see what you mean. Well, how often is that liable to happen?"

"I don't know, but I've been warned that assistant secretaries do dedicate factories and are expected to read a speech. Do you admire Mrs. Roosevelt?"

"Mrs. Roosevelt? Eleanor Roosevelt is a splendid—"

"All right, Creighton. You've answered me."

"But I really do like her."

"Now don't overdo it, Creighton. You've handled it very well."

"Well, she—"

"Don't say any more. I had no right to ask you."

"All right. Then it's agreed. You're coming?"

"Yes."

"Fine. Congratulations, and welcome. Would you like Jean to help Mary find a place to live? She's pretty good at that."

"She's not coming to Washington. I'm going to take a couple of rooms at the Wardman Park. Mary's staying in New York so that we won't have to take our own Jean out of school."

"Oh, I'm sorry to hear that. Mary would have been an addition to the Washington scene."

"Well, she doesn't think so, and by the way, I take a very dim view of the social life here."

"Why? Too much, or too little?"

"Much too much. And the government offices knocking off at four-thirty and five."

"You think they ought to work longer?"

"I sure as hell do. You look out on Constitution Avenue at five-fifteen and you'd never think there was a war going on. Plenty of uniforms, sure. Plenty of those good-looking female marines. But it looks like a college campus."

"Wait till you're here a while," said Duffy. "You're going to want that six o'clock Martini more than you ever did in your life before."

"I'd thought of going on the wagon."

"Don't. And don't feel conscience-stricken. You'll soon find out that you're a better public servant for having had that Martini than if you'd stayed at your desk till nine o'clock.

The hardest thing is getting to that God damn desk at eight o'clock in the morning. I never did that before I came to Washington. By the way, it might be a good idea for you to have a medical check-up."

"What the hell for? I'm all right."

"You're forty-five, you never know where to expect trouble." Alfred was silent, and Duffy continued.

"Well, suit yourself, of course. I just think it's a good idea, but I'm a sort of a health nut. You've probably noticed, I'm very handy with the knife and fork and I'm fond of good wines, but I get a complete going-over twice a year and I'm a great believer in steam baths and massage. You're not going to get in your court tennis here."

"Not unless I go to Aiken or Philadelphia. But I haven't been playing much the last few years. Both my sons can beat me at lawn tennis, and I think Rowland has the makings of a court tennis player."

"Well, Sandy Duffy still boxes. Or I guess he does. He got his wings just the other day, and now he's a naval aviator."

"Where's he stationed?"

"Pensacola, but I don't think he'll be there much longer. He thinks North Island will be his next stop, and then a carrier."

"Good for him."

"And thanks to you. Do you still carry that scar?"

"Oh, sure."

"I often look at that boy, especially when he was the Yale middleweight champion, and think how close he came to the next world."

"I don't even remember much about it any more, except that it was a mighty cold day."

"If you get down to Pensacola I wish you'd take a look at Sandy. You haven't seen him these past couple of years. He's hefty, like his mother and I, but he's a bull-ox for strength, and very fast on his feet. Not handsome, but a face you'd trust."

"Oh, I remember him very well."

"If anything happened to him it'd be the end of me, you can be sure of that. I wouldn't let him know that. I said to him when he won the Yale tournament, 'I can still pin your ears back,' and he just laughed at me, knowing damn well I wouldn't last two rounds with him."

"You know, Creighton, I've never heard you talk like this before."

"You wouldn't now if you didn't have a son learning to fly. That puts us in the same boat. Oh, I've got a stake in this war, too, Alfred."

"Well, if I go to Pensacola I'll be sure to look him up. Or I might even see him out at North Island. Do you remember my friend Lex Porter? He's at North Island. Administrative officer with a fighter group and he might be there when Sandy reports."

"Hell, I guess I knew Lex Porter before you did."

"Yes, I guess you did, come to think of it."

"I was born in Oyster Bay, you know. I've known those people all my life. This may seem odd to you, but my father considered James D. MacHardie a newcomer. My father had the second Rolls-Royce on the North Shore. I'm not sure who had the first, whether it was Payne Whitney or Clarence Mackay. Oh, we had all those things, but we never got anywhere socially because the women didn't approve of my mother. She was an Irish immigrant girl and she drank her tea out of her saucer. But Mrs. MacHardie drank hers out of a bottle, and it wasn't tea."

"I never knew that."

"Not many people do know it, and those who did pretended they didn't, either out of politeness or because it was a very sensitive point with James D. But she was a lush right out of Dickens, and nobody ever understood why, because the old man worshipped her. You can still see where the iron bars were on some of the second-story windows. Take a look the next time you're invited for one of those MacHardie weekends."

Here, in this town and at this time, Alfred found that he was liking Creighton Duffy. Of all times and places he would have least expected to like him. It would not last, but that it could happen at all was phenomenal. He had known this man for twenty years, had begun the acquaintance as dramatically as possible, and thought there was no more to know. But he had found out more about him as a man in one conversation than in all the previous years. A man at the Racquet Club had said it: "You never know the holes in the lining of the other fellow's coat." That had an Irish sound to it, and it came quickly to mind now.

"I haven't been very observant," said Alfred.

"Nobody sees everything," said Duffy. "And Alfred, I know we aren't palsy-walsy, but I'd like you to know that I feel partly responsible for your coming down here, and therefore if there's anything I can do for you while you're here, just say the word. And you can trust me."

"Can I?"

Duffy grinned. "Well, this is a rat-race here, you know, and to have a rat-race you first have to have rats. We all have a bit of rat in us, and you should be able to decide where and how much you want to trust me. You can be serenely confident that I'm not going to do anything for you that's liable to get *me* in trouble, but I *can* get things done. I'd have been out of here long ago if I'd seen I wasn't getting anywhere. I never get to

731

drive, but Daddy lets me hold the slack end of the reins. Remember when you were a kid?"

"I must have been a born conservative, Creighton. My biggest kick was putting my foot on the brake."

"That's in character, all right," said Duffy. "Speaking of our boyhood, I see a Port Jefferson friend of yours now and then. I naturally don't mean Port Jefferson. I mean Port Johnson."

"Who's that?"

"Tom Rothermel. He had a government job for a while, but now he's in the C. I. O."

"Where he rightly belongs."

"True. I gather that you were friends when you were young, but there was a parting of the ways."

"Yes, he took the fork to the left. So much so that I've lost him."

"Well, if I were you, I'd find him again. You don't have to do anything that goes against the grain, but more and more people in Washington are trying to get to know Tom, and you already do. Don't pass up that advantage. I can see why you'd think Tom was a little prick. He's very cocky, and I guess a prick should be cocky. But he typifies the younger element at the C. I. O. You can love a man like Phil Murray, but it's the Tom Rothermels you're going to have to do business with, now and after the war. And I'll give you another piece of advice. Don't ever forget that this war is going to end."

"Why do you say that?"

"I'll tell you why. The unions aren't forgetting it."

"That's still a little cryptic."

"Only because you haven't thought about it. Management has plenty of men thinking about what's going to happen after the war. You know better than I do that every time we design a new bomber and put it up in the air, there are guys at Douglas and Lockheed who are giving *some* little thought to how many seats those bombers could hold, how many paid passengers. It's only natural, and I don't think it's a crime, not as long as the Air Force is getting the immediate benefit. Of course it's a great break for the aviation industry to have Uncle Sugar pay for getting the bugs out of those big planes. So you can't really blame labor for looking ahead, too."

"How are they looking ahead?"

"If this war lasts five years you're going to have to join a union to get in the F. B. I."

Alfred laughed.

"Well, I'm exaggerating, but in some of the European countries the government employes are all organized, and don't forget that the Civil Service amounts to a union. Here's the difference between the Phil Murrays and the Tom Rothermels. Phil Murray would try to avoid a strike if he were

732

convinced that it hurt the war effort. Phil Murray is a good American. Tom Rothermel would pull the electricians out during the bombing of New York, if he thought he'd gain an advantage for the union. I've spent many hours with that guy. He looks upon this war as a fight between fascism and capitalism, with capitalism so close to fascism that it's dog-eat-dog. The main war is between fascistic capital on the one side, and labor, socialistic labor, on the other. That's what Tom Rothermel thinks."

"I've been having a hard time trying to discover what *you* think."

"After an evening with Tom Rothermel I have a hard time myself. I'm a Roosevelt man."

"And that covers everything?"

"It covers my confusion, and I'm not going to get arrested for it."

"Do you know what I think? I think your man is in so deep that he couldn't get out if he wanted to, and I think he wants to, but he's so God damn stubborn and arrogant that he's not even going to try to do what he'd like to. And that's one of the reasons I don't like him. Having heard me say that, you're at liberty to withdraw the job offer."

"Oh, it's a familiar complaint."

"Is Tom Rothermel a communist?"

Duffy thought a moment. "I somehow doubt it, if you mean does he belong to a cell and carry a card. I think Tom is too sophisticated to be a party member. The CP boys would probably call him a deviationist, because he doesn't automatically follow the morning line, as you might call it. In Russia he'd probably be shot for getting too far ahead of the pack. They don't like that. Party discipline is very important because a guy like Tom Rothermel, an eager beaver, can spring something before the party is ready. You can see why that would be. A guy climbs over the parapet and starts shooting and a whole attack is ruined. However, there is very little danger that Tom Rothermel will ever be called *anti*-communist. Tom is the clean-shaven, Hart, Schaffner & Marx version of the Bolshevik with the bomb and the sparkling fuse in his pocket. You remember the cartoons. The world seemed a lot simpler then, didn't it?"

"It wasn't, though. The guy with the whiskers and the bomb never existed, but those damn cartoons made people look for the whiskers and the bombs. It was much easier to recognize a capitalist or a crooked politician. They all looked like Boies Penrose."

"Well, they couldn't have picked a better model. The Penroses had their day, and now it's Tom Rothermel's turn."

"Oh, you think they're going to have their turn?"

733

"That was a slip, and I don't often make that kind of a slip. Yes, I think they're going to have their day. The New Deal was part of it."

"The New Deal will collapse after the war."

"Oh, you're so wrong. There's so much written into the law of the land now that we'd have to begin all over again with the Articles of Confederation. Yes, the Tom Rothermels will be having their turn. Union fascism. Then the dictatorship of the proletariat. Then the women will take over, then the gigolos. then the fairies and Lesbians, then nothing for a while till Nature's had time to develop a new species of ape."

"I thought you were a Catholic."

"I am. This will be a Catholic ape."

"How is your Catholic ape going to learn all about Christ and the Pope?"

"Oh, he'll be a super-ape, able to read Latin at birth. He'll dig up all the records under the ruins of the Vatican and start reading it all and say, 'Boy, this is for me.'"

"Time I was getting back to the hotel. Your mind is beginning to wander."

"That eight o'clock comes early. Goodnight, Alfred."

"Goodnight, Creighton."

"I had a very pleasant evening."

"So did I. Very."

In the weeks between that conversation and the press interview Alfred saw Creighton Duffy only twice, both times briefly, and as he reconsidered the reporter's question as to his being a Creighton Duffy man, he found that it was quite as easy to revert to his former appraisal of him and to be uninfluenced by the warmth of that conversation. But if Duffy was using him. he was quite prepared to use Duffy, and the opportunity to do so came soon.

Alfred had not been in on the three-cornered negotiations for the E-1-FX, but he was given a quick briefing by Captain John J. Joralemon. the officer who had acted for the Navy. Joralemon's report was as candid as could be expected in the circumstances; he protected himself against responsibility for a project that had not been a conspicuous success, and at the same time Alfred detected a tendency to be protective of Larry Von Elm. Alfred then concluded that Joralemon and Von Elm were working together. had worked together, and would go on working together, and that they were two against the one of the Sierra people. It was therefore Alfred's duty to talk to the Sierra people, and he accordingly flew to California. He was accompanied by his aide, Lieutenant Commander Frank W. Wilson, U. S. N.. and for three days Alfred talked to the officials of Sierra, foremen, designers, mechanics, publicity men, and almost anyone else he happened to think of. They were all agreed that the E-1-FX was a fine airplane, and Alfred knew that he was up against a conspiracy to tell him nothing. On the afternoon that he was to return to Washington he called in the president of Sierra, a man named Wilmer ("Bill") Hanniford, an old Army flyer, barnstormer and mail pilot who was obviously fronting for the money men of Sierra. The corporation had put an office at Alfred's disposal, and Alfred did not for a moment forget that they had had ample opportunity to bug the office with hidden microphones and that every word spoken in that office was being taken down.

"Well, Bill," said Alfred. "All I've been able to find out is that the E-1-FX is a crackerjack airplane that would do everything but fly."

Hanniford smiled. "You're kind of rough on it, Mr. Secretary."

"That's all I've been able to get out of your people."

"I'm sure they told you all they knew. They were instructed to be cooperative."

"Were they? Some of them behaved as though they didn't quite believe my credentials."

"Oh, I don't think it was that so much as they never talked to anybody high up before. They froze at the stick, you might say."

"Well, I have a boss, too, and when I go back to Washington I'll have to report the failure of a mission."

"I'm sorry to hear that," said Hanniford, without any discernible sorrow.

"I'm going to make one more little effort."

"Okay. What's that?"

"I'll give you one hour to produce the test pilot who's been so damn busy ever since I've been in California."

Hanniford was disturbed. "Gosh, I don't know if I can produce him in an hour. I don't have any idea where he is."

"You have an hour to find out and bring him here. He's made himself scarce for three days, and if you don't know where your test pilots are for three days at a time, you're in the wrong business, and don't think *that* won't be in my report."

"All right, sir, I'll see if I can find him."

"And don't waste too much time calling your backers. Do this on your own responsibility and explain it to them later."

Hanniford's face reddened and he turned his back on Alfred to avoid charging him. The test pilot appeared in twenty minutes. He was a deeply sunburned man with a waxed moustache and a livid scar on his forehead. "You asked to

735

see me, sir? My name is Jerry Kelly. Test pilot."

Alfred leaned forward and shook hands. "Glad to know you. Let's go for a walk."

"How do you mean a walk?"

"You know, where you put one foot in front of the other and find yourself in motion. I'd like to have a private conversation with you, and I have an idea this office isn't as private as I'd like."

Kelly grinned. "Whatever you say."

They left the office and walked until they came upon a small tractor standing outside a hangar. "All right, Kelly. All you can give me on the E-1-FX."

Kelly talked for half an hour, chain smoking and linking his thumbs to make the gestures of a flying airplane. He spoke rapidly, in a deep voice and with a slight stammer, so full of his subject that a fast stenographer could not have taken down what he said. But he was unquestionably honest and even beyond that, honorable. "I heard you were here. I was kinda sore you didn't even send for me."

"I asked for you the day I got here. They said you were out in the Valley, whatever that means."

"I was, but not all day."

"You're not worried about your job, are you?"

"Are you kidding? I can get a job anywhere in the country."

"Good. Well, thanks very much. You've been the only help I got here."

"It's a good airplane, but they hurried it a little. They want to get into production and start getting their dough back. That's all it is."

"What if the Navy had okayed it?"

"The Navy couldn't have okayed it, Mr. Eaton. I have a boy in the Navy and anything gets past me is ready to fly."

"You don't look old enough to have a boy in the Navy."

"Don't let the sunburn fool you. Although that's what I have it for. My kid and I double-date sometimes."

"Where's his mother?"

"Oh, I been married four times. God damn it, no, I been married five times. I just got divorced this year. What do you want me to tell Hanniford?"

"Tell him you told me the truth about the E-1-FX. I don't care what you tell him. I only care what you tell me. Where's your boy stationed?"

"Oh, he's on the Big E. He's a j. g. Norton Kelly. Look him up if you get out that way. He's one hell of a kid, let me tell you. He'll look at a dame and she'll practically say, 'All right, kid, where do we do it?' Oh, a wild man. You know something? I let him solo when he was fifteen years of age. He had over six hundred hours logged when he joined the Navy, but I told him, I said, 'If they find that out you're gonna be an instructor. Don't even tell them you were up in the Goodyear blimp, for Christ's sake.' At that he almost washed out. They thought anybody flew an airplane the way he did with eight or ten hours, they thought he was crazy."

"Well, I have to get back. But thanks a lot, Kelly."

"Here, let's take this thing and ride back. Okay?"

"Sure."

"You been checked out in one of these?"

"No, you better drive."

The Assistant Secretary of the Navy thereupon rode back to the office on a small yellow tractor, pursued part of the way by a profane man in a white coverall. Alfred began to enjoy his job.

He flew down to North Island late that afternoon and checked in at the Coronado. He pulled rank and took Sandy Duffy to dinner. Sandy was a rather phlegmatic young man who was enough older than Rowland Eaton to make the remark, "Let's see, Rowland would be a senior this year, wouldn't he?" seem insufferably patronizing. It was not a successful evening, but Alfred had kept his promise.

When he got back to Washington his private secretary, Miss Canfield, whom he had brought down from MacHardie & Company, told him that, among other people, Larry Von Elm had been telephoning. "Only telephoning? I thought he'd have a cot set up in the hall. Well, let's let him stew one more night," said Alfred. "Meanwhile, will you get me Mr. Duffy?"

"Creighton," he said, when the connection was made, "I took your son to dinner two nights ago. I was in North Island."

"That was damn nice of you, Alfred. You didn't have to do that."

"But I more or less promised you I'd give him a personal inspection. He looks well. Very anxious to see some action—"

"God, I hate that word."

"Yes, but they're men on their own now. He sent his love to Jean and you, and his grandfather."

"Did you see him fly?"

"No, but I know he can. His commanding officer told me Sandy's one of the best men he has. Thought you'd be pleased to know that. Creighton, would you like to have a drink with me, say about six-thirty at my hotel? Come to my room?"

"Six-thirty will be fine."

Alfred was dictating personal correspondence to Miss Canfield when Duffy appeared at the hotel. "Do you mind if I finish this one letter? Martini?"

"You finish your letter. I'll make the Martinis," said Duffy.

Alfred resumed dictation, but he watched Duffy, who was preparing the drinks while also frankly taking in the details of the apartment. Alfred finished, thanked Miss Canfield, and said goodnight to her.

"There'll never be any scandal about having *her* in your apartment," said Duffy.

"No, when she begins to look good, I've been here too long."

"I see you haven't got the usual picture of F. D. R.," said Duffy.

"No, nor anybody else. Mary and the children, that's all. This may not be the most cheerful apartment, but at least it has nothing to remind me that I'm in Washington. I could just as easily be at the Warwick in Philadelphia." Duffy did not react to the sudden mention of the Warwick, and Alfred was now satisfied that he had not heard of the picture-taking raid.

"The telephone, the bathtub, the donnicker and the bed. That's all I want in a hotel room," said Duffy.

"The donnicker?"

"The crapper. Hotels waste a lot of money trying to make things pretty for me. I like home too much."

"You continually surprise me. I thought you went to '21' and El Morocco every night of your life."

"But not to sleep. The big problem for Jean when we moved to Washington was getting a mattress big enough for the two of us. You've seen our hay in New York and in the country. It was easy enough to have a big bed made, but that mattress we finally got here cost me six hundred dollars. No, it was six-fifty. Well, what's on your mind, Alfred?"

"You remember our conversation about Tom Rothermel?"

"I remember it."

"I am taking your advice. Will you invite me to dinner the next time you have him?"

"Sure, but I don't understand why you have to go to all this trouble. I'm delighted to have a cocktail with you, but you could have asked me that over the phone."

"No, I couldn't. All my incoming and outgoing calls are monitored and I just don't like the idea of having it on the record that my office, not I personally, but my office wanted to arrange to get together with Tom Rothermel. If I happen to see Tom at your house, that's one thing. But I don't think the Assistant Secretary of the Navy should have a meeting originate in his office. It may seem like hair-splitting, and it probably is, but I'll be damned if I'll dignify Tom Rothermel at a cost of dignity to the Navy. He's in no position to grant us favors."

"He isn't?"

Alfred grinned. "God damn you, Creighton, of course he is, and that's what I hate about it."

"Well, then, why don't you face it?"

"Never."

738

"A big word. I think it was one of the Shuberts said about Sam H. Harris. 'We'll never use that son of a bitch again— till we need him.' No, it was Sam Harris and George M. Cohan, talking about some actor. But you get my point."

"Only too well. But I don't subscribe to it. I'm all for using Tom, but one use at a time. I don't want to grant him permanent authority."

"You're too late. He has it. What's more, he'll see through your being at my house when he is. He won't think it's an accident."

"Let him think what he pleases. At least he won't be able to say the Navy sought him out."

"The Navy already has, more than once."

"All right, then, the Assistant Secretary of the Navy hasn't. This particular Assistant Secretary of the Navy," said Alfred. "This would be a fairly logical meeting. You've found out that Tom and I grew up in the same small town, and you thought it would be a nice idea to stage a reunion at your house."

"Oh, sure. It happens all the time, here. This is a funny town. It's a city of strangers, new strangers all the time, whenever there's a congressional election, and especially now, with all the big government agencies, Army and Navy. Every train brings newcomers, and most of them are here to stay, at least for the duration. Even the ousted congressmen don't go home unless they have to. But because it *is* a city of strangers, they all take advantage of even the slightest acquaintance out of the past. Loneliness, partly, and of course the practical reason. Contacts. If you've met Hopkins once, that's a contact, and you can always remind him of it. If you see him a lot, it's a better contact, naturally. But once is enough to be able to tell your boss. Build up your contacts, get to know all these strangers, and a mediocre guy can make a pretty good living here the rest of his life. Washington used to be a place you never went to if you didn't have to. People in your spot avoided it as much as they could. But now it's the place where things are happening, where things originate. I hear '21' is thinking of opening a branch down here. They'd make millions. And Society is flocking here. I know a woman who moved here ostensibly to be near her son. *Her son is at Fort Benning, Georgia,* and when he's shipped out do you think she's going to move back to New York? Her husband stays in New York, her son has never been inside her house, but she had to have some excuse. She'd give the Democratic party a hundred thousand dollars if her husband could have a job like yours."

"Too bad I can't name my successor. Maybe I'd make a deal with her. God knows how long I'm going to last here."

"But you've begun to like it, haven't you?"

"Yes, I have."

"It has a weird effect on you. I've tried cases before the Supreme Court, so I've been coming here for a good many years, but I always got the next train home. Now—well, Jean went out and had a look at a place near Middleburg. I may be here a long time."

"I don't think I'll get rooted here."

"Probably not. You have a big job waiting for you in New York."

"Is that what they call here a fishing expedition, Creighton?"

"My wife and her father are still on speaking terms, don't forget that."

"There are others who have earned that job and are more entitled to it."

"True, but I never hear their names mentioned. No rumors about them. Plenty of rumors about you, and you're the man I'm going to cultivate. It's become almost a point of honor with me to get MacHardie & Company for Mortimer & Miller. I realize it'll never happen while the old man's alive, but we were the lawyers for Ziegler Oil and we didn't do such a bad job there. The old man knows we're good, or he wouldn't have kept us on for Ziegler Oil. It's just that he won't let us handle MacHardie & Company because I married his daughter."

"Naturally you don't expect me to make any comment on that, or any aspect of it."

"No, but when I said a couple of weeks ago that this war isn't going to last forever, and what I told you about industry and labor planning ahead—I'm planning ahead, too."

"You just said, or practically said, you were going to stay in Washington after the war."

"The telephone and the airplane are marvelous inventions. Very quick. And even if I decide to open an office here, it'd be as a partner in Mortimer & Miller. Have you ever thought of the legal entanglements that'll come up as soon as the war's over?"

"Not once."

"You ought to. You owe it to yourself, you owe it to your firm, and you owe it to your country."

"To my country? Well, now let's hear what you have to say on that, and I'm sure it's plenty."

Duffy's little eyes almost disappeared, and he was controlling his anger. "It's plenty, but it won't take long. You have a nickname. I suppose you know that."

"Speedy. Yes, I've heard it."

"So, if you have your wish, this war will end soon, and fast. Then what? Twelve million men and women dumped back into civilian life, industry back on a peacetime basis. And so forth. Are you, in your important position, going to be ready for the reconversion, or how long is it going to take you? The economy is just another John Stuart Mill word for bread-and-butter. Big business, which you're a part of, must be ready to make the reconversion as quick and as painless as possible, or there'll be hell to pay. It'll suit the Tom Rothermels just fine if there's hell to pay. You give me the impression that you're looking down your nose at me because I'm thinking so much about post-war conditions. The truth is I'm a damned sight better American for that than I would be if I only thought of the present and the immediate future."

"I hope we can disagree without your thinking I'm looking down my nose at you. It may be a good thing to have some post-war plans. Probably is. Oh, not probably. It is. But may I ask you this? Before we were actually in the war, when we were theoretically at peace, were you doing as much belligerent thinking, planning for the war, as you are doing peacetime planning now?"

"Everybody knew we were going to get in it."

"Everybody knew nothing of the kind. There were a great many people, not only the German-American Bund people, who resisted every move that pushed us closer to actual fighting."

"I wasn't one of them."

"Are you sure?"

"What are you trying to say? That I was an America Firster?"

"Well, were you?"

"No, I helped to write the over-age destroyer deal."

"That was two years ago. Things had begun to happen then. But where did you stand before that?"

"Oh, no. You're not going to make an America Firster out of me."

"I'm not trying to. I'm only trying to show you that I think you're somewhat premature in your post-war planning. That goes for you, for big business, for labor, and for the guy with the filling-station in Shreveport, Louisiana. I think the government agencies should be working around the clock and not knocking off for these Martinis. I saw a Marine lieutenant at North Island who two years ago was teaching school in Montana. Today he has one eye and one arm. A schoolteacher, mind you, but I'd like Tom Rothermel to hear *him* on the rights of labor and post-war planning."

"Maybe as a favor to you I'd better not have you and Tom Rothermel at the same time."

"Oh, I'm not going to blow my top with Tom. He'd be totally unimpressed by any arguments of mine. Or, for that matter, of the Marine lieutenant's. I figure that I'm just that much smarter than Tom that I can use him. Also, I have a certain advantage over Tom. He wouldn't have got through college if it hadn't been for my grandfather."

"That only makes him hate you the more."

"Of course it does. I know that. But as between Tom and me, not the labor movement and me, but Tom and me, Tom knows that it was my grandfather, and no matter how much he hates me for it, down deep he knows himself to be an ungrateful little prick."

"Tom doesn't believe in gratitude."

"Ah, there you're wrong. He doesn't practice it, and he's contemptuous of it, but I knew Tom for the first twenty years of his life. Karl Marx and some professor at Penn State don't change all that. You doubt me. Well, Tom was always a hustler for money when he was a kid. He earned every penny of it and he worked his ass off earning it, but he was a bright, cheerful kid. Do you know what Tom enjoys most nowadays?"

"Stenographers."

"Oh, sure, but aside from tail and booze he likes to make money. It's a game with him, playing the market, but it's still his fun. That's a carry-over from those dimes and quarters he made when he was a kid. He couldn't have done it then if it hadn't been fun. He worked much harder than was necessary. My point is, he hasn't lost that, and he hasn't lost the habit of saying thank-you. He was always polite, right through to about his junior year in college. Then he stopped acting polite, but it's still with him. It's still with him. He can be snotty with anybody in the world but me. I knew him when he had nice manners."

"I guess I see what you mean, but pardon me if I don't think it's going to work. Not to your advantage. It may work to your disadvantage. Tom hasn't got time for such subtleties."

"When you were in college did you ever lose a fist-fight?"

"Yes," said Duffy. "Two."

"Did you fight them again and win?"

"One of them. I never fought the other guy again."

"Did you win the second fight?"

"No. He licked me again."

"Do you hate that guy?"

"No, as a matter of fact he's a friend of mine."

"That's the situation between Tom and me. No fist-fight, but I had some superiority then, and I still have it. And I wouldn't be surprised if Tom *didn't* hate me."

"You're much too subtle for me. And I have to warn you, you're all wrong about Tom. He's told me about his boyhood days, and *he* doesn't think he had any fun. The picture of Tom, the happy errand boy, may have been right at the time, but the way he paints it now it was child labor at its worst. And as far as playing the market, that's the revolutionary out-smarting the cap-*pittle*-ist. Every dollar he ever made out of the market increased his contempt for the Wall Street blood-suckers."

Alfred nodded slowly. "I suppose so. Your arrangement is much simpler than mine, and probably closer to the truth. But I'm going to give my theory one try, in front of you."

"All right. I'll set it up for you in the next week or so." He rose to leave.

"Thanks for coming. I enjoy talking to you."

"Eye-to-eye, though, Alfred. Not down the patrician schnozzola."

"Patrician? Me? *My* father never looked down his nose at James D. MacHardie."

"Touché," said Duffy, and closed the door behind him.

"I think I can handle you, too," said Alfred, and went to the telephone to place a call to Natalie. There was not much they could say. She told him all that she had been doing, and he told her nothing of what he had been doing or where he had been. The time would come when he would be going overseas, and it was better to form the habit of withholding all information as to his comings and goings. (The old familiar name Raymond would come in handy now.) She promised to come to Washington on the following Saturday afternoon. "Telephone me from the station. If I'm not here, telephone me when you get here, on the house phone. But I'll send you a key tonight, special delivery, so you won't have to hang around downstairs."

In the morning he took a call from Larry Von Elm and agreed to an appointment for that afternoon. At precisely the appointed hour Miss Canfield announced Von Elm, and it was plain to see that Von Elm was agitated, but Alfred was only polite and serene.

"You've given me a bad four days," said Von Elm.

"Have I? How?"

"And not only me. The fellows at Sierra. They don't know where they stand, either."

"Well, now, we'll see if we can show them where they stand," said Alfred. "And you. You know they tried to pull a fast one."

"They're sorry about that. They admit it."

"Oh, they have to admit it. They're not making any big concession by admitting it. If this were private business, and peacetime, I'll tell you where they'd stand. Up to their ears in quicksand, and nobody hearing their cries for help. That's where they'd be anyway if it was up to me. I'm just sore enough at the whole outfit to let them sink. I went out there on official Navy business and they gave me an office and a stenographer, and I was also given strong hints that if I wanted to have my back rubbed by a movie starlet, they could arrange that easily. I suppose that's the way they've always done business and they don't know any other way."

"I'm not apologizing for them. I gave them hell. But they didn't know you."

"That's one of the things that make me sore. They take for granted that I'm like them. But then that business about hiding their test pilot. I'll tell you this much, Larry. That's already in my preliminary report and has been seen by those who ought to know about it. Now aside from some frightened apologies, what have you got to say?"

"Well, first of all, I don't want you to hold it against Bill Hanniford. In fairness to him, he doesn't operate that way."

"He doesn't, but he did."

"The money men. He was acting under their instructions. I know Bill very well, and I assure you, he's more direct than that. When you told him to get the test pilot, he did, and then he called up the others and resigned. You don't know what that means to Bill Hanniford. He's been around airplanes all his life and this is the first time he's ever made any real money, but he resigned."

"He doesn't get an Air Medal for that. Did they accept it?"

"No, but he told them that if they lost out on the contract for trying to pull a fast one on you, he didn't give a damn whether they accepted it or not. He just wasn't going to be there."

"I'm unmoved by Hanniford's sudden piety. He knew he was hired as a front man."

"That's what he was hired for, but he's been more than that. He followed the E-1-FX every step of the way including—and this isn't in his contract—flying it. That's a pretty hot airplane for a man his age to take up, but he did. I don't suppose Kelly told you that?"

"No, he didn't."

"Well, maybe he didn't know it, or maybe he just neglected to tell you. But Bill was determined to do all he could to build a good airplane, and he was there day and night, and you'd never find this out from him. So whatever comes of all this, I don't want you to hold it against Bill."

"It seems to me you're in no position to say you don't want this and you don't want that."

Von Elm looked at him in silence. "Listen, Alfred, a man can only take just so much punishment and then he either fights back or runs away. I've taken about enough from you."

"So long," said Alfred, and picked up some papers out of the plywood tray, and put on his reading glasses.

"Oh, now wait a minute, Alfred."

744

"If you're going to run, run. If you're going to fight, go fight some place else. I'm busy."

"All right, you win."

"What do I win?"

"Whatever you want."

Alfred removed his glasses and laid them on the desk. "Get it through your head, first of all, that when I took this job I made up my mind that I was doing it for one purpose only. To do everything and anything I could to help win this war quickly and decisively. Anything that deflects me from that purpose has to go, or I go. A clear example of what I mean was hiding that test pilot. When I was in North Island I made up my mind that if Sierra ever got another nickel from the Navy, the Navy would have my resignation. That is how I felt about that bunch. I know their situation. If they don't get the contract they'll be out of business in about two weeks. As far as I'm concerned, they deserve to be. I wasn't there as a guy named Eaton. I was there for the Navy, an accredited representative of the Navy, with rank that I happen to respect because the most I ever made before was lieutenant. I frankly don't give a damn how much punishment you can or can't endure. At the moment I'm only interested in the fighter program. I'm particularly not interested in *your* health and welfare because I hadn't even taken this job before you told the press that you and I had been in business together. In the first place, that was not true. You were a salaried employe. In the second place, you deliberately created a false impression with the press. In the third place, I insisted on giving the Navy all the records of the Nassau Aeronautical Corporation, which I had kept in storage for twenty years, thank God. What's more, I insisted they be examined before I was sworn in."

"I talked to one reporter and happened to mention that I'd known you years ago. That's all there was to that."

"Not quite all, but never mind. The point is that you at your end and the Sierra boys at their end seem to like fast ones. I don't. As a result of my experience with you, everything you and they do from now on is going to be scrutinized so carefully that you're not going to be able to get away with anything. I can tell you now that Sierra is getting the contract for the E-2-FX, but the only way you'll be able to get away with any fast ones will be to do something so crooked that you'll be liable to criminal prosecution."

"Do the Sierra people know they've got the contract?"

"Yes, Larry. They know. You are not going to have the privilege of telling them, and possibly implying that you swung it. I told them before you came in here. I also gave them a few plain truths, such as I've been giving you. I talked to Hanniford, and I gave it to him very straight. I anticipate no further trouble there. I quite agree with you about Hanniford, but I wanted to hear all you had to say about him. My impression is that the next time those money men ask him to pull a fast one, he may take a shot at them. He knew God damn well that his lifelong reputation was on the table. That's all for today, Larry."

"Thanks," said Von Elm, and left.

But it was not quite all for the day. At six-thirty Alfred went to the Mayflower to meet Harrison Potts, the Republican senator from Pennsylvania, who was taking him to a small senatorial gathering in a mezzanine suite. Potts was late, and Alfred went to the newsstand and bought a Washington paper and leaned against a pillar near the registration desk. As luck, good or bad, would have it, he saw Larry Von Elm, holding a woman's arm and propelling her to the elevator. When they reached the elevators Alfred got a better look at her. It was Clemmie Shreve Hennessey Porter. "Oh, no," said Alfred, and his pain was real.

It was a new social experience to watch Tom Rothermel with Jean MacHardie Duffy. There was not much novelty to be expected of Jean Duffy; she had abandoned all hope of winning her private war against fat and she no longer deprived herself of the pleasures of the table and the bar. Creighton Duffy had never objected to her eating and drinking but only to her disposition during the few periods of dieting and abstinence that she had imposed upon herself, and it had pleased her that he had at such times missed her as his eating and drinking companion. In normal times they would go to the good restaurants and order completely different meals, and she would scoop up a sauce and present it to him, saying, "Taste this, darling. This is really tops," or he would slice off a morsel of nearly-raw venison and feed it to her for her appreciation. His favorite sommeliers fell into two groups: the young men, who made no suggestions whatever because they respected his abundant knowledge of wines, and the older men, who liked to discuss wines with him because he respected their superior knowledge. About wines he was a show-off but not a snob, and if he was in a mood for a domestic draught beer he had that and not a wine or an imported German *brau*. There was real love in his wife's acceptance of his choices of food and drink for her, and he would often call a restaurant at three o'clock in the afternoon to order their dinners for the evening. It was only natural that at home (although never in public) she would sometimes top off a satisfactory meal with a good cigar, which she had learned to hold without awkward daintiness or irritating affectation. One of the pleasant things about being the daughter of James D. MacHardie was that she could

746

light her cigar without apology or explanation. In public, however, and as Duffy had pointed out to her, not everyone in the restaurant would know that she was MacHardie's daughter, and the cigar would only annoy strangers unnecessarily.

And it was not in her make-up to annoy people. She laughed a lot and smiled more. She was a jovial woman, and the quality had been brought out by Duffy in their perfect marriage. The MacHardie money had got her nothing but duty dances as a debutante, but Creighton Duffy wooed her with second helpings of ice cream and cake, and she had won him by devouring them. She became a Catholic (as she would have become a Mohammedan) because he asked her to, and the loneliness of her first eighteen years vanished and the memory of it followed soon. They had each other, and it became increasingly unimportant that no one else wanted either one of them. Then after Duffy had begun to be a success they became something of an institution and their joint independence of others was forgiven. They became popular, without having to resort to guile, to strenuous sports, to intellectual pose, or to reducing exercises. Jean could sight-read sheet music, which she played confidently and well, with a ragtime swing, but it was her only accomplishment. She had few ideas that could not be immediately traced to Duffy, and when he changed his, she changed hers. She would hate a man or woman on no more than Duffy's say-so, and he was wise enough not to tamper with the pity and affection and dutiful love she felt for her father. The slaps and ticklings that stimulated them in their love-making had never gone past the danger point, and when love-making had exhausted them they slept like enormous, untroubled infants until time for their next feeding.

Tom Rothermel's violent hatred of the rich had been directed at many men and women who had far less money than Jean Duffy, but this well-conditioned hatred of the rich did not respond to the single stimulus of Jean's money. In all respects she was too likable: there was her friendliness, which was available to everyone; her appearance, which belonged with her friendliness and separated her from the thin, cruel aristocrats; her appetite for food and drink, which put him in mind of Rothermel cousins who made eating an athletic contest; and even her piano-playing and singing, which obviously were simple pleasures for her but were also appealing in a quite literal sense of wanting to be liked. Instead of the thin, cruel aristocrat who would delight in starving the tenantry, she had turned out to be this cheerful, ordinary fat woman, much more like real people than the Johnsons, the Van Peltzes and the Eatons he had grown up with. As he grew to know Jean MacHardie Duffy a little better he also began in retrospect to see the Johnsons and Van Peltzes and Eatons as spurious aristocrats having not nearly the wealth that Jean had, but putting on the airs of the gentry with their coachmen and their condescension as they did their shopping in Lower Montgomery Street. Such reconsiderations of the important people he had known as a boy made his retroactive judgment of them even more severe than it had begun to be in the second half of his life, and money, in Jean's special case, was not to be held against her. She had, moreover, married Duffy, who not only was "a sort of a" New Dealer, but was also an Irish Catholic. The term was, for Tom Rothermel, pleonastic: if you said Irish, you automatically meant Catholic; if you said Catholic, you could also have said Irish. Tom had no use for them, whatever they were called. But he accepted them for what they were not: they were *not* Van Peltzes or Eatons. All Irish, and therefore all Catholics, properly belonged in the servant class and were therefore, in the view Tom held in the years after Penn State, members of the proletariat. The Catholics had a grievance, all Catholics had a grievance, and Duffy was a Catholic and therefore logically a New Dealer, along with the labor leaders who belonged to Duffy's church. The grievance was that they were not Johnsons, Eatons, or Van Peltzes, and Jean MacHardie Duffy had cast her lot with the potentially proletarians by marrying Duffy and joining his church. On more familiar ground, in the labor movement, Tom Rothermel distrusted the Catholics among the leaders, partly because of his native distrust of Catholics and partly because in his own faction the Catholics were regarded as conservatives and secretly anti-communist. Tom had been admittedly opposed to the Ku Klux Klan, but he had been tolerant of his many Rothermel cousins in the organization who had been active in anti-Catholic fraternal orders before the Klan made its Pennsylvania appearance in the nineteen-twenties. Since local Klan activity had been directed largely against Catholics and was chiefly political, Tom's opposition to it was vehement where it concerned lynching of distant Negroes, but there was no serious Negro problem in Pennsylvania (with the exception of the southeast) and in the towns where Tom worked, the Jews were so overwhelmingly outnumbered that they were not a considerable factor in the economic or political life. Tom's opposition to the Klan was therefore not likely to involve any local situation, and his anti-Catholicism had existed long before the Klan suddenly spread from the Democratic South to the Republican North. He considered Creighton Duffy's Catholicism as having been atoned for by his associating himself with the New Deal, as he considered Jean Duffy's wealth atoned for by her marrying Duffy. In the crisis that he was doing everything he could to hasten, Tom would have liquidated both Duffys, but for the present they were providing him with his first intimate study of the living habits of the very rich, and they were doing it without his having to apologize to his revolutionary principles.

Until he began to be invited by the Duffys he never had been in a private house where men functioned as servants, and the Duffys' Bruce Barrett was unreal to him. "You don't have to call me sir," he said to Barrett on an early visit.

"It's customary, sir. Habit, you might say," said Barrett.

"Oh, then it doesn't mean anything?"

"Oh, I didn't say quite that, sir. In the Army, where I was for twelve years, a man said 'sir' to all officers alike, but there was a rather nice thing about it. The same 'sir' to a well-liked colonel as to a major one might feel different to."

"Well, I'll win you over," said Tom.

"Very good, sir. Will there be anything else, sir?"

Tom soon saw that the imperturbable Barrett said 'sir' to him as often as he said it to any other guest of the Duffys, whether it was a general or one of the society men who came to the Duffy parties, but then he next realized that some of the society men would exchange a few words with Barrett and during the exchanges Barrett would momentarily lose the look of impersonal respect that he habitually affected.

"Bruce, I saw your old sidekick Arthur Bundy a couple of weeks ago."

"Oh, you did, sir? Was this in Philadelphia, sir?" Barrett's face was relaxed and smiling.

"No, he's back in New York. He's tending bar at the St. Regis."

"At the St. Regis. Well, I daresay Mr. Astor can afford it, if you know what I mean, sir."

"I know exactly what you mean. I couldn't afford him, good as he was."

"Good as he was, no sir. I helped Arthur many's the time, but he had the fatal weakness. Surprising he's working so near liquor."

"Shortage of bartenders, I guess."

"No doubt, sir. No doubt. Well, thank you, sir. And a pleasant evening to you, sir."

Barrett then turned to Tom and the impersonal respect was back on his face, colder than any snub Tom had ever received from one of the society men, but with nothing in word or expression that could be complained of. Then when he realized that Bruce Barrett would often carry on a relaxed conversation with Creighton Duffy, his employer, Tom was confused. It would be a quick exchange, sometimes unintelligible to Tom, but for a brief moment Duffy and Barrett would be two men working together on a problem and Barrett would be respect-

749

ing what Duffy was saying and Duffy respectfully depending on Barrett to carry out instructions capably. These conversations confused Tom until he came to understand their larger implications: that Duffy as an employer had earned Barrett's respect in matters on which Barrett was an authority. They were men together, just as Barrett and the men of the Arthur Bundy conversation had been men together, with one having more money and other saying "sir," and the two keeping a precise distance that was no measure of one's respect for the other. The man with the money and the man saying "sir" understood each other, liked each other, and observed rules that kept the relationship successful. Tom Rothermel knew then that he never could have such a relationship with a Bruce Barrett, and with that discovery he had another look at Creighton Duffy and saw him for an enemy.

But the world was peopled with enemies of Tom Rothermel, and Creighton Duffy was particularly well qualified for reclassification. It had been much more difficult to accept Duffy than it now became to hate him, a rich Irish-Catholic lawyer whom Tom immediately began to suspect as a saboteur of the New Deal. Tom told himself that the confusion was not new; the confusion had been there all the time, while he tried to overlook Duffy's palpable bad points in an effort to fit him into the New Deal organization. As soon as he discovered that Duffy was at his ease with a servant and therefore, in Tom's view, a member of the ruling class, his only regret was that he had deceived himself, and since no one else had known of this self-deception, he let himself off easy, grateful that he had found out in time that Duffy was a potential saboteur of the New Deal and a crafty, treacherous operator. His less than harsh judgment of himself was also commingled with relief for his narrow escape, for while Tom Rothermel was expediently not a Communist party member, he was subject to the party discipline and punishment, and the mortal sin of misleading others like himself was absolved only in rare instances. The tactic of the time was the classic one: the party turned informer on members and sympathizers whose bad judgment had been costly. And while Tom, who was not a fool, did not delude himself about the harmlessness of his F.B.I. dossier, he was positive that the government files would have been enriched by information from party sources. And he was far from ready to lose standing with the party or to be discredited at the union. Tom was a very ambitious man, and his ambitions could not afford a break with the party while the Soviet Union was an ally of the country. Later, when this war interval was concluded, would come the opportunity to proceed with his plan for a western revolution that would function on at

750

least equal terms with the eastern, then to overtake and pass the men of the Kremlin. As a native American, fifth or sixth generation, and a college graduate who had spent years in corporation business, Tom was secretly contemptuous of the whimsically murderous Stalin and his button-nosed sycophants. He did not object to assassination or execution or any other capital punishment on humanitarian grounds, since he recognized the need for killing men in certain cases. But an assassination signified a transaction that had failed, and to Tom's way of thinking it was wasteful to kill off all the electrical engineers because a power plant had not met the demands of politicians. It was all right to reduce them in rank, it was all right to punish them, but a brain that had been stopped by a bullet was stopped forever. He could not believe that a hundred Russian engineers would band together to sabotage a power plant; he believed too firmly in the industrial spy system to accept that possibility. They would not get very far in the United States, and in the Soviet Union they would be detected overnight. Therefore, why the wholesale killings? The only excuse for them he could think of was that the man responsible for their efficiency was passing the blame on to them, and if he made his purge bloody enough he might appear to have discovered a gigantic plot against the People and in so doing have earned himself the Hero's medal. Tom was reconciled to the Asiatics' low appraisal of human life, but he was extremely disappointed in their wastage of brains.

Tom knew that his own brains would be spattered against a wall if he gave utterance to such thoughts in Russia, and he was careful not to speak out in Washington, where his life was not in immediate danger, but where his future depended on his handling of the present. It is worth noting that in the Washington of the time Tom was as careful of what he said at a Duffy dinner party as he was at the study meetings he attended in apartments in the opposite compass-point section of the capital.

In deference to the war effort the Duffy dinners were briefer than they had been in peacetime, and the black market filet mignon was preceded by only one course and followed by one other, after which the gentlemen went to the library for their choice of cognac, Asbach, kirsch, Benedictine, Cointreau, Drambuie, Fundador, crème de menthe, and coffee with sugar or, for those who had formed the new habit, saccharin. On the night of his prearranged meeting with Tom, Alfred was seated on Jean's right, but throughout the meal Tom, who was three persons to Jean's left, used Alfred's presence to speak quite entertainingly of his Horatio Algerian boyhood. He would mention the name of a Port Johnson merchant and say,

"You remember him, Alfred," thus in effect forcing Alfred to corroborate a story that he had not yet told and that Alfred did not always believe when it was told. He would tell how much money he had been paid, and anticipate any slight defense of the merchants by saying, with elaborate sarcasm, "Of course fifteen cents was a lot of money in those days. I considered myself highly paid." At one point he annoyed Alfred by describing him as a boy in a velvet suit and silver buckles on his shoes, but Alfred held his temper. "Those were my work clothes," said Alfred. "I usually wore satin breeches and gold buckles." It was Tom's turn to be annoyed because he had inadvertently put his audience, composed of men who had had to wear velvet suits, on Alfred's side, when his purpose had been to ridicule him. Tom was also completely unfair about the Eaton mill until Alfred inserted a question: "And do you remember those machine guns?"

"What machine guns? Heavens!" said Jean Duffy.

"Oh, on payday, my father used to wait till the men got their money, then he'd let fly the machine guns and mow them down. Didn't he, Tom?"

"If he didn't it was because he didn't think of it," said Tom.

"Was your father really like that, Alfred? He sounds like Mr. Frick," said Jean.

"Sure. He'd mow them down and take their money away. How else could we afford gold buckles for my pumps?" Alfred allowed himself to be baited by Tom, put up a superficially good-humored defense, and was careful to let Tom dominate the conversation. He knew he would get nowhere with Tom if he offered no resistance, but he controlled his resistance so that Tom had no reason to lose face. To Alfred the fascinating thing was Tom's concentration on Jean and his ignoring of the others, including his host. Alfred had expected to see Creighton Duffy included as an ally, and he was mystified by Tom's playing solely to Jean. There were three other women at dinner, two wives of men present and one young woman whose absent husband was in State, and all three were more attractive than otherwise, but Tom made no effort in their direction. It was obvious that there was no romantic activity involving Tom and Jean, but it was equally obvious that Tom wanted to please her and there was more to it than a wish to remain on the Duffys' dinner lists.

After dinner, in the library, Tom was a disappointment. He contributed nothing to the conversation and almost belligerently withdrew from it, as though to declare himself in opposition to the others. He stood with his back turned, taking down and replacing the owner's hand-tooled volumes, and participated with the others only in their return to the sittingroom, where he immediately seated himself beside Jean and spoke to no one but her until one of the men announced that it was ten-thirty and that he had to go home. The others left, Tom among them, and Alfred stayed.

"You didn't get very far with Rothermel. I'm sorry," said Duffy.

"Neither did you. Only Jean," said Alfred.

"Oh, I always have fun with him," said Jean. "But why was he so strange with you, dear? Have you had a spat?"

"Not that I know of. He's been that way the last few times he's been here. He's probably moody. Or else I can't do anything for him at the moment. But he sure wasn't buttering you up, Alfred."

"No, he wasn't, was he?"

"You two underestimate him. He saw through your plan. He said to me after dinner, he liked you when you were boys together in Pennsylvania, but you'd never had anything in common since then. He said you were practically a stranger to him now."

"Well, that ought to cement my relations with the N. A. M."

"National Association of Manufacturers," said Duffy. "I didn't want Jean to think you were mixed up with what her father calls the New Deal alphabet soup."

"By the way, Alfred, have you heard anything from anybody at MacHardie & Company?"

"Not lately."

"Well, it isn't serious, but Father had a slight chill the day before yesterday and he's been taken to Harkness. Just as a precautionary measure. I spoke to Mr. Hasbrouck early this evening."

"Hasbrouck? Is he is charge?"

"I guess so. Is he, Creighton?"

"Apparently, yes."

"That's interesting. I'm sorry I didn't know about your father, Jean. I'll have Mary send him some flowers."

"No, don't, Alfred," said Duffy. "I spoke to Percy, too, and Mr. MacHardie isn't at Harkness under his real name."

"Oh, you spoke to Percy, too?"

"Yes."

"I didn't know you and Percy were such buddies."

"Hardly buddies, but better friends than we used to be."

"Well, that's interesting, too," said Alfred.

"He'll be down here next Tuesday, if you'd like to see him."

"I'll be out of town Tuesday."

On his way home Alfred pondered the possibly accidental news about the friendship between Duffy and Hasbrouck. Duffy was certainly ready to have it known to Alfred, but whether Hasbrouck was ready was another matter. There were various reasons why Hasbrouck had taken over during the old man's illness, but the one Alfred least liked was the one he guessed was the true one: Hasbrouck had got more capital and was preparing to use it to strengthen his position in the firm. New York and MacHardie & Company had seemed very far away in recent weeks, but they were in his thoughts that night as he went to his rooms at the hotel. And after he had turned out the light he had an unaccountable spasm of loneliness that was as severe as any he had felt since his early days at Princeton. He reached out to telephone Natalie, but remembered that she was working at Travelers Aid. He wondered if Roosevelt ever felt this way.

Everything was fogged in from Cape May to Nova Scotia. Alfred's train was more than two hours late arriving at Penn Station and three hours late leaving New Haven. At New London he could barely make out the outlines of a submarine in the Thames and at Providence he could not see the Biltmore Hotel. A Navy car met him at Back Bay and took almost a half hour to transport him to the Somerset Club. He gave his name to the club servant, who took his bag and handed him the guest card made out to Mr. A. Eaton at the request of Mr. John Warren. He went up the stairs and back to his room, which looked down on the courtyard which he vaguely recalled as an area known to members as "the Bricks."

"Will you get me Trowbridge 6-0626, please?" he said into the telephone, and waited. "May I speak to Mr. Warren, please? Mr. Warren? Alfred Eaton."

"Oh, yes. Don't imagine you flew today."

"No, and my train was over three hours late."

"Bird-walking weather, eh? Well, I'll be right over."

In the next half hour Alfred, alone in this quiet club, and then in the company of Jack Warren, was as far removed from his job and the privileges of rank as he had been since taking the oath. If the aging Irish servants knew he was Assistant Secretary of the Navy, they did not show it. He was Mr. Eaton, guest of Mr. Warren and having guest status but *not* member status. It was a contrast to the saluting by the marines and the "Mr. Secretary" by the civilians in the Navy Building, and it was a relief.

Alfred was at the cigar counter when Warren entered the club, wearing an old British warm and a hat with a narrow, turned-up brim. A servant came out of the cloakroom and took Warren's coat and hat and Warren, with a look of concern, said: "Good evening, my dear boy. You've had your dinner?"

"On the train. It's nice to see you, Mr. Warren."

"Thank you. Shall we go in here? You've been in this den of iniquity before, haven't you?"

"Yes. Several times. You got me my first guest card here."

"Oh, yes, a long time ago. I wasn't sure. Well, we seem to have the place to ourselves. I usually sit over there near the window. Stand, to be truthful. I stand there and look down Beacon Street and watch the progress of my friends, huffing and puffing their way up the hill. Always give them a minute or two to get their breath after they get here. It's truly remarkable what habit will do. I know damn well that they can get to Number 42, but if they had to go one house beyond, they'd never make it. Extra exertion would tell on them, and we'd lose some of our most valuable members. And I'm only half joking, Alfred. Well, I hope you noticed—in your honor?" He tapped his necktie, the red and blue of the Racquet & Tennis Club.

"I did, immediately."

"I had it on my mind to resign after old Fritz Thornton died. He got me in there, as he did several other New York clubs that he was interested in and that I wasn't interested in one bit. But I said to myself, what the devil, I might as well stay in for the few years that are left me. Some of those New York codgers won't have any other way of knowing I've cashed in my chips if they don't see it on the bulletin board. I thought I'd bring my obituary up to date one day last summer, and I discovered I hadn't done a damn thing worth mentioning in the past ten years. Isn't that awful? Are you in *Who's Who*, Alfred? I'm sure you are."

"Yes."

"Well, now you've got something worthwhile for the next issue. Your new job, and a son in the Navy. Are you going to see him while you're here?"

"I just missed him. He's in Florida. And I don't think I'd have seen him even if he'd still been at Squantum. It would have embarrassed him. It would have embarrassed me, too, I suppose."

"Then I won't get to see the young man who's marrying my cousin?

"No, sir, I'm afraid not."

"But you still want to see my young cousin?"

"Oh, I do indeed."

"Then you still want to have lunch tomorrow?"

"Yes. I don't know when I'll be up this way again. I'm here on Navy business, of course. While I'm here I'll put in an appearance at Dartmouth, the Navy Yard, and Squantum, and on the way back, at Quonset. Other places, too, but that'll give you an idea. However, I wanted to see you and have dinner with you, and I could have if it hadn't been for that damned fog."

"It was very nice of you to think of me. I don't see why you shouldn't give some thought to becoming a member here. I have quite a credit accumulating in this place. The last time I put a man up was twenty years ago, so think it over, and if you're interested, we'll get the wheels in motion."

"That's very nice of you, but I wouldn't like to be put up here while I have this Navy title. In Washington it's different, but elsewhere there might be the thought that I was using the Navy for selfish purposes."

"I assure you, Alfred, that your Navy title wouldn't carry any weight here, so don't let that bother you. And you might want to have this for after the war. The war isn't going to last forever."

"So people keep telling me."

"Well, you're in a position to know, but they don't last forever, do they?"

"No, but this looks like a long one. Speaking unofficially, of course."

"Yes. I hear very good things about that boy of yours, to change the subject slightly, but not altogether. Had you thought of having him go in with you after the war?"

"I'd like him to finish Harvard and then go to the Law School, if he could get in."

"Oh, well now that's the sort of thing I wanted to hear. Although I notice you haven't said yes or no to my question. But if he came back and finished at Harvard and then took the degree in law, he'd have a rather wide acquaintance in Boston, and I know that it's a matter of some concern, the next generation. Question of new blood, and if your boy and Sadie tie the knot, he'd have a future here. Of course I didn't go to Groton. Was there a Groton then? I don't think so. No, of course not. After you've reached eighty the memory lets you down sometimes. I was saying?"

"New blood in Boston, and my son's marriage." Alfred noticed what he had not noticed before: that Warren's white shirt was fresh from the drawer. It was more than possible that the old man had been in bed, retired for the night, and Alfred was touched. It was going on eleven o'clock, but Jack Warren had got out of bed, dressed, and come here to talk, and would not think of mentioning what he had done.

"Yes. Well, now you see our trouble here is that we haven't been producing enough sons, or I should say, grandsons. And if our young men insist on going away, then we have to bring in new blood. When did your family leave Boston?"

"They never lived here."

756

"But the name is familiar to me. Didn't we speak of this before?"

"Very likely. I think my great-grandfather came from up this way."

"Yes. Well then you see your son would be bringing back some of the good *old* blood as well as the new."

"Well, it's quite possible. I never knew my Grandfather Eaton, but I know the name is fairly common in New England, and I've always had the impression we had our roots here."

"I know a very reliable man who looks into such matters, if you'd like to have his name. I'll send it to you. I'll think of his name in the morning. Now if you don't mind, Alfred, I'm *not* going to have lunch with you tomorrow. It would be much easier for you and for my young cousin if it were just the two of you. I honestly don't really know her very well. I knew her father, and her mother is more closely related to me than her father. But you have things to talk about that don't concern me and I'd feel like an intruder. So I'm going to beg off tomorrow. Are you comfortable here?"

"Very. I'm in Room 27, complete with bathrobe and bedroom slippers."

"Hope the bathrobe fits. There've been some complaints from fellows your height. Then I think I'll have them call me a taxicab."

Alfred had a cab sent for and waited with the old man until it arrived. Jack Warren was frail and exquisitely neat and very tired, and when he left the club Alfred thought sadly of the ending of a life that had been lived with such attention to the enjoyment of living, now restricted to a flat around the corner that probably contained the souvenirs that were never looked at, and to a club from which Warren could observe the signs of the end in the fatigue of his friends. Alfred slowly mounted the stairs and for the second time in a week he was attacked by loneliness. He wrote a four-page love letter to Natalie and destroyed it because he was afraid it would depress her needlessly, but it had a cathartic effect on his loneliness and he went to sleep in good season. After all, love letters were an art form, and he had some vague recollection that Aristotle and Dorothy Parker believed in art as a form of catharsis. He dreamed of Sadie Warren whose face was Natalie's.

Her face was not Natalie's. Her eyes were dark, like Natalie's (and like Mary's and Victoria Dockwiler's), but they were to see with and to think through; intelligent eyes rather than the eyes of an ensemble of beauty. She was shorter than he had expected her to be, and her lips moved quickly and constantly over her strong, large, white teeth. She spoke with

757

natural precision and animation and assurance, and he guessed that she would sail boats against men on equal terms and that she played good tennis. He was already sure about the tennis; that much had been told him. She was a healthy girl, but it was not until she removed her raincoat and draped it over the back of her chair that he was ready to give his son good marks for picking women. She was wearing two matching sweaters and as she threw back her shoulders to unburden herself of the mackintosh Alfred had a quick look at the outlines of her breasts. He was agreeably startled and had to remind himself that he was there as the father of his son only. Even the nipples showed under the cashmere, revealing the nervous excitement she was trying to cover with animated chatter. He knew that in her quick look at him she found him attractive for his age and he knew also that he could be in love with her for at least one afternoon, but not much more.

"So you're Sadie."

"I'm Sadie."

"Well, I liked what I knew before, and now I like what I see." He steadfastly kept his gaze above her chin.

"Thank you. I do, too, if that isn't fresh."

"Not a bit fresh. Wait till Rowland's my age and you'll see how pleased he'll be to get compliments from attractive young women."

"And the heck of it is, he will, too. Get compliments. He's going to be like you. Age well."

"Thank you. What's the latest scuttlebutt?"

"Well, I had a letter from him this morning. He'll get his wings in about seven more weeks, I think, if all goes well, and then I guess he'll have some leave, although we don't know how much. If it's very little, I'll go to Florida. My family will raise the dickens about that, you may be sure, but he'll be allowed to get married then and I don't intend to come back from Florida a young old maid."

"Do you think he's weakening in his high resolve?"

"Yes, I sort of do. Little things in his letters. I know that he misses me much more, and he speaks, uh, enviously of a trainee he knows who *is* married. Secretly, of course, but not a very well-kept secret."

"You don't think you may be crowding him a little?"

"Mr. Eaton, if I go to Florida that's the same as announcing that I'm going to sleep with him, isn't it? Which, by the way, I have."

"Remember, I didn't ask you that, Sadie."

"I know you didn't, but I'm telling you to get you completely on my side. I'm not a girl that sleeps with boys. I never have, except Rowland. Well, if I publicly declare that I'm

758

going to sleep with him, marriage or no marriage, all right, it's crowding him, but he's going to marry me anyway, after the war, so what earthly difference does it make if he marries me now or later? Except to me. It makes a lot of difference to me. I want to start a baby, but I don't want a little b, a. s, t, a, r, d. Oh, he makes me very cross sometimes. Are you stubborn?"

"Uh, yes, I can be. I have been."

"I knew he got it from somewhere. Of course I am, too."

"Well, I'm on your side. I've been from the start. Now that I've met you I think he'd be a damn fool not to marry you."

"He isn't a damn fool, but he can be very stuffy. You're not stuffy, are you? Not from what I've been able to gather."

"I'm *sort of* stuffy. What have you gathered about me?"

"Oh, well, weren't you, uh, rather wild before you got married? I understand that you and a Mr. Porter used to give wild parties in New York. Now I *heard* that from a friend of my mother's who went to Groton with Mr. Porter, and I ought to explain that my mother's friend is really stuffy, *really* stuffy. Is there any truth in it?"

"What would your guess be?"

"I would guess that there was some truth in it."

"Why?"

"Just a guess. I'll bet I understand you a lot better than Rowland does."

"I'm sure you do."

She looked at him steadily for a moment.

"Go on, what are you thinking? Tell me," he said.

"I wouldn't dare. Because if I was wrong you'd never speak to me again."

"I'll always speak to you. What were you thinking?"

"Well, you won't take offense? It's really meant as a compliment."

"I won't take offense."

"Well—I wouldn't be surprised if you'd been unfaithful to Mrs. Eaton."

"Why wouldn't you be surprised?"

"Well, that's one of the differences I notice between you and Rowland. Rowland never went on any wild parties, but you did, and you're much more sophisticated than he is. Even now."

"Even now? At my age?"

"Yes. Rowland never sees another girl, but you've seen every good-looking woman or girl in this room, and they've seen you. I wouldn't like that if Rowland did it, but he never would. I know exactly what I want out of life and so does Rowland."

"And I don't?"

"That's getting too complicated. But it's nothing against you, Mr. Eaton. You're a ladies' man, and Rowland is a born husband."

"Where did you ever get that expression, ladies' man?"

"I don't know, but I didn't want to say wolf, because you're not a wolf."

"No, I'm not a wolf. I may have had some lupine tendencies, but as I understand the wolf, he doesn't stop at tendencies. With him it's a full-time occupation. Am I right?"

"Right. Actually my conception of a wolf is that he does a lot more howling than he does biting."

"Well, I suppose we ought to leave that just where it is," said Alfred.

She smiled. "Yes, I think we'd better." In three sentences they had covered and disposed of the subject of her physical attraction, accidentally, but with good humor and with mutual understanding. They were friends now, tacitly but frankly conceding the sexual attraction, and in agreement that though it was there, they never would do anything about it. It would make their future encounters innocent but not numb and (although he did not appreciate this at the moment) enable her to understand him in his relationship with Mary, and him to understand her in her relationship with Rowland. He was quite sure that this girl, with her directness, would soon guess accurately the status of himself and Mary and even surmise that there was a Natalie. They finished their lunch and she walked with him to the Navy car. They had agreed that it was a little too soon for an exchange of family visits and for the time being she would handle the whole problem of Rowland's stubbornness herself.

He took her hand, which was strong but surprisingly small, and said, "Do I kiss you goodbye?"

"In front of all these people, of course."

He bent down and kissed her.

"You're an attractive man, Mr. Eaton."

"I feel attractive, Sadie. Thanks."

In the car he said to the aide, Wilson: "Girl's going to marry my son."

"Good deal," said Wilson. "Four-oh."

"I think so," said Alfred.

There were items to be read on the trip to Hanover, but they lay there in his lap, in their smooth, heavy composition folders, and he gazed out the car window at the rolling Massachusetts–New Hampshire countryside, thinking of the things that were in back of his son's life that his son would never know of: the passion that had created him, the care that had protected him from ugliness, the worries and satisfactions and rewards of directing him toward the final independence that he had now achieved, the things that only

760

a father could know that he had not learned from his own father, that he could not pass on to his son. The boy was honorable, dignified, rather humorless, but safe, and if the relationship had always been slightly formal, it was better to have had it that way than to have him come to this stage of independence incapable of independence, and unable to transfer dependence to a dependable young woman like Sadie Warren. Best of all, whatever the boy thought of him, Alfred was pleased that he had brought him this far without weakening his spirit as his father had weakened his own. There was sufficient evidence that the boy knew he was loved; the boy's self-confidence and dignity were evidence enough. From somewhere—and he could not immediately place it—he thought of the words, "This is my beloved son, in whom I am well pleased." There was more that he could not remember, and that he was afraid might change the present application of the words, but they were apt for now. He would try to get closer to his other son and to his daughter, too.

He passed the next few days and nights in the First and Third Naval Districts in what he called assistant-secretarial boot training, which consisted of listening and looking, shaking hands, placing his hat over his heart, requesting permission to board the ship, and relieving his superiors of the ceremonial and morale chores that he had been assured meant a great deal. In his own active naval career he had never met anyone of higher rank than captain and had gone through the war believing that the assistant secretary came from Oyster Bay. But this was a bigger war and paradoxically men of his status were expected to waste more time in foolishness than they had in 1917. At Quonset and at Dartmouth he had had to keep a straight face while looking down from a platform into the faces of men with whom he had played bottle pool at the Racquet Club. He had not the slightest doubt that they respected him more as a pool-player and MacHardie partner than as the recipient of the official attentions due his rank. Men he had known, who were approximately his own age, were being trained for posts that would soon put them under fire, and even when he got out to the Pacific, as he was scheduled to do, *he* would always be able to get home. Since that was the case he invariably declined when the commanding officers offered him the opportunity to forgather informally with friends at the various installations, and he wryly comforted himself with the assurance that it was better for them in the long run. He was not going to have the "trade school boys" of Annapolis pass the word that he was overfriendly to the ninety-day wonders of the U. S. N. R. They had convinced him in Washington that it was as important to him as to the

761

men to learn his way about, hence his invention of the term assistant-secretarial boot training. He did not believe them, but their suggestions carried the weight of orders, and he did as he was told. Wilson, with the chicken-guts on his shoulder and the Annapolis ring on his finger, tried to create a quasi-social atmosphere in the late afternoon and evening get-togethers and the higher brass luncheons, but Alfred would not play. He would accept the inevitable cocktail, but he would not finish it, and he was genuinely shocked to discover how frequently it happened that very recent commanders, captains and rear admirals would try to maneuver the conversation in the direction of MacHardie & Company and their own special qualifications for civilian jobs came peacetime. They all were willing to start at $25,000 a year. (Vice admirals would come a little higher.) It was his first disillusionment, and when he got back to Washington he told Forrestal that he was thinking of having a MacHardie & Company house flag embossed on his Navy stationery. Forrestal pulled on his pipe and laughed. "They're not all like that," he said. "But I don't say there aren't some."

"Then for Christ's sake fix it so I can see the others," said Alfred.

"Keep your shirt on," said Forrestal.

The almost simultaneous naval defeat of the Japanese in the Solomons and Eisenhower's invasion of North Africa, within less than a year of the attack on Pearl Harbor and so soon after all the news from Guadalcanal had been discouraging, revived the civilian bluster about a short war. This was especially true on the Atlantic Coast, where the citizens without personal identification with the Marine Corps were inclined to consider the entire Guadalcanal operation as characteristically brave but of questionable military significance. The enormity of the Japanese successes was lost upon these citizens. They believed that the Japs had had a string of easy victories over undefended or weakly defended small island paradises that were inhabited by English wastrels in crumpled linen suits and brown girls with firm young breasts who would swim out to offer themselves at the monthly arrival of the mail packet. The theory was that the victories had been so easy that the retaking of the islands could be accomplished with little resistance and in our own good time. Even after what the Japanese had demonstrated at Pearl Harbor there were millions of Americans who could not concede that Japan was a first-rate naval power, and the distances that the Japanese had covered in their victories had little meaning. As late as September the narrow escape at Port Moresby was underestimated. What was New Guinea but an island that had been named for its silhouette on the map, and which seemed to be sitting on top of Australia? Australia was a name they could recognize, but Australia seemed safe enough. Australia was a continent, populated by hard workers, good swimmers, the best tennis players, and men who could lick the Japs. There was the theory that the Japs had overextended themselves (which may have been true enough when they reached the neighborhood of Port Moresby), and that as soon as the European operations were well in hand, the American Navy would concentrate on the Pacific theater, destroy the Japanese fleet, and allow the Australians and American marines to mop up the Japs in the islands of the easy victories. Momentarily the war was almost over before it had really begun, and the sour ones who argued otherwise were accused of pessimism, militarism, and anti-Russianism, the last because of the insistent communist propaganda for the second front. Even marines like Alfred's Montana schoolteacher had difficulty in trying to convince marines in stateside training that every gyrene could not positively lick three Japs in hand-to-hand encounter.

The letdown following the good news of mid-November was the cause of the first overt quarrel Alfred had with Mary during the years of their mannerly antagonism. At irregular intervals—irregular for security reasons, so that he was not expected to telephone her at stated times—he would talk with her and with his daughter. The conversations with Mary were agreeable enough, confined to household news and problems and a carefully limited quantity of small talk. During this conversation in the third week of November Mary made her domestic report and then said: "Is there any chance that Rowland will get home for Thanksgiving?"

"I shouldn't think so. He's just finished fifteen hours of instrument flying and they accepted him for fighter training. That means he's right in the middle of operational flying, very tough, and I don't think he'd *want* to leave."

"But you could arrange it."

"Oh, no."

"Yes you could. Stop leaning over backwards. All you'd have to do is make one telephone call."

"Oh, I could. But I certainly won't. What the hell is Thanksgiving? Wait till we really have something to be thankful for."

"Well, we have. That's why I'd like him to come home. We could have his girl come down from Boston, and even you might show up. Everybody says the war'll be over in a year."

"Jesus H. Christ! Where do you get your information?"

"Why it's common knowledge."

"I've never heard anything so stupid in my life."

"You just want him to stay in the Navy to get his commission."

"Will you stop that talk? When did the Germans surrender?"

"They will, any minute."

"Then we went to a lot of unnecessary trouble landing those men in Africa, didn't we?"

"That's why they're going to surrender."

"It sounds to me as though you had a new boy friend, a military expert. Well, tell him for me he's wrong. And you're not helping your son by repeating such crap. Rowland's war hasn't even begun."

"Then you refuse to be helpful."

"He'll get some leave when he gets his wings."

"I repeat, you refuse to be helpful?"

"I'm not going to ask for any special consideration for my son."

"Blah blah blah blah blah. No wonder they call you Speedy. Goodnight."

He signaled the operator without replacing the phone, and in a minute or two he was speaking to Natalie. "A slight change in plans, you'll be glad to hear. You don't have to come to Washington this weekend. I'm going to New York."

"Oh, good. And stay here?"

"Friday at Seventy-second Street, Saturday at Fifty-fifth."

He then telephoned Percy Hasbrouck and asked him to arrange a luncheon at the office for Friday. "I'd appreciate it if you'd invite about ten of the top men from the biggest banks. This isn't MacHardie & Company business, but I'd like to have the luncheon there because I don't want to have it at one of the clubs. And you invite the men personally, will you please? In other words, not through their secretaries."

"This sounds urgent, Alfred."

"It is. And I'll sign for the lunch. It's my own affair."

"I gather you're going to make a speech."

"Sort of, but not a stand-up speech, so have them put up the round table."

Six MacHardie partners, including Alfred, and nine men from other banking houses sat down at twelve-thirty to the one dish, liver and bacon and mashed potatoes, and as soon as the two waiters left the room Alfred began to speak. "Gentlemen, I first want to thank you for coming here, obviously breaking other engagements on short notice. All of you, I know from experience, are used to talking business through lunch, and I only wish I could talk to you one at a time. But I hope you'll feel that that's the atmosphere I'm trying to simulate here today. Informal. Interrupt when you feel like it. Make any comments that occur to you.

"Now then. I am very much disturbed, I can't tell you how disturbed I am, by the kind of talk that's going around about this war. I'll be brief, and it's all too easy. In the last week

764

or so, ever since General Eisenhower landed in North Africa and we had some success in the Solomon Islands, I've been hearing that we've broken the back of this war. I think I know why. It's the first time we've had good news from both east *and* west, and we've been starving for it. We were embarrassed by Pearl Harbor, and we've been embarrassed by strong hints from our European allies that history is repeating itself. You all remember, 'You're coming over when it's all over,' from the last war. The only trouble with that is that it's a little too early, in my opinion, for our allies to make that accusation again, and that leads me to one point, namely, that the war in Europe is going to take a long time.

"The war in the Pacific is going to take longer.

"I speak to you today not in my official capacity. Percy will tell you that this is a private luncheon, I'm paying the bill, which is always a pleasure when it involves such distinguished company. And I shall be very careful not to reveal any military secrets. However, both in my official position and as a member of this community and with some good old Pennsylvania common sense, I can speak pretty frankly without telling you anything that I'm sworn not to tell you. I have brought with me two maps, one of Europe, the other of what the cartographers call Oceania. Does anybody remember dancing to the 'Oceania Roll'? Thought so. Well, here's the map of Europe, with enough of North Africa showing to show you where we are now. Here is what Mr. Churchill calls the soft underbelly of Europe. Italy. France. Here are Spain and Portugal. The Low Countries. I know you're all familiar with these countries, and I'm not trying to give you a geography lesson. But here, for instance, are Spain and Portugal, no help at all to us. Spain particularly is neutral on the enemy's side and in my personal opinion that could have been averted, but that's spilt milk. Germany is going to defend Italy to the last Italian, and France started this war as a fourth-rate military power and is now hardly more than an allied sympathizer. I promised to be brief, so I won't go into the tragedy of France.

"Now in the back of your minds is, of course, Russia. The Russian army. The Russian winter. But there are not going to be any Russians at whatever spot we pick to attack the European continent. Common sense, whether it's Pennsylvania common sense or Nassau County common sense, or Bronx common sense, will tell you that it's up to us and the British. Gentlemen, it is going to be bloody and costly and long.

"The most disturbing, alarming chatter that I've heard had to do with surrender. I've heard it from women and men. It appears, gentlemen, that now that we have succeeded in landing in Africa, the Germans would like to withdraw. That's one of the rumors. The Germans are satisfied that we can invade the continent of Europe, therefore, rather than risk military defeat, they will withdraw, not all the way back to where they started from. Oh, not quite that. They will hold on to everything in France that is north of a line drawn from Havre to Strasbourg and Stuttgart. As you see, that will allow the French to have Paris, which is a very big, face-saving gesture of the Germans, but on the German side of that line will be Verdun. Also, of course, Belgium and Holland. And, naturally, Denmark. That, according to what I've been hearing, is Germany's price for withdrawing.

"There are people who say it isn't too big a price. But those people live in this country. Still, the idea is to convince some of our people that it'd be better that way than to engage in a war on the continent of Europe. And some of them seem to *be* convinced, or damn near it." Alfred paused. He did not expect any of the men to speak up; they were eating and listening, turning their gaze on him while chewing their food, but paying attention to his remarks. The faster or lighter eaters sat quietly attentive, and he continued.

"Gentlemen, the theory that I've been advancing to you has no basis in fact. It is all rumor. In spite of what you may hear from Stockholm or Lisbon, or from the Stork Club, the Germans do not want to withdraw on anything like the terms I have stated. I must ask you to take my word for that, and I shall now commit one indiscretion. What I am about to say is unofficial and does not come through government intelligence channels. But it's something for you to think about. It's more than that. It's in the nature of a warning.

"In our government there are already plans on what should be done to the Germans after the war. They are drastic plans that would reduce a defeated Germany from an industrial country to a severely controlled agricultural country. There's been so much talk about these plans that a great many people seem to think they represent our government's policy. Well, I'm not on the policy-making level; but I've expressed myself to my superiors as opposed to these plans, and I know it's no secret that Mr. Churchill is opposed to them. But in any event, because there's been so much talk, and because so many people think that we intend to destroy the German industrial potential, certain extremely misguided people in and out of our government have given Hitler his most effective internal propaganda weapon. Hitler is now able to tell his big industry and his people that they must win or be obliterated. He hasn't had to use that *yet*. Germany is at the moment winning this war, as far as it has gone. But later, when things begin to get tough at home as a result of defeats in the field and the enormous cost to the German people, he only has to remind them that no matter how bad things may be, they're going to be a hell of a sight worse if they lose.

"We at home here are no longer worried about the possibility of Hitler's old plan. You remember that one. Subdue North Africa and start taking over this hemisphere by way of Brazil. If that really was Hitler's dream, he's had to wake up. And I don't want to imply for one second that we're not going to win in Europe. But I want to state, practically to swear to you, that we have one hell of a war left in Europe. And I'm a *Navy* man. Not an Army man. I'm giving it to you as straight as I can, but that's not nearly as straight as an Army man could. They know what we're in for.

"I now speak for *my* team. Unofficially, but as sincerely as I am able. Here is the map of Oceania. Here is Tokyo. Here is Pearl Harbor. Here is Port Moresby. Gentlemen, some of you are interested in shipping, some of you in aviation. All of you have done some traveling. Does any of you think the Japanese are going to be dislodged by a few regiments of marines with some air support? Do you as business men, who are as new to the word logistics as I am, do you realize what the Japanese have done? I don't have to sell you this so-called 'other war.' All you have to do is look at the map and *see* what they've done in a year's time.

"And I assure you, gentlemen, the Japanese are not going to surrender any more than the Germans are. They'll fight after we've defeated the Germans. And that concludes my monologue. I welcome any and all questions and I'll try to be as frank as my circumstances permit."

There was a silence. He knew he was bound to have stepped on some toes in this group, which included men who had had business acquaintances in German industry and others who were as much at home in London as in New York, and others who worked in New York but had never truly left the Middle West. Alfred waited for Percy Hasbrouck to break the silence, but it was Don Shanley who spoke up.

"As a sort of a co-host here, I'd like to express my pride in my partner, Alfred Eaton. I don't say I agree with him all up and down the line, but he has shaken my complacency."

Immediately there were murmurs and mutterings in an approving tone, and at the sound of their own voices the men became articulate.

"Suppose we have the dishes cleared away and coffee and dessert brought in," said Hasbrouck. "That will give us all a chance to formulate our questions? Okay, gentlemen?"

The waiters functioned efficiently and departed promptly. Hasbrouck, after his cowardly silence, now became chairman. "Who would like to be first? Ed?"

"Yes. I liked what Alfred said, or at least the way he said it. But he could have had me in mind when he mentioned Stockholm, because the information *I* get from there is that the Germans *have* made overtures to us. I wish Alfred would say a little more about that."

"As much as I can. It isn't taken seriously in Washington," said Alfred.

"Yeah, but what the hell is? I'd like to know. Supposing a German did want to seriously discuss a—French word—rapprochement—would anybody pay any attention to him down there? Or *is* it the policy to wipe Germany off the face of the earth?"

"There have been so-called feelers, Ed," said Alfred. "I can only repeat that they're not taken seriously. They are considered to be fishing expeditions, and they would be dangerous if they were taken seriously, because there are a lot of very nervous men in London who are looking for the first hint of appeasement. As to our policy of punishment, I don't think it goes up as high as Roosevelt."

"How does anybody know what he thinks?" said someone.

"Paul? You had a question?" said Hasbrouck.

"Yes. I wanted to ask Alfred the same thing that's on all our minds. What is his estimate of how long it will take to defeat Germany? If that's permissible."

"I thought that would be the first question," said Alfred, smiling. "I'm so afraid that I might inadvertently say something I shouldn't that I'll have to call the question un-permissible."

"I was afraid of that," said Paul.

"However, if you stop to think of it, and in spite of what I say about its being a long war, the modern all-out war uses up men and matériel so fast that I'll guess under ten years."

"Thanks, that's a *lot* of help," said Paul.

"George?" said Hasbrouck.

"Thank you, Percy. Thank you. Now *I* heard the very strangest rumor that I've ever heard in my life. I've lived a long time and I've seen and heard a great many strange and awful and peculiar things. Now please don't anyone interrupt me, because I have to get this clear in my own mind. I see Tom over there thinking he knows what I'm going to say, but he doesn't. Tom thinks I'm going to say something he told me about, but he's wrong. This is something I haven't disscussed with Tom. I don't distrust Tom, but I do distrust myself. But I don't distrust my patriotism. It's just that I distrust my ignorance, and possibly Alfred can enlighten me."

"I'll try."

"Well. Could you possibly tell me why, with all the money we're spending for bigger aeroplanes, bigger ships, bigger this, bigger that, bigger the other thing, why would Franklin Roosevelt want to spend—now listen to this, you fellows—why would he want to spend money to study the *atom!* The tiniest thing there is!"

"Oh, it's just something to keep Eleanor occupied."

"No. I don't think so. My granddaughter is engaged—or I guess you'd call it engaged—to a young man. But that's neither here nor there. I just thought I'd ask you what the *atom* has to do with the war."

"I don't know a thing about it," said Alfred.

"Chemical warfare, no doubt," said Hasbrouck.

"An interesting possibility," said George. "Sorry I interrupted."

"I have a question of my own, while I think of it," said Hasbrouck. "I think it's of general interest, or I'd save it."

"Fire away," said Alfred.

"Well, assuming that we invade the continent of Europe and wage a successful campaign, and assuming that the Germans see the light and do want to negotiate a peace—what is going to happen to Mr. Hitler?"

"In what way, Percy? Do you mean are we going to dicker with him, or are we going to kick him out and then dicker?" said Alfred.

"Well, either way," said Hasbrouck.

"My answer, which is an informed guess, and worth just that, is that our government will never do business with Hitler. I would say that we might do business with the German General Staff, or with whoever supplants Hitler and his crowd, but never with Hitler or the top Nazis. Even if we wanted to, which we don't, our allies wouldn't hold still for it, and I wouldn't blame them. My own guess, *un*-informed, is that as soon as we put together a bunch of victories and are really headed for German soil, the German General Staff will liquidate Hitler. However, I've been wrong before about the German General Staff, as Don will tell you, so don't take my word for that. Anyway, here we are, gentlemen, falling back into the kind of thinking that I earnestly urge you to put aside. I have just said 'put together a bunch of victories.' That, at the moment, is the worst kind of anticipation and wishful thinking. I have one son in the Navy, and another son who is fifteen. If you want to know what I think, I can tell you that in every letter to my younger son I try to say something about physical fitness. Calisthenics, and track. Endurance stuff. I want him to get himself into such good shape that when he's drafted he's not going to be soft. Now, you can figure out from that that I don't expect this war to be over for at least three years."

"Three years, for Christ's sake?" said the man named Ed.

"That's my guess as to the minimum," said Alfred. "And that's with luck, good planning, sacrifice, and God's help."

They looked at him as though he had announced a punishment which some of them felt they deserved and others considered to be unjust and unusual, and which all of them felt it would be useless to appeal. Hasbrouck, who was quick to sense majority reactions, put on an expression to match the gloomiest at the table, and chose his words with the care of a man who wants everyone to remember that he had chosen his words with care: "Alfred—Alfred has spoken with such finality that—that we must all give thoughtful consideration—thoughtful consideration—to what he's told us. And if I'm any judge, if my own reaction is any indication, I'd say that we all feel that this would be the right moment to adjourn this little get-together. Unless, of course, there are any more questions."

"I'm still willing to answer questions, but I'd prefer to limit them to questions that won't draw encouragement from the answers, if that isn't too confusing."

"I say thanks for the lunch, Alfred," said Ed. "But you haven't made it easy to digest. Not with that bitter pill you served along with it."

There was mild, assenting laughter upon that comment, and the men rose and soon all outsiders had gone. Hasbrouck put out his hand to say goodbye to Alfred. "All in all, a good speech," he said. "And in wartime it never does any harm to make that kind of a speech."

"Do you think I went to all this trouble to make quote that kind of a speech unquote, Percy?"

"Well, we haven't won the war by a long shot, but we haven't lost it, either."

"No, we haven't won it, and we haven't lost it. But I'd like to know where you think we've begun to fight it."

"I rather resent that question," said Hasbrouck, carefully smiling.

"I know, but answer it."

"Now I *do* resent it."

"All right, but I'm still waiting for an answer."

"Oh, now just a *second*, please."

"No, and don't make any remarks about my official position."

"You're quite right. I was going to remind you that you have certain temporary advantages."

"Percy, my temporary advantages have nothing to do with your ability or inability to answer my question. I asked you where you think we've begun to fight this war. Well, where? Landing troops in North Africa? A few naval battles in the Pacific? How many inches of territory have we re-occupied?

770

How many divisions have we landed in France? Who's having dinner at the Paris Ritz tonight? How many oil tankers did we lose in the western Atlantic *today?* I said the western Atlantic, within a hundred miles of the Jersey coast? You resent my questions? I resent your patronizing brush-off of what I was trying to tell these men today. Thoughtful consideration, my ass. File and forget. I had them *thinking* for fifteen seconds, and then you sabotaged me right on my own home ground. If it *is* my own home ground."

"*If* it is your own home ground. You have a point there."

"So I've heard. I'm going to find out a little more about *that* while I'm in New York. But I'm not going to ask *you* any more questions. You don't like questions, Percy."

"Then I suggest you put your questions to any of the partners you see here. They have the same answers I'd give you."

"I suggest you go jump in the lake."

"Oho, no, Alfred. That's your specialty. That's how you got here in the first place. Now you'll have to excuse me, but the other partners, *full* partners, will tell you all you want to know."

He marched out, and Alfred gazed about him at the Mac-Hardie & Company partners who were present. In three seconds he knew that his career at MacHardie & Company was ended.

They all, in their turn, saw that he knew it, and Don Shanley spoke up. "Gentlemen," said Shanley, "I've been closer to Alfred than any of the rest of you. Therefore, I think it's up to me."

"*Et tu, Brute,*" said Alfred.

"Hardly as bad as that, Alfred," said Shanley, hurt by the implied accusation of treachery.

"Nothing like," said William Zabriskie Kingsley. "Gentlemen, Don *has* been closer to Alfred. Why don't we let Don explain it to Alfred alone, and then if Alfred wants to talk about it later, we'll all be at our desks."

"I won't be at my desk," said Guy Titterton. "I'm on duty at four o'clock. My Civil Air Patrol. I know about those submarines, Alfred. They got a tanker yesterday, off Asbury Park, New Jersey."

"Not supposed to say that, Guy," said Alfred.

"I know, but I'm afraid some of these fellows think I'm a damned old show-off, flying a flivver plane at my age."

"The C. A. P. is God damn important work," said Alfred.

"We hope so," said Titterton. "In any event, I'm off. But anything Don says is okay with me. Nice to have seen you, Alfred. Good-speech."

Rough, tough old Titterton had spoken the first and, so far, the only warmly friendly words of the meeting, and Alfred

771

shook hands and thanked him. "Happy landings," said Alfred.

Frederick Cross got up. "Well, I'll be here all afternoon if you want to see me, Alfred."

"So will I," said Kingsley, and left with Cross.

Shanley, when he and Alfred were alone, reached for the nickel-plated Thermos and said, "More coffee, Alfred?"

"Sure."

Shanley poured the coffee, poured some for himself and broke a lump of sugar in two and dropped a half into the cup.

"I'll take the other half," said Alfred.

"Share and share alike," said Shanley. "Seems rather meaningless at the moment, doesn't it?"

"It holds good for a lump of sugar."

"I want to call your attention to the way Guy Titterton spoke to you. He happened to do most of the talking, but that's the way the others feel, except Percy. But it shouldn't come as any news to you that you get in Percy's hair. I think I may have put you on the alert a long time ago, but even then it shouldn't have been a surprise. I am not going to be subversive about Percy. I don't have to be. You've always known that as far back as that Louisiana proposition, you rubbed him the wrong way. My guess is that if it hadn't been the Louisiana thing, it would have been something else. Percy's animosity was a compliment. If you hadn't been a threat, Percy would have been nice to you, but then if you hadn't been a threat you never would have been taken into the firm, if you see what I mean. And you mustn't forget this, Alfred. You never liked Percy."

"Never."

"A natural antagonism that was all right so long as it was kept within bounds. But Mr. MacHardie's failing health happened to more or less coincide with your taking the job in Washington, and Percy saw his opportunity. He went out and got more money, and now he's in control."

"In control? He is?"

"Well, he is, and he isn't. At this moment he has more capital in MacHardie & Company than any other individual except Mr. MacHardie himself. Any three of us have more than Percy has, but not any two. And Percy has Fritz Cross, Bill Kingsley, and Steve Van Ingen going along with him."

"Van Ingen doesn't surprise me, but—"

"Billy Kingsley and Fritz Cross like you, but they don't want a fight, and they go along with Percy because you've taken a leave of absence to work for the government. By one of those ironies of fate, that fine speech you made today just about cooked your goose."

"Of course it did."

"As soon as you began talking about a long war, I had a

772

look at Billy and Fritz and I knew what they were thinking. The more successfully you argued your case against letting down the war effort, the stronger you were making Percy's position. It always comes down to dollars and cents, Alfred. You know that. I have all the money I want or will ever need, and I have no children, but all the others have children and grandchildren, and they're letting Percy take over.

"As a matter of fact, the days of MacHardie & Company are numbered. We're an anachronism today. As soon as Mr. MacHardie passes on—which I'm told won't be very far in the future—MacHardie & Company will cease to function as a private bank. We're going to incorporate and expand. We're going to start dying off pretty soon, and you know what the inheritance taxes are going to do to private fortunes. Therefore, as soon as Mr. MacHardie dies, as I say, we cease to be, and those of us who survive Mr. MacHardie will start a new business, inviting the public to come in. Everybody will know who we are. The old MacHardie & Company partnership. But it won't be MacHardie & Company. I doubt if we'll even be MacHardie & Company Incorporated."

"Hasbrouck & Van Ingen, Incorporated."

Shanley smiled. "The name Hasbrouck will most likely be in there somewhere."

Alfred, who had been making a piston-like motion with a lead pencil, held the pencil still and read the name stamped on it: " 'MacHardie & Company.' You know, Don, my mind refuses to accept all this. I knew there was something cooking. I meant to find out what it was, but now I find that I'm out on my ass, which isn't as much of a shock as it should be after twenty years, but somehow I thought MacHardie & Company would go on forever."

"What does go on forever, Alfred? Be glad that this is happening while you're still a young man. And be gladder still that it happened before you took over. You're young, you're serving your country. When the war's over you'll be able to look around and decide what you'd like to do."

"Just another Navy officer looking for a good job."

"Hardly that."

"As to my being young. Forty-five isn't young. It's only younger than fifty, not really young."

"Oh, I agree. It's old if you're going to die at forty-six, but you ought to be around for twenty more years at least."

"But at fifty I'll be looking for something to do."

"You think the war will last five more years?"

"Close to it."

"I would like to say this, in fairness to Percy—"

"Oh, by all means let's be fair to Percy."

"This thing came to a head today by accident. Percy was

773

going to tell you the whole story, and you were going to be offered stock in the new corporation, and a directorship. Percy doesn't underestimate your ability. Or, for that matter, your standing in the financial community. It's just that he never wanted to be in an inferior position to you. This whole thing blew up today because you both lost your tempers. You gave it to him about as hard as you could. Short of accusing him of treason."

"I'm glad I did. I don't think I could have listened to his suave explanation of what he was doing while my back was turned. I'd much rather have it the way it was."

"Oh, I suppose you'd have had to tell him off sometime, but he did intend to put the whole thing on the table."

"What actually happens to me now?"

"Well, I suppose what will happen will be up to the lawyers and won't happen overnight. But you'll get a good fair price for getting out. You won't lose money. I would think that in a case like this you'll stay on the books as a limited partner until the end of our fiscal year, then there'll be a distribution of profits to you as limited partner, and whatever money and legal arrangements as will be necessary to terminate your connection with the firm. It all may take some time and I imagine that the longer it takes, the better for your tax position. I don't know. You'll work that out with your own lawyers and Mortimer & Miller."

"Mortimer & Miller? Duffy's firm!"

"Representing Percy. MacHardie & Company still retain Pickett, McKinstry, Livingston, Chase & McDonald, but I have a feeling not for long."

"Well, isn't that cozy? Then I don't suppose there's any point in my going to see Mr. MacHardie."

"You have to, as a courtesy. I'm old enough to insist on your doing that. You'd really displease me if you didn't. Displease and disappoint me. But I warn you, don't go there prepared to have a knock-down drag-out. Wait till you see him."

"He's that bad?"

"I don't know what's keeping him alive. I never question the mercy of God, but when I see someone in that condition I wonder."

"Well, Don. What do I do next? Clean out my desk? I did clean it out when I went to Washington."

"Your desk will be there until your resignation is announced. You know how punctilious we are here. Incidentally, if you'd like to have the desk when you leave—"

"What on earth for?"

Shanley smiled. "Haven't you any sentiment?"

"Dollars and cents, my friend. And I'll let Percy have the

774

desk to keep his throat-gargles in. By the way, I said I'd pay for this lunch today."

"You still have a commissary account. All those things are just the same. The only difference is that you're not—"

"The only difference is, as I said before, I'm out on my ass. I'm the most limited limited partner in town."

"I don't have to say that I hope this leaves us, you and me, where we've always been."

"If I ever start a business of my own you know who's going to be the first man I ask to go in with me."

"Well, if you don't mind a partner who creaks at the joints."

"No creaking where it counts," said Alfred, tapping his head and his heart.

"Go away, now. I'm Irish, and we *are* sentimental."

Mary was not at the apartment, but she arrived there shortly after Alfred, accompanied by their daughter Jean. The girl greeted her father generously and, as was their custom when the children were present, Mary presented her cheek for Alfred's kiss. "We've been to Schwarz's" said Mary.

"Let me tell him," said Jean, and did until she was taken away for her supper.

"How are you?" said Mary.

"Well, for one thing, I'm a free agent in Wall Street."

"How is that?"

"It seems that Percy Hasbrouck has become the king pin at MacHardie & Company, and shortly after the first of the year I shall no longer be a partner."

"You won't be anything?"

"An ex-partner."

"You don't seem very worried."

"I'm not. It won't make much difference in our scale of living. I may even stand to gain a little, temporarily, so don't you worry."

"I never have. I've never worried about money. I took it for granted when I was a girl. Daddy was Daddy, and like all daddies he had money. Then when I married you and I found out a little more about it, I had every confidence in your ability to make it. I always have had."

"Why, thank you."

"It's an odd thing, isn't it? I spend a lot of money on clothes and other things, and you've given me a lot of jewelry, but I've never wanted more than we had or you earned at any given time."

"No, you've been very good about that. Well, I just wanted you to know, we won't have to give up anything."

"But aren't you at all upset about the firm, leaving it after so long? You were going to succeed Mr. MacHardie, weren't you?"

"I thought so, but nobody's really going to succeed him. They're all ready to incorporate as soon as he dies, which I'm told is going to be very soon. When MacHardie & Company fold, there'll only be Brown-Harriman left of the old private banking firms. Hasbrouck, of course, will become an investment banking corporation, and in a way it's a break for me to get out intact. I'll explain it to you if you like."

"You know it's no use. You've tried before."

"Well, just that getting out now I'll—this is oversimplifying, but that's all right—I'll take more money with me than I would if we weren't having a wartime prosperity. You understand that much."

"I suppose I do. Is this confidential?"

"Yes. At least they'll try to keep it so, and I'm not going to blab it around. But these things leak out, so I suppose it'll be in the *Journal* on Monday."

"What are your plans?"

"To go on working for the government as long as they want me. After that, who knows? I'll play a lot of golf and eat a lot of lunch and then go into some business."

"Do you feel that you got a screwing?"

"I got a bit of a screwing, but if I hadn't lost my temper it would have been a more gradual process leading to the same conclusion. With the old gentleman out of the driver's seat there never would have been room for Percy and me both. I was fixing to kick his ass out, after the war, but he beat me to it. Luckily I have plenty to do, so I'm not going to brood much over it."

"Did Percy do anything unethical?"

"Well, your father would probably consider it unethical. My Grandfather Johnson would. But on the other hand, I think my father would probably consider it just being tough in business. My father and Percy weren't a bit alike, but they saw business the same way."

"What do *you* think?"

"Well, let's just say that my being in Washington didn't turn out to be a disadvantage for Percy. I don't *think* I'd have done the same thing if our circumstances had been reversed, but I might have. You think I'm a son of a bitch anyway, so I'm not going to plead my case very eloquently."

"Oh, you're a son of a bitch, but I think you're very ethical in business."

"Well, thanks for that much. I gather you're having some people in for dinner."

She smiled. "We were having the Hasbroucks, but she called up and left a message. She said she was sure I'd understand. I thought I understood in an understanding way, but now I realize she meant much more than that."

"We should have had them and invited George S. Kaufman and Edna Ferber. Too bad. Who else?"

"Just the Wellses."

"Oh, Christ. Let's take them to '21' and get rid of them early."

"I can get out of it entirely if you like. People don't mind nowadays, especially since you're the Assistant Secretary."

"Oh, let's take them to '21.' Save you some food points, won't it?"

"Yes, but don't think for a minute I don't deal in the black market, because I do."

"I'd rather not hear about it. When did you start getting so chummy with the Wellses?"

"Last summer, at East Hampton."

"Oh, yes. Well, I think I'll take a bath."

"If you decide to take a nap I'll call you at seven-thirty."

She came into his room shortly after seven-thirty and stood beside his bed. He opened his eyes. "Seven-thirty?" he said.

"Yes. Parker's here, but Nancy couldn't make it."

"Parker? Parker Wells. Oh, Nancy couldn't make it? Well, why don't you and Parker go out and have dinner and I'll have some scrambled eggs here?"

"Because I'm not going to have dinner with Parker alone."

"Good Lord, why not?"

"Because Nancy wouldn't like it."

"Good Lord. All right, I'll get dressed. Ask Thomas to bring me a Coke with a lot of ice in it."

He drank the Coca-Cola while he was dressing, and went out to join Mary and Parker Wells. "Hello, Parker."

"Hello, Alfred," said Wells, rising and shaking hands.

"Sorry Nancy couldn't make it."

"I know. Wisdom tooth."

"God, she's young."

"No, not that young. But it never gave her any trouble before, then it began to act up a couple of days ago, and she finally had to have it out this morning."

"Well, I'm sorry to hear it. What's new with you?"

"Oh, there's nothing new in our business. Everybody wants to advertise but we can't get a third of it published. Nowadays the guys on the magazines and the newspapers sit back and take their revenge. We solicit them now, they do us a favor by accepting our ads."

Wells was from Chicago by way of Dartmouth, still somewhat impressed by the authentic New York society background of his wife's family. She was a Bogardus, a niece of the MacHardie partner Stephen Van Ingen, and she had prevailed upon the male members of her family to get Parker into the Racquet and the Union clubs. She had also, in a small way, changed her husband's name. At Oak Park High and at Dartmouth he had been Fred P. Wells, but she had made the wedding invitations read Frederick Parker Wells, which was then truncated to Parker Wells. He was in no immediate or remote danger from the draft, since his age was forty-two, and in his medical history there was a record of *encephalitis lethargica* which, however, was interpreted by Nancy to mean a fractured skull from a skiing accident. Wells had started his New York life as a clean-cut young resident of the Murray Hill Allerton House and Nancy had been overlooked by the young men of her own set. She easily won him away from the Chicago girl whom he more or less planned to marry, and he was pleased to discover that he could sleep with a girl whose family had a butler and a liveried chauffeur. She lent him the money for the engagement ring and did not ask its repayment when her father gave the delighted bridegroom a wedding present of $50,000. It had always been that way with Nancy: if it was hers, it was the best or it was going to be made to seem like the best; she enjoyed her new Dartmouth partisanship over Harvard, the alma mater of her father and her uncles, and the advertising business became, in her conversation, the most fascinating occupation in the catalog of man's endeavor. She even encouraged Parker's slight idiosyncrasies of dress (after he was securely in the Racquet and the Union), which included hand-painted neckties and grosgrain evening shoes and one of the earliest if not the first plaid dinner jacket ever seen on Long Island. Nancy and Parker had one child, a daughter, who from the age of three was predictably so hopelessly homely that the child was given riding lessons and horses until, at the earliest possible date, she was entered in boarding-school and a sort of oblivion.

Parker, with some considerable assistance from Nancy and her father, bought into the advertising agency that had been his only employment since college, and as a vice-president and director he became a high-level representative of the agency in dealing with clients' complaints that would not involve the possible loss of billings. He spoke of himself as a trouble-shooter, and his work consisted of traveling to the clients' main offices, accompanied by the account executive, and promising to give the complaints the highest priority. He did no harm, and the fact of his being a vice-president and director and higher-echelon than the account executive showed at least that the agency was taking the complaint seriously.

He had discovered rather early in his marriage to Nancy that it was not necessary to invent elaborate lies to cover his infidelities. She had the husband she was terrified of not getting, and nothing short of bringing a whore to their apartment was likely to break up the marriage. Such misconduct was not probable, since the agency maintained, full-time, a large suite in an apartment-hotel in the Sixties, where it was possible for two executives to have assignations simultaneously without encountering each other, so long as arrangements had been made beforehand. It was there that Parker had his meetings with Mary.

"Did Mary tell you we're going to '21'?" said Alfred. "Maybe we ought to call up for a table. I don't go there much."

"I do," said Wells. "We won't have any trouble, and we wouldn't anyway. They know you."

They got a broken-down taxi and were driven to the restaurant and after a cocktail at the bar they were given the first available table in the front room upstairs. Except for the incidence of uniforms the crowd was the usual mixture of society, café society, the movies, the theater, and the arts and letters. They ordered roast beef and beer, and smiled and nodded to the people they knew or thought they knew. Some men smiled and nodded at Alfred without his genuine recognition of them in turn, but he was getting accustomed to that. Wells excused himself to visit at two other tables, at one of which there were two of the non-recognized men, and when he came back he said, "Alfred, you see the elderly man in the brown suit over against the wall? That's D. B. Spratling, chairman of the board of Spratling Mills."

"It is?" said Alfred.

"Yes, you know, Spratling Mills. Flour."

"Yes, I know Spratling Mills. St. Paul."

"Right. I was just wondering if you'd mind going over and saying hello to the old boy."

"Are you kidding? Of course I'd mind."

"He'd appreciate it."

"Would he really? Well, you'd better tell him not to wait till I get there, because it's going to be a long, long wait." It was amusing to watch Wells's avoidance of Spratling's smiling and then unsmiling and finally frowning stare. In time he got the point and when he paid his bill and left he did not stop at Alfred's table or say goodnight to Wells. Wells got up and followed him downstairs.

"I've disappointed your friend," said Alfred. "Now he's explaining to the old fart that I was *going* to come over after dinner. I know that type so well."

"Which type?"

"Well, both types. But I was speaking of Spratling. He's so used to kinging it in St. Paul that he expects the same ass-kissing here. And he gets it, too, from people like Wells."

Wells returned.

"What did you tell him, Parker?" said Alfred.

"Tell who?"

"Mr. Spratling."

"Oh, let's drop it, shall we?" said Mary.

"In a minute," said Alfred. "I'd like to know how Parker got out of the spot he got himself into. What made you think I'd ever pay court to that old fluff?"

"I thought you might want to."

"Why?"

"Well, you're a business man and he's a business man."

"Oh, and you thought it'd be nice if you brought us together. It wasn't because the old man would have liked to have the Assistant Secretary of the Navy paying his respects to the chairman of Spratling Crunchies?"

"Don't get sore about it. If I made a mistake, I apologize."

"Okay. We've got that straight. I'll arrange my own introductions."

"Oh, for heaven's sake."

"Christ, I didn't mean any harm, and there wouldn't have been any harm in it. This war isn't going to last forever."

"Oh, now let's hear about that," said Alfred.

"I give up," said Mary.

"Too easily," said Alfred. "What about this war, Parker?"

"Well, of course I don't have the pipelines that you have, but almost everybody I talk to says the war will be over in a year."

"Oh?"

"Yes. There's a very strong rumor that when What's His Name Eisenhower landed the army in Africa, right away the Germans started negotiations through the neutral countries. Sweden and Switzerland. If we'll guarantee not to invade France, they'll get out of France, or most of it. That's common knowledge."

"It is? Well, I must say I've heard it before. In almost those same words."

"You did?"

"Absolutely. Ask Mary."

He did not have to look at Mary to feel the malevolence of her gaze.

"Oh, then you believe the rumor?"

"I didn't say that. Far from it. But I did say I'd heard the rumor in almost exactly those words. Your words, Parker."

Mary turned to Wells. "Don't you see what he's doing? He's making a damn fool of you."

"I fail to see that," said Wells. "How? I usually know when a man is trying to make a fool out of me."

"You didn't this time, though, Parker," said Alfred.

"About what? Everybody's heard that rumor."

"The more you say, the worse fool you make of yourself. It has nothing to do with the war."

"He's trying to tell you that he knows you and I are having an affair!" said Mary.

"Yes. And of course enjoying the act you've been putting on," said Alfred.

"When did you tell him?" said Wells.

"I didn't. You did."

"Mary, we're too subtle for him," said Alfred.

"I don't know what you mean by subtle, but you're right about Mary and I."

"Of course I am."

"Well, what's so subtle about that? What are you going to do about it?"

"Not a damn thing. What are *you?*"

"What am I? What do you mean, what am I?"

"Going to do about it? Are you going to ask Nancy for a divorce so that you can propose honorable marriage to Mary?"

Wells looked quickly at Mary and away from her. "That's none of your damn business."

"Well, you got out of that one, as long as I don't ask it again. Maybe I will ask it again. Are you going to ask Nancy for a divorce?"

"I told you it was none of your God damn business."

"Well, how about if I ask you one that *is* my business. Did you ask Mary to marry you?"

"Yes."

"Oh, you did?"

"No, you didn't. We never discussed marriage," said Mary.

"Well, I ask you now."

"And what is your answer, Mary?" said Alfred.

"My answer is that I hate both of you, despise you."

"There goes your proposal, Parker. But at least now she can't say you weren't a gentleman. And that's what you are. Gentleman by act of Bogardus."

"Why don't you hit him?" said Mary to Wells.

"Because he isn't sure. Old Amos Bogardus never told him what to do in a case like this. Besides, they might bar him from '21' and then where would he go?"

"Will you please go? Will you please get out of here?" Mary said to Wells.

"Well, now you *know* what to do when *that* happens. The lady asked you to go, so as a gentleman you go. Goodnight." Alfred looked down at his food and cut a slice of beef. Wells got up and left.

"He wasn't your type, Mary."

She put back her head and laughed. "Ho! My type!"

"He wasn't. Oh, I admit I don't know what is, but not a cheap, low-grade son of a bitch like that. You can do much better."

"Yes, and I've done much worse."

"But you shouldn't. As a former friend of yours I want to see you do better."

The waiter captain stood at the table. "Mr. Wells is not coming back? Something wrong?"

"Nothing wrong, but Mr. Wells isn't coming back, thank you," said Alfred. The captain summoned the bus boy and Wells's place was cleared.

"You can take these things away, too. And just bring us some coffee. Two demi-tasse," said Alfred.

"Kind of a rough day all around," he said.

She was not listening to him. "Hm?"

"I said it was kind of a rough day all around, for both of us."

"I wonder if that woman really loves you. If I thought I could get away with it I'd poison you."

"What the hell for? You asked for this thing tonight, if that's what's eating you. You know who my girl is, and she never appears in your life. Just by accident I find out you've been sleeping with a cheap bastard that's kind of a comedy character around New York. I gave it to him good because I was sore at you. And you're sore at me because you saw him at his worst, and I really didn't have to do a damn thing to make him look bad."

"Let's go home. I want to talk to you. If I stay another minute I'll scream."

They got another wartime taxi, one that had to proceed in second gear or coast in neutral for a block at a time. "It's a disgrace, askin' people to ride in a heap like this here," said the driver. "But everything's priorities, and it's gonna be a long war, brother. You take it from me."

"For that you get a dollar tip," said Alfred. "No, here's five. Keep the change."

From the apartment he telephoned the Navy and made his whereabouts known to an orderly, and then had a conversation with Miss Canfield at her apartment. Mary put on a night-gown and bathrobe, and he changed to pajamas and bathrobe. "Would you like a drink?"

"No thanks," she said. "Let's get to the point."

"All right."

"This business today, downtown. If you're through with MacHardie & Company, then MacHardie & Company is no reason for not getting a divorce."

"It hasn't been for some time."

"I know, but one thing at a time. The only other reason is Jean, isn't that so?"

"Yes."

"If it's going to be such a long war, you're going to be away from home most of the time, aren't you?"

"It certainly looks that way."

"And Jean isn't going to be seeing much of you."

"I'm afraid not."

"I can see you're getting ready to interrupt me, but please don't."

"All right."

"Then she's going to grow up with me and not with you, anyway, so why can't we get a divorce? There's every reason to, and practically no reason not to."

"Are you finished?"

"Go ahead. Oh, before you do, one thing more. Jean is happy with me. Now go ahead."

"Of course she's happy with you. Now of course I'd like to be free to marry Natalie, and my first impulse is to jump at any chance to get a divorce. But whether I'm here every night to tuck Jean into bed or to see her off to school every morning—my physical presence, or absence, is one thing. Her knowledge that you and I were no longer married is something else again. The boys know that all is not well. Even Alex knows, and Rowland's known for several years. They don't say anything, but they know. I don't think Jean does know. My guess is that the way you and I behave in front of her is her idea of the way parents behave. Stiffly polite, rather impersonal. Certainly no demonstrations of affection. But if you told her that you and I were getting a divorce, that I was never coming home again, I'm afraid it would have a seriously bad effect on her sense of security. A young girl needs a father almost as much as she needs a mother. She needs both, and grandparents, too. And brothers and sisters. But if, for instance, you were to die, I'd quit the Navy job and come back to New York. I could do that if we weren't divorced. I could do it anyway, and would, but it wouldn't be as successful after a divorce."

"Are you planning to have me die at some early date?"

"I'm not planning to poison you."

"Touché."

"Yes. But I haven't finished, if you don't mind. As much as I'd like to have a divorce, for that one reason—Natalie—I don't want it now. With me out of the picture, how would Jean be brought up? You don't bring men here now, but how do I know you wouldn't if we were divorced?"

"You'd have only my word for that."

"Which you might mean at the time you gave it, but how long before you'd let one stay one night, then a couple of nights? The kind of guy I know about—Roper and this really cheesy Wells—would have no scruples about the effect on a young girl. And God knows what else you've been sleeping with if they were worse than Wells. Some of those bisexuals you met through Sage Rimmington, I suppose. How long before one of them, just for the fun of it, decided to corrupt Jean? What would you do if one of them did try to corrupt Jean?"

"I'd kill him."

"You'd kill him." He nodded. "And what would your defense be? That you killed a man because he had corrupted your nine- or ten-year-old daughter. *That's* getting her off to a good start in life. People would never have any trouble remembering her after that. No, ma'am. As long as I'm nominally your husband I can drop in here any hour of the day or night, announced or unannounced, expected or unexpected, and if things don't look right to me, I can do something about it."

"Feeling this way about me, I'm amazed that you let me see her at all."

"That shouldn't be hard to understand, if you'd just think back over what I've been saying. As long as I'm your husband, there are some restraints. That's aside from whatever love you may have for Jean. But one of these days you're going to meet a guy that'll put you in such a spin that you won't give a damn about Jean or yourself or anything else. And it'll probably be some no-good bastard that you won't be able to dominate. You're about due for one of those. You're forty-one."

"Men are important to me, but not one man."

"You're due. By the way, we never got around to why you suddenly want a divorce. You got somebody picked out for the next sleeping partner? You want to marry somebody?"

"Just what I was hoping you'd ask me. No. Obviously I've dropped Mr. Wells after tonight, but I have no one else picked out. That's why this seemed to be a good time to bring up divorce. When there is nobody else. No matter who I picked, you'd find some objection to him."

"It probably wouldn't be hard."

"It would be very easy, for you. No, my dear, today seemed like a good opportunity. You're through at MacHardie & Company, and I don't like this so-called marriage any more than you do. I might want to marry somebody else, somebody that you wouldn't think was half-bad, but a lot of men who like me keep their distance because of you. Either they like you, or they respect you, or they're afraid of you."

"Afraid of me? Why?"

"You and MacHardie & Company, and the United States Navy. Oh, hell, there aren't many men the right age who want to go through all the mess and incovenience of two divorces. And yet some of them would make perfectly good husbands for me, if I were free. There are men who know their wives are having affairs, but they don't want to disrupt their lives. But if they knew I was free, they might have one more go at marriage with me.

"Also, as you so graciously pointed out, I'm forty-one, and I can add. I'll be fifty when Jean is eighteen, and there are more widows than there are widowers. If we wait nine more God-awful years it's not going to be as easy to get a husband as it might be now, and I don't intend to live alone in my fifties and sixties and seventies. Not if I can help it."

"Well, why do you have affairs with people like Wells?"

"That was sex."

"Wells?"

"Oh, you Racquet Club snobs may not invite him to sit down, but he's very much in demand with some of your wives."

"That's obvious, in one case."

"You people will never learn. Men like Parker and Larry Von Elm soon find out that people like you and Lex Porter can't stand them. So they have no compunctions about going after your women."

"Yes, and what you women never learn is that we do know that about Wells and Von Elm. We know it instinctively, and that's why we don't like them in the first place. Parker Wells stands out like a spotted horse. He'd always do something wrong, say something wrong, wear something wrong. Tonight he did all three, and he married Nancy Bogardus after no one that knew her would. You don't wound me by calling me a snob. I've never denied it. As long as people like Parker Wells are not snobs, I want to be one."

"Oh, all right. Stop beating a dead horse. You've made up your mind to continue this ridiculous marriage."

"At least until Jean goes to boarding-school."

"Four more years, probably, at the earliest. All right, you've said your say. But it isn't necessarily the final word."

"If it isn't, it'll do."

"So you seem to think. But I've told you that I would like to have a divorce. I *offered* it to you. Easy. Quiet, No fuss. No mess. Just remember that."

"Got some deep dark plan, Mary?"

"I haven't, but you can be sure I'll work on one."

"Well, I suppose I'm being threatened, so I guess I'll have to threaten right back." He leaned forward and pointed a finger at her. "Don't try to get at me through Natalie, because if you do, if any mud lands on her, by the time I'm through with you *Sage Rimmington* won't speak to you."

"Drink Moxie."

"What?"

"Just an ad for a soft drink. That's all the effect you have on me. I don't like people pointing their fingers at me."

"You'll like it a hell of a sight less."

He retired to his room and the Navy folders, but he could not concentrate on them and he could not sleep. But he did become unconscious for minutes at a time, convinced only by the clock that he had slept.

He said goodbye to his daughter, who was at breakfast, and left the apartment without waiting for a cup of coffee. At Natalie's he let himself in with his key. She sat up in her bed, not thoroughly awake. "Don't wake up. I'm getting into bed with you," he said.

She lay back drowsily until he had his arms around her. They made sex for its own sake, with terms of endearment but no speeches of love. Their need was great and concurrent, their love was reassured and renewed, and they went to sleep in peace.

They were awakened by the air-raid warning test. "One o'clock?" he said.

"Yes. Do you want to sleep some more, or shall we have some breakfast?"

"I'm hungry."

"So am I. I've had almost fifteen hours' sleep. I didn't know I could sleep that long."

"You probably can't, without Dr. Eaton's Magic Formula."

"I needed Dr. Eaton's Magic Formula. You always seem to know how I want it. This morning I just wanted—well, the way it was. You came at me like a drunken miner, and I loved it."

"A drunken miner?"

"I told you. I've seen them. No preliminaries. Me, woman. You, man. You put thing in me, and *whee!*"

"You're in a very good mood this morning, Miss Benziger."

"Why not? What do you want for breakfast? How would you like some scrapple?"

"You really have some?"

"Yes. And it doesn't use up many points."

"Fine. And ketchup?"

"And ketchup. Would you like it crisp around the edges?"

"Crisp around the edges. Why don't I start the coffee while you go to the bathroom?"

"Don't you like my hair this way? It's the new slattern effect. Very popular with some of my regulars. Yes, you start the coffee. But I'd appreciate it if you'd put something on."

"I'm temporarily harmless."

"Nevertheless, please put something on. A pair of shorts, anyway."

"You're overdressed."

"Listen, you drunken miner. You didn't even give me a chance to take off my nightgown."

"Well, I rolled it up."

"No you *didn't. I* did."

He laughed. "As a matter of fact, you did."

After breakfast he read the newspaper until she finished with the dishes. "How did your talk go at the office?" she said.

"It went so well that except for my job with the government, I'm out of work." He put down the paper. "Things always happen to me in pairs and triples. I guess they do to everybody. One thing leads to another, or leads out of another. That's where we make a mistake in planning only one thing at a time. I should know better by this time, but I still go on planning one thing, and out of it comes something else besides. For instance, when I went to see your father, and met you Yesterday I'd concentrated my planning on what I was going to say to the luncheon group, and the only other thing I'd half planned was to have a casual but probing conversation with Hasbrouck. Well, I'll give you the whole story."

He did so, and as he finished she said: "As a practical, Pennsylvania Dutch girl, how is this going to affect you financially?"

"By the time the tax lawyers work it out, it may be to my advantage."

"Then you're not worried?"

"I wouldn't have to worry anyway, Natalie. I could stop work and it wouldn't have much effect on the way I live. I won't be giving Princeton any new dormitories, but I never intended to. I'm worth all told about $3,000,000. Somewhat less, but more than two. If the mill hadn't folded I'd be worth an awful lot more, especially now, but I certainly can't complain, and I'm not worried. But I'm very grateful for you."

"Why?"

"Because I'm sore and I'm disappointed. I had one ambition, as you know. I wanted to succeed Mr. MacHardie. That's the disappointment. I'm sore because I blew my top and I mishandled Percy Hasbrouck. Now I have another story for you. Two stories, really. About Mary."

He told, as separate stories, the events at "21" and the conversation at home. Natalie was the only person in the world to whom he was truthful beyond the point of self-preservation, and he did not leave out the exchange of threats between Mary and himself. It had taken fully a half hour for

him to tell the two stories, and she had been so silent throughout that she was accustomed to it, but he was not.

"Well?" he said.

"What?"

"Quite a glob of stuff to think about, isn't it?"

"Oh. Why haven't I said anything? Because I don't know
where to start. You shouldn't have reminded Mary of her age,
and I don't think it was a good idea to hammer away at what
a cheap person Mr. Wells is. A woman is more liable to resent
criticism of her lovers than of her husband."

"Oh, I don't believe that for a minute. I've heard women
defend men that I know they despised, but they happened to
be married to them."

"That's defending the home, the marriage. I said women
resent criticism of their lovers. I didn't say they defended their
lovers. I put up with a lot from Ben, but I always defended
him. If anybody had criticized you I might not have defended
you, but I'd have been seething inside. A woman's lover is a
much more personal choice than her husband. There are a lot
of reasons why a woman might marry a man, I mean reasons
that aren't as personal as her reasons for choosing a certain
man to be her lover. In some ways, and in some cases, a woman
can be more loyal to a lover than to a man she genuinely
loves."

"How do you feel about Sterling Calthorp?"

"I have nothing against him. I know that makes you angry,
and it does no good to tell you that I love you and I never
loved him, but whenever you ask me a question, I tell you the
truth. I had an affair with Sterling Calthorp, the affair came to
an end and maybe it never should have happened at all. Well,
of course it shouldn't, really. But it did. It'll never start up
again, but it did happen, and I don't really like it when you
turn your big guns on Sterling. I ended the affair. There's no
need for you to remind me of my mistake. But that isn't what
we were talking about. We got on the subject because I think
you made a mistake with Mary. It was bad psychology to
talk about her age and her cheap lover. You're going to have
trouble with Mary."

"I may have trouble with you, too, if you insist on defending
Sterling Calthorp."

"Yes, you may. If I'm to be made to feel guilty about
Sterling it won't be because of you, but because of Ben. Ben
was my husband, Ben was the man I was being unfaithful to.
I've given up everyone and everything for you, because I love
you, because you're the only man I ever loved and ever will
love. But be careful."

"Is that a warning?"

"Yes. Yes it is. I'm only four years younger than Mary,
788

and I could be facing the same future. I expect to marry you some day, and I live now as though I were married to you. I'm strictly *strictly* faithful to you, I arrange my life with you uppermost in my mind, I'm alone a good deal of the time because I don't want it any other way. But don't do things or say things that will make me unhappy and feel sorry for myself. Don't get me started brooding over some of the possibilities in my future."

"Such as."

"Well, such as the fact that I have nine years to wait, too, and all the things that can happen in nine years. I don't want to think about them enough to talk about them, so don't make me."

"Then you have been brooding?"

"Not exactly brooding, but I *have* thought how terribly much I've come to count on seeing you. Visiting Day. Yes, like Visiting Day at boarding-school, prison."

He got up and looked out the window. "Things don't happen in two's and three's any more. They happen in four's. I wonder what will be next." He turned and saw that she was looking at the wall opposite to her. "Would you just as soon I went back to Washington this afternoon?"

"I'd hate it."

"But I think I'd better. I'm not going to be very good company. Maybe I could go to Washington and do some work this afternoon and tonight, and come back tomorrow."

"I want to do what you want to do. I'm ashamed of myself. You came to me because you love me and know I love you, and I gave you no comfort. Don't go, Raymond. I'd rather have you sit here and read than have you leave me now. I won't bother you. I won't talk. But stay, will you please? I have a *lot* of books I know you haven't had time to read."

He smiled. "Of course I'll stay."

She got up and walked to the bookshelf and was reaching for some books when he put his arm about her shoulders. "Always come to me. That's the wonderful thing, that I know you're going to," she said, without looking at him.

"What have you got that will improve my disposition? 'How to Behave Like a Mature Human Being'?"

She started to answer him and the telephone rang. "Who on earth?" she said, and crossed the room to the desk. "Hello?"

"Mrs. Eustace? This is Mary Eaton. I would like you to give Alfred a message. Will you please tell him to come home immediately? It's urgent. Very urgent. If he's not there and you know where he is, will you get the message to him as soon as possible? Thank you." Mary then hung up.

Natalie turned and faced Alfred: "That was Mary. There's something wrong. I'll try to tell you exactly what she said:

789

'Mrs. Eustace, this is Mary Eaton. Please give Alfred this message. Ask him to come home immediately. Very urgent. If he isn't there but you know where to find him, pass the message on to him as soon as possible.' Then she thanked me and hung up. Darling, this *is* urgent. It wasn't snooping. It wasn't angry. Whatever it is, it's more important than her jealousy or anything else, and you've got to go immediately."

"I'll call her."

"No. Go. She doesn't want you to call her. I *know* that. Will you let me know as soon as you can? It's bad, and I'm worried."

"I'll let you know the minute I can." He put on his necktie and jacket and overcoat.

"You'd better take your brief case. You may not be coming back here." She kissed him. "I love you, darling, I wish I could go with you."

He got a taxi and was at the apartment in less than ten minutes. Mary was sitting alone in the library, smoking a cigarette and staring at the floor. She looked up when he came in but did not speak. Instead she picked up a telegram and handed it to him. It was addressed to Mary and read:

I DEEPLY REGRET TO INFORM YOU THAT YOUR SON ENSIGN ROW-LAND EATON USNR DIED HERE TODAY FROM INJURIES RECEIVED IN A TRAINING ACCIDENT. TELEGRAPH BUREAU OF MEDICINE AND SURGERY, NAVY DEPARTMENT, WASHINGTON, D. C., IMMEDIATELY WHETHER YOU DESIRE REMAINS INTERRED IN NAVAL OR NATIONAL CEMETERY OR SENT HOME. IF INTERRED BY NAVY ALL EXPENSES WILL BE PAID. IF SENT HOME EXPENSES OF PREPARATION, EN-CASEMENT, AND TRANSPORTATION WILL BE PREPAID AND REASON-ABLE NECESSARY FUNERAL EXPENSES NOT EXCEEDING $50 REIMBURSED ON APPLICATION TO BUREAU OF MEDICINE AND SURGERY, NAVY DEPARTMENT. ESCORT OF ONE PERSON WILL ACCOMPANY REMAINS HOME IF REQUESTED. SINCEREST SYMPA-THY EXTENDED. LETTER FOLLOWS.

(SIGNED) WALTER B. GANS, CAPTAIN, USN

"Good Christ! When did this come?"

"About fifteen minutes ago. Twenty minutes ago," said Mary. "It might have been twenty-five minutes ago. I didn't look at the clock. I was sitting here when Thomas brought it to me, and I telephoned Mrs. Eustace right away."

Alfred sat down. "It doesn't say much."

"Letter follows."

"Well, we won't wait for that. I'll call the Navy in Washington and get put through to Captain Gans at Jacksonville, or else get a message to him and have him call me here. Are you all right?"

"Oh, I'm all right," she said.

"Have you told anyone?"

"You. No one else."

"The servants don't know."

"No. If you're wondering about Jean, she's at a birthday party."

Thomas entered the library: "Long distance call for you, sir. Captain Gans of the Navy calling and wishes to speak to you personally. He says it's urgent and official, I believe he said."

"Thank you. I'll take it in here. That's all, Thomas." The butler left and Alfred said: "Do you want to listen in on the extension?"

She shook her head, and Alfred picked up the telephone. "Eaton speaking, go ahead with Captain Gans."

"Gans here, Mr. Secretary. Have you received our telegram?"

"Yes I have, Captain, but that's all. You confirm the telegram, I suppose."

"Yes sir, I'm very sorry to say I do. I have the preliminary reports of two eyewitnesses and the medical officer in charge. Shall I read you the reports verbatim or would you rather I gave you the gist of what happened?"

"Give me the gist of it now, Captain."

"Well, Ensign Eaton, Rowland, that is, took off at about 1100 hours this morning in an F3F, that's the Grumman biplane that he's been doing dive-bomber training in. He and some other trainees were dropping smoke bombs on a target marked out in a swamp, a safe distance from Jacksonville. It was a flight consisting of an instructor leading nine officer trainees. I have the instructor, Lieutenant Cooper, in my outer office right now and you can talk to him if you care to, but I'm afraid there isn't much to say. Rowland made two successful passes at the target, but then on the third he went into his dive and never pulled out of it. Death was instantaneous. It couldn't have been any other way, if you'll excuse the details."

"I want all the details I can get, Captain."

"Yes sir. Well, he crashed and the plane caught fire and Lieutenant Cooper radioed for the crash wagon and the ambulance, giving the exact position of the crash, but he wouldn't have had to because I sent my exec over to have a look from the air and he said you could see the smoke almost from here as soon as you gained a little altitude. About fifteen miles from here, I should imagine. It took a little time to get to the airplane because of the ground conditions there. Swamp, you know."

"What about my son?"

"He was burned beyond recognition, I regret to say. But positively identified. We made a special effort to recover the uh, body, the uh, remains and the natives did a very good job of that. The remains were brought back here, sir, but I'm afraid it will be impossible to, uh, for the undertaker to reconstruct the, uh, features. The medical officers can give you a full report of their findings, but of course in cases of this kind, where the man fails to pull out of a dive, they don't have too much to go on. In other words, we probably never will know exactly what was the cause of the crash, whether it was a blackout or engine failure or what. The airplane was okayed at oh-nine hundred this morning and Rowland was with it from that time on, so apparently he was satisfied with the way it was performing. I can also tell you that he was known as a very careful, conscientious officer and well liked by the ground crew. I'm sorry to say I didn't know him personally, although I knew he was your son, but he was very well liked here."

"He was very well liked here, too, Captain."

"Pardon?"

"Nothing."

"If there's anything we can do here, sir, you've only to say the word. We've tried to think of everything. I'll be able to send you full reports from the men in the flight, and the natives, the medical officers. Do you want the remains sent to New York? You can let me know when you decide and we'll do whatever you say."

"I'll let you know, and meanwhile I want to thank you and your officers and men for the great kindness and consideration you've shown both Mrs. Eaton and myself. I appreciate your extra efforts in our behalf and I'll write you a letter to that effect when I get back to Washington."

"Well, I have a son, Mr. Secretary, and I know how a father would feel at a time like this."

"Is your son in the Navy?"

"No sir, he's still in high school."

"I see. Well, thank you, Captain. If I think of anything I'll call you."

He replaced the phone and looked across the room at Mary.

"That's the way you sound as Assistant Secretary. I never heard you being Assistant Secretary before. You're very good at it. Did he have anything to say?"

"It was very tough on him, and he did it very well."

"Well, maybe you can promote him to commander or something."

"He's been a commander. In the Navy captain is higher than commander."

"Would you like to go back to Mrs. Eustace now?"

"Mary, Rowland was our son. Do you want to hear what the captain told me?"

"All right," she said.

792

She listened, but how much she was taking in he could not tell. She asked no questions, and at the end of his recital her expression did not change. Then he saw that where she was sitting placed her in a position facing a cabinet-size photograph of Rowland in the shirt, pants, and socks of the Harvard freshman crew. He had not noticed the relative positions of Mary's chair and the photograph, and he wondered if she had taken her position deliberately.

Instinct, and Mary's impassivity, warned him against any show of tenderness or pity, although pity for her was what he felt now more than the sorrow that he knew was gestating in himself. "We might as well let Thomas know. The telephone's going to start ringing any minute, and it'll be ringing the rest of the day. If you have any calls, make them on my phone in my room. When people call do you want to speak to anybody?"

"Of course I do. If they're nice enough to call."

"Right. What about Jean?"

"Let her enjoy her party as long as she can."

"You don't think we ought to call the people where she is and let them know?"

"No. She was crazy about Rowland, and I want to put off her knowing as long as I can."

"Do you want me to go and bring her home when the party's over?"

"And tell her about her brother?"

"Yes."

"If you did you'd be sorry."

"Why?"

"You'd have a hysterical child on your hands. She doesn't know you."

"Jean doesn't know me?"

"She knows Thomas much better than she knows you. You're going to find that out. You've never fed her or been with her when she was sick or any of those things."

"If that's the case I know why. It's no accident."

"You've been so busy, Alfred."

"So have you, I'm beginning to realize. Have you worked on Alex, too, or is it all right if I call him?"

"Call him, but he'll want to speak to me."

"You've done quite a job."

"I had to. Some day you were going to threaten me with taking the children away from me, but you never did anything about *them*. You didn't make them want to come to you, rely on you. If you ever took them away from me, they'd run away from you, back to me. I just loved it last night when you prattled on about a daughter needing a father and grandfather and the rest of it. What a child needs is what a child

793

has gotten used to, and they never got used to you. Your home isn't here. Your home is in bed with Mrs. Eustace. I guess the difference between you and me, Alfred, is that I always came back here and made a home for the children, and you've always been impatient to get away. Whatever I've done, the children thought of me as the home, not you. They knew your thoughts were some place else."

"They've been made to think that."

"A little. But I didn't have any trouble. You cooperated."

"There's another difference between you and me. I'd never rub your nose in it at a time like this. I came home knowing only that you were in some kind of trouble. That's *all* I knew. That's all you told Mrs. Eustace. I came here because *you* were in trouble. Some day think of the kinds of trouble you could have been in. But I came, didn't I? *I* was in a little trouble yesterday, but you didn't give a damn. Not even a polite damn. Yesterday I lost out on something I'd been working toward for nearly twenty years. Today I've lost my son, and you take the occasion to tell me I've also lost my younger son and my daughter. Thanks, Mary. But some day you'll need me. There'll be something that I, and no one else, can do for you. I don't know what it'll be, but I hope you forget this day and ask me, and when you do, *I'll* remember this day. I'll remember my pity for you, and my wanting to help you—and your evil joy in what you've been doing to me.

"Telephone your father," he said.

THE PUBLIC RELATIONS OFFICER at Lee Field released the news of the death of Ensign Eaton at 1600 hours, and twenty minutes later the President of the United States was speaking to Mary Eaton. He knew what to say, he knew when to stop, but the effect of that voice and the easy precision of the enunciation, which she had previously heard only on the radio, was more shattering than the news itself. She had never seen Roosevelt, she had heard few good words for him, she had never questioned the unfavorable opinions of him; but as he spoke to her, saying the plain but rightly chosen words of sympathy from "myself and my wife," it was as though the words were coming not through the telephone but out of the air about her and from God, like some divine, mysterious message in a Biblical legend. Her own training in manners enabled her to make the proper responses and at the end to say "Thank you, Mr. President." But then she went to her room and darkened it and wept, afraid of death, of sin, of

God, of her solitude, of love, and of the faces of her son that looked down at her; changing, unsmiling faces in flying helmet; in the brown hat with the tan edging to the brim; bareheaded with the crew cut. The new fear of the changing faces was caused not by any disapproval in his expression but by the renewal of anguish that came with every newly remembered face. The boy did not smile, the boy did not frown, the dignity that he had always shown was there but now genuine and softened and still. She stared into the total darkness and waited for him to speak, to move his lips in speech or in a smile, or for a brightness to come into his eyes. But then she remembered: he was dead. He was not in torment; he was dead. He was not seeing her; he was dead. She was not seeing him; she was seeing what he had been, now purified of the virus of life, never again to breathe, to speak, to eat, to stir a woman, to laugh or to suffer. Not even to hope or to fear. He was dead and there never would be any answer from him, and she respected this dead man who had so completely made her understand for the first time that living was febrile and insatiable and that all death and all deaths brought peace onward from the end.

And now there was peace for her, for in the darkened room she had been given confirmation of her disbelief in love, which more than ever she saw as an impossible state of self-deception, of easy and stupid self-deception. Whom could she not live without? She could not live without food and drink, she demanded the soft scratching of her sensuality, but someone would provide these, and if not someone, then someone else. And if no one, then death.

She got up and raised the window-shades, but it was already dark outside and she turned on a light and lowered the shades and closed the draperies and took off her dress and washed her face and put on her make-up and dressed again and went out to the library. Her father was there, coughing up a deep deposit of phlegm and Jean was watching the near-paroxysm with frowning fascination. Alfred was on the telephone, nodding to some long-winded caller.

"Oh, my," said St. John, with tears in his eyes from his effort. "Terribly sorry." He patted his chest and immediately commenced another siege.

"Didn't you *get* it, Grandfather?" said the child.

"Kleenex, please," said St. John.

"In the lavatory, there's a whole box. Get it for Grandfather, and then I think it's time for your supper," said Mary.

"Oh, can't I stay up?"

"You may stay up till nine, but I want you to go in and have your supper."

"Kleenex," said St. John.

"Hurry, now. Don't stand there when I tell you to do something."

"I'm sor-ry," said the child.

Alfred hung up the telephone. "That was my dear, embarrassed friend Billy Kingsley. Love and sympathy to you. The telegrams have started. Apparently it was on the radio. We're going to have to get somebody from the office. It's Saturday and they're closed but since old Billy offered to do anything at all, I took him at his word and he'll have somebody here from the stenographer pool tomorrow. I haven't opened any of the telegrams, but I suppose I'd better. They may not all be about Rowland. Some are for you, some are for me, most of them are addressed to both of us."

"I suppose I should make a list of them."

"Just save them and give them to the girl tomorrrow."

St. John emptied his mouth in the Kleenex and said, "It *was* on the radio. I heard it on the five o'clock news. But think of Mr. Roosevelt calling you himself. Whatever you may think of him, he is a warmhearted sort. I went to that wedding, you know."

"You did? I never knew you knew him," said Mary.

"Oh, I don't mean his wedding. I meant the son that married one of the du Pont girls."

"Excuse me," said Mary. "I want to see if that kid is eating her supper."

St. John addressed Alfred: "Proud of that girl, Alfred."

"You have every right to be."

"Was that the only time she broke up? When F. D. R. called?"

"The only time."

"It did her good. It was coming. She was too tense. A storm was brewing, and good heavens, when the President of the United States calls up. What are the plans?"

"The funeral plans?"

"Yes."

"They're going to take him to Port Johnson and the funeral will be there."

"You have the family plot there, haven't you, I seem to recall?"

"Yes. My father and my Grandfather and Grandmother Eaton, my brother, all buried there."

"Oh, and that's where you and Mary will be."

"I expect so."

"I want to be cremated."

"All right."

"What?"

"I said all right."

"Well, not today, though." The old man chuckled. "You

sounded as if I'd asked you to get me a drink of water or something."

"I'm sorry, Mr. St. John. I must have been goofing off."

"Well, you have a thousand-and-one things on your mind. When are the ceremonies taking place?"

"Tuesday at noon."

"A military service, I suppose."

"No. Very definitely not."

"But the boy died in the service of his country."

"He did, but he wouldn't look at it that way. It's going to be family only. All his friends are scattered all over the globe. Navy. Army. Marine Corps. You say you heard it on the five o'clock news?"

"Yes. I think you were taking a call on the phone in your room."

"Yes. If you'll excuse me, I have to make another call. Tell Mary I'm calling Sadie Warren."

"Sadie Warren. Does Mary know who that is?"

"She'll know."

Alfred went to his bedroom and put in the call to Sadie. "Sadie? This is Alfred Eaton."

"I know. I heard. I didn't know whether to call you or to wait, then I thought it was better to wait."

"Did you hear it on the radio?"

"Mother did. I was out skating. She told me when I got home. I called the radio station and they were very nice. They read it to me, so I was sure. I do send you and Mrs. Eaton my love and sympathy. And Alex and Jean."

"Sadie?"

"Yes?"

"You're a wonderful girl."

"Please don't say that, Mr. Eaton."

"I'm glad I know you, and I'm glad Rowland knew you."

"I know how you feel, and I've been thinking about you."

"I wanted to tell you, the funeral is Tuesday noon in Port Johnson, Pennsylvania. That's my home town. It will be private, but I consider you probably closer to Rowland than any of us, so if you want to come, I'll tell you how to get there."

"Thank you, but not now. Later, I want to go there and see the place. But I don't want to go to the funeral."

"I understand. But I'll write you next week, all the information I have or will have then. And I'll tell you how to get to Port Johnson. My mother lives there, and I have a younger sister I think you'd like. Not really young, but she's a good person and you two would like each other. Is there anything you'd like me to do?"

"There is one thing."

"Anything at all."

"Will they send you his things?"

"Yes. They're probably on the way now. Should get here by Monday."

"Could I have his wings? I promise I won't wear them. But I'd like to have them, unless Mrs. Eaton wants them."

"I'll send them to you special-delivery Monday."

"There's something else I'd like you to do. Will you burn my letters?"

"Of course."

"I've already burned his. To anyone else our letters might seem dirty, but they weren't to us. They were just what we felt."

"They'll have your return address on the envelope, won't they?"

"My name and address."

"I'll burn them, all letters from you. Unread. And don't let's lose touch with each other, Sadie. I wish you'd write to me if you ever feel like it. The Wardman Park Hotel, Washington, D. C."

"Thank you. I was going to ask you if I could. Goodbye, Mr. Eaton."

"Goodbye, Sadie."

He sat beside the telephone, wondering now what she would do, what exactly she would do in the next sixty seconds, tonight, tomorrow, next week on Tuesday morning, next summer. She would help her mother with supper (did they really eat baked beans every Saturday night?). She would try to read until a suitable hour before retiring. She would go to bed, and she would not sleep, and perhaps then she would weep and later her mother would come in and sit with her, because he had the impression that there was a closeness between her and her mother. Tomorrow she would go to church, perhaps go skating, and when it began to grow dark she would go home and her mother would have the things Sadie liked for tea. But then, *then,* it would hit her. The lovely dark evening of a New England town and the strong feeling of homes to be lived in that familiarity had not dulled for her. She was a Yankee girl who was going to reconvert his son to the Yankee ways that he, Alfred Eaton, alone of his line had been ignorant of, deprived of by his own father.

He began to be afraid of the surprise moment when *he* would crack, as Mary had cracked after the conversation with the President. Roosevelt had spoken to him, too, in another, later call, thus graciously keeping the calls separate and that much more meaningful. But Roosevelt's call to Alfred was complimentary but less perturbing than it had been to Mary; he had met and talked with the President perhaps a dozen times, and he looked upon Roosevelt as neither an ogre nor a disembodied voice. Roosevelt's gift in that respect was that he was able, when he so chose, to talk easily with almost any man, while unable to establish such rapport with most women. Consequently, Alfred had been comforted by Roosevelt's call, where Mary had been bewildered. Alfred had seen Mary crack, he had imagined the moment of Sadie's cracking, but he could not fortify himself against his own attack of inner horror and grief. The elements were there, and he knew it, but he became so vigilant against the attack that he created an impression of a cold calm that he did not feel.

He hired two limousines to make the trip to Port Johnson with Mary, Alex, Jean, and Eugene St. John in one car and himself, Alex Thornton (representing the Porter and Thornton families) and Thomas in the other. They set out early Tuesday morning and arrived at the farm before eleven o'clock. The casket had been sent to the church, where it awaited the funeral party. Sally had seen to everything, following Alfred's telephoned instructions, but she could not have anticipated the confusion caused by Martha Eaton, who was now seventy-one years old, normally confined to the house, but determined to assign the mourners to the various automobiles and pews.

"Mary and Alfred will go in the first car, and so will Mr. St. John and I. The surviving grandparents. That's the way it should be in church, too. Alex and Jean and Sally and Mr. Thornton in the second car and the second pew, and Sally's children and the servants in the next car and the third pew. It's lucky we're such a small family. I've asked absolutely no one else to come to the church, but there'll be some nosy-parkers there, you can be sure of that."

"Mother, there's a young officer that came from Jacksonville, escorting the body. I want him to be with us," said Alfred.

"Do you know him? If not, he can sit on the other side of the aisle. We can't make any exceptions."

"I didn't know him, but Rowland did. They picked a man who was a friend of Rowland's."

"I have friends here in Port Johnson where I've lived for seventy-one years, but I've told them they couldn't come. Why should a total stranger—"

"He isn't a total stranger, Mother," said Alfred. At the church he introduced himself to the young man, an Ensign Longfellow, from Boston, a member of Rowland's Harvard class as well as his fighter trainee group. Longfellow was unhappy, uncomfortable, ill at ease, and almost pleaded with Alfred to be excused from returning to the farm for the post-funeral luncheon. Alfred excused him, and Martha had had her way.

The numerous curious sat in the rear of the church, separated from the funeral party by rows of vacant pews, but as the mourners left the church Martha, holding St. John's arm, glared at the uninvited and made those whose eyes she met turn their faces away. At the cemetery she saw a firing squad of American Legionnaires in highly polished tin helmets and blue uniforms under civilian overcoats. She left St. John and walked over to the nearest Legionnaire.

"You're not going to shoot those guns off, are you?"

"That's what we're here for, Mrs. Eaton. We're the honor guard, from the Legion."

"I don't want any shooting, and I won't have it. What's your name?"

"Theodore Rothermel."

"Oh, yes. You're from Eckburg, not even from Port Johnson. Well, there's to be no shooting."

Rothermel looked inquiringly to Alfred, who shook his head, and there was no volley over the grave. The clergyman, a stranger to Alfred, spoke his holy words into the cold breeze and gulped the December air so that he seemed to be speaking from a great distance and saying things that did not reach or even belong to the ceremony. At the lowering of the casket it happened, the surprise attack that Alfred had been dreading. With no more than a second's warning, he vomited. He clapped his hand to his mouth and walked hurriedly away and emptied his mouth and waited. He put his hand, blindly through tearful eyes, on the nearest monument to steady himself against the dizziness and when his eyes cleared he realized that he had unintentionally desecrated his father's grave.

Longfellow came to his side. "Can I help you, sir?"

"Thanks, I think I'll be all right," whispered Alfred.

"Mummy, Father's sick," said Jean. "He threw up."

The clergyman signified by a bow to Mary and Martha that the ceremony was at an end and Mary went and stood silently beside Alfred. The clergyman joined them and with practiced but genuine concern led Alfred to an iron chair. "Thank you, I'll be all right," said Alfred.

"Stay where you are till you feel better," said Martha. "The rest of you get in your cars."

Alfred could not keep from looking at the others, all of them singly, and receiving their stares at him. Only Alex Thornton did not look at him; the others by their stares exposed their reactions to his weakness; curiosity and some pity on the part of the Legionnaires; fascination and some fear on the part of Jean; worry, by Sally and St. John; and in the eyes of Mary and Alex nothing but disgust. He marked that. Mary had indeed taken Alex away from him.

"I'll stay here with you, Ma," said Alex.

"No, you go with Jean."

"We're all going the way we came," said Alfred. "I'll sit in the front seat and get some air. We can put the window up between the front and the back." His manner was commanding, and Martha did not protest. It was her first defeat of the day.

Alfred sat beside the driver. He took off his hat and let the cold air revive him. At the farm he gargled with a mouth wash. The dizziness had not all left him, but he rejoined the others. Luncheon, with cocktails for the grownups, took slightly more than an hour, and then Martha had her second defeat of the day. The New York party, with the exception of Alfred, went back to New York. "I don't want the children to miss any more school," said Mary. "We'll try to get over at Christmastime. Only about another week."

"Well, I didn't get much chance to see anybody. What are *you* going to do?" Martha asked Alfred.

"A Navy car is coming out from Philadelphia and then I'm going on to Washington, by train. I've been away five days."

The others departed and Alfred was alone with his mother.

"Your father did exactly the same thing when William died."

"Oh, come on, Mother. He didn't."

"I didn't say he did it at the cemetery. But he did here, in the house. On that rug over by the window. I didn't have the rug there then, but that's the rug."

"Ay, there's the rug."

"What?"

"Shakespeare, Mother. 'To sleep, perchance to dream, ay, there's the rug.'"

"You pick an odd time to make jokes."

"I pick an odd time to do a lot of things."

"What's the matter with you? You look awful, not because you were sick. You did anyway. And don't tell me it's working too hard."

"I've never said that in my life. I like to work."

"Oh, where have I heard *those* words before? What's the trouble between you and Mary? Has she got somebody, or have you? Or both?"

"We haven't got each other, you must know that."

"Anybody could tell that."

"I begin to see certain similarities between my father and me."

She laughed. "Oh, my. When did you catch on to that?"

"I haven't caught on to it yet, but I see certain similarities in our lives."

"In your lives? In yourselves, you mean. It isn't in your lives that it counts, it's in your two selves. The older you get the more like him you are."

"Rubbish, Mother, rubbish."

"Rubbish, is it? Lives don't make lives, it's people that make lives. Don't talk about lives, talk about people. You're like your father more and more every day."

"You don't see me every day, and when you do see me you look for similarities between my father and me. You ignore the differences."

"There aren't any differences that matter. I tried to warn you years ago."

"Oh, was that a warning? You mean that stuff about my being cruel to women?"

She seemed to be ignoring him. "When you were a boy I was always afraid that some day your father would try to take you and the girls away from me."

"Really? Now this is fascinating."

"Oh, I don't want your sarcasm."

"But it is fascinating."

"I was going to tell you something, but Lord deliver me from your sarcasm. We can't have a sensible conversation without you getting sarcastic."

"The one time I wasn't sarcastic I get accused of it anyway. How can I win?"

"You're treating Mary the way your father treated me."

"What makes you so sure of that?"

"Your father had his whores. I guess you have, too."

"No."

"We never saw William. They just put him in the coffin and we never saw him."

He waited. He was not sure, but he thought he could understand her mind's working. For a few minutes she would be brilliantly in the present, penetrating, observant, instinctively aware. Then her mind would tire, and she would almost visibly slide back into the past, finding things in the past that were closely identical with things of the forgotten present. He remembered that William *had* been put in a sealed coffin as prescribed by law for victims of spinal meningitis.

"That wasn't William today, Mother," he said, gently.

"I know. They said it was, but it wasn't. They took William to the university. *I* know. They do that for the medical students. When they hang people, too. The medical students operate on them. If they'd asked me I would have given them permission, but they never ask. They do it without telling you." This, apparently, was a conversation she had had with his father in 1908.

"Mother?"

"Yes, dear."

"Are you tired?"

"Yes."

"Let me take you upstairs and you can lie down for a while."

"I don't want you to take me upstairs," she said.

There was a slight emphasis on her pronunciation of the word *you,* and in an instant he realized that in the rapid changes that were going on in her mind he had lost his identity; she did not know who he was. This was confirmed by her next speech: "Tell *Miss Trimingham* to help me upstairs."

"Of course. Just you sit there and I'll get her for you."

He stepped out into the hall and called out, "Miss Trimingham?"

Trimingham appeared from the diningroom side of the house. "Mother wants you to help her upstairs," he said, carefully, distinctly. Then, quickly in a whisper: "She doesn't know who I am."

Trimingham nodded.

"Up we go," she said to Martha. "Time for our nap."

Martha rose and walked past Alfred without appearing to notice him. Trimingham came downstairs in about fifteen minutes. "She didn't know you? She does that oftener nowadays," said the nurse. "It used to be she'd go off on a tangent. That often used to happen. But this past year or so she just doesn't know who you are, or anybody, whether they're there or not. Last night she had to be up early and ready to go to William's funeral. *William's.* And she has you mixed up with your father sometimes. But other times she's as smart as a whip, doesn't miss a trick. Still and all, she's healthy, considering."

"Considering what, Miss Trimingham?"

"That when I first came here she wasn't given long to live."

"And wouldn't have, without you to take care of her."

"Thank you. But not all the credit goes to me. A lot of them want to live for some *reas*on. You don't always find out what the reason is, but they have one. I had one with cancer that the doctors gave her six weeks. Six months she hung on, because she wanted to see her first grandchild. That's not the case here, but I wouldn't be surprised to see her reach eighty. That is, if she has to wait that long."

"For whatever she's waiting for?"

"Yes. For whatever she's waiting for. Maybe *she's* waiting for a *great*-grandchild."

"She could have had one in another year. My son was engaged to be married."

"Tragic. But then the next boy, Mr. Alex. If he married

803

young. But I don't have any reason to say it's a great-grandchild she's waiting for. It could be something entirely different."

"Still, it would be a nice thing to keep alive for."

"Yes. Yes it would. But do you mind if I say something? As a nurse?"

"Go right ahead."

"At the cemetery. You vomited blood. Do you know that?"

"No, did I?"

"You did. In my opinion you ought to tell your doctor when you get home. Didn't you ever vomit blood before?"

"I haven't vomited at all since I don't know when."

"Then it's only the beginning. I mean, you're in the early stages of a peptic ulcer. At least that's probably what it is. That's for your doctor to say, but that's what I'd say it is."

"I'll make an appointment when I'm in New York again."

"Don't they have doctors in Washington?"

He laughed.

"Laugh," she said. "But you'd like to see your great-grandchildren, wouldn't you? You won't if you neglect a peptic ulcer. I could tell you other things that would frighten you, but you're an educated man. You don't have to be frightened into taking care of yourself, do you?"

"No, not really. I'll have some X-rays taken in Washington. We have a very good hospital down there."

"You have more than one, but they can't do you any good if you don't go to them. I'm speaking as a nurse, of course."

"You're speaking as a good human being. Thank you."

In the evening, when he got to the hotel, Natalie was there, completely to his surprise. She was sitting on the sofa, reading a magazine. He put down his Gladstone and attaché case and laid his overcoat and hat on top of them. "I wouldn't even let myself pray that you'd be here," he said. "On the way from Philadelphia I just said, 'I wish Natalie could be there when I get there.' And here you are." They held each other close, loving but without passion.

"I've wanted to be with you since Saturday," she said.

"I know. I could feel that."

"But this was one time you had to be with Mary."

"Mary and I are through," he said.

"That's an odd thing to say."

"No. There's always been the possibility that you'd get discouraged. Fed up. And who could blame you? If that had happened, it was conceivable that she and I might have said, 'Well, we're not young any more. We might as well try to make the best of a bad bargain.' It was conceivable. But now it isn't. From now on it's going to be hard to be even polite to her. She's done a job on the younger children, Alex especially, and now for the first time in my life I have no home. I've been trying all the way from Philadelphia to find the right words for it, and now out they come. I have no home."

She smiled. "I know how it is."

"Yes," he said. "That's true, isn't it? You haven't had a home, and that never occurred to me. It never occurred to me till tonight that I *had* one. *Had* had one. And bad as it was, I had. That's a hell of a thing, to discover what you've had only by discovering that you haven't got it any more. I wonder what other things I have that I don't know about. It isn't just a matter of taking something for granted. When you take something for granted that usually means you know it's there but kind of neglect it. But I'd never before thought about my home as a home. I was brought up not to say home when I meant house. Westerners always say home when they mean house. Maybe it isn't only Westerners. It's probably in the same category as saying lady for woman."

"Well, now you can begin to think of Fifty-fifth Street as your home. But don't deceive yourself. You're still going to think of where Mary and the children are as your home, the home you lost. You and I are just going to have our own home together, in ourselves."

"Yes. But it's become very important to me now to have a home, a real establishment, with you. I mean marriage. I'm ready to do an about-face as far as a divorce is concerned."

"Oh, let's go slowly now," she said.

"No. Have I told you the nickname they gave me down here?"

"Nickname?"

"Speedy. I'm called Speedy. I'm trying to win the war too fast, all by myself."

"The war hasn't been going on as long as this marriage. Maybe you'll win the war before you—well, I'd hardly say *win* this marriage."

"Win which marriage?" he asked. "The one to Mary, or the one to you, that I want."

"I'm very pleased that you've said these things to me. I needed them. But now that you've said them, let's for God's sake make haste slowly. I'm satisfied now. I really am. I feel now that we will get married, that I will be your wife and that you'll be my husband. This is what I've wanted more than anything else in life, to be married to you, and I'm a firm believer in that theory that you almost always get what you want most. But getting this close to it, so that I can almost see it, touch it, I'd be willing to give it up if it's going to cost too much."

"It won't cost any more than it has."

"Maybe not, but I'd be willing to give up what we've paid,

805

and take something else. I'd rather go on this way than—oh, I'm afraid."

"You're superstitious, that's all."

"Yes, probably. But whether it's superstitious or not, or whatever it is, I'm afraid."

"Come out and say what you're thinking."

"All right. I'm worried about you. Will you do me a favor? Will you go see a doctor?"

"Why?"

"For two reasons. First, because you ought to, after the strain you've been through lately, just the past week or so. The other reason, you haven't been looking well. And when you told me a minute ago that they nicknamed you Speedy, that obviously means that you've been working too hard."

"What else?"

"Last Saturday. When you can't be relaxed with me, what relaxation do you get? On Saturday we got into a quarrel that wasn't over anything new. Sterling Calthorp. I'm not passing the blame for that quarrel on to you, but I'm not taking it all myself. It isn't a matter of blaming anyone. It's just that you aren't able to relax with me, and you always used to. Do you know what it could be?"

"What?"

"It could be something very small. Like a tooth, or an ingrown toenail. Something like that. Open your mouth. Let me see your teeth."

He opened his mouth and she examined his teeth. "I don't see anything, but the dentist might."

"I have teeth like my father's. I hardly ever get a cavity."

"But you may have some abscess that you don't know about."

"Would you like to have a look at my toenails?"

"I will in a few minutes. You're not getting a hemorrhoid?"

"No."

"But you see what I mean by this unromantic questioning? You ought to have a complete checkup and I'll bet they'd find some little thing that you don't know about. Ordinarily it wouldn't bother you and doesn't now, but you've been pushing yourself and when a man or a woman gets overtired, the small thing gets bigger."

"When I'm overtired my small thing doesn't get bigger."

"I *knew* you were going to say that, as soon as I said it, I thought 'What an opening!'"

"How is your opening, dear?"

"Oh, all right. But now promise me you'll have a checkup."

"All right."

"No, not all right. I want you to promise."

"All right. I promise."

"When?"

"Well, I'll make an appointment to see Doc Tinkham."

"He's your New York doctor. Couldn't you see someone down here?"

"I could, but Don has my complete record for the past fifteen years. It'd be much easier all around if I saw him."

"Well, just so you see him, and don't put it off."

"Speaking of putting things off, do you have to go back to New York tomorrow?"

"Yes. In the morning. I want to get back before noon. We've never been so busy. It's really awful. We can sell anything. Everybody has money, and they'll pay the most ungodly prices for things they wouldn't look at twice in normal times. We're already twice as big as last Christmas. You know a lot of women who used to go abroad every year, now they can't, and there aren't many places they want to go to in this country, so they've had that money accumulating, and they *have* to spend it some way. Every single day a customer will try to bribe me to hold out something nice and expensive for her. Of course nothing's coming from Paris, and that's a good thing in a way. They're finding out that there are a few American designers. But the designers have found it out, too, and all the little fairies have begun to demand prices that Molyneux wouldn't have asked five years ago. You ought to see them."

"I suppose I ought to," he said, pretending to be serious. "As a well-rounded man, I suppose I ought to. Do you recommend any particular one?"

"What?"

"Of course I'm not particularly well-rounded where they'd like me to be."

"Oh, you. I thought you were suddenly getting interested in the shop. As a matter of fact, you're not so clever. They don't seem to go for the well-rounded man. All those that I know like men about your build. A little *younger*, of course. But the fat ones are the fairies, and they don't like other fat ones."

"Something I've often wondered about. Don't they ever make passes at you? They're supposed to have a more acute sense of beauty than the rest of us, and God knows you're beautiful. And they must see a lot of models without any clothes on. I should think that might stir them up a little."

"I'll tell you about that. I know a little pansy named Chuck Slawter, a hat designer, and he's so pretty that you can't believe it. Well, a model named Tee, she doesn't work for us and I only know her as Tee, but anyway she's pretty queer herself, but she decided she wanted to have an affair with Chuck. So she got him tight one night and got him into bed with her and made him screw her. He actually did, the regular thing. But then when it was over he was completely sober, completely, and he ran out of the bedroom and she went in after him and he was sitting there. When she started to walk over to where he was sitting he screamed at her, 'Don't come near me. Please don't come near me.' And then after a while he said to her, 'You must never do that again, Tee. If I'd stayed in that room I would have killed you. You're not even safe now. But never do that again.' She's a terrible girl anyway, and it would have served her right, or at least I couldn't have found him guilty if he'd murdered her. Oh, they walk in and out of the models' room and some of the girls are sitting with nothing on but panty-girdles and never bother to cover up their fronts. Just go on smoking, talking. One time I did walk in on a model making a pass at another model, but some of those high-fashion models are so undernourished that they're unbalanced. They really don't know what they're doing. They burst into tears over nothing at all. You always have to tell them everything twice. And they get lost. I know one that got lost going from Fifty-second and Madison to Fifty-seventh between Madison and Park. If she has a date with a photographer she has to have the address printed on a piece of paper and takes a taxi. They never eat."

"What happens to them?"

"They die. If they keep at it long enough and don't marry and start eating, they get tuberculosis and die. Some of the lucky ones start fainting on jobs after living on nothing but coffee or tea without sugar or cream, and they go back to Indiana and get some food. But nobody can go on for long, living the way some of those girls do."

"I always thought you'd be a good model."

"Me? I'm too fat. I have a thirty-seven bust and thirty-nine hips. I could model some things, but not high-fashion originals. I eat more for breakfast than most of those girls eat all day."

"By the way, Fatso, have you had your dinner?"

"No, and I've been wondering when you'd finally take the hint."

"We'll see if they haven't got a leaf of lettuce and some Melba toast for you. Hot water with lemon, dear heart?"

"Don't you like me this way?"

"I like you, but I've just begun to realize that there's quite a lot of you. Thirty-nine hips, eh? Thirty-seven bust?"

"You've never known me when my bust wasn't nearly thirty-seven."

"I haven't? What about the hips?"

"Thirty-seven when I first met you. I added two inches sitting and waiting for you, Mr. Smarty."

"Do you know that I love you, even with your big fat ass?"

"Then will you please send down for that leaf of lettuce

and tell them to put some prime ribs of beef on top of it? If you're going to make cracks about my figure, I have to have the strength to endure them. What are you going to have to sustain you?"

"I'm not hungry."

"You pig. You ate on the train?"

"No, but I'm not hungry. I'll have a chicken sandwich. Glass of milk."

"Are you going to pose for those new uniforms? I don't think much of the color, by the way. Filling-station grey, isn't it?"

"There's a reason for that color, but it's a military secret. If you insist on knowing, all right. It's to match a certain admiral's eyes."

"Well, probably better than taking the color of *your* eyes at this moment."

"What *is* the color of my eyes, dear?"

"At this moment, an interesting mixture of yellow where they should be white, and underneath, circles of black with grey pouches."

"We're back on health again."

"No. You've promised, so I'm not going to pursue the subject."

"Good. Would you like to know what my job entails?"

"I've often wondered."

"Sit still, and I'll see if I can find the paper that has my duties all written down."

"Order dinner for Fatso first, will you please?"

"All right." He telephoned the order, carefully enunciating his name and room number to the steward so that the roast beef would be forthcoming, and then probed in his desk until he found the papers he wanted. "Here we are," he said.

He took an easy chair and prepared to read from several documents. "I never bothered to learn this by heart, although I suppose I should have. It's a memorandum from the office of the Secretary of the Navy, dated August twenty-third, 1940, and the subject is the allocation of duties and responsibilities of the Secretary, Under Secretary, and Assistant Secretary. I know my part of it, though, and that's what you're interested in. I am responsible for the Shore Establishments Division, Civil Employees, Labor Liaison, Shore Station Development Board, Army and Navy Munitions Board, and the Chief Clerk's Office. The Assistant Secretary used to be responsible for Commissioned and Enlisted Personnel, but this year they changed that. They took it away from my job and gave it to the Secretary, probably on the theory that he had nothing to do, don't you suppose?

"Would you like to know my salary? I get $9,000 a year.

Don't ask me how they arrive at those salaries, any of them. The Secretary gets fifteen thousand. The Undersecretary gets a thousand more than I do. I figured it out one day that the reason the salaries are so low is that some devious character said to himself, 'If we offer a $100,000-a-year man $15,000, he'll either finish up the work and get out quick, or he'll turn crooked and we'll throw him into the clink. Either way, he won't hang around here lousing up things for us professionals."

"I want to know why you suddenly felt you had to tell me about your work?"

"Simple. I wanted to show you that whether I'm conscientious or not, there's plenty to be done. The job is a busy one. And I can be asked to do things that aren't on my list of duties. For instance, it says here, 'The Assistant Secretary of the Navy shall perform such duties as may be prescribed by the Secretary of the Navy or required by law.' Then it says, 'The Assistant Secretary of the Navy for Air shall be charged with the supervision of naval aeronautics and the coordination of its activities with other governmental agencies and, in addition, such other duties as may be assigned to him by the Secretary of the Navy.' Well, it wasn't really my job to go to California on that E-1-FX mishmash. That's normally part of the Assistant Secretary for Air's job. But I was sent because I knew Von Elm.

"Let's see what else you might like to know. I am assigned a black Buick sedan, 1941 model, and I also rate use of a Douglas R4D or a Lockheed R50. With the black sedan goes a black chauffeur and a relief driver if necessary. They're civilians. The airplane pilots and crews are regular Navy or Marine Corps personnel.

"It's really the life of Riley, isn't it? But I'm not being sarcastic. I like it. I'm doing something."

At the office the next day he was stopped by acquaintances and by total strangers who tried to tell him they were sorry for the death of his son. The fact surprised him. He had not thought so many people would know about Rowland, and he even detected a special man-to-man sympathy in the look of the Marine Corps guards and orderlies. Alfred had no decoration to wear in his lapel for his World War I service; he had never applied for his Victory Medal, and he had not joined the American Legion or the Military Order. But on Saturday he had immediately inherited a sort of invisible gold star; the Washington papers had run photographs of Rowland as a Harvard oarsman which made his death more poignant than if the pictures had been the usual collar-and-tie cuts. Alfred was warmed and touched by the kindness of so many people. He was not accustomed to personal gestures by strangers, but for a week or more he would know by the way a man looked at him and hesitated that the man was going to yield to the impulse to come to him and shake his hand. Junior officers, Waves, marines and unknown civilian employes of the Navy were suddenly related to him through the death of a young man whose existence had been unknown to some of them a fortnight ago. The mail was plentiful, the letters were in the thousands; from parents, from Navy men, from Harvard and Groton men, from Princeton and Yale men, from young girls in California and small boys in Ohio, from almost everyone who had ever gone to Knox School and from places like Eckburg and Eck Mills and Rothermel Landing and Prosperity, as well as from Their Britannic Majesties and the Allied brass and Mr. Churchill and three former governors of Pennsylvania and six hundred men and women of Wall Street and Sterling Calthorp and a woman who said she had asked him to have a drink one time after a football game in Gibbsville, Pennsylvania; and close to five hundred letters from Philadelphia and Wilmington and one from a former bellboy in a New Orleans hotel and a man named Joseph B. Chapin, whom he had met on a train, and one in an almost illegibly tiny hand from Jack Warren on Somerset Club stationery and a postcard from a former paid hand on Fritz Thornton's boat and a very gentle note from the snippy woman reporter who had annoyed him in his first press conference. There was an odd absence of hatred in the letters, virtually no mention of the Germans and the Japs, and only a little of the glory of dying for one's country, but there was a frequently recurring reference to the tragedy of waste of a young life, due, surely, to the non-combat character of the fatality. As he read samplings of the stacks of mail Alfred guessed that the letters would have been different for a combat casualty: as though glory was reward enough, but that a special sadness was reserved for death without glory. It was remarkable, too, that not one in a hundred of the letters had been written by acquaintances of Rowland's. They came to *him*, Rowland's father, and they were for him and for his loss.

It was not easy to get back to the work routine, and Alfred thought it might be a good idea to take an inspection trip, but it would be the same wherever he went officially, and he could not ask for time off. The work had piled up. One of the first men to call at his office in person was Creighton Duffy. "I've been to London, just got back," he said. "I can't tell you—Jean has been inconsolable. She tried to go to the funeral, you know, but I don't blame you for keeping it private. How is Mary? Jean spoke to her on the phone and she said Mary's bearing up wonderfully, but is she all right?"

"She's bearing up wonderfully, as Jean said," said Alfred.

"You ought to keep an eye on Mary."

"Why?" It was simply not possible that Duffy was warning him about Mary's extra-marital activities, but the thought crossed Alfred's mind.

"Well, you know how they are. Show nothing, but they store up their emotions until there has to be an explosion."

It was indeed possible that Duffy was doing exactly what Alfred thought he could not do. He was doing it obliquely, putting it on a basis of unexpressed grief, but he was doing it just the same.

"She did let go once, when the President telephoned. But she's a very strong woman, Mary. Very self-reliant."

"Your mention of the President—I had another reason for taking up your time today. I heard you really gave it to those Wall Street boys last week. Do you know where I heard that?"

"Well, logically I would say you heard it from your great friend Percy Hasbrouck."

"I'll have to take that up on our own time. I know you think Percy and I've been playing footie under the table—"

"Yes, I think so, Creighton. But go on."

"I heard it from the President himself. He was so delighted, it gave him more pleasure than anything he's heard in a long while."

"Well, I'm glad it had that effect on him. That wasn't my purpose, but *I* hope it has some effect on the men at the luncheon."

"What he liked most about it was that you went ahead and did it on your own. Let's see, it was Friday you gave your talk. He heard about it Sunday. Had all the names of the men who were there and I imagine a pretty accurate report of what you said. Now do you think you could take a swing around the country doing the same thing? Possibly larger groups of men like those you talked to. They'd take it from you where they wouldn't take it from—well, me, or some New Dealer or even an admiral or a general. The great value of having you do it would be in the fact that nobody suspects *you* of being a New Dealer or even a particular admirer of the President. What would you think of that idea?"

"When the President, or rather, when Franklin D. Roosevelt, not just any president, asks you what you think of an idea like that, you know he approves of it and he's just telling you gracefully to go on out and do it. Is that a pretty fair estimate of the situation?"

Duffy smiled judiciously. "Pretty fair."

"I thought so. Well, I said in the beginning I'd do what I was told."

"If you're thinking about your work here, that can be taken care of. Just means more work for the other men of your rank."

"Or of some reasonably intelligent j. g.'s. I put in at least an hour a day signing my name where somebody tells me to."

"You'd still have to do that, I'm afraid, even if you were on the road. Stuff that has to have your signature would be flown to you wherever you happened to be. But it's okay for me to start setting up meetings in the key cities? As I see it, they should be mostly big men in industry and business. Not the newspaper editors, clergymen, people like that. We want the factory and business men to feel that they're being considered separately. We get those other guys in there and it's just another Red Cross drive. And we're perfectly willing to supply you with all the material you'll need, even if it means relaxing some security restrictions. Naturally there won't be any Top Secret stuff, but you'll be talking to men who already have classified information through their own work, and you'll have to give those men some hard facts and figures. If you feel it'd be helpful, we could bring back anyone from the forward area. Not somebody like Nimitz or Mitscher. They're a little too busy. But if you thought you needed a marine from Guadal, or somebody off a carrier, you know, to dramatize your story. Although there again I think the men you'll be talking to get enough of that, and what we want is not only the immediate effect, but having them know that a man like you feels the way you do. I'd like every man that hears you to feel that business is in the government, not only that the government is in business."

"That's rather neatly put, but the less I say about the government being in business, the better. They know only too damn well that the government's in business. With both feet."

"Well, looking at it from their point of view, you're right."

"Looking at it from *my* point of view, too, Creighton. I'm not going to say anything I don't believe."

"You won't be asked to. When would be the earliest you could start?"

"I could start tomorrow. You arrange for the meetings. I'll leave whenever I'm told to."

"Great. Splendid. It's going to be a tough grind. You'll be in almost every state in the Union before you're through."

"I will?"

"Yes. It won't only be Pittsburgh and Detroit. Los Angeles and Chicago. It'll be Wichita and Toledo and Sandusky and smaller places. We're going to aim first at the towns where there's been noticeable slowing-down of production, and some of your audiences are going to be hostile for just that reason

813

They'll know that you're not there to give them a Navy 'E' and occasionally I imagine you're going to have to control your temper when they start defending themselves."

"You know the risk you're running. I could do a lot of harm."

"Some harm will be done. We concede that. But we count on you."

"I'll be a son of a bitch if this isn't funny."

"What is?"

"This 'we' talk. You and the Old Boy himself, I suppose. You've really been having a high old time for yourself, haven't you? You've been working hand in glove with Percy Hasbrouck, and at—"

"I'll discuss that with you some other time, Alfred."

"There's nothing to discuss. I just want to say, you've been working with Percy to give me a royal screwing, and you've succeeded. And then you come to my office with orders from on high that I have to obey or quit. But I'm not going to quit. I'm not going to think about it now, but after the war I'm going to have to put you back in your place."

"You can try."

"I think I can do better than that, Creighton."

"Well, you're not going to make me lose *my* temper, Alfred. I'd lose more than my temper if I did. I admit I suggested you for this job. I don't mean the job of Assistant Secretary, although I did that. I mean the swing around the country. And that's a compliment. It's a job you can do that I don't know anybody that could do better. I have a stake in this war, too, don't forget."

"You mean your son."

"I mean my son."

"I was somehow hoping we'd be able to get through this discussion without mentioning our sons, but I guess that's the real reason you picked me for this tour. Come on, Duffy, for once in your life, tell the plain truth. Did you say anything to Roosevelt about my son's death in relation to this tour?"

"That's nothing to be ashamed of. Yes, I did."

"And what did Roosevelt say?"

"I'm not privileged to repeat what he said."

"Only when it suits your purpose. Well, now we can proceed. I'm a government official who is going to use his son's death to wake up American industry. All right. There's something a little disgusting about it, but I don't suppose the boy would mind, so why should I? Is there anything else you'd like? A book of Navy matches? A date with a Wave, for Tom Rothermel? I don't want you to go away empty-handed. But I *do* want you to go away."

Duffy rose. "I'm looking forward to after the war just as

814

much as you are," he said. "I've taken an awful lot of shit from you over the years."

"Oh, you mustn't think that, Creighton. That was just the way I felt about you from the very first time I ever saw you."

"Mutual, I assure you," said Duffy, and left.

Alfred got home for Christmas Day, but was back in Washington that night, ready to take off the next morning for the first leg of his centipedal tour of the country. He was gone for two months, missed, he knew, by no one but Natalie. There was nothing unusual about his not seeing Alex, holed up at Groton for the post-holiday weeks, but he had no hope that his postcards to the boy would be welcomed or retained. The worst moments of his family relations were during his twice-weekly telephone calls. Jean would come to the telephone and make no effort to have a conversation; as soon as he had run out of questions she would say, with no attempt to disguise her relief, "Now do you want to talk to Mummy again?" The calls were an ordeal for the child; for her father they were that and an exercise in futility besides. He made each call with the hope that something pleasant might have happened that day that would put the child in such good humor that not even the sound of his voice would change it, but since she always knew that it was he who had caused her to be summoned to the telephone, she always had time to adjust her manner to the same degree of politeness-without-warmth that was maintained throughout all their conversations. He had now no curiosity about how Mary had effected the change in the child's attitude. But he resolutely continued to make the calls so that Mary could not take further advantage of his *not* making them. At Christmas the child had been unable to repulse him entirely; she was not vicious, she was not evil, she was not cruel. She had shown pleasure in his Christmas presents: a rebuilt, repainted, renickeled English bicycle for the country; a gold locket with a thin golden chain; a boy's wrist-watch. All surprises that he had kept secret from Mary. But before he left for his plane ride to Washington the child had taken the presents back to her own room and out of her mother's disapproving sight. He had made more fuss than was necessary over the child's present to him, a water color she had done in art class, and he guessed that his enthusiasm for the gift had pricked the child's conscience. In any event she was not there to say goodbye when he left. The boy Alex, more sophisticated, uttered the proper words of thanks for the hard-to-obtain hockey skates and the gift certificate on J. Press, but there was nothing apologetic in his apology: "I didn't have a chance to get you anything," which was such a calculated cut and deliberate lie that Alfred wanted to slap him hard. But Mary was witness to that moment and Alfred

815

said, "Oh, I didn't expect anything from you, son," and allowed Mary to enjoy her few seconds of victory before he added: "I got a nice present from Rowland, and that was enough." Alex immediately burst into tears and left the room, ashamed of his lie, ashamed of the unfavorable comparison of his own and his brother's conduct.

"You hateful creature. You didn't get a present from Rowland," said Mary.

"But I did. He must have ordered it weeks ago. I'm wearing it." He looked down at the gold tie clasp with a superimposed miniature Navy cap device. He took it off and held it out toward her. "Want to read the inscription? Nothing sentimental. 'To Lieutenant R. A. Eaton USNRF from Ensign R. Eaton USNR.' I wasn't going to mention it, but you asked for it. You were so God damn smug. You've got what you've got, Mary. You've done what you've done, but when you try to take everything, you lose." He replaced the tie clasp. "You couldn't stop this, and it turns out to be the best Christmas present I ever had. I'm going to wear it as long as I live, and you'll never be able to get your hooks on it." He was deliberately cruel; he had known all day that Mary had received no present from Rowland, and for that reason he had intended to say nothing about the tie clasp, but she had taken such pleasure in Alex's ungracious performance that he returned cruelty for cruelty and without regret . . .

He knew that Mary would never forgive him for his refusal to wangle a Thanksgiving leave for Rowland, and it was easy for her to be unforgiving after it turned out that it would have been her last look at their son. The marriage was now in a state of putrefaction, the only word he could find for it, and on his tour of the country he gave some thought each day to all the details of a divorce. In past angers at Mary he had thought of divorce as the obvious if undesirable solution to immediate or long-lasting unhappiness. But now he was beginning to think of it repeatedly as his only chance of survival. Now it seemed there was nothing to save but himself, and in the lowest stages of his depressions he even wondered if it was not too late for that. He had arrived at a state in which he could look back with some calm and fail to find evidence that he had escaped the consequences of this bad marriage and its hypocritically expedient continuance. He had always thought of "the marriage" and "Mary" as synonymous, interchangeable terms; but now he was succeeding in thinking of the marriage as a bad relationship in which he was equally one of two principals. It was not a matter of fixing blame or of sharing it or of refusing to accept it. Rather it was a reconsideration of a relationship and its potentialities for actual danger to life itself. There was danger to the woman, to Mary, in the things that could happen to her, but he no longer cared what happened to her, and what happened to her separately could no longer affect him. But where happenings to her likewise affected him he was in danger. As a principal in the relationship he had already avoided his responsibility to himself, had compromised where compromise was cowardly and easier, and had lived those many years with that guilty knowledge which he palliated by self-righteous, second-hand, contemptible slogans in support of the marital institution. He had once believed, without serious inquiry, that the maintenance of an unsuccessful marriage was contributary to character, a valuable discipline, a strengthening self-denial. But now he rejected all that: a continuing act of hypocrisy in one mental process made hypocrisy less unacceptable in others; valuable discipline was stubbornness; strengthening self-denial was autogenous justification. Over and over again he picked flaws in the marriage that had not stopped at being imperfections in the relationship: they had had their bad effect on him as a man and, through him, unfortunate effects on other people. The principal victim was, of course, the woman he loved. He really had no one else in the world, but to suit the convenience of himself as partner in a bad marriage he had driven her into a bad marriage of her own and thus, indirectly, created a bad marriage for Ben Eustace, who was unfit for marriage to anyone and grotesquely unsuitable as husband for Natalie. Thus her affair with Sterling Calthorp was no one's fault but his own; he could even see that Sterling Calthorp was enough like him in personality and appearance to make Natalie accept him as a substitute. Much as he hated to think of Natalie coupled in bed with Calthorp, he could in imagination read her thoughts during the sexual act, noticing Calthorp's similarities to Alfred and his differences from Ben, the significant similarity to Alfred and difference from Ben being in the achievement of orgasm. She had told him, in semi-clinical fashion, many details of Ben's love-making, a dreadful story of perversions, fetishes and masturbation that were followed by shame, weeping, and talk of suicide. She had not, on the other hand, told him any of the details of her affair with Calthorp beyond the statement that it had been sexually satisfactory to her and therefore, Alfred inferred, a short-lived duplication of her relationship with him, but without love. There was no apparent damage to Natalie as a result of her experiences with Ben or her sex matches with Calthorp; she had seen rough and raw sex in the mountains of Pennsylvania while still a virgin. But marriage to Ben had not been what a girl like Natalie would hope for, and if injury was not apparent it had nonetheless occurred. Likewise, an affair with Sterling Calthorp might not have been injurious in other circumstances, but they

817

had not been other circumstances; they had been the circumstances that obtained at the time of the affair, namely, a sexual need that had to be attended to under surreptitious conditions of double adultery, anaesthetized love for one man and relief from the passionate abuse of another who happened to be her husband. Alfred had never known any woman who could come out of such experiences without injury, and the injury to the girl he had first known in Mountain City was not hard to imagine. The fact that it had to be imagined, that she did not complain, spoke well for her courage and dignity, but ideally there would have been no such demands on her courage or her dignity. The truth was that the mere contracting of a marriage to a man like Ben Eustace was injury enough for a girl who had had her hopes and dreams, and the affair with Calthorp was a smaller part of the larger injury, but as such no less harmful. And it could have been prevented.

There was more. As his mistress—or as anyone's mistress—she had had to qualify her admiration for her father. She had taken a decision which her father never would have sanctioned, and therefore she had had to bring her admiration of him to a halt at that point at which he, if he had known, would have begun to disapprove. It mattered little that her father never had known; her feelings for him—reciprocated—had been so real that the reality continued after her father's death, and the only way she could avoid a fancied quarrel with him was to pretend that a fact was the truth; that the fact of his death was truly an end to her relationship with him. Natalie, to be sure, had never said any of this to Alfred, but he could think as she thought, just as she could think as he did, and one of the major elements of the soul of Natalie Benziger was her appreciation of her father. Her recognition of her father's goodness may even have been the first evidence of her sophistication as it was surely evidence of her wisdom. Wisdom without sophistication would not have made her aware of his goodness. Alfred's own fondness for Ralph Benziger made Natalie's intelligent appreciation of the man an admirable quality and an enthusiasm to be shared. He had always wanted Benziger's approval, and sometimes he thought he might still earn it.

But Benziger's forgiveness would have to come first. Benziger had not become a symbol of Alfred's conscience, but Alfred often judged his own acts by Benziger's standards, which were tolerant, uncomplicated, and uncompromising. By those standards Alfred knew that he would have been summarily and severely judged. For fifteen years he had been the man whom Natalie loved, and regardless of the interruptions, he could not conscientiously claim to have made the strongest effort to convince Natalie of the futility of her love.

The act of separation had been Natalie's out of desperation and misery. Ralph Benziger would have said there was no place in their lives for any love or hope of love. But the affair had been resumed, and now Natalie was close to forty, completely his mistress, of necessity childless and approaching a time when childlessness was likely to be her permanent condition. Moreover, men died at forty-five, and death was a greater factor with each succeeding year, so that each succeeding year increased the probability of Natalie's being left with only a brother whom she seldom saw, and no one to talk to in the dark of night, no one to kiss or to ask for a kiss....

The tour was going well, by and large, and was in its seventh week. In the beginning there had been resistance, then slowly but perceptibly the resistance had decreased, not because of Alfred's talks: the kind of men he was speaking to were not likely to have their minds changed in one ninety-minute speech, no matter who made it. But after Christmas the country seemed to be more willing to admit that the New Year and all of the year would be a time of war and that talk of peace under any conditions was a foolish rejection of the facts. At the end of January Alfred was able to report to Washington that his audiences were not only with him, but sometimes a little ahead of him in a desire to get on with the war, and he questioned the advisability of continuing the tour. The reply was smarter than he had expected it to be: he was told that other reports had pronounced the tour an official and personal success, that the men he had spoken to were pleased that the Navy had taken the trouble to send him out to speak so candidly and forthrightly. Washington agreed with Alfred that the tone of his talks could be changed, that it was probably no longer necessary to use the Dutch-uncle approach, but he was advised that as a good-will gesture and a stimulant to high-level morale, the tour was too effective to be discontinued. Men from the cities he had visited were inevitably talking to men in cities he was yet to visit, and the Navy did not want local pride to be affronted by ending the tour at the halfway point. Indeed, after the first few weeks there had been some industrialist snobbery in the matter of invitations to the talks, and not only was attendance close to 100%, but in several instances men who had not been invited made it plain that they wanted to be invited, and additions were made to the original lists. The Navy kept Alfred supplied with information that was not being printed in the newspapers; in the second week in January he was given some details of the Roosevelt-Churchill meeting at Casablanca that betrayed no secrets but made his audiences feel that he was keeping in touch with grand strategy and therefore was not merely giving them canned propaganda that had been prepared months earlier.

Later in the month he was permitted to give some figures on the first Air Force raids over Germany, which he did with gracious credit to the Air Force while not failing to remind his audience that he was a Navy man, making the point that the Navy was happy to call attention to the deeds of the Air Force. "If the cavalry won a victory, we'd be proud of that, too. Although it may interest you gentlemen to know that we probably have more men on horseback than the entire Army. I don't mean horse-marines. You see, we use horses in the Coast Guard, patrolling beaches," he explained. The speeches were honest and firm, humorous without frivolity, and respectful without obsequiousness. In the first weeks at almost every talk there was at least one heckler, sometimes a victim of Martinis, but more usually an unreconciled Roosevelt-hater or a New Yorker-hater. When Alfred was heckled he would ask the man to stand up and repeat his question or his comment, and he would allow a silence to ensue before answering the man. During the silence the man would become embarrassed and either sit down or rephrase his question so that Alfred was able to say, "My dear sir, I'll be glad to answer one question at a time, if I can." But even in those audiences in which admiration for Roosevelt was non-existent, there would be a sense of good manners and fair play, and often the other men would tell their townsman to sit down and shut up. When the questions were put in a way that indicated that the man wanted to know something, Alfred answered as best he could, and if the questions carried an attack on Roosevelt, Alfred's reply would make mention of "the well-established fact that I am not a member of the President's party, and no one knows it better than Mr. Roosevelt himself. When you go to get your draft card you don't say whether you're a Republican or a Single Taxer, and without taking any poll, I'd guess that there aren't ten admirals in the whole Navy who could be called Roosevelt Democrats. And don't even ask me for *their* names."

They did not consider Alfred "one of them"; he was a New Yorker who did not happen to drop his r's, but his suits and his haberdashery were not like theirs, he was taller than most of them and thinner, and he had refinements of manner that many of the men recognized as having been part of their own equipment in their youth, but which they had started shedding in their twenties and had lost entirely in their thirties, largely through association with other men who had never had them at all. The manner was on display during his speeches, during which he showed no fear and no tendency to assume another manner more in conformity with theirs. He had a rich manner that could not be bought late in life, but it was not reserved for the rich or the important, and the men he talked to from the platform or later were proud enough of their own success to see the differences between Alfred and themselves without wanting to change themselves or him. They were all of them successful Americans, good at judging their own kind, and by choice keeping to their own kind while remaining unresentful of the refinements they saw in the men now represented by Alfred Eaton.

He was always asked to join a group after one of his talks, and he always declined, using a Washington telephone call as his excuse, an excuse which was not only acceptable but subtly complimentary. In most of the cities he gave his talk at the good men's club but spent the night in the best hotel. For the first time in his middle years he was concerned about expenses; the Navy share of his hotel bills and other expenditures was fractional and the trip was costing him between $500 and $1,000 a week, while the expense of the apartment at the Wardman Park went on. His aide, Wilson, was in no position to afford his own share of the hotel bills and Alfred paid those as well. Wilson was something of a problem. He knew the Navy and protocol and he was efficient, but Alfred had already discovered that in every new city at the first opportunity Wilson was busy "lining up something." He was especially successful with women room clerks, telephone operators, cocktail lounge waitresses, and girls who sat at the automobile-rental desks, apparently having developed a standard fast technique that was based on a limited time for a few drinks and a visit to his room, all without leaving the hotel. He was a man of medium height, with tight curly brown hair and large front teeth. He was separated from his wife, who taught school in Trenton, New Jersey, and who would not give him a divorce because she was a Catholic, but in so doing she protected him from the more badly smitten room clerks and telephone operators. He had been a fair halfback at the Naval Academy and had the Purple Heart from the Battle of Coral Sea, and having won his Annapolis "A" and given his blood in a wound that had left a sizable gouge in his right calf, he was content to do his aide work to the best of his ability and to make up for several months of celibacy in the Pacific.

"Wilson, your love life is your own business, but you got your wires crossed tonight," said Alfred one night.

"Sir, I don't understand what the Secretary is inferring."

"A gorgeous piece of telephone operator knocked on my door at a little after eleven."

"Oh, Christ. I beg your pardon, sir. That was my fault."

"You're damn right it was. You stood her up, I guess. She knocked on the door and I got out of bed and let her in. She asked where you were, and then she wanted to stay. Let's have no more of that, Wilson."

Wilson was no companion. Alfred often felt as far away

from home—whatever home was—as anyone in the forward area. He could have flown back to Washington on weekends, but instead he stayed in hotel rooms, working, reading, sleeping. Natalie came to see him at the end of the first month while he was in Minneapolis. He told Wilson to report to him on Monday morning, which gave the lovers most of two days and all of two nights together. "Is this going to be all right, I mean from your official point of view?" she said.

"Nobody cares any more. This is wartime. Finally."

"How is it going?"

"They tell me it's going very well," he said, and related some of the Washington information and decision.

"You needed that," she said.

"How did you know? I didn't know it myself, but you did. Yes, I needed it badly. You can do almost everything for me, but you can't tell me officially that I've done a good job. They have. But I sure needed a little pat on the head. This trip has reminded me of the stories I used to hear about the Triangle Club trips, but without the fun. And God *knows*, twenty-five years too late. Other times I felt like a traveling salesman, but with Wilson getting the nooky. And still other times it reminded me of when I first met you and I was staying at that hotel in Gibbsville."

"Don't you see *anybody?*"

"Socially? No. When I get to a town I usually find a message to call somebody I knew at Princeton, but it's never anyone I knew very well and sometimes it's a guy I can't remember at all. After all, I wasn't there very long. I'm *ex*-'19, you know. How are you?"

"Frozen. God, it's cold out here."

"It's the Fitzgerald country. Do you remember his stories about the girls at the country club? Always seemed to be in front of a big fireplace. I wish this room had a fireplace."

"Would be nice. I'm going to take a hot bath and see if that will thaw me out."

"Would you like me to scrub your back?"

"You can get in the tub with me if you like. But that wasn't very successful when we tried it. Do you remember?"

"Sure. Thirteenth Street. There was hardly room for you in that tub. This one is bigger, but I guess I'll let you scrub your own back."

"I'm always willing to try, said she, meekly."

"No. I think you're really an old-fashioned girl."

"Not dull, I hope."

"If dull is what you are, dull is what I want."

"I still don't want to be dull." She knelt before him and put her hands under his thighs. "Does M'sieu think little Kiki ees dull, hein?"

822

"Go on, take your bath."

"For one sousand franc little Kiki will geef M'sieu a new srill."

"Cut it out, will you?"

"Five hondred franc?"

"Cut it out!" He was laughing.

"No? Sen I do it for nossing, yes?"

"If you're going to take your bath, you'd better do it now."

"You make me take bass? Bath? Bass? I am not dairtee. I am co-vair wiss perfume."

"Yeah. Chanel soixante-neuf."

"Oh, you shock! Kiki go home."

"Heap big American soldier wait for squaw on bed. How's that for getting you out of this French thing?"

She stood up. "Maybe I didn't want to get out of it. But I know where I'm not wanted."

"And I know where you *are* wanted." He reached out to touch her.

"Hands off the merchandise. If you can't make up your mind when it's offered to you, you just have to wait your turn. Do you know what I'd like? I'd like a drink. Have you any whiskey?"

"You would? I have bourbon and Scotch."

"I'd like a bourbon and some water."

"Now or when you finish your bath?"

"Oh, you know me. It'll take me that long to finish it. I'll have it now. I'm cold and I'm shaky after that plane trip."

"You had a bad flight?"

"Oh, I might as well tell you. You know, I don't usually get frightened on planes, but this time I was. Bumpy. Then about ten minutes before we landed, the hostess told us that there was a little engine trouble, and of course we all looked out the window but the shades were drawn. Wartime. When we finally did land, one of the motors was on fire."

He took her in his arms. "You shouldn't hold these things in. I tell you everything. You must tell me."

She shook her head. "I don't know how to."

"Just do," he said.

"I'll be all right. Just give me a drink. All the way from the airport I kept thinking, what if we'd crashed and I'd been killed? All the publicity. You'd claim my body, I know, but everybody'd know what I was here for——and my brother and his family——and oh, you know all the rest of it. And what it would do to you. Two deaths in a little over a month. Hold me. Tell me you love me."

"I love you, you're all I love."

"You're all I love. I need you."

"I know."

"A minute ago, when you told me to go away, I almost cried. Playing a silly game, I almost cried."

"Never go. Will you promise never to go?"

"I love you. I'm all right now. Just give me that drink."

She stayed in the bathroom for half an hour and he thought of the loneliness of her life, and, in a natural sequence, the loneliness of his life if it had to be lived without her. Then, as though it were the normal, orderly procedure for a Saturday afternoon, he put in a long distance call to Rex Easterday, a lawyer whom he knew so slightly that he could not even remember the full name of Easterday's firm. But he did not bother to call Easterday's office; it would not be open. He gave the number of the restaurant "21," and in a few minutes Easterday was speaking: "Now who is this, please?" said Easterday.

"This is Alfred Eaton."

"*The* Alfred Eaton? MacHardie & Company?"

"I'm that Alfred Eaton, yes, Mr. Easterday."

"How did you track me down here?"

"Just a hunch. That only times I've ever been there on a Saturday, you were always there. Are you speaking from a table or a booth?"

"Oh, I never speak from a table. I don't believe in letting anyone know the least thing about my business, Mr. Eaton. I've overheard too many interesting things here myself. What can I do for you?"

"I would like you to represent me in a suit for divorce."

"Yes."

"Are you available?"

"I am, under certain conditions."

"The conditions being monetary?"

"Naturally, but there are others. I'd have to hear the whole story, and I don't think you want to tell it to me over the telephone. I'm having a party this afternoon and it's probably going to last well into the night, but I could see you tomorrow."

"No, I'm in Minneapolis."

"Oh, you're calling from Minneapolis, Minnesota. But there must be some urgency to this or you'd wait till Monday."

"There is, and there isn't."

"Then let me ask you one or two questions. Has there been any other lawyer in this case?"

"No."

"I know MacHardie & Company are represented by Pickett, McKinstry, Livingston, Chase & McDonald. Have you consulted them?"

"No."

"Then I take it you came to me on your own."

"Correct."

"And what about Mrs. Eaton? Who are her attorneys?"

"She has none. I've just made up my mind to take this action, and I haven't spoken to her."

"How very wise you are, Mr. Eaton. Now, I take it that you are the one instituting the divorce proceedings? You know the New York State laws, of course."

"Put it this way. We've talked about it in the past, but at the moment I'm originating the proceedings. I want the divorce."

"Does she? Mrs. Eaton? As soon as she hires a lawyer he's probably going to make sounds like opposing the divorce, you anticipate that, of course."

"More or less. I'm prepared for some unpleasantness, one way or another."

"Counsel for Mrs. Eaton will see to it that this costs you a lot of money. I gather you don't want the *Daily News* to have a field day on this."

"I have three—two children, and the less notoriety the better."

"And in view of your position in the government, of course. Now, Mr. Eaton, I have a reputation for performing miracles, but there aren't any miracles in the practice of law. That's point one. Point two, although I'm known as a divorce lawyer, I always say to my clients, are you sure you want this divorce? With a man like you, you wouldn't have got as far as phoning me without making up your mind, but I still ask the question. You're sure you want to go ahead with it?"

"Quite sure."

"Then that's all we ought to discuss now."

"You'll take the case?"

"I'll take the case."

"What about your fee?"

"It may be as high as $25,000. It may be less. It won't be more. You may find that Mrs. Eaton's lawyer will cost you more than I do."

"I'm prepared to provide for Mrs. Eaton and the children."

"Well, let's not start by being over-generous, let's not give them a blank cheque. Will you telephone me next week, before you say anything to Mrs. Eaton?"

"Could you meet me in Wichita, Kansas, next Tuesday?"

"Wichita, Kansas."

"Or Fort Worth, Texas, next Wednesday?"

"I see. You're doing one-night stands. Nothing intended by that remark. I have a lot of theatrical people. Yes, I could meet you in Fort Worth."

"Fine. Thank you. Will you want a retainer now?"

"Let's wait and see what you have left. Pleasure to talk to you. Goodbye, Mr. Eaton."

"Goodbye, Mr. Easterday."

Natalie had come in the room toward the end of the conversation.

"The only Easterday I know of is a lawyer. He has an account at the shop," said Natalie, rubbing her back hair with a towel.

"That's the one," said Alfred. They looked at each other for a long and silent moment. Finally he nodded. "It's what you think."

"You're going to get a divorce," she said, making it more a statement than a question.

"Yes."

She crossed the room and sat beside him on the bed and took his hand and kissed it, and rubbed the back of it against her cheek.

"I always knew. I often doubted, but I *always* knew. The man of my life. What suddenly made you do it? The airplane?"

"Yes. The airplane, and thinking that on another Saturday Rowland went out to fly, probably had things planned for that night. Probably had a date to telephone his girl . . . The life I've made you lead. My own life without you."

"And in a way there really isn't anything left for us but marriage, is there? I don't want to make marriage sound like a last resort. I meant that—well, it is a last resort, isn't it? Oh, I'm incoherent today. But do you know what I mean?"

"Yes. We have to get married or die without it."

"Still not exactly it, but closer than I came. There's one other thing. I'm strongly tempted to go back in the bathroom and remove my safeguard. I want to start having a baby."

"No, let's do it right," he said. "We've always been so damn careful, and this divorce may take a little time."

"You're absolutely right," she said, and laughed. "It was sort of my way of celebrating."

"I did this without consulting you. Are you prepared for a rugged time? Mary might get very tough."

"She'd better not," said Natalie. "I've heard things about Mary that not even you know."

"There are lots of things I don't know. But why didn't you tell me?"

"You knew enough, none of it through me. You wouldn't have liked me if I'd told you. I wouldn't have liked myself. But I wouldn't hesitate to use anything now. My little fairies, they love Mary, but they just can't be loyal to any woman. We'll be all right, don't worry about it."

"I know we will. We are now. Positive action."

"Do you know what would be nice? If we just pulled down those shades and turned out the light and had a wonderful, beautiful sleep. And then I could wake up and it would still be true. Shall we just sleep?"

"There isn't a chance."

She laughed. "No, I guess not. But I may freeze up on you, now that's it's almost legal."

"There's evidence to the contrary."

"Isn't he clever, this man? Can't keep anything from him."

Easterday's advice when he met Alfred in Fort Worth was to say and do nothing until the tour was completed and Alfred could talk to Mary in person. Accordingly, Alfred went to New York in the middle of March and after dinner in the apartment he closed the library door and said: "This is going to be a long one, I have a feeling."

"Oh, dear."

"Yes. Without any preamble, or funny stories, I would like to have a divorce."

"All right."

"You're going to be nice about it?"

"Yes. Shall I use those pictures you had taken with Mrs. Eustace in Philadelphia?"

"Oh, you're *not* going to be nice."

"You want the divorce, and that's what the grounds are in New York."

"You wouldn't go to Reno?"

"Why should I?"

"Well, aside from all other considerations, money."

"I'll get that anyway, won't I?"

"Not if I do the suing."

"On what grounds?"

"On what grounds? Well, there's that fine, upstanding member of the medical profession, Jim Roper. There's that other feeler of the public pulse, Mr. Parker Wells. In between them, God knows how many boys and maybe even a few girls, judging by the company you keep. I want this divorce, and I'm going to get it, Mary."

"My terms are a million dollars, and some publicity for Mrs. Eustace."

"Why the publicity for Mrs. Eustace?"

"Just because I hate her."

"I thought you didn't. I remember a conversation we had, a long time ago."

"Forget it. I've *learned* to hate her, and it wasn't hard. It was bad enough when she married poor Ben Eustace, but then having an affair with Red Calthorp all the time she was married to Ben, or didn't you know about Red Calthorp?"

"Yes, I knew about Red Calthorp. I'm a little surprised that you did."

"Why are you surprised? I got my information from the

827

same person that told me you'd had an affair with Clemmie Shreve. In other words, Clemmie Shreve. The wife of your best friend. Now sleeping with Larry Von Elm and I don't know who else. But the only one that will make any difference to Lex Porter is you, dear boy. So before you start smearing me, think what I have to smear you back with. If I know Lex Porter, he'd actually want to kill you and Clemmie, and even if he didn't, just think of the hell that would break loose."

"Did Clemmie by any chance tell you *when* I slept with her?"

"Yes. Just before she married Lex, but that's not going to make him feel more kindly toward you. You might at least have warned your best friend that he was marrying a tramp."

"You use such strange words."

"I get it. But I'm not a tramp."

"Well, we won't go into, what do you call them, semantics. I guess I have nothing more to say. My lawyer told me to be very careful what I said."

"Oh, you have a lawyer? My, my."

"Rex Easterday."

"Heard of him, but I'm not afraid of him. I'm sure any smart shyster can make it very difficult for you."

"But at least he'd be doing it as a job. You'd be doing it out of some strange vindictiveness."

"She's a hypocrite."

"No, she's not a hypocrite. And she protected you for God knows how long, but I won't tell you about that. You don't deserve to know it. As of tomorrow, then, I move out of here. All future contacts with me will be through Easterday."

"What about bills? What about money?"

"What money?"

"Upkeep of the apartment? Alex's bills, Jean's. The servants."

"You'll have to speak to Easterday about that. I'll give you his card."

"I'm not going to call up any lawyer for money."

"Well, you suit yourself about that. Tomorrow morning all charge accounts will be notified that I am closing them out as of *today*. Letters and cheques went out this afternoon, so don't hurry down to Cartier's. From now on you will have to do everything through Easterday. Just a matter of accounting. Perfectly legitimate. A man can close out his charge accounts any time he feels like it. He can sell his car for the OPA price, which I expect to do. He can do all sorts of things that his wife may not like. Resign from the Maidstone Club, for instance, which would probably mean that his wife would have to get on a waiting-list to get back in."

"Yes, and he can resign from the United States Government, too."

"Yes, he can. Oh, he's thought of all the angles that his wife's likely to think of, plus a little help from Rex Easterday, a very smart, very learned lawyer, with a terrific record for winning divorce cases."

"There's less than $4,000 in the bank."

"If you mean at MacHardie & Company, the joint account, there's less than that. There's nothing. I closed it. You have your own checking account at the Corn Exchange, but I believe that's something like $641.42. You go ahead and be tough. Live that way for a while. You had your chance to be decent and reasonable, now you can sweat it out."   •

She stared straight down at the rug in front of her feet.

"You win," she said.

"Don't tell me. Tell Easterday. You could have behaved like a decent human being, and I wouldn't have had to do any of those things or make any threats. And I could have revoked all those suspensions of charge accounts. But I knew what you were going to do, and *I* don't *win. You lose.* You lose the last bit of respect I had for you. I'm through." He left the library and went back to his own room. He thought he heard her going out, closing the apartment door, but he did not investigate. He had said more than he had intended to say, lost his temper, and got into the kind of bitter exchange he had been determined (and advised) to avoid. Her hauteur was not without its attractive features in the days when he knew that a quarrel could easily end in ardent love-making; on such occasions her indifference or her cold anger gave him, and her, the illusion of modified rape, and he sometimes suspected that deliberately or semi-deliberately she had provoked quarrels for just such simulated excitement. But he now sincerely believed that apart from his love for Natalie, his hostility toward Mary had become so deep and so thorough that in attractiveness she was sexless, and her femininity no more than a difference from him which gave her protection against physical violence. Her femininity had made her like a crippled man, who could be abusive and insulting and cruel without the risk of a beating, and thus her beauty joined with her femininity as negative characteristics of the total person. There had often been violence in their love-making, having to do with urgency or with sensuality, but it had been controlled violence for the sake of pleasure. In the present state of their relationship he had no significant desire to do violence on her, controlled or uncontrolled. It was almost the final evidence of his feeling for her that he wanted to slap her face but then immediately turn away from her in disgust. He had slapped other faces in the same gesture of contempt—or had he? He could not remember if he had, but it was the *kind* of thing he could have done and forget, as he now wanted to do to her and forget her. He did not seek for a more abstruse definition of his feeling than contempt. He did not even want to hate her. He wanted *not* to hate her. He wanted her to vanish from his life and from his thoughts, and he had the good fortune to have an intelligence that told him that that would not occur. He could not completely emasculate himself against one woman, but since he had been faithful to Natalie for so long a time, he was as sure that his practical, working contempt for Mary would endure as he was that his fidelity to Natalie was secure.

He had not given enough to the younger children, and it disturbed him to wonder about that, to find an answer to the question whether he had loved them less and had given less because of a lesser love. It was an examination that was hopeless, in that he could not be sure of his entire truthfulness with himself. The resulting present condition, however, was some evidence against him, and he knew it. It would not have been quite so easy for Mary to take them out of—to use a phrase of the time—his sphere of influence if he had been productive of more love for them. There were, in March of 1943, children of the ages of his children who had not even seen their fathers in more than a year's time, but seemed to love them nonetheless. There were other children in other times who had loved their fathers in spite of sternness and even cruelty, and Alfred had not been cruel or cruelly stern. It appeared, then, that he could convict himself of inadequate love for the younger children and that his punishment was just what he was getting: the loss of them to Mary. He could not do a remote reasoning with them, in which he would try to explain how much as well as how less than sufficiently he loved them. It was not a thing that could be explained remotely or directly. But it was a sad thing now, and potentially tragic for the future, for he did love the children—Jean was a beauty with charm, Alex was an independent mind and an attractive boy—and it was almost predictable now that they would grow up to think of him as formally their father, but humanly the former husband of their mother, a man who had left her and them for another woman *and for nothing else*. They would have to live a long time themselves before they would understand with any tolerance that there was anything on his side to be understood. As to the near future, he could not in honesty deny that regardless of the private mess that Mary had made of her own life, she had been and was a competent, successful mother. Soon it would be impossible for her to do Alex much harm; he was sophisticated and intelligent, and he was away at school. Alfred also conceded that in the matter of experience and information, Mary was qualified to be a vigilant guardian of her daughter. So far there had been no signs of early cynicism or premature sophistication in Jean; in all respects she seemed to be average, and Mary apparently had doled out sexual information as it became necessary as indicated by Jean's questions, so that the child had rudimentary instruction in the processes of reproduction but had not been told about sexual pleasure for its own sake. On the record, on the state of the children's bodies and minds, Alfred had no valid excuse to take them away from her.

In that respect he had followed Easterday's advice; to say nothing whatever about custody of the children. Easterday's strategy at this stage was to be as uncommunicative as possible in the circumstances, to withhold information that might be the basis of later negotiations. Easterday was himself a volubly uncommunicative man; in their two lengthy conferences Alfred had a strong suspicion that the lawyer had gone to some trouble to find out on his own a great deal more about Mary and about Alfred than was to be inferred from anything he actually said. He frequently expressed his admiration of good taste, which Alfred listened to with a straight face while ignoring the lawyer's rings, watches—he wore two—and neckties, and habits of speech that reminded Alfred of the magazine stories by Arthur Kober. Whenever he had to interrupt Alfred he would say, "Permit me if I may," without ever specifying what permission he sought. "Permit me if I may, but on the subject of custody of these minor children, namely, Alexander Porter Eaton, infant, residing gwith parents at said address, and Yoojeenie Eaton, infant, likewise residing gwith parents, same address, let us make has'e slowly. To put it in the vernacular, Alfred, we don't want to tip our mitt. Give nothing now, let the generosity come later," Easterday had said. Alfred, however, did not deceive himself; the unmentioned children probably had been so much on Mary's mind that to bring them into the discussion would have been an act of supererogation, which she was willing to spare him. In any event, he was already reconciled to the loss of them, and whatever Rex Easterday could gain for him in the way of visiting days would be welcome, but Alfred was already planning to invoke that right judiciously. It could easily turn into the most perilous factor in his future relationships with his children—or it could be, carefully planned, a joy.

On his last night in this room he could get sentimental over the children, but otherwise he felt no regret. He had adjusted his reading lamp so that outside the range of its illumination he could see only outlines of furniture, and might as well have been in any of the fifty hotel rooms he had slept in in recent months. Tentatively he planned to put his books and pictures and knickknacks in storage in New York; he still wanted nothing in Washington that would imply permanent residence —and then he began to think about Washington and the divorce and their relation, one to another. So far, those who knew anything at all about the divorce plans were Natalie, Mary, Easterday, and Easterday's private secretary. The news, Easterday had warned him, could be bottled up no longer; the gossip columnists would have it within forty-eight hours as a result of the letters to credit managers. Easterday advised him to answer "No comment" to all newspaper questions, and to stick to it, no matter how insistently and adroitly the reporters asked for more. Above all, Easterday cautioned him not to come forward with denials of inaccuracies in the first stories, regardless of how malicious, untrue or distorted they might seem or of whom they mentioned by name or innuendo. "When the proper time gets here, I'll handle the press boys," said Easterday. As he thought of the newspaper publicity he was reminded of a night long ago, the night before he was to play a high-stake golf match with a man who was suspected of cheating but had never been caught. It was not, in other words, an ordinary match, but he had let himself in for it, he could not default—and he lost fairly and decisively to a better golfer, who had not had to cheat. He had never played the man again, but he often wondered whether the man's dubious reputation was not as good as a four-stroke advantage over men who played according to the rules.

He had given a lot of thought to Washington and the possible consequences of the divorce, and he had always come back to the same restful conclusion: whatever they did was up to them. He then fell asleep and was awakened much later by plumbing noises; the flushing of the toilet and the thundering cascade of water in a tub. He looked at his watch: it was four-thirty. She was a damned fool, and for one second he pitied her. But then he recalled that she had not used the telephone before leaving the house and that therefore wherever she had gone, to whom she had gone, she must have been expected; and if not expected, so sure of her welcome that she had not hesitated. She had gone there as he might have gone to Natalie's flat in Fifty-fifth Street.

He fell asleep again, but he awoke again at a few minutes past five, and knew there was to be no more sleep for him. He went back to the kitchen and started some coffee, shaved while the water was boiling and returned to the kitchen and made some toast while the coffee was dripping through. It was early for the household, and he had been walking around in his pajama pants and bare feet, and he turned in embarrassment when the pantry door at his back swung open. He did not like to be seen undressed. But it was not one of the servants: it was Mary in a dressing-gown over her nightgown.

"Good morning," she said.

"Good morning."

"I heard the water running in your bathroom."

"I did in yours, about three-quarters of an hour ago."

"Yes, I took a bath when I got home. Is there enough coffee for me to have a cup? If not, I can make some more."

"Do you want coffee? You won't be able to go back to sleep."

"I won't now anyway. I'll see Jean off to school and then go back to bed."

"Yes, there's enough. One cup's all I want."

"Are you sure? That cup doesn't hold as much as the big ones you got from the Harvard Club."

"I'll be drinking coffee all day. They'll have it on the plane. The Navy lives on coffee."

"If you're wondering why I came out here, I don't know."

"I'm sure I don't. I told you to get in touch with Easterday."

"I'm a bit hung over. I went and had a talk with Jim Roper, and I drank more than I like to."

"You're awfully candid."

"Oh, heavens, Alfred. Jim is a fairy. If you sued me and named Jim you'd have half of New York laughing at you."

"He wasn't always."

"As a matter of fact, he was. Oh, I slept with him, yes, but that was years ago. Jim is like a sister to me. He is! I'm not saying anything behind his back. He said it first."

"He's that far gone?"

"He's as far as you can go without wearing dresses."

"Then I guess he does that, too."

"I don't know. Probably. But don't start saying things against him. He's on your side."

"That's a friend I always wanted. Jim Roper."

"Well, he's not exactly on your side. But he advised me to go ahead with the divorce, go to Reno, make no fuss, and forget you."

"That last remark makes me laugh," he said. "Forget me?"

"That's what he said. Put you out of my life. Find another man, marry him, and lose myself in a new life so that you won't be able to upset me. I'm quoting Jim."

"Well, you'd decided that last night, I thought."

"Not all of it. But Jim made me see, or tried to make me see, that you were a constant reminder of a big defeat and that as long as I had that reminder, I'd be unhappy. Makes sense. Our marriage *was* a defeat for me and if we're divorced maybe I will forget you. So you can tell your Mr. Easterday that I'm going to be as nice as pie. You can tell him that today, and you can tell him to get me a lawyer. I still want a million dollars, and I have to have custody of the children, but you can come and see them. So there it is, all settled. As far as I'm concerned, the divorce is granted. You're free, I'm free."

"I can hardly believe my ears."

"Aren't you going to say thank-you? You usually have such good manners."

"I do thank you."

She took off her wedding ring and placed it on the table. "I'll never wear *that* again. What do people do with old wedding rings when they've been divorced? I can't give it to Alex for his wife."

"Have it melted down and made into something else."

"Yes, if I can think of something. You know, you have a very good build for a man your age."

"Thank you. So have you."

"Yes, I was thinking. Would you like to go back to my room? I promise you it wouldn't mean anything. I wouldn't hold it over you."

"Are you seducing me, Mary?"

"Well, I'm not doing it very well, but you're sitting here practically naked." She reached over and put her hand on his chest and slowly moved it downward, stopping at the string of his pajama pants, and holding her hand there. "Is anything happening?"

"Yes."

"Yes," she said. "Before anybody comes in." She got up and left the room and he followed her. She did all the preliminary love-making, prolonging it because of and in spite of his impatience, but when he was inside her he took control and brought her near to climax twice before giving one of their old signals for total release. She shouted and would not let him go until she could no longer keep him with her, then she lay back with her eyes open, staring at the ceiling and with a smile on her lips. "Oh, that was wonderful," she said. She did not seem necessarily to be talking to him.

"But as you said, it didn't mean anything," he said.

"I'm not so sure of that now."

He thought, but did not say, "I am." She could think what she pleased, but he would avoid antagonizing her until the divorce papers were signed. It was bad enough now, to have this new sense of having just lost Natalie, as though Natalie knew what had happened. He had done everything wrong, and if Mary wanted to be a bitch she could recite everything he had said and done that was wrong, but all his fresh guilt was in this brutal infidelity to Natalie. And brutal it was, all of it; the manner of his love-making with Mary, which was not disagreeable to her but made him shameful in his own estimation; and the disloyalty to Natalie in letting Mary know that she could lead him into her bed on any terms.

"Where are you going?" she said, holding out her hand.

"I'm going to take a shower, get dressed, and go downtown

to 90 Church Street. Then I'm going to talk to Easterday, then take a plane to Washington." He tried to be matter-of-fact in the hope that the same casualness would be communicated to her.

"Aren't you going to see Mrs. Eustace today?"

"I won't have a chance to."

"Well, at least I'm glad of that." She drew the sheet over her figure.

"I'm not a superman," he said.

"I disagree. I'm sure you stayed with her sometime yesterday, but I wouldn't have known it this morning."

"I surprised myself," he said.

"But you shouldn't have been surprised. If 'way back we'd agreed on what kind of people we are, that we can't help wanting other people, we could have saved ourselves a lot of unhappiness."

"I'm afraid I have different ideas about marriage."

"But you haven't. You'd like to have, but didn't you feel a while ago that you were all-but married to Mrs. Eustace?"

"Yes."

"But then you made wonderful love to me. So where does that leave your ideas about marriage?"

"Where they always were. On a pedestal, except when I knocked them off, or you did."

"Yes, and that's where they belong. On a pedestal. They don't belong in bed. All right, go take your shower. And don't torment yourself. I'm not going to tell Mrs. Eustace that her boy friend gave me a good screw. You're great in the hay, but you're an awful sissy."

"I'm inclined to agree with you."

"Put your pants on, honey, you're no use to me now." She pulled the bedclothes over her shoulder and lay on her right side. "Open the windows before you leave, will you, please?"

He wanted to laugh at her. As the enemy of marriage she was the strongest argument in its favor; and as the advocate of her own way of life she was a sermon against it. It had taken the second half of his life for him to see that he was married to the true sister of a girl in London who was the quintessence of excitement at the first half. There were differences; nothing was ever quite the same as anything else; he had been deceived for hours by Betty (last name long since forgotten), years by Mary; and at forty-five, almost forty-six, he would not allow himself to be deceived by Betty or by Mary; but Mary was Betty and Betty was Mary and he found himself, at this early hour, trying to edit the poet of Empire: "I learned about women from Judy O'Grady/ and her sister under the skin."

He finished his chores at 90 Church Street and was driven to

Easterday's office on Fifth Avenue. He could not compel himself to make a candid report of all that had occurred, but concentrated his remarks on Mary's agreeing to be cooperative. It made a fairly long story and Easterday listened, nodding now and then, tapping his fingers on the arms of his Supreme Court-like chair.

"All finished, Alfred?" said Easterday.

"Well, I could give you a lot more, but—"

"Permit me if I may, Alfred." He reached out and picked up a bronze desk calendar. "March, 1943, this little device proclaims. August, 1943, I shall attain the age of forty-eight, the good Lord permitting. My no doubt theatrical gesture serves a useful purpose, namely, I wasn't born yesterday, Alfred. You're holding gout on me, Alfred."

"Yes, I am."

"One doesn't listen to thousands upon thousands of words of testimony without developing the instinct for the ring gof truth. I've often sat in a courtroom, listening to a witness testify, and suddenly my ears perk up and I say to myself, 'This son of a bitch is lying.' You understand I'm not calling you a son of a bitch or a liar. You are a gentleman, and I trust I am also. But you have not given me a straight story, whatever your reasons may be. Now is it all right if I help you a little, nudge you a little?"

"Go ahead. I deserve it."

"I'm a man, too, you know. Considerably fond of the fair sex. So—did you by any chance have sexual relations with Mrs. Eaton at any time within the past twenty-four hours?"

"Yes, I did."

"Normal. Exceedingly attractive woman. I understand perfectly how these things happen. But you must know enough law to realize, Alfred, your moment of pleasure jeopardizes certain aspects of our case. Some judges would hold that your connubial relations have the effect of condoning past acts of Mrs. Eaton's of which you have knowledge. In other words, if we take that tact, we have to start as of today. However, let us forget about the law and turn our thoughts toward psychology and psychological strategy, Alfred. *I* say, we better move swiftly. I say we get Mrs. Eaton on the earliest possible train to Reno, before anything happens to change her mind. What could happen? Well, I must speak as one man of the world to another, Alfred. Mrs. Eaton may at this very moment be wishing you were in bed with her and there was a song by the title 'Wishing Will Make It So.' You will not get the lady on a train to Reno if she has the female desire to go to bed with you. This I know, believe me, Alfred. They will stall, they will delay." He was interrupted by the inter-office

phone. "Who is it? You know I don't want to be disturbed . . .
Oh, very good. Put her on . . . The lady we were just analyzing
. . . Yes, Mrs. Eaton. I would of known anyway, Mrs. Eaton. I
often admired you from afar in such places as the '21' Club
and the Colony Restaurant . . . I do. Yes, I have already seen
Alfred and I believe he is on his way to Washington by air . . .
You could indeed. Three o'clock on the dot, Mrs. Eaton.
Charming to speak with you . . . Well, so far so good, Alfred.
She'll be coming to my office at three o'clock. She had an
affable sound to her voice and I only hope it lasts through
lunch. I've seen too many ladies change from affable to hell-
cats after taking too many Martini cocktails. I'll be on the
phone to you tonight at your hotel. Meanwhile, if you want no
more hitches, please don't get alone with Mrs. Eaton. This
lady is a powerhouse, I could tell it over the phone, just those
few words."

There was nothing in the afternoon papers about the separation, nor in the early editions of the morning papers that
Alfred had sent to his room. He was resolved to volunteer no
information to anyone in Washington. In the evening Easterday telephoned: Mary would leave for Reno after the spring
school vacations. She wanted a million dollars and custody of
the children, ownership of the apartment in Seventy-second
Street and the house in East Hampton, the Buick limousine-
sedan and the Ford station wagon. She would sue on grounds
of incompatibility and mental cruelty, and she agreed to an un-
published decree. Meanwhile Alfred was to restore the household charge accounts and deposit $10,000 in her Corn Ex-
change account. "I have a confession to make to you, Alfred,"
said Easterday. "I never sent out those letters and cheques
yesterday."

"You son of a gun. Why?"

"Well, I wanted you to *think* I had so you could talk convincingly, but they don't do much good. She could open
accounts anywhere in New York on her name alone, and you'd
of been stuck in the end, so why tell every son of a bitch in
town that you're getting a divorce?"

"Thank you, Rex, I'm glad you did that."

"I knew you would be. Those bed-and-board notices, they're
not for nice people."

"Well, you're a pretty God damn nice fellow yourself."

"In there trying."

But the news was in the Monday morning papers, and Alfred was pleased that he had taken two hours to compose the
letter to Alex which would have reached him before the
Boston or New York papers reached the Rector's breakfast
table.

Dear Alex:

I would like you, upon opening this letter, to look around you and see whether you are going to be interrupted while reading it, and if so, to postpone reading it until you can be alone for a few minutes. You will infer from that suggestion that this is a letter of more than usual importance, and it is.

It is the sad purpose of my letter to tell you that your Mother and I have come to a parting of the ways and that at some time in the very near future she will begin suit for divorce. As you see, I am writing to you from Washington and for the time being at least, these rooms will be my home. As you will learn from your Mother (if you have not already), she intends to go to Reno, Nevada, after the spring holiday, there to establish legal residence necessary to obtain a Nevada divorce. The grounds for her divorce will be "mental cruelty" and "incompatibility of temperament" and although those terms are often meaningless except in a court of law, they do happen to state the case with some degree of accuracy. For you must have known for some time that your Mother and I, while maintaining outward appearances of a reasonably happily married couple, have, in fact, been incompatible. Many years ago, before your sister was born, we reached an impasse and almost separated then, but we decided to give it another try and for a while it worked out successfully. Unfortunately, however, the differences between us were so deep-rooted that the reconciliation did not last and in recent years ours has been, to use the hackneyed phrase, a marriage in name only.

You may, quite rightly, consider that I am being somewhat evasive in stating my case. It is natural for you to suspect that one of us or both of us have fallen in love with someone else. In my case that is true. I have been in love with a fine woman whose name is Mrs. Natalie Benziger Eustace, the widow of a Philadelphian. She, too, is a Pennsylvanian whom I first met about fifteen years ago and quite frankly I have been in love with her almost from the first moment I met her. But I do not want you to think of her as the villainess in a bad movie. The differences between your Mother and me had existed and been known to both of us before I met Mrs. Eustace (who was then Miss Benziger). I have no desire, furthermore, to imply even slightly that I regard your Mother as a villainess, or that I regard myself as a villain. If you have not already been in love and fallen out of it, the time will come when you will understand that that can happen. Your reasons for falling out of love will be your own reasons and probably totally different from mine, but at least you will see that it can happen. Even Rowland, who had he lived was going to marry that fine girl, Sadie Warren, had, I am quite sure, been attracted to other girls before he fell in love with Sadie. It is not always love when we think it is, and it does not always last even when it was. In the case of your Mother and me, it did not last. It did not survive the strain that was caused by our different outlooks on life and marriage. I am quite willing to take my share of the blame so long as in doing so I do not create the impression that some of *my* blame is also to be shared by Mrs. Eustace. She sent me away twice, but I went back to her because I did and do love her. As to your Mother, I do not know whether she has or has not any romantic interest, but I have no doubt that so attractive a woman, with so many admirers, will in due time remarry and I trust that the man she chooses will be acceptable to you without entirely taking my place in your life.

I have been very careful in this letter to avoid an apologetic tone. You are old enough now to know that marriages do fail; you have seen it happen among the parents of your friends. I would not be sincere if I took an apologetic tone or even made the chivalrous gesture of taking complete blame for the failure of my marriage. Such a gesture, if it were not based on conviction, would be an insult to your intelligence, for which I have great respect. However, I am also aware of the fact that for some time you and I have not been as close as we were in the past. I am not very happy about that, but it is something fathers have to face; the sons tend to drift away from their fathers, often at a time when the passage of years might be expected to cause them to enjoy each other's company. I hope that after the immediate effect of this news has begun to wear off, you and I can reestablish a cordial, friendly relationship based on mature understanding and mutual affection. Your Mother has agreed that I am to see you and Jean at certain intervals, but it is not my intention to insist on carrying out that agreement to the letter. I much prefer to leave some of those arrangements to you, or, in other words, to have you express the desire to see me. It should be obvious to you that such meetings cannot come too often for me, that I will write to you and see you as often as you like. I realize that that may be making it difficult for you, but all your life you have been able to ask me for anything and I want you to go on feeling that that, at least, has not changed.

Except for my absence on your school vacations, your life will not be affected by what has happened to your parents. You will stay at Groton, your finances will be the same as usual, you will continue to live in the apartment on 72nd Street and spend your summers at East Hampton. I suppose you would not call this a very warm letter, but you have almost reached an age where you could enlist in the Navy and thus assume some of the responsibilities of a full-grown man, and I have therefore tried to keep my words on the man-to-man level. But underneath it all I have the same love for you that I've always had and always will have and no words of a judge in Reno can ever change that. I am, as always,

> Your loving
> Father

The letter itself had not pleased Alfred, but he knew that whatever he said would be subject to the quick intelligence and wry comments of the boy and his present mood. Sentiment was out, self-abnegation could do lasting harm to him, to Natalie, and to the boy; and to pretend that he had not noticed Alex's indifference (if that was not too weak a word) would be to admit an insensitivity that did not exist or a willingness to trade respect for affection, which would result in the loss of both. The boy was alert and incisive and in all probability in for some disillusionment by his mother, and when that occurred, Alfred wanted Alex to be able to turn to him with confidence in his father's strength and dependability. With that his intention and purpose, Alfred had sent off the letter in spite of its business-like tone. Then, when he had mailed the letter, he had a feeling that he had performed an act of wisdom.

Wilson telephoned him at six o'clock on the Monday morning. "I called you a half an hour early, sir, because of what's in the papers. Commander Dantzig in the PRO's office wants to know how you intend to handle it."

"Tell Dantzig for the present any statement will have to come from my attorney, Rex Easterday, in New York. Otherwise I'll have no comment and I want the Navy kept out of it as much as possible. It has nothing whatever to do with the Navy, and if Dantzig isn't authorized to say any more than that, they'll stop bothering him *and* the Navy."

"Dantzig suggested maybe a press conference."

"Thank Dantzig for his suggestion and tell him it's rejected. I know Dantzig wants to keep on their right side, but I've anticipated all this and my mind is made up. If anything is going to be given to the press, it'll come from Mr. Easterday."

Not a soul of any rank or rating mentioned the news of the divorce throughout the day, and Alfred was almost relieved when at the end of the day his secretary said: "I'm sorry about the news that was in the paper."

"Thank you. Not surprised, though?"

Miss Canfield smiled. "Surprised? Oh, come on, Mr. Eaton. I wouldn't have been surprised three or four years ago."

"Aren't you the wise one, though? What else do you know?"

"Well, for two years I've known the lady's name."

"How?"

"You don't make many slips, but in my job I'm very likely to be there when you make them."

"Come on. Don't hold out."

"Well, you chartered a boat two summers ago, I think it was."

"And?"

"And the lady left her purse with her driver's license and other identification on the boat. The boat people returned it to you here, and I sent it to the address on Fifty-fifth Street."

"And never said anything to me."

"You were away, in Washington, I think."

"But why didn't you say anything to me?"

"Oh, you'd have been upset."

840

"There's nobody like you. What were the other slips?"

"One. She must have paid you for something. There was a cheque for something like, let me see, oh, something like $44.26. I guess you figured that you were safe as long as there were no cheques made out to her and signed by you, but you gave me the cheque with several others and I deposited it, and I said to myself, 'Hmm, I remember *that* name.' Would you mind my asking what was that cheque for? It was such an odd sum, it's always piqued my curiosity."

"It was for her half of something. I bought something and paid for it, and she reimbursed me for her half. Something I paid cash for. Oh, I know! Now we're getting into some intimate details, Miss Canfield."

"Oh, excuse me."

"It was for a record player. She didn't want it and I did, but she wouldn't let me pay the whole bill. Your memory is good. It came to about $90 plus tax."

"She must be a nice woman."

"You have my word for that. You'll meet her in a little while. After Mrs. Eaton graduates from Reno. That's where she's going in a few weeks. And by the way, whatever happens here, I hope you're going to stay on with me. In other words, if I become persona non grata here, I hope you're going back to New York with me."

"That's for sure. The work here is interesting, but there's nothing to do at night. In New York I could go to the theater, and go see my sister in Brooklyn, and I had my friends. But in Washington if you're not in the Waves or the Wacs a single woman my age might as well be resigned to it."

"Yes, I should imagine it'd get pretty tedious. But save your strength. You'll need it when I start my own business."

"That I'll really take an interest in. At MacHardie & Company things were sort of cut and dried, but starting a new business should be inspiring. I'll really like that. All new partners, new personnel. And even you, you'll have a new wife, won't you?"

"God willing."

"I'm really looking forward to after the war—in spite of your speeches, Mr. Eaton."

"This may happen before the war's over."

"No, the scuttlebutt—"

"The *what?*"

"Yes, I say that and 'squared away.' But I refuse to say deck for floor. Anyhow, the scuttlebutt today was that the divorce isn't going to affect you with the Navy. You're only doing what a lot of the brass would like to do, and may have to if their wives catch on. So they don't dare crack down on you, at least that's the word today, for fear it would set a precedent. Some of the brass at CINCPAC are really living it up, I hear."

"You may not say deck for floor, but you talk Navy talk. Well, permission granted, if you want to leave the ship, and thanks for a pleasant conversation."

She grinned at him. "Say, you're entitled to eight side-boys. Why don't you get one of them for me?"

"Good*night*, Miss Canfield."

The quasi-official view of the divorce news was, as often happened, precisely that predicted in the scuttlebutt. "They're trying to ignore it the way they would if I had a boil on my nose," he said to Miss Canfield, when the newspapers reported Mary's departure for Reno. The Washington hostesses became more persistent in their efforts to change his anti-social habits, and he was quite sure he detected something extra in the glances of the Waves he passed in the corridors. But he contrived to be out of town on Navy business during most of Mary's residence period in Reno, and he was actually in Los Angeles on the day the divorce was granted in May.

There was no "Hollywood angle" to his divorce, but he was nevertheless amused by the fact that after finishing lunch in the executives' diningroom at a studio, he was completely ignored by the studio press agent who wanted the two admirals in the luncheon party to pose for photographs with the male and female stars of a spy picture. The admirals obliged while the Assistant Secretary waited in his car, with Wilson on the front seat. "Wilson, you ought to be out there," said Alfred.

"Sir, I don't want any pictures with movie gals. I got me that little old ex-wife in Trenton, New Jersey. Only separated. She sees my picture in the paper with one of these broads and up goes the dough I have to pay her. Oh, I got something lined up, but there won't be any pictures. Sir, look at Admiral Quinn. I don't think Mrs. Quinn's going to like that, either. I know Mrs. Quinn."

"Well, then make a note of this. Ask these people to use some discretion about the pictures they send out."

"Yes sir. And they'll cooperate."

"You bet they'll cooperate. They want a lot of Navy film for their picture. No, I don't think Mrs. Quinn would be too pleased. Who's the actress?"

"Don't you know her? She's that French actress from, as they'd say in France, the Departmong of the Gowanus."

"The Gowanus Canal?"

"Yes sir. Good old Brooklyn. Colette Sauvoir."

"Looks French from here."

"Well . . . ?" said Wilson.

"No thanks."

842

"It's D-Day for the Secretary."

"D-Day? Oh, yes. Still no thanks. I only know a few words in Gowanus."

Wilson laughed. "Very good. A few words in Gowanus. Huh, huh, huh."

"That's quite a hunk of woman," said Quinn, when they were under way. "But just between you and me and the bedpost, she's no more French than I am. I happen to speak pretty good French, so I rattled off a few sentences and I was much too fast for her."

"Harry, what you asked her was probably too fast in any language," said Strove, the other admiral.

"Could be. Could be. But eventually I got the right answer, and that's what counts, n'est-çe pas, Mr. Secretary?"

"Absolument, Mon Admiral," said Alfred. "Decidement."

He dropped the admirals at an office building in downtown Los Angeles, as uninterested in what they were doing there as they were in him (having been quietly assured by Wilson that Eaton's visit need not concern them). They bored him, he bored them, and he was tired. He had not yet received word that the divorce had gone through; the Reno attorney who was Easterday's correspondent was instructed to telephone Easterday, and Easterday was to send Alfred a telegram to the Navy Building in Washington, which Miss Canfield would forward to Alfred at the Beverly Hills Hotel. Mary had been so docile throughout the weeks of conferences with Easterday and the residence in Reno that now that the waiting was reduced to a few hundreds of minutes, the tension was compressed and increasing.

The admirals had climbed over him and disappeared, and Wilson, who liked to sit in the rear seat with the Assistant Secretary, was waiting on the curb with the door hanging open. "Oh, sorry, Wilson. Get in."

"Aye, aye, sir," said Wilson.

"How far is it to Oceanside?" said Alfred.

"Sailor, how far is it to Oceanside?"

"A good eighty miles from here, sir," said the driver.

"A good eighty miles," said Wilson.

"And it's ten past four," said Alfred. "I'm afraid I'm going to have to disappoint the marines."

"There was no special time for your arrival there, sir," said Wilson. "It was left at some time late this afternoon."

"I know it was, and at the moment I'm glad it was. We'd be two hours on the road, and I don't like to interrupt the marines at their chow."

"No sir," said Wilson.

"Although of course you could point out to me that there won't be any chow-line on those beach landings."

"No sir. Combat conditions."

"So in that respect it wouldn't make any difference what time I got there."

"No sir."

"What's that general's name again?"

"Major General Irving K. Robert, USMC, sir."

"I'll end the suspense, Wilson. Take me back to the hotel, and my compliments to General Robert. I'll try to get down there tomorrow."

"Aye, aye, sir."

Alfred's name was not publicly registered at the hotel; it was necessary to call him by room number; but messages were taken by the operator on an as-if-and-when basis, and relayed to him through the assistant manager and Wilson. Thus it was that there was a telegram from Easterday in the same batch with a message to call a New York number which Alfred recognized as Natalie's. The telegram read:

MISSION ACCOMPLISHED ON SKED AND ACCORDING TO PLAN (SIGNED) REX

He put off telephoning Natalie until he had dismissed Wilson for the night, and in the meantime a telegram arrived from Reno via Washington:

MRS. ST. JOHN EATON—NO SIG.

He wondered about that: had Mary's succinctness been caused by the wartime regulation against congratulatory telegrams, or had she really had an inspiration? He decided to be gracious, in the circumstances, and credit her with an inspiration. After all, she was under no obligation to telegraph him anything, and she surely had noticed that the divorce was granted only a week short of their twenty-third wedding anniversary.

He had not seen Natalie since the last morning with Mary. He lied to Natalie: he told her that Easterday had advised him against being alone with any woman until the decree was made final. The truth was that he was afraid his guilt would be apparent to Natalie the moment she saw him, and, with more craftiness, he was certain that if she did not detect guilt, she would in any event see and feel some change in him that would puzzle her and worry her, and in the process of trying to make him unburden himself she would accidentally force a confession. And he knew himself and her: he knew that his shame and guilt were dangerous, in that no matter how much she might be disposed to forgive him for an act that was hardly more than functional, she would be compelled by the sincerity of his regret to consider the act on his own terms: he had

844

been unfaithful to her. And there was closely following that the fear that she would quite consistently maintain that it would mean nothing if once or twice during the divorcing period she should go to bed with Sterling Calthorp or anyone else who answered the functional need. She *would not* so argue, his judgment of her told him, but she *could* so argue, and an admission of guilt left him weak and vulnerable, subject to her whim, her kindness, and her love. She had never been unfaithful to him; marriage to Ben Eustace and the affair with Calthorp had taken place before mutual fidelity had been tacitly agreed upon. He had often thought that in the future they would date their marriage not from the legal transaction but from the beginning of their second affair, which deserved a better word than *affair* had come to mean. He could never explain to her that their relationship had been a continuous one made exciting by climaxes of love-making but never descending to the low that he had felt toward Mary on the last morning. Natalie might know all that, but she would need to be told and have every right to be told, and she would want to be told, but he could only hear the impotence of his explanation. And he had never learned to plead.

He wished that he could explain to Natalie that the half-hour with Mary could as easily have belonged with the un-counted and forgotten sex matches with other women in other times. But that was not so; the lie was too big. Mary had touched him and made him a liar to himself; he was not invulnerable to her and he was not even immune to a self-contained desire of her. Easterday was perceptive and right, as much in what he did not say as in what he said, for Easterday had implied that Alfred was potentially a willing partner to a repetition of the act. Regardless of his regret and his determination to avoid what the Roman Church called the occasion of sin, Alfred recognized as a fact Mary's special and unique talent for creating in him the desire that correspondingly was all she offered. In a sense, then, she was triumphant in her denial of love's existence; she could produce in him the same functional expression of love that was as much as she asked for while rejecting love itself. And thus, finally, in their last moment together, she had had him in her own way and not in the way that he had tried to force upon her. It was more than the casual piece of tail that he had pretended to believe it to be. Final or not, she had shown him that he could want to make love to her and with her at the very moment of his new and confident independence, with scorn for her and love of Natalie on his side. And Mary would go on knowing that so long as the three of them and she and any one of them lived.

A well-fed chief yeoman took dictation for Alfred until a few minutes past six. Alfred let him and Wilson go for the night, and as soon as he was sure that Wilson was not up to his old trick of returning for something he had deliberately forgotten, Alfred called Natalie.

"Hello?" she said.

"Name the day," he said.

"Isn't it wonderful? There's something in the late afternoon papers. Just a paragraph, but it's all there. Are you having champagne?"

"Not till I see you. How are you?"

"How are *you?* Have you had any last-minute misgivings?"

"I had some last-hour jitters."

"So did I. You mean, that something might go wrong?"

"Yes."

"Well, she's probably just as glad to be free as you are."

"I hope she is. I hope she finds a guy quickly and marries him. Some fairly reliable guy. I don't want her to marry somebody that'll take her for a lot of dough and then have her come to me."

"I know I shouldn't ask, but are you anywhere near here?"

"No. I'm in California, but I'll see you Sunday, if that's okay with you."

"It'll be okay with me."

"I'd be in a hell of a spot if it wasn't. Seriously, give some thought to my first remark. About naming the day."

"We'll talk about that Sunday."

"But let's not put it off any longer than we have to. All we want is a civil ceremony."

"That's all I want, but I was thinking of how much notice I ought to give at the shop, and where we're going to live and all those things."

"Okay. I'll see you Sunday, and I love you."

"I love you, and I won't set foot outside till you get here. Goodnight, my love."

"Goodnight." It was still bright daylight where he was, and probably not yet dark in New York, but it was the right word to say.

It came upon him that he had not been so alone in twenty-three years. He was wifeless and in effect childless, his mother was measurably 3,000 miles away and immeasurably remote by the state of her mind and of her feelings for him. One sister was in India, the other in Pennsylvania, and both had their own lives and interests. His best friend was aboard a carrier in the Pacific, and Alfred was already apprehensive about Lex. That friendship was over, enduring only until poor, foolish little Clemmie risked her own life and turned the friendship into hatred by a single, petulant remark. The scene was as clear as though it had already happened, and the inevitability of it was as relentless as death itself. Clemmie could avoid personal danger by an action that Alfred doubted she would take: if she would tell Lex by letter that she had fallen in love with another man and wanted a divorce, Lex might give his consent. She could then marry and stay away from Lex. That, too, was the only possible way out of Lex's discovery of Clemmie's single night with Alfred. But Clemmie did not want to be married to anyone else; Lex Porter was rich enough and he had the Porter social position that she would lose upon divorcing him. But none of that would happen. The first time Lex got leave he would ask her the same question that was being asked a million times a year: had she been faithful? She would lie, and now he would know she lied, and in the quarrel that ensued she would stop lying and tell too much truth, and if Lex did not kill her then, it would be a miracle.

It was odd, Alfred told himself, how he had become convinced that his best friend was capable of murder. He had known that Lex had deliberately killed at least two men. It was kill or be killed, in aerial dog-fights, but Lex had once told him that in both cases he had got close enough to the German pilots to see their faces. He had missed one of them on the first pass, turned and banked and gone into pursuit of the German until he was again in range, then shot him in the head with a burst from the Lewis gun. His second kill was faster, but it had been deliberate and he had seen the German's face in spite of goggles and helmet. Lex had come down out of a cloud less than a hundred feet above the German, who looked up and died with the incredulous, startled expression still on his face. In telling the stories Lex had referred to both Germans as "the poor son of a bitch" but there was no pity in the phrase, and if there was ever any regret, Alfred had not known it. Lex was a man of cold violence, willing to take his own chances but not to be satisfied with an uncompleted fight. No woman who came to the Gramercy Park apartment was allowed to change her mind after she got there, and with Clemmie on the ranch he probably had been passionate but not ardent. He undoubtedly thought he loved Clemmie and, in his way, did. In any case, she was his wife, and his inadequacy for her was obviously serious enough to make her take the risks she must have known she was taking. It was almost a certainty that Lex and Alfred would have a bloody fist-fight that would last as long as their middle-aged strength, and it could happen anywhere. But a fist-fight was not a murder.

When he got back to Washington Alfred found a letter from Sally on the pile of personal mail.

Alfred dear:

Can't tell when my important brother will get to Port Johnson again, so I am writing you now. The good news first, or I think it's good news. Our Florence Nightingale sister is on her way home—*a bride!* She is a bride unaccompanied by husband, but husband has left a little souvenir in the reproductive organs. Yes, Constance is married and pregnant and politely kicked out of the Red Cross. (Don't ask me whether married & pregnant is the right order—I may have it in reverse.) She fell in love with a Lt. Col. William J. Day, who was stationed in India with the Air Corps, at a place called Assam. No cracks, please. They were married about a month ago as far as I have been able to discern from her tiny handwriting on V-mail stationery. She is gloriously happy and I am too. Anything is better than that Philadelphia romance I am sure you will agree. Of course having a child at her age is risky (just turned 41) but well worth the chance for Constance, who I always thought would be a wonderful mother. Mr. Day, or I should call him Lieutenant Colonel Day, writes for the movies. He is a year younger than C. and went to the University of Washington. Has had two novels published but C. did not give the titles and they are not listed in the P. J. library files.

The other news is not bad but is on the unpleasant side. Some fool from the paper called up and asked Mother about your divorce, the first she had heard of it. La Trimingham is usually more efficient than that but she let the reporter speak to Mother, who threatened to have the man fired, denied everything, etc. I know you told her Mary was in Reno but she forgets things. I am telling you this in case you happen to telephone or come home, you will understand her attitude. She is getting very old. Fun for a while but when her mind begins to wander it is pathetic.

I want to hear all about your divorce and future plans so here's hoping you do get home soon. Meanwhile, with all love,

Ever,
Sally

There was other mail, and there was a problem in etiquette: whether to send flowers to Mary in New York. He decided against it.

THE FURNISHED HOUSE they rented belonged to an Army colonel who had a rich wife, who was more concerned with what happened to her Meissen pieces and her husbands' Meissonier than with any supra-OPA rental arrangements. The colonel was at Schofield, sitting out his buck general's star, and his lady was back home in Louisville with her railroad bonds and whiskey shares. The covenant between the Alfred Eatons and

848

the Colonel Farridees was enough like the Jagger's Cove agreement to prompt Alfred to tell Natalie about it before signing. "I see what you mean," said Natalie. "But I'm not that superstitious, so let's grab it." The fact that Alfred was Assistant Secretary of the Navy cut no ice with Mrs. Colonel Farridee, but a warm recommendation from Templeton Avirett and Natalie's being a sister alumna of Miss Baldwin's School clinched the deal, with a payment of three months' rent in advance and some complicated provisions for insurance, inventories, restrictions on the use of certain sets of china, exclusion of any and all animals, and a gentlemen's agreement covering the smoking of cigars in the sittingroom and in Mrs. Colonel Farridee's bedroom. "I don't know how we're going to break that news to Jean Duffy," said Alfred. "I guess I just don't offer her a cigar, and hope she doesn't bring any of her own."

"It's going to raise hell with me," said Natalie. "*I* was thinking of taking up cigars. Especially since Lucky Strike green has gone to war. Cigarettes don't taste the same as they used to."

"You'd look well with a cigar."

"Yes, I know. Or is that a crack about my moustache?"

"I wouldn't go and make any crack about your moustache, sweetie-pie. I'm just jealous because I can't grow as good a one."

She swung a slap at him and missed.

There was a fair amount of semi-official entertaining for the new Mrs. Eaton, and the verdict was that she was an addition to the Washington-Georgetown scene. She was handsome enough for the most discriminating men, and she was Alfred's wife so quickly after his divorce that the women gratifyingly guessed at the truth of her previous relationship with him. A few of the women had known Natalie in Philadelphia, but Natalie had never been in Society. Ben Eustace's connections had been solid and good, but by the time he married Natalie he was no longer in a position where his connections automatically assured acceptance of an upstate girl without connections of her own. The Philadelphia expatriates recalled that there had been *some* talk about Natalie Eustace and Red Calthorp, but the revived gossip on that score was fairly gentle since Red Calthorp was either related to or had been said to have had relations with several of the women, and they all had to think twice before speaking. And in any event, Natalie's quick marriage to Alfred was enough to account for her recent activities in the adultery line.

A considerable number of the Washington-Georgetown women had fled the Washington summer, and the entertaining was for that reason as well as for the war reason informal and easy. The dinners were small and simple, and invariably the drop-in trade, as it was called, of men and women who arrived after dinner, brought more people than had sat at table. Also, partly as a consequence of the war, the ages of the guests at any party ranged from the low twenties to the low seventies, with hardly any distinction of intimacy between very young brides and recent grandmothers. They shared a genuine interest and concern in each other's absent husbands and sons and a woman's face was often the brightest at a party because she had just received two or three long-awaited V-mails. Natalie soon caught on to the slightly defensive attitude of women whose husbands were "cooped up in Washington" on desk jobs, the swivel-chair commanders and filing-corps majors. Her brother, Ralph Benziger, Junior, was an Air Force major who did all his flying while reading contracts and the transcripts of courts-martial, and she had no one closer than a second cousin from Fort Penn, Pennsylvania, who was being shot at by the enemy. But many of the wives did not know what their husbands were doing, and did not know where they went when they went overseas for weeks or months without leaving an APO number. These were the wives of the O. S. S. men, and there were enough of them to give a sort of blanket protection to all the wives whose husbands were not in infantry battalions or destroyer-escorts. A woman whose husband had an innocuous job in Interior was surprised and delighted when her husband came home with the Medaille Militaire, and a woman whose son had never been in uniform quietly drank herself into a stupor every night because she knew (and everyone else knew) that he had been last seen parachuting over northern Italy, now seven months ago. They could not say he was dead, they would not say he was alive.

For lack of a good reason to dislike her, and because she was restful to the eye and friendly, the women accepted Natalie on a wartime basis, on the same basis that most of them had had to qualify when they first moved to Washington. "You're a great success," said Alfred one night.

"Well—a success so far," she said. "I think I'll have one or two friends when we leave here. You forget, this is a new experience for me. When I was first married to Ben we had to go through quite a lot of family-dinner-party kind of thing. And some of them put it off as long as they could. They knew Ben better than I did, and they wondered why I'd married him. Then after they'd done their duty by the family, *kerplunk!* We were dropped. Sink or swim. Make your own way. And of course Ben made his own way to the Racquet Club bar and more or less stayed there. Here I'm your wife, attractive man, important job, and I think a lot of them respect me because you gave so much money to Mary. These people are pretty wise about money and they know you're not a billionaire."

"Still a millionaire, kid. That aint tin."

"No, but they know you gave up half of what you had—"

"Not quite."

"Let me make my point. They know I love you. They all know that. But they know you love me, too, or you wouldn't have given up seven-sixteenths of what you had to marry me. *And* you're not so Texas rich that I married you for your money. Of course they also know you didn't marry me for *my* money."

"It may turn out that way."

"Anyway, I'm glad they like me. It's nice to be liked, and I always have been except for Philadelphia while I was married to Ben. I've always gotten along well with people."

"Yes. I wonder why it is, when underneath it all you're such a reptilian character. If they only knew what a devious, Machiavellian woman you are."

"Don't say that. You'll make me cry. Honestly."

"Are you serious? I believe you are."

"I am. I couldn't bear to find out that I was different from the way I think I am."

"Then do you want an expert to tell you what you are?"

"You?"

"Yes."

"All right."

"I think you're the nicest woman I ever knew. One of the very few genuinely nice men *or* women I've ever known. I've known you for sixteen years, and I've never known you to do anything mean and I don't think you've ever thought a mean thought. I think you're probably the most honest person I've ever known, even including your father. It was always a toss-up in my mind whether your father or James MacHardie was the most honest person I'd ever met, but actually you are. I think you've managed to be all these things in spite of some big disappointments. In life. In love. In me. In people as a whole. In the Divine scheme of things. I think you started life as a cheerful, quite lovable kid and you kept it through puberty and adolescence, in spite of all the things you saw in the bushes around Mountain City and the pretty shocking things you'd be exposed to in a mining town. Also, in spite of the shocking things that happened to you with Ben and probably the other men in your life. I think you have real courage to do some of the things you've done and some of the things you didn't do. In addition to all that you're a feast to the eye, and you're the only woman I've ever known who could be in one woman all that I want and need in a woman. I'm sorry for the bad times I've given you, and I'm sorry that

I didn't have enough in myself to keep from giving you those bad times. I don't know what made you what you are. Your father's greatness and your mother's beauty, of course, but there must have been a great-grandfather or a great-great-grandmother somewhere that handed something down to you. It's something more than your father or your mother had, and your brother hasn't got it. I'd trust my life to your quickest instinct, because I know it'd be right. And I do trust my life to something that isn't a quick instinct, your love and your decency and patience and understanding. And I have only one thing more to add. You're a lady."

"God. God. Oh, my love. My dear sweet love. I shouldn't cry. But I have to. No woman ever had anything so beautiful said to her."

"There's no poetry in me, my dear. It's only what I think of you."

They sat together, with her under his arm, until the shuddering of her breath ended her weeping. She sat up and looked at him and smiled. "You'll never lose me now," she said.

"Was I going to?"

"No, but now you couldn't. I didn't know you loved me that much."

"You didn't? No, I guess you didn't. But I do."

"Some day I'll tell you how I love you. Not now, though. I couldn't do it justice."

He stood up. "Guess it's time to put the cat out."

"What cat?"

"Just an expression."

"Oh. I know what you're doing."

"What?"

"You're returning to the prosaic things of life. But I'll never forget what you said to me tonight. And do you know, there's only one person I could ever tell it to."

"Good God, who's that?"

"If we had a daughter. I'd like to tell it to our daughter the first time she ever confided in me that she was in love."

"Well, as I said, I guess it's time to put the cat out. Whatever happens after that, I'm not responsible for."

"All right, if you're not too tired."

Most mornings they did not even have breakfast together. He rose at six-thirty, usually having shaved before going to bed, and she would prepare breakfast for him and one or two other men whom he had invited for breakfast appointments. The orange juice was at the places at table, the coffee was in a Thermos jug, and the eggs on toast were kept warm in an electric chafing-dish on the sideboard. Natalie did not appear. Her Negro cook-maid reported in mid-afternoon and stayed through dinner, if dinner was not too late, in which case the woman went home and left the dishes for Natalie. After breakfast Natalie was left alone until lunchtime and she passed the mornings at dusting Mrs. Colonel Farridee's figurines and decorative dishes and pillboxes; at marketing; at the telephone; and at reading every bit of war news that concerned the Navy, which at that time was brief. She had no compunction about her failure to sign on with any of the women's volunteer war activities. She luxuriated in her first home with Alfred and in this substitute for a wedding trip. Their marriage at Elkton, Maryland, was performed by a Baptist minister but was entirely devoid of religious circumstance and except for the clergyman and the words he read, it was kept strictly to the legal essentials of a civil ceremony. Their first two weeks were at Alfred's apartment in the Wardman Park, until, largely through the good work of Templeton Avirett, they saw the Farridee house. Major Ralph Benziger, Junior, announced the marriage of his sister, Mrs. Natalie Benziger Eustace, and every trivial thing she did had meaning for Natalie because the big thing that had meant so much for so long was now in the real present instead of the improbable future. She was made happy by the small things that continually reminded her of the real present; the routine tasks of running a household were a grown-up version of playing with dolls, and she admitted it to herself and to her husband. "I'm very glad we have so many stairs," she told him.

"It is a change from living in an apartment. Apartments can get uninteresting if you've been brought up in a three-story house, with attic and cellar."

"I wasn't thinking of that so much as my figure."

"Do we have to talk about your figger, my dear? After all, married only such a short while. Certain reticences, you know. Period of getting acquainted. Intimate side of marriage. Things better left unsaid. Familiarity. Illusions. One shouldn't say cock in front of the little woman."

"What I was thinking of—and you *shouldn't* say cock in front of the little woman—was that if it weren't for the stairs, I'd begin to worry about my weight. At the shop I walked miles every day, and I was on my feet most of the time."

"Yes, that almost follows, doesn't it? If you walked miles, you'd have to be on your feet a good deal of the time. You're not a knee-walker, like certain Hindu sects, or a hand-walker. Or are you? Can you walk on your hands?"

"I could at one time."

"And drink a glass of water?"

"What?"

"Walk on your hands and drink a glass of water at one time. It's a good trick if you can do it."

"Do you know who you don't remind me of?"

"No, my dear."

"Soames Forsyte. When you try an English accent the Port Johnson, Pennsylvania, comes out like an I-don't-know-what."

"Oh, you can't let me down that way. Finish the simile. Like what? Like a set of false teeth? Like one of Jean Duffy's jugs? Like the pants of a blue serge suit? Like money from home?"

"No. Like an I-don't-know-what. Do you think I *am* putting on weight?"

"You're relentless. Where?"

"Where I don't want to."

"How can I tell when you're sitting down?"

"Well have you *noticed* that I was?"

"No, but I don't get back there very often."

"Stop it! I think I am putting on some. I can't tell by the bathroom scales. According to them I weigh a hundred and five, and I haven't weighed that since I was twelve."

"The Farridees are notorious for short weight. But don't worry, the Better Business Bureau has been notified. What the hell's all this talk about your weight, anyway?"

"I think I'm putting on weight, that's all, and I don't want to."

"Well, just cut out those starchy foods and banana splits. You're going to have a hickey for the Junior Prom, so don't say I didn't warn you."

"How much do you weigh?"

"About one eighty-eight. How much do you?"

"That's the trouble. I don't know. I weighed a hundred and thirty-one before we were married, on my scales at Fifty-fifth Street. But those scales are still in New York, so I can't tell whether I've gained or not."

"Well, start going by the scales here. You said you weighed a hundred and five?"

"Yes."

"Well, keep weighing yourself and see if you notice any difference."

"That might work out."

"Sure it will. There's only one thing wrong with my suggestion."

"What?"

"Well, according to those scales *I* weigh a hundred and five. But still—"

"I'm going to buy some new scales."

"Somehow I could see that coming, from way the hell out in left field. How about a tape measure?"

854

"I'm going to look around again and see if Mrs. F didn't leave one somewhere. I have looked several times, but I must have looked in the wrong places."

"Very likely. Here's a quarter. Why don't you buy a new one? If her tape measure is no more reliable than her scales, you'll never settle it, and I can see you're mighty worried."

"Well, I'm not really worried, but I don't want to get fat."

"You'll never get fat."

"You won't, but I might. Women do."

"Well, maybe I'd like you fat. Don't worry about it."

"You'd like me fat? Did you ever have an affair with a fat girl?"

"How fat?"

"Well, I don't know Mrs. Duffy, but as fat as you say she is."

"No. But I have laid some that were a great deal bulkier than you."

"But I'm not bulky. At least not yet."

"Well, when you start getting too bulky, I'll let you know."

"Will you promise?"

"Yes."

"Of course I'll know, when my clothes don't fit me."

"And *I'll* know when your clothes don't fit you."

"Oh, don't talk like a husband on the radio. Don't forget, I still get almost everything wholesale. And really wholesale, not just a discount. You know, I could probably get some things for *you* wholesale."

"Thanks, but I doubt it. Anyway, I don't need anything. I have all the suits I'll ever need. Overcoats. Shoes."

"I've never spent much money on clothes. Caroline English and I used to have the same clothes allowance, and I always came out a little ahead and she was always a little behind. *Don't bother*. I know. Little behind. You didn't say it, but you were going to."

"*You* said it."

"I'm really quite thrifty. That's my German ancestry, I suppose. Do you realize that the money I'm getting for the apartment is almost as much as I gave up by quitting the shop?"

"You may be thrifty, but you're wrong as hell about that. You got five hundred a month salary. Right? You get three hundred for the apartment."

"But the three hundred is all clear. You pay my bills."

"Oh. By the way, I'm going to try to work out something to start giving you money while I'm alive."

"Still alive? What kind of talk is that?"

"Practical talk. You know, I didn't actually hand over a

million dollars to Mary. She'll get a million, but she hasn't got it all at once. I'll explain it to you sometime. Meanwhile I want to have my tax man figure out the best way to give you some dough that won't be subject to inheritance taxes."

"Wait till after the war. You're going to need cash when you start the new business."

"Yes, but I'm still going to give you some every year."

"Don't you get a pension from the government?"

"Ha ha ha. Sardonic laughter. No. When I leave the government I even have to buy my office chair. If I want it."

"I'll buy it for a present, for our new house. Where shall we have our house?"

"In one of the medium-income sections of Hoboken. I don't know. Have you any ideas?"

"Some. A place near the water, because you miss sailing."

"Connecticut or Long Island."

"Not too far from New York, and not fashionable. When you're sixty I'd like you to retire from Wall Street. Not to quit work, but to start a new business that you could manage at home."

"That may happen long before I'm sixty. I may be weaving baskets for the State. Isn't that what they do in prison?"

"Now that's a fancy new thought. I've thought about you under all sorts of circumstances, but I never pictured you in prison."

"That's a chance you take whenever you handle other people's money. I think you have a low opinion of Wall Street. That's why you want me to retire from it."

"I honestly don't know what my opinion of Wall Street is. I probably distrust the whole idea of it because I'm a small-town girl, and I often saw my father go to work in boots and a miner's cap with a safety lamp on it."

"Whenever I saw your father he was dressed like a successful banker, or thereabouts."

"His taste in clothes improved after Ralph came home from college, then when Ralph left home—my father never seemed to care much about clothes."

"They didn't matter."

"No. But to get back to what we were talking about. If you don't want to retire, I'll give up now trying to make you. I just thought it would be nice to have that as a goal. We could spend more time together. I just don't want you to go on working hard. I know you'd like to get the new business started, and see it successful, but then what?"

"Think back. You know what my trouble is. I wanted to be the head man at MacHardie & Company, and that's out. Eaton & Company Incorporated would never be as important as MacHardie & Company, but it would be my baby.

And I just might persuade Alex to come in with me when he's ready."

"Oh, don't count on that. Not from all you've told me about him. I don't think he'll go into any business. At least not stocks and bonds or banking."

"He has expensive tastes, and that's where the money is. Right now it's writing. He thinks he wants to be a writer. But before that it was music and somewhere along the line it was painting."

"That's what I mean, though. He sounds more artistic than business-like."

"But he's not. If he wanted to do any of those things he'd have stuck to it and by this time made his choice. The fact is, boys nowadays seem to get exposed to more general culture than when I was his age, and for a while it's writing, then painting, then music. A little of each, and it doesn't do them any harm, so long as they don't kid themselves. But Alex doesn't quite fit in with the others. You see, he happens to be pretty good at math. So many of them want to write or something like that because they hate math, not because they really love literature or painting or music. So whatever he does, I think math will enter into it. You don't need to be a math shark in Wall Street. There are plenty of accountants and statisticians there who'll never make more than $25,000 a year, and most of them don't make anything like that. But if you're in a business like the one I'm hoping to start, the math will help you. It'd be a great advantage, put it that way, whereas the lack of it isn't fatal. The kind of math that he's good at isn't arithmetic. It's way beyond arithmetic. It would be entirely wasted on small business. That's arithmetic. But in really big business, a mathematically-minded man can clean up. I'm told that J. P. Morgan, the one that died before World War One, was a real mathematician. Unfortunately, you have touched on something that is quite true about a boy like Alex. Or let's put it this way, if Alex, who is a born mathematician, gets into it more deeply, then mathematics can be just as, uh, forbidding to a business career as if he'd really had a talent for writing or the artistic stuff. Mathematics then becomes an art, or an art form, and money ceases to mean a God damn thing. He'd go around with the ass out of his pants just like any sculptor or painter. I don't think Alex is all that good, but it could happen. The Morgan I spoke of, his father made his bundle in fire insurance, but he started out with stage coaches and hotels. In other words, the original rich Morgan was rich, all right, but it was the next generation, J. P., who was the born mathematician and used his talent for—oh, Christ. What wasn't he in? Munitions. Gold. Railroads. Maybe that's what will happen to Alex. I've made money, my father made money, both my grandfathers did all right. But none of us had that genius for it that Mr. Morgan had. Maybe Alex has."

"Is that what you want for him?"

"If he wants it, you're God damn right it is. If Alex Eaton wants to make twice as much money as Andrew Mellon, that's all right with me. This thing about only being able to ride in one car at a time, wearing one suit at a time, that's vinegar talk. That's the excuse of the guys that didn't make it or know damn well they never can. It's *my* excuse. I've got by on a first-rate intelligence without real brilliance, hard work, some personality, some independence that MacHardie encouraged, and an ardent desire to make more money than my old man made. Maybe I didn't set my sights high enough, but maybe I set them exactly as accurately as I could shoot. I know now and I've really known for a couple of years that I'll never be one of the five or ten biggest men in my field. So I'm going to have one more whack at it, and then maybe that place in Connecticut will look awfully good to me.

"I could never have told you this before we were married, it's so terribly personal. But when I took this Navy job I was proud of myself. Do you know why? Because I was giving up X years of my best chance to be a big shot. I could never say this to anyone but you. I'm convinced that this war will take another four or five years, and during that time I'll be completely out of touch with what I'm best at and spent my life doing. If I ever had a real chance, it was now. My experience, my age, my contacts, my day-to-day knowledge of what was going on. I was just about right if I was ever going to be. Not too young, not too old, not a failure, not too much of a success. And do you know what convinces me that I'm right?"

"What?"

"The fact that soon as I started making plans to come here, Percy Hasbrouck moved in. *He* knew I was ready, and he knew it was now or never for him. Well, I didn't take that into consideration at the time. That's second-guessing on Percy and the situation. But I did know that if I came down here for five years, I'd never get those years back, and I could almost surely say bye-bye to my big ambitions."

"Are you sorry?"

"If I was, I stopped being. The day Rowland was killed. I made my decision because I love my country. That isn't the reason now. It's because I love my son and I can't bear to think that he's dead. It's as if by working here I was. somehow keeping him alive. But I could never tell any of that to anyone but you. It's the most personal thing I've ever told anyone, and I'm amazed that I let it come out, even to you."

"But you did," she said, and rubbed the back of his hand. "You know, we knew each other so well, and we were so much in love. The sex has always been wonderful, and some of the difficult times were cruel but made us close. And yet in these three months I've really begun to realize that all the other time was like a long engagement. Is that why I wanted to be married so much? Because I knew that there was so much more? *You* are so much more. God *knows* I've been in love with you, but I'm only beginning to know the man I've been in love with. And don't misunderstand this, but I'm only beginning to know what it is to be in love."

"You're right. Everything else seems like kid stuff."

"Yes. Are you going to work tonight?"

"For about an hour or so."

"Well, I think I'll retire. Will you outen the lights?"

"I'll outen the lights."

She kissed him and left him.

He set up one of Mrs. Colonel Farridee's sturdy bridge tables and on it placed a tablet of lined yellow paper, a fistful of Navy pencils, and a dozen composition folders. He stood a floor lamp so that it illuminated the contents of the table, and switched off the other lamps. He worked for about an hour, stopped for a cigarette and was about to resume when the doorbell rang. His watch said ten-twenty, an unusual hour for callers.

He went to the door and in the light from the hall he saw a man in naval officer's blues, but he could not immediately identify the man or his rank. "Good evening," said Alfred.

"Lieutenant Commander Porter would like to pay his respects to the Assistant Secretary," said the man, saluting.

"Lieutenant Commander Po—Lex! For Christ's sake! Come in!"

Lex Porter entered, and Alfred saw that he limped and was carrying a walking-stick. They shook hands and embraced, and as they did Alfred got a whiff of whiskey, but Lex's mood seemed to be an affable one with perhaps a touch of diffidence or restraint. In any case, Alfred quickly dismissed the thought that Lex was on a mission of revenge, and relaxed in the pleasure of seeing his best friend. "Come on back where I can get a look at you," he said. He led Lex to the sitting-room and turned on some lights.

"Home work? I don't want to snafu any Navy business."

"Forget it. I was just finishing up. What's the walking-stick? Are you out of uniform? No, you've got a Purple Heart. What happened to you?"

"Oh, I dropped a cocktail shaker on my big toe."

"Oh, come off it. What did happen?"

"Well, I guess you didn't know I was on the *Tuscarora*."

"The jeep carrier. You took a fish," said Alfred. "Is that when you got it?"

"No, then we had a visit from a kamikaze on the way back to Pearl. He didn't do much damage to the ship because the boys on the fives were shooting better that day, but he came in sort of wobbly and hit us, and I got some old Sixth Avenue 'L' track in my foot. They say I may have led my last cotillion."

"How bad is it?"

"Oh, not bad. What the limeys used to call a blighty wound. I've had one operation and they're probably going to do another, but I'll be all right."

"What else have you got there? You've got a Silver Star."

"That was for destroying Navy property."

"What?"

"Well, another guy and I pushed a plane off the flight deck. The kamikaze had put it on fire, so we dumped it."

"I'll have to get the report on all this. I'm obviously not going to get it from you. How about a drink?"

"Well of course. I didn't come here to waste my time. Scotch, if you have any."

Alfred made the drinks. "How long have you been in these parts?"

"I got in yesterday. Here. I got home about two weeks ago, then I came down here yesterday."

"Is Clemmie with you?"

"No, she stayed in New York with Mother. Where's *your* wife? I want to meet her."

"I'll call her."

"No, not if she's in bed. I'm going to be here for a week or so, then I think they're going to send me to New York for the next operation."

"She wants to see you."

"I'll come in tomorrow, if I may. I've been paying some unofficial calls."

"You seem all right to me."

"Let's wait till tomorrow. I'll be bright and hung over. I can't tell you how sorry I was about Rowland."

"It was tough."

"I guess it still is. Well, God bless him." He raised his glass and drank. "I'm a little embarrassed, Alfred, and I might as well tell you why. I don't want you to think, or your *wife* to think it meant anything, but Clemmie and I spent last weekend with Mary, in East Hampton."

"Well, why shouldn't you? You knew Mary before I did."

"Oh, you know why I shouldn't. I don't want your wife to think my going there first meant anything."

"Hell, she wouldn't think that. Mary and Clemmie have

860

been seeing a lot of each other, and you live in New York. What the hell?"

"Well, I'm going to make it clear to Natalie."

"You don't have to do that."

"*I* feel I have to, so I'm going to. This is an attractive layout you've got here."

"Belongs to an Army colonel named Farridee. Actually I think it belongs to his wife, although it's in his name. He's at Schofield, or was the last I heard."

"That's a tough war there. Those Jap prisoners. They may take over any minute. Oh, shit, I've got nothing to be sore about. I'm home, and I'll probably be a civilian as soon as they fix up my foot. How do you like the job?"

"My job? Oh, it's all right. I don't envy you your Purple Heart but I'd like to have the Silver Star."

"Actually I hear you're doing a great job."

"Is there anybody in Washington they don't say that about? 'He's doing a terrific job.' Anything this side of high treason is a terrific job."

"Well, I'm glad to hear you say that. You haven't lost your sour old perspective."

"There are a lot of things to be sour about, but I wouldn't tell you about them. Bad for morale."

"If you don't mind my saying so, you don't look so good."

"For forty-six?"

"Christ, that aint old. You ought to get a load of some of those Seabees."

"I have. But they're out in the open air."

"Where the temperature gets to 130 Fahrenheit."

"They sweat it out. I don't even get to sweat any more. But I do as I'm told. Somebody has to make the chewing-gum or we'd lose the war. That's what I keep telling myself."

"If you want my candid opinion, nobody over thirty ought to be in uniform. Let the young ones do the fighting and we'll stay home and do the fucking."

They talked for two hours, and Lex drank three drinks to every one of Alfred's. At one o'clock Alfred said, "What time do you have to get back to the hospital?"

"I'm not going back to the hospital. I have a date with a senator's girl friend. When she gets through tickling him with a feather, he goes home and I move in."

"You made fast time."

"Yep. I met her this afternoon at a cocktail party. I took one look at that shape and I said, 'Dear one, you could do a lot for Navy War Relief.' She looked at me and didn't say anything and I thought she was going to haul off and poke me, but then she said, '*I'm* interested.' "

"Do you know anything about her?"

"All I need to know. She's about thirty-five or so, divorced, has an apartment that the senator pays for, and she works in some department store. The senator has first call on her, but I don't imagine that's very often. He's sixty-five anyway."

"Well, watch your step."

"On account of Clemmie?"

"Naturally."

"Clemmie. That's really something, that Clemmie. I don't think I was out of the country before she started cheating on me. I know you're going to think I'm a shit before I get through telling you about Clemmie, but Clemmie asked me for a divorce before I went away. She was quite frank about it. She said all the other women were making impossible promises, but she wasn't going to, so rather than have me pass up anything because I thought she was staying pure, why not give her a divorce and then if we still liked each other after the war, get married again. Well, what the hell. No children. She had a point. But I said, 'I'll play it your way, but why bother about a divorce?' I don't think she was absolutely faithful to me before the war, but I couldn't prove anything and at that time I didn't want to. I was pretty stuck on her. I was in love with the little—well, what the hell.

"But it's one thing to know about it, and another thing to see it with your own eyes. And that, my friend, is where you're going to think I'm a shit.

"Last weekend. East Hampton. Your house, or Mary's house. I took a nap after lunch. We had the corner bedroom above the patio. I woke up around four o'clock and I could hear the ocean and a few birds, but otherwise not a sound. And then I heard some voices down on the patio and I went to the window and looked down and little Clemmie was there in her bathing suit, stretched out on one of those beach chairs, and I was just about to call down to her to fix me a Collins and I heard her say, 'Darling, will you reach me those matches?' And then I saw that she wasn't alone. This young man went over and stood beside her and lit her cigarette, but while he was lighting the cigarette she put her hand on his hip and he kept standing there and she worked her way around until she had her hand on top of his fly, and I heard her say, 'Do you like that?' and he laughed, and I think he said, 'Do you?' And she said, 'I think I might, but I can't tell this way.' So damned if she didn't get up and look around, took off her bathing suit and put on a beach robe, lay down on the beach chair again and she screwed him while he still had his pants on. Isn't she something? Mary could have walked in on them. One of the maids. Your daughter. Me. Anybody. She just got the urge, he was there, and that was that."

"What did you do?"

862

"Me? Well, then she came upstairs, all wrapped up in her beach robe, and hiding the bathing suit underneath it and headed for the bathroom. I'll tell you what I did. I let her get past me and then I yanked the beach robe off her and tossed her on the bed. It was that or go attack one of your maids, or Mary."

"But what about the guy? Did you do anything to him?"

"No."

"And I guess I know why."

"You think you do?"

"Yes. Because the guy was my son, your namesake. Was it?"

"Yes."

"Well, it'll probably do him more good than harm."

"You're not sore?"

"I have no right to be. I got off to an early start myself. But I'm surprised that you weren't sore."

"I was. But I was more hot nuts than sore."

"What was her reaction?"

"She didn't know how to take it. She wasn't sure I'd seen anything."

"Didn't you finally admit that you had?"

"No."

"That isn't like you."

"I know it isn't. And if it had been anybody but your kid I'd probably have given her, and him, a good thumping around. I *was* pretty God damn sore. I haven't gone into all the details. But your kid is now one of the best educated boys at my old school, as of last Saturday."

"When I was his age I went around thinking I was the only guy that really knew about women. Do you know why I think a lot of guys had some experience but didn't admit it?"

"No."

"Because when you and I were growing up we were under a sort of Y. M. C. A. morality that had us believing that every guy had to be as virginal as the girl he married. I think the women spread that propaganda, then they all got sore as hell because their husbands were no good in the hay."

"Well, a lot of guys were virgins, and their women did get sore, and promptly went out and slept with guys that were a little older and more experienced. I tell you, Eaton boy, the women run the God damn country, and as far as I'm concerned, they always will, as long as they've got that little fur piece. I trust that the senator's girl friend has had it marcelled, because dear one, here I come." He stood up.

"I'll call Veteran for a taxi."

"No Navy car for the wounded sailor?"

"No Navy car till Oh-800."

"Your company, delightful as it may be, doesn't offer the

proper consolation for the jolly tar. I therefore request permission to leave the ship."

"Permission granted as soon as the taxi gets here." Alfred telephoned, and a taxi was promised in five minutes.

"Shall I tell Natalie you'll be in tomorrow about six-thirty? We're going out to dinner, but we can make some plans tomorrow about having a party for you. Or maybe we'd better wait till Clemmie comes down."

"Clemmie isn't coming down. I have her stashed away at Mother's for when I go to New York. Oh, speaking of New York, do you ever see our old chum Larry Von Elm? I know you never p'ticly liked Larry, but I had a letter from some guy asking me if I'd write a letter for Larry at the Racquet. Is that a good idea?"

"No."

"You don't think I ought to write a letter for old Larry?"

"No."

"He must be coming up in the world, though. He knows people at the Racquet Club that I don't know. I never heard of this fellow, whatever his name was."

"There are guys in the Racquet Club now that never heard of *you*. You're just a name in the book, with Buffalo, Wyoming, after it."

"Well, if that's what it's come to, why not let old Larry in?"

"Do me a favor and don't write a letter for Von Elm."

"Oh, all right, if you feel that strongly about it. Why? Is he a crook or something?"

"He's something. Just don't write a letter for him. There's your taxi."

"Where's my taxi?"

"Car outside. See you tomorrow."

"Thanks, old boy. Good to see you, damned if it isn't."

Even at a ratio of 1 to 3, and not nearly so strong, the drinks that Alfred had taken with Lex were beyond his recent capacity and he went to bed slightly drunk for the first time in years. He was careful not to awaken Natalie, and when he opened his eyes in the morning she was standing over him, frowning and worried.

"Darling, is there anything wrong?" she said.

"Oh, Lord, is there!"

"Why did you get drunk after I went to bed?"

He sat up. "You mustn't worry," he said. "I'm not turning into a solitary lush. I had a visitor. Lex Porter."

"Oh, that's better."

"You mustn't worry about me, Natalie. *We're all right.*"

"Thank God. I'll get you some coffee while you're shaving. You didn't shave before you went to bed."

"You mustn't worry. You mustn't jump to conclusions."
864

"I know. It's so good, I can't get used to it," she said. "And when I smelled that whiskey this morning . . ."

"Bring me a Coke with a lot of ice and I'll tell you about my evening while the coffee's boiling."

She sat on the top of the tub while he shaved and gave her a considerably censored account of Lex's visit, with no mention whatever of Clemmie's adventure with Alex. He had not decided what to tell her about that.

"Do you still like him as much as ever?"

"Lex? You're so acute. No, I guess I don't, but I'll continue to like him better than any other friend my own age. And he's going to need a friend."

"Why?"

"Oh, he just is. It's too long to go into it now. I have the feeling that he's just where he was when he came back from the first war, but this is twenty-four years later. Lex belonged in an entirely different era, when knights were bold and so forth. I'll tell you when we have more time."

They were on their way to dinner the next night. "Well, what did you think of him?"

"Lex Porter?"

"Yes."

"Would you like me to tell you in one word?"

"All right."

"Dissipated."

"Is that all?"

"It's not all, but it's all that matters at the moment. To him or to me. The charm isn't there. Not now. I'll say one thing for him. He made me feel like a respectable old married woman. That's new for me, and I like it. But he wasn't at all interested in me, except to see what I was like. He knows that he could never sleep with me, whether he actually wanted to or not, so he immediately lost interest. And you were right this morning. He is going to need a friend. Seeing him for the first time, you know, I just see a middle-aged man with bloodshot eyes and that quick sizing-up that women get to know. Will she, or won't she? And when you send back the answer, *no,* you've insulted his virility. Of course his manners were perfect. A great credit to old Pillsbury."

"Who's Pillsbury?"

"Isn't he the headmaster at Groton?"

"Peabody. The Rector."

"Well, anyway, the breeding is there. Unmistakably a gentleman. But he's a tomcat and maybe it's only temporary, but I don't think he cares about anything else, and that's not very attractive when you're meeting a man for the first time, middle-aged. Clemmie Shreve is the perfect wife for him."

Alfred laughed. "Well, you've done a job on him, all right."

"I'll do a job on anybody whenever you ask me what I think. And I do a job on him because I don't want our marriage to be looked down on by a man like that. You admire him, and probably envy him some things, but you're twice the man he is in spite of all his medals and his Groton and rich uncles. You could have gone to Groton if your father hadn't been such a son of a bitch, and your father was certainly a better man than *his* father. And I'll bet your mother is more of a person than his mother. And I like a man to work."

"Lex worked. That ranch was tough work."

"It was no work at all. It comes under the head of sport. So does war, for that matter."

"No, war doesn't come under the head of sport."

"There I disagree entirely. War comes under the head of sport. It's dirty, but so is football if it rained that morning, and the boredom and physical discomfort? Don't most sports have that? I've known a few boys that rowed on crews, and could anything be more boring or tedious or exhausting than that? Would you like to be fighting a war all the time?"

"No—and I suspect a trap."

"Well, why not? Because you know darn well it's a game, a sport. It isn't a lifetime occupation. You were right about something else this morning. You said Lex should have lived in the days of the pluméd knights on their chargers and so forth. Right. He should have. Between games he isn't so much."

"But we need men like him when the games start."

"Do we? I doubt it. There were only two men in Gibbsville that won the Congressional Medal of Honor. One was a doctor, and the other was a schoolteacher. I have to admit, one was a Navy doctor but in peacetime he didn't loaf around. He attended to sick people. I say war is sport, and sport isn't the kind of thing a man spends his life on."

"But when you go in for a sport, you want to win."

"Naturally. But when you take a job in Wall Street you want to win, too. Or if you're a farmer, you want to win over the weather and the insects. We all want to win."

"You're not going to agree with me, but the Lex Porters are needed to remind us of the fact that there is war and there is sport."

"I don't consider that much of an argument."

He laughed. "I don't either, but I can't match your eloquence tonight."

"It isn't eloquence. It's trying to show you that you and men like you should never be beholden to people like Lex Porter. Good God, I was married to a football hero. Men like Lex Porter aren't total strangers to me, you know. I went to school with a girl from Kentucky and she used to say that such-and-such a year was Man o' War's year, or Sir Barton's year. Whoever won the Derby."

"She never said Man o' War's year. He never won the Derby."

"That's how much I know about it. The only reason I remember Sir Barton was because she had a picture of him in her room. Anyway, that's how she remembered years. Ben Eustace remembered them by whoever was captain of Penn. And my *brother* went to Cornell, so I was a great help."

"Well, here we are. I just want to remind you before we go in. The Aviretts are Southerners, and they don't consider war a sport."

"Yes, a war they never saw, and that never should have been fought."

"And I also have to remind you that—"

"That you are the Assistant Secretary of the Navy and that we are at war."

"Exactly," he said. "And one thing more."

"More?"

"Yes. I love you and I'm glad you're my wife."

"Oh, *well.*"

He rang the doorbell and as they waited to be admitted he said: "What if I'd been a ten-goal polo player? Would you feel the same way about war and games?"

"A polo player never would have come to Mountain City, and anyway it's not a fair question."

Dinner at the Aviretts' was a properly cooked meal of ham and four vegetables and a custard, followed by a long segregation of the sexes, followed by unsuccessful efforts on the part of the host to keep his eyes open during the mixed-company conversation. There were ten guests, and the hostess maintained that precisely equal distribution of hospitality that showed plainly that it was a party of her husband's and not of her own. "Everything beautifully done," said Natalie on the way home. "That was her best flat silver, but I'll bet it was the second-best set of china. Poor woman. Am I going to have to give that kind of a party? Can't we always squeeze in two people that we really like?"

"We'll worry about that when we have to," said Alfred. "Do you feel terribly sentimental about Labor Day? Would you cry your eyes out if I have to leave you on that occasion?"

"You're going to be away Monday?"

"Yes. I'm going around slowing up production. I have to make three very dull but fortunately very short speeches. Newport News, and—Good Lord, I've forgotten where the others are. By the way, are you interested in a diamond wrist-watch?"

"Sir?"

"Oh, not me. When I can't get it for nothin' I don't want it. And that's a big lie. But next year, after we've been married six months or so, you can christen a ship, and usually the sponsor gets a trinket such as a diamond wrist-watch. Theoretically the shipbuilder pays for it. In the long run, of course, the taxpayer does. Mary got a gold cigarette case last year."

"Why did you have to spoil it? I never owned a diamond wrist-watch."

"I should have kept my big mouth shut."

"Is it ethical?"

"It's the custom. It may make you a little happier to know that Mary's ship is now lying in sixty fathoms of water off the Jersey coast. That's how much luck she brought it."

"I'm sorry for the men that were drowned. Was it torpedoed?"

"Yes."

"Well, let's be nice and say we can't blame Mary."

"All right. Let's be nice."

"Let's not waste our time, is what I really mean. She'll be hitting back at you one of these days."

"She'll probably try. Through the children."

"She's done that. I think your relations with the children are going to start getting better."

"Well, they couldn't be much worse."

"They could be a *lot* worse. They're bad now because Mary had a chance to work on them. But you didn't do anything to deserve it. You didn't do anything nasty to them or mean. And I'll bet you anything they'll begin to miss you and start thinking. I won't say it's going to happen next week, but don't be discouraged."

On the following evening he said to her: "You must have Gipsy blood or something. Read this. It's from Alex." He handed her a piece of notepaper from the house in East Hampton.

Dear Father:
   I am writing to ask you if you will please continue writing to me at school as you did last year and other years. Probably I wil not see you before Xmas, if then, but I would like very much to hear from you and get your advice, etc. I discussed this with Ma and she has no objection. I look forward to hearing from you when you have time.

                                   Your loving son,
                                   Alex

"That kid's in a tough spot," said Natalie. "The worst of it is, he knows it. That's one thing you've got to do every week, and I'll remind you. First, sit down this minute and answer him, now."

"I'll answer him, but later."

"No, darling. *Now*. Don't you *see?* You must do it this minute and I'll take it out to the mail-box tonight. He wrote this letter, let's see, two days ago, plus today, plus tomorrow. It'll be five days between his writing and hearing from you. That's a long time for a boy to wait for an answer to a letter like this. Do you know why I'm so insistent? Because you mustn't risk a repetition of the dreadful agony *you* went through with *your* father."

"I think he might have said something about you. Best wishes or something."

"Oh, the hell with that. He probably showed the letter to Mary and was being over-tactful. Anyway, he hasn't met me. As a matter of fact, if you don't answer him promptly, he'd have every right to think I was to blame."

Alfred nodded. "You know, you're all right. You really are." He went to the desk and wrote a note:

Dear Alex:
    I was delighted to hear from you and needless to say, I was hoping that we could resume our correspondence when you go back to G. S. I would have missed our letters, yours to me and mine to you, as I get a lot out of writing to my son that I don't get out of writing to other people. I will try to maintain a schedule of once a week, but if I am dilatory you can blame the Navy. I expect to be out of the country in the not too distant future, so if there is a period without a letter, you will know why without my telling you at the time. Natalie joins me in wishing you good luck at school. Always,
                              Your loving Father

Natalie read it and shook her head. "Everything is all right except I don't want you to mention me at all. Later, when he's at school, but not now. It'll only irritate Mary, and what's the use? Copy it over and leave out the part about me. By the way, what's this about leaving the country?"

"It's indefinite, but I've been at them for months and they may send me. I don't know when."

"Will I be told?"

"Well, I can't help it if I talk in my sleep, and you happen to be awake and listening."

"Do you know—suddenly, for the first time, I have a different feeling about the war. You mean you'd go to the Pacific?"

"That's where I want to go."

"How long would you be gone?"

"Two or three weeks."

She nodded. "This is it. This is the thing that a million women have had to face, and I never understood it before. I'm not dramatizing it, and I won't be messy. But now I know what it's like. The absolutely cold terror that I never understood before. You going away."

"And coming right back."

"I *know* that. But I'm just telling you what I feel, it's an experience like—it's the difference between necking and going all the way. It's really that big an experience. And I'm *not* going to be stupid or hysterical. You know that. And don't misunderstand me. I'm very glad for you. I wouldn't stop you if I could. Only—well, don't start commuting between here and there. I'll never get used to it. How do you feel about it?"

"You mean am I scared? I guess I am. I'll tell you a former secret. You know when the krauts got Leslie Howard?"

"Yes."

"That was a case of mistaken identity. They knew there was a V. I. P. flying in that area, and they made a guess that it was Churchill. They got Howard. If it *had* been Churchill, they'd have got him. So when I go away, if you know any Japanese spies, tell them Roosevelt's with me. They won't believe you, and I'll come back safe and sound."

"Well, it'd be no fun if you weren't a little scared."

"That's right. And I'd much rather commute, as you call it, than stand up before a lot of riveters in their lunch hour, handing them patriotic platitudes. While they're thinking, 'Who the hell is this jerk?' "

"Truthfully, can you tell me how close you are to going away?"

"I'm having my shots next week. That's all I know."

She was silent.

"Now don't worry," he said.

"I'm not. Honestly. I'm just making a decision."

"What kind of a decision."

"Sh-h-h. I'm thinking." She took a deep breath and said: "The decision is in the positive. I was trying to decide whether to tell you something or not. I've decided I will."

"Good."

"You remember our discussion about my getting fat?"

"Yes."

"Have you also noticed that I've been available for the art of love without any five-day interruptions?"

"I did notice that. Are you trying to tell me that you're pregnant?"

"I'm trying to be as subtle about it as I can."

"Well, for God's sake. You are?"

"Mm-hmm. Good and."

870

"Like what?"

"Two months."

"September, October, November, December, January, February, March. You mean you're going to have a baby in March?"

"Or February, that's undecided."

"Well, for God's sake. That's wonderful. That's wonderful. You're really going to have a baby."

"That's what the doctor says."

"You and I, having a baby. That's really wonderful."

"Aren't you going to kiss me?"

"Of course." He kissed her. "This is the first time you've ever been pregnant?"

"Yes . . . No, I have to tell you the truth. I had an abortion when I was married to Ben. I didn't want his child, and he didn't either. It was—I don't want to talk about it."

"I don't either, and I'm sorry. I wasn't digging, I was thinking of you, having the experience for the first time. When did you find out? Today?"

"This afternoon."

"What do you want, a boy or a girl?"

"A boy, to make up for Rowland."

"You always say the right thing. So do I want a boy, but I want whatever we have. Ours."

"Well, we won't be having many, so we're probably going to have to be satisfied with this one."

"I'll be satisfied."

"Let's not tell anybody. I don't want to tell anybody till it gets noticeable."

"It'll probably be noticeable on me, but not on my belly. In my face. Am I beaming, the way I feel?"

"You never beam."

"Let's have some champagne."

"If you want some, I'll take a sip, but I'm on the wagon, no smoking, diet, and certain other unpleasant things I have to watch."

"What?"

"*Constipation.* Why did you make me say it? Horrible word."

"You must pardon my looking at you this way, but I'm expecting to see you swell up, and you don't."

"But I'll bet I do. The doctor assures me I'm a born breeder. He says he isn't too worried about my age. He says there *is* a possibility of a Caesarean, but it's too early to tell."

"Just imagine. I wonder when it was."

"Do you mean which night? We were pretty active for a while."

"What do you mean, for a while? I think we still are. A lot of guys my age are strictly Sunday morning. You wanted this baby, didn't you?"

"I've done nothing to stop it since the night we got back from Elkton. I think it must have something to do with our being so relaxed, after all those years."

"You know, I don't know the first thing about that. You hear all sorts of theories. Oh, I know what I wanted to ask you. Why were you making a big decision about telling me?"

"I wasn't sure I wanted to tell you before you went away or keep it till you came back."

"Oh, I'm glad you didn't wait. While I think of it." He wrote some words on a piece of notepaper. "Call Jemima and ask her to come and witness this. It's a very simple will. 'I leave everything to my wife, Natalie B. Eaton.' It protects you. I'll have them draw up a better one, but meanwhile you have this so I don't die intestate in the meanwhile."

"I don't like to complain, but you don't seem very excited about this news."

"Do you know why?"

"No."

"Because it's more than exciting news."

"Still you could show a *little* excitement."

"Honestly, it's too good for that. I'm forty-six. I don't say yip-ee. I never was much for that. But in my mind and in my heart, my whole outlook on life is changed. For the next seven months every minute, every second, my child is growing inside you. This minute. I love my other children, Natalie, but I never loved their mother as I have, and do, you. This is a very special child. It's your first, and probably our only one. Don't feel let down if I don't behave like a young father. Please don't."

"Sorry. I just thought you might show a little more enthusiasm. Maybe I shouldn't ask you this, but *you* want the child, don't you?"

"Don't ever doubt that. Let me tell you something about yourself, so you'll understand how you feel."

"So I'll understand how I feel?"

"Yes. You've just had the news that I'm going away, and you found that out on top of your own news. Either one of those developments is enough for one day, but you had both. That's why you're over-sensitive about my taking this so calmly. I understand that, but maybe you don't."

"Old Man Wisdom."

"All right. I should have got *something* out of being married for twenty-three years. If I hadn't, I wouldn't be any good at all. And I think I am pretty good. At least I'm good

872

enough for you to want to have my child. I call that pretty good."

"You should have been a lawyer."

"I beg your pardon. I am a lawyer. At least I studied law. I'm not a lawyer. Natalie, don't be sore at me. Blow your top, and you will, but don't get sore at me."

She was silent.

"How is your bosom? Sensitive?"

"Oh, don't talk about my bosom. Yes, very sensitive. Don't be so expert."

"I've decided what to call the baby."

"You've decided?"

"Yes. Ralph Benziger Eaton."

She looked at him coldly and then laughed. "All right. You're so God damned nice, I give up. I can't stay cross with you. But you really could have shown a little more enthusiasm. You could have *pretended*."

"With you? And have you sit there and think, 'What is he making a horse's ass of himself for? Putting on an act.' "

"A woman likes to see her husband make a horse's ass of himself."

"Not deliberately. She may like it when he's being pompous and accidentally deflates himself. But you wouldn't want me to make an ass of myself by doing something phony, that you knew was phony and I knew was phony, and each knew that the other knew that each knew that the other knew and so forth. Luckily, I'm not on the wagon and I'm going to have a drink. Luckily, I won't have to call Jemima for some ice."

"There's plenty of ice in the bucket."

"But I won't need it. I'll just let you dip your finger in my drink. That'll cool it plenty."

She tried not to smile, but he saw that she was all right again, and he came over from the liquor-stand and kissed her cheek and she reached up and squeezed his hand. All the strain and hostilities and exchanges of hurt were over, and coincidentally they both drew long breaths and sighed. The coincidence amused them both, and they were able to look at each other and see love and feel the beauty of it.

"Do you realize he won't be twenty-one till 1965?" she said.

"Let me see how that would figure. If he graduated from college at twenty-two, that would be 1966. Daddy would be going back to his forty-seventh reunion. Which reminds me that next year will be my twenty-fifth, and I've heard a small rumor that Princeton is going to give me an honorary degree."

"Really? Where did you hear that?"

"Templeton Avirett. He's getting one. He's not a Princeton man, but he's a distinguished lawyer, friend of Woodrow Wilson's. He deserves it. A damned sight more than I do. Anyway, one of the trustees, a friend of his, told him he was getting one and so was I."

"Well, aren't you pleased?"

"Sure I'm pleased. I went through an anti-collegiate period, including Princeton, but I had to admit that I always looked to see how the basketball team made out against Lehigh, and the names of the girls at House Party. I'm fond of the place."

"You're telling *me."*

"I've been conjuring up a pretty picture for next June. You'll be sitting there on the platform, with all the faculty and trustees, distinguished guests, receivers of honorary degrees. And you'll be in the very front row. I don't know if that's how it's done, but I'm creating a picture."

"Yes. Go on."

"Then my name is called. 'Raymond Alfred Eaton, ex-member of the Class of 1919,' and there I am in cap and gown, standing there while the president reads the citation. And of course you'll have the baby on your lap."

"Will I? Go on."

"And just in the middle of the citation, the baby gets hungry, you open your dress and give him the right one. Imagine the cheers that will go up from the Class of 1919?"

"Really!"

"The only time in the history of Princeton. Man celebrating his twenty-fifth reunion, getting an honorary degree, and his wife is nursing a brand-new child. Why, say, that baby will steal the show. Not to mention my wife, of course, giving my lecherous classmates a perfectly platonic look at her bosom."

"You'd approve of that, would you?"

"Only for that one occasion, of course. But it should entitle the boy to a scholarship, don't you think?"

"Oh, by all means."

"Of course if you have to change him at that particular moment, that wouldn't be so good. That might seem to reflect on the whole ceremony, or my eligibility."

"But if I do agree to cooperate in this adorable picture at Princeton, will you promise me something in exchange?"

"Naturally."

"They don't give degrees at my alma mater, but you could make the commencement address with your fly open."

"Baccalaureate sermon would be better. And why just my fly open? I could wear my L. D. gown and nothing underneath, and from time to time just accidentally swing it open for the full treatment."

"No, I don't think I'd like that. These girls are four years younger than a college graduating class. It's all right to prom-

874

ise them a full life in the world they're about to enter, but I don't think you ought to promise them all *that*."

"Perhaps you're right, my dear. Just the open fly."

"That's enough for them."

"Are you counting on me to be standing on a platform?"

"Yes."

"Looking down into the smiling bosoms of the sweet girl graduates?"

"I hadn't thought of that."

"Because in that case—"

"I see exactly what you mean. I release you from your promise. I think that might cause talk."

"It just might. It might put me in some demand as a commencement speaker at girls' schools, but I'm sure they don't pay very high fees. And any other arrangement would be quite exhausting."

"Well, the only other arrangement that *you* can think of."

"Precisely."

"I want to tell you something."

"What?"

"I never want to be with anyone but you."

THE PLANE was airborne and they—Alfred and Wilson and a chief yeoman who had been with them all day—unfastened their seat belts. "Headed for the barn," said Alfred. "Be home in time for dinner."

"Easily, sir. It was a good day, though," said Wilson.

It had been a good day: three speeches at three plants, two on Long Island, the third in Bayonne, New Jersey. There had been plenty to talk about and not much time to say it in. The British and Canadians, under General Eisenhower, had come near the instep of the Italian boot at Messina, General MacArthur had landed some Australians on New Guinea, Berlin had been hit by 1,000 tons of bombs in twenty minutes, and it was still close enough to the fourth anniversary of Hitler's invasion of Poland to get in a few words about that. Compliments to workers in war plants were not the easiest part of Alfred's job, but he had been able to get by with a minimum of those and to point to the results of their work.

"In a minute or so we'll be flying over my alma mater," he said.

"Princeton, sir," said Wilson.

"And a few minutes later to the west, another alma mater, the prep school I went to, except that it doesn't exist any

875

more. And if we changed our course a little, I could show you the old homestead. Are we on automatic pilot?"

"Yes sir, but we can change our course."

"No, let's get home," said Alfred.

"Cup of coffee, sir?" said the chief.

"No thanks. Oh, all right, I don't want to fall asleep."

He took the coffee and had not finished it when Wilson answered the buzzer of the inter-com. "Where?" he said, to the pilot or co-pilot. "Thanks."

"The pilot said to look down to the left. It looks like a train accident. He's going to circle for a better look. Look down there at the railroad tracks, sir."

On the second time around Alfred saw the toy train, the first half standing on the tracks, but the cars of the second half lay across the tracks and on top of each other. "Co-pilot says it could be the Congressional. He thinks it is. The pilot says no," said Wilson.

"Jesus, I hope not," said Alfred. "For the sake of the people in those rear cars."

"Not so good for the ones in the forward cars, either. We can find out."

"We'll find out soon enough. We can't do anything. Let's go home."

He was home before nine o'clock and Natalie told him she had heard on the radio that the advance Congressional had been wrecked and at least a hundred persons killed.

"Anyone we know?" he said.

"Not that I've heard."

"I saw it from the air. There'll be at least a hundred."

In the morning the number of dead was lessened, but the accident ceased to be a matter of statistical interest when they read the list of the killed. There, in 6½ point Ionic type caps, was the name: "PORTER, LT. CDR. A. T., USNR, New York City, age 46, recently returned from Pacific for treatment of injuries received in combat aboard a U. S. Navy carrier. Porter, a graduate of Groton School and Princeton University, was decorated for bravery in both World Wars. His nearly decapitated body was found in the wreckage of the club car. Surviving is his wife, the former Miss Clementine Hennessey, of Philadelphia."

Alfred looked at Natalie, who was ready to receive his look with sympathy and love. "Lex," he said.

"There's too much detail for it to be a mistake."

"It's Lex, all right. In a lousy train accident. Not kidnapping Tojo. In a lousy train wreck in Frankford. You know where Frankford is."

"Yes."

"About as unglamorous as a place can get. What was he

doing going to New York? Oh, I know. He was supposed to go and see about an operation on his foot." He looked at the newspaper again and re-read the brief item. "That's a nice touch. 'Nearly decapitated.' I hope they keep that out of the New York papers."

"How did they know all that about him so soon?"

"Identification tag, and then check with the Navy." He began to read intently.

"What?" she said.

"I guess he wasn't traveling alone. 'STAHLMYER, Mrs. Cora B., age 40, Washington, D. C., former secretary to U. S. Senator Peter D. Carriman (D., Mont.), saleswoman, Woodward & Lothrop.' That was Lex's new girl friend. 'Fractured skull, internal injuries. Body recovered from club car. Surviving is one daughter, Mrs. Lloyd R. Hinkle, 6488 Cottage Grove Ave., Chicago.'"

"Do you know it was his girl friend?"

"I didn't know her name, but the other facts fit. Yes, I'm sure. I wonder how long it took. Not long for Lex, I guess, from this description. Probably not long for her. Well, maybe they were sitting in the bar car, whizzing along, drinking it up. *Maybe* they never knew what happened. I hope not. I've got to do something. I don't know exactly what, but this is one time when it's an advantage to be able to give orders. Poor old Clemmie."

"Poor old Clemmie?"

"Yes. I don't like her, but it's all over for her. Everybody knew she was cheating on Lex, and she won't be able to get anybody to listen now. And she'll *want* to talk about Lex."

"Well, let her talk to Mary."

"Mary won't listen," he said. "I can't believe that this world hasn't got Lex any more. Indestructible. All that energy, that vitality. I suppose it's a violent death, to be killed in a train wreck, but I wish he'd been able to sneak off with a fighter plane and buzz the Imperial Palace. That would have been the way for him, not sitting having drinks in a comfortable, safe Pullman car. No, it's wrong. That'd be all right for me, but not for Lex."

"Don't say things like that."

"Safe Pullman car. Christ, only a week ago there was that accident on the Lackawanna, upstate New York. Something like thirty killed in that. Wasn't much of an end for Mrs. Stahlmyer, either. She was being kept by the senator, and now he's off the hook, the hypocritical son of a bitch. He's a friend of Creighton Duffy's and Tom Rothermel's. And Hopkins' and F. D. R.'s. But not mine. He got himself on the record with a few slightly insulting questions before I was confirmed."

"I know it's foolish to suggest it, but I wish you could stay home today."

"I'd really like to, but I've got too damn many things to do. Sweetheart, when I start to cry I'll just go in my little can. At least I rate my own private head. I haven't begun to feel grief so far. More anger. Maybe I'll save up the grief till I get home tonight. Special treat for you."

"I hope you do. Well, there's your car. And you didn't eat much breakfast."

"You go back to bed. We'll probably have to go to New York for the funeral, and I want you to get a lot of rest."

They flew to New York early Thursday morning in a commercial airliner, and went directly to Mrs. Porter's house. The funeral had been announced as private, flowers to be omitted, but Alfred was astonished to see only Mrs. Porter, Elizabeth, Alexander Thornton, and Clemmie at the house, and, as he passed the diningroom, to notice that places were laid for only six. He had expected that there would be polite pressure on Mrs. Porter—or her own inclination—that would cause her to relax somewhat the announcement of privacy. At the church, as at Rowland's funeral, there were people in the back pews, and he recognized some of them: old Grotties and their wives, all now middle-aged, and he spotted a barman from the Racquet Club and a few men who had known Lex through college, club, or sports, but the chief mourners all sat in one pew and rode in one car. Mary was not there. The service took less than twenty minutes and there was no music. Except for the forbidden flowers there was something almost furtive about the ceremony, the ride out to Long Island and the burial service, and the ride back. Then somewhere—at the cemetery, or in the New York-bound limousine—Alfred discovered that there was no warmth between any two of this little group, excepting only that between Natalie and himself. Mother, sister, wife, uncle, each had his thoughts and emotions toward the man who was represented by the casket, but the politeness of all of them among themselves was hardly more than a substitute for hostility. He felt them, each of them, all of them, turning to him for some warming human intercourse, but never seeking it among those others. Then partly, and later fully, he began to understand that it was not so much hostility—although there was some of that—as fear, and the fear was of death and was an omnipotent reality, to the aging, aged mother and uncle, to the middle-aged and aging wife and sister. There was no young person there to offer by his young presence some implied defiance of age and inevitability. Natalie was the youngest, but not young enough to qualify. But then what was Lex? A middle-aged man; and those people

878

in the back pews had been appropriately distant from what was so accurately called the remains of their dashing friend and of their own youth. Alfred had decided against asking Mary to send Alex to the funeral, and the decision had turned out to be a good one. Youth did not belong here. An old young man was dead, and he was reminder enough of all that died with him, that had died years ago.

Luncheon after the funeral was a purely social occasion, as though Mrs. Porter had brought together a few friends to meet Natalie. There were cocktails, vichyssoise, prosciutto ham and melon, ice cream with a sauce of melted chocolate and Kirsch, and a light white wine that went down like water, followed by an almost complete offering of liqueurs. Natalie's topics, since she became the object of attention, were the house in Washington and domestic problems and some mention of her career as a *vendeuse*. The men and women did not separate for coffee; Alexander put his arm in Alfred's and said, "Oh, very well. We'll bear with you. But Alfred and I are going to the club."

"I'm afraid not, sir. I have to get back this afternoon."

"This afternoon?" There was some desperation in the old man's voice, which Alfred guessed was caused by a desire to talk about Lex, or, quite as likely, by loneliness—or both. Alfred was tempted to stay over. He was fond of the old man, the inoffensive, homosexual aesthete, with his beautifully cut double-breasted blue linen suit, fine white broadcloth shirt, black silk necktie, black wax calf shoes, and Legion of Honor rosette, which no one would ever mistake for a military-division award. He was a correspondent of Beerbohm and Berenson and had known Oscar Wilde, but he was not so finally *fin de siècle* as those unhappy younger men and women in the back pews of the church.

"I'd like to stay over," said Alfred. "But my time isn't my own. Is there any chance you'll be coming to Washington? How about the Mellon Gallery?"

"How about the Louvre? Those barbarians are keeping me away from the Louvre, but I'd be no more at home in Washington. No, thank you, Alfred. I have a Daumier that saves me the trouble of going to Washington. But I should like to sit down and have a chat with you—and this charming, quite beautiful lady. Natalie is your name? You should have children. I take it you have none."

"I have none, but I couldn't agree with you more."

"Natalie. Birth. But I wonder if you know what it means even before that?"

"Yes, I do, Mr. Thornton." She smiled.

He smiled. "Good for you! Good for you!"

"What *does* it mean?" said Alfred.

"I only know because it's my name and naturally I looked it up."

"Oh. I thought I'd met a young woman in this day and age who knew her Latin. Oh, you've let me down."

"Well, what does it mean?" said Alfred.

"You'll find out, you'll find out," said the old man. "Won't he?"

"Yes, he will," said Natalie.

The old man nodded, enormously pleased with the private joke. " I'm *sure* he will."

The other three, the mother, the sister, the widow, sat silent and bored by their exclusion from the only conversation in the room, and Alfred saw that they would not make any further efforts in Natalie's direction. "I don't think we'll even sit down, Mrs. Porter. I really have to get back."

"I understand, Alfred. It was very good of you to come, and you, too, Mrs. Eaton. I hope Alfred will bring you here again. Alfred, wouldn't you like to stay here when you're in New York? We have so much room. Alexander doesn't want me to sell until after the war."

"Let's not go into real estate, Mother. Alfred has to catch a train."

"Oh, not a train!" said Mrs. Porter.

"A plane," said Alfred. "Thank you very much, Mrs. Porter. Clemmie, let us hear from you. And goodbye, Elizabeth."

They left the house and went to a drug store. "I have tentative reservations on four flights. I'll cancel three, maybe all four. I don't mind bumping two people on a Washington flight. Unless you want to stay over." He entered the telephone booth.

"And leave you? Today? Stay close to me."

"Good."

They took a taxi to the airport, where a plane was held for them. "God damn airlines object to competition from NATS, and I guess I don't blame them, but then they can't object if I make them wait five minutes. Right?"

"Right," she said.

They fastened their seat belts. "All right. What does Natalie mean?"

"Buttocks."

"Buttocks? Behind? Derrière?"

"*Nates.* Means buttocks."

"Oh, the old man loved you for that," said Alfred. "Of course I do too, but not for quite the same reason."

"He was lovely. But the others? I never heard a single mention of Lex's name. That's carrying the stiff upper lip too far. As though he'd embarrassed them."

"He had, in a way. He was responsible for Clemmie's being there."

"At least she was the only one that showed any emotion."

"If she did, I didn't see it."

"She did. On the way back in the car, she looked out the window and she was crying. I saw her."

"Fear, I guess. She hasn't got much of a future."

"Who in that group has?"

"Who in most groups that age?"

"We have."

"Yes, but we're not typical. Do you mind if I have a cigarette?"

"No, but why don't you take a nap instead?"

"That's a better idea. If I can work this seat."

"Push the button for the stewardess."

"I can work it."

"I want her to bring you a blanket."

"How about you?"

"I'll read. But you get a nap. I'll get a real nap when we get home."

The stewardess gave him a blanket and he reclined. "I'm going to miss that guy," he said.

"Yes," said Natalie, and watched him until he slept.

And watched him when he awoke, that day and other days and nights. She watched him asleep and awake, making himself attractive to other people, relaxing into the easy naturalness of the quiet moments at home with her, responding to her need of him and his of her that were so often simultaneous in onset and continuing—sometimes through a delay of hours —until opportunity at last was attained. At first she thought this new vigil was a result of the accident to Lex and a concern for a dramatic effect on Alfred, but as the weeks passed and her watchfulness continued she knew that there was another reason that was not love alone, although it was a part of love, and not her pregnancy, although it was a part of that state. It could have happened, this watchfulness, without the accident to Lex or without her pregnancy; it was a concentration of concern for him and rejection of interest in others. She had never felt this way about any man, never even about Alfred. It was so simple: she wanted no one else now; she could not again take pleasure in herself or anyone else but him; the random curiosities and lusts of the other years, acted upon or denied, would henceforth be small and impossible in this final and total absorption in this one man. All other men reminded her of him, and they were not him. *He* was no other man. The frenzy of the bed was now no longer governed by the urgencies of convenience, nights or hours stolen from his regular life and snatched often as not at moments that gave no time for preparation, for leisure, for the hidden sensuality in plain companionship. But she would not dismiss fear of the future, not a Clemmie Porter's fear of an empty future but a fear of the loss of a minute, a year, or a decade in a future of abundance. All the things of their joined lives were small now, but their joined life was great and needed all the small things. There must be no incompleteness, no doles of deed or thought to others, nothing of anything to anyone who was not them.

He would have to go away soon, and the history of men at war and the official communiqués in the morning newspaper said that there was a factual probability that he could be killed, that he could lose his life. But if that happened, at that very moment her own life would end, notwithstanding the beating of her heart. His coming absence would be a sadness as his going away every morning was a sadness, measured these days by hours, measured sometime in the future by weeks. But the sadness ended at the sound of his voice or his footsteps; as it did every day, it would do so again. It was not a destructiveness sadness; it always went away.

Early in October she knew that he had been given a date for his departure. "You're getting ready to go away, aren't you?" she said, one evening.

"Yes. Getting ready. How do you know?"

"Because I'm a spy."

He shook his head. "You could have a desk in the Navy Building and it wouldn't do you much good. Not as a spy. There's nothing on paper. So, how did you guess?"

"Well, you've been getting home a little later. Not very much later, fifteen or twenty minutes past your usual time."

"And?"

"And you don't ride all the way home in your car."

"Very good. Go on."

"*I've* come to the conclusion that you probably leave the office about the same time as usual, *but* somewhere along the way you get out and walk. Why? To get some exercise, to exercise your legs."

"Very good. Absolutely correct. Two miles a day. And I've been swimming in a pool every day. The day before yesterday I swam the length of the pool forty-four times, exactly half a mile. No speed, but no floating. Straight, easy swimming. I'm playing tennis with Forrestal on Sunday."

"Well, that means you're not leaving before Sunday. Are you going to tell me when you leave?"

"Oh, sure. But you're not going to tell anybody which way I'm headed. Nobody will ask you, but if the subject comes up, if we're invited out, just say we have another engagement. Or that I'm out of town for a few days. Use your own judgment."

"How much *can* you tell me?"

"Theoretically, nothing. I think I'll be gone about three weeks. If it turns out to be more than four, I'll get word to you. As to where I'm going, I can't tell you that, because it's not only me that's involved."

"But are you allowed to say it's the Pacific?"

"I'm not allowed to say it, but I am saying it, to you. But you won't hear from me. When I leave, it'll be absolute silence till I get back. There are reasons for that. I'm not just being stuffy."

"Are you going to let me know ahead of time, that you're leaving?"

He shook his head. "The night before. I won't, in other words, just disappear. But I won't give you advance warning. Some night I'll tell you, and the next morning I'll be off. I hope it won't be too tough on you. Maybe you'd like to go away while I'm gone, or have somebody here."

"No. I'd rather stay right here alone, take my constitutional for the baby and read *The Robe*."

"*The Robe?* What do you want to read that for?"

"I don't. Maybe I'll give *War and Peace* another try. I'd ask your sister Constance to come stay with me, but two pregnant women, both pregnant rather late—no, I don't think we'd be at our best."

"I'm glad of that. I don't want Constance here. Nor Sally, nor my mother. Nor my children."

"Why not?"

"If it's all right with you, I don't want anybody from the past. I have to say a brutal thing, but I have to say it. If Lex had lived, he'd have become a nuisance. I'd loved Lex in exactly the way I should have loved my brother."

"I hardly ever remember your brother as a person, that you knew him. I always think of him as symbol of what went on between you and your father."

"Well, that's what he's become, in thirty-five years, but I knew him, and I'm sure we would have grown up miles apart. But I was talking about Lex. I have to explain that remark. In spite of how I felt about him, all the signs pointed to his becoming a nuisance, a middle-aged drunk, a middle-aged lecher. And I was in no way responsible for that and to have taken any responsibility for it would have been phony on my part, and resented by him the moment he caught on. We had a friendship and it was a permanent institution, but in recent years neither of us had paid any tribute to the friendship. It was like people belonging to a church but never going there. That's pretty good. It's the way I am about my mother and sisters. We belong to the same family, but we go our separate ways, by choice, and because life is like that. Men and women my age may be members of a family as they would be members of a church or a club, but a church or a club they don't use much. And they're only *members* of a family. They can't be considered as inseparable parts of a family. People don't think that way. They think and behave as individuals first, and as units of a family second—and a bad second. The connection between an individual and his relatives is all surrounded with flowers and vines that obscure the essential facts. A man's or a woman's principal connection is with his wife or husband. Since I'm a man I'll stick to the male side of it. A man's principal human connection is with his woman, the female in his cave, that he fucks and finds food for, and drives off other males from. Next in order of importance are the young that he and the woman produce. As to brothers and sisters, he's compatible with them if he's lucky, and fond of them to the point of calling it love. If he isn't lucky, he fights with them over the food the father brings to the cave, and they fight with him over the mother's and father's attentions. But there I get into something else. I want to get back to the relations between parents and children. Parents have a natural protective instinct for their young children, but we've gone on for thousands of years thinking that it lasts, and it doesn't. At least it doesn't necessarily. It isn't an elemental instinct. The female parent in time takes her teats away from the child and makes him go on out and pull down a deer, and that *is* an elemental instinct. The desire to go on feeding and training the child is civilized and part of basic civilization, but it isn't an elemental thing, and I'm trying to examine all this as an anthropologist. You didn't know I was an anthropologist, did you?"

"I still don't, but go on, Professor."

"Well, not to discourage the expectant mother, but I do feel that our children disappoint us because we demand too much. We demand something that isn't there basically. Respect and gratitude. You see, I discovered, in my researches for the Peabody Museum, that at just about the same moment in the history of mankind that parents began to extend the period of feeding and housing the little pricks, the parents also began to invent such things as respect and gratitude, especially respect. Respect is a phenomenon of civilization, like the handkerchief, the knife and fork, toilet paper, and so on. Gratitude is closer to basic, but if you examine gratitude very closely, as I did in 1885, when I was studying at Heidelberg and doing my famous researches—gratitude is just a refinement of the instinct for self-preservation."

"Now how do you figure that, Doctor?"

"The professor's going to make you stay after class if you keep interrupting, and you know what the professor always makes you do."

"But I like to do it."

"Yes, so the boys tell me. Now I've lost the thread of my discourse."

"Respect and gratitude, Herr Professor."

"Oh, yes. You like after schule, fraulein?"

"Ja."

"Well, you were asking me how or why I believe that gratitude is a refinement of the instinct of self-preservation. The answer involves a certain scientific cynicism. You see, the little bastards, and they were, because this was pre-sacramental days—they got the parents to keep on feeding them and housing them, and they did it by buttering up the old boy and his woman. Toadying to him. Taking the ticks out of his hairy chest, or her hairy—chest. That was the beginning of gratitude. But then as civilization became more as we know it, gratitude was expressed in certain purrings and grunts, the prehistoric thank-you and what-a-wonderful-poppa. It was only a matter of two or three hundred thousand years before the little bastards were actually saying thank-you and bowing and curtseying. That is a short history of respect and gratitude. Shall I continue?"

"Pray do."

"Actually it was all a digression. I was attempting to be very wise about the family versus the individual."

"And why Lex would have become a nuisance, with which, by the way, I agree."

"Well, I guess I got on that because I compared my feelings for Lex with my feelings for my brother. You see, I believe that there is no law in nature that says you have to love your brother, and that in civilization we get into a lot of trouble because we've come to believe that there *is* such a law."

"There is. It's called Christianity."

"It was probably something else before it was Christianity, but I'm trying to talk as a scientist. If you bring religion and politics into it, I'll give you Cain and Abel. I can't handle Christianity and science in the limited time at my disposal, such as twenty or thirty years. But anyway, there is no *natural* law that says brother has to love brother. If they get along, that's fine. But if they don't, why try to force them to behave unnaturally? Why should my brother William love me when he didn't even like me? If we'd been living in a cave, he'd have broken my skull with a club, or I'd have cut his throat with a sharp stone."

"But civilization kept you from doing that."

"From doing that, yes. But we'd have done the modern version of it. We'd have competed, and loathed each other. I am very distrustful of forced love. At the moment it's Hitler and the Germans saying, 'You love me, God damn you, or I'll blow you off the face of the earth.' But that's what will always happen when you try to force people to love you. You may argue that you're a nice guy and people ought to love you, but if they don't, they don't, and if you try to make them love you, you're going to make them hate you. One of the *good* things about civilization, about being what we call ladies and gentlemen, is that a lady or a gentleman doesn't force himself on anyone. And that isn't only good manners. That's God damn sound practice.

"And therefore, I admit to you frankly that I was not going to try to force an old friendship on Lex. Lex would have known that he had become a nuisance, and he would have been very resentful of any effort on my part to try to rehabilitate him. He would have been a damned sight better off knowing that if he wanted help, he could depend on me, but he'd have had a much better chance of rehabilitation if he'd ignored me and kept his self-respect by not calling for help. I know that. I don't advance it as a general rule of conduct. Maybe it's a good one, maybe not, but it would have been the right one for Lex. Until he was able to appear here with his self-respect completely restored, he didn't really want to come here."

"I agree with you. And I think I know why you don't want your mother and your sisters here."

"Why?"

"You want them to live their own lives."

"No. I want you and me to live our own lives. Our own life. We're no good to anyone else if we're not good for ourselves. Your father and mother were good for each other, and were good for and to other people. My father and mother are perfect examples of the opposite. No good for each other, terrible with other people. My father was a stupid, bulldozer of a man. My mother caused one man to commit suicide, and I don't know what other harm she's done, but I'm sure it's plenty."

"Well, they bred you."

"Below the belt, they bred me. Whatever good you see in me, I can thank my grandfather, and a coachman, and a wonderful girl named Norma Budd. And then, later in life, your father, and you. Sometime I'll tell you the story of my life, but that doesn't come under the head of anthropology. More a-pology than anthropology. What are you thinking?"

"Oh, about us, naturally. All those years when we thought

we were so much in love. But we always had our eye on the clock."

After he had become settled in Washington—now almost a year ago—Alfred had looked and listened, and he had been unable to discover any higher post that he would want that he could reasonably expect to have offered him. There were a couple of Cabinet jobs that he was sure he could perform more efficiently than the incumbents, but even if Roosevelt and Hopkins and the Democrats had seen fit to elevate him to Cabinet rank—a fantastically unlikely prospect—the jobs themselves were too civilian. In the job he held he could pretend that he was back in the Navy. As Secretary of the Treasury, for example, he would not even have charge of the Coast Guard, which for the duration had been taken from Treasury and placed under Navy. And he had not the slightest reason to hope that he would get any higher in the armed forces' departments. He therefore resigned himself to the job he had and permanently dismissed all present and future temptation to play politics. Once he had made that decision, he felt a relief that surprised him—but that warned him how close he had come and how much the temptation to play politics had been in his secret thoughts. He congratulated himself as from a narrow escape, while chiding himself for encouraging a weakness. He then became happier in his job because he was doing it better, and even the newspaper men, who were an unforgiving lot, conceded that he could be included among the public servants who had a sense of "mission," of "dedication," and who were efficient and innocent of self-aggrandizement. His relations with the press improved only to the extent that they did not worsen; but a few individual newspaper men, speaking as individuals and not as members of the pack, and not speaking to other newspaper men, went so far as to say that Eaton was a well-mannered Ickes and that the country could use a hundred more like him.

Alfred made no friendships among the reporters and they knew only through the grapevine that he had his private convictions and *in camera* controversies, some of which strictly speaking were none of his business. He deplored Hopkins' magazine article predicting an end to the war in 1945; he spoke out in meeting against Morgenthau's plan to reduce the German populace to a nation of small farmers; he opposed lifting of any of the gas rationing and food rationing restrictions; he made several attempts to have big league baseball suspended for the duration; in a moment of supreme anger he proposed that men who struck a war plant should lose their ration coupons; and he solemnly suggested that one group of airplane manufacturers be drafted and sent to Kiska, where

887

there were not even any Japs to talk to. His constant refusal to carry his defeats to friendly reporters, or to leak information to anti-administration publishers, made him a man to be trusted in the Department and with the trust went respect, since as a Republican it was often difficult for him to keep his mouth shut.

The atmosphere, then, in the autumn of 1943, was as pleasant as he could hope for. He was known, and knew that he was known, as a man who was taking a sub-Cabinet job as seriously as a Cabinet official. Washington was full of men who talked so much about their passion for anonymity that they had become famous for it, but Alfred remained anonymously anonymous and saved his passion for Natalie. He was quite aware that his job demanded no unique qualifications and that he was not uniquely qualified to hold the job, but the job was there and it did require a lot of work, and he was doing it. When the war ended he would get out, sped on his way by a letter commencing "Dear Alfred" and signed by Roosevelt, who never had and never would call him Alfred, and the letter, suitably framed, would take its honored place on the mantelpiece with the Princeton honorary degree that he would get in June. He would probably be in his sixties before the son he hoped for would have any curiosity about the letter and the diploma. Well, there would not be much to tell, but there would be nothing to be ashamed of.

He went home one evening and Natalie was in the sittingroom, transferring ice cubes from a glass pitcher to an aluminum bucket. She turned, looked at him, and said: "You're leaving tomorrow."

"How did you know?"

"I don't know. I think there was something more deliberate in your footsteps. A tiny fraction of a second slower. I've noticed it before when you've had something you didn't want to tell me."

"What have I not wanted to tell you? I can't remember any such times."

"You didn't always know about them. But they'd come out in conversation. Things you didn't want to discuss, but then did."

" 'The ploughman homeward plods his weary way.' I guess he plodded because he didn't want to tell the Missus he was taking off for far parts."

" 'And leaves the world to darkness and to me.' Oh, I'm not gloomy. Why do I say that?"

"Pay no attention to the words. It's a lovely poem, musically. You could almost tell it was autumn by the sounds. I hope it *was* autumn, my favorite season."

"Mine is spring."

"Women's is always spring."

"Is men's always autumn?"

"I haven't the faintest idea. It probably changes with age, but I think mine's always been autumn. I like sadness."

"Yes, I know you do."

"Sweet sadness. You'll never catch me saying, 'Hence loathed melancholy.' Look at us. We're autumn."

"I don't consider myself autumn."

"But *we're* autumn. I think we are. We're certainly not spring. You are, individually. You're having a baby. But you and I aren't spring. We're calm and peaceful autumn. Quiet, and not glary. Rich brown, and gold."

"And silv'ry threads among the? No thank you."

"Well, as I say, you're a pregnant woman."

"Yes, and I certainly knew it today."

"Oh?"

"Seasick. I've been crossing the Channel all day."

"Are you all right now?"

"I think so. This is really probably a very good time for you to be absent. You've never seen me upchuck, and I never want you to. Will you remember that? Don't follow me into the bathroom. I'd much rather be alone."

"Darling, I love you dearly, but you're not going to have any trouble keeping me out of the bathroom when you're snapping the cookies, as we used to say."

"Good. What would you like to do on your last night?"

"Try to pretend that it isn't my last night."

"Is that what you'd like to do, or are you telling me to do that?"

"That's what I'd like to do. But I guess that's as impossible for you as it is for me. If we were real drawing-room people, I suppose we could."

"You're much more drawing-room than I am. Here's a drink for you."

"Are you having one?"

"I'm having iced tea with lemon and very little sugar. The only thing I seem to be able to hold down."

"Why am I more drawing-room than you are?" he said. "My mind goes back to plays by Noel Coward and Philip Barry, and when I think of the men in those plays I'm not so sure I like being a drawing-room type."

"You're not. But you're more so than I am. You have much more poise than I have, and you're very sophisticated, at least in manner."

"Only since I've been wearing double-breasted suits. You have plenty of poise."

"Not really. When you get rich again, don't count on me

to be a society hostess. I'd be a good airline hostess, but not society. I wouldn't even be a good airline hostess any more. My behind has gotten too big."

"Your *nates*."

"Yes, my *nates*."

"The only time I'm ever tempted to be unfaithful to you is on a commercial airplane. Those nice, round little bottoms. I wonder how many times a year they get goosed."

"By the passengers or by the pilots?"

"Oh, I imagine the pilots do very well. I was thinking of the passengers. I'm sure they're not all as well-behaved as I am."

"You're much too sophisticated to goose an airline hostess."

"There you're right. The kind of sophisticated I am, I wouldn't goose anybody. I've never goosed anybody."

"Me."

"That's not a real goose."

"No, it isn't really."

"A real goose is grabbing yourself a real, honest feel with a dame you don't know very well or don't know at all. Women call it pinching, when it happens to them in Italy, but I'm sure the Italians aren't satisfied with a mere pinch. I mean a nice handful of ass, squeezed enough to be noticeable without hurting. And if the lady in question happens to be standing still, the gentleman can work his way under and forward, to headquarters. Has that ever happened to you?"

"Yes. And I've never been in Italy. It happened to me in a wholesale house on Seventh Avenue, in New York City, U. S. A. In an elevator. Horrible little man, I didn't even notice him till he began goosing me."

"What did you do?"

"I looked down at the floor and made sure where his feet were, and then I came down on his foot with a spike heel and he *screamed* with pain. I really ground my heel in him, and I just turned and smiled at him."

"And said, 'Oh, I'm so sorry.' "

"I did not. Just smiled."

"Everybody in the elevator knew what had happened, of course."

"Of course. Especially the elevator operator. He was a colored man and he roared with laughter without even turning around. Then when we were getting off he said to me, 'Nice going, lady. Nice going.' Have you ever been goosed by a girl?"

"Not goosed. I got the frontal attack one time. One night at the theater. A girl, a woman, about thirty. Absolute stranger. I began getting the knee against my right leg, so I moved my leg. The show, by the way, was *Anything Goes,* which seems appropriate."

"Who were you with?"

"Mary. But I wasn't sitting with her. We were with another couple, I forget who."

"Did she stop, then? This woman?"

"Oh, no. We four went out for a drink, and then when we came back I *was* sitting with Mary and I began to get the knee again, and I thought, 'What the hell? This dame means it.' So I didn't budge. And then I began to get the hand."

"Did she ever get to headquarters?"

"Yes. She sort of circled around, got her hand on it, and then stopped completely. Suddenly. I guess she came."

"I guess she did. What about you? Did you cooperate?"

"Yes."

"How?"

"I held my hat and coat over her hand."

"Did you suffer later?"

"As a matter of fact I was a little tight and we four walked over to '21' and when we sat down, there, across the room, was my friend. I'd never seen her before or the guy she was with, but she gave me a kind of a half smile. The '21' people seemed to know them. I guess they were from out-of-town. Guy was obviously her husband. A Yale type, I would say. Bald-headed, nice-looking dinner jacket as I remember, and she looked like a youngish, Junior League housewife, country club. Several people I knew stopped and said hello to them. They left before we did, and I've never seen her from that day to this."

"But she left an impression. You'd know her if you saw her again."

"In the dark. I'd recognize that touch."

"Do you suppose she made a habit of it? Or was it you?"

"I think she made a habit of it, quite seriously. I think she probably picked out guys that wouldn't make any kind of a fuss. But she knew damn well that I'd never seen her before, and I could tell by the way she smiled in '21' that we had our little secret. If I wanted to collect, I could have. Otherwise, a friendly little feel between two nice people."

"Awfully nice people."

"Oh, I don't claim that I was ravished. I'd heard other guys telling about the same kind of experience, but it'd never happened to me. That was almost ten years ago."

"What would you do if you met her at a dinner party?"

"Well, the first thing I'd do would be to slip in and change the place cards, to make sure I had her on my right."

"Why not your left? She's worked the right side."

"Because I dress on the left and I wouldn't want to make it too easy for her. After all, she's neglected me for ten years."

"And you want to play hard to get."

"Exactly. I'm no pushover."

"Well, I'm terribly glad to hear that."

"Why? Were you beginning to have your doubts?"

"Not about you, dear. But I don't trust women."

"I know. I'm putty in their hands."

"I don't think putty is the right word."

"No, maybe not. Maybe not."

"Why didn't you ever tell me about that before?"

"Why didn't you tell me about the guy in the elevator?"

"I don't know."

"I do."

"Why?"

"Because before we were married, although we had a lot of fun, still we were very serious most of the time."

"Yes, we were."

"As you said a while ago, we always had one eye on the clock, always a train to catch, or some lie to live up to. We're in a relaxed phase now, and I like it much better."

"So do I."

He smiled. "I know we're not relaxed just now, but I'll be back very soon. I was thinking what hell it would be if I were going away and we weren't married. This way at least everything can go through channels. I *can* get word to you through an office-messenger, and later I'll give you the dope on how you can reach me if you have to. Have you thought any more of what you're going to do while I'm away? You haven't got an old family servant you could have come and stay with you? Or some friend like Caroline English?"

"I really will be much happier alone."

"I don't like your being alone in the house at night."

"Jemima says she'll stay any night I want her to, except Saturday. Saturday night she says she *allocates* that to her friend. He's a car-cleaner on the B & O. Walter. Walter's married and has five children, but he just won't tolerate her giving Saturday night to anyone else."

"Walter's absolutely right. But try to get someone for Saturdays, and have Jemima the other nights."

"All right."

"And you know where I keep that .38."

"I'm not afraid of being alone. You forget Mountain City."

"I'll never forget Mountain City."

"Are you all packed?"

"It'll take me fifteen minutes, tops."

"Do you wear a uniform?"

"Later I do, a sort of uniform. Khaki pants and shirt and

cap. Black necktie part of the time, no necktie the rest of the time. I wear an ordinary business suit when I leave. I was advised to buy shirts here, apparently a shortage out yonder. Taking a pair of loafers with me, and I get skivvies later. Probably take a bottle of Scotch, maybe two. I'll have plenty of room in my flight kit."

"Not room enough for me, though."

"No. Not this time. Some time, after the war."

"Well, at least you'll get a big welcome out there."

"Why?"

"Your thing in the paper today about keeping the Navy separate. What is it—unification?"

"Unification. Unifornication. In which the Navy gets a screwing by the Air Force, and MacArthur. They sure picked a hell of a time to try to take over the Navy, but they're hard at it, and they're going to keep on trying."

"But my man isn't going to let them."

"Your man is going to do everything he can to stop them, you can be damn sure of that."

"You love the Navy."

"Yes, I love the Navy."

"Have you ever wondered why?"

"Wondered, thought about it, and came up with an answer."

"All right. What's the answer?"

"Actually several answers. We lived too far up-river to have a real boat, such as a cabin cruiser."

"Don't forget, I lived on the same river, or near it."

"That's true, you did. My, we have that in common, and I never thought of it. Well, you know how the river is at Port Johnson. It doesn't get good for another ten or fifteen miles. Therefore I had the usual landlubber's love of boats. Any boat. All boats. Then when I got to know Lex and the Thorntons, I took to their boats like a duck to water. That's pretty good, isn't it? I took to boats like a duck to water. They never had to tell me anything twice. Fritz Thornton was a strong believer in heredity and he was convinced I was descended from New England sea captains. He may have been right. Well, then came the war and I joined the Navy, like a duck to water. But then the whole thing changed. It's hard to explain, because I've never tried. But when I went to sea as an ensign it was the first time I was ever really on my own, the first time I ever really earned any money that didn't have some family connection. I earned money, I was given responsibility not only for property and equipment, but for men's lives. If I failed in my job, a lot of men might die. Also, I was responsible for their behavior, their conduct, in other matters that weren't life or death, but were of major importance to them. If I didn't give a man my permission, he couldn't go ashore and get drunk

893

and get laid. That's God damn important, especially when some of the men are fifteen or twenty years older than you are, and you're just a young prick that hasn't even finished college. It gave me some spine, as my grandfather used to say. I think it made me realize that no matter how young I was, I was old enough to take part in life and death, and I *think* I realized that I could never get any older than that. Wiser, maybe, but not older. And it was important for me to get old, *that* old. I had to get out of boyhood. My boyhood was misery, miserable. Maturity seemed very attractive, and as a matter of fact, it is. But especially so to me at that age. Well, what made it possible? The Navy. A vague institution known as the Navy. Not Josephus Daniels. Not Admiral Sims. Not John Paul Jones. Not League Island or Pelham Bay, and not even the ships themselves. 'What *is* the Navy?' I used to ask myself. The Navy is the chiefs, the chief petty officers, some people say. But that's balls, too. If that were true, there wouldn't be so many mustangs."

"What are mustangs?"

"Chiefs that get wartime commissions. If the Navy were chiefs, they'd be indispensable and they wouldn't get commissions. Well, what was it then? I knew a lot of things that it wasn't, but I had a hard time trying to find out what it was."

"And what is it?"

"Oh, I knew you'd ask that, and my answer isn't as good as I'd like it to be. But I'll risk it. The answer is me, multiplied by all the guys like me who are attracted to it, some because they started out by liking boats and the sea, some because they knocked up a girl in their home town and ran away and joined the Navy. Whatever the reason guys like me get attracted to it. Then we find that the life includes a lot of hard work, some of it dull, some of it dirty, some of it dangerous. A lot of it surrounded by rules and regulations and a lingo that seems like so much horse-shit. But then you begin to realize that a lot of the rules and even the small courtesies have good solid reason for being there. You do certain things certain ways because in the long run they've been proven to be the best ways. Even the lingo serves a purpose. The deck is the floor, a flight of steps is a ladder. But if you get in the habit of calling things by the names the Navy calls them, you're continually reminded of the fact that you're in the Navy, and that's important not to forget. Because presumably you have to think and react as a Navy man does, and you won't react quickly if you aren't constantly reminded of the fact, consciously or subconsciously."

"You, you. What about you?"

"Me multiplied. There comes a time, weeks or months, when the indoctrination takes effect, catches hold of you.

894

Boot camp, or whatever. But you've been absorbed, without realizing it. You've been baptized, tattooed. You're like those babies that have a complete change of blood by transfusion. Now the Navy still doesn't mean Daniels or a certain ship or a shore station or certain foolish customs. But you are Daniels, you are the ship, you talk that foolish language. You may not have rank, you may despise your commanding officer, hate the food, rebel at the discipline. But you are it and it is you. Whatever you were before, or whatever you become later, I believe it can only happen once. It's like belonging to a religion that hasn't got a god. It's this vague thing called the Navy, and you, and you are the Navy. All by yourself on a train, you are the Navy. With a thousand guys on the deck of a battlewagon, posing for a picture by Mole & Thomas, you are the Navy, even if all you are is part of the letter W in War Bonds. But I think it's never stronger than when you're alone with civilians, or non-Navy people. That's when you become the whole God damn Navy, when the width of your pants means one thing and the buttons mean something else. Well, finally, a million guys, living and dead, have felt that way. A million me's. We may get sick of the sight of each other, and do, but we've poured some kind of spiritual energy into this vague thing called the Navy, and there it is, forever. We can't get it back. It can't be gotten back. Maybe it can be compared to sperm, except that sperm, as you're perfectly well aware at the moment, comes back as a child. This is a spiritual thing, a spiritual investment, like the prayers that the Catholics offer for something that they don't want for themselves. Well, finally, double-finally, we've helped to create a completely vague, intangible thing called the Navy, just as intangible whether it's a yeoman's pencil or a torpedo bomber. It's not dependent on being tangible or human, but it is tangible and it is human, and I for one love it. I've got you nowhere. It'd be so much easier to tell you why I love you."

"And yet—would it?"

"You did that very well, not long ago," she said.

"But the words didn't tell it. I can tell you what you are and what you're not, but do I finally tell you why I love you? No. Do I know? Do I *have* to know? No. I don't have to know why I love you."

"Ah, but it's nice to hear you try."

"Is it? I suppose it is. But you've never really tried, and I know it just as well."

"I'm glad the Navy isn't a woman."

"I'm glad you know that it isn't a woman. At least I didn't make that mistake. It isn't a man, either. It's as sexless as a cloud. Good Lord! I'm off again, trying to explain the inexplicable."

"Well, maybe you should have been a musician. Debussy explained clouds."

"Oho, my dear wife. You are so wrong. The passing of clouds, but not clouds."

"I stand corrected and rightly so."

"Let's play it and see."

"It's there, in among Mrs. Colonel Farridee's records, but Mrs. Colonel didn't leave us any needles."

"Well, she did leave us forks, her second best, so how about having some dinner?"

They went to the diningroom and were served by Jemima, whose real name was Jemima.

"Jemima, you're going to take excellent care of Mrs. Eaton while I'm gone."

"Try. Yes sir. That you can be sure of. Having difficulty getting food into her now, but that'll all iron itself out. That's the ways of nature, Mr. Eaton, the ways of nature."

"I'm glad you're going to be here at night."

"Leavin' out Saturday. I got that allocated. But you only be gone two or three Saturdays."

"Oh?"

"How I know that? Watchin'. I work for a great many transient government folks in *my* time. They don't tell us much, so *we* gotta *guess*. You aint goin' for no two-three days, but you aint goin' for no month. Watchin' and guessin'. I take good care of her."

"I'm sure you will."

"U. S. Navy take care of you, Jemima Pilkington take care of Mizz Eaton. Fair exchange, no robbery. You washes the one hand with the other. Yes sir."

In the morning he was awake before the alarm clock, set for five o'clock, went off. He put off the alarm, dressed quietly, and when he heard the car outside he sat on the edge of her bed and spoke her name. She opened her eyes. "Goodbye, my love," he said.

"Goodbye," she said.

"Go back to sleep," he whispered.

She nodded and put her arms about his neck and kissed him. He moved silently out of the room while she was still half asleep.

THE NOTE accompanying the flowers was written in a hand scarcely larger than if it had been done on a typewriter, but it was fascinatingly legible. It read:

Dear Mrs. Eaton:
I trust you will pardon this forwardness by an individual who is a stranger to yourself but not to your husband. Am

896

proud to state that I am an old friend of Alfred Eaton and only regret that my visit to Washington had to come at a time when he is absent. I had hoped to be able to have a chat with Alfred and to meet his charming wife. I shall endeavor to plan my next trip North so as to coincide with Alfred's presence here. Meanwhile, I trust you will convey to him my highest personal regards and for yourself my every wish for a long and happy voyage on the sea of matrimony with my old shipmate and friend.

Sincerely yours,
Jack Tom Smith

P. S.: Should Alfred return sooner than anticipated, I shall be at the Mayflower until late afternoon tomorrow.

J. T. S.

The flowers were two dozen long-stem American Beauties. She telephoned Jack Tom Smith to thank him and found herself inviting him for a drink that same afternoon. He appeared punctually, wearing the white fedora and black boots she had expected he might wear, and a somewhat modified version of the stock-feeder's suit and a black string tie. The jacket of the suit had buttoned flaps for the breast pockets, from which seams were stitched that led down to the slanting lower pockets. She was very self-conscious about the suit and tie until she realized that he was not. He moved slowly and quietly, which to her was surprising in a man so thin and quick-looking. His nose, his lips, his jaw and his eyes seemed to have been drawn with a sharp pen and as though the artist had been frugal of ink.

"What can I give you to drink?" she said.

"Any kind of whiskey, ma'am."

"Bourbon?"

"It's my preference, but anything at all."

"Bourbon and branch water?"

"Branch water, ma'am?"

"Isn't that what they say in Texas?"

"Yes, ma'am, you often do hear that in Texas."

"You don't mind if I have a glass of iced tea? I'm not drinking till after I've had my baby."

"I surely want to be one of the first to congratulate you. I couldn't have told it."

"Thank you. At least I *take* it as a compliment."

"It was so intended." He took his drink and raised his glass. "To you, ma'am, and the little fellow, and his daddy."

"Thank you for all three of us," she said.

When he sat down across the room from her he did so with grace and assurance and slowly she began to understand

897

that this was one of the most assured men she had ever met. He looked about him at the furniture and small objects in the room, exhibiting no more interest in one thing than in another, but neither giving nor withholding approval.

"Do you get to Washington very often?" she said.

"Not very. Very seldom. You come from Pennsylvania, I believe."

"A little town called Mountain City."

"Then I'm not giving offense to say what I heard. This town is a madhouse run by the inmates. That's what a man said to me today. This is my first stopover since Alfred took office. As a rule I have m' lawyers save me the trouble, but that aint always feasible."

"Alfred will be sorry to have missed you."

"No sorrier than I am. I'd like very much to have a chat with Alfred. Are you acquainted with a man named Lawrence Von Elm?"

"I know who he is."

"You acquainted with another man named Thomas Rothermel?"

"I know who he is, too."

"Creighton Duffy?"

"I *have* met *him.* Yes."

"No friends of Alfred's, either one of 'em, and I came to tell him so. If Alfred don't know it, it's time he did, ma'am, and I'm telling you not because I want to trouble you, but so Alfred'll be told by someone he trusts, and told quickly."

"Well, I don't think he trusts either of *those* men very much."

"I sincerely hope not. When Alfred gets back I'd be much obliged if you'd tell him to get in touch with me and I'll fly up to Washington for a chat." He stood up.

"You're not leaving?"

"Yes, ma'am, I am. You were very kind to invite me to your very delightful home."

"Before you go, do you think you could tell me a little more about Mr. Duffy and the other two? Alfred will ask me."

"I'd be pleased to tell you all I know, if you think it'd do any good. But do you have enough background information to know what I'd be talking about? For instance, you know what Von Elm does for a livin'? And Rothermel? I gather you do know what Duffy does?"

"Von Elm is in the aviation business. Rothermel is a union official, and Duffy is a New Deal lawyer. I know a little more than that, I suppose, but is that enough?"

"I reckon it'll be enough. Right now I don't know where Rothermel fits in with the other two, but politics the way they run them in this town, you never know who's scratchin' whose back. You describe Duffy as a New Deal lawyer, but I wouldn't call him that. He is a lawyer, and he sure aint *anti*-New Deal, but New Deal lawyer is a term I don't think describes him. He's a Wall Street lawyer tied up with the New Deal and married to a rich woman. New Deal lawyer to me means a $7,000 man with a lot more say than he's entitled to. Duffy's no $7,000 man, if you see what I mean."

"I see exactly what you mean. He's not a do-gooder."

"He *is* a do-gooder. Or a talk-gooder. I guess I don't make the distinction clear, and maybe it aint worth botherin' to make clear, Here's what I mean, if the New Deal collapses, Duffy will be back in Wall Street, but not making any itty-bitty $7,000 a year the way he would if he was a New Deal lawyer."

"Please sit down and have another drink."

"No thank you, ma'am. I got a lot of places to go to and I gotta take a drink every place I go. I got about six drinks facin' me before I get my dinner. I'll drink along with any man, but if I'm doin' business with him I don't like to give him a nine-drink advantage."

"I never thought of it that way."

"I'm sure you never had to. I like my whiskey, but I want to keep on liking it, and I'd sure get to hate it if it cost me an awl well, even an awl well I didn't have. *Specially* an awl well I didn't have. This evening I'm having dinner with a man's got awl wells I don't have but I'd like to have. Well, about these friends of Alfred's. Von Elm is looking for capital and he got sicked on to me by Duffy. Von Elm didn't know it, but I was ready to back Alfred over twenty years ago when Von Elm was just a $75-a-week draughtsman and working for Alfred and poor old Lex Porter. So I knew about Von Elm from 'way back, but he didn't know me. I just remembered that Alfred didn't think much of him as a business man, whether he was a good draughtsman or not. I know Duffy and Duffy knows me because I *have* to know men high up in government, and Duffy has to know campaign contributors. But Duffy didn't know I was a friend of Alfred's. He just sent me a little message saying there was a fellow he wanted me to meet, and it was Von Elm.

"I went by Duffy's for dinner last night and there was Von Elm and this rabid communist Rothermel. A rabid communist. He never said anything that was any different from the commies, and it took me all evening to figure out why Duffy would have him in his house. I may be *slow* sometimes, but a lot of men got poor awful quick because they thought I was stupid. I aint stupid, ma'am. They was just the four of us men at Duffy's home, and when we finally got up from a meal would have foundered a horse, Duffy made the preliminary remarks, then Von Elm told about *his* big dreams and how much he needed, and I came near asking what was Rothermel doing there, not saying anything, but not trying to hide that he was thick as thieves with the other two. Then I caught on. He was practically guaranteeing the sucker, me, that Von Elm didn't have to worry about labor troubles. Mind you, he never said it, but he knew the whole picture *and he was there.* You don't bring a union boss to a meeting like that unless you have your good reasons to. In my experience, the union people are the *last* you invite to a meeting like that. So I thought, well, why don't I ask a few dumb questions? They're after me for money, they *expect* some questions. So I did. I asked a few questions any itty-bitty child would ask, and while they were falling over themselves giving me the easy answers, I just casually said, 'I'm mighty glad to see that Brother Rothermel is taking the right interest in this proposition.' And Duffy and Rothermel nodded and Duffy said, 'We all understand each other. Labor has to be in on the ground floor now'days.' And I thought to myself, 'Brother Duffy, you don't just have Brother Rothermel in on the ground floor. You got him in the wine cellar with the only key, and if you don't watch out he's gonna turn off your water supply and bank your furnace,' because despite what Brother Duffy may think, Brother Rothermel don't like him worth a dang. Duffy thinks he's arranging the whole deal, but those two Dutchmen are going to give that Irisher a—well, they're going to cut him up between them and toss him to the vultures. But I just sat there and made faces like a greedy promoter, and I said when did they expect to get moving on all this. I said I happen to know that there's been cutbacks in production on a lot of war stuff, and they were laying off people in a lot of plants, and government lawyers were going all over the country adjusting war contracts. I said by the look of things, it wouldn't be very wise to tie up any large sum of money in the expectation of military contracts. On the other hand, I said, 'You gentlemen will understand my confusion, because I have the information that anybody can get from the Commerce Department and the newspapers. War production is slowing down. But contrariwise, we hear it's going to take several years to finish this war. What was a poor ignorant Texas business man supposed to believe?"

" 'Oh, you've been listening to people like Speedy Eaton,' said Duffy.

" 'Speedy Eaton?' I said. 'I never even heard of him.'

" 'That's Alfred Eaton, the Assistant Secretary of the Navy,' said Duffy. 'That so-and-so, all he does is go around frightening people.'

" 'He's a fascist,' said Rothermel. 'A fascist and a labor-
900

busting fink. His latest is to try to take away the working man's ration cards.'

" 'I forgot that,' said Duffy.

" 'You oughtn't to had,' said Rothermel. 'You told me.'

" 'Well, Mr. Smith isn't interested in Speedy. He wants to get some straight facts,' said Duffy. 'The facts are, Mr. Smith,' he said, 'war production is off, but we're not interested in war production. We're thinking in terms of post-war.' So I told him so were Douglas and Lockheed and Boeing and all of them. What did Duffy's particular setup have to offer? And that's where Duffy was very careful. 'In this room,' he said, 'are represented know-how, by Larry Von Elm, ideal labor relations, by Tom Rothermel, and financing, by you.' And I asked him what he represented, didn't he represent anything? And he said to me did I see those two telephones on the desk? And I said I did. And he said did I see the white one, the one that was painted white? And I said I couldn't miss it, it looked so sanitary. And he said where did I suppose that phone connected with? And I said well, I guessed a white phone might very likely connect with a white *house*. And he said, 'I represent connections, Mr. Smith, and they not all by telephone and they not all to the same place.'

"Mrs. Eaton, if I was Alfred, I'd get out of this place so fast I wouldn't even wait to hear the door slam. That's an unholy alliance, ma'am, and the old saying was touch pitch and ye shall be defiled. Von Elm is nothing. I don't think Von Elm can see past a million dollars, which he don't rightly have. I looked him up. But away from money he's a qualified, fairly competent man in his field, and he sure makes a fine threesome with the other two."

"What are *you* going to do, Mr. Smith, if I may ask?"

"Ma'am, I told you so much already, you can ask me anything. What am I gonna do? Well, I'm a party contributor, so Duffy has to be polite to me for a while. I don't have a little old white phone, but I do have a few friends that go back to my granddaddy, and got as *good* as white phones. As to Brother Rothermel, he looked right at me when he called Alfred a labor-bustin' fascist fink. He knew I fought every union there was for me to fight, and he knows I'll go on fightin' them as long as I got title to an acre of land or a thirsty steer. If Brother Rothermel wants to play management by day and talk commie by night, it'll be with somebody else paying for it, not me. I don't worry about me. Where I come from lo'alty to a friend is our religion, not the Baptist church, and I could no more leave this town without warning Alfred than I could refuse another little toddy if you invited me to have one. I'll make it quick, this one, and I'll have branch water the next place I go to."

"But don't make it quick," she said, as he poured himself some whiskey.

"Believe me, I don't like to. But I'm past due at two places. I just got this to say. I saw Alfred last winter when he was down our way, and he looked tard, but he was a new man, and I surmised it was being so enthusiastic for his job. But now I can see it wasn't only that. Not meaning to get personal, or fresh, but it wasn't the job, it was you."

"Thank you, Mr. Smith."

"I mean it. And I prove I mean it by telling you as much as I have just the same as I would Alfred. I knew after I was here five minutes that it was just as necessary for you to know all this as it was Alfred. You mustn't let patriotism keep him from getting out of here. He has ideals, that man. Don't ask me what they are, but you can tell when a man has them, and he has, but these thieves and double-crossers can ruin him."

"It's going to be very hard to get him out of here. Probably impossible."

"Not impossible, hard maybe, but not impossible. And whatever way you manage it, it'll be worth it. I tell you what is impossible. To get a whole new set of beliefs when you're past forty-five years of age. Ideals, anyway. You can get new beliefs, but not ideals. I only started with a few, maybe only one. If you like a man, consider him your friend. If he double-crosses you, get away from him quick. *You* were wrong, and *he'll* be wrong *again*. Leastways, he'll never be right again, not with *you*. Having no further truck with him is best for all concerned. Raymond Alfred Eaton has been my friend for twenty-five years and I expect him to be for twenty-five more, and then if he wants to he can draw up a new contract. But I won't need one."

"You know his name is Raymond. I call him that."

"At home I got a scrapbook about him. We don't get to meet but only every five or ten years maybe, but I got newspaper clippings at home going back to when he used to play that indoor tennis? Court tennis? And social events he attended. He don't know any of this, but I'm telling you because that's what one man thinks of your husband."

"You must have had some misgivings about me."

"Well, I couldn't judge you till I met you, but I guess I wasn't bowled over when you and Mary got a divorce. 'Nough said, on that."

"Are you married?"

"I'm a four-time loser, Mrs. Eaton."

"Natalie."

"Natalie. Thank you, Natalie. I've been to the altar, or at any rate the parson, four times. I'm not made for marriage, Natalie, but I keep marryin' girls that ought to have more sense. Only two of them married me for my money. The other two thought they could hobble me, but I wouldn't hobble. I got three children and no two of them by the same mother. Strangers to each other and strangers to me. I don't feel right about them. I feel as if I ought to apologize to them for doing their mother a dirty trick. I swear. All three being raised by stepfathers and one of them thinks the stepfather is his real daddy. *I* sure as hell won't disillusion the poor little fellow. But all three of them each has a million dollars in a Houston bank, and I'll let that one little fellow's stepfather explain it when he's twenty-one. But maybe there's some hope for me, I keep telling myself. My granddaddy took his third wife when he was sixty-nine years of age and fathered my half-uncle two days after his seventieth birthday. Only trouble with that is, Granddaddy was a real family man all his life. Eight children by his first wife, none by his second. Too old. And one by his third."

"How old was his second wife?"

"Oh, she must have been—I guess she was around his age."

"You don't guess anything of the kind, but you're being very tactful."

"I swear. She was around sixty-five or so."

"All right. I won't pursue it."

"Nowheres near as young as you, if that's what you're thinking."

"Thank you. That's what I *was* thinking."

"No, nowheres near. Well, Natalie. It's been a great honor and privilege as well as a pleasure to have a chat with you. And remember, tell Alfred I'll fly back here the minute he gives me the signal."

"You're a very good friend, Jack."

"Jack Tom. I wasn't even christened John or Thomas. Jack Tom."

"Jack Tom. Be sure and let us know when you're coming to Washington again."

"Natalie, truthfully, I'm hoping you won't be in Washington the next time I'm here."

"Well, who can tell?"

"Who can tell is right. Well, if you can't tell the one way, you can't tell the other, so maybe you will get him away. Then I hope you and Alfred and the baby will come have a visit with me."

"I've never been to Texas."

"Well, it wasn't exactly Texas I was thinking of. Not that I'm ashamed of Texas, mind you. No ma'am. But I was thinking of California."

"Oh, you have a place there, too?"

"Truthfully I'm there as much as I am home. Fact is, you

could call it my second home. Being in the awl business."

"Isn't there enough oil business in Texas?"

"Natalie, there isn't enough awl business anywhere for me. If the awl business took me to Patagonia, I'd go. And I may, 'cause it's there, so I'm told. But I want you and Alfred and the baby to come have a long visit with me in Beverly Hills. I got a place there you wouldn't think was possible."

"I've always thought anything was possible in California."

"I meant from the standpoint of peace and quiet. Way high up, and the only traffic is the airplanes flying over you. And yet hardly more than a rifle shot from Prince Mike Romanoff's saloon. Less'n fifteen minutes from the hairdresser and all the stores. But so quiet if you didn't have those airplanes to remind you, you'd forget you were so close to two million people. You'd like it. All you'd *ever* want to *read*. A nice pool, naturally, and two tennis courts. I could turn the guest cottage into a nursery in no time. It's *got* its own kitchen and all. The only thing I don't have is a yacht landing. That I must apologize for."

"How inconsiderate of you. Why did you skimp on that?"

He smiled. "Found out it cost too much to move the Pacific Ocean, even for a vulgar awl-rich Texan. Also, if I did it, then all the other rich Texans out there would want to do it too. Seriously, I want you to keep it in mind, because some day you may own it."

"How would that come about?"

"Oh, I got some ideas, just between us. There's a lot of real money floating around underneath the ground, and id be a good thing for money if a fellow like Alfred would show us how to spend it."

"You mean you want him to go in with you?"

"I mean exactly and precisely nothing else. But first you have a long visit and see if you like it. Then if you like it I won't have to do much convincing to Alfred."

"Wrong. He's the only one to convince. What he does and where we live are two things that are entirely up to him to decide."

"I'da stayed married to two of my wives if they'da left that decision up to me. But one of them wanted to live in New York City and the other wanted to live in Paris, France. Paris, France! She *come* from Paris, Texas! . . . Natalie, this time I mean it. Goodnight, and thank you kindly."

"Thank you, Jack Tom."

She experienced painless guilt for a new affectionate disloyalty to Alfred. Jack Tom Smith had put into words several of the hopes that she had refused to put into any form. Secretly she had hoped Alfred would begin to think about leaving Washington, to return to work elsewhere than in New York.

She had partially abandoned the Connecticut plan; New York was too near; it was neither a fresh start nor a change of scene, and she could not believe that New York would be stimulating or enjoyable. She had never met anyone like Jack Tom Smith, and he was still so strange to her that she was rather ashamed to find that she could resist his sincerity as well as his lavish generosity while she instinctively trusted him. He was a foreigner; much more a foreigner than the Poles and Lithuanians she had known as a girl. He was an Anglo-Saxon, but as unlike the Anglo-Saxon Alfred Eaton as the simple similarities of facial appearance would allow. She had never listened very carefully when Alfred had told her, once in a while, about his enormously wealthy friend Jack Tom Smith, but she recalled now that even as he spoke of Jack Tom, Alfred had seemed to be on the defensive about him and for him, as though any unfavorable comments on Jack Tom's wealth would be countered by Alfred's praise of him as a man and as a friend. It was quite possible, she thought, that Jack Tom liked being accepted by Alfred as Alfred had liked being accepted by Lex; but Alfred was more understanding of Jack Tom than Lex had been of Alfred or —poor Lex—of anyone. Lex could take admiration in stride; to Alfred it was more personal and therefore more precious, especially when with the admiration went affection. It was nice to know now that Alfred's warmer consideration was appreciated. It was very nice to know that one's husband could and did inspire such lo'alty among men. It was the more valuable because the admiration, the affection, the approval had been freely bestowed by men who were themselves, at least in Alfred's opinion (since she had not even seen most of them), admirable men and because he had not made deliberate effort to gain such approval. Raymond Johnson. Eugene St. John. Ralph Benziger. Don Shanley. James MacHardie. Lex Porter. Jack Tom Smith. They stacked up very well against Creighton Duffy, Larry Von Elm, Tom Rothermel and Jim Roper. Alexander Thornton certainly canceled out Percy Hasbrouck, and she had no doubt that George Fry had been a better man than Charles Frolick. Natalie had not blindly assumed all of Alfred's likes and dislikes, feuds and friendships: if Lex Porter had lived he would have become something worse than the nuisance Alfred had called him. But in the new comradeship of their young marriage Natalie saw men as Alfred saw them and oftener and oftener she agreed with what he saw. It was very nice indeed that so many men likewise saw her husband as she did.

And yet he was a private man; not merely a private citizen, but a private man. He was working for the government, but he was not a government man, nor a public man. He was a personal man, extremely sparing in friendship he gave and correspondingly limited in friendship given. His office, his title, his job were, so to speak, public property, but while occupying them he had not proceeded to identification of man with job, which was the Washington procedure. He was still Alfred, or Speedy, Eaton, holding a certain job, but only in the sense of doing certain work as holder of the job. He was not precisely the Assistant Secretary of the Navy, but rather Alfred Eaton doing certain work, whether as lieutenant junior grade or as a member of Roosevelt's Cabinet or in the sub-Cabinet rank he actually held. After his recovery from the brief attack of envy, in which he had made his own estimate of some of the men more highly placed, he had behaved creditably and consistently. He was entitled to certain ruffles and flourishes, but he accepted them, as it were, in the name of the job and even in the names of the men who had held and would hold the job, which was just as well, since he was often saluted by admirals and cooks who could not have supplied his first name, if, indeed, they had been able to supply his last. He could quite as easily, or more easily, have gone about the performance of his duties without the title and rights and privileges, since he invariably spoke in the language of his experience and conducted himself as a civilian to whom the Navy had given authority but no uniform. He was always prepared to invoke his authority when he saw fit, but on such occasions he was only calling upon the Navy for authority and not exercising authority of his own as implied in the expression "pulling rank" or the rule implied in the tradition that "rank has its privileges." As a personal man, as a private man, he had thus kept free of intra-service entanglements and governmental involvements, and he was as free to go as they were free to dismiss him.

These were the thoughts of Natalie in the aftermath of Jack Tom's warning. Alfred was not going to resign for the insufficient reasons Jack Tom had given, but if there were more and better reasons, she was quite happy in the knowledge that she and Alfred could be packed and gone in two or three trunks and twenty-four hours. And she now knew with a suddenness that was not startling that they had entered the final phase of their Washington sojourn.

As though to put an end to what was more than a phase of Alfred's career, James D. MacHardie died of a coronary thrombosis in the Harkness Pavilion. Natalie noted with some irony and bitterness that the *Herald Tribune* and the *Times* printed lists of the men who had been *invited* to serve as honorary pallbearers, and Alfred Eaton, Assistant Secretary of the Navy, was one of them. No such invitation had been seen by Miss Canfield or by Natalie. Miss Canfield, as usual, had it all figured out: "I'll bet Mr. Shanley put Mr. Eaton's name on the list, and *that Mr. Hasbrouck* wouldn't send the telegram." Miss Canfield, as it transpired, was correct.

His hair was cut a trifle shorter than the length he usually preferred. His face and hands were lightly tanned, and he had a rash between his fingers. His eyes were in shadow, as they got when he had missed sleep. But he was standing there before her. "Yes, it's me," he said.

"Darling!"

"Don't jump up, now. It isn't good for you."

But she stood up and embraced him. "How did you get in? What's the matter with your fingers? How long have you been standing here? Oh, you're back, and that's the best thing. Hold me, kiss me. Tell me you love me."

"I love you. Do you love me?"

"*Yes,* I love you. So much I can't ever tell you. I can never tell you how much. Oh, darling, darling. My husband. You're home."

"Ah, I missed you."

"Did you? I missed you."

"Are you all right? Is everything going well?"

"Everything seems to be going beautifully. Are *you* all right? What happened to your hands?"

"It's a rash you get. Everybody gets it, then it goes away. This'll be gone in a day or two. Do you realize that yesterday morning I was at Pearl Harbor? You don't realize it, but I was."

"But you're all right?"

"Of course I'm all right. I'm tired. I didn't sleep well last night or the night before. I sat up most of the night, night before last, gabbing and having drinks, and I guess the night before last I didn't sleep much either. As a matter of fact, I've sort of lost count of the last few days and nights. Let me see. I flew back to Pearl. That sounds as though I had a Jewish mistress, but I haven't. I haven't talked to another woman since—yes I have. I went to a dinner party the night before last. Oh, the hell. I have so much to tell you, it'll be months."

"Were you in danger?"

"For two hours. Otherwise, not really, except the same kind of danger that I was in in the first war. Submarines. Well, maybe planes. But hidden submarines and hidden planes that I don't even know were there. I saw some action. That was the two hours. Otherwise it was a yachting trip, a 27,000-ton yacht. And some smaller ones. I couldn't begin to tell you any of it, and I'm not going to try now. Oh, I'll fill you full of it in weeks to come, but not now. How about a drink? How about a Scotch and water for the old man?"

"You're tanned."

"Listen, I played tennis! I've been on a yachting trip. Come to think of it, I *was* in danger. I went surf-riding and I God damn near got my block knocked off. No more surf-riding for me. It's too late for me to start being a beach boy."

"How did you get in the house? I looked up, and there you were."

"I let myself in very quietly. Did I startle you?"

"I guess you did, but pleasantly."

"How is your passenger?"

"My passenger? Oh, the baby? Well, heavy. And I feel as though my cheeks were puffed out sometimes. I'd hate to tell you what I weigh."

"Has the doctor said anything about curtailing our activities?"

"He said not to, as long as I wanted to."

"I hope you want to, because I do."

"Oho, do I want to? Just wait till I get you in bed."

"Well, do we have to wait?"

"Yes, you have your drink and a cigarette, and I'll bet you want a bath."

"The last bath I had was in the Hawaiian Islands."

"You must have come right home."

"I haven't even checked in with the Navy. Oh, they know I'm here, but I came here straight from the plane."

"Did you see a lot of people you know?"

"On the trip? A fair number. What have you being doing? Have you been bored?"

"Not a bit. I haven't seen many people, but I haven't been bored."

Here they came to the conversational impasse that occurs when two intimates have too much to talk about, where any topic, large or small, would be covered in such detail and at such length that they hesitated to select any. When they resumed speaking they both spoke at once: "I brought you a couple of presents," he said, and she said: "Jack Tom Smith called on me." And he said: "Jack Tom was here?" and she said: "Did you bring them with you?"

"I'll take command," he said. "Let's forget about the presents and Jack Tom. Let's just be you and me and take our clothes off and just wallow in each other."

"That's what I want."

They went to their room and dropped their clothes on the floor, and they made love so quickly that when it was over they laughed.

"That must have set some kind of a record," he said.

"I couldn't have waited another second," she said.

"Obviously I couldn't, and didn't. Was it all right for you?"

908

"Oh, *was* it? Twice."

"Really?"

"Honestly. As soon as I felt you, and then when you did. I've been in a *state.*"

"So have I. The carrier I was on, they had a sort of a news-sheet that was mimeographed every day, and every day they reported how much fresh water'd been used the day before. '*Too much!*' it always said. 'Yesterday we used 12,000 gallons. *Too much!*' Well, do you know whose fault that was? Yours. I kept thinking about you and I took too many showers. I saw a letter that had to be censored. A fighter pilot was writing to his girl and he said, 'They say we're 4,000 miles from home. I wish my thing was 4,000 miles and eight inches long so it could be in you this minute.' Had to be censored on account of the 4,000 miles. But that was how *I* felt. Now tell me how *you* felt."

"Wanting to be at the opposite end of the 4,000 miles and eight inches."

"Thanks for the compliment."

"What did you do all day? What did you do at night?"

"Answered bugle calls. Reveille. 'Heave out and trice up.' General quarters. Torpedo defense. I watched a couple of thousand take-offs and landings. I took naps. I stood in the dark, just like the first war, literally unable to see my hand in front of my eyes. But the sea was never as rough as the Atlantic. Oh, it gets rough. But not while I was there. Oh, I have a thousand things to tell you."

"What about the time it was dangerous?"

"When we have more time."

"Did you see anybody get killed?"

"Yes."

"Just answer this one more question and I'll stop. Could you have been killed?"

"Yes, all of us could."

"That's all I'll ask you. I just wanted to know that my prayers did some good. I prayed."

"I'm glad you did. I didn't exactly pray. I don't know how. I've never been very close to the Old Gentleman and I didn't think it was proper to start off by asking Him a lot of favors."

"*I* never hesitated."

"I went to several services and Masses, for kids that had been killed. I didn't think much of the ministers, but I did get something out of sitting there with those young guys. They were awfully young, but they had a better feeling for religion than I had. One day after a service a fighter pilot came to me and said, 'Sir, I knew Rowland. I was terribly sorry when he got it.' He'd known Rowland in college. I thought it was awfully nice of him to come up and speak to me that way. It made me feel much closer to all of them, and I guess they may have felt a little closer to me. Kids are awfully nice if they know you're in trouble. And these were kids. I've often said myself that we ought not to call them kids when they're doing a man's job, but Christ, they *were* kids. I'd watch them before take-offs. I'd be standing on the island, the superstructure, and I'd look down at a kid in an F-4-F, a Grumman fighter, for instance. The airplane looks like a sporty job, especially compared to the torpedo planes and the dive bombers. But then you'd see this kid, all alone, and small, and the plane looked enormous. I remember thinking one day that they reminded me of young knights mounted on Percherons that were covered with armor. You know, how they used to get those big horses and cover them with armor? But these kids had no armor. They had their planes, but they themselves carried a .38 in a shoulder holster and a sheath knife and a pocket knife like a scout knife, and a whistle, a compass. On safety pins. All full of very important gadgets but they always made me think of scouts, Boy Scouts. And I'd think of all they'd had to learn in the past year or so, all the concentrated knowledge and training. 'Pilots, man your planes!' And they'd climb up in the planes and they'd shoot off the starter and the propeller would begin to whirl and all the colors of the rainbow would be in there where the propeller blades were spinning. Some atmospheric freak. And the kids would yell to the mechanical crew and it was a God damn serious thing, very little joking. And that's when they stopped being kids, when they'd stare at the flight deck officer for the signal to take off, the wings unfolding, and you'd watch the plane moving forward on the flight deck and I'd find myself trying to pull the plane off the deck and into the air. And of course once in a while I didn't pull hard enough. The plane would go all the way forward and off the deck and wobble, and fall into the water."

"Then you'd stop?"

"The hell we did. If the kid was lucky and the carrier missed him and his plane, maybe he'd be picked up later by a destroyer, but he had to be awfully lucky."

"You mean they didn't stop the ship?"

"No. The carrier's probably going at twenty-seven knots. Planes on a carrier have to take off into the wind, except the night fighters, that are catapulted. I'm not sure whether the carrier alters its course for them or not. Probably not. But in the daytime the planes are supposed to be airborne before they reach the forward end of the flight deck, and in any case, the carrier keeps right on going. An Essex class carrier can turn like a motorboat, but the whole point is to get a deckload of airplanes into the air as quickly as possible, and they can't stop for one airplane. Or two. Or three. You must remember that more than half of that whole top deck is covered with planes, some of them carrying bombs and torpedoes. Their wings are up in the air, folded upward until they begin to move into position to take off. It's a matter of seconds for each plane, once he gets the signal. If he goes into the drink there's already another plane, maybe two, in the air above where he went in. Let me tell you something, my wife. These are wonderful men, and God damn it, they're all wonderful. A flight deck officer is working under pressure you can't believe *and* if he's careless for a fraction of a second, he can be blown into a propeller and that's it for him. As long as I live I never hope to see a finer combination of efficiency and quick thinking and guts than the take-off of a deckload of airplanes. Yes, I will. And I have. *Landing* those same planes. But I don't want to talk about that now."

"But you do."

"No, I don't. I want to be home with you."

"For a while. And then you want to go out again."

"Yes. How did you know?"

"How did I *know?* Oh, my dear. I think you're going to apply for a commission."

"No. But I do want to go out again."

"And you should. But will you wait till after I discharge my passenger?"

"Of course I will."

"Then I'll have company."

"Maybe I won't want to go."

"You will."

"How about Jemima? Did she take good care of you?"

"Very good. Even stayed one Saturday night. Did you know about Mr. MacHardie?"

"I read about it. What do you know about it?"

"No more than you do, but I imagine Miss Canfield will have all the dope. I want to tell you about Jack Tom's visit, but later."

"How did you like him?"

"I couldn't help liking anybody that's so infatuated with you."

"Well-l-l. Is that true?"

"Guess not. But I liked Jack Tom. It wasn't so much liking him as what he said. I don't like that kind of looks, and his clothes are dreadful, and even his manner. He gives you, or at least me, the impression that he has no respect for anything because it can all be bought. But he was here one day, I guess for over a half an hour, and before he was finished talking, I trusted him. That's a strange thing to say. That I trusted him. Maybe because when I first saw him I didn't trust him."

"Trust him how? Did you think he was going to make a pass at you?"

"Not a pass, but it wouldn't have surprised me if he had *said* to me, 'Let's go to bed,' without making a pass. I'm still convinced that's the way he'd be with a woman. But never with me, never with your wife. Oh, I might as well tell you all about his visit. Have a fresh drink and sit back. It's a long story, and I don't want to omit anything."

Several times she wished she had not begun the story; it was obvious that his mind was at work and that sleep would be difficult for him now, but she continued all the way through to Jack Tom's departure. Alfred lit another cigarette.

"Thanks, my dear. That was a thorough job and it wasn't easy. It's very interesting to me that Jack Tom is so anxious to have me quit. Tell you why it's interesting. It means that there's so much more that he didn't want to tell you or have time to tell you. And the purpose of telling you as much as he did was not to be informative but to be emphatic, insistent on my quitting. It must be pretty awful. He left out a lot about himself, the machinations and pressures that got him to go to Duffy's house. Jack Tom doesn't like to go out with what he would call society folks, and the Duffys would be considered society folks. Then on the face of it, there's no reason why I should quit any more than the Secretary or anybody else higher or of equal rank with me. Am I involved in this thing without knowing it? That's something I must find out. *Jesus!*"

"What?"

"I have a hunch. Will you hand me that address book like a good little wife?"

He turned the pages quickly and found his number. He picked up the telephone and put in a person-to-person call to Alexander Thornton. "It's Mr. Eaton," he said, presently. "Uncle Alex? I hate to bother you like this. I know you usually lie down before dinner, but this wouldn't wait. You're an executor of Lex's estate, are you not? . . . That's what I thought. What I wanted to know is whether you've come across any indication that Lex had any financial transactions with Larry Von Elm. Lawrence B. Von Elm. He was with Lex and me in the Nassau Aeronau—you do? You did? How recently was that? It must have been late August or early September. I see. Oh, really, as much as that? I didn't realize Lex had so much loose cash. You say $200,000. Did you happen to notice whether the names Creighton Duffy and Thomas Rothermel appeared in any of the correspondence?

R, o, t, h, e, r, m, e, l. Roth-er-mel. I didn't think it would but I asked anyway. And you say Duffy's name didn't appear, but there was some correspondence with Mortimer & Miller. You have a very good memory. That *is* Duffy's firm. What? I beg your pardon? No I didn't. I had no idea. No, I'd have asked about him if I'd known, but I didn't know *he* was mixed up in it at all. That's *very* interesting. She's fine. Studying her Latin so she won't disappoint you again. I will, thank you, and from both of us. I hope so, very soon. Goodbye."

"Lex was in it? That was your hunch?"

"That's all it was. A hunch. I don't even know how it came to me, although I'm beginning to. Yes, Lex was in it for $200,000. Von Elm hasn't lost any time. They incorporated last summer. But the big news, that I almost hung up without getting, the real surprise package in this Jack Horner pie is none other than my dear friend and great admirer, Mr. Percy Hasbrouck. *Now* I know why old Jack Tom wants me to quit. It stinks to him, and it stinks to me. Do you realize how close I am to every one of those bastards? I come from the same town and more or less grew up with Rothermel. I got my job with MacHardie by saving Duffy's kid from drowning and the kid was MacHardie's grandson. I was associated over twenty years ago with Von Elm and gave him his first aviation job. I was a co-partner with Percy Hasbrouck and saw him every day for years. And Lex Porter was my best friend, best man, godfather to my son, and his widow seems to be my ex-wife's closest friend.

"Do you realize the spot I'm in, without having done a God damn thing? Everything I do and don't do now becomes subject to the most thorough, the most cynical, skeptical investigation at any time in the future, any time. Five years from now. One year from now. Any time. For example, what if I were to say that a certain war plant should be closed down, for good, honest, economy reasons? Fine. But what if Duffy and Von Elm were to buy that plant at the kind of marked-down prices that such plants will be going for? See? Or, on the other hand, what if I said that another plant should be kept going? Then suppose the Duffy-Von Elm group bought *that* plant? I could be accused of having kept the plant going at government expense and wasting government money in order to keep the plant at peak efficiency. Those are two examples. I make in the course of my job hundreds of major and minor decisions that almost always cost the government some money, sometimes quite big money, and I often put my signature to letters and contracts that I simply have no time to read. But if one of those letters or contracts later turns out to be profitable to Duffy and Von Elm and Hasbrouck and Rothermel—I can see some congressmen sneering at me and ticking off my connections with those boys. As a matter of fact, I could go to prison. Speedy Eaton. Was he in a hurry to win the war, or was he in a hurry to get rich? Everything I do becomes suspect. Last winter, when I went around making those speeches, telling business and industry to forget about post-war and concentrate on the immediate problem. A lot of men didn't like those speeches and didn't like me for making them. Can you imagine them rubbing their hands when I'm called up before Congress? If I can be shown to have connections with the Duffy outfit, and I certainly can, those business men that I attacked so rudely can accuse me of trying to keep them from making post-war plans, while I was busy making them for myself.

"It's perfect. I can't win. I'm through."

"No you're not."

"Yes, dear, I am. For a number of reasons, but one of the worst is that I won't be able to trust myself. I mean, I won't be efficient because I'll have to consider everything I do and don't do in the light of the interpretation that may be put on it in the future. Don't you see that?"

"I see it, but I don't agree with it. Everybody knows you're a man of honor and integrity."

"Who knows that? Not the people who are going to be suspicious, not the eager-beaver congressman, having a Roman holiday with a Wall Street crook. And do you think I'm going to get any break in or from the press?"

"You have to fight."

"Fight what, with what? The most awful irony now is that I haven't even got a good reason for resigning. I'll think of one, but if I resigned tomorrow, everybody'd wonder why. Who turned on the heat? Why does Speedy Eaton quit without any apparent reason? This is the most perfect trap an innocent man ever got into. There's that word innocent. I'm already pleading not-guilty, and I hate it. Jesus H. Christ! Those bastards have fixed me better than they could have planned it in a thousand years. By quitting I would be doing the most honorable thing I've ever done in my whole life, and there's nothing else I can do with honor. But the moment I quit I expose myself, I raise questions, I create suspicions.

"And remember this, my dear. I can't go to the Attorney General and say, 'Old Pal, a certain banker, a certain lawyer, a certain aviation designer, and a certain labor leader are going into business together, and because of that I have to resign.' They're doing nothing illegal—so far—and as to ethics, well, that's too childish to comment on. I gain one thing by resigning, and that is, I will no longer be in a position where I could possibly do the government any harm, and I won't be in a position where every act is subject to scrutiny.

914

However, I must avoid even the remotest business connection with Duffy, Hasbrouck, Von Elm or Rothermel. Ever."

"I want to ask you one thing," said Natalie. "Why are you so sure that your associations with them are going to make you look guilty?"

"Know your men. They're not going to do anything that's going to land them in jail, not if they can help it. But they're going to cut corners, they're going to bend the law. Sooner or later they're going to get into some kind of difficulty, and when they do, I don't want to have to defend myself for my innocence. I am so God damn innocent, actually, that I might be a little better off if I had maybe one slightly questionable action to explain. People do not believe in total innocence. They don't even like it in business and politics. I just thought of another ironic touch."

"What?"

"Duffy and those guys don't even know that they're giving me hell."

"Well, that's a *small* satisfaction."

"Yes. Well, now I must start thinking of a good reason for resigning."

"Take your time, though. At least time is on your side."

"It isn't, though. I want to get out quick. If you want to know the truth, I don't even want to go to the office tomorrow."

"Then don't." She kissed him and rubbed her cheek against his. "Why don't you have a good nap and we'll have something on a tray later. You need the sleep."

"All right."

She covered him with the bedclothes and went downstairs for a few hours. At nine-thirty she went upstairs again and he was not in the bed. The bathroom door was open and she spoke his name, but when he did not answer she went in and saw him lying on the floor in blood and vomit, and unconscious. "Oh, God! What have they done to you?"

THEY WERE INSTALLED in Jack Tom's house within three weeks of the night of Alfred's massive hemorrhage and so great was the power of the sun that after the fourth week they found it easy to pretend that they had begun another life. The sun was everywhere, even in dark corners it was never more than a step or two away and it became welcome, for they were unaccustomed to the clamminess of California houses in the winter months. They stayed out of doors as much as they could between sunup and sundown, and then they would go inside and read and rest until the sun came up again and they could lead their terrace life. From the terrace they looked out upon the strange un-urban city, with the palms of Beverly Hills in the foreground, the stands of oil derricks to the west and the south and the patches of blue water in the distance; and everywhere the working people's little white houses and tan houses that were more comfortable than tents but served the same purpose for this huge camp at the edge of the Pacific Ocean.

Sometimes through a freak of sound they would hear a single airplane insistently and impatiently warming up on one of the fields in the valley behind them, and from the boulevards would come the *whooshing* of the motor traffic a mile below them, but the quiet was next to the sun in its permeating presence, and next after the quiet was the sense of remoteness from people. The last fifty yards of Jack Tom's driveway was so steep that no car could make it without changing gear; it had been planned that way to give the second warning of visitors, and farther down the driveway a treadle across the width of the road gave the first warning of the approach of a motor vehicle. But they had no visitors, only Alfred's doctor and Natalie's doctor.

The permanent household staff consisted of a couple, Anton and Marie Schaftman, Swiss nationals who were indistinguishable from Germans and whose passport Alfred did not ask to see; and a gardener, John Drood, an elderly Englishman who seldom exchanged two words with Anton and Marie. All three were lifelong members of the servant class, knowledgeable and efficient. In peacetime there were a chauffeur, a chambermaid and a waitress; at the moment there was no extra help, and the Eatons made very little extra work for the Schaftmans. Alfred's physician, a man named Daley, who had postponed retirement from practice when the country entered the war, usually stopped in on his way to the office or on his way home, and usually stayed about ten minutes. Natalie's doctor came to see her every third day. He was tiny, young, and brisk. "Dr. Middleton avoids looking me straight in the eye, and I think I know why," she told Alfred.

"I do, too. *He* knows that's not the place to look for a tiny hand or a tiny head. You can't fool him."

"Stop. No, he's afraid that if I really look at him I'm going to burst out laughing. He's almost a midget. When he's examining me I can see the top of his head and it's too ridiculous."

"Well, my advice to you is, you'd better count after he leaves. He may get lost down there, the way sponges get lost during an operation. Missing: one small obstetrician, last seen entering—"

"Never mind, never mind, never mind. I guess I'm lucky to have him."

"*I'm* the one that's lucky to have him. I wouldn't know how to deliver a baby. I wouldn't want to try."

Their conversation now was continuous. They were physically apart only for minutes at a time, and when the one rejoined the other the separation had only stored up things to say. He was chair-ridden; he was compelled to keep his right leg on a leg-rest because of the phlebitis that followed the hemorrhages, and the calf was wrapped in what he called a spiral puttee. He was on a soft diet, he could not smoke, and conversation and reading became more important to him than he had known they could be. But conversation with Natalie always superseded reading; there was no reading that he would not drop to talk to her. In the sun he began to relax more fully than ever before, and from the terrace of Jack Tom's establishment he looked out and saw, not the oil derricks and patches of the Pacific, but the meetings and separations, the joinings and partings of himself and the men and women and children who made his life whatever it was. (Much of this he told Natalie, as much as he could, and more that he could reveal than he could explicitly tell, for there was not all the time in the world. There never is, in one life.)

They had, now, such happiness as was theirs alone; not happiness in degree, but in richness that could not be measured against the happiness of any other two. It was peculiarly their own because they were now peculiarly their own, in the great fact of their common presence which owed itself to all the millions of minutes since their common presence came into being in the doorway of a pleasant house in a very small town in Pennsylvania. Here on another mountaintop they could see their happiness beginning that far back, and he could see that for him it had even begun in the loneliness and misery of the years before that, when there had not been anyone so fully matched to him. Viewing her, too, on this terrace but from this terrace, he could see her entrance into his life as coming not a moment too soon, for it could have come too soon. A year earlier would have been too soon—indeed, in the factual chronology of his life, one week might have been too soon. But there she had been, and here she was, with him, and if he said it aloud and it ended, it was still forever the truth. But he did not say it. The sun was warm, and it was so easy to sleep.

He slept, this day, and she rested a light blanket over him and she stood watching him for a moment, the face now still, but the lines and wrinkles now white and deep in the tan motionless skin. She moved a chair so that she could sit where she could watch him, and she watched *over* him. It was that: watched over him, Biblical language, just as it was Biblical language that they half jokingly but only half jokingly used when they spoke of her as "awaiting her time." In spite of the modernity of their surroundings and the electricity of the household equipment she easily put herself and him into a much earlier time and an alien place. They were, to be sure, the aliens, in a place that was foreign to her and in which her only other human contacts were with two German Swiss, an Englishman who said "aye" for yes, and two medical practitioners who likewise had a language of their own.

His sleep was a deep one, his breathing eager and hungry, his body starved for the nourishment of air and rest and consuming it by the mouthful. It was often like that. Small exertion cost him all his resources of strength. They had been here now two weeks, and it was only too apparent that the blood that had been put back in him by transfusion had served no more than the emergency purpose of keeping him alive. From a walk to the bathroom he would return unsteady on his feet and seat himself in the beach chair with his hands hanging down over the arms, smiling to reassure her but unable to deny his weakness. As she now watched over him his hand, that had been lying on his chest over the blanket, moved until it fell at his side. She put the hand back on his lap and covered him again without disturbing the voracious, cadenced breathing.

He would be safe for a while, and she went inside and got pen and writing paper for the difficult letter she had to write: the reply to a letter from his mother asking for all information. It was a difficult letter because Martha Eaton's letter had been hardly more than an admission of curiosity, interest, but not concern. "Answer the old girl when you feel like it," he had said. "But don't be any more cordial to her than she was to you. Just be factual. Anything else would be lost on her."

Natalie put the notepaper on the iron-and-glass table and wrote: "Dear Mrs. Eaton—" It was as far as she got. She looked at the fountain pen in her hand and knew it to be a fountain pen, but she did not see her hand. None of the objects about her had changed, she could see them all with fine clarity and she could see her sleeping husband; but the simple ability to see and to recognize Alfred and all the objects about them was being overwhelmed by an attack of such terror that she sat in horror and fascination as it reached totality. There was no time-length for the onset of her terror and it immediately was converted into fear when it was fol-

918

lowed by the real, the physical alarm from the bottom of her belly. The baby had started to come and there was no doubt about it.

She stood up, cautiously but compulsively, and she was wet and hurting. She was afraid to move, afraid to take the steps that would bring her to the house, but she took them and in her bedroom she rang the bell for Marie Schaftman and took off her dress and lay on the bed.

"Yes, ma'am?" said Marie Schaftman, the servant, but then Marie Schaftman, the woman, saw what was happening. "Mein Gott im Himmel. Is coming the chilt. Lie down and push. I call the doctor."

"No, stay with me. No, yes, call him. No, don't go. Stay with me."

"Yes, I stay, I stay."

The little white thing came out of her, slowly and steadily, and Marie Schaftman shook her head. "So little. Deat."

"No! Please, no!"

Marie Schaftman nodded. "I cut the string." She did so, with the scissors of a desk set. She wrapped the little white thing in a Turkish towel and got it out of sight, in the bathroom.

"It's dead, my baby's dead?"

"I'm sorry," said Marie Schaftman. She made a circular gesture about her head. "The string. Now rest. Please rest. More is to come. I call Dr. Middleton."

Middleton was there in less than an hour. He did what had to be done for Natalie, and telephoned the undertaker to come and take away Baby Eaton, male.

Middleton sat with her. "Mr. Eaton's asleep out on the terrace. He doesn't know about this?"

"No."

"Do you want me to tell him? I think it might be easier for both of you if I did. It would be."

"Yes, I guess it would," said Natalie. "Yes, please do, Dr. Middleton. It would be much easier for him. And I know it'll be much easier for me. What will you say to him?"

"Simply that you've had the baby and that it was born dead, strangled by the cord. It was alive two days ago, I know that. But it died before it was born. I asked the woman, the maid. She could tell by the cord. You can, you know. But probably you don't want to talk about it."

"Was it something I did wrong?"

"Absolutely not, Mrs. Eaton, and put that thought out of your mind. The baby himself did it, moving around. It happens, oh, once in two or three thousand cases."

"Was it because I'm too old?"

"No. It's an absolutely unpredictable accident. If it hadn't happened, you could have counted on having a normal child and a normal delivery. That sounds foolish, but it's the truth. It's a big 'if' now, to you, but that's what accidents are, I guess. Big 'if's.' "

"Am I going to have to stay in bed?"

"I'd stay in bed for a couple of days, but you won't have to stay any longer than that. I'll give you some medicine that will stop the milk forming in your breasts. You'll have to take that now and every day for the next ten days, but of course I'll be in to see you this evening and every day. I don't think I'll try to get you a nurse. It's almost hopeless, and this woman, the maid, she's had experience, with children of her own and with other mothers."

"I'm a mother?"

"Yes, you're a mother. You're legally a mother, Mrs. Eaton. That's the way it appears on the death certificate."

She laughed unhappily. "Nowhere else, though."

"Try not to think of the baby as a baby, Mrs. Eaton. This sounds cold-blooded to you, probably, but it never was a baby, you know. Oh—you're not a Catholic, are you? A Roman Catholic?"

"No."

"They would have a different view of it, but since you're not one, try to think of the baby as just what it was. Flesh and blood, yes, but something that literally never saw this world. I've only known you a few weeks, but in my profession you can tell a lot about a person in a very short time. Oh, there'll be a letdown. I won't deny that. Nature punishes all imperfections. But Nature compensates, too, Mrs. Eaton. You'll find that out, too. Will you try to think of the pregnancy as a failure but yourself as not a failure? Will you promise me that?"

"Yes, Doctor, I'll try."

"Because there was no failure on your part. Your pregnancy was the victim of an unpredictable accident. That's the only sensible way a sensible woman can look at it. Okay?"

"Thank you."

"Now I think I'd better go speak to Mr. Eaton, then I won't be back until nine, nine-thirty this evening."

"Very well."

"Shall I send for the maid, or would you rather be alone for a few minutes? Only a few minutes, though, Mrs. Eaton."

"Two minutes? Five minutes?"

He looked at his wrist-watch. "I'll keep your husband with me for five minutes. You're entitled to that."

"God, you're a nice man," she said. She suddenly began to cry softly, and he left her.

There was often rain and there were days when they could not go out on the terrace at all, but they did not miss the sun, and when the weather was fair and bright they would dress in their smartest country clothes—flannels, cashmeres, home-spuns, tweeds—and make each visit to the terrace more an occasion than a habit. They were getting well, gaining strength, and the source of all strength was now an undependable, capricious factor in their lives, reduced to the power to decide whether they had lunch indoors or out, but hardly more than that. They now no longer spoke of sopping up the sun, of basking in it. If it stayed hidden, they dismissed it. What they had taken from the sun in the beginning they now could get from each other and could give to each other. This was a period in which their love was demonstrated in smiles, in silences, in the spoken word, and in the gestures of good manners. The period was part of the process of recovery for both; in Natalie's case it had begun with his tenderness and good manners after his five minutes with Dr. Middleton, and the strength he lacked at the time returned in another form: the reliability of his tenderness and good manners, which for her became a strength. It was as much as he had to offer, and it was always there. It was even more necessary in that period than their infinitely living love; she was in need of his thoughtfulness and gentleness more than of their joint love, which always led to and from passion, which was for the moment denied them and of which she had a temporary fear. The cool, wise words of Dr. Middleton would come back to her and shorten her sessions with melancholia, but sadness would come to her without warning and she would weep. There was an evening, before dinner, when she was sitting at her dressing-table looking at herself in the mirror. She took down her brassière and watched her reflected image as she moved her hands gently down her breasts, and became aware that Alfred was standing in the doorway.

"I would like to kiss them," he said.

She shook her head. "Not yet," she said.

"Oh I knew that," he said. "But I would like to."

"Then do," she said.

"No," he said. "Look."

She looked down and the nipples were hard and extended.

"We'd never stop," he said.

"No," she said, and smiled and covered herself, and he went away, closing the door behind him. She wept a little then, but he had made her remember her breasts as something other than symbols of the dead baby.

The pain in his leg was less severe and he moved about with more freedom and ease. They played two-handed card games and he tried to teach her to shoot pool, but so much standing and walking was exhausting and they changed to darts and the pinball machine from a sitting position. In Jack Tom's basement was the inevitable, and inevitably named, rumpus room, which contained an extensive sampling of the wares offered by Kerr's, Abercrombie & Fitch, the Brunswick-Balke-Collender firms, and a few items from Lillywhite's of London. The room was an arsenal—eight shotguns, fifteen rifles and carbines, forty-one hand guns, a Tommy gun, sixteen dirks, daggers, knives and bayonets, three bows and two unopened boxes of arrows—and a saloon, pool hall, gymnasium, and gambling joint. There were also an upright piano and a set of snare and bass drums, complete with cymbals and hi-hat.

Their host had stayed away; they had not seen him at any time, and they had had only two telephone calls from him. In the course of the second call Alfred told Jack Tom that the baby was born dead, and Jack Tom's immediate response was to offer them his house in Palm Springs, to get away from unhappy surroundings; but Alfred in turn urged Jack Tom to come and visit them in Beverly Hills, since he had felt that Jack Tom was staying away out of delicate consideration for Natalie's pregnancy. Between them they agreed that it was more desirable to remain in Beverly Hills and for Jack Tom to start using his guest cottage instead of the hotel that Alfred correctly guessed he had been staying at. Accordingly, Jack Tom told them he would arrive during the first week in January and would stay a few days at the guest house, but that he would have dinner with them the first night only.

The precursor of his arrival was a colored man named Jim, a valet-chauffeur who apparently was a full-time servant of Jack Tom's as distinguished from the Schaftmans, who took care of the needs of the Beverly Hills establishment but were not suitable for the nighttime activities of Mr. Smith. Jim came to the house in a rental Cadillac sedan, paid his respects to the Eatons and the Schaftmans, and then retired to the guest house, which had been kept locked throughout the Eatons' stay. Jack Tom himself turned up before dinner, had a bath, put on an ordinary blue suit and an ordinary white shirt and ordinary black bow tie, and joined the Eatons in the livingroom. The Texas cattleman was left somewhere behind; this Jack Tom was J. T. Smith, Esquire, a thin, middle-aged man of no noticeable eccentricity of manner or attire. There was something about the way he entered the house, hatless, that Natalie mentioned later, as though he had dropped in while strolling about his vast estate—which, indeed, was a true statement. But it was the absence of a hat that made the difference.

"How they treating you?" he said.

"Oh, Marie and Anton?" said Natalie. "Wonderfully. I'll be forever grateful to Marie, especially. You know she helped me, of course."

"M'rie's a good woman," he said, nodding. "Anton's all right, too. They been with me for six-seven years, I guess I told you. I can go away and forget everything, and when I come back it'll all be just right, just like I never left it. I told 'em when I hard them, I said, I'm gonna pay you high wages because I don't like totin'. My Jim, he totes, because he was brought up to and id take the fun out of life if he didn't tote and knock down here and there. But that's all right for a Neggra. In a white man it's trying to get the best of you, and when a white man tries to get the best of me, underhanded-like, then old Jack Tom just naturally has to dig down in the trick-bag and see what dirty tricks he can extract.

"Apropos of which, Alfred, I met up with Mr. Creighton Duffy recently. Natalie, you'll be hearing from Mrs. Duffy, as I took the liberty of telling her your sad news."

"I have heard from her. A very nice note."

"Good enough. Unfortunately, Alfred, you're going to hear from Duffy, maybe even have a visit from him. He knew where you were, although I didn't tell him, and he's coming out this way and said he'd like to see you. It wasn't my place to tell him to stay the hell away from you, so you got that to look forward to. As far as I'm concerned, don't think you have to see him on account of me."

"Oh, it might be interesting. I'll see him. Have you given him a no on the setup with Hasbrouck and Von Elm?"

"And Rothermel? Don't leave him out. No, I haven't given him an anything, yes or no. He'll get his no when I've found out all I can without committing myself. He doesn't know me very well. If I like a deal, I like it from the beginning. Sometimes I go from maybe to yes, but I hardly ever go from no to yes, and this was no from the beginning. As I said to Natalie a while back, this was an unholy alliance and I never did like the ring of it, the look of it or the smell of it. You know why Duffy wants to see you, don't you?"

"I can guess. He wants to know whether I'm going to keep on a leave of absence, or resign. He wants to start playing politics with my job."

"Your husband claims he don't know anything about politics, but don't you believe him, Natalie. Yes, that's what he wants, Alfred, and that's why I specially wanted to chat with you before he gets here. *I don't* know anything about politics, but I do have sense enough to go to a wise old friend of my granddaddy's for my advice. My advice to you, Alfred, which is second-hand, is—well, first of all, do you intend to resign?"

"Yes. There's no use kidding myself in any way. It's going to be a long pull to get my health back, and the other reasons for resigning are just as true now as they were originally."

"Good. Well, my friend says for you to get in your resignation before Duffy sees you. Get your letter to Mr. Roosevelt as quick as you can. Then Duffy can't claim to have any part of your resigning, and you on the other hand can always say that you never even talked to Duffy about it."

"I'll write the resignation tonight."

"I'm glad of that. Duffy won't be out here for another week or two, and by that time the whole thing'll be wrapped up and put away."

"Why would Duffy want to say he influenced Alfred to resign?" said Natalie. "I thought it would be just the opposite."

"Shall I tell her, or you?" said Alfred.

"You go ahead," said Jack Tom.

"Well, if he came out and saw me and then I resigned, he could go back to the politicians, the party, and say he got rid of me and created a vacancy for some deserving Democrat or some high-minded Republican. In either case, he shows his power, his value to the party. Is that about it, Jack Tom?"

"That's about it. And of course there's more, the unpleasant side in the future. For instance, supposing there's some funny stuff later on and they want to implicate Alfred. Duffy can always say, 'Why I went out to California and I made that fellow Eaton resign.' He might want to do that to save his own hide if the going ever gets rough. You see, Natalie, if he could say that, it might sort of break the connection between his crowd and this scoundrel you're married to."

"I have some Navy stationery. I'll write the President tonight."

"Good enough," said Jack Tom. They continued their conversation as they went in to dinner. "What does old Doc Daley have to say?"

"Oh, he never says much. When my leg gets a little better I'm going to have to go to New York and see my own doctor."

"But you'll come back here, I hope. Why don't you rent this place from me for a year?"

"Well, I admit I've thought about it. Natalie and I have discussed it a couple of times."

"You can stay as long as you like. You know that, but I know you and pretty soon you're not going to feel right about it. How about five hundred a month?"

"That's pretty low for this place."

"Well, it is and it isn't. I never *have* rented it to anybody and I *could* get more. But in the first place, I'm not out to make a profit on my friends, and the second place, I couldn't be as sure of anybody else as I am of you and Natalie, and the third place, I'd like to keep the guest cottage for myself. So you wouldn't be getting the full value. Tell you what I'll do, Alfred. I told Natalie, some day I'd like to see you own this place. You like it, and id be a good investment. But supposin' I rent it to you for a year at five hundred, option to renew at the same figure for two more years, and then if you want to buy any time, apply the rent to the purchase price."

"Have you any idea now what the purchase price would be?"

"You'll be able to afford it. You're coming in with me, Alfred."

"I am? I'm complimented, but what would I do? I don't know anything about the oil business."

"You know some, and I have a place picked out for you in my organization. You might as well get some of this money, my friend. What did I say to you, Natalie?"

"I think it was that Alfred—it would be a good thing for money if Alfred would show you how to spend it. But that doesn't seem like a very polite statement for me to make. Not true, either, when I see what you've done here."

"I can't take credit for this place. I had a lady from back East furnish it, and a fellow here in L.A. was the architect. Get good people is my way of doing things, and that's why I want *this* man in my organization. We got a pretty high-class group of men. We got a Porcellian from Harvard and two Death's Head from Yale on our board. The awl company, that is. We got a seven-goal man and a former eight-goal man and me, I'm down to no handicap because I had to either give up polo or my Wife Number Three was going to leave me. So I gave up polo and then she gave up me. All our fellows belong to the California Club, most of them did belong to Midwick, and two belong to the Pacific Union. You'll be right at home, Alfred. I could even put you up for the Petroleum Club, but I bet you never even heard of that."

"Sure I have. It's in Houston. Oh, I'm interested. But I don't know what I'd do. I don't think the oil business is as simple as you make it out to be."

"If you're inarrested, that's all I want to know now."

"It wouldn't be for a year, though, Jack Tom."

"Well, all right, but why not?"

"Because I'd want my successor in the Navy to renew the contracts I'd made with your company. In other words, I'd want it on the record that the Navy went on doing business with your company although I was no longer there."

"My friend, you never have to worry about that angle. We do twice as much business with the Air Force. You know dang well we couldn't do more business with the Navy because we didn't have the awl. You're in the clear there before you even get started. But I respect your feelings and I respect you for having them. Natalie, you got to admit it, you can't help admiring this old scoundrel."

"I admire him."

"Yes, on due consideration I'd call that the understatement of the century, and I'll even let you go ahead and pick your century. *God* bless the world for nice people."

"For *all* nice people," said Natalie, very directly to Jack Tom.

They saw him only at breakfast during the next two days, and on the third day, before they were up, the house had been filled with flowers and plants that had not been raised by John Drood. At Natalie's place at the breakfast table was a note: "Bless the world for nice people. Off to the bad lands. See you soon. (Signed) J.T.S."

There were telephone calls from the White House and the Navy, asking Alfred if he had any particular points he wanted made in the announcement of his resignation, but when he told them that his letter to Roosevelt spoke for itself, it was made the first item on the President's next press conference; copies were distributed, along with copies of the President's letter of acceptance, which began "Dear Alfred," and went on to thank him for his valued and valuable service to the country, regretting his illness and trusting that upon his recovery he could be called upon for assistance in the Department which he had so ably served. It was a gracious letter, and had all the finality that could be expressed in a communication that closed "Cordially yours." Since the resignation had not been unexpected—Alfred's death had been expected and obituaries prepared only a few weeks previously—the newspapers and magazines noted the resignation for the record and kept the news stories brief. In the Washington chatter columns Alfred was treated as a casualty of wartime overwork, in the Republican press; and as the former occupant of a new vacancy that should be filled by a true supporter of the administration, in the Democratic. In both cases he was as far removed from Washington as he had ever hoped to be. For a week after Roosevelt's letter he tried to express his feelings to Natalie. "I think I have a guilty conscience," he said. "I half want to go back. I have freedom that I don't want. I'm so used to harness that I'm uncomfortable without it."

"Don't borrow trouble, as my mother used to say. You got out of this with honor and respect. Roosevelt didn't have to write you as nice a letter as that if he didn't mean it."

"It isn't Roosevelt. It's leaving the Navy, I guess."

"Oh, you'll never leave the Navy, and you don't have to. Good Lord, you've given one son to the Navy, and you very nearly gave yourself."

"I didn't give a son to the Navy, Natalie. That's Gold Star

926

Mother talk. No mother or father ever gave her son to the Navy, and that includes the Sullivans, who have a destroyer named after *their* sons. The parent has no claim on the Navy or the Army because a son was killed in uniform. The son may have given his life to the Navy, but that's an entirely different matter. God deliver me from Gold Star Mothers. And as far as I'm concerned, I must have been enjoying myself or I wouldn't have this desire to go back."

"All right, but don't accuse me of being a Gold Star Mother."

"I'm sorry I jumped you. I just feel so strongly about people who capitalize on their sons' death. I've met a great many of them, and I think all the good ones stay home. That's where the English have it on us. I understand that if you get the Victoria Cross you can always get a job as a bus driver. But if they have a Gold Star Mothers organization, I never heard of it. If your son is killed, honor him, but don't demand anything for yourself."

"I wouldn't know."

"I'm sorry. I'm tactless because I'm innocent. I was not in any way comparing you to a Gold Star Mother."

"Or any other kind of a mother."

"Oh, Lord."

"Yes, oh, Lord." She left him to go inside, but she turned around and came back, and when she saw the misery in his face she suddenly realized that she had overpunished a man who was almost totally defenseless. There had been other times when he had not defended but she had always recognized his temporary use of passive resistance as tactical and often humorous, the device of letting her blow off steam. Not so now; he failed to defend because almost literally he could not stand up to her. It was all there in his face—but it was *not* all there in his face. It was in his hands as well, hands that had not altered in size or even, possibly, in immediate muscular strength; but that had lately lain loosely spread as to the fingers and browned but browned dry in the sun.

"Did you forget something?" he said. "Do you want to tell me off some more?"

"I forgot that I love you," she said. "We're both on edge." She grasped the hand he reached out to her and she sat beside him, but she saw that their small crisis had taken so much of him that he had only been able to anticipate more punishment.

"Thank the Lord for nice people," he said.

"I wasn't very nice."

"You came back," he said. "Are we getting tired of this place?"

"Maybe. But we've been through a hell of a lot. It isn't the place. I can't think of any place that would be better than this."

"Neither can I, or I was going to suggest going away. Is there any value in the idea of your going away or my going away?"

"From each other? Separately?"

"Yes—I hope you say no."

"I couldn't stand it for one night."

"I wouldn't want to try."

"Good. Then we can forget about that."

"It seems to me I'm taking too long getting well. You've had a worse time than I had, the emotional experience as well as the physical. But you're better. There's no doubt about it, women are stronger. I wonder about Daley. Don't you think I ought to have another doctor? I don't know a damn thing about doctors. I've hardly ever been sick before."

"Your friend Tinkham recommended him."

"But I don't seem to be getting anywhere."

"You did get somewhere. You got out of the hospital. This is what they call the long pull. No, I don't think another doctor is the answer. Or moving. Rest and milk and probanthine and those pills I always call Jealousy. I did have one thought, though."

"What's that?"

"There must be some books you could read—"

"I read—"

"Now hold still till I finish. Books about the oil business. Something like 'Introduction to the Petroleum Industry' or some whole stack of books for the layman. A history of the oil business."

"To bone up for my job with Jack Tom?"

"Yes. In a year you could learn a lot through reading that you won't have time for later. And you don't mind plowing through that kind of reading."

"It might be worthwhile. Might also completely discourage me from wanting to take the job, whatever it may be."

"Well, that would be worthwhile, too. You'd have the best of reasons for not wanting to take the job."

"How do you feel about my working for Jack Tom?"

"That depends entirely on how you feel a year or six months from now. I'm glad you said you wouldn't be ready for a year, because I want you to have a good long loaf, and it'll give you time to decide what you really want to do. Jack Tom isn't the only one that'll offer you a job. And you may want to go out on your own."

"Naturally that's my first choice and always has been, to start something of my own. I'd be very happy to let Jack Tom put in some money, but I've only really had three jobs and they were all for someone else. Nassau Aeronautical was never really my baby. MacHardie & Company. And the Navy.

928

Branch banking is the big thing out here, but I might want to start a bank in some small town and, as they say, see what happens. I've also been thinking about after the war and small boats. I have a feeling that there's going to be a lot of activity in that field. Sail and power. You have no idea, for instance, the kind of power they can build into an outboard motor these days. You think of outboards as those crazy things you see in the newsreels. Cypress Gardens. Or a fisherman putt-putting in an eight-foot flat-bottom rowboat. They have outboards right now that could supply the power for our old friend the Staten Island ferry. Johnson Sea Horse. We use them in the Navy. Well, just imagine the difference that's going to make in the cost of a small cabin cruiser, if you can build it for an outboard instead of an inboard."

"A big difference?"

"Well, as if your grandmother's Pierce-Arrow had been run by a Smith Motor Wheel. You remember the Red Bugs?"

"I remember the Red Bugs, but my grandmother never had a Pierce-Arrow."

"I never even had a grandmother, that I remember. Every boy ought to have at least one grandmother, if only to show him that sex isn't everything."

"I know. Every girl, too. I had a grandmother, and that's why I never got interested in sex."

"I didn't need one. I just didn't like it. My whole feeling has always been, if you want to wrestle, wrestle. But all that other stuff just wears you out. And it isn't real wrestling."

"Oh, I've done some real wrestling with boys."

"Black Belt?"

"You mean Harlem? No."

"No, Black Belt is judo. It's a rank. Don't ask me any more."

"I will about boats. Would you like to start a boat factory?"

"Oh, I'm not at all sure what I'd like to do. But something on my own, if I can. I'm almost forty-seven. Forty-eight before I get going on something. Fifty doesn't look so old to somebody my age, but most people aren't my age. They're younger. And fifty looks pretty old to them."

"Yes, but don't forget that most of the men who have money would consider you a young man."

"No. Not most of them. Most of the men with money and making money, are my age and younger. That's why I'm wondering about taking a whole year out to loaf."

"Don't call it loafing. Call it looking around."

He smiled and shook his head. "*They* don't call it loafing, *or* looking around. They call it out-of-a-job. With the men I've known, you go right from one job to another, without any time in between. Not even one day, sometimes. My busi-

929

ness acquaintances take a dim view of a guy that's months without a job. I did myself. Whenever a guy stopped working at one place and didn't start some place else right away, I used to wonder whether he wasn't awful damn lucky to get the next job. 'Well, the Yale gang finally got together and found something for good old Archie Busby.' God, I'd hate that. I just don't want to be Archie Busby, for Jack Tom Smith or any son of a bitch anywhere, nohow. If I start being an Archie Busby, will you tell me?"

"You never will be."

"Will you tell me? Will you promise? As my wife? It'll be much better in the long run if you tell me."

"Who on earth is Archie Busby?"

"A symbol. He was a real person. But he's a symbol of all the Yale guys and Princeton guys and Racquet Club and Jekyll Island and Links Club nice-guys that for some reason or other didn't quite make it. Forty. Forty-five. Fifty. Along in there they get let out just when they most need some reassurance. They sit around the club, they go to the ball game when the Giants are in town. I've watched them for twenty years. They start drinking in the daytime. Some of them play bridge for high stakes, or backgammon. Or they play the market, although not that so much because they want to have nothing but winners there. Bad enough to have everybody know you're out of a job without having them hear you've lost your touch downtown. That would really cook you. But they're always around, professional Yale men or Princeton men. Reunions. Games. Professional uncles, too. And if somebody wants somebody to drive their car to Florida, they call up an Archie Busby and think they're doing him a favor. And in a way they are. It makes him feel useful. But then the next step down is when they start pimping, and being extra man at dinner parties and leaving their wives at home. I actually saw Archie Busby going to Brooks Brothers to get an evening shirt before the store closed, not for himself, but for some young snot-nose downtown that knew Archie had nothing better to do. And he *didn't* have anything better to do."

"But then what happened to him?"

"He got a job. The Yale gang got together and they found something for good old Arch."

"What?"

"You know my friend Don Shanley?"

"Yes."

"Don and some other Elis got Archie a job with a rubber company in Akron, Ohio. He was put in charge of a fleet of cars that went all over the country testing tires. He was back in New York in six months and about two weeks after he got back he jumped in front of a subway train. And Archie wasn't broke. Archie left over $300,000, and his wife had some money. And he wasn't a *bad* guy. He wasn't a prick, or mean. But he was forty-five, all right, and he was sort of getting in the way. They wanted his office for some younger guy, that's about what it amounted to. So they gave him a dinner, and a silver tray, and turned him loose. And he couldn't get used to it."

"Tragic story," said Natalie.

"I should have told it to you without the end, the subway part."

"It was tragic enough without that."

"Ah, but that's why you're my girl. You know it was. But I have told that story a couple of times without the end, just to get people's reactions. They didn't think it was tragic. At least two men said Archie must have been a bum, and one said he wished he'd get the sack so he could lead that kind of a life."

"When did you tell the story?"

"Oh—seven or eight years ago, it must have been. Archie's been dead at least that long."

"I was wondering why you never told it to me. The only man I ever knew that committed suicide was Julian English."

"Yes, I remember him."

"But after he died I used to think back and there were things we should have known, recognized."

"Such as?"

"Oh—little things, but so many of them examples of self-destruction. Insulting important people. His drinking. Fast driving. You'd have had to know him. But heavens, he's been dead fourteen years and you hardly ever hear his name mentioned any more. But Mr. Busby was different."

"Completely. He was perfectly satisfied with life. Probably too much so."

"There's no such thing as too much so. It's the only life we have, and we've got to be satisfied with it."

"Archie wasn't. Neither was your friend English. However, it is the only life we have."

"As I wasn't the first to say."

"But I'm glad to hear you say it," he said. "I know you've been depressed."

"Never that depressed, though. Not enough to commit suicide. I have too much with you. When you die, or I die, we can't help that. But I'd never want to die while you're still alive."

"I don't think *I* would while *you* are."

"I'd like that a little more affirmatively, please."

"Give me a small kiss before I sack out."

She kissed his mouth gently.

"I've been wondering about the raveled sleeve of care," he said. "Do you suppose the sleeve was on a bolero, and that's what made Ravel ravel—I'm sleepy."

Often during the Fifty-fifth Street phase of their love affair she had observed that he had an unconscious trick of revealing his own concerns by discussing similar problems pertaining to problems of other men. The habit of the trick had stayed with him during their married life, and the story of Archie Busby now explained some of his silences on the terrace, when he appeared to be about to doze off but, as she knew, was actually in deep thought. In spite of the near-completeness of their communication, there were things he seldom discussed: delicacy, tact, reticence, guilt, and even the fear of being a bore kept him silent on some subjects. He spoke of Mary and the children only enough to dispel any suspicion of secretiveness. But his utter contempt for the cult of the bisexual woman was no more than a substitute for a free and candid expression of his contempt for Mary, which he hid now because she had the children and he could not even admit to Natalie that Mary was potentially dangerous. Likewise in other matters he was indirect and evasive and devious, usually with laudable purpose, but making it sometimes difficult for Natalie to know what he was thinking. She knew, for example, that he had provided generously for her in his will, but he had an aversion to the slightest mention of it because—and this she knew without reason—he would leave her more money than she had inherited from her father, and he was so careful to preserve her admiration of Ralph Benziger that he would not deliberately provide such a contrast. He was a subtle man, and no one else had ever understood that. But his subtlety did not often mislead her, and his story of Archie Busby troubled her because she realized that it stated a possibility that was troublous to him. It was fear growing out of weakness, not unrelated to the defenselessness she had just discovered, and a fear that was of itself so strong that he could beg her to warn him if she saw signs of his becoming, as he said, an Archie Busby. And in her heart, in her secret mind, she knew that the danger already existed. It was something too subtle for them to share, and she wondered how much of this new problem he had begun to recognize or how much his outspoken discussion of it as a problem was only fear of a condition thus far unrelated to himself.

She could never, of course, do what he had asked; she could never warn him. To warn him would be such cruelty as she could not inflict on this man, for by the act of warning him she would be showing him that he himself had failed to recognize the signs, and failure to recognize the signs would be, to this man, as bad as to find himself in the condition he dreaded. Her first efforts would be toward the gradual but thorough immolation of Jack Tom's kindness and his specific offer of a job. It was an immediately gratifying decision; it was something to do that was totally destructive and at the same time happily corrective. And in the end she knew that her husband would have retained Jack Tom's respect, which was so rarely given to any man that it was uniquely valuable. Her decision was gratifying, too, because whether Alfred knew it or not—and he would not—his problem was taken care of.

Creighton Duffy, who turned up two weeks after Jack Tom's visit, made a few attempts to continue the relationship as it functioned in Washington, where the White House connection carried higher authority than any mere portfolio. But Alfred would have none of it. He asked a few polite questions about Washington as though he and Duffy were two men who had known each other in a foreign land to which the one would return while the other had outgrown it. Duffy understood what was happening, but he could not antagonize the house guest of the man whose financial backing he was eager to have. Duffy left after lunch, having undertaken to perform various small chores for Alfred and Natalie that would be performed efficiently and reluctantly.

"You were at your worst, your absolute, snooty, delightful worst," said Natalie.

"Me? I? Feigning innocence. Sure I was. The whole visit was a total loss for old Creighton. But he'd told Jack Tom he was coming, so he had to show up. And I'd made up my mind what to do if he started pulling rank, and he lost no time there. He had one hell of a nerve, though, bringing the cigarette box." Alfred referred to a silver cigarette box engraved with the signatures of his superiors and associates in the Department of the Navy. "He has no official Navy connection. I'd much rather have had a delegation of Waves, or female marines. They could have brought their bathing suits."

"Maybe they'll turn up when you get your medal."

"I doubt it. I mean I doubt if I'll get a medal."

But a few weeks later a party headed by an admiral and including Alfred's former aide, Wilson, appeared by appointment and gave him the Legion of Merit, which Alfred characterized to Natalie as not so good as the Distinguished Service Medal and a hell of a lot better than nothing. "You can now write *finis* to my naval career," he said. "The verdict is not guilty, but pay the costs. But I'm glad Wilson brought my flag. I really wanted that more than the medal. I was hoping I'd get the D. S. M., and I was afraid I wouldn't get the Legion of Merit. But the flag really belongs to me, and I'm just so stubborn I wouldn't have put in for it."

933

"Why wouldn't you, if it was yours?"

"If they'd forgotten me that quickly, I'd have said the hell with them."

"Have you been brooding about that?"

"Yes, I have. Which for some reason reminds me, the real estate people have finally agreed to get us off the hook on the Farridee house. We lose two months' rent, but Mrs. Colonel has kindly consented to tear up the lease. Now the next problem, in the same mail, is do we want to sign the lease for this place?"

"That's entirely up to you."

"No, now don't say that. I'm asking you for *your* opinion, *your* wishes."

"Well, we couldn't do better if we're going to stay in California."

"And do you *want* to stay in California?"

"Yes, I think I do."

"Then I'll sign it. I agree with you. Even if I don't go to work for Jack Tom I'd like to stay here. I frankly don't want to move again for a while. In another month or so we can begin to see some people, so it won't be so boring for you, and I suppose some time this summer we ought to go East for a week or two. By that time I'll have any number of things to do in New York, and I'll have to go to Port Johnson, you and I, and spend one night there."

He continued adding to the list of the things there would be to do on the Eastern trip, and there were so many of them —some of which he rejected in passing—that she knew his strength was returning. He had never before broached the subject of seeing California people or, by implication, of wanting to enter into a social life. She decided that the visits from Duffy and the admiral had removed some of the unfinished recent past, and that he now would begin to take a more active part in the life that had been kept out by Jack Tom's high paling fences. It was reassuring, but it was a time for caution.

IN THE MORNING they would be home—home, that is, in California. They were in the dip down from Colorado into New Mexico and every few minutes they could hear a little boy in the next compartment saying: "Mummy, *there's* a cowboy. Mummy, I just saw another cowboy."

"Yes, dear."

934

"Mummy, I just saw *two* cowboys."

"Mm-hmm."

"But you didn't look."

"I'm trying to write a letter to Daddy. I'll tell him you saw two cowboys."

"No, I saw twelve. Tell him I saw twelve. I counted them. No, no, now it's thirteen! I just saw another."

"I think I'll just tell him you've been seeing a lot of cowboys. What else shall I tell him, from you?"

"Tell him to bring me back a Japanese sword."

"I did tell him that long ago."

"But I don't want him to forget."

"He won't forget, but all right, I'll remind him again. Wouldn't you like to tell him something, not just ask him for something?"

"I don't know what to tell him."

"Tell him you miss him."

"But I don't miss him, Mum-my. *I* don't miss him. I never saw him."

"You did, too, but you don't remember. He misses you."

"Yes, but he remembers me and I don't remember him."

"Well, you would miss him if you remembered him. You can be damn sure of that."

"Grandmother doesn't want you to say damn in front of me."

"Oh, don't be such a little prig."

The child bawled. "You called me a prig, and I don't know what that is."

"Then stop crying, if you don't know what it is."

"It wasn't nice, I could tell."

"No, it wasn't nice, and if you don't stop bawling I'll close the door and you won't be able to see out on both sides."

"I don't care. You called me something."

"Oh, for Christ's sake, shut up." She closed the door to the passageway, and Natalie and Alfred could hear only their voices.

"That's the very pretty blonde," said Natalie.

"I noticed her at Fort Madison. She looks the way Clemmie Shreve used to, but taller. Vuitton bags. Must be in the chips."

"Oho. Plenty. I know where that suit came from. Four hundred dollars."

"Very attractive."

"The little boy must be about four."

"Four or five. Where are they going and what are they doing?"

"You mean my dear Watson?"

"Yes."

"Well, she's a New York girl. She has that Spence-Chapin accent. But she may be from some other Eastern city. Some Philadelphia girls talk that way. Husband is in the Pacific."

"In the Navy or the Marines. The kid wants one of those kamikaze swords. And if the father's been gone so long that the kid doesn't know him, he's either a marine or he's been on a ship. Not a naval aviator. I don't think he'd have been out there that long if he'd been a naval aviator, not without getting back. And I don't think this man ever got stateside."

"Why? I have a theory, but what's yours?"

"Well, I think the mother is cranky because——"

"That's what I think, too. Because she's been faithful to him."

"Yes. Anything else?"

"Oh—they've been spending the summer with her mother."

"The swearing, yes."

"And this is just a guess, but I'm sure they're going to visit another grandmother or somebody like that, in California. In the hope that husband will get some leave, but not too confident, or she wouldn't be writing that kind of letter."

"Oh? What kind of letter?"

"Sort of a duty letter, don't you think? She wanted to get some fresh ideas from the child, instead of just the same old thing. But if she had any hope of seeing her husband soon—well, I know what kind of letter I'd write if I hadn't seen you for several years. I wouldn't need any help from a child if I thought I was going to see you soon."

"Do you remember those pictures? We should have saved some for our old age?"

"The hotel pictures? What ever made you think of them? My shape was much better then."

"I was thinking about some of *our* letters. I don't think I'd show them to the bishop, if I knew any bishop. In logical sequence I thought of the French postcards we posed for."

"It wasn't so funny at the time."

"It certainly was not. Now it all seems so long ago."

"Yes. All of it. Still, it's all much more vivid than this trip. I don't mean just the nude snapshots. I mean all those years. Thirteenth Street, and Ben, and the time I met you and Mary at Penn Station. But the past two weeks—I couldn't tell you which night we went to the Shanleys' or what night we went anywhere."

"I might be able to, with an effort. But I've been wondering on the train—was this trip necessary? What did it accomplish?"

"What it was supposed to, didn't it? We saw your mother——"

"A mild disaster. Sucking her hollow tooth and trying to warn you against me."

"Well, she got nowhere with that, and I knew it was coming. But you saw your children."

"Yes, and learned that my son and I get along fine as pen pals, but in person, nothing to say."

"But you couldn't accomplish much in two meetings. And you were pleased with Jean."

"But also disappointed. I wanted her to ask to meet you."

"Well, so did I, but since she didn't, we'll just have to wait."

"No, I think you were wrong in insisting on her making the first request. She's too young, and much too loyal to Mary. I should have gotten you together."

"No. People don't like each other just because you may want them to, especially under those circumstances."

"Well, at least Don Tinkham says I'll live."

"If you take care of yourself."

"Yes, but of course you don't need a doctor to tell you that. I didn't. God almighty! The guys I knew in business. 'Well, Alfred old boy, you look a lot better than I expected. You must have had a rough time.' Those little bluebirds of happiness. I wanted to tell some of them they didn't look so God damn good themselves. They've all reached the age where one year makes a hell of a lot of difference in how a guy looks, but they see each other all the time and they don't notice it. But I noticed it. Some of those I hadn't seen since I went to Washington—if I'd told them how they looked to me."

"Then you think the trip was a waste?"

"By and large, I do. I think it did you good, but I'm glad it's over."

She looked out at unreeling New Mexico in an effort to be casual, but she trembled as she asked him: "You wouldn't like to work back there again?"

"Not the way I feel now," he said, and her relief lasted only until he added: "Not that anybody asked me to." He made the statement with such dull factuality that she realized he was not yet conscious of his disappointment. This time he was not being devious or reticent; he had not even known that he had hoped for some offers, and now he was simply stating a fact. But his opinion of the trip as a whole had been prejudiced by the failure of his friends to want him and to tell him so. She chose her next words with extreme care.

"Well, I'm really glad you let them know that," she said.

"Know what?"

"That you didn't want to go back to Wall Street."

He hesitated, and she knew he was trying to be honest but instinctively trying to protect himself at the same time. "I didn't let them know," he said. "At least not by anything I said."

"Oh, you don't always have to say things, Raymond. You get your points across. I was thinking of that time Creighton Duffy came to lunch. You were never actually rude to him, but you couldn't have been more devastating if you'd thrown a pie in his face."

"That face would look good covered with custard," he said.

She relaxed; for the moment the danger had passed.

Late the next morning they got off the train at Pasadena and were met by Jack Tom's Jim in a rental Cadillac. They got a surprising smile from the blond young mother from the adjoining compartment, who was met by a man, unmistakably her father, in frontier pants and modified sombrero, who took her to an old Buick station wagon which had El Rancho de Los Tres Piños painted on the doors. "That man went to Harvard and I've met him," said Alfred. "I guess she must have known who we were."

"From your picture, probably."

"From our luggage tags, more likely. I wish we'd had more curiosity about her. I'm sure I know that man, and he looks like a nice guy."

"Well, if we remember the name of the ranch, we can ask."

Jim, looking into the rear-vision mirror said: "I can tell you the gentleman's name, Mizz Eaton. That's Mr. F. F. Warren, and I know him on account of how he work with Mr. Jack Tom, no less. You might say him and Mr. Jack Tom, they partners. Yes ma'am, partners."

"Thank you, Jim."

"Yes ma'am. Mr. Jack Tom, he go dove-shootin' out to Mr. Warren's ranch, way, way, *way* out, maybe a hundred miles from here. They got a *long* ride ahead of them, we only got a little-bitty ride. Oh, it's too lonesome out there, for me. I'm a town boy. Mm-*hmm*."

"Now do you remember him?" said Natalie.

"Sure," said Alfred. "I met him the first time in London. In 1918. He was in the Navy, too. Since then I've seen him in New York a half a dozen times. I guess he came close to being what they call a relative by marriage. Through Sadie Warren."

"That was one thing we meant to do and didn't. I wish we had."

"See Sadie Warren? Well, it wasn't our fault and it wasn't hers. Why particularly do you wish we'd seen her?"

"Oh—you like her, and I think I would. You always perk up when you talk about her."

"Now don't get any ideas."

"Why not? I don't see anything wrong in your finding her as attractive as Rowland did. Of course I can say that at this

938

safe distance. I might not be so generous if she were going to be around."

"Well, I guess we'll send her a Christmas present, then in a year or so a wedding present, then Christmas cards, then nothing."

"I suppose so."

After Labor Day they had another visit from Jack Tom, a somewhat longer one, in the course of which he gave a large dinner party at the main house and Natalie and Alfred were introduced to their first sampling of Los Angeles society. For this occasion Jack Tom resumed his position as host, and he did it well. In accordance with a California custom the men wore dark business suits and the women wore evening dresses and jewelry. Four Olvera Street Hawaiians sang and played at the pool, a comfortable distance from the house and terrace, and the Schaftmans retired to their quarters while the catering service attended to the preparation and serving of the food and drink. There were thirty guests, of whom twenty-eight were married couples, and one divorcee and her lover. Some of the men had gone to college in the East, but except for those few women who had not always lived in California, the women were locally educated—Marlborough, Westlake, Sacred Heart. The women, all older than Natalie, knew the minutest details of each other's lives, past and present. All of them had been abroad many times, but always in the company of at least one other Los Angeles-Pasadena couple. They had all stayed at the same hotels—the George Cinq, the Savoy, Shepheard's, Raffles. They could, and did, remember a pink dress that Molyneux had sold one of them in 1927, and the original setting of a ruby that was being worn that night. At this dinner party the timely topic was education: every mother at the party had at least one child going back East to prep school or college: Foxcroft, Farmington, St. Timothy's, St. Mark's, St. George's, Pomfret, Choate, Hotchkiss and Canterbury; Yale, Princeton, Dartmouth and Williams; Vassar, Wellesley, Smith and Radcliffe. None of the sons was going to his father's prep school; the Culver man was sending his son to Lawrenceville, the Lawrenceville man was sending his son to St. Paul's. It was remarkable how often the mothers had been intended for Foxcroft, but had not gone because it was so much more of a trip in those days.

The men were all brown, or red, from the sun; the women were uniformly pale, were not just losing their tan; they had never had one, and they told Natalie that they envied her her tan, but the sun did awful things to their skin. They spoke the truth, since in several cases the skin had been tightened by surgery.

Natalie recognized all their names; they were the same names that day after day, including Sunday—especially including Sunday—appeared *en bloc* in the Los Angeles society pages. Among them there was a uniform adoption of the custom of three names: Mrs. William Joseph Smith, Mrs. Arthur Snyder Taylor, Mrs. Henry Brown Shillington, although it was permissible to use the style Mrs. W. Joseph Smith, Mrs. A. Snyder Taylor, Mrs. H. Brown Shillington. They were also fond of 2d, which had more chic than 3d, which had incomparably more chic than Jr. Among the children the names Jill and Peter were having a vogue, so that in conversation the mothers frequently said "your Jill and my Jill." They avoided saying "my Peter and your Peter" since there was a phallic connotation, of which they were all privately aware. But in four hours with these women Natalie did not hear a single naughty word, although three of the women got tight and noisy. She did, however, hear scandalous items of news about other women, especially women who were residents of San Francisco or New York, or were movie actresses. The casual positiveness of the gossip appalled Natalie. Not one of the women defended or even questioned the veracity of the gossip. There was one correction. When one woman said, "I hear she's having an affair with Sage Rimmington," a second woman said, "Oh, that's over. Sage is having an affair with that girl, What's Her Name, that's playing in the Pacific Southwest. A very good doubles player."

"I'll say she is," said another woman. "Oh, maybe Natalie knows Sage. Did you ever know Sage Rimmington back East? She came from Wilmington originally."

"I never knew her. I met her, that's all," said Natalie.

At first, at cocktails and during the long meal, she had pitied these women for their fading prettiness in its contrast with the general vigor of their husbands, for the emptiness of their lives and their frightened interdependence among their own group, for the inquisitive lechery of their husbands toward her. The men had given her looks that they could not take back, and that had implicitly stated that the wives were unimportant. But after dinner, alone with the women, Natalie dismissed her pity and for the first time since she had become Alfred's wife she became afraid of what such a group could do with the facts of her life. These women frightened her by their glib viciousness. They would first want to find out whether Jack Tom's generosity had as much to do with a friendship for Alfred as for something else with her. And since most of them obviously knew Sage Rimmington, they would ask Sage what she knew about Mrs. Alfred Eaton. The present Mrs. Alfred Eaton.

When they all went home Natalie had fourteen more or

less definite invitations to lunch or dinner; one woman was leaving for the East to put her daughter in school. Jack Tom was pleased with Natalie's impression on his guests. "They're the people get things done in this town," he said. "I got another group I'd like you to meet, but I'll have them next time I get out here."

In their room at last and in their beds they could have a free discussion of the dinner guests. Natalie made her report and asked Alfred for his.

"What did the boys talk about? Well, of course we had to observe the ritual. The toast to the King."

"The toast to the King? I don't understand that."

"Oh, sure you do. 'May the son of a bitch rot in hell.' "

"Oh, you talked about the President."

"Exactly. I don't like him any better than they do, but good Lord. We have him, we're stuck with him, and it's gotten to be such a bore. And two of them were very tentative about me, oh, very. 'Mr. Eaton, how did a man like you happen to get mixed up with him in the first place?' It was that little guy that carried his head way back on his shoulders. I think he wears a toupee. His name is Orville Reichler, J. Orville Reichler. I thought, 'Now you little prick, who do you think you are, putting me on the stand at a party like this, in front of a lot of guys I've just met?' "

"So you let him have it."

"Did I? 'Well, Mr. Reichler,' I said. 'First I'd have to understand clearly and exactly what you mean by mixed up. For me it carries a rather unpleasant connotation. As for example, mixed up in a scandal, or a crooked deal. You never say a man was mixed up in the construction of a cathedral, for instance. Or that he was mixed up in the discovery of a cure for cancer. And I don't think anybody would ever say when I was a banker that I was *mixed up* in an enterprise. At least he wouldn't say it to me.' "

"What happened?"

"Dead silence, which I broke. 'You see, Mr. Reichler, I haven't the slightest intention of being put on the defensive about my having been Assistant Secretary of the Navy. I'm sure that wasn't your intention, either. But all the same, as a stranger in this part of the country, I do find myself somewhat on the defensive, possibly because we attach different meanings to the expression, mixed up. Now if you simply mean, how did I happen to take the job, I can answer that quickly. I was in the Navy in the first war and I've always been very fond of the Navy and still am. So that when the job was offered, I snatched it. Aside from sea duty in a combat ship, for which they want younger men, I couldn't think of a wartime job I'd rather have had. Now as to Mr. Roosevelt, I merely made the decision that a lot of men like me made. If he, a Democrat, was willing to let me, a very staunch, anti-New Deal Republican, have the job, we were even. In fact, on a basis of, well, good manners, and mutual trust, he made a better showing than I did. He could just as easily have given the job to a Republican who wasn't as anti-New Deal as I was, and thereby made the bi-partisan gesture. I didn't intend to make a speech, but this happens to be a very influential group of men here tonight, and you've given me an opportunity to tell how I happened to take the job, and at the same time, make it clear that I wouldn't for one second think of apologizing for taking it. I'd still be there if I hadn't had a hemorrhage, Mr. Reichler.' "

"What then?"

"Well, by that time some of them were enjoying what I was doing to Reichler. I would guess, although I don't know, that Reichler is one of those little guys that goes to work on people, and I suppose out here he's important enough to get away with it. It just happened to be Reichler, of course. All the others felt the same way, but I flatter myself that some of them were glad it was Reichler getting his nose rubbed in it and not they. They're not cowards, not those guys, they're tough. But the tougher the guy, the less he likes to be made a horse's ass of, especially in front of his best buddies."

"Mrs. Reichler invited us to dinner."

"Oh, Reichler, the little prick, he backtracked and got very chummy. But of course he'll knife me if he ever gets the chance."

"What else did you talk about."

"Pussy."

"Pussy Who?"

"Snatch, dearie. Tail."

"Oh. *You* did, too?"

"Oh, yes. Apparently there's a woman here who's a real virtuoso with the electric vibrator. Is virtuoso feminine? I know it's its own reward."

"Oh, my."

"Anyway, any time I want to get fixed up, I can get her number from at least five of them. And there's another one that just came to town. Only two of them knew her, and what she does they're not telling. They're saving her for a surprise when some of the boys go gunning in the High Sierras. There's a man that wasn't here tonight, and they're all looking forward to his meeting with the new girl."

"Will they see it?"

"Of course. That's half the fun. He's the ex-husband of the Mrs. Gratwin that *was* here tonight. They're going to pretend that the new girl's car breaks down, just before they arrive at the camp where they hunt. They persuade her to spend the night at the camp and she pretends to pass out on one drink. Supposed to be a country girl. So they put her to bed and then they let nature take its course. Apparently Gratwin will go for anything female and they're counting on him to sneak into the room with the girl, thinking she's an appleknocker. And that's when the fun begins."

"Well, I guess I don't object to that so much. He has it coming to him."

"He never gets suspicious, either. One time they had a girl go to his apartment dressed as a policewoman. She was pretending to be checking on a maid that used to work for him. First she had a cigarette and then a couple of drinks and finally got in the hay with him. She was still there when he went to his office in the morning, and when he came home that evening, there were two big trunks in the bedroom. He asked what the hell? And she said she was moving in, and if he wanted to make any trouble, she could make just as much for him, because the Vice Squad knew all about him. He went to his lawyer, who was in on the joke, and the lawyer advised him to sit tight for a day or two but under no circumstances to make another pass at the girl. Well, that advice was not heeded and Gratwin had visions of the newspapers when he married a policewoman."

"They go to such trouble. What happened?"

"Oh, they made him sweat it out for three days and the third day she wasn't there when he came home, but some of his friends dropped in and presented him with a pair of handcuffs and an old-time police helmet. For a while they called him Sergeant. I guess he must be one of the all-time chumps."

"And what else did you talk about?"

"Golf, and fishing. We've been invited to join a couple of golf clubs. I may want to do that. Wouldn't you like to play?"

"Yes, I think it would be fun. But don't ask me to fish. I did that in the Poconos and a couple of times at Barnegat with Ben. I'd much rather play golf."

"I won't ask you to fish, but *I* may have to. All these red-blooded Americans tonight were fishermen."

"Why do you say you may *have* to?"

"I don't know. It just seems to be part of their life."

"The whores are, too, but you're not going to have to do that," she said. "You're not going to have to do anything you don't want to do. That's the wonderful position you're in."

"One more Gratwin story?"

"Oh, I like them. They make such an ass of him, these stories."

"The boys chartered a small cruiser and got six or seven whores to go aboard and head for Catalina. Then the boys in their own boat went out a little later, and one of them, looking through the binoculars, said, 'Good Lord, what do I see?' And handed Gratwin the glass and there were six dames, absolutely bare-ass, all over the cruiser. Gratwin persuaded his boat to go after them, but when they got close the owner refused to go any closer, but he said Gratwin could borrow the tender. So Gratwin got in the tender, which had an outboard motor, and went after the cruiser, which was just drifting. When he got close the naked girls waved him off and screamed, but he kept coming and then they all pulled revolvers, loaded with blanks, of course, and started shooting at him. He started to make his way back to the big boat but they put on speed and for a while Gratwin was left alone in the channel in the outboard. Then after about a half an hour the boys came back for him."

"They chartered a boat and hired those girls just for that?"

"Oh, come. The girls went on the big boat later."

"What does Gratwin do for a living?"

"Real estate. He sold Jack Tom this house, or the land and the house that was on it originally."

"And he was married to that quite lovely-looking woman that came with that insipid man. Why does a woman like that have such poor taste in men? But who am I to talk? I married Ben. And I suppose she's fifty, and lonely, and this is the land of youth. The young girls here are so pretty, I've never seen so many beautiful figures. But something happens. Do you suppose it's the sun? Shall I start carrying a parasol?"

"Carry it, in case of mashers, but don't open it. You've never looked better in your life."

"Thank you, my dear."

The days, and then the weeks and months moved along through the autumn and their second winter and second spring, the spring of 1945. They were still a novelty to the Los Angeles-Pasadena-Santa Barbara rich, and on one day during the Christmas holidays they were able to make a selection from among twenty-eight invitations to cocktail parties. By this time they were in the New York Social Register, with Jack Tom's address. There was no Los Angeles edition of the Social Register, but an extraordinary number of Los Angeles women bought the New York edition, and in the society columns Alfred and Natalie were invariably referred to as "the former Assistant Secretary of the Navy and his charming wife, the Socially-Registered Alfred and Natalie Eaton, who plan to make the Southland their permanent home." Alfred alone was sometimes referred to as the handsome member of the posh or swank New York Racquet & Tennis Club and of the ultra-conservative Union Club, and Natalie was called a Junior Leaguer, which was pure invention. "They could say that I was a former member of the waiting-list for the Acorn Club, but that was as far as I got. I've never thought of that. I wonder what happened there. Do you suppose they just crossed out my name? Ben's aunt put me up. Do you suppose she then turned around and blackballed me? Should I be indignant, Mr. Posh Swank Racquet Club?"

"Yes, I think so."

"Maybe I ought to go back to Philadelphia and picket the place."

"I don't know. You know the saying, it won't get well if you picket."

"Where did you hear that? You didn't make it up."

"Oh, in our mad whirl. It seems to me we're going to an awful lot of parties, doesn't it you?"

It seemed so to her, but she was willing to go along with whatever he did in such matters. "Too many, do you think?"

"I don't know. Too many, or I wouldn't be raising the question."

"Well, we can easily fix that. We can cut down the number. Ration ourselves. Or stop entirely. We were here for ten or eleven months without ever going to or giving a party."

"Oh, I don't want to stop entirely, but it might be a sensible plan to say no to any more cocktail parties. We've met enough people now to know which ones we like, which ones we want to see. Although I'll be the first to admit, we do see people that we don't necessarily like. That's my doing. I know by now who the men are that run this town, and most of them seem to like us, and whatever I eventually do, I want them in my corner. *If* I ever do anything besides play golf and bridge."

It was the first time he had expressed any concern about the present pattern of his life, but it was also the last time he discussed a curtailment of their social schedule. As the date for renewal of their lease grew near, he arranged to have a chat with Jack Tom on one of Jack Tom's quick visits.

The two men sat at the pool in their Hawaiian-print bathing trunks one Sunday afternoon while Natalie, forewarned, had retired for a nap. "Jack Tom, you've been very good about not pressing me on the subject of the job. I appreciate that, as I appreciate everything else, but the year's up and I think you're entitled to your answer."

"No hurry. All in good time."

"Well, what it comes down to, and the only really important factor, is, do I want to work for someone else, or do I want to work for myself."

"And then I know your answer."

"I'm sure you do. I've discussed this with Natalie often and at great length, but I always come around to saying the same things. I've never been my own boss. No matter how much authority I was given, how much responsibility and even dignity, the trappings, I was still accountable to at least one other man, and that man always had the right to veto anything I did. Although James MacHardie, in the last five or six years I was with him, practically gave me carte-blanche. So, in another two years I'll be fifty. I'm closer to fifty than I am to anything else but forty-nine, and I'd very much like to find a business that I could buy and make into something, or start one from the ground up. I think you understand that."

"Listen, Alfred, I had a hunch you were thinking along these lines. If id been any other way you'uda told me by now. Sure I understand. Understand? Hell, you're only doing what every man wants to do, every man I'd like to have in my organization. I wouldn't want a man that didn't have spunk and ineetiative. However, I owe it to my associates here and now to say to you, every man in my organization—on the directorship level, that is—every one of them did make good on his own. They all had their own business, or else, like in the case of Fritz Warren, taking care of his money was a full-time occupation. They're all in with me because our kind of awl business is big awl business. We don't figger to put the Rockefellers out of commission, least not yet. But you know we're pretty big. Call us a big small outfit, or a small big outfit. Well, I'm not one of those Armenians or Greeks that can do it all like running a kingdom. We have problems they don't have. Tax problems, government regulations. And when we want a new lease we can't send out a troop of Texas Rangers and shoot up the bastards that won't sign. The foreigners can do that, we can't. And as far as me being the chairman of the board, I'm entitled to that for one reason and one reason only—I started the company. But some hot little bitch might stick a knife into me one of these nights, and the next day there'd be a new chairman. And any man on my board would be a good one, every bit as good if not a hell of a sight better than me. I won't kid you. If you came in tomorrow and I got cut up tomorrow night, you wouldn't get chairman of the board Tuesday morning. You wouldn't want it, with as little experience as you had. But maybe the next time around you *would* get chairman, and meanwhile you'd be making a pisspot full of money and maybe having a little fun. However, your mind is made up and I bow to it with deep respect and no change in our friendship. I don't want to sound like that letter you got from Franklin D. Roozavelt, but I would like to feel that I could kinda hash things over with you, just as a friend, and I'd always like to feel I could send you a cheque for your advice."

"My advice is yours for the asking, and the pleasure of talking to you."

"No, I'd like to see some money change hands. You might

946

just off-hand make a suggestion that I could turn into a million dollars or more. Well, I'll be the judge of that when the time comes. Now meantime, I'm hoping you're going to renew your lease here."

"I'd like to."

"I was hoping so. I'm getting the altar-itch again, Alfred, and the poor unfortunate young lady says she won't live in any house where I ever bedded down with another woman. So you can figure to have this house—oh, if she sticks it out five years that'll be as much as I can ask. And any time you want to buy this place, you and I can work out something. My tax law'r may even want me to take a little loss on it. I don't know. So I guess we settled a lot of business for the Lord's Day."

"Well, I hope as satisfactorily to you as to me."

"Don't you fret over that, Alfred. You oughta sometime see me gettin' out of something I don't want to do."

"How about this new girl of yours? Natalie would like to hear about that." Alfred summoned Natalie, who had not slept a wink. She came down to the pool and sat with them.

"Jack Tom is our landlord for another year. It's all settled."

"I'm so pleased," she said.

"But he has other news."

"Another poor unfortunate young lady has promised to be my bride. They never learn."

"Who is she? Tell us about her?"

"Well, she's a Pi Phi from Stanford—"

"That's good, I hope," said Alfred.

"Oh, very good," said Natalie. "You don't read the local papers carefully enough."

"Second Pi Phi I been married to. Cupid's arrow, I guess. Their pin is an arrow, case you didn't know that, *and* you didn't. Her folks are from up North, Marin County. Daddy's retired. *Was* in the shipping business. Mother come from Iowa."

"Is it all right for me to ask how old she is?" said Natalie.

"Well, she's young enough so she'll tell it, but so young I'm almost ashamed to. She's twenty-three, and looks every bit of nineteen. She's been down here making like she was taking her Master's at U. C. L. A., but since I knew her she's been studying sociology at Ciro's and Romanoff's. Well, I guess you don't have to do all your studying on Central Avenue. Anybody can study the poor people. So I'm a little over twice her age and I can't do the rumba, but she was married once before to a fuhtball player—"

"As who wasn't?" said Natalie.

"Well, I didn't mean anything by that, Natalie. But she was, and she says she's marrying me because a man's been married four times, he's proved he isn't very positive about his likes and dislikes, and he aint gonna expect everything in one woman. She fractures me, this young lady. Nothin' she says is like anything anybody else says. I went to Brock's and bought her a little diamond bracelet and when I gave it to her she said what did I want to give her a diamond bracelet for? And I said didn't she ever hear of a man giving a girl a present? She sure did, she said, 'But why are you giving it to me? People are gonna ask me what I got it for, and you gotta tell me what I'm supposed to tell them. I'm not gonna think up any answers,' she says. She said she was perfectly willing to tell people it was the usual reason why an old man gave a young girl a diamond bracelet, but that was for me to decide. So I took back the diamond bracelet and bought her an engagement ring. Then when I gave her that she said, 'Okay, now you can go back and get the bracelet. From now on, I'll take anything you give me.' "

"She sounds like quite a girl," said Natalie.

"She fractures me. Always calls me Jackson-Tomson. She says I'm too old to be called Jack Tom. And she won't call me Jack because that means money in slang, and she says she don't need any reminders that I got plenty of money. Every waiter and orchestra leader and blond whore in L. A. knows I got money."

"She also sounds as if she had a great deal of sense," said Alfred.

"Listen, if she stays married to me till she's thirty you just watch what she does with money. We don't get to have a serious chat very often, but she said to me one night, 'Is all you want to do make it?' She wants me to get together ten or twenty of the best doctors in the world and find out from them one disease that's almost licked, and go after that one disease, instead of trying to spread the money around here and there. Then if we lick that one disease, go after another."

"How does she know such things, spending all her time in Ciro's?" said Natalie.

"Reads, I guess. She's very near-sighted and she wears glasses as thick as a window when she reads, but she says she reads because she likes to be alone in the daytime. I think she likes to be alone so she can read. Same difference. But she hates to be alone at night, and that's why she goes to night clubs."

"Does she want children?" said Natalie.

"She says she won't have any children till she has a look at my children by the other wives, and she and I have to both go on the wagon for a year before we have any. She fractures me, and it was all for laughs the first couple months, but I think I'm in love for the first time in my silly life."

"What's her name?" said Alfred.

"Henrietta McCandless. Known as Mickey, but lately I been calling her Henrietta. That's sure a sign of something, or I'm an old rubber boot."

"When are you getting married?"

"She says she'll give me plenty of warning. Three days. If I can't be ready to marry her in three days, the deal's off, she says. That'll give me all the time I need to fly back here if I'm in New York, and then we hop over to Nevada some place. No best man, no maid of honor. She says she had one big wedding and the engagement parties lasted longer than the marriage. So you can see, I gotta be ready at a moment's notice." He smiled rather proudly. "You know what I gave her? I went and ordered a fraternity pin. I'm a Beta, and I don't guess I've owned a badge since I was in school. But I went and bought one and gave it to her. She wears it, too. She said to me, 'You would join a lodge that has a diamond in the pin.' Fractures me, I swear."

The soon following news that Jack Tom and Miss McCandless had eloped to Carson City was thus no surprise at all to Alfred and Natalie, and they looked forward to meeting her, but for months they heard nothing from Jack Tom and saw in the newspapers only small items reporting that he and his bride were living in New York. The people that Alfred and Natalie saw at the cocktail and dinner parties—an undiminished program in spite of Alfred's talk of curtailment— usually expected the Eatons to have some report of the Smiths; but of at least equal conversational interest was the ending of the war in Europe. Briefly at cocktail parties, and in the more extended conversations at dinner parties it was generally agreed that the Japanese would hold out a little longer, to gain whatever could be salvaged in the time remaining before massive movements of troops from the European theater would commence, westward, at which point the Japanese would sue for an armistice and settle for surrender to Douglas MacArthur, and the marines would undertake the task of mopping up the hold-outs on the scattered islands of the Pacific. In any event the war in the Pacific would be over before the end of the year. Occasionally at these parties there would be a Navy officer who would attempt to cast some doubt on the total reliability of the predictions, but his conservatism, which was called pessimism, was unwelcome in this otherwise conservative society. And, of course, as it turned out, the Navy officer was wrong. The war was over on 14 August 1945, and many of the women were looking forward to their first trip in the *Lurline* in years and years.

The immediate lifting of restrictions on the sale of gasoline affected the life of every man, woman and child in the most motorized city in the world. Its effect on the lives of Natalie and Alfred was, for the moment negligible, since they had depended upon taxicabs and rented cars for their transportation. But within a week of V-J Day Alfred heard from Jack Tom Smith for the first time since his marriage, and the effect was far from negligible. The note was written in San Francisco, and it read:

Dear Alfred:

Henrietta and I have been hoping to get to see Natalie and yourself and I feel somewhat remiss in not writing you sooner. However, you no doubt can guess how tied up I have been these past couple of months and we did not even get a chance to visit Mr. and Mrs. McCandless 'til last week. We had a pleasant visit with them at their home and are now in San Francisco for a few days. I am writing you now because since they took off gas rationing I have a Rolls that was in dead storage through the war which I have ordered put back in running order. It is a convertible I had built in England before the War and for a Rolls is almost brand new, about 8,000 mi. I have rec'd word that it is now back in running order & if you and Natalie felt like it you could get it out of the garage and drive it up here and the four of us could have a few days in S. F. and all drive back to L. A. together. We have some friends on the Peninsula you would like and this town is really jumping now. You could easily make it in one day. If this appeals to you, call my Jim and tell him to have the car delivered to you and either phone me or send me a wire saying when to expect you, preferably the 20th or 21st. Looking forward to seeing you both,

As ever,
Jack Tom

"What a guy, I never even knew he had a Rolls, although why anything like that should surprise me, I don't know." He spoke while Natalie was reading the note.

"What do you think?" he said. "It might be fun."

She was sickened and wanted to scream, "No! No!" But he had read into the letter only a request by a friend for a small favor which was more than balanced by the pleasure of driving a fine car. *Now* was the time for caution, to stifle the thought of Archie Busby going to Brooks for somebody's evening shirt.

"Well, I don't know," she said.

"You're not in favor of it?"

"Oh, I don't think I'd mind the trip, although it is pretty long. I suppose we could spell each other in the driving, and I've never driven a Rolls."

"Well then what *do* you object to?" he said. "Is it something to do with Jack Tom's wife?"

"Yes," she said. "I'd rather wait and meet her when we're

950

not tired from such a long drive. I want to be at my best when I see her for the first time. It's not only feminine vanity. I don't think I'd be much good all the time we were there. I still don't snap back to normal the way I could a few years ago, without the right amount of sleep . . . Let's not."

"He'll be disappointed, but all right. I'll send him a day letter. I'll tell him my leg is bothering me and it's too long a trip."

"You don't have to say anything about your leg. Why don't you say we've invited people for dinner for the twenty-first? And let's make it the truth by inviting some people."

"It might *be* quite an exhausting trip, at that. It's close to five hundred miles."

"Too much for one day, Rolls or no Rolls."

He had inadvertently provided her with a good excuse by mentioning Henrietta Smith, and the present danger had passed. But she saw clearly enough that he did not recognize the signs, the Archie Busby signs, and she also saw now that her prescience was correct; that to direct his attention to a sign would be an act of cruelty that she could not inflict on this man, ever. In that respect the course of their relationship was established: she would guide him as though he had lost his sight, and she would refrain from describing the ugly things that in his blindness he did not see. It was not surprising that in the nights that followed she enjoyed a deeper satisfaction from his fondness for her breasts.

She had agreed, promised him, not to attempt another pregnancy. "I ask you selfishly," he had said, when they could again make love. "All selfishly. I don't want you to die before I do, and you could. Is that as plain and unembellished a statement as I could make? I'll plead guilty to selfishness."

"Well, so will I. I'm not eager to have a baby right away, and maybe by the time I am, I won't be able to. All right, I promise."

She was never completely reconciled to the childlessness of their marriage, but his real and present need of her—no less real and no less present for his unconsciousness of it—compensated her and made her think of little Doctor Middleton, still a comical figure in his burrowing, but the tallest and wisest of men in the lowest depths of her life. What strange things, she thought, we are grateful for! He had given her five minutes in which to weep. Would anyone else have had such beautiful courtesy? . . .

Henrietta and Jack Tom Smith arrived in the cream-colored Rolls during the second week of September, and in the very first minutes of conversation Natalie elicited the admission that *they* had not driven the car from San Francisco. Henrietta, in a sleeveless white lawn dress and bright yellow babushka, wasted little time on Natalie. A man of any age could interest Henrietta, but no woman of any age could interest her for long. She pointed at Alfred with an empty cigarette holder and said: "My father said you made one hell of a speech one time when you were in San Francisco."

"Well, thank you. That's very nice of him," said Alfred.

"He really did say that, too," said Jack Tom. "I was there when he said it."

She turned slowly and looked down at her husband, who was sitting Indian style at the edge of the pool. "Now who asked you for corroboration? Eaton didn't think I was lying to him. I don't have to butter him up, and don't always be getting into everybody's act. As I was saying, my father thought your speech was the only thing like it he heard during the whole war that made any sense. Not like the rest of the crap that came out of Washington."

"Well, not everybody felt the way your father did."

"That's why he liked it. My father's like me, or I guess I'm like him. Either way, we don't like people that are afraid to say what they think. And coming from you, a Wall Street robber baron—oh, the Pacific Union boys didn't like you at all. That's not a labor union, Mrs. Eaton. Anything but."

"Oh, I've heard of it. Since I've been living out *here*," said Natalie.

Henrietta studied Natalie with a slight increase in respect. "Oh, you read that line very nicely. I got it."

"I was *sure* you *would*," said Natalie.

"Yeah, and I got that one, too," said Henrietta. She smiled at Natalie, without any friendliness, but as an indication of not uncomplimentary recognition.

"Now can I say something?" said Jack Tom.

"If you've got something to say, go ahead."

"It's a question I wanted to ask Alfred. It's big stuff. It's gonna be a weighty decision."

"I'll bet," said Henrietta. "Such as, do we go to Mike's or Perino's."

"Bigger'n that. Alfred, Fritz Warren—I saw him yesterday at a meeting—he said to tell you a young cousin of his that you know is coming out to visit him and Annabella, and he wants to know what would be a good night for Natalie and you. Any night the week after next."

"Any night would suit us. Can't we telephone him?"

Jack Tom shook his head. "He's out on his boat and it doesn't have but a small receiving set you can't talk on."

"Anything else'd be a sheer waste of money for that man," said Henrietta. "You know the Warrens? Fritz, and that dried-up codfish he's married to, Annabella?"

"We've met them twice. I didn't think she was a dried-up codfish, though," said Natalie.

"She's a good fifty-five, and if she uses anything but saddle soap on that complexion she's throwing Warren's money away. Why do you like her?" said Henrietta.

"Well, I wouldn't say she was a friend of mine, on the strength of two meetings, but I do say I liked what I saw of her."

"Yes, I could have guessed that, but my question was why?"

"Do you want me to list what I considered her attractive features?"

"Sure," said Henrietta. "We certainly won't be all day on that."

"Well, she's a lady," said Natalie, pausing to give Henrietta every opportunity.

"Glub glub. A lady."

"She's devoted to her husband, and he is to her."

"Touching. Touching."

"And with that straight black hair and high cheekbones, she looks like an Indian."

"You mean the way an Easterner thinks an Indian ought to look. I've known more Indians than you have, Mrs. Eaton."

"I'm sure you have, and I admit that that's what I meant. An idealized Indian. But I don't think that's so bad."

"Also, you didn't specify squaw or brave. You can't like flat-chested women. You're not one."

"Honey, you're gettin' too personal," said Jack Tom.

"If I am, Mrs. Eaton can tell me so. Mrs. Eaton and I understand one another. So you like her because she looks like an Indian and she's a lady. You know, I guess those are some of the reasons why I don't like her. How do you like her, Eaton?"

"Very much. I think she's very attractive, and I don't even agree with you about the flat-chested."

"Well, maybe you know something I don't know," said Henrietta.

"Now, honey. Take it easy."

"Only what I could see in an evening dress. She's rather well developed, if I'm any judge."

"And I'll bet you are, too. Or were."

"I gotta take you outa here before these good people lose patience with you."

"Well, put your gun away, I'll go quietly."

"You're not really going? We're expecting you to stay for lunch," said Natalie.

"Thanks, but Jackson–Tomson is showing me around this afternoon."

"I don't know that I will if this is the way you're gonna behave."

"Well, mercy me, don't break my heart. I want to ask Mrs. Eaton a favor. Would you show me the house?"

Natalie, surprised, said, "Gladly. Come with me."

Together they walked up the slowly winding stone steps to the main house, and when they got inside the girl sat down and looked up at Natalie. She did not speak.

"Are you feeling all right?" said Natalie, genuinely concerned.

Suddenly the girl put her face in her hands, but she did not cover her eyes and she did not weep. "Jesus, what am I going to do?"

"Are you in some kind of trouble? Can I help you?"

"Am I in trouble? That's just what I am. That's what the servant-girls call it. I'm knocked up. This son of a bitch has got me pregnant, four months gone, and I can't stand the sight of him. I didn't want to have a baby, and he knew that, but he fixed me. He made me take a chance, and I lost. Now I'm having a baby by a man that I'm going to walk out on."

"But why are you telling me all this?"

"Because I can't tell any of my friends, but I knew I could tell you."

"Why me?"

"This will give you a laugh. The only other person I wanted to tell was Annabella Warren. Now do you see why?"

"I think so."

"Somebody that instinct told me I could trust. But Annabella didn't like me. She thought I was cheap. I knew you didn't think I was cheap."

"It may work out. You're going to have the baby, I hope."

"I'll have the baby. I want that. But it's not going to work out. You wonder why I married him. Because I wasn't as smart as he was, and $40,000,000 is a lot of money. He let me have my own way in everything before we were married. If he hadn't I wouldn't have gone out with him. I'm not poor, and I had plenty of people to take me out. But here was the famous Jack Tom Smith, jumping whenever I cracked the whip, and I thought that was the way it was going to be. But I was wrong. The other women—well, that's insulting, but I can understand it. If you give a hat-check girl a hundred dollars for nothing, just because she has pretty legs, she's going to be looking for five hundred and *she's* going to go on the make. That happened, a month after we were married."

"And he gave her five hundred dollars?"

"He gave her nothing, except a lay."

"He told you about it?"

"Yes. I asked him and he said yes. And that's where he was so smart. He acted as if we'd agreed on that."

"You, too? Could you sleep with anyone you felt like?"

"Well, that wasn't straightened out, because I don't sleep around. I'm not promiscuous. I was married before, and I've had more than one affair, but I wasn't promiscuous and he was. And here I am, twenty-three, married twice, pregnant, and getting ready to take a powder. A great start in life for somebody that wanted to—oh, hell."

"Wanted to what, Henrietta?"

"I wanted to study medicine, but my mother screamed at that. Not with laughter, either. Horror. And then I went to college, and I was pretty, and I was pinned three times before I got married. And *he* wasn't ready to get married, either."

"You haven't said a word about love."

"I don't know anything about love. I can tell you a lot about sex, and jealousy. But the boys don't think about love, and the girls are afraid that if they talk about love to the boys, the boys will call them sissies, and they'll be unpopular."

"But don't you believe in love?"

"Well, if I do—Jack Tom Smith said he was in love with me. That's not much of a recommendation for it. I suppose you do believe in it."

"More than anything."

"Oh, I guess every young girl starts out believing in it, but the boys frighten us out of it. I guess one thing is that I've never had any respect for any boy I went out with. *Or* got in bed with. And I've never admired any of them. They just don't *know* anything, and if *you* do, they try to make it seem like a disease. Not even a disease. An eccentricity. A phony pose. And the so-called intellectuals are just as bad. Commies. Get all their ideas from the *Daily Worker* or the commies on the faculty. Know-it-alls. And not a bit embarrassed when they're wrong, like that time Stalin and Hitler got palsy-walsy. They'll stomach anything."

"Hey there, little lady, if you're gonna go, these good people want to eat their lunch," Jack Tom's voice came from the terrace.

"Come and see me, Henrietta. We're here every day. I go down to Beverly Hills some mornings, but I wish you'd think of this as a place to come to."

"Don't be surprised if I do. I'd like to."

"We're even in the telephone book."

"Oh, the Great Lubricator wouldn't like that. But maybe he'd think it was all right if you did it. He thinks your husband is un parfait gentilhomme."

"He's right on that. Who is your doctor?"

"A little man named Middleton."

"Oh, good for you. He was my doctor."

"I thought he was just an obstetrician."

"And gynecologist. He is. Don't you know about me?"

Henrietta smiled. "Are there things to know about you? I'll bet there are, but I'll bet they don't get told."

"I'm not a femme fatale. No, I meant my medical history. I lost a baby last year, and Dr. Middleton took care of me. I recommend him highly."

"He has a good reputation among doctors, and they can be mean bastards. But I have a hard time taking him seriously when he's down there looking at my crotch. I see the top of his head and I want to say, 'Don't get lost, boy.' "

Natalie laughed, fully and heartily. "The poor man—because that's exactly what I thought."

"You two ladies got any funny jokes, let us in on them," said Jack Tom, in the doorway.

Henrietta rose and shook hands with Natalie. "I will call you."

"Be long distance, because we're going to New York tomorrow," said Jack Tom.

"It'll be local, because I'm *not* going to New York tomorrow," said Henrietta.

"Suit yourself, honey. You want to turn me loose."

They heard the special music of the Rolls exhaust and Alfred said to Natalie: "Did Henrietta tell you their news?"

"Yes."

"He's overjoyed. He's absolutely convinced it's going to be a boy, and I think he's planning to buy Harvard."

"I'm sorry. I can't make jokes about him."

"Why?"

She repeated the scene with Henrietta.

"Well," said Alfred. "I guess the obvious remark is, she knew what she was getting into."

"I'm on her side."

"Stay out of it."

"You mean, don't see her?"

"See her, but don't take sides."

"I'm sorry, but if I see her, I'm going to let her know I'm on her side. She knows it already."

"*She* does, but he *doesn't*."

"Then I take it you're on his side."

"You would have been until ten minutes ago. She was giving you a going-over. I've known him for twenty-seven years, and we've known her for about twenty-seven minutes."

"And we both know her better in twenty-seven minutes than you know him in twenty-seven years." Then, before she

956

could stop them, the words were out: "What's the matter? Are you afraid of him?"

He took a deep breath and looked at her, and turned and started to leave the room.

"I didn't mean that," she said. "I apologize."

He kept on going and went out and sat in his favorite deck chair in his favorite place for that hour of the day. She watched him from inside the house and she saw that he did a curious thing: he "favored" his right leg, although it had not been hurting him recently, and he otherwise assumed the same attitude he had been accustomed to take fifteen months ago, when he was an invalid. She turned on the radio for what remained of Arturo Toscanini's reading of the First Symphony of Johannes Brahms. She knew at exactly what point on the volume dial the music would sound best on the terrace and she regulated the dial to that point. But she then went to their bedroom and closed the door. She took off her dress and lay on the bed in her slip. She had tried so hard and had been so successful—and then in small anger she had impulsively described to the blind man one of the ugliest sights of all: the reflection of his own self, his uncertainty and his timidity. There was one certainty: that the question of fear would always arise with the mention of Jack Tom's name.

Natalie was already preparing for whatever punishment she would receive: his silence, his sarcasm, his aloof politeness. Once again she had over-punished him and she was more than willing to suffer some if that would restore him some. But soon, and probably very soon, he would set out to prove to her that he was not afraid of Jack Tom, and she had an all but specific premonition that whatever he did for proof would be a mistake. And so it was.

Fritz and Annabella Warren's dinner party was at Romanoff's, in the small diningroom off the front room. Gary Cooper, Spencer Tracy, Antonio Moreno, Irene Dunne, Loretta Young, and Constance Bennett were there to give Sadie Warren some movie names to remember. Robert Benchley, a Harvard classmate of Fritz Warren's, and James Malloy, a novelist whom Sadie admired, were there. The others were naturalized or first-generation Southern Californians whose Somerset-Chilton connections were as active as though they had only moved to Albany. It was not a California party, and except for the presence of the motion picture stars, it could just as well have been held in Calcutta or Viña del Mar or Rochester, Minnesota; and the movie stars came from Montana, Wisconsin, Mexico, Kentucky, Utah and New York.

The movie people present comprised almost the total roster of the Warrens' acquaintances among screen actors. There were some men—directors, producers, writers—whom Fritz Warren knew through polo, fishing, and the Republican party —but over the years their wives had not been compatible with Annabella, and they were not invited to functions at which she officiated. Annabella Warren's effect on Henrietta Smith was typical of her effect on most Pacific Coast women, and they chose to regard her as a frump, a snob, and a freak. To them she was unfeminine with her even stride, black straight hair parted in the middle with a bun in the back, and plain brown felt hats and tweed suits. It irritated them, and had from the beginning of the Warrens' residence in California, that Fritz Warren preferred this odd woman to them, pretended not to understand when they flirted with him, and left them quickly when their flirtatiousness passed the point where it could not fail to be understood. It was impossible for these women to believe that the Warrens could live so close to Los Angeles—a hundred miles was no great distance—without making *some* effort to achieve a position in the social life of the city. If they had been living in an *estancia* in the Argentine or a station in the Australian bush they could not have been more remote and self-sufficient, and it never occurred to the women that that was precisely what the Warrens had hoped to achieve, had come all the way to California to achieve it. It would have been somewhat comforting if the Warrens had bothered to explain that they were no more anxious to avoid Los Angeles society than they had been to pull out of Boston, but the Warrens were done with explaining after they had finished with Louisburg Square. The Warrens could also have explained that they had never been active in society: their social life in Boston had been largely confined to gatherings of their families, which were society enough for non-members but still no more than family parties to the Warrens. (It would have been true, of course, to say that by 1922, when the Warrens moved to California, they would have been at least fifth cousins to nearly everyone present at any Boston party they wanted to attend.)

Fritz and Annabella Warren barely knew their cousin Sadie, had not seen her since her childhood, but their own daughter had seen her and liked her, and had happened to be in Boston shortly after the death of Rowland Eaton. Dorothy Warren Bolling, the young mother who had been on the train with the Eatons, became a friend to her cousin through her own loneliness for her absent husband. James Bolling, gunnery officer aboard an attack transport, lacked sufficient points for an early separation from the Navy, and Dorothy was not present at the party, but she had been responsible for Sadie's visit to the Warrens' ranch. "She needs a change," Dorothy had told Annabella Warren. "I mean needs it." The invitation had gone out forthwith.

It was immediately apparent to Alfred that whether or not a change was needed, a change had occurred. Even allowing for the passage of a couple of years, Sadie had aged. She was a young woman, never again to be called a girl. Her figure was good, and her face was rather more interesting for the loss of the roundness of her cheeks, but the changes in her appearance suggested that she might also have changed in ways that would make it difficult to take up where they had left off. In that respect he guessed wrong.

"It's grand to see you again. Do you mind if I give your husband a kiss, Mrs. Eaton?"

"Not when he's been looking forward to it as much as he has," said Natalie.

"He has? Well then I'm going to give him a big hug for that, too." They embraced, and she said to Natalie: "I'm going to have him for dinner, too."

"Better spread a good sauce over me. I'm pretty stringy," said Alfred.

Sadie quickly looked about her and said: "When I heard Spencer Tracy and Gary Cooper were going to be here, I said to Annabella, for God's sake not to put me next to them. They're my favorites, and Charles Boyer, and I wouldn't know what on earth to talk about."

"We haven't met Charles Boyer, but Cooper and Tracy are easy to talk to," said Alfred. "As a matter of fact, Tracy has a very good sense of humor, dryly sarcastic."

"What about Mr. Cooper?"

"Polite. Very good manners, and *interested,*" said Natalie. "And he remembers you."

"Well, I should think anybody'd remember *you,*" said Sadie.

"You're very generous," said Natalie.

The waiter stopped with a tray full of drinks. "I'll take one of those," said Sadie. She took a Martini, drank half of it quickly and said to the waiter: "You'll be back soon, I hope?"

"Yes ma'am."

To the Eatons she said: "This party terrifies me, except for you two. I'm related to half a dozen people in this room, but I couldn't pick them out. Don't you two drink at all? Neither of you?"

"I do, occasionally, but Alfred is still on the ulcer wagon."

"How can you stand parties without drinking? I'd just shrivel up and hide in a corner. I couldn't face people without"— she stopped and reconsidered the near admission—"at least at parties. I guess I don't really like parties. Or maybe I don't

959

like people. In the mass, that is." The original gaiety disappeared, if it was gaiety, and after hesitating a moment she gulped the rest of her cocktail. "Can I come and spend a night with you before I go home? Just the three of us?"

"You could spend tonight, if you like," said Alfred. "You're not going back to the ranch tonight, are you?"

"No, we're staying at the, I think it's called the Town House. But I'd like to come to your house some other night."

"Any night you pick," said Natalie. "We'd love it."

Annabella came and took her away to be introduced to some new arrivals and they did not speak to her again until they were seated. In the meantime she had had more to drink and said so to Alfred. "This food is coming none too soon," she said. "I'm afraid I've tied one on. Will you protect me from myself? I don't mean my baser instincts. But if you talk to me all through dinner, I won't have to talk to this man on my left, and I think he's one of the cousins."

They had a potage Mongole, which she scooped up hungrily. "That should help," she said. She put her hand on Alfred's under the table. "I said I was nervous about the party, but it wasn't only that. It isn't this party, or any party. I do this all the time. And you know why."

"I'm terribly sorry to hear that. Could I have been any help? Or can I be? You know why I stayed away, don't you?"

"Yes. You wanted me to get him out of my mind and get a new start."

"You're young, Sadie. You still can. And you must."

"Who says I must?"

"Well, I just did."

"I've tried everything. Everything."

"I don't shock that easily, so don't expect me to fall over or get indignant. You had to try to fall in love with someone else and falling in love meant sleeping with him."

"Not him. Them."

"Well, all right. Them. That didn't work, and now you're fed up with it. It wasn't any fun, was it?"

"It wasn't any fun for anybody. Oh, I guess the boy always has *some* pleasure. I didn't fight."

"I think the boys were God damn lucky, and I'm sure they felt that, at least. Did you give any of them a chance to feel any more than that? No, I'll bet."

"How could I, when I didn't feel any more myself?"

"Then you did get something out of it?"

"Well, yes. At the time. At the very moment."

"How many actually were there?"

"Times, or boys? As a matter of fact one wasn't a boy at all. He was the father of a friend of mine. That's why I came out here. I thought it would mean even less to a married man,

960

but he began talking about a divorce, and he couldn't afford all that. And I wasn't the slightest bit in love with him. Or he with me. But he wanted to make up for what he'd missed when he was at Harvard. That's all it was. He was behaving more like an undergraduate than they were themselves. I didn't come out here to forget him. I came out to get away from him."

"The middle-aged surge. We all get it, I guess. It's supposed to be the dying gasp, the final one before we lose our powers."

"But this lasted a year."

"Oh, it isn't just one night. It can last several years."

"Is it usually one girl, or lots of girls?"

"It works both ways."

"This one—I think it may turn out to be several girls. I hope so. It began so—strangely. I've been going to his house for years and spending the night, and his daughter to my house. This one night he just came in the room and got in bed with me and I didn't dare make a sound. It wasn't exactly rape, I couldn't call it that, but I did everything he told me to. The next time I admit I could have locked the door, but I didn't want to. And then I began to meet him in town, willingly. Until he said he wanted to get a divorce and marry me, and that was simply out of the question. I stopped seeing him altogether, but he'd call me up and one time my mother recognized his voice and gave him the devil. She didn't threaten him. She just told him to stop making an ass of himself, and I think that did it. He did stop. She was wonderful with me. She didn't cross-examine me. She just said, ask myself whether I wasn't using unhappiness as an excuse. That's all. 'Ask yourself whether you're not using unhappiness as an excuse.' Didn't say an excuse for what. Then I realized that she'd been making some good guesses about the rest. Then maybe by accident or maybe not, my cousin Dorothy stayed with us a couple of times, and here I am."

"You'll fall in love again, but I think your mother asked a good question."

"Do you think I'm a tramp at heart?"

"No. But it's damn near time you began behaving in a way that doesn't need any excuse. What if you'd been married to Rowland? Would you have behaved this way? I say, no. Are you sore at him or sore at life because you didn't get married?"

"Maybe."

"I think it's more than maybe, Sadie. I think that's what it is. Stop being sore at Rowland, and stop being sore at the world. It's no trick at all for a girl as attractive as you to get men to sleep with her. But this married man sounds to me like a real shit-heel, and I don't think you raised your standards any by having an affair with him. That's what you ought to ask yourself. Ask yourself if it isn't true that every new guy you slept with was a little inferior to the one before him. And also whether it wasn't a little easier every time there was a new guy. I don't know how many there've been, but I'll bet the first one after Rowland was a much nicer guy than your friend's father."

"Much nicer. Maybe too nice. He was a friend of Rowland's."

The woman at Alfred's right said: "Now, Mr. Eaton, you've got to pay some attention to me."

The party went on for several hours. Shortly before eleven Sadie came to Alfred, who was sitting with Annabella and some others, and said: "What is a sneak preview?"

"It's when they show a movie in a theater in Glendale, a movie that hasn't been released. Why?"

"Someone just said the crowd is coming in from the sneak preview, out in the main restaurant. Will you take me there?"

"Sure." He excused himself and took her out to the bar. They sat with their backs to the bar and she watched the stars and producers and agents table-hopping.

"Hi, my friend."

Alfred turned and saw Jack Tom, standing beside him.

"Hello, Jack Tom."

Jack Tom looked at Sadie and whispered: "Who's the dish? Introduce me to the little lady."

Alfred realized that Jack Tom did not understand the circumstances of their being there, and that he believed Alfred and Sadie were out alone. "No," he said.

"No? This something you been keeping on ice? You dog, Alfred. Come on, boy, I gotta meet this."

"No."

"I ain't gonna take no, Alfred."

"Beat it, will you?"

Jack Tom lifted his head as though his chin had been tapped. "Did you tell me to beat it?"

"I did."

Jack Tom took a deep breath. "My friend, you may be awful sorry you said that. Awful sorry. You gonna find that maybe she aint wuth it." He looked at the row of tables, picked one group and slowly ambled over to it. He was loudly welcomed and the group quickly made room for him. Very distinctly he said: "Thank you all. I just been told to beat it. I never been told that before." The men and women at the table stared at Alfred, and in every face there was the same combination of pity and fear for him. He knew some of them, they all knew him, but not one of them gave any sign that he was recognized. The proprietor himself stopped at the table and Jack Tom said, "Mike, I just been told to beat it."

"Come-come, old boy," said Romanoff.

"Who was the pushy man?" said Sadie.

"Let's go back. I may have made a mistake."

"That all depends," said Natalie, in their room that night. "Was he tight?"

"I've never really seen him tight, so I don't know. He holds his liquor very well and always has. No, I don't think he was tight. He'll remember the whole thing."

"Then it was a mistake, if you think offending him was a mistake. Do you think it was a mistake to offend him?"

"I do. If I wanted to show you, and myself, that I'm not afraid of Jack Tom Smith, I probably could have picked a better way, a more sensible way. Maybe a more courageous way."

"Well, then, obviously you apologize."

"Oh, no. I couldn't apologize unless I meant it, and I don't know how sincerely I'd mean it. I might mutter some words apologizing for offending him, but then would I have to admit to myself that I am afraid of him? I don't know. The doubt is there, and would be there, and as long as it is, I won't apologize. Also, knowing him as well as I do, I know what he thinks of apologies."

"Yes. He'd only see it as a sign of weakness. Don't apologize. And there's another perfectly good reason for not apologizing."

"What's that?"

"*He* was wrong."

Alfred's face brightened. "You're right, he was. What the hell am I sweating for?"

"But wait a minute. That isn't to say that he's going to know he was wrong, or admit it. He was only doing what he's done all his life, only this time he did it to you."

"But you make me feel better. He was insolent, therefore I'm in the right. Let him make the first move. And he just might, because he must know by this time that the B-girl was actually Fritz Warren's cousin. He's terribly impressed by Fritz Warren and the P. C."

"What's the P. C.?"

"Porcellian. The fairest jewel in Jack Tom's diadem, a member of The Pork on his board. He will never offend Fritz Warren. He'd give anything to have a son of his in Porcellian. Unfortunately for him, there's nothing he has, or any son of his will have, that will ever get the boy in, but that's not going to keep Jack Tom from trying. I must say that even if I've made jokes all my life about Porcellian, it's nice to know they wouldn't do business with Jack Tom for his whole forty million. Incidentally, that's the figure that Henrietta spoke of. She's wrong. He has much more than forty million."

"That measly little man."

"No. Don't judge him by his small ambitions and his sex life. He has brains, he has physical courage, he makes a religion of loyalty—"

"Not to his women."

"No, but they're not so much women as squaws. As a man I can understand why it's sometimes necessary to lie to a woman. I'm sure I have, back in my shady past. Oh, I know damn well I have. Any man who's slept with more than one or two women in his life, he's had to lie. If you haven't got all year, you're going to have to tell a few lies."

"Oh, we all know that. I was talking about loyalty. Fidelity and respect and some unselfishness."

"Well, his loyalty only operates with men."

"I really hate his money, what it does to other people, letting him get away with just about anything."

"You have a point. When you have as much money as that, nobody can blackmail you. And if a little guy tries to sue you, for anything, you turn your lawyers on him and he'll go broke trying to fight you. Postponements and delays and appeals and all the legal stratagems that a poor man can't afford. Oh, I don't say he's a laudable citizen, but I've often had to force myself to see the good points in other men. Percy Hasbrouck. Creighton Duffy. I've also had to keep my eyes open to the the weaknesses of my friends. The hardest thing of all is to try to render a fair opinion of myself. I went along for years with nothing but a low opinion of myself, and then I began to give myself a little more of the best of it. At this point in my personal history I'm quite thoroughly confused. I wish I had something to do."

"You will have."

"But I don't seem to get started on anything. Look at the things that have been going on in the world this year. When we dropped those atomic bombs on Japan, do you remember almost my first reaction?"

"Well, you said something about thanking God you didn't have to keep that secret any more."

"Exactly. What a small, personal reaction to the biggest thing that's ever happened in the history of the world."

"Is it that?"

"It's incomprehensible. Don't think of it as only a weapon of war. Think of it in the same terms as you would electricity, the world as it was before electricity, and as it's been since."

"I honestly don't think there's been much difference. Men go on fighting over girls and money. Helen of Troy. Cleopatra. Territories. Gold. What was this war fought over? Money. The Germans didn't just want land. They wanted to rule and be rich. And the Japs wanted to rule their half of the world. And why did we fight? For the same reasons we'll always fight, and all countries will always fight. We fight for our national existence, so we're told. But isn't money another word for that?"

"You make it seem so simple. But the next big war just can't happen. It will mean the destruction of the human race."

"Oh, well, now *that's* incomprehensible to me. Germ warfare, I can understand that. But if all that stuff about chain reaction is true, why didn't it start at Hiroshima? And why did it stop? In August, we didn't see the light from the atomic bomb, or hear the noise. Am I just stupid?"

"Never that."

"So the atomic bomb may have been bigger than any other in history, but it wouldn't even have wiped out Los Angeles. Nothing as small as that is going to stop the next war."

"No, but there's another chain reaction."

"What?"

"The scientists didn't stop, even if their bomb did."

"Well, they're people. Why don't they stop?"

"Because they're scientists. Science is their religion and they never have seemed to care much about people."

"Oh, come on, darling. What about the fights against yellow fever, and syphilis and so on?"

"I've never thought that the scientists gave much of a damn about the people involved. As people. A scientist is a fanatic, his religion is the search for information. But it certainly wouldn't surprise me if fifty years from now they rule the world. Maybe a cabinet of scientists, an international cabinet, physicists and biochemists. And then God help the world. If it isn't blown up before then, it will be when they start tiffing among themselves. They're just as bad as any ladies' bridge club. Or, if you prefer, a syndicate of gangsters. The North Side mob muscles into the South Side territory, and the shooting begins. The sad truth I guess is that the human race is made up of people who don't get along very well together. And never will. Come lie in my bed."

She smiled, and got out of her bed and lay down beside him.

"That was the only possible way to end that."

"Yes, the hell with science. We have our art."

"Mm-hmm."

"How'd you like to go for a swim?"

"Now? It'd be terribly cold."

"I guess it would. I was just thinking, we may have to get out of this house, and I'm really going to miss it."

"We have a lease. We wouldn't have to get out till spring."

"But we might want to. Circumstances have changed."

"Yes, but let's not worry about it tonight, and let's not go for a swim. Can't I persuade you that it's much pleasanter here?"

"You're being very persuasive."

"And you're a very cooperative man."

"Yes, I seem to be."

"Will you not get angry if I ask you a question?"

"I'm not inclined to get angry with you at just this moment. What?"

"If you had squaws, plural, and I was one of them, would you have Sadie Warren for another?"

"I might. But I won't. Why?"

"You know the only reason she came to California."

"Yes, I do. But you don't."

"Yes I do. She's in love with you."

"I'm not surprised to hear you say that. But you're wrong."

"Nothing will convince me that I'm wrong. Do you know who else thinks you're attractive?"

"Who?"

"Annabella Warren."

"She would interest me more than Sadie. Sadie is a push-over. I'll tell you all about it tomorrow."

"If you were sure I'd never find out about it would you have an affair with Annabella?"

"You mean if you never found out about it, in your whole life?"

"Yes."

"Or suspected it?"

"Yes."

"And do you mean just sleep with her once, or have a real affair?"

"A real affair."

"No, I wouldn't have an affair with her, not while I'm married to you. But if you change it and ask me if I'd sleep with her maybe once or twice, with an impossible guarantee that you'd never know about it, I'd have to say yes."

"I was sure you'd answer the way you did. I don't mind your thinking she's attractive, as long as you're not going to do anything about it. She is attractive. If I die I give you permission to marry her. She's the only woman I know of that I could stand having you marry. And that I'd feel would be as good a wife to you as I am. Or as I try to be."

"You don't have to qualify those statements. You *are* my wife. But why ask me about these other women?"

"Because I watched them with you tonight, two women as different as could be, and both strongly attracted to you. The one obvious, Sadie. But Annabella, just the rather contented smile whenever she was standing near you, and then the way she'd look, not at you, but down at the floor, when you'd leave her. And I'm sure neither one of you said anything at all personal."

"Build me up, kid. I can use it."

966

"We don't have to live here."

"No."

In the next few days they anticipated some word from Jack Tom: an apology, perhaps, or a friendly gesture without overt apology, or, contrariwise, an unfriendly gesture. But they heard nothing from him. Nor he from them: Alfred considered writing a letter in which he would invite Jack Tom to declare himself in regard to their continued renting of the house; but he held to his determination to wait out the first word from Jack Tom. They heard nothing from Jack Tom but they heard of him. Sadie Warren spent a night with Alfred and Natalie. She and Natalie had a cocktail apiece, dinner moved along with conversation about life in California, and after dinner the threesome sat in the library and kept themselves out of the conversation so that (as Natalie had planned) Sadie went to her room with an impression of the serenity that existed for a happily married couple, who wanted no one else and wanted no one else's problems. At only one point was their conversation out of Natalie's control.

After dinner Sadie said: "I haven't had a chance to tell you, but I met the pushy man, and he owns this house!"

"You met Jack Tom Smith? How did you like him?" said Alfred.

"There isn't much there to like or dislike," said Sadie. "He came out to the ranch on Sunday, and I don't think he was expected. But he arrived in a white Rolls-Royce with his wife and another couple, older. The other man was a partner, too, like Fritz. It was pretty dull, I can tell you. Mr. Smith and Fritz and the other man went off and talked business and Annabella and I just sat there, listening to two women gabbing away about parties. Then the men came back and Mr. Smith said he had tried to wangle an introduction to this little lady, meaning me, but you, Alfred, must have thought he was tight, because you wouldn't introduce him. He said it all in front of everybody, as though he'd been unjustly condemned. And he tried to make it very clear that he'd known I was Fritz's cousin. And that's not true. I heard him call me a dish, and he had no idea who I was. But it was very smart of him to get that idea across, wasn't it? He came right out and said, 'I'm afraid Alfred Eaton thought I was on the make for Miss Warren, and Alfred should be more sure of his facts before he misjudges an old friend.' The other woman, whose name I never got, said that the Eatons were very high-hat anyway, and all you two did was go to parties and act superior. I thought you'd like to know that. Annabella stepped in and said she considered the Eatons a great addition to Southern California, and she hoped people would do everything they could to make you want to stay. The woman was about to say some more and I saw Annabella look

967

at her, practically saying, 'If you open your mouth again about the Eatons, you'll find out that I much prefer them to you.' "

"People named Davis? Did he wear a Stetson and a fringed buckskin jacket?" said Alfred.

"Yes, and a sombrero, pure white."

"Ralph Davis and Betty-Ann."

"Yes. Betty-Ann, and she's over sixty."

"Actually she isn't," said Natalie. "But she had her face lifted, one of the early ones, and I guess they didn't know so much about it then. She usually manages to mention that I was a salesgirl in New York. Which of course I was. Waited on her many times, before she was Mrs. Davis. How did you like Mrs. Smith? Henrietta?"

"I thought she was a show-off. One of those people that reads *Time* every week and tries to hold everybody spellbound with how much she knows."

"She's better than that, Sadie, but I know what you mean," said Natalie.

"That was a darn nice thing of Annabella to say," said Alfred.

"Annabella! She thinks you two are the most attractive people she knows."

"She doesn't know us very *well*," said Alfred.

"Maybe not, but she certainly doesn't want you to leave California."

Alfred heard more of Annabella's admiration for "the Eatons" when a few days after Sadie's overnight visit, Fritz Warren invited him to lunch at a place called the Cock 'n' Bull, which featured pewter tankards. "I've heard some talk that you were thinking of leaving California," said Fritz. "I hope there's no truth in it."

"Well, there's always been more than a grain of truth in it," said Alfred. "It's high time I stopped being an invalid and got to work."

"Are you interested in buying a ranch? I know a good one that's going on the market shortly. It's about thirty miles from us. The owner died, and the widow doesn't like the life."

"I don't know enough about it, Fritz, and I could lose my shirt and maybe even ruin a good ranch. I was thinking of a business."

"Banking?"

"I had thought of that, but I've given that up. Too many things against it. The big ones like Gianini's and the Security-First National, they'd make it pretty tough for a stranger to go into a small town and open up, even if I could get a charter. I also thought of going into the small boat business, and I haven't altogether given that up."

"Small boats on a small scale?"

968

"Well, I'd start small. But I've already found out that a lot of other fellows have had the same idea, and for a while there's going to be some overcrowding, with the usual result."

"Were you going to do that here, or in the East?"

"In the East, more likely. Where did you hear that we were leaving California?"

"Jack Tom Smith. Has there been any trouble there, Alfred? I feel I can ask you that, as a friend of both parties."

"Yes, there has been."

"But you'd rather not talk about it. Well, I don't want to stick my nose in it. I was sure there was, because he seems rather hurt that you've been talking about leaving California without telling him. That's his version."

"That certainly is his version. It's a case of the wish being father to the thought."

"Oh? Well, now, I don't want to pursue this, if you don't care to, but I don't like to be told something that isn't the truth. Jack Tom's version is that you're fed up with the place and have been saying so to everybody but him, and he considers that disloyal."

"Jack Tom is indulging in pure fantasy."

"I'm on one of his boards, as you know, but Annabella's been wanting me to quit for years. I'm not one of the working directors and Annabella's always said I shouldn't serve if I'm to be just a figurehead. But it's been a profitable, interesting sinecure. However, I don't like to be lied to. Obviously I am being lied to, therefore being used, therefore have probably been used before without catching on."

"Jack Tom is very much annoyed with me in a matter that has nothing to do with business. Bear that in mind, Fritz."

"I shall, but possibly not the way you intended. I'm a fairly smart business man but I'm not *in* business. We made up our minds twenty years ago and have never regretted our decision, Annabella and I. Tranquillity. Now when a business association can become a hazard to our tranquillity, it must be got rid of. It isn't a question of honesty or ethics. I didn't put my name on Jack Tom's board without making some inquiries, and he's honest. But I don't like it any better when a man lies to me, simply because there doesn't happen to be a dollar made or lost. I can protect myself in dollar matters, but in other matters it's not always so easy. I'll think this over, but I can almost foretell the result. Meanwhile, to get back to us, there's a great deal of money around, Alfred, waiting for someone to come along with the right proposition. I'm acquainted with a dozen men who have some of that money. So are you. But I've already done business with them and you haven't, so whenever you feel that you'd like to talk to them across a desk, instead of a dinner table, I have my orders to see to it that the Eatons don't leave California." He smiled. "And they're orders that I've accepted with very good grace."

"Thank you."

"But do you mind if I ask you a rather impertinent question?"

"I'll take a chance."

"Do you feel that you have to go into business? A man can keep busy without going into business, you know. I put in a fourteen-hour day every day, but I only spend one afternoon a week at my desk, even with the blasted forms the government makes us farmers fill out."

"My trouble is I can't make up my mind."

"Oh, now you certainly know that any damn fool can make up his mind. It's how you make up your mind, what you make up your mind to."

"Yes, but nobody can accuse me of being hasty. I've wasted almost two years out here."

"I still say you're better off coasting than going into something that wasn't suitable. You have, as I see it, only one worry."

"Which is?"

"Well, all the young fellows who were in the war, every one of them that's worth his salt has some ideas for the post-war period. Fellows our age will be competing with them."

"I found that out already, in the boat business."

"Even in my business, which isn't even a proper business. I've had several offers to buy the ranch. And I know of other businesses where they've swung into action while they were still in uniform. They all seem to want to have something of their own. The good ones. The others, that I don't think so much of, they want to sign lifetime contracts, for security, with the big corporations. That's where the war, Army life, Navy life, had one of its worst effects. Killed initiative. Is that strange, coming from me? Not so very. It took a hell of a lot of a certain kind of initiative for us to pull out of Boston." He smiled. "Whenever we have to return there for a wedding or funeral there are always some of our relatives to say, 'You'll be back.' I'll be back, to be sure, but I'll be embalmed first."

It was entertaining to sit with this man, who still got his town clothes from a Cambridge tailor and wore a polka-dot blue and white bow tie and a heavy gold watch-chain and brown hat with the brim turned up all around—and happily proclaimed his abandonment of the life to which he was born. Life on the reclaimed desert, in the sun and heat and wind, had done to his appearance just what the sun and wind and spray would have done if he had stayed home. His close-cropped white hair and brown skin were the same, except that the upper part of his forehead showed lighter where he had habitually worn a Stetson, but tennis, bareheaded, had darkened even that lighter part. He had a gift for cordiality without incurring obligations that was a mark of his breed, and Alfred guessed that Fritz Warren had come this far in age without a single close friendship, albeit with perhaps two dozen good friends who felt the same way about him; usher friends, cousin friends, club friends, godfather friends, pallbearer friends, but no intimate. Alfred knew exactly where he stood with Fritz Warren: as a Princeton man he had a status that was as unchangeable as if he were of another nationality, but as the father of a boy who was reasonably presumed to have been headed for the Porcellian, he was regarded as entitled to a special category of his own. He would have liked to be a close friend of Fritz Warren's, but Fritz Warren had gone as far as he ever would in that direction. And on the way home Alfred, taking a long look at himself, realized that he himself no longer had much to offer in the creation of a close friendship. In place of a friendship he would have to make-do with the friends he had.

One morning a few weeks after the Warrens' party at Romanoff's Alfred was lying awake in bed, waiting for the small cup of coffee that Marie Schaftman brought daily. The quiet was shattered by a noise that was like a machine gun heard close to. It was a pneumatic hammer, recognizably, and when Marie came in he asked her, "Are we doing some construction work?"

"There's men on the drifeway."

"On the driveway? What are they doing? Our driveway?"

"Yes sir. I don't know."

"They must have the wrong place." He drank his coffee quickly and put on a pair of slacks and a polo shirt and went out to the men with the hammer.

"Hold it, hold it," he said. "What goes on?"

"We got orders to cut up this road."

"Now wait a second. Who gave you the orders, and are you sure you have the right place?" said Alfred. "What address were you given?"

"This address, 1666 Spiral Drive, Beverly Hills. Smith."

"I think the Smith is what threw you. That's the address, all right, but you'd better come in and call your office and find out which Smith you're looking for."

"Jack Tom Smith, the oil man. I worked here before," said the older of the men.

"What are you doing? It's the right place, all right."

"We got orders to cut up this road. I think he's gonna get rid of the concrete and put in asphalt."

"I'm the tenant, and I don't know anything about that."

"Well, all I know, we got two days to chop it up."

"Do you work for a paving firm?"

"No, we work for a general contractor."

"I see. And the firm that does the paving comes in the day after tomorrow. Now take a look up there, in that garage. You see two cars there, don't you?"

"I see a 60-Special and I see a '38 Pontiac."

"Did you see them before you started chopping up this driveway?"

"I took notice to them, yeah."

"But you didn't bother to notify anybody in this house. How do you expect a car to get over that rubble?"

"Well, I guess you could make it, but we were told to go right to work."

"By whom?"

"By the boss. He said orders were to get up here and start chopping."

"What's his name and what's your office phone?"

"Crestview 9-8811. Spurley & Company, and ask for Joe Delgado, he's our foreman."

Natalie had joined Alfred during the exchange. "Ask them if they'll stop long enough to get the cars out on the street."

"I won't ask them, I'll tell them. You with the drill, break up those big chunks so we can get our cars out of here, and then don't do any more chopping till I've spoken to your boss."

"I'll get the Cadillac and you tell Anton to get the other car," said Natalie. In a lowered tone she said, "You know, of course, what's happening."

"I can make a pretty God damn good guess."

Telephone calls to the Spurley company, to Jack Tom's downtown office and to his Los Angeles attorneys provided all the essential information. It seemed, according to an attorney who admitted he had been expecting a call, that there was nothing in the Eatons' lease that said that Mr. Smith was prevented from making improvements on the property while they occupied it. Mr. Smith intended to make extensive improvements, of which a new driveway was only the first. He intended also to enlarge the swimming pool, to change the location of one of the tennis courts, and, later, to rearrange the terrace.

"All these improvements," said Alfred. "They'll naturally necessitate frequent use of the pneumatic hammer."

"Naturally. And a bulldozer," said the attorney.

"Very well thought out," said Alfred. "Of course I could get an injunction."

"You probably could. If you *wanted* to."

"But you're counting on my not wanting to."

972

"I didn't say that, Mr. Eaton."

"No, and you never suggested that if we wanted to get out of the lease, we could."

"No I didn't, but are you suggesting that you do want to get out of the lease?"

"I'm not sure. We may want to stick it out here till the lease is up in March."

"That's entirely up to you, Mr. Eaton. You have that right."

"Is this call being monitored?"

"Yes sir, every word we've spoken since you gave your name to our operator."

"I see. I thought as much. Well, you tell Jack Tom Smith, hereinafter referred to as that horse's ass, that I will talk to my own attorneys today and that said horse's ass need expect no trouble from us. We no longer have any desire to live in that said horse's ass's house or even to have any communication with that said horse's ass, which will be our principal reason for consulting our attorneys. You see what I've done, don't you? I've made it impossible to have a complete record of this conversation without repeated identification of Jack Tom Smith as a horse's ass. I'm sure Jack Tom Smith won't enjoy having a record of his being called a horse's ass. And now if you'd care to say something to wind up the conversation, the record will be complete."

"I have no more to say to you, Mr. Eaton," said the bewildered attorney, and Alfred replaced the telephone.

Natalie laughed. "Jack Tom'll smash that record the first time he hears it. He couldn't stand having—just having that lawyer hear you will drive him crazy. It really puts the lawyer in quite a spot."

"My heart bleeds for that lawyer. He was so God damn arrogant," said Alfred. He took her arm and they went out. "Do you know what I'm going to miss most?"

"What?"

"The terrace. In some ways we got closer there than anywhere else. The long stories I told you."

"And I told you."

"Not so many. The terrace was *my* platform. I had to tell you everything that ever happened to me. I'm not sure why. You knew nearly everything."

"No. A great deal I didn't know."

"Was it because I'd just been so close to checking out for good?"

"Probably."

"Or would I have told you anyhow? No. I was immobilized, and I had a captive audience. And the time was just right. The right time to look back, I guess."

"I guess so."

"It would have been a good place to talk about the future, but I never did, much."

She hesitated. "Oh, well, it isn't easy to talk about the future."

"It isn't easy if you're not sure of it, and who is, at my age? I was pretty sure of it at one time."

"And did you talk about it?"

"Not much."

"There you are."

"Yes, there I am. There I am, all right. And what are we going to do about it?"

"About what?"

"Natalie, Natalie. My good wife."

She embraced his arm with both of hers.

"Let's get out of here today," he said. "Let's not spend another night here. You don't want to wake up tomorrow with that noise, do you?"

"No. Do you want to go to a hotel?"

"I want to go to a hotel, and the next two days—it shouldn't take more—we can get ready to leave California. Is that all right with you?"

"Completely. Where shall we go?"

"Well, I guess New York, for a while. I can start looking around."

"Yes," she said. She looked up quickly, and then away, and pressed her cheek to his arm. They turned slowly and in step they came in, for the last time, from the terrace.

There are always so many things for a man to do if he does not have to work for a living. If he is taken ill, he can go to California to recuperate, and when he is well again, or at least as well as he can ever reasonably hope to be, he can try to interest himself in some activity that he can engage in with pleasure and profit. If he decides to leave California, he can go back to New York, where there are many, many things to be done, especially after an absence of two years from the city in which he has spent most of his life. In 1946 there was the problem of finding an apartment, which was no easy problem and could take weeks that ran into months. There were family and friends to see, and there were plays to be seen. Then, with the coming of mild weather a man who did not have to go to an office five days a week could drive out to the North Shore of Long Island and take advantage of the almost deserted golf courses, and if a friend wanted to steal an afternoon off in the middle of the week, it was pleasant to play golf with a man for a change, instead of one's wife. On rainy days it was pleasant to go lunch at a club and while away the afternoon at bottle-pool and backgammon in the company of other men who did not have to work for a living. True, nearly all of them drank, and the older ones were usually quite drunk before evening, but a man began to feel that they depended upon him and really missed him on days when he had gone to the golf course.

Any day was easy to fill with human contacts and conversations that were substantially on the good-humored side, and besides golf and the indoor games, there were often deviations from the routine that were in the nature of surprises. There was always a baseball game in New York or Brooklyn, and there was horse-racing every day but Sunday. Repeated visits to the ball parks and the race tracks stimulated an interest in the newspaper articles covering those activities and thus added an hour to the time one gave to morning reading. The mornings were, in fact, the idlest time of day, best for writing letters, seeing dentists and tailors and shirtmakers. The active part of the day really began at noon, before which a man did not like to go to the club. But if it was not quite right to get there before noon, it was inconsiderate to get there much later, for it was plain to see that a man's friends depended upon him to be there earlier than the rest of the crowd. A man's friends could become nervous and quite irritable at having to drink alone, even though one did not join them in a drink. They did not realize how much they had come to depend on one, but for one to be there partook of some of the nature of a duty. A friend who had not long to live was a responsibility; it was surely a decent thing, if not one's actual duty, to accept the responsibility . . .

In the evenings early that spring, after they had settled in their small, easy-to-run apartment in East Seventy-eighth Street, Natalie would prepare and serve the dinner and listen to Alfred's report on his day. In the beginning the names of the men were new to her, but she soon could follow his stories without having to ask who the men were. They were few in number, ten at most, and she would know that Tom was seventy and Stewart was deaf and Ted was dying of cancer and Bud was the great Yale pitcher who had known Samuel Eaton and Morrie was the one who always swam in the ocean on New Year's Day. At first she had not bothered to remember them individually, but as she heard their names again and again she understood their importance to Alfred. They were his life now, they were the men he saw.

It was running from the truth to think otherwise. Alfred had spoken and continued to speak of the spring and the fall: people now were planning their summers; in the fall, which for New York even more than for any other city was the beginning of a new year, he would one day walk into an office and hang up his hat. But men whom she knew he had counted on had seen him or entertained them while they were still living in the hotel, and then had not seen him again, unless they ran into him at one of the clubs. They had paid their respects, they had fulfilled their obligations, but then they had vanished—except those few who would telephone him on a Wednesday for a truant afternoon of golf. There had been enough time left before summer for serious conference, but in the middle of March this man whom she loved was already making excuses for them that, she admitted, were likewise excuses for himself. She recognized a sweetness in his kindness to the old men at the clubs, but his sweetness, his kindness, had always been available on call, and had never been the preoccupation of Alfred Eaton of MacHardie & Company or the Department of the Navy. He was neither old enough nor young enough to do what he was doing: he was not young enough to light their cigars, and he was not old enough to share their decrepitude. These men were not Raymond Johnson and Ralph Benziger, for whom he had affection and respect; in his stories about them in the evening he reported their idiosyncrasies and eccentricities and crotchets with humor. Nevertheless, he preferred the easy association with them to the small expense of effort that would put him in the proximity of vitality. On an impulse one day she made an appointment to see Don Shanley, who invited her to lunch at the Biltmore.

When she saw Shanley, who identified her from her description of the clothes she would wear, she decided to say nothing about the age of Alfred's new companions. Shanley was not young, nor middle-aged; he was a well-preserved old man.

"This is an imposition, I know," she said. "But Alfred still considers you one of his best friends."

"That's good. So do I. What's worrying you?"

"I want to know first of all, what are people saying about Alfred? Please tell me the frank, brutal truth."

"Well, you're right. It's brutal. It's brutal truth, and it's brutal the way they express it. They say he's all washed up. They—the more sympathetic ones—say he never got over the death of his son, tried to forget it by working too hard, and finally wrecked his health so badly that it took him two years to be able to see people again."

"Do you subscribe to that?"

He took a long time before answering her. "You've put a lot of trust in me, Mrs. Eaton, and I almost wish you hadn't, because I have to match your trust with equal sincerity. Yes, I do subscribe to it. Some men downtown also point to the fact that Alfred isn't with our new firm as proof that he's through. That isn't the case. You know the complications there, I'm sure. Then there are others who say he was broken up by failure of his marriage. I mention both these items not because I believe there's any truth to them, but to show you that a lot of men are giving a lot of reasons for what they call the collapse of Alfred Eaton."

"What do you believe is the cause?"

"Well, I think there's something in the theory of the fatal accident to young Rowland, followed by overwork and illness. But it's deeper, and I know so little about it that I hesitate to put my thoughts into words."

"Well, please don't hesitate any longer."

"I'm not a Judas, Mrs. Eaton, and I don't like the role, but since I'll probably never see you again, I'll try to find the words. Alfred Eaton was for quite a few years considered one of the fair-haired young men of Wall Street. But in my opinion, he did it all with brains and luck. I don't know why he liked me, but he did, and I liked him very much, but I don't think he gave a damn for anyone else he saw, and I think that's the impression most men got. I must explain to you that when your business is money, you stand to make an enemy every time you go into a deal. Maybe you've swung something that someone else was working on. I couldn't begin to go into the ways you can make enemies in our business, and we all take enemies for granted. In any war, you have to have casualties. But Alfred didn't only make enemies. He failed to do the concomitant thing, which is to make a friend. When I speak of making a friend, I don't mean a pal or a chum, or a blood-brother. I only mean, and should have said, a friendly connection. Mind you, the enemies down there are just like enemies anywhere, but that's why it's important to pick up some friendly connections as you make enemies. Alfred didn't, and consequently people resented him all along the way, and that's why I said he did it all with brains and luck. In the money business you always need friendly connections, or friends, unless you're a genius, and Alfred isn't that. He's a very attractive man with an unattractive outlook on people. Not to me. I like him. I saw a lot of him, by choice, and I enjoyed every minute. But for some reason unknown to me, he gave me his friendship and kept it from everyone else in the firm. You can draw some satisfaction from the fact that he accomplished what he did on merit. But I'm afraid that isn't going to be much help to you now."

"God, what people!"

"No, now you're making a mistake. The very same people would have responded differently to a different outlook. There are men in the financial district without half his brains, making just as much money as he did, without half the effort. They may be mediocrities, Mrs. Eaton, but most people are. You could argue that Alfred is a man of much higher principle than most of them, since he refused to compromise. But business is trade, Mrs. Eaton, and trade is trading. Alfred was really a seller, not a trader. And not a salesman. He sold what he sold because he convinced people that they would be damned fools not to buy. He didn't coax them. That's what salesmen do, they coax, they persuade. Alfred didn't even argue. Now of course we didn't do much actual selling, but I use the term in a slangy sense. We did more buying than selling, but Alfred sold our buying, if you see what I mean."

"What is his future?"

"Downtown? He could get lots of jobs, but he wouldn't take any of them. He'd be a good name on a lot of boards or painted on the window, but most firms wouldn't want to risk letting him handle delicate propositions. He went around the country during the war and in effect told a great many men that they were traitors. Some of them were, but that's the Attorney General's job."

"You're trying to tell me that my husband has an unpleasant personality. Then why did you put up with him?"

"A unique personality. I enjoyed his company because, well, he was probably doing what I'd wanted to do. Luckily you have no financial worries. I did. I worked my way through Yale and I landed in New York with $100 to last me the rest of my life."

"Well, have you any suggestions? Any advice?"

"You won't like it."

"I haven't liked much that you've said, Mr. Shanley."

"Well, it may seem like a tragic waste to you, but I'd encourage him to go on doing what he is doing. He doesn't need money. But I've inquired, and I understand he's just loafing, seeing men at his clubs and not trying to sell them anything. Just taking them for what they are."

"How little you know Alfred Eaton. How little any of you know him."

"I don't deny that. It's what I've been saying. But is he unhappy, and is he going to be happy doing something different?"

"Of course he's unhappy, but he doesn't know it now. You knew a man named Archie Busby."

"I did indeed. I helped to get Archie his last job, Mrs. Eaton. But don't you start comparing Alfred Eaton with Archie Busby, or trying to detect any similarity. There was none. Archie Busby unfortunately one day had to look back on a life of such dull mediocrity that—*his* tragedy was in getting that look at himself. If he'd only been able to last out a few years longer without getting what you might call an outside look . . . Most men are luckier than Archie, they don't get to see themselves that way. As long as they don't, they can go plugging away, never really realizing how dull their lives have been. And Alfred Eaton has certainly not led a dull life."

"But he is now."

"Well, he's fifty or close to it, and he's had one hemorrhage. I wish you'd look at it this way: he'll probably live a lot longer now than if he'd got back into business."

"That's easy for you to say, Mr. Shanley. You won't be there the day he discovers that he's become another Busby."

"I'm distressed, Mrs. Eaton. I wanted to help you, and Alfred, and I seem to have done everything but help you."

He was stating a fact, but he might also have been uttering a prophecy. They continued their lunch with a mutual understanding of the undesirability and uselessness of any further conversation about Alfred, and they shook hands without warmth, without animosity, like two people who had not been able to come to terms and would never negotiate again. A few days later Alfred received a letter from Shanley which he passed over to Natalie at breakfast. "Nice to hear from old Don," he said. "And very tactful of him to write instead of asking me to come downtown. Nice letter."

She read the letter:

Dear Alfred:

A group of New York and Boston friends of Guy Titterton's have gotten together to raise a fund to provide an appropriate memorial and it has been suggested that you might be willing to serve as Honorary Chairman of the Committee. I have been appointed to fill you in on the details and to ask you if you will serve in the aforementioned capacity. As you know, Guy spent over fifty summers on Sisquit Isle, off the Maine coast, and at the time of his death he was most enthusiastic over a project to erect a small hospital on the island, which has doubled in population in recent years but is completely without hospital facilities. Several lives have been lost due to the inaccessibility of the island from the mainland, a condition which Guy had hoped to remedy by the construction and partial endowment of a hospital. The funds were to be raised through subscription by friends of Guy's among New York and Boston yachtsmen who had sailed in those waters or had spent summers there. After his death, however, it was agreed that other friends of Guy's might be invited to subscribe, with the result that a committee is in process of formation to handle the more ambitious project. Your name naturally appeared on the list of prospective contributors and it was then suggested that because of your association with Guy and your interest in sailing, you would be a happy choice as Honorary Chairman. I trust that you will allow me to report back to the others with a favorable reply from you. It will mean a great deal to have your name heading our Committee. I enclose a list of the members, most of whom are known to you.

Meanwhile, kindest personal regards.

As ever
Don Shanley

"Look at that list," said Alfred. "It's got everybody since Sebastian Cabot, at a quick glance. And the New York guys —I recognize four winners of the Bermuda Race. One, two, three of the Block Island Race. One Gibson Island. I don't think there's going to be much trouble raising the money. State Street, Wall Street and Forty-fourth Street."

"What's Forty-fourth Street?"

"New York Yacht Club."

"State Street is Chicago."

"Not in this case. Boston."

"Well, two down and one to go. I guess I'm right on Wall Street. Are you going to take it?"

"Naturally. It'd be churlish to refuse, and I want to do it anyway."

"Then get off your letter to Mr. Shanley right away." She had to give Shanley the benefit of her serious doubt. His intention was presumably good, but she could see the possibility that Shanley was inspired by the wish to keep Alfred at doing nothing, and if that was his intention he would find her opposed to him. Still, she believed that Shanley had been the one to suggest Alfred for the Honorary Chairmanship, and the pleasure it gave Alfred was touching as well as alarming.

She had learned a lesson from her meeting with Shanley. He was a friend of Alfred's, and he had been honest enough in his analysis of Alfred and his position. He had been more honest than she had any right to expect. But she would go to no more friends for advice. Shanley had told her enough, and another meeting with another friend, possibly less discreet than Shanley, would only start the talk that Alfred Eaton's wife was desperately trying to get him something to do. No more friends for advice.

They stayed in town that summer, to the extent at least that they kept the apartment open. They went away every weekend, and on one weekend when there were no invitations, they never left the building and bravely pretended to enjoy the sequestered long days and long nights. The telephone had not rung since Thursday afternoon. Then on Sunday evening it rang, and involuntarily they looked at each other, eagerly. "I'll answer it," he said.

"Hello," he said. "Yes it is. Oh, hello, Don. No, we stayed in town this weekend. How is it out there? I'll bet it is. It's been around ninety here, but we haven't stirred. *Don Shanley. Says there isn't a puff of wind anywhere on the North Shore.* Well, I know how it can get out there. Oh, I wouldn't. The traffic will be frightful tonight. You what? Your brother-in-law. Yes. Yes. Seventy-five. Why, yes, I could do that. No, absolutely. It won't be any trouble at all. No, no. Certainly

980

not. And he *has* the reservation at the Pierre. Oh, I won't miss him."

Natalie listened to his words, and easily supplied most of Shanley's words that she could not hear. It had come, it was here, as she had seen it coming, and the only real surprise was in discovering that in pitying Alfred she could hate him. Not for his weakness—the pity was for that. But for counting on her love to make him believe that his weakness was strength.

"Right away, Don," he said. "See you soon." He hung up and turned to her and he was even able to simulate a small triumph. "Don's brother-in-law. He's seventy-five and partly paralyzed. He's coming in on the nine-forty train from New London, and Don wants me to meet him and see that he gets to the hotel."

"How did he know you were here?"

"Just took a chance."

"At five minutes after nine? What if you hadn't been here? Mr. Shanley wouldn't have been able to get in from the country."

"I didn't ask him that, Natalie."

"Well, I used to do work for the Travelers Aid. Let's go."

"You don't have to go with me."

"Oh, but I do," she said.

"Well, all right. It's something to do."

FINE WORKS OF FICTION AND NON-FICTION AVAILABLE FROM CARROLL & GRAF

☐ O'Hara, John/A RAGE TO LIVE $4.95
☐ O'Hara, John/TEN NORTH FREDERICK $4.50
☐ Proffitt, Nicholas/GARDENS OF STONE $4.50
☐ Purdy, James/CABOT WRIGHT BEGINS $4.50
☐ Rechy, John/BODIES AND SOULS $4.50
☐ Reilly, Sidney/BRITAIN'S MASTER SPY $3.95
☐ Scott, Paul/THE LOVE PAVILION $4.50
☐ Taylor, Peter/IN THE MIRO DISTRICT $3.95
☐ Thirkell, Angela/AUGUST FOLLY $4.95
☐ Thirkell, Angela/CHEERFULNESS BREAKS
  IN $4.95
☐ Thirkell, Angela/HIGH RISING $4.95
☐ Thirkell, Angela/MARLING HALL $4.95
☐ Thirkell, Angela/NORTHBRIDGE RECTORY $5.95
☐ Thirkell, Angela/POMFRET TOWERS $4.95
☐ Thirkell, Angela/WILD STRAWBERRIES $4.95
☐ Thompson, Earl/A GARDEN OF SAND $5.95
☐ Thompson, Earl/TATTOO $6.95
☐ West, Rebecca/THE RETURN OF THE SOLDIER $8.95
☐ Wharton, Williams/SCUMBLER $3.95
☐ Wilder, Thornton/THE EIGHTH DAY $4.95

Available from fine bookstores everywhere or use this coupon for ordering.